# THE STEPHEN CRANE MEGAPACK®

## STEPHEN CRANE

Published by Wildside Press LLC.
www.wildsidebooks.com

# Contents

# STEPHEN CRANE: AN INTRODUCTION

## VINCENT STARRETT

It hardly profits us to conjecture what Stephen Crane might have written about the World War had he lived. Certainly, he would have been in it, in one capacity or another. No man had a greater talent for war and personal adventure, nor a finer art in describing it. Few writers of recent times could so well describe the poetry of motion as manifested in the surge and flow of battle, or so well depict the isolated deed of heroism in its stark simplicity and terror.

To such an undertaking as Henri Barbusse's "Under Fire," that powerful, brutal book, Crane would have brought an analytical genius almost clairvoyant. He possessed an uncanny vision; a descriptive ability photographic in its clarity and its care for minutiae—yet unphotographic in that the big central thing often is omitted, to be felt rather than seen in the occult suggestion of detail. Crane would have seen and depicted the grisly horror of it all, as did Barbusse, but also he would have seen the glory and the ecstasy and the wonder of it, and over that his poetry would have been spread.

While Stephen Crane was an excellent psychologist, he was also a true poet. Frequently his prose was finer poetry than his deliberate essays in poesy. His most famous book, "The Red Badge of Courage," is essentially a psychological study, a delicate clinical dissection of the soul of a recruit, but it is also a *tour de force* of the imagination. When he wrote the book he had never seen a battle: he had to place himself in the situation of another. Years later, when he came out of the Greco-Turkish *fracas*, he remarked to a friend: "*The Red Badge* is all right."

Written by a youth who had scarcely passed his majority, this book has been compared with Tolstoy's "Sebastopol" and Zola's "La Débâcle," and with some of the short stories of Ambrose Bierce. The comparison with Bierce's work is legitimate; with the other books, I think, less so. Tolstoy and Zola see none of the traditional beauty of battle; they apply themselves to a devoted—almost obscene—study of corpses and carnage generally; and they lack the American's instinct for the rowdy commonplace, the natural, the irreverent, which so materially aids his realism. In "The Red Badge of Courage" invariably the tone is kept down where one expects a height: the most heroic deeds are accomplished with studied awkwardness.

Crane was an obscure free-lance when he wrote this book. The effort, he says, somewhere, "was born of pain—despair, almost." It was a better piece of work, however, for that very reason, as Crane knew. It is far from flawless. It has been remarked that it bristles with as many grammatical errors as with bayonets; but it is a big canvas, and I am certain that many of Crane's deviations from the rules of polite rhetoric were deliberate experiments, looking to effect—effect which, frequently, he gained.

Stephen Crane "arrived" with this book. There are, of course, many who never have heard of him, to this day, but there was a time when he was very much talked of. That was in the middle nineties, following publication of "The Red Badge of

Courage," although even before that he had occasioned a brief flurry with his weird collection of poems called "The Black Riders and Other Lines." He was highly praised, and highly abused and laughed at; but he seemed to be "made." We have largely forgotten since. It is a way we have.

Personally, I prefer his short stories to his novels and his poems; those, for instance, contained in "The Open Boat," in "Wounds in the Rain," and in "The Monster." The title-story in that first collection is perhaps his finest piece of work. Yet what is it? A truthful record of an adventure of his own in the filibustering days that preceded our war with Spain; the faithful narrative of the voyage of an open boat, manned by a handful of shipwrecked men. But Captain Bligh's account of *his* small boat journey, after he had been sent adrift by the mutineers of the *Bounty*, seems tame in comparison, although of the two the English sailor's voyage was the more perilous.

In "The Open Boat" Crane again gains his effects by keeping down the tone where another writer might have attempted "fine writing" and have been lost. In it perhaps is most strikingly evident the poetic cadences of his prose: its rhythmic, monotonous flow is the flow of the gray water that laps at the sides of the boat, that rises and recedes in cruel waves, "like little pointed rocks." It is a desolate picture, and the tale is one of our greatest short stories. In the other tales that go to make up the volume are wild, exotic glimpses of Latin-America. I doubt whether the color and spirit of that region have been better rendered than in Stephen Crane's curious, distorted, staccato sentences.

"War Stories" is the laconic sub-title of "Wounds in the Rain." It was not war on a grand scale that Crane saw in the Spanish-American complication, in which he participated as a war correspondent; no such war as the recent horror. But the occasions for personal heroism were no fewer than always, and the opportunities for the exercise of such powers of trained and appreciative understanding and sympathy as Crane possessed, were abundant. For the most part, these tales are episodic, reports of isolated instances—the profanely humorous experiences of correspondents, the magnificent courage of signalmen under fire, the forgotten adventure of a converted yacht—but all are instinct with the red fever of war, and are backgrounded with the choking smoke of battle. Never again did Crane attempt the large canvas of "The Red Badge of Courage." Before he had seen war, he imagined its immensity and painted it with the fury and fidelity of a Verestchagin; when he was its familiar, he singled out its minor, crimson passages for briefer but no less careful delineation.

In this book, again, his sense of the poetry of motion is vividly evident. We see men going into action, wave on wave, or in scattering charges; we hear the clink of their accoutrements and their breath whistling through their teeth. They are not men going into action at all, but men going about their business, which at the moment happens to be the capture of a trench. They are neither heroes nor cowards. Their faces reflect no particular emotion save, perhaps, a desire to get somewhere. They are a line of men running for a train, or following a fire engine, or charging a trench. It is a relentless picture, ever changing, ever the same. But it contains poetry, too, in rich, memorable passages.

In "The Monster and Other Stories," there is a tale called "The Blue Hotel". A Swede, its central figure, toward the end manages to get himself murdered. Crane's description of it is just as casual as that. The story fills a dozen pages of the book; but the social injustice of the whole world is hinted in that space; the upside-downness of creation, right prostrate, wrong triumphant,—a mad, crazy world. The incident of the murdered Swede is just part of the backwash of it all, but it is an illuminating fragment. The Swede was slain, not by the gambler whose knife pierced his thick hide: he was the victim of a condition for which he was no more to blame than the man who stabbed him. Stephen Crane thus speaks through the lips of one of the characters:—

> "We are all in it! This poor gambler isn't even a noun. He is a kind of an adverb. Every sin is the result of a collaboration. We, five of us, have collaborated in the murder of this Swede. Usually there are from a dozen to forty women really involved in every murder, but in this case it seems to be only five men—you, I, Johnnie, Old Scully, and that fool of an unfortunate gambler came merely as a culmination, the apex of a human movement, and gets all the punishment."

And then this typical and arresting piece of irony:—

> "The corpse of the Swede, alone in the saloon, had its eyes fixed upon a dreadful legend that dwelt atop of the cash-machine: 'This registers the amount of your purchase.'"

In "The Monster," the ignorance, prejudice and cruelty of an entire community are sharply focussed. The realism is painful; one blushes for mankind. But while this story really belongs in the volume called "Whilomville Stories," it is properly left out of that series. The Whilomville stories are pure comedy, and "The Monster" is a hideous tragedy.

Whilomville is any obscure little village one may happen to think of. To write of it with such sympathy and understanding, Crane must have done some remarkable listening in Boyville. The truth is, of course, he was a boy himself—"a wonderful boy," somebody called him—and was possessed of the boy mind. These tales are chiefly funny because they are so true—boy stories written for adults; a child, I suppose, would find them dull. In none of his tales is his curious understanding of human moods and emotions better shown.

A stupid critic once pointed out that Crane, in his search for striking effects, had been led into "frequent neglect of the time-hallowed rights of certain words," and that in his pursuit of color he "falls occasionally into almost ludicrous mishap." The smug pedantry of the quoted lines is sufficient answer to the charges, but in support of these assertions the critic quoted certain passages and phrases. He objected to cheeks "scarred" by tears, to "dauntless" statues, and to "terror-stricken" wagons. The very touches of poetic impressionism that largely make for Crane's greatness, are cited to prove him an ignoramus. There is the finest of poetic imagery in the suggestions subtly conveyed by Crane's tricky adjectives, the use of which was as deliberate with him as his choice of a subject. But Crane was an imagist before our modern imagists were known.

This unconventional use of adjectives is marked in the Whilomville tales. In one of them Crane refers to the "solemn odor of burning turnips." It is the most nearly perfect characterization of burning turnips conceivable: can anyone improve upon that "solemn odor"?

Stephen Crane's first venture was "Maggie: A Girl of the Streets." It was, I believe, the first hint of naturalism in American letters. It was not a best-seller; it offers no solution of life; it is an episodic bit of slum fiction, ending with the tragic finality of a Greek drama. It is a skeleton of a novel rather than a novel, but it is a powerful outline, written about a life Crane had learned to know as a newspaper reporter in

New York. It is a singularly fine piece of analysis, or a bit of extraordinarily faithful reporting, as one may prefer; but not a few French and Russian writers have failed to accomplish in two volumes what Crane achieved in two hundred pages. In the same category is "George's Mother," a triumph of inconsequential detail piling up with a cumulative effect quite overwhelming.

Crane published two volumes of poetry—*The Black Riders* and *War is Kind*. Their appearance in print was jeeringly hailed; yet Crane was only pioneering in the free verse that is today, if not definitely accepted, at least more than tolerated. I like the following love poem as well as any rhymed and conventionally metrical ballad that I know:—

> *"Should the wide world roll away,*
> *Leaving black terror,*
> *Limitless night,*
> *Nor God, nor man, nor place to stand*
> *Would be to me essential,*
> *If thou and thy white arms were there*
> *And the fall to doom a long way."*

"If war be kind," wrote a clever reviewer, when the second volume appeared, "then Crane's verse may be poetry, Beardsley's black and white creations may be art, and this may be called a book";—a smart summing up that is cherished by cataloguers to this day, in describing the volume for collectors. Beardsley needs no defenders, and it is fairly certain that the clever reviewer had not read the book, for certainly Crane had no illusions about the kindness of war. The title-poem of the volume is an amazingly beautiful satire which answers all criticism.

> *"Do not weep, maiden, for war is kind.*
> *Because your lover threw wild hands toward the sky*
> *And the affrighted steed ran on alone,*
> *Do not weep.*
> *War is kind.*

> *"Hoarse, booming drums of the regiment,*
> *Little souls who thirst for fight,*
> *These men were born to drill and die.*
> *The unexplained glory flies above them,*
> *Great is the battle-god, and his kingdom—*
> *A field where a thousand corpses lie.*

* * * *

> *"Mother whose heart hung humble as a button*
> *On the bright splendid shroud of your son,*
> *Do not weep.*
> *War is kind."*

Poor Stephen Crane! Like most geniuses, he had his weaknesses and his failings; like many, if not most, geniuses, he was ill. He died of tuberculosis, tragically young. But what a comrade he must have been, with his extraordinary vision, his keen, sardonic comment, his fearlessness and his failings!

Just a glimpse of Crane's last days is afforded by a letter written from England by Robert Barr, his friend—Robert Barr, who collaborated with Crane in "The O' Ruddy," a rollicking tale of old Ireland, or, rather, who completed it at Crane's death, to satisfy his friend's earnest request. The letter is dated from Hillhead, Woldingham, Surrey, June 8, 1900, and runs as follows:—

"My Dear—

"I was delighted to hear from you, and was much interested to see the article on Stephen Crane you sent me. It seems to me the harsh judgment of an unappreciative, commonplace person on a man of genius. Stephen had many qualities which lent themselves to misapprehension, but at the core he was the finest of men, generous to a fault, with something of the old-time recklessness which used to gather in the ancient literary taverns of London. I always fancied that Edgar Allan Poe revisited the earth as Stephen Crane, trying again, succeeding again, failing again, and dying ten years sooner than he did on the other occasion of his stay on earth.

"When your letter came I had just returned from Dover, where I stayed four days to see Crane off for the Black Forest. There was a thin thread of hope that he might recover, but to me he looked like a man already dead. When he spoke, or, rather, whispered, there was all the accustomed humor in his sayings. I said to him that I would go over to the Schwarzwald in a few weeks, when he was getting better, and that we would take some convalescent rambles together. As his wife was listening he said faintly: 'I'll look forward to that,' but he smiled at me, and winked slowly, as much as to say: 'You damned humbug, you know I'll take no more rambles in this world.' Then, as if the train of thought suggested what was looked on before as the crisis of his illness, he murmured: 'Robert, when you come to the hedge—that we must all go over—it isn't bad. You feel sleepy—and—you don't care. Just a little dreamy curiosity—which world you're really in—that's all.'

"Tomorrow, Saturday, the 9th, I go again to Dover to meet his body. He will rest for a little while in England, a country that was always good to him, then to America, and his journey will be ended.

"I've got the unfinished manuscript of his last novel here beside me, a rollicking Irish tale, different from anything he ever wrote before. Stephen thought I was the only person who could finish it, and he was too ill for me to refuse. I don't know what to do about the matter, for I never could work up another man's ideas. Even your vivid imagination could hardly conjecture anything more ghastly than the dying man, lying by an open window overlooking the English channel, relating in a sepulchral whisper the comic situations of his humorous hero so that I might take up the thread of his story.

"From the window beside which I write this I can see down in the valley Ravensbrook House, where Crane used to live and where Harold Frederic, he and I spent many a merry night together. When the Romans occupied Britain, some of their legions, parched with thirst, were wandering about these dry hills with the chance of finding water or perishing. They watched the ravens, and so came to the stream which rises under my place and flows past Stephen's former home; hence the name, Ravensbrook.

"It seems a strange coincidence that the greatest modern writer on war should set himself down where the greatest ancient warrior, Caesar, probably stopped to quench his thirst.

"Stephen died at three in the morning, the same sinister hour which carried away our friend Frederic nineteen months before. At midnight, in Crane's fourteenth-century house in Sussex, we two tried to lure back the ghost of Frederic into that house of ghosts, and to our company, thinking that if reappearing were ever possible so strenuous a man as Harold would somehow shoulder his way past the guards, but he made no sign. I wonder if the less insistent Stephen will suggest some ingenious method by which the two can pass the barrier. I can imagine Harold cursing on the other side, and welcoming the more subtle assistance of his finely fibred friend.

"I feel like the last of the Three Musketeers, the other two gone down in their duel with Death. I am wondering if, within the next two years, I also shall get the challenge. If so, I shall go to the competing ground the more cheerfully that two such good fellows await the outcome on the other side.

"Ever your friend,
"ROBERT BARR."

The last of the Three Musketeers is gone, now, although he outlived his friends by some years. Robert Barr died in 1912. Perhaps they are still debating a joint return.

There could be, perhaps, no better close for a paper on Stephen Crane than the subjoined paragraph from a letter written by him to a Rochester editor:—

"The one thing that deeply pleases me is the fact that men of sense invariably believe me to be sincere. I know that my work does not amount to a string of dried beans—I always calmly admit it—but I also know that I do the best that is in me without regard to praise or blame. When I was the mark for every humorist in the country, I went ahead; and now when I am the mark for only fifty per cent of the humorists of the country, I go ahead; for I understand that a man is born into the world with his own pair of eyes, and he is not at all responsible for his vision—he is merely responsible for his quality of personal honesty. To keep close to this personal honesty is my supreme ambition."

# THE RED BADGE OF COURAGE

## *An Episode of the American Civil War*

### CHAPTER I.

The cold passed reluctantly from the earth, and the retiring fogs revealed an army stretched out on the hills, resting. As the landscape changed from brown to green, the army awakened, and began to tremble with eagerness at the noise of rumors. It cast its eyes upon the roads, which were growing from long troughs of liquid mud to proper thoroughfares. A river, amber-tinted in the shadow of its banks, purled at the army's feet; and at night, when the stream had become of a sorrowful blackness, one could see across it the red, eyelike gleam of hostile camp-fires set in the low brows of distant hills.

Once a certain tall soldier developed virtues and went resolutely to wash a shirt. He came flying back from a brook waving his garment bannerlike. He was swelled with a tale he had heard from a reliable friend, who had heard it from a truthful cavalryman, who had heard it from his trustworthy brother, one of the orderlies at division headquarters. He adopted the important air of a herald in red and gold.

"We're goin' t' move t'morrah—sure," he said pompously to a group in the company street. "We're goin' 'way up the river, cut across, an' come around in behint 'em."

To his attentive audience he drew a loud and elaborate plan of a very brilliant campaign. When he had finished, the blue-clothed men scattered into small arguing groups between the rows of squat brown huts. A negro teamster who had been dancing upon a cracker box with the hilarious encouragement of twoscore soldiers was deserted. He sat mournfully down. Smoke drifted lazily from a multitude of quaint chimneys.

"It's a lie! that's all it is—a thunderin' lie!" said another private loudly. His smooth face was flushed, and his hands were thrust sulkily into his trousers' pockets. He took the matter as an affront to him. "I don't believe the derned old army's ever going to move. We're set. I've got ready to move eight times in the last two weeks, and we ain't moved yet."

The tall soldier felt called upon to defend the truth of a rumor he himself had introduced. He and the loud one came near to fighting over it.

A corporal began to swear before the assemblage. He had just put a costly board floor in his house, he said. During the early spring he had refrained from adding extensively to the comfort of his environment because he had felt that the army might start on the march at any moment. Of late, however, he had been impressed that they were in a sort of eternal camp.

Many of the men engaged in a spirited debate. One outlined in a peculiarly lucid manner all the plans of the commanding general. He was opposed by men who advocated that there were other plans of campaign. They clamored at each other, numbers making futile bids for the popular attention. Meanwhile, the soldier who had fetched the rumor bustled about with much importance. He was continually assailed by questions.

"What's up, Jim?"

"Th' army's goin' t' move."

"Ah, what yeh talkin' about? How yeh know it is?"

"Well, yeh kin b'lieve me er not, jest as yeh like. I don't care a hang."

There was much food for thought in the manner in which he replied. He came near to convincing them by disdaining to produce proofs. They grew excited over it.

There was a youthful private who listened with eager ears to the words of the tall soldier and to the varied comments of his comrades. After receiving a fill of discussions concerning marches and attacks, he went to his hut and crawled through an intricate hole that served it as a door. He wished to be alone with some new thoughts that had lately come to him.

He lay down on a wide bank that stretched across the end of the room. In the other end, cracker boxes were made to serve as furniture. They were grouped about the fireplace. A picture from an illustrated weekly was upon the log walls, and three rifles were paralleled on pegs. Equipments hunt on handy projections, and some tin dishes lay upon a small pile of firewood. A folded tent was serving as a roof. The sunlight, without, beating upon it, made it glow a light yellow shade. A small window shot an oblique square of whiter light upon the cluttered floor. The smoke from the fire at times neglected the clay chimney and wreathed into the room, and this flimsy chimney of clay and sticks made endless threats to set ablaze the whole establishment.

The youth was in a little trance of astonishment. So they were at last going to fight. On the morrow, perhaps, there would be a battle, and he would be in it. For a time he was obliged to labor to make himself believe. He could not accept with assurance an omen that he was about to mingle in one of those great affairs of the earth.

He had, of course, dreamed of battles all his life—of vague and bloody conflicts that had thrilled him with their sweep and fire. In visions he had seen himself in many struggles. He had imagined peoples secure in the shadow of his eagle-eyed prowess. But awake he had regarded battles as crimson blotches on the pages of the past. He had put them as things of the bygone with his thought-images of heavy crowns and high castles. There was a portion of the world's history which he had regarded as the time of wars, but it, he thought, had been long gone over the horizon and had disappeared forever.

From his home his youthful eyes had looked upon the war in his own country with distrust. It must be some sort of a play affair. He had long despaired of witnessing a Greeklike struggle. Such would be no more, he had said. Men were better, or more timid. Secular and religious education had effaced the throat-grappling instinct, or else firm finance held in check the passions.

He had burned several times to enlist. Tales of great movements shook the land. They might not be distinctly Homeric, but there seemed to be much glory in them. He had read of marches, sieges, conflicts, and he had longed to see it all. His busy mind had drawn for him large pictures extravagant in color, lurid with breathless deeds.

But his mother had discouraged him. She had affected to look with some contempt upon the quality of his war ardor and patriotism. She could calmly seat herself and with no apparent difficulty give him many hundreds of reasons why he was of vastly more importance on the farm than on the field of battle. She had had certain ways of expression that told him that her statements on the subject came from a deep conviction. Moreover, on her side, was his belief that her ethical motive in the argument was impregnable.

At last, however, he had made firm rebellion against this yellow light thrown upon the color of his ambitions. The newspapers, the gossip of the village, his own picturings had aroused him to an uncheckable degree. They were in truth fighting finely down there. Almost every day the newspapers printed accounts of a decisive victory.

One night, as he lay in bed, the winds had carried to him the clangoring of the church bell as some enthusiast jerked the rope frantically to tell the twisted news of a great battle. This voice of the people rejoicing in the night had made him shiver in a prolonged ecstasy of excitement. Later, he had gone down to his mother's room and had spoken thus: "Ma, I'm going to enlist."

"Henry, don't you be a fool," his mother had replied. She had then covered her face with the quilt. There was an end to the matter for that night.

Nevertheless, the next morning he had gone to a town that was near his mother's farm and had enlisted in a company that was forming there. When he had returned home his mother was milking the brindle cow. Four others stood waiting. "Ma, I've enlisted," he had said to her diffidently. There was a short silence. "The Lord's will be done, Henry," she had finally replied, and had then continued to milk the brindle cow.

When he had stood in the doorway with his soldier's clothes on his back, and with the light of excitement and expectancy in his eyes almost defeating the glow of regret for the home bonds, he had seen two tears leaving their trails on his mother's scarred cheeks.

Still, she had disappointed him by saying nothing whatever about returning with his shield or on it. He had privately primed himself for a beautiful scene. He had prepared certain sentences which he thought could be used with touching effect. But her words destroyed his plans. She had doggedly peeled potatoes and addressed him as follows: "You watch out, Henry, an' take good care of yerself in this here fighting business—you watch out, an' take good care of yerself. Don't go a-thinkin' you can lick the hull rebel army at the start, because yeh can't. Yer jest one little feller amongst a hull lot of others, and yeh've got to keep quiet an' do what they tell yeh. I know how you are, Henry.

"I've knet yeh eight pair of socks, Henry, and I've put in all yer best shirts, because I want my boy to be jest as warm and comf'able as anybody in the army. Whenever they get holes in 'em, I want yeh to send 'em right-away back to me, so's I kin dern 'em.

"An' allus be careful an' choose yer comp'ny. There's lots of bad men in the army, Henry. The army makes 'em wild, and they like nothing better than the job of leading off a young feller like you, as ain't never been away from home much and has allus had a mother, an' a-learning 'em to drink and swear. Keep clear of them folks, Henry. I don't want yeh to ever do anything, Henry, that yeh would be 'shamed to let me know about. Jest think as if I was a-watchin' yeh. If yeh keep that in yer mind allus, I guess yeh'll come out about right.

"Yeh must allus remember yer father, too, child, an' remember he never drunk a drop of licker in his life, and seldom swore a cross oath.

"I don't know what else to tell yeh, Henry, excepting that yeh must never do no shirking, child, on my account. If so be a time comes when yeh have to be kilt or do a mean thing, why, Henry, don't think of anything 'cept what's right, because there's many a woman has to bear up 'ginst sech things these times, and the Lord'll take keer of us all.

"Don't forgit about the socks and the shirts, child; and I've put a cup of blackberry jam with yer bundle, because I know yeh like it above all things. Good-by, Henry. Watch out, and be a good boy."

He had, of course, been impatient under the ordeal of this speech. It had not been quite what he expected, and he had borne it with an air of irritation. He departed feeling vague relief.

Still, when he had looked back from the gate, he had seen his mother kneeling among the potato parings. Her brown face, upraised, was stained with tears, and her spare form was quivering. He bowed his head and went on, feeling suddenly ashamed of his purposes.

From his home he had gone to the seminary to bid adieu to many schoolmates. They had thronged about him with wonder and admiration. He had felt the gulf now between them and had swelled with calm pride. He and some of his fellows who had donned blue were quite overwhelmed with privileges for all of one afternoon, and it had been a very delicious thing. They had strutted.

A certain light-haired girl had made vivacious fun at his martial spirit, but there was another and darker girl whom he had gazed at steadfastly, and he thought she grew demure and sad at sight of his blue and brass. As he had walked down the path between the rows of oaks, he had turned his head and detected her at a window watching his departure. As he perceived her, she had immediately begun to stare up through the high tree branches at the sky. He had seen a good deal of flurry and haste in her movement as she changed her attitude. He often thought of it.

On the way to Washington his spirit had soared. The regiment was fed and caressed at station after station until the youth had believed that he must be a hero. There was a lavish expenditure of bread and cold meats, coffee, and pickles and cheese. As he basked in the smiles of the girls and was patted and complimented by the old men, he had felt growing within him the strength to do mighty deeds of arms.

After complicated journeyings with many pauses, there had come months of monotonous life in a camp. He had had the belief that real war was a series of death struggles with small time in between for sleep and meals; but since his regiment had come to the field the army had done little but sit still and try to keep warm.

He was brought then gradually back to his old ideas. Greeklike struggles would be no more. Men were better, or more timid. Secular and religious education had effaced the throat-grappling instinct, or else firm finance held in check the passions.

He had grown to regard himself merely as a part of a vast blue demonstration. His province was to look out, as far as he could, for his personal comfort. For recreation he could twiddle his thumbs and speculate on the thoughts which must agitate the minds of the generals. Also, he was drilled and drilled and reviewed, and drilled and drilled and reviewed.

The only foes he had seen were some pickets along the river bank. They were a sun-tanned, philosophical lot, who sometimes shot reflectively at the blue pickets. When reproached for this afterward, they usually expressed sorrow, and swore by their gods that the guns had exploded without their permission. The youth, on guard duty one night, conversed across the stream with one of them. He was a slightly ragged man, who spat skillfully between his shoes and possessed a great fund of bland and infantile assurance. The youth liked him personally.

"Yank," the other had informed him, "yer a right dum good feller." This sentiment, floating to him upon the still air, had made him temporarily regret war.

Various veterans had told him tales. Some talked of gray, bewhiskered hordes who were advancing with relentless curses and chewing tobacco with unspeakable valor; tremendous bodies of fierce soldiery who were sweeping along like the Huns. Others spoke of tattered and eternally hungry men who fired despondent powders. "They'll charge through hell's fire an' brimstone t' git a holt on a haversack, an' sech stomachs ain't a-lastin' long," he was told. From the stories, the youth imagined the red, live bones sticking out through slits in the faded uniforms.

Still, he could not put a whole faith in veterans' tales, for recruits were their prey. They talked much of smoke, fire, and blood, but he could not tell how much might be lies. They persistently yelled "Fresh fish!" at him, and were in no wise to be trusted.

However, he perceived now that it did not greatly matter what kind of soldiers he was going to fight, so long as they fought, which fact no one disputed. There was a more serious problem. He lay in his bunk pondering upon it. He tried to mathematically prove to himself that he would not run from a battle.

Previously he had never felt obliged to wrestle too seriously with this question. In his life he had taken certain things for granted, never challenging his belief in ultimate success, and bothering little about means and roads. But here he was confronted with a thing of moment. It had suddenly appeared to him that perhaps in a battle he might run. He was forced to admit that as far as war was concerned he knew nothing of himself.

A sufficient time before he would have allowed the problem to kick its heels at the outer portals of his mind, but now he felt compelled to give serious attention to it.

A little panic-fear grew in his mind. As his imagination went forward to a fight, he saw hideous possibilities. He contemplated the lurking menaces of the future, and failed in an effort to see himself standing stoutly in the midst of them. He recalled his visions of broken-bladed glory, but in the shadow of the impending tumult he suspected them to be impossible pictures.

He sprang from the bunk and began to pace nervously to and fro. "Good Lord, what's th' matter with me?" he said aloud.

He felt that in this crisis his laws of life were useless. Whatever he had learned of himself was here of no avail. He was an unknown quantity. He saw that he would again be obliged to experiment as he had in early youth. He must accumulate information of himself, and meanwhile he resolved to remain close upon his guard lest those qualities of which he knew nothing should everlastingly disgrace him. "Good Lord!" he repeated in dismay.

After a time the tall soldier slid dexterously through the hole. The loud private followed. They were wrangling.

"That's all right," said the tall soldier as he entered. He waved his hand expressively. "You can believe me or not, jest as you like. All you got to do is to sit down and wait as quiet as you can. Then pretty soon you'll find out I was right."

His comrade grunted stubbornly. For a moment he seemed to be searching for a formidable reply. Finally he said: "Well, you don't know everything in the world, do you?"

"Didn't say I knew everything in the world," retorted the other sharply. He began to stow various articles snugly into his knapsack.

The youth, pausing in his nervous walk, looked down at the busy figure. "Going to be a battle, sure, is there, Jim?" he asked.

"Of course there is," replied the tall soldier. "Of course there is. You jest wait 'til tomorrow, and you'll see one of the biggest battles ever was. You jest wait."

"Thunder!" said the youth.

"Oh, you'll see fighting this time, my boy, what'll be regular out-and-out fighting," added the tall soldier, with the air of a man who is about to exhibit a battle for the benefit of his friends.

"Huh!" said the loud one from a corner.

"Well," remarked the youth, "like as not this story'll turn out jest like them others did."

"Not much it won't," replied the tall soldier, exasperated. "Not much it won't. Didn't the cavalry all start this morning?" He glared about him. No one denied his statement. "The cavalry started this morning," he continued. "They say there ain't hardly any cavalry left in camp. They're going to Richmond, or some place, while we fight all the Johnnies. It's some dodge like that. The regiment's got orders, too. A feller what seen 'em go to headquarters told me a little while ago. And they're raising blazes all over camp—anybody can see that."

"Shucks!" said the loud one.

The youth remained silent for a time. At last he spoke to the tall soldier. "Jim!"

"What?"

"How do you think the reg'ment'll do?"

"Oh, they'll fight all right, I guess, after they once get into it," said the other with cold judgment. He made a fine use of the third person. "There's been heaps of fun poked at 'em because they're new, of course, and all that; but they'll fight all right, I guess."

"Think any of the boys'll run?" persisted the youth.

"Oh, there may be a few of 'em run, but there's them kind in every regiment, 'specially when they first goes under fire," said the other in a tolerant way. "Of course it might happen that the hull kit-and-boodle might start and run, if some big fighting came first-off, and then again they might stay and fight like fun. But you can't bet on nothing. Of course they ain't never been under fire yet, and it ain't likely they'll lick the hull rebel army all-to-oncet the first time; but I think they'll fight better than some, if worse than others. That's the way I figger. They call the reg'ment 'Fresh fish' and everything; but the boys come of good stock, and most of 'em'll fight like sin after they oncet git shootin'," he added, with a mighty emphasis on the last four words.

"Oh, you think you know—" began the loud soldier with scorn.

The other turned savagely upon him. They had a rapid altercation, in which they fastened upon each other various strange epithets.

The youth at last interrupted them. "Did you ever think you might run yourself, Jim?" he asked. On concluding the sentence he laughed as if he had meant to aim a joke. The loud soldier also giggled.

The tall private waved his hand. "Well," said he profoundly, "I've thought it might get too hot for Jim Conklin in some of them scrimmages, and if a whole lot of boys started and run, why, I s'pose I'd start and run. And if I once started to run, I'd run like the devil, and no mistake. But if everybody was a-standing and a-fighting, why, I'd stand and fight. Be jiminey, I would. I'll bet on it."

"Huh!" said the loud one.

The youth of this tale felt gratitude for these words of his comrade. He had feared that all of the untried men possessed a great and correct confidence. He now was in a measure reassured.

# CHAPTER II.

The next morning the youth discovered that his tall comrade had been the fast-flying messenger of a mistake. There was much scoffing at the latter by those who had yesterday been firm adherents of his views, and there was even a little sneering by men who had never believed the rumor. The tall one fought with a man from Chatfield Corners and beat him severely.

The youth felt, however, that his problem was in no wise lifted from him. There was, on the contrary, an irritating prolongation. The tale had created in him a great concern for himself. Now, with the newborn question in his mind, he was compelled to sink back into his old place as part of a blue demonstration.

For days he made ceaseless calculations, but they were all wondrously unsatisfactory. He found that he could establish nothing. He finally concluded that the only way to prove himself was to go into the blaze, and then figuratively to watch his legs to discover their merits and faults. He reluctantly admitted that he could not sit still and with a mental slate and pencil derive an answer. To gain it, he must have blaze, blood, and danger, even as a chemist requires this, that, and the other. So he fretted for an opportunity.

Meanwhile he continually tried to measure himself by his comrades. The tall soldier, for one, gave him some assurance. This man's serene unconcern dealt him a measure of confidence, for he had known him since childhood, and from his intimate knowledge he did not see how he could be capable of anything that was beyond him, the youth. Still, he thought that his comrade might be mistaken about himself. Or, on the other hand, he might be a man heretofore doomed to peace and obscurity, but, in reality, made to shine in war.

The youth would have liked to have discovered another who suspected himself. A sympathetic comparison of mental notes would have been a joy to him.

He occasionally tried to fathom a comrade with seductive sentences. He looked about to find men in the proper mood. All attempts failed to bring forth any statement which looked in any way like a confession to those doubts which he privately acknowledged in himself. He was afraid to make an open declaration of his concern, because he dreaded to place some unscrupulous confidant upon the high plane of the unconfessed from which elevation he could be derided.

In regard to his companions his mind wavered between two opinions, according to his mood. Sometimes he inclined to believing them all heroes. In fact, he usually admitted in secret the superior development of the higher qualities in others. He could conceive of men going very insignificantly about the world bearing a load of courage unseen, and although he had known many of his comrades through boyhood, he began to fear that his judgment of them had been blind. Then, in other moments, he flouted these theories, and assured himself that his fellows were all privately wondering and quaking.

His emotions made him feel strange in the presence of men who talked excitedly of a prospective battle as of a drama they were about to witness, with nothing but eagerness and curiosity apparent in their faces. It was often that he suspected them to be liars.

He did not pass such thoughts without severe condemnation of himself. He dinned reproaches at times. He was convicted by himself of many shameful crimes against the gods of traditions.

In his great anxiety his heart was continually clamoring at what he considered the intolerable slowness of the generals. They seemed content to perch tranquilly on the river bank, and leave him bowed down by the weight of a great problem. He wanted it settled forthwith. He could not long bear such a load, he said. Sometimes his anger at the commanders reached an acute stage, and he grumbled about the camp like a veteran.

One morning, however, he found himself in the ranks of his prepared regiment. The men were whispering speculations and recounting the old rumors. In the gloom before the break of the day their uniforms glowed a deep purple hue. From across the river the red eyes were still peering. In the eastern sky there was a yellow patch like a rug laid for the feet of the coming sun; and against it, black and patternlike, loomed the gigantic figure of the colonel on a gigantic horse.

From off in the darkness came the trampling of feet. The youth could occasionally see dark shadows that moved like monsters. The regiment stood at rest for what seemed a long time. The youth grew impatient. It was unendurable the way these affairs were managed. He wondered how long they were to be kept waiting.

As he looked all about him and pondered upon the mystic gloom, he began to believe that at any moment the ominous distance might be aflare, and the rolling crashes of an engagement come to his ears. Staring once at the red eyes across the river, he conceived them to be growing larger, as the orbs of a row of dragons advancing. He turned toward the colonel and saw him lift his gigantic arm and calmly stroke his mustache.

At last he heard from along the road at the foot of the hill the clatter of a horse's galloping hoofs. It must be the coming of orders. He bent forward, scarce breathing. The exciting clickety-click, as it grew louder and louder, seemed to be beating upon his soul. Presently a horseman with jangling equipment drew rein before the colonel of the regiment. The two held a short, sharp-worded conversation. The men in the foremost ranks craned their necks.

As the horseman wheeled his animal and galloped away he turned to shout over his shoulder, "Don't forget that box of cigars!" The colonel mumbled in reply. The youth wondered what a box of cigars had to do with war.

A moment later the regiment went swinging off into the darkness. It was now like one of those moving monsters wending with many feet. The air was heavy, and cold with dew. A mass of wet grass, marched upon, rustled like silk.

There was an occasional flash and glimmer of steel from the backs of all these huge crawling reptiles. From the road came creakings and grumblings as some surly guns were dragged away.

The men stumbled along still muttering speculations. There was a subdued debate. Once a man fell down, and as he reached for his rifle a comrade, unseeing, trod upon his hand. He of the injured fingers swore bitterly and aloud. A low, tittering laugh went among his fellows.

Presently they passed into a roadway and marched forward with easy strides. A dark regiment moved before them, and from behind also came the tinkle of equipments on the bodies of marching men.

The rushing yellow of the developing day went on behind their backs. When the sunrays at last struck full and mellowingly upon the earth, the youth saw that the landscape was streaked with two long, thin, black columns which disappeared on the brow of a hill in front and rearward vanished in a wood. They were like two serpents crawling from the cavern of the night.

The river was not in view. The tall soldier burst into praises of what he thought to be his powers of perception.

Some of the tall one's companions cried with emphasis that they, too, had evolved the same thing, and they congratulated themselves upon it. But there were others who said that the tall one's plan was not the true one at all. They persisted with other theories. There was a vigorous discussion.

The youth took no part in them. As he walked along in careless line he was engaged with his own eternal debate. He could not hinder himself from dwelling upon it. He was despondent and sullen, and threw shifting glances about him. He looked ahead, often expecting to hear from the advance the rattle of firing.

But the long serpents crawled slowly from hill to hill without bluster of smoke. A dun-colored cloud of dust floated away to the right. The sky overhead was of a fairy blue.

The youth studied the faces of his companions, ever on the watch to detect kindred emotions. He suffered disappointment. Some ardor of the air which was causing the veteran commands to move with glee—almost with song—had infected the new regiment. The men began to speak of victory as of a thing they knew. Also, the tall soldier received his vindication. They were certainly going to come around in behind the enemy. They expressed commiseration for that part of the army which had been left upon the river bank, felicitating themselves upon being a part of a blasting host.

The youth, considering himself as separated from the others, was saddened by the blithe and merry speeches that went from rank to rank. The company wags all made their best endeavors. The regiment tramped to the tune of laughter.

The blatant soldier often convulsed whole files by his biting sarcasms aimed at the tall one.

And it was not long before all the men seemed to forget their mission. Whole brigades grinned in unison, and regiments laughed.

A rather fat soldier attempted to pilfer a horse from a dooryard. He planned to load his knap-sack upon it. He was escaping with his prize when a young girl rushed from the house and grabbed the animal's mane. There followed a wrangle. The young girl, with pink cheeks and shining eyes, stood like a dauntless statue.

The observant regiment, standing at rest in the roadway, whooped at once, and entered whole-souled upon the side of the maiden. The men became so engrossed in this affair that they entirely ceased to remember their own large war. They jeered the piratical private, and called attention to various defects in his personal appearance; and they were wildly enthusiastic in support of the young girl.

To her, from some distance, came bold advice. "Hit him with a stick."

There were crows and catcalls showered upon him when he retreated without the horse. The regiment rejoiced at his downfall. Loud and vociferous congratulations were showered upon the maiden, who stood panting and regarding the troops with defiance.

At nightfall the column broke into regimental pieces, and the fragments went into the fields to camp. Tents sprang up like strange plants. Camp fires, like red, peculiar blossoms, dotted the night.

The youth kept from intercourse with his companions as much as circumstances would allow him. In the evening he wandered a few paces into the gloom. From this little distance the many fires, with the black forms of men passing to and fro before the crimson rays, made weird and satanic effects.

He lay down in the grass. The blades pressed tenderly against his cheek. The moon had been lighted and was hung in a treetop. The liquid stillness of the night enveloping him made him feel vast pity for himself. There was a caress in the soft winds; and the whole mood of the darkness, he thought, was one of sympathy for himself in his distress.

He wished, without reserve, that he was at home again making the endless rounds from the house to the barn, from the barn to the fields, from the fields to the barn, from the barn to the house. He remembered he had often cursed the brindle cow and her mates, and had sometimes flung milking stools. But, from his present point of view, there was a halo of happiness about each of their heads, and he would have sacrificed all the brass buttons on the continent to have been enabled to return to them. He told himself that he was not formed for a soldier. And he mused seriously upon the radical differences between himself and those men who were dodging imp-like around the fires.

As he mused thus he heard the rustle of grass, and, upon turning his head, discovered the loud soldier. He called out, "Oh, Wilson!"

The latter approached and looked down. "Why, hello, Henry; is it you? What you doing here?"

"Oh, thinking," said the youth.

The other sat down and carefully lighted his pipe. "You're getting blue, my boy. You're looking thundering peeked. What the dickens is wrong with you?"

"Oh, nothing," said the youth.

The loud soldier launched then into the subject of the anticipated fight. "Oh, we've got 'em now!" As he spoke his boyish face was wreathed in a gleeful smile, and his voice had an exultant ring. "We've got 'em now. At last, by the eternal thunders, we'll lick 'em good!"

"If the truth was known," he added, more soberly, "*They've* licked *us* about every clip up to now; but this time—this time—we'll lick 'em good!"

"I thought you was objecting to this march a little while ago," said the youth coldly.

"Oh, it wasn't that," explained the other. "I don't mind marching, if there's going to be fighting at the end of it. What I hate is this getting moved here and moved there, with no good coming of it, as far as I can see, excepting sore feet and damned short rations."

"Well, Jim Conklin says we'll get a plenty of fighting this time."

"He's right for once, I guess, though I can't see how it come. This time we're in for a big battle, and we've got the best end of it, certain sure. Gee rod! how we will thump 'em!"

He arose and began to pace to and fro excitedly. The thrill of his enthusiasm made him walk with an elastic step. He was sprightly, vigorous, fiery in his belief in success. He looked into the future with clear, proud eye, and he swore with the air of an old soldier.

The youth watched him for a moment in silence. When he finally spoke his voice was as bitter as dregs. "Oh, you're going to do great things, I s'pose!"

The loud soldier blew a thoughtful cloud of smoke from his pipe. "Oh, I don't know," he remarked with dignity; "I don't know. I s'pose I'll do as well as the rest. I'm going to try like thunder." He evidently complimented himself upon the modesty of this statement.

"How do you know you won't run when the time comes?" asked the youth.

"Run?" said the loud one; "run?—of course not!" He laughed.

"Well," continued the youth, "lots of good-a-'nough men have thought they was going to do great things before the fight, but when the time come they skedaddled."

"Oh, that's all true, I s'pose," replied the other; "but I'm not going to skedaddle. The man that bets on my running will lose his money, that's all." He nodded confidently.

"Oh, shucks!" said the youth. "You ain't the bravest man in the world, are you?"

"No, I ain't," exclaimed the loud soldier indignantly; "and I didn't say I was the bravest man in the world, neither. I said I was going to do my share of fighting—that's what I said. And I am, too. Who are you, anyhow. You talk as if you thought you was Napoleon Bonaparte." He glared at the youth for a moment, and then strode away.

The youth called in a savage voice after his comrade: "Well, you needn't git mad about it!" But the other continued on his way and made no reply.

He felt alone in space when his injured comrade had disappeared. His failure to discover any mite of resemblance in their view points made him more miserable than before. No one seemed to be wrestling with such a terrific personal problem. He was a mental outcast.

He went slowly to his tent and stretched himself on a blanket by the side of the snoring tall soldier. In the darkness he saw visions of a thousand-tongued fear that would babble at his back and cause him to flee, while others were going coolly about their country's business. He admitted that he would not be able to cope with this monster. He felt that every nerve in his body would be an ear to hear the voices, while other men would remain stolid and deaf.

And as he sweated with the pain of these thoughts, he could hear low, serene sentences. "I'll bid five." "Make it six." "Seven." "Seven goes."

He stared at the red, shivering reflection of a fire on the white wall of his tent until, exhausted and ill from the monotony of his suffering, he fell asleep.

## CHAPTER III.

When another night came the columns, changed to purple streaks, filed across two pontoon bridges. A glaring fire wine-tinted the waters of the river. Its rays, shining upon the moving masses of troops, brought forth here and there sudden gleams of silver or gold. Upon the other shore a dark and mysterious range of hills was curved against the sky. The insect voices of the night sang solemnly.

After this crossing the youth assured himself that at any moment they might be suddenly and fearfully assaulted from the caves of the lowering woods. He kept his eyes watchfully upon the darkness.

But his regiment went unmolested to a camping place, and its soldiers slept the brave sleep of wearied men. In the morning they were routed out with early energy, and hustled along a narrow road that led deep into the forest.

It was during this rapid march that the regiment lost many of the marks of a new command.

The men had begun to count the miles upon their fingers, and they grew tired. "Sore feet an' damned short rations, that's all," said the loud soldier. There was perspiration and grumblings. After a time they began to shed their knapsacks. Some tossed them unconcernedly down; others hid them carefully, asserting their plans to return for them at some convenient time. Men extricated themselves from thick shirts. Presently few carried anything but their necessary clothing, blankets, haversacks, canteens, and arms and ammunition. "You can now eat and shoot," said the tall soldier to the youth. "That's all you want to do."

There was sudden change from the ponderous infantry of theory to the light and speedy infantry of practice. The regiment, relieved of a burden, received a new impetus. But there was much loss of valuable knapsacks, and, on the whole, very good shirts.

But the regiment was not yet veteranlike in appearance. Veteran regiments in the army were likely to be very small aggregations of men. Once, when the command had first come to the field, some perambulating veterans, noting the length of their column, had accosted them thus: "Hey, fellers, what brigade is that?" And when the men had replied that they formed a regiment and not a brigade, the older soldiers had laughed, and said, "O Gawd!"

Also, there was too great a similarity in the hats. The hats of a regiment should properly represent the history of headgear for a period of years. And, moreover, there were no letters of faded gold speaking from the colors. They were new and beautiful, and the color bearer habitually oiled the pole.

Presently the army again sat down to think. The odor of the peaceful pines was in the men's nostrils. The sound of monotonous axe blows rang through the forest, and the insects, nodding upon their perches, crooned like old women. The youth returned to his theory of a blue demonstration.

One gray dawn, however, he was kicked in the leg by the tall soldier, and then, before he was entirely awake, he found himself running down a wood road in the midst of men who were panting from the first effects of speed. His canteen banged rhythmically upon his thigh, and his haversack bobbed softly. His musket bounced a trifle from his shoulder at each stride and made his cap feel uncertain upon his head.

He could hear the men whisper jerky sentences: "Say—what's all this—about?" "What th' thunder—we—skedaddlin' this way fer?" "Billie—keep off m' feet. Yeh run—like a cow." And the loud soldier's shrill voice could be heard: "What th' devil they in sich a hurry for?"

The youth thought the damp fog of early morning moved from the rush of a great body of troops. From the distance came a sudden spatter of firing.

He was bewildered. As he ran with his comrades he strenuously tried to think, but all he knew was that if he fell down those coming behind would tread upon him. All his faculties seemed to be needed to guide him over and past obstructions. He felt carried along by a mob.

The sun spread disclosing rays, and, one by one, regiments burst into view like armed men just born of the earth. The youth perceived that the time had come. He was about to be measured. For a moment he felt in the face of his great trial like a babe, and the flesh over his heart seemed very thin. He seized time to look about him calculatingly.

But he instantly saw that it would be impossible for him to escape from the regiment. It inclosed him. And there were iron laws of tradition and law on four sides. He was in a moving box.

As he perceived this fact it occurred to him that he had never wished to come to the war. He had not enlisted of his free will. He had been dragged by the merciless government. And now they were taking him out to be slaughtered.

The regiment slid down a bank and wallowed across a little stream. The mournful current moved slowly on, and from the water, shaded black, some white bubble eyes looked at the men.

As they climbed the hill on the farther side artillery began to boom. Here the youth forgot many things as he felt a sudden impulse of curiosity. He scrambled up the bank with a speed that could not be exceeded by a bloodthirsty man.

He expected a battle scene.

There were some little fields girted and squeezed by a forest. Spread over the grass and in among the tree trunks, he could see knots and waving lines of skirmishers who were running hither and thither and firing at the landscape. A dark battle line lay upon a sunstruck clearing that gleamed orange color. A flag fluttered.

Other regiments floundered up the bank. The brigade was formed in line of battle, and after a pause started slowly through the woods in the rear of the receding skirmishers, who were continually melting into the scene to appear again farther on. They were always busy as bees, deeply absorbed in their little combats.

The youth tried to observe everything. He did not use care to avoid trees and branches, and his forgotten feet were constantly knocking against stones or getting entangled in briers. He was aware that these battalions with their commotions were woven red and startling into the gentle fabric of softened greens and browns. It looked to be a wrong place for a battle field.

The skirmishers in advance fascinated him. Their shots into thickets and at distant and prominent trees spoke to him of tragedies—hidden, mysterious, solemn.

Once the line encountered the body of a dead soldier. He lay upon his back staring at the sky. He was dressed in an awkward suit of yellowish brown. The youth could see that the soles of his shoes had been worn to the thinness of writing paper, and from a great rent in one the dead foot projected piteously. And it was as if fate had betrayed the soldier. In death it exposed to his enemies that poverty which in life he had perhaps concealed from his friends.

The ranks opened covertly to avoid the corpse. The invulnerable dead man forced a way for himself. The youth looked keenly at the ashen face. The wind raised the tawny beard. It moved as if a hand were stroking it. He vaguely desired to walk around and around the body and stare; the impulse of the living to try to read in dead eyes the answer to the Question.

During the march the ardor which the youth had acquired when out of view of the field rapidly faded to nothing. His curiosity was quite easily satisfied. If an intense scene had caught him with its wild swing as he came to the top of the bank, he might have gone roaring on. This advance upon Nature was too calm. He had opportunity to reflect. He had time in which to wonder about himself and to attempt to probe his sensations.

Absurd ideas took hold upon him. He thought that he did not relish the landscape. It threatened him. A coldness swept over his back, and it is true that his trousers felt to him that they were no fit for his legs at all.

A house standing placidly in distant fields had to him an ominous look. The shadows of the woods were formidable. He was certain that in this vista there lurked fierce-eyed hosts. The swift thought came to him that the generals did not know what they were about. It was all a trap. Suddenly those close forests would bristle with rifle barrels. Ironlike brigades would appear in the rear. They were all going to be sacrificed. The generals were stupids. The enemy would presently swallow the whole command. He glared about him, expecting to see the stealthy approach of his death.

He thought that he must break from the ranks and harangue his comrades. They must not all be killed like pigs; and he was sure it would come to pass unless they were informed of these dangers. The generals were idiots to send them marching into a regular pen. There was but one pair of eyes in the corps. He would step forth and make a speech. Shrill and passionate words came to his lips.

The line, broken into moving fragments by the ground, went calmly on through fields and woods. The youth looked at the men nearest him, and saw, for the most part, expressions of deep interest, as if they were investigating something that had fascinated them. One or two stepped with overvaliant airs as if they were already plunged into war. Others walked as upon thin ice. The greater part of the untested men appeared quiet and absorbed. They were going to look at war, the red animal— war, the blood-swollen god. And they were deeply engrossed in this march.

As he looked the youth gripped his outcry at his throat. He saw that even if the men were tottering with fear they would laugh at his warning. They would jeer him, and, if practicable, pelt him with missiles. Admitting that he might be wrong, a frenzied declamation of the kind would turn him into a worm.

He assumed, then, the demeanor of one who knows that he is doomed alone to unwritten responsibilities. He lagged, with tragic glances at the sky.

He was surprised presently by the young lieutenant of his company, who began heartily to beat him with a sword, calling out in a loud and insolent voice: "Come, young man, get up into ranks there. No skulking'll do here." He mended his pace with suitable haste. And he hated the lieutenant, who had no appreciation of fine minds. He was a mere brute.

After a time the brigade was halted in the cathedral light of a forest. The busy skirmishers were still popping. Through the aisles of the wood could be seen the floating smoke from their rifles. Sometimes it went up in little balls, white and compact.

During this halt many men in the regiment began erecting tiny hills in front of them. They used stones, sticks, earth, and anything they thought might turn a bullet. Some built comparatively large ones, while others seemed content with little ones.

This procedure caused a discussion among the men. Some wished to fight like duelists, believing it to be correct to stand erect and be, from their feet to their foreheads, a mark. They said they scorned the devices of the cautious. But the others scoffed in reply, and pointed to the veterans on the flanks who were digging at the ground like terriers. In a short time there was quite a barricade along the regimental fronts. Directly, however, they were ordered to withdraw from that place.

This astounded the youth. He forgot his stewing over the advance movement. "Well, then, what did they march us out here for?" he demanded of the tall soldier. The latter with calm faith began a heavy explanation, although he had been compelled to leave a little protection of stones and dirt to which he had devoted much care and skill.

When the regiment was aligned in another position each man's regard for his safety caused another line of small intrenchments. They ate their noon meal behind a third one. They were moved from this one also. They were marched from place to place with apparent aimlessness.

The youth had been taught that a man became another thing in a battle. He saw his salvation in such a change. Hence this waiting was an ordeal to him. He was in a fever of impatience. He considered that there was denoted a lack of purpose on the part of the generals. He began to complain to the tall soldier. "I can't stand this much longer," he cried. "I don't see what good it does to make us wear out our legs for nothin'." He wished to return to camp, knowing that this affair was a blue demonstration; or else to go into a battle and discover that he had been a fool in his doubts, and was, in truth, a man of traditional courage. The strain of present circumstances he felt to be intolerable.

The philosophical tall soldier measured a sandwich of cracker and pork and swallowed it in a nonchalant manner. "Oh, I suppose we must go reconnoitering around the country jest to keep 'em from getting too close, or to develop 'em, or something."

"Huh!" said the loud soldier.

"Well," cried the youth, still fidgeting, "I'd rather do anything 'most than go tramping 'round the country all day doing no good to nobody and jest tiring ourselves out."

"So would I," said the loud soldier. "It ain't right. I tell you if anybody with any sense was a-runnin' this army it—"

"Oh, shut up!" roared the tall private. "You little fool. You little damn' cuss. You ain't had that there coat and them pants on for six months, and yet you talk as if—"

"Well, I wanta do some fighting anyway," interrupted the other. "I didn't come here to walk. I could 'ave walked to home—'round an' 'round the barn, if I jest wanted to walk."

The tall one, red-faced, swallowed another sandwich as if taking poison in despair.

But gradually, as he chewed, his face became again quiet and contented. He could not rage in fierce argument in the presence of such sandwiches. During his meals he always wore an air of blissful contemplation of the food he had swallowed. His spirit seemed then to be communing with the viands.

He accepted new environment and circumstance with great coolness, eating from his haversack at every opportunity. On the march he went along with the stride of a hunter, objecting to neither gait nor distance. And he had not raised his voice when he had been ordered away from three little protective piles of earth and stone, each of which had been an engineering feat worthy of being made sacred to the name of his grandmother.

In the afternoon the regiment went out over the same ground it had taken in the morning. The landscape then ceased to threaten the youth. He had been close to it and become familiar with it.

When, however, they began to pass into a new region, his old fears of stupidity and incompetence reassailed him, but this time he doggedly let them babble. He was occupied with his problem, and in his desperation he concluded that the stupidity did not greatly matter.

Once he thought he had concluded that it would be better to get killed directly and end his troubles. Regarding death thus out of the corner of his eye, he conceived it to be nothing but rest, and he was filled with a momentary astonishment that he should have made an extraordinary commotion over the mere matter of getting killed. He would die; he would go to some place where he would be understood. It was useless to expect appreciation of his profound and fine senses from such men as the lieutenant. He must look to the grave for comprehension.

The skirmish fire increased to a long chattering sound. With it was mingled faraway cheering. A battery spoke.

Directly the youth would see the skirmishers running. They were pursued by the sound of musketry fire. After a time the hot, dangerous flashes of the rifles were visible. Smoke clouds went slowly and insolently across the fields like observant phantoms. The din became crescendo, like the roar of an oncoming train.

A brigade ahead of them and on the right went into action with a rending roar. It was as if it had exploded. And thereafter it lay stretched in the distance behind a long gray wall, that one was obliged to look twice at to make sure that it was smoke.

The youth, forgetting his neat plan of getting killed, gazed spell bound. His eyes grew wide and busy with the action of the scene. His mouth was a little ways open.

Of a sudden he felt a heavy and sad hand laid upon his shoulder. Awakening from his trance of observation he turned and beheld the loud soldier.

"It's my first and last battle, old boy," said the latter, with intense gloom. He was quite pale and his girlish lip was trembling.

"Eh?" murmured the youth in great astonishment.

"It's my first and last battle, old boy," continued the loud soldier. "Something tells me—"

"What?"

"I'm a gone coon this first time and—and I w-want you to take these here things—to—my—folks." He ended in a quavering sob of pity for himself. He handed the youth a little packet done up in a yellow envelope.

"Why, what the devil—" began the youth again.

But the other gave him a glance as from the depths of a tomb, and raised his limp hand in a prophetic manner and turned away.

## CHAPTER IV.

The brigade was halted in the fringe of a grove. The men crouched among the trees and pointed their restless guns out at the fields. They tried to look beyond the smoke.

Out of this haze they could see running men. Some shouted information and gestured as they hurried.

The men of the new regiment watched and listened eagerly, while their tongues ran on in gossip of the battle. They mouthed rumors that had flown like birds out of the unknown.

"They say Perry has been driven in with big loss."

"Yes, Carrott went t' th' hospital. He said he was sick. That smart lieutenant is commanding 'G' Company. Th' boys say they won't be under Carrott no more if they all have t' desert. They allus knew he was a—"

"Hannises' batt'ry is took."

"It ain't either. I saw Hannises' batt'ry off on th' left not more'n fifteen minutes ago."

"Well—"

"Th' general, he ses he is goin' t' take th' hull cammand of th' 304th when we go inteh action, an' then he ses we'll do sech fightin' as never another one reg'ment done."

"They say we're catchin' it over on th' left. They say th' enemy driv' our line inteh a devil of a swamp an' took Hannises' batt'ry."

"No sech thing. Hannises' batt'ry was 'long here 'bout a minute ago."

"That young Hasbrouck, he makes a good off'cer. He ain't afraid 'a nothin'."

"I met one of th' 148th Maine boys an' he ses his brigade fit th' hull rebel army fer four hours over on th' turnpike road an' killed about five thousand of 'em. He ses one more sech fight as that an' th' war'll be over."

"Bill wasn't scared either. No, sir! It wasn't that. Bill ain't a-gittin' scared easy. He was jest mad, that's what he was. When that feller trod on his hand, he up an' sed that he was willin' t' give his hand t' his country, but he be dumbed if he was goin' t' have every dumb bushwhacker in th' kentry walkin' 'round on it. Se he went t' th' hospital disregardless of th' fight. Three fingers was crunched. Th' dern doctor wanted t' amputate 'm, an' Bill, he raised a heluva row, I hear. He's a funny feller."

The din in front swelled to a tremendous chorus. The youth and his fellows were frozen to silence. They could see a flag that tossed in the smoke angrily. Near it were the blurred and agitated forms of troops. There came a turbulent stream of men across the fields. A battery changing position at a frantic gallop scattered the stragglers right and left.

A shell screaming like a storm banshee went over the huddled heads of the reserves. It landed in the grove, and exploding redly flung the brown earth. There was a little shower of pine needles.

Bullets began to whistle among the branches and nip at the trees. Twigs and leaves came sailing down. It was as if a thousand axes, wee and invisible, were being wielded. Many of the men were constantly dodging and ducking their heads.

The lieutenant of the youth's company was shot in the hand. He began to swear so wondrously that a nervous laugh went along the regimental line. The officer's profanity sounded conventional. It relieved the tightened senses of the new men. It was as if he had hit his fingers with a tack hammer at home.

He held the wounded member carefully away from his side so that the blood would not drip upon his trousers.

The captain of the company, tucking his sword under his arm, produced a handkerchief and began to bind with it the lieutenant's wound. And they disputed as to how the binding should be done.

The battle flag in the distance jerked about madly. It seemed to be struggling to free itself from an agony. The billowing smoke was filled with horizontal flashes.

Men running swiftly emerged from it. They grew in numbers until it was seen that the whole command was fleeing. The flag suddenly sank down as if dying. Its motion as it fell was a gesture of despair.

Wild yells came from behind the walls of smoke. A sketch in gray and red dissolved into a moblike body of men who galloped like wild horses.

The veteran regiments on the right and left of the 304th immediately began to jeer. With the passionate song of the bullets and the banshee shrieks of shells were mingled loud catcalls and bits of facetious advice concerning places of safety.

But the new regiment was breathless with horror. "Gawd! Saunders's got crushed!" whispered the man at the youth's elbow. They shrank back and crouched as if compelled to await a flood.

The youth shot a swift glance along the blue ranks of the regiment. The profiles were motionless, carven; and afterward he remembered that the color sergeant was standing with his legs apart, as if he expected to be pushed to the ground.

The following throng went whirling around the flank. Here and there were officers carried along on the stream like exasperated chips. They were striking about them with their swords and with their left fists, punching every head they could reach. They cursed like highwaymen.

A mounted officer displayed the furious anger of a spoiled child. He raged with his head, his arms, and his legs.

Another, the commander of the brigade, was galloping about bawling. His hat was gone and his clothes were awry. He resembled a man who has come from bed to go to a fire. The hoofs of his horse often threatened the heads of the running men, but they scampered with singular fortune. In this rush they were apparently all deaf and blind. They heeded not the largest and longest of the oaths that were thrown at them from all directions.

Frequently over this tumult could be heard the grim jokes of the critical veterans; but the retreating men apparently were not even conscious of the presence of an audience.

The battle reflection that shone for an instant in the faces on the mad current made the youth feel that forceful hands from heaven would not have been able to have held him in place if he could have got intelligent control of his legs.

There was an appalling imprint upon these faces. The struggle in the smoke had pictured an exaggeration of itself on the bleached cheeks and in the eyes wild with one desire.

The sight of this stampede exerted a floodlike force that seemed able to drag sticks and stones and men from the ground. They of the reserves had to hold on. They grew pale and firm, and red and quaking.

The youth achieved one little thought in the midst of this chaos. The composite monster which had caused the other troops to flee had not then appeared. He resolved to get a view of it, and then, he thought he might very likely run better than the best of them.

## CHAPTER V.

There were moments of waiting. The youth thought of the village street at home before the arrival of the circus parade on a day in the spring. He remembered how he had stood, a small, thrillful boy, prepared to follow the dingy lady upon the white horse, or the band in its faded chariot. He saw the yellow road, the lines of expectant people, and the sober houses. He particularly remembered an old fellow who used to sit upon a cracker box in front of the store and feign to despise such exhibitions. A thousand details of color and form surged in his mind. The old fellow upon the cracker box appeared in middle prominence.

Some one cried, "Here they come!"

There was rustling and muttering among the men. They displayed a feverish desire to have every possible cartridge ready to their hands. The boxes were pulled around into various positions, and adjusted with great care. It was as if seven hundred new bonnets were being tried on.

The tall soldier, having prepared his rifle, produced a red handkerchief of some kind. He was engaged in knitting it about his throat with exquisite attention to its position, when the cry was repeated up and down the line in a muffled roar of sound.

"Here they come! Here they come!" Gun locks clicked.

Across the smoke-infested fields came a brown swarm of running men who were giving shrill yells. They came on, stooping and swinging their rifles at all angles. A flag, tilted forward, sped near the front.

As he caught sight of them the youth was momentarily startled by a thought that perhaps his gun was not loaded. He stood trying to rally his faltering intellect so that he might recollect the moment when he had loaded, but he could not.

A hatless general pulled his dripping horse to a stand near the colonel of the 304th. He shook his fist in the other's face. "You've got to hold 'em back!" he shouted, savagely; "you've got to hold 'em back!"

In his agitation the colonel began to stammer. "A-all r-right, General, all right, by Gawd! We—we'll do our—we-we'll d-d-do—do our best, General." The general made a passionate gesture and galloped away. The colonel, perchance to relieve his feelings, began to scold like a wet parrot. The youth, turning swiftly to make sure that the rear was unmolested, saw the commander regarding his men in a highly regretful manner, as if he regretted above everything his association with them.

The man at the youth's elbow was mumbling, as if to himself: "Oh, we're in for it now! oh, we're in for it now!"

The captain of the company had been pacing excitedly to and fro in the rear. He coaxed in schoolmistress fashion, as to a congregation of boys with primers. His talk was an endless repetition. "Reserve your fire, boys—don't shoot till I tell you—save your fire—wait till they get close up—don't be damned fools—"

Perspiration streamed down the youth's face, which was soiled like that of a weeping urchin. He frequently, with a nervous movement, wiped his eyes with his coat sleeve. His mouth was still a little ways open.

He got the one glance at the foe-swarming field in front of him, and instantly ceased to debate the question of his piece being loaded. Before he was ready to begin—before he had announced to himself that he was about to fight—he threw the obedient, well-balanced rifle into position and fired a first wild shot. Directly he was working at his weapon like an automatic affair.

He suddenly lost concern for himself, and forgot to look at a menacing fate. He became not a man but a member. He felt that something of which he was a part—a regiment, an army, a cause, or a country—was in a crisis. He was welded into a common personality which was dominated by a single desire. For some moments he could not flee no more than a little finger can commit a revolution from a hand.

If he had thought the regiment was about to be annihilated perhaps he could have amputated himself from it. But its noise gave him assurance. The regiment was like a firework that, once ignited, proceeds superior to circumstances until its blazing vitality fades. It wheezed and banged with a mighty power. He pictured the ground before it as strewn with the discomfited.

There was a consciousness always of the presence of his comrades about him. He felt the subtle battle brotherhood more potent even than the cause for which they were fighting. It was a mysterious fraternity born of the smoke and danger of death.

He was at a task. He was like a carpenter who has made many boxes, making still another box, only there was furious haste in his movements. He, in his thought, was careering off in other places, even as the carpenter who as he works whistles and thinks of his friend or his enemy, his home or a saloon. And these jolted dreams were never perfect to him afterward, but remained a mass of blurred shapes.

Presently he began to feel the effects of the war atmosphere—a blistering sweat, a sensation that his eyeballs were about to crack like hot stones. A burning roar filled his ears.

Following this came a red rage. He developed the acute exasperation of a pestered animal, a well-meaning cow worried by dogs. He had a mad feeling against his rifle, which could only be used against one life at a time. He wished to rush forward and strangle with his fingers. He craved a power that would enable him to make a world-sweeping gesture and brush all back. His impotency appeared to him, and made his rage into that of a driven beast.

Buried in the smoke of many rifles his anger was directed not so much against the men whom he knew were rushing toward him as against the swirling battle phantoms which were choking him, stuffing their smoke robes down his parched throat. He fought frantically for respite for his senses, for air, as a babe being smothered attacks the deadly blankets.

There was a blare of heated rage mingled with a certain expression of intentness on all faces. Many of the men were making low-toned noises with their mouths, and these subdued cheers, snarls, imprecations, prayers, made a wild, barbaric song that went as an undercurrent of sound, strange and chantlike with the resounding chords of the war march. The man at the youth's elbow was babbling. In it there was something soft and tender like the monologue of a babe. The tall soldier was swearing in a loud voice. From his lips came a black procession of curious oaths. Of a sudden another broke out in a querulous way like a man who has mislaid his hat. "Well, why don't they support us? Why don't they send supports? Do they think—"

The youth in his battle sleep heard this as one who dozes hears.

There was a singular absence of heroic poses. The men bending and surging in their haste and rage were in every impossible attitude. The steel ramrods clanked and clanged with incessant din as the men pounded them furiously into the hot rifle barrels. The flaps of the cartridge boxes were all unfastened, and bobbed idiotically with each movement. The rifles, once loaded, were jerked to the shoulder and fired without apparent aim into the smoke or at one of the blurred and shifting forms which upon the field before the regiment had been growing larger and larger like puppets under a magician's hand.

The officers, at their intervals, rearward, neglected to stand in picturesque attitudes. They were bobbing to and fro roaring directions and encouragements. The dimensions of their howls were extraordinary. They expended their lungs with prodigal wills. And often they nearly stood upon their heads in their anxiety to observe the enemy on the other side of the tumbling smoke.

The lieutenant of the youth's company had encountered a soldier who had fled screaming at the first volley of his comrades. Behind the lines these two were acting a little isolated scene. The man was blubbering and staring with sheeplike eyes at the lieutenant, who had seized him by the collar and was pommeling him. He drove him back into the ranks with many blows. The soldier went mechanically, dully, with his animal-like eyes upon the officer. Perhaps there was to him a divinity expressed in the voice of the other—stern, hard, with no reflection of fear in it. He tried to reload his gun, but his shaking hands prevented. The lieutenant was obliged to assist him.

The men dropped here and there like bundles. The captain of the youth's company had been killed in an early part of the action. His body lay stretched out in the position of a tired man resting, but upon his face there was an astonished and sorrowful look, as if he thought some friend had done him an ill turn. The babbling man was grazed by a shot that made the blood stream widely down his face. He clapped both hands to his head. "Oh!" he said, and ran. Another grunted suddenly as if he had been struck by a club in the stomach. He sat down and gazed ruefully. In his eyes there was mute, indefinite reproach. Farther up the line a man, standing behind a tree, had had his knee joint splintered by a ball. Immediately he had dropped his rifle and gripped the tree with both arms. And there he remained, clinging desperately and crying for assistance that he might withdraw his hold upon the tree.

At last an exultant yell went along the quivering line. The firing dwindled from an uproar to a last vindictive popping. As the smoke slowly eddied away, the youth saw that the charge had been repulsed. The enemy were scattered into reluctant groups. He saw a man climb to the top of the fence, straddle the rail, and fire a parting shot. The waves had receded, leaving bits of dark *débris* upon the ground.

Some in the regiment began to whoop frenziedly. Many were silent. Apparently they were trying to contemplate themselves.

After the fever had left his veins, the youth thought that at last he was going to suffocate. He became aware of the foul atmosphere in which he had been struggling. He was grimy and dripping like a laborer in a foundry. He grasped his canteen and took a long swallow of the warmed water.

A sentence with variations went up and down the line. "Well, we've helt 'em back. We've helt 'em back; derned if we haven't." The men said it blissfully, leering at each other with dirty smiles.

The youth turned to look behind him and off to the right and off to the left. He experienced the joy of a man who at last finds leisure in which to look about him.

Under foot there were a few ghastly forms motionless. They lay twisted in fantastic contortions. Arms were bent and heads were turned in incredible ways. It seemed that the dead men must have fallen from some great height to get into such positions. They looked to be dumped out upon the ground from the sky.

From a position in the rear of the grove a battery was throwing shells over it. The flash of the guns startled the youth at first. He thought they were aimed directly at him. Through the trees he watched the black figures of the gunners as they worked swiftly and intently. Their labor seemed a complicated thing. He wondered how they could remember its formula in the midst of confusion.

The guns squatted in a row like savage chiefs. They argued with abrupt violence. It was a grim pow-wow. Their busy servants ran hither and thither.

A small procession of wounded men were going drearily toward the rear. It was a flow of blood from the torn body of the brigade.

To the right and to the left were the dark lines of other troops. Far in front he thought he could see lighter masses protruding in points from the forest. They were suggestive of unnumbered thousands.

Once he saw a tiny battery go dashing along the line of the horizon. The tiny riders were beating the tiny horses.

From a sloping hill came the sound of cheerings and clashes. Smoke welled slowly through the leaves.

Batteries were speaking with thunderous oratorical effort. Here and there were flags, the red in the stripes dominating. They splashed bits of warm color upon the dark lines of troops.

The youth felt the old thrill at the sight of the emblem. They were like beautiful birds strangely undaunted in a storm.

As he listened to the din from the hillside, to a deep pulsating thunder that came from afar to the left, and to the lesser clamors which came from many directions, it occurred to him that they were fighting, too, over there, and over there, and over there. Heretofore he had supposed that all the battle was directly under his nose.

As he gazed around him the youth felt a flash of astonishment at the blue, pure sky and the sun gleamings on the trees and fields. It was surprising that Nature had gone tranquilly on with her golden process in the midst of so much devilment.

## CHAPTER VI.

The youth awakened slowly. He came gradually back to a position from which he could regard himself. For moments he had been scrutinizing his person in a dazed way as if he had never before seen himself. Then he picked up his cap from the ground. He wriggled in his jacket to make a more comfortable fit, and kneeling relaced his shoe. He thoughtfully mopped his reeking features.

So it was all over at last! The supreme trial had been passed. The red, formidable difficulties of war had been vanquished.

He went into an ecstasy of self-satisfaction. He had the most delightful sensations of his life. Standing as if apart from himself, he viewed that last scene. He perceived that the man who had fought thus was magnificent.

He felt that he was a fine fellow. He saw himself even with those ideals which he had considered as far beyond him. He smiled in deep gratification.

Upon his fellows he beamed tenderness and good will. "Gee! ain't it hot, hey?" he said affably to a man who was polishing his streaming face with his coat sleeves.

"You bet!" said the other, grinning sociably. "I never seen sech dumb hotness."
He sprawled out luxuriously on the ground. "Gee, yes! An' I hope we don't have no
more fightin' till a week from Monday."

There were some handshakings and deep speeches with men whose features
were familiar, but with whom the youth now felt the bonds of tied hearts. He helped
a cursing comrade to bind up a wound of the shin.

But, of a sudden, cries of amazement broke out along the ranks of the new regiment. "Here they come ag'in! Here they come ag'in!" The man who had sprawled
upon the ground started up and said, "Gosh!"

The youth turned quick eyes upon the field. He discerned forms begin to swell in
masses out of a distant wood. He again saw the tilted flag speeding forward.

The shells, which had ceased to trouble the regiment for a time, came swirling
again, and exploded in the grass or among the leaves of the trees. They looked to be
strange war flowers bursting into fierce bloom.

The men groaned. The luster faded from their eyes. Their smudged countenances
now expressed a profound dejection. They moved their stiffened bodies slowly, and
watched in sullen mood the frantic approach of the enemy. The slaves toiling in the
temple of this god began to feel rebellion at his harsh tasks.

They fretted and complained each to each. "Oh, say, this is too much of a good
thing! Why can't somebody send us supports?"

"We ain't never goin' to stand this second banging. I didn't come here to fight
the hull damn' rebel army."

There was one who raised a doleful cry. "I wish Bill Smithers had trod on my
hand, insteader me treddin' on his'n." The sore joints of the regiment creaked as it
painfully floundered into position to repulse.

The youth stared. Surely, he thought, this impossible thing was not about to happen. He waited as if he expected the enemy to suddenly stop, apologize, and retire
bowing. It was all a mistake.

But the firing began somewhere on the regimental line and ripped along in both
directions. The level sheets of flame developed great clouds of smoke that tumbled
and tossed in the mild wind near the ground for a moment, and then rolled through
the ranks as through a gate. The clouds were tinged an earthlike yellow in the sun-
rays and in the shadow were a sorry blue. The flag was sometimes eaten and lost in
this mass of vapor, but more often it projected, sun-touched, resplendent.

Into the youth's eyes there came a look that one can see in the orbs of a jaded
horse. His neck was quivering with nervous weakness and the muscles of his arms
felt numb and bloodless. His hands, too, seemed large and awkward as if he was
wearing invisible mittens. And there was a great uncertainty about his knee joints.

The words that comrades had uttered previous to the firing began to recur to him.
"Oh, say, this is too much of a good thing! What do they take us for—why don't
they send supports? I didn't come here to fight the hull damned rebel army."

He began to exaggerate the endurance, the skill, and the valor of those who were
coming. Himself reeling from exhaustion, he was astonished beyond measure at
such persistency. They must be machines of steel. It was very gloomy struggling
against such affairs, wound up perhaps to fight until sundown.

He slowly lifted his rifle and catching a glimpse of the thickspread field he
blazed at a cantering cluster. He stopped then and began to peer as best he could
through the smoke. He caught changing views of the ground covered with men who
were all running like pursued imps, and yelling.

To the youth it was an onslaught of redoubtable dragons. He became like the man who lost his legs at the approach of the red and green monster. He waited in a sort of a horrified, listening attitude. He seemed to shut his eyes and wait to be gobbled.

A man near him who up to this time had been working feverishly at his rifle suddenly stopped and ran with howls. A lad whose face had borne an expression of exalted courage, the majesty of he who dares give his life, was, at an instant, smitten abject. He blanched like one who has come to the edge of a cliff at midnight and is suddenly made aware. There was a revelation. He, too, threw down his gun and fled. There was no shame in his face. He ran like a rabbit.

Others began to scamper away through the smoke. The youth turned his head, shaken from his trance by this movement as if the regiment was leaving him behind. He saw the few fleeting forms.

He yelled then with fright and swung about. For a moment, in the great clamor, he was like a proverbial chicken. He lost the direction of safety. Destruction threatened him from all points.

Directly he began to speed toward the rear in great leaps. His rifle and cap were gone. His unbuttoned coat bulged in the wind. The flap of his cartridge box bobbed wildly, and his canteen, by its slender cord, swung out behind. On his face was all the horror of those things which he imagined.

The lieutenant sprang forward bawling. The youth saw his features wrathfully red, and saw him make a dab with his sword. His one thought of the incident was that the lieutenant was a peculiar creature to feel interested in such matters upon this occasion.

He ran like a blind man. Two or three times he fell down. Once he knocked his shoulder so heavily against a tree that he went headlong.

Since he had turned his back upon the fight his fears had been wondrously magnified. Death about to thrust him between the shoulder blades was far more dreadful than death about to smite him between the eyes. When he thought of it later, he conceived the impression that it is better to view the appalling than to be merely within hearing. The noises of the battle were like stones; he believed himself liable to be crushed.

As he ran he mingled with others. He dimly saw men on his right and on his left, and he heard footsteps behind him. He thought that all the regiment was fleeing, pursued by these ominous crashes.

In his flight the sound of these following footsteps gave him his one meager relief. He felt vaguely that death must make a first choice of the men who were nearest; the initial morsels for the dragons would be then those who were following him. So he displayed the zeal of an insane sprinter in his purpose to keep them in the rear. There was a race.

As he, leading, went across a little field, he found himself in a region of shells. They hurtled over his head with long wild screams. As he listened he imagined them to have rows of cruel teeth that grinned at him. Once one lit before him and the livid lightning of the explosion effectually barred the way in his chosen direction. He groveled on the ground and then springing up went careering off through some bushes.

He experienced a thrill of amazement when he came within view of a battery in action. The men there seemed to be in conventional moods, altogether unaware of the impending annihilation. The battery was disputing with a distant antagonist and the gunners were wrapped in admiration of their shooting. They were continually bending in coaxing postures over the guns. They seemed to be patting them on the back and encouraging them with words. The guns, stolid and undaunted, spoke with dogged valor.

The precise gunners were coolly enthusiastic. They lifted their eyes every chance to the smoke-wreathed hillock from whence the hostile battery addressed them. The youth pitied them as he ran. Methodical idiots! Machine-like fools! The refined joy of planting shells in the midst of the other battery's formation would appear a little thing when the infantry came swooping out of the woods.

The face of a youthful rider, who was jerking his frantic horse with an abandon of temper he might display in a placid barnyard, was impressed deeply upon his mind. He knew that he looked upon a man who would presently be dead.

Too, he felt a pity for the guns, standing, six good comrades, in a bold row.

He saw a brigade going to the relief of its pestered fellows. He scrambled upon a wee hill and watched it sweeping finely, keeping formation in difficult places. The blue of the line was crusted with steel color, and the brilliant flags projected. Officers were shouting.

This sight also filled him with wonder. The brigade was hurrying briskly to be gulped into the infernal mouths of the war god. What manner of men were they, anyhow? Ah, it was some wondrous breed! Or else they didn't comprehend—the fools.

A furious order caused commotion in the artillery. An officer on a bounding horse made maniacal motions with his arms. The teams went swinging up from the rear, the guns were whirled about, and the battery scampered away. The cannon with their noses poked slantingly at the ground grunted and grumbled like stout men, brave but with objections to hurry.

The youth went on, moderating his pace since he had left the place of noises.

Later he came upon a general of division seated upon a horse that pricked its ears in an interested way at the battle. There was a great gleaming of yellow and patent leather about the saddle and bridle. The quiet man astride looked mouse-colored upon such a splendid charger.

A jingling staff was galloping hither and thither. Sometimes the general was surrounded by horsemen and at other times he was quite alone. He looked to be much harassed. He had the appearance of a business man whose market is swinging up and down.

The youth went slinking around this spot. He went as near as he dared trying to overhear words. Perhaps the general, unable to comprehend chaos, might call upon him for information. And he could tell him. He knew all concerning it. Of a surety the force was in a fix, and any fool could see that if they did not retreat while they had opportunity—why—

He felt that he would like to thrash the general, or at least approach and tell him in plain words exactly what he thought him to be. It was criminal to stay calmly in one spot and make no effort to stay destruction. He loitered in a fever of eagerness for the division commander to apply to him.

As he warily moved about, he heard the general call out irritably: "Tompkins, go over an' see Taylor, an' tell him not t' be in such an all-fired hurry; tell him t' halt his brigade in th' edge of th' woods; tell him t' detach a reg'ment—say I think th' center'll break if we don't help it out some; tell him t' hurry up."

A slim youth on a fine chestnut horse caught these swift words from the mouth of his superior. He made his horse bound into a gallop almost from a walk in his haste to go upon his mission. There was a cloud of dust.

A moment later the youth saw the general bounce excitedly in his saddle.

"Yes, by heavens, they have!" The officer leaned forward. His face was aflame with excitement. "Yes, by heavens, they've held 'im! They've held 'im!"

He began to blithely roar at his staff: "We'll wallop 'im now. We'll wallop 'im now. We've got 'em sure." He turned suddenly upon an aid: "Here—you—Jones—quick—ride after Tompkins—see Taylor—tell him t' go in—everlastingly—like blazes—anything."

As another officer sped his horse after the first messenger, the general beamed upon the earth like a sun. In his eyes was a desire to chant a paean. He kept repeating, "They've held 'em, by heavens!"

His excitement made his horse plunge, and he merrily kicked and swore at it. He held a little carnival of joy on horseback.

## CHAPTER VII.

The youth cringed as if discovered in a crime. By heavens, they had won after all! The imbecile line had remained and become victors. He could hear cheering.

He lifted himself upon his toes and looked in the direction of the fight. A yellow fog lay wallowing on the treetops. From beneath it came the clatter of musketry. Hoarse cries told of an advance.

He turned away amazed and angry. He felt that he had been wronged.

He had fled, he told himself, because annihilation approached. He had done a good part in saving himself, who was a little piece of the army. He had considered the time, he said, to be one in which it was the duty of every little piece to rescue itself if possible. Later the officers could fit the little pieces together again, and make a battle front. If none of the little pieces were wise enough to save themselves from the flurry of death at such a time, why, then, where would be the army? It was all plain that he had proceeded according to very correct and commendable rules. His actions had been sagacious things. They had been full of strategy. They were the work of a master's legs.

Thoughts of his comrades came to him. The brittle blue line had withstood the blows and won. He grew bitter over it. It seemed that the blind ignorance and stupidity of those little pieces had betrayed him. He had been overturned and crushed by their lack of sense in holding the position, when intelligent deliberation would have convinced them that it was impossible. He, the enlightened man who looks afar in the dark, had fled because of his superior perceptions and knowledge. He felt a great anger against his comrades. He knew it could be proved that they had been fools.

He wondered what they would remark when later he appeared in camp. His mind heard howls of derision. Their density would not enable them to understand his sharper point of view.

He began to pity himself acutely. He was ill used. He was trodden beneath the feet of an iron injustice. He had proceeded with wisdom and from the most righteous motives under heaven's blue only to be frustrated by hateful circumstances.

A dull, animal-like rebellion against his fellows, war in the abstract, and fate grew within him. He shambled along with bowed head, his brain in a tumult of agony and despair. When he looked loweringly up, quivering at each sound, his eyes had the expression of those of a criminal who thinks his guilt and his punishment great, and knows that he can find no words.

He went from the fields into a thick woods, as if resolved to bury himself. He wished to get out of hearing of the crackling shots which were to him like voices.

The ground was cluttered with vines and bushes, and the trees grew close and spread out like bouquets. He was obliged to force his way with much noise. The creepers, catching against his legs, cried out harshly as their sprays were torn from the barks of trees. The swishing saplings tried to make known his presence to the world. He could not conciliate the forest. As he made his way, it was always calling out protestations. When he separated embraces of trees and vines the disturbed foliages waved their arms and turned their face leaves toward him. He dreaded lest these noisy motions and cries should bring men to look at him. So he went far, seeking dark and intricate places.

After a time the sound of musketry grew faint and the cannon boomed in the distance. The sun, suddenly apparent, blazed among the trees. The insects were making rhythmical noises. They seemed to be grinding their teeth in unison. A woodpecker stuck his impudent head around the side of a tree. A bird flew on lighthearted wing.

Off was the rumble of death. It seemed now that Nature had no ears.

This landscape gave him assurance. A fair field holding life. It was the religion of peace. It would die if its timid eyes were compelled to see blood. He conceived Nature to be a woman with a deep aversion to tragedy.

He threw a pine cone at a jovial squirrel, and he ran with chattering fear. High in a treetop he stopped, and, poking his head cautiously from behind a branch, looked down with an air of trepidation.

The youth felt triumphant at this exhibition. There was the law, he said. Nature had given him a sign. The squirrel, immediately upon recognizing danger, had taken to his legs without ado. He did not stand stolidly baring his furry belly to the missile, and die with an upward glance at the sympathetic heavens. On the contrary, he had fled as fast as his legs could carry him; and he was but an ordinary squirrel, too—doubtless no philosopher of his race. The youth wended, feeling that Nature was of his mind. She re-enforced his argument with proofs that lived where the sun shone.

Once he found himself almost into a swamp. He was obliged to walk upon bog tufts and watch his feet to keep from the oily mire. Pausing at one time to look about him he saw, out at some black water, a small animal pounce in and emerge directly with a gleaming fish.

The youth went again into the deep thickets. The brushed branches made a noise that drowned the sounds of cannon. He walked on, going from obscurity into promises of a greater obscurity.

At length he reached a place where the high, arching boughs made a chapel. He softly pushed the green doors aside and entered. Pine needles were a gentle brown carpet. There was a religious half light.

Near the threshold he stopped, horror-stricken at the sight of a thing.

He was being looked at by a dead man who was seated with his back against a columnlike tree. The corpse was dressed in a uniform that once had been blue, but was now faded to a melancholy shade of green. The eyes, staring at the youth, had changed to the dull hue to be seen on the side of a dead fish. The mouth was open. Its red had changed to an appalling yellow. Over the gray skin of the face ran little ants. One was trundling some sort of a bundle along the upper lip.

The youth gave a shriek as he confronted the thing. He was for moments turned to stone before it. He remained staring into the liquid-looking eyes. The dead man and the living man exchanged a long look. Then the youth cautiously put one hand behind him and brought it against a tree. Leaning upon this he retreated, step by step, with his face still toward the thing. He feared that if he turned his back the body might spring up and stealthily pursue him.

The branches, pushing against him, threatened to throw him over upon it. His unguided feet, too, caught aggravatingly in brambles; and with it all he received a subtle suggestion to touch the corpse. As he thought of his hand upon it he shuddered profoundly.

At last he burst the bonds which had fastened him to the spot and fled, unheeding the underbrush. He was pursued by a sight of the black ants swarming greedily upon the gray face and venturing horribly near to the eyes.

After a time he paused, and, breathless and panting, listened. He imagined some strange voice would come from the dead throat and squawk after him in horrible menaces.

The trees about the portal of the chapel moved soughingly in a soft wind. A sad silence was upon the little guarding edifice.

## CHAPTER VIII.

The trees began softly to sing a hymn of twilight. The sun sank until slanted bronze rays struck the forest. There was a lull in the noises of insects as if they had bowed their beaks and were making a devotional pause. There was silence save for the chanted chorus of the trees.

Then, upon this stillness, there suddenly broke a tremendous clangor of sounds. A crimson roar came from the distance.

The youth stopped. He was transfixed by this terrific medley of all noises. It was as if worlds were being rended. There was the ripping sound of musketry and the breaking crash of the artillery.

His mind flew in all directions. He conceived the two armies to be at each other panther fashion. He listened for a time. Then he began to run in the direction of the battle. He saw that it was an ironical thing for him to be running thus toward that which he had been at such pains to avoid. But he said, in substance, to himself that if the earth and the moon were about to clash, many persons would doubtless plan to get upon the roofs to witness the collision.

As he ran, he became aware that the forest had stopped its music, as if at last becoming capable of hearing the foreign sounds. The trees hushed and stood motionless. Everything seemed to be listening to the crackle and clatter and earshaking thunder. The chorus pealed over the still earth.

It suddenly occurred to the youth that the fight in which he had been was, after all, but perfunctory popping. In the hearing of this present din he was doubtful if he had seen real battle scenes. This uproar explained a celestial battle; it was tumbling hordes a-struggle in the air.

Reflecting, he saw a sort of a humor in the point of view of himself and his fellows during the late encounter. They had taken themselves and the enemy very seriously and had imagined that they were deciding the war. Individuals must have supposed that they were cutting the letters of their names deep into everlasting tablets of brass, or enshrining their reputations forever in the hearts of their countrymen, while, as to fact, the affair would appear in printed reports under a meek and immaterial title. But he saw that it was good, else, he said, in battle every one would surely run save forlorn hopes and their ilk.

He went rapidly on. He wished to come to the edge of the forest that he might peer out.

As he hastened, there passed through his mind pictures of stupendous conflicts. His accumulated thought upon such subjects was used to form scenes. The noise was as the voice of an eloquent being, describing.

Sometimes the brambles formed chains and tried to hold him back. Trees, confronting him, stretched out their arms and forbade him to pass. After its previous hostility this new resistance of the forest filled him with a fine bitterness. It seemed that Nature could not be quite ready to kill him.

But he obstinately took roundabout ways, and presently he was where he could see long gray walls of vapor where lay battle lines. The voices of cannon shook him. The musketry sounded in long irregular surges that played havoc with his ears. He stood regardant for a moment. His eyes had an awestruck expression. He gawked in the direction of the fight.

Presently he proceeded again on his forward way. The battle was like the grinding of an immense and terrible machine to him. Its complexities and powers, its grim processes, fascinated him. He must go close and see it produce corpses.

He came to a fence and clambered over it. On the far side, the ground was littered with clothes and guns. A newspaper, folded up, lay in the dirt. A dead soldier was stretched with his face hidden in his arm. Farther off there was a group of four or five corpses keeping mournful company. A hot sun had blazed upon the spot.

In this place the youth felt that he was an invader. This forgotten part of the battle ground was owned by the dead men, and he hurried, in the vague apprehension that one of the swollen forms would rise and tell him to begone.

He came finally to a road from which he could see in the distance dark and agitated bodies of troops, smoke-fringed. In the lane was a blood-stained crowd streaming to the rear. The wounded men were cursing, groaning, and wailing. In the air, always, was a mighty swell of sound that it seemed could sway the earth. With the courageous words of the artillery and the spiteful sentences of the musketry mingled red cheers. And from this region of noises came the steady current of the maimed.

One of the wounded men had a shoeful of blood. He hopped like a schoolboy in a game. He was laughing hysterically.

One was swearing that he had been shot in the arm through the commanding general's mismanagement of the army. One was marching with an air imitative of some sublime drum major. Upon his features was an unholy mixture of merriment and agony. As he marched he sang a bit of doggerel in a high and quavering voice:

> *"Sing a song 'a vic'try,*
> *A pocketful 'a bullets,*
> *Five an' twenty dead men*
> *Baked in a—pie."*

Parts of the procession limped and staggered to this tune.

Another had the gray seal of death already upon his face. His lips were curled in hard lines and his teeth were clinched. His hands were bloody from where he had pressed them upon his wound. He seemed to be awaiting the moment when he should pitch headlong. He stalked like the specter of a soldier, his eyes burning with the power of a stare into the unknown.

There were some who proceeded sullenly, full of anger at their wounds, and ready to turn upon anything as an obscure cause.

An officer was carried along by two privates. He was peevish. "Don't joggle so, Johnson, yeh fool," he cried. "Think m' leg is made of iron? If yeh can't carry me decent, put me down an' let some one else do it."

He bellowed at the tottering crowd who blocked the quick march of his bearers. "Say, make way there, can't yeh? Make way, dickens take it all."

They sulkily parted and went to the roadsides. As he was carried past they made pert remarks to him. When he raged in reply and threatened them, they told him to be damned.

The shoulder of one of the tramping bearers knocked heavily against the spectral soldier who was staring into the unknown.

The youth joined this crowd and marched along with it. The torn bodies expressed the awful machinery in which the men had been entangled.

Orderlies and couriers occasionally broke through the throng in the roadway, scattering wounded men right and left, galloping on followed by howls. The melancholy march was continually disturbed by the messengers, and sometimes by bustling batteries that came swinging and thumping down upon them, the officers shouting orders to clear the way.

There was a tattered man, fouled with dust, blood and powder stain from hair to shoes, who trudged quietly at the youth's side. He was listening with eagerness and much humility to the lurid descriptions of a bearded sergeant. His lean features wore an expression of awe and admiration. He was like a listener in a country store to wondrous tales told among the sugar barrels. He eyed the story-teller with unspeakable wonder. His mouth was agape in yokel fashion.

The sergeant, taking note of this, gave pause to his elaborate history while he administered a sardonic comment. "Be keerful, honey, you'll be a-ketchin' flies," he said.

The tattered man shrank back abashed.

After a time he began to sidle near to the youth, and in a different way try to make him a friend. His voice was gentle as a girl's voice and his eyes were pleading. The youth saw with surprise that the soldier had two wounds, one in the head, bound with a blood-soaked rag, and the other in the arm, making that member dangle like a broken bough.

After they had walked together for some time the tattered man mustered sufficient courage to speak. "Was pretty good fight, wa'n't it?" he timidly said. The youth, deep in thought, glanced up at the bloody and grim figure with its lamblike eyes. "What?"

"Was pretty good fight, wa'n't it?

"Yes," said the youth shortly. He quickened his pace.

But the other hobbled industriously after him. There was an air of apology in his manner, but he evidently thought that he needed only to talk for a time, and the youth would perceive that he was a good fellow.

"Was pretty good fight, wa'n't it?" he began in a small voice, and then he achieved the fortitude to continue. "Dern me if I ever see fellers fight so. Laws, how they did fight! I knowed th' boys'd like when they onct got square at it. Th' boys ain't had no fair chanct up t' now, but this time they showed what they was. I knowed it'd turn out this way. Yeh can't lick them boys. No, sir! They're fighters, they be."

He breathed a deep breath of humble admiration. He had looked at the youth for encouragement several times. He received none, but gradually he seemed to get absorbed in his subject.

"I was talkin' 'cross pickets with a boy from Georgie, onct, an' that boy, he ses, 'Your fellers'll all run like hell when they onct hearn a gun,' he ses. 'Mebbe they will,' I ses, 'but I don't b'lieve none of it,' I ses; 'an' b'jiminey,' I ses back t' 'um, 'mebbe your fellers'll all run like hell when they onct hearn a gun,' I ses. He larfed. Well, they didn't run t' day, did they, hey? No, sir! They fit, an' fit, an' fit."

His homely face was suffused with a light of love for the army which was to him all things beautiful and powerful.

After a time he turned to the youth. "Where yeh hit, ol' boy?" he asked in a brotherly tone.

The youth felt instant panic at this question, although at first its full import was not borne in upon him.

"What?" he asked.

"Where yeh hit?" repeated the tattered man.

"Why," began the youth, "I—I—that is—why—I—"

He turned away suddenly and slid through the crowd. His brow was heavily flushed, and his fingers were picking nervously at one of his buttons. He bent his head and fastened his eyes studiously upon the button as if it were a little problem.

The tattered man looked after him in astonishment.

## CHAPTER IX.

The youth fell back in the procession until the tattered soldier was not in sight. Then he started to walk on with the others.

But he was amid wounds. The mob of men was bleeding. Because of the tattered soldier's question he now felt that his shame could be viewed. He was continually casting sidelong glances to see if the men were contemplating the letters of guilt he felt burned into his brow.

At times he regarded the wounded soldiers in an envious way. He conceived persons with torn bodies to be peculiarly happy. He wished that he, too, had a wound, a red badge of courage.

The spectral soldier was at his side like a stalking reproach. The man's eyes were still fixed in a stare into the unknown. His gray, appalling face had attracted attention in the crowd, and men, slowing to his dreary pace, were walking with him. They were discussing his plight, questioning him and giving him advice.

In a dogged way he repelled them, signing to them to go on and leave him alone. The shadows of his face were deepening and his tight lips seemed holding in check the moan of great despair. There could be seen a certain stiffness in the movements of his body, as if he were taking infinite care not to arouse the passion of his wounds. As he went on, he seemed always looking for a place, like one who goes to choose a grave.

Something in the gesture of the man as he waved the bloody and pitying soldiers away made the youth start as if bitten. He yelled in horror. Tottering forward he laid a quivering hand upon the man's arm. As the latter slowly turned his waxlike features toward him, the youth screamed:

"Gawd! Jim Conklin!"

The tall soldier made a little commonplace smile. "Hello, Henry," he said.

The youth swayed on his legs and glared strangely. He stuttered and stammered. "Oh, Jim—oh, Jim—oh, Jim—"

The tall soldier held out his gory hand. There was a curious red and black combination of new blood and old blood upon it. "Where yeh been, Henry?" he asked. He continued in a monotonous voice, "I thought mebbe yeh got keeled over. There's been thunder t' pay t'-day. I was worryin' about it a good deal."

The youth still lamented. "Oh, Jim—oh, Jim—oh, Jim—"

"Yeh know," said the tall soldier, "I was out there." He made a careful gesture. "An', Lord, what a circus! An', b'jiminey, I got shot—I got shot. Yes, b'jiminey, I got shot." He reiterated this fact in a bewildered way, as if he did not know how it came about.

The youth put forth anxious arms to assist him, but the tall soldier went firmly on as if propelled. Since the youth's arrival as a guardian for his friend, the other wounded men had ceased to display much interest. They occupied themselves again in dragging their own tragedies toward the rear.

Suddenly, as the two friends marched on, the tall soldier seemed to be overcome by a terror. His face turned to a semblance of gray paste. He clutched the youth's arm and looked all about him, as if dreading to be overheard. Then he began to speak in a shaking whisper:

"I tell yeh what I'm 'fraid of, Henry—I'll tell yeh what I 'm 'fraid of. I 'm 'fraid I'll fall down—an' then yeh know—them damned artillery wagons—they like as not'll run over me. That's what I 'm 'fraid of—"

The youth cried out to him hysterically: "I'll take care of yeh, Jim! I'll take care of yeh! I swear t' Gawd I will!"

"Sure—will yeh, Henry?" the tall soldier beseeched.

"Yes—yes—I tell yeh—I'll take care of yeh, Jim!" protested the youth. He could not speak accurately because of the gulpings in his throat.

But the tall soldier continued to beg in a lowly way. He now hung babelike to the youth's arm. His eyes rolled in the wildness of his terror. "I was allus a good friend t' yeh, wa'n't I, Henry? I've allus been a pretty good feller, ain't I? An' it ain't much t' ask, is it? Jest t' pull me along outer th' road? I'd do it fer you, Wouldn't I, Henry?"

He paused in piteous anxiety to await his friend's reply.

The youth had reached an anguish where the sobs scorched him. He strove to express his loyalty, but he could only make fantastic gestures.

However, the tall soldier seemed suddenly to forget all those fears. He became again the grim, stalking specter of a soldier. He went stonily forward. The youth wished his friend to lean upon him, but the other always shook his head and strangely protested. "No—no—no—leave me be—leave me be—"

His look was fixed again upon the unknown. He moved with mysterious purpose, and all of the youth's offers he brushed aside. "No—no—leave me be—leave me be—"

The youth had to follow.

Presently the latter heard a voice talking softly near his shoulders. Turning he saw that it belonged to the tattered soldier. "Ye'd better take 'im outa th' road, pardner. There's a batt'ry comin' helitywhoop down th' road an' he'll git runned over. He's a goner anyhow in about five minutes—yeh kin see that. Ye'd better take 'im outa th' road. Where th' blazes does he git his stren'th from?"

"Lord knows!" cried the youth. He was shaking his hands helplessly.

He ran forward presently and grasped the tall soldier by the arm. "Jim! Jim!" he coaxed, "come with me."

The tall soldier weakly tried to wrench himself free. "Huh," he said vacantly. He stared at the youth for a moment. At last he spoke as if dimly comprehending. "Oh! Inteh th' fields? Oh!"

He started blindly through the grass.

The youth turned once to look at the lashing riders and jouncing guns of the battery. He was startled from this view by a shrill outcry from the tattered man.

"Gawd! He's runnin'!"

Turning his head swiftly, the youth saw his friend running in a staggering and stumbling way toward a little clump of bushes. His heart seemed to wrench itself almost free from his body at this sight. He made a noise of pain. He and the tattered man began a pursuit. There was a singular race.

When he overtook the tall soldier he began to plead with all the words he could find. "Jim—Jim—what are you doing—what makes you do this way—you'll hurt yerself."

The same purpose was in the tall soldier's face. He protested in a dulled way, keeping his eyes fastened on the mystic place of his intentions. "No—no—don't tech me—leave me be—leave me be—"

The youth, aghast and filled with wonder at the tall soldier, began quaveringly to question him. "Where yeh goin', Jim? What you thinking about? Where you going? Tell me, won't you, Jim?"

The tall soldier faced about as upon relentless pursuers. In his eyes there was a great appeal. "Leave me be, can't yeh? Leave me be fer a minnit."

The youth recoiled. "Why, Jim," he said, in a dazed way, "what's the matter with you?"

The tall soldier turned and, lurching dangerously, went on. The youth and the tattered soldier followed, sneaking as if whipped, feeling unable to face the stricken man if he should again confront them. They began to have thoughts of a solemn ceremony. There was something rite-like in these movements of the doomed soldier. And there was a resemblance in him to a devotee of a mad religion, blood-sucking, muscle-wrenching, bone-crushing. They were awed and afraid. They hung back lest he have at command a dreadful weapon.

At last, they saw him stop and stand motionless. Hastening up, they perceived that his face wore an expression telling that he had at last found the place for which he had struggled. His spare figure was erect; his bloody hands were quietly at his side. He was waiting with patience for something that he had come to meet. He was at the rendezvous. They paused and stood, expectant.

There was a silence.

Finally, the chest of the doomed soldier began to heave with a strained motion. It increased in violence until it was as if an animal was within and was kicking and tumbling furiously to be free.

This spectacle of gradual strangulation made the youth writhe, and once as his friend rolled his eyes, he saw something in them that made him sink wailing to the ground. He raised his voice in a last supreme call.

"Jim—Jim—Jim—"

The tall soldier opened his lips and spoke. He made a gesture. "Leave me be— don't tech me—leave me be—"

There was another silence while he waited.

Suddenly, his form stiffened and straightened. Then it was shaken by a pro-longed ague. He stared into space. To the two watchers there was a curious and profound dignity in the firm lines of his awful face.

He was invaded by a creeping strangeness that slowly enveloped him. For a moment the tremor of his legs caused him to dance a sort of hideous hornpipe. His arms beat wildly about his head in expression of implike enthusiasm.

His tall figure stretched itself to its full height. There was a slight rending sound. Then it began to swing forward, slow and straight, in the manner of a falling tree. A swift muscular contortion made the left shoulder strike the ground first.

The body seemed to bounce a little way from the earth. "God!" said the tattered soldier.

The youth had watched, spellbound, this ceremony at the place of meeting. His face had been twisted into an expression of every agony he had imagined for his friend.

He now sprang to his feet and, going closer, gazed upon the pastelike face. The mouth was open and the teeth showed in a laugh.

As the flap of the blue jacket fell away from the body, he could see that the side looked as if it had been chewed by wolves.

The youth turned, with sudden, livid rage, toward the battlefield. He shook his fist. He seemed about to deliver a philippic.

"Hell—"

The red sun was pasted in the sky like a wafer.

## CHAPTER X.

The tattered man stood musing.

"Well, he was reg'lar jim-dandy fer nerve, wa'n't he," said he finally in a little awestruck voice. "A reg'lar jim-dandy." He thoughtfully poked one of the docile hands with his foot. "I wonner where he got 'is stren'th from? I never seen a man do like that before. It was a funny thing. Well, he was a reg'lar jim-dandy."

The youth desired to screech out his grief. He was stabbed, but his tongue lay dead in the tomb of his mouth. He threw himself again upon the ground and began to brood.

The tattered man stood musing.

"Look-a-here, pardner," he said, after a time. He regarded the corpse as he spoke. "He's up an' gone, ain't 'e, an' we might as well begin t' look out fer ol' number one. This here thing is all over. He's up an' gone, ain't 'e? An' he's all right here. Nobody won't bother 'im. An' I must say I ain't enjoying any great health m'self these days."

The youth, awakened by the tattered soldier's tone, looked quickly up. He saw that he was swinging uncertainly on his legs and that his face had turned to a shade of blue.

"Good Lord!" he cried, "you ain't goin' t'—not you, too."

The tattered man waved his hand. "Nary die," he said. "All I want is some pea soup an' a good bed. Some pea soup," he repeated dreamfully.

The youth arose from the ground. "I wonder where he came from. I left him over there." He pointed. "And now I find 'im here. And he was coming from over there, too." He indicated a new direction. They both turned toward the body as if to ask of it a question.

"Well," at length spoke the tattered man, "there ain't no use in our stayin' here an' tryin' t' ask him anything."

The youth nodded an assent wearily. They both turned to gaze for a moment at the corpse.

The youth murmured something.

"Well, he was a jim-dandy, wa'n't 'e?" said the tattered man as if in response.

They turned their backs upon it and started away. For a time they stole softly, treading with their toes. It remained laughing there in the grass.

"I'm commencin' t' feel pretty bad," said the tattered man, suddenly breaking one of his little silences. "I'm commencin' t' feel pretty damn' bad."

The youth groaned. "O Lord!" He wondered if he was to be the tortured witness of another grim encounter.

But his companion waved his hand reassuringly. "Oh, I'm not goin' t' die yit! There too much dependin' on me fer me t' die yit. No, sir! Nary die! I *can't*! Ye'd oughta see th' swad a' chil'ren I've got, an' all like that."

The youth glancing at his companion could see by the shadow of a smile that he was making some kind of fun.

As they plodded on the tattered soldier continued to talk. "Besides, if I died, I wouldn't die th' way that feller did. That was th' funniest thing. I'd jest flop down, I would. I never seen a feller die th' way that feller did.

"Yeh know Tom Jamison, he lives next door t' me up home. He's a nice feller, he is, an' we was allus good friends. Smart, too. Smart as a steel trap. Well, when we was a-fightin' this atternoon, all-of-a-sudden he begin t' rip up an' cuss an' beller at me. 'Yer shot, yeh blamed infernal!'—he swear horrible—he ses t' me. I put up m' hand t' m' head an' when I looked at m' fingers, I seen, sure 'nough, I was shot. I give a holler an' begin t' run, but b'fore I could git away another one hit me in th' arm an' whirl' me clean 'round. I got skeared when they was all a-shootin' b'hind me an' I run t' beat all, but I cotch it pretty bad. I've an idee I'd a' been fightin' yit, if t'was n't fer Tom Jamison."

Then he made a calm announcement: "There's two of 'em—little ones—but they're beginnin' t' have fun with me now. I don't b'lieve I kin walk much furder."

They went slowly on in silence. "Yeh look pretty peek-ed yerself," said the tattered man at last. "I bet yeh've got a worser one than yeh think. Ye'd better take keer of yer hurt. It don't do t' let sech things go. It might be inside mostly, an' them plays thunder. Where is it located?" But he continued his harangue without waiting for a reply. "I see 'a feller git hit plum in th' head when my reg'ment was a-standin' at ease onct. An' everybody yelled out to 'im: Hurt, John? Are yeh hurt much? 'No,' ses he. He looked kinder surprised, an' he went on tellin' 'em how he felt. He sed he didn't feel nothin'. But, by dad, th' first thing that feller knowed he was dead. Yes, he was dead—stone dead. So, yeh wanta watch out. Yeh might have some queer kind 'a hurt yerself. Yeh can't never tell. Where is your'n located?"

The youth had been wriggling since the introduction of this topic. He now gave a cry of exasperation and made a furious motion with his hand. "Oh, don't bother me!" he said. He was enraged against the tattered man, and could have strangled him. His companions seemed ever to play intolerable parts. They were ever upraising the ghost of shame on the stick of their curiosity. He turned toward the tattered man as one at bay. "Now, don't bother me," he repeated with desperate menace.

"Well, Lord knows I don't wanta bother anybody," said the other. There was a little accent of despair in his voice as he replied, "Lord knows I've gota 'nough m' own t' tend to."

The youth, who had been holding a bitter debate with himself and casting glances of hatred and contempt at the tattered man, here spoke in a hard voice. "Good-by," he said.

The tattered man looked at him in gaping amazement. "Why—why, pardner, where yeh goin'?" he asked unsteadily. The youth looking at him, could see that he, too, like that other one, was beginning to act dumb and animal-like. His thoughts seemed to be floundering about in his head. "Now—now—look—a—here, you Tom Jamison—now—I won't have this—this here won't do. Where—where yeh goin'?"

The youth pointed vaguely. "Over there," he replied.

"Well, now look—a—here—now," said the tattered man, rambling on in idiot fashion. His head was hanging forward and his words were slurred. "This thing won't do, now, Tom Jamison. It won't do. I know yeh, yeh pig-headed devil. Yeh wanta go trompin' off with a bad hurt. It ain't right—now—Tom Jamison—it ain't. Yeh wanta leave me take keer of yeh, Tom Jamison. It ain't—right—it ain't—fer yeh t' go—trompin' off—with a bad hurt—it ain't—ain't—ain't right—it ain't."

In reply the youth climbed a fence and started away. He could hear the tattered man bleating plaintively.

Once he faced about angrily. "What?"

"Look—a—here, now, Tom Jamison—now—it ain't—"

The youth went on. Turning at a distance he saw the tattered man wandering about helplessly in the field.

He now thought that he wished he was dead. He believed that he envied those men whose bodies lay strewn over the grass of the fields and on the fallen leaves of the forest.

The simple questions of the tattered man had been knife thrusts to him. They asserted a society that probes pitilessly at secrets until all is apparent. His late companion's chance persistency made him feel that he could not keep his crime concealed in his bosom. It was sure to be brought plain by one of those arrows which cloud the air and are constantly pricking, discovering, proclaiming those things which are willed to be forever hidden. He admitted that he could not defend himself against this agency. It was not within the power of vigilance.

## CHAPTER XI.

He became aware that the furnace roar of the battle was growing louder. Great brown clouds had floated to the still heights of air before him. The noise, too, was approaching. The woods filtered men and the fields became dotted.

As he rounded a hillock, he perceived that the roadway was now a crying mass of wagons, teams, and men. From the heaving tangle issued exhortations, commands, imprecations. Fear was sweeping it all along. The cracking whips bit and horses plunged and tugged. The white-topped wagons strained and stumbled in their exertions like fat sheep.

The youth felt comforted in a measure by this sight. They were all retreating. Perhaps, then, he was not so bad after all. He seated himself and watched the terror-stricken wagons. They fled like soft, ungainly animals. All the roarers and lashers served to help him to magnify the dangers and horrors of the engagement that he might try to prove to himself that the thing with which men could charge him was in truth a symmetrical act. There was an amount of pleasure to him in watching the wild march of this vindication.

Presently the calm head of a forward-going column of infantry appeared in the road. It came swiftly on. Avoiding the obstructions gave it the sinuous movement of a serpent. The men at the head butted mules with their musket stocks. They prodded teamsters indifferent to all howls. The men forced their way through parts of the dense mass by strength. The blunt head of the column pushed. The raving teamsters swore many strange oaths.

The commands to make way had the ring of a great importance in them. The men were going forward to the heart of the din. They were to confront the eager rush of the enemy. They felt the pride of their onward movement when the remainder of the army seemed trying to dribble down this road. They tumbled teams about with a fine feeling that it was no matter so long as their column got to the front in time. This importance made their faces grave and stern. And the backs of the officers were very rigid.

As the youth looked at them the black weight of his woe returned to him. He felt that he was regarding a procession of chosen beings. The separation was as great to him as if they had marched with weapons of flame and banners of sunlight. He could never be like them. He could have wept in his longings.

He searched about in his mind for an adequate malediction for the indefinite cause, the thing upon which men turn the words of final blame. It—whatever it was—was responsible for him, he said. There lay the fault.

The haste of the column to reach the battle seemed to the forlorn young man to be something much finer than stout fighting. Heroes, he thought, could find excuses in that long seething lane. They could retire with perfect self-respect and make excuses to the stars.

He wondered what those men had eaten that they could be in such haste to force their way to grim chances of death. As he watched his envy grew until he thought that he wished to change lives with one of them. He would have liked to have used a tremendous force, he said, throw off himself and become a better. Swift pictures of himself, apart, yet in himself, came to him—a blue desperate figure leading lurid charges with one knee forward and a broken blade high—a blue, determined figure standing before a crimson and steel assault, getting calmly killed on a high place before the eyes of all. He thought of the magnificent pathos of his dead body.

These thoughts uplifted him. He felt the quiver of war desire. In his ears, he heard the ring of victory. He knew the frenzy of a rapid successful charge. The music of the trampling feet, the sharp voices, the clanking arms of the column near him made him soar on the red wings of war. For a few moments he was sublime.

He thought that he was about to start for the front. Indeed, he saw a picture of himself, dust-stained, haggard, panting, flying to the front at the proper moment to seize and throttle the dark, leering witch of calamity.

Then the difficulties of the thing began to drag at him. He hesitated, balancing awkwardly on one foot.

He had no rifle; he could not fight with his hands, said he resentfully to his plan. Well, rifles could be had for the picking. They were extraordinarily profuse.

Also, he continued, it would be a miracle if he found his regiment. Well, he could fight with any regiment.

He started forward slowly. He stepped as if he expected to tread upon some explosive thing. Doubts and he were struggling.

He would truly be a worm if any of his comrades should see him returning thus, the marks of his flight upon him. There was a reply that the intent fighters did not care for what happened rearward saving that no hostile bayonets appeared there. In the battle-blur his face would, in a way be hidden, like the face of a cowled man.

But then he said that his tireless fate would bring forth, when the strife lulled for a moment, a man to ask of him an explanation. In imagination he felt the scrutiny of his companions as he painfully labored through some lies.

Eventually, his courage expended itself upon these objections. The debates drained him of his fire.

He was not cast down by this defeat of his plan, for, upon studying the affair carefully, he could not but admit that the objections were very formidable.

Furthermore, various ailments had begun to cry out. In their presence he could not persist in flying high with the wings of war; they rendered it almost impossible for him to see himself in a heroic light. He tumbled headlong.

He discovered that he had a scorching thirst. His face was so dry and grimy that he thought he could feel his skin crackle. Each bone of his body had an ache in it, and seemingly threatened to break with each movement. His feet were like two sores. Also, his body was calling for food. It was more powerful than a direct hunger. There was a dull, weight like feeling in his stomach, and, when he tried to walk, his head swayed and he tottered. He could not see with distinctness. Small patches of green mist floated before his vision.

While he had been tossed by many emotions, he had not been aware of ailments. Now they beset him and made clamor. As he was at last compelled to pay attention to them, his capacity for self-hate was multiplied. In despair, he declared that he was not like those others. He now conceded it to be impossible that he should ever become a hero. He was a craven loon. Those pictures of glory were piteous things. He groaned from his heart and went staggering off.

A certain mothlike quality within him kept him in the vicinity of the battle. He had a great desire to see, and to get news. He wished to know who was winning.

He told himself that, despite his unprecedented suffering, he had never lost his greed for a victory, yet, he said, in a half-apologetic manner to his conscience, he could not but know that a defeat for the army this time might mean many favorable things for him. The blows of the enemy would splinter regiments into fragments. Thus, many men of courage, he considered, would be obliged to desert the colors and scurry like chickens. He would appear as one of them. They would be sullen brothers in distress, and he could then easily believe he had not run any farther or faster than they. And if he himself could believe in his virtuous perfection, he conceived that there would be small trouble in convincing all others.

He said, as if in excuse for this hope, that previously the army had encountered great defeats and in a few months had shaken off all blood and tradition of them, emerging as bright and valiant as a new one; thrusting out of sight the memory of disaster, and appearing with the valor and confidence of unconquered legions. The shrilling voices of the people at home would pipe dismally for a time, but various generals were usually compelled to listen to these ditties. He of course felt no compunctions for proposing a general as a sacrifice. He could not tell who the chosen for the barbs might be, so he could center no direct sympathy upon him. The people were afar and he did not conceive public opinion to be accurate at long range. It was quite probable they would hit the wrong man who, after he had recovered from his amazement would perhaps spend the rest of his days in writing replies to the songs of his alleged failure. It would be very unfortunate, no doubt, but in this case a general was of no consequence to the youth.

In a defeat there would be a roundabout vindication of himself. He thought it would prove, in a manner, that he had fled early because of his superior powers of perception. A serious prophet upon predicting a flood should be the first man to climb a tree. This would demonstrate that he was indeed a seer.

A moral vindication was regarded by the youth as a very important thing. Without salve, he could not, he thought, wear the sore badge of his dishonor through life. With his heart continually assuring him that he was despicable, he could not exist without making it, through his actions, apparent to all men.

If the army had gone gloriously on he would be lost. If the din meant that now his army's flags were tilted forward he was a condemned wretch. He would be compelled to doom himself to isolation. If the men were advancing, their indifferent feet were trampling upon his chances for a successful life.

As these thoughts went rapidly through his mind, he turned upon them and tried to thrust them away. He denounced himself as a villain. He said that he was the most unutterably selfish man in existence. His mind pictured the soldiers who would place their defiant bodies before the spear of the yelling battle fiend, and as he saw their dripping corpses on an imagined field, he said that he was their murderer.

Again he thought that he wished he was dead. He believed that he envied a corpse. Thinking of the slain, he achieved a great contempt for some of them, as if they were guilty for thus becoming lifeless. They might have been killed by lucky chances, he said, before they had had opportunities to flee or before they had been really tested. Yet they would receive laurels from tradition. He cried out bitterly that their crowns were stolen and their robes of glorious memories were shams. However, he still said that it was a great pity he was not as they.

A defeat of the army had suggested itself to him as a means of escape from the consequences of his fall. He considered, now, however, that it was useless to think of such a possibility. His education had been that success for that mighty blue machine was certain; that it would make victories as a contrivance turns out buttons. He presently discarded all his speculations in the other direction. He returned to the creed of soldiers.

When he perceived again that it was not possible for the army to be defeated, he tried to bethink him of a fine tale which he could take back to his regiment, and with it turn the expected shafts of derision.

But, as he mortally feared these shafts, it became impossible for him to invent a tale he felt he could trust. He experimented with many schemes, but threw them aside one by one as flimsy. He was quick to see vulnerable places in them all.

Furthermore, he was much afraid that some arrow of scorn might lay him mentally low before he could raise his protecting tale.

He imagined the whole regiment saying: "Where's Henry Fleming? He run, didn't 'e? Oh, my!" He recalled various persons who would be quite sure to leave him no peace about it. They would doubtless question him with sneers, and laugh at his stammering hesitation. In the next engagement they would try to keep watch of him to discover when he would run.

Wherever he went in camp, he would encounter insolent and lingeringly cruel stares. As he imagined himself passing near a crowd of comrades, he could hear some one say, "There he goes!"

Then, as if the heads were moved by one muscle, all the faces were turned toward him with wide, derisive grins. He seemed to hear some one make a humorous remark in a low tone. At it the others all crowed and cackled. He was a slang phrase.

## CHAPTER XII.

The column that had butted stoutly at the obstacles in the roadway was barely out of the youth's sight before he saw dark waves of men come sweeping out of the woods and down through the fields. He knew at once that the steel fibers had been washed from their hearts. They were bursting from their coats and their equipments as from entanglements. They charged down upon him like terrified buffaloes.

Behind them blue smoke curled and clouded above the treetops, and through the thickets he could sometimes see a distant pink glare. The voices of the cannon were clamoring in interminable chorus.

The youth was horrorstricken. He stared in agony and amazement. He forgot that he was engaged in combating the universe. He threw aside his mental pamphlets on the philosophy of the retreated and rules for the guidance of the damned.

The fight was lost. The dragons were coming with invincible strides. The army, helpless in the matted thickets and blinded by the overhanging night, was going to be swallowed. War, the red animal, war, the blood-swollen god, would have bloated fill.

Within him something bade to cry out. He had the impulse to make a rallying speech, to sing a battle hymn, but he could only get his tongue to call into the air: "Why—why—what—what's th' matter?"

Soon he was in the midst of them. They were leaping and scampering all about him. Their blanched faces shone in the dusk. They seemed, for the most part, to be very burly men. The youth turned from one to another of them as they galloped along. His incoherent questions were lost. They were heedless of his appeals. They did not seem to see him.

They sometimes gabbled insanely. One huge man was asking of the sky: "Say, where de plank road? Where de plank road!" It was as if he had lost a child. He wept in his pain and dismay.

Presently, men were running hither and thither in all ways. The artillery booming, forward, rearward, and on the flanks made jumble of ideas of direction. Landmarks had vanished into the gathered gloom. The youth began to imagine that he had got into the center of the tremendous quarrel, and he could perceive no way out of it. From the mouths of the fleeing men came a thousand wild questions, but no one made answers.

The youth, after rushing about and throwing interrogations at the heedless bands of retreating infantry, finally clutched a man by the arm. They swung around face to face.

"Why—why—" stammered the youth struggling with his balking tongue.

The man screamed: "Let go me! Let go me!" His face was livid and his eyes were rolling uncontrolled. He was heaving and panting. He still grasped his rifle, perhaps having forgotten to release his hold upon it. He tugged frantically, and the youth being compelled to lean forward was dragged several paces.

"Let go me! Let go me!"

"Why—why—" stuttered the youth.

"Well, then!" bawled the man in a lurid rage. He adroitly and fiercely swung his rifle. It crushed upon the youth's head. The man ran on.

The youth's fingers had turned to paste upon the other's arm. The energy was smitten from his muscles. He saw the flaming wings of lightning flash before his vision. There was a deafening rumble of thunder within his head.

Suddenly his legs seemed to die. He sank writhing to the ground. He tried to arise. In his efforts against the numbing pain he was like a man wrestling with a creature of the air.

There was a sinister struggle.

Sometimes he would achieve a position half erect, battle with the air for a moment, and then fall again, grabbing at the grass. His face was of a clammy pallor. Deep groans were wrenched from him.

At last, with a twisting movement, he got upon his hands and knees, and from thence, like a babe trying to walk, to his feet. Pressing his hands to his temples he went lurching over the grass.

He fought an intense battle with his body. His dulled senses wished him to swoon and he opposed them stubbornly, his mind portraying unknown dangers and mutilations if he should fall upon the field. He went tall soldier fashion. He imagined secluded spots where he could fall and be unmolested. To search for one he strove against the tide of his pain.

Once he put his hand to the top of his head and timidly touched the wound. The scratching pain of the contact made him draw a long breath through his clinched teeth. His fingers were dabbled with blood. He regarded them with a fixed stare.

Around him he could hear the grumble of jolted cannon as the scurrying horses were lashed toward the front. Once, a young officer on a besplashed charger nearly ran him down. He turned and watched the mass of guns, men, and horses sweeping in a wide curve toward a gap in a fence. The officer was making excited motions with a gauntleted hand. The guns followed the teams with an air of unwillingness, of being dragged by the heels.

Some officers of the scattered infantry were cursing and railing like fishwives. Their scolding voices could be heard above the din. Into the unspeakable jumble in the roadway rode a squadron of cavalry. The faded yellow of their facings shone bravely. There was a mighty altercation.

The artillery were assembling as if for a conference.

The blue haze of evening was upon the field. The lines of forest were long purple shadows. One cloud lay along the western sky partly smothering the red.

As the youth left the scene behind him, he heard the guns suddenly roar out. He imagined them shaking in black rage. They belched and howled like brass devils guarding a gate. The soft air was filled with the tremendous remonstrance. With it came the shattering peal of opposing infantry. Turning to look behind him, he could see sheets of orange light illumine the shadowy distance. There were subtle and sudden lightnings in the far air. At times he thought he could see heaving masses of men.

He hurried on in the dusk. The day had faded until he could barely distinguish place for his feet. The purple darkness was filled with men who lectured and jabbered. Sometimes he could see them gesticulating against the blue and somber sky. There seemed to be a great ruck of men and munitions spread about in the forest and in the fields.

The little narrow roadway now lay lifeless. There were overturned wagons like sun-dried bowlders. The bed of the former torrent was choked with the bodies of horses and splintered parts of war machines.

It had come to pass that his wound pained him but little. He was afraid to move rapidly, however, for a dread of disturbing it. He held his head very still and took many precautions against stumbling. He was filled with anxiety, and his face was pinched and drawn in anticipation of the pain of any sudden mistake of his feet in the gloom.

His thoughts, as he walked, fixed intently upon his hurt. There was a cool, liquid feeling about it and he imagined blood moving slowly down under his hair. His head seemed swollen to a size that made him think his neck to be inadequate.

The new silence of his wound made much worriment. The little blistering voices of pain that had called out from his scalp were, he thought, definite in their expression of danger. By them he believed that he could measure his plight. But when they remained ominously silent he became frightened and imagined terrible fingers that clutched into his brain.

Amid it he began to reflect upon various incidents and conditions of the past. He bethought him of certain meals his mother had cooked at home, in which those dishes of which he was particularly fond had occupied prominent positions. He saw the spread table. The pine walls of the kitchen were glowing in the warm light from the stove. Too, he remembered how he and his companions used to go from the schoolhouse to the bank of a shaded pool. He saw his clothes in disorderly array upon the grass of the bank. He felt the swash of the fragrant water upon his body. The leaves of the overhanging maple rustled with melody in the wind of youthful summer.

He was overcome presently by a dragging weariness. His head hung forward and his shoulders were stooped as if he were bearing a great bundle. His feet shuffled along the ground.

He held continuous arguments as to whether he should lie down and sleep at some near spot, or force himself on until he reached a certain haven. He often tried to dismiss the question, but his body persisted in rebellion and his senses nagged at him like pampered babies.

At last he heard a cheery voice near his shoulder: "Yeh seem t' be in a pretty bad way, boy?"

The youth did not look up, but he assented with thick tongue. "Uh!"

The owner of the cheery voice took him firmly by the arm. "Well," he said, with a round laugh, "I'm goin' your way. Th' hull gang is goin' your way. An' I guess I kin give yeh a lift." They began to walk like a drunken man and his friend.

As they went along, the man questioned the youth and assisted him with the replies like one manipulating the mind of a child. Sometimes he interjected anecdotes. "What reg'ment do yeh b'long teh? Eh? What's that? Th' 304th N' York? Why, what corps is that in? Oh, it is? Why, I thought they wasn't engaged t'-day—they're 'way over in th' center. Oh, they was, eh? Well, pretty nearly everybody got their share 'a fightin' t'-day. By dad, I give myself up fer dead any number 'a times. There was shootin' here an' shootin' there, an' hollerin' here an' hollerin' there, in th' damn' darkness, until I couldn't tell t' save m' soul which side I was on. Sometimes I thought I was sure 'nough from Ohier, an' other times I could 'a swore I was from th' bitter end of Florida. It was th' most mixed up dern thing I ever see. An' these here hull woods is a reg'lar mess. It'll be a miracle if we find our reg'ments t'-night. Pretty soon, though, we'll meet a-plenty of guards an' provost-guards, an' one thing an' another. Ho! there they go with an off'cer, I guess. Look at his hand a-draggin'. He's got all th' war he wants, I bet. He won't be talkin' so big about his reputation an' all when they go t' sawin' off his leg. Poor feller! My brother's got whiskers jest like that. How did yeh git 'way over here, anyhow? Your reg'ment is a long way from here, ain't it? Well, I guess we can find it. Yeh know there was a boy killed in my comp'ny t'-day that I thought th' world an' all of. Jack was a nice feller. By ginger, it hurt like thunder t' see ol' Jack jest git knocked flat. We was a-standin' purty peaceable fer a spell, 'though there was men runnin' ev'ry way all 'round us, an' while we was a-standin' like that, 'long come a big fat feller. He began t' peck at Jack's elbow, an' he ses: 'Say, where's th' road t' th' river?' An' Jack, he never paid no attention, an' th' feller kept on a-peckin' at his elbow an' sayin': 'Say, where's th' road t' th' river?' Jack was a-lookin' ahead all th' time tryin' t' see th' Johnnies comin' through th' woods, an' he never paid no attention t' this big fat feller fer a long time, but at last he turned 'round an' he ses: 'Ah, go t' hell an' find th' road t' th' river!' An' jest then a shot slapped him bang on th' side th' head. He was a sergeant, too. Them was his last words. Thunder, I wish we was sure 'a findin' our reg'ments t'-night. It's goin' t' be long huntin'. But I guess we kin do it."

In the search which followed, the man of the cheery voice seemed to the youth to possess a wand of a magic kind. He threaded the mazes of the tangled forest with a strange fortune. In encounters with guards and patrols he displayed the keenness of a detective and the valor of a gamin. Obstacles fell before him and became of assistance. The youth, with his chin still on his breast, stood woodenly by while his companion beat ways and means out of sullen things.

The forest seemed a vast hive of men buzzing about in frantic circles, but the cheery man conducted the youth without mistakes, until at last he began to chuckle with glee and self-satisfaction. "Ah, there yeh are! See that fire?"

The youth nodded stupidly.

"Well, there's where your reg'ment is. An' now, good-by, ol' boy, good luck t' yeh."

A warm and strong hand clasped the youth's languid fingers for an instant, and then he heard a cheerful and audacious whistling as the man strode away. As he who had so befriended him was thus passing out of his life, it suddenly occurred to the youth that he had not once seen his face.

## CHAPTER XIII.

The youth went slowly toward the fire indicated by his departed friend. As he reeled, he bethought him of the welcome his comrades would give him. He had a conviction that he would soon feel in his sore heart the barbed missiles of ridicule. He had no strength to invent a tale; he would be a soft target.

He made vague plans to go off into the deeper darkness and hide, but they were all destroyed by the voices of exhaustion and pain from his body. His ailments, clamoring, forced him to seek the place of food and rest, at whatever cost.

He swung unsteadily toward the fire. He could see the forms of men throwing black shadows in the red light, and as he went nearer it became known to him in some way that the ground was strewn with sleeping men.

Of a sudden he confronted a black and monstrous figure. A rifle barrel caught some glinting beams. "Halt! halt!" He was dismayed for a moment, but he presently thought that he recognized the nervous voice. As he stood tottering before the rifle barrel, he called out: "Why, hello, Wilson, you—you here?"

The rifle was lowered to a position of caution and the loud soldier came slowly forward. He peered into the youth's face. "That you, Henry?"

"Yes, it's—it's me."

"Well, well, ol' boy," said the other, "by ginger, I'm glad t' see yeh! I give yeh up fer a goner. I thought yeh was dead sure enough." There was husky emotion in his voice.

The youth found that now he could barely stand upon his feet. There was a sudden sinking of his forces. He thought he must hasten to produce his tale to protect him from the missiles already at the lips of his redoubtable comrades. So, staggering before the loud soldier, he began: "Yes, yes. I've—I've had an awful time. I've been all over. Way over on th' right. Ter'ble fightin' over there. I had an awful time. I got separated from th' reg'ment. Over on th' right, I got shot. In th' head. I never see sech fightin'. Awful time. I don't see how I could 'a got separated from th' reg'ment. I got shot, too."

His friend had stepped forward quickly. "What? Got shot? Why didn't yeh say so first? Poor ol' boy, we must—hol' on a minnit; what am I doin'. I'll call Simpson."

Another figure at that moment loomed in the gloom. They could see that it was the corporal. "Who yeh talkin' to, Wilson?" he demanded. His voice was anger-toned. "Who yeh talkin' to? Yeh th' derndest sentinel—why—hello, Henry, you here? Why, I thought you was dead four hours ago! Great Jerusalem, they keep turnin' up every ten minutes or so! We thought we'd lost forty-two men by straight count, but if they keep on a-comin' this way, we'll git th' comp'ny all back by mornin' yit. Where was yeh?"

"Over on th' right. I got separated"—began the youth with considerable glibness.

But his friend had interrupted hastily. "Yes, an' he got shot in th' head an' he's in a fix, an' we must see t' him right away." He rested his rifle in the hollow of his left arm and his right around the youth's shoulder.

"Gee, it must hurt like thunder!" he said.

The youth leaned heavily upon his friend. "Yes, it hurts—hurts a good deal," he replied. There was a faltering in his voice.

"Oh," said the corporal. He linked his arm in the youth's and drew him forward. "Come on, Henry. I'll take keer 'a yeh."

As they went on together the loud private called out after them: "Put 'im t' sleep in my blanket, Simpson. An'—hol' on a minnit—here's my canteen. It's full 'a coffee. Look at his head by th' fire an' see how it looks. Maybe it's a pretty bad un. When I git relieved in a couple 'a minnits, I'll be over an' see t' him."

The youth's senses were so deadened that his friend's voice sounded from afar and he could scarcely feel the pressure of the corporal's arm. He submitted passively to the latter's directing strength. His head was in the old manner hanging forward upon his breast. His knees wobbled.

The corporal led him into the glare of the fire. "Now, Henry," he said, "let's have look at yer ol' head."

The youth sat down obediently and the corporal, laying aside his rifle, began to fumble in the bushy hair of his comrade. He was obliged to turn the other's head so that the full flush of the fire light would beam upon it. He puckered his mouth with a critical air. He drew back his lips and whistled through his teeth when his fingers came in contact with the splashed blood and the rare wound.

"Ah, here we are!" he said. He awkwardly made further investigations. "Jest as I thought," he added, presently. "Yeh've been grazed by a ball. It's raised a queer lump jest as if some feller had lammed yeh on th' head with a club. It stopped a-bleedin' long time ago. Th' most about it is that in th' mornin' yeh'll feel that a number ten hat wouldn't fit yeh. An' your head'll be all het up an' feel as dry as burnt pork. An' yeh may git a lot 'a other sicknesses, too, by mornin'. Yeh can't never tell. Still, I don't much think so. It's jest a damn' good belt on th' head, an' nothin' more. Now, you jest sit here an' don't move, while I go rout out th' relief. Then I'll send Wilson t' take keer 'a yeh."

The corporal went away. The youth remained on the ground like a parcel. He stared with a vacant look into the fire.

After a time he aroused, for some part, and the things about him began to take form. He saw that the ground in the deep shadows was cluttered with men, sprawling in every conceivable posture. Glancing narrowly into the more distant darkness, he caught occasional glimpses of visages that loomed pallid and ghostly, lit with a phosphorescent glow. These faces expressed in their lines the deep stupor of the tired soldiers. They made them appear like men drunk with wine. This bit of forest might have appeared to an ethereal wanderer as a scene of the result of some frightful debauch.

On the other side of the fire the youth observed an officer asleep, seated bolt upright, with his back against a tree. There was something perilous in his position. Badgered by dreams, perhaps, he swayed with little bounces and starts, like an old toddy-stricken grandfather in a chimney corner. Dust and stains were upon his face.

His lower jaw hung down as if lacking strength to assume its normal position. He was the picture of an exhausted soldier after a feast of war.

He had evidently gone to sleep with his sword in his arms. These two had slumbered in an embrace, but the weapon had been allowed in time to fall unheeded to the ground. The brass-mounted hilt lay in contact with some parts of the fire.

Within the gleam of rose and orange light from the burning sticks were other soldiers, snoring and heaving, or lying deathlike in slumber. A few pairs of legs were stuck forth, rigid and straight. The shoes displayed the mud or dust of marches and bits of rounded trousers, protruding from the blankets, showed rents and tears from hurried pitchings through the dense brambles.

The fire crackled musically. From it swelled light smoke. Overhead the foliage moved softly. The leaves, with their faces turned toward the blaze, were colored shifting hues of silver, often edged with red. Far off to the right, through a window in the forest could be seen a handful of stars lying, like glittering pebbles, on the black level of the night.

Occasionally, in this low-arched hall, a soldier would arouse and turn his body to a new position, the experience of his sleep having taught him of uneven and objectionable places upon the ground under him. Or, perhaps, he would lift himself to a sitting posture, blink at the fire for an unintelligent moment, throw a swift glance at his prostrate companion, and then cuddle down again with a grunt of sleepy content.

The youth sat in a forlorn heap until his friend the loud young soldier came, swinging two canteens by their light strings. "Well, now, Henry, ol' boy," said the latter, "we'll have yeh fixed up in jest about a minnit."

He had the bustling ways of an amateur nurse. He fussed around the fire and stirred the sticks to brilliant exertions. He made his patient drink largely from the canteen that contained the coffee. It was to the youth a delicious draught. He tilted his head afar back and held the canteen long to his lips. The cool mixture went caressingly down his blistered throat. Having finished, he sighed with comfortable delight.

The loud young soldier watched his comrade with an air of satisfaction. He later produced an extensive handkerchief from his pocket. He folded it into a manner of bandage and soused water from the other canteen upon the middle of it. This crude arrangement he bound over the youth's head, tying the ends in a queer knot at the back of the neck.

"There," he said, moving off and surveying his deed, "yeh look like th' devil, but I bet yeh feel better."

The youth contemplated his friend with grateful eyes. Upon his aching and swelling head the cold cloth was like a tender woman's hand.

"Yeh don't holler ner say nothin'," remarked his friend approvingly. "I know I'm a blacksmith at takin' keer 'a sick folks, an' yeh never squeaked. Yer a good un, Henry. Most 'a men would a' been in th' hospital long ago. A shot in th' head ain't foolin' business."

The youth made no reply, but began to fumble with the buttons of his jacket.

"Well, come, now," continued his friend, "come on. I must put yeh t' bed an' see that yeh git a good night's rest."

The other got carefully erect, and the loud young soldier led him among the sleeping forms lying in groups and rows. Presently he stooped and picked up his blankets. He spread the rubber one upon the ground and placed the woolen one about the youth's shoulders.

"There now," he said, "lie down an' git some sleep."

The youth, with his manner of doglike obedience, got carefully down like a crone stooping. He stretched out with a murmur of relief and comfort. The ground felt like the softest couch.

But of a sudden he ejaculated: "Hol' on a minnit! Where you goin' t' sleep?"

His friend waved his hand impatiently. "Right down there by yeh."

"Well, but hol' on a minnit," continued the youth. "What yeh goin' t' sleep in? I've got your—"

The loud young soldier snarled: "Shet up an' go on t' sleep. Don't be makin' a damn' fool 'a yerself," he said severely.

After the reproof the youth said no more. An exquisite drowsiness had spread through him. The warm comfort of the blanket enveloped him and made a gentle languor. His head fell forward on his crooked arm and his weighted lids went softly down over his eyes. Hearing a splatter of musketry from the distance, he wondered indifferently if those men sometimes slept. He gave a long sigh, snuggled down into his blanket, and in a moment was like his comrades.

## CHAPTER XIV.

When the youth awoke it seemed to him that he had been asleep for a thousand years, and he felt sure that he opened his eyes upon an unexpected world. Gray mists were slowly shifting before the first efforts of the sun rays. An impending splendor could be seen in the eastern sky. An icy dew had chilled his face, and immediately upon arousing he curled farther down into his blanket. He stared for a while at the leaves overhead, moving in a heraldic wind of the day.

The distance was splintering and blaring with the noise of fighting. There was in the sound an expression of a deadly persistency, as if it had not begun and was not to cease.

About him were the rows and groups of men that he had dimly seen the previous night. They were getting a last draught of sleep before the awakening. The gaunt, careworn features and dusty figures were made plain by this quaint light at the dawning, but it dressed the skin of the men in corpselike hues and made the tangled limbs appear pulseless and dead. The youth started up with a little cry when his eyes first swept over this motionless mass of men, thick-spread upon the ground, pallid, and in strange postures. His disordered mind interpreted the hall of the forest as a charnel place. He believed for an instant that he was in the house of the dead, and he did not dare to move lest these corpses start up, squalling and squawking. In a second, however, he achieved his proper mind. He swore a complicated oath at himself. He saw that this somber picture was not a fact of the present, but a mere prophecy.

He heard then the noise of a fire crackling briskly in the cold air, and, turning his head, he saw his friend pottering busily about a small blaze. A few other figures moved in the fog, and he heard the hard cracking of axe blows.

Suddenly there was a hollow rumble of drums. A distant bugle sang faintly. Similar sounds, varying in strength, came from near and far over the forest. The bugles called to each other like brazen gamecocks. The near thunder of the regimental drums rolled.

The body of men in the woods rustled. There was a general uplifting of heads. A murmuring of voices broke upon the air. In it there was much bass of grumbling oaths. Strange gods were addressed in condemnation of the early hours necessary to correct war. An officer's peremptory tenor rang out and quickened the stiffened movement of the men. The tangled limbs unraveled. The corpse-hued faces were hidden behind fists that twisted slowly in the eye sockets.

The youth sat up and gave vent to an enormous yawn. "Thunder!" he remarked petulantly. He rubbed his eyes, and then putting up his hand felt carefully of the bandage over his wound. His friend, perceiving him to be awake, came from the fire. "Well, Henry, ol' man, how do yeh feel this mornin'?" he demanded.

The youth yawned again. Then he puckered his mouth to a little pucker. His head, in truth, felt precisely like a melon, and there was an unpleasant sensation at his stomach.

"Oh, Lord, I feel pretty bad," he said.

"Thunder!" exclaimed the other. "I hoped ye'd feel all right this mornin'. Let's see th' bandage—I guess it's slipped." He began to tinker at the wound in rather a clumsy way until the youth exploded.

"Gosh-dern it!" he said in sharp irritation; "you're the hangdest man I ever saw! You wear muffs on your hands. Why in good thunderation can't you be more easy? I'd rather you'd stand off an' throw guns at it. Now, go slow, an' don't act as if you was nailing down carpet."

He glared with insolent command at his friend, but the latter answered soothingly. "Well, well, come now, an' git some grub," he said. "Then, maybe, yeh'll feel better."

At the fireside the loud young soldier watched over his comrade's wants with tenderness and care. He was very busy marshaling the little black vagabonds of tin cups and pouring into them the streaming, iron colored mixture from a small and sooty tin pail. He had some fresh meat, which he roasted hurriedly upon a stick. He sat down then and contemplated the youth's appetite with glee.

The youth took note of a remarkable change in his comrade since those days of camp life upon the river bank. He seemed no more to be continually regarding the proportions of his personal prowess. He was not furious at small words that pricked his conceits. He was no more a loud young soldier. There was about him now a fine reliance. He showed a quiet belief in his purposes and his abilities. And this inward confidence evidently enabled him to be indifferent to little words of other men aimed at him.

The youth reflected. He had been used to regarding his comrade as a blatant child with an audacity grown from his inexperience, thoughtless, headstrong, jealous, and filled with a tinsel courage. A swaggering babe accustomed to strut in his own dooryard. The youth wondered where had been born these new eyes; when his comrade had made the great discovery that there were many men who would refuse to be subjected by him. Apparently, the other had now climbed a peak of wisdom from which he could perceive himself as a very wee thing. And the youth saw that ever after it would be easier to live in his friend's neighborhood.

His comrade balanced his ebony coffee-cup on his knee. "Well, Henry," he said, "what d'yeh think th' chances are? D'yeh think we'll wallop 'em?"

The youth considered for a moment. "Day-b'fore-yesterday," he finally replied, with boldness, "you would 'a' bet you'd lick the hull kit-an'-boodle all by yourself."

His friend looked a trifle amazed. "Would I?" he asked. He pondered. "Well, perhaps I would," he decided at last. He stared humbly at the fire.

The youth was quite disconcerted at this surprising reception of his remarks. "Oh, no, you wouldn't either," he said, hastily trying to retrace.

But the other made a deprecating gesture. "Oh, yeh needn't mind, Henry," he said. "I believe I was a pretty big fool in those days." He spoke as after a lapse of years.

There was a little pause.

"All th' officers say we've got th' rebs in a pretty tight box," said the friend, clearing his throat in a commonplace way. "They all seem t' think we've got 'em jest where we want 'em."

"I don't know about that," the youth replied. "What I seen over on th' right makes me think it was th' other way about. From where I was, it looked as if we was gettin' a good poundin' yestirday."

"D'yeh think so?" inquired the friend. "I thought we handled 'em pretty rough yestirday."

"Not a bit," said the youth. "Why, lord, man, you didn't see nothing of the fight. Why!" Then a sudden thought came to him. "Oh! Jim Conklin's dead."

His friend started. "What? Is he? Jim Conklin?"

The youth spoke slowly. "Yes. He's dead. Shot in th' side."

"Yeh don't say so. Jim Conklin.… poor cuss!"

All about them were other small fires surrounded by men with their little black utensils. From one of these near came sudden sharp voices in a row. It appeared that two light-footed soldiers had been teasing a huge, bearded man, causing him to spill coffee upon his blue knees. The man had gone into a rage and had sworn comprehensively. Stung by his language, his tormentors had immediately bristled at him with a great show of resenting unjust oaths. Possibly there was going to be a fight.

The friend arose and went over to them, making pacific motions with his arms. "Oh, here, now, boys, what's th' use?" he said. "We'll be at th' rebs in less'n an hour. What's th' good fightin' 'mong ourselves?"

One of the light-footed soldiers turned upon him red-faced and violent. "Yeh needn't come around here with yer preachin'. I s'pose yeh don't approve 'a fightin' since Charley Morgan licked yeh; but I don't see what business this here is 'a yours or anybody else."

"Well, it ain't," said the friend mildly. "Still I hate t' see—"

There was a tangled argument.

"Well, he—," said the two, indicating their opponent with accusative forefingers.

The huge soldier was quite purple with rage. He pointed at the two soldiers with his great hand, extended clawlike. "Well, they—"

But during this argumentative time the desire to deal blows seemed to pass, although they said much to each other. Finally the friend returned to his old seat. In a short while the three antagonists could be seen together in an amiable bunch.

"Jimmie Rogers ses I'll have t' fight him after th' battle t'-day," announced the friend as he again seated himself. "He ses he don't allow no interferin' in his business. I hate t' see th' boys fightin' 'mong themselves."

The youth laughed. "Yer changed a good bit. Yeh ain't at all like yeh was. I remember when you an' that Irish feller—" He stopped and laughed again.

"No, I didn't use t' be that way," said his friend thoughtfully. "That's true 'nough."

"Well, I didn't mean—" began the youth.

The friend made another deprecatory gesture. "Oh, yeh needn't mind, Henry."

There was another little pause.

"Th' reg'ment lost over half th' men yestirday," remarked the friend eventually. "I thought a course they was all dead, but, laws, they kep' a-comin' back last night until it seems, after all, we didn't lose but a few. They'd been scattered all over, wanderin' around in th' woods, fightin' with other reg'ments, an' everything. Jest like you done."

"So?" said the youth.

## CHAPTER XV.

The regiment was standing at order arms at the side of a lane, waiting for the command to march, when suddenly the youth remembered the little packet enwrapped in a faded yellow envelope which the loud young soldier with lugubrious words had intrusted to him. It made him start. He uttered an exclamation and turned toward his comrade.

"Wilson!"

"What?"

His friend, at his side in the ranks, was thoughtfully staring down the road. From some cause his expression was at that moment very meek. The youth, regarding him with sidelong glances, felt impelled to change his purpose. "Oh, nothing," he said.

His friend turned his head in some surprise, "Why, what was yeh goin' t' say?"

"Oh, nothing," repeated the youth.

He resolved not to deal the little blow. It was sufficient that the fact made him glad. It was not necessary to knock his friend on the head with the misguided packet.

He had been possessed of much fear of his friend, for he saw how easily questionings could make holes in his feelings. Lately, he had assured himself that the altered comrade would not tantalize him with a persistent curiosity, but he felt certain that during the first period of leisure his friend would ask him to relate his adventures of the previous day.

He now rejoiced in the possession of a small weapon with which he could prostrate his comrade at the first signs of a cross-examination. He was master. It would now be he who could laugh and shoot the shafts of derision.

The friend had, in a weak hour, spoken with sobs of his own death. He had delivered a melancholy oration previous to his funeral, and had doubtless in the packet of letters, presented various keepsakes to relatives. But he had not died, and thus he had delivered himself into the hands of the youth.

The latter felt immensely superior to his friend, but he inclined to condescension. He adopted toward him an air of patronizing good humor.

His self-pride was now entirely restored. In the shade of its flourishing growth he stood with braced and self-confident legs, and since nothing could now be discovered he did not shrink from an encounter with the eyes of judges, and allowed no thoughts of his own to keep him from an attitude of manfulness. He had performed his mistakes in the dark, so he was still a man.

Indeed, when he remembered his fortunes of yesterday, and looked at them from a distance he began to see something fine there. He had license to be pompous and veteranlike.

His panting agonies of the past he put out of his sight.

In the present, he declared to himself that it was only the doomed and the damned who roared with sincerity at circumstance. Few but they ever did it. A man with a full stomach and the respect of his fellows had no business to scold about anything that he might think to be wrong in the ways of the universe, or even with the ways of society. Let the unfortunates rail; the others may play marbles.

He did not give a great deal of thought to these battles that lay directly before him. It was not essential that he should plan his ways in regard to them. He had been taught that many obligations of a life were easily avoided. The lessons of yesterday had been that retribution was a laggard and blind. With these facts before him he did not deem it necessary that he should become feverish over the possibilities of the ensuing twenty-four hours. He could leave much to chance. Besides, a faith in himself had secretly blossomed. There was a little flower of confidence growing within him. He was now a man of experience. He had been out among the dragons, he said, and he assured himself that they were not so hideous as he had imagined them. Also, they were inaccurate; they did not sting with precision. A stout heart often defied, and defying, escaped.

And, furthermore, how could they kill him who was the chosen of gods and doomed to greatness?

He remembered how some of the men had run from the battle. As he recalled their terror-struck faces he felt a scorn for them. They had surely been more fleet and more wild than was absolutely necessary. They were weak mortals. As for himself, he had fled with discretion and dignity.

He was aroused from this reverie by his friend, who, having hitched about nervously and blinked at the trees for a time, suddenly coughed in an introductory way, and spoke.

"Fleming!"

"What?"

The friend put his hand up to his mouth and coughed again. He fidgeted in his jacket.

"Well," he gulped, at last, "I guess yeh might as well give me back them letters." Dark, prickling blood had flushed into his cheeks and brow.

"All right, Wilson," said the youth. He loosened two buttons of his coat, thrust in his hand, and brought forth the packet. As he extended it to his friend the latter's face was turned from him.

He had been slow in the act of producing the packet because during it he had been trying to invent a remarkable comment upon the affair. He could conjure nothing of sufficient point. He was compelled to allow his friend to escape unmolested with his packet. And for this he took unto himself considerable credit. It was a generous thing.

His friend at his side seemed suffering great shame. As he contemplated him, the youth felt his heart grow more strong and stout. He had never been compelled to blush in such manner for his acts; he was an individual of extraordinary virtues.

He reflected, with condescending pity: "Too bad! Too bad! The poor devil, it makes him feel tough!"

After this incident, and as he reviewed the battle pictures he had seen, he felt quite competent to return home and make the hearts of the people glow with stories of war. He could see himself in a room of warm tints telling tales to listeners. He could exhibit laurels. They were insignificant; still, in a district where laurels were infrequent, they might shine.

He saw his gaping audience picturing him as the central figure in blazing scenes. And he imagined the consternation and the ejaculations of his mother and the young lady at the seminary as they drank his recitals. Their vague feminine formula for beloved ones doing brave deeds on the field of battle without risk of life would be destroyed.

# CHAPTER XVI.

A sputtering of musketry was always to be heard. Later, the cannon had entered the dispute. In the fog-filled air their voices made a thudding sound. The reverberations were continued. This part of the world led a strange, battleful existence.

The youth's regiment was marched to relieve a command that had lain long in some damp trenches. The men took positions behind a curving line of rifle pits that had been turned up, like a large furrow, along the line of woods. Before them was a level stretch, peopled with short, deformed stumps. From the woods beyond came the dull popping of the skirmishers and pickets, firing in the fog. From the right came the noise of a terrific fracas.

The men cuddled behind the small embankment and sat in easy attitudes awaiting their turn. Many had their backs to the firing. The youth's friend lay down, buried his face in his arms, and almost instantly, it seemed, he was in a deep sleep.

The youth leaned his breast against the brown dirt and peered over at the woods and up and down the line. Curtains of trees interfered with his ways of vision. He could see the low line of trenches but for a short distance. A few idle flags were perched on the dirt hills. Behind them were rows of dark bodies with a few heads sticking curiously over the top.

Always the noise of skirmishers came from the woods on the front and left, and the din on the right had grown to frightful proportions. The guns were roaring without an instant's pause for breath. It seemed that the cannon had come from all parts and were engaged in a stupendous wrangle. It became impossible to make a sentence heard.

The youth wished to launch a joke—a quotation from newspapers. He desired to say, "All quiet on the Rappahannock," but the guns refused to permit even a comment upon their uproar. He never successfully concluded the sentence. But at last the guns stopped, and among the men in the rifle pits rumors again flew, like birds, but they were now for the most part black creatures who flapped their wings drearily near to the ground and refused to rise on any wings of hope. The men's faces grew doleful from the interpreting of omens. Tales of hesitation and uncertainty on the part of those high in place and responsibility came to their ears. Stories of disaster were borne into their minds with many proofs. This din of musketry on the right, growing like a released genie of sound, expressed and emphasized the army's plight.

The men were disheartened and began to mutter. They made gestures expressive of the sentence: "Ah, what more can we do?" And it could always be seen that they were bewildered by the alleged news and could not fully comprehend a defeat.

Before the gray mists had been totally obliterated by the sun rays, the regiment was marching in a spread column that was retiring carefully through the woods. The disordered, hurrying lines of the enemy could sometimes be seen down through the groves and little fields. They were yelling, shrill and exultant.

At this sight the youth forgot many personal matters and became greatly enraged. He exploded in loud sentences. "B'jiminey, we're generaled by a lot 'a lunkheads."

"More than one feller has said that t'-day," observed a man.

His friend, recently aroused, was still very drowsy. He looked behind him until his mind took in the meaning of the movement. Then he sighed. "Oh, well, I s'pose we got licked," he remarked sadly.

The youth had a thought that it would not be handsome for him to freely condemn other men. He made an attempt to restrain himself, but the words upon his tongue were too bitter. He presently began a long and intricate denunciation of the commander of the forces.

"Mebbe, it wa'n't all his fault—not all together. He did th' best he knowed. It's our luck t' git licked often," said his friend in a weary tone. He was trudging along with stooped shoulders and shifting eyes like a man who has been caned and kicked.

"Well, don't we fight like the devil? Don't we do all that men can?" demanded the youth loudly.

He was secretly dumfounded at this sentiment when it came from his lips. For a moment his face lost its valor and he looked guiltily about him. But no one questioned his right to deal in such words, and presently he recovered his air of courage. He went on to repeat a statement he had heard going from group to group at the camp that morning. "The brigadier said he never saw a new reg'ment fight the way we fought yestirday, didn't he? And we didn't do better than many another reg'ment, did we? Well, then, you can't say it's th' army's fault, can you?"

In his reply, the friend's voice was stern. "'A course not," he said. "No man dare say we don't fight like th' devil. No man will ever dare say it. Th' boys fight like hell-roosters. But still—still, we don't have no luck."

"Well, then, if we fight like the devil an' don't ever whip, it must be the general's fault," said the youth grandly and decisively. "And I don't see any sense in fighting and fighting and fighting, yet always losing through some derned old lunkhead of a general."

A sarcastic man who was tramping at the youth's side, then spoke lazily. "Mebbe yeh think yeh fit th' hull battle yestirday, Fleming," he remarked.

The speech pierced the youth. Inwardly he was reduced to an abject pulp by these chance words. His legs quaked privately. He cast a frightened glance at the sarcastic man.

"Why, no," he hastened to say in a conciliating voice, "I don't think I fought the whole battle yesterday."

But the other seemed innocent of any deeper meaning. Apparently, he had no information. It was merely his habit. "Oh!" he replied in the same tone of calm derision.

The youth, nevertheless, felt a threat. His mind shrank from going near to the danger, and thereafter he was silent. The significance of the sarcastic man's words took from him all loud moods that would make him appear prominent. He became suddenly a modest person.

There was low-toned talk among the troops. The officers were impatient and snappy, their countenances clouded with the tales of misfortune. The troops, sifting through the forest, were sullen. In the youth's company once a man's laugh rang out. A dozen soldiers turned their faces quickly toward him and frowned with vague displeasure.

The noise of firing dogged their footsteps. Sometimes, it seemed to be driven a little way, but it always returned again with increased insolence. The men muttered and cursed, throwing black looks in its direction.

In a clear space the troops were at last halted. Regiments and brigades, broken and detached through their encounters with thickets, grew together again and lines were faced toward the pursuing bark of the enemy's infantry.

This noise, following like the yellings of eager, metallic hounds, increased to a loud and joyous burst, and then, as the sun went serenely up the sky, throwing illuminating rays into the gloomy thickets, it broke forth into prolonged pealings. The woods began to crackle as if afire.

"Whoop-a-dadee," said a man, "here we are! Everybody fightin'. Blood an' destruction."

"I was willin' t' bet they'd attack as soon as th' sun got fairly up," savagely asserted the lieutenant who commanded the youth's company. He jerked without mercy at his little mustache. He strode to and fro with dark dignity in the rear of his men, who were lying down behind whatever protection they had collected.

A battery had trundled into position in the rear and was thoughtfully shelling the distance. The regiment, unmolested as yet, awaited the moment when the gray shadows of the woods before them should be slashed by the lines of flame. There was much growling and swearing.

"Good Gawd," the youth grumbled, "we're always being chased around like rats! It makes me sick. Nobody seems to know where we go or why we go. We just get fired around from pillar to post and get licked here and get licked there, and nobody knows what it's done for. It makes a man feel like a damn' kitten in a bag. Now, I'd like to know what the eternal thunders we was marched into these woods for anyhow, unless it was to give the rebs a regular pot shot at us. We came in here and got our legs all tangled up in these cussed briers, and then we begin to fight and the rebs had an easy time of it. Don't tell me it's just luck! I know better. It's this derned old—"

The friend seemed jaded, but he interrupted his comrade with a voice of calm confidence. "It'll turn out all right in th' end," he said.

"Oh, the devil it will! You always talk like a dog-hanged parson. Don't tell me! I know—"

At this time there was an interposition by the savage-minded lieutenant, who was obliged to vent some of his inward dissatisfaction upon his men. "You boys shut right up! There no need 'a your wastin' your breath in long-winded arguments about this an' that an' th' other. You've been jawin' like a lot 'a old hens. All you've got t' do is to fight, an' you'll get plenty 'a that t' do in about ten minutes. Less talkin' an' more fightin' is what's best for you boys. I never saw sech gabbling jackasses."

He paused, ready to pounce upon any man who might have the temerity to reply. No words being said, he resumed his dignified pacing.

"There's too much chin music an' too little fightin' in this war, anyhow," he said to them, turning his head for a final remark.

The day had grown more white, until the sun shed his full radiance upon the thronged forest. A sort of a gust of battle came sweeping toward that part of the line where lay the youth's regiment. The front shifted a trifle to meet it squarely. There was a wait. In this part of the field there passed slowly the intense moments that precede the tempest.

A single rifle flashed in a thicket before the regiment. In an instant it was joined by many others. There was a mighty song of clashes and crashes that went sweeping through the woods. The guns in the rear, aroused and enraged by shells that had been thrown burlike at them, suddenly involved themselves in a hideous altercation with another band of guns. The battle roar settled to a rolling thunder, which was a single, long explosion.

In the regiment there was a peculiar kind of hesitation denoted in the attitudes of the men. They were worn, exhausted, having slept but little and labored much. They rolled their eyes toward the advancing battle as they stood awaiting the shock. Some shrank and flinched. They stood as men tied to stakes.

# CHAPTER XVII.

This advance of the enemy had seemed to the youth like a ruthless hunting. He began to fume with rage and exasperation. He beat his foot upon the ground, and scowled with hate at the swirling smoke that was approaching like a phantom flood. There was a maddening quality in this seeming resolution of the foe to give him no rest, to give him no time to sit down and think. Yesterday he had fought and had fled rapidly. There had been many adventures. For today he felt that he had earned opportunities for contemplative repose. He could have enjoyed portraying to uninitiated listeners various scenes at which he had been a witness or ably discussing the processes of war with other proved men. Too it was important that he should have time for physical recuperation. He was sore and stiff from his experiences. He had received his fill of all exertions, and he wished to rest.

But those other men seemed never to grow weary; they were fighting with their old speed.

He had a wild hate for the relentless foe. Yesterday, when he had imagined the universe to be against him, he had hated it, little gods and big gods; today he hated the army of the foe with the same great hatred. He was not going to be badgered of his life, like a kitten chased by boys, he said. It was not well to drive men into final corners; at those moments they could all develop teeth and claws.

He leaned and spoke into his friend's ear. He menaced the woods with a gesture. "If they keep on chasing us, by Gawd, they'd better watch out. Can't stand *too* much."

The friend twisted his head and made a calm reply. "If they keep on a-chasin' us they'll drive us all inteh th' river."

The youth cried out savagely at this statement. He crouched behind a little tree, with his eyes burning hatefully and his teeth set in a curlike snarl. The awkward bandage was still about his head, and upon it, over his wound, there was a spot of dry blood. His hair was wondrously tousled, and some straggling, moving locks hung over the cloth of the bandage down toward his forehead. His jacket and shirt were open at the throat, and exposed his young bronzed neck. There could be seen spasmodic gulpings at his throat.

His fingers twined nervously about his rifle. He wished that it was an engine of annihilating power. He felt that he and his companions were being taunted and derided from sincere convictions that they were poor and puny. His knowledge of his inability to take vengeance for it made his rage into a dark and stormy specter, that possessed him and made him dream of abominable cruelties. The tormentors were flies sucking insolently at his blood, and he thought that he would have given his life for a revenge of seeing their faces in pitiful plights.

The winds of battle had swept all about the regiment, until the one rifle, instantly followed by others, flashed in its front. A moment later the regiment roared forth its sudden and valiant retort. A dense wall of smoke settled slowly down. It was furiously slit and slashed by the knifelike fire from the rifles.

To the youth the fighters resembled animals tossed for a death struggle into a dark pit. There was a sensation that he and his fellows, at bay, were pushing back, always pushing fierce onslaughts of creatures who were slippery. Their beams of crimson seemed to get no purchase upon the bodies of their foes; the latter seemed to evade them with ease, and come through, between, around, and about with unopposed skill.

When, in a dream, it occurred to the youth that his rifle was an impotent stick, he lost sense of everything but his hate, his desire to smash into pulp the glittering smile of victory which he could feel upon the faces of his enemies.

The blue smoke-swallowed line curled and writhed like a snake stepped upon. It swung its ends to and fro in an agony of fear and rage.

The youth was not conscious that he was erect upon his feet. He did not know the direction of the ground. Indeed, once he even lost the habit of balance and fell heavily. He was up again immediately. One thought went through the chaos of his brain at the time. He wondered if he had fallen because he had been shot. But the suspicion flew away at once. He did not think more of it.

He had taken up a first position behind the little tree, with a direct determination to hold it against the world. He had not deemed it possible that his army could that day succeed, and from this he felt the ability to fight harder. But the throng had surged in all ways, until he lost directions and locations, save that he knew where lay the enemy.

The flames bit him, and the hot smoke broiled his skin. His rifle barrel grew so hot that ordinarily he could not have borne it upon his palms; but he kept on stuffing cartridges into it, and pounding them with his clanking, bending ramrod. If he aimed at some changing form through the smoke, he pulled his trigger with a fierce grunt, as if he were dealing a blow of the fist with all his strength.

When the enemy seemed falling back before him and his fellows, he went instantly forward, like a dog who, seeing his foes lagging, turns and insists upon being pursued. And when he was compelled to retire again, he did it slowly, sullenly, taking steps of wrathful despair.

Once he, in his intent hate, was almost alone, and was firing, when all those near him had ceased. He was so engrossed in his occupation that he was not aware of a lull.

He was recalled by a hoarse laugh and a sentence that came to his ears in a voice of contempt and amazement. "Yeh infernal fool, don't yeh know enough t' quit when there ain't anything t' shoot at? Good Gawd!"

He turned then and, pausing with his rifle thrown half into position, looked at the blue line of his comrades. During this moment of leisure they seemed all to be engaged in staring with astonishment at him. They had become spectators. Turning to the front again he saw, under the lifted smoke, a deserted ground.

He looked bewildered for a moment. Then there appeared upon the glazed vacancy of his eyes a diamond point of intelligence. "Oh," he said, comprehending.

He returned to his comrades and threw himself upon the ground. He sprawled like a man who had been thrashed. His flesh seemed strangely on fire, and the sounds of the battle continued in his ears. He groped blindly for his canteen.

The lieutenant was crowing. He seemed drunk with fighting. He called out to the youth: "By heavens, if I had ten thousand wild cats like you I could tear th' stomach outa this war in less'n a week!" He puffed out his chest with large dignity as he said it.

Some of the men muttered and looked at the youth in awe-struck ways. It was plain that as he had gone on loading and firing and cursing without the proper intermission, they had found time to regard him. And they now looked upon him as a war devil.

The friend came staggering to him. There was some fright and dismay in his voice. "Are yeh all right, Fleming? Do yeh feel all right? There ain't nothin' th' matter with yeh, Henry, is there?"

"No," said the youth with difficulty. His throat seemed full of knobs and burs.

These incidents made the youth ponder. It was revealed to him that he had been a barbarian, a beast. He had fought like a pagan who defends his religion. Regarding it, he saw that it was fine, wild, and, in some ways, easy. He had been a tremendous figure, no doubt. By this struggle he had overcome obstacles which he had admitted to be mountains. They had fallen like paper peaks, and he was now what he called a hero. And he had not been aware of the process. He had slept and, awakening, found himself a knight.

He lay and basked in the occasional stares of his comrades. Their faces were varied in degrees of blackness from the burned powder. Some were utterly smudged. They were reeking with perspiration, and their breaths came hard and wheezing. And from these soiled expanses they peered at him.

"Hot work! Hot work!" cried the lieutenant deliriously. He walked up and down, restless and eager. Sometimes his voice could be heard in a wild, incomprehensible laugh.

When he had a particularly profound thought upon the science of war he always unconsciously addressed himself to the youth.

There was some grim rejoicing by the men.

"By thunder, I bet this army'll never see another new reg'ment like us!"

"You bet!"

> *"A dog, a woman, an' a walnut tree,*
> *Th' more yeh beat 'em, th' better they be!*

That's like us."

"Lost a piler men, they did. If an' ol' woman swep' up th' woods she'd git a dustpanful."

"Yes, an' if she'll come around ag'in in 'bout an' hour she'll git a pile more."

The forest still bore its burden of clamor. From off under the trees came the rolling clatter of the musketry. Each distant thicket seemed a strange porcupine with quills of flame. A cloud of dark smoke, as from smoldering ruins, went up toward the sun now bright and gay in the blue, enameled sky.

## CHAPTER XVIII.

The ragged line had respite for some minutes, but during its pause the struggle in the forest became magnified until the trees seemed to quiver from the firing and the ground to shake from the rushing of the men. The voices of the cannon were mingled in a long and interminable row. It seemed difficult to live in such an atmosphere. The chests of the men strained for a bit of freshness, and their throats craved water.

There was one shot through the body, who raised a cry of bitter lamentation when came this lull. Perhaps he had been calling out during the fighting also, but at that time no one had heard him. But now the men turned at the woeful complaints of him upon the ground.

"Who is it? Who is it?"

"It's Jimmie Rogers. Jimmie Rogers."

When their eyes first encountered him there was a sudden halt, as if they feared to go near. He was thrashing about in the grass, twisting his shuddering body into many strange postures. He was screaming loudly. This instant's hesitation seemed to fill him with a tremendous, fantastic contempt, and he damned them in shrieked sentences.

The youth's friend had a geographical illusion concerning a stream, and he obtained permission to go for some water. Immediately canteens were showered upon him. "Fill mine, will yeh?" "Bring me some, too." "And me, too." He departed, ladened. The youth went with his friend, feeling a desire to throw his heated body onto the stream and, soaking there, drink quarts.

They made a hurried search for the supposed stream, but did not find it. "No water here," said the youth. They turned without delay and began to retrace their steps.

From their position as they again faced toward the place of the fighting, they could of course comprehend a greater amount of the battle than when their visions had been blurred by the hurling smoke of the line. They could see dark stretches winding along the land, and on one cleared space there was a row of guns making gray clouds, which were filled with large flashes of orange-colored flame. Over some foliage they could see the roof of a house. One window, glowing a deep murder red, shone squarely through the leaves. From the edifice a tall leaning tower of smoke went far into the sky.

Looking over their own troops, they saw mixed masses slowly getting into regular form. The sunlight made twinkling points of the bright steel. To the rear there was a glimpse of a distant roadway as it curved over a slope. It was crowded with retreating infantry. From all the interwoven forest arose the smoke and bluster of the battle. The air was always occupied by a blaring.

Near where they stood shells were flip-flapping and hooting. Occasional bullets buzzed in the air and spanged into tree trunks. Wounded men and other stragglers were slinking through the woods.

Looking down an aisle of the grove, the youth and his companion saw a jangling general and his staff almost ride upon a wounded man, who was crawling on his hands and knees. The general reined strongly at his charger's opened and foamy mouth and guided it with dexterous horsemanship past the man. The latter scrambled in wild and torturing haste. His strength evidently failed him as he reached a place of safety. One of his arms suddenly weakened, and he fell, sliding over upon his back. He lay stretched out, breathing gently.

A moment later the small, creaking cavalcade was directly in front of the two soldiers. Another officer, riding with the skillful abandon of a cowboy, galloped his horse to a position directly before the general. The two unnoticed foot soldiers made a little show of going on, but they lingered near in the desire to overhear the conversation. Perhaps, they thought, some great inner historical things would be said.

The general, whom the boys knew as the commander of their division, looked at the other officer and spoke coolly, as if he were criticising his clothes. "Th' enemy's formin' over there for another charge," he said. "It'll be directed against Whiterside, an' I fear they'll break through there unless we work like thunder t' stop them."

The other swore at his restive horse, and then cleared his throat. He made a gesture toward his cap. "It'll be hell t' pay stoppin' them," he said shortly.

"I presume so," remarked the general. Then he began to talk rapidly and in a lower tone. He frequently illustrated his words with a pointing finger. The two infantrymen could hear nothing until finally he asked: "What troops can you spare?"

The officer who rode like a cowboy reflected for an instant. "Well," he said, "I had to order in th' 12th to help th' 76th, an' I haven't really got any. But there's th' 304th. They fight like a lot 'a mule drivers. I can spare them best of any."

The youth and his friend exchanged glances of astonishment.

The general spoke sharply. "Get 'em ready, then. I'll watch developments from here, an' send you word when t' start them. It'll happen in five minutes."

As the other officer tossed his fingers toward his cap and wheeling his horse, started away, the general called out to him in a sober voice: "I don't believe many of your mule drivers will get back."

The other shouted something in reply. He smiled.

With scared faces, the youth and his companion hurried back to the line.

These happenings had occupied an incredibly short time, yet the youth felt that in them he had been made aged. New eyes were given to him. And the most startling thing was to learn suddenly that he was very insignificant. The officer spoke of the regiment as if he referred to a broom. Some part of the woods needed sweeping, perhaps, and he merely indicated a broom in a tone properly indifferent to its fate. It was war, no doubt, but it appeared strange.

As the two boys approached the line, the lieutenant perceived them and swelled with wrath. "Fleming—Wilson—how long does it take yeh to git water, anyhow—where yeh been to."

But his oration ceased as he saw their eyes, which were large with great tales. "We're goin' t' charge—we're goin' t' charge!" cried the youth's friend, hastening with his news.

"Charge?" said the lieutenant. "Charge? Well, b'Gawd! Now, this is real fightin'." Over his soiled countenance there went a boastful smile. "Charge? Well, b'Gawd!"

A little group of soldiers surrounded the two youths. "Are we, sure 'nough? Well, I'll be derned! Charge? What fer? What at? Wilson, you're lyin'."

"I hope to die," said the youth, pitching his tones to the key of angry remonstrance. "Sure as shooting, I tell you."

And his friend spoke in re-enforcement. "Not by a blame sight, he ain't lyin'. We heard 'em talkin'."

They caught sight of two mounted figures a short distance from them. One was the colonel of the regiment and the other was the officer who had received orders from the commander of the division. They were gesticulating at each other. The soldier, pointing at them, interpreted the scene.

One man had a final objection: "How could yeh hear 'em talkin'?" But the men, for a large part, nodded, admitting that previously the two friends had spoken truth.

They settled back into reposeful attitudes with airs of having accepted the matter. And they mused upon it, with a hundred varieties of expression. It was an engrossing thing to think about. Many tightened their belts carefully and hitched at their trousers.

A moment later the officers began to bustle among the men, pushing them into a more compact mass and into a better alignment. They chased those that straggled and fumed at a few men who seemed to show by their attitudes that they had decided to remain at that spot. They were like critical shepherds struggling with sheep.

Presently, the regiment seemed to draw itself up and heave a deep breath. None of the men's faces were mirrors of large thoughts. The soldiers were bended and stooped like sprinters before a signal. Many pairs of glinting eyes peered from the grimy faces toward the curtains of the deeper woods. They seemed to be engaged in deep calculations of time and distance.

They were surrounded by the noises of the monstrous altercation between the two armies. The world was fully interested in other matters. Apparently, the regiment had its small affair to itself.

The youth, turning, shot a quick, inquiring glance at his friend. The latter returned to him the same manner of look. They were the only ones who possessed an inner knowledge. "Mule drivers—hell t' pay—don't believe many will get back." It was an ironical secret. Still, they saw no hesitation in each other's faces, and they nodded a mute and unprotesting assent when a shaggy man near them said in a meek voice: "We'll git swallowed."

## CHAPTER XIX.

The youth stared at the land in front of him. Its foliages now seemed to veil powers and horrors. He was unaware of the machinery of orders that started the charge, although from the corners of his eyes he saw an officer, who looked like a boy a-horseback, come galloping, waving his hat. Suddenly he felt a straining and heaving among the men. The line fell slowly forward like a toppling wall, and, with a convulsive gasp that was intended for a cheer, the regiment began its journey. The youth was pushed and jostled for a moment before he understood the movement at all, but directly he lunged ahead and began to run.

He fixed his eye upon a distant and prominent clump of trees where he had concluded the enemy were to be met, and he ran toward it as toward a goal. He had believed throughout that it was a mere question of getting over an unpleasant matter as quickly as possible, and he ran desperately, as if pursued for a murder. His face was drawn hard and tight with the stress of his endeavor. His eyes were fixed in a lurid glare. And with his soiled and disordered dress, his red and inflamed features surmounted by the dingy rag with its spot of blood, his wildly swinging rifle and banging accouterments, he looked to be an insane soldier.

As the regiment swung from its position out into a cleared space the woods and thickets before it awakened. Yellow flames leaped toward it from many directions. The forest made a tremendous objection.

The line lurched straight for a moment. Then the right wing swung forward; it in turn was surpassed by the left. Afterward the center careered to the front until the regiment was a wedge-shaped mass, but an instant later the opposition of the bushes, trees, and uneven places on the ground split the command and scattered it into detached clusters.

The youth, light-footed, was unconsciously in advance. His eyes still kept note of the clump of trees. From all places near it the clannish yell of the enemy could be heard. The little flames of rifles leaped from it. The song of the bullets was in the air and shells snarled among the tree-tops. One tumbled directly into the middle of a hurrying group and exploded in crimson fury. There was an instant's spectacle of a man, almost over it, throwing up his hands to shield his eyes.

Other men, punched by bullets, fell in grotesque agonies. The regiment left a coherent trail of bodies.

They had passed into a clearer atmosphere. There was an effect like a revelation in the new appearance of the landscape. Some men working madly at a battery were plain to them, and the opposing infantry's lines were defined by the gray walls and fringes of smoke.

It seemed to the youth that he saw everything. Each blade of the green grass was bold and clear. He thought that he was aware of every change in the thin, transparent vapor that floated idly in sheets. The brown or gray trunks of the trees showed each roughness of their surfaces. And the men of the regiment, with their starting eyes and sweating faces, running madly, or falling, as if thrown headlong, to queer, heaped-up corpses—all were comprehended. His mind took a mechanical but firm impression, so that afterward everything was pictured and explained to him, save why he himself was there.

But there was a frenzy made from this furious rush. The men, pitching forward insanely, had burst into cheerings, moblike and barbaric, but tuned in strange keys that can arouse the dullard and the stoic. It made a mad enthusiasm that, it seemed, would be incapable of checking itself before granite and brass. There was the delirium that encounters despair and death, and is heedless and blind to the odds. It is a temporary but sublime absence of selfishness. And because it was of this order was the reason, perhaps, why the youth wondered, afterward, what reasons he could have had for being there.

Presently the straining pace ate up the energies of the men. As if by agreement, the leaders began to slacken their speed. The volleys directed against them had had a seeming windlike effect. The regiment snorted and blew. Among some stolid trees it began to falter and hesitate. The men, staring intently, began to wait for some of the distant walls of smoke to move and disclose to them the scene. Since much of their strength and their breath had vanished, they returned to caution. They were become men again.

The youth had a vague belief that he had run miles, and he thought, in a way, that he was now in some new and unknown land.

The moment the regiment ceased its advance the protesting splutter of musketry became a steadied roar. Long and accurate fringes of smoke spread out. From the top of a small hill came level belchings of yellow flame that caused an inhuman whistling in the air.

The men, halted, had opportunity to see some of their comrades dropping with moans and shrieks. A few lay under foot, still or wailing. And now for an instant the men stood, their rifles slack in their hands, and watched the regiment dwindle. They appeared dazed and stupid. This spectacle seemed to paralyze them, overcome them with a fatal fascination. They stared woodenly at the sights, and, lowering their eyes, looked from face to face. It was a strange pause, and a strange silence.

Then, above the sounds of the outside commotion, arose the roar of the lieutenant. He strode suddenly forth, his infantile features black with rage.

"Come on, yeh fools!" he bellowed. "Come on! Yeh can't stay here. Yeh must come on." He said more, but much of it could not be understood.

He started rapidly forward, with his head turned toward the men. "Come on," he was shouting. The men stared with blank and yokel-like eyes at him. He was obliged to halt and retrace his steps. He stood then with his back to the enemy and delivered gigantic curses into the faces of the men. His body vibrated from the weight and force of his imprecations. And he could string oaths with the facility of a maiden who strings beads.

The friend of the youth aroused. Lurching suddenly forward and dropping to his knees, he fired an angry shot at the persistent woods. This action awakened the men. They huddled no more like sheep. They seemed suddenly to bethink them of their weapons, and at once commenced firing. Belabored by their officers, they began to move forward. The regiment, involved like a cart involved in mud and muddle, started unevenly with many jolts and jerks. The men stopped now every few paces to fire and load, and in this manner moved slowly on from trees to trees.

The flaming opposition in their front grew with their advance until it seemed that all forward ways were barred by the thin leaping tongues, and off to the right an ominous demonstration could sometimes be dimly discerned. The smoke lately generated was in confusing clouds that made it difficult for the regiment to proceed with intelligence. As he passed through each curling mass the youth wondered what would confront him on the farther side.

The command went painfully forward until an open space interposed between them and the lurid lines. Here, crouching and cowering behind some trees, the men clung with desperation, as if threatened by a wave. They looked wild-eyed, and as if amazed at this furious disturbance they had stirred. In the storm there was an ironical expression of their importance. The faces of the men, too, showed a lack of a certain feeling of responsibility for being there. It was as if they had been driven. It was the dominant animal failing to remember in the supreme moments the forceful causes of various superficial qualities. The whole affair seemed incomprehensible to many of them.

As they halted thus the lieutenant again began to bellow profanely. Regardless of the vindictive threats of the bullets, he went about coaxing, berating, and be-damning. His lips, that were habitually in a soft and childlike curve, were now writhed into unholy contortions. He swore by all possible deities.

Once he grabbed the youth by the arm. "Come on, yeh lunkhead!" he roared. "Come on! We'll all git killed if we stay here. We've on'y got t' go across that lot. An' then"—the remainder of his idea disappeared in a blue haze of curses.

The youth stretched forth his arm. "Cross there?" His mouth was puckered in doubt and awe.

"Certainly. Jest 'cross th' lot! We can't stay here," screamed the lieutenant. He poked his face close to the youth and waved his bandaged hand. "Come on!" Presently he grappled with him as if for a wrestling bout. It was as if he planned to drag the youth by the ear on to the assault.

The private felt a sudden unspeakable indignation against his officer. He wrenched fiercely and shook him off.

"Come on yerself, then," he yelled. There was a bitter challenge in his voice.

They galloped together down the regimental front. The friend scrambled after them. In front of the colors the three men began to bawl: "Come on! come on!" They danced and gyrated like tortured savages.

The flag, obedient to these appeals, bended its glittering form and swept toward them. The men wavered in indecision for a moment, and then with a long, wailful cry the dilapidated regiment surged forward and began its new journey.

Over the field went the scurrying mass. It was a handful of men splattered into the faces of the enemy. Toward it instantly sprang the yellow tongues. A vast quantity of blue smoke hung before them. A mighty banging made ears valueless.

The youth ran like a madman to reach the woods before a bullet could discover him. He ducked his head low, like a football player. In his haste his eyes almost closed, and the scene was a wild blur. Pulsating saliva stood at the corners of his mouth.

Within him, as he hurled himself forward, was born a love, a despairing fondness for this flag which was near him. It was a creation of beauty and invulnerability. It was a goddess, radiant, that bended its form with an imperious gesture to him. It was a woman, red and white, hating and loving, that called him with the voice of his hopes. Because no harm could come to it he endowed it with power. He kept near, as if it could be a saver of lives, and an imploring cry went from his mind.

In the mad scramble he was aware that the color sergeant flinched suddenly, as if struck by a bludgeon. He faltered, and then became motionless, save for his quivering knees.

He made a spring and a clutch at the pole. At the same instant his friend grabbed it from the other side. They jerked at it, stout and furious, but the color sergeant was dead, and the corpse would not relinquish its trust. For a moment there was a grim encounter. The dead man, swinging with bended back, seemed to be obstinately tugging, in ludicrous and awful ways, for the possession of the flag.

It was past in an instant of time. They wrenched the flag furiously from the dead man, and, as they turned again, the corpse swayed forward with bowed head. One arm swung high, and the curved hand fell with heavy protest on the friend's unheeding shoulder.

## CHAPTER XX.

When the two youths turned with the flag they saw that much of the regiment had crumbled away, and the dejected remnant was coming slowly back. The men, having hurled themselves in projectile fashion, had presently expended their forces. They slowly retreated, with their faces still toward the spluttering woods, and their hot rifles still replying to the din. Several officers were giving orders, their voices keyed to screams.

"Where in hell yeh goin'?" the lieutenant was asking in a sarcastic howl. And a red-bearded officer, whose voice of triple brass could plainly be heard, was commanding: "Shoot into 'em! Shoot into 'em, Gawd damn their souls!" There was a *melée* of screeches, in which the men were ordered to do conflicting and impossible things.

The youth and his friend had a small scuffle over the flag. "Give it t' me!" "No, let me keep it!" Each felt satisfied with the other's possession of it, but each felt bound to declare, by an offer to carry the emblem, his willingness to further risk himself. The youth roughly pushed his friend away.

The regiment fell back to the stolid trees. There it halted for a moment to blaze at some dark forms that had begun to steal upon its track. Presently it resumed its march again, curving among the tree trunks. By the time the depleted regiment had again reached the first open space they were receiving a fast and merciless fire. There seemed to be mobs all about them.

The greater part of the men, discouraged, their spirits worn by the turmoil, acted as if stunned. They accepted the pelting of the bullets with bowed and weary heads. It was of no purpose to strive against walls. It was of no use to batter themselves against granite. And from this consciousness that they had attempted to conquer an unconquerable thing there seemed to arise a feeling that they had been betrayed. They glowered with bent brows, but dangerously, upon some of the officers, more particularly upon the red-bearded one with the voice of triple brass.

However, the rear of the regiment was fringed with men, who continued to shoot irritably at the advancing foes. They seemed resolved to make every trouble. The youthful lieutenant was perhaps the last man in the disordered mass. His forgotten back was toward the enemy. He had been shot in the arm. It hung straight and rigid. Occasionally he would cease to remember it, and be about to emphasize an oath with a sweeping gesture. The multiplied pain caused him to swear with incredible power.

The youth went along with slipping, uncertain feet. He kept watchful eyes rearward. A scowl of mortification and rage was upon his face. He had thought of a fine revenge upon the officer who had referred to him and his fellows as mule drivers. But he saw that it could not come to pass. His dreams had collapsed when the mule drivers, dwindling rapidly, had wavered and hesitated on the little clearing, and then had recoiled. And now the retreat of the mule drivers was a march of shame to him.

A dagger-pointed gaze from without his blackened face was held toward the enemy, but his greater hatred was riveted upon the man, who, not knowing him, had called him a mule driver.

When he knew that he and his comrades had failed to do anything in successful ways that might bring the little pangs of a kind of remorse upon the officer, the youth allowed the rage of the baffled to possess him. This cold officer upon a monument, who dropped epithets unconcernedly down, would be finer as a dead man, he thought. So grievous did he think it that he could never possess the secret right to taunt truly in answer.

He had pictured red letters of curious revenge. "We *are* mule drivers, are we?" And now he was compelled to throw them away.

He presently wrapped his heart in the cloak of his pride and kept the flag erect. He harangued his fellows, pushing against their chests with his free hand. To those he knew well he made frantic appeals, beseeching them by name. Between him and the lieutenant, scolding and near to losing his mind with rage, there was felt a subtle fellowship and equality. They supported each other in all manner of hoarse, howling protests.

But the regiment was a machine run down. The two men babbled at a forceless thing. The soldiers who had heart to go slowly were continually shaken in their resolves by a knowledge that comrades were slipping with speed back to the lines. It was difficult to think of reputation when others were thinking of skins. Wounded men were left crying on this black journey.

The smoke fringes and flames blustered always. The youth, peering once through a sudden rift in a cloud, saw a brown mass of troops, interwoven and magnified until they appeared to be thousands. A fierce-hued flag flashed before his vision.

Immediately, as if the uplifting of the smoke had been prearranged, the discovered troops burst into a rasping yell, and a hundred flames jetted toward the retreating band. A rolling gray cloud again interposed as the regiment doggedly replied. The youth had to depend again upon his misused ears, which were trembling and buzzing from the *melée* of musketry and yells.

The way seemed eternal. In the clouded haze men became panicstricken with the thought that the regiment had lost its path, and was proceeding in a perilous direction. Once the men who headed the wild procession turned and came pushing back against their comrades, screaming that they were being fired upon from points which they had considered to be toward their own lines. At this cry a hysterical fear and dismay beset the troops. A soldier, who heretofore had been ambitious to make the regiment into a wise little band that would proceed calmly amid the huge-appearing difficulties, suddenly sank down and buried his face in his arms with an air of bowing to a doom. From another a shrill lamentation rang out filled with profane allusions to a general. Men ran hither and thither, seeking with their eyes roads of escape. With serene regularity, as if controlled by a schedule, bullets buffed into men.

The youth walked stolidly into the midst of the mob, and with his flag in his hands took a stand as if he expected an attempt to push him to the ground. He unconsciously assumed the attitude of the color bearer in the fight of the preceding day. He passed over his brow a hand that trembled. His breath did not come freely. He was choking during this small wait for the crisis.

His friend came to him. "Well, Henry, I guess this is good-by—John."

"Oh, shut up, you damned fool!" replied the youth, and he would not look at the other.

The officers labored like politicians to beat the mass into a proper circle to face the menaces. The ground was uneven and torn. The men curled into depressions and fitted themselves snugly behind whatever would frustrate a bullet.

The youth noted with vague surprise that the lieutenant was standing mutely with his legs far apart and his sword held in the manner of a cane. The youth wondered what had happened to his vocal organs that he no more cursed.

There was something curious in this little intent pause of the lieutenant. He was like a babe which, having wept its fill, raises its eyes and fixes upon a distant toy. He was engrossed in this contemplation, and the soft under lip quivered from self-whispered words.

Some lazy and ignorant smoke curled slowly. The men, hiding from the bullets, waited anxiously for it to lift and disclose the plight of the regiment.

The silent ranks were suddenly thrilled by the eager voice of the youthful lieutenant bawling out: "Here they come! Right onto us, b'Gawd!" His further words were lost in a roar of wicked thunder from the men's rifles.

The youth's eyes had instantly turned in the direction indicated by the awakened and agitated lieutenant, and he had seen the haze of treachery disclosing a body of soldiers of the enemy. They were so near that he could see their features. There was a recognition as he looked at the types of faces. Also he perceived with dim amazement that their uniforms were rather gay in effect, being light gray, accented with a brilliant-hued facing. Too, the clothes seemed new.

These troops had apparently been going forward with caution, their rifles held in readiness, when the youthful lieutenant had discovered them and their movement had been interrupted by the volley from the blue regiment. From the moment's glimpse, it was derived that they had been unaware of the proximity of their dark-suited foes or had mistaken the direction. Almost instantly they were shut utterly from the youth's sight by the smoke from the energetic rifles of his companions. He strained his vision to learn the accomplishment of the volley, but the smoke hung before him.

The two bodies of troops exchanged blows in the manner of a pair of boxers. The fast angry firings went back and forth. The men in blue were intent with the despair of their circumstances and they seized upon the revenge to be had at close range. Their thunder swelled loud and valiant. Their curving front bristled with flashes and the place resounded with the clangor of their ramrods. The youth ducked and dodged for a time and achieved a few unsatisfactory views of the enemy. There appeared to be many of them and they were replying swiftly. They seemed moving toward the blue regiment, step by step. He seated himself gloomily on the ground with his flag between his knees.

As he noted the vicious, wolflike temper of his comrades he had a sweet thought that if the enemy was about to swallow the regimental broom as a large prisoner, it could at least have the consolation of going down with bristles forward.

But the blows of the antagonist began to grow more weak. Fewer bullets ripped the air, and finally, when the men slackened to learn of the fight, they could see only dark, floating smoke. The regiment lay still and gazed. Presently some chance whim came to the pestering blur, and it began to coil heavily away. The men saw a ground vacant of fighters. It would have been an empty stage if it were not for a few corpses that lay thrown and twisted into fantastic shapes upon the sward.

At sight of this tableau, many of the men in blue sprang from behind their covers and made an ungainly dance of joy. Their eyes burned and a hoarse cheer of elation broke from their dry lips.

It had begun to seem to them that events were trying to prove that they were impotent. These little battles had evidently endeavored to demonstrate that the men could not fight well. When on the verge of submission to these opinions, the small duel had showed them that the proportions were not impossible, and by it they had revenged themselves upon their misgivings and upon the foe.

The impetus of enthusiasm was theirs again. They gazed about them with looks of uplifted pride, feeling new trust in the grim, always confident weapons in their hands. And they were men.

## CHAPTER XXI.

Presently they knew that no firing threatened them. All ways seemed once more opened to them. The dusty blue lines of their friends were disclosed a short distance away. In the distance there were many colossal noises, but in all this part of the field there was a sudden stillness.

They perceived that they were free. The depleted band drew a long breath of relief and gathered itself into a bunch to complete its trip.

In this last length of journey the men began to show strange emotions. They hurried with nervous fear. Some who had been dark and unfaltering in the grimmest moments now could not conceal an anxiety that made them frantic. It was perhaps that they dreaded to be killed in insignificant ways after the times for proper military deaths had passed. Or, perhaps, they thought it would be too ironical to get killed at the portals of safety. With backward looks of perturbation, they hastened.

As they approached their own lines there was some sarcasm exhibited on the part of a gaunt and bronzed regiment that lay resting in the shade of trees. Questions were wafted to them.

"Where th' hell yeh been?"

"What yeh comin' back fer?"

"Why didn't yeh stay there?"

"Was it warm out there, sonny?"

"Goin' home now, boys?"

One shouted in taunting mimicry: "Oh, mother, come quick an' look at th' so-jers!"

There was no reply from the bruised and battered regiment, save that one man made broadcast challenges to fist fights and the red-bearded officer walked rather near and glared in great swashbuckler style at a tall captain in the other regiment. But the lieutenant suppressed the man who wished to fist fight, and the tall captain, flushing at the little fanfare of the red-bearded one, was obliged to look intently at some trees.

The youth's tender flesh was deeply stung by these remarks. From under his creased brows he glowered with hate at the mockers. He meditated upon a few revenges. Still, many in the regiment hung their heads in criminal fashion, so that it came to pass that the men trudged with sudden heaviness, as if they bore upon their bended shoulders the coffin of their honor. And the youthful lieutenant, recollecting himself, began to mutter softly in black curses.

They turned when they arrived at their old position to regard the ground over which they had charged.

The youth in this contemplation was smitten with a large astonishment. He discovered that the distances, as compared with the brilliant measurings of his mind, were trivial and ridiculous. The stolid trees, where much had taken place, seemed incredibly near. The time, too, now that he reflected, he saw to have been short. He wondered at the number of emotions and events that had been crowded into such little spaces. Elfin thoughts must have exaggerated and enlarged everything, he said.

It seemed, then, that there was bitter justice in the speeches of the gaunt and bronzed veterans. He veiled a glance of disdain at his fellows who strewed the ground, choking with dust, red from perspiration, misty-eyed, disheveled.

They were gulping at their canteens, fierce to wring every mite of water from them, and they polished at their swollen and watery features with coat sleeves and bunches of grass.

However, to the youth there was a considerable joy in musing upon his performances during the charge. He had had very little time previously in which to appreciate himself, so that there was now much satisfaction in quietly thinking of his actions. He recalled bits of color that in the flurry had stamped themselves unawares upon his engaged senses.

As the regiment lay heaving from its hot exertions the officer who had named them as mule drivers came galloping along the line. He had lost his cap. His tousled hair streamed wildly, and his face was dark with vexation and wrath. His temper was displayed with more clearness by the way in which he managed his horse. He jerked and wrenched savagely at his bridle, stopping the hard-breathing animal with a furious pull near the colonel of the regiment. He immediately exploded in reproaches which came unbidden to the ears of the men. They were suddenly alert, being always curious about black words between officers.

"Oh, thunder, MacChesnay, what an awful bull you made of this thing!" began the officer. He attempted low tones, but his indignation caused certain of the men to learn the sense of his words. "What an awful mess you made! Good Lord, man, you stopped about a hundred feet this side of a very pretty success! If your men had gone a hundred feet farther you would have made a great charge, but as it is—what a lot of mud diggers you've got anyway!"

The men, listening with bated breath, now turned their curious eyes upon the colonel. They had a ragamuffin interest in this affair.

The colonel was seen to straighten his form and put one hand forth in oratorical fashion. He wore an injured air; it was as if a deacon had been accused of stealing. The men were wiggling in an ecstasy of excitement.

But of a sudden the colonel's manner changed from that of a deacon to that of a Frenchman. He shrugged his shoulders. "Oh, well, general, we went as far as we could," he said calmly.

"As far as you could? Did you, b'Gawd?" snorted the other. "Well, that wasn't very far, was it?" he added, with a glance of cold contempt into the other's eyes. "Not very far, I think. You were intended to make a diversion in favor of Whiterside. How well you succeeded your own ears can now tell you." He wheeled his horse and rode stiffly away.

The colonel, bidden to hear the jarring noises of an engagement in the woods to the left, broke out in vague damnations.

The lieutenant, who had listened with an air of impotent rage to the interview, spoke suddenly in firm and undaunted tones. "I don't care what a man is—whether he is a general or what—if he says th' boys didn't put up a good fight out there he's a damned fool."

"Lieutenant," began the colonel, severely, "this is my own affair, and I'll trouble you—"

The lieutenant made an obedient gesture. "All right, colonel, all right," he said. He sat down with an air of being content with himself.

The news that the regiment had been reproached went along the line. For a time the men were bewildered by it. "Good thunder!" they ejaculated, staring at the vanishing form of the general. They conceived it to be a huge mistake.

Presently, however, they began to believe that in truth their efforts had been called light. The youth could see this conviction weigh upon the entire regiment until the men were like cuffed and cursed animals, but withal rebellious.

The friend, with a grievance in his eye, went to the youth. "I wonder what he does want," he said. "He must think we went out there an' played marbles! I never see sech a man!"

The youth developed a tranquil philosophy for these moments of irritation. "Oh, well," he rejoined, "he probably didn't see nothing of it at all and got mad as blazes, and concluded we were a lot of sheep, just because we didn't do what he wanted done. It's a pity old Grandpa Henderson got killed yestirday—he'd have known that we did our best and fought good. It's just our awful luck, that's what."

"I should say so," replied the friend. He seemed to be deeply wounded at an injustice. "I should say we did have awful luck! There's no fun in fightin' fer people when everything yeh do—no matter what—ain't done right. I have a notion t' stay behind next time an' let 'em take their ol' charge an' go t' th' devil with it."

The youth spoke soothingly to his comrade. "Well, we both did good. I'd like to see the fool what'd say we both didn't do as good as we could!"

"Of course we did," declared the friend stoutly. "An' I'd break th' feller's neck if he was as big as a church. But we're all right, anyhow, for I heard one feller say that we two fit th' best in th' reg'ment, an' they had a great argument 'bout it. Another feller, 'a course, he had t' up an' say it was a lie—he seen all what was goin' on an' he never seen us from th' beginnin' t' th' end. An' a lot more struck in an' ses it wasn't a lie—we did fight like thunder, an' they give us quite a send-off. But this is what I can't stand—these everlastin' ol' soldiers, titterin' an' laughin', an' then that general, he's crazy."

The youth exclaimed with sudden exasperation: "He's a lunkhead! He makes me mad. I wish he'd come along next time. We'd show 'im what—"

He ceased because several men had come hurrying up. Their faces expressed a bringing of great news.

"O Flem, yeh jest oughta heard!" cried one, eagerly.

"Heard what?" said the youth.

"Yeh jest oughta heard!" repeated the other, and he arranged himself to tell his tidings. The others made an excited circle. "Well, sir, th' colonel met your lieutenant right by us—it was damnedest thing I ever heard—an' he ses: 'Ahem! ahem!' he ses. 'Mr. Hasbrouck!' he ses, 'by th' way, who was that lad what carried th' flag?' he ses. There, Flemin', what d' yeh think 'a that? 'Who was th' lad what carried th' flag?' he ses, an' th' lieutenant, he speaks up right away: 'That's Flemin', an' he's a jimhickey,' he ses, right away. What? I say he did. 'A jim-hickey,' he ses—those 'r his words. He did, too. I say he did. If you kin tell this story better than I kin, go ahead an' tell it. Well, then, keep yer mouth shet. Th' lieutenant, he ses: 'He's a jimhickey,' an' th' colonel, he ses: 'Ahem! ahem! he is, indeed, a very good man t' have, ahem! He kep' th' flag 'way t' th' front. I saw 'im. He's a good un,' ses th' colonel. 'You bet,' ses th' lieutenant, 'he an' a feller named Wilson was at th' head 'a th' charge, an' howlin' like Indians all th' time,' he ses. 'Head 'a th' charge all th' time,' he ses. 'A feller named Wilson,' he ses. There, Wilson, m'boy, put that in a letter an' send it hum t' yer mother, hay? 'A feller named Wilson,' he ses. An' th' colonel, he ses: 'Were they, indeed? Ahem! ahem! My sakes!' he ses. 'At th' head 'a th' reg'ment?' he ses. 'They were,' ses th' lieutenant. 'My sakes!' ses th' colonel. He ses: 'Well, well, well,' he ses, 'those two babies?' 'They were,' ses th' lieutenant. 'Well, well,' ses th' colonel, 'they deserve t' be major generals,' he ses. 'They deserve t' be major-generals.'"

The youth and his friend had said: "Huh!" "Yer lyin', Thompson." "Oh, go t' blazes!" "He never sed it." "Oh, what a lie!" "Huh!" But despite these youthful scoffings and embarrassments, they knew that their faces were deeply flushing from thrills of pleasure. They exchanged a secret glance of joy and congratulation.

They speedily forgot many things. The past held no pictures of error and disappointment. They were very happy, and their hearts swelled with grateful affection for the colonel and the youthful lieutenant.

## CHAPTER XXII.

When the woods again began to pour forth the dark-hued masses of the enemy the youth felt serene self-confidence. He smiled briefly when he saw men dodge and duck at the long screechings of shells that were thrown in giant handfuls over them. He stood, erect and tranquil, watching the attack begin against a part of the line that made a blue curve along the side of an adjacent hill. His vision being unmolested by smoke from the rifles of his companions, he had opportunities to see parts of the hard fight. It was a relief to perceive at last from whence came some of these noises which had been roared into his ears.

Off a short way he saw two regiments fighting a little separate battle with two other regiments. It was in a cleared space, wearing a set-apart look. They were blazing as if upon a wager, giving and taking tremendous blows. The firings were incredibly fierce and rapid. These intent regiments apparently were oblivious of all larger purposes of war, and were slugging each other as if at a matched game.

In another direction he saw a magnificent brigade going with the evident intention of driving the enemy from a wood. They passed in out of sight and presently there was a most awe-inspiring racket in the wood. The noise was unspeakable. Having stirred this prodigious uproar, and, apparently, finding it too prodigious, the brigade, after a little time, came marching airily out again with its fine formation in nowise disturbed. There were no traces of speed in its movements. The brigade was jaunty and seemed to point a proud thumb at the yelling wood.

On a slope to the left there was a long row of guns, gruff and maddened, denouncing the enemy, who, down through the woods, were forming for another attack in the pitiless monotony of conflicts. The round red discharges from the guns made a crimson flare and a high, thick smoke. Occasional glimpses could be caught of groups of the toiling artillerymen. In the rear of this row of guns stood a house, calm and white, amid bursting shells. A congregation of horses, tied to a long railing, were tugging frenziedly at their bridles. Men were running hither and thither.

The detached battle between the four regiments lasted for some time. There chanced to be no interference, and they settled their dispute by themselves. They struck savagely and powerfully at each other for a period of minutes, and then the lighter-hued regiments faltered and drew back, leaving the dark-blue lines shouting. The youth could see the two flags shaking with laughter amid the smoke remnants.

Presently there was a stillness, pregnant with meaning. The blue lines shifted and changed a trifle and stared expectantly at the silent woods and fields before them. The hush was solemn and churchlike, save for a distant battery that, evidently unable to remain quiet, sent a faint rolling thunder over the ground. It irritated, like the noises of unimpressed boys. The men imagined that it would prevent their perched ears from hearing the first words of the new battle.

Of a sudden the guns on the slope roared out a message of warning. A spluttering sound had begun in the woods. It swelled with amazing speed to a profound clamor that involved the earth in noises. The splitting crashes swept along the lines until an interminable roar was developed. To those in the midst of it it became a din fitted to the universe. It was the whirring and thumping of gigantic machinery, complications among the smaller stars. The youth's ears were filled up. They were incapable of hearing more.

On an incline over which a road wound he saw wild and desperate rushes of men perpetually backward and forward in riotous surges. These parts of the opposing armies were two long waves that pitched upon each other madly at dictated points. To and fro they swelled. Sometimes, one side by its yells and cheers would proclaim decisive blows, but a moment later the other side would be all yells and cheers. Once the youth saw a spray of light forms go in houndlike leaps toward the waving blue lines. There was much howling, and presently it went away with a vast mouthful of prisoners. Again, he saw a blue wave dash with such thunderous force against a gray obstruction that it seemed to clear the earth of it and leave nothing but trampled sod. And always in their swift and deadly rushes to and fro the men screamed and yelled like maniacs.

Particular pieces of fence or secure positions behind collections of trees were wrangled over, as gold thrones or pearl bedsteads. There were desperate lunges at these chosen spots seemingly every instant, and most of them were bandied like light toys between the contending forces. The youth could not tell from the battle flags flying like crimson foam in many directions which color of cloth was winning.

His emaciated regiment bustled forth with undiminished fierceness when its time came. When assaulted again by bullets, the men burst out in a barbaric cry of rage and pain. They bent their heads in aims of intent hatred behind the projected hammers of their guns. Their ramrods clanged loud with fury as their eager arms pounded the cartridges into the rifle barrels. The front of the regiment was a smoke-wall penetrated by the flashing points of yellow and red.

Wallowing in the fight, they were in an astonishingly short time resmudged. They surpassed in stain and dirt all their previous appearances. Moving to and fro with strained exertion, jabbering the while, they were, with their swaying bodies, black faces, and glowing eyes, like strange and ugly friends jigging heavily in the smoke.

The lieutenant, returning from a tour after a bandage, produced from a hidden receptacle of his mind new and portentous oaths suited to the emergency. Strings of expletives he swung lashlike over the backs of his men, and it was evident that his previous efforts had in nowise impaired his resources.

The youth, still the bearer of the colors, did not feel his idleness. He was deeply absorbed as a spectator. The crash and swing of the great drama made him lean forward, intent-eyed, his face working in small contortions. Sometimes he prattled, words coming unconsciously from him in grotesque exclamations. He did not know that he breathed; that the flag hung silently over him, so absorbed was he.

A formidable line of the enemy came within dangerous range. They could be seen plainly—tall, gaunt men with excited faces running with long strides toward a wandering fence.

At sight of this danger the men suddenly ceased their cursing monotone. There was an instant of strained silence before they threw up their rifles and fired a plumping volley at the foes. There had been no order given; the men, upon recognizing the menace, had immediately let drive their flock of bullets without waiting for word of command.

But the enemy were quick to gain the protection of the wandering line of fence. They slid down behind it with remarkable celerity, and from this position they began briskly to slice up the blue men.

These latter braced their energies for a great struggle. Often, white clinched teeth shone from the dusky faces. Many heads surged to and fro, floating upon a pale sea of smoke. Those behind the fence frequently shouted and yelped in taunts and gibelike cries, but the regiment maintained a stressed silence. Perhaps, at this new assault the men recalled the fact that they had been named mud diggers, and it made their situation thrice bitter. They were breathlessly intent upon keeping the ground and thrusting away the rejoicing body of the enemy. They fought swiftly and with a despairing savageness denoted in their expressions.

The youth had resolved not to budge whatever should happen. Some arrows of scorn that had buried themselves in his heart had generated strange and unspeakable hatred. It was clear to him that his final and absolute revenge was to be achieved by his dead body lying, torn and gluttering, upon the field. This was to be a poignant retaliation upon the officer who had said "mule drivers," and later "mud diggers," for in all the wild graspings of his mind for a unit responsible for his sufferings and commotions he always seized upon the man who had dubbed him wrongly. And it was his idea, vaguely formulated, that his corpse would be for those eyes a great and salt reproach.

The regiment bled extravagantly. Grunting bundles of blue began to drop. The orderly sergeant of the youth's company was shot through the cheeks. Its supports being injured, his jaw hung afar down, disclosing in the wide cavern of his mouth a pulsing mass of blood and teeth. And with it all he made attempts to cry out. In his endeavor there was a dreadful earnestness, as if he conceived that one great shriek would make him well.

The youth saw him presently go rearward. His strength seemed in nowise impaired. He ran swiftly, casting wild glances for succor.

Others fell down about the feet of their companions. Some of the wounded crawled out and away, but many lay still, their bodies twisted into impossible shapes.

The youth looked once for his friend. He saw a vehement young man, powder-smeared and frowzled, whom he knew to be him. The lieutenant, also, was unscathed in his position at the rear. He had continued to curse, but it was now with the air of a man who was using his last box of oaths.

For the fire of the regiment had begun to wane and drip. The robust voice, that had come strangely from the thin ranks, was growing rapidly weak.

## CHAPTER XXIII.

The colonel came running along back of the line. There were other officers following him. "We must charge'm!" they shouted. "We must charge'm!" they cried with resentful voices, as if anticipating a rebellion against this plan by the men.

The youth, upon hearing the shouts, began to study the distance between him and the enemy. He made vague calculations. He saw that to be firm soldiers they must go forward. It would be death to stay in the present place, and with all the circumstances to go backward would exalt too many others. Their hope was to push the galling foes away from the fence.

He expected that his companions, weary and stiffened, would have to be driven to this assault, but as he turned toward them he perceived with a certain surprise that they were giving quick and unqualified expressions of assent. There was an ominous, clanging overture to the charge when the shafts of the bayonets rattled upon the rifle barrels. At the yelled words of command the soldiers sprang forward in eager leaps. There was new and unexpected force in the movement of the regiment. A knowledge of its faded and jaded condition made the charge appear like a paroxysm, a display of the strength that comes before a final feebleness. The men scampered in insane fever of haste, racing as if to achieve a sudden success before an exhilarating fluid should leave them. It was a blind and despairing rush by the collection of men in dusty and tattered blue, over a green sward and under a sapphire sky, toward a fence, dimly outlined in smoke, from behind which spluttered the fierce rifles of enemies.

The youth kept the bright colors to the front. He was waving his free arm in furious circles, the while shrieking mad calls and appeals, urging on those that did not need to be urged, for it seemed that the mob of blue men hurling themselves on the dangerous group of rifles were again grown suddenly wild with an enthusiasm of unselfishness. From the many firings starting toward them, it looked as if they would merely succeed in making a great sprinkling of corpses on the grass between their former position and the fence. But they were in a state of frenzy, perhaps because of forgotten vanities, and it made an exhibition of sublime recklessness. There was no obvious questioning, nor figurings, nor diagrams. There was, apparently, no considered loopholes. It appeared that the swift wings of their desires would have shattered against the iron gates of the impossible.

He himself felt the daring spirit of a savage religion mad. He was capable of profound sacrifices, a tremendous death. He had no time for dissections, but he knew that he thought of the bullets only as things that could prevent him from reaching the place of his endeavor. There were subtle flashings of joy within him that thus should be his mind.

He strained all his strength. His eyesight was shaken and dazzled by the tension of thought and muscle. He did not see anything excepting the mist of smoke gashed by the little knives of fire, but he knew that in it lay the aged fence of a vanished farmer protecting the snuggled bodies of the gray men.

As he ran a thought of the shock of contact gleamed in his mind. He expected a great concussion when the two bodies of troops crashed together. This became a part of his wild battle madness. He could feel the onward swing of the regiment about him and he conceived of a thunderous, crushing blow that would prostrate the resistance and spread consternation and amazement for miles. The flying regiment was going to have a catapultian effect. This dream made him run faster among his comrades, who were giving vent to hoarse and frantic cheers.

But presently he could see that many of the men in gray did not intend to abide the blow. The smoke, rolling, disclosed men who ran, their faces still turned. These grew to a crowd, who retired stubbornly. Individuals wheeled frequently to send a bullet at the blue wave.

But at one part of the line there was a grim and obdurate group that made no movement. They were settled firmly down behind posts and rails. A flag, ruffled and fierce, waved over them and their rifles dinned fiercely.

The blue whirl of men got very near, until it seemed that in truth there would be a close and frightful scuffle. There was an expressed disdain in the opposition of the little group, that changed the meaning of the cheers of the men in blue. They became yells of wrath, directed, personal. The cries of the two parties were now in sound an interchange of scathing insults.

They in blue showed their teeth; their eyes shone all white. They launched themselves as at the throats of those who stood resisting. The space between dwindled to an insignificant distance.

The youth had centered the gaze of his soul upon that other flag. Its possession would be high pride. It would express bloody minglings, near blows. He had a gigantic hatred for those who made great difficulties and complications. They caused it to be as a craved treasure of mythology, hung amid tasks and contrivances of danger.

He plunged like a mad horse at it. He was resolved it should not escape if wild blows and darings of blows could seize it. His own emblem, quivering and aflare, was winging toward the other. It seemed there would shortly be an encounter of strange beaks and claws, as of eagles.

The swirling body of blue men came to a sudden halt at close and disastrous range and roared a swift volley. The group in gray was split and broken by this fire, but its riddled body still fought. The men in blue yelled again and rushed in upon it.

The youth, in his leapings, saw, as through a mist, a picture of four or five men stretched upon the ground or writhing upon their knees with bowed heads as if they had been stricken by bolts from the sky. Tottering among them was the rival color bearer, whom the youth saw had been bitten vitally by the bullets of the last formidable volley. He perceived this man fighting a last struggle, the struggle of one whose legs are grasped by demons. It was a ghastly battle. Over his face was the bleach of death, but set upon it was the dark and hard lines of desperate purpose. With this terrible grin of resolution he hugged his precious flag to him and was stumbling and staggering in his design to go the way that led to safety for it.

But his wounds always made it seem that his feet were retarded, held, and he fought a grim fight, as with invisible ghouls fastened greedily upon his limbs. Those in advance of the scampering blue men, howling cheers, leaped at the fence. The despair of the lost was in his eyes as he glanced back at them.

The youth's friend went over the obstruction in a tumbling heap and sprang at the flag as a panther at prey. He pulled at it and, wrenching it free, swung up its red brilliancy with a mad cry of exultation even as the color bearer, gasping, lurched over in a final throe and, stiffening convulsively, turned his dead face to the ground. There was much blood upon the grass blades.

At the place of success there began more wild clamorings of cheers. The men gesticulated and bellowed in an ecstasy. When they spoke it was as if they considered their listener to be a mile away. What hats and caps were left to them they often slung high in the air.

At one part of the line four men had been swooped upon, and they now sat as prisoners. Some blue men were about them in an eager and curious circle. The soldiers had trapped strange birds, and there was an examination. A flurry of fast questions was in the air.

One of the prisoners was nursing a superficial wound in the foot. He cuddled it, baby-wise, but he looked up from it often to curse with an astonishing utter abandon straight at the noses of his captors. He consigned them to red regions; he called upon the pestilential wrath of strange gods. And with it all he was singularly free from recognition of the finer points of the conduct of prisoners of war. It was as if a clumsy clod had trod upon his toe and he conceived it to be his privilege, his duty, to use deep, resentful oaths.

Another, who was a boy in years, took his plight with great calmness and apparent good nature. He conversed with the men in blue, studying their faces with his bright and keen eyes. They spoke of battles and conditions. There was an acute interest in all their faces during this exchange of view points. It seemed a great satisfaction to hear voices from where all had been darkness and speculation.

The third captive sat with a morose countenance. He preserved a stoical and cold attitude. To all advances he made one reply without variation, "Ah, go t' hell!"

The last of the four was always silent and, for the most part, kept his face turned in unmolested directions. From the views the youth received he seemed to be in a state of absolute dejection. Shame was upon him, and with it profound regret that he was, perhaps, no more to be counted in the ranks of his fellows. The youth could detect no expression that would allow him to believe that the other was giving a thought to his narrowed future, the pictured dungeons, perhaps, and starvations and brutalities, liable to the imagination. All to be seen was shame for captivity and regret for the right to antagonize.

After the men had celebrated sufficiently they settled down behind the old rail fence, on the opposite side to the one from which their foes had been driven. A few shot perfunctorily at distant marks.

There was some long grass. The youth nestled in it and rested, making a convenient rail support the flag. His friend, jubilant and glorified, holding his treasure with vanity, came to him there. They sat side by side and congratulated each other.

## CHAPTER XXIV.

The roarings that had stretched in a long line of sound across the face of the forest began to grow intermittent and weaker. The stentorian speeches of the artillery continued in some distant encounter, but the crashes of the musketry had almost ceased. The youth and his friend of a sudden looked up, feeling a deadened form of distress at the waning of these noises, which had become a part of life. They could see changes going on among the troops. There were marchings this way and that way. A battery wheeled leisurely. On the crest of a small hill was the thick gleam of many departing muskets.

The youth arose. "Well, what now, I wonder?" he said. By his tone he seemed to be preparing to resent some new monstrosity in the way of dins and smashes. He shaded his eyes with his grimy hand and gazed over the field.

His friend also arose and stared. "I bet we're goin' t' git along out of this an' back over th' river," said he.

"Well, I swan!" said the youth.

They waited, watching. Within a little while the regiment received orders to retrace its way. The men got up grunting from the grass, regretting the soft repose. They jerked their stiffened legs, and stretched their arms over their heads. One man swore as he rubbed his eyes. They all groaned "O Lord!" They had as many objections to this change as they would have had to a proposal for a new battle.

They trampled slowly back over the field across which they had run in a mad scamper.

The regiment marched until it had joined its fellows. The reformed brigade, in column, aimed through a wood at the road. Directly they were in a mass of dust-covered troops, and were trudging along in a way parallel to the enemy's lines as these had been defined by the previous turmoil.

They passed within view of a stolid white house, and saw in front of it groups of their comrades lying in wait behind a neat breastwork. A row of guns were booming at a distant enemy. Shells thrown in reply were raising clouds of dust and splinters. Horsemen dashed along the line of intrenchments.

At this point of its march the division curved away from the field and went winding off in the direction of the river. When the significance of this movement had impressed itself upon the youth he turned his head and looked over his shoulder toward the trampled and *débris*-strewed ground. He breathed a breath of new satisfaction. He finally nudged his friend. "Well, it's all over," he said to him.

His friend gazed backward. "B'Gawd, it is," he assented. They mused.

For a time the youth was obliged to reflect in a puzzled and uncertain way. His mind was undergoing a subtle change. It took moments for it to cast off its battleful ways and resume its accustomed course of thought. Gradually his brain emerged from the clogged clouds, and at last he was enabled to more closely comprehend himself and circumstance.

He understood then that the existence of shot and counter-shot was in the past. He had dwelt in a land of strange, squalling upheavals and had come forth. He had been where there was red of blood and black of passion, and he was escaped. His first thoughts were given to rejoicings at this fact.

Later he began to study his deeds, his failures, and his achievements. Thus, fresh from scenes where many of his usual machines of reflection had been idle, from where he had proceeded sheeplike, he struggled to marshal all his acts.

At last they marched before him clearly. From this present view point he was enabled to look upon them in spectator fashion and to criticise them with some correctness, for his new condition had already defeated certain sympathies.

Regarding his procession of memory he felt gleeful and unregretting, for in it his public deeds were paraded in great and shining prominence. Those performances which had been witnessed by his fellows marched now in wide purple and gold, having various deflections. They went gayly with music. It was pleasure to watch these things. He spent delightful minutes viewing the gilded images of memory.

He saw that he was good. He recalled with a thrill of joy the respectful comments of his fellows upon his conduct.

Nevertheless, the ghost of his flight from the first engagement appeared to him and danced. There were small shoutings in his brain about these matters. For a moment he blushed, and the light of his soul flickered with shame.

A specter of reproach came to him. There loomed the dogging memory of the tattered soldier—he who, gored by bullets and faint for blood, had fretted concerning an imagined wound in another; he who had loaned his last of strength and intellect for the tall soldier; he who, blind with weariness and pain, had been deserted in the field.

For an instant a wretched chill of sweat was upon him at the thought that he might be detected in the thing. As he stood persistently before his vision, he gave vent to a cry of sharp irritation and agony.

His friend turned. "What's the matter, Henry?" he demanded. The youth's reply was an outburst of crimson oaths.

As he marched along the little branch-hung roadway among his prattling companions this vision of cruelty brooded over him. It clung near him always and darkened his view of these deeds in purple and gold. Whichever way his thoughts turned they were followed by the somber phantom of the desertion in the fields. He looked stealthily at his companions, feeling sure that they must discern in his face evidences of this pursuit. But they were plodding in ragged array, discussing with quick tongues the accomplishments of the late battle.

"Oh, if a man should come up an' ask me, I'd say we got a dum good lickin'."

"Lickin'—in yer eye! We ain't licked, sonny. We're goin' down here aways, swing aroun', an' come in behint 'em."

"Oh, hush, with your comin' in behint 'em. I've seen all 'a that I wanta. Don't tell me about comin' in behint—"

"Bill Smithers, he ses he'd rather been in ten hundred battles than been in that heluva hospital. He ses they got shootin' in th' night-time, an' shells dropped plum among 'em in th' hospital. He ses sech hollerin' he never see."

"Hasbrouck? He's th' best off'cer in this here reg'ment. He's a whale."

"Didn't I tell yeh we'd come aroun' in behint 'em? Didn't I tell yeh so? We—"

"Oh, shet yeh mouth!"

For a time this pursuing recollection of the tattered man took all elation from the youth's veins. He saw his vivid error, and he was afraid that it would stand before him all his life. He took no share in the chatter of his comrades, nor did he look at them or know them, save when he felt sudden suspicion that they were seeing his thoughts and scrutinizing each detail of the scene with the tattered soldier.

Yet gradually he mustered force to put the sin at a distance. And at last his eyes seemed to open to some new ways. He found that he could look back upon the brass and bombast of his earlier gospels and see them truly. He was gleeful when he discovered that he now despised them.

With this conviction came a store of assurance. He felt a quiet manhood, nonassertive but of sturdy and strong blood. He knew that he would no more quail before his guides wherever they should point. He had been to touch the great death, and found that, after all, it was but the great death. He was a man.

So it came to pass that as he trudged from the place of blood and wrath his soul changed. He came from hot plowshares to prospects of clover tranquilly, and it was as if hot plowshares were not. Scars faded as flowers.

It rained. The procession of weary soldiers became a bedraggled train, despondent and muttering, marching with churning effort in a trough of liquid brown mud under a low, wretched sky. Yet the youth smiled, for he saw that the world was a world for him, though many discovered it to be made of oaths and walking sticks. He had rid himself of the red sickness of battle. The sultry nightmare was in the past. He had been an animal blistered and sweating in the heat and pain of war. He turned now with a lover's thirst to images of tranquil skies, fresh meadows, cool brooks—an existence of soft and eternal peace.

Over the river a golden ray of sun came through the hosts of leaden rain clouds.

# THE OPEN BOAT

A Tale intended to be after the fact. Being the experience of four men from the sunk steamer "Commodore"

## I

None of them knew the color of the sky. Their eyes glanced level, and were fastened upon the waves that swept toward them. These waves were of the hue of slate, save for the tops, which were of foaming white, and all of the men knew the colors of the sea. The horizon narrowed and widened, and dipped and rose, and at all times its edge was jagged with waves that seemed thrust up in points like rocks. Many a man ought to have a bath-tub larger than the boat which here rode upon the sea. These waves were most wrongfully and barbarously abrupt and tall, and each froth-top was a problem in small-boat navigation.

The cook squatted in the bottom and looked with both eyes at the six inches of gunwale which separated him from the ocean. His sleeves were rolled over his fat forearms, and the two flaps of his unbuttoned vest dangled as he bent to bail out the boat. Often he said: "Gawd! That was a narrow clip." As he remarked it he invariably gazed eastward over the broken sea.

The oiler, steering with one of the two oars in the boat, sometimes raised himself suddenly to keep clear of water that swirled in over the stern. It was a thin little oar and it seemed often ready to snap.

The correspondent, pulling at the other oar, watched the waves and wondered why he was there.

The injured captain, lying in the bow, was at this time buried in that profound dejection and indifference which comes, temporarily at least, to even the bravest and most enduring when, willy nilly, the firm fails, the army loses, the ship goes down. The mind of the master of a vessel is rooted deep in the timbers of her, though he commanded for a day or a decade, and this captain had on him the stern impression of a scene in the greys of dawn of seven turned faces, and later a stump of a top-mast with a white ball on it that slashed to and fro at the waves, went low and lower, and down. Thereafter there was something strange in his voice. Although steady, it was, deep with mourning, and of a quality beyond oration or tears.

"Keep 'er a little more south, Billie," said he.

"'A little more south,' sir," said the oiler in the stern.

A seat in this boat was not unlike a seat upon a bucking broncho, and by the same token, a broncho is not much smaller. The craft pranced and reared, and plunged like an animal. As each wave came, and she rose for it, she seemed like a horse making at a fence outrageously high. The manner of her scramble over these walls of water is a mystic thing, and, moreover, at the top of them were ordinarily these problems in white water, the foam racing down from the summit of each wave, requiring a new leap, and a leap from the air. Then, after scornfully bumping a crest, she would slide, and race, and splash down a long incline, and arrive bobbing and nodding in front of the next menace.

A singular disadvantage of the sea lies in the fact that after successfully surmounting one wave you discover that there is another behind it just as important and just as nervously anxious to do something effective in the way of swamping boats. In a ten-foot dingey one can get an idea of the resources of the sea in the line of waves that is not probable to the average experience which is never at sea in a dingey. As each slatey wall of water approached, it shut all else from the view of the men in the boat, and it was not difficult to imagine that this particular wave was the final outburst of the ocean, the last effort of the grim water. There was a terrible grace in the move of the waves, and they came in silence, save for the snarling of the crests.

In the wan light, the faces of the men must have been grey. Their eyes must have glinted in strange ways as they gazed steadily astern. Viewed from a balcony, the whole thing would doubtless have been weirdly picturesque. But the men in the boat had no time to see it, and if they had had leisure there were other things to occupy their minds. The sun swung steadily up the sky, and they knew it was broad day because the color of the sea changed from slate to emerald-green, streaked with amber lights, and the foam was like tumbling snow. The process of the breaking day was unknown to them. They were aware only of this effect upon the color of the waves that rolled toward them.

In disjointed sentences the cook and the correspondent argued as to the difference between a life-saving station and a house of refuge. The cook had said: "There's a house of refuge just north of the Mosquito Inlet Light, and as soon as they see us, they'll come off in their boat and pick us up."

"As soon as who see us?" said the correspondent.

"The crew," said the cook.

"Houses of refuge don't have crews," said the correspondent. "As I understand them, they are only places where clothes and grub are stored for the benefit of shipwrecked people. They don't carry crews."

"Oh, yes, they do," said the cook.

"No, they don't," said the correspondent.

"Well, we're not there yet, anyhow," said the oiler, in the stern.

"Well," said the cook, "perhaps it's not a house of refuge that I'm thinking of as being near Mosquito Inlet Light. Perhaps it's a life-saving station."

"We're not there yet," said the oiler, in the stern.

## II

As the boat bounced from the top of each wave, the wind tore through the hair of the hatless men, and as the craft plopped her stern down again the spray splashed past them. The crest of each of these waves was a hill, from the top of which the men surveyed, for a moment, a broad tumultuous expanse, shining and wind-riven. It was probably splendid. It was probably glorious, this play of the free sea, wild with lights of emerald and white and amber.

"Bully good thing it's an on-shore wind," said the cook; "If not, where would we be? Wouldn't have a show."

"That's right," said the correspondent.

The busy oiler nodded his assent.

Then the captain, in the bow, chuckled in a way that expressed humor, contempt, tragedy, all in one. "Do you think We've got much of a show now, boys?" said he.

Whereupon the three were silent, save for a trifle of hemming and hawing. To express any particular optimism at this time they felt to be childish and stupid, but they all doubtless possessed this sense of the situation in their mind. A young man thinks doggedly at such times. On the other hand, the ethics of their condition was decidedly against any open suggestion of hopelessness. So they were silent.

"Oh, well," said the captain, soothing his children, "We'll get ashore all right."

But there was that in his tone which made them think, so the oiler quoth: "Yes! If this wind holds!"

The cook was bailing: "Yes! If we don't catch hell in the surf."

Canton flannel gulls flew near and far. Sometimes they sat down on the sea, near patches of brown seaweed that rolled on the waves with a movement like carpets on a line in a gale. The birds sat comfortably in groups, and they were envied by some in the dingey, for the wrath of the sea was no more to them than it was to a covey of prairie chickens a thousand miles inland. Often they came very close and stared at the men with black bead-like eyes. At these times they were uncanny and sinister in their unblinking scrutiny, and the men hooted angrily at them, telling them to be gone. One came, and evidently decided to alight on the top of the captain's head. The bird flew parallel to the boat and did not circle, but made short sidelong jumps in the air in chicken-fashion. His black eyes were wistfully fixed upon the captain's head. "Ugly brute," said the oiler to the bird. "You look as if you were made with a jack-knife." The cook and the correspondent swore darkly at the creature. The captain naturally wished to knock it away with the end of the heavy painter; but he did not dare do it, because anything resembling an emphatic gesture would have capsized this freighted boat, and so with his open hand, the captain gently and carefully waved the gull away. After it had been discouraged from the pursuit the captain breathed easier on account of his hair, and others breathed easier because the bird struck their minds at this time as being somehow grewsome and ominous.

In the meantime the oiler and the correspondent rowed And also they rowed.

They sat together in the same seat, and each rowed an oar. Then the oiler took both oars; then the correspondent took both oars; then the oiler; then the correspondent. They rowed and they rowed. The very ticklish part of the business was when the time came for the reclining one in the stern to take his turn at the oars. By the very last star of truth, it is easier to steal eggs from under a hen than it was to change seats in the dingey. First the man in the stern slid his hand along the thwart and moved with care, as if he were of Sèvres. Then the man in the rowing seat slid his hand along the other thwart. It was all done with most extraordinary care. As the two sidled past each other, the whole party kept watchful eyes on the coming wave, and the captain cried: "Look out now! Steady there!"

The brown mats of seaweed that appeared from time to time were like islands, bits of earth. They were traveling, apparently, neither one way nor the other. They were, to all intents, stationary. They informed the men in the boat that it was making progress slowly toward the land.

The captain, rearing cautiously in the bow, after the dingey soared on a great swell, said that he had seen the light-house at Mosquito Inlet. Presently the cook remarked that he had seen it. The correspondent was at the oars then, and for some reason he too wished to look at the lighthouse, but his back was toward the far shore and the waves were important, and for some time he could not seize an opportunity to turn his head. But at last there came a wave more gentle than the others, and when at the crest of it he swiftly scoured the western horizon.

"See it?" said the captain.

"No," said the correspondent slowly, "I didn't see anything."

"Look again," said the captain. He pointed. "It's exactly in that direction."

At the top of another wave, the correspondent did as he was bid, and this time his eyes chanced on a small still thing on the edge of the swaying horizon. It was precisely like the point of a pin. It took an anxious eye to find a light house so tiny.

"Think we'll make it, captain?"

"If this wind holds and the boat don't swamp, we can't do much else," said the captain.

The little boat, lifted by each towering sea, and splashed viciously by the crests, made progress that in the absence of seaweed was not apparent to those in her. She seemed just a wee thing wallowing, miraculously top-up, at the mercy of five oceans. Occasionally, a great spread of water, like white flames, swarmed into her.

"Bail her, cook," said the captain serenely.

"All right, captain," said the cheerful cook.

### III

It would be difficult to describe the subtle brotherhood of men that was here established on the seas. No one said that it was so. No one mentioned it. But it dwelt in the boat, and each man felt it warm him. They were a captain, an oiler, a cook, and a correspondent, and they were friends, friends in a more curiously iron-bound degree than may be common. The hurt captain, lying against the water-jar in the bow, spoke always in a low voice and calmly, but he could never command a more ready and swiftly obedient crew than the motley three of the dingey. It was more than a mere recognition of what was best for the common safety. There was surely in it a quality that was personal and heartfelt. And after this devotion to the commander of the boat there was this comradeship that the correspondent, for instance, who had been taught to be cynical of men, knew even at the time was the best experience of his life. But no one said that it was so. No one mentioned it.

"I wish we had a sail," remarked the captain. "We might try my overcoat on the end of an oar and give you two boys a chance to rest." So the cook and the correspondent held the mast and spread wide the overcoat. The oiler steered, and the little boat made good way with her new rig. Sometimes the oiler had to scull sharply to keep a sea from breaking into the boat, but otherwise sailing was a success.

Meanwhile the lighthouse had been growing slowly larger. It had now almost assumed color, and appeared like a little grey shadow on the sky. The man at the oars could not be prevented from turning his head rather often to try for a glimpse of this little grey shadow.

At last, from the top of each wave the men in the tossing boat could see land. Even as the lighthouse was an upright shadow on the sky, this land seemed but a long black shadow on the sea. It certainly was thinner than paper. "We must be about opposite New Smyrna," said the cook, who had coasted this shore often in schooners. "Captain, by the way, I believe they abandoned that life-saving station there about a year ago."

"Did they?" said the captain.

The wind slowly died away. The cook and the correspondent were not now obliged to slave in order to hold high the oar. But the waves continued their old impetuous swooping at the dingey, and the little craft, no longer under way, struggled woundily over them. The oiler or the correspondent took the oars again.

Shipwrecks are *à propos* of nothing. If men could only train for them and have them occur when the men had reached pink condition, there would be less drowning at sea. Of the four in the dingey none had slept any time worth mentioning for two days and two nights previous to embarking in the dingey, and in the excitement of clambering about the deck of a foundering ship they had also forgotten to eat heartily.

For these reasons, and for others, neither the oiler nor the correspondent was fond of rowing at this time. The correspondent wondered ingenuously how in the name of all that was sane could there be people who thought it amusing to row a boat. It was not an amusement; it was a diabolical punishment, and even a genius of mental aberrations could never conclude that it was anything but a horror to the muscles and a crime against the back. He mentioned to the boat in general how the amusement of rowing struck him, and the weary-faced oiler smiled in full sympathy. Previously to the foundering, by the way, the oiler had worked double-watch in the engine-room of the ship.

"Take her easy, now, boys," said the captain. "Don't spend yourselves. If we have to run a surf you'll need all your strength, because we'll sure have to swim for it. Take your time."

Slowly the land arose from the sea. From a black line it became a line of black and a line of white, trees and sand. Finally, the captain said that he could make out a house on the shore. "That's the house of refuge, sure," said the cook. "They'll see us before long, and come out after us."

The distant lighthouse reared high. "The keeper ought to be able to make us out now, if he's looking through a glass," said the captain. "He'll notify the life-saving people."

"None of those other boats could have got ashore to give word of the wreck," said the oiler, in a low voice. "Else the lifeboat would be out hunting us."

Slowly and beautifully the land loomed out of the sea. The wind came again. It had veered from the north-east to the south-east. Finally, a new sound struck the ears of the men in the boat. It was the low thunder of the surf on the shore. "We'll never be able to make the lighthouse now," said the captain. "Swing her head a little more north, Billie," said he.

"'A little more north,' sir," said the oiler.

Whereupon the little boat turned her nose once more down the wind, and all but the oarsman watched the shore grow. Under the influence of this expansion doubt and direful apprehension was leaving the minds of the men. The management of the boat was still most absorbing, but it could not prevent a quiet cheerfulness. In an hour, perhaps, they would be ashore.

Their backbones had become thoroughly used to balancing in the boat, and they now rode this wild colt of a dingey like circus men. The correspondent thought that he had been drenched to the skin, but happening to feel in the top pocket of his coat, he found therein eight cigars. Four of them were soaked with sea-water; four were perfectly scathless. After a search, somebody produced three dry matches, and thereupon the four waifs rode impudently in their little boat, and with an assurance of an impending rescue shining in their eyes, puffed at the big cigars and judged well and ill of all men. Everybody took a drink of water.

IV

"Cook," remarked the captain, "there don't seem to be any signs of life about your house of refuge."

"No," replied the cook. "Funny they don't see us!"

A broad stretch of lowly coast lay before the eyes of the men. It was of dunes topped with dark vegetation. The roar of the surf was plain, and sometimes they could see the white lip of a wave as it spun up the beach. A tiny house was blocked out black upon the sky. Southward, the slim lighthouse lifted its little grey length.

Tide, wind, and waves were swinging the dingey northward. "Funny they don't see us," said the men.

The surf's roar was here dulled, but its tone was, nevertheless, thunderous and mighty. As the boat swam over the great rollers, the men sat listening to this roar. "We'll swamp sure," said everybody.

It is fair to say here that there was not a life-saving station within twenty miles in either direction, but the men did not know this fact, and in consequence they made dark and opprobrious remarks concerning the eyesight of the nation's life-savers. Four scowling men sat in the dingey and surpassed records in the invention of epithets.

"Funny they don't see us."

The lightheartedness of a former time had completely faded. To their sharpened minds it was easy to conjure pictures of all kinds of incompetency and blindness and, indeed, cowardice. There was the shore of the populous land, and it was bitter and bitter to them that from it came no sign.

"Well," said the captain, ultimately, "I suppose we'll have to make a try for ourselves. If we stay out here too long, we'll none of us have strength left to swim after the boat swamps."

And so the oiler, who was at the oars, turned the boat straight for the shore. There was a sudden tightening of muscle. There was some thinking.

"If we don't all get ashore—" said the captain. "If we don't all get ashore, I suppose you fellows know where to send news of my finish?"

They then briefly exchanged some addresses and admonitions. As for the reflections of the men, there was a great deal of rage in them. Perchance they might be formulated thus: "If I am going to be drowned—if I am going to be drowned—if I am going to be drowned, why, in the name of the seven mad gods who rule the sea, was I allowed to come thus far and contemplate sand and trees? Was I brought here merely to have my nose dragged away as I was about to nibble the sacred cheese of life? It is preposterous. If this old ninny-woman, Fate, cannot do better than this, she should be deprived of the management of men's fortunes. She is an old hen who knows not her intention. If she has decided to drown me, why did she not do it in the beginning and save me all this trouble? The whole affair is absurd…. But no, she cannot mean to drown me. She dare not drown me. She cannot drown me. Not after all this work." Afterward the man might have had an impulse to shake his fist at the clouds: "Just you drown me, now, and then hear what I call you!"

The billows that came at this time were more formidable. They seemed always just about to break and roll over the little boat in a turmoil of foam. There was a preparatory and long growl in the speech of them. No mind unused to the sea would have concluded that the dingey could ascend these sheer heights in time. The shore was still afar. The oiler was a wily surfman. "Boys," he said swiftly, "she won't live three minutes more, and we're too far out to swim. Shall I take her to sea again, captain?"

"Yes! Go ahead!" said the captain.

This oiler, by a series of quick miracles, and fast and steady oarsmanship, turned the boat in the middle of the surf and took her safely to sea again.

There was a considerable silence as the boat bumped over the furrowed sea to deeper water. Then somebody in gloom spoke. "Well, anyhow, they must have seen us from the shore by now."

The gulls went in slanting flight up the wind toward the grey desolate east. A squall, marked by dingy clouds, and clouds brick-red, like smoke from a burning building, appeared from the south-east.

"What do you think of those life-saving people? Ain't they peaches?'

"Funny they haven't seen us."

"Maybe they think we're out here for sport! Maybe they think we're fishin'. Maybe they think we're damned fools."

It was a long afternoon. A changed tide tried to force them southward, but the wind and wave said northward. Far ahead, where coast-line, sea, and sky formed their mighty angle, there were little dots which seemed to indicate a city on the shore.

"St. Augustine?"

The captain shook his head. "Too near Mosquito Inlet."

And the oiler rowed, and then the correspondent rowed. Then the oiler rowed. It was a weary business. The human back can become the seat of more aches and pains than are registered in books for the composite anatomy of a regiment. It is a limited area, but it can become the theatre of innumerable muscular conflicts, tangles, wrenches, knots, and other comforts.

"Did you ever like to row, Billie?" asked the correspondent.

"No," said the oiler. "Hang it!"

When one exchanged the rowing-seat for a place in the bottom of the boat, he suffered a bodily depression that caused him to be careless of everything save an obligation to wiggle one finger. There was cold sea-water swashing to and fro in the boat, and he lay in it. His head, pillowed on a thwart, was within an inch of the swirl of a wave crest, and sometimes a particularly obstreperous sea came in-board and drenched him once more. But these matters did not annoy him. It is almost certain that if the boat had capsized he would have tumbled comfortably out upon the ocean as if he felt sure that it was a great soft mattress.

"Look! There's a man on the shore!"

"Where?"

"There! See 'im? See 'im?"

"Yes, sure! He's walking along."

"Now he's stopped. Look! He's facing us!"

"He's waving at us!"

"So he is! By thunder!"

"Ah, now we're all right! Now we're all right! There'll be a boat out here for us in half-an-hour."

"He's going on. He's running. He's going up to that house there."

The remote beach seemed lower than the sea, and it required a searching glance to discern the little black figure. The captain saw a floating stick and they rowed to it. A bath-towel was by some weird chance in the boat, and, tying this on the stick, the captain waved it. The oarsman did not dare turn his head, so he was obliged to ask questions.

"What's he doing now?"

"He's standing still again. He's looking, I think.... There he goes again. Toward the house.... Now he's stopped again."

"Is he waving at us?"

"No, not now! he was, though."

"Look! There comes another man!"

"He's running."

"Look at him go, would you."

"Why, he's on a bicycle. Now he's met the other man. They're both waving at us. Look!"

"There comes something up the beach."

"What the devil is that thing?"

"Why it looks like a boat."

"Why, certainly it's a boat."

"No, it's on wheels."

"Yes, so it is. Well, that must be the life-boat. They drag them along shore on a wagon."

"That's the life-boat, sure."

"No, by God, it's—it's an omnibus."

"I tell you it's a life-boat."

"It is not! It's an omnibus. I can see it plain. See? One of these big hotel omnibuses."

"By thunder, you're right. It's an omnibus, sure as fate. What do you suppose they are doing with an omnibus? Maybe they are going around collecting the life-crew, hey?"

"That's it, likely. Look! There's a fellow waving a little black flag. He's standing on the steps of the omnibus. There come those other two fellows. Now they're all talking together. Look at the fellow with the flag. Maybe he ain't waving it."

"That ain't a flag, is it? That's his coat. Why, certainly, that's his coat."

"So it is. It's his coat. He's taken it off and is waving it around his head. But would you look at him swing it."

"Oh, say, there isn't any life-saving station there. That's just a winter resort hotel omnibus that has brought over some of the boarders to see us drown."

"What's that idiot with the coat mean? What's he signaling, anyhow?"

"It looks as if he were trying to tell us to go north. There must be a life-saving station up there."

"No! He thinks we're fishing. Just giving us a merry hand. See? Ah, there, Willie!"

"Well, I wish I could make something out of those signals. What do you suppose he means?"

"He don't mean anything. He's just playing."

"Well, if he'd just signal us to try the surf again, or to go to sea and wait, or go north, or go south, or go to hell—there would be some reason in it. But look at him. He just stands there and keeps his coat revolving like a wheel. The ass!"

"There come more people."

"Now there's quite a mob. Look! Isn't that a boat?"

"Where? Oh, I see where you mean. No, that's no boat."

"That fellow is still waving his coat."

"He must think we like to see him do that. Why don't he quit it? It don't mean anything."

"I don't know. I think he is trying to make us go north. It must be that there's a life-saving station there somewhere."

"Say, he ain't tired yet. Look at 'im wave."

"Wonder how long he can keep that up. He's been revolving his coat ever since he caught sight of us. He's an idiot. Why aren't they getting men to bring a boat out? A fishing boat—one of those big yawls—could come out here all right. Why don't he do something?"

"Oh, it's all right, now."

"They'll have a boat out here for us in less than no time, now that they've seen us."

A faint yellow tone came into the sky over the low land. The shadows on the sea slowly deepened. The wind bore coldness with it, and the men began to shiver.

"Holy smoke!" said one, allowing his voice to express his impious mood, "if we keep on monkeying out here! If we've got to flounder out here all night!"

"Oh, we'll never have to stay here all night! Don't you worry. They've seen us now, and it won't be long before they'll come chasing out after us."

The shore grew dusky. The man waving a coat blended gradually into this gloom, and it swallowed in the same manner the omnibus and the group of people. The spray, when it dashed uproariously over the side, made the voyagers shrink and swear like men who were being branded.

"I'd like to catch the chump who waved the coat. I feel like soaking him one, just for luck."

"Why? What did he do?"

"Oh, nothing, but then he seemed so damned cheerful."

In the meantime the oiler rowed, and then the correspondent rowed, and then the oiler rowed. Grey-faced and bowed forward, they mechanically, turn by turn, plied the leaden oars. The form of the lighthouse had vanished from the southern horizon, but finally a pale star appeared, just lifting from the sea. The streaked saffron in the west passed before the all-merging darkness, and the sea to the east was black. The land had vanished, and was expressed only by the low and drear thunder of the surf.

"If I am going to be drowned—if I am going to be drowned—if I am going to be drowned, why, in the name of the seven mad gods who rule the sea, was I allowed to come thus far and contemplate sand and trees? Was I brought here merely to have my nose dragged away as I was about to nibble the sacred cheese of life?"

The patient captain, drooped over the water-jar, was sometimes obliged to speak to the oarsman.

"Keep her head up! Keep her head up!"

"'Keep her head up,' sir." The voices were weary and low.

This was surely a quiet evening. All save the oarsman lay heavily and listlessly in the boat's bottom. As for him, his eyes were just capable of noting the tall black waves that swept forward in a most sinister silence, save for an occasional subdued growl of a crest.

The cook's head was on a thwart, and he looked without interest at the water under his nose. He was deep in other scenes. Finally he spoke. "Billie," he murmured, dreamfully, "what kind of pie do you like best?"

V

"Pie," said the oiler and the correspondent, agitatedly. "Don't talk about those things, blast you!"

"Well," said the cook, "I was just thinking about ham sandwiches, and—"

A night on the sea in an open boat is a long night. As darkness settled finally, the shine of the light, lifting from the sea in the south, changed to full gold. On the northern horizon a new light appeared, a small bluish gleam on the edge of the waters. These two lights were the furniture of the world. Otherwise there was nothing but waves.

Two men huddled in the stern, and distances were so magnificent in the dingey that the rower was enabled to keep his feet partly warmed by thrusting them under his companions. Their legs indeed extended far under the rowing-seat until they touched the feet of the captain forward. Sometimes, despite the efforts of the tired oarsman, a wave came piling into the boat, an icy wave of the night, and the chilling water soaked them anew. They would twist their bodies for a moment and groan, and sleep the dead sleep once more, while the water in the boat gurgled about them as the craft rocked.

The plan of the oiler and the correspondent was for one to row until he lost the ability, and then arouse the other from his sea-water couch in the bottom of the boat.

The oiler plied the oars until his head drooped forward, and the overpowering sleep blinded him. And he rowed yet afterward. Then he touched a man in the bottom of the boat, and called his name. "Will you spell me for a little while?" he said, meekly.

"Sure, Billie," said the correspondent, awakening and dragging himself to a sitting position. They exchanged places carefully, and the oiler, cuddling down in the sea-water at the cook's side, seemed to go to sleep instantly.

The particular violence of the sea had ceased. The waves came without snarling. The obligation of the man at the oars was to keep the boat headed so that the tilt of the rollers would not capsize her, and to preserve her from filling when the crests rushed past. The black waves were silent and hard to be seen in the darkness. Often one was almost upon the boat before the oarsman was aware.

In a low voice the correspondent addressed the captain. He was not sure that the captain was awake, although this iron man seemed to be always awake. "Captain, shall I keep her making for that light north, sir?"

The same steady voice answered him. "Yes. Keep it about two points off the port bow."

The cook had tied a life-belt around himself in order to get even the warmth which this clumsy cork contrivance could donate, and he seemed almost stove-like when a rower, whose teeth invariably chattered wildly as soon as he ceased his labor, dropped down to sleep.

The correspondent, as he rowed, looked down at the two men sleeping underfoot. The cook's arm was around the oiler's shoulders, and, with their fragmentary clothing and haggard faces, they were the babes of the sea, a grotesque rendering of the old babes in the wood.

Later he must have grown stupid at his work, for suddenly there was a growling of water, and a crest came with a roar and a swash into the boat, and it was a wonder that it did not set the cook afloat in his life-belt. The cook continued to sleep, but the oiler sat up, blinking his eyes and shaking with the new cold.

"Oh, I'm awful sorry, Billie," said the correspondent contritely.

"That's all right, old boy," said the oiler, and lay down again and was asleep.

Presently it seemed that even the captain dozed, and the correspondent thought that he was the one man afloat on all the oceans. The wind had a voice as it came over the waves, and it was sadder than the end.

There was a long, loud swishing astern of the boat, and a gleaming trail of phosphorescence, like blue flame, was furrowed on the black waters. It might have been made by a monstrous knife.

Then there came a stillness, while the correspondent breathed with the open mouth and looked at the sea.

Suddenly there was another swish and another long flash of bluish light, and this time it was alongside the boat, and might almost have been reached with an oar. The correspondent saw an enormous fin speed like a shadow through the water, hurling the crystalline spray and leaving the long glowing trail.

The correspondent looked over his shoulder at the captain. His face was hidden, and he seemed to be asleep. He looked at the babes of the sea. They certainly were asleep. So, being bereft of sympathy, he leaned a little way to one side and swore softly into the sea.

But the thing did not then leave the vicinity of the boat. Ahead or astern, on one side or the other, at intervals long or short, fled the long sparkling streak, and there was to be heard the whirroo of the dark fin. The speed and power of the thing was greatly to be admired. It cut the water like a gigantic and keen projectile.

The presence of this biding thing did not affect the man with the same horror that it would if he had been a picnicker. He simply looked at the sea dully and swore in an undertone.

Nevertheless, it is true that he did not wish to be alone. He wished one of his companions to awaken by chance and keep him company with it. But the captain hung motionless over the water-jar, and the oiler and the cook in the bottom of the boat were plunged in slumber.

### VI

"If I am going to be drowned—if I am going to be drowned—if I am going to be drowned, why, in the name of the seven mad gods who rule the sea, was I allowed to come thus far and contemplate sand and trees?"

During this dismal night, it may be remarked that a man would conclude that it was really the intention of the seven mad gods to drown him, despite the abominable injustice of it. For it was certainly an abominable injustice to drown a man who had worked so hard, so hard. The man felt it would be a crime most unnatural. Other people had drowned at sea since galleys swarmed with painted sails, but still—

When it occurs to a man that nature does not regard him as important, and that she feels she would not maim the universe by disposing of him, he at first wishes to throw bricks at the temple, and he hates deeply the fact that there are no brick and no temples. Any visible expression of nature would surely be pelleted with his jeers.

Then, if there be no tangible thing to hoot he feels, perhaps, the desire to confront a personification and indulge in pleas, bowed to one knee, and with hands supplicant, saying: "Yes, but I love myself."

A high cold star on a winter's night is the word he feels that she says to him. Thereafter he knows the pathos of his situation.

The men in the dingey had not discussed these matters, but each had, no doubt, reflected upon them in silence and according to his mind. There was seldom any expression upon their faces save the general one of complete weariness. Speech was devoted to the business of the boat.

To chime the notes of his emotion, a verse mysteriously entered the correspondent's head. He had even forgotten that he had forgotten this verse, but it suddenly was in his mind.

> *"A soldier of the Legion lay dying in Algiers,*
> *There was a lack of woman's nursing, there was dearth of woman's*
> *tears;*
> *But a comrade stood beside him, and he took that comrade's hand,*
> *And he said: 'I shall never see my own, my native land.'"*

**THE OPEN BOAT** | 97

In his childhood, the correspondent had been made acquainted with the fact that a soldier of the Legion lay dying in Algiers, but he had never regarded the fact as important. Myriads of his school-fellows had informed him of the soldier's plight, but the dinning had naturally ended by making him perfectly indifferent. He had never considered it his affair that a soldier of the Legion lay dying in Algiers, nor had it appeared to him as a matter for sorrow. It was less to him than the breaking of a pencil's point.

Now, however, it quaintly came to him as a human, living thing. It was no longer merely a picture of a few throes in the breast of a poet, meanwhile drinking tea and warming his feet at the grate; it was an actuality—stern, mournful, and fine.

The correspondent plainly saw the soldier. He lay on the sand with his feet out straight and still. While his pale left hand was upon his chest in an attempt to thwart the going of his life, the blood came between his fingers. In the far Algerian distance, a city of low square forms was set against a sky that was faint with the last sunset hues. The correspondent, plying the oars and dreaming of the slow and slower movements of the lips of the soldier, was moved by a profound and perfectly impersonal comprehension. He was sorry for the soldier of the Legion who lay dying in Algiers.

The thing which had followed the boat and waited, had evidently grown bored at the delay. There was no longer to be heard the slash of the cut-water, and there was no longer the flame of the long trail. The light in the north still glimmered, but it was apparently no nearer to the boat. Sometimes the boom of the surf rang in the correspondent's ears, and he turned the craft seaward then and rowed harder. Southward, some one had evidently built a watch-fire on the beach. It was too low and too far to be seen, but it made a shimmering, roseate reflection upon the bluff back of it, and this could be discerned from the boat. The wind came stronger, and sometimes a wave suddenly raged out like a mountain-cat, and there was to be seen the sheen and sparkle of a broken crest.

The captain, in the bow, moved on his water-jar and sat erect. "Pretty long night," he observed to the correspondent. He looked at the shore. "Those life-saving people take their time."

"Did you see that shark playing around?"

"Yes, I saw him. He was a big fellow, all right."

"Wish I had known you were awake."

Later the correspondent spoke into the bottom of the boat.

"Billie!" There was a slow and gradual disentanglement. "Billie, will you spell me?"

"Sure," said the oiler.

As soon as the correspondent touched the cold comfortable sea-water in the bottom of the boat, and had huddled close to the cook's life-belt he was deep in sleep, despite the fact that his teeth played all the popular airs. This sleep was so good to him that it was but a moment before he heard a voice call his name in a tone that demonstrated the last stages of exhaustion. "Will you spell me?"

"Sure, Billie."

The light in the north had mysteriously vanished, but the correspondent took his course from the wide-awake captain.

Later in the night they took the boat farther out to sea, and the captain directed the cook to take one oar at the stern and keep the boat facing the seas. He was to call out if he should hear the thunder of the surf. This plan enabled the oiler and the correspondent to get respite together. "We'll give those boys a chance to get into shape again," said the captain. They curled down and, after a few preliminary chatterings and trembles, slept once more the dead sleep. Neither knew they had bequeathed to the cook the company of another shark, or perhaps the same shark.

As the boat caroused on the waves, spray occasionally bumped over the side and gave them a fresh soaking, but this had no power to break their repose. The ominous slash of the wind and the water affected them as it would have affected mummies.

"Boys," said the cook, with the notes of every reluctance in his voice, "she's drifted in pretty close. I guess one of you had better take her to sea again." The correspondent, aroused, heard the crash of the toppled crests.

As he was rowing, the captain gave him some whisky-and-water, and this steadied the chills out of him. "If I ever get ashore and anybody shows me even a photograph of an oar—"

At last there was a short conversation.

"Billie…. Billie, will you spell me?"

"Sure," said the oiler.

## VII

When the correspondent again opened his eyes, the sea and the sky were each of the grey hue of the dawning. Later, carmine and gold was painted upon the waters. The morning appeared finally, in its splendor, with a sky of pure blue, and the sunlight flamed on the tips of the waves.

On the distant dunes were set many little black cottages, and a tall white windmill reared above them. No man, nor dog, nor bicycle appeared on the beach. The cottages might have formed a deserted village.

The voyagers scanned the shore. A conference was held in the boat. "Well," said the captain, "if no help is coming we might better try a run through the surf right away. If we stay out here much longer we will be too weak to do anything for ourselves at all." The others silently acquiesced in this reasoning. The boat was headed for the beach. The correspondent wondered if none ever ascended the tall wind-tower, and if then they never looked seaward. This tower was a giant, standing with its back to the plight of the ants. It represented in a degree, to the correspondent, the serenity of nature amid the struggles of the individual—nature in the wind, and nature in the vision of men. She did not seem cruel to him then, nor beneficent, nor treacherous, nor wise. But she was indifferent, flatly indifferent. It is, perhaps, plausible that a man in this situation, impressed with the unconcern of the universe, should see the innumerable flaws of his life, and have them taste wickedly in his mind and wish for another chance. A distinction between right and wrong seems absurdly clear to him, then, in this new ignorance of the grave-edge, and he understands that if he were given another opportunity he would mend his conduct and his words, and be better and brighter during an introduction or at a tea.

"Now, boys," said the captain, "she is going to swamp, sure. All we can do is to work her in as far as possible, and then when she swamps, pile out and scramble for the beach. Keep cool now, and don't jump until she swamps sure."

The oiler took the oars. Over his shoulders he scanned the surf. "Captain," he said, "I think I'd better bring her about, and keep her head-on to the seas and back her in."

"All right, Billie," said the captain. "Back her in." The oiler swung the boat then and, seated in the stern, the cook and the correspondent were obliged to look over their shoulders to contemplate the lonely and indifferent shore.

The monstrous in-shore rollers heaved the boat high until the men were again enabled to see the white sheets of water scudding up the slanted beach. "We won't get in very close," said the captain. Each time a man could wrest his attention from the rollers, he turned his glance toward the shore, and in the expression of the eyes during this contemplation there was a singular quality. The correspondent, observing the others, knew that they were not afraid, but the full meaning of their glances was shrouded.

As for himself, he was too tired to grapple fundamentally with the fact. He tried to coerce his mind into thinking of it, but the mind was dominated at this time by the muscles, and the muscles said they did not care. It merely occurred to him that if he should drown it would be a shame.

There were no hurried words, no pallor, no plain agitation. The men simply looked at the shore. "Now, remember to get well clear of the boat when you jump," said the captain.

Seaward the crest of a roller suddenly fell with a thunderous crash, and the long white comber came roaring down upon the boat.

"Steady now," said the captain. The men were silent. They turned their eyes from the shore to the comber and waited. The boat slid up the incline, leaped at the furious top, bounced over it, and swung down the long back of the wave. Some water had been shipped and the cook bailed it out.

But the next crest crashed also. The tumbling, boiling flood of white water caught the boat and whirled it almost perpendicular. Water swarmed in from all sides. The correspondent had his hands on the gunwale at this time, and when the water entered at that place he swiftly withdrew his fingers, as if he objected to wetting them.

The little boat, drunken with this weight of water, reeled and snuggled deeper into the sea.

"Bail her out, cook! Bail her out," said the captain.

"All right, captain," said the cook.

"Now, boys, the next one will do for us, sure," said the oiler. "Mind to jump clear of the boat."

The third wave moved forward, huge, furious, implacable. It fairly swallowed the dingey, and almost simultaneously the men tumbled into the sea. A piece of lifebelt had lain in the bottom of the boat, and as the correspondent went overboard he held this to his chest with his left hand.

The January water was icy, and he reflected immediately that it was colder than he had expected to find it on the coast of Florida. This appeared to his dazed mind as a fact important enough to be noted at the time. The coldness of the water was sad; it was tragic. This fact was somehow so mixed and confused with his opinion of his own situation that it seemed almost a proper reason for tears. The water was cold.

When he came to the surface he was conscious of little but the noisy water. Afterward he saw his companions in the sea. The oiler was ahead in the race. He was swimming strongly and rapidly. Off to the correspondent's left, the cook's great white and corked back bulged out of the water, and in the rear the captain was hanging with his one good hand to the keel of the overturned dingey.

There is a certain immovable quality to a shore, and the correspondent wondered at it amid the confusion of the sea.

It seemed also very attractive, but the correspondent knew that it was a long journey, and he paddled leisurely. The piece of life-preserver lay under him, and sometimes he whirled down the incline of a wave as if he were on a handsled.

But finally he arrived at a place in the sea where travel was beset with difficulty. He did not pause swimming to inquire what manner of current had caught him, but there his progress ceased. The shore was set before him like a bit of scenery on a stage, and he looked at it and understood with his eyes each detail of it.

As the cook passed, much farther to the left, the captain was calling to him, "Turn over on your back, cook! Turn over on your back and use the oar."

"All right, sir." The cook turned on his back, and, paddling with an oar, went ahead as if he were a canoe.

Presently the boat also passed to the left of the correspondent with the captain clinging with one hand to the keel. He would have appeared like a man raising himself to look over a board fence, if it were not for the extraordinary gymnastics of the boat. The correspondent marvelled that the captain could still hold to it.

They passed on, nearer to shore—the oiler, the cook, the captain—and following them went the water-jar, bouncing gaily over the seas.

The correspondent remained in the grip of this strange new enemy—a current. The shore, with its white slope of sand and its green bluff,topped with little silent cottages, was spread like a picture before him. It was very near to him then, but he was impressed as one who in a gallery looks at a scene from Brittany or Holland.

He thought: "I am going to drown? Can it be possible Can it be possible? Can it be possible?" Perhaps an individual must consider his own death to be the final phenomenon of nature.

But later a wave perhaps whirled him out of this small, deadly current, for he found suddenly that he could again make progress toward the shore. Later still, he was aware that the captain, clinging with one hand to the keel of the dingey, had his face turned away from the shore and toward him, and was calling his name. "Come to the boat! Come to the boat!"

In his struggle to reach the captain and the boat, he reflected that when one gets properly wearied, drowning must really be a comfortable arrangement, a cessation of hostilities accompanied by a large degree of relief, and he was glad of it, for the main thing in his mind for some months had been horror of the temporary agony. He did not wish to be hurt.

Presently he saw a man running along the shore. He was undressing with most remarkable speed. Coat, trousers, shirt, everything flew magically off him.

"Come to the boat," called the captain.

"All right, captain." As the correspondent paddled, he saw the captain let himself down to bottom and leave the boat. Then the correspondent performed his one little marvel of the voyage. A large wave caught him and flung him with ease and supreme speed completely over the boat and far beyond it. It struck him even then as an event in gymnastics, and a true miracle of the sea. An over-turned boat in the surf is not a plaything to a swimming man.

The correspondent arrived in water that reached only to his waist, but his condition did not enable him to stand for more than a moment. Each wave knocked him into a heap, and the under-tow pulled at him.

Then he saw the man who had been running and undressing, and undressing and running, come bounding into the water. He dragged ashore the cook, and then waded towards the captain, but the captain waved him away, and sent him to the correspondent. He was naked, naked as a tree in winter, but a halo was about his head, and he shone like a saint. He gave a strong pull, and a long drag, and a bully heave at the correspondent's hand. The correspondent, schooled in the minor formulae, said:

"Thanks, old man." But suddenly the man cried: "What's that?" He pointed a swift finger. The correspondent said: "Go."

In the shallows, face downward, lay the oiler. His forehead touched sand that was periodically, between each wave, clear of the sea.

The correspondent did not know all that transpired afterward. When he achieved safe ground he fell, striking the sand with each particular part of his body. It was as if he had dropped from a roof, but the thud was grateful to him.

It seems that instantly the beach was populated with men with blankets, clothes, and flasks, and women with coffeepots and all the remedies sacred to their minds. The welcome of the land to the men from the sea was warm and generous, but a still and dripping shape was carried slowly up the beach, and the land's welcome for it could only be the different and sinister hospitality of the grave.

When it came night, the white waves paced to and fro in the moonlight, and the wind brought the sound of the great sea's voice to the men on shore, and they felt that they could then be interpreters.

# THE RELUCTANT VOYAGERS

## CHAPTER I

Two men sat by the sea waves.

"Well, I know I'm not handsome," said one gloomily. He was poking holes in the sand with a discontented cane.

The companion was watching the waves play. He seemed overcome with perspiring discomfort as a man who is resolved to set another man right.

Suddenly his mouth turned into a straight line.

"To be sure you are not," he cried vehemently.

"You look like thunder. I do not desire to be unpleasant, but I must assure you that your freckled skin continually reminds spectators of white wall paper with gilt roses on it. The top of your head looks like a little wooden plate. And your figure—heavens!"

For a time they were silent. They stared at the waves that purred near their feet like sleepy sea-kittens.

Finally the first man spoke.

"Well," said he, defiantly, "what of it?"

"What of it?" exploded the other. "Why, it means that you'd look like blazes in a bathing-suit."

They were again silent. The freckled man seemed ashamed. His tall companion glowered at the scenery.

"I am decided," said the freckled man suddenly. He got boldly up from the sand and strode away. The tall man followed, walking sarcastically and glaring down at the round, resolute figure before him.

A bath-clerk was looking at the world with superior eyes through a hole in a board. To him the freckled man made application, waving his hands over his person in illustration of a snug fit. The bath-clerk thought profoundly. Eventually, he handed out a blue bundle with an air of having phenomenally solved the freckled man's dimensions.

The latter resumed his resolute stride.

"See here," said the tall man, following him, "I bet you've got a regular toga, you know. That fellow couldn't tell—"

"Yes, he could," interrupted the freckled man, "I saw correct mathematics in his eyes."

"Well, supposin' he has missed your size. Supposin'—"

"Tom," again interrupted the other, "produce your proud clothes and we'll go in."

The tall man swore bitterly. He went to one of a row of little wooden boxes and shut himself in it. His companion repaired to a similar box.

At first he felt like an opulent monk in a too-small cell, and he turned round two or three times to see if he could. He arrived finally into his bathing-dress. Immediately he dropped gasping upon a three-cornered bench. The suit fell in folds about his reclining form. There was silence, save for the caressing calls of the waves without.

Then he heard two shoes drop on the floor in one of the little coops. He began to clamor at the boards like a penitent at an unforgiving door.

"Tom," called he, "Tom—"

A voice of wrath, muffled by cloth, came through the walls. "You go t' blazes!"

The freckled man began to groan, taking the occupants of the entire row of coops into his confidence.

"Stop your noise," angrily cried the tall man from his hidden den. "You rented the bathing-suit, didn't you? Then—"

"It ain't a bathing-suit," shouted the freckled man at the boards. "It's an auditorium, a ballroom, or something. It isn't a bathing-suit."

The tall man came out of his box. His suit looked like blue skin. He walked with grandeur down the alley between the rows of coops. Stopping in front of his friend's door, he rapped on it with passionate knuckles.

"Come out of there, y' ol' fool," said he, in an enraged whisper. "It's only your accursed vanity. Wear it anyhow. What difference does it make? I never saw such a vain ol' idiot!"

As he was storming the door opened, and his friend confronted him. The tall man's legs gave way, and he fell against the opposite door.

The freckled man regarded him sternly.

"You're an ass," he said.

His back curved in scorn. He walked majestically down the alley. There was pride in the way his chubby feet patted the boards. The tall man followed, weakly, his eyes riveted upon the figure ahead.

As a disguise the freckled man had adopted the stomach of importance. He moved with an air of some sort of procession, across a board walk, down some steps, and out upon the sand.

There was a pug dog and three old women on a bench, a man and a maid with a book and a parasol, a seagull drifting high in the wind, and a distant, tremendous meeting of sea and sky. Down on the wet sand stood a girl being wooed by the breakers.

The freckled man moved with stately tread along the beach. The tall man, numb with amazement, came in the rear. They neared the girl.

Suddenly the tall man was seized with convulsions. He laughed, and the girl turned her head.

She perceived the freckled man in the bathing-suit. An expression of wonderment overspread her charming face. It changed in a moment to a pearly smile.

This smile seemed to smite the freckled man. He obviously tried to swell and fit his suit. Then he turned a shrivelling glance upon his companion, and fled up the beach. The tall man ran after him, pursuing with mocking cries that tingled his flesh like stings of insects. He seemed to be trying to lead the way out of the world. But at last he stopped and faced about.

"Tom Sharp," said he, between his clenched teeth, "you are an unutterable wretch! I could grind your bones under my heel."

The tall man was in a trance, with glazed eyes fixed on the bathing-dress. He seemed to be murmuring: "Oh, good Lord! Oh, good Lord! I never saw such a suit!"

The freckled man made the gesture of an assassin.

"Tom Sharp, you—"

The other was still murmuring: "Oh, good Lord! I never saw such a suit! I never—"

The freckled man ran down into the sea.

# CHAPTER II

The cool, swirling waters took his temper from him, and it became a thing that is lost in the ocean. The tall man floundered in, and the two forgot and rollicked in the waves.

The freckled man, in endeavoring to escape from mankind, had left all save a solitary fisherman under a large hat, and three boys in bathing-dress, laughing and splashing upon a raft made of old spars.

The two men swam softly over the ground swells.

The three boys dived from their raft, and turned their jolly faces shorewards. It twisted slowly around and around, and began to move seaward on some unknown voyage. The freckled man laid his face to the water and swam toward the raft with a practised stroke. The tall man followed, his bended arm appearing and disappearing with the precision of machinery.

The craft crept away, slowly and wearily, as if luring. The little wooden plate on the freckled man's head looked at the shore like a round, brown eye, but his gaze was fixed on the raft that slyly appeared to be waiting. The tall man used the little wooden plate as a beacon.

At length the freckled man reached the raft and climbed aboard. He lay down on his back and puffed. His bathing-dress spread about him like a dead balloon. The tall man came, snorted, shook his tangled locks and lay down by the side of his companion.

They were overcome with a delicious drowsiness. The planks of the raft seemed to fit their tired limbs. They gazed dreamily up into the vast sky of summer.

"This is great," said the tall man. His companion grunted blissfully.

Gentle hands from the sea rocked their craft and lulled them to peace. Lapping waves sang little rippling sea-songs about them. The two men issued contented groans.

"Tom," said the freckled man.

"What?" said the other.

"This is great."

They lay and thought.

A fish-hawk, soaring, suddenly, turned and darted at the waves. The tall man indolently twisted his head and watched the bird plunge its claws into the water. It heavily arose with a silver gleaming fish.

"That bird has got his feet wet again. It's a shame," murmured the tall man sleepily. "He must suffer from an endless cold in the head. He should wear rubber boots. They'd look great, too. If I was him, I'd—Great Scott!"

He had partly arisen, and was looking at the shore.

He began to scream. "Ted! Ted! Ted! Look!"

"What's matter?" dreamily spoke the freckled man. "You remind me of when I put the bird-shot in your leg." He giggled softly.

The agitated tall man made a gesture of supreme eloquence. His companion up-reared and turned a startled gaze shoreward.

"Lord!" he roared, as if stabbed.

The land was a long, brown streak with a rim of green, in which sparkled the tin roofs of huge hotels. The hands from the sea had pushed them away. The two men sprang erect, and did a little dance of perturbation.

"What shall we do? What shall we do?" moaned the freckled man, wriggling fantastically in his dead balloon.

The changing shore seemed to fascinate the tall man, and for a time he did not speak.

Suddenly he concluded his minuet of horror. He wheeled about and faced the freckled man. He elaborately folded his arms.

"So," he said, in slow, formidable tones. "So! This all comes from your accursed vanity, your bathing-suit, your idiocy; you have murdered your best friend."

He turned away. His companion reeled as if stricken by an unexpected arm.

He stretched out his hands. "Tom, Tom," wailed he, beseechingly, "don't be such a fool."

The broad back of his friend was occupied by a contemptuous sneer.

Three ships fell off the horizon. Landward, the hues were blending. The whistle of a locomotive sounded from an infinite distance as if tooting in heaven.

"Tom! Tom! My dear boy," quavered the freckled man, "don't speak that way to me."

"Oh, no, of course not," said the other, still facing away and throwing the words over his shoulder. "You suppose I am going to accept all this calmly, don't you? Not make the slightest objection? Make no protest at all, hey?"

"Well, I—I—" began the freckled man.

The tall man's wrath suddenly exploded. "You've abducted me! That's the whole amount of it! You've abducted me!"

"I ain't," protested the freckled man. "You must think I'm a fool."

The tall man swore, and sitting down, dangled his legs angrily in the water. Natural law compelled his companion to occupy the other end of the raft.

Over the waters little shoals of fish spluttered, raising tiny tempests. Languid jelly-fish floated near, tremulously waving a thousand legs. A row of porpoises trundled along like a procession of cog-wheels. The sky became greyed save where over the land sunset colors were assembling.

The two voyagers, back to back and at either end of the raft, quarrelled at length.

"What did you want to follow me for?" demanded the freckled man in a voice of indignation.

"If your figure hadn't been so like a bottle, we wouldn't be here," replied the tall man.

## CHAPTER III

The fires in the west blazed away, and solemnity spread over the sea. Electric lights began to blink like eyes. Night menaced the voyagers with a dangerous darkness, and fear came to bind their souls together. They huddled fraternally in the middle of the raft.

"I feel like a molecule," said the freckled man in subdued tones.

"I'd give two dollars for a cigar," muttered the tall man.

A V-shaped flock of ducks flew towards Barnegat, between the voyagers and a remnant of yellow sky. Shadows and winds came from the vanished eastern horizon.

"I think I hear voices," said the freckled man.

"That Dollie Ramsdell was an awfully nice girl," said the tall man.

When the coldness of the sea night came to them, the freckled man found he could by a peculiar movement of his legs and arms encase himself in his bathing-dress. The tall man was compelled to whistle and shiver. As night settled finally over the sea, red and green lights began to dot the blackness. There were mysterious shadows between the waves.

"I see things comin'," murmured the freckled man.

"I wish I hadn't ordered that new dress-suit for the hop tomorrow night," said the tall man reflectively.

The sea became uneasy and heaved painfully, like a lost bosom, when little forgotten heart-bells try to chime with a pure sound. The voyagers cringed at magnified foam on distant wave crests. A moon came and looked at them.

"Somebody's here," whispered the freckled man.

"I wish I had an almanac," remarked the tall man, regarding the moon.

Presently they fell to staring at the red and green lights that twinkled about them.

"Providence will not leave us," asserted the freckled man.

"Oh, we'll be picked up shortly. I owe money," said the tall man.

He began to thrum on an imaginary banjo.

"I have heard," said he, suddenly, "that captains with healthy ships beneath their feet will never turn back after having once started on a voyage. In that case we will be rescued by some ship bound for the golden seas of the south. Then, you'll be up to some of your confounded devilment and we'll get put off. They'll maroon us! That's what they'll do! They'll maroon us! On an island with palm trees and sun-kissed maidens and all that. Sun-kissed maidens, eh? Great! They'd—"

He suddenly ceased and turned to stone. At a distance a great, green eye was contemplating the sea wanderers.

They stood up and did another dance. As they watched the eye grew larger.

Directly the form of a phantom-like ship came into view. About the great, green eye there bobbed small yellow dots. The wanderers could hear a far-away creaking of unseen tackle and flapping of shadowy sails. There came the melody of the waters as the ship's prow thrust its way.

The tall man delivered an oration.

"Ha!" he exclaimed, "here come our rescuers. The brave fellows! How I long to take the manly captain by the hand! You will soon see a white boat with a star on its bow drop from the side of yon ship. Kind sailors in blue and white will help us into the boat and conduct our wasted frames to the quarter-deck, where the handsome, bearded captain, with gold bands all around, will welcome us. Then in the hard-oak cabin, while the wine gurgles and the Havanas glow, we'll tell our tale of peril and privation."

The ship came on like a black hurrying animal with froth-filled maw. The two wanderers stood up and clasped hands. Then they howled out a wild duet that rang over the wastes of sea.

The cries seemed to strike the ship.

Men with boots on yelled and ran about the deck. They picked up heavy articles and threw them down. They yelled more. After hideous creakings and flappings, the vessel stood still.

In the meantime the wanderers had been chanting their song for help. Out in the blackness they beckoned to the ship and coaxed.

A voice came to them.

"Hello," it said.

They puffed out their cheeks and began to shout. "Hello! Hello! Hello!"

"Wot do yeh want?" said the voice.

The two wanderers gazed at each other, and sat suddenly down on the raft. Some pall came sweeping over the sky and quenched their stars.

But almost the tall man got up and brawled miscellaneous information. He stamped his foot, and frowning into the night, swore threateningly.

The vessel seemed fearful of these moaning voices that called from a hidden cavern of the water. And now one voice was filled with a menace. A number of men with enormous limbs that threw vast shadows over the sea as the lanterns flickered, held a debate and made gestures.

Off in the darkness, the tall man began to clamor like a mob. The freckled man sat in astounded silence, with his legs weak.

After a time one of the men of enormous limbs seized a rope that was tugging at the stem and drew a small boat from the shadows. Three giants clambered in and rowed cautiously toward the raft. Silver water flashed in the gloom as the oars dipped.

About fifty feet from the raft the boat stopped. "Who er you?" asked a voice.

The tall man braced himself and explained. He drew vivid pictures, his twirling fingers illustrating like live brushes.

"Oh," said the three giants.

The voyagers deserted the raft. They looked back, feeling in their hearts a mite of tenderness for the wet planks. Later, they wriggled up the side of the vessel and climbed over the railing.

On deck they met a man.

He held a lantern to their faces. "Got any chewin' tewbacca?" he inquired.

"No," said the tall man, "we ain't."

The man had a bronze face and solitary whiskers. Peculiar lines about his mouth were shaped into an eternal smile of derision. His feet were bare, and clung handily to crevices.

Fearful trousers were supported by a piece of suspender that went up the wrong side of his chest and came down the right side of his back, dividing him into triangles.

"Ezekiel P. Sanford, capt'in, schooner 'Mary Jones,' of N'yack, N. Y., genelmen," he said.

"Ah!" said the tall man, "delighted, I'm sure."

There were a few moments of silence. The giants were hovering in the gloom and staring.

Suddenly astonishment exploded the captain.

"Wot th' devil—" he shouted. "Wot th' devil yeh got on?"

"Bathing-suits," said the tall man.

## CHAPTER IV

The schooner went on. The two voyagers sat down and watched. After a time they began to shiver. The soft blackness of the summer night passed away, and grey mists writhed over the sea. Soon lights of early dawn went changing across the sky, and the twin beacons on the highlands grew dim and sparkling faintly, as if a monster were dying. The dawn penetrated the marrow of the two men in bathing-dress.

The captain used to pause opposite them, hitch one hand in his suspender, and laugh.

"Well, I be dog-hanged," he frequently said.

The tall man grew furious. He snarled in a mad undertone to his companion. "This rescue ain't right. If I had known—"

He suddenly paused, transfixed by the captain's suspender. "It's goin' to break," cried he, in an ecstatic whisper. His eyes grew large with excitement as he watched the captain laugh. "It'll break in a minute, sure."

But the commander of the schooner recovered, and invited them to drink and eat. They followed him along the deck, and fell down a square black hole into the cabin.

It was a little den, with walls of a vanished whiteness. A lamp shed an orange light. In a sort of recess two little beds were hiding. A wooden table, immovable, as if the craft had been builded around it, sat in the middle of the floor. Overhead the square hole was studded with a dozen stars. A foot-worn ladder led to the heavens.

The captain produced ponderous crackers and some cold broiled ham. Then he vanished in the firmament like a fantastic comet.

The freckled man sat quite contentedly like a stout squaw in a blanket. The tall man walked about the cabin and sniffed. He was angered at the crudeness of the rescue, and his shrinking clothes made him feel too large. He contemplated his unhappy state.

Suddenly, he broke out. "I won't stand this, I tell you! Heavens and earth, look at the—say, what in the blazes did you want to get me in this thing for, anyhow? You're a fine old duffer, you are! Look at that ham!"

The freckled man grunted. He seemed somewhat blissful. He was seated upon a bench, comfortably enwrapped in his bathing-dress.

The tall man stormed about the cabin.

"This is an outrage! I'll see the captain! I'll tell him what I think of—"

He was interrupted by a pair of legs that appeared among the stars. The captain came down the ladder. He brought a coffee pot from the sky.

The tall man bristled forward. He was going to denounce everything.

The captain was intent upon the coffee pot, balancing it carefully, and leaving his unguided feet to find the steps of the ladder.

But the wrath of the tall man faded. He twirled his fingers in excitement, and renewed his ecstatic whisperings to the freckled man.

"It's going to break! Look, quick, look! It'll break in a minute!"

He was transfixed with interest, forgetting his wrongs in staring at the perilous passage.

But the captain arrived on the floor with triumphant suspenders.

"Well," said he, "after yeh have eat, maybe ye'd like t'sleep some! If so, yeh can sleep on them beds."

The tall man made no reply, save in a strained undertone. "It'll break in about a minute! Look, Ted, look quick!"

The freckled man glanced in a little bed on which were heaped boots and oil-skins. He made a courteous gesture.

"My dear sir, we could not think of depriving you of your beds. No, indeed. Just a couple of blankets if you have them, and we'll sleep very comfortable on these benches."

The captain protested, politely twisting his back and bobbing his head. The suspenders tugged and creaked. The tall man partially suppressed a cry, and took a step forward.

The freckled man was sleepily insistent, and shortly the captain gave over his deprecatory contortions. He fetched a pink quilt with yellow dots on it to the freckled man, and a black one with red roses on it to the tall man.

Again he vanished in the firmament. The tall man gazed until the last remnant of trousers disappeared from the sky. Then he wrapped himself up in his quilt and lay down. The freckled man was puffing contentedly, swathed like an infant. The yellow polka-dots rose and fell on the vast pink of his chest.

The wanderers slept. In the quiet could be heard the groanings of timbers as the sea seemed to crunch them together. The lapping of water along the vessel's side sounded like gaspings. A hundred spirits of the wind had got their wings entangled in the rigging, and, in soft voices, were pleading to be loosened.

The freckled man was awakened by a foreign noise. He opened his eyes and saw his companion standing by his couch.

His comrade's face was wan with suffering. His eyes glowed in the darkness. He raised his arms, spreading them out like a clergyman at a grave. He groaned deep in his chest.

"Good Lord!" yelled the freckled man, starting up. "Tom, Tom, what's th' matter?"

The tall man spoke in a fearful voice. "To New York," he said, "to New York in our bathing-suits."

The freckled man sank back. The shadows of the cabin threw mysteries about the figure of the tall man, arrayed like some ancient and potent astrologer in the black quilt with the red roses on it.

## CHAPTER V

Directly the tall man went and lay down and began to groan.

The freckled man felt the miseries of the world upon him. He grew angry at the tall man awakening him. They quarrelled.

"Well," said the tall man, finally, "we're in a fix."

"I know that," said the other, sharply.

They regarded the ceiling in silence.

"What in the thunder are we going to do?" demanded the tall man, after a time. His companion was still silent. "Say," repeated he, angrily, "what in the thunder are we going to do?"

"I'm sure I don't know," said the freckled man in a dismal voice.

"Well, think of something," roared the other. "Think of something, you old fool. You don't want to make any more idiots of yourself, do you?"

"I ain't made an idiot of myself."

"Well, think. Know anybody in the city?"

"I know a fellow up in Harlem," said the freckled man.

"You know a fellow up in Harlem," howled the tall man. "Up in Harlem! How the dickens are we to—say, you're crazy!"

"We can take a cab," cried the other, waxing indignant.

The tall man grew suddenly calm. "Do you know any one else?" he asked, measuredly.

"I know another fellow somewhere on Park Place."

"Somewhere on Park Place," repeated the tall man in an unnatural manner. "Somewhere on Park Place." With an air of sublime resignation he turned his face to the wall.

The freckled man sat erect and frowned in the direction of his companion. "Well, now, I suppose you are going to sulk. You make me ill! It's the best we can do, ain't it? Hire a cab and go look that fellow up on Park—What's that? You can't afford it? What nonsense! You are getting—Oh! Well, maybe we can beg some clothes of the captain. Eh? Did I see 'im? Certainly, I saw 'im. Yes, it is improbable that a man who wears trousers like that can have clothes to lend. No, I won't wear oilskins and a sou'-wester. To Athens? Of course not! I don't know where it is. Do you? I thought not. With all your grumbling about other people, you never know anything important yourself. What? Broadway? I'll be hanged first. We can get off at Harlem, man alive. There are no cabs in Harlem. I don't think we can bribe a sailor to take us ashore and bring a cab to the dock, for the very simple reason that we have nothing to bribe him with. What? No, of course not. See here, Tom Sharp, don't you swear at me like that. I won't have it. What's that? I ain't, either. I ain't. What? I am not. It's no such thing. I ain't. I've got more than you have, anyway. Well, you ain't doing anything so very brilliant yourself—just lying there and cussin'." At length the tall man feigned prodigiously to snore. The freckled man thought with such vigor that he fell asleep.

After a time he dreamed that he was in a forest where bass drums grew on trees. There came a strong wind that banged the fruit about like empty pods. A frightful din was in his ears.

He awoke to find the captain of the schooner standing over him.

"We're at New York now," said the captain, raising his voice above the thumping and banging that was being done on deck, "an' I s'pose you fellers wanta go ashore." He chuckled in an exasperating manner. "Jes' sing out when yeh wanta go," he added, leering at the freckled man.

The tall man awoke, came over and grasped the captain by the throat.

"If you laugh again I'll kill you," he said.

The captain gurgled and waved his legs and arms.

"In the first place," the tall man continued, "you rescued us in a deucedly shabby manner. It makes me ill to think of it. I've a mind to mop you 'round just for that. In the second place, your vessel is bound for Athens, N. Y., and there's no sense in it. Now, will you or will you not turn this ship about and take us back where our clothes are, or to Philadelphia, where we belong?"

He furiously shook the captain. Then he eased his grip and awaited a reply.

"I can't," yelled the captain, "I can't. This vessel don't belong to me. I've got to—"

"Well, then," interrupted the tall man, "can you lend us some clothes?"

"Hain't got none," replied the captain, promptly. His face was red, and his eyes were glaring.

"Well, then," said the tall man, "can you lend us some money?"

"Hain't got none," replied the captain, promptly. Something overcame him and he laughed.

"Thunderation," roared the tall man. He seized the captain, who began to have wriggling contortions. The tall man kneaded him as if he were biscuits. "You infernal scoundrel," he bellowed, "this whole affair is some wretched plot, and you are in it. I am about to kill you."

The solitary whisker of the captain did acrobatic feats like a strange demon upon his chin. His eyes stood perilously from his head. The suspender wheezed and tugged like the tackle of a sail.

Suddenly the tall man released his hold. Great expectancy sat upon his features. "It's going to break!" he cried, rubbing his hands.

But the captain howled and vanished in the sky.

The freckled man then came forward. He appeared filled with sarcasm.

"So!" said he. "So, you've settled the matter. The captain is the only man in the world who can help us, and I daresay he'll do anything he can now."

"That's all right," said the tall man. "If you don't like the way I run things you shouldn't have come on this trip at all."

They had another quarrel.

At the end of it they went on deck. The captain stood at the stern addressing the bow with opprobrious language. When he perceived the voyagers he began to fling his fists about in the air.

"I'm goin' to put yeh off!" he yelled. The wanderers stared at each other.

"Hum," said the tall man.

The freckled man looked at his companion. "He's going to put us off, you see," he said, complacently.

The tall man began to walk about and move his shoulders. "I'd like to see you do it," he said, defiantly.

The captain tugged at a rope. A boat came at his bidding.

"I'd like to see you do it," the tall man repeated, continually. An imperturbable man in rubber boots climbed down in the boat and seized the oars. The captain motioned downward. His whisker had a triumphant appearance.

The two wanderers looked at the boat. "I guess we'll have to get in," murmured the freckled man.

The tall man was standing like a granite column. "I won't," said he. "I won't! I don't care what you do, but I won't!"

"Well, but—" expostulated the other. They held a furious debate.

In the meantime the captain was darting about making sinister gestures, but the back of the tall man held him at bay. The crew, much depleted by the departure of the imperturbable man into the boat, looked on from the bow.

"You're a fool," the freckled man concluded his argument.

"So?" inquired the tall man, highly exasperated.

"So! Well, if you think you're so bright, we'll go in the boat, and then you'll see."

He climbed down into the craft and seated himself in an ominous manner at the stern.

"You'll see," he said to his companion, as the latter floundered heavily down. "You'll see!"

The man in rubber boots calmly rowed the boat toward the shore. As they went, the captain leaned over the railing and laughed. The freckled man was seated very victoriously.

"Well, wasn't this the right thing after all?" he inquired in a pleasant voice. The tall man made no reply.

## CHAPTER VI

As they neared the dock something seemed suddenly to occur to the freckled man.

"Great heavens!" he murmured. He stared at the approaching shore.

"My, what a plight, Tommy!" he quavered.

"Do you think so?" spoke up the tall man. "Why, I really thought you liked it." He laughed in a hard voice. "Lord, what a figure you'll cut."

This laugh jarred the freckled man's soul. He became mad.

"Thunderation, turn the boat around!" he roared. "Turn 'er round, quick! Man alive, we can't—turn 'er round, d'ye hear!"

The tall man in the stern gazed at his companion with glowing eyes.

"Certainly not," he said. "We're going on. You insisted Upon it." He began to prod his companion with words.

The freckled man stood up and waved his arms.

"Sit down," said the tall man. "You'll tip the boat over."

The other man began to shout.

"Sit down!" said the tall man again.

Words bubbled from the freckled man's mouth. There was a little torrent of sentences that almost choked him. And he protested passionately with his hands.

But the boat went on to the shadow of the docks. The tall man was intent upon balancing it as it rocked dangerously during his comrade's oration.

"Sit down," he continually repeated.

"I won't," raged the freckled man. "I won't do anything." The boat wobbled with these words.

"Say," he continued, addressing the oarsman, "just turn this boat round, will you? Where in the thunder are you taking us to, anyhow?"

The oarsman looked at the sky and thought. Finally he spoke. "I'm doin' what the cap'n sed."

"Well, what in th' blazes do I care what the cap'n sed?" demanded the freckled man. He took a violent step. "You just turn this round or—"

The small craft reeled. Over one side water came flashing in. The freckled man cried out in fear, and gave a jump to the other side. The tall man roared orders, and the oarsman made efforts. The boat acted for a moment like an animal on a slackened wire. Then it upset.

"Sit down!" said the tall man, in a final roar as he was plunged into the water. The oarsman dropped his oars to grapple with the gunwale. He went down saying unknown words. The freckled man's explanation or apology was strangled by the water.

Two or three tugs let off whistles of astonishment, and continued on their paths. A man dozing on a dock aroused and began to caper.

The passengers on a ferry-boat all ran to the near railing. A miraculous person in a small boat was bobbing on the waves near the piers. He sculled hastily toward the scene. It was a swirl of waters in the midst of which the dark bottom of the boat appeared, whale-like.

Two heads suddenly came up.

"839," said the freckled man, chokingly. "That's it! 839!"

"What is?" said the tall man.

"That's the number of that feller on Park Place. I just remembered."

"You're the bloomingest—" the tall man said.

"It wasn't my fault," interrupted his companion. "If you hadn't—" He tried to gesticulate, but one hand held to the keel of the boat, and the other was supporting the form of the oarsman. The latter had fought a battle with his immense rubber boots and had been conquered.

The rescuer in the other small boat came fiercely. As his craft glided up, he reached out and grasped the tall man by the collar and dragged him into the boat, interrupting what was, under the circumstances, a very brilliant flow of rhetoric directed at the freckled man. The oarsman of the wrecked craft was taken tenderly over the gunwale and laid in the bottom of the boat. Puffing and blowing, the freckled man climbed in.

"You'll upset this one before we can get ashore," the other voyager remarked.

As they turned toward the land they saw that the nearest dock was lined with people. The freckled man gave a little moan.

But the staring eyes of the crowd were fixed on the limp form of the man in rubber boots. A hundred hands reached down to help lift the body up. On the dock some men grabbed it and began to beat it and roll it. A policeman tossed the spectators about. Each individual in the heaving crowd sought to fasten his eyes on the blue-tinted face of the man in the rubber boots. They surged to and fro, while the policeman beat them indiscriminately.

The wanderers came modestly up the dock and gazed shrinkingly at the throng. They stood for a moment, holding their breath to see the first finger of amazement levelled at them.

But the crowd bended and surged in absorbing anxiety to view the man in rubber boots, whose face fascinated them. The sea-wanderers were as though they were not there.

They stood without the jam and whispered hurriedly.

"839," said the freckled man.

"All right," said the tall man.

Under the pommeling hands the oarsman showed signs of life. The voyagers watched him make a protesting kick at the leg of the crowd, the while uttering angry groans.

"He's better," said the tall man, softly; "let's make off."

Together they stole noiselessly up the dock. Directly in front of it they found a row of six cabs.

The drivers on top were filled with a mighty curiosity. They had driven hurriedly from the adjacent ferry-house when they had seen the first running sign of an accident. They were straining on their toes and gazing at the tossing backs of the men in the crowd.

The wanderers made a little detour, and then went rapidly towards a cab. They stopped in front of it and looked up.

"Driver," called the tall man, softly.

The man was intent.

"Driver," breathed the freckled man. They stood for a moment and gazed imploringly.

The cabman suddenly moved his feet. "By Jimmy, I bet he's a gonner," he said, in an ecstacy, and he again relapsed into a statue.

The freckled man groaned and wrung his hands. The tall man climbed into the cab.

"Come in here," he said to his companion. The freckled man climbed in, and the tall man reached over and pulled the door shut. Then he put his head out the window.

"Driver," he roared, sternly, "839 Park Place—and quick."

The driver looked down and met the eye of the tall man. "Eh?—Oh—839? Park Place? Yessir." He reluctantly gave his horse a clump on the back. As the conveyance rattled off the wanderers huddled back among the dingy cushions and heaved great breaths of relief.

"Well, it's all over," said the freckled man, finally. "We're about out of it. And quicker than I expected. Much quicker. It looked to me sometimes that we were doomed. I am thankful to find it not so. I am rejoiced. And I hope and trust that you—well, I don't wish to—perhaps it is not the proper time to—that is, I don't wish to intrude a moral at an inopportune moment, but, my dear, dear fellow, I think the time is ripe to point out to you that your obstinacy, your selfishness, your villainous temper, and your various other faults can make it just as unpleasant for your ownself, my dear boy, as they frequently do for other people. You can see what you brought us to, and I most sincerely hope, my dear, dear fellow, that I shall soon see those signs in you which shall lead me to believe that you have become a wiser man."

# THE END OF THE BATTLE

## *(Also published as "And If He Wills, We Must Die")*

A sergeant, a corporal, and fourteen men of the Twelfth Regiment of the Line had been sent out to occupy a house on the main highway. They would be at least a half of a mile in advance of any other picket of their own people. Sergeant Morton was deeply angry at being sent on this duty. He said that he was over-worked. There were at least two sergeants, he claimed furiously, whose turn it should have been to go on this arduous mission. He was treated unfairly; he was abused by his superiors; why did any damned fool ever join the army? As for him he would get out of it as soon as possible; he was sick of it; the life of a dog. All this he said to the corporal, who listened attentively, giving grunts of respectful assent. On the way to this post two privates took occasion to drop to the rear and pilfer in the orchard of a deserted plantation. When the sergeant discovered this absence, he grew black with a rage which was an accumulation of all his irritations. "Run, you!" he howled. "Bring them here! I'll show them—"A private ran swiftly to the rear. The remainder of the squad began to shout nervously at the two delinquents, whose figures they could see in the deep shade of the orchard, hurriedly picking fruit from the ground and cramming it within their shirts, next to their skins. The beseeching cries of their comrades stirred the criminals more than did the barking of the sergeant. They ran to rejoin the squad, while holding their loaded bosoms and with their mouths open with aggrieved explanations.

Jones faced the sergeant with a horrible cancer marked in bumps on his left side. The disease of Patterson showed quite around the front of his waist in many protuberances. "A nice pair!" said the sergeant, with sudden frigidity. "You're the kind of soldiers a man wants to choose for a dangerous outpost duty, ain't you?"

The two privates stood at attention, still looking much aggrieved. "We only—" began Jones huskily.

"Oh, you 'only!'" cried the sergeant. "Yes, you 'only.' I know all about that. But if you think you are going to trifle with me—"

A moment later the squad moved on towards its station. Behind the sergeant's back Jones and Patterson were slyly passing apples and pears to their friends while the sergeant expounded eloquently to the corporal. "You see what kind of men are in the army now. Why, when I joined the regiment it was a very different thing, I can tell you. Then a sergeant had some authority, and if a man disobeyed orders, he had a very small chance of escaping something extremely serious. But now! Good God! If I report these men, the captain will look over a lot of beastly orderly sheets and say—'Haw, eh, well, Sergeant Morton, these men seem to have very good re-cords; very good records, indeed. I can't be too hard on them; no, not too hard.'" Continued the sergeant: "I tell you, Flagler, the army is no place for a decent man."

Flagler, the corporal, answered with a sincerity of appreciation which with him had become a science. "I think you are right, sergeant," he answered.

Behind them the privates mumbled discreetly. "Damn this sergeant of ours. He thinks we are made of wood. I don't see any reason for all this strictness when we are on active service. It isn't like being at home in barracks! There is no great harm in a couple of men dropping out to raid an orchard of the enemy when all the world knows that we haven't had a decent meal in twenty days."

The reddened face of Sergeant Morton suddenly showed to the rear. "A little more marching and less talking," he said.

When he came to the house he had been ordered to occupy the sergeant sniffed with disdain. "These people must have lived like cattle," he said angrily. To be sure, the place was not alluring. The ground floor had been used for the housing of cattle, and it was dark and terrible. A flight of steps led to the lofty first floor, which was denuded but respectable. The sergeant's visage lightened when he saw the strong walls of stone and cement. "Unless they turn guns on us, they will never get us out of here," he said cheerfully to the squad. The men, anxious to keep him in an amiable mood, all hurriedly grinned and seemed very appreciative and pleased. "I'll make this into a fortress," he announced. He sent Jones and Patterson, the two orchard thieves, out on sentry-duty. He worked the others, then, until he could think of no more things to tell them to do. Afterwards he went forth, with a major-general's serious scowl, and examined the ground in front of his position. In returning he came upon a sentry, Jones, munching an apple. He sternly commanded him to throw it away.

The men spread their blankets on the floors of the bare rooms, and putting their packs under their heads and lighting their pipes, they lived an easy peace. Bees hummed in the garden, and a scent of flowers came through the open window. A great fan-shaped bit of sunshine smote the face of one man, and he indolently cursed as he moved his primitive bed to a shadier place.

Another private explained to a comrade: "This is all nonsense anyhow. No sense in occupying this post. They—"

"But, of course," said the corporal, "when she told me herself that she cared more for me than she did for him, I wasn't going to stand any of his talk—" The corporal's listener was so sleepy that he could only grunt his sympathy.

There was a sudden little spatter of shooting. A cry from Jones rang out. With no intermediate scrambling, the sergeant leaped straight to his feet. "Now," he cried, "let us see what you are made of! If," he added bitterly, "you are made of anything!"

A man yelled: "Good God, can't you see you're all tangled up in my cartridge belt?"

Another man yelled: "Keep off my legs! Can't you walk on the floor?"

To the windows there was a blind rush of slumberous men, who brushed hair from their eyes even as they made ready their rifles. Jones and Patterson came stumbling up the steps, crying dreadful information. Already the enemy's bullets were spitting and singing over the house.

The sergeant suddenly was stiff and cold with a sense of the importance of the thing. "Wait until you see one," he drawled loudly and calmly, "then shoot."

For some moments the enemy's bullets swung swifter than lightning over the house without anybody being able to discover a target. In this interval a man was shot in the throat. He gurgled, and then lay down on the floor. The blood slowly waved down the brown skin of his neck while he looked meekly at his comrades.

There was a howl. "There they are! There they come!" The rifles crackled. A light smoke drifted idly through the rooms. There was a strong odor as if from burnt paper and the powder of firecrackers. The men were silent. Through the windows and about the house the bullets of an entirely invisible enemy moaned, hummed, spat, burst, and sang.

The men began to curse. "Why can't we see them?" they muttered through their teeth. The sergeant was still frigid. He answered soothingly as if he were directly reprehensible for this behavior of the enemy. "Wait a moment. You will soon be able to see them. There! Give it to them!" A little skirt of black figures had appeared in a field. It was really like shooting at an upright needle from the full length of a ballroom. But the men's spirits improved as soon as the enemy—this mysterious enemy—became a tangible thing, and far off. They had believed the foe to be shooting at them from the adjacent garden.

"Now," said the sergeant ambitiously, "we can beat them off easily if you men are good enough."

A man called out in a tone of quick, great interest. "See that fellow on horseback, Bill? Isn't he on horseback? I thought he was on horseback."

There was a fusilade against another side of the house. The sergeant dashed into the room which commanded the situation. He found a dead soldier on the floor. He rushed out howling: "When was Knowles killed? When was Knowles killed? When was Knowles killed? Damn it, when was Knowles killed?" It was absolutely essential to find out the exact moment this man died. A blackened private turned upon his sergeant and demanded: "How in hell do I know?" Sergeant Morton had a sense of anger so brief that in the next second he cried: "Patterson!" He had even forgotten his vital interest in the time of Knowles' death.

"Yes?" said Patterson, his face set with some deep-rooted quality of determination. Still, he was a mere farm boy.

"Go in to Knowles' window and shoot at those people," said the sergeant hoarsely. Afterwards he coughed. Some of the fumes of the fight had made way to his lungs.

Patterson looked at the door into this other room. He looked at it as if he suspected it was to be his death-chamber. Then he entered and stood across the body of Knowles and fired vigorously into a group of plum trees.

"They can't take this house," declared the sergeant in a contemptuous and argumentative tone. He was apparently replying to somebody. The man who had been shot in the throat looked up at him. Eight men were firing from the windows. The sergeant detected in a corner three wounded men talking together feebly. "Don't you think there is anything to do?" he bawled. "Go and get Knowles' cartridges and give them to somebody who can use them! Take Simpson's too." The man who had been shot in the throat looked at him. Of the three wounded men who had been talking, one said: "My leg is all doubled up under me, sergeant." He spoke apologetically.

Meantime the sergeant was re-loading his rifle. His foot slipped in the blood of the man who had been shot in the throat, and the military boot made a greasy red streak on the floor.

"Why, we can hold this place!" shouted the sergeant jubilantly. "Who says we can't?"

Corporal Flagler suddenly spun away from his window and fell in a heap.

"Sergeant," murmured a man as he dropped to a seat on the floor out of danger, "I can't stand this. I swear I can't. I think we should run away."

Morton, with the kindly eyes of a good shepherd, looked at the man. "You are afraid, Johnston, you are afraid," he said softly. The man struggled to his feet, cast upon the sergeant a gaze full of admiration, reproach, and despair, and returned to his post. A moment later he pitched forward, and thereafter his body hung out of the window, his arms straight and the fists clenched. Incidentally this corpse was pierced afterwards by chance three times by bullets of the enemy.

The sergeant laid his rifle against the stonework of the window-frame and shot with care until his magazine was empty. Behind him a man, simply grazed on the elbow, was wildly sobbing like a girl. "Damn it, shut up!" said Morton, without turning his head. Before him was a vista of a garden, fields, clumps of trees, woods, populated at the time with little fleeting figures.

He grew furious. "Why didn't he send me orders?" he cried aloud. The emphasis on the word "he" was impressive. A mile back on the road a galloper of the Hussars lay dead beside his dead horse.

The man who had been grazed on the elbow still set up his bleat. Morton's fury veered to this soldier. "Can't you shut up? Can't you shut up? Can't you shut up? Fight! That's the thing to do. Fight!"

A bullet struck Morton, and he fell upon the man who had been shot in the throat. There was a sickening moment. Then the sergeant rolled off to a position upon the bloody floor. He turned himself with a last effort until he could look at the wounded who were able to look at him.

"Kim up, the Kickers," he said thickly. His arms weakened and he dropped on his face.

After an interval a young subaltern of the enemy's infantry, followed by his eager men, burst into this reeking interior. But just over the threshold he halted before the scene of blood and death. He turned with a shrug to his sergeant. "God, I should have estimated them at least one hundred strong."

# UPTURNED FACE

"What will we do now?" said the adjutant, troubled and excited.

"Bury him," said Timothy Lean.

The two officers looked down close to their toes where lay the body of their comrade. The face was chalk-blue; gleaming eyes stared at the sky. Over the two upright figures was a windy sound of bullets, and on the top of the hill Lean's prostrate company of Spitzbergen infantry was firing measured volleys.

"Don't you think it would be better—" began the adjutant. "We might leave him until tomorrow."

"No," said Lean. "I can't hold that post an hour longer. I've got to fall back, and we've got to bury old Bill."

"Of course," said the adjutant, at once. "Your men got intrenching tools?"

Lean shouted back to his little line, and two men came slowly, one with a pick, one with a shovel. They started in the direction of the Rostina sharp-shooters. Bullets cracked near their ears. "Dig here," said Lean gruffly. The men, thus caused to lower their glances to the turf, became hurried and frightened merely because they could not look to see whence the bullets came. The dull beat of the pick striking the earth sounded amid the swift snap of close bullets. Presently the other private began to shovel.

"I suppose," said the adjutant, slowly, "we'd better search his clothes for—things."

Lean nodded. Together in curious abstraction they looked at the body. Then Lean stirred his shoulders suddenly, arousing himself.

"Yes," he said, "we'd better see what he's got." He dropped to his knees, and his hands approached the body of the dead officer. But his hands wavered over the buttons of the tunic. The first button was brick-red with drying blood, and he did not seem to dare touch it.

"Go on," said the adjutant, hoarsely.

Lean stretched his wooden hand, and his fingers fumbled the blood-stained buttons. At last he rose with ghastly face. He had gathered a watch, a whistle, a pipe, a tobacco pouch, a handkerchief, a little case of cards and papers. He looked at the adjutant. There was a silence. The adjutant was feeling that he had been a coward to make Lean do all the grisly business.

"Well," said Lean, "that's all, I think. You have his sword and revolver?"

"Yes," said the adjutant, his face working, and then he burst out in a sudden strange fury at the two privates. "Why don't you hurry up with that grave? What are you doing, anyhow? Hurry, do you hear? I never saw such stupid—"

Even as he cried out in his passion the two men were laboring for their lives. Ever overhead the bullets were spitting.

The grave was finished, It was not a masterpiece—a poor little shallow thing. Lean and the adjutant again looked at each other in a curious silent communication.

Suddenly the adjutant croaked out a weird laugh. It was a terrible laugh, which had its origin in that part of the mind which is first moved by the singing of the nerves. "Well," he said, humorously to Lean, "I suppose we had best tumble him in."

"Yes," said Lean. The two privates stood waiting, bent over their implements. "I suppose," said Lean, "it would be better if we laid him in ourselves."

"Yes," said the adjutant. Then apparently remembering that he had made Lean search the body, he stooped with great fortitude and took hold of the dead officer's clothing. Lean joined him. Both were particular that their fingers should not feel the corpse. They tugged away; the corpse lifted, heaved, toppled, flopped into the grave, and the two officers, straightening, looked again at each other—they were always looking at each other. They sighed with relief.

The adjutant said, "I suppose we should—we should say something. Do you know the service, Tim?"

"They don't read the service until the grave is filled in," said Lean, pressing his lips to an academic expression.

"Don't they?" said the adjutant, shocked that he had made the mistake.

"Oh, well," he cried, suddenly, "let us—let us say something—while he can hear us."

"All right," said Lean. "Do you know the service?"

"I can't remember a line of it," said the adjutant.

Lean was extremely dubious. "I can repeat two lines, but—"

"Well, do it," said the adjutant. "Go as far as you can. That's better than nothing. And the beasts have got our range exactly."

Lean looked at his two men. "Attention," he barked. The privates came to attention with a click, looking much aggrieved. The adjutant lowered his helmet to his knee. Lean, bareheaded, he stood over the grave. The Rostina sharpshooters fired briskly.

"Oh, Father, our friend has sunk in the deep waters of death, but his spirit has leaped toward Thee as the bubble arises from the lips of the drowning. Perceive, we beseech, O Father, the little flying bubble, and—".

Lean, although husky and ashamed, had suffered no hesitation up to this point, but he stopped with a hopeless feeling and looked at the corpse.

The adjutant moved uneasily. "And from Thy superb heights—" he began, and then he too came to an end.

"And from Thy superb heights," said Lean.

The adjutant suddenly remembered a phrase in the back part of the Spitzbergen burial service, and he exploited it with the triumphant manner of a man who has recalled everything, and can go on.

"Oh, God, have mercy—"

"Oh, God, have mercy—" said Lean.

"Mercy," repeated the adjutant, in quick failure.

"Mercy," said Lean. And then he was moved by some violence of feeling, for he turned suddenly upon his two men and tigerishly said, "Throw the dirt in."

The fire of the Rostina sharpshooters was accurate and continuous.

* * * *

One of the aggrieved privates came forward with his shovel. He lifted his first shovel-load of earth, and for a moment of inexplicable hesitation it was held poised above this corpse, which from its chalk-blue face looked keenly out from the grave. Then the soldier emptied his shovel on—on the feet.

Timothy Lean felt as if tons had been swiftly lifted from off his forehead. He had felt that perhaps the private might empty the shovel on—on the face. It had been emptied on the feet. There was a great point gained there—ha, ha!—the first shovelful had been emptied on the feet. How satisfactory!

The adjutant began to babble. "Well, of course—a man we've messed with all these years—impossible—you can't, you know, leave your intimate friends rotting on the field. Go on, for God's sake, and shovel, you!"

The man with the shovel suddenly ducked, grabbed his left arm with his right hand, and looked at his officer for orders. Lean picked the shovel from the ground. "Go to the rear," he said to the wounded man. He also addressed the other private. "You get under cover, too; I'll finish this business."

The wounded man scrambled hard still for the top of the ridge without devoting any glances to the direction whence the bullets came, and the other man followed at an equal pace; but he was different, in that he looked back anxiously three times.

This is merely the way—often—of the hit and unhit.

Timothy Lean filled the shovel, hesitated, and then in a movement which was like a gesture of abhorrence he flung the dirt into the grave, and as it landed it made a sound—plop! Lean suddenly stopped and mopped his brow—a tired laborer.

"Perhaps we have been wrong," said the adjutant. His glance wavered stupidly. "It might have been better if we hadn't buried him just at this time. Of course, if we advance tomorrow the body would have been—"

"Damn you," said Lean, "shut your mouth!" He was not the senior officer.

He again filled the shovel and flung the earth. Always the earth made that sound—plop! For a space Lean worked frantically, like a man digging himself out of danger.

Soon there was nothing to be seen but the chalk-blue face. Lean filled the shovel. "Good God," he cried to the adjutant. "Why didn't you turn him somehow when you put him in? This—" Then Lean began to stutter.

The adjutant understood. He was pale to the lips. "Go on, man," he cried, beseechingly, almost in a shout. Lean swung back the shovel. It went forward in a pendulum curve. When the earth landed it made a sound—plop!

# AN EPISODE OF WAR

The lieutenant's rubber blanket lay on the ground, and upon it he had poured the company's supply of coffee. Corporals and other representatives of the grimy and hot-throated men who lined the breastwork had come for each squad's portion.

The lieutenant was frowning and serious at this task of division. His lips pursed as he drew with his sword various crevices in the heap until brown squares of coffee, astoundingly equal in size, appeared on the blanket. He was on the verge of a great triumph in mathematics, and the corporals were thronging forward, each to reap a little square, when suddenly the lieutenant cried out and looked quickly at a man near him as if he suspected it was a case of personal assault. The others cried out also when they saw blood upon the lieutenant's sleeve.

He had winced like a man stung, swayed dangerously, and then straightened. The sound of his hoarse breathing was plainly audible. He looked sadly, mystically, over the breastwork at the green face of a wood, where now were many little puffs of white smoke. During this moment the men about him gazed statue-like and silent, astonished and awed by this catastrophe which happened when catastrophes were not expected—when they had leisure to observe it.

As the lieutenant stared at the wood, they too swung their heads, so that for another instant all hands, still silent, contemplated the distant forest as if their minds were fixed upon the mystery of a bullet's journey.

The officer had, of course, been compelled to take his sword into his left hand. He did not hold it by the hilt. He gripped it at the middle of the blade, awkwardly. Turning his eyes from the hostile wood, he looked at the sword as he held it there, and seemed puzzled as to what to do with it, where to put it. In short, this weapon had of a sudden become a strange thing to him. He looked at it in a kind of stupefaction, as if he had been endowed with a trident, a sceptre, or a spade.

Finally he tried to sheath it. To sheath a sword held by the left hand, at the middle of the blade, in a scabbard hung at the left hip, is a feat worthy of a sawdust ring. This wounded officer engaged in a desperate struggle with the sword and the wobbling scabbard, and during the time of it he breathed like a wrestler.

But at this instant the men, the spectators, awoke from their stone-like poses and crowded forward sympathetically. The orderly-sergeant took the sword and tenderly placed it in the scabbard. At the time, he leaned nervously backward, and did not allow even his finger to brush the body of the lieutenant. A wound gives strange dignity to him who bears it. Well men shy from this new and terrible majesty. It is as if the wounded man's hand is upon the curtain which hangs before the revelations of all existence—the meaning of ants, potentates, wars, cities, sunshine, snow, a feather dropped from a bird's wing; and the power of it sheds radiance upon a bloody form, and makes the other men understand sometimes that they are little. His comrades look at him with large eyes thoughtfully. Moreover, they fear vaguely that the weight of a finger upon him might send him headlong, precipitate the tragedy, hurl him at once into the dim, grey unknown. And so the orderly-sergeant, while sheathing the sword, leaned nervously backward.

There were others who proffered assistance. One timidly presented his shoulder and asked the lieutenant if he cared to lean upon it, but the latter waved him away mournfully. He wore the look of one who knows he is the victim of a terrible disease and understands his helplessness. He again stared over the breastwork at the forest, and then turning went slowly rearward. He held his right wrist tenderly in his left hand as if the wounded arm was made of very brittle glass.

And the men in silence stared at the wood, then at the departing lieutenant—then at the wood, then at the lieutenant.

As the wounded officer passed from the line of battle, he was enabled to see many things which as a participant in the fight were unknown to him. He saw a general on a black horse gazing over the lines of blue infantry at the green woods which veiled his problems. An aide galloped furiously, dragged his horse suddenly to a halt, saluted, and presented a paper. It was, for a wonder, precisely like an historical painting.

To the rear of the general and his staff a group, composed of a bugler, two or three orderlies, and the bearer of the corps standard, all upon maniacal horses, were working like slaves to hold their ground, preserve, their respectful interval, while the shells boomed in the air about them, and caused their chargers to make furious quivering leaps.

A battery, a tumultuous and shining mass, was swirling toward the right. The wild thud of hoofs, the cries of the riders shouting blame and praise, menace and encouragement, and, last the roar of the wheels, the slant of the glistening guns, brought the lieutenant to an intent pause. The battery swept in curves that stirred the heart; it made halts as dramatic as the crash of a wave on the rocks, and when it fled onward, this aggregation of wheels, levers, motors, had a beautiful unity, as if it were a missile. The sound of it was a war-chorus that reached into the depths of man's emotion.

The lieutenant, still holding his arm as if it were of glass, stood watching this battery until all detail of it was lost, save the figures of the riders, which rose and fell and waved lashes over the black mass.

Later, he turned his eyes toward the battle where the shooting sometimes crackled like bush-fires, sometimes sputtered with exasperating irregularity, and sometimes reverberated like the thunder. He saw the smoke rolling upward and saw crowds of men who ran and cheered, or stood and blazed away at the inscrutable distance.

He came upon some stragglers, and they told him how to find the field hospital. They described its exact location. In fact, these men, no longer having part in the battle, knew more of it than others. They told the performance of every corps, every division, the opinion of every general. The lieutenant, carrying his wounded arm rearward, looked upon them with wonder.

At the roadside a brigade was making coffee and buzzing with talk like a girls' boarding-school. Several officers came out to him and inquired concerning things of which he knew nothing. One, seeing his arm, began to scold. "Why, man, that's no way to do. You want to fix that thing." He appropriated the lieutenant and the lieutenant's wound. He cut the sleeve and laid bare the arm, every nerve of which softly fluttered under his touch. He bound his handkerchief over the wound, scolding away in the meantime. His tone allowed one to think that he was in the habit of being wounded every day. The lieutenant hung his head, feeling, in this presence, that he did not know how to be correctly wounded.

The low white tents of the hospital were grouped around an old school-house. There was here a singular commotion. In the foreground two ambulances inter-locked wheels in the deep mud. The drivers were tossing the blame of it back and forth, gesticulating and berating, while from the ambulances, both crammed with wounded, there came an occasional groan. An interminable crowd of bandaged men were coming and going. Great numbers sat under the trees nursing heads or arms or legs. There was a dispute of some kind raging on the steps of the school-house. Sitting with his back against a tree a man with a face as grey as a new army blanket was serenely smoking a corn-cob pipe. The lieutenant wished to rush forward and inform him that he was dying.

A busy surgeon was passing near the lieutenant. "Good-morning," he said, with a friendly smile. Then he caught sight of the lieutenant's arm and his face at once changed. "Well, let's have a look at it." He seemed possessed suddenly of a great contempt for the lieutenant. This wound evidently placed the latter on a very low social plane. The doctor cried out impatiently, "What mutton-head had tied it up that way anyhow?" The lieutenant answered, "Oh, a man."

When the wound was disclosed the doctor fingered it disdainfully. "Humph," he said. "You come along with me and I'll 'tend to you." His voice contained the same scorn as if he were saying, "You will have to go to jail."

The lieutenant had been very meek, but now his face flushed, and he looked into the doctor's eyes. "I guess I won't have it amputated," he said.

"Nonsense, man! Nonsense! Nonsense!" cried the doctor. "Come along, now. I won't amputate it. Come along. Don't be a baby."

"Let go of me," said the lieutenant, holding back wrathfully, his glance fixed upon the door of the old school-house, as sinister to him as the portals of death.

And this is the story of how the lieutenant lost his arm. When he reached home, his sisters, his mother, his wife sobbed for a long time at the sight of the flat sleeve. "Oh, well," he said, standing shamefaced amid these tears, "I don't suppose it matters so much as all that."

# AN EXPERIMENT IN MISERY

It was late at night, and a fine rain was swirling softly down, causing the pavements to glisten with hue of steel and blue and yellow in the rays of the innumerable lights. A youth was trudging slowly, without enthusiasm, with his hands buried deep in his trousers' pockets, toward the downtown places where beds can be hired for coppers. He was clothed in an aged and tattered suit, and his derby was a marvel of dust-covered crown and torn rim. He was going forth to eat as the wanderer may eat, and sleep as the homeless sleep. By the time he had reached City Hall Park he was so completely plastered with yells of "bum" and "hobo," and with various unholy epithets that small boys had applied to him at intervals, that he was in a state of the most profound dejection. The sifting rain saturated the old velvet collar of his overcoat, and as the wet cloth pressed against his neck, he felt that there no longer could be pleasure in life. He looked about him searching for an outcast of highest degree that they too might share miseries, but the lights threw a quivering glare over rows and circles of deserted benches that glistened damply, showing patches of wet sod behind them. It seemed that their usual freights had fled on this night to better things. There were only squads of well-dressed Brooklyn people who swarmed towards the bridge.

The young man loitered about for a time and then went shuffling off down Park Row. In the sudden descent in style of the dress of the crowd he felt relief, and as if he were at last in his own country. He began to see tatters that matched his tatters. In Chatham Square there were aimless men strewn in front of saloons and lodging-houses, standing sadly, patiently, reminding one vaguely of the attitudes of chickens in a storm. He aligned himself with these men, and turned slowly to occupy himself with the flowing life of the great street.

Through the mists of the cold and storming night, the cable cars went in silent procession, great affairs shining with red and brass, moving with formidable power, calm and irresistible, dangerful and gloomy, breaking silence only by the loud fierce cry of the gong. Two rivers of people swarmed along the sidewalks, spattered with black mud, which made each shoe leave a scarlike impression. Overhead elevated trains with a shrill grinding of the wheels stopped at the station, which upon its leglike pillars seemed to resemble some monstrous kind of crab squatting over the street. The quick fat puffings of the engines could be heard. Down an alley there were somber curtains of purple and black, on which street lamps dully glittered like embroidered flowers.

A saloon stood with a voracious air on a corner. A sign leaning against the front of the door-post announced "Free hot soup tonight!" The swing doors, snapping to and fro like ravenous lips, made gratified smacks as the saloon gorged itself with plump men, eating with astounding and endless appetite, smiling in some indescribable manner as the men came from all directions like sacrifices to a heathenish superstition.

Caught by the delectable sign the young man allowed himself to be swallowed. A bartender placed a schooner of dark and portentous beer on the bar. Its monumental form upreared until the froth a-top was above the crown of the young man's brown derby.

"Soup over there, gents," said the bartender affably. A little yellow man in rags and the youth grasped their schooners and went with speed toward a lunch counter, where a man with oily but imposing whiskers ladled genially from a kettle until he had furnished his two mendicants with a soup that was steaming hot, and in which there were little floating suggestions of chicken. The young man, sipping his broth, felt the cordiality expressed by the warmth of the mixture, and he beamed at the man with oily but imposing whiskers, who was presiding like a priest behind an altar. "Have some more, gents?" he inquired of the two sorry figures before him. The little yellow man accepted with a swift gesture, but the youth shook his head and went out, following a man whose wondrous seediness promised that he would have a knowledge of cheap lodging-houses.

On the sidewalk he accosted the seedy man. "Say, do you know a cheap place to sleep?"

The other hesitated for a time, gazing sideways. Finally he nodded in the direction of the street, "I sleep up there," he said, "when I've got the price."

"How much?"

"Ten cents." The young man shook his head dolefully. "That's too rich for me."

At that moment there approached the two a reeling man in strange garments. His head was a fuddle of bushy hair and whiskers, from which his eyes peered with a guilty slant. In a close scrutiny it was possible to distinguish the cruel lines of a mouth which looked as if its lips had just closed with satisfaction over some tender and piteous morsel. He appeared like an assassin steeped in crimes performed awkwardly.

But at this time his voice was tuned to the coaxing key of an affectionate puppy. He looked at the men with wheedling eyes, and began to sing a little melody for charity.

"Say, gents, can't yeh give a poor feller a couple of cents t' git a bed? I got five, and I gits anudder two I gits me a bed. Now, on th' square, gents, can't yeh jest gimme two cents t' git a bed? Now, yeh know how a respecter'ble gentlem'n feels when he's down on his luck, an' I—"

The seedy man, staring with imperturbable countenance at a train which clattered overhead, interrupted in an expressionless voice—"Ah, go t' h—!"

But the youth spoke to the prayerful assassin in tones of astonishment and inquiry. "Say, you must be crazy! Why don't yeh strike somebody that looks as if they had money?"

The assassin, tottering about on his uncertain legs, and at intervals brushing imaginary obstacles from before his nose, entered into a long explanation of the psychology of the situation. It was so profound that it was unintelligible.

When he had exhausted the subject, the young man said to him:

"Let's see th' five cents."

The assassin wore an expression of drunken woe at this sentence, filled with suspicion of him. With a deeply pained air he began to fumble in his clothing, his red hands trembling. Presently he announced in a voice of bitter grief, as if he had been betrayed—"There's on'y four."

"Four," said the young man thoughtfully. "Well, look here, I'm a stranger here, an' if ye'll steer me to your cheap joint I'll find the other three."

The assassin's countenance became instantly radiant with joy. His whiskers quivered with the wealth of his alleged emotions. He seized the young man's hand in a transport of delight and friendliness.

"B' Gawd," he cried, "if ye'll do that, b' Gawd, I'd say yeh was a damned good fellow, I would, an' I'd remember yeh all m' life, I would, b' Gawd, an' if I ever got a chance I'd return the compliment"—he spoke with drunken dignity—"b' Gawd, I'd treat yeh white, I would, an' I'd allus remember yeh."

The young man drew back, looking at the assassin coldly. "Oh, that's all right," he said. "You show me th' joint—that's all you've got t' do."

The assassin, gesticulating gratitude, led the young man along a dark street. Finally he stopped before a little dusty door. He raised his hand impressively. "Look-a-here," he said, and there was a thrill of deep and ancient wisdom upon his face, "I've brought yeh here, an' that's my part, ain't it? If th' place don't suit yeh, yeh needn't git mad at me, need yeh? There won't be no bad feelin', will there?"

"No," said the young man.

The assassin waved his arm tragically, and led the march up the steep stairway. On the way the young man furnished the assassin with three pennies. At the top a man with benevolent spectacles looked at them through a hole in a board. He collected their money, wrote some names on a register, and speedily was leading the two men along a gloom-shrouded corridor.

Shortly after the beginning of this journey the young man felt his liver turn white, for from the dark and secret places of the building there suddenly came to his nostrils strange and unspeakable odors, that assailed him like malignant diseases with wings. They seemed to be from human bodies closely packed in dens; the exhalations from a hundred pairs of reeking lips; the fumes from a thousand bygone debauches; the expression of a thousand present miseries.

A man, naked save for a little snuff-colored undershirt, was parading sleepily along the corridor. He rubbed his eyes, and, giving vent to a prodigious yawn, demanded to be told the time.

"Half-past one."

The man yawned again. He opened a door, and for a moment his form was outlined against a black, opaque interior. To this door came the three men, and as it was again opened the unholy odors rushed out like fiends, so that the young man was obliged to struggle as against an overpowering wind.

It was some time before the youth's eyes were good in the intense gloom within, but the man with benevolent spectacles led him skilfully, pausing but a moment to deposit the limp assassin upon a cot. He took the youth to a cot that lay tranquilly by the window, and showing him a tall locker for clothes that stood near the head with the ominous air of a tombstone, left him.

The youth sat on his cot and peered about him. There was a gas-jet in a distant part of the room, that burned a small flickering orange-hued flame. It caused vast masses of tumbled shadows in all parts of the place, save where, immediately about it, there was a little grey haze. As the young man's eyes became used to the darkness, he could see upon the cots that thickly littered the floor the forms of men sprawled out, lying in deathlike silence, or heaving and snoring with tremendous effort, like stabbed fish.

The youth locked his derby and his shoes in the mummy case near him, and then lay down with an old and familiar coat around his shoulders. A blanket he handed gingerly, drawing it over part of the coat. The cot was covered with leather, and as cold as melting snow. The youth was obliged to shiver for some time on this affair, which was like a slab. Presently, however, his chill gave him peace, and during this period of leisure from it he turned his head to stare at his friend the assassin, whom he could dimly discern where he lay sprawled on a cot in the abandon of a man filled with drink. He was snoring with incredible vigor. His wet hair and beard dimly glistened, and his inflamed nose shone with subdued lustre like a red light in a fog.

Within reach of the youth's hand was one who lay with yellow breast and shoulders bare to the cold drafts. One arm hung over the side of the cot, and the fingers lay full length upon the wet cement floor of the room. Beneath the inky brows could be seen the eyes of the man exposed by the partly opened lids. To the youth it seemed that he and this corpse-like being were exchanging a prolonged stare, and that the other threatened with his eyes. He drew back, watching his neighbor from the shadows of his blanket edge. The man did not move once through the night, but lay in this stillness as of death like a body stretched out expectant of the surgeon's knife.

And all through the room could be seen the tawny hues of naked flesh, limbs thrust into the darkness, projecting beyond the cots; upreared knees, arms hanging long and thin over the cot edges. For the most part they were statuesque, carven, dead. With the curious lockers standing all about like tombstones, there was a strange effect of a graveyard where bodies were merely flung.

Yet occasionally could be seen limbs wildly tossing in fantastic nightmare gestures, accompanied by guttural cries, grunts, oaths. And there was one fellow off in a gloomy corner, who in his dreams was oppressed by some frightful calamity, for of a sudden he began to utter long wails that went almost like yells from a hound, echoing wailfully and weird through this chill place of tombstones where men lay like the dead.

The sound in its high piercing beginnings, that dwindled to final melancholy moans, expressed a red and grim tragedy of the unfathomable possibilities of the man's dreams. But to the youth these were not merely the shrieks of a vision-pierced man: they were an utterance of the meaning of the room and its occupants. It was to him the protest of the wretch who feels the touch of the imperturbable granite wheels, and who then cries with an impersonal eloquence, with a strength not from him, giving voice to the wail of a whole section, a class, a people. This, weaving into the young man's brain, and mingling with his views of the vast and sombre shadows that, like mighty black fingers, curled around the naked bodies, made the young man so that he did not sleep, but lay carving the biographies for these men from his meagre experience. At times the fellow in the corner howled in a writhing agony of his imaginations.

Finally a long lance-point of grey light shot through the dusty panes of the window. Without, the young man could see roofs drearily white in the dawning. The point of light yellowed and grew brighter, until the golden rays of the morning sun came in bravely and strong. They touched with radiant color the form of a small fat man, who snored in stuttering fashion. His round and shiny bald head glowed suddenly with the valor of a decoration. He sat up, blinked at the sun, swore fretfully, and pulled his blanket over the ornamental splendors of his head.

The youth contentedly watched this rout of the shadows before the bright spears of the sun, and presently he slumbered. When he awoke he heard the voice of the assassin raised in valiant curses. Putting up his head, he perceived his comrade seated on the side of the cot engaged in scratching his neck with long finger-nails that rasped like files.

"Hully Jee, dis is a new breed. They've got can-openers on their feet." He continued in a violent tirade.

The young man hastily unlocked his closet and took out his shoes and hat. As he sat on the side of the cot lacing his shoes, he glanced about and saw that daylight had made the room comparatively commonplace and uninteresting. The men, whose faces seemed stolid, serene or absent, were engaged in dressing, while a great crackle of bantering conversation arose.

A few were parading in unconcerned nakedness. Here and there were men of brawn, whose skins shone clear and ruddy. They took splendid poses, standing massively like chiefs. When they had dressed in their ungainly garments there was an extraordinary change. They then showed bumps and deficiencies of all kinds.

There were others who exhibited many deformities. Shoulders were slanting, humped, pulled this way and pulled that way. And notable among these latter men was the little fat man who had refused to allow his head to be glorified. His pudgy form, builded like a pear, bustled to and fro, while he swore in fishwife fashion. It appeared that some article of his apparel had vanished.

The young man attired speedily, and went to his friend the assassin. At first the latter looked dazed at the sight of the youth. This face seemed to be appealing to him through the cloud wastes of his memory. He scratched his neck and reflected. At last he grinned, a broad smile gradually spreading until his countenance was a round illumination. "Hello, Willie," he cried cheerily.

"Hello," said the young man. "Are yeh ready t' fly?"

"Sure." The assassin tied his shoe carefully with some twine and came ambling.

When he reached the street the young man experienced no sudden relief from unholy atmospheres. He had forgotten all about them, and had been breathing naturally, and with no sensation of discomfort or distress.

He was thinking of these things as he walked along the street, when he was suddenly startled by feeling the assassin's hand, trembling with excitement, clutching his arm, and when the assassin spoke, his voice went into quavers from a supreme agitation.

"I'll be hully, bloomin' blowed if there wasn't a feller with a nightshirt on up there in that joint."

The youth was bewildered for a moment, but presently he turned to smile indulgently at the assassin's humor.

"Oh, you're a damned liar," he merely said.

Whereupon the assassin began to gesture extravagantly, and take oath by strange gods. He frantically placed himself at the mercy of remarkable fates if his tale were not true.

"Yes, he did! I cross m' heart thousan' times!" he protested, and at the moment his eyes were large with amazement, his mouth wrinkled in unnatural glee.

"Yessir! A nightshirt! A hully white nightshirt!"

"You lie!"

"No, sir! I hope ter die b'fore I kin git anudder ball if there wasn't a jay wid a hully, bloomin' white nightshirt!"

His face was filled with the infinite wonder of it. "A hully white nightshirt," he continually repeated.

The young man saw the dark entrance to a basement restaurant. There was a sign which read "No mystery about our hash"! and there were other age-stained and world-battered legends which told him that the place was within his means. He stopped before it and spoke to the assassin. "I guess I'll git somethin' t' eat."

At this the assassin, for some reason, appeared to be quite embarrassed. He gazed at the seductive front of the eating place for a moment. Then he started slowly up the street. "Well, good-bye, Willie," he said bravely.

For an instant the youth studied the departing figure. Then he called out, "Hol' on a minnet." As they came together he spoke in a certain fierce way, as if he feared that the other would think him to be charitable. "Look-a-here, if yeh wanta git some breakfas' I'll lend yeh three cents t' do it with. But say, look-a-here, you've gota git out an' hustle. I ain't goin' t' support yeh, or I'll go broke b'fore night. I ain't no millionaire."

"I take me oath, Willie," said the assassin earnestly, "th' on'y thing I really needs is a ball. Me t'roat feels like a fryin'-pan. But as I can't get a ball, why, th' next bes' thing is breakfast, an' if yeh do that for me, b'Gawd, I say yeh was th' whitest lad I ever see."

They spent a few moments in dexterous exchanges of phrases, in which they each protested that the other was, as the assassin had originally said, "a respecter'ble gentlem'n." And they concluded with mutual assurances that they were the souls of intelligence and virtue. Then they went into the restaurant.

There was a long counter, dimly lighted from hidden sources. Two or three men in soiled white aprons rushed here and there.

The youth bought a bowl of coffee for two cents and a roll for one cent. The assassin purchased the same. The bowls were webbed with brown seams, and the tin spoons wore an air of having emerged from the first pyramid. Upon them were black mosslike encrustations of age, and they were bent and scarred from the attacks of long-forgotten teeth. But over their repast the wanderers waxed warm and mellow. The assassin grew affable as the hot mixture went soothingly down his parched throat, and the young man felt courage flow in his veins.

Memories began to throng in on the assassin, and he brought forth long tales, intricate, incoherent, delivered with a chattering swiftness as from an old woman. "—great job out'n Orange. Boss keep yeh hustlin' though all time. I was there three days, and then I went an' ask 'im t' lend me a dollar. 'G-g-go ter the devil,' he ses, an' I lose me job."

"South no good. Damn niggers work for twenty-five an' thirty cents a day. Run white man out. Good grub, though. Easy livin'."

"Yas; useter work little in Toledo, raftin' logs. Make two or three dollars er day in the spring. Lived high. Cold as ice, though, in the winter."

"I was raised in northern N'York. O-a-ah, yeh jest oughto live there. No beer ner whisky, though, way off in the woods. But all th' good hot grub yeh can eat. B'Gawd, I hung around there long as I could till th' ol' man fired me. 'Git t' hell outa here, yeh wuthless skunk, git t' hell outa here, an' go die,' he ses. 'You're a hell of a father,' I ses, 'you are,' an' I quit 'im."

As they were passing from the dim eating place, they encountered an old man who was trying to steal forth with a tiny package of food, but a tall man with an indomitable moustache stood dragon fashion, barring the way of escape. They heard the old man raise a plaintive protest. "Ah, you always want to know what I take out, and you never see that I usually bring a package in here from my place of business."

As the wanderers trudged slowly along Park Row, the assassin began to expand and grow blithe. "B'Gawd, we've been livin' like kings," he said, smacking appreciative lips.

"Look out, or we'll have t' pay fer it t'night," said the youth with gloomy warning.

But the assassin refused to turn his gaze toward the future. He went with a limping step, into which he injected a suggestion of lamblike gambols. His mouth was wreathed in a red grin.

In the City Hall Park the two wanderers sat down in the little circle of benches sanctified by traditions of their class. They huddled in their old garments, slumbrously conscious of the march of the hours which for them had no meaning.

The people of the street hurrying hither and thither made a blend of black figures changing yet frieze-like. They walked in their good clothes as upon important missions, giving no gaze to the two wanderers seated upon the benches. They expressed to the young man his infinite distance from all that he valued. Social position, comfort, the pleasures of living, were unconquerable kingdoms. He felt a sudden awe.

And in the background a multitude of buildings, of pitiless hues and sternly high, were to him emblematic of a nation forcing its regal head into the clouds, throwing no downward glances; in the sublimity of its aspirations ignoring the wretches who may flounder at its feet. The roar of the city in his ear was to him the confusion of strange tongues, babbling heedlessly; it was the clink of coin, the voice if the city's hopes which were to him no hopes.

He confessed himself an outcast, and his eyes from under the lowered rim of his hat began to glance guiltily, wearing the criminal expression that comes with certain convictions.

# THE DUEL THAT WAS NOT FOUGHT

Patsy Tulligan was not as wise as seven owls, but his courage could throw a shadow as long as the steeple of a cathedral. There were men on Cherry Street who had whipped him five times, but they all knew that Patsy would be as ready for the sixth time as if nothing had happened.

Once he and two friends had been away up on Eighth Avenue, far out of their country, and upon their return journey that evening they stopped frequently in saloons until they were as independent of their surroundings as eagles, and cared much less about thirty days on Blackwell's.

On Lower Sixth Avenue they paused in a saloon where there was a good deal of lamp-glare and polished wood to be seen from the outside, and within, the mellow light shone on much furbished brass and more polished wood. It was a better saloon than they were in the habit of seeing, but they did not mind it. They sat down at one of the little tables that were in a row parallel to the bar and ordered beer. They blinked stolidly at the decorations, the bartender, and the other customers. When anything transpired they discussed it with dazzling frankness, and what they said of it was as free as air to the other people in the place.

At midnight there were few people in the saloon. Patsy and his friends still sat drinking. Two well-dressed men were at another table, smoking cigars slowly and swinging back in their chairs. They occupied themselves with themselves in the usual manner, never betraying by a wink of an eyelid that they knew that other folk existed. At another table directly behind Patsy and his companions was a slim little Cuban, with miraculously small feet and hands, and with a youthful touch of down upon his lip. As he lifted his cigarette from time to time his little finger was bended in dainty fashion, and there was a green flash when a huge emerald ring caught the light. The bartender came often with his little brass tray. Occasionally Patsy and his two friends quarrelled.

Once this little Cuban happened to make some slight noise and Patsy turned his head to observe him. Then Patsy made a careless and rather loud comment to his two friends. He used a word which is no more than passing the time of day down in Cherry Street, but to the Cuban it was a dagger-point. There was a harsh scraping sound as a chair was pushed swiftly back.

The little Cuban was upon his feet. His eyes were shining with a rage that flashed there like sparks as he glared at Patsy. His olive face had turned a shade of grey from his anger. Withal his chest was thrust out in portentous dignity, and his hand, still grasping his wine-glass, was cool and steady, the little finger still bended, the great emerald gleaming upon it. The others, motionless, stared at him.

"Sir," he began ceremoniously. He spoke gravely and in a slow way, his tone coming in a marvel of self-possessed cadences from between those lips which quivered with wrath. "You have insult me. You are a dog, a hound, a cur. I spit upon you. I must have some of your blood."

Patsy looked at him over his shoulder.

"What's th' matter wi' che?" he demanded. He did not quite understand the words of this little man who glared at him steadily, but he knew that it was something about fighting. He snarled with the readiness of his class and heaved his shoulders contemptuously. "Ah, what's eatin' yeh? Take a walk! You hain't got nothin' t' do with me, have yeh? Well, den, go sit on yerself."

And his companions leaned back valorously in their chairs, and scrutinized this slim young fellow who was addressing Patsy.

"What's de little Dago chewin' about?"

"He wants t' scrap!"

"What!"

The Cuban listened with apparent composure. It was only when they laughed that his body cringed as if he was receiving lashes. Presently he put down his glass and walked over to their table. He proceeded always with the most impressive deliberation.

"Sir," he began again. "You have insult me. I must have s-s-satisfac-shone. I must have your body upon the point of my sword. In my country you would already be dead. I must have s-s-satisfac-shone."

Patsy had looked at the Cuban with a trifle of bewilderment. But at last his face began to grow dark with belligerency, his mouth curved in that wide sneer with which he would confront an angel of darkness. He arose suddenly in his seat and came towards the little Cuban. He was going to be impressive too.

"Say, young feller, if yeh go shootin' off yer face at me, I'll wipe d' joint wid yeh. What'cher gaffin' about, hey? Are yeh givin' me er jolly? Say, if yeh pick me up fer a cinch, I'll fool yeh. Dat's what! Don't take me fer no dead easy mug." And as he glowered at the little Cuban, he ended his oration with one eloquent word, "Nit!"

The bartender nervously polished his bar with a towel, and kept his eyes fastened upon the men. Occasionally he became transfixed with interest, leaning forward with one hand upon the edge of the bar and the other holding the towel grabbed in a lump, as if he had been turned into bronze when in the very act of polishing.

The Cuban did not move when Patsy came toward him and delivered his oration. At its conclusion he turned his livid face toward where, above him, Patsy was swaggering and heaving his shoulders in a consummate display of bravery and readiness. The Cuban, in his clear, tense tones, spoke one word. It was the bitter insult. It seemed fairly to spin from his lips and crackle in the air like breaking glass.

Every man save the little Cuban made an electric movement. Patsy roared a black oath and thrust himself forward until he towered almost directly above the other man. His fists were doubled into knots of bone and hard flesh. The Cuban had raised a steady finger.

"If you touch me wis your hand, I will keel you."

The two well-dressed men had come swiftly, uttering protesting cries. They suddenly intervened in this second of time in which Patsy had sprung forward and the Cuban had uttered his threat. The four men were now a tossing, arguing; violent group, one well-dressed man lecturing the Cuban, and the other holding off Patsy, who was now wild with rage, loudly repeating the Cuban's threat, and maneuvering and struggling to get at him for revenge's sake.

The bartender, feverishly scouring away with his towel, and at times pacing to and fro with nervous and excited tread, shouted out—

"Say, for heaven's sake, don't fight in here. If yeh wanta fight, go out in the street and fight all yeh please. But don't fight in here."

Patsy knew one only thing, and this he kept repeating:

"Well, he wants t' scrap! I didn't begin dis! He wants t' scrap."

The well-dressed man confronting him continually replied—

"Oh, well, now, look here, he's only a lad. He don't know what he's doing. He's crazy mad. You wouldn't slug a kid like that."

Patsy and his aroused companions, who cursed and growled, were persistent with their argument. "Well, he wants t' scrap!" The whole affair was as plain as daylight when one saw this great fact. The interference and intolerable discussion brought the three of them forward, battleful and fierce.

"What's eatin' you, anyhow?" they demanded. "Dis ain't your business, is it? What business you got shootin' off your face?"

The other peacemaker was trying to restrain the little Cuban, who had grown shrill and violent.

"If he touch me wis his hand I will keel him. We must fight like gentlemen or else I keel him when he touch me wis his hand."

The man who was fending off Patsy comprehended these sentences that were screamed behind his back, and he explained to Patsy.

"But he wants to fight you with swords. With swords, you know."

The Cuban, dodging around the peacemakers, yelled in Patsy's face—

"Ah, if I could get you before me wis my sword! Ah! Ah! A-a-ah!" Patsy made a furious blow with a swift fist, but the peacemakers bucked against his body suddenly like football players.

Patsy was greatly puzzled. He continued doggedly to try to get near enough to the Cuban to punch him. To these attempts the Cuban replied savagely—

"If you touch me wis your hand, I will cut your heart in two piece."

At last Patsy said—"Well, if he's so dead stuck on fightin' wid swords, I'll fight 'im. Soitenly! I'll fight 'im." All this palaver had evidently tired him, and he now puffed out his lips with the air of a man who is willing to submit to any conditions if he can only bring on the row soon enough. He swaggered, "I'll fight 'im wid swords. Let 'im bring on his swords, an' I'll fight 'im 'til he's ready t' quit."

The two well-dressed men grinned. "Why, look here," they said to Patsy, "he'd punch you full of holes. Why he's a fencer. You can't fight him with swords. He'd kill you in 'bout a minute."

"Well, I'll giv' 'im a go at it, anyhow," said Patsy, stouthearted and resolute. "I'll giv' 'im a go at it, anyhow, an' I'll stay wid 'im as long as I kin."

As for the Cuban, his lithe body was quivering in an ecstasy of the muscles. His face radiant with a savage joy, he fastened his glance upon Patsy, his eyes gleaming with a gloating, murderous light. A most unspeakable, animal-like rage was in his expression.

"Ah! ah! He will fight me! Ah!" He bended unconsciously in the posture of a fencer. He had all the quick, springy movements of a skilful swordsman. "Ah, the b-r-r-rute! The b-r-r-rute! I will stick him like a pig!"

The two peacemakers, still grinning broadly, were having a great time with Patsy.

"Why, you infernal idiot, this man would slice you all up. You better jump off the bridge if you want to commit suicide. You wouldn't stand a ghost of a chance to live ten seconds."

Patsy was as unshaken as granite. "Well, if he wants t' fight wid swords, he'll get it. I'll giv' 'im a go at it, anyhow."

One man said—"Well, have you got a sword? Do you know what a sword is? Have you got a sword?"

"No, I ain't got none," said Patsy honestly, "but I kin git one." Then he added valiantly—"An' quick, too."

The two men laughed. "Why, can't you understand it would be sure death to fight a sword duel with this fellow?"

"Dat's all right! See? I know me own business. If he wants t' fight one of dees damn duels, I'm in it, understan'"

"Have you ever fought one, you fool?"

"No, I ain't. But I will fight one, dough! I ain't no muff. If he wants t' fight a duel, by Gawd, I'm wid 'im! D'yeh understan' dat!" Patsy cocked his hat and swaggered. He was getting very serious.

The little Cuban burst out—"Ah, come on, sirs: come on! We can take cab. Ah, you big cow, I will stick you, I will stick you. Ah, you will look very beautiful, very beautiful. Ah, come on, sirs. We will stop at hotel—my hotel. I there have weapons."

"Yeh will, will yeh? Yeh bloomin' little black Dago!" cried Patsy in hoarse and maddened reply to the personal part of the Cuban's speech. He stepped forward. "Git yer damn swords," he commanded. "Git yer swords. Git 'em quick! I'll fight wi' che! I'll fight wid anyt'ing, too! See? I'll fight yeh wid a knife an' fork if yeh say so! I'll fight yer standin' up er sittin' down!" Patsy delivered this intense oration with sweeping, intensely emphatic gestures, his hands stretched out eloquently, his jaw thrust forward, his eyes glaring.

"Ah!" cried the little Cuban joyously. "Ah, you are in very pretty temper. Ah, how I will cut your heart in two piece, my dear, d-e-a-r friend." His eyes, too, shone like carbuncles, with a swift, changing glitter, always fastened upon Patsy's face.

The two peacemakers were perspiring and in despair. One of them blurted out—

"Well, I'll be blamed if this ain't the most ridiculous thing I ever saw."

The other said—"For ten dollars I'd be tempted to let these two infernal blockheads have their duel."

Patsy was strutting to and fro, and conferring grandly with his friends.

"He took me for a muff. He t'ought he was goin' t' bluff me out, talkin' 'bout swords. He'll get fooled." He addressed the Cuban—"You're a fine little dirty picter of a scrapper, ain't che? I'll chew yez up, dat's what I will!"

There began then some rapid action. The patience of well-dressed men is not an eternal thing. It began to look as if it would at last be a fight with six corners to it. The faces of the men were shining red with anger. They jostled each other defiantly, and almost every one blazed out at three or four of the others. The bartender had given up protesting. He swore for a time and banged his glasses. Then he jumped the bar and ran out of the saloon, cursing sullenly.

When he came back with a policeman, Patsy and the Cuban were preparing to depart together. Patsy was delivering his last oration—

"I'll fight yer wid swords! Sure I will! Come ahead, Dago! I'll fight yeh anywheres wid anyt'ing! We'll have a large, juicy scrap, an' don't yeh forgit dat! I'm right wid yez. I ain't no muff! I scrap with a man jest as soon as he ses scrap, an' if yeh wanta scrap, I'm yer kitten. Understan' dat?"

The policeman said sharply—"Come, now; what's all this?" He had a distinctly business air.

The little Cuban stepped forward calmly. "It is none of your business."

The policeman flushed to his ears. "What?"

One well-dressed man touched the other on the sleeve. "Here's the time to skip," he whispered. They halted a block away from the saloon and watched the policeman pull the Cuban through the door. There was a minute of scuffle on the sidewalk, and into this deserted street at midnight fifty people appeared at once as if from the sky to watch it.

At last the three Cherry Hill men came from the saloon, and swaggered with all their old valor toward the peacemakers.

"Ah," said Patsy to them, "he was so hot talkin' about this duel business, but I would a-given 'im a great scrap, an' don't yeh forgit it."

For Patsy was not as wise as seven owls, but his courage could throw a shadow as long as the steeple of a cathedral.

# A DESERTION

The yellow gas-light that came with an effect of difficulty through the dust-stained windows on either side of the door gave strange hues to the faces and forms of the three women who stood gabbling in the hallway of the tenement. They made rapid gestures, and in the background their enormous shadows mingled in terrific conflict.

"Aye, she ain't so good as he thinks she is, I'll bet. He can watch over 'er an' take care of 'er all he pleases, but when she wants t' fool 'im, she'll fool 'im. An' how does he know she ain't foolin' im' now?"

"Oh, he thinks he's keepin' 'er from goin' t' th' bad, he does. Oh, yes. He ses she's too purty t' let run round alone. Too purty! Huh! My Sadie—"

"Well, he keeps a clost watch on 'er, you bet. On'y las' week, she met my boy Tim on th' stairs, an' Tim hadn't said two words to 'er b'fore th' ol' man begin to holler. 'Dorter, dorter, come here, come here!'"

At this moment a young girl entered from the street, and it was evident from the injured expression suddenly assumed by the three gossipers that she had been the object of their discussion. She passed them with a slight nod, and they swung about into a row to stare after her.

On her way up the long flights the girl unfastened her veil. One could then clearly see the beauty of her eyes, but there was in them a certain furtiveness that came near to marring the effects. It was a peculiar fixture of gaze, brought from the street, as of one who there saw a succession of passing dangers with menaces aligned at every corner.

On the top floor, she pushed open a door and then paused on the threshold, confronting an interior that appeared black and flat like a curtain. Perhaps some girlish idea of hobgoblins assailed her then, for she called in a little breathless voice, "Daddie!"

There was no reply. The fire in the cooking-stove in the room crackled at spasmodic intervals. One lid was misplaced, and the girl could now see that this fact created a little flushed crescent upon the ceiling. Also, a series of tiny windows in the stove caused patches of red upon the floor. Otherwise, the room was heavily draped with shadows.

The girl called again, "Daddie!"

Yet there was no reply.

"Oh, Daddie!"

Presently she laughed as one familiar with the humors of an old man. "Oh, I guess yer cussin' mad about yer supper, Dad," she said, and she almost entered the room, but suddenly faltered, overcome by a feminine instinct to fly from this black interior, peopled with imagined dangers.

Again she called, "Daddie!" Her voice had an accent of appeal. It was as if she knew she was foolish but yet felt obliged to insist upon being reassured. "Oh, Daddie!"

Of a sudden a cry of relief, a feminine announcement that the stars still hung, burst from her. For, according to some mystic process, the smoldering coals of the fire went aflame with sudden, fierce brilliance, splashing parts of the walls, the floor, the crude furniture, with a hue of blood-red. And in the light of this dramatic outburst of light, the girl saw her father seated at a table with his back turned toward her.

She entered the room, then, with an aggrieved air, her logic evidently concluding that somebody was to blame for her nervous fright. "Oh, yer on'y sulkin' 'bout yer supper. I thought mebbe ye'd gone somewheres."

Her father made no reply. She went over to a shelf in the corner, and, taking a little lamp, she lit it and put it where it would give her light as she took off her hat and jacket in front of the tiny mirror. Presently she began to bustle among the cooking utensils that were crowded into the sink, and as she worked she rattled talk at her father, apparently disdaining his mood.

"I'd 'a ' come home earlier t'night, Dad, on'y that fly foreman, he kep' me in th' shop 'til half-past six. What a fool! He came t' me, yeh know, an' he ses, 'Nell, I wanta give yeh some brotherly advice.' Oh, I know him an' his brotherly advice. 'I wanta give yeh some brotherly advice. Yer too purty, Nell,' he ses, 't' be workin' in this shop an' paradin' through the streets alone, without somebody t' give yeh good brotherly advice, an' I wanta warn yeh, Nell. I'm a bad man, but I ain't as bad as some, an' I wanta warn yeh.' 'Oh, g'long 'bout yer business,' I ses. I know 'im. He's like all of 'em, on'y he's a little slyer. I know 'im. 'You g'long 'bout yer business,' I ses. Well, he ses after a while that he guessed some evenin' he'd come up an' see me. 'Oh, yeh will,' I ses, 'yeh will? Well, you jest let my ol' man ketch yeh comin' foolin' 'round our place. Yeh'll wish yeh went t' some other girl t' give brotherly advice.' 'What th' 'ell do I care fer yer father?' he ses. 'What's he t' me?' 'If he throws yeh downstairs, yeh'll care for 'im,' I ses. 'Well,' he ses, 'I'll come when 'e ain't in, b' Gawd, I'll come when 'e ain't in.' 'Oh, he's allus in when it means takin' care 'o me,' I ses. 'Don't yeh fergit it, either. When it comes t' takin' care o' his dorter, he's right on deck every single possible time.'"

After a time, she turned and addressed cheery words to the old man. "Hurry up th' fire, Daddie! We'll have supper pretty soon."

But still her father was silent, and his form in its sullen posture was motionless.

At this, the girl seemed to see the need of the inauguration of a feminine war against a man out of temper. She approached him breathing soft, coaxing syllables.

"Daddie! Oh, Daddie! O—o—oh, Daddie!"

It was apparent from a subtle quality of valor in her tones that this manner of onslaught upon his moods had usually been successful, but tonight it had no quick effect. The words, coming from her lips, were like the refrain of an old ballad, but the man remained stolid.

"Daddie! My Daddie! Oh, Daddie, are yeh mad at me, really—truly mad at me!"

She touched him lightly upon the arm. Should he have turned then he would have seen the fresh, laughing face, with dew-sparkling eyes, close to his own.

"Oh, Daddie! My Daddie! Pretty Daddie!"

She stole her arm about his neck, and then slowly bended her face toward his. It was the action of a queen who knows that she reigns notwithstanding irritations, trials, tempests.

But suddenly, from this position, she leaped backward with the mad energy of a frightened colt. Her face was in this instant turned to a grey, featureless thing of horror. A yell, wild and hoarse as a brute-cry, burst from her. "Daddie!" She flung herself to a place near the door, where she remained, crouching, her eyes staring at the motionless figure, spattered by the quivering flashes from the fire. Her arms extended, and her frantic fingers at once besought and repelled. There was in them an expression of eagerness to caress and an expression of the most intense loathing.

And the girl's hair that had been a splendor, was in these moments changed to a disordered mass that hung and swayed in witchlike fashion.

Again, a terrible cry burst from her. It was more than the shriek of agony—it was directed, personal, addressed to him in the chair, the first word of a tragic conversation with the dead.

It seemed that when she had put her arm about its neck, she had jostled the corpse in such a way that now she and it were face to face. The attitude expressed an intention of arising from the table. The eyes, fixed upon hers, were filled with an unspeakable hatred.

* * * *

The cries of the girl aroused thunders in the tenement. There was a loud slamming of doors, and presently there was a roar of feet upon the boards of the stairway. Voices rang out sharply.

"What is it?"

"What's th' matter?"

"He's killin' her!"

"Slug 'im with anythin' yeh kin lay hold of, Jack!"

But over all this came the shrill, shrewish tones of a woman. "Ah, th' damned ol' fool, he's drivin' 'er inteh th' street—that's what he's doin'. He's drivin' 'er inteh th' street."

# A DARK-BROWN DOG

A child was standing on a street-corner. He leaned with one shoulder against a high board fence and swayed the other to and fro, the while kicking carelessly at the gravel.

Sunshine beat upon the cobbles, and a lazy summer wind raised yellow dust which trailed in clouds down the avenue. Clattering trucks moved with indistinctness through it. The child stood dreamily gazing.

After a time, a little dark-brown dog came trotting with an intent air down the sidewalk. A short rope was dragging from his neck. Occasionally he trod upon the end of it and stumbled.

He stopped opposite the child, and the two regarded each other. The dog hesitated for a moment, but presently he made some little advances with his tail. The child put out his hand and called him. In an apologetic manner the dog came close, and the two had an interchange of friendly pattings and waggles. The dog became more enthusiastic with each moment of the interview, until with his gleeful caperings he threatened to overturn the child. Whereupon the child lifted his hand and struck the dog a blow upon the head.

This thing seemed to overpower and astonish the little dark-brown dog, and wounded him to the heart. He sank down in despair at the child's feet. When the blow was repeated, together with an admonition in childish sentences, he turned over upon his back, and held his paws in a peculiar manner. At the same time with his ears and his eyes he offered a small prayer to the child.

He looked so comical on his back, and holding his paws peculiarly, that the child was greatly amused and gave him little taps repeatedly, to keep him so. But the little dark-brown dog took this chastisement in the most serious way and no doubt considered that he had committed some grave crime, for he wriggled contritely and showed his repentance in every way that was in his power. He pleaded with the child and petitioned him, and offered more prayers.

At last the child grew weary of this amusement and turned toward home. The dog was praying at the time. He lay on his back and turned his eyes upon the retreating form.

Presently he struggled to his feet and started after the child. The latter wandered in a perfunctory way toward his home, stopping at times to investigate various matters. During one of these pauses he discovered the little dark-brown dog who was following him with the air of a footpad.

The child beat his pursuer with a small stick he had found. The dog lay down and prayed until the child had finished, and resumed his journey. Then he scrambled erect and took up the pursuit again.

On the way to his home the child turned many times and beat the dog, proclaiming with childish gestures that he held him in contempt as an unimportant dog, with no value save for a moment. For being this quality of animal the dog apologized and eloquently expressed regret, but he continued stealthily to follow the child. His manner grew so very guilty that he slunk like an assassin.

When the child reached his doorstep, the dog was industriously ambling a few yards in the rear. He became so agitated with shame when he again confronted the child that he forgot the dragging rope. He tripped upon it and fell forward.

The child sat down on the step and the two had another interview. During it the dog greatly exerted himself to please the child. He performed a few gambols with such abandon that the child suddenly saw him to be a valuable thing. He made a swift, avaricious charge and seized the rope.

He dragged his captive into a hall and up many long stairways in a dark tenement. The dog made willing efforts, but he could not hobble very skilfully up the stairs because he was very small and soft, and at last the pace of the engrossed child grew so energetic that the dog became panic-stricken. In his mind he was being dragged toward a grim unknown. His eyes grew wild with the terror of it. He began to wiggle his head frantically and to brace his legs.

The child redoubled his exertions. They had a battle on the stairs. The child was victorious because he was completely absorbed in his purpose, and because the dog was very small. He dragged his acquirement to the door of his home, and finally with triumph across the threshold.

No one was in. The child sat down on the floor and made overtures to the dog. These the dog instantly accepted. He beamed with affection upon his new friend. In a short time they were firm and abiding comrades.

When the child's family appeared, they made a great row. The dog was examined and commented upon and called names. Scorn was leveled at him from all eyes, so that he became much embarrassed and drooped like a scorched plant. But the child went sturdily to the center of the floor, and, at the top of his voice, championed the dog. It happened that he was roaring protestations, with his arms clasped about the dog's neck, when the father of the family came in from work.

The parent demanded to know what the blazes they were making the kid howl for. It was explained in many words that the infernal kid wanted to introduce a disreputable dog into the family.

A family council was held. On this depended the dog's fate, but he in no way heeded, being busily engaged in chewing the end of the child's dress.

The affair was quickly ended. The father of the family, it appears, was in a particularly savage temper that evening, and when he perceived that it would amaze and anger everybody if such a dog were allowed to remain, he decided that it should be so. The child, crying softly, took his friend off to a retired part of the room to hobnob with him, while the father quelled a fierce rebellion of his wife. So it came to pass that the dog was a member of the household.

He and the child were associated together at all times save when the child slept. The child became a guardian and a friend. If the large folk kicked the dog and threw things at him, the child made loud and violent objections. Once when the child had run, protesting loudly, with tears raining down his face and his arms outstretched, to protect his friend, he had been struck in the head with a very large saucepan from the hand of his father, enraged at some seeming lack of courtesy in the dog. Ever after, the family were careful how they threw things at the dog. Moreover, the latter grew very skilful in avoiding missiles and feet. In a small room containing a stove, a table, a bureau and some chairs, he would display strategic ability of a high order, dodging, feinting and scuttling about among the furniture. He could force three or four people armed with brooms, sticks and handfuls of coal, to use all their ingenuity to get in a blow. And even when they did, it was seldom that they could do him a serious injury or leave any imprint.

But when the child was present these scenes did not occur. It came to be recognized that if the dog was molested, the child would burst into sobs, and as the child, when started, was very riotous and practically unquenchable, the dog had therein a safeguard.

However, the child could not always be near. At night, when he was asleep, his dark-brown friend would raise from some black corner a wild, wailful cry, a song of infinite loneliness and despair, that would go shuddering and sobbing among the buildings of the block and cause people to swear. At these times the singer would often be chased all over the kitchen and hit with a great variety of articles.

Sometimes, too, the child himself used to beat the dog, although it is not known that he ever had what truly could be called a just cause. The dog always accepted these thrashings with an air of admitted guilt. He was too much of a dog to try to look to be a martyr or to plot revenge. He received the blows with deep humility, and furthermore he forgave his friend the moment the child had finished, and was ready to caress the child's hand with his little red tongue.

When misfortune came upon the child, and his troubles overwhelmed him, he would often crawl under the table and lay his small distressed head on the dog's back. The dog was ever sympathetic. It is not to be supposed that at such times he took occasion to refer to the unjust beatings his friend, when provoked, had administered to him.

He did not achieve any notable degree of intimacy with the other members of the family. He had no confidence in them, and the fear that he would express at their casual approach often exasperated them exceedingly. They used to gain a certain satisfaction in underfeeding him, but finally his friend the child grew to watch the matter with some care, and when he forgot it, the dog was often successful in secret for himself.

So the dog prospered. He developed a large bark, which came wondrously from such a small rug of a dog. He ceased to howl persistently at night. Sometimes, indeed, in his sleep, he would utter little yells, as from pain, but that occurred, no doubt, when in his dreams he encountered huge flaming dogs who threatened him direfully.

His devotion to the child grew until it was a sublime thing. He wagged at his approach; he sank down in despair at his departure. He could detect the sound of the child's step among all the noises of the neighborhood. It was like a calling voice to him.

The scene of their companionship was a kingdom governed by this terrible potentate, the child; but neither criticism nor rebellion ever lived for an instant in the heart of the one subject. Down in the mystic, hidden fields of his little dog-soul bloomed flowers of love and fidelity and perfect faith.

The child was in the habit of going on many expeditions to observe strange things in the vicinity. On these occasions his friend usually jogged aimfully along behind. Perhaps, though, he went ahead. This necessitated his turning around every quarter-minute to make sure the child was coming. He was filled with a large idea of the importance of these journeys. He would carry himself with such an air! He was proud to be the retainer of so great a monarch.

One day, however, the father of the family got quite exceptionally drunk. He came home and held carnival with the cooking utensils, the furniture and his wife. He was in the midst of this recreation when the child, followed by the dark-brown dog, entered the room. They were returning from their voyages.

The child's practised eye instantly noted his father's state. He dived under the table, where experience had taught him was a rather safe place. The dog, lacking skill in such matters, was, of course, unaware of the true condition of affairs. He looked with interested eyes at his friend's sudden dive. He interpreted it to mean: Joyous gambol. He started to patter across the floor to join him. He was the picture of a little dark-brown dog en route to a friend.

The head of the family saw him at this moment. He gave a huge howl of joy, and knocked the dog down with a heavy coffee-pot. The dog, yelling in supreme astonishment and fear, writhed to his feet and ran for cover. The man kicked out with a ponderous foot. It caused the dog to swerve as if caught in a tide. A second blow of the coffee-pot laid him upon the floor.

Here the child, uttering loud cries, came valiantly forth like a knight. The father of the family paid no attention to these calls of the child, but advanced with glee upon the dog. Upon being knocked down twice in swift succession, the latter apparently gave up all hope of escape. He rolled over on his back and held his paws in a peculiar manner. At the same time with his eyes and his ears he offered up a small prayer.

But the father was in a mood for having fun, and it occurred to him that it would be a fine thing to throw the dog out of the window. So he reached down and, grabbing the animal by a leg, lifted him, squirming, up. He swung him two or three times hilariously about his head, and then flung him with great accuracy through the window.

The soaring dog created a surprise in the block. A woman watering plants in an opposite window gave an involuntary shout and dropped a flower-pot. A man in another window leaned perilously out to watch the flight of the dog. A woman who had been hanging out clothes in a yard began to caper wildly. Her mouth was filled with clothes-pins, but her arms gave vent to a sort of exclamation. In appearance she was like a gagged prisoner. Children ran whooping.

The dark-brown body crashed in a heap on the roof of a shed five stories below. From thence it rolled to the pavement of an alleyway.

The child in the room far above burst into a long, dirge-like cry, and toddled hastily out of the room. It took him a long time to reach the alley, because his size compelled him to go downstairs backward, one step at a time, and holding with both hands to the step above.

When they came for him later, they found him seated by the body of his dark-brown friend.

# THE PACE OF YOUTH

## I

Stimson stood in a corner and glowered. He was a fierce man and had indomitable whiskers, albeit he was very small.

"That young tarrier," he whispered to himself. "He wants to quit makin' eyes at Lizzie. This is too much of a good thing. First thing you know, he'll get fired."

His brow creased in a frown, he strode over to the huge open doors and looked at a sign. "Stimson's Mammoth Merry-Go-Round," it read, and the glory of it was great. Stimson stood and contemplated the sign. It was an enormous affair; the letters were as large as men. The glow of it, the grandeur of it was very apparent to Stimson. At the end of his contemplation, he shook his head thoughtfully, determinedly. "No, no," he muttered. "This is too much of a good thing. First thing you know, he'll get fired."

A soft booming sound of surf, mingled with the cries of bathers, came from the beach. There was a vista of sand and sky and sea that drew to a mystic point far away in the northward. In the mighty angle, a girl in a red dress was crawling slowly like some kind of a spider on the fabric of nature. A few flags hung lazily above where the bathhouses were marshalled in compact squares. Upon the edge of the sea stood a ship with its shadowy sails painted dimly upon the sky, and high overhead in the still, sun-shot air a great hawk swung and drifted slowly.

Within the Merry-Go-Round there was a whirling circle of ornamental lions, giraffes, camels, ponies, goats, glittering with varnish and metal that caught swift reflections from windows high above them. With stiff wooden legs, they swept on in a never-ending race, while a great orchestrion clamored in wild speed. The summer sunlight sprinkled its gold upon the garnet canopies carried by the tireless racers and upon all the devices of decoration that made Stimson's machine magnificent and famous. A host of laughing children bestrode the animals, bending forward like charging cavalrymen, and shaking reins and whooping in glee. At intervals they leaned out perilously to clutch at iron rings that were tendered to them by a long wooden arm. At the intense moment before the swift grab for the rings one could see their little nervous bodies quiver with eagerness; the laughter rang shrill and excited. Down in the long rows of benches, crowds of people sat watching the game, while occasionally a father might arise and go near to shout encouragement, cautionary commands, or applause at his flying offspring. Frequently mothers called out: "Be careful, Georgie!" The orchestrion bellowed and thundered on its platform, filling the ears with its long monotonous song. Over in a corner, a man in a white apron and behind a counter roared above the tumult: "Popcorn! Popcorn!"

A young man stood upon a small, raised platform, erected in a manner of a pulpit, and just without the line of the circling figures. It was his duty to manipulate the wooden arm and affix the rings. When all were gone into the hands of the triumphant children, he held forth a basket, into which they returned all save the coveted brass one, which meant another ride free and made the holder very illustrious. The young man stood all day upon his narrow platform, affixing rings or holding forth the basket. He was a sort of general squire in these lists of childhood. He was very busy.

And yet Stimson, the astute, had noticed that the young man frequently found time to twist about on his platform and smile at a girl who shyly sold tickets behind a silvered netting. This, indeed, was the great reason of Stimson's glowering. The young man upon the raised platform had no manner of license to smile at the girl behind the silvered netting. It was a most gigantic insolence. Stimson was amazed at it. "By Jiminy," he said to himself again, "that fellow is smiling at my daughter." Even in this tone of great wrath it could be discerned that Stimson was filled with wonder that any youth should dare smile at the daughter in the presence of the august father.

Often the dark-eyed girl peered between the shining wires, and, upon being detected by the young man, she usually turned her head quickly to prove to him that she was not interested. At other times, however, her eyes seemed filled with a tender fear lest he should fall from that exceedingly dangerous platform. As for the young man, it was plain that these glances filled him with valor, and he stood carelessly upon his perch, as if he deemed it of no consequence that he might fall from it. In all the complexities of his daily life and duties he found opportunity to gaze ardently at the vision behind the netting.

This silent courtship was conducted over the heads of the crowd who thronged about the bright machine. The swift eloquent glances of the young man went noiselessly and unseen with their message. There had finally become established between the two in this manner a subtle understanding and companionship. They communicated accurately all that they felt. The boy told his love, his reverence, his hope in the changes of the future. The girl told him that she loved him, and she did not love him, that she did not know if she loved him. Sometimes a little sign, saying "cashier" in gold letters, and hanging upon the silvered netting, got directly in range and interfered with the tender message.

The love affair had not continued without anger, unhappiness, despair. The girl had once smiled brightly upon a youth who came to buy some tickets for his little sister, and the young man upon the platform, observing this smile, had been filled with gloomy rage. He stood like a dark statue of vengeance upon his pedestal and thrust out the basket to the children with a gesture that was full of scorn for their hollow happiness, for their insecure and temporary joy. For five hours he did not once look at the girl when she was looking at him. He was going to crush her with his indifference; he was going to demonstrate that he had never been serious. However, when he narrowly observed her in secret he discovered that she seemed more blythe than was usual with her. When he found that his apparent indifference had not crushed her he suffered greatly. She did not love him, he concluded. If she had loved him she would have been crushed. For two days he lived a miserable existence upon his high perch. He consoled himself by thinking of how unhappy he was, and by swift, furtive glances at the loved face. At any rate he was in her presence, and he could get a good view from his perch when there was no interference by the little sign: "Cashier."

But suddenly, swiftly, these clouds vanished, and under the imperial blue sky of the restored confidence they dwelt in peace, a peace that was satisfaction, a peace that, like a babe, put its trust in the treachery of the future. This confidence endured until the next day, when she, for an unknown cause, suddenly refused to look at him. Mechanically he continued his task, his brain dazed, a tortured victim of doubt, fear, suspicion. With his eyes he supplicated her to telegraph an explanation. She replied with a stony glance that froze his blood. There was a great difference in their respective reasons for becoming angry. His were always foolish, but apparent, plain as the moon. Hers were subtle, feminine, as incomprehensible as the stars, as mysterious as the shadows at night.

They fell and soared and soared and fell in this manner until they knew that to live without each other would be a wandering in deserts. They had grown so intent upon the uncertainties, the variations, the guessings of their affair that the world had become but a huge immaterial background. In time of peace their smiles were soft and prayerful, caresses confided to the air. In time of war, their youthful hearts, capable of profound agony, were wrung by the intricate emotions of doubt. They were the victims of the dread angel of affectionate speculation that forces the brain endlessly on roads that lead nowhere.

At night, the problem of whether she loved him confronted the young man like a spectre, looming as high as a hill and telling him not to delude himself. Upon the following day, this battle of the night displayed itself in the renewed fervor of his glances and in their increased number. Whenever he thought he could detect that she too was suffering, he felt a thrill of joy.

But there came a time when the young man looked back upon these contortions with contempt. He believed then that he had imagined his pain. This came about when the redoubtable Stimson marched forward to participate.

"This has got to stop," Stimson had said to himself, as he stood and watched them. They had grown careless of the light world that clattered about them; they were become so engrossed in their personal drama that the language of their eyes was almost as obvious as gestures. And Stimson, through his keenness, his wonderful, infallible penetration, suddenly came into possession of these obvious facts. "Well, of all the nerves," he said, regarding with a new interest the young man upon the perch.

He was a resolute man. He never hesitated to grapple with a crisis. He decided to overturn everything at once, for, although small, he was very fierce and impetuous. He resolved to crush this dreaming.

He strode over to the silvered netting. "Say, you want to quit your everlasting grinning at that idiot," he said, grimly.

The girl cast down her eyes and made a little heap of quarters into a stack. She was unable to withstand the terrible scrutiny of her small and fierce father.

Stimson turned from his daughter and went to a spot beneath the platform. He fixed his eyes upon the young man and said—

"I've been speakin' to Lizzie. You better attend strictly to your own business or there'll be a new man here next week." It was as if he had blazed away with a shotgun. The young man reeled upon his perch. At last he in a measure regained his composure and managed to stammer: "A—all right, sir." He knew that denials would be futile with the terrible Stimson. He agitatedly began to rattle the rings in the basket, and pretend that he was obliged to count them or inspect them in some way. He, too, was unable to face the great Stimson.

For a moment, Stimson stood in fine satisfaction and gloated over the effect of his threat.

"I've fixed them," he said complacently, and went out to smoke a cigar and revel in himself. Through his mind went the proud reflection that people who came in contact with his granite will usually ended in quick and abject submission.

## II

One evening, a week after Stimson had indulged in the proud reflection that people who came in contact with his granite will usually ended in quick and abject submission, a young feminine friend of the girl behind the silvered netting came to her there and asked her to walk on the beach after "Stimson's Mammoth Merry-Go-Round" was closed for the night. The girl assented with a nod.

The young man upon the perch holding the rings saw this nod and judged its meaning. Into his mind came an idea of defeating the watchfulness of the redoubtable Stimson. When the Merry-Go-Round was closed and the two girls started for the beach, he wandered off aimlessly in another direction, but he kept them in view, and as soon as he was assured that he had escaped the vigilance of Stimson, he followed them.

The electric lights on the beach made a broad band of tremoring light, extending parallel to the sea, and upon the wide walk there slowly paraded a great crowd, intermingling, intertwining, sometimes colliding. In the darkness stretched the vast purple expanse of the ocean, and the deep indigo sky above was peopled with yellow stars. Occasionally out upon the water a whirling mass of froth suddenly flashed into view, like a great ghostly robe appearing, and then vanished, leaving the sea in its darkness, whence came those bass tones of the water's unknown emotion. A wind, cool, reminiscent of the wave wastes, made the women hold their wraps about their throats, and caused the men to grip the rims of their straw hats. It carried the noise of the band in the pavilion in gusts. Sometimes people unable to hear the music glanced up at the pavilion and were reassured upon beholding the distant leader still gesticulating and bobbing, and the other members of the band with their lips glued to their instruments. High in the sky soared an unassuming moon, faintly silver.

For a time the young man was afraid to approach the two girls; he followed them at a distance and called himself a coward. At last, however, he saw them stop on the outer edge of the crowd and stand silently listening to the voices of the sea. When he came to where they stood, he was trembling in his agitation. They had not seen him.

"Lizzie," he began. "I—"

The girl wheeled instantly and put her hand to her throat.

"Oh, Frank, how you frightened me," she said—inevitably.

"Well, you know, I—I—" he stuttered.

But the other girl was one of those beings who are born to attend at tragedies. She had for love a reverence, an admiration that was greater the more that she contemplated the fact that she knew nothing of it. This couple, with their emotions, awed her and made her humbly wish that she might be destined to be of some service to them. She was very homely.

When the young man faltered before them, she, in her sympathy, actually overestimated the crisis, and felt that he might fall dying at their feet. Shyly, but with courage, she marched to the rescue.

"Won't you come and walk on the beach with us?" she said.

The young man gave her a glance of deep gratitude which was not without the patronage which a man in his condition naturally feels for one who pities it. The three walked on.

Finally, the being who was born to attend at this tragedy said that she wished to sit down and gaze at the sea, alone.

They politely urged her to walk on with them, but she was obstinate. She wished to gaze at the sea, alone. The young man swore to himself that he would be her friend until he died.

And so the two young lovers went on without her. They turned once to look at her.

"Jennie's awful nice," said the girl.

"You bet she is," replied the young man, ardently.

They were silent for a little time.

At last the girl said—

"You were angry at me yesterday."

"No, I wasn't."

"Yes, you were, too. You wouldn't look at me once all day."

"No, I wasn't angry. I was only putting on."

Though she had, of course, known it, this confession seemed to make her very indignant. She flashed a resentful glance at him.

"Oh, you were, indeed?" she said with a great air.

For a few minutes she was so haughty with him that he loved her to madness. And directly this poem, which stuck at his lips, came forth lamely in fragments.

When they walked back toward the other girl and saw the patience of her attitude, their hearts swelled in a patronizing and secondary tenderness for her.

They were very happy. If they had been miserable they would have charged this fairy scene of the night with a criminal heartlessness; but as they were joyous, they vaguely wondered how the purple sea, the yellow stars, the changing crowds under the electric lights could be so phlegmatic and stolid.

They walked home by the lakeside way, and out upon the water those gay paper lanterns, flashing, fleeting, and careering, sang to them, sang a chorus of red and violet, and green and gold; a song of mystic bands of the future.

One day, when business paused during a dull sultry afternoon, Stimson went up town. Upon his return, he found that the popcorn man, from his stand over in a corner, was keeping an eye upon the cashier's cage, and that nobody at all was attending to the wooden arm and the iron rings. He strode forward like a sergeant of grenadiers.

"Where in thunder is Lizzie?" he demanded, a cloud of rage in his eyes.

The popcorn man, although associated long with Stimson, had never got over being dazed.

"They've—they've—gone round to th'—th'—house," he said with difficulty, as if he had just been stunned.

"Whose house?" snapped Stimson.

"Your—your house, I s'pose," said the popcorn man.

Stimson marched round to his home. Kingly denunciations surged, already formulated, to the tip of his tongue, and he bided the moment when his anger could fall upon the heads of that pair of children. He found his wife convulsive and in tears.

"Where's Lizzie?"

And then she burst forth—"Oh—John—John—they've run away, I know they have. They drove by here not three minutes ago. They must have done it on purpose to bid me good-bye, for Lizzie waved her hand sadlike; and then, before I could get out to ask where they were going or what, Frank whipped up the horse."

Stimson gave vent to a dreadful roar.

"Get my revolver—get a hack—get my revolver, do you hear—what the devil—" His voice became incoherent.

He had always ordered his wife about as if she were a battalion of infantry, and despite her misery, the training of years forced her to spring mechanically to obey; but suddenly she turned to him with a shrill appeal.

"Oh, John—not—the—revolver."

"Confound it, let go of me!" he roared again, and shook her from him.

He ran hatless upon the street. There were a multitude of hacks at the summer resort, but it was ages to him before he could find one. Then he charged it like a bull.

"Uptown!" he yelled, as he tumbled into the rear seat.

The hackman thought of severed arteries. His galloping horse distanced a large number of citizens who had been running to find what caused such contortions by the little hatless man.

It chanced as the bouncing hack went along near the lake, Stimson gazed across the calm grey expanse and recognized a color in a bonnet and a pose of a head. A buggy was traveling along a highway that led to Sorington. Stimson bellowed—

"There—there—there they are—in that buggy."

The hackman became inspired with the full knowledge of the situation. He struck a delirious blow with the whip. His mouth expanded in a grin of excitement and joy. It came to pass that this old vehicle, with its drowsy horse and its dusty-eyed and tranquil driver, seemed suddenly to awaken, to become animated and fleet. The horse ceased to ruminate on his state, his air of reflection vanished. He became intent upon his aged legs and spread them in quaint and ridiculous devices for speed. The driver, his eyes shining, sat critically in his seat. He watched each motion of this rattling machine down before him. He resembled an engineer. He used the whip with judgment and deliberation as the engineer would have used coal or oil. The horse clacked swiftly upon the macadam, the wheels hummed, the body of the vehicle wheezed and groaned.

Stimson, in the rear seat, was erect in that impassive attitude that comes sometimes to the furious man when he is obliged to leave the battle to others. Frequently, however, the tempest in his breast came to his face and he howled—

"Go it—go it—you're gaining; pound 'im! Thump the life out of 'im; hit 'im hard, you fool!" His hand grasped the rod that supported the carriage top, and it was clenched so that the nails were faintly blue.

Ahead, that other carriage had been flying with speed, as from realization of the menace in the rear. It bowled away rapidly, drawn by the eager spirit of a young and modern horse. Stimson could see the buggy-top bobbing, bobbing. That little pane, like an eye, was a derision to him. Once he leaned forward and bawled angry sentences. He began to feel impotent; his whole expedition was a tottering of an old man upon a trail of birds. A sense of age made him choke again with wrath. That other vehicle, that was youth, with youth's pace; it was swift-flying with the hope of dreams. He began to comprehend those two children ahead of him, and he knew a sudden and strange awe, because he understood the power of their young blood, the power to fly strongly into the future and feel and hope again, even at that time when his bones must be laid in the earth. The dust rose easily from the hot road and stifled the nostrils of Stimson.

The highway vanished far away in a point with a suggestion of intolerable length. The other vehicle was becoming so small that Stimson could no longer see the derisive eye.

At last the hackman drew rein to his horse and turned to look at Stimson.

"No use, I guess," he said.

Stimson made a gesture of acquiescence, rage, despair. As the hackman turned his dripping horse about, Stimson sank back with the astonishment and grief of a man who has been defied by the universe. He had been in a great perspiration, and now his bald head felt cool and uncomfortable. He put up his hand with a sudden recollection that he had forgotten his hat.

At last he made a gesture. It meant that at any rate he was not responsible.

# A TENT IN AGONY

## A SULLIVAN COUNTY TALE

Four men once came to a wet place in the roadless forest to fish. They pitched their tent fair upon the brow of a pine-clothed ridge of riven rocks whence a bowlder could be made to crash through the brush and whirl past the trees to the lake below. On fragrant hemlock boughs they slept the sleep of unsuccessful fishermen, for upon the lake alternately the sun made them lazy and the rain made them wet. Finally they ate the last bit of bacon and smoked and burned the last fearful and wonderful hoecake.

Immediately a little man volunteered to stay and hold the camp while the remaining three should go the Sullivan county miles to a farmhouse for supplies. They gazed at him dismally. "There's only one of you—the devil make a twin," they said in parting malediction, and disappeared down the hill in the known direction of a distant cabin. When it came night and the hemlocks began to sob they had not returned. The little man sat close to his companion, the campfire, and encouraged it with logs. He puffed fiercely at a heavy built brier, and regarded a thousand shadows which were about to assault him. Suddenly he heard the approach of the unknown, crackling the twigs and rustling the dead leaves. The little man arose slowly to his feet, his clothes refused to fit his back, his pipe dropped from his mouth, his knees smote each other. "Hah!" he bellowed hoarsely in menace. A growl replied and a bear paced into the light of the fire. The little man supported himself upon a sapling and regarded his visitor.

The bear was evidently a veteran and a fighter, for the black of his coat had become tawny with age. There was confidence in his gait and arrogance in his small, twinkling eye. He rolled back his lips and disclosed his white teeth. The fire magnified the red of his mouth. The little man had never before confronted the terrible and he could not wrest it from his breast. "Hah!" he roared. The bear interpreted this as the challenge of a gladiator. He approached warily. As he came near, the boots of fear were suddenly upon the little man's feet. He cried out and then darted around the campfire. "Ho!" said the bear to himself, "this thing won't fight—it runs. Well, suppose I catch it." So upon his features there fixed the animal look of going— somewhere. He started intensely around the campfire. The little man shrieked and ran furiously. Twice around they went.

The hand of heaven sometimes falls heavily upon the righteous. The bear gained.

In desperation the little man flew into the tent. The bear stopped and sniffed at the entrance. He scented the scent of many men. Finally he ventured in.

The little man crouched in a distant corner. The bear advanced, creeping, his blood burning, his hair erect, his jowls dripping. The little man yelled and rustled clumsily under the flap at the end of the tent. The bear snarled awfully and made a jump and a grab at his disappearing game. The little man, now without the tent, felt a tremendous paw grab his coat tails. He squirmed and wriggled out of his coat like a schoolboy in the hands of an avenger. The bear bowled triumphantly and jerked the coat into the tent and took two bites, a punch and a hug before he, discovered his man was not in it. Then he grew not very angry, for a bear on a spree is not a black-haired pirate. He is merely a hoodlum. He lay down on his back, took the coat on his four paws and began to play uproariously with it. The most appalling, blood-curdling whoops and yells came to where the little man was crying in a treetop and froze his blood. He moaned a little speech meant for a prayer and clung convulsively to the bending branches. He gazed with tearful wistfulness at where his comrade, the campfire, was giving dying flickers and crackles. Finally, there was a roar from the tent which eclipsed all roars; a snarl which it seemed would shake the stolid silence of the mountain and cause it to shrug its granite shoulders. The little man quaked and shrivelled to a grip and a pair of eyes. In the glow of the embers he saw the white tent quiver and fall with a crash. The bear's merry play had disturbed the center pole and brought a chaos of canvas upon his head.

Now the little man became the witness of a mighty scene. The tent began to flounder. It took flopping strides in the direction of the lake. Marvellous sounds came from within—rips and tears, and great groans and pants. The little man went into giggling hysterics.

The entangled monster failed to extricate himself before he had walloped the tent frenziedly to the edge of the mountain. So it came to pass that three men, clambering up the hill with bundles and baskets, saw their tent approaching. It seemed to them like a white-robed phantom pursued by hornets. Its moans riffled the hemlock twigs.

The three men dropped their bundles and scurried to one side, their eyes gleaming with fear. The canvas avalanche swept past them. They leaned, faint and dumb, against trees and listened, their blood stagnant. Below them it struck the base of a great pine tree, where it writhed and struggled. The three watched its convolutions a moment and then started terrifically for the top of the hill. As they disappeared, the bear cut loose with a mighty effort. He cast one dishevelled and agonized look at the white thing, and then started wildly for the inner recesses of the forest.

The three fear-stricken individuals ran to the rebuilt fire. The little man reposed by it calmly smoking. They sprang at him and overwhelmed him with interrogations. He contemplated darkness and took a long, pompous puff. "There's only one of me—and the devil made a twin," he said.

# FOUR MEN IN A CAVE

## LIKEWISE FOUR QUEENS, AND A
## SULLIVAN COUNTY HERMIT

The moon rested for a moment on the top of a tall pine on a hill.

The little man was standing in front of the campfire making orations to his companions.

"We can tell a great tale when we get back to the city if we investigate this thing," said he, in conclusion.

They were won.

The little man was determined to explore a cave, because its black mouth had gaped at him. The four men took a lighted pine-knot and clambered over boulders down a hill. In a thicket on the mountainside lay a little tilted hole. At its side they halted.

"Well?" said the little man.

They fought for last place and the little man was overwhelmed. He tried to struggle from under by crying that if the fat, pudgy man came after, he would be corked. But he finally administered a cursing over his shoulder and crawled into the hole. His companions gingerly followed.

A passage, the floor of damp clay and pebbles, the walls slimy, green-mossed, and dripping, sloped downward. In the cave atmosphere the torches became studies in red blaze and black smoke.

"Ho!" cried the little man, stifled and bedraggled, "let's go back." His companions were not brave. They were last. The next one to the little man pushed him on, so the little man said sulphurous words and cautiously continued his crawl.

Things that hung seemed to be on the wet, uneven ceiling, ready to drop upon the men's bare necks. Under their hands the clammy floor seemed alive and writhing. When the little man endeavored to stand erect the ceiling forced him down. Knobs and points came out and punched him. His clothes were wet and mud-covered, and his eyes, nearly blinded by smoke, tried to pierce the darkness always before his torch.

"Oh, I say, you fellows, let's go back," cried he. At that moment he caught the gleam of trembling light in the blurred shadows before him.

"Ho!" he said, "here's another way out."

The passage turned abruptly. The little man put one hand around the corner, but it touched nothing. He investigated and discovered that the little corridor took a sudden dip down a hill. At the bottom shone a yellow light.

The little man wriggled painfully about, and descended feet in advance. The others followed his plan. All picked their way with anxious care. The traitorous rocks rolled from beneath the little man's feet and roared thunderously below him, lesser stone loosened by the men above him, hit him on the back. He gained seemingly firm foothold, and, turning halfway about, swore redly at his companions for dolts and careless fools. The pudgy man sat, puffing and perspiring, high in the rear of the procession. The fumes and smoke from four pine-knots were in his blood. Cinders and sparks lay thick in his eyes and hair. The pause of the little man angered him.

"Go on, you fool!" he shouted. "Poor, painted man, you are afraid."

"Ho!" said the little man. "Come down here and go on yourself, imbecile!"

The pudgy man vibrated with passion. He leaned downward. "Idiot—"

He was interrupted by one of his feet which flew out and crashed into the man in front of and below. It is not well to quarrel upon a slippery incline, when the unknown is below. The fat man, having lost the support of one pillar-like foot, lurched forward. His body smote the next man, who hurtled into the next man. Then they all fell upon the cursing little man.

They slid in a body down over the slippery, slimy floor of the passage. The stone avenue must have wibble-wobbled with the rush of this ball of tangled men and strangled cries. The torches went out with the combined assault upon the little man. The adventurers whirled to the unknown in darkness. The little man felt that he was pitching to death, but even in his convolutions he bit and scratched at his companions, for he was satisfied that it was their fault. The swirling mass went some twenty feet, and lit upon a level, dry place in a strong, yellow light of candles. It dissolved and became eyes.

The four men lay in a heap upon the floor of a grey chamber. A small fire smoldered in the corner, the smoke disappearing in a crack. In another corner was a bed of faded hemlock boughs and two blankets. Cooking utensils and clothes lay about, with boxes and a barrel.

Of these things the four men took small cognisance. The pudgy man did not curse the little man, nor did the little man swear, in the abstract. Eight widened eyes were fixed upon the center of the room of rocks.

A great, gray stone, cut squarely, like an altar, sat in the middle of the floor. Over it burned three candles, in swaying tin cups hung from the ceiling. Before it, with what seemed to be a small volume clasped in his yellow fingers, stood a man. He was an infinitely sallow person in the brown-checked shirt of the ploughs and cows. The rest of his apparel was boots. A long grey beard dangled from his chin. He fixed glinting, fiery eyes upon the heap of men, and remained motionless. Fascinated, their tongues cleaving, their blood cold, they arose to their feet. The gleaming glance of the recluse swept slowly over the group until it found the face of the little man. There it stayed and burned.

The little man shrivelled and crumpled as the dried leaf under the glass.

Finally, the recluse slowly, deeply spoke. It was a true voice from a cave, cold, solemn, and damp.

"It's your ante," he said.

"What?" said the little man.

The hermit tilted his beard and laughed a laugh that was either the chatter of a banshee in a storm or the rattle of pebbles in a tin box. His visitors' flesh seemed ready to drop from their bones.

They huddled together and cast fearful eyes over their shoulders. They whispered.

"A vampire!" said one.

"A ghoul!" said another.

"A Druid before the sacrifice," murmured another.

"The shade of an Aztec witch doctor," said the little man.

As they looked, the inscrutable face underwent a change. It became a livid background for his eyes, which blazed at the little man like impassioned carbuncles. His voice arose to a howl of ferocity. "It's your ante!" With a panther-like motion he drew a long, thin knife and advanced, stooping. Two cadaverous hounds came from nowhere, and, scowling and growling, made desperate feints at the little man's legs. His quaking companions pushed him forward.

Tremblingly he put his hand to his pocket.

"How much?" he said, with a shivering look at the knife that glittered.

The carbuncles faded.

"Three dollars," said the hermit, in sepulchral tones which rang against the walls and among the passages, awakening long-dead spirits with voices. The shaking little man took a roll of bills from a pocket and placed "three ones" upon the altar-like stone. The recluse looked at the little volume with reverence in his eyes. It was a pack of playing cards.

Under the three swinging candles, upon the altar-like stone, the grey beard and the agonized little man played at poker. The three other men crouched in a corner, and stared with eyes that gleamed with terror. Before them sat the cadaverous hounds licking their red lips. The candles burned low, and began to flicker. The fire in the corner expired.

Finally, the game came to a point where the little man laid down his hand and quavered: "I can't call you this time, sir. I'm dead broke."

"What?" shrieked the recluse. "Not call me! Villain Dastard! Cur! I have four queens, miscreant." His voice grew so mighty that it could not fit his throat. He choked wrestling with his lungs for a moment. Then the power of his body was concentrated in a word: "Go!"

He pointed a quivering, yellow finger at a wide crack in the rock. The little man threw himself at it with a howl. His erstwhile frozen companions felt their blood throb again. With great bounds they plunged after the little man. A minute of scrambling, falling, and pushing brought them to open air. They climbed the distance to their camp in furious springs.

The sky in the east was a lurid yellow. In the west the footprints of departing night lay on the pine trees. In front of their replenished camp fire sat John Willerkins, the guide.

"Hello!" he shouted at their approach. "Be you fellers ready to go deer huntin'?"

Without replying, they stopped and debated among themselves in whispers.

Finally, the pudgy man came forward.

"John," he inquired, "do you know anything peculiar about this cave below here?"

"Yes," said Willerkins at once; "Tom Gardner."

"What?" said the pudgy man.

"Tom Gardner."

"How's that?"

"Well, you see," said Willerkins slowly, as he took dignified pulls at his pipe, "Tom Gardner was once a fambly man, who lived in these here parts on a nice leetle farm. He uster go away to the city orften, and one time he got a-gamblin' in one of them there dens. He went ter the dickens right quick then. At last he kum home one time and tol' his folks he had up and sold the farm and all he had in the worl'. His leetle wife she died then. Tom he went crazy, and soon after—"

The narrative was interrupted by the little man, who became possessed of devils.

"I wouldn't give a cuss if he had left me 'nough money to get home on the dog-goned, grey-haired red pirate," he shrilled, in a seething sentence. The pudgy man gazed at the little man calmly and sneeringly.

"Oh, well," he said, "we can tell a great tale when we get back to the city after having investigated this thing."

"Go to the devil," replied the little man.

# THE MESMERIC MOUNTAIN

## A TALE OF SULLIVAN COUNTY

On the brow of a pine-plumed hillock there sat a little man with his back against a tree. A venerable pipe hung from his mouth, and smoke-wreaths curled slowly skyward, he was muttering to himself with his eyes fixed on an irregular black opening in the green wall of forest at the foot of the hill. Two vague wagon ruts led into the shadows. The little man took his pipe in his hands and addressed the listening pines.

"I wonder what the devil it leads to," said he.

A grey, fat rabbit came lazily from a thicket and sat in the opening. Softly stroking his stomach with his paw, he looked at the little man in a thoughtful manner. The little man threw a stone, and the rabbit blinked and ran through an opening. Green, shadowy portals seemed to close behind him.

The little man started. "He's gone down that roadway," he said, with ecstatic mystery to the pines. He sat a long time and contemplated the door to the forest. Finally, he arose, and awakening his limbs, started away. But he stopped and looked back.

"I can't imagine what it leads to," muttered he. He trudged over the brown mats of pine needles, to where, in a fringe of laurel, a tent was pitched, and merry flames caroused about some logs. A pudgy man was fuming over a collection of tin dishes. He came forward and waved a plate furiously in the little man's face.

"I've washed the dishes for three days. What do you think I am—"

He ended a red oration with a roar: "Damned if I do it any more."

The little man gazed dim-eyed away. "I've been wonderin' what it leads to."

"What?"

"That road out yonder. I've been wonderin' what it leads to. Maybe, some discovery or something," said the little man.

The pudgy man laughed. "You're an idiot. It leads to ol' Jim Boyd's over on the Lumberland Pike."

"Ho!" said the little man, "I don't believe that."

The pudgy man swore. "Fool, what does it lead to, then?"

"I don't know just what, but I'm sure it leads to something great or something. It looks like it."

While the pudgy man was cursing, two more men came from obscurity with fish dangling from birch twigs. The pudgy man made an obviously herculean struggle and a meal was prepared. As he was drinking his cup of coffee, he suddenly spilled it and swore. The little man was wandering off.

"He's gone to look at that hole," cried the pudgy man.

The little man went to the edge of the pine-plumed hillock, and, sitting down, began to make smoke and regard the door to the forest. There was stillness for an hour. Compact clouds hung unstirred in the sky. The pines stood motionless, and pondering.

Suddenly the little man slapped his knees and bit his tongue. He stood up and determinedly filled his pipe, rolling his eye over the bowl to the doorway. Keeping his eyes fixed he slid dangerously to the foot of the hillock and walked down the wagon ruts. A moment later he passed from the noise of the sunshine to the gloom of the woods.

The green portals closed, shutting out live things. The little man trudged on alone.

Tall tangled grass grew in the roadway, and the trees bended obstructing branches. The little man followed on over pine-clothed ridges and down through water-soaked swales. His shoes were cut by rocks of the mountains, and he sank ankle-deep in mud and moss of swamps. A curve just ahead lured him miles.

Finally, as he wended the side of a ridge, the road disappeared from beneath his feet. He battled with hordes of ignorant bushes on his way to knolls and solitary trees which invited him. Once he came to a tall, bearded pine. He climbed it, and perceived in the distance a peak. He uttered an ejaculation and fell out.

He scrambled to his feet, and said: "That's Jones's Mountain, I guess. It's about six miles from our camp as the crow flies."

He changed his course away from the mountain, and attacked the bushes again. He climbed over great logs, golden-brown in decay, and was opposed by thickets of dark-green laurel. A brook slid through the ooze of a swamp, cedars and hemlocks hung their spray to the edges of pools.

The little man began to stagger in his walk. After a time he stopped and mopped his brow.

"My legs are about to shrivel up and drop off," he said.… "Still if I keep on in this direction, I am safe to strike the Lumberland Pike before sundown."

He dived at a clump of tag-alders, and emerging, confronted Jones's Mountain.

The wanderer sat down in a clear space and fixed his eyes on the summit. His mouth opened widely, and his body swayed at times. The little man and the peak stared in silence.

A lazy lake lay asleep near the foot of the mountain. In its bed of water-grass some frogs leered at the sky and crooned. The sun sank in red silence, and the shadows of the pines grew formidable. The expectant hush of evening, as if some thing were going to sing a hymn, fell upon the peak and the little man.

A leaping pickerel off on the water created a silver circle that was lost in black shadows. The little man shook himself and started to his feet, crying: "For the love of Mike, there's eyes in this mountain! I feel 'em! Eyes!"

He fell on his face.

When he looked again, he immediately sprang erect and ran.

"It's comin'!"

The mountain was approaching.

The little man scurried, sobbing through the thick growth. He felt his brain turning to water. He vanquished brambles with mighty bounds.

But after a time he came again to the foot of the mountain.

"God!" he howled, "it's been follerin' me." He grovelled.

Casting his eyes upward made circles swirl in his blood.

"I'm shackled I guess," he moaned. As he felt the heel of the mountain about to crush his head, he sprang again to his feet. He grasped a handful of small stones and hurled them.

"Damn you," he shrieked loudly. The pebbles rang against the face of the mountain.

The little man then made an attack. He climbed with hands and feet wildly. Brambles forced him back and stones slid from beneath his feet. The peak swayed and tottered, and was ever about to smite with a granite arm. The summit was a blaze of red wrath.

But the little man at last reached the top. Immediately he swaggered with valor to the edge of the cliff. His hands were scornfully in his pockets.

He gazed at the western horizon, edged sharply against a yellow sky. "Ho!" he said. "There's Boyd's house and the Lumberland Pike."

The mountain under his feet was motionless.

# THE SNAKE

Where the path wended across the ridge, the bushes of huckleberry and sweet fern swarmed at it in two curling waves until it was a mere winding line traced through a tangle. There was no interference by clouds, and as the rays of the sun fell full upon the ridge, they called into voice innumerable insects which chanted the heat of the summer day in steady, throbbing, unending chorus.

A man and a dog came from the laurel thickets of the valley where the white brook brawled with the rocks. They followed the deep line of the path across the ridges. The dog—a large lemon and white setter—walked, tranquilly meditative, at his master's heels.

Suddenly from some unknown and yet near place in advance there came a dry, shrill whistling rattle that smote motion instantly from the limbs of the man and the dog. Like the fingers of a sudden death, this sound seemed to touch the man at the nape of the neck, at the top of the spine, and change him, as swift as thought, to a statue of listening horror, surprise, rage. The dog, too—the same icy hand was laid upon him, and he stood crouched and quivering, his jaw dropping, the froth of terror upon his lips, the light of hatred in his eyes.

Slowly the man moved his hands toward the bushes, but his glance did not turn from the place made sinister by the warning rattle. His fingers, unguided, sought for a stick of weight and strength. Presently they closed about one that seemed adequate, and holding this weapon poised before him the man moved slowly forward, glaring. The dog with his nervous nostrils fairly fluttering moved warily, one foot at a time, after his master.

But when the man came upon the snake, his body underwent a shock as if from a revelation, as if after all he had been ambushed. With a blanched face, he sprang forward and his breath came in strained gasps, his chest heaving as if he were in the performance of an extraordinary muscular trial. His arm with the stick made a spasmodic, defensive gesture.

The snake had apparently been crossing the path in some mystic travel when to his sense there came the knowledge of the coming of his foes. The dull vibration perhaps informed him, and he flung his body to face the danger. He had no knowledge of paths; he had no wit to tell him to slink noiselessly into the bushes. He knew that his implacable enemies were approaching; no doubt they were seeking him, hunting him. And so he cried his cry, an incredibly swift jangle of tiny bells, as burdened with pathos as the hammering upon quaint cymbals by the Chinese at war—for, indeed, it was usually his death-music.

"Beware! Beware! Beware!"

The man and the snake confronted each other. In the man's eyes were hatred and fear. In the snake's eyes were hatred and fear. These enemies maneuvered, each preparing to kill. It was to be a battle without mercy. Neither knew of mercy for such a situation. In the man was all the wild strength of the terror of his ancestors, of his race, of his kind. A deadly repulsion had been handed from man to man through long dim centuries. This was another detail of a war that had begun evidently when first there were men and snakes. Individuals who do not participate in this strife incur the investigations of scientists. Once there was a man and a snake who were friends, and at the end, the man lay dead with the marks of the snake's caress just over his East

Indian heart. In the formation of devices, hideous and horrible, Nature reached her supreme point in the making of the snake, so that priests who really paint hell well fill it with snakes instead of fire. The curving forms, these scintillant coloring create at once, upon sight, more relentless animosities than do shake barbaric tribes. To be born a snake is to be thrust into a place a-swarm with formidable foes. To gain an appreciation of it, view hell as pictured by priests who are really skilful.

As for this snake in the pathway, there was a double curve some inches back of its head, which, merely by the potency of its lines, made the man feel with tenfold eloquence the touch of the death-fingers at the nape of his neck. The reptile's head was waving slowly from side to side and its hot eyes flashed like little murder-lights. Always in the air was the dry, shrill whistling of the rattles.

"Beware! Beware! Beware!"

The man made a preliminary feint with his stick. Instantly the snake's heavy head and neck were bended back on the double curve and instantly the snake's body shot forward in a low, strait, hard spring. The man jumped with a convulsive chatter and swung his stick. The blind, sweeping blow fell upon the snake's head and hurled him so that steel-colored plates were for a moment uppermost. But he rallied swiftly, agilely, and again the head and neck bended back to the double curve, and the steaming, wide-open mouth made its desperate effort to reach its enemy. This attack, it could be seen, was despairing, but it was nevertheless impetuous, gallant, ferocious, of the same quality as the charge of the lone chief when the walls of white faces close upon him in the mountains. The stick swung unerringly again, and the snake, mutilated, torn, whirled himself into the last coil.

And now the man went sheer raving mad from the emotions of his forefathers and from his own. He came to close quarters. He gripped the stick with his two hands and made it speed like a flail. The snake, tumbling in the anguish of final despair, fought, bit, flung itself upon this stick which was taking his life.

At the end, the man clutched his stick and stood watching in silence. The dog came slowly and with infinite caution stretched his nose forward, sniffing. The hair upon his neck and back moved and ruffled as if a sharp wind was blowing, the last muscular quivers of the snake were causing the rattles to still sound their treble cry, the shrill, ringing war chant and hymn of the grave of the thing that faces foes at once countless, implacable, and superior.

"Well, Rover," said the man, turning to the dog with a grin of victory, "we'll carry Mr. Snake home to show the girls."

His hands still trembled from the strain of the encounter, but he pried with his stick under the body of the snake and hoisted the limp thing upon it. He resumed his march along the path, and the dog walked tranquilly meditative, at his master's heels.

# LONDON IMPRESSIONS

## CHAPTER I

London at first consisted of a porter with the most charming manners in the world, and a cabman with a supreme intelligence, both observing my profound ignorance without contempt or humor of any kind observable in their manners. It was in a great resounding vault of a place where there were many people who had come home, and I was displeased because they knew the detail of the business, whereas I was confronting the inscrutable. This made them appear very stony-hearted to the sufferings of one of whose existence, to be sure, they were entirely unaware, and I remember taking great pleasure in disliking them heartily for it. I was in an agony of mind over my baggage, or my luggage, or my—perhaps it is well to shy around this terrible international question; but I remember that when I was a lad I was told that there was a whole nation that said luggage instead of baggage, and my boyish mind was filled at the time with incredulity and scorn. In the present case it was a thing that I understood to involve the most hideous confessions of imbecility on my part, because I had evidently to go out to some obscure point and espy it and claim it, and take trouble for it; and I would rather have had my pockets filled with bread and cheese, and had no baggage at all.

Mind you, this was not at all a homage that I was paying to London. I was paying homage to a new game. A man properly lazy does not like new experiences until they become old ones. Moreover, I have been taught that a man, any man, who has a thousand times more points of information on a certain thing than I have will bully me because of it, and pour his advantages upon my bowed head until I am drenched with his superiority. It was in my education to concede some license of the kind in this case, but the holy father of a porter and the saintly cabman occupied the middle distance imperturbably, and did not come down from their hills to clout me with knowledge. From this fact I experienced a criminal elation. I lost view of the idea that if I had been brow-beaten by porters and cabmen from one end of the United States to the other end I should warmly like it, because in numbers they are superior to me, and collectively they can have a great deal of fun out of a matter that would merely afford me the glee of the latent butcher.

This London, composed of a porter and a cabman, stood to me subtly as a benefactor. I had scanned the drama, and found that I did not believe that the mood of the men emanated unduly from the feature that there was probably more shillings to the square inch of me than there were shillings to the square inch of them. Nor yet was it any manner of palpable warm-heartedness or other natural virtue. But it was a perfect artificial virtue; it was drill, plain, simple drill. And now was I glad of their drilling, and vividly approved of it, because I saw that it was good for me. Whether it was good or bad for the porter and the cabman I could not know; but that point, mark you, came within the pale of my respectable rumination.

I am sure that it would have been more correct for me to have alighted upon St. Paul's and described no emotion until I was overcome by the Thames Embankment and the Houses of Parliament. But as a matter of fact I did not see them for some days, and at this time they did not concern me at all. I was born in London at a railroad station, and my new vision encompassed a porter and a cabman. They deeply absorbed me in new phenomena, and I did not then care to see the Thames Embankment nor the Houses of Parliament. I considered the porter and the cabman to be more important.

## CHAPTER II

The cab finally rolled out of the gas-lit vault into a vast expanse of gloom. This changed to the shadowy lines of a street that was like a passage in a monstrous cave. The lamps winking here and there resembled the little gleams at the caps of the miners. They were not very competent illuminations at best, merely being little pale flares of gas that at their most heroic periods could only display one fact concerning this tunnel—the fact of general direction. But at any rate I should have liked to have observed the dejection of a search-light if it had been called upon to attempt to bore through this atmosphere. In it each man sat in his own little cylinder of vision, so to speak. It was not so small as a sentry-box nor so large as a circus tent, but the walls were opaque, and what was passing beyond the dimensions of his cylinder no man knew.

It was evident that the paving was very greasy, but all the cabs that passed through my cylinder were going at a round trot, while the wheels, shod in rubber, whirred merely like bicycles. The hoofs of the animals themselves did not make that wild clatter which I knew so well. New York in fact, roars always like ten thousand devils. We have ingenuous and simple ways of making a din in New York that cause the stranger to conclude that each citizen is obliged by statute to provide himself with a pair of cymbals and a drum. If anything by chance can be turned into a noise it is promptly turned. We are engaged in the development of a human creature with very large, sturdy, and doubly, fortified ears.

It was not too late at night, but this London moved with the decorum and caution of an undertaker. There was a silence, and yet there was no silence. There was a low drone, perhaps a humming contributed inevitably by closely-gathered thousands, and yet on second thoughts it was to me silence. I had perched my ears for the note of London, the sound made simply by the existence of five million people in one place. I had imagined something deep, vastly deep, a bass from a mythical organ, but found as far as I was concerned, only a silence.

New York in numbers is a mighty city, and all day and all night it cries its loud, fierce, aspiring cry, a noise of men beating upon barrels, a noise of men beating upon tin, a terrific racket that assails the abject skies. No one of us seemed to question this row as a certain consequence of three or four million people living together and scuffling for coin, with more agility, perhaps, but otherwise in the usual way. However, after this easy silence of London, which in numbers is a mightier city, I began to feel that there was a seduction in this idea of necessity. Our noise in New York was not a consequence of our rapidity at all. It was a consequence of our bad pavements.

Any brigade of artillery in Europe that would love to assemble its batteries, and then go on a gallop over the land, thundering and thundering, would give up the idea of thunder at once if it could hear Tim Mulligan drive a beer wagon along one of the side streets of cobbled New York.

## CHAPTER III

Finally a great thing came to pass. The cab horse, proceeding at a sharp trot, found himself suddenly at the top of an incline, where through the rain the pavement shone like an expanse of ice. It looked to me as if there was going to be a tumble. In an accident of such a kind a hansom becomes really a cannon in which a man finds that he has paid shillings for the privilege of serving as a projectile. I was making a rapid calculation of the arc that I would describe in my flight, when the horse met his crisis with a masterly device that I could not have imagined. He tranquilly braced his four feet like a bundle of stakes, and then, with a gentle gaiety of demeanor, he slid swiftly and gracefully to the bottom of the hill as if he had been a toboggan. When the incline ended he caught his gait again with great dexterity, and went pattering off through another tunnel.

I at once looked upon myself as being singularly blessed by this sight. This horse had evidently originated this system of skating as a diversion, or, more probably, as a precaution against the slippery pavement; and he was, of course the inventor and sole proprietor—two terms that are not always in conjunction. It surely was not to be supposed that there could be two skaters like him in the world. He deserved to be known and publicly praised for this accomplishment. It was worthy of many records and exhibitions. But when the cab arrived at a place where some dipping streets met, and the flaming front of a music-hall temporarily widened my cylinder, behold there were many cabs, and as the moment of necessity came the horses were all skaters. They were gliding in all directions. It might have been a rink. A great omnibus was hailed by a hand under an umbrella on the side walk, and the dignified horses bidden to halt from their trot did not waste time in wild and unseemly spasms. They, too, braced their legs and slid gravely to the end of their momentum.

It was not the feat, but it was the word which had at this time the power to conjure memories of skating parties on moonlit lakes, with laughter ringing over the ice, and a great red bonfire on the shore among the hemlocks.

## CHAPTER IV

A Terrible thing in nature is the fall of a horse in his harness. It is a tragedy. Despite their skill in skating there was that about the pavement on the rainy evening which filled me with expectations of horses going headlong. Finally it happened just in front. There was a shout and a tangle in the darkness, and presently a prostrate cab horse came within my cylinder. The accident having been a complete success and altogether concluded, a voice from the side walk said, "*Look* out, now! *Be* more careful, can't you?"

I remember a constituent of a Congressman at Washington who had tried in vain to bore this Congressman with a wild project of some kind. The Congressman eluded him with skill, and his rage and despair ultimately culminated in the supreme grievance that he could not even get near enough to the Congressman to tell him to go to Hades.

This cabman should have felt the same desire to strangle this man who spoke from the sidewalk. He was plainly impotent; he was deprived of the power of looking out. There was nothing now for which to look out. The man on the sidewalk had dragged a corpse from a pond and said to it,

"*Be* more careful, can't you, or you'll drown?" My cabman pulled up and addressed a few words of reproach to the other. Three or four figures loomed into my cylinder, and as they appeared spoke to the author or the victim of the calamity in varied terms of displeasure. Each of these reproaches was couched in terms that defined the situation as impending. No blind man could have conceived that the precipitate phrase of the incident was absolutely closed.

"*Look* out now, cawn't you?" And there was nothing in his mind which approached these sentiments near enough to tell them to go to Hades.

However, it needed only an ear to know presently that these expressions were formulae. It was merely the obligatory dance which the Indians had to perform before they went to war. These men had come to help, but as a regular and traditional preliminary they had first to display to this cabman their idea of his ignominy.

The different thing in the affair was the silence of the victim. He retorted never a word. This, too, to me seemed to be an obedience to a recognized form. He was the visible criminal, if there was a criminal, and there was born of it a privilege for them.

They unfastened the proper straps and hauled back the cab. They fetched a mat from some obscure place of succor, and pushed it carefully under the prostrate thing. From this panting, quivering mass they suddenly and emphatically reconstructed a horse. As each man turned to go his way he delivered some superior caution to the cabman while the latter buckled his harness.

## CHAPTER V

There was to be noticed in this band of rescuers a young man in evening clothes and top-hat. Now, in America a young man in evening clothes and a top-hat may be a terrible object. He is not likely to do violence, but he is likely to do impassivity and indifference to the point where they become worse than violence. There are certain of the more idle phases of civilization to which America has not yet awakened—and it is a matter of no moment if she remains unaware. This matter of hats is one of them. I recall a legend recited to me by an esteemed friend, ex-Sheriff of Tin Can, Nevada. Jim Cortright, one of the best gun-fighters in town, went on a journey to Chicago, and while there he procured a top-hat. He was quite sure how Tin Can would accept this innovation, but he relied on the celerity with which he could get a six-shooter in action. One Sunday Jim examined his guns with his usual care, placed the top-hat on the back of his head, and sauntered coolly out into the streets of Tin Can.

Now, while Jim was in Chicago some progressive citizen had decided that Tin Can needed a bowling alley. The carpenters went to work the next morning, and an order for the balls and pins was telegraphed to Denver. In three days the whole population was concentrated at the new alley betting their outfits and their lives.

It has since been accounted very unfortunate that Jim Cortright had not learned of bowling alleys at his mother's knee or even later in the mines. This portion of his mind was singularly belated. He might have been an Apache for all he knew of bowling alleys.

In his careless stroll through the town, his hands not far from his belt and his eyes going sideways in order to see who would shoot first at the hat, he came upon this long, low shanty where Tin Can was betting itself hoarse over a game between a team from the ranks of Excelsior Hose Company No. 1 and a team composed from the *habitues* of the "Red Light" saloon.

Jim, in blank ignorance of bowling phenomena, wandered casually through a little door into what must always be termed the wrong end of a bowling alley. Of course, he saw that the supreme moment had come. They were not only shooting at the hat and at him, but the low-down cusses were using the most extraordinary and hellish ammunition. Still, perfectly undaunted, however, Jim retorted with his two Colts, and killed three of the best bowlers in Tin Can.

The ex-Sheriff vouched for this story. He himself had gone headlong through the door at the firing of the first shot with that simple courtesy which leads Western men to donate the fighters plenty of room. He said that afterwards the hat was the cause of a number of other fights, and that finally a delegation of prominent citizens was obliged to wait upon Cortright and ask him if he wouldn't take that thing away somewhere and bury it. Jim pointed out to them that it was his hat, and that he would regard it as a cowardly concession if he submitted to their dictation in the matter of his headgear. He added that he purposed to continue to wear his top-hat on every occasion when he happened to feel that the wearing of a top-hat was a joy and a solace to him.

The delegation sadly retired, and announced to the town that Jim Cortright had openly defied them, and had declared his purpose of forcing his top-hat on the pained attention of Tin Can whenever he chose. Jim Cortright's plug hat became a phrase with considerable meaning to it.

However, the whole affair ended in a great passionate outburst of popular revolution. Spike Foster was a friend of Cortright, and one day, when the latter was indisposed, Spike came to him and borrowed the hat. He had been drinking heavily at the "Red Light," and was in a supremely reckless mood. With the terrible gear hanging jauntily over his eye and his two guns drawn, he walked straight out into the middle of the square in front of the Palace Hotel, and drew the attention of all Tin Can by a blood-curdling imitation of the yowl of a mountain lion.

This was when the long suffering populace arose as one man. The top-hat had been flaunted once too often. When Spike Foster's friends came to carry him away they found nearly a hundred and fifty men shooting busily at a mark—and the mark was the hat.

My informant told me that he believed he owed his popularity in Tin Can, and subsequently his election to the distinguished office of Sheriff, to the active and prominent part he had taken in the proceedings.

The enmity to the top-hat expressed by the convincing anecdote exists in the American West at present, I think, in the perfection of its strength; but disapproval is not now displayed by volleys from the citizens, save in the most aggravating cases. It is at present usually a matter of mere jibe and general contempt. The East, however, despite a great deal of kicking and gouging, is having the top-hat stuffed slowly and carefully down its throat, and there now exist many young men who consider that they could not successfully conduct their lives without this furniture.

To speak generally, I should say that the headgear then supplies them with a kind of ferocity of indifference. There is fire, sword, and pestilence in the way they heed only themselves. Philosophy should always know that indifference is a militant thing. It batters down the walls of cities, and murders the women and children amid flames and the purloining of altar vessels. When it goes away it leaves smoking ruins, where lie citizens bayoneted through the throat. It is not a children's pastime like mere highway robbery.

Consequently in America we may be much afraid of these young men. We dive down alleys so that we may not kowtow. It is a fearsome thing.

Taught thus a deep fear of the top-hat in its effect upon youth, I was not prepared for the move of this particular young man when the cab-horse fell. In fact, I grovelled in my corner that I might not see the cruel stateliness of his passing. But in the meantime he had crossed the street, and contributed the strength of his back and some advice, as well as the formal address, to the cabman on the importance of looking out immediately.

I felt that I was making a notable collection. I had a new kind of porter, a cylinder of vision, horses that could skate, and now I added a young man in a top-hat who would tacitly admit that the beings around him were alive. He was not walking a churchyard filled with inferior headstones. He was walking the world, where there were people, many people.

But later I took him out of the collection. I thought he had rebelled against the manner of a class, but I soon discovered that the top-hat was not the property of a class. It was the property of rogues, clerks, theatrical agents, damned seducers, poor men, nobles, and others. In fact, it was the universal rigging. It was the only hat; all other forms might as well be named ham, or chops, or oysters. I retracted my admiration of the young man because he may have been merely a rogue.

## CHAPTER VI

There was a window whereat an enterprising man by dodging two placards and a calendar was entitled to view a young woman. She was dejectedly writing in a large book. She was ultimately induced to open the window a trifle. "What nyme, please?" she said wearily. I was surprised to hear this language from her. I had expected to be addressed on a submarine topic. I have seen shell fishes sadly writing in large books at the bottom of a gloomy acquarium who could not ask me what was my "nyme."

At the end of the hall there was a grim portal marked "lift." I pressed an electric button and heard an answering tinkle in the heavens. There was an upholstered settle near at hand, and I discovered the reason. A deer-stalking peace drooped upon everything, and in it a man could invoke the passing of a lazy pageant of twenty years of his life. The dignity of a coffin being lowered into a grave surrounded the ultimate appearance of the lift. The expert we in America call the elevator-boy stepped from the car, took three paces forward, faced to attention and saluted. This elevator boy could not have been less than sixty years of age; a great white beard streamed towards his belt. I saw that the lift had been longer on its voyage than I had suspected.

Later in our upward progress a natural event would have been an establishment of social relations. Two enemies imprisoned together during the still hours of a balloon journey would, I believe, suffer a mental amalgamation. The overhang of a common fate, a great principal fact, can make an equality and a truce between any pair. Yet, when I disembarked, a final survey of the grey beard made me recall that I had failed even to ask the boy whether he had not taken probably three trips on this lift.

My windows overlooked simply a great sea of night, in which were swimming little gas fishes.

## CHAPTER VII

I have of late been led to reflect wistfully that many of the illustrators are very clever. In an impatience, which was donated by a certain economy of apparel, I went to a window to look upon day-lit London. There were the 'buses parading the streets with the miens of elephants There were the police looking precisely as I had been informed by the prints. There were the sandwich-men. There was almost everything.

But the artists had not told me the sound of London. Now, in New York the artists are able to portray sound because in New York a dray is not a dray at all; it is a great potent noise hauled by two or more horses. When a magazine containing an illustration of a New York street is sent to me, I always know it beforehand. I can hear it coming through the mails. As I have said previously, this which I must call sound of London was to me only a silence.

Later, in front of the hotel a cabman that I hailed said to me—"Are you gowing far, sir? I've got a byby here, and want to giv'er a bit of a blough." This impressed me as being probably a quotation from an early Egyptian poet, but I learned soon enough that the word "byby" was the name of some kind or condition of horse. The cabman's next remark was addressed to a boy who took a perilous dive between the byby's nose and a cab in front. "That's roight. Put your head in there and get it jammed—a whackin good place for it, I should think." Although the tone was low and circumspect, I have never heard a better off-handed declamation. Every word was cut clear of disreputable alliances with its neighbors. The whole thing was clean as a row of pewter mugs. The influence of indignation upon the voice caused me to reflect that we might devise a mechanical means of inflaming some in that constellation of mummers which is the heritage of the Anglo-Saxon race.

Then I saw the drilling of vehicles by two policemen. There were four torrents converging at a point, and when four torrents converge at one point engineering experts buy tickets for another place.

But here, again, it was drill, plain, simple drill. I must not falter in saying that I think the management of the traffic—as the phrase goes—to be distinctly illuminating and wonderful. The police were not ruffled and exasperated. They were as peaceful as two cows in a pasture.

I can remember once remarking that mankind, with all its boasted modern progress, had not yet been able to invent a turnstile that will commute in fractions. I have now learned that 756 rights-of-way cannot operate simultaneously at one point. Right-of-way, like fighting women, requires space. Even two rights-of-way can make a scene which is only suited to the tastes of an ancient public.

This truth was very evidently recognized. There was only one right-of-way at a time. The police did not look behind them to see if their orders were to be obeyed; they knew they were to be obeyed. These four torrents were drilling like four battalions. The two blue-cloth men maneuvered them in solemn, abiding peace, the silence of London.

I thought at first that it was the intellect of the individual, but I looked at one constable closely and his face was as afire with intelligence as a flannel pin-cushion. It was not the police, and it was not the crowd. It was the police and the crowd. Again, it was drill.

## CHAPTER VIII

I have never been in the habit of reading signs. I don't like to read signs. I have never met a man that liked to read signs. I once invented a creature who could play the piano with a hammer, and I mentioned him to a professor in Harvard University whose peculiarity was Sanscrit. He had the same interest in my invention that I have in a certain kind of mustard. And yet this mustard has become a part of me. Or, I have become a part of this mustard. Further, I know more of an ink, a brand of hams, a kind of cigarette, and a novelist than any man living. I went by train to see a friend in the country, and after passing through a patent mucilage, some more hams, a South African Investment Company, a Parisian millinery firm, and a comic journal, I alighted at a new and original kind of corset. On my return journey the road almost continuously ran through soap.

I have accumulated superior information concerning these things, because I am at their mercy. If I want to know where I am I must find the definitive sign. This accounts for my glib use of the word mucilage, as well as the titles of other staples.

I suppose even the Briton in mixing his life must sometimes consult the labels on 'buses and streets and stations, even as the chemist consults the labels on his bottles and boxes. A brave man would possibly affirm that this was suggested by the existence of the labels.

The reason that I did not learn more about hams and mucilage in New York seems to me to be partly due to the fact that the British advertiser is allowed to exercise an unbridled strategy in his attack with his new corset or whatever upon the defensive public. He knows that the vulnerable point is the informatory sign which the citizen must, of course, use for his guidance, and then, with horse, foot, guns, corsets, hams, mucilage, investment companies, and all, he hurls himself at the point.

Meanwhile I have discovered a way to make the Sanscrit scholar heed my creature who plays the piano with a hammer.

# THE SCOTCH EXPRESS

The entrance to Euston Station is of itself sufficiently imposing. It is a high portico of brown stone, old and grim, in form a casual imitation, no doubt, of the front of the temple of Nike Apteros, with a recollection of the Egyptians proclaimed at the flanks. The frieze, where of old would prance an exuberant processional of gods, is, in this case, bare of decoration, but upon the epistyle is written in simple, stern letters the word "EUSTON." The legend reared high by the gloomy Pelagic columns stares down a wide avenue, In short, this entrance to a railway station does not in any way resemble the entrance to a railway station. It is more the front of some venerable bank. But it has another dignity, which is not born of form. To a great degree, it is to the English and to those who are in England the gate to Scotland.

The little hansoms are continually speeding through the gate, dashing between the legs of the solemn temple; the four-wheelers, their tops crowded with luggage, roll in and out constantly, and the footways beat under the trampling of the people. Of course, there are the suburbs and a hundred towns along the line, and Liverpool, the beginning of an important sea-path to America, and the great manufacturing cities of the North; but if one stands at this gate in August particularly, one must note the number of men with gun-cases, the number of women who surely have Tam-o'-Shanters and plaids concealed within their luggage, ready for the moors. There is, during the latter part of that month, a wholesale flight from London to Scotland which recalls the July throngs leaving New York for the shore or the mountains.

The hansoms, after passing through this impressive portal of the station, bowl smoothly across a courtyard which is in the center of the terminal hotel, an institution dear to most railways in Europe. The traveler lands amid a swarm of porters, and then proceeds cheerfully to take the customary trouble for his luggage. America provides a contrivance in a thousand situations where Europe provides a man or perhaps a number of men, and the work of our brass check is here done by porters, directed by the traveler himself. The men lack the memory of the check; the check never forgets its identity. Moreover, the European railways generously furnish the porters at the expense of the traveler. Nevertheless, if these men have not the invincible business precision of the check, and if they have to be tipped, it can be asserted for those who care that in Europe one-half of the populace waits on the other half most diligently and well.

Against the masonry of a platform, under the vaulted arch of the train-house, lay a long string of coaches. They were painted white on the bulging part, which led halfway down from the top, and the bodies were a deep bottle-green. There was a group of porters placing luggage in the van, and a great many others were busy with the affairs of passengers, tossing smaller bits of luggage into the racks over the seats, and bustling here and there on short quests. The guard of the train, a tall man who resembled one of the first Napoleon's veterans, was caring for the distribution of passengers into the various bins. There were no second-class compartments; they were all third and first-class.

The train was at this time engineless, but presently a railway "flier," painted a glowing vermilion, slid modestly down and took its place at the head. The guard walked along the platform, and decisively closed each door. He wore a dark blue uniform thoroughly decorated with silver braid in the guise of leaves. The way of him gave to this business the importance of a ceremony. Meanwhile the fireman had climbed down from the cab and raised his hand, ready to transfer a signal to the driver, who stood looking at his watch. In the interval there had something progressed in the large signal box that stands guard at Euston. This high house contains many levers, standing in thick, shining ranks. It perfectly resembles an organ in some great church, if it were not that these rows of numbered and indexed handles typify something more acutely human than does a keyboard. It requires four men to play this organ-like thing, and the strains never cease. Night and day, day and night, these four men are walking to and fro, from this lever to that lever, and under their hands the great machine raises its endless hymn of a world at work, the fall and rise of signals and the clicking swing of switches.

And so as the vermilion engine stood waiting and looking from the shadow of the curve-roofed station, a man in the signal house had played the notes that informed the engine of its freedom. The driver saw the fall of those proper semaphores which gave him liberty to speak to his steel friend. A certain combination in the economy of the London and Northwestern Railway, a combination which had spread from the men who sweep out the carriages through innumerable minds to the general manager himself, had resulted in the law that the vermilion engine, with its long string of white and bottle-green coaches, was to start forthwith toward Scotland.

Presently the fireman, standing with his face toward the rear, let fall his hand. "All right," he said. The driver turned a wheel, and as the fireman slipped back, the train moved along the platform at the pace of a mouse. To those in the tranquil carriages this starting was probably as easy as the sliding of one's hand over a greased surface, but in the engine there was more to it. The monster roared suddenly and loudly, and sprang forward impetuously. A wrong-headed or maddened draft-horse will plunge in its collar sometimes when going up a hill. But this load of burdened carriages followed imperturbably at the gait of turtles. They were not to be stirred from their way of dignified exit by the impatient engine. The crowd of porters and transient people stood respectful. They looked with the indefinite wonder of the railway-station sight-seer upon the faces at the windows of the passing coaches. This train was off for Scotland. It had started from the home of one accent to the home of another accent. It was going from manner to manner, from habit to habit, and in the minds of these London spectators there surely floated dim images of the traditional kilts, the burring speech, the grouse, the canniness, the oat-meal, all the elements of a romantic Scotland.

The train swung impressively around the signal-house, and headed up a brick-walled cut. In starting this heavy string of coaches, the engine breathed explosively. It gasped, and heaved, and bellowed; once, for a moment, the wheels spun on the rails, and a convulsive tremor shook the great steel frame.

The train itself, however, moved through this deep cut in the body of London with coolness and precision, and the employees of the railway, knowing the train's mission, tacitly presented arms at its passing. To the travelers in the carriages, the suburbs of London must have been one long monotony of carefully made walls of stone or brick. But after the hill was climbed, the train fled through pictures of red habitations of men on a green earth.

But the noise in the cab did not greatly change its measure. Even though the speed was now high, the tremendous thumping to be heard in the cab was as alive with strained effort and as slow in beat as the breathing of a half-drowned man. At the side of the track, for instance, the sound doubtless would strike the ear in the familiar succession of incredibly rapid puffs; but in the cab itself, this land-racer breathes very like its friend, the marine engine. Everybody who has spent time on shipboard has forever in his head a reminiscence of the steady and methodical pounding of the engines, and perhaps it is curious that this relative which can whirl over the land at such a pace, breathes in the leisurely tones that a man heeds when he lies awake at night in his berth.

There had been no fog in London, but here on the edge of the city a heavy wind was blowing, and the driver leaned aside and yelled that it was a very bad day for traveling on an engine. The engine-cabs of England, as of all Europe, are seldom made for the comfort of the men. One finds very often this apparent disregard for the man who does the work—this indifference to the man who occupies a position which for the exercise of temperance, of courage, of honesty, has no equal at the altitude of prime ministers. The American engineer is the gilded occupant of a salon in comparison with his brother in Europe. The man who was guiding this five-hundred-ton bolt, aimed by the officials of the railway at Scotland, could not have been as comfortable as a shrill gibbering boatman of the Orient. The narrow and bare bench at his side of the cab was not directly intended for his use, because it was so low that he would be prevented by it from looking out of the ship's port-hole which served him as a window. The fireman, on his side, had other difficulties. His legs would have had to straggle over some pipes at the only spot where there was a prospect, and the builders had also strategically placed a large steel bolt. Of course it is plain that the companies consistently believe that the men will do their work better if they are kept standing. The roof of the cab was not altogether a roof. It was merely a projection of two feet of metal from the bulkhead which formed the front of the cab. There were practically no sides to it, and the large cinders from the soft coal whirled around in sheets. From time to time the driver took a handkerchief from his pocket and wiped his blinking eyes.

London was now well to the rear. The vermilion engine had been for some time flying like the wind. This train averages, between London and Carlisle forty-nine and nine-tenth miles an hour. It is a distance of 299 miles. There is one stop. It occurs at Crewe, and endures five minutes. In consequence, the block signals flashed by seemingly at the end of the moment in which they were sighted.

There can be no question of the statement that the road-beds of English railways are at present immeasurably superior to the American road-beds. Of course there is a clear reason. It is known to every traveler that peoples of the Continent of Europe have no right at all to own railways. Those lines of travel are too childish and trivial for expression. A correct fate would deprive the Continent of its railways, and give them to somebody who knew about them.

The continental idea of a railway is to surround a mass of machinery with forty rings of ultra-military law, and then they believe they have one complete. The Americans and the English are the railway peoples. That our road-beds are poorer than the English road-beds is because of the fact that we were suddenly obliged to build thousands upon thousands of miles of railway, and the English were obliged to build slowly tens upon tens of miles. A road-bed from New York to San Francisco, with stations, bridges, and crossings of the kind that the London and Northwestern owns from London to Glasgow, would cost a sum large enough to support the German army for a term of years. The whole way is constructed with the care that inspired the creators of some of our now obsolete forts along the Atlantic coast.

An American engineer, with his knowledge of the difficulties he had to encounter—the wide rivers with variable banks, the mountain chains, perhaps the long spaces of absolute desert; in fact, all the perplexities of a vast and somewhat new country—would not dare spend a respectable portion of his allowance on seventy feet of granite wall over a gully, when he knew he could make an embankment with little cost by heaving up the dirt and stones from here and there. But the English road is all made in the pattern by which the Romans built their highways. After England is dead, savants will find narrow streaks of masonry leading from ruin to ruin. Of course this does not always seem convincingly admirable. It sometimes resembles energy poured into a rat-hole. There is a vale between expediency and the convenience of posterity, a mid-ground which enables men surely to benefit the hereafter people by valiantly advancing the present; and the point is that, if some laborers live in unhealthy tenements in Cornwall, one is likely to view with incomplete satisfaction the record of long and patient labor and thought displayed by an eight-foot drain for a nonexistent, impossible rivulet in the North. This sentence does not sound strictly fair, but the meaning one wishes to convey is that if an English company spies in its dream the ghost of an ancient valley that later becomes a hill, it would construct for it a magnificent steel trestle, and consider that a duty had been performed in proper accordance with the company's conscience. But after all is said of it, the accidents and the miles of railway operated in England are not in proportion to the accidents and the miles of railway operated in the United States. The reason can be divided into three parts—older conditions, superior caution, the road-bed. And of these, the greatest is older conditions.

In this flight toward Scotland one seldom encountered a grade crossing. In nine cases of ten there was either a bridge or a tunnel. The platforms of even the remote country stations were all of ponderous masonry in contrast to our constructions of planking. There was always to be seen, as we thundered toward a station of this kind, a number of porters in uniform, who requested the retreat of any one who had not the wit to give us plenty of room. And then, as the shrill warning of the whistle pierced even the uproar that was about us, came the wild joy of the rush past a station. It was something in the nature of a triumphal procession conducted at thrilling speed. Perhaps there was a curve of infinite grace, a sudden hollow explosive effect made by the passing of a signal-box that was close to the track, and then the deadly lunge to shave the edge of a long platform. There were always a number of people standing afar, with their eyes riveted upon this projectile, and to be on the engine was to feel their interest and admiration in the terror and grandeur of this sweep. A boy allowed to ride with the driver of the band-wagon as a circus parade winds through one of our village streets could not exceed for egotism the temper of a new man in the cab of a train like this one. This valkyric journey on the back of the vermilion engine, with the shouting of the wind, the deep, mighty panting of the steed, the gray blur at the track-side, the flowing quicksilver ribbon of the other rails, the sudden clash as a switch intersects, all the din and fury of this ride, was of a splendor that caused one to look abroad at the quiet, green landscape and believe that it was of a phlegm quiet beyond patience. It should have been dark, rain-shot, and windy; thunder should have rolled across its sky.

It seemed, somehow, that if the driver should for a moment take his hands from his engine, it might swerve from the track as a horse from the road. Once, indeed, as he stood wiping his fingers on a bit of waste, there must have been something ludicrous in the way the solitary passenger regarded him. Without those finely firm hands on the bridle, the engine might rear and bolt for the pleasant farms lying in the sunshine at either side.

This driver was worth contemplation. He was simply a quiet, middle-aged man, bearded, and with the little wrinkles of habitual geniality and kindliness spreading from the eyes toward the temple, who stood at his post always gazing out, through his round window, while, from time to time, his hands went from here to there over his levers. He seldom changed either attitude or expression. There surely is no engine-driver who does not feel the beauty of the business, but the emotion lies deep, and mainly inarticulate, as it does in the mind of a man who has experienced a good and beautiful wife for many years. This driver's face displayed nothing but the cool sanity of a man whose thought was buried intelligently in his business. If there was any fierce drama in it, there was no sign upon him. He was so lost in dreams of speed and signals and steam, that one speculated if the wonder of his tempestuous charge and its career over England touched him, this impassive rider of a fiery thing.

It should be a well-known fact that, all over the world, the engine-driver is the finest type of man that is grown. He is the pick of the earth. He is altogether more worthy than the soldier, and better than the men who move on the sea in ships. He is not paid too much; nor do his glories weight his brow; but for outright performance, carried on constantly, coolly, and without elation, by a temperate, honest, clear-minded man, he is the further point. And so the lone human at his station in a cab, guarding money, lives, and the honor of the road, is a beautiful sight. The whole thing is aesthetic. The fireman presents the same charm, but in a less degree, in that he is bound to appear as an apprentice to the finished manhood of the driver. In his eyes, turned always in question and confidence toward his superior, one finds this quality; but his aspirations are so direct that one sees the same type in evolution.

There may be a popular idea that the fireman's principal function is to hang his head out of the cab and sight interesting objects in the landscape. As a matter of fact, he is always at work. The dragon is insatiate. The fireman is continually swinging open the furnace-door, whereat a red shine flows out upon the floor of the cab, and shoveling in immense mouthfuls of coal to a fire that is almost diabolic in its madness. The feeding, feeding, feeding goes on until it appears as if it is the muscles of the fireman's arms that are speeding the long train. An engine running over sixty-five miles an hour, with 500 tons to drag, has an appetite in proportion to this task.

View of the clear-shining English scenery is often interrupted between London and Crew by long and short tunnels. The first one was disconcerting. Suddenly one knew that the train was shooting toward a black mouth in the hills. It swiftly yawned wider, and then in a moment the engine dived into a place inhabitated by every demon of wind and noise. The speed had not been checked, and the uproar was so great that in effect one was simply standing at the center of a vast, black-walled sphere. The tubular construction which one's reason proclaimed had no meaning at all. It was a black sphere, alive with shrieks. But then on the surface of it there was to be seen a little needle-point of light, and this widened to a detail of unreal land-scape. It was the world; the train was going to escape from this cauldron, this abyss of howling darkness. If a man looks through the brilliant water of a tropical pool, he can sometimes see coloring the marvels at the bottom the blue that was on the sky and the green that was on the foliage of this detail. And the picture shimmered in the heat-rays of a new and remarkable sun. It was when the train bolted out into the open air that one knew that it was his own earth.

Once train met train in a tunnel. Upon the painting in the perfectly circular frame formed by the mouth there appeared a black square with sparks bursting from it. This square expanded until it hid everything, and a moment later came the crash of the passing. It was enough to make a man lose his sense of balance. It was a momentary inferno when the fireman opened the furnace door and was bathed in blood-red light as he fed the fires.

The effect of a tunnel varied when there was a curve in it. One was merely whirling then heels over head, apparently in the dark, echoing bowels of the earth. There was no needle-point of light to which one's eyes clung as to a star.

From London to Crew, the stern arm of the semaphore never made the train pause even for an instant. There was always a clear track. It was great to see, far in the distance, a goods train whooping smokily for the north of England on one of the four tracks. The overtaking of such a train was a thing of magnificent nothing for the long-strided engine, and as the flying express passed its weaker brother, one heard one or two feeble and immature puffs from the other engine, saw the fireman wave his hand to his luckier fellow, saw a string of foolish, clanking flat-cars, their freights covered with tarpaulins, and then the train was lost to the rear.

The driver twisted his wheel and worked some levers, and the rhythmical chunking of the engine gradually ceased. Gliding at a speed that was still high, the train curved to the left, and swung down a sharp incline, to move with an imperial dignity through the railway yard at Rugby. There was a maze of switches, innumerable engines noisily pushing cars here and there, crowds of workmen who turned to look, a sinuous curve around the long train-shed, whose high wall resounded with the rumble of the passing express; and then, almost immediately, it seemed, came the open country again. Rugby had been a dream which one could properly doubt. At last the relaxed engine, with the same majesty of ease, swung into the high-roofed station at Crewe, and stopped on a platform lined with porters and citizens. There was instant bustle, and in the interest of the moment no one seemed particularly to notice the tired vermilion engine being led away.

There is a five-minute stop at Crewe. A tandem of engines slip up, and buckled fast to the train for the journey to Carlisle. In the meantime, all the regulation items of peace and comfort had happened on the train itself. The dining-car was in the center of the train. It was divided into two parts, the one being a dining-room for first-class passengers, and the other a dining-room for the third-class passengers. They were separated by the kitchens and the larder. The engine, with all its rioting and roaring, had dragged to Crewe a car in which numbers of passengers were lunching in a tranquility that was almost domestic, on an average menu of a chop and potatoes, a salad, cheese, and a bottle of beer. Betimes they watched through the windows the great chimney-marked towns of northern England. They were waited upon by a young man of London, who was supported by a lad who resembled an American bell-boy. The rather elaborate menu and service of the Pullman dining-car is not known in England or on the Continent. Warmed roast beef is the exact symbol of a European dinner, when one is traveling on a railway.

This express is named, both by the public and the company, the "Corridor Train," because a coach with a corridor is an unusual thing in England, and so the title has a distinctive meaning. Of course, in America, where there is no car which has not what we call an aisle, it would define nothing. The corridors are all at one side of the car. Doors open thence to little compartments made to seat four, or perhaps six, persons. The first-class carriages are very comfortable indeed, being heavily upholstered in dark, hard-wearing stuffs, with a bulging rest for the head. The third-class accommodations on this train are almost as comfortable as the first-class, and attract a kind of people that are not usually seen traveling third-class in Europe. Many people sacrifice their habit, in the matter of this train, to the fine conditions of the lower fare.

One of the feats of the train is an electric button in each compartment. Commonly an electric button is placed high on the side of the carriage as an alarm signal, and it is unlawful to push it unless one is in serious need of assistance from the guard. But these bells also rang in the dining-car, and were supposed to open negotiations for tea or whatever. A new function has been projected on an ancient custom. No genius has yet appeared to separate these two meanings. Each bell rings an alarm and a bid for tea or whatever. It is perfect in theory then that, if one rings for tea, the guard comes to interrupt the murder, and that if one is being murdered, the attendant appears with tea. At any rate, the guard was forever being called from his reports and his comfortable seat in the forward end of the luggage-van by thrilling alarms. He often prowled the length of the train with hardihood and determination, merely to meet a request for a sandwich.

The train entered Carlisle at the beginning of twilight. This is the border town, and an engine of the Caledonian Railway, manned by two men of broad speech, came to take the place of the tandem. The engine of these men of the North was much smaller than the others, but her cab was much larger, and would be a fair shelter on a stormy night. They had also built seats with hooks by which they hang them to the rail, and thus are still enabled to see through the round windows without dislocating their necks. All the human parts of the cab were covered with oilcloth. The wind that swirled from the dim twilight horizon made the warm glow from the furnace to be a grateful thing.

As the train shot out of Carlisle, a glance backward could learn of the faint, yellow blocks of light from the carriages marked on the dimmed ground. The signals were now lamps, and shone palely against the sky. The express was entering night as if night were Scotland.

There was a long toil to the summit of the hills, and then began the booming ride down the slope. There were many curves. Sometimes could be seen two or three signal lights at one time, twisting off in some new direction. Minus the lights and some yards of glistening rails, Scotland was only a blend of black and weird shapes. Forests which one could hardly imagine as weltering in the dewy placidity of evening sank to the rear as if the gods had bade them. The dark loom of a house quickly dissolved before the eyes. A station with its lamps became a broad yellow band that, to a deficient sense, was only a few yards in length. Below, in a deep valley, a silver glare on the waters of a river made equal time with the train. Signals appeared, grew, and vanished. In the wind and the mystery of the night, it was like sailing in an enchanted gloom. The vague profiles of hills ran like snakes across the somber sky. A strange shape boldly and formidably confronted the train, and then melted to a long dash of track as clean as sword-blades.

The vicinity of Glasgow is unmistakable. The flames of pauseless industries are here and there marked on the distance. Vast factories stand close to the track, and reaching chimneys emit roseate flames. At last one may see upon a wall the strong reflection from furnaces, and against it the impish and inky figures of working-men. A long, prison-like row of tenements, not at all resembling London, but in one way resembling New York, appeared to the left, and then sank out of sight like a phantom.

At last the driver stopped the brave effort of his engine The 400 miles were come to the edge. The average speed of forty-nine and one-third miles each hour had been made, and it remained only to glide with the hauteur of a great express through the yard and into the station at Glasgow.

A wide and splendid collection of signal lamps flowed toward the engine. With delicacy and care the train clanked over some switches, passes the signals, and then there shone a great blaze of arc-lamps, defining the wide sweep of the station roof.

Smoothly, proudly, with all that vast dignity which had surrounded its exit from London, the express moved along its platform. It was the entrance into a gorgeous drawing-room of a man that was sure of everything.

The porters and the people crowded forward. In their minds there may have floated dim images of the traditional music-halls, the bobbies, the 'buses, the 'Arrys and 'Arriets, the swells of London.

# THE O'RUDDY: A ROMANCE

## *by Stephen Crane and Robert Barr*

### CHAPTER I

My chieftain ancestors had lived at Glandore for many centuries and were very well known. Hardly a ship could pass the Old Head of Kinsale without some boats putting off to exchange the time of day with her, and our family name was on men's tongues in half the seaports of Europe, I dare say. My ancestors lived in castles which were like churches stuck on end, and they drank the best of everything amid the joyous cries of a devoted peasantry. But the good time passed away soon enough, and when I had reached the age of eighteen we had nobody on the land but a few fisher-folk and small farmers, people who were almost law-abiding, and my father came to die more from disappointment than from any other cause. Before the end he sent for me to come to his bedside.

"Tom," he said, "I brought you into existence, and God help you safe out of it; for you are not the kind of man ever to turn your hand to work, and there is only enough money to last a gentleman five more years.

"The 'Martha Bixby,' she was, out of Bristol for the West Indies, and if it hadn't been for her we would never have got along this far with plenty to eat and drink. However, I leave you, besides the money, the two swords,—the grand one that King Louis, God bless him, gave me, and the plain one that will really be of use to you if you get into a disturbance. Then here is the most important matter of all. Here are some papers which young Lord Strepp gave me to hold for him when we were comrades in France. I don't know what they are, having had very little time for reading during my life, but do you return them to him. He is now the great Earl of Westport, and he lives in London in a grand house, I hear. In the last campaign in France I had to lend him a pair of breeches or he would have gone bare. These papers are important to him, and he may reward you, but do not you depend on it, for you may get the back of his hand. I have not seen him for years. I am glad I had you taught to read. They read considerably in England, I hear. There is one more cask of the best brandy remaining, and I recommend you to leave for England as soon as it is finished. And now, one more thing, my lad, never be civil to a king's officer. Wherever you see a red coat, depend there is a rogue between the front and the back of it. I have said everything. Push the bottle near me."

Three weeks after my father's burial I resolved to set out, with no more words, to deliver the papers to the Earl of Westport. I was resolved to be prompt in obeying my father's command, for I was extremely anxious to see the world, and my feet would hardly wait for me. I put my estate into the hands of old Mickey Clancy, and told him not to trouble the tenants too much over the rent, or they probably would split his skull for him. And I bid Father Donovan look out for old Mickey Clancy, that he stole from me only what was reasonable.

I went to the Cove of Cork and took ship there for Bristol, and arrived safely after a passage amid great storms which blew us so near Glandore that I feared the enterprise of my own peasantry. Bristol, I confess, frightened me greatly. I had not imagined such a huge and teeming place. All the ships in the world seemed to lie there, and the quays were thick with sailor-men. The streets rang with noise. I suddenly found that I was a young gentleman from the country.

I followed my luggage to the best inn, and it was very splendid, fit to be a bishop's palace. It was filled with handsomely dressed people who all seemed to be yelling, "Landlord! landlord!" And there was a little fat man in a white apron who flew about as if he were being stung by bees, and he was crying, "Coming, sir! Yes, madam! At once, your ludship!" They heeded me no more than if I had been an empty glass. I stood on one leg, waiting until the little fat man should either wear himself out or attend all the people. But it was to no purpose. He did not wear out, nor did his business finish, so finally I was obliged to plant myself in his way, but my speech was decent enough as I asked him for a chamber. Would you believe it, he stopped abruptly and stared at me with sudden suspicion. My speech had been so civil that he had thought perhaps I was a rogue. I only give you this incident to show that if later I came to bellow like a bull with the best of them, it was only through the necessity of proving to strangers that I was a gentleman. I soon learned to enter an inn as a drunken soldier goes through the breach into a surrendering city.

Having made myself as presentable as possible, I came down from my chamber to seek some supper. The supper-room was ablaze with light and well filled with persons of quality, to judge from the noise that they were making. My seat was next to a garrulous man in plum-colour, who seemed to know the affairs of the entire world. As I dropped into my chair he was saying—

"—the heir to the title, of course. Young Lord Strepp. That is he—the slim youth with light hair. Oh, of course, all in shipping. The Earl must own twenty sail that trade from Bristol. He is posting down from London, by the way, tonight."

You can well imagine how these words excited me. I half arose from my chair with the idea of going at once to the young man who had been indicated as Lord Strepp, and informing him of my errand, but I had a sudden feeling of timidity, a feeling that it was necessary to be proper with these people of high degree. I kept my seat, resolving to accost him directly after supper. I studied him with interest. He was a young man of about twenty years, with fair unpowdered hair and a face ruddy from a life in the open air. He looked generous and kindly, but just at the moment he was damning a waiter in language that would have set fire to a stone bridge. Opposite him was a clear-eyed soldierly man of about forty, whom I had heard called "Colonel," and at the Colonel's right was a proud, dark-skinned man who kept looking in all directions to make sure that people regarded him, seated thus with a lord.

They had drunk eight bottles of port, and in those days eight bottles could just put three gentlemen in pleasant humour. As the ninth bottle came on the table the Colonel cried—

"Come, Strepp, tell us that story of how your father lost his papers. Gad, that's a good story."

"No, no," said the young lord. "It isn't a good story, and besides my father never tells it at all. I misdoubt it's truth."

The Colonel pounded the table. "'Tis true. 'Tis too good a story to be false. You know the story, Forister?" said he, turning to the dark-skinned man. The latter shook his head.

"Well, when the Earl was a young man serving with the French he rather recklessly carried with him some valuable papers relating to some estates in the North, and once the noble Earl—or Lord Strepp as he was then—found it necessary, after fording a stream, to hang his breeches on a bush to dry, and then a certain black-guard of a wild Irishman in the corps came along and stole—"

But I had arisen and called loudly but with dignity up the long table, "That, sir, is a lie." The room came still with a bang, if I may be allowed that expression. Every one gaped at me, and the Colonel's face slowly went the colour of a tiled roof.

"My father never stole his lordship's breeches, for the good reason that at the time his lordship had no breeches. 'Twas the other way. My father—"

Here the two long rows of faces lining the room crackled for a moment, and then every man burst into a thunderous laugh. But I had flung to the winds my timidity of a new country, and I was not to be put down by these clowns.

"'Tis a lie against an honourable man and my father," I shouted. "And if my father hadn't provided his lordship with breeches, he would have gone bare, and there's the truth. And," said I, staring at the Colonel, "I give the lie again. We are never obliged to give it twice in my country."

The Colonel had been grinning a little, no doubt thinking, along with everybody else in the room, that I was drunk or crazy; but this last twist took the smile off his face clean enough, and he came to his feet with a bound. I awaited him. But young Lord Strepp and Forister grabbed him and began to argue. At the same time there came down upon me such a deluge of waiters and pot-boys, and, may be, hostlers, that I couldn't have done anything if I had been an elephant. They were frightened out of their wits and painfully respectful, but all the same and all the time they were bundling me toward the door. "Sir! Sir! Sir! I beg you, sir! Think of the 'ouse, sir! Sir! Sir! Sir!" And I found myself out in the hall.

Here I addressed them calmly. "Loose me and takes yourselves off quickly, lest I grow angry and break some dozen of these wooden heads." They took me at my word and vanished like ghosts. Then the landlord came bleating, but I merely told him that I wanted to go to my chamber, and if anybody inquired for me I wished him conducted up at once.

In my chamber I had not long to wait. Presently there were steps in the corridor and a knock at my door. At my bidding the door opened and Lord Strepp entered. I arose and we bowed. He was embarrassed and rather dubious.

"Aw," he began, "I come, sir, from Colonel Royale, who begs to be informed who he has had the honour of offending, sir?"

"'Tis not a question for your father's son, my lord," I answered bluntly at last.

"You are, then, the son of The O'Ruddy?"

"No," said I. "I am The O'Ruddy. My father died a month gone and more."

"Oh!" said he. And I now saw why he was embarrassed. He had feared from the beginning that I was altogether too much in the right. "Oh!" said he again. I made up my mind that he was a good lad. "That is dif—" he began awkwardly. "I mean, Mr. O'Ruddy—oh, damn it all, you know what I mean, Mr. O'Ruddy!"

I bowed. "Perfectly, my lord!" I did not understand him, of course.

"I shall have the honour to inform Colonel Royale that Mr. O'Ruddy is entitled to every consideration," he said more collectedly. "If Mr. O'Ruddy will have the goodness to await me here?"

"Yes, my lord." He was going in order to tell the Colonel that I was a gentle-man. And of course he returned quickly with the news. But he did not look as if the message was one which he could deliver with a glib tongue. "Sir," he began, and then halted. I could but courteously wait. "Sir, Colonel Royale bids me say that he is shocked to find that he has carelessly and publicly inflicted an insult upon an unknown gentleman through the memory of the gentleman's dead father. Colonel

Royale bids me to say, sir, that he is overwhelmed with regret, and that far from taking an initial step himself it is his duty to express to you his feeling that his movements should coincide with any arrangements you may choose to make."

I was obliged to be silent for a considerable period in order to gather head and tail of this marvellous sentence. At last I caught it. "At daybreak I shall walk abroad," I replied, "and I have no doubt that Colonel Royale will be good enough to accompany me. I know nothing of Bristol. Any cleared space will serve."

My Lord Strepp bowed until he almost knocked his forehead on the floor. "You are most amiable, Mr. O'Ruddy. You of course will give me the name of some friend to whom I can refer minor matters?"

I found that I could lie in England as readily as ever I did in Ireland. "My friend will be on the ground with me, my lord; and as he also is a very amiable man it will not take two minutes to make everything clear and fair." Me, with not a friend in the world but Father O'Donovan and Mickey Clancy at Glandore!

Lord Strepp bowed again, the same as before. "Until the morning then, Mr. O'Ruddy," he said, and left me.

I sat me down on my bed to think. In truth I was much puzzled and amazed. These gentlemen were actually reasonable and were behaving like men of heart. Neither my books nor my father's stories—great lies, many of them, God rest him!—had taught me that the duelling gentry could think at all, and I was quite certain that they never tried. "You were looking at me, sir?" "Was I, 'faith? Well, if I care to look at you I shall look at you." And then away they would go at it, prodding at each other's bellies until somebody's flesh swallowed a foot of steel. "Sir, I do not like the colour of your coat!" Clash! "Sir, red hair always offends me." Cling! "Sir, your fondness for rabbit-pie is not polite." Clang!

However, the minds of young Lord Strepp and Colonel Royale seemed to be capable of a process which may be termed human reflection. It was plain that the Colonel did not like the situation at all, and perhaps considered himself the victim of a peculiarly exasperating combination of circumstances. That an Irishman should turn up in Bristol and give him the lie over a French pair of breeches must have seemed astonishing to him, notably when he learned that the Irishman was quite correct, having in fact a clear title to speak authoritatively upon the matter of the breeches. And when Lord Strepp learned that I was The O'Ruddy he saw clearly that the Colonel was in the wrong, and that I had a perfect right to resent the insult to my father's memory. And so the Colonel probably said: "Look you, Strepp. I have no desire to kill this young gentleman, because I insulted his father's name. It is out of all decency. And do you go to him this second time and see what may be done in the matter of avoidance. But, mark you, if he expresses any wishes, you of course offer immediate accommodation. I will not wrong him twice." And so up came my Lord Strepp and hemmed and hawed in that way which puzzled me. A pair of thoughtful, honourable fellows, these, and I admired them greatly.

There was now no reason why I should keep my chamber, since if I now met even the Colonel himself there would be no brawling; only bows. I was not, indeed, fond of these latter,—replying to Lord Strepp had almost broken my back; but, any how, more bows were better than more loud words and another downpour of waiters and pot-boys.

But I had reckoned without the dark-skinned man, Forister. When I arrived in the lower corridor and was passing through it on my way to take the air, I found a large group of excited people talking of the quarrel and the duel that was to be fought at daybreak. I thought it was a great hubbub over a very small thing, but it seems that the mainspring of the excitement was the tongue of this black Forister. "Why, the Irish run naked through their native forests," he was crying. "Their sole weapon is the great knotted club, with which, however, they do not hesitate, when in great numbers, to attack lions and tigers. But how can this barbarian face the sword of an officer of His Majesty's army?"

Some in the group espied my approach, and there was a nudging of elbows. There was a general display of agitation, and I marvelled at the way in which many made it to appear that they had not formed part of the group at all. Only Forister was cool and insolent. He stared full at me and grinned, showing very white teeth. "Swords are very different from clubs, great knotted clubs," he said with admirable deliberation.

"Even so," rejoined I gravely. "Swords are for gentlemen, while clubs are to clout the heads of rogues—thus." I boxed his ear with my open hand, so that he fell against the wall. "I will now picture also the use of boots by kicking you into the inn yard which is adjacent." So saying I hurled him to the great front door which stood open, and then, taking a sort of hop and skip, I kicked for glory and the Saints.

I do not know that I ever kicked a man with more success. He shot out as if he had been heaved by a catapult. There was a dreadful uproar behind me, and I expected every moment to be stormed by the waiter-and-pot-boy regiment. However I could hear some of the gentlemen bystanding cry:

"Well done! Well kicked! A record! A miracle!"

But my first hours on English soil contained still other festivities. Bright light streamed out from the great door, and I could plainly note what I shall call the arc or arcs described by Forister. He struck the railing once, but spun off it, and to my great astonishment went headlong and slap-crash into some sort of an upper servant who had been approaching the door with both arms loaded with cloaks, cushions, and rugs.

I suppose the poor man thought that black doom had fallen upon him from the sky. He gave a great howl as he, Forister, the cloaks, cushions, and rugs spread out grandly in one sublime confusion.

Some ladies screamed, and a bold commanding voice said: "In the devil's name what have we here?" Behind the unhappy servant had been coming two ladies and a very tall gentleman in a black cloak that reached to his heels. "What have we here?" again cried this tall man, who looked like an old eagle. He stepped up to me haughtily. I knew that I was face to face with the Earl of Westport.

But was I a man for ever in the wrong that I should always be giving down and walking away with my tail between my legs? Not I; I stood bravely to the Earl:

"If your lordship pleases, 'tis The O'Ruddy kicking a blackguard into the yard," I made answer coolly.

I could see that he had been about to shout for the landlord and more waiters and pot-boys, but at my naming myself he gave a quick stare.

"The O'Ruddy?" he repeated. "Rubbish!"

He was startled, bewildered; but I could not tell if he were glad or grieved.

"'Tis all the name I own," I said placidly. "My father left it me clear, it being something that he could not mortgage. 'Twas on his death-bed he told me of lending you the breeches, and that is why I kicked the man into the yard; and if your lordship had arrived sooner I could have avoided this duel at daybreak, and, any how, I wonder at his breeches fitting you. He was a small man."

Suddenly the Earl raised his hand. "Enough," he said sternly. "You are your father's son. Come to my chamber in the morning, O'Ruddy."

There had been little chance to see what was inside the cloaks of the ladies, but at the words of the Earl there peeped from one hood a pair of bright liquid eyes—God save us all! In a flash I was no longer a free man; I was a dazed slave; the Saints be good to us!

The contents of the other hood could not have been so interesting, for from it came the raucous voice of a bargeman with a cold:

"Why did he kick him? Whom did he kick? Had he cheated at play? Where has he gone?"

The upper servant appeared, much battered and holding his encrimsoned nose.

"My lord—" he began.

But the Earl roared at him,—

"Hold your tongue, rascal, and in future look where you are going and don't get in a gentleman's way."

The landlord, in a perfect anguish, was hovering with his squadrons on the flanks. They could not think of pouncing upon me if I was noticed at all by the great Earl; but, somewhat as a precaution perhaps, they remained in form for attack. I had no wish that the pair of bright eyes should see me buried under a heap of these wretches, so I bowed low to the ladies and to the Earl and passed out of doors. As I left, the Earl moved his hand to signify that he was now willing to endure the attendance of the landlord and his people, and in a moment the inn rang with hurried cries and rushing feet.

As I passed near the taproom window the light fell full upon a railing; just beneath and over this railing hung two men. At first I thought they were ill, but upon passing near I learned that they were simply limp and helpless with laughter, the sound of which they contrived to keep muffled. To my surprise I recognized the persons of young Lord Strepp and Colonel Royale.

## CHAPTER II

The night was growing, and as I was to fight at daybreak I needed a good rest; but I could not forget that in my pride I had told Lord Strepp that I was provided with a friend to attend me at the duel. It was on my mind. I must achieve a friend, or Colonel Royale might quite properly refuse to fight me on the usual grounds that if he killed me there would be present no adherent of my cause to declare that the fight was fair. And any how I had lied so thoroughly to Lord Strepp. I must have a friend.

But how was I to carve a friend out of this black Bristol at such short notice? My sense told me that friends could not be found in the road like pebbles, but some curious feeling kept me abroad, scanning by the light of the lanterns or the torches each face that passed me. A low dull roar came from the direction of the quay, and this was the noise of the sailor-men, being drunk. I knew that there would be none found there to suit my purpose, but my spirit led me to wander so that I could not have told why I went this way or that way.

Of a sudden I heard from a grassy bank beside me the sound of low and strenuous sobbing. I stopped dead short to listen, moved by instinctive recognition. Aye, I was right. It was Irish keening. Some son of Erin was spelling out his sorrow to the darkness with that profound and garrulous eloquence which is in the character of my people.

"Wirra, wirra! Sorrow the day I would be leaving Ireland against my own will and intention, and may the rocks go out to meet the lugger that brought me here! It's beginning to rain, too! Sure it never rains like this in Ireland! And me without a brass penny to buy a bed! If the Saints save me from England, 'tis al—"

"Come out of that, now!" said I.

The monologue ceased; there was a quick silence. Then the voice, much altered, said: "Who calls? 'Tis may be an Irish voice!"

"It is," said I. "I've swallowed as much peat smoke as any man of my years. Come out of that now, and let me have a look at you."

He came trustfully enough, knowing me to be Irish, and I examined him as well as I was able in the darkness. He was what I expected, a bedraggled vagabond with tear-stains on his dirty cheeks and a vast shock of hair which I well knew would look, in daylight, like a burning haycock. And as I examined him he just as carefully examined me. I could see his shrewd blue eyes twinkling.

"You are a red man," said I. "I know the strain; 'tis better than some. Your family must have been very inhospitable people." And then, thinking that I had spent enough time, I was about to give the fellow some coin and send him away. But here a mad project came into my empty head. I had ever been the victim of my powerful impulses, which surge up within me and sway me until I can only gasp at my own con duct. The sight of this red-headed scoundrel had thrust an idea into my head, and I was a lost man.

"Mark you!" said I to him. "You know what I am?"

"'Tis hard to see in the dark," he answered; "but I mistrust you are a gentleman, sir. McDermott of the Three Trees had a voice and a way with him like you, and Father Burk too, and he was a gentleman born if he could only remain sober."

"Well, you've hit it, in the dark or whatever," said I. "I am a gentleman. Indeed I am an O'Ruddy. Have you ever been hearing of my family?"

"Not of your honour's branch of it, sure," he made answer confidently. "But I have often been hearing of the O'Ruddys of Glandore, who are well known to be such great robbers and blackguards that their match is not to be found in all the south of Ireland. Nor in the west, neither, for that matter."

"Aye," said I, "I have heard that that branch of the family was much admired by the peasantry for their qualities. But let us have done with it and speak of other matters. I want a service of you."

"Yes, your honour," said he, dropping his voice. "May be 'twill not be the first time I've been behind a ditch; but the light tonight is very bad unless I am knowing him well, and I would never be forgetting how Tim Malone let fly in the dark of a night like this, thinking it was a bailiff, until she screamed out with the pain in her leg, the poor creature, and her beyond seventy and a good Catholic."

"Come out of it now!" said I impatiently. "You will be behind no ditch." And as we walked back to the inn I explained to my new man the part I wished him to play. He was amazed at it, and I had to explain fifty times; but when it once was established in his red head Paddy was wild with enthusiasm, and I had to forbid him telling me how well he would do it.

I had them give him some straw in the stable, and then retired to my chamber for needed rest. Before dawn I had them send Paddy to me, and by the light of a new fire I looked at him. Ye Saints! What hair! It must have been more than a foot in length, and the flaming strands radiated in all directions from an isolated and central spire which shot out straight toward the sky. I knew what to do with his tatters, but that crimson thatch dumfounded me. However there was no going back now, so I set to work upon him. Luckily my wardrobe represented three generations of O'Ruddy clothes, and there was a great plenty. I put my impostor in a suit of blue velvet with a flowered waistcoat and stockings of pink. I gave him a cocked hat and a fine cloak. I worked with success up to the sword-belt, and there I was checked. I had two swords, but only one belt. However, I slung the sword which King Louis had given my father on a long string from Paddy's neck and sternly bid him keep his cloak tight about him. We were ready.

"Now, Paddy," said I, "do you bow in this manner." I bowed as a gentleman should. But I will not say how I strove with him. I could do little in that brief space. If he remained motionless and kept his tongue still he was somewhat near his part, but the moment he moved he was astonishing. I depended on keeping him under my eye, and I told him to watch me like a cat. "Don't go thinking how grand you are, that way," I cried to him angrily. "If you make a blunder of it, the gentle men will cudgel you, mark you that. Do you as I direct you. And the string, curse you. Mind your cloak!" The villain had bethought him of his flowered waistcoat, and with a comic air flung back his coat to display it. "Take your fingers out of your mouth. Stop scratching your shin with your foot. Leave your hair alone. 'Tis as good and as bad as you can make it. Come along now, and hold your tongue like a graven image if you would not be having me stop the duel to lather you."

We marched in good order out of the inn. We saw our two gentlemen awaiting us, wrapped in their cloaks, for the dawn was cold. They bowed politely, and as I returned their salute I said in a low, quick aside to Paddy:

"Now, for the love of God, bow for your life!"

My intense manner must have frightened the poor thing, for he ducked as swiftly as if he had been at a fair in Ireland and somebody had hove a cobble at his head.

"Come up!" I whispered, choking with rage. "Come up! You'll be breaking your nose on the road."

He straightened himself, looking somewhat bewildered, and said:

"What was it? Was I too slow? Did I do it well?"

"Oh, fine," said I. "Fine. You do it as well as that once more, and you will probably break your own neck, and 'tis not me will be buying masses for your soul, you thief. Now don't drop as if a gamekeeper had shot at you. There is no hurry in life. Be quiet and easy."

"I mistrusted I was going too fast," said he; "but for the life of me I couldn't pull up. If I had been the Dublin mail, and the road thick as fleas with highwaymen, I should have gone through them grand."

My Lord Strepp and Colonel Royale had not betrayed the slightest surprise at the appearance of my extraordinary companion. Their smooth, regular faces remained absolutely imperturbable. This I took to be very considerate of them, but I gave them just a little more than their due, as I afterward perceived when I came to understand the English character somewhat. The great reason was that Paddy and I were foreigners. It is not to be thought that gentlemen of their position would have walked out for a duel with an Englishman in the party of so fantastic an appearance. They would have placed him at once as a person impossible and altogether out of their class. They would have told a lackey to kick this preposterous creation into the horse-pond. But since Paddy was a foreigner he was possessed of some curious license, and his grotesque ways could be explained fully in the simple phrase, "'Tis a foreigner."

So, then, we preceded my Lord Strepp and Colonel Royale through a number of narrow streets and out into some clear country. I chose a fine open bit of green turf as a goodly place for us to meet, and I warped Paddy through the gate and moved to the middle of the field. I drew my sword and saluted, and then turned away. I had told Paddy everything which a heaven-sent sense of instruction could suggest, and if he failed I could do no more than kill him.

After I had kicked him sharply he went aside with Lord Strepp, and they indulged in what sounded like a very animated discussion. Finally I was surprised to see Lord Strepp approaching me. He said:

"It is very irregular, but I seem unable to understand your friend. He has proposed to me that the man whose head is broken first—I do not perfectly understand what he could mean by that; it does not enter our anticipations that a man could possibly have his head broken—he has proposed that the man whose head may be broken first should provide 'lashings'—I feel sure that is the word—lashings of meat and drink at some good inn for the others. Lashings is a word which I do not know. We do not know how to understand you gentlemen when you speak of lashings. I am instructed to meet any terms which you may suggest, but I find that I cannot make myself clear to your friend who speaks of nothing but lashings."

"Sir," said I, as I threw coat and waistcoat on the grass, "my friend refers to a custom of his own country. You will, I feel sure, pardon his misconception of the circumstances. Pray accept my regrets, and, if you please, I am ready."

He immediately signified that his mind was now clear, and that the incident of Paddy's lashings he regarded as closed. As for that flame-headed imp of crime, if I could have got my hands upon him he would have taken a short road to his fathers. Him and his lashings! As I stood there with a black glare at him, the impudent scoundrel repeatedly winked at me with the readable information that if I only would be patient and bide a moment he would compass something very clever. As I faced Colonel Royale I was so wild with thinking of what I would do to Paddy, that, for all I knew, I might have been crossing swords with my mother.

And now as to this duel. I will not conceal that I was a very fine fencer in both the French and Italian manners. My father was in his day one of the finest blades in Paris, and had fought with some of the most skillful and impertinent gentlemen in all France. He had done his best to give me his eye and his wrist, and sometimes he would say that I was qualified to meet all but the best in the world. He commonly made fun of the gentlemen of England, saying that a dragoon was their ideal of a man with a sword; and he would add that the rapier was a weapon which did not lend itself readily to the wood-chopper's art. He was all for the French and Italian schools.

I had always thought that my father's judgment was very good, but I could not help reflecting that if it turned out to be bad I would have a grievance as well as a sword-thrust in the body. Colonel Royale came at me in a somewhat leisurely manner, and, as I said, my mind was so full of rage at Paddy that I met the first of my opponent's thrusts through sheer force of habit. But my head was clear a moment later, and I knew that I was fighting my first duel in England and for my father's honour. It was no time to think of Paddy.

Another moment later I knew that I was the Colonel's master. I could reach him where I chose. But he did not know it. He went on prodding away with a serious countenance, evidently under the impression that he had me hard put to it. He was as grave as an owl-faced parson. And now here I did a sorry thing. I became the victim of another of my mad impulses. I was seized with an ungovernable desire to laugh. It was hideous. But laugh I did, and, of necessity, square in the Colonel's face. And to this day I regret it.

Then the real duel began. At my laugh the Colonel instantly lost his grave air, and his countenance flushed with high, angry surprise. He beset me in a perfect fury, caring no more for his guard than if he had been made of iron. Never have I seen such quick and tremendous change in a man. I had laughed at him under peculiar conditions: very well, then; he was a demon. Thrice my point pricked him to keep him off, and thrice my heart was in my mouth that he would come on regardless. The blood oozed out on his white ruffled shirt; he was panting heavily, and his eyes rolled. He was a terrible sight to face. At last I again touched him, and this time sharply and in the sword arm, and upon the instant my Lord Strepp knocked our blades apart.

"Enough," he cried sternly. "Back, Colonel! Back!"

The Colonel flung himself sobbing into his friend's arms, choking out, "O God, Strepp! I couldn't reach him. I couldn't reach him, Strepp! Oh, my God!"

At the same time I disappeared, so to speak, in the embrace of my red-headed villain, who let out an Irish howl of victory that should have been heard at Glandore. "Be quiet, rascal," I cried, flinging him off. But he went on with his howling until I was obliged forcibly to lead him to a corner of the field, where he exclaimed:

"Oh, your honour, when I seen the other gentleman, all blazing with rage, rush at you that way, and me with not so much as a tuppence for all my service to you excepting these fine clothes and the sword, although I am thinking I shall have little to do with swords if this is the way they do it, I said, 'Sorrow the day England saw me!'"

If I had a fool for a second, Colonel Royale had a fine, wise young man. Lord Strepp was dealing firmly and coolly with his maddened principal.

"I can fight with my left hand," the Colonel was screaming. "I tell you, Strepp, I am resolved! Don't bar my way! I will kill him! I will kill him!"

"You are not in condition to fight," said the undisturbed young man. "You are wounded in four places already. You are in my hands. You will fight no more today."

"But, Strepp!" wailed the Colonel. "Oh, my God, Strepp!"

"You fight no more today," said the young lord.

Then happened unexpected interruptions. Paddy told me afterward that during the duel a maid had looked over a wall and yelled, and dropped a great brown bowl at sight of our occupation. She must have been the instrument that aroused the entire county, for suddenly men came running from everywhere. And the little boys! There must have been little boys from all over England.

"What is it? What is it?"

"Two gentlemen have been fighting!"

"Oh, aye, look at him with the blood on him!"

"Well, and there is young my Lord Strepp. He'd be deep in the matter, I warrant you!"

"Look yon, Bill! Mark the gentleman with the red hair. He's not from these parts, truly. Where, think you, he comes from?"

"'Tis a great marvel to see such hair, and I doubt not he comes from Africa."

They did not come very near, for in those days there was little the people feared but a gentleman, and small wonder. However, when the little boys judged that the delay in a resumption of the fight was too prolonged, they did not hesitate to express certain unconventional opinions and commands.

"Hurry up, now!"

"Go on!"

"You're both afeared!"

"Begin! Begin!"

"Are the gentlemen in earnest?"

"Sirs, do you mean ever to fight again? Begin, begin."

But their enthusiasm waxed high after they had thoroughly comprehended Paddy and his hair.

"You're alight, sir; you're alight!"

"Water! Water!"

"Farmer Pelton will have the officers at you an you go near his hay. Water!"

Paddy understood that they were paying tribute to his importance, and he again went suddenly out of my control. He began to strut and caper and pose with the air of knowing that he was the finest gentleman in England.

"Paddy, you baboon," said I, "be quiet and don't be making yourself a laughing-stock for the whole of them."

But I could give small heed to him, for I was greatly occupied in watching Lord Strepp and the Colonel. The Colonel was listening now to his friend for the simple reason that the loss of blood had made him too weak to fight again. Of a sudden he slumped gently down through Lord Strepp's arms to the ground, and, as the young man knelt, he cast his eyes about him until they rested upon me in what I took to be mute appeal. I ran forward, and we quickly tore his fine ruffles to pieces and succeeded in quite stanching his wounds, none of which were serious. "'Tis only a little blood-letting," said my Lord Strepp with something of a smile. "'Twill cool him, perchance."

"None of them are deep," I cried hastily. "I—"

But Lord Strepp stopped me with a swift gesture. "Yes," he said, "I knew. I could see. But—" He looked at me with troubled eyes. "It is an extraordinary situation. You have spared him, and—he will not wish to be spared, I feel sure. Most remarkable case."

"Well, I won't kill him," said I bluntly, having tired of this rubbish. "Damme if I will!"

Lord Strepp laughed outright. "It is ridiculous," he said. "Do you return, O'Ruddy, and leave me the care of this business. And," added he, with embarrassed manner, "this mixture is full strange; but—I feel sure—any how, I salute you, sir." And in his bow he paid a sensible tribute to my conduct.

Afterward there was nought to do but gather in Paddy and return to the inn. I found my countryman swaggering to and fro before the crowd. Some ignoramus, or some wit, had dubbed him the King of Ireland, and he was playing to the part.

"Paddy, you red-headed scandal," said I, "come along now!"

When he heard me, he came well enough; but I could not help but feel from his manner that he had made a great concession.

"And so they would be taking me for the King of Ireland, and, sure, 'tis an advantage to be thought a king whatever, and if your honour would be easy 'tis you and me that would sleep in the finest beds in Bristol the night, and nothing to do but take the drink as it was handed and—I'll say no more."

A rabble followed us on our way to the inn, but I turned on them so fiercely from time to time that ultimately they ran off. We made direct for my chamber, where I ordered food and drink immediately to be served. Once alone there with Paddy I allowed my joy to take hold on me. "Eh, Paddy, my boy," said I, walking before him, "I have done grand. I am, indeed, one of the finest gentlemen in the world."

"Aye, that's true," he answered, "but there was a man at your back throughout who—"

To his extreme astonishment I buffeted him heavily upon the cheek. "And we'll have no more of that talk," said I.

# CHAPTER III

"Aye!" said Paddy, holding his jowl; "'tis what one gets for serving a gentleman. 'Tis the service of a good truthful blackguard I'd be looking for, and that's true for me."

"Be quiet and mind what I tell you," I cried to him. "I'm uplifted with my success in England, and I won't be hearing anything from you while I am saying that I am one of the grandest gentlemen in all the world. I came over here with papers—papers!" said I; and then I bethought me that I would take the papers and wave them in my hand. I don't know why people wish to wave important documents in their hands, but the impulse came to me. Above all things I wished to take these papers and wave them defiantly, exultantly, in the air. They were my inheritance and my land of promise; they were everything. I must wave them even to the chamber, empty save for Paddy.

When I reached for them in the proper place in my luggage they were gone. I wheeled like a tiger upon Paddy.

"Villain," I roared, grasping him at the throat, "you have them!"

He sank in full surrender to his knees.

"I have, your honour," he wailed; "but, sure, I never thought your honour would care, since one of them is badly worn at the heel, and the other is no better than no boot at all."

I was cooled by the incontestable verity of this man. I sat heavily down in a chair by the fire.

"Aye," said I stupidly, "the boots! I did not mean the boots, although when you took them passes my sense of time. I mean some papers."

"Some papers!" cried he excitedly. "Your honour never thought it would be me that would steal papers? Nothing less than good cows would do my people, and a bit of turf now and then, but papers—"

"Peace!" said I sombrely, and began to search my luggage thoroughly for my missing inheritance. But it was all to no purpose. The papers were not there. I could not have lost them. They had been stolen. I saw my always-flimsy inheritance melt away. I had been, I thought, on the edge of success, but I now had nothing but my name, a successful duel, and a few pieces of gold. I was buried in defeat.

Of a sudden a name shot through my mind. The name of this black Forister was upon me violently and yet with perfect sureness. It was he who had stolen the papers. I knew it. I felt it in every bone. He had taken the papers.

I have since been told that it is very common for people to be moved by these feelings of omen, which are invariably correct in their particulars; but at the time I thought it odd that I should be so certain that Forister had my papers. However, I had no time to waste in thinking. I grasped my pistols. "A black man—black as the devil," cried I to Paddy. "Help me catch a little black man."

"Sure!" said Paddy, and we sallied forth.

In a moment I was below and crying to the landlord in as fine a fury as any noble:

"This villain Forister! And where be he?"

The landlord looked at me with bulging eyes. "Master Forister," he stammered. "Aye—aye—he's been agone these many hours since your lordship kicked him. He took horse, he did, for Bath, he did."

"Horses!" I roared. "Horses for two gentlemen!" And the stableyard, very respectful since my duel, began to ring with cries. The landlord pleaded something about his bill, and in my impatience I hurled to him all of my gold save one piece.

The horses came soon enough, and I leaped into the saddle and was away to Bath after Forister. As I galloped out of the inn yard I heard a tumult behind me, and, looking back, I saw three hostlers lifting hard at Paddy to raise him into the saddle. He gave a despairing cry when he perceived me leaving him at such speed, but my heart was hardened to my work. I must catch Forister.

It was a dark and angry morning. The rain swept across my face, and the wind flourished my cloak. The road, glistening steel and brown, was no better than an Irish bog for hard riding. Once I passed a chaise with a flogging post-boy and steaming nags. Once I overtook a farmer jogging somewhere on a fat mare. Otherwise I saw no travellers.

I was near my journey's end when I came to a portion of the road which dipped down a steep hill. At the foot of this hill was an oak-tree, and under this tree was a man masked and mounted, and in his hand was a levelled pistol.

"Stand!" he said. "Stand!"

I knew his meaning, but when a man has lost a documentary fortune and given an innkeeper all but his last guinea, he is sure to be filled with fury at the appearance of a third and completing misfortune. With a loud shout I drew my pistol and rode like a demon at the highwayman. He fired, but his bullet struck nothing but the flying tails of my cloak. As my horse crashed into him I struck at his pate with my pistol. An instant later we both came a mighty downfall, and when I could get my eyes free of stars I arose and drew my sword. The highwayman sat before me on the ground, ruefully handling his skull. Our two horses were scampering away into the mist.

I placed my point at the highwayman's throat.

"So, my fine fellow," cried I grandly, "you rob well. You are the principal knight of the road of all England, I would dare say, by the way in which an empty pistol overcomes you."

He was still ruefully handling his skull.

"Aye," he muttered sadly, more to himself than to me, "a true knight of the road with seven ballads written of me in Bristol and three in Bath. Ill betide me for not minding my mother's word and staying at home this day. 'Tis all the unhappy luck of Jem Bottles. I should have remained an honest sheep-stealer and never engaged in this dangerous and nefarious game of lifting purses."

The man's genuine sorrow touched me. "Cheer up, Jem Bottles," said I. "All may yet be well. 'Tis not one little bang on the crown that so disturbs you?"

"'Tis not one—no," he answered gloomily; "'tis two. The traveller riding to the east before you dealt me a similar blow—may hell catch the little black devil."

"Black!" cried I. "Forister, for my life!"

"He took no moment to tell me his name," responded the sullen and wounded highwayman. "He beat me out of the saddle and rode away as brisk as a bird. I know not what my mother will say. She be for ever telling me of the danger in this trade, and here come two gentlemen in one day and unhorse me without the profit of a sixpence to my store. When I became a highwayman I thought me I had profited me from the low estate of a sheep-stealer, but now I see that happiness in this life does not altogether depend upon—"

"Enough," I shouted in my impatience. "Tell me of the black man! The black man, worm!" I pricked his throat with my sword very carefully.

"He was black, and he rode like a demon, and he handled his weapons finely," said Jem Bottles. "And since I have told you all I know, please, good sir, move the point from my throat. This will be ill news for my mother."

I took thought with myself. I must on to Bath; but the two horses had long since scampered out of sight, and my pursuit of the papers would make small way afoot.

"Come, Jem Bottles," I cried, "help me to a horse in a comrade's way and for the sake of your mother. In another case I will leave you here a bloody corse. Come; there's a good fellow!"

He seemed moved to help me. "Now, if there comes a well-mounted traveller," he said, brightening, "I will gain his horse for you if I die for it."

"And if there comes no well-mounted traveller?"

"I know not, sir. But—perhaps he will come."

"'Tis a cheap rogue who has but one horse," I observed contemptuously. "You are only a footpad, a simple-minded marquis of the bludgeon."

Now, as I had hoped, this deeply cut his pride.

"Did I not speak of the ballads, sir?" he demanded with considerable spirit. "Horses? Aye, and have I not three good nags hid behind my mother's cottage, which is less than a mile from this spot?"

"Monsieur Jem Bottles," said I, not forgetting the French manners which my father had taught me, "unless you instantly show me the way to these horses I shall cut off your hands, your feet, and your head; and, ripping out your bowels, shall sprinkle them on the road for the first post-horses to mash and trample. Do you understand my intention, Monsieur Jem Bottles?"

"Sir," he begged, "think of my mother!"

"I think of the horses," I answered grimly. "'Tis for you to think of your mother. How could I think of your mother when I wouldn't know her from the Head of Kinsale, if it didn't happen that I know the Head of Kinsale too well to mistake it for anybody's mother?"

"You speak like a man from foreign parts, sir," he rejoined in a meek voice; "but I am able to see that your meaning is serious."

"'Tis so serious," said I, rapping him gently on the head with the butt of my pistol, "that if you don't instantly display a greedy activity you will display a perfect inability to move."

"The speeching is obscure," said he, "but the rap on the head is clear to me. Still, it was not kind of you to hit me on the same spot twice."

He now arose from his mournful seat on the ground, and, still rubbing his pate, he asked me to follow him. We moved from the highway into a very narrow lane, and for some time proceeded in silence.

"'Tis a regular dog's life," spoke Jem Bottles after a period of reflection.

By this time I had grown a strong sympathy for my scoundrel.

"Come, cheer yourself, Jem Bottles," said I. "I have known a lesser ruffian who was hanged until he was dry, whereas you march along the lane with nought to your discouragement but three cracks in your crown."

"'Tis not the cracks in the crown," he answered moodily. "'Tis what my mother will say."

"I had no thought that highwaymen had mothers," said I. I had resolved now to take care of his pride, for I saw that he was bound to be considered a great highwayman, and I did not wish to disturb his feelings until I gained possession of one of the horses. But now he grew as indignant as he dared.

"Mother? Mother, sir? Do you think me an illegitimate child? I say to you flat in your face, even if you kill me the next instant, that I have a mother. Perchance I am not of the lofty gentry who go about beating honest highwaymen to the earth, but

I repulse with scorn any man's suggestion that I am illegitimate. In a quarter of an hour you shall see my mother for yourself."

"Peace, Jem Bottles," said I soothingly. "I took no thought of such a thing. I would be thinking only of the ballads, and how honourable it is that a gallant and dashing life should be celebrated in song. I, for certain, have never done anything to make a pothouse ring with my name, and I liken you to the knights of olden days who tilted in all simple fair bravery without being able to wager a brass farthing as to who was right and who was wrong. Admirable Jem Bottles," I cried enthusiastically, "tell me, if you will, of your glories; tell me with your own tongue, so that when I hear the ballads waxing furious with praise of you, I shall recall the time I marched with your historic person."

"My beginning was without pretence," said the highwayman. "Little Susan, daughter of Farmer Hants, was crossing the fields with a basket of eggs. I, a masked figure, sprang out at her from a thicket. I seized the basket. She screamed. There was a frightful tumult. But in the end I bore away this basket of eight eggs, creeping stealthily through the wood. The next day Farmer Hants met me. He had a long whip. There was a frightful tumult. But he little knew that he was laying with his whip the foundation of a career so illustrious. For a time I stole his sheep, but soon grew weary of this business. Once, after they had chased me almost to Bristol, I was so weary that I resolved to forego the thing entirely. Then I became a highwayman, whom you see before you. One of the ballads begins thus:

> *"What ho! the merry Jem!*
> *Not a pint he gives for them. All his—"*

"Stop," said I, "we'll have it at Dame Bottles's fireside. Hearing songs in the night air always makes me hoarse the next morning."

"As you will," he answered without heat. "We're a'most there."

Soon a lighted window of the highwayman's humble home shone out in the darkness, and a moment later Jem Bottles was knocking at the door. It was immediately opened, and he stalked in with his blood-marks still upon his face. There was a great outcry in a feminine voice, and a large woman rushed forward and flung her arms about the highwayman.

"Oh, Jemmie, my son, my son!" she screamed, "whatever have they done to ye this time?"

"Silence, mother dear," said Bottles. "'Tis nought but a wind-broken bough fallen on my head. Have you no manners? Do you not see the gentleman waiting to enter and warm himself?"

The woman turned upon me, alarmed, but fiery and defiant. After a moment's scrutiny she demanded:

"Oh, ho, and the gentleman had nought to do of course with my Jem's broken head?"

"'Tis a priest but newly arrived from his native island of Asia," said Bottles piously; "and it ill beseems you, mother dear, to be haggling when you might be getting the holy man and I some supper."

"True, Jemmie, my own," responded Dame Bottles. "But there are so many rogues abroad that you must forgive your old mother if she grow often affrighted that her good Jemmie has been misled." She turned to me. "Pardon, my good gentleman," she said almost in tears. "Ye little know what it is to be the mother of a high-spirited boy."

"I can truthfully say that I do not, Dame Bottles," said I, with one of my father's French bows. She was immensely pleased. Any woman may fall a victim to a limber, manly, and courteous bow.

Presently we sat down to a supper of plum-stew and bread. Bottles had washed the blood from his face and now resembled an honest man.

"You may think it strange, sir," said Dame Bottles with some housewifely embarrassment, "that a highwayman of such distinction that he has had written of him in Bristol six ballads—"

"Seven," said the highwayman.

"Seven in Bristol and in Bath two."

"Three," said the highwayman.

"And three in Bath," continued the old woman. "You may think it strange, sir, that a highwayman of such distinction that he has had written of him in Bristol seven ballads, and in Bath three, is yet obliged to sit down to a supper of plum-stew and bread."

"Where is the rest of that cheese I took on last Michaelmas?" demanded Bottles suddenly.

"Jemmie," answered his mother with reproach, "you know you gave the last of it to the crippled shepherd over on the big hill."

"So I did, mother dear," assented the highwayman, "and I regret now that I let no less than three cheeses pass me on the highway because I thought we had plenty at home."

"If you let anything pass on the road because you do not lack it at the moment, you will ultimately die of starvation, Jemmie dear," quoth the mother. "How often have I told you?"

"Aye," he answered somewhat irritably, "you also often have told me to take snuff-boxes."

"And was I at fault," she retorted, "because the cheating avarice of the merchants led them to make sinful, paltry snuff-boxes that were mere pictures of the good old gold and silver? Was it my mischief? Or was it the mischief of the plotting swineherds who now find it to their interest to deal in base and imitative metals?"

"Peace, my mother," said the highwayman. "The gentleman here has not the same interest in snuff-boxes which moves us to loud speech."

"True," said Dame Bottles, "and I readily wish that my Jemmie had no reason to care if snuff-boxes were made from cabbage-leaves."

I had been turning a scheme in my mind, and here I thought I saw my opportunity to introduce it. "Dame Bottles," said I, "your words fit well with the plan which has brought me here to your house. Know you, then, that I am a nobleman—"

"Alack, poor Jemmie!" cried the woman, raising her hands.

"No," said I, "I am not a nobleman rampant. I am a nobleman in trouble, and I need the services of your son, for which I will reward him with such richness that he will not care if they make snuff-boxes out of water or wind. I am in pursuit of a man—"

"The little black man," cried the alert Bottles.

"And I want your son to ride with me to catch this thief. He need never pass through the shadow of the creeping, clanking tree. He will be on an honest hunt to recover a great property. Give him to me. Give him fourteen guineas from his store, and bid us mount his horses and away. Save your son!"

The old woman burst into tears. "Sir," she answered, "I know little of you, but, as near as I can see in the light of this one candle, you are a hangel. Take my boy!

Treat him as you would your own stepson, and if snuff-boxes ever get better I will let you both hear of it."

Less than an hour later Jem Bottles and I were off for Bath, riding two very good horses.

## CHAPTER IV

Now my whole mind was really bent on finding my black Forister, but yet, as Jem Bottles and I rode toward Bath, I thought of a cloaked figure and a pair of shining eyes, and it seemed to me that I recalled the curve of sweet, proud lips. I knew that I should be thinking of my papers, my future; but a quick perversity made me dwell for a long trotting time in a dream of feminine excellence, in a dream of feminine beauty which was both ascetic and deeply sensuous. I know hardly how to say that two eyes, a vision of lips, a conception of a figure, should properly move me as I bounced along the road with Jem Bottles. But it is certain that it came upon me. The eyes of the daughter of the great Earl of Westport had put in chains the redoubtable O'Ruddy. It was true. It was clear. I admitted it to myself. The admission caused a number of reflections to occur in my mind, and the chief of these was that I was a misfortunate wretch.

Jem Bottles recalled me to the immediate business.

"'Tis the lights of Bath, sir," he said, "and if it please you, sir, I shall await you under yonder tree, since the wretched balladists have rendered me so well known in the town that I dare not venture in it for fear of a popular welcome from the people who have no snuff-boxes whatever."

"I will go and listen to the ballads," I replied, "and in the mean time do you await me here under that tree."

So saying I galloped into Bath, my soul sharp to find Forister and to take him by the neck and strangle out of him those papers which were my sole reasons for living. But the landlord of the best inn met me with an unmistakable frankness.

"Mr. Forister?" said he. "Yes, your lordship, but Mr. Forister is gone back to Bristol."

I was so pleased with his calling me "your lordship" that I hesitated a moment. But I was recalled to sense by the thought that although Jem Bottles and I had fifteen guineas between us, he had fourteen and I had the one. Thanking the landlord I galloped out of Bath.

Bottles was awaiting me under the tree. "To Bristol," I cried. "Our chase lies toward Bristol. He has doubled back."

"'Twas while we were at supper," said Bottles, as he cantered up to my shoulder. "I might have had two trials at him if I had not had the honour of meeting your worship. I warrant you, sir, he would not have escaped me twice."

"Think of his crack in your skull, and be content," I replied. "And in the mean time ride for Bristol."

Within five miles of Bristol we came upon a wayside inn in which there was progressing a great commotion. Lights flashed from window to window, and we could hear women howling. To my great surprise Bottles at once became hugely excited.

"Damme, sir," he shouted, "my sweetheart is a chambermaid here, and if she be hurted I will know it."

He spurred valiantly forward, and, after futilely calling to him to check his career, I followed. He leaped from his horse at the door of the inn and bounced into the place, pistol in hand. I was too confused to understand much, but it seemed to my ears that his entrance was hailed with a roar of relief and joy. A stable-boy, fearfully anxious, grasped my bridle, crying, "Go in, sir, in God's name. They will be killing each other." Thinking that, whatever betide, it was proper to be at the back of my friend Bottles, I too sprang from my horse and popped into the inn.

A more unexpected sight never met my experienced gaze. A fat landlady, mark you, was sobbing in the arms of my villainous friend, and a pretty maid was clinging to his arm and screaming. At the same time there were about him a dozen people of both sexes who were yelling,—

"Oh, pray, Master Bottles! Good Master Bottles, do stop them. One is a great Afric chief, red as a fire, and the other is Satan, Satan himself! Oh, pray, good Master Bottles, stop them!"

My fine highwayman was puffed out like a poisoned frog. I had no thought that he could be so grand.

"What is this disturbance?" he demanded in a bass voice.

"O good Master Bottles," clamoured the people. "Satan wishes to kill the Red Giant, who has Satan barred in the best room in the inn. And they make frightful destruction of chairs and tables. Bid them cease, O good Master Bottles!"

From overhead we could hear the sound of blows upon wood mingled with threatening talk.

"Stand aside," said the highwayman in a great gruff voice which made me marvel at him. He unhesitatingly dumped the swooning form of the landlady into another pair of arms, shook off the pretty maid, and moved sublimely upon the foot of the stairs amid exclamations of joy, wonder, admiration, even reverence.

But the voice of an unseen person hailed suddenly from the head of the stairs.

"And if ye have not said enough masses for your heathen soul," remarked the voice, "you would be better mustering the neighbours this instant to go to church for you and bid them do the best they can in a short time. You will never be coming downstairs if you once come up."

Bottles hesitated; the company shuddered out: "'Tis the Red Giant."

"And I would be having one more word with you," continued the unseen person. "I have him here, and here I keep him. 'Tis not me that wants the little black rogue, what with his hammering on the door and his calling me out of my name. 'Tis no work that I like, and I would lever go in and put my heel in his face. But I was told to catch a little black man, and I have him, and him I will keep. 'Tis not me that wished to come here and catch little black men for anybody; but here I am in this foreign country, catching little black men, and I will have no interference."

But here I gave a great call of recognition.

"Paddy!"

I saw the whole thing. This wild-headed Paddy, whom I had told to catch me a little black man, had followed after me toward Bath and somehow managed to barricade in a room the very first man he saw who was small and black. At first I wished to laugh; an instant later I was furious.

"Paddy," I thundered; "come down out of that now! What would you be doing? Come down out of that now!"

The reply was sulky, but unmistakably from Paddy. Most of it was mumbled.

"Sure I've gone and caught as little and as black a man as is in the whole world, and was keeping the scoundrel here safe, and along he comes and tells me to come down out of that now with no more gratitude than if he had given me a gold goose. And yet I fought a duel for him and managed everything so finely that he came away well enough to box me on the ear, which was mere hilarity and means nothing between friends."

Jem Bottles was still halted on the stair. He and all the others had listened to Paddy's speeches in a blank amazement which had much superstition in it.

"Shall I go up, sir?" he asked, not eagerly.

"No," said I. "Leave me to deal with it. I fear a great mistake. Give me ten minutes, and I promise to empty the inn of all uproar."

A murmur of admiration arose, and as the sound leaped about my ears I moved casually and indifferently up against Paddy. It was a grand scene.

"Paddy," I whispered as soon as I had reached a place on the stairs safe from the ears of the people below. "Paddy, you have made a great blunder. You have the wrong man."

"'Tis unlikely," replied Paddy with scorn. "You wait until you see him, and if he is not little and black, then—"

"Yes, yes," said I hastily, "but it was not any little black man at all which I wanted. It was a particular little black man."

"But," said the ruffian brightly, "it would be possible this one will serve your end. He's little and he's black."

At this moment the voice of the captive came intoning through the door of a chamber.

"When I am free I will first cut out your liver and have it grilled, and feed it to you as you are dying."

Paddy had stepped forward and placed his lips within about six inches of one of the panels.

"Come now, be easy!" he said. "You know well that if you should do as you say, I would beat your head that it would have the looks of a pudding fallen from a high window, and that's the truth."

"Open the door, rascal," called the captive, "and we shall see."

"I will be opening no doors," retorted Paddy indignantly. "Remain quiet, you little black devil, or, by the mass, I'll—"

"I'll slice your heart into pieces of paper," thundered Paddy's prisoner, kicking and pounding.

By this time I was ready to interfere. "Paddy," said I, catching him by the shoulder, "you have the wrong man. Leave it to me; mind you, leave it to me."

"He's that small and black you'd think—" he began dejectedly, but I cut him short.

Jem Bottles, unable to endure the suspense, had come up from below. He was still bristling and blustering, as if all the maids were remarking him.

"And why does this fine gentleman kick and pound on the door?" he demanded in a gruff voice loud enough to be heard in all appreciative parts of the inn. "I'll have him out and slit his nose."

The thunder on the door ceased, and the captive observed:

"Ha! another scoundrel! If my ears do not play me false, there are now three waiting for me to kick them to the hangman."

Restraining Paddy and Bottles, who each wished to reply in heroic verse to this sally, I stepped to the door.

"Sir," said I civilly, "I fear a great blunder has been done. I—"

"Why," said the captive with a sneer, "'tis the Irishman! 'Tis the king of the Irelands. Open the door, pig."

My elation knew no bounds.

"Paddy," cried I, "you have the right little black man." But there was no time for celebration. I must first answer my enemy. "You will remember that I kicked you once," said I, "and if you have a memory as long as my finger be careful I do not kick you again, else even people as far away as the French will think you are a meteor. But I would not be bandying words at long range. Paddy, unbar the door."

"If I can," muttered Paddy, fumbling with a lot of machinery so ingenious that it would require a great lack of knowledge to thoroughly understand it. In the mean time we could hear Forister move away from the door, and by the sound of a leisurely scrape of a chair on the floor I judge he had taken his seat somewhere near the centre of the room. Bottles was handling his pistol and regarding me.

"Yes," said I, "if he fires, do you pepper him fairly. Otherwise await my orders. Paddy, you slug, unbar the door."

"If I am able," said Paddy, still muttering and fumbling with his contrivances. He had no sooner mouthed the words than the door flew open as if by magic, and we discovered a room bright with the light of a fire and candles. Forister was seated negligently at a table in the centre of the room. His legs were crossed, but his naked sword lay on the table at his hand. He had the first word, because I was amazed, almost stunned, by the precipitous opening of the door.

"Ho! ho!" he observed frigidly, "'tis indeed the king of the Irelands, accompanied by the red-headed duke who has entertained me for some time, and a third party with a thief's face who handles a loaded pistol with such abandon as leads me to suppose that he once may have been a highwayman. A very pretty band."

"Use your tongue for a garter, Forister," said I. "I want my papers."

## CHAPTER V

"Your 'papers'?" said Forister. "Damn you and your papers. What would I know of your papers?"

"I mean," said I fiercely, "the papers that you stole out of my chamber in the inn at Bristol."

The man actually sank back in his chair and laughed me up to the roof.

"'Papers'!" he shouted. "Here's the king of the Irelands thinking that I have made off with his papers!"

"You choose a good time for laughing," said I, with more sobriety. "In a short time you will be laughing with the back of your head."

He sat up and looked at me with quick decision.

"Now, what is all this rubbish about papers?" he said sharply. "What have I to do with your filthy papers? I had one intention regarding you,—of that I am certain. I was resolved to kill you on the first occasion when we could cross swords, but— 'papers'—faugh! What do you mean?"

The hoarse voice of Jem Bottles broke in from somewhere behind me. "We might easily throw him to the earth and tie him, sir, and then make search of him."

"And you would know how to go about the business, I warrant me," laughed Forister. "You muzzle-faced rogue, you!"

To my astonishment the redoubtable highwayman gave back before the easy disdain of this superior scoundrel.

"My ways may not always have been straight and narrow, master," he rejoined, almost in a whine, "but you have no call to name me muzzle-faced."

Forister turned from him contemptuously and fixed his regard with much enthusiasm upon Paddy.

"Very red," said he. "Very red, indeed. And thick as fagots, too. A very delectable head of hair, fit to be spun into a thousand blankets for the naked savages in heathen parts. The wild forests in Ireland must indeed be dark when it requires a lantern of this measure to light the lonely traveller on his way."

But Paddy was an honest man even if he did not know it, and he at once walked to Forister and held against his ear a fist the size of a pig's hind-leg.

"I cannot throw the talk back to you," he said. "You are too fast for me, but I tell you to your face that you had better change your tongue for a lock of an old witch's hair unless you intend to be battered this moment."

"Peace," said Forister calmly. "I am a man of natural wit, and I would entertain myself. Now, there is your excellent chieftain the king of the Irelands. Him I regard as a very good specimen, whose ancestors were not very long ago swinging by their tails from the lofty palms of Ireland and playing with cocoanuts to and fro." He smiled and leaned back, well satisfied with himself.

All this time I had been silent, because I had been deep in reflection upon Forister. Now I said:

"Forister, you are a great rogue. I know you. One thing is certain. You have not my papers and never did you have them."

He looked upon me with some admiration and cried:

"Aye, the cannibal shows a glimmer of reason. No, I have not your foolish papers, and I only wish I had them in order to hurl the bundle at your damned stupid head."

"For a kicked man you have a gay spirit," I replied. "But at any rate I have no time for you now. I am off to Bristol after my papers, and I only wish for the sake of ease that I had to go no farther than this chamber. Come, Paddy! Come, Jem!"

My two henchmen were manifestly disappointed; they turned reluctantly at my word.

"Have I the leave of one crack at him, your honour?" whispered Paddy earnestly. "He said my head was a lantern."

"No," said I, "leave him to his meditations."

As we passed down the corridor we heard him laugh loudly, and he called out to me,—

"When I come to Bristol I will kill you."

I had more than a mind to go back and stuff this threat into his throat, but I better knew my business, which was to recover the papers.

"Come," said I, and we passed down stairs.

The people of the inn made way for Paddy as if he had been a falling tree, and at the same time they worshipped Jem Bottles for having performed everything. I had some wonder as to which would be able to out-strut the other. I think Jem Bottles won the match, for he had the advantage of being known as one of the most dangerous men in southwestern England, whereas Paddy had only his vanity to help him.

"'Tis all arranged," said Bottles pompously. "Your devil will come forth as quiet as a rabbit."

We ordered our horses, and a small crowd of obsequious stable-boys rushed to fetch them. I marvelled when I saw them lead out Paddy's horse. I had thought from what I perceived over my shoulder when I left Bristol that he would never be able to make half a league in the saddle. Amid the flicker of lanterns, Bottles and I mounted and then I heard Paddy calling to him all the stable-boys:

"Now, when I give the word, you heave for your lives. Stand, you beast! Cannot four of you hold him by the legs? I will be giving the word in a moment. Are you all ready? Well, now, ready again—heave!"

There was a short scuffle in the darkness, and presently Paddy appeared above the heads of the others in the *mêlée*.

"There, now," said he to them, "that was well done. One would easily be telling that I was an ex-trooper of the king." He rode out to us complacently. "'Tis a good horse, if only he steered with a tiller instead of these straps," he remarked, "and he goes well before the wind."

"To Bristol," said I. "Paddy, you must follow as best you may. I have no time to be watching you, although you are interesting."

An unhappy cry came from behind Bottles, and I spurred on, but again I could not wait for my faithful countryman. My papers were still the stake for which I played. However I hoped that Paddy would now give over his ideas about catching little black men.

As we neared Bristol Jem Bottles once more be came backward. He referred to the seven ballads, and feared that the unexpected presence of such a well-known character would create an excitement which would not be easy to cool. So we made a rendezvous under another tree, and I rode on alone. Thus I was separated from both my good companions. However, before parting, I took occasion to borrow five guineas from Jem's store.

I was as weary as a dog, although I had never been told that gentlemen riding amid such adventures were ever aweary. At the inn in Bristol a sleepy boy took my horse, and a sleepy landlord aroused himself as he recognized me.

"My poor inn is at your disposal, sir," he cried as he bowed. "The Earl has inquired for you today, or yesterday, as well as my young Lord Strepp and Colonel Royale."

"Aye?" said I carelessly. "Did they so? Show me to a chamber. I am much en-wearied. I would seek a good bed and a sound sleep, for I have ridden far and done much since last I had repose."

"Yes, sir," said the landlord deferentially.

After a long hard sleep I was aroused by a constant pounding on my door. At my cry a servant entered. He was very abject. "His lordship's valet has been waiting to give you a message from his lordship, sir." I bid him let the valet enter. The man whose heroic nose had borne the brunt of Forister's swift departure from the inn when I kicked him came into my chamber with distinguished grace and dignity and informed me that his noble master cared to see me in his chamber when it would suit my convenience.

Of course the old Earl was after his papers. And what was I to tell him,—that I was all befooled and befuddled?—that after my father had kept these papers for so many years in faithful trust I had lost them on the very brink of deliverance of them to their rightful owner? What was I to speak?

I did not wish to see the Earl of Westport, but some sudden and curious courage forced me into my clothes and out to the corridor. The Earl's valet was waiting there. "I pray you, sir, follow me," he said. I followed him to an expensive part of the inn, where he knocked upon a door. It was opened by a bending serving-man. The room was a kind of parlour, and in it, to my surprise, were Lord Strepp and Colonel Royale. They gazed at me with a surprise equivalent to mine own.

Young Lord Strepp was the first one thoroughly to collect himself. Then he advanced upon me with outstretched hand.

"Mr. O'Ruddy," he cried, "believe me, we are glad to see you. We thought you had gone for all time."

Colonel Royale was only a moment behind his friend, but as he extended his hand his face flushed painfully.

"Sir," he said somewhat formally, "not long ago I lost my temper, I fear. I know I have to thank you for great consideration and generosity. I—I—you—"

Whereupon we both began to stammer and grimace. All the time I was chocking out:

"Pray—pray—, don't speak of it—a—nothing—in truth, you kindly exaggerate—I—"

It was young Lord Strepp who brought us out of our embarrassment. "Here, you two good fellows," he cried heartily, "a glass of wine with you."

We looked gratefully at him, and in the business of filling our glasses we lost our awkwardness. "To you," said Lord Strepp; and as we drained our wine I knew that I had two more friends in England.

During the drinking the Earl's valet had been hovering near my coat-tails. Afterward he took occasion to make gentle suggestion to me:

"His lordship awaits your presence in his chamber, sir, when it pleases you."

The other gentlemen immediately deferred to my obligation, and I followed the valet into a large darkened chamber. It was some moments before my eyes could discover that the Earl was abed. Indeed, a rasping voice from beneath the canopies called to me before I knew that anybody was in the chamber but myself and the valet.

"Come hither, O'Ruddy," called the Earl. "Tompkins, get out! Is it your duty to stand there mummified? Get out!"

The servant hastily withdrew, and I walked slowly to the great man's bedside. Two shining shrewd eyes looked at me from a mass of pillows, and I had a knowledge of an aged face, half smiling and yet satirical, even malignant.

"And so this is the young fortune-hunter from Ireland," he said in a hoarse sick-man's voice. "The young fortune-hunter! Ha! With his worthless papers! Ha!"

"Worthless?" cried I, starting.

"Worthless!" cried the Earl vehemently. He tried to lift himself in his bed, in order to make more emphasis. "Worthless! Nothing but straw—straw—straw!" Then he cackled out a laugh.

And this was my inheritance! I could have sobbed my grief and anger, but I took firm hold on myself and resolved upon another way of dealing with the nobleman.

"My lord," said I coolly, "My father is dead. When he was dying he gave certain papers into my hands,—papers which he had guarded for many years,—and bade me, as his son, to deliver them into the hands of an old friend and comrade; and I come to this old friend and comrade of my father, and he lies back in his bed and cackles at me like a hen. 'Tis a small foot I would have set upon England if I had known more of you, you old skate!"

But still he laughed and cried: "Straw! Straw! Nothing but straw!"

"Well, sir," said I with icy dignity, "I may be a fool of an Irishman with no title save an older one than yours; but I would be deeply sorry if there came a day when I should throw a trust back in the teeth of a dead comrade's son."

"No," said the bright-eyed old man, comforting himself amid his pillows. "Look you, O'Ruddy! You are a rascal! You came over in an attempt to ruin me! I know it!"

I was awed by this accusation. It seemed to me to be too grand, too gorgeous for my personal consumption. I knew not what to do with this colossus. It towered above me in splendour and gilt. I had never expected to be challenged with attempting to ruin earls. My father had often ruined sea-captains, but he never in his life ruined so much as a baronet. It seemed altogether too fine for my family, but I could only blurt weakly, "Yessir." I was much like a lackey.

"Aye," said the old man, suddenly feeble from the excitement, "I see you admit it, you black Irish rogue." He sank back and applied a napkin to his mouth. It seemed to come away stained with blood. "You scoundrel!"

I had a strange cowardly inclination to fling myself upon this ancient survival and squeeze his throat until it closed like a pursel. And my inclination was so strong that I stood like a stone.

The valet opened the door. "If it please your Lordship—Lady Mary," he announced, and stood aside to let a lady pass. The Earl seemed immediately to forget my presence. He began at once to make himself uncomfortable in his bed. Then he cried fretfully: "Come, Mary, what caused you to be so long? Make me easy! Ruffle my pillows! Come, daughter."

"Yes, father," answered a soothing and sweet voice. A gracious figure passed before me and bended over the bed of the Earl. I was near blinded. It was not a natural blindness. It was an artificial blindness which came from my emotion. Was she tall? I don't know. Was she short? I don't know. But I am certain that she was exactly of the right size. She was, in all ways, perfection. She was of such glory, she was so splendid, that my heart ceased to beat. I remained standing like a stone, but my sword scabbard, reminiscent of some movement, flapped gently against my leg. I thought it was a horrible sound. I sought to stay it, but it continued to tinkle, and I remember that, standing there in the room with the old Earl and my love-'til-death, I thought most of my scabbard and its inability to lay quiet at my thigh.

She smoothed his bed and coaxed him and comforted him. Never had I seen such tenderness. It was like a vision of a classic hereafter. In a second I would have exchanged my youth for the position of this doddering old nobleman who spat blood into a napkin.

Suddenly the Earl wheeled his eyes and saw me.

"Ha, Mary!" he cried feebly, "I wish to point out a rogue. There he stands! The O'Ruddy! An Irishman and a fine robber! Mark him well, and keep stern watch of your jewels."

The beautiful young lady turned upon me an affrighted glance. And I stood like a stone.

"Aye," said the old wretch, "keep stern watch of your jewels. He is a very demon for skill. He could take a ring from your finger while you were thinking he was fluttering his hands in the air."

I bowed gallantly to the young lady. "Your rings are safe, my lady. I would ill requite the kindness shown by your father to the son of an old friend if I deprived your white fingers of a single ornament."

"Clever as ever, clever as ever," chuckled the wicked old man.

The young lady flushed and looked first at me and then at her father. I thought her eye, as it rested upon me, was not without some sympathetic feeling. I adored her. All the same I wished to kill her father. It is very curious when one wishes to kill the father of the woman one adores. But I suppose the situation was made more possible for me by the fact that it would have been extremely inexpedient to have killed the Earl in his sick bed. I even grinned at him.

"If you remember my father, your lordship," said I amiably, "despite your trying hard to forget him, you will remember that he had a certain native wit which on occasion led him to be able to frustrate his enemies. It must have been a family trait, for I seem to have it. You are an evil old man! You yourself stole my papers!"

# CHAPTER VI

At first I thought that my speech had given the aged Earl a stroke. He writhed on his bed, and something appeared at his lips which was like froth. His lovely daughter sprang to him with a cry of fear and woe. But he was not dying; he was only mad with rage.

"How dare you? How dare you?" he gasped. "You whelp of Satan!"

"'Tis me that would not be fearing to dare anything," I rejoined calmly. "I would not so. I came here with a mind for fair words, but you have met me with insult and something worse. We cannot talk the thing. We must act it. The papers are yours, but you took them from me unfairly. You may destroy them. Otherwise I will have them back and discover what turned you into a great rogue near the end of your days."

"Hearken!" screamed the Earl. "Hearken! He threatens." The door into the parlour flew open, and Lord Strepp and Colonel Royale appeared on the threshold, their faces blank with wonder.

"Father," cried the young lord, stepping hastily forward, "whatever is wrong?"

"That!" screamed the Earl, pointing a palsied finger at me. "That! He comes here and threatens *me*,—a peer of England."

The Lady Mary spoke swiftly to her brother and the Colonel.

"'Tis a sick man's fancy," she said. "There have been no threats. Father has had a bad day. He is not himself. He talks wildly. He—"

"Mary!" yelled the Earl as well as he was able. "Do you betray me? Do you betray your own father? Oh, a woman Judas and my daughter!"

Lord Strepp and Colonel Royale looked as if their minds were coming apart. They stared at Lady Mary, at the Earl, at me. For my part I remained silent and stiff in a corner, keeping my eye upon the swords of the other gentlemen. I had no doubt but that presently I would be engaged in a desperate attempt to preserve my life. Lady Mary was weeping. She had never once glanced in my direction. But I was thrilling with happiness. She had flung me her feeble intercession even as a lady may fling a bun to a bear in a pit, but I had the remembrance to prize, to treasure, and if both gentlemen had set upon me and the sick Earl had advanced with the warming-pan I believe my new strength would have been able to beat them off.

In the meantime the Earl was screeching meaningless rubbish in which my name, with epithets, occurred constantly. Lady Mary, still weeping, was trying to calm him.

Young Lord Strepp at last seemed to make up his mind. He approached me and remarked:

"An inexplicable situation, Mr. O'Ruddy."

"More to me than to you," I repeated suavely.

"How?" he asked, with less consideration in his manner. "I know nought of this mummery."

"At least I know no more," I replied, still suave.

"How, Mr. O'Ruddy?" he asked, frowning. "I enter and find you wrangling with my father in his sick chamber. Is there to be no word for this?"

"I dare say you will get forty from your father; a hundred, it may be," said I, always pleasant. "But from me you will get none."

He reflected for a moment. "I dare say you understand I will brook no high-handed silence in a matter of this kind. I am accustomed to ask for the reasons for certain kinds of conduct, and of course I am somewhat prepared to see that the reasons are forthcoming."

"Well, in this case, my lord," said I with a smile, "you can accustom yourself to not getting a reason for a certain kind of conduct, because I do not intend to explain myself."

But at this moment our agreeable conversation was interrupted by the old Earl who began to bay at his son. "Arthur, Arthur, fling the rascal out; fling the rascal out! He is an impostor, a thief!" He began to fume and sputter, and threw his arms wildly; he was in some kind of convulsion; his pillows tossed, and suddenly a packet fell from under them to the floor. As all eyes wheeled toward it, I stooped swiftly and picked it up.

"My papers!" said I.

On their part there was a breathless moment of indecision. Then the swords of Lord Strepp and the Colonel came wildly from their scabbards. Mine was whipped out no less speedily, but I took it and flung it on the floor at their feet, the hilt toward them. "No," said I, my hands empty save for the papers, "'tis only that I would be making a present to the fair Lady Mary, which I pray her to receive." With my best Irish bow I extended to the young lady the papers, my inheritance, which had caused her father so much foaming at the mouth.

She looked at me scornfully, she looked at her father, she looked at me pathetically, she looked at her father, she looked at me piteously; she took the papers.

I walked to the lowering and abashed points of the other men's swords, and picked my blade from the floor. I paid no heed to the glittering points which flashed near my eyes. I strode to the door; I turned and bowed; as I did so, I believe I saw something in Lady Mary's eyes which I wished to see there. I closed the door behind me.

But immediately there was a great clamour in the room I had left, and the door was thrown violently open again. Colonel Royale appeared in a high passion:

"No, no, O'Ruddy," he shouted, "you are a gallant gentleman. I would stake my life that you are in the right. Say the word, and I will back you to the end against ten thousand fiends."

And after him came tempestuously young Lord Strepp, white on the lips with pure rage. But he spoke with a sudden steadiness.

"Colonel Royale, it appears," he said, "thinks he has to protect my friend The O'Ruddy from some wrong of my family or of mine?"

The Colonel drew in his breath for a dangerous reply, but I quickly broke in:

"Come, come, gentlemen," said I sharply. "Are swords to flash between friends when there are so many damned scoundrels in the world to parry and pink? 'Tis wrong; 'tis very wrong. Now, mark you, let us be men of peace at least until tomorrow morning, when, by the way, I have to fight your friend Forister."

"Forister!" they cried together. Their jaws fell; their eyes bulged; they forgot everything; there was a silence.

"Well," said I, wishing to reassure them, "it may not be tomorrow morning. He only told me that he would kill me as soon as he came to Bristol, and I expect him tonight or in the morning. I would of course be expecting him to show here as quickly as possible after his grand speech; but he would not be entirely unwelcome, I am thinking, for I have a mind to see if the sword of an honest man, but no fighter, would be able to put this rogue to shame, and him with all his high talk about killing people who have never done a thing in life to him but kick him some number of feet out into the inn yard, and this need never to have happened if he had known enough to have kept his sense of humour to himself, which often happens in this world."

Reflectively, Colonel Royale murmured:

"One of the finest swordsmen in England."

For this I cared nothing.

Reflectively, Lord Strepp murmured: "My father's partner in the shipping trade."

This last made me open my eyes. "Your father's partner in the shipping trade, Lord Strepp? That little black rascal?"

The young nobleman looked sheepish.

"Aye, I doubt not he may well be called a little black rascal, O'Ruddy," he answered; "but in fact he is my father's partner in certain large—fairly large, you know—shipping interests. Of course that is a matter of no consequence to me personally—but—I believe my father likes him, and my mother and my sister are quite fond of him, I think. I, myself, have never been able to quite—quite understand him in certain ways. He seems a trifle odd at moments. But he certainly is a friend of the family."

"Then," said I, "you will not be able to have the felicity of seeing him kill me, Lord Strepp."

"On the contrary," he rejoined considerately, "I would regard it as usual if he asked me to accompany him to the scene of the fight."

His remark, incidentally, that his sister was fond of Forister, filled me with a sudden insolent madness.

"I would hesitate to disturb any shipping trade," I said with dignity. "It is far from me to wish that the commerce of Great Britain should be hampered by sword-thrust of mine. If it would please young Lord Strepp, I could hand my apologies to Forister all tied up in blue-silk ribbon."

But the youthful nobleman only looked at me long with a sad and reproachful gaze.

"O'Ruddy," he said mournfully, "I have seen you do two fine things. You have never seen me do anything. But, know you now, once and for all, that you may not quarrel with me."

This was too much for an Irish heart. I was moved to throw myself on this lad's neck. I wished to swear to him that I was a brother in blood, I wished to cut a vein to give him everlasting strength—but per haps his sister Mary had something to do with this feeling.

Colonel Royale had been fidgeting. Now he said suddenly:

"Strepp, I wronged you. Your pardon, Mr. O'Ruddy; but, damme, Strepp, if I didn't think you had gone wrong for the moment."

Lord Strepp took the offered hand. "You are a stupid old firebrain," he said affectionately to the Colonel.

"Well," said the Colonel jubilantly, "now everything is clear. If Mr. O'Ruddy will have me, I will go with him to meet this Forister; and you, Strepp, will accompany Forister; and we all will meet in a friendly way—ahem!"

"The situation is intimately involved," said Lord Strepp dejectedly. "It will be a ridiculous business—watching each blade lunge toward the breast of a friend. I don't know that it is proper. Royale, let us set ourselves to part these duellists. It is indecent."

"Did you note the manner in which he kicked him out of the inn?" asked the Colonel. "Do you think a few soothing words would calm the mind of one of the finest swordsmen in England?"

I began to do some profound thinking.

"Look you, Colonel," said I. "Do you mean that this wretched little liar and coward is a fine swordsman?"

"I haven't heard what you call him," said the Colonel, "but his sword-play is regular firelight on the wall. However," he added hopefully, "we may find some way to keep him from killing you. I have seen some of the greatest swordsmen lose by chance to a novice. It is something like cards. And yet you are not an ignorant player. That, I, Clarence Royale, know full well. Let us try to beat him."

I remembered Forister's parting sentence. Could it be true that a man I had kicked with such enthusiasm and success was now about to take revenge by killing me? I was really disturbed. I was a very brave youth, but I had the most advanced ideas about being killed. On occasion of great danger I could easily and tranquilly develop a philosophy of avoidance and retirement. I had no antiquated notions about going out and getting myself killed through sheer bull-headed scorn of the other fellow's hurting me. My father had taught me this discretion. As a soldier he claimed that he had run away from nine battles, and he would have run away from more, he said, only that all the others had turned out to be victories for his side. He was admittedly a brave man, but, more than this, he had a great deal of sense. I was the child of my father. It did not seem to me profitable to be killed for the sake of a sentiment which seemed weak and dispensable. This little villain! Should I allow him to gratify a furious revenge because I was afraid to take to my heels? I resolved to have the courage of my emotions. I would run away.

But of all this I said nothing. It passed through my mind like light and left me still smiling gayly at Colonel Royale's observations upon the situation.

"Wounds in the body from Forister," quoth he academically, "are almost certain to be fatal, for his wrist has a magnificent twist which reminds one of a top. I do not know where he learned this wrist movement, but almost invariably it leads him to kill his man. Last year I saw him—I digress. I must look to it that O'Ruddy has quiet, rest, and peace of mind until the morning."

Yes; I would have great peace of mind until the morning! I saw that clearly.

"Well," said I, "at any rate we will know more tomorrow. A good day to you, Lord Strepp, and I hope your principal has no more harm come to him than I care to have come to me, which is precious little, and in which case the two of us will be little hurt."

"Good-bye, O'Ruddy," said the young man.

In the corridor the Colonel slapped my shoulder in a sudden exuberant outburst.

"O'Ruddy," he cried, "the chance of your life! Probably the best-known swordsman in all England! 'Pon my word, if you should even graze him, it would almost make you a peer. If you truly pinked him, you could marry a duchess. My eye, what an opportunity for a young and ambitious man."

"And what right has he to be such a fine swordsman?" I demanded fretfully. "Damn him! 'Tis no right of a little tadpole like him to be a great cut-throat. One could never have told from the look of him, and yet it simply teaches one to be always cautious with men."

The Colonel was bubbling over with good nature, his mind full of the prospective event.

"I saw Ponsonby kill Stewart in their great fight several years agone," he cried, rubbing his hands, "but Ponsonby was no such swordsman as Forister, and I misdoubt me that Stewart was much better than you yourself."

Here was a cheerful butcher. I eyed him coldly.

"And out of this," said I slowly, "comes a vast deal of entertainment for you, and a hole between two ribs for me. I think I need a drink."

"By all means, my boy," he answered, heartily. "Come to my chamber. A quart of port under your waistcoat will cure a certain bilious desire in you to see the worst of things, which I have detected lately in your manner. With grand sport before us, how could you be otherwise than jolly? Ha, Ha!"

So saying, he affectionately took my arm and led me along the corridor.

## CHAPTER VII

When I reached my own chamber I sank heavily into a chair. My brain was in a tumult. I had fallen in love and arranged to be killed in one short day's work. I stared at my image in a mirror. Could I be The O'Ruddy? Perhaps my name was Paddy or Jem Bottles? Could I pick myself out in a crowd? Could I establish my identification? I little knew.

At first I thought of my calm friend who apparently drank blood for his breakfast. Colonel Royale to me was somewhat of a stranger, but his charming willingness to grind the bones of his friends in his teeth was now quite clear. I fight the best swordsman in England as an amusement, a show? I began to see reasons for returning to Ireland. It was doubtful if old Mickey Clancy would be able to take full care of my estate even with the assistance and prevention of Father Donovan. All properties looked better while the real owner had his eye on them. It would be a shame to waste the place at Glandore all for a bit of pride of staying in England. Never a man neglected his patrimony but that it didn't melt down to a kick in the breeches and much trouble in the courts. I perceived, in short, that my Irish lands were in danger. What could endanger them was not quite clear to my eye, but at any rate they must be saved. Moreover it was necessary to take quick measures. I started up from my chair, hastily recounting Jem Bottles's five guineas.

But I bethought me of Lady Mary. She could hardly be my good fairy. She was rather too plump to be a fairy. She was not extremely plump, but when she walked something moved within her skirts. For my part I think little of fairies, who remind me of roasted fowl's wing. Give me the less brittle beauty which is not likely to break in a man's arms.

After all, I reflected, Mickey Clancy could take care quite well of that estate at Glandore; and, if he didn't, Father Donovan would soon bring him to trouble; and, if Father Donovan couldn't, why, the place was worth very little any how. Besides, 'tis a very weak man who cannot throw an estate into the air for a pair of bright eyes.

Aye, and Lady Mary's bright eyes! That was one matter. And there was Forister's bright sword. That was another matter. But to my descendants I declare that my hesitation did not endure an instant. Forister might have an arm so supple and a sword so long that he might be able to touch the nape of his neck with his own point, but I was firm on English soil. I would meet him even if he were a *chevaux de frise*. Little it mattered to me. He might swing the ten arms of an Indian god; he might yell like a gale at sea; he might be more terrible in appearance than a volcano in its passions; still I would meet him.

There was a knock, and at my bidding a servant approached and said: "A gentleman, Mr. Forister, wishes to see you, sir."

For a moment I was privately in a panic. Should I say that I was ill, and then send for a doctor to prove that I was not ill? Should I run straightway and hide under the bed? No!

"Bid the gentleman enter," said I to the servant.

Forister came in smiling, cool and deadly. "Good day to you, Mr. O'Ruddy," he said, showing me his little teeth. "I am glad to see that you are not for the moment consorting with highwaymen and other abandoned characters who might succeed in corrupting your morals, Mr. O'Ruddy. I have decided to kill you, Mr. O'Ruddy. You may have heard that I am the finest swordsman in England, Mr. O'Ruddy?"

I replied calmly: "I have heard that you are the finest swordsman in England, Mr. Forister, whenever better swordsmen have been traveling in foreign parts, Mr. Forister, and when no visitors of fencing distinction have taken occasion to journey here, Mr. Forister."

This talk did not give him pleasure, evidently. He had entered with brave composure, but now he bit his lip and shot me a glance of hatred. "I only wished to announce," he said savagely, "that I would prefer to kill you in the morning as early as possible."

"And how may I render my small assistance to you, Mr. Forister? Have you come to request me to arise at an untimely hour?"

I was very placid; but it was not for him to be coming to my chamber with talk of killing me. Still, I thought that, inasmuch as he was there, I might do some good to myself by irritating him slightly. I continued:

"I today informed my friends—"

"Your friends!" said he.

"My friends," said I. "Colonel Royale in this matter."

"Colonel Royale!" said he.

"Colonel Royale," said I. "And if you are bound to talk more you had best thrust your head from the window and talk to those chimneys there, which will take far more interest in your speech than I can work up. I was telling you that today I informed my friends—then you interrupted me. Well, I informed them—but what the devil I informed them of you will not know very soon. I can promise you, however, it was not a thing you would care to hear with your hands tied behind you."

"Here's a cold man with a belly full of ice," said he musingly. "I have wronged him. He has a tongue on him, he has that. And here I have been judging from his appearance that he was a mere common dolt. And, what, Mr. O'Ruddy," he added, "were you pleased to say to the gentlemen which I would not care to hear with my hands tied behind me?"

"I told them why you took that sudden trip to Bristol," I answered softly.

He fairly leaped in a sudden wild rage. "You—told them?" he stuttered. "You poltroon! 'Twas a coward's work!"

"Be easy," said I, to soothe him. "'Tis no more cowardly than it is for the best swordsman in England to be fighting the worst swordsman in Ireland over a matter in which he is entirely in the wrong, although 'tis not me that cares one way or another way. Indeed, I prefer you to be in the wrong, you little black pig."

"Stop," said he, with a face as white as milk. "You told them—you told them about—about the girl at Bristol?"

"What girl at Bristol?" said I innocently. "'Tis not me to be knowing your wenches in Bristol or otherwheres."

A red flush came into the side of his neck and swelled slowly across his cheeks. "If you've told them about Nell!"

"Nell?" said I. "Nell? Yes, that's the name. Nell. Yes, Nell. And if I told them about Nell?"

"Then," he rejoined solemnly, "I shall kill you ten times if I lose my soul in everlasting hell for it."

"But after I have killed you eleven times I shall go to Bristol and have some sweet interviews with fair Nell," said I. This sting I expected to call forth a terrific outburst, but he remained scowling in dark thought. Then I saw where I had been wrong. This Nell was now more a shame than a sweetheart, and he was afraid that word had been passed by me to the brother of—Here was a chance to disturb him. "When I was making my little joke of you and your flame at Bristol," said I thoughtfully, "I believe there were no ladies present. I don't remember quite. Any how we will let that pass. 'Tis of no consequence."

And here I got him in full cry. "*God rot you!*" he shrieked. His sword sprang and whistled in the air.

"Hold," said I, as a man of peace. "'Twould be murder. My weapon is on the bed, and I am too lazy to go and fetch it. And in the mean time let me assure you that no word has crossed my lips in regard to Nell, your Bristol sweetheart, for the very excellent reason that I never knew of her existence until you yourself told me some moments ago."

Never before had he met a man like me. I thought his under-jaw would drop on the floor.

"Up to a short time ago," said I candidly, "your indecent amours were safe from my knowledge. I can be in the way of putting myself as silent as a turtle when it comes to protecting a man from his folly with a woman. In fact, I am a gentleman. But," I added sternly, "what of the child?"

"The child?" he cried jumping. "May hell swallow you! And what may you know of the child?"

I waved my hand in gentle deprecation of his excitement as I said:

"Peace, Forister; I know nothing of any child. It was only an observation by a man of natural wit who desired to entertain himself. And, pray, how old is the infant?"

He breathed heavily. "You are a fiend," he answered. Keeping his eyes on the floor, he deliberated upon his choice of conduct. Presently he sheathed his sword and turned with some of his old jauntiness toward the door. "Very good," said he. "Tomorrow we shall know more of our own affairs."

"True," I replied.

"We shall learn if slyness and treachery are to be defeated by fair-going and honour."

"True," said I.

"We shall learn if a snake in the grass can with freedom bite the foot of a lion."

"True," said I.

There was a loud jovial clamour at the door, and at my cry it flew open. Colonel Royale entered precipitately, beaming with good humour.

"O'Ruddy, you rascal," he shouted, "I commanded you to take much rest, and here I find—" He halted abruptly as he perceived my other visitor. "And here I find," he repeated coldly, "here I find Mr. Forister."

Forister saluted with finished politeness. "My friend and I," he said, "were discussing the probabilities of my killing him in the morning. He seems to think that he has some small chance for his life, but I have assured him that any real betting man would not wager a grain of sand that he would see the sun go down tomorrow."

"Even so," rejoined the Colonel imperturbably.

"And I also suggested to my friend," pursued Forister, "that tomorrow I would sacrifice my ruffles for him, although I always abominate having a man's life-blood about my wrists."

"Even so," quoth the undisturbed Colonel.

"And further I suggested to my friend that if he came to the ground with a coffin on his back, it might promote expedition after the affair was over."

Colonel Royale turned away with a gesture of disgust.

I thought it was high time to play an ace at Forister and stop his babble, so I said: "And when Mr. Forister had finished his graceful remarks we had some talk regarding Mr. Forister's affairs in Bristol, and I confess I was much interested in hearing about the little—"

Here I stopped abruptly, as if I had been interrupted by Forister; but he had given me no sign but a sickly grin.

"Eh, Forister?" said I. "What's that?"

"I was remarking that I had nothing further to say for the present," he replied, with superb insolence. "For the time I am quite willing to be silent. I bid you a good day, sirs."

## CHAPTER VIII

As the door closed upon Forister, Colonel Royale beat his hand passionately against the wall. "O'Ruddy," he cried, "if you could severely maim that cold-blooded bully, I would be willing to adopt you as my legitimate grandfather. I would indeed."

"Never fear me," said I. "I shall pink him well."

"Aye," said my friend, looking at me mournfully, "I ever feared your Irish light-heartedness. 'Twill not do to be confident. He is an evil man, but a great swordsman. Now I never liked Ponsonby, and Stewart was the most lovable of men; but in the great duel Ponsonby killed—"

"No," I interrupted, "damn the duel between Ponsonby and Stewart. I'm sick of it. This is to be the duel between The O'Ruddy and Forister, and it won't be like the other."

"Eh, well," said the Colonel good-naturedly; "make your mind easy. But I hope to God you lay him flat."

"After I have finished with him," said I in measured tones, "he will be willing to sell himself as a sailor to go to the Indies; only, poor devil, he won't be able to walk, which is always a drawback after a hard fight, since it leaves one man incapable on the ground and thus discloses strong evidence of a struggle."

I could see that Colonel Royale had no admiration for my bragging air, but how otherwise was I to keep up my spirits? With all my discouragements it seemed to me that I was privileged to do a little fine lying. Had my father been in my place, he would have lied Forister into such a corner that the man would be thinking that he had the devil for an opponent. My father knew more about such matters.

Still I could not help but be thinking how misfortunate it was that I had kicked a great swordsman out of this inn at Bristol when he might have been a harmless shoemaker if I had only decent luck. I must make the best of it, and for this my only method was to talk loudly,—to myself, if need be; to others if I could. I was not the kind that is quite unable to say a good word for itself even if I was not able to lie as well as my father in his prime. In his day he could lie the coat off a man's back, or the patches off a lady's cheek, and he could lie a good dog into howling ominously. Still it was my duty to lie as well as I was able.

After a time Lord Strepp was announced and entered. Both he and Colonel Royale immediately stiffened and decided not to perceive each other. "Sir," said Lord Strepp to me, "I have the honour to present my compliments to you, and to request that you join a friend of mine, Mr. Forister, at dawn tomorrow, in the settlement of a certain small misunderstanding."

"Sir," said I, in the same manner, "I am only too happy to have this little matter adjusted."

"And of course the arrangements, sir?"

"For them I may refer you to my friend Colonel Royale."

"Ah," said the young Lord, as if he had never before seen the Colonel.

"I am at your service, sir," said Colonel Royale as if he never in his whole life had heard of Lord Strepp.

Then these two began to salaam one another, and mouth out fool phrases, and cavort and prance and caracole, until I thought them mad. When they departed there was a dreadful scene. Each refused to go through the door before the other. There was a frightful deadlock. They each bowed and scraped and waved their hands, and surrendered the doorway back and forth, until I thought they were to be in my chamber eternally. Lord Strepp gorgeously presented the right of way to Colonel Royale, and the Colonel gorgeously presented the right of way to Lord Strepp. All this time they were bending their backs at each other.

Finally I could stand it no longer. "In God's name," I shouted, "the door is wide enough for the two of you. Take it together. You will go through like grease. Never fear the door. 'Tis a good wide door."

To my surprise, they turned to glance at me and burst into great laughter. Then they passed out amiably enough together. I was alone.

Well, the first thing I did was to think. I thought with all my force. I fancied the top of my skull was coming off. I thought myself into ten thousand intricacies. I thought myself into doom and out of it, and behind it and below it, but I could not think of anything which was of service to me. It seemed that I had come among a lot of mummers, and one of these mummers was resolved to kill me, although I had never even so much as broken his leg. But I remembered my father's word, who had told me that gentlemen should properly kill each other over a matter of one liking oranges and the other not liking oranges. It was the custom among men of position, he had said, and of course a way was not clear to changing this custom at the time. However, I determined that if I lived I would insist upon all these customs being moderated and re-directed. For my part I was willing that any man should like oranges.

I decided that I must go for a walk. To sit and gloom in my room until the time of the great affair would do me no good in any case. In fact it was likely to do me much harm. I went forth to the garden in the rear of the inn. Here spread a lawn more level than a ballroom floor. There was a summer-house and many beds of flowers. On this day there was nobody abroad in the garden but an atrocious parrot, which, balancing on its stick, called out continually raucous cries in a foreign tongue.

I paced the lawn for a time, and then took a seat in the summer-house. I had been there but a moment when I perceived Lady Mary and the Countess come into the garden. Through the leafy walls of the summer-house I watched them as they walked slowly to and fro on the grass. The mother had evidently a great deal to say to the daughter. She waved her arms and spoke with a keen excitement.

But did I overhear anything? I overheard nothing! From what I knew of the proper conduct of the really thrilling episodes of life I judged that I should have been able to overhear almost every word of this conversation. Instead, I could only see the Countess making irritated speech to Lady Mary.

Moreover it was legitimate that I should have been undetected in the summer-house. On the contrary, they were perfectly aware that there was somebody there, and so in their promenade they presented it with a distinguished isolation.

No old maid ever held her ears so wide open. But I could hear nothing but a murmur of angry argument from the Countess and a murmur of gentle objection from Lady Mary. I was in possession of an ideal place from which to overhear conversation. Almost every important conversation ever held had been overheard from a position of this kind. It seemed unfair that I, of all men in literature, should be denied this casual and usual privilege.

The Countess harangued in a low voice at great length; Lady Mary answered from time to time, admitting this and admitting that, protesting against the other. It seemed certain to me that talk related to Forister, although I had no real reason for thinking it. And I was extremely angry that the Countess of Westport and her daughter, Lady Mary Strepp, should talk of Forister.

Upon my indignant meditations the parrot interpolated:

"Ho, ho!" it cried hoarsely. "A pretty lady! A pretty lady! A pretty lady! A pretty lady!—"

Lady Mary smiled at this vacuous repetition, but her mother went into a great rage, opening her old jaws like a maddened horse. "Here, landlord! Here, waiter! Here, anybody!"

So people came running from the inn, and at their head was, truly enough, the landlord. "My lady," he cried panting.

She pointed an angry and terrible finger at the parrot. "When I walk in this garden, am I to be troubled with this wretched bird?"

The landlord almost bit the turf while the servants from the inn grovelled near him. "My lady," he cried, "the bird shall be removed at once." He ran forward. The parrot was chained by its leg to a tall perch. As the innkeeper came away with the entire business, the parrot began to shout: "Old harridan! Old harridan! Old harridan!" The innkeeper seemed to me to be about to die of wild terror. It was a dreadful moment. One could not help but feel sorry for this poor wretch, whose sole offence was that he kept an inn and also chose to keep a parrot in his garden.

The Countess sailed grandly toward the door of the hotel. To the solemn protestations of six or seven servants she paid no heed. At the door she paused and turned for the intimate remark. "I cannot endure parrots," she said impressively. To this dictum the menials crouched.

The servants departed: the garden was now empty save for Lady Mary and me. She continued a pensive strolling. Now, I could see plainly that here fate had arranged for some kind of interview. The whole thing was set like a scene in a theatre. I was undoubtedly to emerge suddenly from the summer-house; the lovely maid would startle, blush, cast down her eyes, turn away. Then, when it came my turn, I would doff my hat to the earth and beg pardon for continuing a comparatively futile existence. Then she would slyly murmur a disclaimer of any ability to criticise my continuation of a comparatively futile existence, adding that she was but an inexperienced girl. The ice thus being broken, we would travel by easy stages into more intimate talk.

I looked down carefully at my apparel and flecked a handkerchief over it. I tilted my hat; I set my hip against my harbour. A moment of indecision, of weakness, and I was out of the summer-house. God knows how I hoped that Lady Mary would not run away.

But the moment she saw me she came swiftly to me. I almost lost my wits.

"'Tis the very gentleman I wished to see," she cried. She was blushing, it is true, but it was evident she intended to say nothing about inexperience or mere weak girls. "I wished to see you because—"she hesitated and then rapidly said: "It was about the papers. I wanted to thank you—I—you have no notion how happy the possession of the papers has made my father. It seemed to have given him new life. I—I saw you throw your sword on the floor with the hilt away from you. And—and then you gave me the papers. I knew you were a gallant gentleman."

All this time, I, in my confusion, was bobbing and murmuring pledges of service. But if I was confused, Lady Mary was soon cool enough in the presence of a simple bog-trotter like me. Her beautiful eyes looked at me reflectively.

"There is only one service I can render you, sir," said she softly. "'Tis advice which would have been useful in saving some men's lives if only they had received it. I mean—don't fight with Forister in the morning. 'Tis certain death."

It was now my turn once more. I drew myself up, and for the first time I looked squarely into her bright eyes.

"My lady," said I, with mournful dignity, "I was filled with pride when you said the good word to me. But what am I to think now? Am I, after all, such a poor stick that, to your mind, I could be advised to sell my honour for a mere fear of being killed?"

Even then I remembered my one-time decision to run away from the duel with Forister; but we will not be thinking of that now.

Tears came into Lady Mary's eyes. "Ah, now, I have blundered," she said. "'Tis what you would say, sir. 'Tis what you would do. I have only made matters worse. A woman's meddling often results in the destruction of those she—those she don't care to have killed."

One would think from the look of this last sentence, that with certain reason I could have felt somewhat elated without being altogether a fool. Lady Mary meant nothing of importance by her speech, but it was a little bit for a man who was hungry to have her think of him. But here I was assailed by a very demon of jealousy and distrust. This beautiful witch had some plan in her head which did not concern my welfare at all. Why should she, a great lady, take any trouble for a poor devil who was living at an inn on money borrowed from a highwayman. I had been highly honoured by an indifferent consideration born of a wish to be polite to a man who had eased the mind of her father. No; I would not deceive myself.

But her tears! Were they marking indifferent consideration? For a second I lost myself in a roseate impossible dream. I dreamed that she had spoken to me because she—

Oh, what folly! Even as I dreamed, she turned to me with splendid carriage, and remarked coldly:

"I did not wish you to suppose that I ever failed to pay a debt. I have paid this one. Proceed now, sir, in your glowing stupidity. I have done."

When I recovered myself she was placidly moving away from me toward the door of the inn.

## CHAPTER IX

I had better be getting to the story of the duel. I have been hanging back with it long enough, and I shall tell it at once. I remember my father saying that the most aggravating creature in life was one who would be keeping back the best part of a story through mere reasons of trickery, although I have seen himself dawdle over a tale until his friends wished to hurl the decanters at him. However, there can be no doubting of the wisdom of my father's remark. Indeed there can be little doubting of the wisdom of anything that my father said in life, for he was a very learned man. The fact that my father did not invariably defer to his own opinions does not alter the truth of those opinions in my judgment, since even the greatest of philosophers is more likely to be living a life based on the temper of his wife and the advice of his physician than on the rules laid down in his books. Nor am I certain that my father was in a regular habit of delaying a story. I only remember this one incident, wherein he was recounting a stirring tale of a fight with a lancer, and just as the lance was within an inch of the paternal breast my father was reminded, by a sight of the walnuts, that Mickey Clancy was not serving the port with his usual rapidity, and so he addressed him. I remember the words well.

"Mickey, you spalpeen," said my father, "would you be leaving the gentlemen as dry as the bottom of Moses' feet when he crossed the Red Sea? Look at O'Mahoney there! He is as thirsty as a fish in the top of a tree. And Father Donovan has had but two small quarts, and he never takes less than five. Bad luck to you, Mickey, if it was a drink for your own stomach, you would be moving faster. Are you wishing to ruin my reputation for hospitality, you rogue you?"

And my father was going on with Mickey, only that he looked about him at this time and discovered his guests all upon their feet, one with the tongs and one with the poker, others with decanters ready to throw.

"What's this?" said he.

"The lance," said they.

"What lance?" said he.

"The lance of the lancer," said they.

"And why shouldn't he have a lance?" said my father. "Faith, 'twould be an odd lancer without a lance!"

By this time they were so angry that Mickey, seeing how things were going, and I being a mere lad, took me from the room. I never heard precisely what happened to the lancer, but he must have had the worst of it, for wasn't my father, seated there at the table, telling the story long years after?

Well, as to my duel with Forister: Colonel Royale was an extremely busy man, and almost tired my life out with a quantity of needless attentions. For my part, I thought more of Lady Mary and the fact that she considered me no more than if I had been a spud. Colonel Royale fluttered about me. I would have gruffly sent him away if it were not that everything he did was meant in kindliness and generous feeling. I was already believing that he did not have more than one brain in his head, but I could not be ungrateful for his interest and enthusiasm in getting me out to be hurt correctly. I understood, long years afterward, that he and Lord Strepp were each so particular in the negotiations that no less than eighteen bottles of wine were consumed.

The morning for the duel dawned softly warm, softly wet, softly foggy. The Colonel popped into my room the moment I was dressed. To my surprise, he was now quite mournful. It was I, now, who had to do the cheering.

"Your spirits are low, Colonel?" said I banteringly.

"Aye, O'Ruddy," he answered with an effort, "I had a bad night, with the gout. Heaven help this devil from getting his sword into your bowels."

He had made the appointment with Strepp, of course, and as we walked toward the ground he looked at me very curiously out of the ends of his eyes. "You know— ah, you have the honour of the acquaintance of Lady Mary Strepp, O'Ruddy?" said he suddenly and nervously.

"I have," I answered, stiffening. Then I said: "And you?"

"Her father and I were friends before either of you were born," he said simply. "I was a cornet in his old regiment. Little Lady Mary played at the knee of the poor young subaltern."

"Oh," said I meanly, "you are, then, a kind of uncle."

"Aye," said he, "a kind of uncle. So much of an uncle," he added with more energy, "that when she gave me this note I thought much of acting like a real uncle. From what I have unfortunately overheard, I suspect that the Earl—aw—disagrees with you on certain points."

He averted his face as he handed me the note, and eagerly I tore it open. It was unsigned. It contained but three words: "God spare you!" And so I marched in a tumult of joy to a duel wherein I was expected to be killed.

I glanced at the Colonel. His countenance was deeply mournful. "'Tis for few girls I would become a dove to carry notes between lovers," he said gloomily. "Damn you for it, O'Ruddy!"

"Nay, Colonel," said I. "'Tis no missive of love. Look you!"

But still he kept his eyes averted. "I judge it was not meant for my eyes," he said, still very gloomy.

But here I flamed up in wrath:

"And would the eye of an angel be allowed to rest upon this paper if it were not fit that it should be so?" I demanded in my anger. "Colonel, am I to hear you bleat about doves and lovers when a glance of your eye will disabuse you? Read!"

He read. "'God spare you!'" he repeated tenderly. Then he addressed me with fine candor. "Aye, I have watched her these many years, O'Ruddy. When she was a babe I have seen her in her little bath. When she was a small girl I have seen her asleep with some trinket clasped in her rosy hand on the coverlet. Since she has been a beautiful young lady I have—but no matter. You come along, named nobody, hail ing from nowhere; and she—she sends me out to deliver her prayer that God may spare you!"

I was awed by this middle-aged sorrow. But, curse him! when she was a babe he had seen her in her little bath, had he? Damn his eyes! He had seen the baby naked in her tiny tub? Damn his eyes again! I was in such a fury that I longed to fight Royale on the spot and kill him, running my sword through his memory so that it would be blotted out forever, and never, never again, even in Paradise, could he recall the image in the little tub.

But the Colonel's next words took the rage out of me.

"Go in, O'Ruddy," he cried heartily. "There is no truer man could win her. As my lady says, 'God spare you!'"

"And if Forister's blade be not too brisk, I will manage to be spared," I rejoined.

"Oh, there is another thing touching the matter," said the Colonel suddenly. "Forister is your chief rival, although I little know what has passed between them. Nothing important, I think, although I am sure Forister is resolved to have her for a bride. Of that I am certain. He is resolved."

"Is he so?" said I.

I was numb and cold for a moment. Then I slowly began to boil, like a kettle freshly placed on the fire. So I was facing a rival? Well, and he would get such a facing as few men had received. And he was my rival and in the breast of my coat I wore a note—"God spare you!" Ha, ha! He little knew the advantages under which he was to play. Could I lose with "God spare you!" against my heart? Not against three Foristers!

But hold! might it not be that the gentle Lady Mary, deprecating this duel and filled with feelings of humanity, had sent us each a note with this fervid cry for God to spare us? I was forced to concede it possible. After all, I perfectly well knew that to Lady Mary I was a mere nothing. Royale's words had been so many plumes in my life's helmet, but at bottom I knew better than to set great store by them. The whole thing was now to hurry to the duelling-ground and see if I could discover from this black Forister's face if he had received a "God spare you!" I took the Colonel's arm and fairly dragged him.

"Damme, O'Ruddy!" said he, puffing; "this can be nought but genuine eagerness."

When we came to the duelling-place we found Lord Strepp and Forister pacing to and fro, while the top of a near-by wall was crowded with pleasant-minded spectators. "Aye, you've come, have ye, sirs?" called out the rabble. Lord Strepp seemed rather annoyed, and Colonel Royale grew red and stepped peremptorily toward the wall, but Forister and I had eyes only for each other. His eye for me was a glad, cruel eye. I have a dim remembrance of seeing the Colonel take his scabbard and incontinently beat many worthy citizens of Bristol; indeed, he seemed to beat every worthy citizen of Bristol who had not legs enough to get away. I could hear them squeaking out protests while I keenly studied the jubilant Forister.

Aye, it was true. He too had a "God spare you!" I felt my blood begin to run hot. My eyes suddenly cleared as if I had been empowered with miraculous vision. My arm became supple as a whip. I decided upon one thing. I would kill Forister.

I thought the Colonel never would give over chasing citizens, but at last he returned breathless, having scattered the populace over a wide stretch of country. The preliminaries were very simple. In a half-minute Forister and I, in our shirts, faced each other.

And now I passed into such a state of fury that I cannot find words to describe it; but, as I have said, I was possessed with a remarkable clearness of vision and strength of arm. These phenomena amaze me even at this day. I was so airy upon my feet that I might have been a spirit. I think great rages work thus upon some natures. Their competence is suddenly made manifold. They live, for a brief space, the life of giants. Rage is destruction active. Whenever anything in this world needs to be destroyed, nature makes somebody wrathful. Another thing that I recall is that I had not the slightest doubt of my ability to kill Forister. There were no more misgivings: no quakings. I thought of the impending duel with delight.

In all my midnight meditations upon the fight I had pictured myself as lying strictly upon the defensive and seeking a chance opportunity to damage my redoubtable opponent. But the moment after our swords had crossed I was an absolute demon of attack. My very first lunge made him give back a long pace. I saw his confident face change to a look of fierce excitement.

There is little to say of the flying, spinning blades. It is only necessary to remark that Forister dropped almost immediately to defensive tactics before an assault which was not only impetuous but exceedingly brilliant, if I may be allowed to say so. And I know that on my left a certain Colonel Royale was steadily growing happier.

The end came with an almost ridiculous swiftness. The feeling of an ugly quivering wrench communicated itself from the point of my sword to my mind; I heard Strepp and Royale cry "Hold!" I saw Forister fall; I lowered my point and stood dizzily thinking. My sight was now blurred; my arm was weak.

My sword had gone deep into Forister's left shoulder, and the bones there had given that hideous feeling of a quivering wrench. He was not injured beyond repair, but he was in exquisite agony. Before they could reach him he turned over on his elbows and managed in some way to fling his sword at me. "Damn your soul!" he cried, and he gave a sort of howl as Lord Strepp, grim and unceremonious, bounced him over again upon his back. In the mean time Colonel Royale was helping me on with my coat and waistcoat, although I hardly knew that either he or the coat or waistcoat were in existence.

I had my usual inclination to go forward and explain to everybody how it all had happened. But Royale took me forcibly by the arm, and we turned our backs on Strepp and Forister and walked toward the inn.

As soon as we were out of their sight, Colonel Royale clasped my hands with rapture. "My boy," he cried, "you are great! You are renowned! You are illustrious! What a game you could give Ponsonby! You would give him such a stir!"

"Never doubt me," said I. "But I am now your legitimate grandfather, and I should be treated with great respect."

When we came near the inn I began to glance up at the windows. I surely expected to see a face at one of them. Certainly she would care to know who was slain or who was hurt. She would be watching, I fondly hoped, to see who returned on his legs. But the front of the inn stared at us, chilly and vacant, like a prison wall.

When we entered, the Colonel bawled lustily for an immediate bottle of wine, and I joined him in its drinking, for I knew that it would be a bellows to my flagging spirits. I had set my heart upon seeing a face at the window of the inn.

## CHAPTER X

And now I found out what it was to be a famous swordsman. All that day the inn seemed to hum with my name. I could not step down a corridor without seeing flocks of servants taking wing. They fled tumultuously. A silly maid coming from a chamber with a bucket saw me and shrieked. She dropped her bucket and fled back into the chamber. A man-servant saw me, gave a low moan of terror, and leaped down a convenient stairway. All attendants scuttled aside.

What was the matter with me? Had I grown in stature or developed a ferocious ugliness? No; I now was a famous swordsman. That was all. I now was expected to try to grab the maids and kiss them wantonly. I now was expected to clout the grooms on their ears if they so much as showed themselves in my sight. In fact, I was now a great blustering, overpowering, preposterous ass.

There was a crowd of people in the coffee-room, but the buzz of talk suddenly ceased as I entered.

"Is this your chair, sir?" said I civilly to a gentleman.

He stepped away from the chair as if it had tried to bite him.

"'Tis at your service, sir!" he cried hastily.

"No," said I, "I would not be taking it if it be yours, for there are just as good chairs in the sea as ever were caught, and it would ill become me to deprive a gentleman of his chair when by exercising a little energy I can gain one for myself, although I am willing to admit that I have a slight hunger upon me. 'Tis a fine morning, sir."

He had turned pale and was edging toward the door. "'Tis at your service, sir," he repeated in a low and frightened voice. All the people were staring at us.

"No, good sir," I remonstrated, stepping forward to explain. "I would not be having you think that I am unable to get a chair for myself, since I am above everything able and swift with my hands, and it is a small thing to get a chair for one's self and not deprive a worthy gentleman of his own."

"I did not think to deprive you, sir," he ejaculated desperately. "The chair is at your service, sir!"

"Plague the man!" I cried, stamping my foot impatiently; and at the stamping of my foot a waiter let fall a dish, some women screamed, three or four people disappeared through the door, and a venerable gentleman arose from his seat in a corner and in a tremulous voice said:

"Sir, let us pray you that there be no bloodshed."

"You are an old fool," said I to him. "How could there be bloodshed with me here merely despising you all for not knowing what I mean when I say it."

"We know you mean what you say, sir," responded the old gentleman. "Pray God you mean peaceably!"

"Hoity-toity!" shouted a loud voice, and I saw a great, tall, ugly woman bearing down upon me from the doorway. "Out of my way," she thundered at a waiter. The man gasped out: "Yes, your ladyship!"

I was face to face with the mother of my lovely Mary.

"Hoity-toity!" she shouted at me again. "A brawler, eh? A lively swordster, hey? A real damn-my-eyes swaggering bully!"

Then she charged upon me. "How dare you brawl with these inoffensive people under the same roof which shelters me, fellow? By my word, I would have pleasure to give you a box on the ear!"

"Madam," I protested hurriedly. But I saw the futility of it. Without devoting further time to an appeal, I turned and fled. I dodged behind three chairs and moved them hastily into a rampart.

"Madam," I cried, feeling that I could parley from my new position, "you labour under a misapprehension."

"Misapprehend me no misapprehensions," she retorted hotly. "How dare you say that I can misapprehend anything, wretch?"

She attacked each flank in turn, but so agile was I that I escaped capture, although my position in regard to the chairs was twice reversed. We performed a series of nimble manœuvres which were characterized on my part by a high degree of strategy. But I found the rampart of chairs an untenable place. I was again obliged hurriedly to retreat, this time taking up a position behind a large table.

"Madam," I said desperately, "believe me, you are suffering under a grave misapprehension."

"Again he talks of misapprehension!"

We revolved once swiftly around the table; she stopped, panting.

"And this is the blusterer! And why do you not stand your ground, coward?"

"Madam," said I with more coolness now that I saw she would soon be losing her wind, "I would esteem it very ungallant behaviour if I endured your attack for even a brief moment. My forefathers form a brave race which always runs away from the ladies."

After this speech we revolved twice around the table. I must in all candour say that the Countess used language which would not at all suit the pages of my true and virtuous chronicle; but indeed it was no worse than I often heard afterward from the great ladies of the time. However, the talk was not always addressed to me, thank the Saints!

After we had made the two revolutions, I spoke reasonably. "Madam," said I, "if we go spinning about the table in this fashion for any length of time, these gawking spectators will think we are a pair of wheels."

"Spectators!" she cried, lifting her old head high. She beheld about seventy-five interested people. She called out loudly to them:

"And is there no gentleman among you all to draw his sword and beat me this rascal from the inn?"

Nobody moved.

"Madam," said I, still reasonable, "would it not be better to avoid a possible scandal by discontinuing these movements, as the tongues of men are not always fair, and it might be said by some—"

Whereupon we revolved twice more around the table.

When the old pelican stopped, she had only enough breath left to impartially abuse all the sight-seers. As her eye fixed upon them, The O'Ruddy, illustrious fighting-man, saw his chance and bolted like a hare. The escape must have formed a great spectacle, but I had no time for appearances. As I was passing out of the door, the Countess, in her disappointed rage, threw a heavy ivory fan after me, which struck an innocent bystander in the eye, for which he apologized.

## CHAPTER XI

I wasted no time in the vicinity of the inn. I decided that an interval spent in some remote place would be consistent with the behaviour of a gentleman.

But the agitations of the day were not yet closed for me. Suddenly I came upon a small, slow-moving, and solemn company of men, who carried among them some kind of a pallet, and on this pallet was the body of Forister. I gazed upon his ghastly face; I saw the large blood blotches on his shirt; as they drew nearer I saw him roll his eyes and heard him groan. Some of the men recognized me, and I saw black looks and straight-pointing fingers. At the rear walked Lord Strepp with Forister's sword under his arm. I turned away with a new impression of the pastime of duelling. Forister's pallor, the show of bloody cloth, his groan, the dark stares of men, made me see my victory in a different way, and I even wondered if it had been absolutely necessary to work this mischief upon a fellow-being.

I spent most of the day down among the low taverns of the sailors, striving to interest myself in a thousand new sights brought by the ships from foreign parts.

But ever my mind returned to Lady Mary, and to my misfortune in being pursued around chairs and tables by my angel's mother. I had also managed to have a bitter quarrel with the noble father of this lovely creature. It was hardly possible that I could be joyous over my prospects.

At noon I returned to the inn, approaching with some display of caution. As I neared it, a carriage followed by some horsemen whirled speedily from the door. I knew at once that Lady Mary had been taken from me. She was gone with her father and mother back to London. I recognized Lord Strepp and Colonel Royale among the horsemen.

I walked through the inn to the garden, and looked at the parrot. My senses were all numb. I stared at the bird as it rolled its wicked eye at me.

"Pretty lady! Pretty lady!" it called in coarse mockery.

"Plague the bird!" I muttered, as I turned upon my heel and entered the inn.

"My bill," said I. "A horse for Bath!" said I.

Again I rode forth on a quest. The first had been after my papers. The second was after my love. The second was the hopeless one, and, overcome by melancholy, I did not even spur my horse swiftly on my mission. There was upon me the deep-rooted sadness which balances the mirth of my people,—the Celtic aptitude for discouragement; and even the keening of old women in the red glow of the peat fire could never have deepened my mood.

And if I should succeed in reaching London, what then? Would the wild savage from the rocky shore of Ireland be a pleasing sight to my Lady Mary when once more amid the glamour and whirl of the fashionable town? Besides, I could no longer travel on the guineas of Jem Bottles. He had engaged himself and his purse in my service because I had told him of a fortune involved in the regaining of certain papers. I had regained those papers, and then coolly placed them as a gift in a certain lovely white hand. I had had no more thought of Jem Bottles and his five guineas than if I had never seen them. But this was no excuse for a gentleman. When I was arrived at the rendezvous I must immediately confess to Jem Bottles, the highwayman, that I had wronged him. I did not expect him to demand satisfaction, but I thought he might shoot me in the back as I was riding away.

But Jem was not at the appointed place under the tree. Not puzzled at this behaviour, I rode on. I saw I could not expect the man to stay for ever under a tree while I was away in Bristol fighting a duel and making eyes at a lady. Still, I had heard that it was always done.

At the inn where Paddy holed Forister, I did not dismount, although a hostler ran out busily. "No," said I. "I ride on." I looked at the man. Small, sharp-eyed, weazened, he was as likely a rascal of a hostler as ever helped a highwayman to know a filled purse from a man who was riding to make arrangements with his creditors.

"Do you remember me?" said I.

"No, sir," he said with great promptitude.

"Very good," said I. "I knew you did. Now I want to know if Master Jem Bottles has passed this way today. A shilling for the truth and a thrashing for a lie."

The man came close to my stirrup. "Master," he said, "I know you to be a friend of him. Well, in day-time he don't ride past our door. There be lanes. And so he ain't passed here, and that's the truth."

I flung him a shilling. "Now," I said, "what of the red giant?"

The man opened his little eyes in surprise. "He took horse with you gentlemen and rode on to Bristol, or I don't know."

"Very good; now I see two very fine horses champing in the yard. And who owns them?"

If I had expected to catch him in treachery I was wrong.

"Them?" said he, jerking his thumb. He still kept his voice lowered. "They belong to two gentlemen who rode out some hours agone along with some great man's carriage. The officer said some pin-pricks he had gotten in a duel had stiffened him, and made the saddle ill of ease with him, and the young lord said that he would stay behind as a companion. They be up in the Colonel's chamber, drinking vastly. But mind your life, sir, if you would halt them on the road. They be men of great spirit. This inn seldom sees such drinkers."

And so Lord Strepp and Colonel Royale were resting at this inn while the carriage of the Earl had gone on toward Bath? I had a mind to dismount and join the two in their roystering, but my eyes turned wistfully toward Bath.

As I rode away I began to wonder what had become of Jem Bottles and Paddy. Here was a fine pair to be abroad in the land. Here were two jewels to be rampaging across the country. Separately, they were villains enough, but together they would overturn England and get themselves hung for it on twin gibbets. I tried to imagine the particular roguery to which they would first give their attention.

But then all thought of the rascals faded from me as my mind received a vision of Lady Mary's fair face, her figure, her foot. It would not be me to be thinking of two such thieves when I could be dreaming of Lady Mary with her soft voice and the clear depth of her eyes. My horse seemed to have a sympathy with my feeling and he leaped bravely along the road. The Celtic melancholy of the first part of the journey had blown away like a sea-mist. I sped on gallantly toward Bath and Lady Mary.

But almost at the end of the day, when I was within a few miles of Bath, my horse suddenly pitched forward onto his knees and nose. There was a flying spray of muddy water. I was flung out of the saddle, but I fell without any serious hurt whatever. We had been ambushed by some kind of deep-sided puddle. My poor horse scrambled out and stood with lowered head, heaving and trembling. His soft nose had been cut between his teeth and the far edge of the puddle. I led him forward, watching his legs. He was lamed. I looked in wrath and despair back at the puddle, which was as plain as a golden guinea on a platter. I do not see how I could have blundered into it, for the daylight was still clear and strong. I had been gazing like a fool in the direction of Bath. And my Celtic melancholy swept down upon me again, and even my father's bier appeared before me with the pale candle-flames swaying in the gusty room, and now indeed my ears heard the loud wailing keen of the old women.

"Rubbish," said I suddenly and aloud, "and is it one of the best swordsmen in England that is to be beaten by a lame horse?" My spirit revived. I resolved to leave my horse in the care of the people of the nearest house and proceed at once on foot to Bath. The people of the inn could be sent out after the poor animal. Wheeling my eyes, I saw a house not more than two fields away, with honest hospitable smoke curling from the chimneys. I led my beast through a hole in the hedge, and I slowly made my way toward it.

Now it happened that my way led me near a haycock, and as I neared this haycock I heard voices from the other side of it. I hastened forward, thinking to find some yokels. But as I drew very close I suddenly halted and silently listened to the voices on the other side.

"Sure, I can read," Paddy was saying. "And why wouldn't I be able? If we couldn't read in Ireland, we would be after being cheated in our rents, but we never pay them any how, so that's no matter. I would be having you to know we are a highly educated people. And perhaps you would be reading it yourself, my man?"

"No," said Jem Bottles, "I be not a great scholar and it has a look of amazing hardness. And I misdoubt me," he added in a morose and envious voice, "that your head be too full of learning."

"Learning!" cried Paddy. "Why wouldn't I be learned, since my uncle was a sexton and had to know one grave from another by looking at the stones so as never to mix up the people? Learning! says you? And wasn't there a convent at Ballygow-agglycuddi, and wasn't Ballygowagglycuddi only ten miles from my father's house, and haven't I seen it many a time?"

"Aye, well, good Master Paddy," replied Jem Bottles, oppressed and sullen, but still in a voice ironic from suspicion, "I never doubt me but what you are a regular clerk for deep learning, but you have not yet read a line from the paper, and I have been waiting this half-hour."

"And how could I be reading?" cried Paddy in tones of indignation. "How could I be reading with you there croaking of this and that and speaking hard of my learning? Bad cess to the paper, I will be after reading it to myself if you are never to stop your clatter, Jem Bottles."

"I be still as a dead rat," exclaimed the astonished highwayman.

"Well, then," said Paddy. "Listen hard, and you will hear such learning as would be making your eyes jump from your head. And 'tis not me either that cares to show my learning before people who are unable to tell a mile-post from a church-tower."

"I be awaiting," said Jem Bottles with a new meekness apparently born of respect for Paddy's eloquence.

"Well, then," said Paddy, pained at these interruptions. "Listen well, and maybe you will gain some learning which may serve you all your life in reading chalk-marks in taprooms; for I see that they have that custom in this country, and 'tis very bad for hard-drinking men who have no learning."

"If you would read from the paper—" began Jem Bottles.

"Now, will you be still?" cried Paddy in vast exasperation.

But here Jem Bottles spoke with angry resolution. "Come, now! Read! 'Tis not me that talks too much, and the day wanes."

"Well, well, I would not be hurried, and that's the truth," said Paddy soothingly. "Listen now." I heard a rustling of paper. "Ahem!" said Paddy, "Ahem! Are ye listening, Jem Bottles?"

"I be," replied the highwayman.

"Ahem!" said Paddy. "Ahem! Are ye listening, Jem Bottles?"

"I be," replied the highwayman.

"Then here's for it," said Paddy in a formidable voice. There was another rustling of paper. Then to my surprise I heard Paddy intone, without punctuation, the following words:

"Dear Sister Mary I am asking the good father to write this because my hand is lame from milking the cows although we only have one and we sold her in the autumn the four shillings you owe on the pig we would like if convenient to pay now owing to the landlord may the plague take him how did your Mickey find the fishing when you see Peggy tell her—"

Here Jem Bottles's voice arose in tones of incredulity.

"And these be the papers of the great Earl!" he cried.

Then the truth flashed across my vision like the lightning. My two madmen had robbed the carriage of the Earl of Westport, and had taken, among other things, the Earl's papers—my papers—Lady Mary's papers. I strode around the haycock.

"Wretches!" I shouted. "Miserable wretches!"

For a time they were speechless. Paddy found his tongue first.

"Aye, 'tis him! 'Tis nothing but little black men and papers with him, and when we get them for him he calls us out of our names in a foreign tongue. 'Tis no service for a bright man," he concluded mournfully.

"Give me the papers," said I.

Paddy obediently handed them. I knew them. They were my papers—Lady Mary's papers.

"And now," said I, eyeing the pair, "what mischief have you two been compassing?"

Paddy only mumbled sulkily. It was something on the difficulties of satisfying me on the subjects of little black men and papers. Jem Bottles was also sulky, but he grumbled out the beginning of an explanation.

"Well, master, I bided under the tree till him here came, and then we together bided. And at last we thought, with the time so heavy, we might better work to handle a purse or two. Thinking," he said delicately, "our gentleman might have need of a little gold. Well, and as we were riding, a good lad from the—your worship knows where—tells us the Earl's carriage is halting there for a time, but will go on later without its escort of two gentlemen; only with servants. And, thinking to do our gentleman a good deed, I brought them to stand on the highway, and then he—"

"And then I," broke in Paddy proudly, "walks up to the carriage-door looking like a king's cruiser, and says I, 'Pray excuse the manners of a self-opinionated man, but I consider your purses would look better in my pocket.' And then there was a great trouble. An old owl of a woman screeched, and was for killing me with a bottle which she had been holding against her nose. But she never dared. And with that an old sick man lifted himself from hundreds of cushions and says he, 'What do you want? You can't have them,' says he, and he keeps clasping his breast. 'First of all,' says I, 'I want what you have there. What I want else I'll tell you at my leisure.' And he was all for mouthing and fuming, but he was that scared he gave me these papers—bad luck to them." Paddy cast an evil eye upon the papers in my hand.

"And then?" said I.

"The driver he tried for to whip up," interpolated Jem Bottles. "He was a game one, but the others were like wet cats."

"And says I," continued Paddy, "'now we will have the gold, if it please you.' And out it came. 'I bid ye a good journey,' says I, and I thought it was over, and how easy it was highwaying, and I liked it well, until the lady on the front seat opens her hood and shows me a prettier face than we have in all Ireland. She clasps two white hands. 'Oh, please Mister Highwayman, my father's papers—' And with that I backs away. 'Let them go,' says I to Jem Bottles, and sick I was of it, and I would be buying masses tonight if I might find a Christian church. The poor lady!"

I was no longer angry with Paddy.

"Aye," said Jem Bottles, "the poor lady was that forlorn!"

I was no longer angry with Jem Bottles.

But I now had to do a deal of thinking. It was plain that the papers were of supreme importance to the Earl. Although I had given them to Lady Mary, they had returned to me. It was fate. My father had taught me to respect these papers, but I now saw them as a sign in the sky.

However, it was hard to decide what to do. I had given the papers to Lady Mary, and they had fled back to me swifter than cormorants. Perhaps it was willed that I should keep them. And then there would be tears in the eyes of Lady Mary, who suffered through the suffering of her father. No; come good, come bad for me, for Jem Bottles, for Paddy, I would stake our fortunes on the act of returning the papers to Lady Mary.

It is the way of Irishmen. We are all of us true philanthropists. That is why we have nothing, although in other countries I have seen philanthropists who had a great deal. My own interest in the papers I staked, mentally, with a glad mind; the minor interests of Jem Bottles and Paddy I staked, mentally, without thinking of them at all. But surely it would be a tribute to fate to give anything to Lady Mary.

I resolved on a course of action. When I aroused to look at my companions I found them seated face to face on the ground like players of draughts. Between them was spread a handkerchief, and on that handkerchief was a heap of guineas. Jem Bottles was saying, "Here be my fingers five times over again." He separated a smaller heap. "Here be my fingers five times over again." He separated another little stack. "And here be my fingers five times over again and two more yet. Now can ye understand?"

"By dad," said Paddy admiringly, "you have the learning this time, Master Bottles. My uncle the sexton could not have done it better."

"What is all this?" said I.

They both looked at me deprecatingly. "'Tis, your honour," began Paddy; "'tis only some little small sum—nothing to be talked of—belonging to the old sick man in the carriage."

"Paddy and Jem Bottles," said I, "I forgive you the taking of the papers. Ye are good men and true. Now we will do great deeds."

## CHAPTER XII

My plans were formed quickly. "We now have a treasure chest of no small dimensions," said I, very complacent, naturally. "We can conquer London with this. Everything is before us. I have already established myself as the grandest swordsman in the whole continent of England. Lately we have gained much treasure. And also I have the papers. Paddy, do you take care of this poor horse. Then follow me into Bath. Jem Bottles, do you mount and ride around the town, for I fear your balladists. Meet me on the London road. Ride slowly on the highway to London, and in due time I will overtake you. I shall pocket a few of those guineas, but you yourself shall be the main treasury. Hold! what of Paddy's hair? Did he rob the Earl with that great flame showing? He dare not appear in Bath."

"'Tis small tribute to my wit, sir," answered Jem Bottles. "I would as soon go poaching in company with a lighthouse as to call a stand on the road with him uncovered. I tied him in cloth until he looked no more like himself than he now does look like a parson."

"Aye," said Paddy in some bad humour, "my head was tied in a bag. My mother would not have known me from a pig going to market. And I would not be for liking it every day. My hair is what the blessed Saints sent me, and I see no such fine hair around me that people are free to throw the laugh at me."

"Peace!" said I.

Their horses were tied in an adjacent thicket. I sent Paddy off with my lame mount, giving him full instructions as to his lies. I and Jem Bottles took the other horses and rode toward Bath.

Where a certain lane turned off from the highway I parted with Jem Bottles, and he rode away between the hedges. I cantered into Bath.

The best-known inn was ablaze with fleeting lights, and people were shouting within. It was some time before I could gain a man to look after my horse. Of him I demanded the reason of the disturbance. "The Earl of Westport's carriage has been robbed on the Bristol road, sir," he cried excitedly. "There be parties starting out. I pray they catch him."

"And who would they be catching, my lad," said I.

"Jem Bottles, damn him, sir," answered the man. "But 'tis a fierce time they will have, for he stands no less than eight feet in his boots, and his eyes are no human eyes, but burn blood-red always. His hands are adrip with blood, and 'tis said that he eats human flesh, sir. He surely is a devil, sir."

"From the description I would be willing to believe it," said I. "However, he will be easy to mark. Such a monster can hardly be mistaken for an honest man."

I entered the inn, while a boy staggered under my valises. I had difficulty in finding the landlord. But in the corridor were a number of travellers, and evidently one had come that day from Bristol, for he suddenly nudged another and hurriedly whispered:

"'Tis him! The great Irish swordsman!"

Then the news spread like the wind, apparently, that the man who had beaten the great Forister was arrived in good health at the inn. There were murmurs, and a great deal of attention, and many eyes. I suddenly caught myself swaggering somewhat. It is hard to be a famous person and not show a great swollen chicken-breast to the people. They are disappointed if you do not strut and step high. "Show me to a chamber," said I splendidly. The servants bowed their foreheads to the floor.

But the great hubbub over the Earl's loss continued without abatement. Gentlemen clanked down in their spurs; there was much talk of dragoons; the tumult was extraordinary. Upstairs the landlord led me past the door of a kind of drawing-room. I glanced within and saw the Earl of Westport gesturing and declaiming to a company of gentlemen. He was propped up in a great arm-chair.

"And why would he be waving his hands that way?" said I to two servants who stood without.

"His lordship has lost many valuable papers at the hands of a miscreant, sir," answered one.

"Is it so?" said I. "Well, then, I would see his lordship."

But here this valet stiffened. "No doubt but what his lordship would be happy to see you, sir," he answered slowly. "Unfortunately, however, he has forbidden me to present strangers to his presence."

"I have very important news. Do not be an idiot," said I. "Announce me. The O'Ruddy."

"The O'Ruggy?" said he.

"The O'Ruddy," said I.

"The O'Rudgy?" said he.

"No," said I, and I told him again. Finally he took two paces within the room and sung out in a loud voice:

"The O'Rubby."

I heard the voice of the sick old Earl calling out from his great chair. "Why, 'tis the Irishman. Bid him enter. I am glad—I am always very glad—ahem!—"

As I strode into the room I was aware of another buzz of talk. Apparently here, too, were plenty of people who knew me as the famous swordsman. The Earl moved his jaw and mumbled.

"Aye," said he at last, "here is The O'Ruddy. And, do you know, Mr. O'Ruddy, I have been foully robbed, and, among other things, have lost your worthless papers?"

"I heard that you had lost them," I answered composedly. "But I refuse to take your word that they are worthless."

Many people stared, and the Earl gave me a firm scowl. But after consideration he spoke as if he thought it well to dissemble a great dislike of me. The many candles burned very brightly, and we could all see each other. I thought it better to back casually toward the wall.

"You never accomplish anything," coughed the sick Earl. "Yet you are for ever prating of yourself. I wish my son were here. My papers are gone. I shall never recover them."

"The papers are in the breast of my coat at this moment," said I coolly.

There was a great tumult. The Earl lost his head and cried:

"Seize him!" Two or three young men took steps toward me. I was back to the wall, and in a leisurely and contemptuous way I drew my sword.

"The first gentleman who advances is a dead man," said I pleasantly.

Some drew away quickly; some hesitated, and then withdrew subtilely. In the mean time the screeches of the Earl mocked them all.

"Aye, the wild Irishman brings you up to a stand, he does! Now who will have at him? In all Bath I have no friend with a stout heart?"

After looking them over I said:

"No, my Lord, you have none."

At this insult the aged peer arose from his chair. "Bring me my sword," he cried to his valet. A hush fell upon us all. We were rendered immovable by the solemn dignity of this proceeding.

It was some time before I could find my tongue.

"And if you design to cross blades with me, you will find me a sad renegade," said I. "I am holding the papers for the hands of their true owner."

"And their true owner?" he demanded.

"Lady Mary Strepp," said I.

He sank back into his seat. "This Irishman's impudence is beyond measuring," he exclaimed. The hurrying valet arrived at that moment with a sword. "Take it away! Take it away!" he cried. "Do I wish valets to be handing swords to me at any time of the day or night?"

Here a belligerent red-faced man disengaged himself abruptly from the group of gentlemen and addressed the Earl. "Westport," said he flatly, "I can ill bear your taunt concerning your Bath friends, and this is not to speak of the insolence of the person yonder."

"Oh, ho!" said I. "Well, and the person yonder remains serene in his insolence."

The Earl, smiling slightly, regarded the new speaker.

"Sir Edmund Flixton was ever a dainty swordsman, picking and choosing like a lady in a flower-bed. Perchance he is anxious to fight the gentleman who has just given Reginald Forister something he will not forget?"

At this Flixton actually turned pale and drew back. Evidently he had not yet heard the news. And, mind you, I could see that he would fight me the next moment. He would come up and be killed like a gentleman. But the name of a great conqueror had simply appalled him and smitten him back.

The Earl was gazing at me with an entirely new expression. He had cleverly eliminated all dislike from his eyes. He covered me with a friendly regard.

"O'Ruddy," he said softly, "I would have some private speech with you. Come into my chamber."

The Earl leaned on the shoulder of his valet and a little fat doctor, and walked painfully into another room. I followed, knowing that I was now to withstand a subtle, wheedling, gentle attempt to gain the papers without the name of Lady Mary being mentioned.

The Earl was slowly lowered into a great chair. After a gasp of relief he devoted a brightening attention to me. "You are not a bad fellow, O'Ruddy," he observed. "You remind me greatly of your father. Aye, he was a rare dog, a rare dog!"

"I've heard him say so, many is the day, sir," I answered.

"Aye, a rare dog!" chuckled the old man. "I have in my memory some brisk pictures of your father with his ready tongue, his what-the-devil-does-it-matter-sir, and that extraordinary swordsmanship which you seem to have inherited."

"My father told me you were great friends in France," I answered civilly, "but from some words you let drop in Bristol I judged that he was mistaken."

"Tut," said the Earl. "You are not out of temper with me, are you, O'Ruddy?"

"With me happily in possession of the papers," I rejoined, "I am in good temper with everybody. 'Tis not for me to lose my good nature when I hold all the cards."

The Earl's mouth quickly dropped to a sour expression, but almost as quickly he put on a pleasant smile. "Aye," he said, nodding his sick head. "Always jovial, always jovial. Precisely like his father. In fact it brings back an old affection."

"If the old affection had been brought back a little earlier, sir," said I, "we all would have had less bother. 'Twas you who in the beginning drew a long face and set a square chin over the business. I am now in the mood to be rather airy."

Our glances blazed across each other.

"But," said the Earl in the gentlest of voices, "you have my papers, O'Ruddy, papers entrusted to you by your dying father to give into the hands of his old comrade. Would you betray such a sacred trust? Could you wanton yourself to the base practices of mere thievery?"

"'Tis not I who has betrayed any trust," I cried boldly. "I brought the papers and wished to offer them. They arrived in your possession, and you cried 'Straw, straw!' Did you not?"

"'Twas an expedient, O'Ruddy," said the Earl.

"There is more than one expedient in the world," said I. "I am now using the expedient of keeping the papers."

And in the glance which he gave me I saw that I had been admitted behind a certain barrier. He was angry, but he would never more attempt to overbear me with grand threats. And he would never more attempt to undermine me with cheap flattery. We had measured one against the other, and he had not come away thinking out of his proportion. After a time he said:

"What do you propose to do, Mr. O'Ruddy?"

I could not help but grin at him. "I propose nothing," said I. "I am not a man for meaning two things when I say one."

"You've said one thing, I suppose?" he said slowly.

"I have," said I.

"And the one thing?" said he.

"Your memory is as good as mine," said I.

He mused deeply and at great length. "You have the papers?" he asked finally.

"I still have them," said I.

"Then," he cried with sudden vehemence, "why didn't you read the papers and find out the truth?"

I almost ran away.

"Your—your lordship," I stammered, "I thought perhaps in London—in London perhaps—I might get a—I would try to get a tutor."

## CHAPTER XIII

"So that is the way of it, is it?" said the Earl, grinning. "And why did you not take it to some clerk?"

"My lord," said I with dignity, "the papers were with me in trust for you. A man may be a gentleman and yet not know how to read and write."

"'Tis quite true," answered he.

"And when I spoke of the tutor in London I did not mean to say that I would use what knowledge he imparted to read your papers. I was merely blushing for the defects in my education, although Father Donovan often said that I knew half as much as he did, poor man, and him a holy father. If you care to so direct me, I can go even now to my chamber and make shift to read the papers."

"The Irish possess a keen sense of honour," said he admiringly.

"We do," said I. "We possess more integrity and perfect sense of honour than any other country in the world, although they all say the same of themselves, and it was my own father who often said that he would trust an Irishman as far as he could see him and no more, but for a foreigner he had only the length of an eyelash."

"And what do you intend with the papers now, O'Ruddy?" said he.

"I intend as I intended," I replied. "There is no change in me."

"And your intentions?" said he.

"To give them into the hands of Lady Mary Strepp and no other," said I boldly.

I looked at him. He looked at me.

"Lady Mary Strepp, my daughter," he said in ironic musing. "Would not her mother do, O'Ruddy?" he asked softly.

I gave a start.

"She is not near?" I demanded, looking from here to there.

He laughed.

"Aye, she is. I can have her here to take the papers in one short moment."

I held up my hands.

"No—no—"

"Peace," said he with a satanic chuckle. "I was only testing your courage."

"My lord," said I gravely, "seeing a bare blade come at your breast is one thing, and running around a table is another, and besides you have no suitable table in this chamber."

The old villain laughed again.

"O'Ruddy," he cried, "I would be a well man if you were always near me. Will I have a table fetched up from below?—'twould be easy."

Here I stiffened.

"My lord, this is frivolity," I declared. "I came here to give the papers. If you do not care to take them in the only way in which I will give them, let us have it said quickly."

"They seem to be safe in your hands at present," he remarked. "Of course after you go to London and get a tutor—ahem!—"

"I will be starting at once," said I, "although Father Donovan always told me that he was a good tutor as tutors went at the time in Ireland. And I want to be saying now, my lord, that I cannot understand you. At one moment you are crying one thing of the papers; at the next moment you are crying another. At this time you are having a laugh with me over them. What do you mean? I'll not stand this shiver-shavering any longer, I'll have you to know. What do you mean?"

He raised himself among his cushions and fixed me with a bony finger.

"What do I mean? I'll tell you, O'Ruddy," said he, while his eyes shone brightly. "I mean that I can be contemptuous of your plot. You will not show these papers to any breathing creature because you are in love with my daughter. Fool, to match your lies against an ex-minister of the King."

My eyes must have almost dropped from my head, but as soon as I recovered from my dumfounderment I grew amazed at the great intellect of this man. I had told nobody, and yet he knew all about it. Yes, I was in love with Lady Mary, and he was as well informed of it as if he had had spies to watch my dreams. And I saw that in many cases a lover was a kind of an ostrich, the bird which buries its head in the sands and thinks it is secure from detection. I wished that my father had told me more about love, for I have no doubt he knew everything of it, he had lived so many years in Paris. Father Donovan, of course, could not have helped me in such instruction. I resolved, any how, to be more cautious in the future, although I did not exactly see how I could improve myself. The Earl's insight was pure mystery to me. I would not be for saying that he practised black magic, but any how, if he had been at Glandore, I would have had him chased through three parishes.

However, the Earl was grinning victoriously, and I saw that I must harden my face to a brave exterior.

"And is it so?" said I. "Is it so?"

"Yes," he said, with his grin.

"And what then?" said I bluntly.

In his enjoyment he had been back again among his cushions.

"'What then? What then?'" he snarled, rearing up swiftly. "Why, then you are an insolent fool: Begone from me! begone! be—" Here some spasm overtook him, a spasm more from rage than from the sickness. He fell back breathless, although his eyes continued to burn at me.

"My lord," said I, bowing, "I will go no poorer than when I came, save that I have lost part of the respect I once had for you."

I turned and left his chamber. Some few gentlemen yet remained in the drawing-room as I passed out into the public part of the inn. I went quietly to a chamber and sat down to think. I was for ever going to chambers and sitting down to think after these talks with the Earl, during which he was for ever rearing up in his chair and then falling back among the cushions.

But here was another tumble over the cliffs, if you like! Here was genuine disaster. I laid my head in my hands and mused before my lonely fire, drinking much and visioning my ruin. What the Earl said was true. There was trouble in the papers for the old nobleman. That he knew. That I knew. And he knew with his devilish wisdom that I would lose my head rather than see her in sorrow. Well, I could bide a time. I would go to London in company with Paddy and Jem Bottles, since they owned all the money, and if three such rogues could not devise something, then I would go away and bury myself in a war in foreign parts, occupying myself in scaling fortresses and capturing guns. These things I know I could have performed magnificently, but from the Earl I had learned that I was an ill man to conduct an affair of the heart.

I do not know how long I meditated, but suddenly there was a great tumult on the stairs near my door. There were the shouts and heavy breathings of men, struggling, and over all rang a screech as from some wild bird. I ran to the door and poked my head discreetly out; for my coat and waistcoat were off as well as my sword, and I wished to see the manner of tumult at a distance before I saw it close. As I thrust forth my head I heard a familiar voice:

"And if ye come closer, ye old hell-cat, 'tis me will be forgetting respect to my four great-grandmothers and braining you. Keep off! Am I not giving ye the word? Keep off!"

Then another familiar voice answered him in a fine high fury. "And you gallows-bird, you gallows-bird, you gallows-bird! You answer me, do you! They're coming, all, even to the hangman! You'll soon know how to dance without a fiddler! Ah, would you? Would you?"

If I had been afflicted with that strange malady of the body which sometimes causes men to fall to the ground and die in a moment without a word, my doom would have been sealed. It was Paddy and Hoity-Toity engaged in animated discussion.

"And if ye don't mind your eye, ye old cormorant—" began Paddy.

"And you would be a highwayman, would you, gallows-bird—" began the Countess.

"Cow—" began Paddy.

Here for many reasons I thought it time to interfere. "Paddy!" I cried. He gave a glance at my door, recognized my face, and, turning quickly, ran through into my chamber. I barred the door even as Hoity-Toity's fist thundered on the oak.

"It's a she-wolf," gasped Paddy, his chest pressing in and out.

"And what did you do to her?" I demanded.

"Nothing but try to run away, sure," said Paddy.

"And why would she be scratching you?"

"She saw me for one of the highwaymen robbing the coach, and there was I, devil knowing what to do, and all the people of the inn trying to put peace upon her, and me dodging, and then—"

"Man," said I, grabbing his arm, "'tis a game that ends on the—"

"Never a bit," he interrupted composedly. "Wasn't the old witch drunk, claws and all, and didn't even the great English lord, or whatever, send his servant to bring her in, and didn't he, the big man, stand in the door and spit on the floor and go in when he saw she was for battering all the servants and using worse talk than the sailors I heard in Bristol? It would not be me they were after, those men running. It would be her. And small power to them, but they were no good at it. I am for taking a stool in my hand—"

"Whist!" said I. "In England they would not be hitting great ladies with stools. Let us hearken to the brawl. She is fighting them finely."

For I had seen that Paddy spoke truth. The noble lady was engaged in battling with servants who had been in pursuit of her when she was in pursuit of Paddy. Never had I seen even my own father so drunk as she was then. But the heart-rending thing was the humble protests of the servants. "Your ladyship! Oh, your ladyship!"—as they came up one by one, or two by two, obeying orders of the Earl, to be incontinently boxed on the ears by a member of a profligate aristocracy. Probably any one of them was strong enough to throw the beldame out at a window. But such was not the manner of the time. One would think they would retreat upon the Earl and ask to be dismissed from his service. But this also was not the manner of the time. No; they marched up heroically and took their cuffs on the head and cried: "Oh, your ladyship! Please, your ladyship!" They were only pretenders in their attacks; all they could do was to wait until she was tired, and then humbly escort her to where she belonged, meanwhile pulling gently at her arms.

"She was after recognizing you then?" said I to Paddy.

"Indeed and she was," said he. He had dropped into a chair and was looking as if he needed a doctor to cure him of exhaustion. "She would be after having eyes like a sea-gull. And Jem Bottles was all for declaring that my disguise was complete, bad luck to the little man."

"Your disguise complete?" said I. "You couldn't disguise yourself unless you stood your head in a barrel. What talk is this?"

"Sure an' I looked no more like myself than I looked like a wild man with eight rows of teeth in his head," said Paddy mournfully. "My own mother would have been after taking me for a horse. 'Tis that old creature with her evil eye who would be seeing me when all the others were blind as bats. I could have walked down the big street in Cork without a man knowing me."

"That you could at any time," said I. The Countess had for some moments ceased to hammer on my door. "Hearken! I think they are managing her."

Either Hoity-Toity had lost heart, or the servants had gained some courage, for we heard them dragging her delicately down the staircase. Presently there was a silence.

After I had waited until this silence grew into the higher silence which seems like perfect safety, I rang the bell and ordered food and drink. Paddy had a royal meal, sitting on the floor by the fireplace and holding a platter on his knee. From time to time I tossed him something for which I did not care. He was very grateful for my generosity. He ate in a barbaric fashion, crunching bones of fowls between his great white teeth and swallowing everything.

I had a mind to discourse upon manners in order that Paddy might not shame me when we came to London; for a gentleman is known by the ways of his servants. If people of quality should see me attended by such a savage they would put me down small. "Paddy," said I, "mend your ways of eating."

"'My ways of eating,' your honour?" said he. "And am I not eating all that I can hold? I was known to be a good man at platter always. Sure I've seen no man in England eat more than me. But thank you kindly, sir."

"You misunderstand me," said I. "I wish to improve your manner of eating. It would not be fine enough for the sight of great people. You eat, without taking breath, pieces as big as a block of turf."

"'Tis the custom in my part of Ireland," answered Paddy.

"I understand," said I. "But over here 'tis only very low people who fall upon their meat from a window above."

"I am not in the way of understanding your honour," said he. "But any how a man may be respectable and yet have a good hunger on him."

## CHAPTER XIV

It had been said that the unexpected often happens, although I do not know what learned man of the time succeeded in thus succinctly expressing a great law and any how it matters little, for I have since discovered that these learned men make one headful of brains go a long way by dint of poaching on each other's knowledge. But the unexpected happened in this case, all true enough whatever.

I was giving my man a bit of a warning.

"Paddy," said I, "you are big, and you are red, and you are Irish; but by the same token you are not the great Fingal, son of lightning. I would strongly give you the word. When you see that old woman you start for the open moors."

"Devil fear me, sir," answered Paddy promptly. "I'll not be stopping. I would be swimming to Ireland before she lays a claw on me."

"And mind you exchange no words with her," said I, "for 'tis that which seems to work most wrongfully upon her."

"Never a word out of me," said he. "I'll be that busy getting up the road."

There was another tumult in the corridor, with the same screeches by one and the same humble protests by a multitude. The disturbance neared us with surprising speed. Suddenly I recalled that when the servant had retired after bringing food and drink I had neglected to again bar the door. I rushed for it, but I was all too late. I saw the latch raise. "Paddy!" I shouted wildly. "Mind yourself!" And with that I dropped to the floor and slid under the bed.

Paddy howled, and I lifted a corner of the valance to see what was transpiring. The door had been opened, and the Countess stood looking into the room. She was no longer in a fiery rage; she was cool, deadly determined, her glittering eye fixed on Paddy. She took a step forward.

Paddy, in his anguish, chanted to himself an Irish wail in which he described his unhappiness. "Oh, mother of me, and here I am caught again by the old hell-cat, and sure the way she creeps toward me is enough to put the fear of God in the heart of a hedge-robber, the murdering old witch. And it was me was living so fine and grand in England and greatly pleased with myself. Sorrow the day I left Ireland; it is, indeed."

She was now close to him, and she seemed to be preparing for one stupendous pounce which would mean annihilation to Paddy. Her lean hands were thrust out, with the fingers crooked, and it seemed to me that her fingers were very long. In despair Paddy changed his tune and addressed her.

"Ah, now, alanna. Sure the kind lady would be for doing no harm? Be easy, now, acushla."

But these tender appeals had no effect. Suddenly she pounced. Paddy roared, and sprang backward with splendid agility. He seized a chair.

Now I am quite sure that before he came to England Paddy had never seen a chair, although it is true that at some time in his life he may have had a peep through a window into an Irish gentleman's house, where there might be a chair if the King's officers in the neighbourhood were not very ambitious and powerful. But Paddy handled this chair as if he had seen many of them. He grasped it by the back and thrust it out, aiming all four legs at the Countess. It was a fine move. I have seen a moderately good swordsman fairly put to it by a pack of scoundrelly drawers who assailed him at all points in this manner.

"An you come on too fast," quavered Paddy, "ye can grab two legs, but there will be one left for your eye and another for your brisket."

However she came on, sure enough, and there was a moment of scuffling near the end of the bed out of my sight. I wriggled down to gain another view, and when I cautiously lifted an edge of the valance my eyes met the strangest sight ever seen in all England. Paddy, much dishevelled and panting like a hunt-dog, had wedged the Countess against the wall. She was pinioned by the four legs of the chair, and Paddy, by dint of sturdily pushing at the chair-back, was keeping her in a fixed position.

In a flash my mind was made up. Here was the time to escape. I scrambled quickly from under the bed. "Bravo, Paddy!" I cried, dashing about the room after my sword, coat, waistcoat, and hat. "Devil a fear but you'll hold her, my bucko! Push hard, my brave lad, and mind your feet don't slip!"

"If your honour pleases," said Paddy, without turning his eyes from his conquest, "'tis a little help I would be wishing here. She would be as strong in the shoulder as a good plough-horse and I am not for staying here for ever."

"Bravo, my grand lad!" I cried, at last finding my hat, which had somehow gotten into a corner. From the door I again addressed Paddy in encouraging speech. "There's a stout-hearted boy for you! Hold hard, and mind your feet don't slip!"

He cast a quick agonized look in my direction, and, seeing that I was about basely to desert him, he gave a cry, dropped the chair, and bolted after me. As we ran down the corridor I kept well in advance, thinking it the best place in case the pursuit should be energetic. But there was no pursuit. When Paddy was holding the Countess prisoner she could only choke and stammer, and I had no doubt that she now was well mastered by exhaustion.

Curiously there was little hubbub in the inn. The fact that the Countess was the rioter had worked in a way to cause people to seek secluded and darkened nooks. However, the landlord raised his bleat at me. "Oh, sir, such a misfortune to befall my house just when so many grand ladies and gentlemen are here."

I took him quietly by the throat and beat his head against the wall, once, twice, thrice.

"And you allow mad ladies to molest your guests, do you?" said I.

"Sir," he stuttered, "could I have caused her to cease?"

"True," I said, releasing him. "But now do as I bid you and quickly. I am away to London. I have had my plenty of you and your mad ladies."

We started bravely to London, but we only went to another and quieter inn, seeking peace and the absence of fear. I may say we found it, and, in a chair before a good fire, I again took my comfort. Paddy sat on the floor, toasting his shins. The warmth passed him into a reflective mood.

"And I know all I need of grand ladies," he muttered, staring into the fire. "I thought they were all for riding in gold coaches and smelling of beautiful flowers, and here they are mad to be chasing Irishmen in inns. I remember old Mag Cooligan fought with a whole regiment of King's troops in Bantry, and even the drums stopped beating, the soldiers were that much interested. But, sure, everybody would be knowing that Mag was no grand lady, although Pat Cooligan, her brother, was pig-killer to half the country-side. I am thinking we were knowing little about grand ladies. One of the soldiers had his head broke by a musket because the others were so ambitious to destroy the old lady, and she scratching them all. 'Twas long remembered in Bantry."

"Hold your tongue about your betters," said I sharply. "Don't be comparing this Mag Cooligan with a real Countess."

"There would be a strange similarity any how," said he. "But, sure, Mag never fought in inns, for the reason that they would not be letting her inside."

"Remember how little you are knowing of them, Paddy," said I. "'Tis not for you to be talking of the grand ladies when you have seen only one, and you would not be knowing another from a fish. Grand ladies are eccentric, I would have you to know. They have their ways with them which are not for omadhauns like you to understand."

"Eccentric, is it?" said he. "I thought it would be some such devilment."

"And I am knowing," said I with dignity, "of one lady so fine that if you don't stop talking that way of ladies I will break your thick skull for you, and it would matter to nobody."

"'Tis an ill subject for discussion, I am seeing that," said Paddy. "But, faith, I could free Ireland with an army of ladies like one I've seen."

"Will you be holding your tongue?" I cried wrathfully.

Paddy began to mumble to himself,—"Bedad, he was under the bed fast enough without offering her a stool by the fire and a small drop of drink which would be no more than decent with him so fond of her. I am not knowing the ways of these people."

In despair of his long tongue I made try to change the talking.

"We are off for London, Paddy. How are you for it?"

"London, is it?" said he warily. "I was hearing there are many fine ladies there."

For the second time in his life I cuffed him soundly on the ear.

"Now," said I, "be ringing the bell. I am for buying you a bit of drink; but if you mention the gentry to me once more in that blackguard way I'll lather you into a resemblance to your grandfather's bones."

After a pleasant evening I retired to bed leaving Paddy snug asleep by the fire. I thought much of my Lady Mary, but with her mother stalking the corridors and her knowing father with his eye wide open, I knew there was no purpose in hanging about a Bath inn. I would go to London, where there were gardens, and walks in the park, and parties, and other useful customs. There I would win my love.

The following morning I started with Paddy to meet Jem Bottles and travel to London. Many surprising adventures were in store for us, but an account of these I shall leave until another time, since one would not be worrying people with too many words, which is a great fault in a man who is recounting his own affairs.

## CHAPTER XV

As we ambled our way agreeably out of Bath, Paddy and I employed ourselves in worthy speech. He was not yet a notable horseman, but his Irish adaptability was so great that he was already able to think he would not fall off so long as the horse was old and tired.

"Paddy," said I, "how would you like to be an Englishman? Look at their cities. Sure, Skibbereen is a mud-pond to them. It might be fine to be an Englishman."

"I would not, your honour," said Paddy. "I would not be an Englishman while these grand—But never mind; 'tis many proud things I will say about the English considering they are our neighbours in one way; I mean they are near enough to come over and harm us when they wish. But any how they are a remarkable hard-headed lot, and in time they may come to something good."

"And is a hard head such a qualification?" said I.

Paddy became academic. "I have been knowing two kinds of hard heads," he said. "Mickey McGovern had such a hard skull on him no stick in the south of Ireland could crack it, though many were tried. And what happened to him? He died poor as a rat. 'Tis not the kind of hard head I am meaning. I am meaning the kind of hard head which believes it contains all the wisdom and honour in the world. 'Tis what I mean. If you have a head like that, you can go along blundering into ditches and tumbling over your own shins, and still hold confidence in yourself. 'Tis not very handsome for other men to see; but devil a bit care you, for you are warm inside with complacence."

"Here is a philosopher, in God's truth," I cried. "And where were you learning all this? In Ireland?"

"Your honour," said Paddy firmly, "you yourself are an Irishman. You are not for saying there is no education in Ireland, for it educates a man to see burning thatches and such like. One of them was my aunt's, Heaven rest her!"

"Your aunt?" said I. "And what of your aunt? What have the English to do with your aunt?"

"That's what she was asking them," said Paddy; "but they burned her house down over a little matter of seventeen years' rent she owed to a full-blooded Irishman, may the devil find him!"

"But I am for going on without an account of your burnt-thatch education," said I. "You are having more than two opinions about the English, and I would be hearing them. Seldom have I seen a man who could gain so much knowledge in so short a space. You are interesting me."

Paddy seemed pleased. "Well, your honour," said he confidentially, "'tis true for you. I am knowing the English down to their toes."

"And if you were an Englishman, what kind of an Englishman would you like to be?" said I.

"A gentleman," he answered swiftly. "A big gentleman!" Then he began to mimic and make gestures in a way that told me he had made good use of his eyes and of the society of underlings in the various inns. "Where's me man? Send me man!

Oh, here you are! And why didn't you know I wanted you? What right have you to think I don't want you? What? A servant dead? Pah! Send it down the back staircase at once and get rid of it. Bedad!" said Paddy enthusiastically, "I could do that fine!" And to prove what he said was true, he cried "Pah!" several times in a lusty voice.

"I see you have quickly understood many customs of the time," said I. "But 'tis not all of it. There are many quite decent people alive now."

"'Tis strange we have never heard tell of them," said Paddy musingly. "I have only heard of great fighters, blackguards, and beautiful ladies, but sure, as your honour says, there must be plenty of quiet decent people somewhere."

"There is," said I. "I am feeling certain of it, although I am not knowing exactly where to lay my hand upon them."

"Perhaps they would be always at mass," said Paddy, "and in that case your honour would not be likely to see them."

"Masses!" said I. "There are more masses said in Ireland in one hour than here in two years."

"The people would be heathens, then?" said Paddy, aghast.

"Not precisely," said I. "But they have reformed themselves several times, and a number of adequate reformations is a fine thing to confuse the Church. In Ireland we are all for being true to the ancient faith; here they are always for improving matters, and their learned men study the Sacred Book solely with a view to making needed changes."

"'Tis heathen they are," said Paddy with conviction. "I was knowing it. Sure, I will be telling Father Corrigan the minute I put a foot on Ireland, for nothing pleases him so much as a good obstinate heathen, and he very near discourses the hair off their heads."

"I would not be talking about such matters," said I. "It merely makes my head grow an ache. My father was knowing all about it; but he was always claiming that if a heathen did his duty by the poor he was as good as anybody, and that view I could never understand."

"Sure, if a heathen gives to the poor, 'tis poison to them," said Paddy. "If it is food and they eat it, they turn black all over and die the day after. If it is money, it turns red-hot and burns a hole in their hand, and the devil puts a chain through it and drags them down to hell, screeching."

"Say no more," said I. "I am seeing you are a true theologian of the time. I would be talking on some more agreeable topic, something about which you know less."

"I can talk of fishing," he answered diffidently. "For I am a great fisherman, sure. And then there would be turf-cutting, and the deadly stings given to men by eels. All these things I am knowing well."

"'Tis a grand lot to know," said I, "but let us be talking of London. Have you been hearing of London?"

"I have been hearing much about the town," said Paddy. "Father Corrigan was often talking of it. He was claiming it to be full of loose women, and sin, and fighting in the streets during mass."

"I am understanding something of the same," I replied. "It must be an evil city. I am fearing something may happen to you, Paddy,—you with your red head as conspicuous as a clock in a tower. The gay people will be setting upon you and carrying you off. Sure there has never been anything like you in London."

"I am knowing how to be dealing with them. It will be all a matter of religious up-bringing, as Father Corrigan was saying. I have but to go to my devotions, and the devil will fly away with them."

"And supposing they have your purse?" said I. "The devil might fly away with them to an ill tune for you."

"When they are flying away with my purse," he replied suggestively, "they will be flying away with little of what could be called my ancestral wealth."

"You are natural rogues," said I, "you and Jem Bottles. And you had best not be talking of religion."

"Sure a man may take the purse of an ugly old sick monkey like him, and still go with an open face to confession," rejoined Paddy, "and I would not be backward if Father Corrigan's church was a mile beyond."

"And are you meaning that Father Corrigan would approve you in this robbery?" I cried.

"Devil a bit he would, your honour," answered Paddy indignantly. "He would be saying to me: 'Paddy, you limb of Satan, and how much did you get?' I would be telling him. 'Give fifteen guineas to the Church, you mortal sinner, and I will be trying my best for you,' he would be saying. And I would be giving them."

"You are saved fifteen guineas by being in England, then," said I, "for they don't do that here. And I am thinking you are traducing your clergy, you vagabond."

"Traducing?" said he. "That would mean giving them money. Aye, I was doing it often. One year I gave three silver shillings."

"You're wrong," said I. "By 'traducing' I mean speaking ill of your priest."

"'Speaking ill of my priest'?" cried Paddy, gasping with amazement. "Sure, my own mother never heard a word out of me!"

"However," said I, "we will be talking of other things. The English land seems good."

Paddy cast his eye over the rainy landscape. "I am seeing no turf for cutting," he remarked disapprovingly, "and the potatoes would not be growing well here. 'Tis a barren country."

At nightfall we came to a little inn which was ablaze with light and ringing with exuberant cries. We gave up our horses and entered. To the left was the closed door of the taproom, which now seemed to furnish all the noise. I asked the landlord to tell me the cause of the excitement.

"Sir," he answered, "I am greatly honoured tonight. Mr. O'Ruddy, the celebrated Irish swordsman, is within, recounting a history of his marvellous exploits."

"Indeed!" said I.

"Bedad!" said Paddy.

## CHAPTER XVI

Paddy was for opening his mouth wide immediately, but I checked him. "I would see this great man," said I to the landlord, "but I am so timid by nature I fear to meet his eagle eye. Is there no way by which we could observe him in secret at our leisure?"

"There be one way," remarked the landlord after deliberation. I had passed him a silver coin. He led us to a little parlour back of the taproom. Here a door opened into the tap itself, and in this door was cut a large square window so that the good man of the inn could sometimes sit at his ease in his great chair in the snug parlour and observe that his customers had only that for which they were paying. It is a very good plan, for I have seen many a worthy man become a rogue merely because nobody was watching him. My father often was saying that if he had not been narrowly eyed all his young life, first by his mother and then by his wife, he had little doubt but what he might have been engaged in dishonest practices sooner or later.

A confident voice was doing some high talking in the taproom. I peered through the window, but at first I saw only a collection of gaping yokels, poor bent men with faces framed in straggly whiskers. Each had a pint pot clutched with a certain air of determination in his right hand.

Suddenly upon our line of vision strode the superb form of Jem Bottles. A short pipe was in his mouth, and he gestured splendidly with a pint pot. "More of the beer, my dear," said he to a buxom maid. "We be all rich in Ireland. And four of them set upon me," he cried again to the yokels. "All noblemen, in fine clothes and with sword-hilts so flaming with jewels an ordinary man might have been blinded. 'Stop!' said I. 'There be more of your friends somewhere. Call them.' And with that—"

"'And with that'?" said I myself, opening the door and stepping in upon him. "'And with that'?" said I again. Whereupon I smote him a blow which staggered him against the wall, holding his crown with both hands while his broken beer-pot rolled on the floor. Paddy was dancing with delight at seeing some other man cuffed, but the landlord and the yokels were nearly dead of terror. But they made no sound; only the buxom girl whimpered.

"There is no cause for alarm," said I amiably. "I was only greeting an old friend. 'Tis a way I have. And how wags the world with you, O'Ruddy?"

"I am not sure for the moment," replied Jem Bottles ruefully. "I must bide till it stops spinning."

"Truth," cried I. "That would be a light blow to trouble the great O'Ruddy. Come now; let us have the pots filled again, and O'Ruddy shall tell us more of his adventures. What say you, lads?"

The yokels had now recovered some of their senses, and they greeted my plan with hoarse mutterings of hasty and submissive assent.

"Begin," said I sternly to the highwayman. He stood miserably on one foot. He looked at the floor; he looked at the wall; from time to time he gave me a sheep's glance. "Begin," said I again. Paddy was wild with glee. "Begin," said I for the third time and very harshly.

"I—" gulped out the wretched man, but he could get no further.

"I am seeing I must help you," said I. "Come now, when did you learn the art of sticadoro proderodo sliceriscum fencing?"

Bottles rolled the eyes of despair at me, but I took him angrily by the shoulder. "Come now; when did you learn the art of sticadoro proderodo sliceriscum fencing?"

Jem Bottles staggered, but at last he choked out: "My mother taught me." Here Paddy retired from the room, doubled in a strong but soundless convulsion.

"Good," said I. "Your mother taught you. We are making progress any how. Your mother taught you. And now tell me this: When you slew Cormac of the Cliffs, what passado did you use? Don't be stuttering. Come now; quick with you; what passado did you use? What passado?"

With a heroism born of a conviction that in any event he was a lost man, Jem Bottles answered: "A blue one."

"Good," I cried cheerfully. "'A blue one'! We are coming on fine. He killed Cormac with a blue passado. And now I would be asking you—"

"Master," interrupted the highwayman with sudden resolution. "I will say no more. I have done. You may kill me an it pleases you."

Now I saw that enough was enough. I burst into laughter and clapped him merrily on the shoulder. "Be cheery, O'Ruddy," I cried. "Sure an Irishman like you ought to be able to look a joke in the face." He gave over his sulks directly, and I made him buy another pint each for the yokels. "'Twas dry work listening to you and your exploits, O'Ruddy," said I.

Later I went to my chamber, attended by my followers, having ordered roast fowls and wine to be served as soon as possible. Paddy and Jem Bottles sat on stools one at each side of the fireplace, and I occupied a chair between them.

Looking at my two faithful henchmen, I was suddenly struck by the thought that they were not very brisk servants for a gentleman to take to fashionable London. I had taken Paddy out of his finery and dressed him in a suit of decent brown; but his hair was still unbarbered, and I saw that unless I had a care his appearance would greatly surprise and please London. I resolved to have him shorn at the first large town.

As for Jem Bottles, his clothes were well enough, and indeed he was passable in most ways unless it was his habit, when hearing a sudden noise, to take a swift dark look to the right and to the left. Then, further, people might shrewdly note his way of always sitting with his back to the wall and his face to the door. However, I had no doubt of my ability to cure him of these tricks as soon as he was far enough journeyed from the scenes of his earlier activity.

But the idea I entertained at this moment was more to train them to be fine grand servants, such as I had seen waiting on big people in Bath. They were both willing enough, but they had no style to them. I decided to begin at once and see what I could teach them.

"Paddy," said I, taking off my sword and holding it out to him. "My sword!"

Paddy looked at it. "It is, sir," he answered respectfully.

"Bad scran to you, Paddy!" I cried angrily. "I am teaching you your duties. Take the sword! In both hands, mind you! Now march over and lay it very tenderly on the stand at the head of the bed. There now!"

I now turned my attention to Jem Bottles.

"Bottles," said I peremptorily, "my coat and waistcoat."

"Yes, sir," replied Bottles quickly, profiting by Paddy's lesson.

"There now," said I, as Bottles laid the coat and waistcoat on a dresser. "'Tis a good beginning. When supper comes I shall teach you other duties."

The supper came in due course, and after the inn's man had gone I bid Jem and Paddy stand one on either side of my chair and a little way back. "Now," said I, "stand square on your feet, and hold your heads away high, and stick your elbows out a little, and try to look as if you don't know enough to tell fire from water. Jem Bottles has it. That's it! Bedad! look at the ignorance on him! He's the man for you, Paddy! Wake up now, and look stupid. Am I not telling you?"

"Begor!" said Paddy dejectedly, "I feel like the greatest omadhaun in all the west country, and if that is not being stupid enough for your honour I can do no better."

"Shame to you, Paddy, to let an Englishman beat you so easily," said I. "Take that grin off your face, you scoundrel! Now," I added, "we are ready to begin. Wait, now. You must each have something to hold in your fist. Let me be thinking. There's only one plate and little of anything else. Ah, I have it! A bottle! Paddy, you shall hold one of the bottles. Put your right hand underneath it, and with your left hand hold it by the neck. But keep your elbows out. Jem, what the devil am I to give you to hold? Ah, I have it! Another bottle! Hold it the same as Paddy. Now! Stand square on your feet, and hold your heads away high, and stick your elbows out a little, and look stupid. I am going to eat my supper."

I finished my first and second bottles with the silence only broken by the sound of my knife-play and an occasional restless creaking of boots as one of my men slyly shifted his position. Wishing to call for my third bottle, I turned and caught them exchanging a glance of sympathetic bewilderment. As my eye flashed upon them, they stiffened up like grenadier recruits.

But I was not for being too hard on them at first. "'Tis enough for one lesson," said I. "Put the bottles by me and take your ease."

With evident feelings of relief they slunk back to the stools by the fire, where they sat recovering their spirits.

After my supper I sat in the chair toasting my shins and lazily listening to my lads finishing the fowls. They seemed much more like themselves, sitting there grinding away at the bones and puffing with joy. In the red firelight it was such a scene of happiness that I misdoubted for a moment the wisdom of my plan to make them into fine grand numskulls.

I could see that all men were not fitted for the work. It needed a beefy person with fat legs and a large amount of inexplicable dignity, a regular God-knows-why loftiness. Truth, in those days, real talent was usually engaged in some form of rascality, barring the making of books and sermons. When one remembers the impenetrable dulness of the great mass of the people, the frivolity of the gentry, the arrogance and wickedness of the court, one ceases to wonder that many men of taste took to the highway as a means of recreation and livelihood. And there I had been attempting to turn my two frank rascals into the kind of sheep-headed rubbish whom you could knock down a great staircase, and for a guinea they would say no more. Unless I was the kicker, I think Paddy would have returned up the staircase after his assailant. Jem Bottles probably would have gone away nursing his wrath and his injury, and planning to waylay the kicker on a convenient night. But neither would have taken a guinea and said no more. Each of these simple-hearted reprobates was too spirited to take a guinea for a kick down a staircase.

Any how I had a mind that I could be a gentleman true enough without the help of Jem and Paddy making fools of themselves. I would worry them no more.

As I was musing thus my eyes closed from a sense of contented weariness, but I was aroused a moment later by hearing Paddy address Jem Bottles in a low voice. "'Tis you who are the cool one, Jem!" said he with admiration, "trying to make them think you were *him*!" Here I was evidently indicated by a sideways bob of the head. "Have you not been seeing the fine ways of him? Sure, be looking at his stride and his habit of slatting people over the head, and his grand manners with his food. You are looking more like a candlestick than you are looking like him. I wonder at you."

"But I befooled them," said Bottles proudly. "I befooled them well. It was Mr. O'Ruddy here, and Mr. O'Ruddy there, and the handsome wench she gave me many a glance of her eye, she did."

"Sorrow the day for her, then," responded Paddy, "and if you would be cozening the girls in the name of *him* there, he will be cozening you, and I never doubt it."

"'Twas only a trick to make the time go easy, it was," said Bottles gloomily. "If you remember, Master Paddy, I have spent the most of my new service waiting under oak-trees; and I will not be saying that it rained always, but oft-times it did rain most accursedly."

## CHAPTER XVII

We rode on at daybreak. At the first large village I bid a little man cut Paddy's hair, and although Paddy was all for killing the little man, and the little man twice ran away, the work was eventually done, for I stood over Paddy and threatened him. Afterward the little boys were not so anxious to hoot us through the streets, calling us Africans. For it must be recalled that at this time there was great curiosity in the provinces over the Africans, because it was known that in London people of fashion often had African servants; and although London cared nothing for the provinces, and the provinces cared nothing for London, still the rumour of the strange man interested the country clodhopper so greatly that he called Paddy an African on principle, in order that he might blow to his neighbours that he had seen the fascinating biped. There was no general understanding that the African was a man of black skin; it was only understood that he was a great marvel. Hence the urchins in these far-away villages often ran at the heels of Paddy's horse, yelling.

In time the traffic on the highway became greatly thickened, and several times we thought we were entering London because of the large size and splendour of the towns to which we came. Paddy began to fear the people had been deceiving us as to the road, and that we had missed London entirely. But finally we came to a river with hundreds of boats upon it, and there was a magnificent bridge, and on the other bank was a roaring city, and through the fog the rain came down thick as the tears of the angels. "That's London," said I.

We rode out upon the bridge, all much interested, but somewhat fearful, for the noise of the city was terrible. But if it was terrible as we approached it, I hesitate to say what it was to us when we were once fairly in it. "Keep close to me," I yelled to Paddy and Jem, and they were not unwilling. And so we rode into this pandemonium, not having the least idea where we were going.

As we progressed I soon saw what occasioned the major part of the noise. Many heavy carts thundered slowly through the narrow, echoing streets, bumping their way uproariously over a miserable pavement. Added to this, of course, were the shrill or hoarse shouts of the street vendors and the apprentices at the shop-doors. To the sky arose an odour almost insupportable, for it was new to us all.

The eaves of the houses streamed with so much water that the sidewalks were practically untenable, although here and there a hardy wayfarer strode on regardless of a drenched cloak, probably being too proud to take to the street. Once our travel was entirely blocked by a fight. A butcher in a bloody apron had dashed out of his shop and attacked the driver of a brewer's sledge. A crowd gathered miraculously and cheered on this spectacle; women appeared at all the windows; urchins hooted; mongrel dogs barked. When the butcher had been worsted and chased back into his shop by the maddened brewer we were allowed to pursue our journey.

I must remark that neither of these men used aught but his hands. Mostly their fists were doubled, and they dealt each other sounding, swinging blows; but there was some hair-pulling, and when the brewer had the butcher down I believe the butcher tried to bite his opponent's ear. However they were rather high-class for their condition. I found out later that at this time in the darker parts of London the knife was a favourite weapon of the English and was as rampant as ever it is in the black alleys of an Italian city. It was no good news for me, for the Irish had long been devoted to the cudgel.

When I wish for information I always prefer making the request to a gentleman. To have speech of a boor is well enough if he would not first study you over to find, if he can, why you want the information, and, after a prolonged pause, tell you wrong entirely. I perceived a young gentleman standing in under a porch and ogling a window on the opposite side of the way. "Sir," said I, halting my horse close to him, "would you be so kind as to point to a stranger the way to a good inn?" He looked me full in the face, spat meaningly in the gutter, and, turning on his heel, walked away. And I will give oath he was not more than sixteen years old.

I sat stiff in the saddle; I felt my face going hot and cold. This new-feathered bird with a toy sword! But to save me, as it happened, from a preposterous quarrel with this infant, another man came along the sidewalk. He was an older man, with a grave mouth and a clean-cut jowl. I resolved to hail him. "And now my man," said I under my breath, "if you are as bad as the other, by the mass, I'll have a turnover here with you, London or no London."

Then I addressed him. "Sir—" I began. But here a cart roared on my other side, and I sat with my mouth open, looking at him. He smiled a little, but waited courteously for the hideous din to cease. "Sir," I was enabled to say at last, "would you be so kind as to point to a stranger the way to a good inn?" He scanned me quietly, in order, no doubt, to gain an idea what kind of inn would suit my condition. "Sir," he answered, coming into the gutter and pointing, "'tis this way to Bishopsgate Street, and there you will see the sign of the 'Pig and Turnip,' where there is most pleasurable accommodation for man and beast, and an agreeable host." He was a shop-keeper of the city of London, of the calm, steady breed that has made successive kings either love them or fearingly hate them,—the bone and the sinew of the great town.

I thanked him heartily, and we went on to the "Pig and Turnip." As we clattered into the inn yard it was full of people mounting and dismounting, but there seemed a thousand stable-boys. A dozen flung themselves at my horse's head. They quite lifted me out of the saddle in their great care that I should be put to no trouble. At the door of the inn a smirking landlord met me, bowing his head on the floor at every backward pace, and humbly beseeching me to tell how he could best serve me. I told him, and at once there was a most pretentious hubbub. Six or eight servants began to run hither and yon. I was delighted with my reception, but several days later I discovered they had mistaken me for a nobleman of Italy or France, and I was expected to pay extravagantly for graceful empty attentions rather than for sound food and warm beds.

This inn was so grand that I saw it would no longer do for Paddy and Jem to be sleeping in front of my fire like big dogs, so I nodded assent when the landlord asked if he should provide lodgings for my two servants. He packed them off somewhere, and I was left lonely in a great chamber. I had some fears having Paddy long out of my sight, but I assured myself that London had such terrors for him he would not dare any Irish mischief. I could trust Jem Bottles to be discreet, for he had learned discretion in a notable school.

Toward the close of the afternoon, the rain ceased, and, attiring myself for the street and going to the landlord, I desired him to tell me what interesting or amusing walk could now conveniently be taken by a gentleman who was a stranger to the sights of London. The man wagged his head in disapproval.

"'Twill be dark presently, sir," he answered, "and I would be an ill host if I did not dissuade a perfect stranger from venturing abroad in the streets of London of a night-time."

"And is it as bad as that?" I cried, surprised.

"For strangers, yes," said he. "For they be for ever wandering, and will not keep to the three or four streets which be as safe as the King's palace. But if you wish, sir, I will provide one man with a lantern and staff to go before you, and another man with lan tern and staff to follow. Then, with two more stout lads and your own servants, I would venture—"

"No, no!" I cried, "I will not head an army on a night march when I intended merely an evening stroll. But how, pray you, am I to be entertained otherwise than by going forth?"

The innkeeper smiled with something like pity.

"Sir, every night there meets here such a company of gay gentlemen, wits and poets, as would dazzle the world did it but hear one half of what they say over their pipes and their punch. I serve the distinguished company myself, for I dare trust nobody's care in a matter so important to my house; and I assure you, sir, I have at times been so doubled with mirth there was no life in me. Why, sir, Mr. Fullbil himself comes here at times!"

"Does he, indeed?" I cried, although I never had heard of the illustrious man.

"Indeed and he does, sir," answered the innkeeper, pleased at my quick appreciation of this matter. "And then there is goings on, I warrant me. Mr. Bobbs and the other gentlemen will be in spirits."

"I never doubt you," said I. "But is it possible for a private gentleman of no wit to gain admittance to this distinguished company?"

"Doth require a little managing, sir," said he, full of meaning.

"Pray you manage it then," said I, "for I have nought to do in London for at least two days, and I would be seeing these famous men with whose names my country rings."

Early in the evening the innkeeper came to me, much pleased. "Sir, the gentlemen bid me bring you their compliments, and I am to say they would be happy to have a pleasure in the honour of your presence. Mr. Fullbil himself is in the chair tonight. You are very fortunate, sir."

"I am," said I. "Lead away, and let us hope to find the great Fullbil in high feather."

## CHAPTER XVIII

The innkeeper led me down to a large room the door of which he had flung open with a flourish. "The furrin' gentleman, may it please you, sirs," he announced, and then retired.

The room was so full of smoke that at first I could see little, but soon enough I made out a long table bordered with smoking and drinking gentlemen. A hoarse voice, away at the head of the board, was growling some words which convulsed most of the gentlemen with laughter. Many candles burned dimly in the haze.

I stood for a moment, doubtful as to procedure, but a gentleman near the foot of the table suddenly arose and came toward me with great frankness and good nature. "Sir," he whispered, so that he would not interrupt the growls at the farther end of the room, "it would give me pleasure if you would accept a chair near me."

I could see that this good gentleman was moved solely by a desire to be kind to a stranger, and I, in another whisper, gave my thanks and assent to his plan. He placed me in a chair next his own. The voice was still growling from the head of the table.

Very quickly my eyes became accustomed to the smoke, especially after I was handed a filled clay pipe by my new and excellent friend. I began to study the room and the people in it. The room was panelled in new oak, and the chairs and table were all of new oak, well carved. It was the handsomest room I had ever been in.

Afterward I looked toward the growl. I saw a little old man in a chair much too big for him, and in a wig much too big for him. His head was bent forward until his sharp chin touched his breast, and out from under his darkling brows a pair of little eyes flashed angrily and arrogantly. All faces were turned toward him, and all ears were open to his growls. He was the king; it was Fullbil.

His speech was all addressed to one man, and I looked at the latter. He was a young man with a face both Roman and feminine; with that type of profile which is possessed by most of the popular actors in the reign of His Majesty of today. He had luxuriant hair, and, stung by the taunts of Fullbil, he constantly brushed it nervously from his brow while his sensitive mouth quivered with held-in retorts. He was Bobbs, the great dramatist.

And as Fullbil growled, it was a curiously mixed crowd which applauded and laughed. There were handsome lordlings from the very top of London cheek by cheek with sober men who seemed to have some intellectual occupation in life. The lordlings did the greater part of the sniggering. In the meantime everybody smoked hard and drank punch harder. During occasional short pauses in Fullbil's remarks, gentlemen passed ecstatic comments one to another.—"Ah, this is indeed a mental feast!"—"Did ye ever hear him talk more wittily?"—"Not I, faith; he surpasses even himself!"—"Is it not a blessing to sit at table with such a master of learning and wit?"—"Ah, these are the times to live in!"

I thought it was now opportune to say something of the same kind to my amiable friend, and so I did it. "The old corpse seems to be saying a prayer," I remarked. "Why don't he sing it?"

My new friend looked at me, all agape, like a fish just over the side of the boat. "'Tis Fullbil, the great literary master—" he began; but at this moment Fullbil, having recovered from a slight fit of coughing, resumed his growls, and my friend subsided again into a worshipping listener.

For my part I could not follow completely the words of the great literary master, but I construed that he had pounced upon the drama of the time and was tearing its ears and eyes off.

At that time I knew little of the drama, having never read or seen a play in my life; but I was all for the drama on account of poor Bobbs, who kept chewing his lip and making nervous movements until Fullbil finished, a thing which I thought was not likely to happen before an early hour of the morning. But finish he did, and immediately Bobbs, much impassioned, brought his glass heavily down on the table in a demand for silence. I thought he would get little hearing, but, much to my surprise, I heard again the ecstatic murmur: "Ah, now, we shall hear Bobbs reply to Fullbil!"—"Are we not fortunate?"—"Faith, this will be over half London tomorrow!"

Bobbs waited until this murmur had passed away. Then he began, nailing an impressive forefinger to the table:

"Sir, you have been contending at some length that the puzzling situations which form the basis of our dramas of the day could not possibly occur in real life because five minutes of intelligent explanation between the persons concerned would destroy the silly mystery before anything at all could happen. Your originality, sir, is famous—need I say it?—and when I hear you champion this opinion in all its majesty of venerable age and general acceptance I feel stunned by the colossal imbecile strength of the whole proposition. Why, sir, you may recall all the mysterious murders which occurred in England since England had a name. The truth of them remains in unfathomable shadow. But, sir, any one of them could be cleared up in five minutes' intelligent explanation. Pontius Pilate could have been saved his blunder by far, far, far less than five minutes of intelligent explanation. But—mark ye!—but who has ever heard five minutes of intelligent explanation? The complex interwoven mesh of life constantly, eternally, prevents people from giving intelligent explanations. You sit in the theatre, and you say to yourself: 'Well, I could mount the stage, and in a short talk to these people I could anticipate a further continuation of the drama.' Yes, you could; but you are an outsider. You have no relations with these characters. You arise like an angel. Nobody has been your enemy; nobody has been your mistress. You arise and give the five minutes' intelligent explanation; bah! There is not a situation in life which does not need five minutes' intelligent explanation; but it does not get it."

It could now be seen that the old man Fullbil was simply aflame with a destructive reply, and even Bobbs paused under the spell of this anticipation of a gigantic answering. The literary master began very deliberately.

"My good friend Bobbs," said he, "I see your nose gradually is turning red."

The drama immediately pitched into oblivion. The room thundered with a great shout of laughter that went to the ceiling. I could see Bobbs making angry shouts against an invulnerable bank of uncontrolled merriment. And amid his victory old Fullbil sat with a vain smile on his cracked lips.

My excellent and adjacent friend turned to me in a burst of enthusiasm.

"And did you ever hear a thing so well turned? Ha, ha! 'My good friend Bobbs,' quoth he, 'I see your nose gradually is turning red.' Ha, ha, ha! By my King, I have seldom heard a wittier answer."

"Bedad!" said I, somewhat bewildered, but resolved to appreciate the noted master of wit, "it stamped the drama down into the ground. Sure, never another play will be delivered in England after that tremendous overthrow."

"Aye," he rejoined, still shuddering with mirth, "I fail to see how the dramatists can survive it. It was like the wit of a new Shakespeare. It subsided Bobbs to nothing. I would not be surprised at all if Bobbs now entirely quit the writing of plays, since Fullbil's words so closely hit his condition in the dramatic world. A dangerous dog is this Fullbil."

"It reminds me of a story my father used to tell—" I began.

"Sir," cried my new friend hastily, "I beg of you! May I, indeed, insist? Here we talk only of the very deepest matters."

"Very good, sir," I replied amiably. "I will appear better, no doubt, as a listener; but if my father was alive—"

"Sir," beseeched my friend, "the great Fancher, the immortal critic, is about to speak."

"Let him," said I, still amiable.

A portly gentleman of middle age now addressed Bobbs amid a general and respectful silence.

"Sir," he remarked, "your words concerning the great age of what I shall call the five-minutes-intelligent-explanation theory was first developed by the Chinese, and is contemporaneous, I believe, with their adoption of the custom of roasting their meat instead of eating it raw."

"Sir, I am interested and instructed," rejoined Bobbs.

Here old Fullbil let go two or three growls of scornful disapproval.

"Fancher," said he, "my delight in your company is sometimes dimmed by my appreciation of your facilities for being entirely wrong. The great theory of which you speak so confidently, sir, was born no earlier than seven o'clock on the morning of this day. I was in my bed, sir; the maid had come in with my tea and toast. 'Stop,' said I, sternly. She stopped. And in those few moments of undisturbed reflection, sir, the thought came to life, the thought which you so falsely attribute to the Chinese, a savage tribe whose sole distinction is its ability to fly kites.”

After the murmurs of glee had died away, Fancher answered with spirit:

“Sir, that you are subject to periods of reflection I will not deny, I cannot deny. Nor can I say honour ably that I give my support to our dramatic friend’s defence of his idea. But, sir, when you refer to the Chinese in terms which I cannot but regard as insulting, I am prepared, sir, to—”

There were loud cries of “Order! Order! Order!” The wrathful Fancher was pulled down into his chair by soothful friends and neighbours, to whom he gesticulated and cried out during the uproar.

I looked toward old Fullbil, expecting to see him disturbed, or annoyed, or angry. On the contrary he seemed pleased, as a little boy who had somehow created a row.

“The excellent Fancher,” said he, “the excellent Fancher is wroth. Let us proceed, gentlemen, to more friendly topics. You, now, Doctor Chord, with what new thing in chemics are you ready to astound us?”

The speech was addressed to a little man near me, who instantly blushed crimson, mopping his brow in much agitation, and looked at the table, unable for the moment to raise his eyes or speak a word.

“One of the greatest scientists of the time,” said my friend in my ear.

“Sir,” faltered the little man in his bashfulness, “that part of the discourse which related to the flying of kites has interested me greatly, and I am ready to contend that kites fly, not, as many say, through the influence of a demon or spirit which inhabits the materials, but through the pressure of the wind itself.”

Fancher, now himself again, said:

“I wish to ask the learned doctor whether he refers to Chinese kites?”

The little man hurriedly replied that he had not Chinese kites in his mind at all.

“Very good, then,” said the great critic. “Very good.”

“But, sir,” said Fullbil to little Chord, “how is it that kites may fly without the aid of demons or spirits, if they are made by man? For it is known, sir, that man may not move in the air without the aid of some devilish agency, and it is also known that he may not send aloft things formed of the gross materials of the earth. How, then, can these kites fly virtuously?”

There was a general murmur of approbation of Fullbil’s speech, and the little doctor cast down his eyes and blushed again, speechless.

It was a triumph for Fullbil, and he received the congratulations of his friends with his faint vain smile implying that it was really nothing, you know, and that he could have done it much better if he had thought that anybody was likely to heed it.

The little Doctor Chord was so downtrodden that for the remainder of the evening he hardly dared to raise his eyes from the table, but I was glad to see him apply himself industriously to the punch.

To my great alarm Fullbil now said: “Sirs, I fear we have suffered ourselves to forget we have with us tonight a strange gentleman from foreign parts. Your good fortune, sir,” he added, bowing to me over his glass. I bowed likewise, but I saw his little piggish eyes looking wickedly at me. There went a titter around the board, and I understood from it that I was the next victim of the celebrated Fullbil.

“Sir,” said he, “may I ask from what part of Italy do you come?”

“I come from Ireland, sir,” I answered decently.

He frowned. “Ireland is not in Italy, sir,” said he. “Are you so good as to trifle with me, sir?”

“I am not, sir,” said I.

All the gentlemen murmured; some looked at me with pity, some with contempt. I began to be frightened until I remembered that if I once drew my sword I could chase the whole roomful of philosophy into the next parish. I resolved to put on a bold front.

"Probably, sir," observed Fullbil, "the people of Ireland have heard so much of me that I may expect many visits from Irish gentlemen who wish to hear what my poor mind may develop in regard to the only true philosophy of life?"

"Not in the least, sir," I rejoined. "Over there they don't know you are alive, and they are not caring."

Consternation fell upon that assembly like snow from a roof. The gentlemen stared at me. Old Fullbil turned purple at first, but his grandeur could not be made to suffer long or seriously from my impudence. Presently he smiled at me,—a smile confident, cruel, deadly.

"Ireland is a great country, sir," he observed.

"'Tis not so great as many people's ignorance of it," I replied bluntly, for I was being stirred somewhat.

"Indeed!" cried Fullbil. Then he triumphantly added: "Then, sir, we are proud to have among us one so manifestly capable of giving us instruction."

There was a loud shout of laughter at this sally, and I was very uncomfortable down to my toes; but I resolved to hold a brave face, and pretended that I was not minding their sneers. However, it was plain enough that old Fullbil had made me the butt of the evening.

"Sir," said the dramatist Bobbs, looking at me, "I understand that in Ireland pigs sit at table with even the best families."

"Sir," said the critic, Fancher, looking at me, "I understand that in Ireland the chastity of the women is so great that no child is born without a birthmark in the shape of the initials of the legal husband and father."

"Sir," said old Fullbil, "I understand that in Ireland people go naked when it rains, for fear of wetting their clothes."

Amid the uproarious merriment provoked by their speeches I sat in silence. Suddenly the embarrassed little scientist, Doctor Chord, looked up at me with a fine friendly sympathy. "A glass with you, sir," he said, and as we nodded our heads solemnly over the rims I felt that there had come to my help one poor little frightened friend. As for my first acquaintance, he, seeing me attacked not only by the redoubtable Fullbil, but also by the formidable Bobbs and the dangerous Fancher, had immediately begun to pretend that never in his life had he spoken to me.

Having a great knowledge of Irish character I could see that trouble was brewing for somebody, but I resolved to be very backward, for I hesitated to create a genuine disturbance in these philosophical circles. However, I was saved this annoyance in a strange manner. The door opened, and a newcomer came in, bowing right and left to his acquaintances, and finally taking a seat near Fullbil. I recognized him instantly; he was Sir Edmund Flixton, the gentleman who had had some thought of fighting me in Bath, but who had refrained from it upon hearing that I had worsted Forister.

However, he did not perceive me at that time. He chattered with Fullbil, telling him evidently some very exciting news, for I heard the old man ejaculate. "By my soul, can it be possible?" Later Fullbil related some amusing things to Flixton, and, upon an inquiry from Flixton, I was pointed out to him. I saw Flixton's face change; he spoke hastily to old Fullbil, who turned pale as death. Swiftly some bit of information flashed around the board, and I saw men's eyes open wide and white as they looked at me.

I have said it was the age of bullies. It was the age when men of physical prowess walked down the street shouldering lesser men into the gutter, and the lesser men had never a word to say for themselves. It was the age when if you expressed opinions contrary to those of a bully he was confidently expected to kill you or somehow maltreat you.

Of all that company of genius there now seemed to be only one gentleman who was not a-tremble. It was the little scientist Doctor Chord. He looked at me with a bright and twinkling eye; suddenly he grinned broadly. I could not but burst into laughter when I noted the appetite with which he enjoyed the confusion and alarm of his friends.

"Come, Fullbil! Come, Bobbs! Come, Fancher! Where are all your pretty wits?" he cried; for this timid little man's impudence increased mightily amid all this helpless distress. "Here's the dignity and power of learning of you, in God's truth. Here's knowledge enthroned, fearless, great! Have ye all lost your tongues?"

And he was for going on to worry them, but that I called out to him,—

"Sir," said I mildly, "if it please you, I would not have the gentlemen disturbed over any little misunderstanding of a pleasant evening. As regards quarrelling, I am all milk and water myself. It reminds me of an occasion in Ireland once when—" Here I recounted a story which Father Donovan always began on after more than three bottles, and to my knowledge he had never succeeded in finishing it. But this time I finished it. "And," said I, "the fellow was sitting there drinking with them, and they had had good fun with him, when of a sudden he up and spoke. Says he: ''Tis God's truth I never expected in all my life to be an evening in the company of such a lot of scurvy rat-eaters,' he says to them. 'And,' says he, 'I have only one word for that squawking old masquerading peacock that sits at the head of the table,' says he. 'What little he has of learning I could put in my eye without going blind,' says he. 'The old curmudgeon!' says he. And with that he arose and left the room, afterward becoming the King of Galway and living to a great age."

This amusing tale created a sickly burst of applause, in the midst of which I bowed myself from the room.

## CHAPTER XIX

On my way to my chamber I met the innkeeper and casually asked him after Paddy and Jem. He said that he would send to have word of them and inform me as soon as possible. Later a drawer came to my door and told me that Paddy and Jem, with three men-servants of gentlemen sleeping at the inn, had sallied out to a mug-house.

"Mug-house?" said I. "What in the devil's name is a mug-house?"

"Mug-house, sir?" said the man, staring. "Mug-house? Why, sir, 'tis—'tis a form of amusement, sir."

"It is, is it?" said I. "Very good. And does any one here know to what mug-house they went?"

"The 'Red Slipper,' I think, sir," said the man.

"And how do I get to it?" said I.

"Oh, sir," he cried, "'tis impossible!"

"Is it?" said I. "And why is it? The innkeeper said the same to me, and I would like to hear all the reasons."

"Sir," said the man, "when it becometh dark in London there walk abroad many men of evil minds who are no respecters of persons, but fall upon whomsoever they, may, beating them sorely, having no regard for that part of the Holy Book in which it is written—"

"Let go," said I. "I see what you mean." I then bade him get for me a stout lad with a cudgel and a lantern and a knowledge of the whereabouts of the "Red Slipper."

I, with the stout lad, had not been long in the street before I understood what the landlord and the waiter had meant. In fact we were scarce out of the door before the man was menacing with his cudgel two human vultures who slunk upon us out of the shadow. I saw their pale, wicked, snarling faces in the glow of the lantern.

A little later a great shindy broke out in the darkness, and I heard voices calling loudly for a rally in the name of some guild or society. I moved closer, but I could make out little save that it was a very pretty fight in which a company of good citizens were trying to put to flight a band of roughs and law-breakers. There was a merry rattling of sticks. Soon enough, answering shouts could be heard from some of the houses, and with a great slamming of doors men rushed out to do battle for the peace of the great city. Meanwhile all the high windows had been filled with night-capped heads, and some of these people even went so far as to pour water down upon the combatants. They also sent down cat-calls and phrases of witty advice. The sticks clattered together furiously; once a man with a bloody face staggered past us; he seemed to have been whacked directly on the ear by some uneducated person. It was as fine a shindy as one could hope to witness, and I was deeply interested.

Then suddenly a man called out hoarsely that he had been stabbed—murdered. There were yells from the street and screams from the windows. My lantern-bearer plucked me madly by the sleeve. I understood him, and we hastily left the neighbourhood.

I may tell now what had happened and what followed this affair of the night. A worthy citizen had been stabbed to death indeed. After further skirmishes his comrade citizens had taken several wretches into custody. They were tried for the murder and all acquitted save one. Of this latter it was proven that the brawl had started through his attempt to gain the purse of a passing citizen, and forthwith he was sentenced to be hanged for murder. His companion rascals were sent to prison for long terms on the expectation that one of them really might have been the murderer.

We passed into another street, where each well-lighted window framed one or more painted hussies who called out in jocular obscenity, but when we marched stiffly on without replying their manner changed, and they delivered at us volley after volley of language incredibly foul. There were only two of these creatures who paid no heed, and their indifference to us was due to the fact that they were deeply engaged in a duel of words, exchanging the most frightful, blood-curdling epithets. Confident drunken men jostled us from time to time, and frequently I could see small, ashy-faced, ancient-eyed youths dodging here and there with food and wine. My lantern-bearer told me that the street was not quite awake; it was waiting for the outpourings from the taverns and mug-houses. I bade him hurry me to the "Red Slipper" as soon as possible, for never have I had any stomach for these tawdry evils, fit as they are only for clerks and sailors.

We came at length to the creaking sign of the "Red Slipper." A great noise came from the place. A large company was roaring out a chorus. Without many words I was introduced into the room in which the disturbance was proceeding. It was blue with smoke, and the thundering chorus was still unfinished. I sank unnoticed into a quiet corner.

I was astonished at the appearance of the company. There were many men who looked like venerable prelates, and many men who looked like the heads of old and noble houses. I laughed in my sleeve when I remembered I had thought to find Paddy and Jem here. And at the same time I saw them up near the head of the table, if it please you. Paddy had his hand on the shoulder of a bishop, and Jem was telling some tale into the sympathetic ear of a marquis. At least this is the way matters appeared to my stupefied sense.

The singing ceased, and a distinguished peer at my elbow resumed a talk which evidently had been broken by the chorus:

"And so the Duke spoke with somewhat more than his accustomed vigour," said the distinguished peer.

My worst suspicions were confirmed. Here was a man talking of what had been said by a duke. I cast my eye toward my happy pair of rogues and wondered how I could ever extricate them from their position.

Suddenly there was a loud pounding upon the table, and in the ensuing quiet the grave and dignified voice of the chairman could be heard:

"Gentlemen," he said, "we crave your attention to a song by Mr. John Snowden."

Whereupon my very own Jem Bottles arose amid a burst of applause, and began to sing a ballad which had been written in Bristol or Bath in celebration of the notorious scoundrel Jem Bottles.

Here I could see that if impudence could serve us we would not lack success in England. The ballad was answered with wild cheers of appreciation. It was the great thing of the evening. Jem was strenuously pressed to sing again, but he buried his face in his mug and modestly refused. However, they devoted themselves to his chorus and sang it over and over with immense delight. I had never imagined that the nobility were so free and easy.

During the excitement over Jem's ballad I stole forward to Paddy. "Paddy," I whispered, "come out of this now. 'Tis no place for you here among all these reverend fathers and gentlemen of title. Shame on you!"

He saw my idea in a flash.

"Whist, sir," he answered. "There are being no reverend fathers or gentlemen of title here. They are all after being footmen and valets."

I was extremely vexed with myself. I had been in London only a brief space; and Paddy had been in the city no longer. However, he had already managed his instruction so well that he could at once tell a member of the gentry from a servant. I admired Paddy's cleverness, but at the same time I felt a certain resentment against the prelates and nobles who had so imposed upon me.

But, to be truthful, I have never seen a finer display of manners. These menials could have put courtiers to the blush. And from time to time somebody spoke out loud and clear an opinion pilfered verbatim from his master. They seldom spoke their own thoughts in their own way; they sent forth as their own whatever they could remember from the talk of their masters and other gentlemen. There was one man who seemed to be the servant of some noted scholar, and when he spoke the others were dumfounded into quiet.

"The loriot," said he with a learned frown, "is a bird. If it is looked upon by one who has the yellow jaundice, the bird straightway dies, but the sick person becomes well instantly. 'Tis said that lovage is used, but I would be luctuous to hear of anybody using this lothir weed, for 'tis no pentepharmacon, but a mere simple and not worth a caspatory."

This utterance fairly made their eyes bulge, and they sat in stunned silence. But I must say that there was one man who did not fear.

"Sir," said Paddy respectfully, but still with his own dignity, "I would be hearing more of this bird, and we all would be feeling honoured for a short description."

"In color he is ningid," said the learned valet.

"Bedad!" cried Paddy. "That's strange!"

"'Tis a question full of tenebrosity," remarked the other leaning back in his chair. "We poor scholars grow madarosis reflecting upon it. However, I may tell you that the bird is simous; yblent in the sunlight, but withal strenuous-eyed; its blood inclined to intumescence. However, I must be breviloquent, for I require an enneadecaterides to enumerate the true qualities of the loriot."

"By gor!" said Paddy, "I'll know that bird if I see him ten years from now. Thank you kindly, sir. But we would be late for breakfast if you took the required time; and that's true for me."

Afterward I reflected that I had attended the meetings of two scholarly bodies in this one evening, but for the life of me I couldn't decide which knew the least.

## CHAPTER XX

By the following Sunday I judged that the Earl of Westport and his family had returned to London, and so I walked abroad in the hopes of catching a glimpse of some of them among the brilliant gentry who on this day thronged the public gardens. I had both Jem Bottles and Paddy accompany me, for I feared that they would get into mischief if I left them to themselves. The innkeeper had told me that Kensington Gardens was the place where the grand people mostly chose to walk and flirt and show their clothes on a clear Sunday. It was a long way to these Gardens, but we footed out bravely, although we stopped once to see a fight between five drunken apprentices, as well as several times for much-needed refreshment.

I had no idea that the scene at the Gardens would be so splendid. Outside, the road was a block of gleaming chariots and coaches with servants ablaze in their liveries. Here I left Paddy and Jem to amuse themselves as suited them.

But the array of carriages had been only a forecast of what my eyes would encounter in the Garden itself. I was involved at once in a swarm of fashionable people. My eyes were dazzled with myriad colours, and my nostrils, trained as they were to peat smoke, were saluted by a hundred delicious perfumes. Priceless silks and satins swept against my modest stockings.

I suffered from my usual inclination to run away, but I put it down with an iron will. I soon found a more retired spot from which I could review the assemblage at something like my leisure. All the highly fashionable flock knew each other intimately, it appeared, and they kept off with figurative pikes attempts of a certain class not quite so high and mighty, who seemed for ever trying to edge into situations which would benefit them on the social ladder. Their failures were dismal, but not so dismal as the heroic smiles with which they covered their little noiseless defeats.

I saw a lady, sumptuously arrayed, sweep slowly along with her daughter, a beautiful girl who greatly wished to keep her eyes fixed on the ground. The mother glanced everywhere with half-concealed eagerness and anxiety. Once she bowed impressively to a dame with a cold, pale aristocratic face, around whom were gathered several officers in the uniform of His Majesty's Guards. The grand dame lifted her lorgnette and stared coolly at that impressive bow; then she turned and said something amusing to one of the officers, who smilingly answered. The mother, with her beautiful daughter, passed on, both pairs of eyes now on the ground.

I had thought the rebuff would settle this poor misguided creature, but in the course of an hour I saw three more of her impressive bows thrown away against the icy faces of other women. But as they were leaving the Gardens they received attention from members of the very best society. One lordling nudged another lordling, and they stared into the face of the girl as if she had been a creature of the street. Then they leisurely looked her up and down from head to toe. No tailor could have taken her measurements so completely. Afterward they grinned at each other, and one spoke behind his hand, his insolent speculative eyes fixed on the retiring form of the girl. This was the social reward of the ambitious mother.

It has always been clear to me why the women turn out in such cohorts to any sort of a function. They wish to see the frocks, and they are insistent that their own frocks shall be seen. Moreover they take great enjoyment in hating such of their enemies as may come under their notice. They never have a really good time; but of this fact they are not aware, since women are so constituted that they are able to misinterpret almost every one of their emotions.

The men, knowing something of their own minds at times, stealthily avoid such things unless there are very special reasons. In my own modest experience I have seen many a popular hostess hunting men with a net. However it was plain why so many men came to Kensington Gardens on a Sunday afternoon. It was the display of feminine beauty. And when I say "display" I mean it. In my old age the fashion balloons a lady with such a sweep of wires and trellises that no Irishman could marry her because there is never a door in all Ireland through which his wife could pass. In my youth, however, the fashion required all dresses to be cut very low, and all skirts to cling so that if a four-legged woman entered a drawing-room everybody would know it. It would be so easy to count them. At present a woman could have eight legs and nobody be the wiser.

It was small wonder that the men came to ogle at Kensington Gardens on a fine Sunday afternoon. Upon my word, it was worth any young gentleman's time. Nor did the beauties blush under the gaze of banks of fastidious beaus who surveyed them like men about to bid at a horse-fair. I thought of my father and how he would have enjoyed the scene. I wager he would have been a gallant with the best of them, bowing and scraping, and dodging ladies' skirts. He would have been in his very element.

But as for me I had come to gain a possible glimpse of Lady Mary. Beyond that I had no warm interest in Kensington Gardens. The crowd was too high and fine; many of the people were altogether too well bred. They frightened me.

However, I turned my head by chance to the left, and saw near me a small plain man who did not frighten me at all. It was Doctor Chord, the little scientist. He was alone and seemed to be occupied in studying the crowd. I moved over to him.

"A good day to you, sir," I said, extending my hand.

When he recognized me, his face broke into a beaming smile.

"Why, sir," he cried, "I am very glad to see you, sir. Perchance, like me, you have come here for an hour's quiet musing on fashionable folly."

"That's it, sir," said I. "You've hit it exactly."

I have said that he was a bashful man, but it seemed that his timidity was likely to show itself only in the presence of other great philosophers and scientists. At any rate, he now rattled on like a little engine, surveying the people keenly and discoursing upon their faults.

"There's the old Marquis of Stubblington," observed my friend. "He beats his wife with an ebony stick. 'Tis said she always carries a little bottle of liniment in the pocket of her skirt. Poor thing, her only pleasure in life is to talk scandal; but this she does on such a heroic scale that it occupies her time completely. There is young Lord Gram walking again with that soap-boiler and candle-maker. 'Tis disgraceful! The poor devil lends Gram money, and Gram repays him by allowing him to be seen in his company. Gram gambles away the money, but I don't know what the soap-boiler does with his distinguished honours. However, you can see that the poor wretch is delighted with his bargain. There are the three Banellic girls, the most ill-tempered, ugly cats in England. But each will have a large marriage portion, so they have no fears, I warrant me. I wonder the elder has the effrontery to show her face here so soon if it is true that the waiting-woman died of her injuries. Little Wax is talking to them. He needs one of those marriage portions. Aye, he needs all three, what with his very boot-maker almost inclined to be insolent to him. I see that foreign count is talking to the Honourable Mrs. Trasky. He is no more nor less than a gambler by trade, and they say he came here from Paris because he was caught cheating there, and was kicked and caned with such intense publicity that he was forced to leave in the dead of night. However, he found many young birds here eager to be plucked and devoured. 'Tis little they care, so long as they may play till dawn. Did you hear about Lady Prefent? She went after her son to the Count's rooms at night. In her younger days she lived rather a gay life herself, 'tis rumoured, and so she was not to be taken by her son's lies as to where he spent his evenings and his money. Ha, I see the Countess Cheer. There is a citadel of virtue! It has been stormed and taken so many times that I wonder it is not in ruins, and yet here it is defiant, with banners flying. Wonderful. She—"

"Hold!" I cried. "I have enough. I would have leave to try and collect my wits. But one thing I would know at once. I thought you were a shy scholar, and here you clatter away with the tongue of an old rake. You amaze me. Tell me why you do this? Why do you use your brain to examine this muck?"

"'Tis my recreation," he answered simply. "In my boyhood I was allowed no games, and in the greater part of my manhood I have been too busy. Of late years I have more leisure, and I often have sought here a little innocent amusement, something to take one's mind off one's own affairs, and yet not of such an arduous nature as would make one's head tired."

"By my faith, it would make my head tired," I said. "What with remembering the names of the people and all the different crimes, I should go raving mad." But what still amazed me was the fact that this little man, habitually meek, frightened and easily trodden down in most ordinary matters, should be able to turn himself upon occasion into a fierce and howling wolf of scandal, baying his betters, waiting for the time when an exhausted one fell in the snow, and then burying his remorseless teeth in him. What a quaint little Doctor Chord.

"But tell me truly," said I. "Is there no virtuous lady or honest gentleman in all this great crowd?"

He stared, his jaw dropping. "Strap me, the place is full of them," he ejaculated. "They are as thick as flies in a fish-market."

"Well, then," said I, "let us talk of them. 'Tis well to furbish and burnish our minds with tales of rectitude and honour."

But the little Doctor was no longer happy. "There is nought to say," he answered gloomily. "They are as quiet as Bibles. They make no recreation for me. I have scant interest in them."

"Oh, you little rogue, you!" I cried. "What a precious little bunch of evil it is! 'They make no recreation for me,' quoth he. Here's a great, bold, outspoken monster. But, mark you, sir, I am a younger man, but I too have a bold tongue in my head, and I am saying that I have friends among ladies in London, and if I catch you so much as whispering their names in your sleep, I'll cut off your ears and eat them. I speak few words, as you may have noted, but I keep my engagements, you little brew of trouble, you!"

"Strap me," whimpered the little Doctor, plucking feverishly at the buttons of his coat, rolling his eyes wildly, not knowing at all what he did. "The man's mad! The man's mad!"

"No," said I, "my blood is cold, very cold."

The little Doctor looked at me with the light of a desperate inspiration in his eye. "If your blood is cold, sir," said he, "I can recommend a gill of port wine."

I needs must laugh. "Good," I cried, "and you will join me."

## CHAPTER XXI

I don't know if it was the gill of comforting port, but at any rate I was soon enough convinced that there was no reason for speaking harshly to Doctor Chord. It served no purpose; it accomplished nothing. The little old villain was really as innocent as a lamb. He had no dream of wronging people. His prattle was the prattle of an unsophisticated maiden lady. He did not know what he was talking. These direful intelligences ran as easily off his tongue as water runs off the falling wheel. When I had indirectly informed him that he was more or less of a dangerous scandal-monger, he had cried: "The man is mad!" Yes; he was an innocent old thing.

But then it is the innocent old scandal-mongers, poor placid-minded well-protected hens, who are often the most harmful. The vicious gabblers defeat themselves very often. I remember my father once going to a fair and kissing some girls there. He kissed them all turn by turn, as was his right and his duty, and then he returned to a girl near the head of the list and kissed her five times more because she was the prettiest girl in all Ireland, and there is no shame to him there. However, there was a great hullabaloo. The girls who had been kissed only once led a regular crusade against the character of this other girl, and before long she had a bad name, and the odious sly lads with no hair on their throats winked as she passed them, and numerous mothers thanked God that their daughters were not fancied by the lord of that region. In time these tales came to the ears of my father, and he called some of his head men to meet him in the dining-room.

"I'll have no trifling," said he. "The girl is a good girl for all I know, and I have never seen her before or since. If I can trace a bad word to any man's mouth, I'll flog him till he can't move. 'Tis a shame taking away the girl's name for a few kisses by the squire at a fair with everybody looking on and laughing. What do you blackguards mean?"

Every man in the dining-room took oath he had never said a word, and they all spoke truth. But the women clamoured on without pausing for wind, and refused to take word of the men-folk, who were gifted with the power of reason. However, the vicious people defeated themselves in time. People began to say to a lass who had been kissed only once: "Ah, now, you would be angry because you were not getting the other five." Everything seemed to grow quiet, and my father thought no more about it, having thought very little about it in the first place save enough to speak a few sharp words. But, would you believe it, there was an old woman living in a hovel not a mile from the castle, who kept up the scandal for twelve more months. She had never been married, and, as far as any one knew, she had never wished to be. She had never moved beyond Father Donovan's church in one direction and a little peat-heap in the other direction. All her days she had seen nothing but the wind-swept moors, and heard nothing but the sea lashing the black rocks. I am mistaken; once she came to the castle, hearing that my mother was ill. She had a remedy with her, poor soul, and they poured it in the ashes when her back was turned. My mother bade them give her some hot porridge and an old cloth gown of her own to take home. I remember the time distinctly. Well, this poor thing couldn't tell between a real sin and an alligator. Bony, withered, aged, this crone might have been one of the highest types of human perfection. She wronged nobody; she had no power to wrong. Nobody wronged her; it was never worth it. She really was at peace with all the world. This obeys the most exalted injunctions. Every precept is kept here. But this tale of the Squire and the girl took root in her head. She must have been dazzled by the immensity of the event. It probably appealed to her as would a grand picture of the burning of Rome or a vivid statue of Lot's wife turning to look back. It reached the dimensions of great history. And so this old woman, who had always lived the life of a nun, dreamed of nothing but the colossal wrong which had come within her stunted range of vision. Before and after church she talked of no other thing for almost eighteen months. Finally my father in despair rode down to her little cottage.

"Mollie," said he, calling from the road, "Mollie, come out." She came out.

"Mollie," said my father, "you know me?"

"Ay," said she, "you are The O'Ruddy, and you are a rogue."

"True for you, Mollie," said my father pleasantly. "You know it and I know it. I am indeed a grand rogue. But why would you be tearing to tatters the name of that poor girl in Ballygoway?"

"'Tis not me that has said more than three words," she cried, astonished, "and before I speak ill of anybody I hope the devil flies away with me."

Well, my father palavered on for a long time, telling her that he would take away the pension of twenty-five shillings a year which he had given her because he by accident had shot her second cousin in the leg twelve years before that time. She steadfastly answered that she would never speak ill of anybody; but the girl was a brazen-faced wench, and he was no better. My father came away, and I have no doubt the scandal would still be alive if the old woman had not died, may the saints rest her!

And so I was no longer angry with Doctor Chord, but spoke to him pleasantly.

"Come," said I, "I would have you point me out the great swordsmen, if it pleases you. I am eager to see them, and the talk will be cleanly, also."

"Aye," said my friend. "Nothing could give me more pleasure. And now, look you! The tall, straight, grave young man there is Ponsonby, who flashes the wisest blade in England unless Reginald Forister is better. Any how, Forister is not here today. At least I don't see him. Ponsonby fought his last duel with a gentleman named Vellum because Vellum said flatly that Mrs. Catherine Wainescorte was a—"

"Stop there," said I, "and get to the tale of the fighting."

"Well, Ponsonby won without difficulty," said the Doctor; "but it is said that he took an unfair advantage—"

"Stop again!" I cried. "Stop again! We will talk no more of swordsmen. Somehow I have lost my interest. I am put to it to think of a subject for talk, and we may have to do with a period of silence, but that will do your jaw no injury at any rate."

But I was mistaken in thinking that the little man could forego his recreation for more than a moment. Suddenly he burst out with a great spleen:

"Titles!" he cried. "Empty titles! husks, husks, husks! 'Tis all they care for, this mob! Honourable manhood goes a-begging while the world worships at the feet of pimply lords! Pah! Lovely girls, the making of fine wives and mothers, grow old while the world worships at the feet of some old horse-headed duchess! Pah! Look at those pick-thanks and flatterers, cringing at the boots of the people of fashion. Upon my life, before I would so demean myself, I—" he ceased suddenly, his eye having caught sight of some people in the crowd. "Ah," said he, while a singularly vain and fatuous smile settled upon his countenance. "Ah, the Countess of Westport and her charming daughter, the Lady Mary, have arrived. I must go and speak to them." My eye had followed his glance quickly enough you may be sure. There, true enough, was the formidable figure of the old Countess, and at her side was the beautiful Lady Mary.

With an absent-minded murmur of apology, Doctor Chord went mincing toward them, his face still spread with its idiotic smile.

He cantered up to them with the grace of a hobbled cow. I expected him to get a rebuff that would stun him into the need of a surgeon, but to my surprise the Countess received him affably, bending her head to say some gracious words. However, I had more eyes for Lady Mary than for the capers of little Chord.

It was a great joy to be able to look at her. I suffered from a delicious trembling, and frequently my vision became dim purely from the excitement. But later I was moved by another profound emotion. I was looking at her; I must have her look at me. I must learn if her eye would light, if her expression would change, when she saw me. All this sounds very boyish, but it is not necessary to leave it out for that reason, because, as my father often said, every Irishman is a boy until he has grandchildren. I do not know if he was perfectly right in this matter, but it is a certain advantage in a love affair to have the true boyish ardour which is able to enshrine a woman in one's heart to the exclusion of everything, believing her to be perfection and believing life without her a hell of suffering and woe. No man of middle-aged experience can ever be in love. He may have his illusions. He may think he is in love. A woman may gain the power to bind him hand and foot and drag him wherever she listeth, but he is not in love. That is his mistaken idea. He is only misinterpreting his feelings. But, as my father said, it is very different with Irishmen, who are able to remain in love to a very great age. If you will note, too, climatic conditions and other unpleasant matters have practically no effect upon them; so little, indeed, that you may find streets named after the main Italian cities, and many little German children speak with a slight brogue. My father often said that one great reason for an Irishman's successes with the ladies was his perfect willingness to get married. He was seldom to be seen scouting for advantages in intrigue. If the girl be willing, be she brown, yellow, or white, he was always for the priest and the solemn words. My father also contended that in every marriage contracted on the face of the earth in which neither maid nor man could understand the other's national speech, the bridegroom was an Irishman. He was the only man who was able to make delightful love with the aid of mere signals.

However I must be going on with my story, although it is a great pleasure to talk of my country-men. They possess a singular fascination for me. I cannot forget that I too am an Irishman.

The little Doctor was still saying agreeable things; Lady Mary was smiling in gentle amusement. As I moved out to catch Lady Mary's eye, I did not at all lose sight of the fact that if the pugnacious mother of my *innamorata* took one glimpse of me there might result a scene which could end in nothing but my ignominious flight. I edged toward the group, advancing on the Countess's port quarter as she was talking animately over her starboard bow at the entranced little Doctor. At times Lady Mary looked about her, still smiling her smile, which no doubt was born of the ridiculous performances of Chord. Once I thought she looked squarely at me, and my heart beat like a drum so loudly that I thought people must hear. But her glance wandered on casually over the throng, and then I felt truly insignificant, like a man who could hide behind the nail of his own thumb.

Perceiving that I was so insignificant, I judged it prudent as well as advantageous to advance much closer. Suddenly Lady Mary's clear virgin eye met mine,—met it fully.

Now, I don't know what was in this glance we exchanged. I have stopped myself just on the verge of a full explanation of the thrills, quivers, hopes, fears, and dreams which assailed me as I looked back into the beautiful face of Lady Mary. I was also going to explain how the whole scene appeared. But I can see soon enough that my language would not be appropriate to the occasion. But any how we looked each other point-blank in the eye. It was a moment in which that very circling of the earth halted, and all the suns of the universe poised, ready to tumble or to rise. Then Lady Mary lowered her glance, and a pink blush suffused her neck and cheek.

The Countess, Lady Mary, and Doctor Chord moved slowly on through the throng, and I followed. The great question now was whether Lady Mary would look back. If she looked back, I would feel that I was making grand way with her. If she did not look back, I would know myself as a lost man. One can imagine how eagerly I watched her. For a long time it was plain that she had no intention whatever of looking back. I lugubriously arranged my complete downfall. Then, at the very moment of my despair, she gazed studiously off to her extreme left for a certain time, and then suddenly cast one short glance behind her. Only heaven knows what value I placed upon this brief look. It appeared for the moment to me that I had won her, won everything. I bravely forged ahead until I was quite insistently under the eye of Lady Mary, and then she again looked toward me, but it was a look so repelling and frigid that it went through me as if I had been a paper ring in the circus. I slunk away through the crowd, my thoughts busy with trying to find out what had happened to me.

For three minutes I was a miserable human being. At the end of that time I took heart again. I decided that Lady Mary had frowned at me because she was afraid that she had been too good to me with her look and smile. You know what I mean. I have seen a young girl give a young man a flower, and at the very next moment be seemingly willing to give her heart's blood to get that flower back, overcome with panic terror that she had passed—in his opinion, mind you—beyond the lines of best behaviour. Well I said to myself that Lady Mary had given me the hard look for similar reasons. It was rational to make this judgment, for certainly she had no cause for an active dislike. I had never been even so much as a nuisance to her.

Fortified with these philosophic decisions, I again followed the trio, and I was just in time to find Chord handing them into a splendid chariot. I stood out boldly, for I knew if I could not get one more look from Lady Mary I would die.

Seated beside her mother, her eye wandered eagerly over the crowd. I was right, by the saints! She was looking for me.

And now here come the stupid laws of convention. Could I yell? Could I even throw my hat in the air to guide her eye aright? No! I was doomed to stand there as still as a bottle on a shelf.

But she saw me! It was at the very last moment. There was no time for coquetry. She allowed her glance to linger, and God knows what we said to each other in this subtle communication through all the noise and hubbub of the entrance place. Then suddenly the coachman's reins tightened; there were some last bows; the chariot whirled away.

## CHAPTER XXII

Chord ambled back, very proud indeed, and still wearing his fatuous smile. He was bursting with a sense of social value, and to everybody he seemed to be saying, "Did you see me?" He was overjoyed to find me waiting for him. He needed a good listener at once. Otherwise he would surely fly to pieces.

"I have been talking to the Countess of Westport and her daughter, Lady Mary Strepp," he said pompously. "The Countess tells that the Earl has been extremely indisposed during their late journey in the West."

He spoke of the Earl's illness with an air of great concern, as if the news had much upset him. He pretended that the day was quite over-gloomed for him. Dear, dear! I doubted if he would be able to eat any supper.

"Have a drop of something, old friend," said I sympathetically. "You can't really go on this way. 'Twill ruin your nerves. I am surprised that the Countess did not break the news to you more gently. She was very inconsiderate, I am sure."

"No, no, don't blame the poor lady," cried Chord. "She herself was quite distracted. The moment she saw me she ran to me—did you see her run to me?"

"I did that," said I with emphasis.

"Aye, she ran to me," said the little fool, "and says she, 'Oh, my dear Doctor, I must tell you at once the condition of the Earl.' And when I heard everything I was naturally cut up, as you remarked, being an old friend of the family, ahem!—yes, an old friend of the family."

He rattled on with his nonsensical lies, and in the mean time I made up my mind to speak plainly to him, as I intended to make him of great service to me.

"Stop a moment," said I good-naturedly. "I will hear no more of this rubbish from you, you impudent little impostor. You care no more for the Earl of Westport's illness than you do for telling the truth, and I know how much you care for that. Listen to me, and I'll see if I can't knock some sense into your little addled head. In the first place the Earl of Westport and my father were old friends and companions-in-arms in the service of the French king, and I came over from Ireland especially to take a dying message and a token from my father to the Earl. That is all you need know about that; but I would have you leave off your prate of your friend the Earl of Westport, for I understand full well you couldn't distinguish between him and a church door, although 'tis scandalously little you know of church doors. So we will stop there on that point. Then I will go on to the next point. The next point is that I am going to marry Lady Mary Strepp."

The little Doctor had been choking and stuttering in a great spasm, but my last point bid fair to flatten him out on the floor. I took the overpowered philosopher and led or carried him to another drink.

"Stap me!" he cried again and again. "The man is mad!"

I surveyed him with a bland smile.

"Let it sink into you," said I soothingly. "Don't snarl and wrangle at it. It is all heaven's truth, and in time you will come to your senses and see what I am telling you."

Well, as soon as he had fully recovered his wind, he fell upon me with thousands of questions; for one may see that he would have plenty of interest in the matter as soon as he was assured that there was much veracity involved in one way or another in my early statement. His questions I answered as it pleased me, but I made clear enough to him that, although Lady Mary was well disposed toward me, neither her father nor her mother would even so much as look at me if I applied for a position as under-footman, I was that low in their estimate.

"However," said I, "I can rearrange all that very easily. And now, my bucko, here is where your fortune meets mine. You are fitted by nature more to attend other people's affairs than to take a strict interest in your own. All kinds of meddling and interference come easily to you. Well, then, here is a chance to exercise your gifts inoffensively, and yet in a way which may make two people happy for life. I will tell you now that I don't even know where is the Earl's town house. There is where your importance appears at once. You must show me the house. That is the first thing. After that we will arrange all the details about ladders and garden walls, and, mayhap, carrier doves. As for your reward, it will appear finally in the shape of a bowing recognition by people of fashion, which is what you most desire in the world, you funny little man."

Again I had stunned him. For a time I could see his brain swimming in a perfect sea of bewilderment. But, as before, sense gradually came to him, and he again volleyed questions at me. But what stuck in his crop was the thought that Lady Mary could prefer me. He tried his best to believe it, but he would always end up by saying: "Well, *if* Lady Mary cares for you, the affair is not too difficult." Or, "Well, if you are *sure* Lady Mary loves you—" I could have broken his head a thousand times.

"Bad luck to you, Doctor," I cried. "Don't you know such croaking would spoil the peace of any true lover? Is ever any worthy man able not to be anxious in such matters? 'Tis only foppery coxcombs who have great confidence, and they are usually misled, thank the Lord! Be quiet, now, and try to take everything for granted."

Then the spirit of the adventure came upon him, and he was all for it, heels over head. As I told him, this sort of meddling was his proper vocation. He who as a recreation revelled in the mere shadows of the intrigues of people of quality was now really part of one, an actor in it, the repository of its deep secret. I had to curb his enthusiasm. He had such a sense of the importance of my news, and of his distinction in having heard it, that I think he wanted to tell the secret to the entire world.

As soon as the afternoon grew late I suggested a walk to that part of London in which was situated the Earl's town house. I did not see why we should not be moving at once on the campaign. The Doctor assented, and we went forth to look for Paddy and Jem Bottles. We found them at an ale-house which was the resort of the chairmen, footmen, and coachmen of the grand people. The two rogues had evidently passed a pleasant afternoon. Jem Bottles was still making love to a very pretty girl, some part of whose easy affection or interest he had won; and Paddy, it seems, had had a rip-roaring fight with two lackeys, worsted them with despatch, and even pursued them some distance. To my stern interrogation in regard to the pretty girl, Jem Bottles stoutly rejoined that she was his second cousin whom he had not seen for many years. To this I made no reply, for it does no good to disturb the balance of a good liar. If at times he is led to tell the truth, he becomes very puzzling. In all the years Jem Bottles has been in my service I have never reprimanded him for lying. I would confuse matters to no purpose, inasmuch as I understand him perfectly.

"And how," said I to Paddy, "did you come to engage in this disgraceful brawl of a Sunday?"

"Your honour," answered Paddy, "there was two of these men with fat legs came here, and says one, looking hard at me, 'Here's a furriner,' he says. 'Furriner yourself, you fish-faced ditch-lurker,' says I, and with that he takes up his fists and hits me a knock. There was a little shindy, and afterward they ran away bawling, and I was pursuing them, only I feared to lose my way in these strange parts."

The walk to Lord Westport's house was a long one. It seemed that he had built a great new mansion at a place outside of the old city gates, where other nobles and great brewers had built fine houses, surrounding them all with splendid gardens.

One must not suppose that I had any idea of taking the mansion by storm. My first idea was to dream a lover's dream as I gazed upon the abode of my treasure. This, I believe, is a legitimate proceeding in all careers. Every lover worthy of the name is certain to pilgrimage, muffled in his cloak, to moon over the home of his adored one. Otherwise there can be no real attachment.

In the second place I wished to develop certain plans for gaining speech of Lady Mary. I will not deny that I purposed on a near day to scale the garden wall and hold speech of my sweetheart as she walked alone among the flowers. For my success I depended upon the absolute conventionality of the idea. In all history no lover has even been chased out of a garden by an under-gardener with a hoe.

When we arrived at the house I found that it was indeed a gorgeous mansion. It was surrounded on all sides by high brick walls, but through the elaborate tracery of one of the iron-work gates I saw Lady Mary's home standing among sweeping green lawns.

We reconnoitred all sides, and at the back I found a lonely avenue lined with oaks. Here a small door pierced the wall for the use apparently of the gardeners or grooms. I resolved that here I would make my attack.

As we passed the iron gates on our way back to town, we saw window after window light up with a golden radiance. I wondered which part of that vast edifice hid the form of my Mary.

I had asked Doctor Chord to sup with me at the inn, and on the way thither he proved somewhat loquacious.

"I see in you, sir," said he, "a certain instinct of true romance which is infrequently encountered in this humdrum commercial age. Allow me to express to you, sir, my warm admiration. I did not think that a gallant of this humdrum commercial age could prove such a free spirit. In this humdrum commercial age—"

"I am an Irishman," said I, "and in Ireland we are always humdrum, but we are never commercial, for the reason that we have not the tools."

"Aye," said he, "you must be a great people. Strangely enough, you are the first Irishman I have ever seen, although I have seen many blackamoors. However, I am edified to find you a gentleman of great learning and experience. In this humdrum commercial age—"

"Let go," said I. "I can do very well without your opinion as to my learning and experience. In regard to this being a humdrum commercial age you will find that all ages say the same thing of themselves. I am more interested in the winning of Lady Mary."

"'Twas to that subject I was just about to turn the talk," said the Doctor. "I need not express again to you the interest I feel; and if it is true, as you say, that Lady Mary really loves you—"

"May the devil fly away with you," I cried in a great rage. "Are you never to have done? You are an old frog. I asked you to help me, and you do nothing but dispirit me with these doubts. I'll not put up with it."

"I am very sorry to displease you, sir," answered my friend. "If you examine my intentions with a dispassionate eye, sir, I am convinced you will have found nothing in me which should properly cause these outbursts of disapprobation. When I say, 'If Lady Mary really loves you,' I am referring to the strange mishaps and misconstructions which attend human thought at all times, and when I say—"

"Let go again," I cried. "When I misunderstand you, don't enlighten me; for I find these explanations very hard to bear."

To my surprise the little man answered with great spirit: "I am unable to gain any approval for my deep interest in your affairs, sir," he cried. "Perchance, it would be better if I could affect a profound indifference. I am certainly at a loss for words when each sentence of mine is made the subject of wrathful objection."

"You are right," said I. "But you will understand how ten thousand emotions beset and haggle a lover, and I believe he always revenges himself upon his dearest friends. Forgive me!"

"With all my heart!" answered the little Doctor. "I am aware, sir, that at the present time you are in many ways like a highly-tightened fiddle, which any breeze frets into murmurings. Now, being absolutely certain of the devotion of your beloved, you naturally—"

"By the ten lame pipers of Ballydehob," I shouted, "let go of that talk. I can't be having it. I warn ye. 'Tis either a grave for me, or quiet for you, and I am thinking it is quiet for you."

"Inasmuch," said the Doctor, "as my most judi cious speeches seem to inflame your passions, sir, I am of the opinion that a perfect silence on my part becomes almost necessary, and, to further this end, I would recommend that you refrain from making interrogations, or otherwise promulgating opportunities, when an expression of candid opinion seems expected and desired."

"You've hit it," said I. "We will have no more interrogations. However, I would much like to know how you became so intimate with Lord Westport's family."

Doctor Chord blushed with something of his earlier manner. "'Tis a matter which I did not expect to have leap at me out of the darkness in this fashion," he said bashfully. "However, I am convinced of how well you know these people, and I will traffic no more with hollow pretence. As you know, I deal much in chemical knowledge, which I am able to spread to almost every branch of human use and need."

"'Tis an ill work," said I slowly. "I doubt if Father Donovan would care to hear you be speaking in this way. He always objected to scientific improvements as things which do harm to the Church."

"In regard to the estimable friend you mention," said the Doctor, "I unhesitatingly state my profound assurances of respect."

"Quite so," I answered. "He will be pleased to hear of it. And now we will return to the other matter."

"I will obediently proceed," said he. "Five years back the Countess of Westport was thrown from her carriage. Physicians rushed to her rescue. I too appeared, being for the time out for a walk. They wished to immediately bleed her, but I waved them aside and, recognizing me as a figure in the street world of science, they fell back abashed. I prescribed a small drink of hot rum. The lady took it. Almost immediately she recovered. She offered me a guinea. I refused curtly. She inquired here and there for my condition. Afterward she apologized to me for not offering me more than a guinea. Since that time we have been warm friends. She knows me as a great scientist who came to her assistance in time of trouble when numerous quacks wished to bleed her, and I overpowered them and gave her a drink of rum. 'Tis true that after she reached her own bed the Earl's physician bled her, but she did not seem to appreciate it although he drew twenty-five ounces, I think. But she has remained always grateful for the hot rum."

## CHAPTER XXIII

At supper that evening Doctor Chord amplified some of his views "A few staunch retainers could quickly aid you to scale the walls of the castle," said he. "But I have forgotten," he added blankly. "'Tis not a castle. 'Tis a house."

"If you would take some of these ancient ideas and bury them in the garden," said I, "they might grow in time to be some kind of turnip or other valuable food. But at the present moment they do not seem to me to serve much purpose. Supposing that the house is not a castle? What of that?"

"Castles—" said he. "Castles lend themselves—"

"Castles!" I cried. "Have done with castles! All castles may be Jews, as you say. But this is a house."

"I remarked that it was a house," he answered gently. "It was that point that I was making."

"Very good," said I. "We will now proceed to define matters. Do you know if Lady Mary walks in the garden? It is absolutely necessary that Lady Mary should walk in the garden."

"She does," he replied at once. "At this season of the year Lady Mary walks in the garden on every fine day at ten of the clock."

"Then," I cried, smiting the table, "our course is clear; I feel elate. My only regret is that my father is not here to give me a word now and then, for 'tis a game he would know down to the ground."

"Although I am not your father," said Doctor Chord modestly, "I may be able to suggest some expedient way of gaining entrance to the castle."

"House," said I.

"House," said he.

"However," said I, "we must lower ourselves to extremely practical matters. Can you climb a tree?"

"A tree?" said he. "Climb a tree? Strap me!"

"'Tis all very well to strap yourself in this fashion," said I rather warmly; "but the climbing of trees appears here as an important matter. In my part of Ireland there are few trees, and so climbing trees did not enter into my education. However, I am willing to attempt the climbing of a tree for the sake of my true love, and if I fall—how high is this wall? Do you remember?"

"'Twas at least ten feet," answered the Doctor. "And there is a murderous row of spikes at the top. But," he added, "the more spikes and all that make them the more convinced that the garden is perfectly safe from intrusion."

"That's a world of sense out of you," I cried. "The spikes convince them the garden is safe from intrusion, and so they give over their watchfulness. So now in the morning we will go there, and I will climb one of the oak-trees bordering the wall—may the saints aid me!"

"You were asking if I could climb a tree," remarked the Doctor. "I will point out to you that it is a question of no importance. It is you yourself who must climb the tree; for even if I succeeded in the arduous and painful task I could not pay your vows to Lady Mary, and for such purpose primarily the tree is to be climbed."

"True for you, Doctor," I answered with a sigh. "True for you. I must climb the tree. I can see that. I had some thought of making Paddy climb it, but, as you say, a man must do his own love-making, and by the same token I would break the head of any one who tried to do it for me. I would that! In this world people must climb their own trees. Now that I think of it seriously, it was ridiculous in me to plan that Paddy should climb the tree."

"'Second thoughts are always best,'" said the little Doctor piously. "'Tis a phrase from one of the greatest writers of the day. And at any rate I myself, because of age and debility, would not be able to climb a tree."

"Let us say no more of it," said I. "I see my mistake. But tell me one thing. I know you are a man with a great deal on your mind. Can you spare the time for this adventure?"

But on this point the Doctor was very clear and emphatic. I think if I had said he could not have a place in the plot he would have died immediately of a broken heart.

"'Tis true I have not yet finished my treatise proving that the touchstone is fallible," he cried eagerly; "but it would give me pleasure to delay the work indefinitely if in the meantime I can be of assistance."

"That is a man's talk," I said. "Well, then, in the morning we will go forth to do or die. And now a glass to success."

That night I slept very heartily, for some of my father's soldier training is in my veins, and on the eve of a hard or precarious work I am always able to get sound rest. My father often said that on the night before a battle in which he would stand seventy-seven chances of being killed he always slept like a dog in front of the fire.

At dawn I was up and ready. My first move was to have Paddy and Jem sent to me, and to give them such information as would lead them to an intelligent performance of their duties during the day. "Mind ye now," said I, "here's where the whole thing may be won or lost. There is a lovely lady inside the walls of that garden which I was showing you yesterday. She lives in the big house. She is the lady who made you feel ashamed when you took the old Earl's—well, never mind! I hope we are all properly repentant over it. However, I had better be getting on with the matter in hand. She lives there, and if I can find no way to gain speech of her we all three of us will have to take to the thickets, and that's the truth."

"If I could but lay my fingers on her throttle," said Jem Bottles in a blood-curdling voice, "she soon enough would—"

"Stop!" I cried. "You misunderstood me!"

"Aye, he does," spoke in Paddy. "But I know what your honour is meaning. You are meaning that the young lady—aye, didn't I see her, and didn't she give me a look of her eye? Aye, I know what your honour is meaning."

"You are knowing it precisely," said I. "The young lady is more to me than three Irelands. You understand? Well, then, in the first place I must gain speech of her. Today we march out and see what I can accomplish by climbing trees. In the meantime you two are to lay in waiting and assist me when necessary."

"I am foreseeing that everything will be easy," cried Paddy jubilantly.

"You are an Irishman," I responded in anger.

"Aye," he replied bitterly, "and another is within reach of my stick if it weren't for my respect for my betters, although such a thing never could happen, please God!"

"No bold talk," said I. "You may do that after." I bade Jem Bottles load his pistols and carry them handy, but to keep them well concealed. Paddy preferred to campaign with only a stout stick. I took one pistol, and of course my sword.

These preparations deeply stirred Jem Bottles and Paddy.

"Your honour," said Paddy, "if I see a man pulling you by the leg when you would be climbing the tree, may I hit him one lick?"

"Aye," growled Jem Bottles, "and if I get a pistol against his head, he'll find out the difference between gunpowder and sand."

"Stop," I cried. "You have the wrong idea entirely. This talk of carnage startles me and alarms me. Remember we are in London. In London even the smallest massacre arouses great excitement. There are to be no killings, and even no sound thrashings. It is all to be done with dainty gloves. Neither one of the pair of you looks fitted for the work, but I am obliged to make you serve by hook or crook. 'Tis too late to scour the country looking for good com rades. I must put up with you, since I can get no better."

They were well pleased at the prospect of spirited adventures, although Paddy made some complaints because there was no chance of a great ogre whom he could assail. He wished to destroy a few giants in order to prove his loyalty to the cause. However, I soothed him out of this mood, showing him where he was mistaken, and presently we were all prepared and only waited for the coming of Doctor Chord.

When the little philosopher appeared, however, I must truly say that I fell back a-gasping. He had tied some sort of a red turban about his head, and pulled a black cocked hat down over it until his left eye was wickedly shaded. From beneath his sombre cloak a heavy scabbard protruded. "I have come; I am ready," said he in a deep voice.

"Bedad, you have!" cried I, sinking into a chair. "And why didn't a mob hang you on the road, little man? How did you reach here safely? London surely never could stand two glimpses of such a dangerous-looking pirate. You would give a sedan-chair the vapours."

He looked himself over ruefully. "'Tis a garb befitting the dangerous adventure upon which I engaged," said he, somewhat stiff in the lip.

"But let me make known to you," I cried, "that when a man wears a garb befitting his adventure he fails surely. He should wear something extraneous. When you wish to do something evil, you put on the coat of a parson. That is the clever way. But here you are looking like a gallows-bird of the greatest claim for the rope. Stop it; take off the red thing, tilt your hat until you look like a gentleman, and let us go to our adventure respectably."

"I was never more surprised in my life," said he sincerely. "I thought I was doing a right thing in thus arraying myself for an experience which cannot fail to be thrilling and mayhap deadly. However, I see you in your accustomed attire, and in the apparel of your men-servants I see no great change from yesterday. May I again suggest to you that the adventure upon which we proceed may be fraught with much danger?"

"A red rag around your temples marks no improvement in our risks," said I. "We will sally out as if we were off to a tea-party. When my father led the forlorn hope at the storming of Würstenhausenstaffenberg, he wore a lace collar, and he was a man who understood these matters. And I may say that I wish he was here. He would be a great help."

In time the Doctor removed his red turban and gradually and sadly emerged from the more sanguine part of his paraphernalia and appeared as a simple little philosopher. Personally I have no objection to a man looking like a brigand, but my father always contended that clothes serve no purpose in real warfare. Thus I felt I had committed no great injustice in depriving Chord of his red turban.

We set out. I put much faith in the fact that we had no definite plans, but to my great consternation Doctor Chord almost at once began to develop well-laid schemes. As we moved toward the scene of our adventure he remarked them to me.

"First of all," said he, "a strong party should be stationed at the iron gates, not only to prevent a sally of the garrison, but to prevent an intrepid retainer from escaping and alarming the city. Furthermore—"

"My gallant warrior," said I, interrupting him, "we will drop this question to the level of a humdrum commercial age. I will try to compass my purpose by the simple climbing of a tree, and to that end all I could need from you is a stout lift and a good word. Then we proceed in the established way of making signs over a wall. All this I explained to you fully. I would not have you think I am about to bombard my lady-love's house."

With a countenance of great mournfulness he grumbled: "No fascines have been prepared."

"Very good," said I. "I will climb the tree without the aid of fascines."

As luck would have it, there was a little inn not very far from the Earl's house and on the lonely avenue lined with oaks. Here I temporarily left Jem Bottles and Paddy, for I feared their earnestness, which was becoming more terrible every minute. In order to keep them pacified I gave instructions that they should keep a strict watch up the avenue, and if they saw any signs of trouble they were to come a-running and do whatever I told them. These orders suggested serious business to their minds, and so they were quite content. Their great point was that if a shindy was coming they had a moral right to be mixed up in it.

Doctor Chord and I strolled carelessly under the oaks. It was still too early for Lady Mary's walk in the garden, and there was an hour's waiting to be worn out. In the mean time I was moved to express some of my reflections.

"'Tis possible—nay, probable—that this is a bootless quest," said I dejectedly. "What shadow of an assurance have I that Lady Mary will walk in the garden on this particular morning? This whole thing is absolute folly."

"At any rate," said the Doctor, "now that you already have walked this great distance, it will be little additional trouble to climb a tree."

He had encouraged me to my work at exactly the proper moment.

"You are right," said I, taking him warmly by the hand, "I will climb the tree in any case."

As the hour approached we began to cast about for the proper oak. I am sure they were all the same to me, but Doctor Chord was very particular.

"'Tis logical to contend," said he, "that the question of the girth of the tree will enter importantly into our devices. For example, if a tree be so huge that your hands may not meet on the far side of it, a successful ascension will be impossible. On the other hand, a very slim tree is like to bend beneath your weight, and even precipitate you heavily to the ground, which disaster might retard events for an indefinite period."

"Science your science, then," said I. "And tell me what manner of tree best suits the purpose of a true lover."

"A tree," said the Doctor, "is a large vegetable arising with one woody stem to a considerable height. As to the appearance and quality of a tree, there are many diversifications, and this fact in itself consti tutes the chief reason for this vegetable being of such great use to the human family. Ships are made of nought but trees, and if it were not for ships we would know but little of the great world of which these English islands form less than a half. Asia itself is slightly larger than all Scotland, and if it were not for the ships we would be like to delude ourselves with the idea that we and our neighbours formed the major part of the world."

With such wise harangues the Doctor entertained my impatience until it was time for me to climb a tree. And when this time came I went at my work without discussion or delay.

"There," said I resolutely, "I will climb this one if it kills me."

I seized the tree; I climbed. I will not say there was no groaning and puffing, but any how I at last found myself astride of a branch and looking over the wall into the Earl of Westport's garden.

But I might have made myself less labour and care by having somebody paint me a large landscape of this garden and surveyed it at my leisure. There I was high in a tree, dangling my legs, and staring at smooth lawns, ornamental copses, and brilliant flower-beds without even so much as a dog to enliven the scene. "O'Ruddy," said I to myself after a long time, "you've hung yourself here in mid-air like a bacon to a rafter, and I'll not say much to you now. But if you ever reach the ground without breaking your neck, I'll have a word with you, for my feelings are sorely stirred."

I do not know how long I sat in the tree engaged in my bitter meditation. But finally I heard a great scudding of feet near the foot of the tree, and I then saw the little Doctor bolting down the road like a madman, his hat gone, his hair flying, while his two coat-tails stuck out behind him straight as boards.

My excitement and interest in my ally's flight was so great that I near fell from my perch. It was incomprehensible that my little friend could dust the road at such speed. He seemed only to touch the ground from time to time. In a moment or two he was literally gone, like an arrow shot from the bow.

But upon casting my bewildered glance downward I found myself staring squarely into the mouth of a blunderbuss. The mouth of this blunderbuss, I may say, was of about the width of a fair-sized water-pitcher; in colour it was bright and steely. Its appearance attracted me to such an extent that I lost all idea of the man behind the gun. But presently I heard a grim, slow voice say,—

"Climb down, ye thief."

The reason for little Doctor Chord's hasty self-removal from the vicinity was now quite clear, and my interest in his departure was no longer speculative.

## CHAPTER XXIV

"Climb down, ye thief," said the grim, slow voice again. I looked once more into the mouth of the blunderbuss. I decided to climb. If I had had my two feet square on the ground, I would have taken a turn with this man, artillery or no artillery, to see if I could get the upper hand of him. But neither I nor any of my ancestors could ever fight well in trees. Foliage incommodes us. We like a clear sweep for the arm, and everything on a level space, and neither man in a tree. However, a sensible man holds no long discussions with a blunderbuss. I slid to the ground, arriving in a somewhat lacerated state. I thereupon found that the man behind the gun was evidently some kind of keeper or gardener. He had a sour face deeply chiselled with mean lines, but his eyes were very bright, the lighter parts of them being steely blue, and he rolled the pair of them from behind his awful weapon.

"And for whom have you mistaken me, rascal?" I cried as soon as I had come ungracefully to the ground and found with whom I had to deal.

"Have mistaken ye for naught," replied the man proudly. "Ye be the thief of the French pears, ye be."

"French pears—French—French what?" I cried.

"Ay, ye know full well," said he, "and now ye'll just march."

Seeing now plainly that I was in the hands of one of Lord Westport's gardeners, who had mistaken me for some garden-thief for whom he had been on the look-out, I began to expostulate very pointedly. But always this man stolidly faced me with the yawning mouth of the blunderbuss.

"And now ye'll march," said he, and despite everything I marched. I marched myself through the little door in the wall, and into the gardens of the Earl of West-port. And the infernal weapon was clamped against the small of my back.

But still my luck came to me even then, like basket falling out of a blue sky. As, in obedience to my captor's orders, I rounded a bit of shrubbery, I came face to face with Lady Mary. I stopped so abruptly that the rim of the on-coming blunderbuss must have printed a fine pink ring on my back. I lost all intelligence. I could not speak. I only knew that I stood before the woman I loved, while a man firmly pressed the muzzle of a deadly firearm between my shoulder-blades. I flushed with shame, as if I really had been guilty of stealing the French pears.

Lady Mary's first look upon me was one of pure astonishment. Then she quickly recognized the quaint threat expressed in the attitude of the blunderbuss.

"Strammers," she cried, rushing forward, "what would you be doing to the gentleman?"

"'Tis no gentleman, your la'ship," answered the man confidently. "He be a low-born thief o' pears, he be."

"Strammers!" she cried again, and wrested the blunderbuss from his hands. I will confess that my back immediately felt easier.

"And now, sir," she said, turning to me haughtily, "you will please grant me an explanation of to what my father is indebted for this visit to his private grounds?"

But she knew; no fool of a gardener and a floundering Irishman could keep pace with the nimble wits of a real woman. I saw the pink steal over her face, and she plainly appeared not to care for an answer to her peremptory question. However, I made a grave reply which did not involve the main situation.

"Madam may have noticed a certain deluded man with a bell-mouthed how-itzer," said I. "His persuasions were so pointed and emphatic that I was induced to invade these gardens, wherein I have been so unfortunate as to disturb a lady's privacy,—a thing which only causes me the deepest regret."

"He be a pear-thief," grumbled Strammers from a distance. "Don't ye take no word o' his, your la'ship, after me bringing 'im down from out a tree."

"From out a tree?" said Lady Mary, and she looked at me, and I looked at her.

"The man is right, Lady Mary," said I significantly. "I was in a tree looking over the garden wall."

"Strammers," said she with decision, "wait for me in the rose-garden, and speak no single word to anybody until I see you again. You have made a great mistake."

The man obediently retired, after saluting me with an air of slightly dubious apology. He was not yet convinced that I had not been after his wretched French pears.

But with the withdrawal of this Strammers Lady Mary's manner changed. She became frightened and backed away from me, still holding the gardener's blunder-buss.

"O sir," she cried in a beautiful agitation, "I beg of you to leave at once. Oh, please!"

But here I saw it was necessary to treat the subject in a bold Irish way.

"I'll not leave, Lady Mary," I answered. "I was brought here by force, and only force can make me withdraw."

A glimmer of a smile came to her face, and she raised the blunderbuss, pointing it full at my breast. The mouth was still the width of a water-jug, and in the fair inexperienced hands of Lady Mary it was like to go off at any moment and blow a hole in me as big as a platter.

"Charming mistress," said I, "shoot!"

For answer she suddenly flung the weapon to the grass, and, burying her face in her hands, began to weep. "I'm afraid it's l-l-loaded," she sobbed out.

In an instant I was upon my knees at her side and had taken her hand. Her fingers resisted little, but she turned away her head.

"Lady Mary," said I softly, "I'm a poor devil of an Irish adventurer, but—I love you! I love you so that if I was dead you could bid me rise! I am a worthless fellow; I have no money, and my estate you can hardly see for the mortgages and trouble upon it; I am no fine suitor, but I love you more than them all; I do, upon my life!"

"Here approaches Strammers in quest of his blunderbuss," she answered calmly. "Perhaps we had better give it to him."

I sprang to my feet, and, sure enough, the thick-headed ninepin of a gardener was nearing us.

"Don't ye trust 'im, your la'ship!" he cried. "I caught 'im in a tree, I did, and he be a bad lot!"

Lady Mary quelled him, and he at once went away with his blunderbuss, still muttering his many doubts. But still one cannot drop a love declaration and pick it up again with the facility of a tailor resuming his work on a waistcoat. One can't say: "Where was I? How far had I gone before this miserable interruption came?" In a word I found mysef stammering and stuttering and wasting moments too precious for words.

"Lady Mary—" I began. "Lady Mary—I love you, Lady Mary! Lady Mary—"

It was impossible for me to depart from this rigmarole and express the many things with which my heart was full. It was a maddening tongue-tie. The moments seemed for me the crisis of my existence, and yet I could only say, "Lady Mary, I love you!" I know that in many cases this statement has seemed to be sufficient, but as a matter of fact I was full of things to say, and it was plain to me that I was losing everything through the fact that my silly tongue clung to the roof of my mouth.

I do not know how long the agony endured, but at any rate it was ended by a thunderous hammering upon the little door in the garden-wall. A high Irish voice could be heard:

"And if ye be not leaving him out immediately, we will be coming over the wall if it is ten thousand feet high, ye murdering rogues."

Lady Mary turned deadly pale. "Oh, we are lost," she cried.

I saw at once that the interview was ended. If I remained doughtily I remained stupidly. I could come back some other day. I clutched Lady Mary's hand and kissed it. Then I ran for the door in the garden wall. In a moment I was out, and I heard her frantically bolting the door behind me.

I confronted Paddy and Jem. Jem had in his hands a brace of pistols which he was waving determinedly. Paddy was wetting his palms and resolutely swinging a club. But when they saw me their ferocity gave way to an outburst of affectionate emotion. I had to assert all my mastership to keep Paddy from singing. He would sing. Sure, if they had never heard an Irish song it was time they did.

"Paddy," said I, "my troubles are on me. I wish to be thinking. Remain quiet."

Presently we reached the little inn, and from there the little Doctor Chord flew out like a hawk at a sparrow.

"I thought you were dead," he shouted wildly. "I thought you were dead."

"No," said I, "I am not dead, but I am very thirsty." And, although they were murmuring this thing and that thing, I would have no word with them until I was led to the parlour of the inn and given a glass.

"Now," said I, "I penetrated to the garden and afterwards I came away and I can say no more."

The little Doctor was very happy and proud.

"When I saw the man with the blunderbuss," he recounted, "I said boldly: 'Sirrah, remove that weapon! Exclude it from the scene! Eliminate it from the situation!' But his behaviour was extraordinary. He trained the weapon in such a manner that I myself was in danger of being eliminated from the situation. I instantly concluded that I would be of more benefit to the cause if I temporarily abandoned the vicinity and withdrew to a place where the climatic conditions were more favourable to prolonged terms of human existence."

"I saw you abandoning the vicinity," said I, "and I am free to declare that I never saw a vicinity abandoned with more spirit and finish."

"I thank you for your appreciation," said the Doctor simply. Then he leaned to my ear and whispered, barring his words from Jem and Paddy, who stood respectfully near our chairs. "And the main object of the expedition?" he asked. "Was there heavy firing and the beating down of doors? And I hope you took occasion to slay the hideous monster who flourished the blunderbuss? Imagine my excitement after I had successfully abandoned the vicinity! I was trembling with anxiety for you. Still, I could adopt no steps which would not involve such opportunities for instant destruction that the thought of them brought to mind the most horrible ideas. I pictured myself lying butchered, blown to atoms by a gardener's blunderbuss. Then the spirit of self-sacrifice arose in me, and, as you know, I sent your two servants to your rescue."

The little man was looking through the window at this moment. Suddenly he started back, flinging up his hands.

"My soul, he is again upon us," he cried.

I hastily followed his glance, and saw the man Strammers making peaceful way toward the inn. Apparently he was going to the taproom for an early pint. The Doctor flurried and dove until I checked him in fear that he would stand on his head in the fireplace.

"No," said I, "calm yourself. There will be no blunderbusses. On the other hand, I see here a great chance for a master-stroke. Be quiet now, and try to hold yourself in a chair and see me deal with the situation. When it comes to a thing like this, it is all child's play for me. Paddy," said I. "Jem," said I, "there is a gardener in the taproom. Go and become his warm friends. You know what I mean. A tuppence here and there won't matter. But, of course, always treat him with the profound consideration which is due to so distinguished a gardener."

They understood me at once and grinned. But even then I was struck with their peculiar reasons for understanding at once. Jem Bottles understood at once because he had been a highwayman; Paddy understood at once because he was an Irishman.

One had been all his life a rogue; the other had been born on an intelligent island. And so they comprehended me with equal facility.

They departed on their errand, and when I turned I found myself in the clutches of a maddened Doctor Chord.

"Monster," he screamed, "you have ordered him to be killed!"

"Whist," said I, "it would never do to order him to be killed. He is too valuable."

## CHAPTER XXV

"You appear more at your ease when you are calm," said I to the Doctor as I squashed him into a chair. "Your ideas of murder are juvenile. Gardeners are murdered only by other gardeners, over some question of a magnolia-tree. Gentlemen of position never murder gardeners."

"You are right, sir," he responded frankly. "I see my mistake. But really, I was convinced that something dreadful was about to happen. I am not familiar with the ways of your nationality, sir, and when you gave the resolute directions to your men it was according to my education to believe that something sinister was at hand, although no one could regret more than I that I have made this foolish mistake."

"No," said I, "you are not familiar with the ways of my nationality, and it will require an indefinite number of centuries to make your country-men understand the ways of my nationality; and when they do they will only pretend that after great research they have discovered something very evil indeed. However, in this detail, I am able to instruct you fully. The gardener will not be murdered. His fluency with a blunderbuss was very annoying, but in my opinion it was not so fluent as to merit death."

"I confess," said Doctor Chord, "that all peoples save my own are great rascals and natural seducers. I cannot change this national conviction, for I have studied politics as they are known in the King's Parliament, and it has been thus proved to me."

"However, the gardener is not to be murdered," said I, "and although I am willing to cure you in that particular ignorance I am not willing to take up your general cure as a life work. A glass of wine with you."

After we had adjusted this slight misunderstanding we occupied our seats comfortably before the fire. I wished to give Paddy and Jem plenty of time to conciliate Strammers, but I must say that the wait grew irksome. Finally I arose and went into the corridor and peered into the taproom. There were Paddy and Jem with their victim, the three of them seated affectionately in a row on a bench, drinking from quart pots of ale. Paddy was clapping the gardener on the shoulder.

"Strammers," he cried, "I am thinking more of you than of my cousin Mickey, who was that gay and that gallant it would make you wonder, although I am truthful in saying they killed him for the peace of the parish. But he had the same bold air with him, and devil the girl in the country-side but didn't know who was the lad for her."

Strammers seemed greatly pleased, but Jem Bottles evinced deep disapproval of Paddy's Celtic methods.

"Let Master Strammers be," said he. "He be a-wanting a quiet draught. Let him have his ale with no talking here and there."

"Ay," said Strammers, now convinced that he was a great man and a philosopher, "a quiet draught o' old ale be a good thing."

"True for you, Master Strammers," cried Paddy enthusiastically. "It is in the way of being a good thing. There you are now. Ay, that's it. A good thing! Sure."

"Ay," said Strammers, deeply moved by this appreciation, which he had believed should always have existed. "Ay, I spoke well."

"Well would be no name for it," responded Paddy fervidly. "By gor, and I wish you were knowing Father Corrigan. He would be the only man to near match you. 'A quiet draught o' old ale is a good thing,' says you, and by the piper 'tis hard to say Father Corrigan could have done it that handily. 'Tis you that are a wonderful man."

"I have a small way o' my own," said Strammers, "which even some of the best gardeners has accounted most wise and humorous. The power o' good speech be a great gift." Whereupon the complacent Strammers lifted his arm and buried more than half his face in his quart pot.

"It is," said Paddy earnestly. "And I'm doubting if even the best gardeners would be able to improve it. And says you: 'A quiet draught o' old ale is a good thing,' 'Twould take a grand gardener to beat that word."

"And besides the brisk way of giving a word now and then," continued the deluded Strammers, "I am a great man with flowers. Some of the finest beds in London are there in my master's park."

"Are they so?" said Paddy. "I would be liking to see them."

"And ye shall," cried the gardener with an outburst of generous feeling. "So ye shall. On a Sun day we may stroll quietly and decently in the gardens, and ye shall see."

Seeing that Paddy and Jem were getting on well with the man, I returned to Doctor Chord.

"'Tis all right," said I. "They have him in hand. We have only to sit still, and the whole thing is managed."

Later I saw the three men in the road, Paddy and Jem embracing the almost tearful Strammers. These farewells were touching. Afterward my rogues appeared before me, each with a wide grin.

"We have him," said Paddy, "and 'tis us that has an invitation to come inside the wall next Sunday. 'I have some fine flowers in the gardens,' said he. 'Have you so?' said I. 'Well, then, 'tis myself will be breaking your head if you don't leave us inside to see them.' 'Master Paddy,' said he, 'you are a gentleman, or if not you are very like one, and you and your handsome friend, Master Jem, as well as another friend or two, is welcome to see the gardens whenever I can make certain the master and mistress is out.' And with that I told him he could go home."

"You are doing well," I said, letting the scoundrel see in my face that I believed his pleasant tale, and he was so pleased that he was for going on and making a regular book out of it. But I checked him. "No," said I. "I am fearing that I would become too much interested and excited. I am satisfied with what you've been telling me. 'Twas more to my mind to have beaten that glass-eyed man, but we have taken the right course. And now we will be returning to where we lodge."

During the walk back to the "Pig and Turnip" Doctor Chord took it upon himself to discourse in his usual style upon the recent events. "Of course, sir, I would care to hear of the tragic scenes which must have transpired soon after I—I—"

"Abandoned the vicinity?" said I.

"Precisely," he responded. "Although I was not in the exact neighbourhood during what must have been a most tempestuous part of your adventure, I can assure you I had lost none of my former interest in the affair."

"I am believing you," said I; "but let us talk now more of the future. I am much absorbed in the future. It appears to me that it will move at a rapid pace."

I did not tell him about my meeting with Lady Mary, because I knew, if occasion arose, he would spread the news over half London. No consideration would have been great enough to bridle the tongue of the little gossip from use of the first bit of news which he had ever received warm from the fire. Besides, after his behaviour in front of the enemy, I was quite certain that an imparting of my news could do nothing in the way of impairing his inefficiency. Consequently it was not necessary to trouble him with dramatic details.

"As to the part of the adventure which took place in the garden, you are consistently silent, I observe, sir," said the Doctor.

"I am," said I. "I come of a long line of silent ancestors. My father was particularly notable in this respect."

"And yet, sir," rejoined the Doctor, "I had gained an impression that your father was quite willing to express himself in a lofty and noble manner on such affairs as attracted his especial notice."

"He was that," said I, pleased. "He was indeed. I am only wishing I had his talent for saying all that was in his mind so fast that even the priest could not keep up with him, and goodness knows Father Donovan was no small talker."

"You prove to me the limitations of science, sir," said he. "Although I think I may boast of some small education of a scientific nature, I think I will require some time for meditation and study before I will be able to reconcile your last two statements."

"'Tis no matter," I cried amiably. "Let it pass."

For the rest of that week there was conference following conference at the "Pig and Turnip" and elsewhere. My three companions were now as eager as myself for the advent of the critical Sunday when I, with Paddy and Jem, were to attempt our visit to Strammers's flower-gardens. I had no difficulty in persuading the Doctor that his services would be invaluable at another place; for the memory of the blunderbuss seemed to linger with him. I had resolved to disguise myself slightly, for I had no mind to have complications arising from this gardener's eyes. I think a little disguise is plenty unless one stalks mysteriously and stops and peers here and there. A little unostentatious minding of one's own affairs is a good way to remain undiscovered. Then nobody looks at you and demands: "Who is this fellow?" My father always said that when he wished to disguise himself he dressed as a common man, and although this gained him many a hard knock of the fist and blow of the stick from people who were really his inferiors, he found his disguise was perfection. However, my father only disguised when on some secret mission from King Louis, for it does not become a gentleman to accept a box on the ears from anybody unless it is in the service of his sovereign.

I remember my father saying also these tours as a common man taught him he must ever afterward ride carefully through the streets of villages and towns. He was deeply impressed by the way in which men, women, and children had to scud for their lives to keep from under the hoofs of the chargers of these devil-may-care gentlemen who came like whirlwinds through narrow crowded streets. He himself often had to scramble for his life, he said.

However, that was many years back, and I did not fear any such adventures in my prospective expedition. In such a case I would have trembled for what might happen. I have no such philosophy of temper as had my father. I might take the heel of a gay cavalier and throw him out of the saddle, and then there would be a fine uproar. However, I am quite convinced that it is always best to dodge. A good dodger seldom gets into trouble in this world, and lives to a green old age, while the noble patriot and others of his kind die in dungeons. I remember an honest man who set out to reform the parish in the matter of drink. They took him and—but, no matter; I must be getting on with the main tale.

## CHAPTER XXVI

On Saturday night I called the lads to my room and gave them their final instructions.

"Now, you rogues," said I to them, "let there be no drinking this night, and no trapesing of the streets, getting your heads broke just at the critical moment; for, as my father used to say, although a broken head is merrily come by, a clear head's worth two of it when business is to be transacted. So go to your beds at once, the two of you, if there's any drinking to be done, troth it's myself that'll attend to it."

With that I drove them out and sat down to an exhilarating bottle, without ever a thought of where the money was to come from to pay for it. It is one of the advantages of a public house frequented by the nobility that if you come to it with a bold front, and one or two servants behind your back, you have at least a clear week ahead before they flutter the show of a bill at you and ask to see the colour of your gold in exchange for their ink and paper.

My father used to say that a gentleman with money in his pocket might economize and no disgrace to him; but when stomach and purse are both empty, go to the best house in the town, where they will feed you, and lodge you, and drink you, before asking questions. Indeed I never shed many salt tears over the losses of a publican, for he shears so closely those sheep that have plenty of wool that he may well take care of an innocent lamb like myself, on which the crop is not yet grown.

I was drinking quietly and thinking deeply on the wisdom of my father, who knew the world better than ever his son will know it, when there was an unexpected knock at the door, and in walked Doctor Chord. I was not too pleased to see the little man, for I had feared he had changed his mind and wanted to come with us in the morning, and his company was something I had no desire for. He was a coward in a pinch, and a distrustful man in peace, ever casting doubt on the affection I was sure sometimes that Lady Mary held for me; and if he wasn't talking about that, sure he went rambling on,—great discourses on science which held little interest for a young man so deeply in love as I was. The proper study of mankind is womankind, said a philosopher that my father used to quote with approval, but whose name I'm forgetting at this moment. Nevertheless I welcomed the little Doctor and said to him:

"Draw you up a chair, and I'll draw out a cork."

The little man sat him down, and I placed an open bottle nice and convenient to his elbow.

Whether it was the prospect of good wine, or the delight of better company, or the thought of what was going to happen on the morrow, I could not tell; but it seemed to me the little Doctor laboured under a great deal of excitement, and I became more and more afraid that he would insist on bearing us company while the Earl and the Countess were away at church. Now it was enough to have on my hands two such models of stupidity as Paddy and Jem without having to look after Doctor Chord as well, and him glancing his eyes this way and that in apprehension of a blunderbuss.

"Have you made all your plans, O'Ruddy?" he inquired, setting down his cup a good deal emptier than when he lifted it.

"I have," said I.

"Are you entirely satisfied with them?" he continued.

"My plans are always perfect plans," I replied to him, "and trouble only comes in the working of them. When you have to work with such raw material as I have to put up with, the best of plans have the unlucky habit of turning round and hitting you in the eye."

"Do you expect to be hit in the eye tomorrow?" asked the Doctor, very excited, which was shown by the rattle of the bottle against the lip of his cup.

"I'm only sure of one thing for tomorrow," said I, "and that is the certainty that if there's blunder to be made one or other of my following will make it. Still, I'm not complaining, for it's good to be certain of something."

"What's to be your mode of procedure?" said the Doctor, giving me a touch of his fine language.

"We wait in the lane till the church bells have stopped ringing, then Paddy and Jem go up to the little door in the wall, and Paddy knocks nice and quietly, in the expectation that the door will be opened as quietly by Strammers, and thereupon Jem and Paddy will be let in."

"But won't ye go in with them?" inquired the little Doctor very hurriedly.

"Doctor Chord," said I, lifting up my cup, "I have the honour to drink wine with you, and to inform you that it's myself that's outlining the plan."

"I beg your pardon for interrupting," said the Doctor; then he nodded to me as he drank.

"My two villains will go in alone with Strammers, and when the door is bolted, and they have passed the time of day with each other, Paddy will look around the garden and exclaim how it excels all the gardens that ever was, including that of Eden; and then Jem will say what a pity it was they couldn't have their young friend outside to see the beauty of it. It is my expectation that Strammers will rise to this, and request the pleasure of their young friend's company; but if he hesitates Paddy will say that the young friend outside is a free-handed Irishman who would no more mind a shilling going from his pocket into that of another man than he would the crooking of an elbow when a good drink is to be had. But be that as it may, they're to work me in through the little door by the united diplomacy of England and Ireland, and, once inside of the walls, it is my hope that I can slip away from them and see something of the inside of the house as well."

"And you have the hope that you'll find Lady Mary in the withdrawing-room," said the Doctor.

"I'll find her," says I, "if she's in the house; for I'm going from room to room on a tour of inspection to see whether I'll buy the mansion or not."

"It's a very good plan," said the Doctor, drawing the back of his hand across his lips. "It's a very good plan," he repeated, nodding his head several times.

"Now, by the Old Head of Kinsale, little man," said I, "what do you mean by that remark and that motion of the head? What's wrong with the plan?"

"The plan's a good one, as I have said," reiterated the Doctor. But I saw there was something on his mind, and told him so, urging him to be out with it.

"Do you think," said I, "that Lady Mary will be in church with her father and mother?"

"I do not," muttered the Doctor, cautiously bringing his voice down to a whisper; "but I want to warn you that there's danger here in this room while you're lurking around my Earl's palace."

"How can danger harm me here when I am somewhere else?" I asked.

A very mysterious manner fell upon the little man, and he glanced, one after the other, at the four corners of the room, as if he heard a mouse moving and wanted to detect it. Then he looked sternly at the door, and I thought he was going to peer up the chimney, but instead he leaned across the table and said huskily,—

"The papers!"

"What papers?" I asked, astonished.

"Your thoughts are so intent on the young lady that you forget everything else. Have you no recollection of the papers the Earl of Westport is so anxious to put himself in possession of?"

I leaned back in my chair and gazed steadily at Chord; but his eyes would not bring themselves to meet mine, and so he made some pother about filling up his cup again, with the neck of the bottle trembling on the edge, as if its teeth were chattering.

Now my father used to say when a man is afraid to meet your eye, be prepared to have him meet your fist. I disremembered saying anything to the Doctor about these same papers, which, truth to tell, I had given but little thought to recently, with other things of more importance to crowd them out of mind.

"How come you to know anything about the papers?" I said at last.

"Oh, your memory is clean leaving you!" cried the little Doctor, as if the cup of wine he drank had brought back his courage to him. "You told me all about the papers when we were in Kensington Gardens."

"If I did," says I, "then I must have further informed you that I gave them as a present to Lady Mary herself. Surely I told you that?"

"You told me that, of course; but I thought you said they had come back into your possession again. If I'm wrong, it's no matter at all, and there's nothing to be said about them. I'm merely speaking to you by way of a friend, and I thought if you had the papers here in your room it was very unsafe to leave them unprotected by yourself or some one you can trust. I was just speaking as your well-wisher, for I don't want to hear you crying you are robbed, and us at our wit's end not getting either the thief or the booty."

He spoke with great candour and good humour, and the only thing that made me suspicious at first was that for the life of me I could not ever remember mentioning the papers to him, yet it was very likely that I did; for, as my father used to say, an Irishman talks more than the recording angel can set down in his busiest day, and therefore it is lucky that everything he says is not held against him. It seemed to me that we talked more of scandal than of papers in the park, but still I might be mistaken.

"Very good, Doctor," I cried, genially. "The papers it is, and, true for you, the Earl would like to get his old claws on them. Have you any suggestions to make?"

"Well, it seems to me, O'Ruddy, that if the Earl got wind of them it would be the easiest thing in the world to have your apartment rifled during your absence."

"That is true enough," I agreed, "so what would you do about the papers if you were in my boots?"

"If I had a friend I could trust," said Doctor Chord slowly, "I would give the papers to him and tell him to take good care of them."

"But why not carry them about in my own pocket?" I asked.

"It seemed to me they were not any too safe last time they were there," said the Doctor, pleasantly enough. "You see, O'Ruddy, you're a marked man if once the Earl gets wind of your being in town. To carry the papers about on your own person would be the unsafest thing you could do, ensuring you a stab in the back, so that little use you'd have for the papers ever after. I have no desire to be mixed further in your affairs than I am at the present moment, but nevertheless I could easily take charge of the packet for you; then you would know where it was."

"But would I be sure to know where *you* were?" said I, my first suspicion of him returning to me.

The little Doctor laughed.

"I am always very easily found," he said; "but when I offered to take the papers it was merely in case a stranger like yourself should not have a faster friend beside him than I am. If you have any such, then I advise you to give custody of the papers to him."

"I have no real friend in London that I know of," said I, "but Paddy."

"The very thing," cried the Doctor, joyously, at once putting to rest all my doubts concerning him. "The very thing. I would give the papers to Paddy and tell him to protect them with his life. I'm sure he'll do it, and you'll know where to find both them and him when you want them. But to go away from the 'Pig and Turnip' right across to the other end of the town, taking your two servants with you, leaving nobody to guard papers that are of importance to you, strikes me as the height of folly. I'll just fill up another cup, and so bid you good-night, and good luck for the morrow."

And with that the little man drained the bottle, taking his leave with great effusion, and begging my pardon for even so much as mentioning the papers, saying they had been on his mind for the last day or two, and, feeling friendly toward me, he wished to warn me not to leave them carelessly about.

After he left I thought a good deal about what the Doctor had said, and I wondered at myself that I had ever misdoubted him; for, although he was a man given greatly to talk, yet he had been exceedingly friendly with me from the very first night I had met him, and I thought shame of myself that I was losing trust in my fellow man here in this great city of Lon don, because in Ireland we trust each other entirely; and indeed we are under some compulsion in that same matter, for there is so little money about that if you do not take a man's word now and then there's nothing else for you to take.

## CHAPTER XXVII

I slept well that night, and it was broad daylight when I awoke. A most beautiful morning it seemed to me, and just the time for a lonely stroll in the beautiful gardens, so long as there was some one with you that you thought a great deal of. I made a good breakfast, and then took out the papers and placed them on the table before me. They were all safe so far. I could not comprehend how the Earl would know anything of my being in London, unless, indeed, he caught sight of me walking in his own gardens with his own daughter, and then, belike, he was so jealous a man that he would maybe come to the conclusion I was in London as well as himself.

After breakfast Paddy and Jem came in, looking as bold as Blarney Castle; and when I eyed them both I saw that neither one nor the other was a fit custodian for papers that might make the proudest Earl in England a poor man or a rich man, depending which way they went. So I put the documents in my own pocket without more ado, and gave up my thoughts to a pleasanter subject. I changed my mind about a disguise, and put on my back the best clothes that I had to wear. I wished I had the new suits I had been measured for, but the spalpeen of a tailor would not let me have them unless I paid him some of the money they cost. When I came to think over it I saw that Strammers would surely never recognize me as a gay spark of fashion when he had merely seen me once before, torn and ragged, coming down from a tree on top of his blunderbuss. So I instructed Paddy to say that he and Jem were servants of the best master in the world, who was a great lover of gardens; that he was of immense generosity, and if Strammers allowed him to come into the gardens by the little door he would be a richer man when the door was opened than he would be if he kept it shut. I had been long enough in London to learn the golden method of persuasion; any how I could not bring myself to the chance of meeting with my lady, and me dressed worse than one of her own servants.

We were all in the lane when the church bells ceased to ring, and if any one had seen us he would simply have met a comely young Irish gentleman taking the air of a Sunday morning with two faithful servants at his heels. I allowed something like ten impatient minutes to crawl past me, and then, as the lane was clear and every one for the church within its walls, I tipped a nod to Paddy, and he, with Jem by his side, tapped lightly at the door, while I stood behind the trunk of the tree up which I had climbed before. There was no sign of Doctor Chord in the vicinity, and for that I was thankful, because up to the last moment I feared the little man could not help intruding himself on what was somebody else's business.

The door was opened with some caution, letting Paddy and Jem enter; then it was closed, and I heard the bolts shot into their places. But I was speedily to hear more than bolts that Sunday morning. There was a sound of thumping sticks, and I heard a yell that might well have penetrated to the "Pig and Turnip" itself, although it was miles away. I knew Paddy's cry, and next there came some good English cursing from Jem Bottles, while a shrill voice called out:—

"Catch the red-haired one; he's the villain we want!"

In the midst of various exclamations, maledictions, and other constructions of speech, mingled, I thought, with laughter, I flung my shoulder against the door, but I might as well have tried to batter down the wall itself. The door was as firm as Macgillicuddy Reeks. I know when I am beat as well as the next man, and, losing no more time there, I ran as fast as I could along the wall, out of the lane, and so to the front of the house. The main entrance was protected by great gates of wrought iron, which were opened on occasion by a man in a little cubby of a cabin that stood for a porter's lodge. The man wasn't there, and the gates were locked; but part of one of the huge wings of wrought iron was a little gate that stood ajar. This I pushed open, and, unmolested, stepped inside.

The trees and shrubbery hid from me the scene that was taking place inside the little wooden door. I dashed through the underbrush and came to the edge of a broad lawn, and there was going on as fine a scrimmage as any man could wish to see. Jem Bottles had his back against the wooden door, and was laying about him with a stout stick; half a dozen tall fellows in livery making a great show of attack, but keeping well out of range of his weapon. Poor Paddy had the broad of his back on the turf, and it looked like they were trying to tear the clothes off him, for another half-dozen were on top of him; but I can say this in his favour, Paddy was using his big feet and doing great execution with them. Every now and then he planted a boot in the well-fed front of a footman or under-gardener, and sent him flying. The whole household seemed to be present, and one could hardly believe there was such a mob in a single mansion. The Earl of Westport was there, and who stood beside him but that little villain, Doctor Chord.

But it was the Countess herself that was directing operations. She had an ebony stick in her hands, and when Paddy kicked one of her underlings the vigorous old lady smote the overturned servant to make him to the fray again. It was an exciting scene, and Donnybrook was nothing to it. Their backs were all toward me, and I was just bubbling with joy to think what a surprise I was about to give them,—for I drew my sword and had a yell of defiance on my lips,—when a cry that nobody paid the least attention to turned my mind in another direction entirely.

One of the first-floor windows was open, and over the sill leaned Lady Mary herself, her face aflush with anger.

"Father! Mother!" she cried. "Are not you ashamed of yourselves, making this commotion on a Sunday morning? Call the servants away from there! Let the two poor men go! Oh, shame, shame upon you."

She wrung her hands, but, as I was saying, nobody paid the slightest heed to her, and I doubt if any of them heard her, for Paddy was not keeping silence by any manner of means. He was taking the worst of all the blows that fell on him in a vigorous outcry.

"Murther! murther!" he shouted. "Let me on me feet, an' I'll knock yez all into the middle of county Clare."

No one, however, took advantage of this generous offer, but they kept as clear as they could of his miscellaneous feet, and the Countess poked him in the ribs with the point of her ebony stick whenever she wasn't laying it over the backs of her servants.

Now, no man can ever say that I was a laggard when a good old-fashioned contest was going on, and the less indolence was observable on my own part when friends of mine were engaged in the fray. Sure I was always eager enough, even when it was a stranger's debate, and I wonder what my father would think of me now, to see me veer from the straight course of battle and thrust my unstruck sword once more into its scabbard. It was the face in the window that made me forget friend and foe alike. Lady Mary was the only member of the household that was not on the lawn, and was protesting unheard against the violence to two poor men who were there because they had been invited to come by the under-gardener.

I saw in the twinkling of an eye that the house had been deserted on the first outcry. Doors were left wide open for the whole world to enter. I dodged behind the trees, scuttled up the gravelled driveway, leaped the stone steps three at a time, and before you could say "Ballymuggins" I was in the most superb hall in which I ever set my foot. It was a square house with the stairway in the middle. I kept in my mind's eye the direction of the window in which Lady Mary had appeared. Quick as a bog-trotter responds to an invitation to drink, I mounted that grand stairway, turned to my right, and came to a door opposite which I surmised was the window through which Lady Mary was leaning. Against this door I rapped my knuckles, and speedily I heard the sweet voice of the most charming girl in all the world demand with something like consternation in its tones,—

"Who is there?"

"It's me, Lady Mary!" said I. "The O'Ruddy, who begs the privilege of a word with you."

I heard the slam of a window being shut, then the sound of a light step across the floor, and after that she said with a catch in her voice,—

"I'll be pleased you should come in, Mr. O'Ruddy."

I tried the door, but found it locked.

"How can I come in, Lady Mary," says I, "if you've got bolts held against me?"

"There are no bolts," said Lady Mary; "the key should be on the outside. I am locked in. Look for the key and open the door."

Was ever a more delightful sentence spoken to a man? My heart was in my throat with joy. I glanced down, and there, sure enough, stuck the key. I turned it at once, then pulled it out of the lock and opened the door.

"Lady Mary," says I, "with your permission, it seems to me a door should be locked from the inside."

With that I thrust the key through the far side of the door, closed it, and locked it. Then I turned round to face her.

The room, it was plain to be seen, was the parlour of a lady,—a boudoir, as they call it in France, a word that my father was very fond of using, having caught it when he was on the campaign in that delightful country. The boudoir was full of confections and charming little dainties in the way of lace, and easy chairs, and bookcases, and little writing-desks, and a work-basket here and there; but the finest ornament it possessed was the girl who now stood in the middle of the floor with a frown on her brow that was most becoming. Yes, there was a frown on her brow, although I expected a smile on her lips because of the cordial invitation she had given me to come in.

It would seem to either you or me that if a lady suffered the indignity of being locked in her room, just as if she was a child of six years old, she would welcome with joy the person who came and released her. Now, my father, who was the wisest man since Solomon,—and indeed, as I listened to him, I've often thought that Solomon was overpraised,—my father used to say there was no mystery at all about women. "You just think," he would say, "of what a sensible man would do on a certain occasion; then configure out in your mind the very opposite, and that's what a woman will do." A man who had been imprisoned would have held out his hand and have said, "God bless you, O'Ruddy; but I'm glad to see you." And here stood this fine lady in the middle of her room, looking at me as if I were the dirt beneath her feet, and had forced my way into her presence, instead of being invited like a man of honour to enter.

"Well, Mr. O'Ruddy," she said, throwing back her head, haughty-like, "Why do you stand dallying in a lady's bower when your followers are being beaten on the lawn outside?"

I cannot give you Lady Mary's exact words, for I was so astonished at their utterance; but I give you a very good purport of them.

"Is it the beating of my men?" I said. "Troth, that's what I pay them for. And whoever gives them a good drubbing saves me the trouble. I saw they had Paddy down on the turf, but he's a son of the ould sod, and little he'll mind being thrown on his mother. But if it's Jem Bottles you're anxious about, truth to tell I'm more sorry for those that come within range of his stick than for Jem with his back to the wall. Bottles can take care of himself in any company, for he's a highwayman in an excellent way of business."

I always like to mention anything that's in favour of a man, and so I told her what profession Bottles followed. She gave a toss of her head, and gave me a look that had something like contempt in it, which was far from being pleasant to endure. Then she began walking up and down the room, and it was plain to see that my Lady was far from being pleased with me.

"Poor fellows! Poor faithful fellows! That's what comes of having a fool for a master."

"Indeed, your ladyship," said I, drawing myself up to my full height, which wasn't so very much short of the door itself, "there are worse things than blows from a good honest cudgel. You might better say, 'This is what comes to a master with two fools for servants.'"

"And what comes to a master?" she demanded. "Sure no one asks you to be here."

"That shows how short your ladyship's memory is," said I with some irritation. "Father Donovan used to tell me that the shortest thing in the world was the interval between an insult and a blow in Ireland, but I think a lady's memory is shorter still. 'Turn the key and come in,' says you. What is that, I would like to know, but an invitation."

It appeared to me that she softened a bit, but she continued her walk up and down the room and was seemingly in great agitation. The cries outside had stopped, but whether they had murdered both Jem Bottles and Paddy I had no means at that moment of knowing, and I hope the two will forgive me when I say that my thoughts were far from them.

"You will understand," said Lady Mary, speaking still with resentment in her voice, "that the papers you held are the key to the situation. Have you no more sense than to trust them to the care of a red-headed clown from whom they can be taken as easy as if they were picked up off the street?"

"Indeed, believe me, Lady Mary, that no red-headed clown has any papers of mine."

"Indeed, and I think you speak the true word there. The papers are now in my father's possession, and he will know how to take care of them."

"Well, he didn't know that the last time he had them," I cried, feeling angry at these unjust accusations, and not being able to bear the compliment to the old man, even if he was an Earl. "The papers," said I, "are as easily picked from me as from the street, like you were saying just now; but it isn't a pack of overfed flunkeys that will lift them from me. Lady Mary, on a previous occasion I placed the papers in your hands; now, with your kind permission, I lay them at your feet,"—and, saying this with the most courteous obeisance, I knelt with one knee on the floor and placed the packet of papers where I said I would place them.

Now, ever since that, the Lady Mary denies that she kicked them to the other end of the room. She says that as she was walking to and fro the toe of her foot touched the packet and sent it spinning; and, as no real Irishman ever yet contradicted a lady, all I will say is that the precious bundle went hurtling to the other end of the room, and it is very likely that Lady Mary thought the gesture of her foot a trifle too much resembled an action of her mother, the Countess, for her manner changed in the twinkling of an eye, and she laughed like her old self again.

"Mr. O'Ruddy," she said, "you put me out of all patience. You're as simple as if you came out of Ireland yesterday."

"It's tolerably well known," said I, "by some of your expert swordsmen, that I came out the day before."

Again Lady Mary laughed.

"You're not very wise in the choice of your friends," she said.

"I am, if I can count you as one of them," I returned.

She made no direct reply to this, but continued:

"Can't you see that that little Doctor Chord is a traitor? He has been telling my father all you have been doing and all you have been planning, and he says you are almost simple enough to have given the papers into his own keeping no longer ago than last night."

"Now, look you, Lady Mary, how much you misjudged me. The little villain asked for the papers, but he didn't get them; then he advised me to give them to a man I could trust, and when I said the only man I could trust was red-headed Paddy out yonder, he was delighted to think I was to leave them in his custody. But you can see for yourself I did nothing of the kind, and if your people thought they could get anything out of Paddy by bad language and heroic kicks they were mistaken."

At that moment we had an interruption that brought our conversation to a standstill and Lady Mary to the door, outside which her mother was crying,—

"Mary, Mary! where's the key?"

"Where should it be?" said Lady Mary, "but in the door."

"It is not in the door," said the Countess wrathfully, shaking it as if she would tear it down.

"It is in the door," said Lady Mary positively; and quite right she was, for both of us were looking at it.

"It is not in the door," shouted her mother. "Some of the servants have taken it away."

Then we heard her calling over the banisters to find out who had taken away the key of Lady Mary's room. There was a twinkle in Mary's eye, and a quiver in the corners of her pretty mouth that made me feel she would burst out laughing, and indeed I had some ado to keep silence myself.

"What have you done with those two poor wretches you were maltreating out in the garden?" asked Lady Mary.

"Oh, don't speak of them," cried the Countess, evidently in no good humour. "It was all a scandal for nothing. The red-headed beast did not have the papers. That little fool, Chord, has misled both your father and me. I could wring his neck for him, and now he is palavering your father in the library and saying he will get the papers himself or die in the attempt. It serves us right for paying attention to a babbling idiot like him. I said in the first place that that Irish baboon of an O'Ruddy was not likely to give them to the ape that follows him."

"Tare-an-ounds!" I cried, clenching my fists and making for the door; but Lady Mary rattled it so I could not be heard, and the next instant she placed her snow-flake hand across my mouth, which was as pleasant a way of stopping an injudicious utterance as ever I had been acquainted with.

"Mary," said the Countess, "your father is very much agitated and disappointed, so I'm taking him out for a drive. I have told the butler to look out for the key, and when he finds it he will let you out. You've only yourself to blame for being locked in, because we expected the baboon himself and couldn't trust you in his presence."

It was now Lady Mary's turn to show confusion at the old termagant's talk, and she coloured as red as a sunset on the coast of Kerry. I forgave the old hag her discourteous appellation of "baboon" because of the joyful intimation she gave me through the door that Lady Mary was not to be trusted when I was near by. My father used to say that if you are present when an embarrassment comes to a lady it is well not to notice it, else the embarrassment will be transferred to yourself. Remembering this, I pretended not to see Lady Mary's flaming cheeks, and, begging her pardon, walked up the room and picked from the corner the bundle of papers which had, somehow or other come there, whether kicked or not. I came back to where she was standing and offered them to her most respectfully, as if they, and not herself, were the subject of discussion.

"Hush," said Lady Mary in a whisper; "sit down yonder and see how long you can keep quiet."

She pointed to a chair that stood beside a beautifully polished table of foreign wood, the like of which I had never seen before, and I, wishing very much to please her, sat down where she told me and placed the bundle of papers on the table. Lady Mary tiptoed over, as light-footed as a canary-bird, and sat down on the opposite side of the table, resting her elbows on the polished wood, and, with her chin in her hands, gazed across at me, and a most bewildering scrutiny I found it, rendering it difficult for me to keep quiet and seated, as she had requested. In a minute or two we heard the crunch of wheels on the gravel in front, then the carriage drove off, and the big gates clanked together.

Still Lady Mary poured the sunshine of her eyes upon me, and I hope and trust she found me a presentable young man, for under the warmth of her look my heart began to bubble up like a pot of potatoes on a strong fire.

"You make me a present of the papers, then?" said Lady Mary at last.

"Indeed and I do, and of myself as well, if you'll have me. And this latter is a thing I've been trying to say to you every time I met you, Mary acushla, and no sooner do the words come to my lips than some doddering fool interrupts us; but now, my darling, we are alone together, in that lover's paradise which is always typified by a locked door, and at last I can say the things—"

Just here, as I mentioned the word "door," there came a rap at it, and Lady Mary started as if some one had fired a gun.

"Your ladyship," said the butler, "I cannot find the key. Shall I send for a locksmith?"

"Oh, no," said Lady Mary, "do not take the trouble. I have letters to write, and do not wish to be disturbed until my mother returns."

"Very good, your ladyship," returned the butler, and he walked away.

"A locksmith!" said Lady Mary, looking across the table at me.

"Love laughs at them," said I.

Lady Mary smiled very sweetly, but shook her head.

"This is not a time for laughter," she said, "but for seriousness. Now, I cannot risk your staying here longer, so will tell you what I have to say as quickly as possible. Your repeatedly interrupted declaration I take for truth, because the course of true love never did run smooth. Therefore, if you want me, you must keep the papers."

At this I hastily took the bundle from the table and thrust it in my pocket, which action made Lady Mary smile again.

"Have you read them?" she asked.

"I have not."

"Do you mean to say you have carried these papers about for so long and have not read them?"

"I had no curiosity concerning them," I replied. "I have something better to look at," I went on, gazing across at her; "and when that is not with me the memory of it is, and it's little I care for a pack of musty papers and what's in them."

"Then I will tell you what they are," said Lady Mary. "There are in that packet the title-deeds to great estates, the fairest length of land that lies under the sun in Sussex. There is also a letter written by my father's own hand, giving the property to your father."

"But he did not mean my father to keep it," said I.

"No, he did not. He feared capture, and knew the ransom would be heavy if they found evidence of property upon him. Now all these years he has been saying nothing, but collecting the revenues of this estate and using them, while another man had the legal right to it."

"Still he has but taken what was his own," said I, "and my father never disputed that, always intending to come over to England and return the papers to the Earl; but he got lazy-like, by sitting at his own fireside, and seldom went farther abroad than to the house of the priest; but his last injunctions to me were to see that the Earl got his papers, and indeed he would have had them long since if he had but treated me like the son of an old friend."

"Did your father mention that the Earl would give you any reward for returning his property to him?"

"He did not," I replied with indignation. "In Ireland, when a friend does a friend's part, he doesn't expect to be paid for it."

"But don't you expect a reward for returning them?"

"Lady Mary," said I, "do you mean to be after insulting me? These papers are not mine, but the Earl of Westport's, and he can have them without saying as much as 'Thank you kindly' for them."

Lady Mary leaned back in her chair and looked at me with half-closed eyes, then she stretched forth her hand and said:

"Give me the papers."

"But it's only a minute since," I cried, perplexed, "that you held them to be the key of the situation, and said if I didn't keep them I would never get you."

"Did I say that?" asked Lady Mary with the innocence of a three-year-old child. "I had no idea we had come to such a conclusion. Now do you want a little advice about those same papers?"

"As long as the advice comes from you, Mary darling, I want it on any subject."

"You have come into England brawling, sword-playing, cudgel-flinging, and never till this moment have you given a thought to what the papers are for. These papers represent the law."

"Bad cess to it," said I. "My father used to say, have as little to do with the law as possible, for what's the use of bringing your man into the courts when a good shillelah is speedier and more satisfactory to all concerned."

"That may be true in Ireland, but it is not true in England. Now, here is my advice. You know my father and mother, and if you'll just quit staring your eyes out at me, and think for a minute, you may be able to tell when you will get their consent to pay your addresses to me without interruption." Here she blushed and looked down.

"Indeed," said I, "I don't need to take my eyes from you to answer *that* question. It'll be the afternoon following the Day of Judgment."

"Very well. You must then stand on your rights. I will give you a letter to a man in the Temple, learned in the law. He was legal adviser to my aunt, who left me all her property, and she told me that if I ever was in trouble I was to go to him; but instead of that I'll send my trouble to him with a letter of introduction. I advise you to take possession of the estate at Brede, and think no more of giving up the papers to my father until he is willing to give you something in return. You may then ask what you like of him; money, goods, or a farm,"—and again a bright red colour flooded her cheeks. With that she drew toward her pen and paper and dashed off a letter which she gave to me.

"I think," she said, "it would be well if you left the papers with the man in the Temple; he will keep them safely, and no one will suspect where they are; while, if you need money, which is likely, he will be able to advance you what you want on the security of the documents you leave with him."

"Is it money?" said I, "sure I couldn't think of drawing money on property that belongs to your good father, the Earl."

"As I read the papers," replied Lady Mary, very demurely, casting down her eyes once more, "the property does not belong to my good father, the Earl, but to the good-for-nothing young man named O'Ruddy. I think that my father, the Earl, will find that he needs your signature before he can call the estate his own once more. It may be I am wrong, and that your father, by leaving possession so long in the hands of the Earl, may have forfeited his claim. Mr. Josiah Brooks will tell you all about that when you meet him in the Temple. You may depend upon it that if he advances you money your claim is good, and, your claim being good, you may make terms with even so obstreperous a man as my father."

"And if I make terms with the father," I cried, "do you think his comely daughter will ratify the bargain?"

Lady Mary smiled very sweetly, and gave me the swiftest and shyest of glances across the table from her speaking eyes, which next instant were hidden from me.

"May be," she said, "the lawyer could answer that question."

"Troth," I said, springing to my feet, "I know a better one to ask it of than any old curmudgeon poring over dry law-books, and the answer I'm going to have from your own lips."

Then, with a boldness that has ever characterized the O'Ruddys, I swung out my arms and had her inside o' them before you could say Ballymoyle. She made a bit of a struggle and cried breathlessly:

"I'll answer, if you'll sit in that chair again."

"It's not words," says I, "I want from your lips, but this,"—and I smothered a little shriek with one of the heartiest kisses that ever took place out of Ireland itself, and it seemed to me that her struggle ceased, or, as one might say, faded away, as my lips came in contact with hers; for she suddenly weakened in my arms so that I had to hold her close to me, for I thought she would sink to the floor if I did but leave go, and in the excitement of the moment my own head was swimming in a way that the richest of wine had never made it swim before. Then Lady Mary buried her face in my shoulder with a little sigh of content, and I knew she was mine in spite of all the Earls and Countesses in the kingdom, or estates either, so far as that went. At last she straightened up and made as though she would push me from her, but held me thus at arms' length, while her limpid eyes looked like twin lakes of Killarney on a dreamy misty morning when there's no wind blowing.

"O'Ruddy," she said, solemnly, with a little catch in her voice, "you're a bold man, and I think you've no doubt of your answer; but what has happened makes me the more anxious for your success in dealing with those who will oppose both your wishes and mine. My dear lover, is what I call you now; you have come over in tempestuous fashion, with a sword in your hand, striving against every one who would stand up before you. After this morning, all that should be changed, for life seems to have become serious and momentous. O'Ruddy, I want your actions to be guided, not by a drawn sword, but by religion and by law."

"Troth, Mary acushla, an Irishman takes to religion of his own nature, but I much misdoubt me if it comes natural to take to the law."

"How often have you been to mass since you came to England, O'Ruddy?"

"How often?" says I, wrinkling my brow, "indeed you mean, how many times?"

"Yes; how many times?"

"Now, Mary, how could you expect me to be keeping count of them?"

"Has your attendance, then, been so regular?"

"Ah, Mary, darling; it's not me that has the face to tell you a lie, and yet I'm ashamed to say that I've never set foot in a church since I crossed the channel, and the best of luck it is for me that good old Father Donovan doesn't hear these same words."

"Then you will go to church this very day and pray for heaven's blessing on both of us."

"It's too late for the mass this Sunday, Mary, but the churches are open, and the first one I come to will have me inside of it."

With that she drew me gently to her, and herself kissed me, meeting none of that resistance which I had encountered but a short time before; and then, as bitter ill luck would have it, at this delicious moment we were startled by the sound of carriage-wheels on the gravel outside.

"Oh!" cried Lady Mary in a panic; "how time has flown!"

"Indeed," said I, "I never knew it so fast before."

And she, without wasting further time in talking, unlocked the door, whipped out the key, and placed it where I had found it in the beginning. She seemed to think of everything in a moment, and I would have left her letter and the papers on the table if it hadn't been for that cleverest of all girls, who, besides her lips of honey, had an alert mind, which is one of the things appreciated in Ireland. I then followed her quickly down a narrow back stairway and out into a glass house, where a little door at the end led us into a deliciously shaded walk, free from all observation, with a thick screen of trees on the right hand and the old stone wall on the left.

Here I sprang quickly to overtake her, but she danced away like a fairy in the moonlight, throwing a glance of mischief over her shoulder at me, with her finger on her lips. It seemed to me a pity that so sylvan a dell should merely be used for the purposes of speed, but in a jiffy Mary was at the little door in the wall and had the bolts drawn back, and I was outside before I understood what had happened, listening to bolts being thrust back again, and my only consolation was the remembrance of a little dab at my lips as I passed through, as brief and unsatisfactory as the peck of a sparrow.

## CHAPTER XXVIII

It was a beautiful day, as lovely as any an indulgent Providence had ever bestowed upon an unthankful generation.

Although I wished I had had an hour or two to spend with Mary wandering up and down that green alley through which we had rushed with such indecent haste, all because two aged and angry members of the nobility might have come upon us, yet I walked through the streets of London as if I trod on the air, and not on the rough cobble-stones of the causeway. It seemed as if I had suddenly become a boy again, and yet with all the strength and vigour of a man, and I was hard put to it not to shout aloud in the sunlight, or to slap on the back the slow and solemn Englishmen I met, who looked as if they had never laughed in their lives. Sure it's a very serious country, this same land of England, where their dignity is so oppressive that it bows down head and shoulders with thinking how grand they are; and yet I'll say nothing against them, for it was an Englishwoman that made me feel like a balloon. Pondering over the sobriety of the nation, I found myself in the shadow of a great church, and, remembering what my dear Mary had said, I turned and went in through the open door, with my hat in my hand. It was a great contrast to the bright sunlight I had left, and to the busy streets with their holiday-making people. There were only a few scattered here and there in the dim silence of the church, some on their knees, some walking slowly about on tiptoe, and some seated meditating in chairs. No service was going forward, so I knelt down in the chapel of Saint Patrick himself; I bowed my head and thanked God for the day and for the blessing that had come with it. As I said, I was like a boy again, and to my lips, too long held from them, came the prayers that had been taught me. I was glad I had not forgotten them, and I said them over and over with joy in my heart. As I raised my head, I saw standing and looking at me a priest, and, rising to my feet, I made my bow to him, and he came forward, recognizing me before I recognized him.

"O'Ruddy," he said, "if you knew the joy it gives to my old heart to meet you in this sacred place and in that devout attitude, it would bring some corresponding happiness to yourself."

"Now by the piper that played before Moses, Father Donovan, and is this yourself? Sure I disrecognized you, coming into the darkness, and me just out of the glare beyond,"—and I took his hand in both of mine and shook it with a heartiness he had not met since he left the old turf. "Sure and there's no one I'd rather meet this day than yourself,"—and with that I dropped on one knee and asked for his blessing on me and mine.

As we walked out of the church together, his hand resting on my shoulder, I asked how such a marvel came to pass as Father Donovan, who never thought to leave Ireland, being here in London. The old man said nothing till we were down the steps, and then he told me what had happened.

"You remember Patsy O'Gorman," he said.

"I do that," I replied, "and an old thief of the world and a tight-fisted miser he is."

"Whist," said Father Donovan, quietly crossing himself. "O'Gorman is dead and buried."

"Do you tell me that!" said I, "then rest his soul. He would be a warm man and leave more money than my father did, I'm thinking."

"Yes, he left some money, and to me he left three hundred pounds, with the request that I should accomplish the desire of my life and take the pilgrimage to Rome."

"The crafty old chap, that same bit of bequestration will help him over many a rough mile in purgatory."

"Ah, O'Ruddy, it's not our place to judge. They gave a harder name to O'Gorman than he deserved. Just look at your own case. The stories that have come back to Ireland, O'Ruddy, just made me shiver. I heard that you were fighting and brawling through England, ready to run through any man that looked cross-eyed at you. They said that you had taken up with a highwayman; that you spent your nights in drink and breathing out smoke; and here I find you, a proper young man, doing credit to your country, meeting you, not in a tavern, but on your knees with bowed head in the chapel of Saint Patrick, giving the lie to the slanderer's tongue."

The good old man stopped in our walk, and with tears in his eyes shook hands with me again, and I had not the heart to tell him the truth.

"Ah well," I said, "Father Donovan, I suppose nobody, except yourself, is quite as good as he thinks, and nobody, including myself, is as bad as he appears to be. And now, Father Donovan, where are you stopping, and how long will you be in London?"

"I am stopping with an old college friend, who is a priest in the church where I found you. I expect to leave in a few days' time and journey down to the seaport of

Rye, where I am to take ship that will land me either in Dunkirk or in Calais. From there I am to make my way to Rome as best I can."

"And are you travelling alone?"

"I am that, although, by the blessing of God, I have made many friends on the journey, and every one I met has been good to me."

"Ah, Father Donovan, you couldn't meet a bad man if you travelled the world over. Sure there's some that carry such an air of blessedness with them that every one they meet must, for very shame, show the best of his character. With me it's different, for it seems that where there's contention I am in the middle of it, though, God knows, I'm a man of peace, as my father was before me."

"Well," said Father Donovan slowly, but with a sweet smile on his lip, "I suppose the O'Ruddys were always men of peace, for I've known them before now to fight hard enough to get it."

The good father spoke a little doubtfully, as if he were not quite approving of our family methods, but he was a kindly man who always took the most lenient view of things. He walked far with me, and then I turned and escorted him to the place where he resided, and, bidding good-bye, got a promise from him that he would come to the "Pig and Turnip" a day later and have a bite and sup with me, for I thought with the assistance of the landlord I could put a very creditable meal before him, and Father Donovan was always one that relished his meals, and he enjoyed his drink too, although he was set against too much of it. He used to say, "It's a wise drinker that knows when geniality ends and hostility begins, and it's just as well to stop before you come to the line."

With this walking to and fro the day was near done with when I got back to the "Pig and Turnip" and remembered that neither a bit of pig nor a bit of turnip had I had all that long day, and now I was ravenous. I never knew anything make me forget my appetite before; but here had I missed my noonday meal, and not in all my life could I overtake it again. Sure there was many an experience crowded together in that beautiful Sunday, so, as I passed through the entrance to the inn I said to the obsequious landlord:

"For the love of Heaven, get placed on my table all you have in the house that's fit to eat, and a trifle of a bottle or two, to wash it down with."

So saying, I passed up the creaking old oaken stair and came to my room, where I instantly remembered there was something else I had forgotten. As I opened the door there came a dismal groan from Paddy, and something that sounded like a wicked oath from Jem Bottles. Poor lads! that had taken such a beating that day, such a cudgelling for my sake; and here I stood at my own door in a wonder of amazement, and something of fright, thinking I had heard a banshee wail. The two misused lads had slipped out of my memory as completely as the devil slipped off Macgillicuddy Reeks into the pond beneath when Saint Patrick had sent the holy words after him.

"Paddy," said I, "are you hurted? Where is it you're sore?"

"Is it sore?" he groaned. "Except the soles of my feet, which they couldn't hit with me kickin' them, there isn't an inch of me that doesn't think it's worse hurted than the rest."

"It's sorry I am to hear that," I replied, quite truthfully, "and you, Jem, how did you come off?"

"Well, I gave a better account of myself than Paddy here, for I made most of them keep their distance from me; but him they got on the turf before you could say

Watch me eye, and the whole boiling of them was on top of him in the twinkling of the same."

"The whole boiling of them?" said I, as if I knew nothing of the occurrence, "then there was more than Strammers to receive you?"

"More!" shouted Jem Bottles, "there was forty if there was one."

Paddy groaned again at the remembrance, and moaned out:

"The whole population of London was there, and half of it on top of me before I could wink. I thought they would strip the clothes off me, and they nearly did it."

"And have you been here alone ever since? Have you had nothing to eat or drink since you got back?"

"Oh," said Jem, "we had too much attention in the morning, and too little as the day went on. We were expecting you home, and so took the liberty of coming up here and waiting for you, thinking you might be good enough to send out for some one who would dress our wounds; but luckily that's not needed now."

"Why is it not needed?" I asked. "I'll send at once.

"Oh, no," moaned Paddy, "there was one good friend that did not forget us."

"Well," said Jem, "he seemed mighty afeerd of coming in. I suppose he thought it was on his advice that we went where we did, and he was afeerd we thought badly of him for it; but of course we had no blame to put on the poor little man."

"In Heaven's name, who are you talking of?" said I.

"Doctor Chord," answered Jem. "He put his head inside the door and inquired for us, and inquired specially where you were; but that, of course, we couldn't tell him. He was very much put out to find us mis-handled, and he sent us some tankards of beer, which are now empty, and we're waiting for him because he promised to come back and attend to our injuries."

"Then you didn't see Doctor Chord in the gardens?"

"In what gardens?" asked Bottles.

"You didn't see him among that mob that set on you?"

"No fear," said Jem, "wherever there is a scrimmage Doctor Chord will keep away from it."

"Indeed and in that you're wrong," said I. "Doctor Chord has been the instigator of everything that has happened, and he stood in the background and helped to set them on."

Paddy sat up with wild alarm in his eyes.

"Sure, master," says he, "how could you see through so thick a wall as that?"

"I did not see through the wall at all; I was in the house. When you went through the back door, I went through the front gate, and what I am telling you is true. Doctor Chord is the cause of the whole commotion. That's why he was afraid to come in the room. He thought perhaps you had seen him, and, finding you had not, he'll be back here again when everything is over. Doctor Chord is a traitor, and you may take my word for that."

Paddy rose slowly to his feet, every red hair in his head bristling with scorn and indignation; but as he stood erect he put his hand to his side and gave a howl as he limped a step or two over the floor.

"The black-hearted villain," he muttered through his teeth. "I'll have his life."

"You'll have nothing of the sort," said I, "and we'll get some good attendance out of him, for he's a skillful man. When he has done his duty in repairing what he has inflicted upon you, then you can give him a piece of your mind."

"I'll give him a piece of my boot; all that's left of it," growled Jem Bottles, scowling.

"You may take your will of him after he has put some embrocation on your bruises," said I; and as I was speaking there came a timorous little knock at the door.

"Come in," I cried, and after some hesitation the door opened, and there stood little Doctor Chord with a big bottle under his arm. I was glad there was no supper yet on the table, for if there had been I must have asked the little man to sit down with me, and that he would do without a second's hesitation, so I could not rightly see him maltreated who had broken a crust with me.

He paid no attention to Jem or Paddy at first, but kept his cunning little eye on me.

"And where have you been today, O'Ruddy?" he asked.

"Oh," said I, "I accompanied these two to the door in the wall, and when they got through I heard yells fit to make a hero out of a nigger; but you know how stout the bolts are and I couldn't get to them, so I had just to go out of hearing of their bellowings. On the way back I happened to meet an old friend of mine, Father Donovan, and—"

Here Paddy, forgetting his good manners, shouted out:

"Thank God there's a holy father in this hole of perdition; for I know I'm goin' t' die tomorrow at the latest."

"Stop your nonsense," said I. "You'll have to hold on to life at least a day longer; for the good father is not coming here until two days are past. You're more frightened than hurt, and the Doctor here has a lotion that will make you meet the priest as a friend and not as a last counsellor."

"As I was saying, Doctor Chord, I met Father Donovan, and we strolled about the town, so that I have only now just come in. The father is a stranger in London, on a pilgrimage to Rome. And sure I had to show him the sights."

"It was a kindly action of you," said Doctor Chord, pulling the cork of the medicine-bottle. "Get those rags off," he called to Paddy, "and I'll rub you down as if you were the finest horse that ever followed the hounds."

There was a great smell of medicine in the air as he lubricated Paddy over the bruised places; then Jem Bottles came under his hands, and either he was not so much hurt as Paddy was, or he made less fuss about it, for he glared at the Doctor all the time he was attending him, and said nothing.

It seemed an inhospitable thing to misuse a man who had acted the good Samaritan so arduously as the little Doctor with three quarters of his bottle gone, but as he slapped the cork in it again I stepped to the door and turned the key. Paddy was scowling now and then, and groaning now and again, when the cheerful Doctor said to him, as is the way with physicians when they wish to encourage a patient:

"Oh, you're not hurt nearly as bad as you think you are. You'll be a little sore and stiff in the morning, that's all, and I'll leave the bottle with you."

"You've never rubbed me at all on the worst place," said Paddy angrily.

"Where was that?" asked Doctor Chord,—and the words were hardly out of his mouth when Paddy hit him one in the right eye that sent him staggering across the room.

"There's where I got the blow that knocked me down," cried Paddy.

Doctor Chord threw a wild glance at the door, when Jem Bottles, with a little run and a lift of his foot, gave him one behind that caused the Doctor to turn a somersault.

"Take that, you thief," said Jem; "and now you've something that neither of us got, because we kept our faces to the villains that set on us."

Paddy made a rush, but I cried:

"Don't touch the man when he's down."

"Sure," says Paddy, "that's when they all fell on me."

"Never strike a man when he's down," I cried.

"Do ye mean to say we shouldn't hit a man when he's down?" asked Jem Bottles.

"You knew very well you shouldn't," I told him. "Sure you've been in the ring before now."

"That I have," shouted Bottles, pouncing on the unfortunate Doctor. He grabbed him by the scruff of the neck and flung him to his feet, then gave him a bat on the side of the head that sent him reeling up toward the ceiling again.

"That's enough, Jem," I cautioned him.

"I'm not only following the Doctor," said Jem, "but I'm following the Doctor's advice. He told us to take a little gentle exercise and it would allay the soreness."

"The exercise you're taking will not allay the soreness on the Doctor's part. Stop it, Jem! Now leave him alone, Paddy; he's had enough to remember you by, and to learn that the way of the traitor is the rocky road to Dublin. Come now, Doctor, the door is open; get out into the passage as quick as you can, and I hope you have another bottle of that excellent lotion at home."

The threatening attitude of both Jem and Paddy seemed to paralyse the little man with fear, and he lay on the boards glaring up at them with terror in his eyes.

"I'm holding the door open for you," said I, "and remember I may not be able to hold Paddy and Jem as easily as I hold the door; so make your escape before they get into action again."

Doctor Chord rolled himself over quickly, but, not daring to get on his feet, trotted out into the passage like a big dog on his hands and knees; and just then a waiter, coming up with a tray and not counting on this sudden apparition in the hallway, fell over him; and if it were not for my customary agility and presence of mind in grasping the broad metal server, a good part of my supper would have been on the floor. The waiter luckily leaned forward when he found himself falling, holding the tray high over his head, and so, seizing it, I saved the situation and the supper.

"What are ye grovelling down there for, ye drunken beast?" shouted the angry waiter, as he came down with a thud. "Why don't you walk on your two feet like a Christian?"

Doctor Chord took the hint and his departure, running along the passage and stumbling down the stairway like a man demented. When he got down into the courtyard he shook his fist at my window and swore he would have the law of us; but I never saw the little man again, although Paddy and Jem were destined to meet him once more, as I shall tell later on.

The supper being now laid, I fell at it and I dis-remember having ever enjoyed a meal more in my life. I sent Paddy and Jem to their quarters with food and a bottle of good wine to keep them company, and I think they deserved it, for they said the lotion the Doctor had put on the outside of them was stinging, so they thought there should be something in the inside to counteract the inconvenience.

I went to sleep the moment I touched the pillow, and dreamed I was in the most umbrageous lover's walk that ever was, overhung with green branches through which the sunlight flickered, and closed in with shrubbery. There I chased a flying nymph that always just eluded me, laughing at me over her shoulder and putting her finger to her lips, and at last, when I caught her, it turned out to be Doctor Chord, whereupon I threw him indignantly into the bushes, and then saw to my dismay it was the Countess. She began giving her opinion of me so vigorously that I awoke and found it broad daylight.

After a comforting and sustaining breakfast I sent for Paddy and Jem, both of whom came in limping.

"Are you no better this morning?" I asked them.

"Troth, we're worse," said Paddy with a most dismal look on his face.

"I'm sorry to hear it," said I; "but I think the trouble will wear off today if you lie snug and quiet in the inn. Here's this bottle of embrocation, or what is left of it, so you may take it with you and divide it fairly between you, remembering that one good rub deserves another, and that our chief duty on this earth is to help our fellow man; and as there's nothing like easy employment for making a man forget his tribulations, Jem will rub Paddy, and Paddy will rub Jem, and thus, God blessing you both, you will pass the time to your mutual benefit."

"Yer honour," sniffed Jem Bottles, "I like your own prescriptions better than Doctor Chord's. I have but small faith in the liniment; the bottle of wine you gave us last night—and I wish it had been as double as it made us see—was far better for our trouble than this stuff."

"I doubt it, Jem," said I, "for you're worse this morning than you were last night; so I'll change the treatment and go back to Doctor Chord's remedy, for sure the Doctor is a physician held in high esteem by the nobility of London. But you're welcome to a double mug of beer at my expense, only see that you don't take too much of that."

"Yer honour," said Jem, "it's only when we're sober that we fall upon affliction. We had not a drop to drink yesterday morning, and see what happened us."

"It would have made no differ," I said, "if you had been as tipsy as the Earl himself is when dinner's over. Trust in Providence, Jem, and rub hard with the liniment, and you'll be a new man by the morrow morn."

With this I took my papers and the letter of introduction, and set out as brave as you please to find the Temple, which I thought would be a sort of a church, but which I found to be a most sober and respectable place very difficult for a stranger to find his way about in. But at last I came to the place where Mr. Josiah Brooks dispensed the law for a consideration to ignorant spalpeens like myself, that was less familiar with the head that had a gray wig on than with cracking heads by help of a good shillelah that didn't know what a wig was. As it was earlier in the morning than Mr. Brooks's usual hour I had to sit kicking my heels in a dismal panelled anteroom till the great lawyer came in. He was a smooth-faced serious-looking man, rather elderly, and he passed through the anteroom without so much as casting a look at me, and was followed by a melancholy man in rusty black who had told me to take a chair, holding in his hand the letter Lady Mary had written. After a short time the man came out again, and, treating me with more deference than when he bade me be seated, asked me kindly if I would step this way and Mr. Brooks would see me.

"You are Mr. O'Ruddy, I take it," he said in a tone which I think he thought was affable.

"I am."

"Have you brought with you the papers referred to in this letter?"

"I have."

And with that I slammed them down on the table before him. He untied the bundle and sorted out the different documents, apparently placing them in their right order. After this he adjusted his glasses more to his liking and glanced over the papers rapidly until he came to one that was smaller than the rest, and this he read through twice very carefully. Then he piled them up together at his right hand very neatly, for he seemed to have a habit of old maid's precision about him. He removed his glasses and looked across the table at me.

"Are you the son of the O'Ruddy here mentioned?"

"I am."

"His eldest son?"

"His only son."

"You can prove that, I suppose?"

"Troth, it was never disputed."

"I mean there would be no difficulty in getting legal and documentary proof."

"I think not, for my father said after my first fight, that it might be questioned whether I was my mother's son or no,—there was no doubt that I was his."

The legal man drew down his brows at this, but made no comment as, in tones that betrayed little interest in the affair, he demanded:

"Why did your father not claim this property during his lifetime?"

"Well, you see, Mr. Brooks, my father was an honest man, and he never pretended the property was his. From what I remember of his conversation on the subject the Earl and him was in a tight place after a battle in France, and it was thought they would both be made prisoners. The Earl had his deeds with him, and if he were caught the enemy would demand a large ransom for him, for these would show him to be a man of property. So he made the estate over to my father, and my father ran the risk of being captured and taken for the Earl of Westport. Now that I have been made happy by the acquaintance of his lordship, I'm thinking that if my father had fallen into the hands of the enemy he might have remained there till this day without the Earl raising a hand to help him. Nobody in England would have disputed the Earl's ownership of his own place, which I understand has been in his family for hundreds of years, so they might very well have got on without the deeds, as in fact they have done. That's all I know about it."

"Then, sir," said Mr. Brooks, "do you intend to contest the ownership of the property on the strength of these documents?"

"I do," said I firmly.

"Very well. You must leave them with me for a few days until I get opinion upon them. I may say I have grave doubts of your succeeding in such litigation unless you can prove that your father gave reasonable consideration for the property made over to him."

"Troth, he'd no consideration to give except his own freedom and the loan of a pair of breeches, and it seems that the Earl never troubled his head whether he gave the first-named or not. He might have given his life for all the thanks his son got from my Lord of Westport."

"From a rapid glance at these instruments I can see that they may be of great value to his lordship, but I doubt their being of any value at all to you; in fact you might find the tables turned upon you, and be put in the position of a fraudulent claimant or a levier of blackmail."

"It's not blackmail I'm going to levy at all," cried I, "but the whitest of white mail. I have not the slightest intention of going into the courts of law; but, to tell you the plain truth about it, Lady Mary and me are going to get married in spite of all the Earls that ever drank, or all the Countesses that ever scolded. Now this dear girl has a great confidence in you, and she has sent me to you to find what's best to be done. I want nothing of this property at all. Sure I've estates enough of my own in Ireland, and a good castle forby, save that the roof leaks a little in places; but a bundle of straw will soon set that to rights, only old Patsy is so lazy through not getting his money regular. Now it struck me that if I went boldly to Brede Castle, or whatever it is, and took possession of it, there would first be the finest scrimmage any man ever saw outside of Ireland, and after that his lordship the Earl would say to me,—

"'O'Ruddy, my boy, my limbs are sore; can't we crack a bottle instead of our heads over this, and make a compromise?'

"'Earl of Westport,' I'll say to him, 'a bottle will be but the beginning of it. We'll sit down at a table and settle this debate in ten minutes if you're reasonable.'

"He'll not be reasonable, of course, but you see what I have in my mind."

"Brede Place," said the lawyer slowly, "is not exactly a castle, but it's a very strong house and might be held by a dozen determined men against an army."

"Then once let me get legally inside, and I'll hold it till the Earl gets more sense in his head than is there at the present moment."

"Possession," said Mr. Brooks, "is nine points of the law."

"It is with a woman," said I, thinking of something else.

"It is with an estate," answered Josiah severely.

"True for you," I admitted, coming back to the point at issue, for it was curious, in spite of the importance of the interview, how my mind kept wandering away to a locked room in the Earl of Westport's house, and to a shady path that ran around the edge of his garden.

"I intend to get possession of the Brede estate if I have to crack the crown of every man at present upon it. But I am an Irishman, and therefore a person of peace, and I wish to crack the crowns in accordance with the law of England, so I come to you for directions how it should be done."

"It is not my place," said Brooks, looking very sour, "to counsel a man to break either heads or the law. In fact it is altogether illegal to assault another unless you are in danger of your own life."

"The blessing of all the Saints be upon you," said I, "yet, ever since I set foot in this land, coming across the boiling seas, entirely to do a kindness to the Earl of Westport, I have gone about in fear of my life."

"You have surely not been assaulted?" demanded Mr. Brooks, raising his eyebrows in surprise.

"Assaulted, is it? I have been set upon in every manner that is possible for a peace-lover to be interfered with. To tell you the truth, no longer ago than yesterday morning, as quiet and decent a Sunday as ever came down on London, my two innocent servants, garrulous creatures that wouldn't hurt a fly, were lured into the high walled garden of the Earl of Westport to see the flowers which both of them love, and there they were pounced upon by the whole body-guard of my lord the Earl, while himself and his quiet-mannered Countess were there to urge them on. Doctor Chord, a little snobbish creature, basking in the smiles of their noble countenances, stood by and gave medical advice showing where best to hit the poor innocent unfortunates that had fallen into their hands."

"Tut, tut!" said Josiah Brooks, his face frowning like a storm-cloud over the hills of Donegal. "If such is indeed the case, an action would lie—"

"Oh, well and as far as that goes, so would Doctor Chord, and all the rest that was there. My poor lads lie now, bruised and sore, in the upper rooms of the stable at the 'Pig and Turnip.' They want no more action, I can tell you, nor lying either."

"You can prove, then," said the lawyer, "that you have suffered violence from the outset."

"Indeed and I could."

"Well, well, we must look into the matter. You recite a most curious accumulation of offences, each of which bears a serious penalty according to the law of England. But there is another matter mentioned in Lady Mary's letter which is even more grave than any yet alluded to."

"And what is that?" I asked in surprise.

"She says that she wishes to have advanced to you, upon the security of these papers, five hundred golden guineas."

"Do you tell me that now?" I cried with delight. "Sure I have always said that Mary was the most sensible girl within the boundaries of this realm."

"That may all be; but women, you see, know little of money or the methods of obtaining it."

"You're right in that," I admitted. "It's the other end of the stick they hold; they know a good deal of the way of spending it."

"You will understand," went on Mr. Brooks, "that if money is to be raised on the security of these documents, your rights in possessing them must be severely scrutinized, while—you will pardon my saying so—the security of your estates in Ireland might be looked at askance by the money-lenders of London."

"Oh, don't let the estates in Ireland trouble you, for the money-lenders of Dublin have already mortgaged them a foot deep. You can raise little on my estates in Ireland but the best turf you ever burned, and that's raised with a spade."

"Very well," said Josiah Brooks, gathering up the papers and tying them together with a bit of red ribbon which he took out of his drawer, ignoring the Irish cord that had held them through all their emergencies. "Very well, I shall seek advice and let you know the result."

"Seek advice," I cried. "Sure a man of your attainments doesn't need to seek advice of any one. Aren't you learned in the law yourself?"

"I must have counsel's opinion," said Josiah solemnly, as if he were speaking of the decisions of Providence.

"Well, you astonish me, Mr. Brooks, for I thought you knew it all, and that's why I came to you; but perhaps it's only your own modesty that makes you reluctant to speak of your attainments, though I suppose what you really mean is that you want to take a pipe in your mouth and a glass of good liquor at your elbow and read the papers at your leisure."

Mr. Josiah Brooks was a solemn man, and he did not appear to relish the picture I so graphically drew of him, when in truth I was thinking only of his own comfort; so I changed the subject with an alertness of mind which perhaps he was incapable of appreciating.

"How far from London is this estate of Brede?" I asked, "and how do you get to it?"

"It is fifty or sixty miles away," he said, "and lies in the county of Sussex, close to the sea, but not on it. If you wish to visit Brede estate," he went on, as if I had not been telling him I was going to do that very thing in force, "if you wish to visit Brede estate, the best plan is to go to Rye and there engage a guide who will lead you to it."

"Rye," said I in astonishment, wondering where I had heard the name before; then, suddenly remembering, I said:

"Rye is a seaport town, is it not?"

"It is," agreed Mr. Brooks.

"Rye is the spot," rejoined I, "where Father Donovan will embark on his pilgrimage to Rome. Sure, and I'm glad to hear that, for the good old man and I will travel there together, and the blessing of Providence will surround me, which I hope will be helpful if the Earl's cut-throats bar the way, as is more than likely."

"Very well, Mr. O'Ruddy, as you are doubtless impatient to know the result, you may call upon me tomorrow afternoon at four o'clock, and I may be in a position to give you more information than I can offer at present."

I took that as a dismissal, and, getting up, shook him warmly by the hand, although his arm was as stiff as a pump handle, and he seemed to take little pleasure in the farewell. And so I left the Temple, that was as lonely as the road between Innishannon and the sea, and trudged out into Fleet Street, which was as lively as Skibbereen Fair. I was so overjoyed to find that my journey lay in the same direction as Father Donovan's that I tramped on westward till after some trouble I found the priest's house in which he was stopping, to tell the good father that I would go part of the way to Rome with him. He was indeed delighted to see me, and introduced me to his host, Father Kilnane, nearly as fine a man and as good a priest as Father Donovan himself.

We had dinner there all together at mid-day, and I invited Father Donovan to come out and see the town with me, which he did. The peaceful father clung to my arm in a kind of terror at what he was witnessing, for he was as innocent of the ways of a big town as if he had been a gossoon from a hedge-school in Ireland. Yet he was mightily interested in all he saw, and asked me many thousand questions that day, and if I did not know the correct answer to them, it made no differ to Father Donovan, for he did not know the answer himself and took any explanation as if it was as true as the gospels he studied and preached.

Daylight was gone before we got back to the house he lodged in, and nothing would do but I must come in and have a bit of supper, although I told him that supper would be waiting for me at the "Pig and Turnip." It had been agreed between us that we would travel together as far as Rye, and that there I should see him off on his tempestuous voyage to Dunkirk or Calais, as the case might be. The old man was mightily delighted to find that our ways lay together through the south of England. He was pleased to hear that I had determined on my rights through the courts of law, with no more sword-playing and violence, which, to tell the truth, until it reached its height, the old man was always against; although, when a quarrel came to its utmost interesting point, I have seen Father Donovan fidget in his cassock, and his eyes sparkle with the glow of battle, although up till then he had done his best to prevent the conflict.

It was getting late when I neared the "Pig and Turnip," and there was a good deal of turmoil in the streets. I saw one or two pretty debates, but, remembering my new resolution to abide by law and order, I came safely past them and turned up the less-frequented street that held my inn, when at the corner, under the big lamp, a young man with something of a swagger about him, in spite of the meanness of his dress, came out from the shadow of the wall and looked me hard in the face.

"Could you direct me, sir, to a hostelry they call the 'Pig and Turnip'?" he asked with great civility.

"If you will come with me," said I, "I'll bring you to the place itself, for that's where I'm stopping."

"Is it possible," he said, "that I have the honour of addressing The O'Ruddy?"

"That great privilege is yours," said I, coming to a standstill in the middle of the street, as I saw the young man had his sword drawn and pressed close against his side to allay suspicion. I forgot all about law and order, and had my own blade free of the scabbard on the instant; but the young man spoke smoothly and made no motion of attack, which was very wise of him.

"Mr. O'Ruddy," he says, "we are both men of the world and sensible men and men of peace. Where two gentlemen, one down on his luck and the other in prosperity, have a private matter to discuss between them, I think this discussion should take place quietly and in even tones of voice."

"Sir," said I, giving my sword-hand a little shake, so that the weapon settled down into its place, "Sir, you express my sentiments exactly, and as you are a stranger to me perhaps you will be good enough to announce the subject that concerns us."

"I may say at the outset," he remarked almost in a whisper, so polite he was, "that I have eight good swordsmen at my back, who are not visible until I give the signal; therefore you see, sir, that your chances are of the slightest if I should be compelled to call upon them. I know the fame of The O'Ruddy as a swordsman, and you may take it as a compliment, sir, that I should hesitate to meet you alone. So much for saving my own skin, but I am a kindly man and would like to save your skin as well. Therefore if you will be kind enough to hand to me the papers which you carry in your pocket, you will put me under strong obligations, and at the same time sleep peaceably tonight at the 'Pig and Turnip' instead of here in the gutter, to be picked up by the watch, for I can assure you, sir, as a man that knows the town, the watch will not be here to save you whatever outcry you may make."

"I am obliged to you, sir, for your discourse and your warning, to both of which I have paid strict attention; and in the interests of that peace which we are each of us so loath to break I may announce to you that the papers you speak of are not in my possession."

"Pardon me, sir, but they must be; for we have searched your room thoroughly, and we have also searched your servants."

"A thief of the night," cried I with mighty indignation, "may easily search an honest man's room; and his poor servants, beaten and bruised by your master's orders, would fall easy victims to the strength and numbers of your ruffians; but you will find it a difficult matter to search me."

"Sir," he replied, bowing as polite as Palermo, "I grieve to state that you are in error. The searching of both your servants and your rooms was accomplished, not through the employment of force, but by the power of money. Your servants insisted they had nothing on their persons but liniment, and they accepted one gold piece each to allow me to verify their statements. Another gold piece gave me, for a time, the freedom of your room. If you have not the papers upon you, then there is no harm in allowing me to run my hand over your clothes, because the package is a bulky one and I will speedily corroborate your statement."

"Sir," said I, not to be outdone in courtesy by this gentleman of the gutter, "I will tell you truthfully that I have nothing on me but my sword, and to that you are quite welcome if you leave to me the choice of which end I hold and which I present to you,"—and with that I sprang with my back to the wall, under the lamp, leaving myself partially in shadow, but having spread in front of me a semicircle of light which any assailant attacking must cross, or indeed remain in its effulgence if he would keep free of the point of my blade.

"It grieves me to find that you are a man of violence," replied the scoundrel in the mildest of tones, "and you will bear witness afterward that I did my best to keep you from harm."

"I freely acknowledge it now," said I. "Bring on your men."

To tell the truth, I had no belief at all in the existence of his force, and thought he was playing a game on me, hoping to take me unawares; for if the man knew anything at all he must have known what a swordsman I was, and it was no charge of cowardice against him that he was loath to come to close quarters with me. I speedily discovered, however, that all he said was true; for he gave a low whistle, and out of the darkness instantly sprang seven or eight as malicious-looking villains as a man would care to see, each one with a sword in his hand.

As many erroneous and exaggerated accounts of this encounter have been given in the coffee-houses, and even in the public prints, it is well that I should now tell the truth about it. No man that has the hang of his blade need fear the onset of a mob except in one case, and that is this,—if the whole eight set upon me at once with every sword extended, there was a chance that though I might, by great expertness, disable half of them, the other half would run me through. But it should never be forgotten that these men were fighting for money, and I was fighting for my life, and that makes all the difference in the world. Each man makes a show of attack, but he holds off, hoping that one of the others will dare to thrust. This is fatal to success, but not necessarily fatal to their intended victim. An active man with a wall at his back can generally account for all that comes in front of him if he is deeply in earnest and has not too much liquor in him. It astonished London that I was able to defeat eight men, each one of whom was armed as efficiently as myself; but, as my father used to say, if you are not wholly taken up with the determination to have a man's life, you may pink him in what spot you choose if you give a little thought to the matter. The great object is the disarming of the enemy. Now, if you give a man a jab in the knuckles, or if you run your blade delicately up his arm from the wrist to the elbow, this is what happens. The man involuntarily yells out, and as involuntarily drops his sword on the flags. If you prick a man on the knuckle-bone, he will leave go his sword before he has time to think, it being an action entirely unconscious on his part, just like winking your eye or drawing your breath; yet I have seen men run through the body who kept sword in hand and made a beautiful lunge with it even as they staggered across the threshold of death's door.

Now I had no desire for any of these men's lives, but I determined to have their swords. I glittered my own shining blade before their eyes, flourishing a semicircle with it, and making it dart here and there like the tongue of an angry snake; and instantly every man in front of me felt uncomfortable, not knowing where the snake was going to sting, and then, as I said before, they were fighting for money and not for honour. When I had dazzled their eyes for a moment with this sword-play and bewildered their dull brains, I suddenly changed my tactics and thrust forward quicker than you can count one, two, three, four, five, six, seven, eight,—and each man was holding a bleeding fist to his mouth, while the swords clattered on the cobbles like hail on the copper roof of a cathedral. It was the most beautiful and complete thing I ever saw. I then swept the unarmed men back a pace or two with a flirt of my weapon, and walked up the pavement, kicking the swords together till they lay in a heap at my feet. The chief ruffian stood there dazed, with his sword still in his hand, for he had stepped outside the circle, he acting as captain, and depending on the men to do the work.

"Drop that," I shouted, turning on him, and he flung his sword in the street as if it was red hot.

"Sir," said I to him, "a sword in your hand is merely an inconvenience to you; see if you don't look better with an armful of them. Pick up these nine blades in a bundle and walk on before me to the 'Pig and Turnip.' When we come into the courtyard of that tavern, you are to turn round and make me the lowest bow you can without rubbing your nose against the pavement. Then you will say, as gracefully as the words can be uttered:

"'Mr. O'Ruddy,' you say, 'these swords are yours by right of conquest. You have defeated nine armed men tonight in less than as many minutes, so I present you with the spoil.' Then you will bow to the people assembled in the courtyard,—for there is aways a mob of them there, late and early,—and you will make another low obeisance to me. If you do all this acceptably to my sense of politeness, I will let you go unmolested; but if you do otherwise, I will split your gullet for you."

"Sir," said the captain, "I accept your terms."

With that he stooped and picked up the bundle of weapons, marching on stolidly before me till he came to the "Pig and Turnip." All the rest had disappeared in the darkness, and had gone to their dens, very likely to nurse sore knuckles and regret the loss of good stout blades.

Our coming to the tavern caused a commotion, as you may well imagine; and although I don't make too much of the encounter, yet it is my belief that such an incident never happened in London before. The captain carried out his part of the presentation with an air of deference and a choice of good language that charmed me; then he backed out under the archway to the street, bowing six or seven times as he went. I had never any fault to find with the man's manner. Paddy and Jem, now seemingly quite recovered from their misusage of Sunday, stood back of the group with eyes and mouths open, gazing upon me with an admiration I could not but appreciate.

"Come out of that," said I, "and take this cutlery up to my room," and they did.

I sat down at the table and wrote a letter to Mr. Brooks.

"Sir," said I in it, "I don't know whether I am plaintiff or defendant in the suit that's coming on, but whichever it is here's a bundle of legal evidence for your use. You mentioned the word 'violence' to me when I had the pleasure of calling on you. This night I was set upon by nine ruffians, who demanded from me the papers now in your possession. I took their knives from them, so they would not hurt themselves or other people, and I send you these knives to be filed for reference."

I tied up the swords in two bundles, and in the morning sent Paddy and Jem off with them and the letter to the Temple, which caused great commotion in that peaceable quarter of the city, and sent forth the rumour that all the lawyers were to be at each other's throats next day.

## CHAPTER XXX

In the afternoon I went slowly to the Temple, thinking a good deal on the way. It's truth I tell, that in spite of the victory of the night before I walked to the Temple rather downhearted. Whether Josiah Brooks was an attorney, or a barrister, or a solicitor, or a plain lawyer, I don't know to this day, and I never could get my mind to grasp the distinction that lies between those names in that trade; but whichever it was it seemed to me he was a cold, unenthusiastic man, and that he thought very little indeed of my game. There is small pleasure in litigation in England as compared with the delight of the law in the old Ark. If I had gone to see a lawyer in Dublin or Cork he would have been wild with excitement before I had got half through my story. He would have slapped me on the back and shook me by the hand, and cried "Whurroo" at the prospect of a contest. My quarrel would have been his before I had been ten minutes in his presence, and he would have entered into the spirit of the fight as if he were the principal in it instead of merely acting for him; but in this gloomy country of England, where they engage upon a lawsuit, not with delight, but as if they were preparing for a funeral; there is no enjoyment in the courts at all at all. I wished I could transfer the case to the old turf, where there is more joy in being defeated than there is in winning in England; for I have seen the opposing lawyers rise from the most gentlemanly and elegant language you ever heard to a heated debate; then fling books at each other, and finally clench, while the judge stood up and saw fair play. But this man Brooks was so calm and collected and uninterested that he fairly discouraged me, and I saw that I was going to get neither the money I needed nor the support I expected from him.

As I went up his dark stairway in the Temple and came to the passage that led to the outer room, I saw standing in a corner the two bundles of swords I had sent him, as if he had cast them out, which indeed he had done. After some delay in the outer room, the melancholy man in rusty black asked me, would I go in, and there sat Josiah Brooks at his table as if he had never left it since I took my departure the day before. He looked across at me with a scrutiny which seemed to be mingled with dislike and disapproval.

"Mr. O'Ruddy," he said, quiet-like, "it is not customary to send to a law office a number of swords, which are entirely out of place in such rooms. They have been counted and are found to number nine. I shall be obliged if you sign this receipt for them, accept delivery of the same, and remove them from the premises at your earliest convenience."

So I signed the receipt without a word and handed it back to him. Then I said,—

"I will send my servant for the swords as soon as I return to the inn."

He inclined his head the merest trifle, drew some papers toward him, and adjusted his glasses.

"It is my duty to tell you, Mr. O'Ruddy, that if you go into the courts with this case you will assuredly be defeated, and the costs will follow. There is also a possibility that when the civil proceedings are determined a criminal action against yourself may ensue."

"I told you, sir," said I, with my heart sinking, "I had no intention of troubling the courts at all at all. In the land I come from we are more inclined to settle a case with a good stout blackthorn than with the aid of a lawyer's wig. These papers say in black and white that I am the owner of Brede estate, and I intend to take possession of it."

"It is only right to add," continued Brooks, with that great air of calm I found so exasperating, "it is only right to add that you are in a position to cause great annoyance to the Earl of Westport. You can at least cast doubt on his title to the estate; and he stands this jeopardy, that if contrary to opinion your cause should prove successful,—and we must never forget that the law is very uncertain,—the Earl would have to account for the moneys he has drawn from the estate, which would run into many thousands of pounds, and, together with the loss of the property, would confront his lordship with a most serious situation. Your case, therefore, though weak from a strictly legal point of view, is exceptionally strong as a basis for compromise."

These words cheered me more than I can say, and it is an extraordinary fact that his frozen, even tone, and his lack of all interest in the proceedings had an elevating effect upon my spirits which I could not have believed possible.

"As it is a compromise that I'm after," said I, "what better case can we want?"

"Quite so," he resumed; "but as there is no encouragement in the strictly legal aspect of the plea, you will understand that no money-lender in London will advance a farthing on such unstable security. Even though I am acting in your interests, I could not take the responsibility of advising any capitalist to advance money on such uncertain tenure.”

This threw me into the depths again; for, although I never care to meet trouble half way, I could not conceal from myself the fact that my bill at the “Pig and Turnip” had already reached proportions which left me no alternative but to slip quietly away in liquidation of the account. This was a thing I never liked to do; and when I am compelled to make that settlement I always take note of the amount, so that I may pay it if I am ever that way again and have more money than I need at the moment. Even if I succeeded in getting away from the inn, what could I do at Brede with no money at all?—for in that part of the country they would certainly look upon the Earl of Westport as the real owner of the property, and on me as a mere interloper; and if I could not get money on the documents in London, there was little chance of getting credit even for food at Brede.

“It is rather a blue look-out then,” said I as cheerfully as I could.

“From a legal standpoint it is,” concurred Mr. Brooks, as unconcerned as if his own payment did not depend on my raising the wind with these papers. “However, I have been instructed by a person who need not be named, who has indeed stipulated that no name shall be mentioned, to advance you the sum of five hundred guineas, which I have here in my drawer, and which I will now proceed to count out to you if you, in the mean time, will sign this receipt, which acquits me of all responsibility and certifies that I have handed the money over to you without rebate or reduction.”

And with that the man pulled open a drawer and began to count out the glittering gold.

I sprang to my feet and brought my fist down on the table with a thump. “Now, by the Great Book of Kells, what do you mean by chopping and changing like a rudderless lugger in a ten-knot breeze? If the expedition is possible, and you had the money in your drawer all the time, why couldn’t you have spoken it out like a man, without raising me to the roof and dropping me into the cellar in the way you’ve done?”

The man looked unruffled across the table at me. He pushed a paper a little farther from him, and said without any trace of emotion:

“Will you sign that receipt at the bottom, if you please?”

I sat down and signed it, but I would rather have jabbed a pen between his close-set lips to give him a taste of his own ink. Then I sat quiet and watched him count the gold, placing it all in neat little pillars before him. When it was finished, he said:

“Will you check the amount?”

“Is that gold mine?” I asked him.

“It is,” he replied.

So I rose up without more ado and shovelled it into my pockets, and he put the receipt into the drawer after reading it over carefully, and arched his eyebrows without saying anything when he saw me pocket the coins uncounted.

“I wish you good afternoon,” said I.

“I have to detain you one moment longer,” he replied. “I have it on the most trustworthy information that the Earl of Westport is already aware of your intention to proceed to the country estate alleged to be owned by him. Your outgoings and incomings are watched, and I have to inform you that unless you proceed to Rye with extreme caution there is likelihood that you may be waylaid, and perchance violence offered to you.”

“In that case I will reap a few more swords; but you need not fear, I shall not trouble you with them.”

"They are out of place in a solicitor's chamber," he murmured gently. "Is there anything further I can do for you?"

"Yes," I said, "there is one thing more. I would be obliged if you could make me a bundle of legal-looking papers that are of no further use to you: a sheet of that parchment, and some of the blue stuff like what I carried. The Earl seems determined to have a packet of papers from me, and I would like to oblige him, as he's going to be my father-in-law, although he doesn't know it. I'd like some writing on these papers,—Latin for preference."

Josiah Brooks thought steadily for a few moments, then he called out and the melancholy rusty man came in. He took a few instructions and went out again. After a long time he entered once more and placed on the table a packet I would have sworn was my own. This the lawyer handed to me without a word, and the rusty man held open the door for me. So, with the bogus papers in my pocket, not to mention the genuine gold, I took my leave of Josiah and the Temple.

As soon as I was outside I saw at once that there was no time to be lost. If the Earl had guessed my intention, as was hinted, what would he do? Whenever I wish to answer a question like that to myself, I think what would I do if I were in the position of the other man. Now what I would have done, was this, if I were the Earl of Westport. I would send down to Brede all the ruffians at my disposal and garrison the house with them; and if the Earl did this, I would be on the outside, and he on the inside with advantage over me accordingly. Most men fight better behind stone walls than out in the open; and, besides, a few men can garrison a barracks that five hundred cannot take by assault. However, as it turned out, I was crediting the Earl with brains equal to my own, which in truth neither he nor any of his followers had below their bonnets. He trusted to intercepting me on the highway, just as if he hadn't already failed in that trick. But it takes a score of failures to convince an Englishman that he is on the wrong track altogether, while an Irishman has so many plans in his head that there's never time to try one of them twice in succession. But if I was wrong about the Earl, I was right about his daughter, when I suspected that she gave the lawyer the information about the Earl's knowledge of my plans, and I was also right when I credited the dear girl with drawing on her own funds to give me the golden guineas,—"and may each one of them," said I to myself, "prove a golden blessing on her head."

At any rate, there was no time to be lost, so I made straight to Father Donovan and asked him would he be ready to begin the journey to Rye after an early breakfast with me at the "Pig and Turnip."

You never saw a man in your life so delighted at the prospect of leaving London as was Father Donovan, and indeed I was glad to get away from the place myself. The good father said the big town confused him; and, although he was glad to have seen it, he was more happy still to get out of it and breathe a breath of fresh country air once more. So it was arranged that he would come to the "Pig and Turnip" next morning between six and seven o'clock. I then turned back to the shop of a tailor who for a long time had had two suits of clothing waiting for me that were entirely elegant in their design. The tailor, however, would not take the word of a gentleman that payment would follow the delivery of the costumes; for a little later would be more convenient for me to give him the money, and this made me doubt, in spite of the buttons and gold lace, if the garments were quite the fashionable cut, because a tailor who demands money on the spot shows he is entirely unaccustomed to deal with the upper classes; but I needed these clothes, as the two suits I possessed were getting a little the worse for wear.

When I went into his shop he was inclined to be haughty, thinking I had come to ask credit again; but when he saw the glitter of the money the man became obsequious to a degree that I never had witnessed before. I was affable to him, but distant; and when he offered me everything that was in his shop, I told him I would take time and consider it. He sent a servant following behind me with the goods, and so I came once more to the "Pig and Turnip," where I ordered Paddy and Jem to go to the Temple and fetch away the swords.

There seemed to be a pleased surprise on the face of the landlord when I called for my bill and paid it without question, chiding him for his delay in not sending it before. I engaged a horse for Father Donovan to ride on the following morning, and ordered breakfast ready at six o'clock, although I gave my commands that I was to be wakened an hour before daylight.

I spent the rest of the day in my room with Paddy and Jem, trying to knock into their heads some little notion of geography, wishing to make certain that they would sooner or later arrive in Rye without stumbling in on Belfast while on the way. My own knowledge of the face of the country was but meagre, so the landlord brought in a rough map of the south of England, and I cautioned the lads to get across London Bridge and make for the town of Maidstone, from where they could go due south, and if they happened on the coast they were to inquire for Rye and stay there until further orders. Jem Bottles, who thought he had brains in his head, said he would not be so open in telling every one we were going to Rye if he was me, because he was sure the Earl had people on the look-out, and money was plenty with his lordship. If every one knew when we were taking our departure, there would be no difficulty in following us and overcoming us on some lonely part of the road.

"Jem," said I, "that's all very true; but when they attacked us before they got very little change for their trouble; and if you are afraid of some slight commotion on the road, then you can stay back here in London."

"I am not afraid at all," said Jem, "but if there's anything particular you would like to see in Rye, there's no use in blocking the road to it."

"Sure, Jem, then be quiet about it."

Turning to the landlord, who was standing by, I said to him:

"My men fear we are going to be intercepted, so I think if I began the journey some time before daylight, and they followed me soon after, I might slip away unnoticed."

The landlord scratched his head and crinkled up his brow, for to think was unusual with him.

"I don't see," he said at last, "what you have to gain by going separately. It seems to me it would be better to go in a body, and then, if you are set on, there are three instead of one."

"Very well," said I, "I'll take your caution into consideration, and act upon it or not as seems best when the time comes."

I told Paddy and Jem to sleep that night on the floor of my own room, and cautioned them to wake me an hour before daylight at the latest. Jem slept through until I had to kick him into consciousness; but poor Paddy, on the other hand, wakened me four times during the night,—the first time two hours after I had gone to sleep, and I could have cudgelled him for his pains, only I knew the lad's intentions were good. The last time I could stand it no longer, although it was still earlier than the hour I had said, so I got up and dressed myself in one of my new suits.

"And here, Paddy," said I, "you will wear the costume I had on yesterday."

"I couldn't think of it," said Paddy, drawing back from the grandeur.

"You are not to think, you impudent gossoon, but to do as I tell you. Put them on, and be as quick as you can."

"Troth, yer honour," said Paddy, still shrinking from them, "they're too grand for the likes o' me, an' few will be able to tell the differ atween us."

"You conceited spalpeen, do ye think there's no difference between us but what the clothes make? Get into them. I intend certain other people to take you for me in the dark, and I can warrant you these clothes, grand as you think them, will be very soundly beaten before this day is done with."

"Ochone, ochone," moaned Paddy, "am I to get another beating already, and some of the bruises not yet off my flesh?"

"Put on the coat now, and don't do so much talking. Sure it's all in the day's work, and I promise you before long you'll have your revenge on them."

"It's not revenge I'm after," wailed Paddy, "but a whole skin."

"Now you're transformed into a gentleman," said I, "and many a lad would take a beating for the privilege of wearing such gorgeous raiment. Here is a packet of paper that you're to keep in your pocket till it's taken away from you. And now I'll help you to saddle the horse, and once you're across London Bridge you'll likely come upon Maidstone and Rye some time in your life, for you can't get back over the river again except by the same bridge, so you'll know it when you come to it."

And so I mounted Paddy in the courtyard; the sleepy watchman undid the bolts in the big gate in the archway; and my man rode out into the darkness in no very cheerful humour over his journey. I came back and took forty winks more in the arm-chair, then, with much difficulty, I roused Jem Bottles. He also, without a murmur, but with much pride in his dressing, put on the second of my discarded suits, and seemed to fancy himself mightily in his new gear. With plenty of cord I tied and retied the two bundles of swords and placed them across the horse in front of his saddle, and it was not yet daylight when Jem jingled out into the street like a moving armoury. Two huge pistols were in his holsters, loaded and ready to his hand.

"By the Saints," said Jem proudly, "the man that meddles with me shall get hot lead or cold steel for his breakfast," and with that he went off at a canter, waking the echoes with the clash of his horse's shoes on the cobble-stones.

I went up stairs again and threw myself down on the bed and slept peacefully with no Paddy to rouse me until half-past-six, when a drawer knocked at the door and said that a priest that was downstairs would be glad to see me. I had him up in a jiffy, and a hot breakfast following fast on his heels, which we both laid in in quantities, for neither of us knew where our next meal was to be. However, the good father paid little thought to the future as long as the present meal was well served and satisfactory. He had no more idea than a spring lamb how we were to get to Rye, but thought perhaps a coach set out at that hour in the morning. When I told him I had a horse saddled and waiting for him, he was pleased, for Father Donovan could scamper across the country in Ireland with the best of them. So far as I could judge, the coast was clear, for every one we met between the "Pig and Turnip" and the bridge seemed honest folk intent on getting early to their work. It was ten minutes past seven when we clattered across the bridge and set our faces toward Rye.

## CHAPTER XXXI

Looking back over my long life I scarcely remember any day more pleasant than that I spent riding side by side with Father Donovan from London to Rye. The fine old man had a fund of entertaining stories, and although I had heard them over and over again there was always something fresh in his way of telling them, and now and then I recognized a narrative that had once made two separate stories, but which had now become welded into one in the old man's mind. There was never anything gloomy in these anecdotes, for they always showed the cheerful side of life and gave courage to the man that wanted to do right; for in all of Father Donovan's stories the virtuous were always made happy. We talked of our friends and acquaintances, and if he ever knew anything bad about a man he never told it; while if I mentioned it he could always say something good of him to balance it, or at least to mitigate the opinion that might be formed of it. He was always doing some man a good turn or speaking a comforting word for him.

"O'Ruddy," he said, "I spent most of the day yesterday writing letters to those that could read them in our part of Ireland, setting right the rumours that had come back to us, which said you were fighting duels and engaged in brawls, but the strangest story of all was the one about your forming a friendship with a highwayman, who, they said, committed robberies on the road and divided the spoil with you, and here I find you without a servant at all at all, leading a quiet, respectable life at a quiet, respectable inn. It's not even in a tavern that I first come across you, but kneeling devoutly, saying a prayer in your mother church. I see you leaving your inn having paid your bill like a gentleman, when they said you took night-leave of most of the hostelries in England. Dear me, and there was the landlord bowing to you as if you were a prince, and all his servants in a row with the utmost respect for you. Ah, O'Ruddy, it's men like you that gives the good name to Ireland, and causes her to be looked up to by all the people of the world."

I gave Father Donovan heartfelt thanks for his kindness, and prayed to myself that we would not come upon Jem Bottles on the road, and that we would be left unmolested on our journey until we saw the sea-coast. Of course, if we were set upon, it would not be my fault, and it's not likely he would blame me; but if we came on Bottles, he was inclined to be very easy in conversation, and, in spite of my warnings, would let slip words that would shock the old priest. But when a day begins too auspiciously, its luck is apt to change before the sun sets, as it was with me.

It was nearing mid-day, and we were beginning to feel a trifle hungry, yet were in a part of the country that gave little promise of an inn, for it was a lonely place with heath on each side of the road, and, further on, a bit of forest. About half-way through this wooded plain an astonishing sight met my eyes. Two saddled horses were tied to a tree, and by the side of the road appeared to be a heap of nine or ten saddles, on one of which a man was sitting, comfortably eating a bit of bread, while on another a second man, whose head was tied up in a white cloth, lay back in a recumbent position, held upright by the saddlery. Coming closer, I was disturbed to see that the man eating was Jem Bottles, while the other was undoubtedly poor Paddy, although his clothes were so badly torn that I had difficulty in recognizing them as my own. As we drew up Jem stood and saluted with his mouth full, while Paddy groaned deeply. I was off my horse at once and ran to Paddy.

"Where are ye hurted?" said I.

"I'm killed," said Paddy.

"I've done the best I could for him," put in Jem Bottles. "He'll be all right in a day or two."

"I'll not," said Paddy, with more strength than one would suspect; "I'll not be all right in a day or two, nor in a week or two, nor in a month or two, nor in a year or two; I'm killed entirely."

"You're not," said Bottles. "When I was on the highway I never minded a little clip like that."

"Hush, Bottles," said I, "you talk altogether too much. Paddy," cried I, "get on your feet, and show yer manners here to Father Donovan."

Paddy got on his feet with a celerity which his former attitude would not have allowed one to believe possible.

"My poor boy!" said the kindly priest; "who has misused you?" and he put his two hands on the sore head.

"About two miles from here," said Paddy, "I was set on by a score of men—"

"There was only nine of them," interrupted Jem, "count the saddles."

"They came on me so sudden and unexpected that I was off my horse before I knew there was a man within reach. They had me down before I could say my prayers, and cudgelled me sorely, tearing my clothes, and they took away the packet of papers you gave me, sir. Sure I tried to guard it with my life, an' they nearly took both."

"I am certain you did your best, Paddy," said I; "and it's sorry I am to see you injured."

"Then they rode away, leaving me, sore wounded, sitting on the side of the road," continued Paddy. "After a while I come to myself, for I seemed dazed; and, my horse peacefully grazing beside me, I managed to get on its back, and turned toward London in the hope of meeting you; but instead of meeting you, sir, I came upon Jem with his pile of saddles, and he bound up my head and did what he could to save me, although I've a great thirst on me at this moment that's difficult to deal with."

"There's a ditch by the side of the road," said the priest.

"Yes," said Paddy sadly; "I tried some of that."

I went to my pack on the horse and took out a bottle and a leather cup. Paddy drank and smacked his lips with an ecstasy that gave us hope for his ultimate recovery. Jem Bottles laughed, and to close his mouth I gave him also some of the wine.

"I hope," said Father Donovan with indignation, "that the miscreant who misused you will be caught and punished."

"I punished them," said Jem, drawing the back of his hand across his mouth.

"We'll hear about it another time," said I, having my suspicions.

"Let the good man go on," begged Father Donovan, who is not without human curiosity.

Jem needed no second bidding.

"Your Reverence," he said, "I was jogging quietly on as a decent man should, when, coming to the edge of this forest, I saw approach me a party of horsemen, who were very hilarious and laughed loudly. If you look up and down the road and see how lonely it is, and then look at the wood, with no hedge between it and the highway, you'll notice the place was designed by Providence for such a meeting."

"Sure the public road is designed as a place for travellers to meet," said the father, somewhat bewildered by the harangue.

"Your Reverence is right, but this place could not afford better accommodation if I had made it myself. I struck into the wood before they saw me, tore the black lining from my hat, punched two holes in it for the eyes, and tied it around my forehead, letting it hang down over my face; then I primed my two pistols and waited for the gentlemen. When they were nearly opposite, a touch of the heels to my horse's flank was enough, and out he sprang into the middle of the road.

"'Stand and deliver!' I cried, pointing the pistols at them, the words coming as glibly to my lips as if I had said them no later ago than yesterday. 'Stand and deliver, ye—'" and here Jem glibly rattled out a stream of profane appellatives which was disgraceful to listen to.

"Tut, tut, Jem," I said, "you shouldn't speak like that. Any way we'll hear the rest another time."

"That's what I called them, sir," said Jem, turning to me with surprise, "you surely would not have me tell an untruth."

"I wouldn't have you tell anything. Keep quiet. Father Donovan is not interested in your recital."

"I beg your pardon, O'Ruddy," said Father Donovan, looking at me reproachfully; "but I am very much interested in this man's narrative."

"As any good man should be," continued Jem, "for these were arrant scoundrels; one of them I knew, and his name is Doctor Chord. He fell off his horse on the roadway at once and pleaded for mercy. I ordered the others instantly to hold their hands above their heads, and they did so, except one man who began fumbling in his holster, and then, to show him what I could do with a pistol, I broke his wrist. At the sound of the shot the horses began to plunge, nearly trampling Doctor Chord into the dust.

"'Clasp your hands above your heads, ye—'"

Here went on another stream of terrible language again, and in despair I sat down on the pile of saddles, allowing things to take their course. Jem continued:

"The lesson of the pistol was not misread by my gentlemen, when they noticed I had a second loaded one; so, going to them one after the other I took their weapons from them and flung them to the foot of that tree, where, if you look, you may see them now. Then I took a contribution from each one, just as you do in church, your Reverence. I'm sure you have a collection for the poor, and that was the one I was taking up this day. I have not counted them yet," said the villain turning to me, "but I think I have between sixty and seventy guineas, which are all freely at your disposal, excepting a trifle for myself and Paddy there. There's no plaster like gold for a sore head, your Reverence. I made each one of them dismount and take off his saddle and throw it in the pile; then I had them mount again and drove them with curses toward London, and very glad they were to escape."

"He did not get the papers again," wailed Paddy, who was not taking as jubilant a view of the world as was Jem at that moment.

"I knew nothing of the papers," protested Bottles. "If you had told me about the papers, I would have had them, and if I had been carrying the papers these fellows would not have made away with them."

"Then," said the horrified priest, "you did not commit this action in punishment for the injury done to your friend? You knew nothing of that at the time. You set on these men thinking they were simple travellers."

"O, I knew nothing of what happened to Paddy till later, but you see, your Reverence, these men themselves were thieves and robbers. In their case it was nine men against one poor half-witted Irish lad—"

"Half-witted yourself," cried Paddy angrily.

"But you, sir," continued his Reverence, "were simply carrying out the action of a highwayman. Sir, you *are* a highwayman."

"I was, your Reverence, but I have reformed."

"And this pile of saddles attests your reformation!" said the old man, shaking his head.

"But you see, your Reverence, this is the way to look at it—"

"Keep quiet, Jem!" cried I in disgust.

"How can I keep quiet," urged Bottles, "when I am unjustly accused? I do not deny that I was once a highwayman, but Mr. O'Ruddy converted me to better ways—"

"Highways," said Paddy, adding, with a sniff, "Half-witted!"

"Your Reverence, I had no more intention of robbing those men than you have at this moment. I didn't know they were thieves themselves. Then what put it into my head to jump into the wood and on with a mask before you could say, Bristol town? It's the mysterious ways of Providence, your Reverence. Even I didn't understand it at the time, but the moment I heard Paddy's tale I knew at once I was but an instrument in the hand of Providence, for I had not said, 'Stand and deliver!' this many a day, nor thought of it."

"It may be so; it may be so," murmured the priest, more to himself than to us; but I saw that he was much troubled, so, getting up, I said to Paddy:

"Are you able to ride farther on today?"

"If I'd another sup from the cup, sir, I think I could," whereat Jem Bottles laughed again, and I gave them both a drink of wine.

"What are you going to do with all this saddlery?" said I to Bottles.

"I don't know anything better than to leave it here; but I think, your honour, the pistols will come handy, for they're all very good ones, and Paddy and me can carry them between us, or I can make two bags from these leather packs, and Paddy could carry the lot in them, as I do the swords."

"Very well," I said. "Make your preparations as quickly as you can and let us be off, for this latest incident, in spite of you, Jem, may lead to pursuit and get us into trouble before we are ready for it."

"No fear, sir," said Jem confidently. "One thief does not lay information against another. If they had been peaceable travellers, that would be another thing; but, as I said, Providence is protecting us, no doubt because of the presence of his Reverence here, and not for our own merits."

"Be thankful it is the reward of some one else's merits you, reap, Bottles, instead of your own. No more talk now, but to horse and away."

For some miles Father Donovan rode very silently. I told him something of my meeting with Jem Bottles and explained how I tried to make an honest man of him, while this was the first lapse I had known since his conversion. I even pretended that I had some belief in his own theory of the interposition of Providence, and Father Donovan was evidently struggling to acquire a similar feeling, although he seemed to find some difficulty in the contest. He admitted that this robbery appeared but even justice; still he ventured to hope that Jem Bottles would not take the coincidence as a precedent, and that he would never mistake the dictates of Providence for the desires of his own nature.

"I will speak with the man later," he said, "and hope that my words will make some impression upon him. There was a trace of exaltation in his recital that showed no sign of a contrite spirit."

On account of the delay at the roadside it was well past twelve o'clock before we reached Maidstone, and there we indulged in a good dinner that put heart into all of us, while the horses had time to rest and feed. The road to Rye presented no difficulties whatever, but under ordinary conditions I would have rested a night before travelling to the coast. There would be a little delay before the Earl discovered the useless nature of the papers which he had been at such expense to acquire, but after the discovery there was no doubt in my mind that he would move upon Brede as quickly as horses could carry his men, so I insisted upon pressing on to Rye that night, and we reached the town late with horses that were very tired. It was a long distance for a man of the age of Father Donovan to travel in a day, but he stood the journey well, and enjoyed his supper and his wine with the best of us.

We learned that there was no boat leaving for France for several days, and this disquieted me, for I would have liked to see Father Donovan off early next morning, for I did not wish to disclose my project to the peace-loving man. I must march on Brede next day if I was to get there in time, and so there was no longer any possibility of concealing my designs. However, there was no help for it, and I resolved to be up bright and early in the morning and engage a dozen men whom I could trust to stand by me. I also intended to purchase several cartloads of provisions, so that if a siege was attempted we could not be starved out. All this I would accomplish at as early an hour as possible, get the carts on their way to Brede, and march at the head of the men myself; so I went to bed with a somewhat troubled mind, but fell speedily into a dreamless sleep nevertheless, and slept till broad daylight.

## CHAPTER XXXII

I found Rye a snug little town, and so entirely peaceable-looking that when I went out in the morning I was afraid there would be nobody there who would join me in the hazardous task of taking possession of the place of so well-known a man as the Earl of Westport. But I did not know Rye then as well as I do now: it proved to be a great resort for smugglers when they were off duty and wished to enjoy the innocent relaxation of a town after the comparative loneliness of the sea-coast, although, if all the tales they tell me are true, the authorities sometimes made the sea-shore a little too lively for their comfort. Then there were a number of seafaring men looking for a job, and some of them had the appearance of being pirates in more prosperous days.

As I wandered about I saw a most gigantic ruffian, taking his ease with his back against the wall, looking down on the shipping.

"If that man's as bold as he's strong," said I to myself, "and I had half a dozen more like him, we'd hold Brede House till the day there's liberty in Ireland;" so I accosted him.

"The top o' the morning to you," said I genially.

He eyed me up and down, especially glancing at the sword by my side, and then said civilly:

"The same to you, sir. You seem to be looking for some one?"

"I am," said I, "I'm looking for nine men."

"If you'll tell me their names I'll tell you where to find them, for I know everybody in Rye."

"If that's the case you'll know their names, which is more than I do myself."

"Then you're not acquainted with them?"

"I am not; but if you'll tell me your name I think then I'll know one of them."

There was a twinkle in his eye as he said:

"They call me Tom Peel."

"Then Tom," said I, "are there eight like you in the town of Rye?"

"Not quite as big perhaps," said Tom, "but there's plenty of good men here, as the French have found out before now,—yes, and the constables as well. What do you want nine men for?"

"Because I have nine swords and nine pistols that will fit that number of courageous subjects."

"Then it's not for the occupation of agriculture you require them?" said Peel with the hint of a laugh. "There's a chance of a cut in the ribs, I suppose, for swords generally meet other swords."

"You're right in that; but I don't think the chance is very strong."

"And perhaps a term in prison when the scrimmage is ended?"

"No fear of that at all at all; for if any one was to go to prison it would be me, who will be your leader, and not you, who will be my dupes, do you see?"

Peel shrugged his shoulders.

"My experience of the world is that the man with gold lace on his coat goes free, while they punish the poor devil in the leather jacket. But, turn the scheme out bad or ill, how much money is at the end of it?"

"There'll be ten guineas at the end of it for each man, win or lose."

"And when will the money be paid?"

"Half before you leave Rye, the other half in a week's time, and perhaps before,—a week's time at the latest; but I want men who will not turn white if a blunderbuss happens to go off."

The rascallion smiled and spat contemptuously in the dust before him.

"If you show me the guineas," said he, "I'll show you the men."

"Here's five of them, to begin with, that won't be counted against you. There'll be five more in your pocket when we leave Rye, and a third five when the job's ended."

His big hand closed over the coins.

"I like your way of speaking," he said. "Now where are we to go?"

"To the strong house of Brede, some seven or eight miles from here. I do not know how far exactly, nor in what direction."

"I am well acquainted with it," said Peel. "It was a famous smuggler's place in its time."

"I don't mean a smuggler's place," said I. "I am talking of the country house of the Earl of Westport."

"Yes, curse him, that's the spot I mean. Many a nobleman's house is put to purposes he learns little of, although the Earl is such a scoundrel he may well have been in with the smugglers and sold them to the government."

"Did he sell them?"

"Somebody sold them."

There was a scowl on Peel's face that somehow encouraged me, although I liked the look of the ruffian from the first.

"You're an old friend of his lordship's, then?" said I.

"He has few friends in Rye or about Rye. If you're going to do anything against Westport, I'll get you a hundred men for nothing if there's a chance of escape after the fight."

"Nine men will do me, if they're the right stuff. You will have good cover to sleep under, plenty to eat and drink, and then I expect you to hold Brede House against all the men the Earl of Westport can bring forward."

"That's an easy thing," said Peel, his eye lighting up. "And if worse comes to the worst I know a way out of the house that's neither through door or window nor up a chimney. Where will I collect your men?"

"Assemble them on the road to Brede, quietly, about half a mile from Rye. Which direction is Brede from here?"

"It lies to the west, between six and seven miles away as the crow flies."

"Very well, collect your men as quickly as you can, and send word to me at the 'Anchor.' Tell your messenger to ask for The O'Ruddy."

Now I turned back to the tavern sorely troubled what I would do with Father Donovan. He was such a kindly man that he would be loath to shake hands with me at the door of the inn, as he had still two or three days to stop, so I felt sure he would insist on accompanying me part of the way. I wished I could stop and see him off on his ship; but if we were to get inside of Brede's House unopposed, we had to act at once. I found Paddy almost recovered from the assault of the day before. He had a bandage around his forehead, which, with his red hair, gave him a hideous appearance, as if the whole top of his head had been smashed. Poor Paddy was getting so used to a beating each day that I wondered wouldn't he be lonesome when the beatings ceased and there was no enemy to follow him.

Father Donovan had not yet appeared, and the fire was just lit in the kitchen to prepare breakfast, so I took Jem and Paddy with me to the eating shop of the town, and there a sleepy-looking shop-keeper let us in, mightily resenting this early intrusion, but changed his demeanour when he understood the size of the order I was giving him, and the fact that I was going to pay good gold; for it would be a fine joke on The O'Ruddy if the Earl surrounded the house with his men and starved him out. So it was no less than three cartloads of provisions I ordered, though one of them was a cartload of drink, for I thought the company I had hired would have a continuous thirst on them, being seafaring men and smugglers, and I knew that strong, sound ale was brewed in Rye.

The business being finished, we three went back to the "Anchor," and found an excellent breakfast and an excellent man waiting for me, the latter being Father Donovan, although slightly impatient for closer acquaintance with the former.

When breakfast was done with, I ordered the three horses saddled, and presently out in the courtyard Paddy was seated on his nag with the two sacks of pistols before him, and Jem in like manner with his two bundles of swords. The stableman held my horse, so I turned to Father Donovan and grasped him warmly by the hand.

"A safe journey across the Channel to you, Father Donovan, and a peaceful voyage from there to Rome, whichever road you take. If you write to me in the care of the landlord of this inn I'll be sending and sending till I get your letter, and when you return I'll be standing and watching the sea, at whatever point you land in England, if you'll but let me know in time. And so good-bye to you, Father Donovan, and God bless you, and I humbly beseech your own blessing in return."

The old man's eyes grew wider and wider as I went on talking and talking and shaking him by the hand.

"What's come over you, O'Ruddy?" he said, "and where are you going?"

"I am taking a long journey to the west and must have an early start."

"Nonsense," cried Father Donovan, "it's two or three days before I can leave this shore, so I'll accompany you a bit of the way."

"You mustn't think of it, Father, because you had a long day's ride yesterday, and I want you to take care of yourself and take thought on your health."

"Tush, I'm as fresh as a boy this morning. Landlord, see that the saddle is put on that horse I came into Rye with."

The landlord at once rushed off and gave the order, while I stood there at my wit's end.

"Father Donovan," said I, "I'm in great need of haste at this moment, and we must ride fast, so I'll just bid good-bye to you here at this comfortable spot, and you'll sit down at your ease in that big arm-chair."

"I'll do nothing of the kind, O'Ruddy. What's troubling you, man? and why are you in such a hurry this morning, when you said nothing of it yesterday?"

"Father, I said nothing of it yesterday, but sure I acted it. See how we rode on and on in spite of everything, and did the whole journey from London to Rye between breakfast and supper. Didn't that give you a hint that I was in a hurry?"

"Well, it should have done, it should have done, O'Ruddy; still, I'll go a bit of the way with you and not delay you."

"But we intend to ride very fast, Father."

"Ah, it's an old man you're thinking I'm getting to be. Troth, I can ride as fast as any one of the three of you, and a good deal faster than Paddy."

At this moment the landlord came bustling in.

"Your Reverence's horse is ready," he said.

And so there was nothing for it but to knock the old man down, which I hadn't the heart to do. It is curious how stubborn some people are; but Father Donovan was always set in his ways, and so, as we rode out of Rye to the west, with Paddy and Jem following us, I had simply to tell his Reverence all about it, and you should have seen the consternation on his countenance.

"Do you mean to tell me you propose to take possession of another man's house and fight him if he comes to claim his own?"

"I intend that same thing, your Reverence;" for now I was as stubborn as the old gentleman himself, and it was not likely I was going to be put off my course when I remembered the happiness that was ahead of me; but there's little use in trying to explain to an aged priest what a young man is willing to do for the love of the sweetest girl in all the land.

"O'Ruddy," he said, "you'll be put in prison. It's the inside of a gaol, and not the inside of a castle, you'll see. It's not down the aisle of a church you'll march with your bride on your arm, but its hobbling over the cobbles of a Newgate passage you'll go with manacles on your legs. Take warning from me, my poor boy, who would be heart-broken to see harm come to you, and don't run your neck into the hangman's noose, thinking it the matrimonial halter. Turn back while there's yet time, O'Ruddy."

"Believe me, Father Donovan, it grieves me to refuse you anything, but I cannot turn back."

"You'll be breaking the law of the land."

"But the law of the land is broken every day in our district of Ireland, and not too many words said about it."

"Oh, O'Ruddy, that's a different thing. The law of the land in Ireland is the law of the alien."

"Father, you're not logical. It's the alien I'm going to fight here,"—but before the father could reply we saw ahead of us the bulky form of Tom Peel, and ranged alongside of the road, trying to look very stiff and military-like, was the most awkward squad of men I had ever clapped eyes on; but determined fellows they were, as I could see at a glance when I came fornenst them, and each man pulled a lock of his hair by way of a salute.

"Do you men understand the use of a sword and a pistol?" said I.

The men smiled at each other as though I was trying some kind of a joke on them.

"They do, your honour," answered Tom Peel on their behalf. "Each one of them can sling a cutlass to the king's taste, and fire a pistol without winking, and there are now concealed in the hedge half a dozen blunderbusses in case they should be needed. They make a loud report and have a good effect on the enemy, even when they do no harm.”

“Yes, we’ll have the blunderbusses,” said I, and with that the men broke rank, burst through the hedge, and came back with those formidable weapons. “I have ammunition in the carts,” I said, “did you see anything of them?”

“The carts have gone on to the west, your honour; but we’ll soon overtake them,” and the men smacked their lips when they thought of the one that had the barrels in it. Now Paddy came forward with the pistols, and Bottles followed and gave each man a blade, while I gave each his money.

“O dear! O dear!” groaned Father Donovan.

“There’s just a chance we may be attacked before we get to Brede, and, Father, though I am loath to say good-bye, still it must be said. It’s rare glad I’ll be when I grip your hand again.”

“All in good time; all in good time,” said Father Donovan; “I’ll go a bit farther along the road with you and see how your men march. They would fight better and better behind a hedge than in the open, I’m thinking.”

“They’ll not have to fight in the open, Father,” said I, “but they’ll be comfortably housed if we get there in time. Now, Peel, I make you captain of the men, as you’ve got them together, and so, Forward, my lads.”

They struck out along the road, walking a dozen different kinds of steps, although there were only nine of them; some with the swords over their shoulders, some using them like walking-sticks, till I told them to be more careful of the points; but they walked rapidly and got over the ground, for the clank of the five guineas that was in each man’s pocket played the right kind of march for them.

“Listen to reason, O’Ruddy, and even now turn back,” said Father Donovan.

“I’ll not turn back now,” said I, “and, sure, you can’t expect it of me. You’re an obstinate man yourself, if I must say so, Father.”

“It’s a foolhardy exploit,” he continued, frowning. “There’s prison at the end of it for some one,” he murmured.

“No, it’s the House of Brede, Father, that’s at the end of it.”

“Supposing the Earl of Westport brings a thousand men against you,—what are you going to do?”

“Give them the finest fight they have ever seen in this part of England.”

In spite of himself I saw a sparkle in Father Donovan’s eye. The nationality of him was getting the better of his profession.

“If it were legitimate and lawful,” at last he said, “it would be a fine sight to see.”

“It will be legitimate and lawful enough when the Earl and myself come to terms. You need have no fear that we’re going to get into the courts, Father.”

“Do you think he’ll fight?” demanded the father suddenly, with a glint in his eyes that I have seen in my own father’s when he was telling us of his battles in France.

“Fight? Why of course he’ll fight, for he’s as full of malice as an egg’s full of meat; but nevertheless he’s a sensible old curmudgeon, when the last word’s said, and before he’ll have it noised over England that his title to the land is disputed he’ll give me what I want, although at first he’ll try to master me.”

“Can you depend on these men?”

“I think I can. They’re old smugglers and pirates, most of them.”

“I wonder who the Earl will bring against you?” said Father Donovan, speaking more to himself than to me. “Will it be farmers or regular soldiers?”

“I expect they will be from among his own tenantry; there’s plenty of them, and they’ll all have to do his bidding.”

"But that doesn't give a man courage in battle?"

"No, but he'll have good men to lead them, even if he brings them from London."

"I wouldn't like to see you attacked by real soldiers; but I think these men of yours will give a good account of themselves if there's only peasantry brought up against them. Sure, the peasantry in this country is not so warlike as in our own,"—and there was a touch of pride in the father's remark that went to my very heart.

After riding in silence for a while, meditating with head bowed, he looked suddenly across at me, his whole face lighted up with delicious remembrance.

"Wouldn't you like to have Mike Sullivan with you this day," he cried, naming the most famous fighter in all the land, noted from Belfast to our own Old Head of Kinsale.

"I'd give many a guinea," I said, "to have Mike by my side when the Earl comes on."

The old father suddenly brought down his open hand with a slap on his thigh.

"I'm going to stand by you, O'Ruddy," he said.

"I'm glad to have your blessing on the job at last, Father," said I; "for it was sore against me to go into this business when you were in a contrary frame of mind."

"You'll not only have my blessing, O'Ruddy, but myself as well. How could I sail across the ocean and never know which way the fight came out? and then, if it is to happen in spite of me, the Lord pity the frailness of mankind, but I'd like to see it. I've not seen a debate since the Black Fair of Bandon."

By this time we had overtaken the hirelings with their carts, and the men were swinging past them at a good pace.

"Whip up your horses," said I to the drivers, "and get over the ground a little faster. It's not gunpowder that's in those barrels, and when we reach the house there will be a drink for every one of you."

There was a cheer at this, and we all pushed on with good hearts. At last we came to a lane turning out from the main road, and then to the private way through fields that led to Brede House. So far there had been no one to oppose us, and now, setting spurs to our horses, we galloped over the private way, which ran along the side of a gentle hill until one end of the mansion came into view. It seemed likely there was no suspicion who we were, for a man digging in the garden, stood up and took off his cap to us. The front door looked like the Gothic entrance of a church, and I sprang from my horse and knocked loudly against the studded oak. An old man opened the door without any measure of caution, and I stepped inside. I asked him who he was, and he said he was the caretaker.

"How many beside yourself are in this house?"

He said there was only himself, his wife, and a kitchen wench, and two of the gardeners, while the family was in London.

"Well," said I, "I'd have you know that I'm the family now, and that I'm at home. I am the owner of Brede estate."

"You're not the Earl of Westport!" said the old man, his eyes opening wide.

"No, thank God, I'm not!"

He now got frightened and would have shut the door, but I gently pushed him aside. I heard the tramp of the men, and, what was more, the singing of a sea song, for they were nearing the end of their walk and thinking that something else would soon pass their lips besides the tune. The old man was somewhat reassured when he saw the priest come in; but dismay and terror took hold of him when the nine men with their blunderbusses and their swords came singing around a corner of the house and drew up in front of it. By and by the carts came creaking along, and then every man turned to and brought the provisions inside of the house and piled them up in the kitchen in an orderly way, while the old man, his wife, the wench, and the two gardeners stood looking on with growing signs of panic upon them.

"Now, my ancient caretaker," said I to the old man, in the kindest tones I could bring to my lips, so as not to frighten him more than was already the case, "what is the name of that little village over yonder?" and I pointed toward the west, where, on the top of a hill, appeared a church and a few houses.

"That, sir," he said, with his lips trembling, "is the village of Brede."

"Is there any decent place there where you five people can get lodging; for you see that this house is now filled with men of war, and so men of peace should be elsewhere? Would they take you in over at the village?"

"Yes, sir, it is like they would."

"Very well. Here is three guineas to divide among you, and in a week or thereabouts you will be back in your own place, so don't think disaster has fallen on you."

The old man took the money, but seemed in a strange state of hesitancy about leaving.

"You will be unhappy here," I said, "for there will be gun-firing and sword-playing. Although I may not look it, I am the most bloodthirsty swordsman in England, with a mighty uncertain temper on me at times. So be off, the five of you!"

"But who is to be here to receive the family?" he asked.

"What family?"

"Sir, we had word last night that the Earl of Westport and his following would come to this house today at two of the clock, and we have much ado preparing for them; for the messenger said that he was bringing many men with him. I thought at first that you were the men, or I would not have let you in."

"Now the Saints preserve us," cried I, "they'll be on us before we get the windows barricaded. Tom Peel," I shouted, "set your men to prepare the defence at once, and you'll have only a few hours to do it in. Come, old man, take your wife and your gardeners, and get away."

"But the family, sir, the family," cried the old man, unable to understand that they should not be treated with the utmost respect.

"I will receive the family. What is that big house over there in the village?"

"The Manor House, sir."

"Very well, get you gone, and tell them to prepare the Manor House for the Earl of Westport and his following; for he cannot lodge here tonight,"—and with that I was compelled to drag them forth, the old woman crying and the wench snivelling in company. I patted the ancient wife on the shoulder and told her there was nothing to be feared of; but I saw my attempt at consolation had little effect.

Tom Peel understood his business; he had every door barred and stanchioned, and the windows protected, as well as the means to his hand would allow. Up stairs he knocked out some of the diamond panes so that the muzzle of a blunderbuss would go through. He seemed to know the house as if it was his own; and in truth the timbers and materials for defence which he conjured up from the ample cellars or pulled down from the garret seemed to show that he had prepared the place for defence long since.

"Your honour," he said, "two dangers threaten this house which you may not be aware of."

"And what are those, Tom?" I asked.

"Well, the least serious one is the tunnel. There is a secret passage from this house down under the valley and out and up near the church. If it was not guarded they could fill this house unknown to you. I will stop this end of it with timber if your honour gives the word. There's not many knows of it, but the Earl of Westport is certain to have the knowledge, and some of his servants as well."

"Lead me to this tunnel, Tom," said I, astonished at his information.

We came to a door in one of the lower rooms that opened on a little circular stone stairway, something like a well, and, going down to the bottom, we found a tunnel in which a short man could stand upright.

"Thunder and turf, Tom!" said I, "what did they want this for?"

"Well, some thought it was to reach the church, but no one ever lived in this house that was so anxious to get to church that he would go underground to it. Faith, they've been a godless lot in Brede Place until your honour came, and we were glad to see you bring a priest with you. It put new heart in the men; they think he'll keep off Sir Goddard Oxenbridge."

"Does he live near here? What has he to do with the place?"

"He is dead long since, sir, and was owner of this house. Bullet wouldn't harm him, nor steel cut him, so they sawed him in two with a wooden saw down by the bridge in front. He was a witch of the very worst kind, your honour. You hear him groaning at the bridge every night, and sometimes he walks through the house himself in two halves, and then every body leaves the place. And that is our most serious danger, your honour. When Sir Goddard takes to groaning through these rooms at night, you'll not get a man to stay with you, sir; but as he comes up from the pit by the will of the Devil we expect his Reverence to ward him off."

Now this was most momentous news, for I would not stop in the place myself if a ghost was in the habit of walking through it; but I cheered up Tom Peel by telling him that no imp of Satan could appear in the same county as Father Donovan, and he passed on the word to the men, to their mighty easement.

We had a splendid dinner in the grand hall, and each of us was well prepared for it; Father Donovan himself, standing up at the head of the table, said the holy words in good Latin, and I was so hungry that I was glad the Latins were in the habit of making short prayers.

Father Donovan and I sat at table with a bottle for company, and now that he knew all about the situation, I was overjoyed to find him an inhabitant of the same house; for there was no gentleman in all the company, except himself, for me to talk with.

Suddenly there was a blast of a bugle, and a great fluttering outside. The lower windows being barricaded, it was not possible to see out of them, and I was up the stair as quick as legs could carry me; and there in front were four horses harnessed to a great carriage, and in it sat the old Earl and the Countess, and opposite them who but Lady Mary herself, and her brother, Lord Strepp. Postilions rode two of the horses, and the carriage was surrounded by a dozen mounted men.

Everybody was looking at the house and wondering why nobody was there to welcome them, and very forbidding this stronghold must have seemed to those who expected to find the doors wide open when they drove up. I undid the bolts of one of the diamond-paned windows, and, throwing it open, leaned with my arms on the sill, my head and shoulders outside.

"Good day to your ladyship and your lordship," I cried,—and then all eyes were turned on me,—"I have just this day come into my inheritance, and I fear the house is not in a state to receive visitors. The rooms are all occupied by desperate men and armed; but I have given orders to your servants to prepare the Manor House in the village for your accommodation; so, if you will be so good as to drive across the valley, you will doubtless meet with a better reception than I can give you at this moment. When you come again, if there are no ladies of the party, I can guarantee you will have no complaint to make of the warmth of your reception."

His lordship sat dumb in his carriage, and for once her ladyship appeared to find difficulty in choosing words that would do justice to her anger. I could not catch a glimpse of Lady Mary's face at all at all, for she kept it turned toward the village; but young Lord Strepp rose in the carriage, and, shaking his fist at me, said:

"By God, O'Ruddy, you shall pay for this;" but the effect of the words was somewhat weakened by reason that his sister, Lady Mary, reached out and pulled him by the coat-tails, which caused him to be seated more suddenly than he expected; then she gave me one rapid glance of her eye and turned away her face again.

Now his lordship, the great Earl of Westport, spoke, but not to me.

"Drive to the village," he said to the postilions; then horsemen and carriage clattered down the hill.

We kept watch all that night, but were not molested. In the southern part of the house Father Donovan found a well-furnished chapel, and next morning held mass there, which had a very quieting effect on the men, especially as Oxenbridge had not walked during the night. The only one of them who did not attend mass was Jem Bottles, who said he was not well enough and therefore would remain on watch. Just as mass was finished Jem appeared in the gallery of the chapel and shouted excitedly:

"They're coming, sir; they're coming!"

I never before saw a congregation dismiss themselves so speedily. They were at their posts even before Tom Peel could give the order. The opposing party was leaving the village and coming down the hill when I first caught sight of them from an upper window. There seemed somewhere between half a dozen and a dozen horsemen, and behind them a great mob of people on foot that fairly covered the hillside. As they crossed the brook and began to come up, I saw that their leader was young Lord Strepp himself, and Jem whispered that the horsemen behind him were the very men he had encountered on the road between London and Maidstone. The cavalry were well in advance, and it seemed that the amateur infantry took less and less pleasure in their excursion the nearer they drew to the gloomy old house, so much so that Lord Strepp turned back among them and appeared to be urging them to make haste. However, their slow progress may be explained by the fact that a certain number of them were carrying a huge piece of timber, so heavy that they had to stagger along cautiously.

"That," said Tom Peel, who stood at my elbow, "is to batter in the front door and take us by storm. If you give the word, your honour, we can massacre the lot o' them before they get three blows struck."

"Give command to the men, Peel," said I, "not to shoot any one if they can help it. Let them hold their fire till they are within fifty yards or so of the front, then pass the word to fire into the gravel of the terrace; and when you shoot let every man yell as if he were a dozen, and keep dead silence till that moment. I'll hold up my hand when I want you to fire."

There was a deep stillness over all the beautiful landscape. The bushes and the wood, however, were an exception to this, although the songs of the birds among the trees and singing of the larks high in the air seemed not to disturb the silence; but the whole air of the country-side was a suggestion of restful peace, at great variance with the designs of the inhabitants, who were preparing to attack each other.

Father Donovan stood beside me, and I saw his lips moving in prayer; but his eyes were dancing with irredeemable delight, while his breath came quick and expectant.

"I'm afraid those chaps will run at the first volley," he said, smiling at me. "They come on very slowly and must be a great trial to the young lord that's leading them."

It was indeed a trial to the patience of all of us, for the time seemed incredibly long till they arrived at the spot where I had determined they should at least hear the report of the blunderbusses, although I hoped none of them would feel the effects of the firing. Indeed, the horsemen themselves, with the exception of Lord Strepp, appeared to take little comfort in their position, and were now more anxious to fall behind and urge on the others on foot than to lead the band with his lordship.

I let them all get very close, then held up my hand, and you would think pandemonium was let loose. I doubt if all the cannon in Cork would have made such a noise, and the heathen Indians we read of in America could not have given so terrifying a yell as came from my nine men. The blunderbusses were more dangerous than I supposed, and they tore up the gravel into a shower of small stones that scattered far and wide, and made many a man fall down, thinking he was shot. Then the mob ran away with a speed which made up for all lost time coming the other direction. Cries of anguish were heard on every side, which made us all laugh, for we knew none of them were hurted. The horses themselves seemed seized with panic; they plunged and kicked like mad, two riders being thrown on the ground, while others galloped across the valley as if they were running away; but I suspect that their owners were slyly spurring them on while pretending they had lost control of them. Lord Strepp and one or two others, however, stood their ground, and indeed his lordship spurred his horse up opposite the front door. One of my men drew a pistol, but I shouted at him:

"Don't shoot at that man, whatever he does," and the weapon was lowered.

I opened the window and leaned out.

"Well, Lord Strepp," cried I, "'tis a valiant crowd you have behind you."

"You cursed highwayman," he cried, "what do you expect to make by this?"

"I expect to see some good foot-racing; but you are under an error in your appellation. I am not a highwayman; it is Jem Bottles here who stopped nine of your men on the Maidstone road and piled their saddles by the side of it. Is it new saddlery you have, or did you make a roadside collection?"

"I'll have you out of that, if I have to burn the house over your head."

"I'll wager you'll not get any man, unless it's yourself, to come near enough to carry a torch to it. You can easily have me out of this without burning the house. Tell your father I am ready to compromise with him."

"Sir, you have no right in my father's house; and, to tell you the truth, I did not expect such outlawry from a man who had shown himself to be a gentleman."

"Thank you for that, Lord Strepp; but, nevertheless, tell your father to try to cultivate a conciliatory frame of mind, and let us talk the matter over as sensible men should."

"We cannot compromise with you, O'Ruddy," said Lord Strepp in a very determined tone, which for the first time made me doubt the wisdom of my proceedings; for of course it was a compromise I had in mind all the time, for I knew as well as Father Donovan that if he refused to settle with me my position was entirely untenable.

"We cannot compromise with you," went on the young man. "You have no right, legal or moral, to this place, and you know it. I have advised my father to make no terms with you. Good day to you, sir."

And with that he galloped off, while I drew a very long face as I turned away.

"Father Donovan," I said, when I had closed the window, "I am not sure but your advice to me on the way here was nearer right than I thought at the time."

"Oh, not a bit of it," cried Father Donovan cheerfully. "You heard what the young man said, that he had advised his father not to make any terms with you. Very well, that means terms have been proposed already; and this youth rejects the wisdom of age, which I have known to be done before."

"You think, then, they will accept a conference?"

"I am sure of it. These men will not stand fire, and small blame to them. What chance have they? As your captain says, he could annihilate the lot of them before they crushed in the front door. The men who ran away have far more sense than that brainless spalpeen who led them on, although I can see he is brave enough. One or two more useless attacks will lead him to a more conciliatory frame of mind, unless he appeals to the law, which is what I thought he would do; for I felt sure a sheriff would be in the van of attack. Just now you are opposed only to the Earl of Westport; but, when the sheriff comes on, you're fornenst the might of England."

This cheered me greatly, and after a while we had our dinner in peace. The long afternoon passed slowly away, and there was no rally in the village, and no sign of a further advance; so night came on and nothing had been done. After supper I said good-night to Father Donovan, threw myself, dressed as I was, on the bed, and fell into a doze. It was toward midnight when Tom Peel woke me up; that man seemed to sleep neither night nor day; and there he stood by my bed, looking like a giant in the flicker of the candle-light.

"Your honour," he said, "I think there's something going on at the mouth of the tunnel. Twice I've caught the glimpse of a light there, although they're evidently trying to conceal it."

I sat up in bed and said:

"What do you propose to do?"

"Well, there's a man inside here that knows the tunnel just as well as I do,—every inch of it,—and he's up near the other end now. If a company begins coming in, my man will run back without being seen and let us know. Now, sir, shall I timber this end, or shall we deal with them at the top of the stair one by one as they come up. One good swordsman at the top of the stair will prevent a thousand getting into the house."

"Peel," said I, "are there any stones outside, at the other end of the tunnel?"

"Plenty. There's a dyke of loose stones fronting it."

"Very well; if your man reports that any have entered the tunnel, they'll have left one or two at the other end on guard; take you five of your most trusted men, and go you cautiously a roundabout way until you are within striking distance of the men on guard. Watch the front upper windows of this house; and if you see two lights displayed, you will know they are in the tunnel. If you waited here till your man comes back, you would be too late; so go now, and, if you see the two lights, overpower the men at the mouth of the tunnel unless they are too many for you. If they are, then there's nothing to do but retreat. When you have captured the guard, make them go down into the tunnel; then you and your men tear down the dyke and fill the hole full of stones; I will guard this end of the passage."

Tom Peel pulled his forelock and was gone at once, delighted with his task. I knew that if I got them once in the tunnel there would no longer be any question of a compromise, even if Lord Strepp himself was leading them. I took two lighted candles with me and sat patiently at the head of the stone stairway that led, in circular fashion, down into the depths. Half an hour passed, but nothing happened, and I began to wonder whether or not they had captured our man, when suddenly his face appeared.

"They are coming, sir," he cried, "by the dozen. Lord Strepp is leading them."

"Will they be here soon, do you think?"

"I cannot tell. First I saw torches appear, then Lord Strepp came down and began giving instructions, and, after counting nearly a score of his followers, I came back as quick as I could."

"You've done nobly," said I. "Now stand here with this sword and prevent any man from coming up."

I took one of the candles, leaving him another, and lighted a third. I went up the stair and set them in the front window; then I opened another window and listened. The night was exceedingly still,—not even the sound of a cricket to be heard. After a few minutes, however, there came a cry, instantly smothered, from the other side of the valley; another moment and I heard the stones a rolling, as if the side of a wall had tumbled over, which indeed was the case; then two lights were shown on the hill and were waved up and down; and although Peel and I had arranged no signal, yet this being the counterpart of my own, I took to signify that they had been successful, so, leaving the candles burning there, in case there might have been some mistake, I started down the stair to the man who was guarding the secret passage.

"Has anything happened?"

"Nothing, sir."

I think the best part of an hour must have passed before there was sign or sound. Of course I knew if the guards were flung down the hole, they would at once run after their comrades and warn them that both ends of the tunnel were in our possession. I was well aware that the imprisoned men might drag away the stones and ultimately win a passage out for themselves; but I trusted that they would be panic-stricken when they found themselves caught like rats in a trap. In any case it would be very difficult to remove stones from below in the tunnel, because the space was narrow and few could labour at a time; then there was every chance that the stones might jam, when nothing could be done. However, I told the man beside me to go across the valley and ask Peel and his men to pile on rocks till he had a great heap above the entrance, and, if not disturbed, to work till nearly daylight, so I sat on the top of the circular stair step with my rapier across my knees, waiting so long that I began to fear they all might be smothered, for I didn't know whether the stopping of air at one end would prevent it coming in at the other, for I never heard my father say what took place in a case like that. Father Donovan was in bed and asleep, and I was afraid to leave the guarding of the stair to any one else. It seemed that hours and hours passed, and I began to wonder was daylight never going to come, when the most welcome sound I ever heard was the well-known tones of a voice which came up from the bottom of the well.

"Are you there, Mr. O'Ruddy?"

There was a subdued and chastened cadence in the inquiry that pleased me.

"I am, and waiting for you."

"May I come up?"

"Yes, and very welcome; but you'll remember, Lord Strepp, that you come up as a prisoner."

"I quite understand that, Mr. O'Ruddy."

So, as I held the candle, I saw the top of his head coming round and round and round, and finally he stood before me stretching out his sword, hilt forward.

"Stick it in its scabbard," said I, "and I'll do the same with mine." Then I put out my hand, "Good morning to your lordship," I said. "It seems to me I've been waiting here forty days and forty nights. Will you have a sup of wine?"

"I would be very much obliged to you for it, Mr. O'Ruddy."

With that I called the nearest guard and bade him let nobody up the stair without my knowing it.

"I suppose, my lord, you are better acquainted with this house than I am; but I know a spot where there's a drop of good drink."

"You have discovered the old gentleman's cellar, then?"

"Indeed, Lord Strepp, I have not. I possess a cellar of my own. It's you that's my guest, and not me that's yours on this occasion."

I poured him out a flagon, and then one for myself, and as we stood by the table I lifted it high and said:

"Here's to our better acquaintance."

His lordship drank, and said with a wry face, as he put down the mug:

"Our acquaintance seems to be a somewhat tempestuous one; but I confess, Mr. O'Ruddy, that I have as great a respect for your generalship as I have for your swordsmanship. The wine is good and revivifying. I've been in that accursed pit all night, and I came to this end of it with greater reluctance than I expected to when I entered the other. We tried to clear away the stones; but they must have piled all the rocks in Sussex on top of us. Are your men toiling there yet?"

"Yes, they're there, and I gave them instructions to work till daylight."

"Well, Mr. O'Ruddy, my poor fellows are all half dead with fright, and they fancy themselves choking; but although the place was foul enough when we entered it, I didn't see much difference at the end. However, I did see one thing, and that was that I had to come and make terms. I want you to let the poor devils go, Mr. O'Ruddy, and I'll be parole that they won't attack you again."

"And who will give his parole that Lord Strepp will not attack me again?"

"Well, O'Ruddy,"—I took great comfort from the fact that he dropped the Mr.— "Well, O'Ruddy, you see we cannot possibly give up this estate. You are not legally entitled to it. It is ours and always has been."

"I'm not fighting for any estate, Lord Strepp."

"Then, in Heaven's name, what are you fighting for?"

"For the consent of the Earl and Countess of Westport to my marriage with Lady Mary, your sister."

Lord Strepp gave a long whistle; then he laughed and sat down in the nearest chair.

"But what does Mary say about it?" he asked at last.

"The conceit of an Irishman, my lord, leads me to suspect that I can ultimately overcome any objections she may put forward."

"Oho! that is how the land lies, is it? I'm a thick-headed clod, or I would have suspected something of that sort when Mary pulled me down so sharply as I was cursing you at the front door." Then, with a slight touch of patronage in his tone, he said:

"There is some difference in the relative positions of our families, Mr. O'Ruddy."

"Oh, I'm quite willing to waive that," said I. "Of course it isn't usual for the descendant of kings, like myself, to marry a daughter of the mere nobility; but Lady Mary is so very charming that she more than makes up for any discrepancy, whatever may be said for the rest of the family."

At this Lord Strepp threw back his head and laughed again joyously, crying,—

"King O'Ruddy, fill me another cup of your wine, and I'll drink to your marriage."

We drank, and then he said:

"I'm a selfish beast, guzzling here when those poor devils think they're smothering down below. Well, O'Ruddy, will you let my unlucky fellows go?"

"I'll do that instantly," said I, and so we went to the head of the circular stair and sent the guard down to shout to them to come on, and by this time the daylight was beginning to turn the upper windows grey. A very bedraggled stream of badly frightened men began crawling up and up and up the stairway, and as Tom Peel had now returned I asked him to open the front door and let the yeomen out. Once on the terrace in front, the men seemed not to be able to move away, but stood there drawing in deep breaths of air as if they had never tasted it before. Lord Strepp, in the daylight, counted the mob, asking them if they were sure every one had come up, but they all seemed to be there, though I sent Tom Peel down along the tunnel to find if any had been left behind.

Lord Strepp shook hands most cordially with me at the front door.

"Thank you for your hospitality, O'Ruddy," he said, "although I came in by the lower entrance. I will send over a flag of truce when I've seen my father; then I hope you will trust yourself to come to the Manor House and have a talk with him."

"I'll do it with pleasure," said I.

"Good morning to you," said Lord Strepp.

"And the top o' the morning to you, which is exactly what we are getting at this moment, though in ten minutes I hope to be asleep."

"So do I," said Lord Strepp, setting off at a run down the slope.

## CHAPTER XXXIII

Once more I went to my bed, but this time with my clothes off, for if there was to be a conference with the Earl and the Countess at the Manor House, not to speak of the chance of seeing Lady Mary herself, I wished to put on the new and gorgeous suit I had bought in London for that occasion, and which had not yet been on my back. I was so excited and so delighted with the thought of seeing Lady Mary that I knew I could not sleep a wink, especially as daylight was upon me, but I had scarcely put my head on the pillow when I was as sound asleep as any of my ancestors, the old Kings of Kinsale. The first thing I knew Paddy was shaking me by the shoulder just a little rougher than a well-trained servant should.

"Beggin' your pardon," says he, "his lordship, the great Earl of Westport, sends word by a messenger that he'll be pleased to have account with ye, at your early convenience, over at the Manor House beyond."

"Very well, Paddy," said I, "ask the messenger to take my compliments to the Earl and say to him I will do myself the honour of calling on him in an hour's time. Deliver that message to him; then come back and help me on with my new duds."

When Paddy returned I was still yawning, but in the shake of a shillelah he had me inside the new costume, and he stood back against the wall with his hand raised in amazement and admiration at the glory he beheld. He said after that kings would be nothing to him, and indeed the tailor had done his best and had won his guineas with more honesty than you'd expect from a London tradesman. I was quietly pleased with the result myself.

I noticed with astonishment that it was long after mid-day, so it occurred to me that Lord Strepp must have had a good sleep himself, and sure the poor boy needed it, for it's no pleasure to spend life underground till after you're dead, and his evening in the tunnel must have been very trying to him, as indeed he admitted to me afterward that it was.

I called on Father Donovan, and he looked me over from head to foot with wonder and joy in his eye.

"My dear lad, you're a credit to the O'Ruddys," he said, "and to Ireland," he said, "and to the Old Head of Kinsale," he said.

"And to that little tailor in London as well," I replied, turning around so that he might see me the better.

In spite of my chiding him Paddy could not contain his delight, and danced about the room like an overgrown monkey.

"Paddy," said I, "you're making a fool of yourself."

Then I addressed his Reverence.

"Father Donovan," I began, "this cruel war is over and done with, and no one hurt and no blood shed, so the Earl—"

At this moment there was a crash and an unearthly scream, then a thud that sounded as if it had happened in the middle of the earth. Father Donovan and I looked around in alarm, but Paddy was nowhere to be seen. Toward the wall there was a square black hole, and, rushing up to it, we knew at once what had happened. Paddy had danced a bit too heavy on an old trap-door, and the rusty bolts had broken. It had let him down into a dungeon that had no other entrance; and indeed this was a queer house entirely, with many odd nooks and corners about it, besides the disadvantage of Sir Goddard Oxenbridge tramping through the rooms in two sections.

"For the love of Heaven and all the Saints," I cried down this trap-door, "Paddy, what has happened to you?"

"Sure, sir, the house has fallen on me."

"Nothing of the kind, Paddy. The house is where it always was. Are you hurted?"

"I'm dead and done for completely this time, sir. Sure I feel I'm with the angels at last."

"Tut, tut, Paddy, my lad; you've gone in the wrong direction altogether for them."

"Oh, I'm dying, and I feel the flutter of their wings," and as he spoke two or three ugly blind bats fluttered up and butted their stupid heads against the wall.

"You've gone in the right direction for the wrong kind of angels, Paddy; but don't be feared, they're only bats, like them in my own tower at home, except they're larger."

I called for Tom Peel, as he knew the place well.

"Many a good cask of brandy has gone down that trap-door," said he, "and the people opposite have searched this house from cellar to garret and never made the discovery Paddy did a moment since."

He got a stout rope and sent a man down, who found Paddy much more frightened than hurt. We hoisted both of them up, and Paddy was a sight to behold.

"Bad luck to ye," says I; "just at the moment I want a presentable lad behind me when I'm paying my respects to the Earl of Westport, you must go diving into the refuse heap of a house that doesn't belong to you, and spoiling the clothes that does. Paddy, if you were in a seven years' war, you would be the first man wounded and the last man killed, with all the trouble for nothing in between. Is there anything broken about ye?"

"Every leg and arm I've got is broken," he whimpered, but Father Donovan, who was nearly as much of a surgeon as a priest, passed his hand over the trembling lad, then smote him on the back, and said the exercise of falling had done him good.

"Get on with you," said I, "and get off with those clothes. Wash yourself, and put on the suit I was wearing yesterday, and see that you don't fall in the water-jug and drown yourself."

I gave the order for Tom Peel to saddle the four horses and get six of his men with swords and pistols and blunderbusses to act as an escort for me.

"Are you going back to Rye, your honour?" asked Peel.

"I am not. I am going to the Manor House."

"That's but a step," he cried in surprise.

"It's a step," said I, "that will be taken with dignity and consequence."

So, with the afternoon sun shining in our faces, we set out from the house of Brede, leaving but few men to guard it. Of course I ran the risk that it might be taken in our absence; but I trusted the word of Lord Strepp as much as I distrusted the designs of his father and mother, and Strepp had been the captain of the expedition against us; but if I had been sure the mansion was lost to me, I would have evaded none of the pomp of my march to the Manor House in the face of such pride as these upstarts of Westports exhibited toward a representative of a really ancient family like the O'Ruddy. So his Reverence and I rode slowly side by side, with Jem and Paddy, also on horseback, a decent interval behind us, and tramping in their wake that giant, Tom Peel, with six men nearly as stalwart as himself, their blunderbusses over their shoulders, following him. It struck panic in the village when they saw this terrible array marching up the hill toward them, with the sun glittering on us as if we were walking jewellery. The villagers, expecting to be torn limb from limb, scuttled away into the forest, leaving the place as empty as a bottle of beer after a wake. Even the guards around the Manor House fled as we approached it, for the fame of our turbulence had spread abroad in the land. Lord Strepp tried to persuade them that nothing would happen to them, for when he saw the style in which we were coming he was anxious to make a show from the Westport side and had drawn up his men in line to receive us. But we rode through a silent village that might have been just sacked by the French. I thought afterward that this desertion had a subduing effect on the old Earl's pride, and made him more easy to deal with. In any case his manner was somewhat abated when he received me. Lord Strepp himself was there at the door, making excuses for the servants, who he said had gone to the fields to pick berries for their supper. So, leaving Paddy to hold one horse and Jem the other, with the seven men drawn up fiercely in front of the Manor House, Father Donovan and myself followed Lord Strepp into a large room, and there, buried in an arm-chair, reclined the aged Earl of Westport, looking none too pleased to meet his visitors. In cases like this it's as well to be genial at the first, so that you may remove the tension in the beginning.

"The top of the morning—I beg your pardon—the tail of the afternoon to you, sir, and I hope I see you well."

"I am very well," said his lordship, more gruffly than politely.

"Permit me to introduce to your lordship, his Reverence, Father Donovan, who has kindly consented to accompany me that he may yield testimony to the long-standing respectability of the House of O'Ruddy."

"I am pleased to meet your Reverence," said the Earl, although his appearance belied his words. He wasn't pleased to meet either of us, if one might judge by his lowering countenance, in spite of my cordiality and my wish to make his surrender as easy for him as possible.

I was disappointed not to see the Countess and Lady Mary in the room, for it seemed a pity that such a costume as mine should be wasted on an old cur mudgeon, sitting with his chin in his breast in the depths of an easy-chair, looking daggers though he spoke dumplings.

I was just going to express my regret to Lord Strepp that no ladies were to be present in our assemblage, when the door opened, and who should sail in, like a full-rigged man-o'-war, but the Countess herself, and Lady Mary, like an elegant yacht floating in tow of her. I swept my bonnet to the boards of the floor with a gesture that would have done honour to the Court of France; but her Ladyship tossed her nose higher in the air, as if the man-o'-war had encountered a huge wave. She seated herself with emphasis on a chair, and says I to myself, "It's lucky for you, you haven't Paddy's trap-door under you, or we'd see your heels disappear, coming down like that."

Lady Mary very modestly took up her position standing behind her mother's chair, and, after one timid glance at me, dropped her eyes on the floor, and then there were some moments of silence, as if every one was afraid to begin. I saw I was going to have trouble with the Countess, and although I think it will be admitted by my enemies that I'm as brave a man as ever faced a foe, I was reluctant to throw down the gage of battle to the old lady.

It was young Lord Strepp that began, and he spoke most politely, as was his custom.

"I took the liberty of sending for you, Mr. O'Ruddy, and I thank you for responding so quickly to my invitation. The occurrences of the past day or two, it would be wiser perhaps to ignore—"

At this there was an indignant sniff from the Countess, and I feared she was going to open her batteries, but to my amazement she kept silent, although the effort made her red in the face.

"I have told my father and mother," went on Lord Strepp, "that I had some conversation with you this morning, and that conditions might be arrived at satisfactory to all parties concerned. I have said nothing to my parents regarding the nature of these conditions, but I gained their consent to give consideration to anything you might say, and to any proposal you are good enough to make."

The old gentleman mumbled something incomprehensible in his chair, but the old lady could keep silence no longer.

"This is an outrage," she cried, "the man's action has been scandalous and unlawful. If, instead of bringing those filthy scoundrels against our own house, those cowards that ran away as soon as they heard the sound of a blunderbuss, we had all stayed in London, and you had had the law of him, he would have been in gaol by this time and not standing brazenly there in the Manor House of Brede."

And after saying this she sniffed again, having no appreciation of good manners.

"Your ladyship has been misinformed," I said with extreme deference. "The case is already in the hands of dignified men of law, who are mightily pleased with it."

"Pleased with it, you idiot," she cried. "They are pleased with it simply because they know somebody will pay them for their work, even it's a beggar from Ireland, who has nothing on him but rags."

"Your ladyship," said I, not loath to call attention to my costume, "I assure you these rags cost golden guineas in London."

"Well, you will not get golden guineas from Brede estate," snapped her ladyship.

"Again your ladyship is misinformed. The papers are so perfect, and so well do they confirm my title to this beautiful domain, that the money-lenders of London simply bothered the life out of me trying to shovel gold on me, and both his lordship and your ladyship know that if a title is defective there is no money to be lent on it."

"You're a liar," said the Countess genially, although the Earl looked up in alarm when I mentioned that I could draw money on the papers. Again I bowed deeply to her ladyship, and, putting my hands in my pockets, I drew out two handfuls of gold, which I strewed up and down the floor as if I were sowing corn, and each guinea was no more than a grain of it.

"There is the answer to your ladyship's complimentary remark," said I with a flourish of my empty hands; and, seeing Lady Mary's eyes anxiously fixed on me, I dropped her a wink with the side of my face farthest from the Countess, at which Lady Mary's eyelids drooped again. But I might have winked with both eyes for all the Countess, who was staring like one in a dream at the glittering pieces that lay here and there and gleamed all over the place like the little yellow devils they were. She seemed struck dumb, and if anyone thinks gold cannot perform a miracle, there is the proof of it.

"Is it gold?" cried I in a burst of eloquence that charmed even myself, "sure I could sow you acres with it by the crooking of my little finger from the revenues of my estate at the Old Head of Kinsale."

"O'Ruddy, O'Ruddy," said Father Donovan very softly and reprovingly, for no one knew better than him what my ancestral revenues were.

"Ah well, Father," said I, "your reproof is well-timed. A man should not boast, and I'll say no more of my castles and my acres, though the ships on the sea pay tribute to them. But all good Saints preserve us, Earl of Westport, if you feel proud to own this poor estate of Brede, think how little it weighed with my father, who all his life did not take the trouble to come over and look at it. Need I say more about Kinsale when you hear that? And as for myself, did I attempt to lay hands on this trivial bit of earth because I held the papers? You know I tossed them into your daughter's lap because she was the finest-looking girl I have seen since I landed on these shores."

"Well, well, well, well," growled the Earl, "I admit I have acted rashly and harshly in this matter, and it is likely I have done wrong to an honourable gentleman, therefore I apologize for it. Now, what have you to propose?"

"I have to propose myself as the husband of your daughter, Lady Mary, and as for our dowry, there it is on the floor for the picking up, and I'm content with that much if I get the lady herself."

His lordship slowly turned his head around and gazed at his daughter, who now was looking full at me with a frown on her brow. Although I knew I had depressed the old people, I had an uneasy feeling that I had displeased Lady Mary herself by my impulsive action and my bragging words. A curious mildness came into the harsh voice of the old Earl, and he said, still looking at his daughter:

"What does Mary say to this?"

The old woman could not keep her eyes from the gold, which somehow held her tongue still, yet I knew she was hearing every word that was said, although she made no comment. Lady Mary shook herself, as if to arouse herself from a trance, then she said in a low voice:

"I can never marry a man I do not love."

"What's that? what's that?" shrieked her mother, turning fiercely round upon her, whereat Lady Mary took a step back. "Love, love? What nonsense is this I hear? You say you will not marry this man to save the estate of Brede?"

"I shall marry no man whom I do not love," repeated Lady Mary firmly.

As for me, I stood there, hat in hand, with my jaw dropped, as if Sullivan had given me a stunning blow in the ear; then the old Earl said sternly:

"I cannot force my daughter: this conference is at an end. The law must decide between us."

"The law, you old dotard," cried the Countess, rounding then on him with a suddenness that made him seem to shrink into his shell. "The law! Is a silly wench to run us into danger of losing what is ours? He *shall* marry her. If you will not force her, then I'll coerce her;" and with that she turned upon her daughter, grasped her by her two shoulders and shook her as a terrier shakes a rat. At this Lady Mary began to weep, and indeed she had good cause to do so.

"Hold, madam," shouted I, springing toward her. "Leave the girl alone. I agree with his lordship, no woman shall be coerced on account of me."

My intervention turned the Countess from her victim upon me.

"You agree with his lordship, you Irish baboon? Don't think she'll marry you because of any liking for you, you chattering ape, who resemble a monkey in a show with those trappings upon you. She'll marry you because I say she'll marry you, and you'll give up those papers to me, who have sense enough to take care of them. If I have a doddering husband, who at the same time lost his breeches and his papers, I shall make amends for his folly."

"Madam," said I, "you shall have the papers; and as for the breeches, by the terror you spread around you, I learn they are already in your possession."

I thought she would have torn my eyes out, but I stepped back and saved myself.

"To your room, you huzzy," she cried to her daughter, and Mary fled toward the door. I leaped forward and opened it for her. She paused on the threshold, pretending again to cry, but instead whispered:

"My mother is the danger. Leave things alone," she said quickly. "We can easily get poor father's consent."

With that she was gone. I closed the door and returned to the centre of the room.

"Madam," said I, "I will not have your daughter browbeaten. It is quite evident she refuses to marry me."

"Hold your tongue, and keep to your word, you idiot," she rejoined, hitting me a bewildering slap on the side of the face, after which she flounced out by the way her daughter had departed.

The old Earl said nothing, but gazed gloomily into space from out the depths of his chair. Father Donovan seemed inexpressibly shocked, but my Lord Strepp, accustomed to his mother's tantrums, laughed outright as soon as the door was closed. All through he had not been in the least deceived by his sister's pretended reluctance, and recognized that the only way to get the mother's consent was through opposition. He sprang up and grasped me by the hand and said:

"Well, O'Ruddy, I think your troubles are at an end, or," he cried, laughing again, "just beginning, but you'll be able to say more on that subject this time next year. Never mind my mother; Mary is, and always will be, the best girl in the world."

"I believe you," said I, returning his handshake as cordially as he had bestowed it.

"Hush!" he cried, jumping back into his seat again. "Let us all look dejected. Hang your head, O'Ruddy!" and again the door opened, this time the Countess leading Lady Mary, her long fingers grasping that slim wrist.

"She gives her consent," snapped the Countess, as if she were pronouncing sentence. I strode forward toward her, but Mary wrenched her wrist free, slipped past me, and dropped at the feet of Father Donovan, who had risen as she came in.

"Your blessing on me, dear Father," she cried, bowing her head, "and pray on my behalf that there may be no more turbulence in my life."

The old father crossed his hands on her shapely head, and for a moment or two it seemed as if he could not command his voice, and I saw the tears fill his eyes. At last he said simply and solemnly:—

"May God bless you and yours, my dear daughter."

* * * *

We were married by Father Donovan with pomp and ceremony in the chapel of the old house, and in the same house I now pen the last words of these memoirs, which I began at the request of Lady Mary herself, and continued for the pleasure she expressed as they went on. If this recital is disjointed in parts, it must be remembered I was always more used to the sword than to the pen, and that it is difficult to write with Patrick and little Mary and Terence and Kathleen and Michael and Bridget and Donovan playing about me and asking questions, but I would not have the darlings sent from the room for all the writings there is in the world.

# A MAN AND SOME OTHERS

## I

Dark mesquit spread from horizon to horizon. There was no house or horseman from which a mind could evolve a city or a crowd. The world was declared to be a desert and unpeopled. Sometimes, however, on days when no heat-mist arose, a blue shape, dim, of the substance of a spectre's veil, appeared in the south-west, and a pondering sheep-herder might remember that there were mountains.

In the silence of these plains the sudden and childish banging of a tin pan could have made an iron-nerved man leap into the air. The sky was ever flawless; the manoeuvring of clouds was an unknown pageant; but at times a sheep-herder could see, miles away, the long, white streamers of dust rising from the feet of another's flock, and the interest became intense.

Bill was arduously cooking his dinner, bending over the fire, and toiling like a blacksmith. A movement, a flash of strange colour, perhaps, off in the bushes, caused him suddenly to turn his head. Presently hearose, and, shading his eyes with his hand, stood motionless and gazing. He perceived at last a Mexican sheep-herder winding through the brush toward his camp.

"Hello!" shouted Bill.

The Mexican made no answer, but came steadily forward until he was within some twenty yards. There he paused, and, folding his arms, drew himself up in the manner affected by the villain in the play. His serape muffled the lower part of his face, and his great sombrero shaded his brow. Being unexpected and also silent, he had something of the quality of an apparition; moreover, it was clearly his intention to be mysterious and devilish.

The American's pipe, sticking carelessly in the corner of his mouth, was twisted until the wrong side was uppermost, and he held his frying-pan poised in the air. He surveyed with evident surprise this apparition in the mesquit. "Hello, José!" he said; "what's the matter?"

The Mexican spoke with the solemnity of funeral tollings: "Beel, you mus' geet off range. We want you geet off range. We no like. Un'erstan'? We no like."

"What you talking about?" said Bill. "No like what?"

"We no like you here. Un'erstan'? Too mooch. You mus' geet out. We no like. Un'erstan'?"

"Understand? No; I don't know what the blazes you're gittin' at." Bill's eyes wavered in bewilderment, and his jaw fell. "I must git out? I must git off the range? What you givin' us?"

The Mexican unfolded his serape with his small yellow hand. Upon his face was then to be seen a smile that was gently, almost caressingly murderous. "Beel," he said, "geet out!"

Bill's arm dropped until the frying-pan was at his knee. Finally he turned again toward the fire. "Go on, you dog-gone little yaller rat!" he said over his shoulder. "You fellers can't chase me off this range. I got as much right here as anybody."

"Beel," answered the other in a vibrant tone, thrusting his head forward and moving one foot, "you geet out or we keel you."

"Who will?" said Bill.

"I—and the others." The Mexican tapped his breast gracefully.

Bill reflected for a time, and then he said: "You ain't got no manner of license to warn me off'n this range, and I won't move a rod. Understand? I've got rights, and I suppose if I don't see 'em through, no one is likely to give me a good hand and help me lick you fellers, since I'm the only white man in half a day's ride. Now, look; if you fellers try to rush this camp, I'm goin' to plug about fifty percent of the gentlemen present, sure. I'm goin' in for trouble, an' I'll git a lot of you. 'Nuther thing: if I was a fine valuable caballero like you, I'd stay in the rear till the shootin' was done, because I'm goin' to make a particular p'int of shootin' you through the chest." He grinned affably, and made a gesture of dismissal.

As for the Mexican, he waved his hands in a consummate expression of indifference. "Oh, all right," he said. Then, in a tone of deep menace and glee, he added: "We will keel you eef you no geet. They have decide'."

"They have, have they?" said Bill. "Well, you tell them to go to the devil!"

## II

Bill had been a mine-owner in Wyoming, a great man, an aristocrat, one who possessed unlimited credit in the saloons down the gulch. He had the social weight that could interrupt a lynching or advise a bad man of the particular merits of a remote geographical point. However, the fates exploded the toy balloon with which they had amused Bill, and on the evening of the same day he was a professional gambler with ill-fortune dealing him unspeakable irritation in the shape of three big cards whenever another fellow stood pat. It is well here to inform the world that Bill considered his calamities of life all dwarfs in comparison with the excitement of one particular evening, when three kings came to him with criminal regularity against a man who always filled a straight. Later he became a cow-boy, more weirdly abandoned than if he had never been an aristocrat. By this time all that remained of his former splendour was his pride, or his vanity, which was one thing which need not have remained. He killed the foreman of the ranch over an inconsequent matter as to which of them was a liar, and the midnight train carried him eastward. He became a brakeman on the Union Pacific, and really gained high honours in the hobo war that for many years has devastated the beautiful railroads of our country. A creature of ill-fortune himself, he practised all the ordinary cruelties upon these other creatures of ill-fortune. He was of so fierce a mien that tramps usually surrendered at once whatever coin or tobacco they had in their possession; and if afterward he kicked them from the train, it was only because this was a recognized treachery of the war upon the hoboes. In a famous battle fought in Nebraska in 1879, he would have achieved a lasting distinction if it had not been for a deserter from the United States army. He was at the head of a heroic and sweeping charge, which really broke the power of the hoboes in that country for three months; he had already worsted four tramps with his own coupling-stick, when a stone thrown by the ex-third baseman of F Troop's nine laid him flat on the prairie, and later enforced a stay in the hospital in Omaha. After his recovery he engaged with other railroads, and shuffled cars in countless yards. An order to strike came upon him in Michigan, and afterward the vengeance of the railroad pursued him until he assumed a name. This mask is like the darkness in which the burglar chooses to move. It destroys many of the healthy fears. It is a small thing, but it eats that which we call our conscience. The conductor of No. 419 stood in the caboose within two feet of Bill's nose, and called him a liar. Bill requested him to use a milder term. He had not bored the foreman of Tin Can

Ranch with any such request, but had killed him with expedition. The conductor seemed to insist, and so Bill let the matter drop.

He became the bouncer of a saloon on the Bowery in New York. Here most of his fights were as successful as had been his brushes with the hoboes in the West. He gained the complete admiration of the four clean bar-tenders who stood behind the great and glittering bar. He was an honoured man. He nearly killed Bad Hennessy, who, as a matter of fact, had more reputation than ability, and his fame moved up the Bowery and down the Bowery.

But let a man adopt fighting as his business, and the thought grows constantly within him that it is his business to fight. These phrases became mixed in Bill's mind precisely as they are here mixed; and let a man get this idea in his mind, and defeat begins to move toward him over the unknown ways of circumstances. One summer night three sailors from the U.S.S. *Seattle* sat in the saloon drinking and attending to other people's affairs in an amiable fashion. Bill was a proud man since he had thrashed so many citizens, and it suddenly occurred to him that the loud talk of the sailors was very offensive. So he swaggered upon their attention, and warned them that the saloon was the flowery abode of peace and gentle silence. They glanced at him in surprise, and without a moment's pause consigned him to a worse place than any stoker of them knew. Whereupon he flung one of them through the side door before the others could prevent it. On the sidewalk there was a short struggle, with many hoarse epithets in the air, and then Bill slid into the saloon again. A frown of false rage was upon his brow, and he strutted like a savage king. He took a long yellow night-stick from behind the lunch-counter, and started importantly toward the main doors to see that the incensed seamen did not again enter.

The ways of sailormen are without speech, and, together in the street, the three sailors exchanged no word, but they moved at once. Landsmen would have required two years of discussion to gain such unanimity. In silence, and immediately, they seized a long piece of scantling that lay handily. With one forward to guide the battering-ram, and with two behind him to furnish the power, they made a beautiful curve, and came down like the Assyrians on the front door of that saloon.

Mystic and still mystic are the laws of fate. Bill, with his kingly frown and his long night-stick, appeared at precisely that moment in the doorway. He stood like a statue of victory; his pride was at its zenith; and in the same second this atrocious piece of scantling punched him in the bulwarks of his stomach, and he vanished like a mist. Opinions differed as to where the end of the scantling landed him, but it was ultimately clear that it landed him in south-western Texas, where he became a sheep-herder.

The sailors charged three times upon the plate-glass front of the saloon, and when they had finished, it looked as if it had been the victim of a rural fire company's success in saving it from the flames. As the proprietor of the place surveyed the ruins, he remarked that Bill was a very zealous guardian of property. As the ambulance surgeon surveyed Bill, he remarked that the wound was really an excavation.

**III**

As his Mexican friend tripped blithely away, Bill turned with a thoughtful face to his frying-pan and his fire. After dinner he drew his revolver from its scarred old holster, and examined every part of it. It was the revolver that had dealt death to the foreman, and it had also been in free fights in which it had dealt death to several or none. Bill loved it because its allegiance was more than that of man, horse, or dog. It questioned neither social nor moral position; it obeyed alike the saint and the assassin. It was the claw of the eagle, the tooth of the lion, the poison of the snake; and when he swept it from its holster, this minion smote where he listed, even to the battering of a far penny. Wherefore it was his dearest possession, and was not to be exchanged in south-western Texas for a handful of rubies, nor even the shame and homage of the conductor of No. 419.

During the afternoon he moved through his monotony of work and leisure with the same air of deep meditation. The smoke of his supper-time fire was curling across the shadowy sea of mesquit when the instinct of the plainsman warned him that the stillness, the desolation, was again invaded. He saw a motionless horseman in black outline against the pallid sky. The silhouette displayed serape and sombrero, and even the Mexican spurs as large as pies. When this black figure began to move toward the camp, Bill's hand dropped to his revolver.

The horseman approached until Bill was enabled to see pronounced American features, and a skin too red to grow on a Mexican face. Bill released his grip on his revolver.

"Hello!" called the horseman.

"Hello!" answered Bill.

The horseman cantered forward. "Good evening," he said, as he again drew rein.

"Good evenin'," answered Bill, without committing himself by too much courtesy.

For a moment the two men scanned each other in a way that is not ill-mannered on the plains, where one is in danger of meeting horse-thieves or tourists.

Bill saw a type which did not belong in the mesquit. The young fellow had invested in some Mexican trappings of an expensive kind. Bill's eyes searched the outfit for some sign of craft, but there was none. Even with his local regalia, it was clear that the young man was of a far, black Northern city. He had discarded the enormous stirrups of his Mexican saddle; he used the small English stirrup, and his feet were thrust forward until the steel tightly gripped his ankles. As Bill's eyes travelled over the stranger, they lighted suddenly upon the stirrups and the thrust feet, and immediately he smiled in a friendly way. No dark purpose could dwell in the innocent heart of a man who rode thus on the plains.

As for the stranger, he saw a tattered individual with a tangle of hair and beard, and with a complexion turned brick-colour from the sun and whisky. He saw a pair of eyes that at first looked at him as the wolf looks at the wolf, and then became childlike, almost timid, in their glance. Here was evidently a man who had often stormed the iron walls of the city of success, and who now sometimes valued himself as the rabbit values his prowess.

The stranger smiled genially, and sprang from his horse. "Well, sir, I suppose you will let me camp here with you tonight?"

"Eh?" said Bill.

"I suppose you will let me camp here with you tonight?"

Bill for a time seemed too astonished for words. "Well,"—he answered, scowling in inhospitable annoyance—"well, I don't believe this here is a good place to camp tonight, mister."

The stranger turned quickly from his saddle-girth.

"What?" he said in surprise. "You don't want me here? You don't want me to camp here?"

Bill's feet scuffled awkwardly, and he looked steadily at a cactus plant. "Well, you see, mister," he said, "I'd like your company well enough, but—you see, some of these here greasers are goin' to chase me off the range tonight; and while I might like a man's company all right, I couldn't let him in for no such game when he ain't got nothin' to do with the trouble."

"Going to chase you off the range?" cried the stranger.

"Well, they said they were goin' to do it," said Bill.

"And—great heavens! will they kill you, do you think?"

"Don't know. Can't tell till afterwards. You see, they take some feller that's alone like me, and then they rush his camp when he ain't quite ready for 'em, and ginerally plug 'im with a sawed-off shot-gun load before he has a chance to git at 'em. They lay around and wait for their chance, and it comes soon enough. Of course a feller alone like me has got to let up watching some time. Maybe they ketch 'im asleep. Maybe the feller gits tired waiting, and goes out in broad day, and kills two or three just to make the whole crowd pile on him and settle the thing. I heard of a case like that once. It's awful hard on a man's mind—to git a gang after him."

"And so they're going to rush your camp tonight?" cried the stranger. "How do you know? Who told you?"

"Feller come and told me."

"And what are you going to do? Fight?"

"Don't see nothin' else to do," answered Bill gloomily, still staring at the cactus plant.

There was a silence. Finally the stranger burst out in an amazed cry. "Well, I never heard of such a thing in my life! How many of them are there?"

"Eight," answered Bill. "And now look-a-here; you ain't got no manner of business foolin' around here just now, and you might better lope off before dark. I don't ask no help in this here row. I know your happening along here just now don't give me no call on you, and you better hit the trail."

"Well, why in the name of wonder don't you go get the sheriff?" cried the stranger.

"Oh, hell!" said Bill.

## IV

Long, smoldering clouds spread in the western sky, and to the east silver mists lay on the purple gloom of the wilderness.

Finally, when the great moon climbed the heavens and cast its ghastly radiance upon the bushes, it made a new and more brilliant crimson of the campfire, where the flames capered merrily through its mesquit branches, filling the silence with the fire chorus, an ancient melody which surely bears a message of the inconsequence of individual tragedy—a message that is in the boom of the sea, the sliver of the wind through the grass-blades, the silken clash of hemlock boughs.

No figures moved in the rosy space of the camp, and the search of the moonbeams failed to disclose a living thing in the bushes. There was no owl-faced clock to chant the weariness of the long silence that brooded upon the plain.

The dew gave the darkness under the mesquit a velvet quality that made air seem nearer to water, and no eye could have seen through it the black things that moved like monster lizards toward the camp. The branches, the leaves, that are fain to cry out when death approaches in the wilds, were frustrated by these uncanny bodies gliding with the finesse of the escaping serpent. They crept forward to the last point where assuredly no frantic attempt of the fire could discover them, and there they paused to locate the prey. A romance relates the tale of the black cell hidden deep in the earth, where, upon entering, one sees only the little eyes of snakes fixing him in menaces. If a man could have approached a certain spot in the bushes, he would not have found it romantically necessary to have his hair rise. There would have been a sufficient expression of horror in the feeling of the death-hand at the nape of his neck and in his rubber knee-joints.

Two of these bodies finally moved toward each other until for each there grew out of the darkness a face placidly smiling with tender dreams of assassination. "The fool is asleep by the fire, God be praised!" The lips of the other widened in a grin of affectionate appreciation of the fool and his plight. There was some signaling in the gloom, and then began a series of subtle rustlings, interjected often with pauses, during which no sound arose but the sound of faint breathing.

A bush stood like a rock in the stream of firelight, sending its long shadow backward. With painful caution the little company travelled along this shadow, and finally arrived at the rear of the bush. Through its branches they surveyed for a moment of comfortable satisfaction a form in a grey blanket extended on the ground near the fire. The smile of joyful anticipation fled quickly, to give place to a quiet air of business. Two men lifted shot-guns with much of the barrels gone, and sighting these weapons through the branches, pulled trigger together.

The noise of the explosions roared over the lonely mesquit as if these guns wished to inform the entire world; and as the grey smoke fled, the dodging company back of the bush saw the blanketed form twitching; whereupon they burst out in chorus in a laugh, and arose as merry as a lot of banqueters. They gleefully gestured congratulations, and strode bravely into the light of the fire.

Then suddenly a new laugh rang from some unknown spot in the darkness. It was a fearsome laugh of ridicule, hatred, ferocity. It might have been demoniac. It smote them motionless in their gleeful prowl, as the stern voice from the sky smites the legendary malefactor. They might have been a weird group in wax, the light of the dying fire on their yellow faces, and shining athwart their eyes turned toward the darkness whence might come the unknown and the terrible.

The thing in the grey blanket no longer twitched; but if the knives in their hands had been thrust toward it, each knife was now drawn back, and its owner's elbow was thrown upward, as if he expected death from the clouds.

This laugh had so chained their reason that for a moment they had no wit to flee. They were prisoners to their terror. Then suddenly the belated decision arrived, and with bubbling cries they turned to run; but at that instant there was a long flash of red in the darkness, and with the report one of the men shouted a bitter shout, spun once, and tumbled headlong. The thick bushes failed to impede the route of the others.

The silence returned to the wilderness. The tired flames faintly illumined the blanketed thing and the flung corpse of the marauder, and sang the fire chorus, the ancient melody which bears the message of the inconsequence of human tragedy.

V

"Now you are worse off than ever," said the young man, dry-voiced and awed.

"No, I ain't," said Bill rebelliously. "I'm one ahead."

After reflection, the stranger remarked, "Well, there's seven more."

They were cautiously and slowly approaching the camp. The sun was flaring its first warming rays over the grey wilderness. Upreared twigs, prominent branches, shone with golden light, while the shadows under the mesquit were heavily blue.

Suddenly the stranger uttered a frightened cry. He had arrived at a point whence he had, through openings in the thicket, a clear view of a dead face.

"Gosh!" said Bill, who at the next instant had seen the thing; "I thought at first it was that there José. That would have been queer, after what I told 'im yesterday."

They continued their way, the stranger wincing in his walk, and Bill exhibiting considerable curiosity.

The yellow beams of the new sun were touching the grim hues of the dead Mexican's face, and creating there an inhuman effect, which made his countenance more like a mask of dulled brass. One hand, grown curiously thinner, had been flung out regardlessly to a cactus bush.

Bill walked forward and stood looking respectfully at the body. "I know that feller; his name is Miguel. He—"

The stranger's nerves might have been in that condition when there is no backbone to the body, only a long groove. "Good heavens!" he exclaimed, much agitated; "don't speak that way!"

"What way?" said Bill. "I only said his name was Miguel."

After a pause the stranger said:

"Oh, I know; but—" He waved his hand. "Lower your voice, or something. I don't know. This part of the business rattles me, don't you see?"

"Oh, all right," replied Bill, bowing to the other's mysterious mood. But in a moment he burst out violently and loud in the most extraordinary profanity, the oaths winging from him as the sparks go from the funnel.

He had been examining the contents of the bundled grey blanket, and he had brought forth, among other things, his frying-pan. It was now only a rim with a handle; the Mexican volley had centered upon it. A Mexican shot-gun of the abbreviated description is ordinarily loaded with flat-irons, stove-lids, lead pipe, old horseshoes, sections of chain, window weights, railroad sleepers and spikes, dumb-bells, and any other junk which may be at hand. When one of these loads encounters a man vitally, it is likely to make an impression upon him, and acooking-utensil may be supposed to subside before such an assault of curiosities.

Bill held high his desecrated frying-pan, turning it this way and that way. He swore until he happened to note the absence of the stranger. A moment later he saw him leading his horse from the bushes. In silence and sullenly the young man went about saddling the animal. Bill said, "Well, goin' to pull out?"

The stranger's hands fumbled uncertainly at the throat-latch. Once he exclaimed irritably, blaming the buckle for the trembling of his fingers. Once he turned to look at the dead face with the light of the morning sun upon it. At last he cried, "Oh, I know the whole thing was all square enough—couldn't be squarer—but—somehow or other, that man there takes the heart out of me." He turned his troubled face for another look. "He seems to be all the time calling me a—he makes me feel like a murderer."

"But," said Bill, puzzling, "you didn't shoot him, mister; I shot him."

"I know; but I feel that way, somehow. I can't get rid of it."

Bill considered for a time; then he said diffidently, "Mister, you're a eddycated man, ain't you?"

"What?"

"You're what they call a—a eddycated man, ain't you?"

The young man, perplexed, evidently had a question upon his lips, when there was a roar of guns, bright flashes, and in the air such hooting and whistling as would come from a swift flock of steam-boilers. The stranger's horse gave a mighty, convulsive spring, snorting wildly in its sudden anguish, fell upon its knees, scrambled afoot again, and was away in the uncanny death run known to men who have seen the finish of brave horses.

"This comes from discussin' things," cried Bill angrily.

He had thrown himself flat on the ground facing the thicket whence had come the firing. He could see the smoke winding over the bush-tops. He lifted his revolver, and the weapon came slowly up from the ground and poised like the glittering crest of a snake. Somewhere on his face there was a kind of smile, cynical, wicked, deadly, of a ferocity which at the same time had brought a deep flush to his face, and had caused two upright lines to glow in his eyes.

"Hello, José!" he called, amiable for satire's sake. "Got your old blunderbusses loaded up again yet?"

The stillness had returned to the plain. The sun's brilliant rays swept over the sea of mesquit, painting the far mists of the west with faint rosy light, and high in the air some great bird fled toward the south.

"You come out here," called Bill, again addressing the landscape, "and I'll give you some shootin' lessons. That ain't the way to shoot." Receiving no reply, he began to invent epithets and yell them at the thicket. He was something of a master of insult, and, moreover, he dived into his memory to bring forth imprecations tarnished with age, unused since fluent Bowery days. The occupation amused him, and sometimes he laughed so that it was uncomfortable for his chest to be against the ground.

Finally the stranger, prostrate near him, said wearily, "Oh, they've gone."

"Don't you believe it," replied Bill, sobering swiftly. "They're there yet—every man of 'em."

"How do you know?"

"Because I do. They won't shake us so soon. Don't put your head up, or they'll get you, sure."

Bill's eyes, meanwhile, had not wavered from their scrutiny of the thicket in front. "They're there all right; don't you forget it. Now you listen." So he called out: "José! Ojo, José! Speak up, *hombre*! I want have talk. Speak up, you yaller cuss, you!"

Whereupon a mocking voice from off in the bushes said, "Señor?"

"There," said Bill to his ally; "didn't I tell you? The whole batch." Again he lifted his voice. "José—look—ain't you gittin' kinder tired? You better go home, you fellers, and git some rest."

The answer was a sudden furious chatter of Spanish, eloquent with hatred, calling down upon Bill all the calamities which life holds. It was as if some one had suddenly enraged a cageful of wild cats. The spirits of all the revenges which they had imagined were loosened at this time, and filled the air.

"They're in a holler," said Bill, chuckling, "or there'd be shootin'."

Presently he began to grow angry. His hidden enemies called him nine kinds of coward, a man who could fight only in the dark, a baby who would run from the shadows of such noble Mexican gentlemen, a dog that sneaked. They described the affair of the previous night, and informed him of the base advantage he had taken of their friend. In fact, they in all sincerity endowed him with every quality which he no less earnestly believed them to possess. One could have seen the phrases bite him as he lay there on the ground fingering his revolver.

## VI

It is sometimes taught that men do the furious and desperate thing from an emotion that is as even and placid as the thoughts of a village clergyman on Sunday afternoon. Usually, however, it is to be believed that a panther is at the time born in the heart, and that the subject does not resemble a man picking mulberries.

"B' G—!" said Bill, speaking as from a throat filled with dust, "I'll go after 'em in a minute."

"Don't you budge an inch!" cried the stranger, sternly. "Don't you budge!"

"Well," said Bill, glaring at the bushes—"well—"

"Put your head down!" suddenly screamed the stranger, in white alarm. As the guns roared, Bill uttered a loud grunt, and for a moment leaned panting on his elbow, while his arm shook like a twig. Then he upreared like a great and bloody spirit of vengeance, his face lighted with the blaze of his last passion. The Mexicans came swiftly and in silence.

The lightning action of the next few moments was of the fabric of dreams to the stranger. The muscular struggle may not be real to the drowning man. His mind may be fixed on the far, straight shadows back of the stars, and the terror of them. And so the fight, and his part in it, had to the stranger only the quality of a picture half drawn. The rush of feet, the spatter of shots, the cries, the swollen faces seen like masks on the smoke, resembled a happening of the night.

And yet afterward certain lines, forms, lived out so strongly from the incoherence that they were always in his memory.

He killed a man, and the thought went swiftly by him, like the feather on the gale, that it was easy to kill a man.

Moreover, he suddenly felt for Bill, this grimy sheep-herder, some deep form of idolatry. Bill was dying, and the dignity of last defeat, the superiority of him who stands in his grave, was in the pose of the lost sheep-herder.

The stranger sat on the ground idly mopping the sweat and powder-stain from his brow. He wore the gentle idiot smile of an aged beggar as he watched three Mexicans limping and staggering in the distance. He noted at this time that one who still possessed a serape had from it none of the grandeur of the cloaked Spaniard, but that against the sky the silhouette resembled a cornucopia of childhood's Christmas.

They turned to look at him, and he lifted his weary arm to menace them with his revolver. They stood for a moment banded together, and hooted curses at him.

Finally he arose, and, walking some paces, stooped to loosen Bill's grey hands from a throat. Swaying as if slightly drunk, he stood looking down into the still face.

Struck suddenly with a thought, he went about with dulled eyes on the ground, until he plucked his gaudy blanket from where it lay dirty from trampling feet. He dusted it carefully, and then returned and laid it over Bill's form. There he again stood motionless, his mouth just agape and the same stupid glance in his eyes, when all at once he made a gesture of fright and looked wildly about him.

He had almost reached the thicket when he stopped, smitten with alarm. A body contorted, with one arm stiff in the air, lay in his path. Slowly and warily he moved around it, and in a moment the bushes, nodding and whispering, their leaf-faces turned toward the scene behind him, swung and swung again into stillness and the peace of the wilderness.

# THE BRIDE COMES TO YELLOW SKY

I

The great Pullman was whirling onward with such dignity of motion that a glance from the window seemed simply to prove that the plains of Texas were pouring eastward. Vast flats of green grass, dull-hued spaces of mesquit and cactus, little groups of frame houses, woods of light and tender trees, all were sweeping into the east, sweeping over the horizon, a precipice.

A newly-married pair had boarded this train at San Antonio. The man's face was reddened from many days in the wind and sun, and a direct result of his new black clothes was that his brick-coloured hands were constantly performing in a most conscious fashion. From time to time he looked down respectfully at his attire. He sat with a hand on each knee, like a man waiting in a barber's shop. The glances he devoted to other passengers were furtive and shy.

The bride was not pretty, nor was she very young. She wore a dress of blue cashmere, with small reservations of velvet here and there, and with steel buttons abounding. She continually twisted her head to regard her puff-sleeves, very stiff, straight, and high. They embarrassed her. It was quite apparent that she had cooked, and that she expected to cook, dutifully. The blushes caused by the careless scrutiny of some passengers as she had entered the car were strange to see upon this plain, under-class countenance, which was drawn in placid, almost emotionless lines.

They were evidently very happy. "Ever been in a parlour-car before?" he asked, smiling with delight.

"No," she answered; "I never was. It's fine, ain't it?"

"Great. And then, after a while, we'll go forward to the diner, and get a big lay-out. Finest meal in the world. Charge, a dollar."

"Oh, do they?" cried the bride. "Charge a dollar? Why, that's too much—for us—ain't it, Jack?"

"Not this trip, anyhow," he answered bravely. "We're going to go the whole thing."

Later, he explained to her about the train. "You see, it's a thousand miles from one end of Texas to the other, and this train runs right across it, and never stops but four times."

He had the pride of an owner. He pointed out to her the dazzling fittings of the coach, and, in truth, her eyes opened wider as she contemplated the sea-green figured velvet, the shining brass, silver, and glass, the wood that gleamed as darkly brilliant as the surface of a pool of oil. At one end a bronze figure sturdily held a support for a separated chamber, and at convenient places on the ceiling were frescoes in olive and silver.

To the minds of the pair, their surroundings reflected the glory of their marriage that morning in San Antonio. This was the environment of their new estate, and the man's face, in particular, beamed with an elation that made him appear ridiculous to the negro porter. This individual at times surveyed them from afar with an amused and superior grin. On other occasions he bullied them with skill in ways that did not make it exactly plain to them that they were being bullied. He subtly used all the manners of the most unconquerable kind of snobbery. He oppressed them, but of this oppression they had small knowledge, and they speedily forgot that unfrequently a number of travellers covered them with stares of derisive enjoyment. Historically there was supposed to be something infinitely humorous in their situation.

"We are due in Yellow Sky at 3.42," he said, looking tenderly into her eyes.

"Oh, are we?" she said, as if she had not been aware of it.

To evince surprise at her husband's statement was part of her wifely amiability. She took from a pocket a little silver watch, and as she held it before her, and stared at it with a frown of attention, the new husband's face shone.

"I bought it in San Anton' from a friend of mine," he told her gleefully.

"It's seventeen minutes past twelve," she said, looking up at him with a kind of shy and clumsy coquetry.

A passenger, noting this play, grew excessively sardonic, and winked at himself in one of the numerous mirrors.

At last they went to the dining-car. Two rows of negro waiters in dazzling white suits surveyed their entrance with the interest, and also the equanimity, of men who had been forewarned. The pair fell to the lot of a waiter who happened to feel pleasure in steering them through their meal. He viewed them with the manner of a fatherly pilot, his countenance radiant with benevolence. The patronage entwined with the ordinary deference was not palpable to them. And yet as they returned to their coach they showed in their faces a sense of escape.

To the left, miles down a long purple slope, was a little ribbon of mist, where moved the keening Rio Grande. The train was approaching it at an angle, and the apex was Yellow Sky. Presently it was apparent that as the distance from Yellow Sky grew shorter, the husband became commensurately restless. His brick-red hands were more insistent in their prominence. Occasionally he was even rather absent-minded and far away when the bride leaned forward and addressed him.

As a matter of truth, Jack Potter was beginning to find the shadow of a deed weigh upon him like a leaden slab. He, the town-marshal of Yellow Sky, a man known, liked, and feared in his corner, a prominent person, had gone to San Antonio to meet a girl he believed he loved, and there, after the usual prayers, had actually induced her to marry him without consulting Yellow Sky for any part of the transaction. He was now bringing his bride before an innocent and unsuspecting community.

Of course, people in Yellow Sky married as it pleased them in accordance with a general custom, but such was Potter's thought of his duty to his friends, or of their idea of his duty, or of an unspoken form which does not control men in these matters, that he felt he was heinous. He had committed an extraordinary crime. Face to face with this girl in San Antonio, and spurred by his sharp impulse, he had gone headlong over all the social hedges. At San Antonio he was like a man hidden in the dark. A knife to sever any friendly duty, any form, was easy to his hand in that remote city. But the hour of Yellow Sky, the hour of daylight, was approaching.

He knew full well that his marriage was an important thing to his town. It could only be exceeded by the burning of the new hotel. His friends would not forgive him. Frequently he had reflected upon the advisability of telling them by telegraph, but a new cowardice had been upon him. He feared to do it. And now the train was hurrying him toward a scene of amazement, glee, reproach. He glanced out of the window at the line of haze swinging slowly in toward the train.

Yellow Sky had a kind of brass band which played painfully to the delight of the populace. He laughed without heart as he thought of it. If the citizens could dream of his prospective arrival with his bride, they would parade the band at the station, and escort them, amid cheers and laughing congratulations, to his adobe home.

He resolved that he would use all the devices of speed and plainscraft in making the journey from the station to his house. Once within that safe citadel, he could issue some sort of a vocal bulletin, and then not go among the citizens until they had time to wear off a little of their enthusiasm.

The bride looked anxiously at him. "What's worrying you, Jack?"

He laughed again. "I'm not worrying, girl. I'm only thinking of Yellow Sky."

She flushed in comprehension.

A sense of mutual guilt invaded their minds, and developed a finer tenderness. They looked at each other with eyes softly aglow. But Potter often laughed the same nervous laugh. The flush upon the bride's face seemed quite permanent.

The traitor to the feelings of Yellow Sky narrowly watched the speeding landscape.

"We're nearly there," he said.

Presently the porter came and announced the proximity of Potter's home. He held a brush in his hand, and, with all his airy superiority gone, he brushed Potter's new clothes, as the latter slowly turned this way and that way. Potter fumbled out a coin, and gave it to the porter as he had seen others do. It was a heavy and muscle-bound business, as that of a man shoeing his first horse.

The porter took their bag, and, as the train began to slow, they moved forward to the hooded platform of the car. Presently the two engines and their longstring of coaches rushed into the station of Yellow Sky.

"They have to take water here," said Potter, from a constricted throat, and in mournful cadence as one announcing death. Before the train stopped his eye had swept the length of the platform, and he was glad and astonished to see there was no one upon it but the station-agent, who, with a slightly hurried and anxious air, was walking toward the water-tanks. When the train had halted, the porter alighted first and placed in position a little temporary step.

"Come on, girl," said Potter, hoarsely.

As he helped her down, they each laughed on a false note. He took the bag from the negro, and bade his wife cling to his arm. As they slunk rapidly away, his hang-dog glance perceived that they were unloading the two trunks, and also that the station-agent, far ahead, near the baggage-car, had turned, and was running toward him, making gestures. He laughed, and groaned as he laughed, when he noted the first effect of his marital bliss upon Yellow Sky. He gripped his wife's arm firmly to his side, and they fled. Behind them the porter stood chuckling fatuously.

## II

The California Express on the Southron Railway was due at Yellow Sky in twenty-one minutes. There were six men at the bar of the Weary Gentleman saloon. One was a drummer, who talked a great deal and rapidly; three were Texans, who did not care to talk at that time; and two were Mexican sheep-herders, who did not talk as a general practice in the Weary Gentleman saloon. The bar-keeper's dog lay on the board-walk that crossed in front of the door. His head was on his paws, and he glanced drowsily here and there with the constant vigilance of a dog that is kicked on occasion. Across the sandy street were some vivid green grass plots, so wonderful in appearance amid the sands that burned near them in a blazing sun, that they caused a doubt in the mind. They exactly resembled the grass-mats used to represent lawns on the stage. At the cooler end of the railway-station a man without a coat sat in a tilted chair and smoked his pipe. The fresh-cut bank of the Rio Grande circled near the town, and there could be seen beyond it a great plum-coloured plain of mesquit.

Save for the busy drummer and his companions in the saloon, Yellow Sky was dozing. The new-comer leaned gracefully upon the bar, and recited many tales with the confidence of a bard who has come upon a new field.

"And at the moment that the old man fell down-stairs, with the bureau in his arms, the old woman was coming up with two scuttles of coal, and, of course—"

The drummer's tale was interrupted by a young man who suddenly appeared in the open door. He cried—

"Scratchy Wilson's drunk, and has turned loose with both hands."

The two Mexicans at once set down their glasses, and faded out of the rear entrance of the saloon.

The drummer, innocent and jocular, answered—

"All right, old man. S'pose he has. Come and have a drink, anyhow."

But the information had made such an obvious cleft in every skull in the room, that the drummer was obliged to see its importance. All had become instantly morose.

"Say," said he, mystified, "what is this?"

His three companions made the introductory gesture of eloquent speech, but the young man at the door forestalled them.

"It means, my friend," he answered, as he came into the saloon, "that for the next two hours this town won't be a health resort."

The bar-keeper went to the door, and locked and barred it. Reaching out of the window, he pulled in heavy wooden shutters and barred them. Immediately a solemn, chapel-like gloom was upon the place. The drummer was looking from one to another.

"But say," he cried, "what is this, anyhow? You don't mean there is going to be a gun-fight?"

"Don't know whether there'll be a fight or not," answered one man grimly. "But there'll be some shootin'—some good shootin'."

The young man who had warned them waved his hand. "Oh, there'll be a fight, fast enough, if any one wants it. Anybody can get a fight out there in the street. There's a fight just waiting."

The drummer seemed to be swayed between the interest of a foreigner, and a perception of personal danger.

"What did you say his name was?" he asked.

"Scratchy Wilson," they answered in chorus.

"And will he kill anybody? What are you going to do? Does this happen often? Does he rampage round like this once a week or so? Can he break in that door?"

"No, he can't break down that door," replied the bar-keeper. "He's tried it three times. But when he comes you'd better lay down on the floor, stranger. He's dead sure to shoot at it, and a bullet may come through."

Thereafter the drummer kept a strict eye on the door. The time had not yet been called for him to hug the floor, but as a minor precaution he sidled near to the wall.

"Will he kill anybody?" he said again.

The men laughed low and scornfully at the question.

"He's out to shoot, and he's out for trouble. Don't see any good in experimentin' with him."

"But what do you do in a case like this? What do you do?"

A man responded—"Why, he and Jack Potter—"

But, in chorus, the other men interrupted—"Jack Potter's in San Anton'."

"Well, who is he? What's he got to do with it?"

"Oh, he's the town-marshal. He goes out and fights Scratchy when he gets on one of these tears."

"Whow!" said the drummer, mopping his brow. "Nice job he's got."

The voices had toned away to mere whisperings. The drummer wished to ask further questions, which were born of an increasing anxiety and bewilderment, but when he attempted them, the men merely looked at him in irritation, and motioned him to remain silent. A tense waiting hush was upon them. In the deep shadows of the room their eyes shone as they listened for sounds from the street. One man made three gestures at the bar-keeper, and the latter, moving like a ghost, handed him a glass and a bottle. The man poured a full glass of whisky, and set down the bottle noiselessly. He gulped the whisky in a swallow, and turned again toward the door in immovable silence. The drummer saw that the bar-keeper, without a sound, had taken a Winchester from beneath the bar. Later, he saw this individual beckoning to him, so he tip-toed across the room.

"You better come with me back of the bar."

"No, thanks," said the drummer, perspiring. "I'd rather be where I can make a break for the back-door."

Whereupon the man of bottles made a kindly but peremptory gesture. The drummer obeyed it, and finding himself seated on a box, with his head below the level of the bar, balm was laid upon his soul at sight of various zinc and copper fittings that bore a resemblance to plate armour. The bar-keeper took a seat comfortably upon an adjacent box.

"You see," he whispered, "this here Scratchy Wilson is a wonder with a gun—a perfect wonder—and when he goes on the war-trail, we hunt our holes—naturally. He's about the last one of the old gang that used to hang out along the river here. He's a terror when he's drunk. When he's sober he's all right—kind of simple— wouldn't hurt a fly—nicest fellow in town. But when he's drunk—whoo!"

There were periods of stillness.

"I wish Jack Potter was back from San Anton'," said the bar-keeper. "He shot Wilson up once—in the leg—and he would sail in and pull out the kinks in this thing."

Presently they heard from a distance the sound of a shot, followed by three wild yells. It instantly removed a bond from the men in the darkened saloon. There was a shuffling of feet. They looked at each other.

"Here he comes," they said.

### III

A man in a maroon-coloured flannel shirt, which had been purchased for purposes of decoration, and made, principally, by some Jewish women on the east side of New York, rounded a corner and walked into the middle of the main street of Yellow Sky. In either hand the man held a long, heavy blue-black revolver. Often he yelled, and these cries rang through a semblance of a deserted village, shrilly flying over the roofs in a volume that seemed to have no relation to the ordinary vocal strength of a man. It was as if the surrounding stillness formed the arch of a tomb over him. These cries of ferocious challenge rang against walls of silence. And his boots had red tops with gilded imprints, of the kind beloved in winter by little sledging boys on the hillsides of New England.

The man's face flamed in a rage begot of whisky. His eyes, rolling and yet keen for ambush, hunted the still door-ways and windows. He walked with the creeping movement of the midnight cat. As it occurred to him, he roared menacing information. The long revolvers in his hands were as easy as straws; they were moved with an electric swiftness. The little fingers of each hand played sometimes in a musician's way. Plain from the low collar of the shirt, the cords of his neck straightened and sank as passion moved him. The only sounds were his terrible invitations. The calm adobes preserved their demeanour at the passing of this small thing in the middle of the street.

There was no offer of fight—no offer of fight. The man called to the sky. There were no attractions. He bellowed and fumed and swayed his revolver here and everywhere.

The dog of the bar-keeper of the Weary Gentleman saloon had not appreciated the advance of events. He yet lay dozing in front of his master's door. At sight of the dog, the man paused and raised his revolver humorously. At sight of the man, the dog sprang up and walked diagonally away, with a sullen head and growling. The man yelled, and the dog broke into a gallop. As it was about to enter an alley, there was a loud noise, a whistling, and something spat the ground directly before it. The dog screamed, and, wheeling in terror, galloped headlong in a new direction. Again there was a noise, a whistling, and sand was kicked viciously before it. Fear-stricken, the dog turned and flurried like an animal in a pen. The man stood laughing, his weapons at his hips.

Ultimately the man was attracted by the closed door of the Weary Gentleman saloon. He went to it, and, hammering with a revolver, demanded drink.

The door remaining imperturbable, he picked a bit of paper from the walk, and nailed it to the framework with a knife. He then turned his back contemptuously upon this popular resort, and, walking to the opposite side of the street and spinning there on his heel quickly and lithely, fired at the bit of paper. He missed it by a half-inch. He swore at himself, and went away. Later, he comfortably fusiladed the windows of his most intimate friend. The man was playing with this town. It was a toy for him.

But still there was no offer of fight. The name of Jack Potter, his ancient antagonist, entered his mind, and he concluded that it would be a glad thing if he should go to Potter's house, and, by bombardment, induce him to come out and fight. He moved in the direction of his desire, chanting Apache scalp music.

When he arrived at it, Potter's house presented the same still, calm front as had the other adobes. Taking up a strategic position, the man howled a challenge. But this house regarded him as might a great stone god. It gave no sign. After a decent wait, the man howled further challenges, mingling with them wonderful epithets.

Presently there came the spectacle of a man churning himself into deepest rage over the immobility of a house. He fumed at it as the winter wind attacks a prairie cabin in the north. To the distance there should have gone the sound of a tumult like the fighting of two hundred Mexicans. As necessity bade him, he paused for breath or to reload his revolvers.

IV

Potter and his bride walked sheepishly and with speed. Sometimes they laughed together shamefacedly and low.

"Next corner, dear," he said finally.

They put forth the efforts of a pair walking bowed against a strong wind. Potter was about to raise a finger to point the first appearance of the new home, when, as they circled the corner, they came face to face with a man in a maroon-coloured shirt, who was feverishly pushing cartridges into a large revolver. Upon the instant the man dropped this revolver to the ground, and, like lightning, whipped another from its holster. The second weapon was aimed at the bridegroom's chest.

There was a silence. Potter's mouth seemed to be merely a grave for his tongue. He exhibited an instinct to at once loosen his arm from the woman's grip, and he dropped the bag to the sand. As for the bride, her face had gone as yellow as old cloth. She was a slave to hideous rites, gazing at the apparitional snake.

The two men faced each other at a distance of three paces. He of the revolver smiled with a new and quiet ferocity. "Tried to sneak up on me!" he said. "Tried to sneak up on me!" His eyes grew more baleful. As Potter made a slight movement, the man thrust his revolver venomously forward. "No; don't you do it, Jack Potter. Don't you move a finger towards a gun just yet. Don't you move an eyelash. The time has come for me to settle with you, and I'm going to do it my own way, and loaf along with no interferin'. So if you don't want a gun bent on you, just mind what I tell you."

Potter looked at his enemy. "I ain't got a gun on me, Scratchy," he said. "Honest, I ain't." He was stiffening and steadying, but yet somewhere at the back of his mind a vision of the Pullman floated—the sea-green figured velvet, the shining brass, silver, and glass, the wood that gleamed as darkly brilliant as the surface of a pool of oil—all the glory of their marriage, the environment of the new estate.

"You know I fight when it comes to fighting, Scratchy Wilson, but I ain't got a gun on me. You'll have to do all the shootin' yourself."

His enemy's face went livid. He stepped forward, and lashed his weapon to and fro before Potter's chest.

"Don't you tell me you ain't got no gun on you, you whelp. Don't tell me no lie like that. There ain't a man in Texas ever seen you without no gun. Don't take me for no kid."

His eyes blazed with light and his throat worked like a pump.

"I ain't takin' you for no kid," answered Potter. His heels had not moved an inch backward. "I'm takin' you for a damned fool. I tell you I ain't got a gun, and I ain't. If you're goin' to shoot me up, you'd better begin now. You'll never get a chance like this again."

So much enforced reasoning had told on Wilson's rage. He was calmer.

"If you ain't got a gun, why ain't you got a gun?" he sneered. "Been to Sunday school?"

"I ain't got a gun because I've just come from San Anton' with my wife. I'm married," said Potter. "And if I'd thought there was going to be any galoots like you prowling around when I brought my wife home, I'd had a gun, and don't you forget it."

"Married!" said Scratchy, not at all comprehending.

"Yes, married! I'm married," said Potter, distinctly.

"Married!" said Scratchy; seeming for the first time he saw the drooping drowning woman at the other man's side. "No!" he said. He was like a creature allowed a glimpse of another world. He moved a pace backward, and his arm with the revolver dropped to his side. "Is this—is this the lady?" he asked.

"Yes, this is the lady," answered Potter.

There was another period of silence.

"Well," said Wilson at last, slowly, "I s'pose it's all off now?"
"It's all off if you say so, Scratchy. You know I didn't make the trouble."
Potter lifted his valise.
"Well, I 'low it's off, Jack," said Wilson. He was looking at the ground. "Married!" He was not a student of chivalry; it was merely that in the presence of this foreign condition he was a simple child of the earlier plains. He picked up his starboard revolver, and placing both weapons in their holsters, he went away. His feet made funnel-shaped tracks in the heavy sand.

# THE WISE MEN

They were youths of subtle mind. They were very wicked according to report, and yet they managed to have it reflect great credit upon them. They often had the well-informed and the great talkers of the American colony engaged in reciting their misdeeds, and facts relating to their sins were usually told with a flourish of awe and fine admiration.

One was from San Francisco and one was from New York, but they resembled each other in appearance. This is an idiosyncrasy of geography.

They were never apart in the City of Mexico, at any rate, excepting perhaps when one had retired to his hotel for a respite, and then the other was usually camped down at the office sending up servants with clamorous messages. "Oh, get up and come on down."

They were two lads—they were called the kids—and far from their mothers. Occasionally some wise man pitied them, but he usually was alone in his wisdom. The other folk frankly were transfixed at the splendour of the audacity and endurance of these kids.

"When do those boys ever sleep?" murmured a man as he viewed them entering a café about eight o'clock one morning. Their smooth infantile faces looked bright and fresh enough, at any rate. "Jim told me he saw them still at it about 4.30 this morning."

"Sleep!" ejaculated a companion in a glowing voice. "They never sleep! They go to bed once in every two weeks." His boast of it seemed almost a personal pride.

"They'll end with a crash, though, if they keep it up at this pace," said a gloomy voice from behind a newspaper.

The Café Colorado has a front of white and gold, in which is set larger plate-glass windows than are commonly to be found in Mexico. Two little wings of willow flip-flapping incessantly serve as doors. Under them small stray dogs go furtively into the café, and are shied into the street again by the waiters. On the side-walk there is always a decorative effect of loungers, ranging from the newly-arrived and superior tourist to the old veteran of the silver mines bronzed by violent suns. They contemplate with various shades of interest the show of the street—the red, purple, dusty white, glaring forth against the walls in the furious sunshine.

One afternoon the kids strolled into the Café Colorado. A half-dozen of the men who sat smoking and reading with a sort of Parisian effect at the little tables which lined two sides of the room, looked up and bowed smiling, and although this coming of the kids was anything but an unusual event, at least a dozen men wheeled in their chairs to stare after them. Three waiters polished tables, and moved chairs noisily, and appeared to be eager. Distinctly these kids were of importance.

Behind the distant bar, the tall form of old Pop himself awaited them smiling with broad geniality. "Well, my boys, how are you?" he cried in a voice of profound solicitude. He allowed five or six of his customers to languish in the care of Mexican bartenders, while he himself gave his eloquent attention to the kids, lending all the dignity of a great event to their arrival. "How are the boys today, eh?"

"You're a smooth old guy," said one, eying him. "Are you giving us this welcome so we won't notice it when you push your worst whisky at us?"

Pop turned in appeal from one kid to the other kid. "There, now, hear that, will you?" He assumed an oratorical pose. "Why, my boys, you always get the best that this house has got."

"Yes, we do!" The kids laughed. "Well, bring it out, anyhow, and if it's the same you sold us last night, we'll grab your cash register and run."

Pop whirled a bottle along the bar and then gazed at it with a rapt expression. "Fine as silk," he murmured. "Now just taste that, and if it isn't the best whisky you ever put in your face, why I'm a liar, that's all."

The kids surveyed him with scorn, and poured their allowances. Then they stood for a time insulting Pop about his whisky. "Usually it tastes exactly like new parlour furniture," said the San Francisco kid. "Well, here goes, and you want to look out for your cash register."

"Your health, gentlemen," said Pop with a grand air, and as he wiped his bristling grey moustaches he wagged his head with reference to the cash register question. "I could catch you before you got very far."

"Why, are you a runner?" said one derisively.

"You just bank on me, my boy," said Pop, with deep emphasis. "I'm a flier."

The kids sat down their glasses suddenly and looked at him. "You must be," they said. Pop was tall and graceful and magnificent in manner, but he did not display those qualities of form which mean speed in the animal. His hair was grey; his face was round and fat from much living. The buttons of his glittering white waistcoat formed a fine curve, so that if the concave surface of a piece of barrel-hoop had been laid against Pop it would have touched every button. "You must be," observed the kids again.

"Well, you can laugh all you like, but—no jolly now, boys, I tell you I'm a winner. Why, I bet you I can skin anything in this town on a square go. When I kept my place in Eagle Pass there wasn't anybody who could touch me. One of these sure things came down from San Anton'. Oh, he was a runner he was. One of these people with wings. Well, I skinned 'im. What? Certainly I did. Never touched me."

The kids had been regarding him in grave silence, but at this moment they grinned, and said quite in chorus, "Oh, you old liar!"

Pop's voice took on a whining tone of earnestness. "Boys, I'm telling it to you straight. I'm a flier."

One of the kids had had a dreamy cloud in his eye and he cried out suddenly— "Say, what a joke to play this on Freddie."

The other jumped ecstatically. "Oh, wouldn't it though. Say he wouldn't do a thing but howl! He'd go crazy."

They looked at Pop as if they longed to be certain that he was, after all, a runner. "Now, Pop, on the level," said one of them wistfully, "can you run?"

"Boys," swore Pop, "I'm a peach! On the dead level, I'm a peach."

"By golly, I believe the old Indian can run," said one to the other, as if they were alone in confidence.

"That's what I can," cried Pop.

The kids said—"Well, so long, old man." They went to a table and sat down. They ordered a salad. They were always ordering salads. This was because one kid had a wild passion for salads, and the other didn't care. So at any hour of the day they might be seen ordering a salad. When this one came they went into a sort of executive session. It was a very long consultation. Men noted it. Occasionally the kids laughed in supreme enjoyment of something unknown. The low rumble of wheels came from the street. Often could be heard the parrot-like cries of distant vendors. The sunlight streamed through the green curtains, and made little amber-coloured flitterings on the marble floor. High up among the severe decorations of the ceiling—reminiscent of the days when the great building was a palace—a small white butterfly was wending through the cool air spaces. The long billiard hall led back to a vague gloom. The balls were always clicking, and one could see countless crooked elbows. Beggars slunk through the wicker doors, and were ejected by the nearest waiter. At last the kids called Pop to them.

"Sit down, Pop. Have a drink." They scanned him carefully. "Say now, Pop, on your solemn oath, can you run?"

"Boys," said Pop piously, and raising his hand, "I can run like a rabbit."

"On your oath?"

"On my oath."

"Can you beat Freddie?"

Pop appeared to look at the matter from all sides. "Well, boys, I'll tell you. No man is ever cock-sure of anything in this world, and I don't want to say that I can best any man, but I've seen Freddie run, and I'm ready to swear I can beat him. In a hundred yards I'd just about skin 'im neat—you understand, just about neat. Freddie is a good average runner, but I—you understand—I'm just—a little—bit—better." The kids had been listening with the utmost attention. Pop spoke the latter part slowly and meanfully. They thought he intended them to see his great confidence.

One said—"Pop, if you throw us in this thing, we'll come here and drink for two weeks without paying. We'll back you and work a josh on Freddie! But O!—if you throw us!"

To this menace Pop cried—"Boys, I'll make the run of my life! On my oath!"

The salad having vanished, the kids arose. "All right, now," they warned him. "If you play us for duffers, we'll get square. Don't you forget it."

"Boys, I'll give you a race for your money. Book on that. I may lose—understand, I may lose—no man can help meeting a better man. But I think I can skin him, and I'll give you a run for your money, you bet."

"All right, then. But, look here," they told him, "you keep your face closed. Nobody gets in on this but us. Understand?"

"Not a soul," Pop declared. They left him, gesturing a last warning from the wicker doors.

In the street they saw Benson, his cane gripped in the middle, strolling through the white-clothed jabbering natives on the shady side. They semaphored to him eagerly. He came across cautiously, like a man who ventures into dangerous company.

"We're going to get up a race. Pop and Fred. Pop swears he can skin 'im. This is a tip. Keep it dark. Say, won't Freddie be hot?"

Benson looked as if he had been compelled to endure these exhibitions of insanity for a century. "Oh, you fellows are off. Pop can't beat Freddie. He's an old bat. Why, it's impossible. Pop can't beat Freddie."

"Can't he? Want to bet he can't?" said the kids. "There now, let's see—you're talking so large."

"Well, you—"

"Oh, bet. Bet or else close your trap. That's the way."

"How do you know you can pull off the race? Seen Freddie?"

"No, but—"

"Well, see him then. Can't bet with no race arranged. I'll bet with you all right—all right. I'll give you fellows a tip though—you're a pair of asses. Pop can't run any faster than a brick school-house."

The kids scowled at him and defiantly said—"Can't he?" They left him and went to the Casa Verde. Freddie, beautiful in his white jacket, was holding one of his innumerable conversations across the bar. He smiled when he saw them. "Where you boys been?" he demanded, in a paternal tone. Almost all the proprietors of American cafés in the city used to adopt a paternal tone when they spoke to the kids.

"Oh, been 'round,'" they replied.

"Have a drink?" said the proprietor of the Casa Verde, forgetting his other social obligations. During the course of this ceremony one of the kids remarked—

"Freddie, Pop says he can beat you running."

"Does he?" observed Freddie without excitement. He was used to various snares of the kids.

"That's what. He says he can leave you at the wire and not see you again."

"Well, he lies," replied Freddie placidly.

"And I'll bet you a bottle of wine that he can do it, too."

"Rats!" said Freddie.

"Oh, that's all right," pursued a kid. "You can throw bluffs all you like, but he can lose you in a hundred yards' dash, you bet."

Freddie drank his whisky, and then settled his elbows on the bar.

"Say, now, what do you boys keep coming in here with some pipe-story all the time for? You can't josh me. Do you think you can scare me about Pop? Why, I know I can beat him. He can't run with me. Certainly not. Why, you fellows are just jollying me."

"Are we though!" said the kids. "You daren't bet the bottle of wine."

"Oh, of course I can bet you a bottle of wine," said Freddie disdainfully. "Nobody cares about a bottle of wine, but—"

"Well, make it five then," advised one of the kids.

Freddie hunched his shoulders. "Why, certainly I will. Make it ten if you like, but—"

"We do," they said.

"Ten, is it? All right; that goes." A look of weariness came over Freddie's face. "But you boys are foolish. I tell you Pop is an old man. How can you expect him to run? Of course, I'm no great runner, but then I'm young and healthy and—and a pretty smooth runner too. Pop is old and fat, and then he doesn't do a thing but tank all day. It's a cinch."

The kids looked at him and laughed rapturously. They waved their fingers at him. "Ah, there!" they cried. They meant that they had made a victim of him.

But Freddie continued to expostulate. "I tell you he couldn't win—an old man like him. You're crazy. Of course, I know you don't care about ten bottles of wine, but, then—to make such bets as that. You're twisted."

"Are we, though?" cried the kids in mockery. They had precipitated Freddie into a long and thoughtful treatise on every possible chance of the thing as he saw it. They disputed with him from time to time, and jeered at him. He laboured on through his argument. Their childish faces were bright with glee.

In the midst of it Wilburson entered. Wilburson worked; not too much, though. He had hold of the Mexican end of a great importing house of New York, and as he was a junior partner, he worked. But not too much, though. "What's the howl?" he said.

The kids giggled. "We've got Freddie rattled."

"Why," said Freddie, turning to him, "these two Indians are trying to tell me that Pop can beat me running."

"Like the devil," said Wilburson, incredulously.

"Well, can't he?" demanded a kid.

"Why, certainly not," said Wilburson, dismissing every possibility of it with a gesture. "That old bat? Certainly not. I'll bet fifty dollars that Freddie—"

"Take you," said a kid.

"What?" said Wilburson, "that Freddie won't beat Pop?"

The kid that had spoken now nodded his head.

"That Freddie won't beat Pop?" repeated Wilburson.

"Yes. It's a go?"

"Why, certainly," retorted Wilburson. "Fifty? All right."

"Bet you five bottles on the side," ventured the other kid.

"Why, certainly," exploded Wilburson wrathfully. "You fellows must take me for something easy. I'll take all those kinds of bets I can get. Cer—tain—ly."

They settled the details. The course was to be paced off on the asphalt of one of the adjacent side-streets, and then, at about eleven o'clock in the evening, the match would be run. Usually in Mexico the streets of a city grow lonely and dark but a little after nine o'clock. There are occasional lurking figures, perhaps, but no crowds, lights and noise. The course would doubtless be undisturbed. As for the policeman in the vicinity, they—well, they were conditionally amiable.

The kids went to see Pop; they told him of the arrangement, and then in deep tones they said, "Oh, Pop, if you throw us!"

Pop appeared to be a trifle shaken by the weight of responsibility thrust upon him, but he spoke out bravely. "Boys, I'll pinch that race. Now you watch me. I'll pinch it."

The kids went then on some business of their own, for they were not seen again till evening. When they returned to the neighbourhood of the Café Colorado the usual stream of carriages was whirling along the calle. The wheels hummed on the asphalt, and the coachmen towered in their great sombreros. On the sidewalk a gazing crowd sauntered, the better class self-satisfied and proud, in their Derby hats and cut-away coats, the lower classes muffling their dark faces in their blankets, slipping along in leather sandals. An electric light sputtered and fumed over the throng. The afternoon shower had left the pave wet and glittering. The air was still laden with the odour of rain on flowers, grass, leaves.

In the Café Colorado a cosmopolitan crowd ate, drank, played billiards, gossiped, or read in the glaring yellow light. When the kids entered a large circle of men that had been gesticulating near the bar greeted them with a roar.

"Here they are now!"

"Oh, you pair of peaches!"

"Say, got any more money to bet with?" Colonel Hammigan, grinning, pushed his way to them. "Say, boys, we'll all have a drink on you now because you won't have any money after eleven o'clock. You'll be going down the back stairs in your stocking feet."

Although the kids remained unnaturally serene and quiet, argument in the Café Colorado became tumultuous. Here and there a man who did not intend to bet ventured meekly that perchance Pop might win, and the others swarmed upon him in a whirlwind of angry denial and ridicule.

Pop, enthroned behind the bar, looked over at this storm with a shadow of anxiety upon his face. This widespread flouting affected him, but the kids looked blissfully satisfied with the tumult they had stirred.

Blanco, honest man, ever worrying for his friends, came to them. "Say, you fellows, you aren't betting too much? This thing looks kind of shaky, don't it?"

The faces of the kids grew sober, and after consideration one said—"No, I guess we've got a good thing, Blanco. Pop is going to surprise them, I think."

"Well, don't—"

"All right, old boy. We'll watch out."

From time to time the kids had much business with certain orange, red, blue, purple, and green bills. They were making little memoranda on the back of visiting cards. Pop watched them closely, the shadow still upon his face. Once he called to them, and when they came he leaned over the bar and said intensely—"Say, boys, remember, now—I might lose this race. Nobody can ever say for sure, and if I do, why—"

"Oh, that's all right, Pop," said the kids, reassuringly. "Don't mind it. Do your derndest, and let it go at that."

When they had left him, however, they went to a corner to consult. "Say, this is getting interesting. Are you in deep?" asked one anxiously of his friend.

"Yes, pretty deep," said the other stolidly. "Are you?"

"Deep as the devil," replied the other in the same tone.

They looked at each other stonily and went back to the crowd. Benson had just entered the café. He approached them with a gloating smile of victory. "Well, where's all that money you were going to bet?"

"Right here," said the kids, thrusting into their waistcoat pockets.

At eleven o'clock a curious thing was learned. When Pop and Freddie, the kids and all, came to the little side street, it was thick with people. It seemed that the news of this race had spread like the wind among the Americans, and they had come to witness the event. In the darkness the crowd moved, mumbling in argument.

The principals—the kids and those with them—surveyed this scene with some dismay. "Say—here's a go." Even then a policeman might be seen approaching, the light from his little lantern flickering on his white cap, gloves, brass buttons, and on the butt of the old-fashioned Colt's revolver which hung at his belt. He addressed Freddie in swift Mexican. Freddie listened, nodding from time to time. Finally Freddie turned to the others to translate. "He says he'll get into trouble if he allows this race when all this crowd is here."

There was a murmur of discontent. The policeman looked at them with an expression of anxiety on his broad, brown face.

"Oh, come on. We'll go hold it on some other fellow's beat," said one of the kids. The group moved slowly away debating. Suddenly the other kid cried, "I know! The Paseo!"

"By jiminy," said Freddie, "just the thing. We'll get a cab and go out to the Paseo. S-s-h! Keep it quiet; we don't want all this mob."

Later they tumbled into a cab—Pop, Freddie, the kids, old Colonel Hammigan and Benson. They whispered to the men who had wagered, "The Paseo." The cab whirled away up the black street. There were occasional grunts and groans, cries of "Oh, get off me feet," and of "Quit! you're killing me." Six people do not have fun in one cab. The principals spoke to each other with the respect and friendliness which comes to good men at such times. Once a kid put his head out of the window and looked backward. He pulled it in again and cried, "Great Scott! Look at that, would you!"

The others struggled to do as they were bid, and afterwards shouted, "Holy smoke! Well, I'll be blowed! Thunder and turf!"

Galloping after them came innumerable cabs, their lights twinkling, streaming in a great procession through the night.

"The street is full of them," ejaculated the old colonel.

The Paseo de la Reforma is the famous drive of the city of Mexico, leading to the Castle of Chapultepec, which last ought to be well known in the United States.

It is a fine broad avenue of macadam with a much greater quality of dignity than anything of the kind we possess in our own land. It seems of the old world, where to the beauty of the thing itself is added the solemnity of tradition and history, the knowledge that feet in buskins trod the same stones, that cavalcades of steel thundered there before the coming of carriages.

When the Americans tumbled out of their cabs the giant bronzes of Aztec and Spaniard loomed dimly above them like towers. The four roads of poplar trees rustled weirdly off there in the darkness. Pop took out his watch and struck a match. "Well, hurry up this thing. It's almost midnight."

The other cabs came swarming, the drivers lashing their horses, for these Americans, who did all manner of strange things, nevertheless always paid well for it. There was a mighty hubbub then in the darkness. Five or six men began to pace the distance and quarrel. Others knotted their handkerchiefs together to make a tape. Men were swearing over bets, fussing and fuming about the odds. Benson came to the kids swaggering. "You're a pair of asses." The cabs waited in a solid block down the avenue. Above the crowd the tall statues hid their visages in the night.

At last a voice floated through the darkness. "Are you ready there?" Everybody yelled excitedly. The men at the tape pulled it out straight. "Hold it higher, Jim, you fool," and silence fell then upon the throng. Men bended down trying to pierce the deep gloom with their eyes. From out at the starting point came muffled voices. The crowd swayed and jostled.

The racers did not come. The crowd began to fret, its nerves burning. "Oh, hurry up," shrilled some one.

The voice called again—"Ready there?"

Everybody replied—"Yes, all ready. Hurry up!"

There was a more muffled discussion at the starting point. In the crowd a man began to make a proposition. "I'll bet twenty—" but the crowd interrupted with a howl. "Here they come!" The thickly-packed body of men swung as if the ground had moved. The men at the tape shouldered madly at their fellows, bawling, "Keep back! Keep back!"

From the distance came the noise of feet pattering furiously. Vague forms flashed into view for an instant. A hoarse roar broke from the crowd. Menbended and swayed and fought. The kids back near the tape exchanged another stolid look. A white form shone forth. It grew like a spectre. Always could be heard the wild patter. A scream broke from the crowd. "By Gawd, it's Pop! Pop! Pop's ahead!"

The old man spun towards the tape like a madman, his chin thrown back, his grey hair flying. His legs moved like oiled machinery. And as he shot forward a howl as from forty cages of wild animals went toward the imperturbable chieftains in bronze. The crowd flung themselves forward. "Oh, you old Indian! You savage! Did anybody ever see such running?"

"Ain't he a peach! Well!"

"Where's the kids? H-e-y, kids!"

"Look at him, would you? Did you ever think?" These cries flew in the air blended in a vast shout of astonishment and laughter.

For an instant the whole tragedy was in view. Freddie, desperate, his teeth shining, his face contorted, whirling along in deadly effort, was twenty feet behind the tall form of old Pop, who, dressed only in his—only in his underclothes—gained with each stride. One grand insane moment, and then Pop had hurled himself against the tape—victor!

Freddie, fallen into the arms of some men, struggled with his breath, and at last managed to stammer—

"Say, can't—can't—that old—old—man run!"

Pop, puffing and heaving, could only gasp—"Where's my shoes? Who's got my shoes?"

Later Freddie scrambled panting through the crowd, and held out his hand. "Good man, Pop!" And then he looked up and down the tall, stout form. "Hell! who would think you could run like that?"

The kids were surrounded by a crowd, laughing tempestuously.

"How did you know he could run?"

"Why didn't you give me a line on him?"

"Say—great snakes!—you fellows had a nerve to bet on Pop."

"Why, I was cock-sure he couldn't win."

"Oh, you fellows must have seen him run before."

"Who would ever think it?"

Benson came by, filling the midnight air with curses. They turned to jibe him.

"What's the matter, Benson?"

"Somebody pinched my handkerchief. I tied it up in that string. Damn it."

The kids laughed blithely. "Why, hello! Benson," they said.

There was a great rush for cabs. Shouting, laughing, wondering, the crowd hustled into their conveyances, and the drivers flogged their horses toward the city again.

"Won't Freddie be crazy! Say, he'll be guyed about this for years."

"But who would ever think that old tank could run so?"

One cab had to wait while Pop and Freddie resumed various parts of their clothing.

As they drove home, Freddie said—"Well, Pop, you beat me."

Pop said—"That's all right, old man."

The kids, grinning, said—"How much did you lose, Benson?"

Benson said defiantly—"Oh, not so much. How much did you win?"

"Oh, not so much."

Old Colonel Hammigan, squeezed down in a corner, had apparently been reviewing the event in his mind, for he suddenly remarked, "Well, I'm damned!"

They were late in reaching the Café Colorado, but when they did, the bottles were on the bar as thick as pickets on a fence.

# THE FIVE WHITE MICE

Freddie was mixing a cock-tail. His hand with the long spoon was whirling swiftly, and the ice in the glass hummed and rattled like a cheap watch. Over by the window, a gambler, a millionaire, a railway conductor, and the agent of a vast American syndicate were playing seven-up. Freddie surveyed them with the ironical glance of a man who is mixing a cock-tail.

From time to time a swarthy Mexican waiter came with his tray from the rooms at the rear, and called his orders across the bar. The sounds of the indolent stir of the city, awakening from its siesta, floated over the screens which barred the sun and the inquisitive eye. From the far-away kitchen could be heard the roar of the old French *chef*, driving, herding, and abusing his Mexican helpers.

A string of men came suddenly in from the street. They stormed up to the bar. There were impatient shouts. "Come now, Freddie, don't stand there like a portrait of yourself. Wiggle!" Drinks of many kinds and colours, amber, green, mahogany, strong and mild, began to swarm upon the bar with all the attendants of lemon, sugar, mint and ice. Freddie,with Mexican support, worked like a sailor in the provision of them, sometimes talking with that scorn for drink and admiration for those who drink which is the attribute of a good bar-keeper.

At last a man was afflicted with a stroke of dice-shaking. A herculean discussion was waging, and he was deeply engaged in it, but at the same time he lazily flirted the dice. Occasionally he made great combinations. "Look at that, would you?" he cried proudly. The others paid little heed. Then violently the craving took them. It went along the line like an epidemic, and involved them all. In a moment they had arranged a carnival of dice-shaking with money penalties and liquid prizes. They clamorously made it a point of honour with Freddie that he should play and take his chance of sometimes providing this large group with free refreshment. With bended heads like football players, they surged over the tinkling dice, jostling, cheering, and bitterly arguing. One of the quiet company playing seven-up at the corner table said profanely that the row reminded him of a bowling contest at a picnic.

After the regular shower, many carriages rolled over the smooth calle, and sent a musical thunder through the Casa Verde. The shop-windows became aglow with light, and the walks were crowded with youths, callow and ogling, dressed vainly according to superstitious fashions. The policemen had muffled themselves in their gnome-like cloaks, and placed their lanterns as obstacles for the carriages in the middle of the street. The city of Mexico gave forth the deep organ-mellow tones of its evening resurrection.

But still the group at the bar of the Casa Verde were shaking dice. They had passed beyond shaking for drinks for the crowd, for Mexican dollars, for dinners, for the wine at dinner. They had even gone to the trouble of separating the cigars and cigarettes from the dinner's bill, and causing a distinct man to be responsible for them. Finally they were aghast. Nothing remained in sight of their minds which even remotely suggested further gambling. There was a pause for deep consideration.

"Well—"

"Well—"

A man called out in the exuberance of creation. "I know! Let's shake for a box tonight at the circus! A box at the circus!" The group was profoundly edified. "That's it! That's it! Come on now! Box at the circus!" A dominating voice cried—"Three dashes—high man out!" An American, tall, and with a face of copper red from the rays that flash among the Sierra Madres and burn on the cactus deserts, took the little leathern cup and spun the dice out upon the polished wood. A fascinated assemblage hung upon the bar-rail. Three kings turned their pink faces upward. The tall man flourished the cup, burlesquing, and flung the two other dice. From them he ultimately extracted one more pink king. "There," he said. "Now, let's see! Four kings!" He began to swagger in a sort of provisional way.

The next man took the cup, and blew softly in the top of it. Poising it in his hand, he then surveyed the company with a stony eye and paused. They knew perfectly well that he was applying the magic of deliberation and ostentatious indifference, but they could not wait in tranquillity during the performance of all these rites. They began to call out impatiently. "Come now—hurry up." At last the man, with a gesture that was singularly impressive, threw the dice. The others set up a howl of joy. "Not a pair!" There was another solemn pause. The men moved restlessly. "Come, now, go ahead!" In the end, the man, induced and abused, achieved something that was nothing in the presence of four kings. The tall man climbed on the foot-rail and leaned hazardously forward. "Four kings! My four kings are good to go out," he bellowed into the middle of the mob, and although in a moment he did pass into the radiant region of exemption, he continued to bawl advice and scorn.

The mirrors and oiled woods of the Casa Verde were now dancing with blue flashes from a great buzzing electric lamp. A host of quiet members of the Anglo-Saxon colony had come in for their pre-dinner cock-tails. An amiable person was exhibiting to some tourists this popular American saloon. It was a very sober and respectable time of day. Freddie reproved courageously the dice-shaking brawlers, and, in return, he received the choicest advice in a tumult of seven combined vocabularies. He laughed; he had been compelled to retire from the game, but he was keeping an interested, if furtive, eye upon it.

Down at the end of the line there was a youth at whom everybody railed for his flaming ill-luck. At each disaster, Freddie swore from behind the bar in a sort of affectionate contempt. "Why, this kid has had no luck for two days. Did you ever see such throwin'?"

The contest narrowed eventually to the New York kid and an individual who swung about placidly on legs that moved in nefarious circles. He had a grin that resembled a bit of carving. He was obliged to lean down and blink rapidly to ascertain the facts of his venture, but fate presented him with five queens. His smile did not change, but he puffed gently like a man who has been running.

The others, having emerged unscathed from this part of the conflict, waxed hilarious with the kid. They smote him on either shoulders. "We've got you stuck for it, kid! You can't beat that game! Five queens!"

Up to this time the kid had displayed only the temper of the gambler, but the cheerful hoots of the players, supplemented now by a ring of guying non-combatants, caused him to feel profoundly that it would be fine to beat the five queens. He addressed a gambler's slogan to the interior of the cup.

> *"Oh, five white mice of chance,*
> *Shirts of wool and corduroy pants,*
> *Gold and wine, women and sin,*
> *All for you if you let me come in—*
> *Into the house of chance."*

Flashing the dice sardonically out upon the bar, he displayed three aces. From two dice in the next throw he achieved one more ace. For his last throw, he rattled the single dice for a long time. He already had four aces; if he accomplished another one, the five queens were vanquished and the box at the circus came from the drunken man's pocket. All the kid's movements were slow and elaborate. For the last throw he planted the cup bottom-down on the bar with the one dice hidden under it. Then he turned and faced the crowd with the air of a conjuror or a cheat.

"Oh, maybe it's an ace," he said in boastful calm. "Maybe it's an ace."

Instantly he was presiding over a little drama in which every man was absorbed. The kid leaned with his back against the bar-rail and with his elbows upon it.

"Maybe it's an ace," he repeated.

A jeering voice in the background said—"Yes, maybe it is, kid!"

The kid's eyes searched for a moment among the men. "I'll bet fifty dollars it is an ace," he said.

Another voice asked—"American money?"

"Yes," answered the kid.

"Oh!" There was a genial laugh at this discomfiture. However, no one came forward at the kid's challenge, and presently he turned to the cup. "Now, I'll show you." With the manner of a mayor unveiling a statue, he lifted the cup. There was revealed naught but a ten-spot. In the roar which arose could be heard each man ridiculing the cowardice of his neighbour, and above all the din rang the voice of Freddie be-rating every one. "Why, there isn't one liver to every five men in the outfit. That was the greatest cold bluff I ever saw worked. He wouldn't know how to cheat with dice if he wanted to. Don't know the first thing about it. I could hardly keep from laughin' when I seen him drillin' you around. Why, I tell you, I had that fifty dollars right in my pocket if I wanted to be a chump. You're an easy lot—"

Nevertheless the group who had won in the theatre-box game did not relinquish their triumph. They burst like a storm about the head of the kid, swinging at him with their fists. "'Five white mice'!" they quoted, choking. "'Five white mice'!"

"Oh, they are not so bad," said the kid.

Afterward it often occurred that a man would jeer a finger at the kid and derisively say—"'Five white mice.'"

On the route from the dinner to the circus, others of the party often asked the kid if he had really intended to make his appeal to mice. They suggested other animals—rabbits, dogs, hedgehogs, snakes, opossums. To this banter the kid replied with a serious expression of his belief in the fidelity and wisdom of the five white mice. He presented a most eloquent case, decorated with fine language and insults, in which he proved that if one was going to believe in anything at all, one might as well choose the five white mice. His companions, however, at once and unanimously pointed out to him that his recent exploit did not place him in the light of a convincing advocate.

The kid discerned two figures in the street. They were making imperious signs at him. He waited for them to approach, for he recognized one as the other kid—the Frisco kid: there were two kids. With the Frisco kid was Benson. They arrived almost breathless. "Where you been?" cried the Frisco kid. It was an arrangement that upon a meeting the one that could first ask this question was entitled to use a tone of limitless injury. "What you been doing? Where you going? Come on with us. Benson and I have got a little scheme."

The New York kid pulled his arm from the grapple of the other. "I can't. I've got to take these sutlers to the circus. They stuck me for it shaking dice at Freddie's. I can't, I tell you."

The two did not at first attend to his remarks. "Come on! We've got a little scheme."

"I can't. They stuck me. I've got to take'm to the circus."

At this time it did not suit the men with the scheme to recognize these objections as important. "Oh, take'm some other time. Well, can't you take'm some other time? Let 'em go. Damn the circus. Get cold feet. What did you get stuck for? Get cold feet."

But despite their fighting, the New York kid broke away from them. "I can't, I tell you. They stuck me." As he left them, they yelled with rage. "Well, meet us, now, do you hear? In the Casa Verde as soon as the circus quits! Hear?" They threw maledictions after him.

In the city of Mexico, a man goes to the circus without descending in any way to infant amusements, because the Circo Teatro Orrin is one of the best in the world, and too easily surpasses anything of the kind in the United States, where it is merely a matter of a number of rings, if possible, and a great professional agreement to lie to the public. Moreover, the American clown, who in the Mexican arena prances and gabbles, is the clown to whom writers refer as the delight of their childhood, and lament that he is dead. At this circus the kid was not debased by the sight of mournful prisoner elephants and caged animals forlorn and sickly. He sat in his box until late, and laughed and swore when past laughing at the comic foolish-wise clown.

When he returned to the Casa Verde there was no display of the Frisco kid and Benson. Freddie was leaning on the bar listening to four men terribly discuss a question that was not plain. There was a card-game in the corner, of course. Sounds of revelry pealed from the rear rooms.

When the kid asked Freddie if he had seen his friend and Benson, Freddie looked bored. "Oh, yes, they were in here just a minute ago, but I don't know where they went. They've got their skates on. Where've they been? Came in here rolling across the floor like two little gilt gods. They wobbled around for a time, and then Frisco wanted me to send six bottles of wine around to Benson's rooms, but I didn't have anybody to send this time of night, and so they got mad and went out. Where did they get their loads?"

In the first deep gloom of the street the kid paused a moment debating. But presently he heard quavering voices. "Oh, kid! kid! Com'ere!" Peering, he recognized two vague figures against the opposite wall. He crossed the street, and they said— "Hello-kid."

"Say, where did you get it?" he demanded sternly. "You Indians better go home. What did you want to get scragged for?" His face was luminous with virtue.

As they swung to and fro, they made angry denials. "We ain' load'! We ain' load'. Big chump. Comonangetadrink."

The sober youth turned then to his friend. "Hadn't you better go home, kid? Come on, it's late. You'd better break away."

The Frisco kid wagged his head decisively. "Got take Benson home first. He'll be wallowing around in a minute. Don't mind me. I'm all right."

"Cerly, he's all right," said Benson, arousing from deep thought. "He's all right. But better take'm home, though. That's ri—right. He's load'. But he's all right. No need go home any more'n you. But better take'm home. He's load'." He looked at his companion with compassion. "Kid, you're load'."

The sober kid spoke abruptly to his friend from San Francisco. "Kid, pull yourself together, now. Don't fool. We've got to brace this ass of a Benson all the way home. Get hold of his other arm."

The Frisco kid immediately obeyed his comrade without a word or a glower. He seized Benson and came to attention like a soldier. Later, indeed, he meekly ventured—"Can't we take cab?" But when the New York kid snapped out that there were no convenient cabs he subsided to an impassive silence. He seemed to be reflecting upon his state, without astonishment, dismay, or any particular emotion. He submitted himself woodenly to the direction of his friend.

Benson had protested when they had grasped his arms. "Washa doing?" he said in a new and guttural voice. "Washa doing? I ain' load'. Comonangetadrink. I—"

"Oh, come along, you idiot," said the New York kid. The Frisco kid merely presented the mien of a stoic to the appeal of Benson, and in silence dragged away at one of his arms. Benson's feet came from that particular spot on the pavement with the reluctance of roots and also with the ultimate suddenness of roots. The three of them lurched out into the street in the abandon of tumbling chimneys. Benson was meanwhile noisily challenging the others to produce any reasons for his being taken home. His toes clashed into the kerb when they reached the other side of the calle, and for a moment the kids hauled him along with the points of his shoes scraping musically on the pavement. He balked formidably as they were about to pass the Casa Verde. "No! No! Leshavanothdrink! Anothdrink! Onemore!"

But the Frisco kid obeyed the voice of his partner in a manner that was blind but absolute, and they scummed Benson on past the door. Locked together the three swung into a dark street. The sober kid's flank was continually careering ahead of the other wing. He harshly admonished the Frisco child, and the latter promptly improved in the same manner of unthinking complete obedience. Benson began to recite the tale of a love affair, a tale that didn't even have a middle. Occasionally the New York kidswore. They toppled on their way like three comedians playing at it on the stage.

At midnight a little Mexican street burrowing among the walls of the city is as dark as a whale's throat at deep sea. Upon this occasion heavy clouds hung over the capital and the sky was a pall. The projecting balconies could make no shadows.

"Shay," said Benson, breaking away from his escort suddenly, "what want gome for? I ain't load'. You got reg'lar spool-fact'ry in your head—you N' York kid there. Thish oth' kid, he's mos' proper shober, mos' proper shober. He's drunk, but—but he's shober."

"Ah, shup up, Benson," said the New York kid. "Come along now. We can't stay here all night." Benson refused to be corralled, but spread his legs and twirled like a dervish, meanwhile under the evident impression that he was conducting himself most handsomely. It was not long before he gained the opinion that he was laughing at the others. "Eight purple dogsh—dogs! Eight purple dogs. Thas what kid'll see in the morn'. Look ou' for 'em. They—"

As Benson, describing the canine phenomena, swung wildly across the sidewalk, it chanced that three other pedestrians were passing in shadowy rank. Benson's shoulder jostled one of them.

A Mexican wheeled upon the instant. His hand flashed to his hip. There was a moment of silence, during which Benson's voice was not heard raised in apology. Then an indescribable comment, one burning word, came from between the Mexican's teeth.

Benson, rolling about in a semi-detached manner, stared vacantly at the Mexican, who thrust his lean face forward while his fingers played nervously at his hip. The New York kid could not follow Spanish well, but he understood when the Mexican breathed softly: "Does the señor want to fight?"

Benson simply gazed in gentle surprise. The woman next to him at dinner had said something inventive. His tailor had presented his bill. Something had occurred which was mildly out of the ordinary, and his surcharged brain refused to cope with it. He displayed only the agitation of a smoker temporarily without a light.

The New York kid had almost instantly grasped Benson's arm, and was about to jerk him away, when the other kid, who up to this time had been an automaton, suddenly projected himself forward, thrust the rubber Benson aside, and said—"Yes."

There was no sound nor light in the world. The wall at the left happened to be of the common prison-like construction—no door, no window, no opening at all. Humanity was enclosed and asleep. Into the mouth of the sober kid came a wretched bitter taste as if it had filled with blood. He was transfixed as if he was already seeing the lightning ripples on the knife-blade.

But the Mexican's hand did not move at that time. His face went still further forward and he whispered—"So?" The sober kid saw this face as if he and it were alone in space—a yellow mask smiling in eager cruelty, in satisfaction, and above all it was lit with sinister decision. As for the features, they were reminiscent of an unplaced, a forgotten type, which really resembled with precision those of a man who had shaved him three times in Boston in 1888. But the expression burned his mind as sealing-wax burns the palm, and fascinated, stupefied, he actually watched the progress of the man's thought toward the point where a knife would be wrenched from its sheath. The emotion, a sort of mechanical fury, a breeze made by electric fans, a rage made by vanity, smote the dark countenance in wave after wave.

Then the New York kid took a sudden step forward. His hand was at his hip. He was gripping there a revolver of robust size. He recalled that upon its black handle was stamped a hunting scene in which a sportsman in fine leggings and a peaked cap was taking aim at a stag less than one-eighth of an inch away.

His pace forward caused instant movement of the Mexicans. One immediately took two steps to face him squarely. There was a general adjustment, pair and pair. This opponent of the New York kid was a tall man and quite stout. His sombrero was drawn low over his eyes. His serape was flung on his left shoulder. His back was bended in the supposed manner of a Spanish grandee. This concave gentleman cut a fine and terrible figure. The lad, moved by the spirits of his modest and perpendicular ancestors, had time to feel his blood roar at sight of the pose.

He was aware that the third Mexican was over on the left fronting Benson, and he was aware that Benson was leaning against the wall sleepily and peacefully eying the convention. So it happened that these six men stood, side fronting side, five of them with their right hands at their hips and with their bodies lifted nervously, while the central pair exchanged a crescendo of provocations. The meaning of their words rose and rose. They were travelling in a straight line toward collision.

The New York kid contemplated his Spanish grandee. He drew his revolver upward until the hammer was surely free of the holster. He waited immovable and watchful while the garrulous Frisco kid expended two and a half lexicons on the middle Mexican.

The eastern lad suddenly decided that he was going to be killed. His mind leaped forward and studied the aftermath. The story would be a marvel of brevity when first it reached the far New York home, written in a careful hand on a bit of cheap paper, topped and footed and backed by the printed fortifications of the cable company. But they are often as stones flung into mirrors, these bits of paper upon which are laconically written all the most terrible chronicles of the times. He witnessed the uprising of his mother and sister, and the invincible calm of his hard-mouthed old father, who would probably shut himself in his library and smoke alone. Then his father would come, and they would bring him here and say—"This is the place." Then, very likely, each would remove his hat. They would stand quietly with their hats in their hands for a decent minute. He pitied his old financing father, unyielding and millioned, a man who commonly spoke twenty-two words a year to his beloved son. The kid understood it at this time. If his fate was not impregnable, he might have turned out to be a man and have been liked by his father.

The other kid would mourn his death. He would be preternaturally correct for some weeks, and recite the tale without swearing. But it would not bore him. For the sake of his dead comrade he would be glad to be preternaturally correct, and to recite the tale without swearing.

These views were perfectly stereopticon, flashing in and away from his thought with an inconceivable rapidity until after all they were simply one quick dismal impression. And now here is the unreal real: into this kid's nostrils, at the expectant moment of slaughter, had come the scent of new-mown hay, a fragrance from a field of prostrate grass, a fragrance which contained the sunshine, the bees, the peace of meadows, and the wonder of a distant crooning stream. It had no right to be supreme, but it was supreme, and he breathed it as he waited for pain and a sight of the unknown.

But in the same instant, it may be, his thought flew to the Frisco kid, and it came upon him like a flicker of lightning that the Frisco kid was not going to be there to perform, for instance, the extraordinary office of respectable mourner. The other kid's head was muddled, his hand was unsteady, his agility was gone. This other kid was facing the determined and most ferocious gentleman of the enemy. The New York kid became convinced that his friend was lost. There was going to be a screaming murder. He was so certain of it that he wanted to shield his eyes fromsight of the leaping arm and the knife. It was sickening, utterly sickening. The New York kid might have been taking his first sea-voyage. A combination of honourable manhood and inability prevented him from running away.

He suddenly knew that it was possible to draw his own revolver, and by a swift manoeuvre face down all three Mexicans. If he was quick enough he would probably be victor. If any hitch occurred in the draw he would undoubtedly be dead with his friends. It was a new game; he had never been obliged to face a situation of this kind in the Beacon Club in New York. In this test, the lungs of the kid still continued to perform their duty.

> *"Oh, five white mice of chance,*
> *Shirts of wool and corduroy pants,*
> *Gold and wine, women and sin,*
> *All for you if you let me come in—*
> *Into the house of chance."*

He thought of the weight and size of his revolver, and dismay pierced him. He feared that in his hands it would be as unwieldy as a sewing-machine for this quick work. He imagined, too, that some singular providence might cause him to lose his grip as he raised his weapon. Or it might get fatally entangled in the tails of his coat. Some of the eels of despair lay wet and cold against his back.

But at the supreme moment the revolver came forth as if it were greased and it arose like a feather. This somnolent machine, after months of repose, was finally looking at the breasts of men.

Perhaps in this one series of movements, the kid had unconsciously used nervous force sufficient to raise a bale of hay. Before he comprehended it he was standing behind his revolver glaring over the barrel at the Mexicans, menacing first one and then another. His finger was tremoring on the trigger. The revolver gleamed in the darkness with a fine silver light.

The fulsome grandee sprang backward with a low cry. The man who had been facing the Frisco kid took a quick step away. The beautiful array of Mexicans was suddenly disorganized.

The cry and the backward steps revealed something of great importance to the New York kid. He had never dreamed that he did not have a complete monopoly of all possible trepidations. The cry of the grandee was that of a man who suddenly sees a poisonous snake. Thus the kid was able to understand swiftly that they were all human beings. They were unanimous in not wishing for too bloody combat. There was a sudden expression of the equality. He had vaguely believed that they were not going to evince much consideration for his dramatic development as an active factor. They even might be exasperated into an onslaught by it. Instead, they had respected his movement with a respect as great even as an ejaculation of fear and backward steps. Upon the instant he pounced forward and began to swear, unreeling great English oaths as thick as ropes, and lashing the faces of the Mexicans with them. He was bursting with rage, because these men had not previously confided to him that they were vulnerable. The whole thing had been an absurd imposition. Hehad been seduced into respectful alarm by the concave attitude of the grandee. And after all there had been an equality of emotion, an equality: he was furious. He wanted to take the serape of the grandee and swaddle him in it.

The Mexicans slunk back, their eyes burning wistfully. The kid took aim first at one and then at another. After they had achieved a certain distance they paused and drew up in a rank. They then resumed some of their old splendour of manner. A voice hailed him in a tone of cynical bravado as if it had come from between lips of smiling mockery. "Well, señor, it is finished?"

The kid scowled into the darkness, his revolver drooping at his side. After a moment he answered—"I am willing." He found it strange that he should be able to speak after this silence of years.

"Good-night, señor."

"Good-night."

When he turned to look at the Frisco kid he found him in his original position, his hand upon his hip. He was blinking in perplexity at the point from whence the Mexicans had vanished.

"Well," said the sober kid crossly, "are you ready to go home now?"

The Frisco kid said—"Where they gone?" His voice was undisturbed but inquisitive.

Benson suddenly propelled himself from his dreamful position against the wall. "Frishco kid's all right. He's drunk's fool and he's all right. But you New York kid, you're shober." He passed into a state of profound investigation. "Kid shober 'cause didn't go with us. Didn't go with us 'cause went to damn circus. Went to damn circus 'cause lose shakin' dice. Lose shakin' dice 'cause—what make lose shakin' dice, kid?"

The New York kid eyed the senile youth. "I don't know. The five white mice, maybe."

Benson puzzled so over this reply that he had to be held erect by his friends. Finally the Frisco kid said—"Let's go home."

Nothing had happened.

# FLANAGAN AND HIS SHORT FILIBUSTERING ADVENTURE

## I

"I have got twenty men at me back who will fight to the death," said the warrior to the old filibuster.

"And they can be blowed for all me," replied the old filibuster. "Common as sparrows. Cheap as cigarettes. Show me twenty men with steel clamps on their mouths, with holes in their heads where memory ought to be, and I want 'em. But twenty brave men merely? I'd rather have twenty brave onions."

Thereupon the warrior removed sadly, feeling that no salaams were paid to valour in these days of mechanical excellence.

Valour, in truth, is no bad thing to have when filibustering; but many medals are to be won by the man who knows not the meaning of "pow-wow," before or afterwards. Twenty brave men with tongues hung lightly may make trouble rise from the ground like smoke from grass, because of their subsequent fiery pride; whereas twenty cow-eyed villains who accept unrighteous and far-compelling kicks as they do the rain from heaven may halo the ultimate history of an expedition with gold, and plentifully bedeck their names, winning forty years of gratitude from patriots, simply by remaining silent. As for the cause, it may be only that they have no friends or other credulous furniture.

If it were not for the curse of the swinging tongue, it is surely to be said that the filibustering industry, flourishing now in the United States, would be pie. Under correct conditions, it is merely a matter of dealing with some little detectives whose skill at search is rated by those who pay them at a value of twelve or twenty dollars each week. It is nearly axiomatic that normally a twelve dollar per week detective cannot defeat a one hundred thousand dollar filibustering excursion. Against the criminal, the detective represents the commonwealth, but in this other case he represents his desire to show cause why his salary should be paid. He represents himself merely, and he counts no more than a grocer's clerk.

But the pride of the successful filibuster often smites him and his cause like an axe, and men who have not confided in their mothers go prone with him. It can make the dome of the Capitol tremble and incite the Senators to over-turning benches. It can increase the salaries of detectives who could not detect the location of a pain in the chest. It is a wonderful thing, this pride.

Filibustering was once such a simple game. It was managed blandly by gentle captains and smooth and undisturbed gentlemen, who at other times dealt inlaw, soap, medicine, and bananas. It was a great pity that the little cote of doves in Washington were obliged to rustle officially, and naval men were kept from their berths at night, and sundry Custom House people got wiggings, all because the returned adventurer pow-wowed in his pride. A yellow and red banner would have been long since smothered in a shame of defeat if a contract to filibuster had been let to some admirable organization like one of our trusts.

And yet the game is not obsolete. It is still played by the wise and the silent men whose names are not display-typed and blathered from one end of the country to the other.

There is in mind now a man who knew one side of a fence from the other side when he looked sharply. They were hunting for captains then to command the first vessels of what has since become a famous little fleet. One was recommended to this man, and he said, "Send him down to my office and I'll look him over." He was an attorney, and he liked to lean back in his chair, twirl a paper-knife, and let the other fellow talk.

The sea-faring man came and stood and appeared confounded. The attorney asked the terrible first question of the filibuster to the applicant. He said, "Why do you want to go?"

The captain reflected, changed his attitude three times, and decided ultimately that he didn't know. He seemed greatly ashamed. The attorney, looking at him, saw that he had eyes that resembled a lambkin's eyes.

"Glory?" said the attorney at last.

"No-o," said the captain.

"Pay?"

"No-o. Not that so much."

"Think they'll give you a land grant when they win out?"

"No; never thought."

"No glory; no immense pay; no land grant. What are you going for, then?"

"Well, I don't know," said the captain, with his glance on the floor and shifting his position again. "I don't know. I guess it's just for fun mostly." The attorney asked him out to have a drink.

When he stood on the bridge of his out-going steamer, the attorney saw him again. His shore meekness and uncertainty were gone. He was clear-eyed and strong, aroused like a mastiff at night. He took his cigar out of his mouth and yelled some sudden language at the deck.

This steamer had about her a quality of unholy mediæval disrepair, which is usually accounted the principal prerogative of the United States Revenue Marine. There is many a seaworthy ice-house if she were a good ship. She swashed through the seas as genially as an old wooden clock, burying her head under waves that came only like children at play, and, on board, it cost a ducking to go from anywhere to anywhere.

The captain had commanded vessels that shore-people thought were liners; but when a man gets the ant of desire-to-see-what-it's-like stirring in his heart, he will wallow out to sea in a pail. The thing surpasses a man's love for his sweetheart. The great tank-steamer *Thunder-Voice* had long been Flanagan's sweetheart, but he was far happier off Hatteras watching this wretched little portmanteau boom down the slant of a wave.

The crew scraped acquaintance one with another gradually. Each man came ultimately to ask his neighbour what particular turn of ill-fortune or inherited deviltry caused him to try this voyage. When one frank, bold man saw another frank, bold man aboard, he smiled, and they became friends. There was not a mind on board the ship that was not fastened to the dangers of the coast of Cuba, and taking wonder at this prospect and delight in it. Still, in jovial moments they termed each other accursed idiots.

At first there was some trouble in the engine-room, where there were many steel animals, for the most part painted red and in other places very shiny—bewildering, complex, incomprehensible to any one who don't care, usually thumping, thumping, thumping with the monotony of a snore.

It seems that this engine was as whimsical as a gas-meter. The chief engineer was a fine old fellow with a grey moustache, but the engine told him that it didn't intend to budge until it felt better. He came to the bridge and said, "The blamed old thing has laid down on us, sir."

"Who was on duty?" roared the captain.

"The second, sir."

"Why didn't he call you?"

"Don't know, sir." Later the stokers had occasion to thank the stars that they were not second engineers.

The *Foundling* was soundly thrashed by the waves for loitering while the captain and the engineers fought the obstinate machinery. During this wait on the sea, the first gloom came to the faces of the company. The ocean is wide, and a ship is a small place for the feet, and an ill ship is worriment. Even when she was again under way, the gloom was still upon the crew. From time to time men went to the engine-room doors, and looking down, wanted to ask questions of the chief engineer, who slowly prowled to and fro, and watched with careful eye his red-painted mysteries. No man wished to have a companion know that he was anxious, and so questions were caught at the lips. Perhaps none commented save the first mate, who remarked to the captain, "Wonder what the bally old thing will do, sir, when we're chased by a Spanish cruiser?"

The captain merely grinned. Later he looked over the side and said to himself with scorn, "Sixteen knots! sixteen knots! Sixteen hinges on the inner gates of Hades! Sixteen knots! Seven is her gait, and nine if you crack her up to it."

There may never be a captain whose crew can't sniff his misgivings. They scent it as a herd scents the menace far through the trees and over the ridges. A captain that does not know that he is on a foundering ship sometimes can take his men to tea and buttered toast twelve minutes before the disaster, but let him fret for a moment in the loneliness of his cabin, and in no time it affects the liver of a distant and sensitive seaman. Even as Flanagan reflected on the *Foundling*, viewing her as a filibuster, word arrived that a winter of discontent had come to the stoke-room.

The captain knew that it requires sky to give a man courage. He sent for a stoker and talked to him on the bridge. The man, standing under the sky, instantly and shamefacedly denied all knowledge of the business; nevertheless, a jaw had presently to be broken by a fist because the *Foundling* could only steam nine knots, and because the stoke-room has no sky, no wind, no bright horizon.

When the *Foundling* was somewhere off Savannah a blow came from the northeast, and the steamer, headed south-east, rolled like a boiling potato. The first mate was a fine officer, and so a wave crashed him into the deck-house and broke his arm. The cook was a good cook, and so the heave of the ship flung him heels over head with a pot of boiling water, and caused him to lose interest in everything save his legs. "By the piper," said Flanagan to himself, "this filibustering is no trick with cards."

Later there was more trouble in the stoke-room. All the stokers participated save the one with a broken jaw, who had become discouraged. The captain had an excellent chest development. When he went aft, roaring, it was plain that a man could beat carpets with a voice like that one.

II

One night the *Foundling* was off the southern coast of Florida, and running at half-speed towards the shore. The captain was on the bridge. "Four flashes at intervals of one minute," he said to himself, gazing steadfastly towards the beach. Suddenly a yellow eye opened in the black face of the night, and looked at the *Foundling* and closed again. The captain studied his watch and the shore. Three times more the eye opened and looked at the *Foundling* and closed again. The captain called to the vague figures on the deck below him. "Answer it." The flash of a light from the bow of the steamer displayed for a moment in golden colour the crests of the inriding waves.

The *Foundling* lay to and waited. The long swells rolled her gracefully, and her two stub masts reaching into the darkness swung with the solemnity of batons timing a dirge. When the ship had left Boston she had been as encrusted with ice as a Dakota stage-driver's beard, but now the gentle wind of Florida softly swayed the lock on the forehead of the coatless Flanagan, and he lit a new cigar without troubling to make a shield of his hands.

Finally a dark boat came plashing over the waves. As it came very near, the captain leaned forward and perceived that the men in her rowed like seamstresses, and at the same time a voice hailed him in bad English. "It's a dead sure connection," said he to himself.

At sea, to load two hundred thousand rounds of rifle ammunition, seven hundred and fifty rifles, two rapid-fire field guns with a hundred shells, forty bundles of machetes, and a hundred pounds of dynamite, from yawls, and by men who are not born stevedores, and in a heavy ground swell, and with the searchlight of a United States cruiser sometimes flashing like lightning in the sky to the southward, is no business for a Sunday-school class. When at last the *Foundling* was steaming for the open over the grey sea at dawn, there was not a man of the forty come aboard from the Florida shore, nor of the fifteen sailed from Boston, who was not glad, standing with his hair matted to his forehead with sweat, smiling at the broad wake of the *Foundling* and the dim streak on the horizon which was Florida.

But there is a point of the compass in these waters men call the north-east. When the strong winds come from that direction they kick up a turmoil that is not good for a *Foundling* stuffed with coals and war-stores. In the gale which came, this ship was no more than a drunken soldier.

The Cuban leader, standing on the bridge with the captain, was presently informed that of his men, thirty-nine out of a possible thirty-nine were sea-sick. And in truth they were sea-sick. There are degrees in this complaint, but that matter was waived between them. They were all sick to the limits. They strewed the deck in every posture of human anguish, and when the *Foundling* ducked and water came sluicing down from the bows, they let it sluice. They were satisfied if they could keep their heads clear of the wash; and if they could not keep their heads clear of the wash, they didn't care. Presently the *Foundling* swung her course to the south-east, and the waves pounded her broadside. The patriots were all ordered below decks, and there they howled and measured their misery one against another. All day the*Foundling* plopped and floundered over a blazing bright meadow of an ocean whereon the white foam was like flowers.

The captain on the bridge mused and studied the bare horizon. "Hell!" said he to himself, and the word was more in amazement than in indignation or sorrow. "Thirty-nine sea-sick passengers, the mate with a broken arm, a stoker with a broken jaw, the cook with a pair of scalded legs, and an engine likely to be taken with all these diseases, if not more! If I get back to a home port with a spoke of the wheel gripped in my hands, it'll be fair luck!"

There is a kind of corn-whisky bred in Florida which the natives declare is potent in the proportion of seven fights to a drink. Some of the Cuban volunteers had had the forethought to bring a small quantity of this whisky aboard with them, and being now in the fire-room and sea-sick, feeling that they would not care to drink liquor for two or three years to come, they gracefully tendered their portions to the stokers. The stokers accepted these gifts without avidity, but with a certain earnestness of manner.

As they were stokers, and toiling, the whirl of emotion was delayed, but it arrived ultimately, and with emphasis. One stoker called another stoker a weird name, and the latter, righteously inflamed at it, smote his mate with an iron shovel, and the man fell headlong over a heap of coal, which crashed gently while piece after piece rattled down upon the deck.

A third stoker was providently enraged at the scene, and assailed the second stoker. They fought for some moments, while the sea-sick Cubans sprawledon the deck watched with languid rolling glances the ferocity of this scuffle. One was so indifferent to the strategic importance of the space he occupied that he was kicked on the shins.

When the second engineer came to separating the combatants, he was sincere in his efforts, and he came near to disabling them for life.

The captain said, "I'll go down there and—" But the leader of the Cubans restrained him. "No, no," he cried, "you must not. We must treat them like children, very gently, all the time, you see, or else when we get back to a United States port they will—what you call? Spring? Yes, spring the whole business. We must—jolly them, you see?"

"You mean," said the captain thoughtfully, "they are likely to get mad, and give the expedition dead away when we reach port again unless we blarney them now?"

"Yes, yes," cried the Cuban leader, "unless we are so very gentle with them they will make many troubles afterwards for us in the newspapers and then in court."

"Well, but I won't have my crew—" began the captain.

"But you must," interrupted the Cuban, "you must. It is the only thing. You are like the captain of a pirate ship. You see? Only you can't throw them overboard like him. You see?"

"Hum," said the captain, "this here filibustering business has got a lot to it when you come to look it over."

He called the fighting stokers to the bridge, and the three came, meek and considerably battered. He was lecturing them soundly but sensibly, when he suddenly tripped a sentence and cried—"Here! Where's that other fellow? How does it come he wasn't in the fight?"

The row of stokers cried at once eagerly, "He's hurt, sir. He's got a broken jaw, sir."

"So he has; so he has," murmured the captain, much embarrassed.

And because of all these affairs, the *Foundling* steamed toward Cuba with its crew in a sling, if one may be allowed to speak in that way.

### III

At night the *Foundling* approached the coast like a thief. Her lights were muffled, so that from the deck the sea shone with its own radiance, like the faint shimmer of some kinds of silk. The men on deck spoke in whispers, and even down in the fire-room the hidden stokers working before the blood-red furnace doors used no words and walked on tip-toe. The stars were out in the blue-velvet sky, and their light with the soft shine of the sea caused the coast to appear black as the side of a coffin. The surf boomed in low thunder on the distant beach.

The *Foundling's* engines ceased their thumping for a time. She glided quietly forward until a bell chimed faintly in the engine-room. Then she paused with a flourish of phosphorescent waters.

"Give the signal," said the captain. Three times a flash of light went from the bow. There was a moment of waiting. Then an eye like the one on the coast of Florida opened and closed, opened and closed, opened and closed. The Cubans, grouped in a great shadow on deck, burst into a low chatter of delight. A hiss from their leader silenced them.

"Well?" said the captain.

"All right," said the leader.

At the giving of the word it was not apparent that any one on board of the *Foundling* had ever been sea-sick. The boats were lowered swiftly—too swiftly. Boxes of cartridges were dragged from the hold and passed over the side with a rapidity that made men in the boats exclaim against it. They were being bombarded. When a boat headed for shore its rowers pulled like madmen. The captain paced slowly to and fro on the bridge. In the engine-room the engineers stood at their station, and in the stoke-hold the firemen fidgeted silently around the furnace doors.

On the bridge Flanagan reflected. "Oh, I don't know!" he observed. "This fili-bustering business isn't so bad. Pretty soon it'll be off to sea again with nothing to do but some big lying when I get into port."

In one of the boats returning from shore came twelve Cuban officers, the greater number of them convalescing from wounds, while two or three of them had been ordered to America on commissions from the insurgents. The captain welcomed them, and assured them of a speedy and safe voyage.

Presently he went again to the bridge and scanned the horizon. The sea was lonely like the spaces amid the suns. The captain grinned and softly smote his chest. "It's dead easy," he said.

It was near the end of the cargo, and the men were breathing like spent horses, although their elation grew with each moment, when suddenly a voice spoke from the sky. It was not a loud voice, but the quality of it brought every man on deck to full stop and motionless, as if they had all been changed to wax. "Captain," said the man at the masthead, "there's a light to the west'ard, sir. Think it's a steamer, sir."

There was a still moment until the captain called, "Well, keep your eye on it now." Speaking to the deck, he said, "Go ahead with your unloading."

The second engineer went to the galley to borrow a tin cup. "Hear the news, second?" asked the cook. "Steamer coming up from the west'ard."

"Gee!" said the second engineer. In the engine-room he said to the chief, "Steamer coming up from the west'ard, sir." The chief engineer began to test vari-ous little machines with which his domain was decorated. Finally he addressed the stoke-room. "Boys, I want you to look sharp now. There's a steamer coming up to the west'ard."

"All right, sir," said the stoke-room.

From time to time the captain hailed the masthead. "How is she now?"

"Seems to be coming down on us pretty fast, sir."

The Cuban leader came anxiously to the captain. "Do you think we can save all the cargo? It is rather delicate business. No?"

"Go ahead," said Flanagan. "Fire away! I'll wait."

There continued the hurried shuffling of feet on deck, and the low cries of the men unloading the cargo. In the engine-room the chief and his assistant were staring at the gong. In the stoke-room the firemen breathed through their teeth. A shovel slipped from where it leaned against the side and banged on the floor. The stokers started and looked around quickly.

Climbing to the rail and holding on to a stay, the captain gazed westward. A light had raised out of the deep. After watching this light for a time he called to the Cuban leader. "Well, as soon as you're ready now, we might as well be skipping out."

Finally, the Cuban leader told him, "Well, this is the last load. As soon as the boats come back you can be off."

"Shan't wait for all the boats," said the captain. "That fellow is too close." As the second boat came aboard, the *Foundling* turned, and like a black shadow stole seaward to cross the bows of the oncoming steamer. "Waited about ten minutes too long," said the captain to himself.

Suddenly the light in the west vanished. "Hum!" said Flanagan, "he's up to some meanness." Every one outside of the engine-rooms was set on watch. The *Foundling*, going at full speed into the north-east, slashed a wonderful trail of blue silver on the dark bosom of the sea.

A man on deck cried out hurriedly, "There she is, sir." Many eyes searched the western gloom, and one after another the glances of the men found a tiny shadow on the deep with a line of white beneath it. "He couldn't be heading better if he had a line to us," said Flanagan.

There was a thin flash of red in the darkness. It was long and keen like a crimson rapier. A short, sharp report sounded, and then a shot whined swiftly in the air and blipped into the sea. The captain had been about to take a bite of plug tobacco at the beginning of this incident, and his arm was raised. He remained like a frozen figure while the shot whined, and then, as it blipped into the sea, his hand went to his mouth and he bit the plug. He looked wide-eyed at the shadow with its line of white.

The senior Cuban officer came hurriedly to the bridge. "It is no good to surrender," he cried. "They would only shoot or hang all of us."

There was another thin red flash and a report. A loud whirring noise passed over the ship.

"I'm not going to surrender," said the captain, hanging with both hands to the rail. He appeared like a man whose traditions of peace are clinched in his heart. He was as astonished as if his hat had turned into a dog. Presently he wheeled quickly and said—"What kind of a gun is that?"

"It is a one-pounder," cried the Cuban officer. "The boat is one of those little gunboats made from a yacht. You see?"

"Well, if it's only a yawl, he'll sink us in five more minutes," said Flanagan. For a moment he looked helplessly off at the horizon. His under-jaw hung low. But a moment later, something touched him, like a stiletto point of inspiration. He leaped to the pilothouse and roared at the man at the wheel. The *Foundling* sheered suddenly to starboard, made a clumsy turn, and Flanagan was bellowing through the tube to the engine-room before everybody discovered that the old basket was heading straight for the Spanish gun-boat. The ship lunged forward like a draught-horse on the gallop.

This strange manoeuvre by the *Foundling* first dealt consternation on board of the *Foundling*. Men instinctively crouched on the instant, and then swore their supreme oath, which was unheard by their own ears.

Later the manoeuvre of the *Foundling* dealt consternation on board of the gunboat. She had been going victoriously forward dim-eyed from the fury of her pursuit. Then this tall threatening shape had suddenly loomed over her like a giant apparition.

The people on board the *Foundling* heard panic shouts, hoarse orders. The little gunboat was paralyzed with astonishment.

Suddenly Flanagan yelled with rage and sprang for the wheel. The helmsman had turned his eyes away. As the captain whirled the wheel far to starboard he heard a crunch as the *Foundling*, lifted on a wave, smashed her shoulder against the gunboat, and he saw shooting past a little launch sort of a thing with men on her that ran this way and that way. The Cuban officers, joined by the cook and a seaman, emptied their revolvers into the surprised terror of the seas.

There was naturally no pursuit. Under comfortable speed the *Foundling* stood to the northwards.

The captain went to his berth chuckling. "There, by God!" he said. "There now!"

## IV

When Flanagan came again on deck, the first mate, his arm in a sling, walked the bridge. Flanagan was smiling a wide smile. The bridge of the *Foundling* was dipping afar and then afar. With each lunge of the little steamer the water seethed and boomed alongside, and the spray dashed high and swiftly.

"Well," said Flanagan, inflating himself, "we've had a great deal of a time, and we've come through it all right, and thank Heaven it is all over."

The sky in the north-east was of a dull brick-red in tone, shaded here and there by black masses that billowed out in some fashion from the flat heavens.

"Look there," said the mate.

"Hum!" said the captain. "Looks like a blow, don't it?"

Later the surface of the water rippled and flickered in the preliminary wind. The sea had become the colour of lead. The swashing sound of the waves on the sides of the *Foundling* was now provided with some manner of ominous significance. The men's shouts were hoarse.

A squall struck the *Foundling* on her starboard quarter, and she leaned under the force of it as if she were never to return to the even keel. "I'll be glad when we get in," said the mate. "I'm going to quit then. I've got enough."

"Hell!" said the beaming Flanagan.

The steamer crawled on into the north-west. The white water, sweeping out from her, deadened the chug-chug-chug of the tired old engines.

Once, when the boat careened, she laid her shoulder flat on the sea and rested in that manner. The mate, looking down the bridge, which slanted more than a coal-shute, whistled softly to himself. Slowly, heavily, the *Foundling* arose to meet another sea.

At night waves thundered mightily on the bows of the steamer, and water lit with the beautiful phosphorescent glamour went boiling and howling along deck.

By good fortune the chief engineer crawled safely, but utterly drenched, to the galley for coffee. "Well, how goes it, chief?" said the cook, standing with his fat arms folded in order to prove that he could balance himself under any conditions.

The engineer shook his head dejectedly. "This old biscuit-box will never see port again. Why, she'll fall to pieces."

Finally at night the captain said, "Launch the boats." The Cubans hovered about him. "Is the ship going to sink?" The captain addressed them politely. "Gentlemen, we are in trouble, but all I ask of you is that you just do what I tell you, and no harm will come to anybody."

The mate directed the lowering of the first boat, and the men performed this task with all decency, like people at the side of a grave.

A young oiler came to the captain. "The chief sends word, sir, that the water is almost up to the fires."

"Keep at it as long as you can."

"Keep at it as long as we can, sir?"

Flanagan took the senior Cuban officer to the rail, and, as the steamer sheered high on a great sea, showed him a yellow dot on the horizon. It was smaller than a needle when its point is towards you.

"There," said the captain. The wind-driven spray was lashing his face. "That's Jupiter Light on the Florida coast. Put your men in the boat we've just launched, and the mate will take you to that light."

Afterwards Flanagan turned to the chief engineer. "We can never beach," said the old man. "The stokers have got to quit in a minute." Tears were in his eyes.

The *Foundling* was a wounded thing. She lay on the water with gasping engines, and each wave resembled her death-blow.

Now the way of a good ship on the sea is finer than sword-play. But this is when she is alive. If a time comes that the ship dies, then her way is the way of a floating old glove, and she has that much vim, spirit, buoyancy. At this time many men on the *Foundling* suddenly came to know that they were clinging to a corpse.

The captain went to the stoke-room, and what he saw as he swung down the companion suddenly turned him hesitant and dumb. Water was swirling to and fro with the roll of the ship, fuming greasily around half-strangled machinery that still attempted to perform its duty. Steam arose from the water, and through its clouds shone the red glare of the dying fires. As for the stokers, death might have been with silence in this room. One lay in his berth, his hands under his head, staring moodily at the wall. One sat near the foot of the companion, his face hidden in his arms. One leaned against the side and gazed at the snarling water as it rose, and its mad eddies among the machinery. In the unholy red light and grey mist of this stifling dim Inferno they were strange figures with their silence and their immobility. The wretched *Foundling* groaned deeply as she lifted, and groaned deeply as she sank into the trough, while hurried waves then thundered over her with the noise of landslides. The terrified machinery was making gestures.

But Flanagan took control of himself suddenly. Then he stirred the fire-room. The stillness had been so unearthly that he was not altogether inapprehensive of strange and grim deeds when he charged into them; but precisely as they had submitted to the sea so they submitted to Flanagan. For a moment they rolled their eyes like hurt cows, but they obeyed the Voice. The situation simply required a Voice.

When the captain returned to the deck the hue of this fire-room was in his mind, and then he understood doom and its weight and complexion.

When finally the *Foundling* sank she shifted and settled as calmly as an animal curls down in the bush grass. Away over the waves two bobbing boats paused to witness this quiet death. It was a slow manoeuvre, altogether without the pageantry of uproar, but it flashed pallor into the faces of all men who saw it, and they groaned when they said, "There she goes!" Suddenly the captain whirled and knocked his hand on the gunwale. He sobbed for a time, and then he sobbed and swore also.

* * * *

There was a dance at the Imperial Inn. During the evening some irresponsible young men came from the beach bringing the statement that several boatloads of people had been perceived off shore. It was a charming dance, and none cared to take time to believe this tale. The fountain in the court-yard splashed softly, and couple after couple paraded through the aisles of palms, where lamps with red shades threw a rose light upon the gleaming leaves. The band played its waltzes slumberously, and its music came faintly to the people among the palms.

Sometimes a woman said—"Oh, it is not really true, is it, that there was a wreck out at sea?"

A man usually said—"No, of course not."

At last, however, a youth came violently from the beach. He was triumphant in manner. "They're out there," he cried. "A whole boat-load!" He received eager attention, and he told all that he supposed. His news destroyed the dance. After a time the band was playing beautifully to space. The guests had hurried to the beach. One little girl cried, "Oh, mamma, may I go too?" Being refused permission she pouted.

As they came from the shelter of the great hotel, the wind was blowing swiftly from the sea, and at intervals a breaker shone livid. The women shuddered, and their bending companions seized the opportunity to draw the cloaks closer.

"Oh, dear!" said a girl; "supposin' they were out there drowning while we were dancing!"

"Oh, nonsense!" said her younger brother; "that don't happen."

"Well, it might, you know, Roger. How can you tell?"

A man who was not her brother gazed at her then with profound admiration. Later, she complained of the damp sand, and, drawing back her skirts, looked ruefully at her little feet.

A mother's son was venturing too near to the water in his interest and excitement. Occasionally she cautioned and reproached him from the background.

Save for the white glare of the breakers, the sea was a great wind-crossed void. From the throng of charming women floated the perfume of many flowers. Later there floated to them a body with a calm face of an Irish type. The expedition of the *Foundling* will never be historic.

# HORSES

Richardson pulled up his horse, and looked back over the trail where the crimson serape of his servant flamed amid the dusk of the mesquit. The hills in the west were carved into peaks, and were painted the most profound blue. Above them the sky was of that marvellous tone of green—like still, sun-shot water—which people denounce in pictures.

José was muffled deep in his blanket, and his great toppling sombrero was drawn low over his brow. He shadowed his master along the dimming trail in the fashion of an assassin. A cold wind of the impending night swept over the wilderness of mesquit.

"Man," said Richardson in lame Mexican as the servant drew near, "I want eat! I want sleep! Understand—no? Quickly! Understand?"

"Si, señor," said José, nodding. He stretched one arm out of his blanket and pointed a yellow finger into the gloom. "Over there, small village. Si, señor."

They rode forward again. Once the American's horse shied and breathed quiveringly at something which he saw or imagined in the darkness, and therider drew a steady, patient rein, and leaned over to speak tenderly as if he were addressing a frightened woman. The sky had faded to white over the mountains, and the plain was a vast, pointless ocean of black.

Suddenly some low houses appeared squatting amid the bushes. The horsemen rode into a hollow until the houses rose against the sombre sundown sky, and then up a small hillock, causing these habitations to sink like boats in the sea of shadow.

A beam of red firelight fell across the trail. Richardson sat sleepily on his horse while his servant quarrelled with somebody—a mere voice in the gloom—over the price of bed and board. The houses about him were for the most part like tombs in their whiteness and silence, but there were scudding black figures that seemed interested in his arrival.

José came at last to the horses' heads, and the American slid stiffly from his seat. He muttered a greeting, as with his spurred feet he clicked into the adobe house that confronted him. The brown stolid face of a woman shone in the light of the fire. He seated himself on the earthen floor and blinked drowsily at the blaze. He was aware that the woman was clinking earthenware, and hieing here and everywhere in the manoeuvres of the housewife. From a dark corner there came the sound of two or three snores twining together.

The woman handed him a bowl of tortillas. She was a submissive creature, timid and large-eyed. She gazed at his enormous silver spurs, his large and impressive revolver, with the interest and admirationof the highly-privileged cat of the adage. When he ate, she seemed transfixed off there in the gloom, her white teeth shining.

José entered, staggering under two Mexican saddles, large enough for building-sites. Richardson decided to smoke a cigarette, and then changed his mind. It would be much finer to go to sleep. His blanket hung over his left shoulder, furled into a long pipe of cloth, according to the Mexican fashion. By doffing his sombrero, unfastening his spurs and his revolver belt, he made himself ready for the slow, blissful twist into the blanket. Like a cautious man he lay close to the wall, and all his property was very near his hand.

The mesquit brush burned long. José threw two gigantic wings of shadow as he flapped his blanket about him—first across his chest under his arms, and then around his neck and across his chest again—this time over his arms, with the end tossed on his right shoulder. A Mexican thus snugly enveloped can nevertheless free his fighting arm in a beautifully brisk way, merely shrugging his shoulder as he grabs for the weapon at his belt. (They always wear their serapes in this manner.)

The firelight smothered the rays which, streaming from a moon as large as a drum-head, were struggling at the open door. Richardson heard from the plain the fine, rhythmical trample of the hoofs of hurried horses. He went to sleep wondering who rode so fast and so late. And in the deep silence the pale rays of the moon must have prevailed against the red spears of the fire until the room was slowly flooded to its middle with a rectangle of silver light.

Richardson was awakened by the sound of a guitar. It was badly played—in this land of Mexico, from which the romance of the instrument ascends to us like a perfume. The guitar was groaning and whining like a badgered soul. A noise of scuffling feet accompanied the music. Sometimes laughter arose, and often the voices of men saying bitter things to each other, but always the guitar cried on, the treble sounding as if some one were beating iron, and the bass humming like bees. "Damn it—they're having a dance," he muttered, fretfully. He heard two men quarrelling in short, sharp words, like pistol shots; they were calling each other worse names than common people know in other countries. He wondered why the noise was so loud. Raising his head from his saddle pillow, he saw, with the help of the valiant moonbeams, a blanket hanging flat against the wall at the further end of the room. Being of opinion that it concealed a door, and remembering that Mexican drink made men very drunk, he pulled his revolver closer to him and prepared for sudden disaster.

Richardson was dreaming of his far and beloved north.

"Well, I would kill him, then!"

"No, you must not!"

"Yes, I will kill him! Listen! I will ask this American beast for his beautiful pistol and spurs and money and saddle, and if he will not give them—you will see!"

"But these Americans—they are a strange people. Look out, señor."

Then twenty voices took part in the discussion. They rose in quavering shrillness, as from men badly drunk. Richardson felt the skin draw tight around his mouth, and his knee-joints turned to bread. He slowly came to a sitting posture, glaring at the motionless blanket at the far end of the room. This stiff and mechanical movement, accomplished entirely by the muscles of the waist, must have looked like the rising of a corpse in the wan moonlight, which gave everything a hue of the grave.

My friend, take my advice and never be executed by a hangman who doesn't talk the English language. It, or anything that resembles it, is the most difficult of deaths. The tumultuous emotions of Richardson's terror destroyed that slow and careful process of thought by means of which he understood Mexican. Then he used his instinctive comprehension of the first and universal language, which is tone. Still, it is disheartening not to be able to understand the detail of threats against the blood of your body.

Suddenly, the clamour of voices ceased. There was a silence—a silence of decision. The blanket was flung aside, and the red light of a torch flared into the room. It was held high by a fat, round-faced Mexican, whose little snake-like moustache was as black as his eyes, and whose eyes were black as jet. He was insane with the wild rage of a man whose liquor is dully burning at his brain. Five or six of his fellows crowded after him. The guitar, which had been thrummed doggedly during the time of the high words, now suddenly stopped. They contemplated each other. Richardson sat very straight and still, his right hand lost in his blanket. The Mexicans jostled in the light of the torch, their eyes blinking and glittering.

The fat one posed in the manner of a grandee. Presently his hand dropped to his belt, and from his lips there spun an epithet—a hideous word which often foreshadows knife-blows, a word peculiarly of Mexico, where people have to dig deep to find an insult that has not lost its savour. The American did not move. He was staring at the fat Mexican with a strange fixedness of gaze, not fearful, not dauntless, not anything that could be interpreted. He simply stared.

The fat Mexican must have been disconcerted, for he continued to pose as a grandee, with more and more sublimity, until it would have been easy for him to have fallen over backward. His companions were swaying very drunkenly. They still blinked their little beady eyes at Richardson. Ah, well, sirs, here was a mystery! At the approach of their menacing company, why did not this American cry out and turn pale, or run, or pray them mercy? The animal merely sat still, and stared, and waited for them to begin. Well, evidently he was a great fighter! Or perhaps he was an idiot? Indeed, this was an embarrassing situation, for who was going forward to discover whether he was a great fighter or an idiot?

To Richardson, whose nerves were tingling and twitching like live wires, and whose heart jolted inside him, this pause was a long horror; and for these men, who could so frighten him, there began to swell in him a fierce hatred—a hatred that made him long to be capable of fighting all of them, a hatred that made him capable of fighting all of them. A 44-calibre revolver can make a hole large enough for little boys to shoot marbles through; and there was a certain fat Mexican with a moustache like a snake who came extremely near to have eaten his last tomale merely because he frightened a man too much.

José had slept the first part of the night in his fashion, his body hunched into a heap, his legs crooked, his head touching his knees. Shadows had obscured him from the sight of the invaders. At this point he arose, and began to prowl quakingly over toward Richardson, as if he meant to hide behind him.

Of a sudden the fat Mexican gave a howl of glee. José had come within the torch's circle of light. With roars of ferocity the whole group of Mexicans pounced on the American's servant. He shrank shuddering away from them, beseeching by every device of word and gesture. They pushed him this way and that. They beat him with their fists. They stung him with their curses. As he grovelled on his knees, the fat Mexican took him by the throat and said—"I am going to kill you!" And continually they turned their eyes to see if they were to succeed in causing the initial demonstration by the American. But he looked on impassively. Under the blanket his fingers were clenched, as iron, upon the handle of his revolver.

Here suddenly two brilliant clashing chords from the guitar were heard, and a woman's voice, full of laughter and confidence, cried from without—"Hello! hello! Where are you?" The lurching company of Mexicans instantly paused and looked at the ground. One said, as he stood with his legs wide apart in order to balance himself—"It is the girls. They have come!" He screamed in answer to the question of the woman—"Here!" And without waiting he started on a pilgrimage toward the blanket-covered door. One could now hear a number of female voices giggling and chattering.

Two other Mexicans said—"Yes, it is the girls! Yes!" They also started quietly away. Even the fat Mexican's ferocity seemed to be affected. He looked uncertainly at the still immovable American. Two of his friends grasped him gaily—"Come, the girls are here! Come!" He cast another glower at Richardson. "But this—," he began. Laughing, his comrades hustled him toward the door. On its threshold, and holding back the blanket, with one hand, he turned his yellow face with a last challenging glare toward the American. José, bewailing his state in little sobs of utter despair and woe, crept to Richardson and huddled near his knee. Then the cries of the Mexicans meeting the girls were heard, and the guitar burst out in joyous humming.

The moon clouded, and but a faint square of light fell through the open main door of the house. The coals of the fire were silent, save for occasional sputters. Richardson did not change his position. He remained staring at the blanket which hid the strategic door in the far end. At his knees José was arguing, in a low, aggrieved tone, with the saints. Without, the Mexicans laughed and danced, and—it would appear from the sound—drank more.

In the stillness and the night Richardson sat wondering if some serpent-like Mexican were sliding towards him in the darkness, and if the first thing he knew of it would be the deadly sting of a knife. "Sssh," he whispered, to José. He drew his revolver from under the blanket, and held it on his leg. The blanket over the door fascinated him. It was a vague form, black and unmoving. Through the opening it shielded were to come, probably, threats, death. Sometimes he thought he saw it move. As grim white sheets, the black and silver of coffins, all the panoply of death, affect us, because of that which they hide, so this blanket, dangling before a hole in an adobe wall, was to Richardson a horrible emblem, and a horrible thing in itself. In his present mood he could not have been brought to touch it with his finger.

The celebrating Mexicans occasionally howled in song. The guitarist played with speed and enthusiasm. Richardson longed to run. But in this vibrating and threatening gloom his terror convinced him that a move on his part would be a signal for the pounce of death. José, crouching abjectly, mumbled now and again. Slowly, and ponderous as stars, the minutes went.

Suddenly Richardson thrilled and started. His breath for a moment left him. In sleep his nerveless fingers had allowed his revolver to fall and clang upon the hard floor. He grabbed it up hastily, and his glance swept apprehensively over the room. A chill blue light of dawn was in the place. Every outline was slowly growing; detail was following detail. The dread blanket did not move. The riotous company had gone or fallen silent. He felt the effect of this cold dawn in his blood. The candour of breaking day brought his nerve. He touched José. "Come," he said. His servant lifted his lined yellow face, and comprehended. Richardson buckled on his spurs and strode up; José obediently lifted the two great saddles. Richardson held two bridles and a blanket on his left arm; in his right hand he had his revolver. They sneaked toward the door.

The man who said that spurs jingled was insane. Spurs have a mellow clash—clash—clash. Walking in spurs—notably Mexican spurs—you remind yourself vaguely of a telegraphic linesman. Richardson was inexpressibly shocked when he came to walk. He sounded to himself like a pair of cymbals. He would have known of this if he had reflected; but then, he was escaping, not reflecting. He made a gesture of despair, and from under the two saddles José tried to make one of hopeless horror. Richardson stooped, and with shaking fingers unfastened the spurs. Taking them in his left hand, he picked up his revolver, and they slunk on toward the door. On the threshold he looked back. In a corner he saw, watching him with large eyes, the Indian man and woman who had been his hosts. Throughout the night they had made no sign, and now they neither spoke nor moved. Yet Richardson thought he detected meek satisfaction at his departure.

The street was still and deserted. In the eastern sky there was a lemon-coloured patch. José had picketed the horses at the side of the house. As the two men came round the corner Richardson's beast set up a whinny of welcome. The little horse had heard them coming. He stood facing them, his ears cocked forward, his eyes bright with welcome.

Richardson made a frantic gesture, but the horse, in his happiness at the appearance of his friends, whinnied with enthusiasm. The American felt that he could have strangled his well-beloved steed. Upon the threshold of safety, he was being betrayed by his horse, his friend! He felt the same hate that he would have felt for a dragon. And yet, as he glanced wildly about him, he could see nothing stirring in the street, nothing at the doors of the tomb-like houses.

José had his own saddle-girth and both bridles buckled in a moment. He curled the picket-ropes with a few sweeps of his arm. The American's fingers, however, were shaking so that he could hardly buckle the girth. His hands were in invisible mittens. He was wondering, calculating, hoping about his horse. He knew the little animal's willingness and courage under all circumstances up to this time; but then— here it was different. Who could tell if some wretched instance of equine perversity was not about to develop? Maybe the little fellow would not feel like smoking over the plain at express speed this morning, and so he would rebel, and kick, and be wicked. Maybe he would be without feeling of interest, and run listlessly. All riders who have had to hurry in the saddle know what it is to be on a horse who does not understand the dramatic situation. Riding a lame sheep is bliss to it. Richardson, fumbling furiously at the girth, thought of these things.

Presently he had it fastened. He swung into the saddle, and as he did so his horse made a mad jump forward. The spurs of José scratched and tore the flanks of his great black beast, and side by side the two horses raced down the village street. The American heard his horse breathe a quivering sigh of excitement. Those four feet skimmed. They were as light as fairy puff balls. The houses glided past in a moment, and the great, clear, silent plain appeared like a pale blue sea of mist and wet bushes. Above the mountains the colours of the sunlight were like the first tones, the opening chords of the mighty hymn of the morning.

The American looked down at his horse. He felt in his heart the first thrill of confidence. The little animal, unurged and quite tranquil, moving his ears this way and that way with an air of interest in the scenery, was nevertheless bounding into the eye of the breaking day with the speed of a frightened antelope. Richardson, looking down, saw the long, fine reach of forelimb as steady as steel machinery. As the ground reeled past, the long, dried grasses hissed, and cactus plants were dull blurs. A wind whirled the horse's mane over his rider's bridle hand.

José's profile was lined against the pale sky. It was as that of a man who swims alone in an ocean. His eyes glinted like metal, fastened on some unknown point ahead of him, some fabulous place of safety. Occasionally his mouth puckered in a little unheard cry; and his legs, bended back, worked spasmodically as his spurred heels sliced his charger's sides.

Richardson consulted the gloom in the west for signs of a hard-riding, yelling cavalcade. He knew that, whereas his friends the enemy had not attacked him when he had sat still and with apparent calmness confronted them, they would take furiously after him now that he had run from them—now that he had confessed himself the weaker. Their valour would grow like weeds in the spring, and upon discovering his escape they would ride forth dauntless warriors. Sometimes he was sure he saw them. Sometimes he was sure he heard them. Continually looking backward over his shoulder, he studied the purple expanses where the night was marching away. José rolled and shuddered in his saddle, persistently disturbing the stride of the black horse, fretting and worrying him until the white foam flew, and the great shoulders shone like satin from the sweat.

At last, Richardson drew his horse carefully down to a walk. José wished to rush insanely on, but the American spoke to him sternly. As the two paced forward side by side, Richardson's little horse thrust over his soft nose and inquired into the black's condition.

Riding with José was like riding with a corpse. His face resembled a cast in lead. Sometimes he swung forward and almost pitched from his seat. Richardson was too frightened himself to do anything but hate this man for his fear. Finally, he issued a mandate which nearly caused José's eyes to slide out of his head and fall to the ground, like two coins:—"Ride behind me—about fifty paces."

"Señor—" stuttered the servant. "Go," cried the American furiously. He glared at the other and laid his hand on his revolver. José looked at his master wildly. He made a piteous gesture. Then slowly he fell back, watching the hard face of the American for a sign of mercy. But Richardson had resolved in his rage that at any rate he was going to use the eyes and ears of extreme fear to detect the approach of danger; so he established his panic-stricken servant as a sort of outpost.

As they proceeded, he was obliged to watch sharply to see that the servant did not slink forward and join him. When José made beseeching circles in the air with his arm, he replied by menacingly gripping his revolver. José had a revolver too; nevertheless it was very clear in his mind that the revolver was distinctly an American weapon. He had been educated in the Rio Grande country.

Richardson lost the trail once. He was recalled to it by the loud sobs of his servant.

Then at last José came clattering forward, gesticulating and wailing. The little horse sprang to the shoulder of the black. They were off.

Richardson, again looking backward, could see a slanting flare of dust on the whitening plain. He thought that he could detect small moving figures in it.

José's moans and cries amounted to a university course in theology. They broke continually from his quivering lips. His spurs were as motors. Theyforced the black horse over the plain in great headlong leaps. But under Richardson there was a little insignificant rat-coloured beast who was running apparently with almost as much effort as it takes a bronze statue to stand still. The ground seemed merely something to be touched from time to time with hoofs that were as light as blown leaves. Occasionally Richardson lay back and pulled stoutly at the bridle to keep from abandoning his servant. José harried at his horse's mouth, flopped about in the saddle, and made his two heels beat like flails. The black ran like a horse in despair.

Crimson serapes in the distance resemble drops of blood on the great cloth of plain. Richardson began to dream of all possible chances. Although quite a humane man, he did not once think of his servant. José being a Mexican, it was natural that he should be killed in Mexico; but for himself, a New Yorker—! He remembered all the tales of such races for life, and he thought them badly written.

The great black horse was growing indifferent. The jabs of José's spurs no longer caused him to bound forward in wild leaps of pain. José had at last succeeded in teaching him that spurring was to be expected, speed or no speed, and now he took the pain of it dully and stolidly, as an animal who finds that doing his best gains him no respite. José was turned into a raving maniac. He bellowed and screamed, working his arms and his heels like one in a fit. He resembled a man on a sinking ship, who appeals to the ship. Richardson, too, cried madly to the black horse. The spirit of the horse responded to these calls, and quivering and breathing heavily he made a great effort, a sort of a final rush, not for himself apparently, but because he understood that his life's sacrifice, perhaps, had been invoked by these two men who cried to him in the universal tongue. Richardson had no sense of appreciation at this time—he was too frightened; but often now he remembers a certain black horse.

From the rear could be heard a yelling, and once a shot was fired—in the air, evidently. Richardson moaned as he looked back. He kept his hand on his revolver. He tried to imagine the brief tumult of his capture—the flurry of dust from the hoofs of horses pulled suddenly to their haunches, the shrill, biting curses of the men, the ring of the shots, his own last contortion. He wondered, too, if he could not somehow manage to pelt that fat Mexican, just to cure his abominable egotism.

It was José, the terror-stricken, who at last discovered safety. Suddenly he gave a howl of delight and astonished his horse into a new burst of speed. They were on a little ridge at the time, and the American at the top of it saw his servant gallop down the slope and into the arms, so to speak, of a small column of horsemen in grey and silver clothes. In the dim light of the early morning they were as vague as shadows, but Richardson knew them at once for a detachment of Rurales, that crack cavalry corps of the Mexican army which polices the plain so zealously, being of themselves the law and the arm of it—a fierce and swift-moving body that knows little of prevention but much of vengeance. They drew up suddenly, and the rows of great silver-trimmed sombreros bobbed in surprise.

Richardson saw José throw himself from his horse and begin to jabber at the leader. When he arrived he found that his servant had already outlined the entire situation, and was then engaged in describing him, Richardson, as an American señor of vast wealth, who was the friend of almost every governmental potentate within two hundred miles. This seemed profoundly to impress the officer. He bowed gravely to Richardson and smiled significantly at his men, who unslung their carbines.

The little ridge hid the pursuers from view, but the rapid thud of their horses' feet could be heard. Occasionally they yelled and called to each other. Then at last they swept over the brow of the hill, a wild mob of almost fifty drunken horsemen. When they discerned the pale-uniformed Rurales, they were sailing down the slope at top speed.

If toboggans half-way down a hill should suddenly make up their minds to turn round and go back, there would be an effect something like that produced by the drunken horsemen. Richardson saw the Rurales serenely swing their carbines forward, and, peculiar-minded person that he was, felt his heart leap into his throat at the prospective volley. But the officer rode forward alone.

It appeared that the man who owned the best horse in this astonished company was the fat Mexican with the snaky moustache, and, in consequence, this gentleman was quite a distance in the van. He tried to pull up, wheel his horse, and scuttle back over the hill as some of his companions had done, but the officer called to him in a voice harsh with rage. "—!" howled the officer. "This señor is my friend, the friend of my friends. Do you dare pursue him, —? —! —! —! —!" These dashes represent terrible names, all different, used by the officer.

The fat Mexican simply grovelled on his horse's neck. His face was green: it could be seen that he expected death. The officer stormed with magnificent intensity: "—!—!—!" Finally he sprang from his saddle, and, running to the fat Mexican's side, yelled—"Go!" and kicked the horse in the belly with all his might. The animal gave a mighty leap into the air, and the fat Mexican, with one wretched glance at the contemplative Rurales, aimed his steed for the top of the ridge. Richardson gulped again in expectation of a volley, for—it is said—this is a favourite method for disposing of objectionable people. The fat, green Mexican also thought that he was to be killed on the run, from the miserable look he cast at the troops. Nevertheless, he was allowed to vanish in a cloud of yellow dust at the ridge-top.

José was exultant, defiant, and, oh! bristling with courage. The black horse was drooping sadly, his nose to the ground. Richardson's little animal, with his ears bent forward, was staring at the horses of the Rurales as if in an intense study. Richardson longed for speech, but he could only bend forward and pat the shining, silken shoulders. The little horse turned his head and looked back gravely.

# DEATH AND THE CHILD

## I

The peasants who were streaming down the mountain trail had in their sharp terror evidently lost their ability to count. The cattle and the huge round bundles seemed to suffice to the minds of the crowd if there were now two in each case where there had been three. This brown stream poured on with a constant wastage of goods and beasts. A goat fell behind to scout the dried grass and its owner, howling, flogging his donkeys, passed far ahead. A colt, suddenly frightened, made a stumbling charge up the hill-side. The expenditure was always profligate and always unnamed, unnoted. It was as if fear was a river, and this horde had simply been caught in the torrent, man tumbling over beast, beast over man, as helpless in it as the logs that fall and shoulder grindingly through the gorges of a lumber country. It was a freshet that might sear the face of the tall quiet mountain; it might draw a livid line across the land, this downpour of fear with a thousand homes adrift in the current—men, women, babes, animals. From it there arose a constant babble of tongues, shrill, broken, and sometimes choking as from men drowning. Many made gestures, painting their agonies on the air with fingers that twirled swiftly.

The blue bay with its pointed ships and the white town lay below them, distant, flat, serene. There was upon this vista a peace that a bird knows when high in the air it surveys the world, a great calm thing rolling noiselessly toward the end of the mystery. Here on the height one felt the existence of the universe scornfully defining the pain in ten thousand minds. The sky was an arch of stolid sapphire. Even to the mountains raising their mighty shapes from the valley, this headlong rush of the fugitives was too minute. The sea, the sky, and the hills combined in their grandeur to term this misery inconsequent. Then too it sometimes happened that a face seen as it passed on the flood reflected curiously the spirit of them all and still more. One saw then a woman of the opinion of the vaults above the clouds. When a child cried it cried always because of some adjacent misfortune, some discomfort of a pack-saddle or rudeness of an encircling arm. In the dismal melody of this flight there were often sounding chords of apathy. Into these preoccupied countenances, one felt that needles could be thrust without purchasing a scream. The trail wound here and there as the sheep had willed in the making of it.

Although this throng seemed to prove that the whole of humanity was fleeing in one direction—with every tie severed that binds us to the soil—a young man was walking rapidly up the mountain, hastening to a side of the path from time to time to avoid some particularly wide rush of people and cattle. He looked at everything in agitation and pity. Frequently he called admonitions to maniacal fugitives, and at other moments he exchanged strange stares with the imperturbable ones. They seemed to him to wear merely the expressions of so many boulders rolling down the hill. He exhibited wonder and awe with his pitying glances.

Turning once toward the rear, he saw a man in the uniform of a lieutenant of infantry marching the same way. He waited then, subconsciously elate at a prospect of being able to make into words the emotion which heretofore had only been expressed in the flash of eyes and sensitive movements of his flexible mouth. He spoke to the officer in rapid French, waving his arms wildly, and often pointing with a dramatic finger. "Ah, this is too cruel, too cruel, too cruel. Is it not? I did not think it would be as bad as this. I did not think—God's mercy—I did not think at all. And yet I am a Greek. Or at least my father was a Greek. I did not come here to fight. I am really a correspondent, you see? I was to write for an Italian paper. I have been educated in Italy. I have spent nearly all my life in Italy. At the schools and universities! I knew nothing of war! I was a student—a student. I came here merely because my father was a Greek, and for his sake I thought of Greece—I loved Greece. But I did not dream—"

He paused, breathing heavily. His eyes glistened from that soft overflow which comes on occasion to the glance of a young woman. Eager, passionate, profoundly moved, his first words, while facing the procession of fugitives, had been an active definition of his own dimension, his personal relation to men, geography, life. Throughout he had preserved the fiery dignity of a tragedian.

The officer's manner at once deferred to this outburst. "Yes," he said, polite but mournful, "these poor people! These poor people! I do not know what is to become of these poor people."

The young man declaimed again. "I had no dream—I had no dream that it would be like this! This is too cruel! Too cruel! Now I want to be a soldier. Now I want to fight. Now I want to do battle for the land of my father." He made a sweeping gesture into the north-west.

The officer was also a young man, but he was very bronzed and steady. Above his high military collar of crimson cloth with one silver star upon it, appeared a profile stern, quiet, and confident, respecting fate, fearing only opinion. His clothes were covered with dust; the only bright spot was the flame of the crimson collar. At the violent cries of his companion he smiled as if to himself, meanwhile keeping his eyes fixed in a glance ahead.

From a land toward which their faces were bent came a continuous boom of artillery fire. It was sounding in regular measures like the beating of a colossal clock, a clock that was counting the seconds in the lives of the stars, and men had time to die between the ticks. Solemn, oracular, inexorable, the great seconds tolled over the hills as if God fronted this dial rimmed by the horizon. The soldier and the correspondent found themselves silent. The latter in particular was sunk in a great mournfulness, as if he had resolved willy-nilly to swing to the bottom of the abyss where dwell secrets of his kind, and had learned beforehand that all to be met there was cruelty and hopelessness. A strap of his bright new leather leggings came unfastened, and he bowed over it slowly, impressively, as one bending over the grave of a child.

Then suddenly, the reverberations mingled until one could not separate an explosion from another, and into the hubbub came the drawling sound of a leisurely musketry fire. Instantly, for some reason of cadence, the noise was irritating, silly, infantile. This uproar was childish. It forced the nerves to object, to protest against this racket which was as idle as the din of a lad with a drum.

The lieutenant lifted his finger and pointed. He spoke in vexed tones, as if he held the other man personally responsible for the noise. "Well, there!" he said. "If you wish for war you now have an opportunity magnificent."

The correspondent raised himself upon his toes. He tapped his chest with gloomy pride. "Yes! There is war! There is the war I wish to enter. I fling myself in. I am a Greek, a Greek, you understand. I wish to fight for my country. You know the way. Lead me. I offer myself." Struck by a sudden thought he brought a case from his pocket, and extracting a card handed it to the officer with a bow. "My name is Peza," he said simply.

A strange smile passed over the soldier's face. There was pity and pride—the vanity of experience—and contempt in it. "Very well," he said, returning the bow. "If my company is in the middle of the fight I shall be glad for the honour of your companionship. If my company is not in the middle of the fight—I will make other arrangements for you."

Peza bowed once more, very stiffly, and correctly spoke his thanks. On the edge of what he took to be a great venture toward death, he discovered that he was annoyed at something in the lieutenant's tone. Things immediately assumed new and extraordinary proportions. The battle, the great carnival of woe, was sunk at once to an equation with a vexation by a stranger. He wanted to ask the lieutenant what was his meaning. He bowed again majestically; the lieutenant bowed. They flung a shadow of manners, of capering tinsel ceremony across a land that groaned, and it satisfied something within themselves completely.

In the meantime, the river of fleeing villagers had changed to simply a last dropping of belated creatures, who fled past stammering and flinging their hands high. The two men had come to the top of the great hill. Before them was a green plain as level as an inland sea. It swept northward, and merged finally into a length of silvery mist. Upon the near part of this plain, and upon two grey treeless mountains at the side of it, were little black lines from which floated slanting sheets of smoke. It was not a battle to the nerves. One could survey it with equanimity, as if it were a tea-table; but upon Peza's mind it struck a loud clanging blow. It was war. Edified, aghast, triumphant, he paused suddenly, his lips apart. He remembered the pageants of carnage that had marched through the dreams of his childhood. Love he knew that he had confronted, alone, isolated, wondering, an individual, an atom taking the hand of a titanic principle. But, like the faintest breeze on his forehead, he felt here the vibration from the hearts of forty thousand men.

The lieutenant's nostrils were moving. "I must go at once," he said. "I must go at once."

"I will go with you wherever you go," shouted Peza loudly.

A primitive track wound down the side of the mountain, and in their rush they bounded from here to there, choosing risks which in the ordinary caution of man would surely have seemed of remarkable danger. The ardour of the correspondent surpassed the full energy of the soldier. Several times he turned and shouted, "Come on! Come on!"

At the foot of the path they came to a wide road, which extended toward the battle in a yellow and straight line. Some men were trudging wearily to the rear. They were without rifles; their clumsy uniforms were dirty and all awry. They turned eyes dully aglow with fever upon the pair striding toward the battle. Others were bandaged with the triangular kerchief upon which one could still see through bloodstains the little explanatory pictures illustrating the ways to bind various wounds. "Fig. 1."—"Fig. 2."—"Fig. 7."

Mingled with the pacing soldiers were peasants, indifferent, capable of smiling, gibbering about the battle, which was to them an ulterior drama. A man was leading a string of three donkeys to the rear, and at intervals he was accosted by wounded or fevered soldiers, from whom he defended his animals with ape-like cries and mad gesticulation. After much chattering they usually subsided gloomily, and allowed him to go with his sleek little beasts unburdened. Finally he encountered a soldier who walked slowly with the assistance of a staff. His head was bound with a wide bandage, grimey from blood and mud. He made application to the peasant, and immediately they were involved in a hideous Levantine discussion. The peasant whined and clamoured, sometimes spitting like a kitten. The wounded soldier jawed on thunderously, his great hands stretched in claw-like graspings over the peasant's head. Once he raised his staff and made threat with it. Then suddenly the row was at an end. The other sick men saw their comrade mount the leading donkey and at once begin to drum with his heels. None attempted to gain the backs of the remaining animals. They gazed after them dully. Finally they saw the caravan outlined for a moment against the sky. The soldier was still waving his arms passionately, having it out with the peasant.

Peza was alive with despair for these men who looked at him with such doleful, quiet eyes. "Ah, my God!" he cried to the lieutenant, "these poor souls! These poor souls!"

The officer faced about angrily. "If you are coming with me there is no time for this." Peza obeyed instantly and with a sudden meekness. In the moment some portion of egotism left him, and he modestly wondered if the universe took cognizance of him to an important degree. This theatre for slaughter, built by the inscrutable needs of the earth, was an enormous affair, and he reflected that the accidental destruction of an individual, Peza by name, would perhaps be nothing at all.

With the lieutenant he was soon walking along behind a series of little crescent-shape trenches, in which were soldiers, tranquilly interested, gossiping with the hum of a tea-party. Although these men were not at this time under fire, he concluded that they were fabulously brave. Else they would not be so comfortable, so at home in their sticky brown trenches. They were certain to be heavily attacked before the day was old. The universities had not taught him to understand this attitude.

At the passing of the young man in very nice tweed, with his new leggings, his new white helmet, his new field-glass case, his new revolver holster, the soiled soldiers turned with the same curiosity which a being in strange garb meets at the corners of streets. He might as well have been promenading a populous avenue. The soldiers volubly discussed his identity.

To Peza there was something awful in the absolute familiarity of each tone, expression, gesture. These men, menaced with battle, displayed the curiosity of the café. Then, on the verge of his great encounter toward death, he found himself extremely embarrassed, composing his face with difficulty, wondering what to do with his hands, like a gawk at a levée.

He felt ridiculous, and also he felt awed, aghast, at these men who could turn their faces from the ominous front and debate his clothes, his business. There was an element which was new born into his theory of war. He was not averse to the brisk pace at which the lieutenant moved along the line.

The roar of fighting was always in Peza's ears. It came from some short hills ahead and to the left. The road curved suddenly and entered a wood. The trees stretched their luxuriant and graceful branches over grassy slopes. A breeze made all this verdure gently rustle and speak in long silken sighs. Absorbed in listening to the hurricane racket from the front, he still remembered that these trees were growing, the grass-blades were extending according to their process. He inhaled a deep breath of moisture and fragrance from the grove, a wet odour which expressed all the opulent fecundity of unmoved nature, marching on with her million plans for multiple life, multiple death.

Further on, they came to a place where the Turkish shells were landing. There was a long hurtling sound in the air, and then one had sight of a shell. To Peza it was of the conical missiles which friendly officers had displayed to him on board warships. Curiously enough, too, this first shell smacked of the foundry, of men with smudged faces, of the blare of furnace fires. It brought machinery immediately into his mind. He thought that if he was killed there at that time it would be as romantic, to the old standards, as death by a bit of falling iron in a factory.

<h2 style="text-align:center">II</h2>

A child was playing on a mountain and disregarding a battle that was waging on the plain. Behind him was the little cobbled hut of his fled parents. It was now occupied by a pearl-coloured cow that stared out from the darkness thoughtful and tender-eyed. The child ran to and fro, fumbling with sticks and making great machinations with pebbles. By a striking exercise of artistic license the sticks were ponies, cows, and dogs, and the pebbles were sheep. He was managing large agricultural and herding affairs. He was too intent on them to pay much heed to the fight four miles away, which at that distance resembled in sound the beating of surf upon rocks. However, there were occasions when some louder outbreak of that thunder stirred him from his serious occupation, and he turned then a questioning eye upon the battle, a small stick poised in his hand, interrupted in the act of sending his dog after his sheep. His tranquillity in regard to the death on the plain was as invincible as that of the mountain on which he stood.

It was evident that fear had swept the parents away from their home in a manner that could make them forget this child, the first-born. Nevertheless, the hut was clean bare. The cow had committed no impropriety in billeting herself at the domicile of her masters. This smoke-coloured and odorous interior contained nothing as large as a humming-bird. Terror had operated on these runaway people in its sinister fashion, elevating details to enormous heights, causing a man to remember a button while he forgot a coat, overpowering every one with recollections of a broken coffee-cup, deluging them with fears forthe safety of an old pipe, and causing them to forget their first-born. Meanwhile the child played soberly with his trinkets.

He was solitary; engrossed in his own pursuits, it was seldom that he lifted his head to inquire of the world why it made so much noise. The stick in his hand was much larger to him than was an army corps of the distance. It was too childish for the mind of the child. He was dealing with sticks.

The battle lines writhed at times in the agony of a sea-creature on the sands. These tentacles flung and waved in a supreme excitement of pain, and the struggles of the great outlined body brought it nearer and nearer to the child. Once he looked at the plain and saw some men running wildly across a field. He had seen people chasing obdurate beasts in such fashion, and it struck him immediately that it was a manly thing which he would incorporate in his game. Consequently he raced furiously at his stone sheep, flourishing a cudgel, crying the shepherd calls. He paused frequently to get a cue of manner from the soldiers fighting on the plain. He reproduced, to a degree, any movements which he accounted rational to his theory of sheep-herding, the business of men, the traditional and exalted living of his father.

<h2 style="text-align:center">III</h2>

It was as if Peza was a corpse walking on the bottom of the sea, and finding there fields of grain, groves, weeds, the faces of men, voices. War, a strange employment of the race, presented to him a scene crowded with familiar objects which wore the livery of their commonness, placidly, undauntedly. He was smitten with keen astonishment; a spread of green grass lit with the flames of poppies was too old for the company of this new ogre. If he had been devoting the full lens of his mind to this phase, he would have known he was amazed that the trees, the flowers, the grass, all tender and peaceful nature had not taken to heels at once upon the outbreak of battle. He venerated the immovable poppies.

The road seemed to lead into the apex of an angle formed by the two defensive lines of the Greeks. There was a straggle of wounded men and of gunless and jaded men. These latter did not seem to be frightened. They remained very cool, walking with unhurried steps and busy in gossip. Peza tried to define them. Perhaps during the fight they had reached the limit of their mental storage, their capacity for excitement, for tragedy, and had then simply come away. Peza remembered his visit to a certain place of pictures, where he had found himself amid heavenly skies and diabolic midnights—the sunshine beating red upon desert sands, nude bodies flung to the shore in the green moon-glow, ghastly and starving men clawing at a wall in darkness, a girl at herbath with screened rays falling upon her pearly shoulders, a dance, a funeral, a review, an execution, all the strength of argus-eyed art: and he had whirled and whirled amid this universe with cries of woe and joy, sin and beauty piercing his ears until he had been obliged to simply come away. He remembered that as he had emerged he had lit a cigarette with unction and advanced promptly to a café. A great hollow quiet seemed to be upon the earth.

This was a different case, but in his thoughts he conceded the same causes to many of these gunless wanderers. They too may have dreamed at lightning speed until the capacity for it was overwhelmed. As he watched them, he again saw himself walking toward the café, puffing upon his cigarette. As if to reinforce his theory, a soldier stopped him with an eager but polite inquiry for a match. He watched the man light his little roll of tobacco and paper and begin to smoke ravenously.

Peza no longer was torn with sorrow at the sight of wounded men. Evidently he found that pity had a numerical limit, and when this was passed the emotion became another thing. Now, as he viewed them, he merely felt himself very lucky, and beseeched the continuance of his superior fortune. At the passing of these slouched and stained figures he now heard a reiteration of warning. A part of himself was appealing through the medium of these grim shapes. It was plucking at his sleeve and pointing, telling him to beware; and so it had come to pass that he cared for the implacable misery of these soldiers only as he would have cared for the harms of broken dolls. His whole vision was focussed upon his own chance.

The lieutenant suddenly halted. "Look," he said. "I find that my duty is in another direction. I must go another way. But if you wish to fight you have only to go forward, and any officer of the fighting line will give you opportunity." He raised his cap ceremoniously; Peza raised his new white helmet. The stranger to battles uttered thanks to his chaperon, the one who had presented him. They bowed punctiliously, staring at each other with civil eyes.

The lieutenant moved quietly away through a field. In an instant it flashed upon Peza's mind that this desertion was perfidious. He had been subjected to a criminal discourtesy. The officer had fetched him into the middle of the thing, and then left him to wander helplessly toward death. At one time he was upon the point of shouting at the officer.

In the vale there was an effect as if one was then beneath the battle. It was going on above somewhere. Alone, unguided, Peza felt like a man groping in a cellar. He reflected too that one should always see the beginning of a fight. It was too difficult to thus approach it when the affair was in full swing. The trees hid all movements of troops from him, and he thought he might be walking out to the very spot which chance had provided for the reception of a fool. He asked eager questions of passing soldiers. Some paid no heed to him; others shook their heads mournfully. They knew nothing save that war was hard work. If they talked at all it was in testimony of having fought well, savagely. Theydid not know if the army was going to advance, hold its ground, or retreat; they were weary.

A long pointed shell flashed through the air and struck near the base of a tree, with a fierce upheaval, compounded of earth and flames. Looking back, Peza could see the shattered tree quivering from head to foot. Its whole being underwent a convulsive tremor which was an exhibition of pain, and, furthermore, deep amazement. As he advanced through the vale, the shells continued to hiss and hurtle in long low flights, and the bullets purred in the air. The missiles were flying into the breast of an astounded nature. The landscape, bewildered, agonized, was suffering a rain of infamous shots, and Peza imagined a million eyes gazing at him with the gaze of startled antelopes.

There was a resolute crashing of musketry from the tall hill on the left, and from directly in front there was a mingled din of artillery and musketry firing. Peza felt that his pride was playing a great trick in forcing him forward in this manner under conditions of strangeness, isolation, and ignorance. But he recalled the manner of the lieutenant, the smile on the hill-top among the flying peasants. Peza blushed and pulled the peak of his helmet down on his forehead. He strode onward firmly. Nevertheless he hated the lieutenant, and he resolved that on some future occasion he would take much trouble to arrange a stinging social revenge upon that grinning jackanapes. It did not occur to him until later that he was now going to battle mainly because at a previous time a certain man had smiled.

## IV

The road curved round the base of a little hill, and on this hill a battery of mountain guns was leisurely shelling something unseen. In the lee of the height the mules, contented under their heavy saddles, were quietly browsing the long grass. Peza ascended the hill by a slanting path. He felt his heart beat swiftly; once at the top of the hill he would be obliged to look this phenomenon in the face. He hurried, with a mysterious idea of preventing by this strategy the battle from making his appearance a signal for some tremendous renewal. This vague thought seemed logical at the time. Certainly this living thing had knowledge of his coming. He endowed it with the intelligence of a barbaric deity. And so he hurried; he wished to surprise war, this terrible emperor, when it was growling on its throne. The ferocious and horrible sovereign was not to be allowed to make the arrival a pretext for some fit of smoky rage and blood. In this half-lull, Peza haddistinctly the sense of stealing upon the battle unawares.

The soldiers watching the mules did not seem to be impressed by anything august. Two of them sat side by side and talked comfortably; another lay flat upon his back staring dreamily at the sky; another cursed a mule for certain refractions. Despite their uniforms, their bandoliers and rifles, they were dwelling in the peace of hostlers. However, the long shells were whooping from time to time over the brow of the hill, and swirling in almost straight lines toward the vale of trees, flowers, and grass. Peza, hearing and seeing the shells, and seeing the pensive guardians of the mules, felt reassured. They were accepting the condition of war as easily as an old sailor accepts the chair behind the counter of a tobacco-shop. Or, it was merely that the farm-boy had gone to sea, and he had adjusted himself to the circumstances immediately, and with only the usual first misadventures in conduct. Peza was proud and ashamed that he was not of them, these stupid peasants, who, throughout the world, hold potentates on their thrones, make statesmen illustrious, provide generals with lasting victories, all with ignorance, indifference, or half-witted hatred, moving the world with the strength of their arms and getting their heads knocked together in the name of God, the king, or the Stock Exchange; immortal, dreaming, hopeless asses who surrender their reason to the care of a shining puppet, and persuade some toy to carry their lives in his purse. Peza mentally abased himself before them, and wished to stir them with furious kicks.

As his eyes ranged above the rim of the plateau, he saw a group of artillery officers talking busily. They turned at once and regarded his ascent. A moment later a row of infantry soldiers in a trench beyond the little guns all faced him. Peza bowed to the officers. He understood at the time that he had made a good and cool bow, and he wondered at it, for his breath was coming in gasps, he was stifling from sheer excitement. He felt like a tipsy man trying to conceal his muscular uncertainty from the people in the street. But the officers did not display any knowledge. They bowed. Behind them Peza saw the plain, glittering green, with three lines of black marked upon it heavily. The front of the first of these lines was frothy with smoke. To the left of this hill was a craggy mountain, from which came a continual dull rattle of musketry. Its summit was ringed with the white smoke. The black lines on the plain slowly moved. The shells that came from there passed overhead with the sound of great birds frantically flapping their wings. Peza thought of the first sight of the sea during a storm. He seemed to feel against his face the wind that races over the tops of cold and tumultuous billows.

He heard a voice afar off—"Sir, what would you?" He turned, and saw the dapper captain of the battery standing beside him. Only a moment had elapsed. "Pardon me, sir," said Peza, bowing again. The officer was evidently reserving his bows; he scanned the new-comer attentively. "Are you a correspondent?" he asked. Peza produced a card. "Yes, I came as a correspondent," he replied, "but now, sir, I have other thoughts. I wish to help. You see? I wish to help."

"What do you mean?" said the captain. "Are you a Greek? Do you wish to fight?"

"Yes, I am a Greek. I wish to fight." Peza's voice surprised him by coming from his lips in even and deliberate tones. He thought with gratification that he was behaving rather well. Another shell travelling from some unknown point on the plain whirled close and furiously in the air, pursuing an apparently horizontal course as if it were never going to touch the earth. The dark shape swished across the sky.

"Ah," cried the captain, now smiling, "I am not sure that we will be able to accommodate you with a fierce affair here just at this time, but—" He walked gaily to and fro behind the guns with Peza, pointing out to him the lines of the Greeks, and describing his opinion of the general plan of defence. He wore the air of an amiable host. Other officers questioned Peza in regard to the politics of the war. The king, the ministry, Germany, England, Russia, all these huge words were continually upon their tongues. "And the people in Athens? Were they—" Amid this vivacious babble Peza, seated upon an ammunition box, kept his glance high, watching the appearance of shell after shell. These officers were like men who had been lost for days in the forest. They were thirsty for any scrap of news. Nevertheless, one of them would occasionally dispute their informant courteously. What would Servia have to say to that? No, no, France and Russia could never allow it. Peza was elated. The shells killed no one; war was not so bad. He was simply having coffee in the smoking-room of some embassy where reverberate the names of nations.

A rumour had passed along the motley line of privates in the trench. The new arrival with the clean white helmet was a famous English cavalry officer come to assist the army with his counsel. They stared at the figure of him, surrounded by officers. Peza, gaining sense of the glances and whispers, felt that his coming was an event.

Later, he resolved that he could with temerity do something finer. He contemplated the mountain where the Greek infantry was engaged, and announced leisurely to the captain of the battery that he thought presently of going in that direction and getting into the fight. He re-affirmed the sentiments of a patriot. The captain seemed surprised. "Oh, there will be fighting here at this knoll in a few minutes," he said orientally. "That will be sufficient? You had better stay with us. Besides, I have been ordered to resume fire." The officers all tried to dissuade him from departing. It was really not worth the trouble. The battery would begin again directly. Then it would be amusing for him.

Peza felt that he was wandering with his protestations of high patriotism through a desert of sensible men. These officers gave no heed to his exalted declarations. They seemed too jaded. They were fighting the men who were fighting them. Palaver of the particular kind had subsided before their intense pre-occupation in war as a craft. Moreover, many men had talked in that manner and only talked.

Peza believed at first that they were treating him delicately. They were considerate of his inexperience. War had turned out to be such a gentle business that Peza concluded he could scorn this idea. He bade them a heroic farewell despite their objections.

However, when he reflected upon their ways afterward, he saw dimly that they were actuated principally by some universal childish desire for a spectatorof their fine things. They were going into action, and they wished to be seen at war, precise and fearless.

<h1 style="text-align:center">V</h1>

Climbing slowly to the high infantry position, Peza was amazed to meet a soldier whose jaw had been half shot away, and who was being helped down the sheep track by two tearful comrades. The man's breast was drenched with blood, and from a cloth which he held to the wound drops were splashing wildly upon the stones of the path. He gazed at Peza for a moment. It was a mystic gaze, which Peza withstood with difficulty. He was exchanging looks with a spectre; all aspect of the man was somehow gone from this victim. As Peza went on, one of the unwounded soldiers loudly shouted to him to return and assist in this tragic march. But even Peza's fingers revolted; he was afraid of the spectre; he would not have dared to touch it. He was surely craven in the movement of refusal he made to them. He scrambled hastily on up the path. He was running away.

At the top of the hill he came immediately upon a part of the line that was in action. Another battery of mountain guns was here firing at the streaks of black on the plain. There were trenches filled with men lining parts of the crest, and near the base were other trenches, all crashing away mightily. The plain stretched as far as the eye can see, and from wheresilver mist ended this emerald ocean of grass, a great ridge of snow-topped mountains poised against a fleckless blue sky. Two knolls, green and yellow with grain, sat on the prairie confronting the dark hills of the Greek position. Between them were the lines of the enemy. A row of trees, a village, a stretch of road, showed faintly on this great canvas, this tremendous picture, but men, the Turkish battalions, were emphasized startlingly upon it. The ranks of troops between the knolls and the Greek position were as black as ink.

The first line of course was muffled in smoke, but at the rear of it battalions crawled up and to and fro plainer than beetles on a plate. Peza had never understood that masses of men were so declarative, so unmistakable, as if nature makes every arrangement to give information of the coming and the presence of destruction, the end, oblivion. The firing was full, complete, a roar of cataracts, and this pealing of connected volleys was adjusted to the grandeur of the far-off range of snowy mountains. Peza, breathless, pale, felt that he had been set upon a pillar and was surveying mankind, the world. In the meantime dust had got in his eye. He took his handkerchief and mechanically administered to it.

An officer with a double stripe of purple on his trousers paced in the rear of the battery of howitzers. He waved a little cane. Sometimes he paused in his promenade to study the field through his glasses. "A fine scene, sir," he cried airily, upon the approach of Peza. It was like a blow in the chest to the wide-eyed volunteer. It revealed to him a point of view."Yes, sir, it is a fine scene," he answered. They spoke in French. "I am happy to be able to entertain monsieur with a little practice," continued the officer. "I am firing upon that mass of troops you see there a little to the right. They are probably forming for another attack." Peza smiled; here again appeared manners, manners erect by the side of death.

The right-flank gun of the battery thundered; there was a belch of fire and smoke; the shell flung swiftly and afar was known only to the ear in which rang a broadening hooting wake of sound. The howitzer had thrown itself backward convulsively, and lay with its wheels moving in the air as a squad of men rushed toward it. And later, it seemed as if each little gun had made the supreme effort of its being in each particular shot. They roared with voices far too loud, and the thunderous effort caused a gun to bound as in a dying convulsion. And then occasionally one was hurled with wheels in air. These shuddering howitzers presented an appearance of so many cowards always longing to bolt to the rear, but being implacably held to their business by this throng of soldiers who ran in squads to drag them up again to their obligation. The guns were herded and cajoled and bullied interminably. One by one, in relentless program, they were dragged forward to contribute a profound vibration of steel and wood, a flash and a roar, to the important happiness of man.

The adjacent infantry celebrated a good shot with smiles and an outburst of gleeful talk.

"Look, sir," cried an officer to Peza. Thin smoke was drifting lazily before Peza, and dodging impatiently he brought his eyes to bear upon that part of the plain indicated by the officer's finger. The enemy's infantry was advancing to attack. From the black lines had come forth an inky mass which was shaped much like a human tongue. It advanced slowly, casually, without apparent spirit, but with an insolent confidence that was like a proclamation of the inevitable.

The impetuous part was all played by the defensive side. Officers called, men plucked each other by the sleeve; there were shouts, motions, all eyes were turned upon the inky mass which was flowing toward the base of the hills, heavily, languorously, as oily and thick as one of the streams that ooze through a swamp.

Peza was chattering a question at every one. In the way, pushed aside, or in the way again, he continued to repeat it. "Can they take the position? Can they take the position? Can they take the position?" He was apparently addressing an assemblage of deaf men. Every eye was busy watching every hand. The soldiers did not even seem to see the interesting stranger in the white helmet who was crying out so feverishly.

Finally, however, the hurried captain of the battery espied him and heeded his question. "No, sir! no, sir! It is impossible," he shouted angrily. His manner seemed to denote that if he had sufficient time he would have completely insulted Peza. The latter swallowed the crumb of news without regard to the coating of scorn, and, waving his hand in adieu, he began to run along the crest of the hill toward the part of the Greek line against which the attack was directed.

VI

Peza, as he ran along the crest of the mountain, believed that his action was receiving the wrathful attention of the hosts of the foe. To him then it was incredible foolhardiness thus to call to himself the stares of thousands of hateful eyes. He was like a lad induced by playmates to commit some indiscretion in a cathedral. He was abashed; perhaps he even blushed as he ran. It seemed to him that the whole solemn ceremony of war had paused during this commission. So he scrambled wildly over the rocks in his haste to end the embarrassing ordeal. When he came among the crowning rifle-pits filled with eager soldiers he wanted to yell with joy. None noticed him save a young officer of infantry, who said—"Sir, what do you want?" It was obvious that people had devoted some attention to their own affairs.

Peza asserted, in Greek, that he wished above everything to battle for the fatherland. The officer nodded; with a smile he pointed to some dead men covered with blankets, from which were thrust upturned dusty shoes.

"Yes, I know, I know," cried Peza. He thought the officer was poetically alluding to the danger.

"No," said the officer at once. "I mean cartridges—a bandolier. Take a bandolier from one of them."

Peza went cautiously toward a body. He moved a hand toward the corner of a blanket. There he hesitated, stuck, as if his arm had turned to plaster. Hearing a rustle behind him he spun quickly. Three soldiers of the close rank in the trench were regarding him. The officer came again and tapped him on the shoulder. "Have you any tobacco?" Peza looked at him in bewilderment. His hand was still extended toward the blanket which covered the dead soldier. "Yes," he said, "I have some tobacco." He gave the officer his pouch. As if in compensation, the other directed a soldier to strip the bandolier from the corpse. Peza, having crossed the long cartridge belt on his breast, felt that the dead man had flung his two arms around him.

A soldier with a polite nod and smile gave Peza a rifle, a relic of another dead man. Thus, he felt, besides the clutch of a corpse about his neck, that the rifle was as inhumanly horrible as a snake that lives in a tomb. He heard at his ear something that was in effect like the voices of those two dead men, their low voices speaking to him of bloody death, mutilation. The bandolier gripped him tighter; he wished to raise his hands to his throat like a man who is choking. The rifle was clammy; upon his palms he felt the movement of the sluggish currents of a serpent's life; it was crawling and frightful.

All about him were these peasants, with their interested countenances, gibbering of the fight. From time to time a soldier cried out in semi-humorous lamentations descriptive of his thirst. One bearded man sat munching a great bit of hard bread. Fat, greasy, squat, he was like an idol made of tallow. Peza felt dimly that there was a distinction between this man and a young student who could write sonnets and play the piano quite well. This old blockhead was coolly gnawing at the bread, while he, Peza, was being throttled by a dead man's arms.

He looked behind him, and saw that a head by some chance had been uncovered from its blanket. Two liquid-like eyes were staring into his face. The head was turned a little sideways as if to get better opportunity for the scrutiny. Peza could feel himself blanch; he was being drawn and drawn by these dead men slowly, firmly down as to some mystic chamber under the earth where they could walk, dreadful figures, swollen and blood-marked. He was bidden; they had commanded him; he was going, going, going.

When the man in the new white helmet bolted for the rear, many of the soldiers in the trench thought that he had been struck, but those who had been nearest to him knew better. Otherwise they would have heard the silken sliding tender noise of the bullet and the thud of its impact. They bawled after him curses, and also outbursts of self-congratulation and vanity. Despite the prominence of the cowardly part, they were enabled to see in this exhibition a fine comment upon their own fortitude. The other soldiers thought that Peza had been wounded somewhere in the neck, because as he ran he was tearing madly at the bandolier, the dead man's arms. The soldier with the bread paused in his eating and cynically remarked upon the speed of the runaway.

An officer's voice was suddenly heard calling out the calculation of the distance to the enemy, the readjustment of the sights. There was a stirring rattle along the line. The men turned their eyes to the front. Other trenches beneath them to the right were already heavily in action. The smoke was lifting toward the blue sky. The soldier with the bread placed it carefully on a bit of paper beside him as he turned to kneel in the trench.

## VII

In the late afternoon, the child ceased his play on the mountain with his flocks and his dogs. Part of the battle had whirled very near to the base of his hill, and the noise was great. Sometimes he could see fantastic smoky shapes which resembled the curious figures in foam which one sees on the slant of a rough sea. The plain indeed was etched in white circles and whirligigs like the slope of a colossal wave. The child took seat on a stone and contemplated the fight. He was beginning to be astonished; he had never before seen cattle herded with such uproar. Lines of flame flashed out here and there. It was mystery.

Finally, without any preliminary indication, he began to weep. If the men struggling on the plain had had time and greater vision, they could have seen this strange tiny figure seated on a boulder, surveying them while the tears streamed. It was as simple as some powerful symbol.

As the magic clear light of day amid the mountains dimmed the distances, and the plain shone as a pallid blue cloth marked by the red threads of the firing, the child arose and moved off to the unwelcoming door of his home. He called softly for his mother, and complained of his hunger in the familiar formula. The pearl-coloured cow, grinding her jaws thoughtfully, stared at him with her large eyes. The peaceful gloom of evening was slowly draping the hills.

The child heard a rattle of loose stones on the hillside, and facing the sound, saw a moment later a man drag himself up to the crest of the hill and fall panting. Forgetting his mother and his hunger, filled with calm interest, the child walked forward and stood over the heaving form. His eyes too were now large and inscrutably wise and sad like those of the animal in the house.

After a silence he spoke inquiringly. "Are you a man?"

Peza rolled over quickly and gazed up into the fearless cherubic countenance. He did not attempt to reply. He breathed as if life was about to leave his body. He was covered with dust; his face had been cut in some way, and his cheek was ribboned with blood. All the spick of his former appearance had vanished in a general dishevelment, in which he resembled a creature that had been flung to and fro, up and down, by cliffs and prairies during an earthquake. He rolled his eye glassily at the child.

They remained thus until the child repeated his words. "Are you a man?"

Peza gasped in the manner of a fish. Palsied, windless, and abject, he confronted the primitive courage, the sovereign child, the brother of the mountains, the sky and the sea, and he knew that the definition of his misery could be written on a grass-blade.

# THE MEN IN THE STORM

The blizzard began to swirl great clouds of snow along the streets, sweeping it down from the roofs, and up from the pavements, until the faces of pedestrians tingled and burned as from a thousand needle-prickings. Those on the walks huddled their necks closely in the collars of their coats, and went along stooping like a race of aged people. The drivers of vehicles hurried their horses furiously on their way. They were made more cruel by the exposure of their position, aloft on high seats. The street cars, bound up town, went slowly, the horses slipping and straining in the spongy brown mass that lay between the rails. The drivers, muffled to the eyes, stood erect, facing the wind, models of grim philosophy. Overhead trains rumbled and roared, and the dark structure of the elevated railroad, stretching over the avenue, dripped little streams and drops of water upon the mud and snow beneath.

All the clatter of the street was softened by the masses that lay upon the cobbles, until, even to one who looked from a window, it became important music, a melody of life made necessary to the ear by the dreariness of the pitiless beat and sweep of the storm. Occasionally one could see black figures of men busily shovelling the white drifts from the walks. The sounds from their labour created new recollections of rural experiences which every man manages to have in a measure. Later, the immense windows of the shops became aglow with light, throwing great beams of orange and yellow upon the pavement. They were infinitely cheerful, yet in a way they accentuated the force and discomfort of the storm, and gave a meaning to the pace of the people and the vehicles, scores of pedestrians and drivers, wretched with cold faces, necks and feet, speeding for scores of unknown doors and entrances, scattering to an infinite variety of shelters, to places which the imagination made warm with the familiar colours of home.

There was an absolute expression of hot dinners in the pace of the people. If one dared to speculate upon the destination of those who came trooping, he lost himself in a maze of social calculation; he might fling a handful of sand and attempt to follow the flight of each particular grain. But as to the suggestion of hot dinners, he was in firm lines of thought, for it was upon every hurrying face. It is a matter of tradition; it is from the tales of childhood. It comes forth with every storm.

However, in a certain part of a dark west-side street, there was a collection of men to whom these things were as if they were not. In this street was located a charitable house, where for five cents the homeless of the city could get a bed at night, and in the morning coffee and bread.

During the afternoon of the storm, the whirling snows acted as drivers, as men with whips, and at half-past three the walk before the closed doors of the house was covered with wanderers of the street, waiting. For some distance on either side of the place they could be seen lurking in the doorways and behind projecting parts of buildings, gathering in close bunches in an effort to get warm. A covered wagon drawn up near the curb sheltered a dozen of them. Under the stairs that led to the elevated railway station, there were six or eight, their hands stuffed deep in their pockets, their shoulders stooped, jiggling their feet. Others always could be seen coming, a strange procession, some slouching along with the characteristic hopeless gait of professional strays, some coming with hesitating steps, wearing the air of men to whom this sort of thing was new.

It was an afternoon of incredible length. The snow, blowing in twisting clouds, sought out the men in their meagre hiding-places, and skilfully beat in among them, drenching their persons with showers of fine stinging flakes. They crowded together, muttering, and fumbling in their pockets to get their red inflamed wrists covered by the cloth.

New-comers usually halted at one end of the groups and addressed a question, perhaps much as a matter of form, "Is it open yet?"

Those who had been waiting inclined to take the questioner seriously and became contemptuous. "No; do yeh think we'd be standin' here?"

The gathering swelled in numbers steadily and persistently. One could always see them coming, trudging slowly through the storm.

Finally, the little snow plains in the street began to assume a leaden hue from the shadows of evening. The buildings upreared gloomily save where various windows became brilliant figures of light, that made shimmers and splashes of yellow on the snow. A street lamp on the curb struggled to illuminate, but it was reduced to impotent blindness by the swift gusts of sleet crusting its panes.

In this half-darkness, the men began to come from their shelter places and mass in front of the doors of charity. They were of all types, but the nationalities were mostly American, German, and Irish. Many were strong, healthy, clear-skinned fellows, with that stamp of countenance which is not frequently seen upon seekers after charity. There were men of undoubted patience, industry, and temperance, who, in time of ill-fortune, do not habitually turn to rail at the state of society, snarling at the arrogance of the rich, and bemoaning the cowardice of the poor, but who at these times are apt to wear a sudden and singular meekness, as if they saw the world's progress marching from them, and were trying to perceive where they had failed, what they had lacked, to be thus vanquished in the race. Then there were others of the shifting, Bowery element, who were used to paying ten cents for a place to sleep, but who now came here because it was cheaper.

But they were all mixed in one mass so thoroughly that one could not have discerned the different elements, but for the fact that the labouring men, for the most part, remained silent and impassive in the blizzard, their eyes fixed on the windows of the house, statues of patience.

The sidewalk soon became completely blocked by the bodies of the men. They pressed close to one another like sheep in a winter's gale, keeping one another warm by the heat of their bodies. The snow came down upon this compressed group of men until, directly from above, it might have appeared like a heap of snow-covered merchandise, if it were not for the fact that the crowd swayed gently with a unanimous, rhythmical motion. It was wonderful to see how the snow lay upon the heads and shoulders of these men, in little ridges an inch thick perhaps in places, the flakes steadily adding drop and drop, precisely as they fall upon the unresisting grass of the fields. The feet of the men were all wet and cold, and the wish to warm them accounted for the slow, gentle, rhythmical motion. Occasionally some man whose ear or nose tingled acutely from the cold winds would wriggle down until his head was protected by the shoulders of his companions.

There was a continuous murmuring discussion as to the probability of the doors being speedily opened. They persistently lifted their eyes towards the windows. One could hear little combats of opinion.

"There's a light in th' winder!"

"Naw; it's a reflection f'm across th' way."

"Well, didn't I see 'em light it?"

"You did?"

"I did!"

"Well, then, that settles it!"

As the time approached when they expected to be allowed to enter, the men crowded to the doors in an unspeakable crush, jamming and wedging in a way that it seemed would crack bones. They surged heavily against the building in a powerful wave of pushing shoulders. Once a rumour flitted among all the tossing heads.

"They can't open th' door! Th' fellers er smack up agin 'em."

Then a dull roar of rage came from the men on the outskirts; but all the time they strained and pushed until it appeared to be impossible for those that they cried out against to do anything but be crushed into pulp.

"Ah, git away f'm th' door!"

"Git outa that!"

"Throw 'em out!"

"Kill 'em!"

"Say, fellers, now, what th' 'ell? G've 'em a chance t' open th' door!"

"Yeh dam pigs, give 'em a chance t' open th' door!"

Men in the outskirts of the crowd occasionally yelled when a boot-heel of one of trampling feet crushed on their freezing extremities.

"Git off me feet, yeh clumsy tarrier!"

"Say, don't stand on me feet! Walk on th' ground!"

A man near the doors suddenly shouted—"O-o-oh! Le' me out—le' me out!" And another, a man of infinite valour, once twisted his head so as to half face those who were pushing behind him. "Quit yer shovin', yeh"—and he delivered a volley of the most powerful and singular invective, straight into the faces of the men behind him. It was as if he was hammering the noses of them with curses of triple brass. His face, red with rage, could be seen upon it, an expression of sublime disregard of consequences. But nobody cared to reply to his imprecations; it was too cold. Many of them snickered, and all continued to push.

In occasional pauses of the crowd's movement the men had opportunities to make jokes; usually grim things, and no doubt very uncouth. Nevertheless, they were notable—one does not expect to find the quality of humour in a heap of old clothes under a snow-drift.

The winds seemed to grow fiercer as time wore on. Some of the gusts of snow that came down on the close collection of heads, cut like knives and needles, and the men huddled, and swore, not like dark assassins, but in a sort of American fashion, grimly and desperately, it is true, but yet with a wondrous under-effect, indefinable and mystic, as if there was some kind of humour in this catastrophe, in this situation in a night of snow-laden winds.

Once the window of the huge dry-goods shop across the street furnished material for a few moments of forgetfulness. In the brilliantly-lighted space appeared the figure of a man. He was rather stout and very well clothed. His beard was fashioned charmingly after that of the Prince of Wales. He stood in an attitude of magnificent reflection. He slowly stroked his moustache with a certain grandeur of manner, and looked down at the snow-encrusted mob. From below, there was denoted a supreme complacence in him. It seemed that the sight operated inversely, and enabled him to more clearly regard his own delightful environment.

One of the mob chanced to turn his head, and perceived the figure in the window. "Hello, lookit 'is whiskers," he said genially.

Many of the men turned then, and a shout went up. They called to him in all strange keys. They addressed him in every manner, from familiar and cordial greetings, to carefully-worded advice concerning changes in his personal appearance. The man presently fled, and the mob chuckled ferociously, like ogres who had just devoured something.

They turned then to serious business. Often they addressed the stolid front of the house.

"Oh, let us in fer Gawd's sake!"

"Let us in, or we'll all drop dead!"

"Say, what's th' use o' keepin' us poor Indians out in th' cold?"

And always some one was saying, "Keep off my feet."

The crushing of the crowd grew terrific toward the last. The men, in keen pain from the blasts, began almost to fight. With the pitiless whirl of snow upon them, the battle for shelter was going to the strong. It became known that the basement door at the foot of a little steep flight of stairs was the one to be opened, and they jostled and heaved in this direction like labouring fiends. One could hear them panting and groaning in their fierce exertion.

Usually some one in the front ranks was protesting to those in the rear—"O-o-ow! Oh, say now, fellers, let up, will yeh? Do yeh wanta kill somebody!"

A policeman arrived and went into the midst of them, scolding and be-rating, occasionally threatening, but using no force but that of his hands and shoulders against these men who were only struggling to get in out of the storm. His decisive tones rang out sharply—"Stop that pushin' back there! Come, boys, don't push! Stop that! Here you, quit yer shovin'! Cheese that!"

When the door below was opened, a thick stream of men forced a way down the stairs, which were of an extraordinary narrowness, and seemed only wide enough for one at a time. Yet they somehow went down almost three abreast. It was a difficult and painful operation. The crowd was like a turbulent water forcing itself through one tiny outlet. The men in the rear, excited by the success of the others, made frantic exertions, for it seemed that this large band would more than fill the quarters, and that many would be left upon the pavements. It would be disastrous to be of the last, and accordingly men with the snow biting their faces, writhed and twisted with their might. One expected that from the tremendous pressure, the narrow passage to the basement door would be so choked and clogged with human limbs and bodies that movement would be impossible. Once indeed the crowd was forced to stop, and a cry went along that a man had been injured at the foot of the stairs. Butpresently the slow movement began again, and the policeman fought at the top of theflight to ease the pressure of those that were going down.

A reddish light from a window fell upon the faces of the men, when they, in turn, arrived at the last three steps, and were about to enter. One could then note a change of expression that had come over their features. As they stood thus upon the threshold of their hopes, they looked suddenly contented and complacent. The fire had passed from their eyes and the snarl had vanished from their lips. The very force of the crowd in the rear, which had previously vexed them, was regarded from another point of view, for it now made it inevitable that they should go through the little doors into the place that was cheery and warm with light.

The tossing crowd on the sidewalk grew smaller and smaller. The snow beat with merciless persistence upon the bowed heads of those who waited. The wind drove it up from the pavements in frantic forms of winding white, and it seethed in circles about the huddled forms passing in one by one, three by three, out of the storm.

# AN OMINOUS BABY

A baby was wandering in a strange country. He was a tattered child with a frowsled wealth of yellow hair. His dress, of a checked stuff, was soiled, and showed the marks of many conflicts, like the chain-shirt of a warrior. His sun-tanned knees shone above wrinkled stockings, which he pulled up occasionally with an impatient movement when they entangled his feet. From a gaping shoe there appeared an array of tiny toes.

He was toddling along an avenue between rows of stolid brown houses. He went slowly, with a look of absorbed interest on his small flushed face. His blue eyes stared curiously. Carriages went with a musical rumble over the smooth asphalt. A man with a chrysanthemum was going up steps. Two nursery maids chatted as they walked slowly, while their charges hobnobbed amiably between perambulators. A truck wagon roared thunderously in the distance.

The child from the poor district made his way along the brown street filled with dull grey shadows. High up, near the roofs, glancing sun-rays changed cornices to blazing gold and silvered the fronts of windows. The wandering baby stopped and stared at the two children laughing and playing in their carriages among the heaps of rugs and cushions. He braced his legs apart in an attitude of earnest attention. His lower jaw fell, and disclosed his small, even teeth. As they moved on, he followed the carriages with awe in his face as if contemplating a pageant. Once one of the babies, with twittering laughter, shook a gorgeous rattle at him. He smiled jovially in return.

Finally a nursery maid ceased conversation and, turning, made a gesture of annoyance.

"Go 'way, little boy," she said to him. "Go 'way. You're all dirty."

He gazed at her with infant tranquillity for a moment, and then went slowly off dragging behind him a bit of rope he had acquired in another street. He continued to investigate the new scenes. The people and houses struck him with interest as would flowers and trees. Passengers had to avoid the small, absorbed figure in the middle of the sidewalk. They glanced at the intent baby face covered with scratches and dust as with scars and with powder smoke.

After a time, the wanderer discovered upon the pavement a pretty child in fine clothes playing with a toy. It was a tiny fire-engine, painted brilliantly in crimson and gold. The wheels rattled as its small owner dragged it uproariously about by means of a string. The babe with his bit of rope trailing behind him paused and regarded the child and the toy. For a long while he remained motionless, save for his eyes, which followed all movements of the glittering thing. The owner paid no attention to the spectator, but continued his joyous imitations of phases of the career of a fire-engine. His gleeful baby laugh rang against the calm fronts of the houses. After a little the wandering baby began quietly to sidle nearer. His bit of rope, now forgotten, dropped at his feet. He removed his eyes from the toy and glanced expectantly at the other child.

"Say," he breathed softly.

The owner of the toy was running down the walk at top speed. His tongue was clanging like a bell and his legs were galloping. He did not look around at the coaxing call from the small tattered figure on the curb.

The wandering baby approached still nearer, and presently spoke again.

"Say," he murmured, "le' me play wif it?"

The other child interrupted some shrill tootings. He bended his head and spoke disdainfully over his shoulder.

"No," he said.

The wanderer retreated to the curb. He failed to notice the bit of rope, once treasured. His eyes followed as before the winding course of the engine, and his tender mouth twitched.

"Say," he ventured at last, "is dat yours?"

"Yes," said the other, tilting his round chin. He drew his property suddenly behind him as if it were menaced. "Yes," he repeated, "it's mine."

"Well, le' me play wif it?" said the wandering baby, with a trembling note of desire in his voice.

"No," cried the pretty child with determined lips. "It's mine. My ma-ma buyed it."

"Well, tan't I play wif it?" His voice was a sob. He stretched forth little covetous hands.

"No," the pretty child continued to repeat. "No, it's mine."

"Well, I want to play wif it," wailed the other. A sudden fierce frown mantled his baby face. He clenched his fat hands and advanced with a formidable gesture. He looked some wee battler in a war.

"It's mine! It's mine," cried the pretty child, his voice in the treble of outraged rights.

"I want it," roared the wanderer.

"It's mine! It's mine!"

"I want it!"

"It's mine!"

The pretty child retreated to the fence, and there paused at bay. He protected his property with outstretched arms. The small vandal made a charge. There was a short scuffle at the fence. Each grasped the string to the toy and tugged. Their faces were wrinkled with baby rage, the verge of tears. Finally, the child in tatters gave a supreme tug and wrenched the string from the other's hands. He set off rapidly down the street, bearing the toy in his arms. He was weeping with the air of a wronged one who has at last succeeded in achieving his rights. The other baby was squalling lustily. He seemed quite helpless. He rung his chubby hands and railed.

After the small barbarian had got some distance away, he paused and regarded his booty. His little form curved with pride. A soft, gleeful smile loomedthrough the storm of tears. With great care he prepared the toy for travelling. He stopped a moment on a corner and gazed at the pretty child, whose small figure was quivering with sobs. As the latter began to show signs of beginning pursuit, the little vandal turned and vanished down a dark side street as into a cavern.

# A GREAT MISTAKE

An Italian kept a fruit-stand on a corner where he had good aim at the people who came down from the elevated station, and at those who went along two thronged streets. He sat most of the day in a backless chair that was placed strategically.

There was a babe living hard by, up five flights of stairs, who regarded this Italian as a tremendous being. The babe had investigated this fruit-stand. It had thrilled him as few things he had met with in his travels had thrilled him. The sweets of the world had laid there in dazzling rows, tumbled in luxurious heaps. When he gazed at this Italian seated amid such splendid treasures, his lower lip hung low and his eyes, raised to the vendor's face, were filled with deep respect, worship, as if he saw omnipotence.

The babe came often to this corner. He hovered about the stand and watched each detail of the business. He was fascinated by the tranquillity of the vendor, the majesty of power and possession. At times he was so engrossed in his contemplation that people, hurrying, had to use care to avoid bumping him down.

He had never ventured very near to the stand. It was his habit to hang warily about the curb. Even there he resembled a babe who looks unbidden at a feast of gods.

One day, however, as the baby was thus staring, the vendor arose, and going along the front of the stand, began to polish oranges with a red pocket handkerchief. The breathless spectator moved across the side walk until his small face almost touched the vendor's sleeve. His fingers were gripped in a fold of his dress.

At last, the Italian finished with the oranges and returned to his chair. He drew a newspaper printed in his language from behind a bunch of bananas. He settled himself in a comfortable position, and began to glare savagely at the print. The babe was left face to face with the massed joys of the world. For a time he was a simple worshipper at this golden shrine. Then tumultuous desires began to shake him. His dreams were of conquest. His lips moved. Presently into his head there came a little plan. He sidled nearer, throwing swift and cunning glances at the Italian. He strove to maintain his conventional manner, but the whole plot was written upon his countenance.

At last he had come near enough to touch the fruit. From the tattered skirt came slowly his small dirty hand. His eyes were still fixed upon the vendor. His features were set, save for the under lip, which had a faint fluttering movement. The hand went forward.

Elevated trains thundered to the station and the stairway poured people upon the sidewalks. There was a deep sea roar from feet and wheels going ceaselessly. None seemed to perceive the babe engaged in a great venture.

The Italian turned his paper. Sudden panic smote the babe. His hand dropped, and he gave vent to a cry of dismay. He remained for a moment staring at the vendor. There was evidently a great debate in his mind. His infant intellect had defined this Italian. The latter was undoubtedly a man who would eat babes that provoked him. And the alarm in the babe when this monarch had turned his newspaper brought vividly before him the consequences if he were detected. But at this moment the vendor gave a blissful grunt, and tilting his chair against a wall, closed his eyes. His paper dropped unheeded.

The babe ceased his scrutiny and again raised his hand. It was moved with supreme caution toward the fruit. The fingers were bent, claw-like, in the manner of great heart-shaking greed. Once he stopped and chattered convulsively, because the vendor moved in his sleep. The babe, with his eyes still upon the Italian, again put forth his hand, and the rapacious fingers closed over a round bulb.

And it was written that the Italian should at this moment open his eyes. He glared at the babe a fierce question. Thereupon the babe thrust the round bulb behind him, and with a face expressive of the deepest guilt, began a wild but elaborate series of gestures declaring his innocence. The Italian howled. He sprang to his feet, and with three steps overtook the babe. He whirled him fiercely, and took from the little fingers a lemon.

# AN ELOQUENCE OF GRIEF

The windows were high and saintly, of the shape that is found in churches. From time to time a policeman at the door spoke sharply to some incoming person. "Take your hat off!" He displayed in his voice the horror of a priest when the sanctity of a chapel is defied or forgotten. The court-room was crowded with people who sloped back comfortably in their chairs, regarding with undeviating glances the procession and its attendant and guardian policemen that moved slowly inside the spear-topped railing. All persons connected with a case went close to the magistrate's desk before a word was spoken in the matter, and then their voices were toned to the ordinary talking strength. The crowd in the court-room could not hear a sentence; they could merely see shifting figures, men that gestured quietly, women that sometimes raised an eager eloquent arm. They could not always see the judge, although they were able to estimate his location by the tall stands surmounted by white globes that were at either hand of him. And so those who had come for curiosity's sweet sake wore an air of being in wait for a cry of anguish, some loud painful protestation that would bring the proper thrill to their jaded, world-weary nerves—wires that refused to vibrate for ordinary affairs.

Inside the railing the court officers shuffled the various groups with speed and skill; and behind the desk the magistrate patiently toiled his way through mazes of wonderful testimony.

In a corner of this space, devoted to those who had business before the judge, an officer in plain clothes stood with a girl that wept constantly. None seemed to notice the girl, and there was no reason why she should be noticed, if the curious in the body of the court-room were not interested in the devastation which tears bring upon some complexions. Her tears seemed to burn like acid, and they left fierce pink marks on her face. Occasionally the girl looked across the room, where two well-dressed young women and a man stood waiting with the serenity of people who are not concerned as to the interior fittings of a jail.

The business of the court progressed, and presently the girl, the officer, and the well-dressed contingent stood before the judge. Thereupon two lawyers engaged in some preliminary fire-wheels, which were endured generally in silence. The girl, it appeared, was accused of stealing fifty dollars' worth of silk clothing from the room of one of the well-dressed women. She had been a servant in the house.

In a clear way, and with none of the ferocity that an accuser often exhibits in a police-court, calmly and moderately, the two young women gave theirtestimony. Behind them stood their escort, always mute. His part, evidently, was to furnish the dignity, and he furnished it heavily, almost massively.

When they had finished, the girl told her part. She had full, almost Afric, lips, and they had turned quite white. The lawyer for the others asked some questions, which he did—be it said, in passing—with the air of a man throwing flower-pots at a stone house.

It was a short case and soon finished. At the end of it the judge said that, considering the evidence, he would have to commit the girl for trial. Instantly the quick-eyed court officer began to clear the way for the next case. The well-dressed women and their escort turned one way and the girl turned another, toward a door with an austere arch leading into a stone-paved passage. Then it was that a great cry rang through the court-room, the cry of this girl who believed that she was lost.

The loungers, many of them, underwent a spasmodic movement as if they had been knived. The court officers rallied quickly. The girl fell back opportunely for the arms of one of them, and her wild heels clicked twice on the floor. "I am innocent! Oh, I am innocent!"

People pity those who need none, and the guilty sob alone; but innocent or guilty, this girl's scream described such a profound depth of woe—it was so graphic of grief, that it slit with a dagger's sweep the curtain of common-place, and disclosed the gloom-shrouded spectre that sat in the young girl's heart so plainly, in so universal a tone of the mind, that aman heard expressed some far-off midnight terror of his own thought.

The cries died away down the stone-paved passage. A patrol-man leaned one arm composedly on the railing, and down below him stood an aged, almost toothless wanderer, tottering and grinning.

"Plase, yer honer," said the old man as the time arrived for him to speak, "if ye'll lave me go this time, I've niver been dhrunk befoor, sir."

A court officer lifted his hand to hide a smile.

# THE AUCTION

Some said that Ferguson gave up sailoring because he was tired of the sea. Some said that it was because he loved a woman. In truth it was because he was tired of the sea and because he loved a woman.

He saw the woman once, and immediately she became for him the symbol of all things unconnected with the sea. He did not trouble to look again at the grey old goddess, the muttering slave of the moon. Her splendours, her treacheries, her smiles, her rages, her vanities, were no longer on his mind. He took heels after a little human being, and the woman made his thought spin at all times like a top; whereas the ocean had only made him think when he was on watch.

He developed a grin for the power of the sea, and, in derision, he wanted to sell the red and green parrot which had sailed four voyages with him. The woman, however, had a sentiment concerning the bird's plumage, and she commanded Ferguson to keep it in order, as it happened, that she might forget to put food in its cage.

The parrot did not attend the wedding. It stayed at home and blasphemed at a stock of furniture, bought on the installment plan, and arrayed for the reception of the bride and groom.

As a sailor, Ferguson had suffered the acute hankering for port; and being now always in port, he tried to force life to become an endless picnic. He was not an example of diligent and peaceful citizenship. Ablution became difficult in the little apartment, because Ferguson kept the wash-basin filled with ice and bottles of beer: and so, finally, the dealer in second-hand furniture agreed to auction the household goods on commission. Owing to an exceedingly liberal definition of a term, the parrot and cage were included. "On the level?" cried the parrot, "On the level? On the level? On the level?"

On the way to the sale, Ferguson's wife spoke hopefully. "You can't tell, Jim," she said. "Perhaps some of 'em will get to biddin', and we might get almost as much as we paid for the things."

The auction room was in a cellar. It was crowded with people and with house furniture; so that as the auctioneer's assistant moved from one piece to another he caused a great shuffling. There was an astounding number of old women in curious bonnets. The rickety stairway was thronged with men who wished to smoke and be free from the old women. Two lamps made all the faces appear yellow as parchment. Incidentally they could impart a lustre of value to very poor furniture.

The auctioneer was a fat, shrewd-looking individual, who seemed also to be a great bully. The assistant was the most imperturbable of beings, moving withthe dignity of an image on rollers. As the Fergusons forced their way down the stairway, the assistant roared: "Number twenty-one!"

"Number twenty-one!" cried the auctioneer. "Number twenty-one! A fine new handsome bureau! Two dollars? Two dollars is bid! Two and a half! Two and a half! Three? Three is bid. Four! Four dollars! A fine new handsome bureau at four dollars! Four dollars! Four dollars! F-o-u-r d-o-l-l-a-r-s! Sold at four dollars."

"On the level?" cried the parrot, muffled somewhere among furniture and carpets. "On the level? On the level?" Every one tittered.

Mrs. Ferguson had turned pale, and gripped her husband's arm. "Jim! Did you hear? The bureau—four dollars—"

Ferguson glowered at her with the swift brutality of a man afraid of a scene. "Shut up, can't you!"

Mrs. Ferguson took a seat upon the steps; and hidden there by the thick ranks of men, she began to softly sob. Through her tears appeared the yellowish mist of the lamplight, streaming about the monstrous shadows of the spectators. From time to time these latter whispered eagerly: "See, that went cheap!" In fact when anything was bought at a particularly low price, a murmur of admiration arose for the successful bidder.

The bedstead was sold for two dollars, the mattresses and springs for one dollar and sixty cents. This figure seemed to go through the woman's heart. There was derision in the sound of it. She bowed her head in her hands. "Oh, God, a dollar-sixty! Oh, God, a dollar-sixty!"

The parrot was evidently under heaps of carpet, but the dauntless bird still raised the cry, "On the level?"

Some of the men near Mrs. Ferguson moved timidly away upon hearing her low sobs. They perfectly understood that a woman in tears is formidable.

The shrill voice went like a hammer, beat and beat, upon the woman's heart. An odour of varnish, of the dust of old carpets, assailed her and seemed to possess a sinister meaning. The golden haze from the two lamps was an atmosphere of shame, sorrow, greed. But it was when the parrot called that a terror of the place and of the eyes of the people arose in her so strongly that she could not have lifted her head any more than if her neck had been of iron.

At last came the parrot's turn. The assistant fumbled until he found the ring of the cage, and the bird was drawn into view. It adjusted its feathers calmly and cast a rolling wicked eye over the crowd.

> *"Oh, the good ship Sarah sailed the seas,*
> *And the wind it blew all day—"*

This was the part of a ballad which Ferguson had tried to teach it. With a singular audacity and scorn, the parrot bawled these lines at the auctioneer as if it considered them to bear some particular insult.

The throng in the cellar burst into laughter. The auctioneer attempted to start the bidding, and the parrot interrupted with a repetition of the lines. It swaggered to and fro on its perch, and gazed at the faces of the crowd, with so much rowdy understanding and derision that even the auctioneer could not confront it. The auction was brought to a halt; a wild hilarity developed, and every one gave jeering advice.

Ferguson looked down at his wife and groaned. She had cowered against the wall, hiding her face. He touched her shoulder and she arose. They sneaked softly up the stairs with heads bowed.

Out in the street, Ferguson gripped his fists and said: "Oh, but wouldn't I like to strangle it!"

His wife cried in a voice of wild grief: "It—it m—made us a laughing-stock in—in front of all that crowd!"

For the auctioning of their household goods, the sale of their home—this financial calamity lost its power in the presence of the social shame contained in a crowd's laughter.

# A DETAIL

The tiny old lady in the black dress and curious little black bonnet had at first seemed alarmed at the sound made by her feet upon the stone pavements. But later she forgot about it, for she suddenly came into the tempest of the Sixth Avenue shopping district, where from the streams of people and vehicles went up a roar like that from headlong mountain torrents.

She seemed then like a chip that catches, recoils, turns and wheels, a reluctant thing in the clutch of the impetuous river. She hesitated, faltered, debated with herself. Frequently she seemed about to address people; then of a sudden she would evidently lose her courage. Meanwhile the torrent jostled her, swung her this and that way.

At last, however, she saw two young women gazing in at a shop-window. They were well-dressed girls; they wore gowns with enormous sleeves that made them look like full-rigged ships with all sails set. They seemed to have plenty of time; they leisurely scanned the goods in the window. Other people had made the tiny old woman much afraid because obviously they were speeding to keep such tremendously important engagements. She went close to the girls and peered in at the same window. She watched them furtively for a time. Then finally she said—

"Excuse me!"

The girls looked down at this old face with its two large eyes turned towards them.

"Excuse me, can you tell me where I can get any work?"

For an instant the two girls stared. Then they seemed about to exchange a smile, but, at the last moment, they checked it. The tiny old lady's eyes were upon them. She was quaintly serious, silently expectant. She made one marvel that in that face the wrinkles showed no trace of experience, knowledge; they were simply little, soft, innocent creases. As for her glance, it had the trustfulness of ignorance and the candour of babyhood.

"I want to get something to do, because I need the money," she continued since, in their astonishment, they had not replied to her first question. "Of course I'm not strong and I couldn't do very much, but I can sew well; and in a house where there was a good many men folks, I could do all the mending. Do you know any place where they would like me to come?"

The young women did then exchange a smile, but it was a subtle tender smile, the edge of personal grief.

"Well, no, madame," hesitatingly said one of them at last; "I don't think I know any one."

A shade passed over the tiny old lady's face, a shadow of the wing of disappointment.

"Don't you?" she said, with a little struggle to be brave, in her voice.

Then the girl hastily continued—"But if you will give me your address, I may find some one, and if I do, I will surely let you know of it."

The tiny old lady dictated her address, bending over to watch the girl write on a visiting card with a little silver pencil. Then she said—

"I thank you very much." She bowed to them, smiling, and went on down the avenue.

As for the two girls, they walked to the curb and watched this aged figure, small and frail, in its black gown and curious black bonnet. At last, the crowd, the innumerable wagons, intermingling and changing with uproar and riot, suddenly engulfed it.

# MAGGIE: A GIRL OF THE STREETS

## CHAPTER I

A very little boy stood upon a heap of gravel for the honor of Rum Alley. He was throwing stones at howling urchins from Devil's Row who were circling madly about the heap and pelting at him.

His infantile countenance was livid with fury. His small body was writhing in the delivery of great, crimson oaths.

"Run, Jimmie, run! Dey'll get yehs," screamed a retreating Rum Alley child.

"Naw," responded Jimmie with a valiant roar, "dese micks can't make me run."

Howls of renewed wrath went up from Devil's Row throats. Tattered gamins on the right made a furious assault on the gravel heap. On their small, convulsed faces there shone the grins of true assassins. As they charged, they threw stones and cursed in shrill chorus.

The little champion of Rum Alley stumbled precipitately down the other side. His coat had been torn to shreds in a scuffle, and his hat was gone. He had bruises on twenty parts of his body, and blood was dripping from a cut in his head. His wan features wore a look of a tiny, insane demon.

On the ground, children from Devil's Row closed in on their antagonist. He crooked his left arm defensively about his head and fought with cursing fury. The little boys ran to and fro, dodging, hurling stones and swearing in barbaric trebles.

From a window of an apartment house that upreared its form from amid squat, ignorant stables, there leaned a curious woman. Some laborers, unloading a scow at a dock at the river, paused for a moment and regarded the fight. The engineer of a passive tugboat hung lazily to a railing and watched. Over on the Island, a worm of yellow convicts came from the shadow of a building and crawled slowly along the river's bank.

A stone had smashed into Jimmie's mouth. Blood was bubbling over his chin and down upon his ragged shirt. Tears made furrows on his dirt-stained cheeks. His thin legs had begun to tremble and turn weak, causing his small body to reel. His roaring curses of the first part of the fight had changed to a blasphemous chatter.

In the yells of the whirling mob of Devil's Row children there were notes of joy like songs of triumphant savagery. The little boys seemed to leer gloatingly at the blood upon the other child's face.

Down the avenue came boastfully sauntering a lad of sixteen years, although the chronic sneer of an ideal manhood already sat upon his lips. His hat was tipped with an air of challenge over his eye. Between his teeth, a cigar stump was tilted at the angle of defiance. He walked with a certain swing of the shoulders which appalled the timid. He glanced over into the vacant lot in which the little raving boys from Devil's Row seethed about the shrieking and tearful child from Rum Alley.

"Gee!" he murmured with interest. "A scrap. Gee!"

He strode over to the cursing circle, swinging his shoulders in a manner which denoted that he held victory in his fists. He approached at the back of one of the most deeply engaged of the Devil's Row children.

"Ah, what deh hell," he said, and smote the deeply-engaged one on the back of the head. The little boy fell to the ground and gave a hoarse, tremendous howl. He scrambled to his feet, and perceiving, evidently, the size of his assailant, ran quickly off, shouting alarms. The entire Devil's Row party followed him. They came to a stand a short distance away and yelled taunting oaths at the boy with the chronic sneer. The latter, momentarily, paid no attention to them.

"What deh hell, Jimmie?" he asked of the small champion.

Jimmie wiped his blood-wet features with his sleeve.

"Well, it was dis way, Pete, see! I was goin' teh lick dat Riley kid and dey all pitched on me."

Some Rum Alley children now came forward. The party stood for a moment exchanging vainglorious remarks with Devil's Row. A few stones were thrown at long distances, and words of challenge passed between small warriors. Then the Rum Alley contingent turned slowly in the direction of their home street. They began to give, each to each, distorted versions of the fight. Causes of retreat in particular cases were magnified. Blows dealt in the fight were enlarged to catapultian power, and stones thrown were alleged to have hurtled with infinite accuracy. Valor grew strong again, and the little boys began to swear with great spirit.

"Ah, we blokies kin lick deh hull damn Row," said a child, swaggering.

Little Jimmie was striving to stanch the flow of blood from his cut lips. Scowling, he turned upon the speaker.

"Ah, where deh hell was yeh when I was doin' all deh fightin?" he demanded. "Youse kids makes me tired."

"Ah, go ahn," replied the other argumentatively.

Jimmie replied with heavy contempt. "Ah, youse can't fight, Blue Billie! I kin lick yeh wid one han'."

"Ah, go ahn," replied Billie again.

"Ah," said Jimmie threateningly.

"Ah," said the other in the same tone.

They struck at each other, clinched, and rolled over on the cobble stones.

"Smash 'im, Jimmie, kick deh damn guts out of 'im," yelled Pete, the lad with the chronic sneer, in tones of delight.

The small combatants pounded and kicked, scratched and tore. They began to weep and their curses struggled in their throats with sobs. The other little boys clasped their hands and wriggled their legs in excitement. They formed a bobbing circle about the pair.

A tiny spectator was suddenly agitated.

"Cheese it, Jimmie, cheese it! Here comes yer fader," he yelled.

The circle of little boys instantly parted. They drew away and waited in ecstatic awe for that which was about to happen. The two little boys fighting in the modes of four thousand years ago, did not hear the warning.

Up the avenue there plodded slowly a man with sullen eyes. He was carrying a dinner pail and smoking an apple-wood pipe.

As he neared the spot where the little boys strove, he regarded them listlessly. But suddenly he roared an oath and advanced upon the rolling fighters.

"Here, you Jim, git up, now, while I belt yer life out, you damned disorderly brat."

He began to kick into the chaotic mass on the ground. The boy Billie felt a heavy boot strike his head. He made a furious effort and disentangled himself from Jimmie. He tottered away, damning.

Jimmie arose painfully from the ground and confronting his father, began to curse him. His parent kicked him. "Come home, now," he cried, "an' stop yer jawin', er I'll lam the everlasting head off yehs."

They departed. The man paced placidly along with the apple-wood emblem of serenity between his teeth. The boy followed a dozen feet in the rear. He swore luridly, for he felt that it was degradation for one who aimed to be some vague soldier, or a man of blood with a sort of sublime license, to be taken home by a father.

## CHAPTER II

Eventually they entered into a dark region where, from a careening building, a dozen gruesome doorways gave up loads of babies to the street and the gutter. A wind of early autumn raised yellow dust from cobbles and swirled it against an hundred windows. Long streamers of garments fluttered from fire-escapes. In all unhandy places there were buckets, brooms, rags and bottles. In the street infants played or fought with other infants or sat stupidly in the way of vehicles. Formidable women, with uncombed hair and disordered dress, gossiped while leaning on railings, or screamed in frantic quarrels. Withered persons, in curious postures of submission to something, sat smoking pipes in obscure corners. A thousand odors of cooking food came forth to the street. The building quivered and creaked from the weight of humanity stamping about in its bowels.

A small ragged girl dragged a red, bawling infant along the crowded ways. He was hanging back, baby-like, bracing his wrinkled, bare legs.

The little girl cried out: "Ah, Tommie, come ahn. Dere's Jimmie and fader. Don't be a-pullin' me back."

She jerked the baby's arm impatiently. He fell on his face, roaring. With a second jerk she pulled him to his feet, and they went on. With the obstinacy of his order, he protested against being dragged in a chosen direction. He made heroic endeavors to keep on his legs, denounce his sister and consume a bit of orange peeling which he chewed between the times of his infantile orations.

As the sullen-eyed man, followed by the blood-covered boy, drew near, the little girl burst into reproachful cries. "Ah, Jimmie, youse bin fightin' agin."

The urchin swelled disdainfully.

"Ah, what deh hell, Mag. See?"

The little girl upbraided him, "Youse allus fightin', Jimmie, an' yeh knows it puts mudder out when yehs come home half dead, an' it's like we'll all get a poundin'."

She began to weep. The babe threw back his head and roared at his prospects.

"Ah, what deh hell!" cried Jimmie. "Shut up er I'll smack yer mout'. See?"

As his sister continued her lamentations, he suddenly swore and struck her. The little girl reeled and, recovering herself, burst into tears and quaveringly cursed him. As she slowly retreated her brother advanced dealing her cuffs. The father heard and turned about.

"Stop that, Jim, d'yeh hear? Leave yer sister alone on the street. It's like I can never beat any sense into yer damned wooden head."

The urchin raised his voice in defiance to his parent and continued his attacks. The babe bawled tremendously, protesting with great violence. During his sister's hasty manoeuvres, he was dragged by the arm.

Finally the procession plunged into one of the gruesome doorways. They crawled up dark stairways and along cold, gloomy halls. At last the father pushed open a door and they entered a lighted room in which a large woman was rampant.

She stopped in a career from a seething stove to a pan-covered table. As the father and children filed in she peered at them.

"Eh, what? Been fightin' agin, by Gawd!" She threw herself upon Jimmie. The urchin tried to dart behind the others and in the scuffle the babe, Tommie, was knocked down. He protested with his usual vehemence, because they had bruised his tender shins against a table leg.

The mother's massive shoulders heaved with anger. Grasping the urchin by the neck and shoulder she shook him until he rattled. She dragged him to an unholy sink, and, soaking a rag in water, began to scrub his lacerated face with it. Jimmie screamed in pain and tried to twist his shoulders out of the clasp of the huge arms.

The babe sat on the floor watching the scene, his face in contortions like that of a woman at a tragedy. The father, with a newly-ladened pipe in his mouth, crouched on a backless chair near the stove. Jimmie's cries annoyed him. He turned about and bellowed at his wife:

"Let the damned kid alone for a minute, will yeh, Mary? Yer allus poundin' 'im. When I come nights I can't git no rest 'cause yer allus poundin' a kid. Let up, d'yeh hear? Don't be allus poundin' a kid."

The woman's operations on the urchin instantly increased in violence. At last she tossed him to a corner where he limply lay cursing and weeping.

The wife put her immense hands on her hips and with a chieftain-like stride approached her husband.

"Ho," she said, with a great grunt of contempt. "An' what in the devil are you stickin' your nose for?"

The babe crawled under the table and, turning, peered out cautiously. The ragged girl retreated and the urchin in the corner drew his legs carefully beneath him.

The man puffed his pipe calmly and put his great mudded boots on the back part of the stove.

"Go teh hell," he murmured, tranquilly.

The woman screamed and shook her fists before her husband's eyes. The rough yellow of her face and neck flared suddenly crimson. She began to howl.

He puffed imperturbably at his pipe for a time, but finally arose and began to look out at the window into the darkening chaos of back yards.

"You've been drinkin', Mary," he said. "You'd better let up on the bot', ol' woman, or you'll git done."

"You're a liar. I ain't had a drop," she roared in reply.

They had a lurid altercation, in which they damned each other's souls with frequence.

The babe was staring out from under the table, his small face working in his excitement.

The ragged girl went stealthily over to the corner where the urchin lay.

"Are yehs hurted much, Jimmie?" she whispered timidly.

"Not a damn bit! See?" growled the little boy.

"Will I wash deh blood?"

"Naw!"

"Will I—"

"When I catch dat Riley kid I'll break 'is face! Dat's right! See?"

He turned his face to the wall as if resolved to grimly bide his time.

In the quarrel between husband and wife, the woman was victor. The man grabbed his hat and rushed from the room, apparently determined upon a vengeful drunk. She followed to the door and thundered at him as he made his way down stairs.

She returned and stirred up the room until her children were bobbing about like bubbles.

"Git outa deh way," she persistently bawled, waving feet with their dishevelled shoes near the heads of her children. She shrouded herself, puffing and snorting, in a cloud of steam at the stove, and eventually extracted a frying-pan full of potatoes that hissed.

She flourished it. "Come teh yer suppers, now," she cried with sudden exasperation. "Hurry up, now, er I'll help yeh!"

The children scrambled hastily. With prodigious clatter they arranged themselves at table. The babe sat with his feet dangling high from a precarious infant chair and gorged his small stomach. Jimmie forced, with feverish rapidity, the grease-enveloped pieces between his wounded lips. Maggie, with side glances of fear of interruption, ate like a small pursued tigress.

The mother sat blinking at them. She delivered reproaches, swallowed potatoes and drank from a yellow-brown bottle. After a time her mood changed and she wept as she carried little Tommie into another room and laid him to sleep with his fists doubled in an old quilt of faded red and green grandeur. Then she came and moaned by the stove. She rocked to and fro upon a chair, shedding tears and crooning miserably to the two children about their "poor mother" and "yer fader, damn 'is soul."

The little girl plodded between the table and the chair with a dish-pan on it. She tottered on her small legs beneath burdens of dishes.

Jimmie sat nursing his various wounds. He cast furtive glances at his mother. His practised eye perceived her gradually emerge from a muddled mist of sentiment until her brain burned in drunken heat. He sat breathless.

Maggie broke a plate.

The mother started to her feet as if propelled.

"Good Gawd," she howled. Her eyes glittered on her child with sudden hatred. The fervent red of her face turned almost to purple. The little boy ran to the halls, shrieking like a monk in an earthquake.

He floundered about in darkness until he found the stairs. He stumbled, panic-stricken, to the next floor. An old woman opened a door. A light behind her threw a flare on the urchin's quivering face.

"Eh, Gawd, child, what is it dis time? Is yer fader beatin' yer mudder, or yer mudder beatin' yer fader?"

## CHAPTER III

Jimmie and the old woman listened long in the hall. Above the muffled roar of conversation, the dismal wailings of babies at night, the thumping of feet in unseen corridors and rooms, mingled with the sound of varied hoarse shoutings in the street and the rattling of wheels over cobbles, they heard the screams of the child and the roars of the mother die away to a feeble moaning and a subdued bass muttering.

The old woman was a gnarled and leathery personage who could don, at will, an expression of great virtue. She possessed a small music-box capable of one tune, and a collection of "God bless yehs" pitched in assorted keys of fervency. Each day she took a position upon the stones of Fifth Avenue, where she crooked her legs under her and crouched immovable and hideous, like an idol. She received daily a small sum in pennies. It was contributed, for the most part, by persons who did not make their homes in that vicinity.

Once, when a lady had dropped her purse on the sidewalk, the gnarled woman had grabbed it and smuggled it with great dexterity beneath her cloak. When she was arrested she had cursed the lady into a partial swoon, and with her aged limbs, twisted from rheumatism, had almost kicked the stomach out of a huge policeman whose conduct upon that occasion she referred to when she said: "The police, damn 'em."

"Eh, Jimmie, it's cursed shame," she said. "Go, now, like a dear an' buy me a can, an' if yer mudder raises 'ell all night yehs can sleep here."

Jimmie took a tendered tin-pail and seven pennies and departed. He passed into the side door of a saloon and went to the bar. Straining up on his toes he raised the pail and pennies as high as his arms would let him. He saw two hands thrust down and take them. Directly the same hands let down the filled pail and he left.

In front of the gruesome doorway he met a lurching figure. It was his father, swaying about on uncertain legs.

"Give me deh can. See?" said the man, threateningly.

"Ah, come off! I got dis can fer dat ol' woman an' it 'ud be dirt teh swipe it. See?" cried Jimmie.

The father wrenched the pail from the urchin. He grasped it in both hands and lifted it to his mouth. He glued his lips to the under edge and tilted his head. His hairy throat swelled until it seemed to grow near his chin. There was a tremendous gulping movement and the beer was gone.

The man caught his breath and laughed. He hit his son on the head with the empty pail. As it rolled clanging into the street, Jimmie began to scream and kicked repeatedly at his father's shins.

"Look at deh dirt what yeh done me," he yelled. "Deh ol' woman 'ill be raisin' hell."

He retreated to the middle of the street, but the man did not pursue. He staggered toward the door.

"I'll club hell outa yeh when I ketch yeh," he shouted, and disappeared.

During the evening he had been standing against a bar drinking whiskies and declaring to all comers, confidentially: "My home reg'lar livin' hell! Damndes' place! Reg'lar hell! Why do I come an' drin' whisk' here thish way? 'Cause home reg'lar livin' hell!"

Jimmie waited a long time in the street and then crept warily up through the building. He passed with great caution the door of the gnarled woman, and finally stopped outside his home and listened.

He could hear his mother moving heavily about among the furniture of the room. She was chanting in a mournful voice, occasionally interjecting bursts of volcanic wrath at the father, who, Jimmie judged, had sunk down on the floor or in a corner.

"Why deh blazes don' chere try teh keep Jim from fightin'? I'll break her jaw," she suddenly bellowed.

The man mumbled with drunken indifference. "Ah, wha' deh hell. W'a's odds? Wha' makes kick?"

"Because he tears 'is clothes, yeh damn fool," cried the woman in supreme wrath.

The husband seemed to become aroused. "Go teh hell," he thundered fiercely in reply. There was a crash against the door and something broke into clattering fragments. Jimmie partially suppressed a howl and darted down the stairway. Below he paused and listened. He heard howls and curses, groans and shrieks, confusingly in chorus as if a battle were raging. With all was the crash of splintering furniture. The eyes of the urchin glared in fear that one of them would discover him.

Curious faces appeared in doorways, and whispered comments passed to and fro. "Ol' Johnson's raisin' hell agin."

Jimmie stood until the noises ceased and the other inhabitants of the tenement had all yawned and shut their doors. Then he crawled upstairs with the caution of an invader of a panther den. Sounds of labored breathing came through the broken door-panels. He pushed the door open and entered, quaking.

A glow from the fire threw red hues over the bare floor, the cracked and soiled plastering, and the overturned and broken furniture.

In the middle of the floor lay his mother asleep. In one corner of the room his father's limp body hung across the seat of a chair.

The urchin stole forward. He began to shiver in dread of awakening his parents. His mother's great chest was heaving painfully. Jimmie paused and looked down at her. Her face was inflamed and swollen from drinking. Her yellow brows shaded eyelids that had brown blue. Her tangled hair tossed in waves over her forehead. Her mouth was set in the same lines of vindictive hatred that it had, perhaps, borne during the fight. Her bare, red arms were thrown out above her head in positions of exhaustion, something, mayhap, like those of a sated villain.

The urchin bended over his mother. He was fearful lest she should open her eyes, and the dread within him was so strong, that he could not forbear to stare, but hung as if fascinated over the woman's grim face.

Suddenly her eyes opened. The urchin found himself looking straight into that expression, which, it would seem, had the power to change his blood to salt. He howled piercingly and fell backward.

The woman floundered for a moment, tossed her arms about her head as if in combat, and again began to snore.

Jimmie crawled back in the shadows and waited. A noise in the next room had followed his cry at the discovery that his mother was awake. He grovelled in the gloom, the eyes from out his drawn face riveted upon the intervening door.

He heard it creak, and then the sound of a small voice came to him. "Jimmie! Jimmie! Are yehs dere?" it whispered. The urchin started. The thin, white face of his sister looked at him from the door-way of the other room. She crept to him across the floor.

The father had not moved, but lay in the same death-like sleep. The mother writhed in uneasy slumber, her chest wheezing as if she were in the agonies of strangulation. Out at the window a florid moon was peering over dark roofs, and in the distance the waters of a river glimmered pallidly.

The small frame of the ragged girl was quivering. Her features were haggard from weeping, and her eyes gleamed from fear. She grasped the urchin's arm in her little trembling hands and they huddled in a corner. The eyes of both were drawn, by some force, to stare at the woman's face, for they thought she need only to awake and all fiends would come from below.

They crouched until the ghost-mists of dawn appeared at the window, drawing close to the panes, and looking in at the prostrate, heaving body of the mother.

## CHAPTER IV

The babe, Tommie, died. He went away in a white, insignificant coffin, his small waxen hand clutching a flower that the girl, Maggie, had stolen from an Italian.

She and Jimmie lived.

The inexperienced fibres of the boy's eyes were hardened at an early age. He became a young man of leather. He lived some red years without laboring. During that time his sneer became chronic. He studied human nature in the gutter, and found it no worse than he thought he had reason to believe it. He never conceived a respect for the world, because he had begun with no idols that it had smashed.

He clad his soul in armor by means of happening hilariously in at a mission church where a man composed his sermons of "yous." While they got warm at the stove, he told his hearers just where he calculated they stood with the Lord. Many of the sinners were impatient over the pictured depths of their degradation. They were waiting for soup-tickets.

A reader of words of wind-demons might have been able to see the portions of a dialogue pass to and fro between the exhorter and his hearers.

"You are damned," said the preacher. And the reader of sounds might have seen the reply go forth from the ragged people: "Where's our soup?"

Jimmie and a companion sat in a rear seat and commented upon the things that didn't concern them, with all the freedom of English gentlemen. When they grew thirsty and went out their minds confused the speaker with Christ.

Momentarily, Jimmie was sullen with thoughts of a hopeless altitude where grew fruit. His companion said that if he should ever meet God he would ask for a million dollars and a bottle of beer.

Jimmie's occupation for a long time was to stand on streetcorners and watch the world go by, dreaming blood-red dreams at the passing of pretty women. He menaced mankind at the intersections of streets.

On the corners he was in life and of life. The world was going on and he was there to perceive it.

He maintained a belligerent attitude toward all well-dressed men. To him fine raiment was allied to weakness, and all good coats covered faint hearts. He and his order were kings, to a certain extent, over the men of untarnished clothes, because these latter dreaded, perhaps, to be either killed or laughed at.

Above all things he despised obvious Christians and ciphers with the chrysanthemums of aristocracy in their button-holes. He considered himself above both of these classes. He was afraid of neither the devil nor the leader of society.

When he had a dollar in his pocket his satisfaction with existence was the greatest thing in the world. So, eventually, he felt obliged to work. His father died and his mother's years were divided up into periods of thirty days.

He became a truck driver. He was given the charge of a painstaking pair of horses and a large rattling truck. He invaded the turmoil and tumble of the down-town streets and learned to breathe maledictory defiance at the police who occasionally used to climb up, drag him from his perch and beat him.

In the lower part of the city he daily involved himself in hideous tangles. If he and his team chanced to be in the rear he preserved a demeanor of serenity, crossing his legs and bursting forth into yells when foot passengers took dangerous dives beneath the noses of his champing horses. He smoked his pipe calmly for he knew that his pay was marching on.

If in the front and the key-truck of chaos, he entered terrifically into the quarrel that was raging to and fro among the drivers on their high seats, and sometimes roared oaths and violently got himself arrested.

After a time his sneer grew so that it turned its glare upon all things. He became so sharp that he believed in nothing. To him the police were always actuated by malignant impulses and the rest of the world was composed, for the most part, of despicable creatures who were all trying to take advantage of him and with whom, in defense, he was obliged to quarrel on all possible occasions. He himself occupied a down-trodden position that had a private but distinct element of grandeur in its isolation.

The most complete cases of aggravated idiocy were, to his mind, rampant upon the front platforms of all the street cars. At first his tongue strove with these beings, but he eventually was superior. He became immured like an African cow. In him grew a majestic contempt for those strings of street cars that followed him like intent bugs.

He fell into the habit, when starting on a long journey, of fixing his eye on a high and distant object, commanding his horses to begin, and then going into a sort of a trance of observation. Multitudes of drivers might howl in his rear, and passengers might load him with opprobrium, he would not awaken until some blue policeman turned red and began to frenziedly tear bridles and beat the soft noses of the responsible horses.

When he paused to contemplate the attitude of the police toward himself and his fellows, he believed that they were the only men in the city who had no rights. When driving about, he felt that he was held liable by the police for anything that might occur in the streets, and was the common prey of all energetic officials. In revenge, he resolved never to move out of the way of anything, until formidable circumstances, or a much larger man than himself forced him to it.

Foot-passengers were mere pestering flies with an insane disregard for their legs and his convenience. He could not conceive their maniacal desires to cross the streets. Their madness smote him with eternal amazement. He was continually storming at them from his throne. He sat aloft and denounced their frantic leaps, plunges, dives and straddles.

When they would thrust at, or parry, the noses of his champing horses, making them swing their heads and move their feet, disturbing a solid dreamy repose, he swore at the men as fools, for he himself could perceive that Providence had caused it clearly to be written, that he and his team had the unalienable right to stand in the proper path of the sun chariot, and if they so minded, obstruct its mission or take a wheel off.

And, perhaps, if the god-driver had an ungovernable desire to step down, put up his flame-colored fists and manfully dispute the right of way, he would have probably been immediately opposed by a scowling mortal with two sets of very hard knuckles.

It is possible, perhaps, that this young man would have derided, in an axle-wide alley, the approach of a flying ferry boat. Yet he achieved a respect for a fire engine. As one charged toward his truck, he would drive fearfully upon a sidewalk, threatening untold people with annihilation. When an engine would strike a mass of blocked trucks, splitting it into fragments, as a blow annihilates a cake of ice, Jimmie's team could usually be observed high and safe, with whole wheels, on the sidewalk. The fearful coming of the engine could break up the most intricate muddle of heavy vehicles at which the police had been swearing for the half of an hour.

A fire engine was enshrined in his heart as an appalling thing that he loved with a distant dog-like devotion. They had been known to overturn street-cars. Those leaping horses, striking sparks from the cobbles in their forward lunge, were creatures to be ineffably admired. The clang of the gong pierced his breast like a noise of remembered war.

When Jimmie was a little boy, he began to be arrested. Before he reached a great age, he had a fair record.

He developed too great a tendency to climb down from his truck and fight with other drivers. He had been in quite a number of miscellaneous fights, and in some general barroom rows that had become known to the police. Once he had been arrested for assaulting a Chinaman. Two women in different parts of the city, and entirely unknown to each other, caused him considerable annoyance by breaking forth, simultaneously, at fateful intervals, into wailings about marriage and support and infants.

Nevertheless, he had, on a certain star-lit evening, said wonderingly and quite reverently: "Deh moon looks like hell, don't it?"

## CHAPTER V

The girl, Maggie, blossomed in a mud puddle. She grew to be a most rare and wonderful production of a tenement district, a pretty girl.

None of the dirt of Rum Alley seemed to be in her veins. The philosophers up-stairs, down-stairs and on the same floor, puzzled over it.

When a child, playing and fighting with gamins in the street, dirt disguised her. Attired in tatters and grime, she went unseen.

There came a time, however, when the young men of the vicinity said: "Dat Johnson goil is a puty good looker." About this period her brother remarked to her: "Mag, I'll tell yeh dis! See? Yeh've edder got teh go teh hell or go teh work!" Whereupon she went to work, having the feminine aversion of going to hell.

By a chance, she got a position in an establishment where they made collars and cuffs. She received a stool and a machine in a room where sat twenty girls of various shades of yellow discontent. She perched on the stool and treadled at her machine all day, turning out collars, the name of whose brand could be noted for its irrelevancy to anything in connection with collars. At night she returned home to her mother.

Jimmie grew large enough to take the vague position of head of the family. As incumbent of that office, he stumbled up-stairs late at night, as his father had done before him. He reeled about the room, swearing at his relations, or went to sleep on the floor.

The mother had gradually arisen to that degree of fame that she could bandy words with her acquaintances among the police-justices. Court-officials called her by her first name. When she appeared they pursued a course which had been theirs for months. They invariably grinned and cried out: "Hello, Mary, you here again?" Her grey head wagged in many a court. She always besieged the bench with voluble excuses, explanations, apologies and prayers. Her flaming face and rolling eyes were a sort of familiar sight on the island. She measured time by means of sprees, and was eternally swollen and dishevelled.

One day the young man, Pete, who as a lad had smitten the Devil's Row urchin in the back of the head and put to flight the antagonists of his friend, Jimmie, strutted upon the scene. He met Jimmie one day on the street, promised to take him to a boxing match in Williamsburg, and called for him in the evening.

Maggie observed Pete.

He sat on a table in the Johnson home and dangled his checked legs with an enticing nonchalance. His hair was curled down over his forehead in an oiled bang. His rather pugged nose seemed to revolt from contact with a bristling moustache of short, wire-like hairs. His blue double-breasted coat, edged with black braid, buttoned close to a red puff tie, and his patent-leather shoes looked like murder-fitted weapons.

His mannerisms stamped him as a man who had a correct sense of his personal superiority. There was valor and contempt for circumstances in the glance of his eye. He waved his hands like a man of the world, who dismisses religion and philosophy, and says "Fudge." He had certainly seen everything and with each curl of his lip, he declared that it amounted to nothing. Maggie thought he must be a very elegant and graceful bartender.

He was telling tales to Jimmie.

Maggie watched him furtively, with half-closed eyes, lit with a vague interest.

"Hully gee! Dey makes me tired," he said. "Mos' e'ry day some farmer comes in an' tries teh run deh shop. See? But dey gits t'rowed right out! I jolt dem right out in deh street before dey knows where dey is! See?"

"Sure," said Jimmie.

"Dere was a mug come in deh place deh odder day wid an idear he wus goin' teh own deh place! Hully gee, he wus goin' teh own deh place! I see he had a still on an' I didn' wanna giv 'im no stuff, so I says: 'Git deh hell outa here an' don' make no trouble,' I says like dat! See? 'Git deh hell outa here an' don' make no trouble'; like dat. 'Git deh hell outa here,' I says. See?"

Jimmie nodded understandingly. Over his features played an eager desire to state the amount of his valor in a similar crisis, but the narrator proceeded.

"Well, deh blokie he says: 'T'hell wid it! I ain' lookin' for no scrap,' he says (See?), 'but' he says, 'I'm 'spectable cit'zen an' I wanna drink an' purtydamnsoon, too.' See? 'Deh hell,' I says. Like dat! 'Deh hell,' I says. See? 'Don' make no trouble,' I says. Like dat. 'Don' make no trouble.' See? Den deh mug he squared off an' said he was fine as silk wid his dukes (See?) an' he wanned a drink damnquick. Dat's what he said. See?"

"Sure," repeated Jimmie.

Pete continued. "Say, I jes' jumped deh bar an' deh way I plunked dat blokie was great. See? Dat's right! In deh jaw! See? Hully gee, he t'rowed a spittoon true deh front windee. Say, I taut I'd drop dead. But deh boss, he comes in after an' he says, 'Pete, yehs done jes' right! Yeh've gota keep order an' it's all right.' See? 'It's all right,' he says. Dat's what he said."

The two held a technical discussion.

"Dat bloke was a dandy," said Pete, in conclusion, "but he hadn' oughta made no trouble. Dat's what I says teh dem: 'Don' come in here an' make no trouble,' I says, like dat. 'Don' make no trouble.' See?"

As Jimmie and his friend exchanged tales descriptive of their prowess, Maggie leaned back in the shadow. Her eyes dwelt wonderingly and rather wistfully upon Pete's face. The broken furniture, grimey walls, and general disorder and dirt of her home of a sudden appeared before her and began to take a potential aspect. Pete's aristocratic person looked as if it might soil. She looked keenly at him, occasionally, wondering if he was feeling contempt. But Pete seemed to be enveloped in reminiscence.

"Hully gee," said he, "dose mugs can't phase me. Dey knows I kin wipe up deh street wid any t'ree of dem."

When he said, "Ah, what deh hell," his voice was burdened with disdain for the inevitable and contempt for anything that fate might compel him to endure.

Maggie perceived that here was the beau ideal of a man. Her dim thoughts were often searching for far away lands where, as God says, the little hills sing together in the morning. Under the trees of her dream-gardens there had always walked a lover.

## CHAPTER VI

Pete took note of Maggie.

"Say, Mag, I'm stuck on yer shape. It's outa sight," he said, parenthetically, with an affable grin.

As he became aware that she was listening closely, he grew still more eloquent in his descriptions of various happenings in his career. It appeared that he was invincible in fights.

"Why," he said, referring to a man with whom he had had a misunderstanding, "dat mug scrapped like a damn dago. Dat's right. He was dead easy. See? He tau't he was a scrapper. But he foun' out diff'ent! Hully gee."

He walked to and fro in the small room, which seemed then to grow even smaller and unfit to hold his dignity, the attribute of a supreme warrior. That swing of the shoulders that had frozen the timid when he was but a lad had increased with his growth and education at the ratio of ten to one. It, combined with the sneer upon his mouth, told mankind that there was nothing in space which could appall him. Maggie marvelled at him and surrounded him with greatness. She vaguely tried to calculate the altitude of the pinnacle from which he must have looked down upon her.

"I met a chump deh odder day way up in deh city," he said. "I was goin' teh see a frien' of mine. When I was a-crossin' deh street deh chump runned plump inteh me, an' den he turns aroun' an' says, 'Yer insolen' ruffin,' he says, like dat. 'Oh, gee,' I says, 'oh, gee, go teh hell and git off deh eart',' I says, like dat. See? 'Go teh hell an' git off deh eart',' like dat. Den deh blokie he got wild. He says I was a contempt'ble scoun'el, er somet'ing like dat, an' he says I was doom' teh everlastin' pe'dition an' all like dat. 'Gee,' I says, 'gee! Deh hell I am,' I says. 'Deh hell I am,' like dat. An' den I slugged 'im. See?"

With Jimmie in his company, Pete departed in a sort of a blaze of glory from the Johnson home. Maggie, leaning from the window, watched him as he walked down the street.

Here was a formidable man who disdained the strength of a world full of fists. Here was one who had contempt for brass-clothed power; one whose knuckles could defiantly ring against the granite of law. He was a knight.

The two men went from under the glimmering street-lamp and passed into shadows.

Turning, Maggie contemplated the dark, dust-stained walls, and the scant and crude furniture of her home. A clock, in a splintered and battered oblong box of varnished wood, she suddenly regarded as an abomination. She noted that it ticked raspingly. The almost vanished flowers in the carpet-pattern, she conceived to be newly hideous. Some faint attempts she had made with blue ribbon, to freshen the appearance of a dingy curtain, she now saw to be piteous.

She wondered what Pete dined on.

She reflected upon the collar and cuff factory. It began to appear to her mind as a dreary place of endless grinding. Pete's elegant occupation brought him, no doubt, into contact with people who had money and manners. It was probable that he had a large acquaintance of pretty girls. He must have great sums of money to spend.

To her the earth was composed of hardships and insults. She felt instant admiration for a man who openly defied it. She thought that if the grim angel of death should clutch his heart, Pete would shrug his shoulders and say: "Oh, ev'ryt'ing goes."

She anticipated that he would come again shortly. She spent some of her week's pay in the purchase of flowered cretonne for a lambrequin. She made it with infinite care and hung it to the slightly-careening mantel, over the stove, in the kitchen. She studied it with painful anxiety from different points in the room. She wanted it to look well on Sunday night when, perhaps, Jimmie's friend would come. On Sunday night, however, Pete did not appear.

Afterward the girl looked at it with a sense of humiliation. She was now convinced that Pete was superior to admiration for lambrequins.

A few evenings later Pete entered with fascinating innovations in his apparel. As she had seen him twice and he had different suits on each time, Maggie had a dim impression that his wardrobe was prodigiously extensive.

"Say, Mag," he said, "put on yer bes' duds Friday night an' I'll take yehs teh deh show. See?"

He spent a few moments in flourishing his clothes and then vanished, without having glanced at the lambrequin.

Over the eternal collars and cuffs in the factory Maggie spent the most of three days in making imaginary sketches of Pete and his daily environment. She imagined some half dozen women in love with him and thought he must lean dangerously toward an indefinite one, whom she pictured with great charms of person, but with an altogether contemptible disposition.

She thought he must live in a blare of pleasure. He had friends, and people who were afraid of him.

She saw the golden glitter of the place where Pete was to take her. An entertainment of many hues and many melodies where she was afraid she might appear small and mouse-colored.

Her mother drank whiskey all Friday morning. With lurid face and tossing hair she cursed and destroyed furniture all Friday afternoon. When Maggie came home at half-past six her mother lay asleep amidst the wreck of chairs and a table. Fragments of various household utensils were scattered about the floor. She had vented some phase of drunken fury upon the lambrequin. It lay in a bedraggled heap in the corner.

"Hah," she snorted, sitting up suddenly, "where deh hell yeh been? Why deh hell don' yeh come home earlier? Been loafin' 'round deh streets. Yer gettin' teh be a reg'lar devil."

When Pete arrived Maggie, in a worn black dress, was waiting for him in the midst of a floor strewn with wreckage. The curtain at the window had been pulled by a heavy hand and hung by one tack, dangling to and fro in the draft through the cracks at the sash. The knots of blue ribbons appeared like violated flowers. The fire in the stove had gone out. The displaced lids and open doors showed heaps of sullen grey ashes. The remnants of a meal, ghastly, like dead flesh, lay in a corner. Maggie's red mother, stretched on the floor, blasphemed and gave her daughter a bad name.

## CHAPTER VII

An orchestra of yellow silk women and bald-headed men on an elevated stage near the centre of a great green-hued hall, played a popular waltz. The place was crowded with people grouped about little tables. A battalion of waiters slid among the throng, carrying trays of beer glasses and making change from the inexhaustible vaults of their trousers pockets. Little boys, in the costumes of French chefs, paraded up and down the irregular aisles vending fancy cakes. There was a low rumble of conversation and a subdued clinking of glasses. Clouds of tobacco smoke rolled and wavered high in air about the dull gilt of the chandeliers.

The vast crowd had an air throughout of having just quitted labor. Men with calloused hands and attired in garments that showed the wear of an endless trudge for a living, smoked their pipes contentedly and spent five, ten, or perhaps fifteen cents for beer. There was a mere sprinkling of kid-gloved men who smoked cigars purchased elsewhere. The great body of the crowd was composed of people who showed that all day they strove with their hands. Quiet Germans, with maybe their wives and two or three children, sat listening to the music, with the expressions of happy cows. An occasional party of sailors from a war-ship, their faces pictures of sturdy health, spent the earlier hours of the evening at the small round tables. Very infrequent tipsy men, swollen with the value of their opinions, engaged their companions in earnest and confidential conversation. In the balcony, and here and there below, shone the impassive faces of women. The nationalities of the Bowery beamed upon the stage from all directions.

Pete aggressively walked up a side aisle and took seats with Maggie at a table beneath the balcony.

"Two beehs!"

Leaning back he regarded with eyes of superiority the scene before them. This attitude affected Maggie strongly. A man who could regard such a sight with indifference must be accustomed to very great things.

It was obvious that Pete had been to this place many times before, and was very familiar with it. A knowledge of this fact made Maggie feel little and new.

He was extremely gracious and attentive. He displayed the consideration of a cultured gentleman who knew what was due.

"Say, what deh hell? Bring deh lady a big glass! What deh hell use is dat pony?"

"Don't be fresh, now," said the waiter, with some warmth, as he departed.

"Ah, git off deh eart'," said Pete, after the other's retreating form.

Maggie perceived that Pete brought forth all his elegance and all his knowledge of high-class customs for her benefit. Her heart warmed as she reflected upon his condescension.

The orchestra of yellow silk women and bald-headed men gave vent to a few bars of anticipatory music and a girl, in a pink dress with short skirts, galloped upon the stage. She smiled upon the throng as if in acknowledgment of a warm welcome, and began to walk to and fro, making profuse gesticulations and singing, in brazen soprano tones, a song, the words of which were inaudible. When she broke into the swift rattling measures of a chorus some half-tipsy men near the stage joined in the rollicking refrain and glasses were pounded rhythmically upon the tables. People leaned forward to watch her and to try to catch the words of the song. When she vanished there were long rollings of applause.

Obedient to more anticipatory bars, she reappeared amidst the half-suppressed cheering of the tipsy men. The orchestra plunged into dance music and the laces of the dancer fluttered and flew in the glare of gas jets. She divulged the fact that she was attired in some half dozen skirts. It was patent that any one of them would have proved adequate for the purpose for which skirts are intended. An occasional man bent forward, intent upon the pink stockings. Maggie wondered at the splendor of the costume and lost herself in calculations of the cost of the silks and laces.

The dancer's smile of stereotyped enthusiasm was turned for ten minutes upon the faces of her audience. In the finale she fell into some of those grotesque attitudes which were at the time popular among the dancers in the theatres up-town, giving to the Bowery public the phantasies of the aristocratic theatre-going public, at reduced rates.

"Say, Pete," said Maggie, leaning forward, "dis is great."

"Sure," said Pete, with proper complacence.

A ventriloquist followed the dancer. He held two fantastic dolls on his knees. He made them sing mournful ditties and say funny things about geography and Ireland.

"Do dose little men talk?" asked Maggie.

"Naw," said Pete, "it's some damn fake. See?"

Two girls, on the bills as sisters, came forth and sang a duet that is heard occasionally at concerts given under church auspices. They supplemented it with a dance which of course can never be seen at concerts given under church auspices.

After the duettists had retired, a woman of debatable age sang a negro melody. The chorus necessitated some grotesque waddlings supposed to be an imitation of a plantation darkey, under the influence, probably, of music and the moon. The audience was just enthusiastic enough over it to have her return and sing a sorrowful lay, whose lines told of a mother's love and a sweetheart who waited and a young man who was lost at sea under the most harrowing circumstances. From the faces of a score or so in the crowd, the self-contained look faded. Many heads were bent forward with eagerness and sympathy. As the last distressing sentiment of the piece was brought forth, it was greeted by that kind of applause which rings as sincere.

As a final effort, the singer rendered some verses which described a vision of Britain being annihilated by America, and Ireland bursting her bonds. A carefully prepared crisis was reached in the last line of the last verse, where the singer threw out her arms and cried, "The star-spangled banner." Instantly a great cheer swelled from the throats of the assemblage of the masses. There was a heavy rumble of booted feet thumping the floor. Eyes gleamed with sudden fire, and calloused hands waved frantically in the air.

After a few moments' rest, the orchestra played crashingly, and a small fat man burst out upon the stage. He began to roar a song and stamp back and forth before the foot-lights, wildly waving a glossy silk hat and throwing leers, or smiles, broadcast. He made his face into fantastic grimaces until he looked like a pictured devil on a Japanese kite. The crowd laughed gleefully. His short, fat legs were never still a moment. He shouted and roared and bobbed his shock of red wig until the audience broke out in excited applause.

Pete did not pay much attention to the progress of events upon the stage. He was drinking beer and watching Maggie.

Her cheeks were blushing with excitement and her eyes were glistening. She drew deep breaths of pleasure. No thoughts of the atmosphere of the collar and cuff factory came to her.

When the orchestra crashed finally, they jostled their way to the sidewalk with the crowd. Pete took Maggie's arm and pushed a way for her, offering to fight with a man or two.

They reached Maggie's home at a late hour and stood for a moment in front of the gruesome doorway.

"Say, Mag," said Pete, "give us a kiss for takin' yeh teh deh show, will yer?"

Maggie laughed, as if startled, and drew away from him.

"Naw, Pete," she said, "dat wasn't in it."

"Ah, what deh hell?" urged Pete.

The girl retreated nervously.

"Ah, what deh hell?" repeated he.

Maggie darted into the hall, and up the stairs. She turned and smiled at him, then disappeared.

Pete walked slowly down the street. He had something of an astonished expression upon his features. He paused under a lamp-post and breathed a low breath of surprise.

"Gawd," he said, "I wonner if I've been played fer a duffer."

## CHAPTER VIII

As thoughts of Pete came to Maggie's mind, she began to have an intense dislike for all of her dresses.

"What deh hell ails yeh? What makes yeh be allus fixin' and fussin'? Good Gawd," her mother would frequently roar at her.

She began to note, with more interest, the well-dressed women she met on the avenues. She envied elegance and soft palms. She craved those adornments of person which she saw every day on the street, conceiving them to be allies of vast importance to women.

Studying faces, she thought many of the women and girls she chanced to meet, smiled with serenity as though forever cherished and watched over by those they loved.

The air in the collar and cuff establishment strangled her. She knew she was gradually and surely shrivelling in the hot, stuffy room. The begrimed windows rattled incessantly from the passing of elevated trains. The place was filled with a whirl of noises and odors.

She wondered as she regarded some of the grizzled women in the room, mere mechanical contrivances sewing seams and grinding out, with heads bended over their work, tales of imagined or real girlhood happiness, past drunks, the baby at home, and unpaid wages. She speculated how long her youth would endure. She began to see the bloom upon her cheeks as valuable.

She imagined herself, in an exasperating future, as a scrawny woman with an eternal grievance. Too, she thought Pete to be a very fastidious person concerning the appearance of women.

She felt she would love to see somebody entangle their fingers in the oily beard of the fat foreigner who owned the establishment. He was a detestable creature. He wore white socks with low shoes. When he tired of this amusement he would go to the mummies and moralize over them.

Usually he submitted with silent dignity to all which he had to go through, but, at times, he was goaded into comment.

"What deh hell," he demanded once. "Look at all dese little jugs! Hundred jugs in a row! Ten rows in a case an' 'bout a t'ousand cases! What deh blazes use is dem?"

Evenings during the week he took her to see plays in which the brain-clutching heroine was rescued from the palatial home of her guardian, who is cruelly after her bonds, by the hero with the beautiful sentiments. The latter spent most of his time out at soak in pale-green snow storms, busy with a nickel-plated revolver, rescuing aged strangers from villains.

Maggie lost herself in sympathy with the wanderers swooning in snow storms beneath happy-hued church windows. And a choir within singing "Joy to the World." To Maggie and the rest of the audience this was transcendental realism. Joy always within, and they, like the actor, inevitably without. Viewing it, they hugged themselves in ecstatic pity of their imagined or real condition.

The girl thought the arrogance and granite-heartedness of the magnate of the play was very accurately drawn. She echoed the maledictions that the occupants of the gallery showered on this individual when his lines compelled him to expose his extreme selfishness.

Shady persons in the audience revolted from the pictured villainy of the drama. With untiring zeal they hissed vice and applauded virtue. Unmistakably bad men evinced an apparently sincere admiration for virtue.

The loud gallery was overwhelmingly with the unfortunate and the oppressed. They encouraged the struggling hero with cries, and jeered the villain, hooting and calling attention to his whiskers. When anybody died in the pale-green snow storms, the gallery mourned. They sought out the painted misery and hugged it as akin.

In the hero's erratic march from poverty in the first act, to wealth and triumph in the final one, in which he forgives all the enemies that he has left, he was assisted by the gallery, which applauded his generous and noble sentiments and confounded the speeches of his opponents by making irrelevant but very sharp remarks. Those actors who were cursed with villainy parts were confronted at every turn by the gallery. If one of them rendered lines containing the most subtle distinctions between right and wrong, the gallery was immediately aware if the actor meant wickedness, and denounced him accordingly.

The last act was a triumph for the hero, poor and of the masses, the representative of the audience, over the villain and the rich man, his pockets stuffed with bonds, his heart packed with tyrannical purposes, imperturbable amid suffering.

Maggie always departed with raised spirits from the showing places of the melodrama. She rejoiced at the way in which the poor and virtuous eventually surmounted the wealthy and wicked. The theatre made her think. She wondered if the culture and refinement she had seen imitated, perhaps grotesquely, by the heroine on the stage, could be acquired by a girl who lived in a tenement house and worked in a shirt factory.

## CHAPTER IX

A group of urchins were intent upon the side door of a saloon. Expectancy gleamed from their eyes. They were twisting their fingers in excitement.

"Here she comes," yelled one of them suddenly.

The group of urchins burst instantly asunder and its individual fragments were spread in a wide, respectable half circle about the point of interest. The saloon door opened with a crash, and the figure of a woman appeared upon the threshold. Her grey hair fell in knotted masses about her shoulders. Her face was crimsoned and wet with perspiration. Her eyes had a rolling glare.

"Not a damn cent more of me money will yehs ever get, not a damn cent. I spent me money here fer t'ree years an' now yehs tells me yeh'll sell me no more stuff! T'hell wid yeh, Johnnie Murckre! 'Disturbance'? Disturbance be damned! T'hell wid yeh, Johnnie—"

The door received a kick of exasperation from within and the woman lurched heavily out on the sidewalk.

The gamins in the half-circle became violently agitated. They began to dance about and hoot and yell and jeer. Wide dirty grins spread over each face.

The woman made a furious dash at a particularly outrageous cluster of little boys. They laughed delightedly and scampered off a short distance, calling out over their shoulders to her. She stood tottering on the curb-stone and thundered at them.

"Yeh devil's kids," she howled, shaking red fists. The little boys whooped in glee. As she started up the street they fell in behind and marched uproariously. Occasionally she wheeled about and made charges on them. They ran nimbly out of reach and taunted her.

In the frame of a gruesome doorway she stood for a moment cursing them. Her hair straggled, giving her crimson features a look of insanity. Her great fists quivered as she shook them madly in the air.

The urchins made terrific noises until she turned and disappeared. Then they filed quietly in the way they had come.

The woman floundered about in the lower hall of the tenement house and finally stumbled up the stairs. On an upper hall a door was opened and a collection of heads peered curiously out, watching her. With a wrathful snort the woman confronted the door, but it was slammed hastily in her face and the key was turned.

She stood for a few minutes, delivering a frenzied challenge at the panels.

"Come out in deh hall, Mary Murphy, damn yeh, if yehs want a row. Come ahn, yeh overgrown terrier, come ahn."

She began to kick the door with her great feet. She shrilly defied the universe to appear and do battle. Her cursing trebles brought heads from all doors save the one she threatened. Her eyes glared in every direction. The air was full of her tossing fists.

"Come ahn, deh hull damn gang of yehs, come ahn," she roared at the spectators. An oath or two, cat-calls, jeers and bits of facetious advice were given in reply. Missiles clattered about her feet.

"What deh hell's deh matter wid yeh?" said a voice in the gathered gloom, and Jimmie came forward. He carried a tin dinner-pail in his hand and under his arm a brown truckman's apron done in a bundle. "What deh hell's wrong?" he demanded.

"Come out, all of yehs, come out," his mother was howling. "Come ahn an' I'll stamp her damn brains under me feet."

"Shet yer face, an' come home, yeh damned old fool," roared Jimmie at her. She strided up to him and twirled her fingers in his face. Her eyes were darting flames of unreasoning rage and her frame trembled with eagerness for a fight.

"T'hell wid yehs! An' who deh hell are yehs? I ain't givin' a snap of me fingers fer yehs," she bawled at him. She turned her huge back in tremendous disdain and climbed the stairs to the next floor.

Jimmie followed, cursing blackly. At the top of the flight he seized his mother's arm and started to drag her toward the door of their room.

"Come home, damn yeh," he gritted between his teeth.

"Take yer hands off me! Take yer hands off me," shrieked his mother.

She raised her arm and whirled her great fist at her son's face. Jimmie dodged his head and the blow struck him in the back of the neck. "Damn yeh," gritted he again. He threw out his left hand and writhed his fingers about her middle arm. The mother and the son began to sway and struggle like gladiators.

"Whoop!" said the Rum Alley tenement house. The hall filled with interested spectators.

"Hi, ol' lady, dat was a dandy!"

"T'ree to one on deh red!"

"Ah, stop yer damn scrappin'!"

The door of the Johnson home opened and Maggie looked out. Jimmie made a supreme cursing effort and hurled his mother into the room. He quickly followed and closed the door. The Rum Alley tenement swore disappointedly and retired.

The mother slowly gathered herself up from the floor. Her eyes glittered menacingly upon her children.

"Here, now," said Jimmie, "we've had enough of dis. Sit down, an' don' make no trouble."

He grasped her arm, and twisting it, forced her into a creaking chair.

"Keep yer hands off me," roared his mother again.

"Damn yer ol' hide," yelled Jimmie, madly. Maggie shrieked and ran into the other room. To her there came the sound of a storm of crashes and curses. There was a great final thump and Jimmie's voice cried: "Dere, damn yeh, stay still." Maggie opened the door now, and went warily out. "Oh, Jimmie."

He was leaning against the wall and swearing. Blood stood upon bruises on his knotty fore-arms where they had scraped against the floor or the walls in the scuffle. The mother lay screeching on the floor, the tears running down her furrowed face.

Maggie, standing in the middle of the room, gazed about her. The usual upheaval of the tables and chairs had taken place. Crockery was strewn broadcast in fragments. The stove had been disturbed on its legs, and now leaned idiotically to one side. A pail had been upset and water spread in all directions.

The door opened and Pete appeared. He shrugged his shoulders. "Oh, Gawd," he observed.

He walked over to Maggie and whispered in her ear. "Ah, what deh hell, Mag? Come ahn and we'll have a hell of a time."

The mother in the corner upreared her head and shook her tangled locks.

"Teh hell wid him and you," she said, glowering at her daughter in the gloom. Her eyes seemed to burn balefully. "Yeh've gone teh deh devil, Mag Johnson, yehs knows yehs have gone teh deh devil. Yer a disgrace teh yer people, damn yeh. An' now, git out an' go ahn wid dat doe-faced jude of yours. Go teh hell wid him, damn yeh, an' a good riddance. Go teh hell an' see how yeh likes it."

Maggie gazed long at her mother.

"Go teh hell now, an' see how yeh likes it. Git out. I won't have sech as yehs in me house! Get out, d'yeh hear! Damn yeh, git out!"

The girl began to tremble.

At this instant Pete came forward. "Oh, what deh hell, Mag, see," whispered he softly in her ear. "Dis all blows over. See? Deh ol' woman 'ill be all right in deh mornin'. Come ahn out wid me! We'll have a hell of a time."

The woman on the floor cursed. Jimmie was intent upon his bruised fore-arms. The girl cast a glance about the room filled with a chaotic mass of debris, and at the red, writhing body of her mother.

"Go teh hell an' good riddance."

She went.

## CHAPTER X

Jimmie had an idea it wasn't common courtesy for a friend to come to one's home and ruin one's sister. But he was not sure how much Pete knew about the rules of politeness.

The following night he returned home from work at rather a late hour in the evening. In passing through the halls he came upon the gnarled and leathery old woman who possessed the music box. She was grinning in the dim light that drifted through dust-stained panes. She beckoned to him with a smudged forefinger.

"Ah, Jimmie, what do yehs t'ink I got onto las' night. It was deh funnies' t'ing I ever saw," she cried, coming close to him and leering. She was trembling with eagerness to tell her tale. "I was by me door las' night when yer sister and her jude feller came in late, oh, very late. An' she, the dear, she was a-cryin' as if her heart would break, she was. It was deh funnies' t'ing I ever saw. An' right out here by me door she asked him did he love her, did he. An' she was a-cryin' as if her heart would break, poor t'ing. An' him, I could see by deh way what he said it dat she had been askin' orften, he says: 'Oh, hell, yes,' he says, says he, 'Oh, hell, yes.'"

Storm-clouds swept over Jimmie's face, but he turned from the leathery old woman and plodded on up-stairs.

"Oh, hell, yes," called she after him. She laughed a laugh that was like a prophetic croak. "'Oh, hell, yes,' he says, says he, 'Oh, hell, yes.'"

There was no one in at home. The rooms showed that attempts had been made at tidying them. Parts of the wreckage of the day before had been repaired by an unskilful hand. A chair or two and the table, stood uncertainly upon legs. The floor had been newly swept. Too, the blue ribbons had been restored to the curtains, and the lambrequin, with its immense sheaves of yellow wheat and red roses of equal size, had been returned, in a worn and sorry state, to its position at the mantel. Maggie's jacket and hat were gone from the nail behind the door.

Jimmie walked to the window and began to look through the blurred glass. It occurred to him to vaguely wonder, for an instant, if some of the women of his acquaintance had brothers.

Suddenly, however, he began to swear.

"But he was me frien'! I brought 'im here! Dat's deh hell of it!"

He fumed about the room, his anger gradually rising to the furious pitch.

"I'll kill deh jay! Dat's what I'll do! I'll kill deh jay!"

He clutched his hat and sprang toward the door. But it opened and his mother's great form blocked the passage.

"What deh hell's deh matter wid yeh?" exclaimed she, coming into the rooms.

Jimmie gave vent to a sardonic curse and then laughed heavily.

"Well, Maggie's gone teh deh devil! Dat's what! See?"

"Eh?" said his mother.

"Maggie's gone teh deh devil! Are yehs deaf?" roared Jimmie, impatiently.

"Deh hell she has," murmured the mother, astounded.

Jimmie grunted, and then began to stare out at the window. His mother sat down in a chair, but a moment later sprang erect and delivered a maddened whirl of oaths. Her son turned to look at her as she reeled and swayed in the middle of the room, her fierce face convulsed with passion, her blotched arms raised high in imprecation.

"May Gawd curse her forever," she shrieked. "May she eat nothin' but stones and deh dirt in deh street. May she sleep in deh gutter an' never see deh sun shine agin. Deh damn—"

"Here, now," said her son. "Take a drop on yourself."

The mother raised lamenting eyes to the ceiling.

"She's deh devil's own chil', Jimmie," she whispered. "Ah, who would t'ink such a bad girl could grow up in our fambly, Jimmie, me son. Many deh hour I've spent in talk wid dat girl an' tol' her if she ever went on deh streets I'd see her damned. An' after all her bringin' up an' what I tol' her and talked wid her, she goes teh deh bad, like a duck teh water."

The tears rolled down her furrowed face. Her hands trembled.

"An' den when dat Sadie MacMallister next door to us was sent teh deh devil by dat feller what worked in deh soap-factory, didn't I tell our Mag dat if she—"

"Ah, dat's annuder story," interrupted the brother. "Of course, dat Sadie was nice an' all dat—but—see—it ain't dessame as if—well, Maggie was diff'ent—see—she was diff'ent."

He was trying to formulate a theory that he had always unconsciously held, that all sisters, excepting his own, could advisedly be ruined.

He suddenly broke out again. "I'll go t'ump hell outa deh mug what did her deh harm. I'll kill 'im! He t'inks he kin scrap, but when he gits me a-chasin' 'im he'll fin' out where he's wrong, deh damned duffer. I'll wipe up deh street wid 'im."

In a fury he plunged out of the doorway. As he vanished the mother raised her head and lifted both hands, entreating.

"May Gawd curse her forever," she cried.

In the darkness of the hallway Jimmie discerned a knot of women talking volubly. When he strode by they paid no attention to him.

"She allus was a bold thing," he heard one of them cry in an eager voice. "Dere wasn't a feller come teh deh house but she'd try teh mash 'im. My Annie says deh shameless t'ing tried teh ketch her feller, her own feller, what we useter know his fader."

"I could a' tol' yehs dis two years ago," said a woman, in a key of triumph. "Yessir, it was over two years ago dat I says teh my ol' man, I says, 'Dat Johnson girl ain't straight,' I says. 'Oh, hell,' he says. 'Oh, hell.' 'Dat's all right,' I says, 'but I know what I knows,' I says, 'an' it 'ill come out later. You wait an' see,' I says, 'you see.'"

"Anybody what had eyes could see dat dere was somethin' wrong wid dat girl. I didn't like her actions."

On the street Jimmie met a friend. "What deh hell?" asked the latter.

Jimmie explained. "An' I'll t'ump 'im till he can't stand."

"Oh, what deh hell," said the friend. "What's deh use! Yeh'll git pulled in! Everybody 'ill be onto it! An' ten plunks! Gee!"

Jimmie was determined. "He t'inks he kin scrap, but he'll fin' out diff'ent."

"Gee," remonstrated the friend. "What deh hell?"

## CHAPTER XI

On a corner a glass-fronted building shed a yellow glare upon the pavements. The open mouth of a saloon called seductively to passengers to enter and annihilate sorrow or create rage.

The interior of the place was papered in olive and bronze tints of imitation leather. A shining bar of counterfeit massiveness extended down the side of the room. Behind it a great mahogany-appearing sideboard reached the ceiling. Upon its shelves rested pyramids of shimmering glasses that were never disturbed. Mirrors set in the face of the sideboard multiplied them. Lemons, oranges and paper napkins, arranged with mathematical precision, sat among the glasses. Many-hued decanters of liquor perched at regular intervals on the lower shelves. A nickel-plated cash register occupied a position in the exact centre of the general effect. The elementary senses of it all seemed to be opulence and geometrical accuracy.

Across from the bar a smaller counter held a collection of plates upon which swarmed frayed fragments of crackers, slices of boiled ham, dishevelled bits of cheese, and pickles swimming in vinegar. An odor of grasping, begrimed hands and munching mouths pervaded.

Pete, in a white jacket, was behind the bar bending expectantly toward a quiet stranger. "A beeh," said the man. Pete drew a foam-topped glassful and set it dripping upon the bar.

At this moment the light bamboo doors at the entrance swung open and crashed against the siding. Jimmie and a companion entered. They swaggered unsteadily but belligerently toward the bar and looked at Pete with bleared and blinking eyes.

"Gin," said Jimmie.

"Gin," said the companion.

Pete slid a bottle and two glasses along the bar. He bended his head sideways as he assiduously polished away with a napkin at the gleaming wood. He had a look of watchfulness upon his features.

Jimmie and his companion kept their eyes upon the bartender and conversed loudly in tones of contempt.

"He's a dindy masher, ain't he, by Gawd?" laughed Jimmie.

"Oh, hell, yes," said the companion, sneering widely. "He's great, he is. Git onto deh mug on deh blokie. Dat's enough to make a feller turn hand-springs in 'is sleep."

The quiet stranger moved himself and his glass a trifle further away and maintained an attitude of oblivion.

"Gee! ain't he hot stuff!"

"Git onto his shape! Great Gawd!"

"Hey," cried Jimmie, in tones of command. Pete came along slowly, with a sullen dropping of the under lip.

"Well," he growled, "what's eatin' yehs?"

"Gin," said Jimmie.

"Gin," said the companion.

As Pete confronted them with the bottle and the glasses, they laughed in his face. Jimmie's companion, evidently overcome with merriment, pointed a grimy forefinger in Pete's direction.

"Say, Jimmie," demanded he, "what deh hell is dat behind deh bar?"

"Damned if I knows," replied Jimmie. They laughed loudly. Pete put down a bottle with a bang and turned a formidable face toward them. He disclosed his teeth and his shoulders heaved restlessly.

"You fellers can't guy me," he said. "Drink yer stuff an' git out an' don' make no trouble."

Instantly the laughter faded from the faces of the two men and expressions of offended dignity immediately came.

"Who deh hell has said anyt'ing teh you," cried they in the same breath.

The quiet stranger looked at the door calculatingly.

"Ah, come off," said Pete to the two men. "Don't pick me up for no jay. Drink yer rum an' git out an' don' make no trouble."

"Oh, deh hell," airily cried Jimmie.

"Oh, deh hell," airily repeated his companion.

"We goes when we git ready! See!" continued Jimmie.

"Well," said Pete in a threatening voice, "don' make no trouble."

Jimmie suddenly leaned forward with his head on one side. He snarled like a wild animal.

"Well, what if we does? See?" said he.

Dark blood flushed into Pete's face, and he shot a lurid glance at Jimmie.

"Well, den we'll see whose deh bes' man, you or me," he said.

The quiet stranger moved modestly toward the door.

Jimmie began to swell with valor.

"Don' pick me up fer no tenderfoot. When yeh tackles me yeh tackles one of deh bes' men in deh city. See? I'm a scrapper, I am. Ain't dat right, Billie?"

"Sure, Mike," responded his companion in tones of conviction.

"Oh, hell," said Pete, easily. "Go fall on yerself."

The two men again began to laugh.

"What deh hell is dat talkin'?" cried the companion.

"Damned if I knows," replied Jimmie with exaggerated contempt.

Pete made a furious gesture. "Git outa here now, an' don' make no trouble. See? Youse fellers er lookin' fer a scrap an' it's damn likely yeh'll fin' one if yeh keeps on shootin' off yer mout's. I know yehs! See? I kin lick better men dan yehs ever saw in yer lifes. Dat's right! See? Don' pick me up fer no stuff er yeh might be jolted out in deh street before yeh knows where yeh is. When I comes from behind dis bar, I t'rows yehs bote inteh deh street. See?"

"Oh, hell," cried the two men in chorus.

The glare of a panther came into Pete's eyes. "Dat's what I said! Unnerstan'?"

He came through a passage at the end of the bar and swelled down upon the two men. They stepped promptly forward and crowded close to him.

They bristled like three roosters. They moved their heads pugnaciously and kept their shoulders braced. The nervous muscles about each mouth twitched with a forced smile of mockery.

"Well, what deh hell yer goin' teh do?" gritted Jimmie.

Pete stepped warily back, waving his hands before him to keep the men from coming too near.

"Well, what deh hell yer goin' teh do?" repeated Jimmie's ally. They kept close to him, taunting and leering. They strove to make him attempt the initial blow.

"Keep back, now! Don' crowd me," ominously said Pete.

Again they chorused in contempt. "Oh, hell!"

In a small, tossing group, the three men edged for positions like frigates contemplating battle.

"Well, why deh hell don' yeh try teh t'row us out?" cried Jimmie and his ally with copious sneers.

The bravery of bull-dogs sat upon the faces of the men. Their clenched fists moved like eager weapons.

The allied two jostled the bartender's elbows, glaring at him with feverish eyes and forcing him toward the wall.

Suddenly Pete swore redly. The flash of action gleamed from his eyes. He threw back his arm and aimed a tremendous, lightning-like blow at Jimmie's face. His foot swung a step forward and the weight of his body was behind his fist. Jimmie ducked his head, Bowery-like, with the quickness of a cat. The fierce, answering blows of him and his ally crushed on Pete's bowed head.

The quiet stranger vanished.

The arms of the combatants whirled in the air like flails. The faces of the men, at first flushed to flame-colored anger, now began to fade to the pallor of warriors in the blood and heat of a battle. Their lips curled back and stretched tightly over the gums in ghoul-like grins. Through their white, gripped teeth struggled hoarse whisperings of oaths. Their eyes glittered with murderous fire.

Each head was huddled between its owner's shoulders, and arms were swinging with marvelous rapidity. Feet scraped to and fro with a loud scratching sound upon the sanded floor. Blows left crimson blotches upon pale skin. The curses of the first quarter minute of the fight died away. The breaths of the fighters came wheezingly from their lips and the three chests were straining and heaving. Pete at intervals gave vent to low, labored hisses, that sounded like a desire to kill. Jimmie's ally gibbered at times like a wounded maniac. Jimmie was silent, fighting with the face of a sacrificial priest. The rage of fear shone in all their eyes and their blood-colored fists swirled.

At a tottering moment a blow from Pete's hand struck the ally and he crashed to the floor. He wriggled instantly to his feet and grasping the quiet stranger's beer glass from the bar, hurled it at Pete's head.

High on the wall it burst like a bomb, shivering fragments flying in all directions. Then missiles came to every man's hand. The place had heretofore appeared free of things to throw, but suddenly glass and bottles went singing through the air. They were thrown point blank at bobbing heads. The pyramid of shimmering glasses, that had never been disturbed, changed to cascades as heavy bottles were flung into them. Mirrors splintered to nothing.

The three frothing creatures on the floor buried themselves in a frenzy for blood. There followed in the wake of missiles and fists some unknown prayers, perhaps for death.

The quiet stranger had sprawled very pyrotechnically out on the sidewalk. A laugh ran up and down the avenue for the half of a block.

"Dey've trowed a bloke inteh deh street."

People heard the sound of breaking glass and shuffling feet within the saloon and came running. A small group, bending down to look under the bamboo doors, watching the fall of glass, and three pairs of violent legs, changed in a moment to a crowd.

A policeman came charging down the sidewalk and bounced through the doors into the saloon. The crowd bended and surged in absorbing anxiety to see.

Jimmie caught first sight of the on-coming interruption. On his feet he had the same regard for a policeman that, when on his truck, he had for a fire engine. He howled and ran for the side door.

The officer made a terrific advance, club in hand. One comprehensive sweep of the long night stick threw the ally to the floor and forced Pete to a corner. With his disengaged hand he made a furious effort at Jimmie's coat-tails. Then he regained his balance and paused.

"Well, well, you are a pair of pictures. What in hell yeh been up to?"

Jimmie, with his face drenched in blood, escaped up a side street, pursued a short distance by some of the more law-loving, or excited individuals of the crowd.

Later, from a corner safely dark, he saw the policeman, the ally and the bartender emerge from the saloon. Pete locked the doors and then followed up the avenue in the rear of the crowd-encompassed policeman and his charge.

On first thoughts Jimmie, with his heart throbbing at battle heat, started to go desperately to the rescue of his friend, but he halted.

"Ah, what deh hell?" he demanded of himself.

# CHAPTER XII

In a hall of irregular shape sat Pete and Maggie drinking beer. A submissive orchestra dictated to by a spectacled man with frowsy hair and a dress suit, industriously followed the bobs of his head and the waves of his baton. A ballad singer, in a dress of flaming scarlet, sang in the inevitable voice of brass. When she vanished, men seated at the tables near the front applauded loudly, pounding the polished wood with their beer glasses. She returned attired in less gown, and sang again. She received another enthusiastic encore. She reappeared in still less gown and danced. The deafening rumble of glasses and clapping of hands that followed her exit indicated an overwhelming desire to have her come on for the fourth time, but the curiosity of the audience was not gratified.

Maggie was pale. From her eyes had been plucked all look of self-reliance. She leaned with a dependent air toward her companion. She was timid, as if fearing his anger or displeasure. She seemed to beseech tenderness of him.

Pete's air of distinguished valor had grown upon him until it threatened stupendous dimensions. He was infinitely gracious to the girl. It was apparent to her that his condescension was a marvel.

He could appear to strut even while sitting still and he showed that he was a lion of lordly characteristics by the air with which he spat.

With Maggie gazing at him wonderingly, he took pride in commanding the waiters who were, however, indifferent or deaf.

"Hi, you, git a russle on yehs! What deh hell yehs lookin' at? Two more beehs, d'yeh hear?"

He leaned back and critically regarded the person of a girl with a straw-colored wig who upon the stage was flinging her heels in somewhat awkward imitation of a well-known danseuse.

At times Maggie told Pete long confidential tales of her former home life, dwelling upon the escapades of the other members of the family and the difficulties she had to combat in order to obtain a degree of comfort. He responded in tones of philanthropy. He pressed her arm with an air of reassuring proprietorship.

"Dey was damn jays," he said, denouncing the mother and brother.

The sound of the music which, by the efforts of the frowsy-headed leader, drifted to her ears through the smoke-filled atmosphere, made the girl dream. She thought of her former Rum Alley environment and turned to regard Pete's strong protecting fists. She thought of the collar and cuff manufactory and the eternal moan of the proprietor: "What een hell do you sink I pie fife dolla a week for? Play? No, py damn." She contemplated Pete's man-subduing eyes and noted that wealth and prosperity was indicated by his clothes. She imagined a future, rose-tinted, because of its distance from all that she previously had experienced.

As to the present she perceived only vague reasons to be miserable. Her life was Pete's and she considered him worthy of the charge. She would be disturbed by no particular apprehensions, so long as Pete adored her as he now said he did. She did not feel like a bad woman. To her knowledge she had never seen any better.

At times men at other tables regarded the girl furtively. Pete, aware of it, nodded at her and grinned. He felt proud.

"Mag, yer a bloomin' good-looker," he remarked, studying her face through the haze. The men made Maggie fear, but she blushed at Pete's words as it became apparent to her that she was the apple of his eye.

Grey-headed men, wonderfully pathetic in their dissipation, stared at her through clouds. Smooth-cheeked boys, some of them with faces of stone and mouths of sin, not nearly so pathetic as the grey heads, tried to find the girl's eyes in the smoke wreaths. Maggie considered she was not what they thought her. She confined her glances to Pete and the stage.

The orchestra played negro melodies and a versatile drummer pounded, whacked, clattered and scratched on a dozen machines to make noise.

Those glances of the men, shot at Maggie from under half-closed lids, made her tremble. She thought them all to be worse men than Pete.

"Come, let's go," she said.

As they went out Maggie perceived two women seated at a table with some men. They were painted and their cheeks had lost their roundness. As she passed them the girl, with a shrinking movement, drew back her skirts.

## CHAPTER XIII

Jimmie did not return home for a number of days after the fight with Pete in the saloon. When he did, he approached with extreme caution.

He found his mother raving. Maggie had not returned home. The parent continually wondered how her daughter could come to such a pass. She had never considered Maggie as a pearl dropped unstained into Rum Alley from Heaven, but she could not conceive how it was possible for her daughter to fall so low as to bring disgrace upon her family. She was terrific in denunciation of the girl's wickedness.

The fact that the neighbors talked of it, maddened her. When women came in, and in the course of their conversation casually asked, "Where's Maggie dese days?" the mother shook her fuzzy head at them and appalled them with curses. Cunning hints inviting confidence she rebuffed with violence.

"An' wid all deh bringin' up she had, how could she?" moaningly she asked of her son. "Wid all deh talkin' wid her I did an' deh t'ings I tol' her to remember? When a girl is bringed up deh way I bringed up Maggie, how kin she go teh deh devil?"

Jimmie was transfixed by these questions. He could not conceive how under the circumstances his mother's daughter and his sister could have been so wicked.

His mother took a drink from a squdgy bottle that sat on the table. She continued her lament.

"She had a bad heart, dat girl did, Jimmie. She was wicked teh deh heart an' we never knowed it."

Jimmie nodded, admitting the fact.

"We lived in deh same house wid her an' I brought her up an' we never knowed how bad she was."

Jimmie nodded again.

"Wid a home like dis an' a mudder like me, she went teh deh bad," cried the mother, raising her eyes.

One day, Jimmie came home, sat down in a chair and began to wriggle about with a new and strange nervousness. At last he spoke shamefacedly.

"Well, look-a-here, dis t'ing queers us! See? We're queered! An' maybe it 'ud be better if I—well, I t'ink I kin look 'er up an'—maybe it 'ud be better if I fetched her home an'—"

The mother started from her chair and broke forth into a storm of passionate anger.

"What! Let 'er come an' sleep under deh same roof wid her mudder agin! Oh, yes, I will, won't I? Sure? Shame on yehs, Jimmie Johnson, for sayin' such a t'ing teh yer own mudder—teh yer own mudder! Little did I t'ink when yehs was a babby playin' about me feet dat ye'd grow up teh say sech a t'ing teh yer mudder—yer own mudder. I never taut—"

Sobs choked her and interrupted her reproaches.

"Dere ain't nottin' teh raise sech hell about," said Jimmie. "I on'y says it 'ud be better if we keep dis t'ing dark, see? It queers us! See?"

His mother laughed a laugh that seemed to ring through the city and be echoed and re-echoed by countless other laughs. "Oh, yes, I will, won't I! Sure!"

"Well, yeh must take me fer a damn fool," said Jimmie, indignant at his mother for mocking him. "I didn't say we'd make 'er inteh a little tin angel, ner nottin', but deh way it is now she can queer us! Don' che see?"

"Aye, she'll git tired of deh life atter a while an' den she'll wanna be a-comin' home, won' she, deh beast! I'll let 'er in den, won' I?"

"Well, I didn' mean none of dis prod'gal bus'ness anyway," explained Jimmie.

"It wasn't no prod'gal dauter, yeh damn fool," said the mother. "It was prod'gal son, anyhow."

"I know dat," said Jimmie.

For a time they sat in silence. The mother's eyes gloated on a scene her imagination could call before her. Her lips were set in a vindictive smile.

"Aye, she'll cry, won' she, an' carry on, an' tell how Pete, or some odder feller, beats 'er an' she'll say she's sorry an' all dat an' she ain't happy, she ain't, an' she wants to come home agin, she does."

With grim humor, the mother imitated the possible wailing notes of the daughter's voice.

"Den I'll take 'er in, won't I, deh beast. She kin cry 'er two eyes out on deh stones of deh street before I'll dirty deh place wid her. She abused an' ill-treated her own mudder—her own mudder what loved her an' she'll never git anodder chance dis side of hell."

Jimmie thought he had a great idea of women's frailty, but he could not understand why any of his kin should be victims.

"Damn her," he fervidly said.

Again he wondered vaguely if some of the women of his acquaintance had brothers. Nevertheless, his mind did not for an instant confuse himself with those brothers nor his sister with theirs. After the mother had, with great difficulty, suppressed the neighbors, she went among them and proclaimed her grief. "May Gawd forgive dat girl," was her continual cry. To attentive ears she recited the whole length and breadth of her woes.

"I bringed 'er up deh way a dauter oughta be bringed up an' dis is how she served me! She went teh deh devil deh first chance she got! May Gawd forgive her."

When arrested for drunkenness she used the story of her daughter's downfall with telling effect upon the police justices. Finally one of them said to her, peering down over his spectacles: "Mary, the records of this and other courts show that you are the mother of forty-two daughters who have been ruined. The case is unparalleled in the annals of this court, and this court thinks—"

The mother went through life shedding large tears of sorrow. Her red face was a picture of agony.

Of course Jimmie publicly damned his sister that he might appear on a higher social plane. But, arguing with himself, stumbling about in ways that he knew not, he, once, almost came to a conclusion that his sister would have been more firmly good had she better known why. However, he felt that he could not hold such a view. He threw it hastily aside.

## CHAPTER XIV

In a hilarious hall there were twenty-eight tables and twenty-eight women and a crowd of smoking men. Valiant noise was made on a stage at the end of the hall by an orchestra composed of men who looked as if they had just happened in. Soiled waiters ran to and fro, swooping down like hawks on the unwary in the throng; clattering along the aisles with trays covered with glasses; stumbling over women's skirts and charging two prices for everything but beer, all with a swiftness that blurred the view of the cocoanut palms and dusty monstrosities painted upon the walls of the room. A bouncer, with an immense load of business upon his hands, plunged about in the crowd, dragging bashful strangers to prominent chairs, ordering waiters here and there and quarreling furiously with men who wanted to sing with the orchestra.

The usual smoke cloud was present, but so dense that heads and arms seemed entangled in it. The rumble of conversation was replaced by a roar. Plenteous oaths heaved through the air. The room rang with the shrill voices of women bubbling o'er with drink-laughter. The chief element in the music of the orchestra was speed. The musicians played in intent fury. A woman was singing and smiling upon the stage, but no one took notice of her. The rate at which the piano, cornet and violins were going, seemed to impart wildness to the half-drunken crowd. Beer glasses were emptied at a gulp and conversation became a rapid chatter. The smoke eddied and swirled like a shadowy river hurrying toward some unseen falls. Pete and Maggie entered the hall and took chairs at a table near the door. The woman who was seated there made an attempt to occupy Pete's attention and, failing, went away.

Three weeks had passed since the girl had left home. The air of spaniel-like dependence had been magnified and showed its direct effect in the peculiar off-handedness and ease of Pete's ways toward her.

She followed Pete's eyes with hers, anticipating with smiles gracious looks from him.

A woman of brilliance and audacity, accompanied by a mere boy, came into the place and took seats near them.

At once Pete sprang to his feet, his face beaming with glad surprise.

"By Gawd, there's Nellie," he cried.

He went over to the table and held out an eager hand to the woman.

"Why, hello, Pete, me boy, how are you," said she, giving him her fingers.

Maggie took instant note of the woman. She perceived that her black dress fitted her to perfection. Her linen collar and cuffs were spotless. Tan gloves were stretched over her well-shaped hands. A hat of a prevailing fashion perched jauntily upon her dark hair. She wore no jewelry and was painted with no apparent paint. She looked clear-eyed through the stares of the men.

"Sit down, and call your lady-friend over," she said cordially to Pete. At his beckoning Maggie came and sat between Pete and the mere boy.

"I thought yeh were gone away fer good," began Pete, at once. "When did yeh git back? How did dat Buff'lo bus'ness turn out?"

The woman shrugged her shoulders. "Well, he didn't have as many stamps as he tried to make out, so I shook him, that's all."

"Well, I'm glad teh see yehs back in deh city," said Pete, with awkward gallantry.

He and the woman entered into a long conversation, exchanging reminiscences of days together. Maggie sat still, unable to formulate an intelligent sentence upon the conversation and painfully aware of it.

She saw Pete's eyes sparkle as he gazed upon the handsome stranger. He listened smilingly to all she said. The woman was familiar with all his affairs, asked him about mutual friends, and knew the amount of his salary.

She paid no attention to Maggie, looking toward her once or twice and apparently seeing the wall beyond.

The mere boy was sulky. In the beginning he had welcomed with acclamations the additions.

"Let's all have a drink! What'll you take, Nell? And you, Miss what's-your-name. Have a drink, Mr. —, you, I mean."

He had shown a sprightly desire to do the talking for the company and tell all about his family. In a loud voice he declaimed on various topics. He assumed a patronizing air toward Pete. As Maggie was silent, he paid no attention to her. He made a great show of lavishing wealth upon the woman of brilliance and audacity.

"Do keep still, Freddie! You gibber like an ape, dear," said the woman to him. She turned away and devoted her attention to Pete.

"We'll have many a good time together again, eh?"

"Sure, Mike," said Pete, enthusiastic at once.

"Say," whispered she, leaning forward, "let's go over to Billie's and have a he-luva time."

"Well, it's dis way! See?" said Pete. "I got dis lady frien' here."

"Oh, t'hell with her," argued the woman.

Pete appeared disturbed.

"All right," said she, nodding her head at him. "All right for you! We'll see the next time you ask me to go anywheres with you."

Pete squirmed.

"Say," he said, beseechingly, "come wid me a minit an' I'll tell yer why."

The woman waved her hand.

"Oh, that's all right, you needn't explain, you know. You wouldn't come merely because you wouldn't come, that's all there is of it."

To Pete's visible distress she turned to the mere boy, bringing him speedily from a terrific rage. He had been debating whether it would be the part of a man to pick a quarrel with Pete, or would he be justified in striking him savagely with his beer glass without warning. But he recovered himself when the woman turned to renew her smilings. He beamed upon her with an expression that was somewhat tipsy and inexpressibly tender.

"Say, shake that Bowery jay," requested he, in a loud whisper.

"Freddie, you are so droll," she replied.

Pete reached forward and touched the woman on the arm.

"Come out a minit while I tells yeh why I can't go wid yer. Yer doin' me dirt, Nell! I never taut ye'd do me dirt, Nell. Come on, will yer?" He spoke in tones of injury.

"Why, I don't see why I should be interested in your explanations," said the woman, with a coldness that seemed to reduce Pete to a pulp.

His eyes pleaded with her. "Come out a minit while I tells yeh."

The woman nodded slightly at Maggie and the mere boy, "'Scuse me."

The mere boy interrupted his loving smile and turned a shrivelling glare upon Pete. His boyish countenance flushed and he spoke, in a whine, to the woman:

"Oh, I say, Nellie, this ain't a square deal, you know. You aren't goin' to leave me and go off with that duffer, are you? I should think—"

"Why, you dear boy, of course I'm not," cried the woman, affectionately. She bended over and whispered in his ear. He smiled again and settled in his chair as if resolved to wait patiently.

As the woman walked down between the rows of tables, Pete was at her shoulder talking earnestly, apparently in explanation. The woman waved her hands with studied airs of indifference. The doors swung behind them, leaving Maggie and the mere boy seated at the table.

Maggie was dazed. She could dimly perceive that something stupendous had happened. She wondered why Pete saw fit to remonstrate with the woman, pleading for forgiveness with his eyes. She thought she noted an air of submission about her leonine Pete. She was astounded.

The mere boy occupied himself with cock-tails and a cigar. He was tranquilly silent for half an hour. Then he bestirred himself and spoke.

"Well," he said, sighing, "I knew this was the way it would be." There was another stillness. The mere boy seemed to be musing.

"She was pulling m'leg. That's the whole amount of it," he said, suddenly. "It's a bloomin' shame the way that girl does. Why, I've spent over two dollars in drinks tonight. And she goes off with that plug-ugly who looks as if he had been hit in the face with a coin-die. I call it rocky treatment for a fellah like me. Here, waiter, bring me a cock-tail and make it damned strong."

Maggie made no reply. She was watching the doors. "It's a mean piece of business," complained the mere boy. He explained to her how amazing it was that anybody should treat him in such a manner. "But I'll get square with her, you bet. She won't get far ahead of yours truly, you know," he added, winking. "I'll tell her plainly that it was bloomin' mean business. And she won't come it over me with any of her 'now-Freddie-dears.' She thinks my name is Freddie, you know, but of course it ain't. I always tell these people some name like that, because if they got onto your right name they might use it sometime. Understand? Oh, they don't fool me much."

Maggie was paying no attention, being intent upon the doors. The mere boy relapsed into a period of gloom, during which he exterminated a number of cock-tails with a determined air, as if replying defiantly to fate. He occasionally broke forth into sentences composed of invectives joined together in a long string.

The girl was still staring at the doors. After a time the mere boy began to see cobwebs just in front of his nose. He spurred himself into being agreeable and insisted upon her having a charlotte-russe and a glass of beer.

"They's gone," he remarked, "they's gone." He looked at her through the smoke wreaths. "Shay, lil' girl, we mightish well make bes' of it. You ain't such bad-lookin' girl, y'know. Not half bad. Can't come up to Nell, though. No, can't do it! Well, I should shay not! Nell fine-lookin' girl! F—i—n—ine. You look damn bad longsider her, but by y'self ain't so bad. Have to do anyhow. Nell gone. On'y you left. Not half bad, though."

Maggie stood up.

"I'm going home," she said.

The mere boy started.

"Eh? What? Home," he cried, struck with amazement. "I beg pardon, did hear say home?"

"I'm going home," she repeated.

"Great Gawd, what hava struck," demanded the mere boy of himself, stupefied.

In a semi-comatose state he conducted her on board an up-town car, ostentatiously paid her fare, leered kindly at her through the rear window and fell off the steps.

## CHAPTER XV

A forlorn woman went along a lighted avenue. The street was filled with people desperately bound on missions. An endless crowd darted at the elevated station stairs and the horse cars were thronged with owners of bundles.

The pace of the forlorn woman was slow. She was apparently searching for some one. She loitered near the doors of saloons and watched men emerge from them. She scanned furtively the faces in the rushing stream of pedestrians. Hurrying men, bent on catching some boat or train, jostled her elbows, failing to notice her, their thoughts fixed on distant dinners.

The forlorn woman had a peculiar face. Her smile was no smile. But when in repose her features had a shadowy look that was like a sardonic grin, as if some one had sketched with cruel forefinger indelible lines about her mouth.

Jimmie came strolling up the avenue. The woman encountered him with an aggrieved air.

"Oh, Jimmie, I've been lookin' all over fer yehs—," she began.

Jimmie made an impatient gesture and quickened his pace.

"Ah, don't bodder me! Good Gawd!" he said, with the savageness of a man whose life is pestered.

The woman followed him along the sidewalk in somewhat the manner of a suppliant.

"But, Jimmie," she said, "yehs told me ye'd—"

Jimmie turned upon her fiercely as if resolved to make a last stand for comfort and peace.

"Say, fer Gawd's sake, Hattie, don' foller me from one end of deh city teh deh odder. Let up, will yehs! Give me a minute's res', can't yehs? Yehs makes me tired, allus taggin' me. See? Ain' yehs got no sense. Do yehs want people teh get onto me? Go chase yerself, fer Gawd's sake."

The woman stepped closer and laid her fingers on his arm. "But, look-a-here—"

Jimmie snarled. "Oh, go teh hell."

He darted into the front door of a convenient saloon and a moment later came out into the shadows that surrounded the side door. On the brilliantly lighted avenue he perceived the forlorn woman dodging about like a scout. Jimmie laughed with an air of relief and went away.

When he arrived home he found his mother clamoring. Maggie had returned. She stood shivering beneath the torrent of her mother's wrath.

"Well, I'm damned," said Jimmie in greeting.

His mother, tottering about the room, pointed a quivering forefinger.

"Lookut her, Jimmie, lookut her. Dere's yer sister, boy. Dere's yer sister. Lookut her! Lookut her!"

She screamed in scoffing laughter.

The girl stood in the middle of the room. She edged about as if unable to find a place on the floor to put her feet.

"Ha, ha, ha," bellowed the mother. "Dere she stands! Ain' she purty? Lookut her! Ain' she sweet, deh beast? Lookut her! Ha, ha, lookut her!"

She lurched forward and put her red and seamed hands upon her daughter's face. She bent down and peered keenly up into the eyes of the girl.

"Oh, she's jes' dessame as she ever was, ain' she? She's her mudder's purty dar-lin' yit, ain' she? Lookut her, Jimmie! Come here, fer Gawd's sake, and lookut her."

The loud, tremendous sneering of the mother brought the denizens of the Rum Alley tenement to their doors. Women came in the hallways. Children scurried to and fro.

"What's up? Dat Johnson party on anudder tear?"

"Naw! Young Mag's come home!"

"Deh hell yeh say?"

Through the open door curious eyes stared in at Maggie. Children ventured into the room and ogled her, as if they formed the front row at a theatre. Women, without, bended toward each other and whispered, nodding their heads with airs of profound philosophy. A baby, overcome with curiosity concerning this object at which all were looking, sidled forward and touched her dress, cautiously, as if investigating a red-hot stove. Its mother's voice rang out like a warning trumpet. She rushed forward and grabbed her child, casting a terrible look of indignation at the girl.

Maggie's mother paced to and fro, addressing the doorful of eyes, expounding like a glib showman at a museum. Her voice rang through the building.

"Dere she stands," she cried, wheeling suddenly and pointing with dramatic finger. "Dere she stands! Lookut her! Ain' she a dindy? An' she was so good as to come home teh her mudder, she was! Ain' she a beaut'? Ain' she a dindy? Fer Gawd's sake!"

The jeering cries ended in another burst of shrill laughter.

The girl seemed to awaken. "Jimmie—"

He drew hastily back from her.

"Well, now, yer a hell of a t'ing, ain' yeh?" he said, his lips curling in scorn. Radiant virtue sat upon his brow and his repelling hands expressed horror of con-tamination.

Maggie turned and went.

The crowd at the door fell back precipitately. A baby falling down in front of the door, wrenched a scream like a wounded animal from its mother. Another woman sprang forward and picked it up, with a chivalrous air, as if rescuing a human being from an oncoming express train.

As the girl passed down through the hall, she went before open doors framing more eyes strangely microscopic, and sending broad beams of inquisitive light into the darkness of her path. On the second floor she met the gnarled old woman who possessed the music box.

"So," she cried, "'ere yehs are back again, are yehs? An' dey've kicked yehs out? Well, come in an' stay wid me teh-night. I ain' got no moral standin'."

From above came an unceasing babble of tongues, over all of which rang the mother's derisive laughter.

## CHAPTER XVI

Pete did not consider that he had ruined Maggie. If he had thought that her soul could never smile again, he would have believed the mother and brother, who were pyrotechnic over the affair, to be responsible for it.

Besides, in his world, souls did not insist upon being able to smile. "What deh hell?"

He felt a trifle entangled. It distressed him. Revelations and scenes might bring upon him the wrath of the owner of the saloon, who insisted upon respectability of an advanced type.

"What deh hell do dey wanna raise such a smoke about it fer?" demanded he of himself, disgusted with the attitude of the family. He saw no necessity for anyone's losing their equilibrium merely because their sister or their daughter had stayed away from home.

Searching about in his mind for possible reasons for their conduct, he came upon the conclusion that Maggie's motives were correct, but that the two others wished to snare him. He felt pursued.

The woman of brilliance and audacity whom he had met in the hilarious hall showed a disposition to ridicule him.

"A little pale thing with no spirit," she said. "Did you note the expression of her eyes? There was something in them about pumpkin pie and virtue. That is a peculiar way the left corner of her mouth has of twitching, isn't it? Dear, dear, my cloud-compelling Pete, what are you coming to?"

Pete asserted at once that he never was very much interested in the girl. The woman interrupted him, laughing.

"Oh, it's not of the slightest consequence to me, my dear young man. You needn't draw maps for my benefit. Why should I be concerned about it?"

But Pete continued with his explanations. If he was laughed at for his tastes in women, he felt obliged to say that they were only temporary or indifferent ones.

The morning after Maggie had departed from home, Pete stood behind the bar. He was immaculate in white jacket and apron and his hair was plastered over his brow with infinite correctness. No customers were in the place. Pete was twisting his napkined fist slowly in a beer glass, softly whistling to himself and occasionally holding the object of his attention between his eyes and a few weak beams of sunlight that had found their way over the thick screens and into the shaded room.

With lingering thoughts of the woman of brilliance and audacity, the bartender raised his head and stared through the varying cracks between the swaying bamboo doors. Suddenly the whistling pucker faded from his lips. He saw Maggie walking slowly past. He gave a great start, fearing for the previously-mentioned eminent respectability of the place.

He threw a swift, nervous glance about him, all at once feeling guilty. No one was in the room.

He went hastily over to the side door. Opening it and looking out, he perceived Maggie standing, as if undecided, on the corner. She was searching the place with her eyes.

As she turned her face toward him Pete beckoned to her hurriedly, intent upon returning with speed to a position behind the bar and to the atmosphere of respectability upon which the proprietor insisted.

Maggie came to him, the anxious look disappearing from her face and a smile wreathing her lips.

"Oh, Pete—," she began brightly.

The bartender made a violent gesture of impatience.

"Oh, my Gawd," cried he, vehemently. "What deh hell do yeh wanna hang aroun' here fer? Do yeh wanna git me inteh trouble?" he demanded with an air of injury.

Astonishment swept over the girl's features. "Why, Pete! yehs tol' me—"

Pete glanced profound irritation. His countenance reddened with the anger of a man whose respectability is being threatened.

"Say, yehs makes me tired. See? What deh hell deh yeh wanna tag aroun' atter me fer? Yeh'll git me inteh trouble wid deh ol' man an' dey'll be hell teh pay! If he sees a woman roun' here he'll go crazy an' I'll lose me job! See? Yer brudder come in here an' raised hell an' deh ol' man hada put up fer it! An' now I'm done! See? I'm done."

The girl's eyes stared into his face. "Pete, don't yeh remem—"

"Oh, hell," interrupted Pete, anticipating.

The girl seemed to have a struggle with herself. She was apparently bewildered and could not find speech. Finally she asked in a low voice: "But where kin I go?"

The question exasperated Pete beyond the powers of endurance. It was a direct attempt to give him some responsibility in a matter that did not concern him. In his indignation he volunteered information.

"Oh, go teh hell," cried he. He slammed the door furiously and returned, with an air of relief, to his respectability.

Maggie went away.

She wandered aimlessly for several blocks. She stopped once and asked aloud a question of herself: "Who?"

A man who was passing near her shoulder, humorously took the questioning word as intended for him.

"Eh? What? Who? Nobody! I didn't say anything," he laughingly said, and continued his way.

Soon the girl discovered that if she walked with such apparent aimlessness, some men looked at her with calculating eyes. She quickened her step, frightened. As a protection, she adopted a demeanor of intentness as if going somewhere.

After a time she left rattling avenues and passed between rows of houses with sternness and stolidity stamped upon their features. She hung her head for she felt their eyes grimly upon her.

Suddenly she came upon a stout gentleman in a silk hat and a chaste black coat, whose decorous row of buttons reached from his chin to his knees. The girl had heard of the Grace of God and she decided to approach this man.

His beaming, chubby face was a picture of benevolence and kind-heartedness. His eyes shone good-will.

But as the girl timidly accosted him, he gave a convulsive movement and saved his respectability by a vigorous side-step. He did not risk it to save a soul. For how was he to know that there was a soul before him that needed saving?

## CHAPTER XVII

Upon a wet evening, several months after the last chapter, two interminable rows of cars, pulled by slipping horses, jangled along a prominent side-street. A dozen cabs, with coat-enshrouded drivers, clattered to and fro. Electric lights, whirring softly, shed a blurred radiance. A flower dealer, his feet tapping impatiently, his nose and his wares glistening with rain-drops, stood behind an array of roses and chrysanthemums. Two or three theatres emptied a crowd upon the storm-swept pavements. Men pulled their hats over their eyebrows and raised their collars to their ears. Women shrugged impatient shoulders in their warm cloaks and stopped to arrange their skirts for a walk through the storm. People having been comparatively silent for two hours burst into a roar of conversation, their hearts still kindling from the glowings of the stage.

The pavements became tossing seas of umbrellas. Men stepped forth to hail cabs or cars, raising their fingers in varied forms of polite request or imperative demand. An endless procession wended toward elevated stations. An atmosphere of pleasure and prosperity seemed to hang over the throng, born, perhaps, of good clothes and of having just emerged from a place of forgetfulness.

In the mingled light and gloom of an adjacent park, a handful of wet wanderers, in attitudes of chronic dejection, was scattered among the benches.

A girl of the painted cohorts of the city went along the street. She threw changing glances at men who passed her, giving smiling invitations to men of rural or untaught pattern and usually seeming sedately unconscious of the men with a metropolitan seal upon their faces.

Crossing glittering avenues, she went into the throng emerging from the places of forgetfulness. She hurried forward through the crowd as if intent upon reaching a distant home, bending forward in her handsome cloak, daintily lifting her skirts and picking for her well-shod feet the dryer spots upon the pavements.

The restless doors of saloons, clashing to and fro, disclosed animated rows of men before bars and hurrying barkeepers.

A concert hall gave to the street faint sounds of swift, machine-like music, as if a group of phantom musicians were hastening.

A tall young man, smoking a cigarette with a sublime air, strolled near the girl. He had on evening dress, a moustache, a chrysanthemum, and a look of ennui, all of which he kept carefully under his eye. Seeing the girl walk on as if such a young man as he was not in existence, he looked back transfixed with interest. He stared glassily for a moment, but gave a slight convulsive start when he discerned that she was neither new, Parisian, nor theatrical. He wheeled about hastily and turned his stare into the air, like a sailor with a search-light.

A stout gentleman, with pompous and philanthropic whiskers, went stolidly by, the broad of his back sneering at the girl.

A belated man in business clothes, and in haste to catch a car, bounced against her shoulder. "Hi, there, Mary, I beg your pardon! Brace up, old girl." He grasped her arm to steady her, and then was away running down the middle of the street.

The girl walked on out of the realm of restaurants and saloons. She passed more glittering avenues and went into darker blocks than those where the crowd travelled.

A young man in light overcoat and derby hat received a glance shot keenly from the eyes of the girl. He stopped and looked at her, thrusting his hands in his pockets and making a mocking smile curl his lips. "Come, now, old lady," he said, "you don't mean to tel me that you sized me up for a farmer?"

A labouring man marched along; with bundles under his arms. To her remarks, he replied, "It's a fine evenin', ain't it?"

She smiled squarely into the face of a boy who was hurrying by with his hands buried in his overcoat pockets, his blonde locks bobbing on his youthful temples, and a cheery smile of unconcern upon his lips. He turned his head and smiled back at her, waving his hands.

"Not this eve—some other eve!"

A drunken man, reeling in her pathway, began to roar at her. "I ain' ga no money!" he shouted, in a dismal voice. He lurched on up the street, wailing to himself: "I ain' ga no money. Ba' luck. Ain' ga no more money."

The girl went into gloomy districts near the river, where the tall black factories shut in the street and only occasional broad beams of light fell across the pavements from saloons. In front of one of these places, whence came the sound of a violin vigorously scraped, the patter of feet on boards and the ring of loud laughter, there stood a man with blotched features.

Further on in the darkness she met a ragged being with shifting, bloodshot eyes and grimy hands.

She went into the blackness of the final block. The shutters of the tall buildings were closed like grim lips. The structures seemed to have eyes that looked over them, beyond them, at other things. Afar off the lights of the avenues glittered as if from an impossible distance. Street-car bells jingled with a sound of merriment.

At the feet of the tall buildings appeared the deathly black hue of the river. Some hidden factory sent up a yellow glare, that lit for a moment the waters lapping oilily against timbers. The varied sounds of life, made joyous by distance and seeming unapproachableness, came faintly and died away to a silence.

## CHAPTER XVIII

In a partitioned-off section of a saloon sat a man with a half dozen women, gleefully laughing, hovering about him. The man had arrived at that stage of drunkenness where affection is felt for the universe.

"I'm good f'ler, girls," he said, convincingly. "I'm damn good f'ler. An'body treats me right, I allus trea's zem right! See?"

The women nodded their heads approvingly. "To be sure," they cried out in hearty chorus. "You're the kind of a man we like, Pete. You're outa sight! What yeh goin' to buy this time, dear?"

"An't'ing yehs wants, damn it," said the man in an abandonment of good will. His countenance shone with the true spirit of benevolence. He was in the proper mode of missionaries. He would have fraternized with obscure Hottentots. And above all, he was overwhelmed in tenderness for his friends, who were all illustrious.

"An't'ing yehs wants, damn it," repeated he, waving his hands with beneficent recklessness. "I'm good f'ler, girls, an' if an'body treats me right I—here," called he through an open door to a waiter, "bring girls drinks, damn it. What 'ill yehs have, girls? An't'ing yehs wants, damn it!"

The waiter glanced in with the disgusted look of the man who serves intoxicants for the man who takes too much of them. He nodded his head shortly at the order from each individual, and went.

"Damn it," said the man, "we're havin' heluva time. I like you girls! Damn'd if I don't! Yer right sort! See?"

He spoke at length and with feeling, concerning the excellencies of his assembled friends.

"Don' try pull man's leg, but have a heluva time! Das right! Das way teh do! Now, if I sawght yehs tryin' work me fer drinks, wouldn' buy damn t'ing! But yer right sort, damn it! Yehs know how ter treat a f'ler, an' I stays by yehs 'til spen' las' cent! Das right! I'm good f'ler an' I knows when an'body treats me right!"

Between the times of the arrival and departure of the waiter, the man discoursed to the women on the tender regard he felt for all living things. He laid stress upon the purity of his motives in all dealings with men in the world and spoke of the fervor of his friendship for those who were amiable. Tears welled slowly from his eyes. His voice quavered when he spoke to them.

Once when the waiter was about to depart with an empty tray, the man drew a coin from his pocket and held it forth.

"Here," said he, quite magnificently, "here's quar'."

The waiter kept his hands on his tray.

"I don' want yer money," he said.

The other put forth the coin with tearful insistence.

"Here, damn it," cried he, "tak't! Yer damn goo' f'ler an' I wan' yehs tak't!"

"Come, come, now," said the waiter, with the sullen air of a man who is forced into giving advice. "Put yer mon in yer pocket! Yer loaded an' yehs on'y makes a damn fool of yerself."

As the latter passed out of the door the man turned pathetically to the women.

"He don' know I'm damn goo' f'ler," cried he, dismally.

"Never you mind, Pete, dear," said a woman of brilliance and audacity, laying her hand with great affection upon his arm. "Never you mind, old boy! We'll stay by you, dear!"

"Das ri'," cried the man, his face lighting up at the soothing tones of the woman's voice. "Das ri', I'm damn goo' f'ler an' w'en anyone trea's me ri', I treats zem ri'! Shee!"

"Sure!" cried the women. "And we're not goin' back on you, old man."

The man turned appealing eyes to the woman of brilliance and audacity. He felt that if he could be convicted of a contemptible action he would die.

"Shay, Nell, damn it, I allus trea's yehs shquare, didn' I? I allus been goo' f'ler wi' yehs, ain't I, Nell?"

"Sure you have, Pete," assented the woman. She delivered an oration to her companions. "Yessir, that's a fact. Pete's a square fellah, he is. He never goes back on a friend. He's the right kind an' we stay by him, don't we, girls?"

"Sure," they exclaimed. Looking lovingly at him they raised their glasses and drank his health.

"Girlsh," said the man, beseechingly, "I allus trea's yehs ri', didn' I? I'm goo' f'ler, ain' I, girlsh?"

"Sure," again they chorused.

"Well," said he finally, "le's have nozzer drink, zen."

"That's right," hailed a woman, "that's right. Yer no bloomin' jay! Yer spends yer money like a man. Dat's right."

The man pounded the table with his quivering fists.

"Yessir," he cried, with deep earnestness, as if someone disputed him. "I'm damn goo' f'ler, an' w'en anyone trea's me ri', I allus trea's—le's have nozzer drink."

He began to beat the wood with his glass.

"Shay," howled he, growing suddenly impatient. As the waiter did not then come, the man swelled with wrath.

"Shay," howled he again.

The waiter appeared at the door.

"Bringsh drinksh," said the man.

The waiter disappeared with the orders.

"Zat f'ler damn fool," cried the man. "He insul' me! I'm ge'man! Can' stan' be insul'! I'm goin' lickim when comes!"

"No, no," cried the women, crowding about and trying to subdue him. "He's all right! He didn't mean anything! Let it go! He's a good fellah!"

"Din' he insul' me?" asked the man earnestly.

"No," said they. "Of course he didn't! He's all right!"

"Sure he didn' insul' me?" demanded the man, with deep anxiety in his voice.

"No, no! We know him! He's a good fellah. He didn't mean anything."

"Well, zen," said the man, resolutely, "I'm go' 'pol'gize!"

When the waiter came, the man struggled to the middle of the floor.

"Girlsh shed you insul' me! I shay damn lie! I 'pol'gize!"

"All right," said the waiter.

The man sat down. He felt a sleepy but strong desire to straighten things out and have a perfect understanding with everybody.

"Nell, I allus trea's yeh shquare, din' I? Yeh likes me, don' yehs, Nell? I'm goo' f'ler?"

"Sure," said the woman of brilliance and audacity.

"Yeh knows I'm stuck on yehs, don' yehs, Nell?"

"Sure," she repeated, carelessly.

Overwhelmed by a spasm of drunken adoration, he drew two or three bills from his pocket, and, with the trembling fingers of an offering priest, laid them on the table before the woman.

"Yehs knows, damn it, yehs kin have all got, 'cause I'm stuck on yehs, Nell, damn't, I—I'm stuck on yehs, Nell—buy drinksh—damn't—we're havin' heluva time—w'en anyone trea's me ri'—I—damn't, Nell—we're havin' heluva—time."

Shortly he went to sleep with his swollen face fallen forward on his chest.

The women drank and laughed, not heeding the slumbering man in the corner. Finally he lurched forward and fell groaning to the floor.

The women screamed in disgust and drew back their skirts.

"Come ahn," cried one, starting up angrily, "let's get out of here."

The woman of brilliance and audacity stayed behind, taking up the bills and stuffing them into a deep, irregularly-shaped pocket. A guttural snore from the recumbent man caused her to turn and look down at him.

She laughed. "What a damn fool," she said, and went.

The smoke from the lamps settled heavily down in the little compartment, obscuring the way out. The smell of oil, stifling in its intensity, pervaded the air. The wine from an overturned glass dripped softly down upon the blotches on the man's neck.

## CHAPTER XIX

In a room a woman sat at a table eating like a fat monk in a picture.

A soiled, unshaven man pushed open the door and entered.

"Well," said he, "Mag's dead."

"What?" said the woman, her mouth filled with bread.

"Mag's dead," repeated the man.

"Deh hell she is," said the woman. She continued her meal. When she finished her coffee she began to weep.

"I kin remember when her two feet was no bigger dan yer t'umb, and she weared worsted boots," moaned she.

"Well, whata dat?" said the man.

"I kin remember when she weared worsted boots," she cried.

The neighbors began to gather in the hall, staring in at the weeping woman as if watching the contortions of a dying dog. A dozen women entered and lamented with her. Under their busy hands the rooms took on that appalling appearance of neatness and order with which death is greeted.

Suddenly the door opened and a woman in a black gown rushed in with outstretched arms. "Ah, poor Mary," she cried, and tenderly embraced the moaning one.

"Ah, what ter'ble affliction is dis," continued she. Her vocabulary was derived from mission churches. "Me poor Mary, how I feel fer yehs! Ah, what a ter'ble affliction is a disobed'ent chil'."

Her good, motherly face was wet with tears. She trembled in eagerness to express her sympathy. The mourner sat with bowed head, rocking her body heavily to and fro, and crying out in a high, strained voice that sounded like a dirge on some forlorn pipe.

"I kin remember when she weared worsted boots an' her two feets was no bigger dan yer t'umb an' she weared worsted boots, Miss Smith," she cried, raising her streaming eyes.

"Ah, me poor Mary," sobbed the woman in black. With low, coddling cries, she sank on her knees by the mourner's chair, and put her arms about her. The other women began to groan in different keys.

"Yer poor misguided chil' is gone now, Mary, an' let us hope it's fer deh bes'. Yeh'll fergive her now, Mary, won't yehs, dear, all her disobed'ence? All her t'ankless behavior to her mudder an' all her badness? She's gone where her ter'ble sins will be judged."

The woman in black raised her face and paused. The inevitable sunlight came streaming in at the windows and shed a ghastly cheerfulness upon the faded hues of the room. Two or three of the spectators were sniffling, and one was loudly weeping. The mourner arose and staggered into the other room. In a moment she emerged with a pair of faded baby shoes held in the hollow of her hand.

"I kin remember when she used to wear dem," cried she. The women burst anew into cries as if they had all been stabbed. The mourner turned to the soiled and unshaven man.

"Jimmie, boy, go git yer sister! Go git yer sister an' we'll put deh boots on her feets!"

"Dey won't fit her now, yeh damn fool," said the man.

"Go git yer sister, Jimmie," shrieked the woman, confronting him fiercely.

The man swore sullenly. He went over to a corner and slowly began to put on his coat. He took his hat and went out, with a dragging, reluctant step.

The woman in black came forward and again besought the mourner.

"Yeh'll fergive her, Mary! Yeh'll fergive yer bad, bad, chil'! Her life was a curse an' her days were black an' yeh'll fergive yer bad girl? She's gone where her sins will be judged."

"She's gone where her sins will be judged," cried the other women, like a choir at a funeral.

"Deh Lord gives and deh Lord takes away," said the woman in black, raising her eyes to the sunbeams.

"Deh Lord gives and deh Lord takes away," responded the others.

"Yeh'll fergive her, Mary!" pleaded the woman in black. The mourner essayed to speak but her voice gave way. She shook her great shoulders frantically, in an agony of grief. Hot tears seemed to scald her quivering face. Finally her voice came and arose like a scream of pain.

"Oh, yes, I'll fergive her! I'll fergive her!"

# THE PRICE OF THE HARNESS

I

Twenty-five men were making a road out of a path up the hillside. The light batteries in the rear were impatient to advance, but first must be done all that digging and smoothing which gains no encrusted medals from war. The men worked like gardeners, and a road was growing from the old pack-animal trail.

Trees arched from a field of guinea-grass which resembled young wild corn. The day was still and dry. The men working were dressed in the consistent blue of United States regulars. They looked indifferent, almost stolid, despite the heat and the labour. There was little talking. From time to time a Government pack-train, led by a sleek-sided tender bell-mare, came from one way or the other way, and the men stood aside as the strong, hard, black-and-tan animals crowded eagerly after their curious little feminine leader.

A volunteer staff-officer appeared, and, sitting on his horse in the middle of the work, asked the sergeant in command some questions which were apparently not relevant to any military business. Men straggling along on various duties almost invariably spun some kind of a joke as they passed.

A corporal and four men were guarding boxes of spare ammunition at the top of the hill, and one of the number often went to the foot of the hill swinging canteens.

The day wore down to the Cuban dusk, in which the shadows are all grim and of ghostly shape. The men began to lift their eyes from the shovels and picks, and glance in the direction of their camp. The sun threw his last lance through the foliage. The steep mountain-range on the right turned blue and as without detail as a curtain. The tiny ruby of light ahead meant that the ammunition-guard were cooking their supper. From somewhere in the world came a single rifle-shot.

Figures appeared, dim in the shadow of the trees. A murmur, a sigh of quiet relief, arose from the working party. Later, they swung up the hill in an unformed formation, being always like soldiers, and unable even to carry a spade save like United States regular soldiers. As they passed through some fields, the bland white light of the end of the day feebly touched each hard bronze profile.

"Wonder if we'll git anythin' to eat," said Watkins, in a low voice.

"Should think so," said Nolan, in the same tone. They betrayed no impatience; they seemed to feel a kind of awe of the situation.

The sergeant turned. One could see the cool grey eye flashing under the brim of the campaign hat. "What in hell you fellers kickin' about?" he asked. They made no reply, understanding that they were being suppressed.

As they moved on, a murmur arose from the tall grass on either hand. It was the noise from the bivouac of ten thousand men, although one saw practically nothing from the low-cart roadway. The sergeant led his party up a wet clay bank and into a trampled field. Here were scattered tiny white shelter tents, and in the darkness they were luminous like the rearing stones in a graveyard. A few fires burned blood-red, and the shadowy figures of men moved with no more expression of detail than there is in the swaying of foliage on a windy night.

The working party felt their way to where their tents were pitched. A man suddenly cursed; he had mislaid something, and he knew he was not going to find it that night. Watkins spoke again with the monotony of a clock, "Wonder if we'll git anythin' to eat."

Martin, with eyes turned pensively to the stars, began a treatise. "Them Spaniards—"

"Oh, quit it," cried Nolan. "What th' piper do you know about th' Spaniards, you fat-headed Dutchman? Better think of your belly, you blunderin' swine, an' what you're goin' to put in it, grass or dirt."

A laugh, a sort of a deep growl, arose from the prostrate men. In the meantime the sergeant had reappeared and was standing over them. "No rations tonight," he said gruffly, and turning on his heel, walked away.

This announcement was received in silence. But Watkins had flung himself face downward, and putting his lips close to a tuft of grass, he formulated oaths. Martin arose and, going to his shelter, crawled in sulkily. After a long interval Nolan said aloud, "Hell!" Grierson, enlisted for the war, raised a querulous voice. "Well, I wonder when we *will* git fed?"

From the ground about him came a low chuckle, full of ironical comment upon Grierson's lack of certain qualities which the other men felt themselves to possess.

## II

In the cold light of dawn the men were on their knees, packing, strapping, and buckling. The comic toy hamlet of shelter-tents had been wiped out as if by a cyclone. Through the trees could be seen the crimson of a light battery's blankets, and the wheels creaked like the sound of a musketry fight. Nolan, well gripped by his shelter tent, his blanket, and his cartridge-belt, and bearing his rifle, advanced upon a small group of men who were hastily finishing a can of coffee.

"Say, give us a drink, will yeh?" he asked, wistfully. He was as sad-eyed as an orphan beggar.

Every man in the group turned to look him straight in the face. He had asked for the principal ruby out of each one's crown. There was a grim silence. Then one said, "What fer?" Nolan cast his glance to the ground, and went away abashed.

But he espied Watkins and Martin surrounding Grierson, who had gained three pieces of hard-tack by mere force of his audacious inexperience. Grierson was fending his comrades off tearfully.

"Now, don't be damn pigs," he cried. "Hold on a minute." Here Nolan asserted a claim. Grierson groaned. Kneeling piously, he divided the hard-tack with minute care into four portions. The men, who had had their heads together like players watching a wheel of fortune, arose suddenly, each chewing. Nolan interpolated a drink of water, and sighed contentedly.

The whole forest seemed to be moving. From the field on the other side of the road a column of men in blue was slowly pouring; the battery had creaked on ahead; from the rear came a hum of advancing regiments. Then from a mile away rang the noise of a shot; then another shot; in a moment the rifles there were drumming, drumming, drumming. The artillery boomed out suddenly. A day of battle was begun.

The men made no exclamations. They rolled their eyes in the direction of the sound, and then swept with a calm glance the forests and the hills which surrounded them, implacably mysterious forests and hills which lent to every rifle-shot the ominous quality which belongs to secret assassination. The whole scene would have spoken to the private soldiers of ambushes, sudden flank attacks, terrible disasters, if it were not for those cool gentlemen with shoulder-straps and swords who, the private soldiers knew, were of another world and omnipotent for the business.

The battalions moved out into the mud and began a leisurely march in the damp shade of the trees. The advance of two batteries had churned the black soil into a formidable paste. The brown leggings of the men, stained with the mud of other days, took on a deeper colour. Perspiration broke gently out on the reddish faces. With his heavy roll of blanket and the half of a shelter-tent crossing his right shoulder and under his left arm, each man presented the appearance of being clasped from behind, wrestler fashion, by a pair of thick white arms.

There was something distinctive in the way they carried their rifles. There was the grace of an old hunter somewhere in it, the grace of a man whose rifle has become absolutely a part of himself. Furthermore, almost every blue shirt sleeve was rolled to the elbow, disclosing fore-arms of almost incredible brawn. The rifles seemed light, almost fragile, in the hands that were at the end of these arms, never fat but always with rolling muscles and veins that seemed on the point of bursting. And another thing was the silence and the marvellous impassivity of the faces as the column made its slow way toward where the whole forest spluttered and fluttered with battle.

Opportunely, the battalion was halted a-straddle of a stream, and before it again moved, most of the men had filled their canteens. The firing increased. Ahead and to the left a battery was booming at methodical intervals, while the infantry racket was that continual drumming which, after all, often sounds like rain on a roof. Directly ahead one could hear the deep voices of field-pieces.

Some wounded Cubans were carried by in litters improvised from hammocks swung on poles. One had a ghastly cut in the throat, probably from a fragment of shell, and his head was turned as if Providence particularly wished to display this wide and lapping gash to the long column that was winding toward the front. And another Cuban, shot through the groin, kept up a continual wail as he swung from the tread of his bearers. "Ay—ee! Ay—ee! Madre mia! Madre mia!" He sang this bitter ballad into the ears of at least three thousand men as they slowly made way for his bearers on the narrow wood-path. These wounded insurgents were, then, to a large part of the advancing army, the visible messengers of bloodshed and death, and the men regarded them with thoughtful awe. This doleful sobbing cry—"Madre mia"—was a tangible consequent misery of all that firing on in front into which the men knew they were soon to be plunged. Some of them wished to inquire of the bearers the details of what had happened; but they could not speak Spanish, and so it was as if fate had intentionally sealed the lips of all in order that even meagre information might not leak out concerning this mystery—battle. On the other hand, many unversed private soldiers looked upon the unfortunate as men who had seen thousands maimed and bleeding, and absolutely could not conjure any further interest in such scenes.

A young staff-officer passed on horseback. The vocal Cuban was always wailing, but the officer wheeled past the bearers without heeding anything. And yet he never before had seen such a sight. His case was different from that of the private soldiers. He heeded nothing because he was busy—immensely busy and hurried with a multitude of reasons and desires for doing his duty perfectly. His whole life had been a mere period of preliminary reflection for this situation, and he had no clear idea of anything save his obligation as an officer. A man of this kind might be stupid; it is conceivable that in remote cases certain bumps on his head might be composed entirely of wood; but those traditions of fidelity and courage which have been handed to him from generation to generation, and which he has tenaciously preserved despite the persecution of legislators and the indifference of his country, make it incredible that in battle he should ever fail to give his best blood and his best thought for his general, for his men, and for himself. And so this young officer in the shapeless hat and the torn and dirty shirt failed to heed the wails of the wounded man, even as the pilgrim fails to heed the world as he raises his illumined face toward his purpose—rightly or wrongly, his purpose—his sky of the ideal of duty; and the wonderful part of it is, that he is guided by an ideal which he has himself created, and has alone protected from attack. The young man was merely an officer in the United States regular army.

The column swung across a shallow ford and took a road which passed the right flank of one of the American batteries. On a hill it was booming and belching great clouds of white smoke. The infantry looked up with interest. Arrayed below the hill and behind the battery were the horses and limbers, the riders checking their pawing mounts, and behind each rider a red blanket flamed against the fervent green of the bushes. As the infantry moved along the road, some of the battery horses turned at the noise of the trampling feet and surveyed the men with eyes as deep as wells, serene, mournful, generous eyes, lit heart-breakingly with something that was akin to a philosophy, a religion of self-sacrifice—oh, gallant, gallant horses!

"I know a feller in that battery," said Nolan, musingly. "A driver."

"Dam sight rather be a gunner," said Martin.

"Why would ye?" said Nolan, opposingly.

"Well, I'd take my chances as a gunner b'fore I'd sit way up in th' air on a raw-boned plug an' git shot at."

"Aw—" began Nolan.

"They've had some losses t'-day all right," interrupted Grierson.

"Horses?" asked Watkins.

"Horses and men too," said Grierson.

"How d'yeh know?"

"A feller told me there by the ford."

They kept only a part of their minds bearing on this discussion because they could already hear high in the air the wire-string note of the enemy's bullets.

**III**

The road taken by this battalion as it followed other battalions is something less than a mile long in its journey across a heavily-wooded plain. It is greatly changed now,—in fact it was metamorphosed in two days; but at that time it was a mere track through dense shrubbery, from which rose great dignified arching trees. It was, in fact, a path through a jungle.

The battalion had no sooner left the battery in rear when bullets began to drive overhead. They made several different sounds, but as these were mainly high shots it was usual for them to make the faint note of a vibrant string, touched elusively, half-dreamily.

The military balloon, a fat, wavering, yellow thing, was leading the advance like some new conception of war-god. Its bloated mass shone above the trees, and served incidentally to indicate to the men at the rear that comrades were in advance. The track itself exhibited for all its visible length a closely-knit procession of soldiers in blue with breasts crossed with white shelter-tents. The first ominous order of battle came down the line. "Use the cut-off. Don't use the magazine until you're ordered." Non-commissioned officers repeated the command gruffly. A sound of clicking locks rattled along the columns. All men knew that the time had come.

The front had burst out with a roar like a brush-fire. The balloon was dying, dying a gigantic and public death before the eyes of two armies. It quivered, sank, faded into the trees amid the flurry of a battle that was suddenly and tremendously like a storm.

The American battery thundered behind the men with a shock that seemed likely to tear the backs of their heads off. The Spanish shrapnel fled on a line to their left, swirling and swishing in supernatural velocity. The noise of the rifle bullets broke in their faces like the noise of so many lamp-chimneys or sped overhead in swift cruel spitting. And at the front the battle-sound, as if it were simply music, was beginning to swell and swell until the volleys rolled like a surf.

The officers shouted hoarsely, "Come on, men! Hurry up, boys! Come on now! Hurry up!" The soldiers, running heavily in their accoutrements, dashed forward. A baggage guard was swiftly detailed; the men tore their rolls from their shoulders as if the things were afire. The battalion, stripped for action, again dashed forward.

"Come on, men! Come on!" To them the battle was as yet merely a road through the woods crowded with troops, who lowered their heads anxiously as the bullets fled high. But a moment later the column wheeled abruptly to the left and entered a field of tall green grass. The line scattered to a skirmish formation. In front was a series of knolls treed sparsely like orchards; and although no enemy was visible, these knolls were all popping and spitting with rifle-fire. In some places there were to be seen long grey lines of dirt, intrenchments. The American shells were kicking up reddish clouds of dust from the brow of one of the knolls, where stood a pagoda-like house. It was not much like a battle with men; it was a battle with a bit of charming scenery, enigmatically potent for death.

Nolan knew that Martin had suddenly fallen. "What—" he began.

"They've hit me," said Martin.

"Jesus!" said Nolan.

Martin lay on the ground, clutching his left forearm just below the elbow with all the strength of his right hand. His lips were pursed ruefully. He did not seem to know what to do. He continued to stare at his arm.

Then suddenly the bullets drove at them low and hard. The men flung themselves face downward in the grass. Nolan lost all thought of his friend. Oddly enough, he felt somewhat like a man hiding under a bed, and he was just as sure that he could not raise his head high without being shot as a man hiding under a bed is sure that he cannot raise his head without bumping it.

A lieutenant was seated in the grass just behind him. He was in the careless and yet rigid pose of a man balancing a loaded plate on his knee at a picnic. He was talking in soothing paternal tones.

"Now, don't get rattled. We're all right here. Just as safe as being in church.... They're all going high. Don't mind them.... Don't mind them.... They're all going high. We've got them rattled and they can't shoot straight. Don't mind them."

The sun burned down steadily from a pale blue sky upon the crackling woods and knolls and fields. From the roar of musketry it might have been that the celestial heat was frying this part of the world.

Nolan snuggled close to the grass. He watched a grey line of intrenchments, above which floated the veriest gossamer of smoke. A flag lolled on a staff behind it. The men in the trench volleyed whenever an American shell exploded near them. It was some kind of infantile defiance. Frequently a bullet came from the woods directly behind Nolan and his comrades. They thought at the time that these bullets were from the rifle of some incompetent soldier of their own side.

There was no cheering. The men would have looked about them, wondering where was the army, if it were not that the crash of the fighting for the distance of a mile denoted plainly enough where was the army.

Officially, the battalion had not yet fired a shot; there had been merely some irresponsible popping by men on the extreme left flank. But it was known that the lieutenant-colonel who had been in command was dead—shot through the heart—and that the captains were thinned down to two. At the rear went on a long tragedy, in which men, bent and hasty, hurried to shelter with other men, helpless, dazed, and bloody. Nolan knew of it all from the hoarse and affrighted voices which he heard as he lay flattened in the grass. There came to him a sense of exultation. Here, then, was one of those dread and lurid situations, which in a nation's history stand out in crimson letters, becoming a tale of blood to stir generation after generation. And he was in it, and unharmed. If he lived through the battle, he would be a hero of the desperate fight at —; and here he wondered for a second what fate would be pleased to bestow as a name for this battle.

But it is quite sure that hardly another man in the battalion was engaged in any thoughts concerning the historic. On the contrary, they deemed it ill that they were being badly cut up on a most unimportant occasion. It would have benefited the conduct of whoever were weak if they had known that they were engaged in a battle that would be famous for ever.

**IV**

Martin had picked himself up from where the bullet had knocked him and addressed the lieutenant. "I'm hit, sir," he said.

The lieutenant was very busy. "All right, all right," he said, just heeding the man enough to learn where he was wounded. "Go over that way. You ought to see a dressing-station under those trees."

Martin found himself dizzy and sick. The sensation in his arm was distinctly galvanic. The feeling was so strange that he could wonder at times if a wound was really what ailed him. Once, in this dazed way, he examined his arm; he saw the hole. Yes, he was shot; that was it. And more than in any other way it affected him with a profound sadness.

As directed by the lieutenant, he went to the clump of trees, but he found no dressing-station there. He found only a dead soldier lying with his face buried in his arms and with his shoulders humped high as if he were convulsively sobbing. Martin decided to make his way to the road, deeming that he thus would better his chances of getting to a surgeon. But he suddenly found his way blocked by a fence of barbed wire. Such was his mental condition that he brought up at a rigid halt before this fence, and stared stupidly at it. It did not seem to him possible that this obstacle could be defeated by any means. The fence was there, and it stopped his progress. He could not go in that direction.

But as he turned he espied that procession of wounded men, strange pilgrims, that had already worn a path in the tall grass. They were passing through a gap in the fence. Martin joined them. The bullets were flying over them in sheets, but many of them bore themselves as men who had now exacted from fate a singular immunity. Generally there were no outcries, no kicking, no talk at all. They too, like Martin, seemed buried in a vague but profound melancholy.

But there was one who cried out loudly. A man shot in the head was being carried arduously by four comrades, and he continually yelled one word that was terrible in its primitive strength,—"Bread! Bread! Bread!" Following him and his bearers were a limping crowd of men less cruelly wounded, who kept their eyes always fixed on him, as if they gained from his extreme agony some balm for their own sufferings.

"Bread! Give me bread!"

Martin plucked a man by the sleeve. The man had been shot in the foot, and was making his way with the help of a curved, incompetent stick. It is an axiom of war that wounded men can never find straight sticks.

"What's the matter with that feller?" asked Martin.

"Nutty," said the man.

"Why is he?"

"Shot in th' head," answered the other, impatiently.

The wail of the sufferer arose in the field amid the swift rasp of bullets and the boom and shatter of shrapnel. "Bread! Bread! Oh, God, can't you give me bread? Bread!" The bearers of him were suffering exquisite agony, and often they exchanged glances which exhibited their despair of ever getting free of this tragedy. It seemed endless.

"Bread! Bread! Bread!"

But despite the fact that there was always in the way of this crowd a wistful melancholy, one must know that there were plenty of men who laughed, laughed at their wounds whimsically, quaintly inventing odd humours concerning bicycles and cabs, extracting from this shedding of their blood a wonderful amount of material for cheerful badinage, and, with their faces twisted from pain as they stepped, they often joked like music-hall stars. And perhaps this was the most tearful part of all.

They trudged along a road until they reached a ford. Here under the eave of the bank lay a dismal company. In the mud and in the damp shade of some bushes were a half-hundred pale-faced men prostrate. Two or three surgeons were working there. Also, there was a chaplain, grim-mouthed, resolute, his surtout discarded. Overhead always was that incessant maddening wail of bullets.

Martin was standing gazing drowsily at the scene when a surgeon grabbed him. "Here, what's the matter with you?" Martin was daunted. He wondered what he had done that the surgeon should be so angry with him.

"In the arm," he muttered, half-shamefacedly.

After the surgeon had hastily and irritably bandaged the injured member he glared at Martin and said, "You can walk all right, can't you?"

"Yes, sir," said Martin.

"Well, now, you just make tracks down that road."

"Yes, sir." Martin went meekly off. The doctor had seemed exasperated almost to the point of madness.

The road was at this time swept with the fire of a body of Spanish sharpshooters who had come cunningly around the flanks of the American army, and were now hidden in the dense foliage that lined both sides of the road. They were shooting at everything. The road was as crowded as a street in a city, and at an absurdly short range they emptied their rifles at the passing people. They were aided always by the over-sweep from the regular Spanish line of battle.

Martin was sleepy from his wound. He saw tragedy follow tragedy, but they created in him no feeling of horror.

A man with a red cross on his arm was leaning against a great tree. Suddenly he tumbled to the ground, and writhed for a moment in the way of a child oppressed with colic. A comrade immediately began to bustle importantly. "Here," he called to Martin, "help me carry this man, will you?"

Martin looked at him with dull scorn. "I'll be damned if I do," he said. "Can't carry myself, let alone somebody else."

This answer, which rings now so inhuman, pitiless, did not affect the other man. "Well, all right," he said. "Here comes some other fellers." The wounded man had now turned blue-grey; his eyes were closed; his body shook in a gentle, persistent chill.

Occasionally Martin came upon dead horses, their limbs sticking out and up like stakes. One beast mortally shot, was besieged by three or four men who were trying to push it into the bushes, where it could live its brief time of anguish without thrashing to death any of the wounded men in the gloomy procession.

The mule train, with extra ammunition, charged toward the front, still led by the tinkling bell-mare.

An ambulance was stuck momentarily in the mud, and above the crack of battle one could hear the familiar objurgations of the driver as he whirled his lash.

Two privates were having a hard time with a wounded captain, whom they were supporting to the rear. He was half cursing, half wailing out the information that he not only would not go another step toward the rear, but that he was certainly going to return at once to the front. They begged, pleaded at great length as they continually headed him off. They were not unlike two nurses with an exceptionally bad and headstrong little duke.

The wounded soldiers paused to look impassively upon this struggle. They were always like men who could not be aroused by anything further.

The visible hospital was mainly straggling thickets intersected with narrow paths, the ground being covered with men. Martin saw a busy person with a book and a pencil, but he did not approach him to become officially a member of the hospital. All he desired was rest and immunity from nagging. He took seat painfully under a bush and leaned his back upon the trunk. There he remained thinking, his face wooden.

V

"My Gawd," said Nolan, squirming on his belly in the grass, "I can't stand this much longer."

Then suddenly every rifle in the firing line seemed to go off of its own accord. It was the result of an order, but few men heard the order; in the main they had fired because they heard others fire, and their sense was so quick that the volley did not sound too ragged. These marksmen had been lying for nearly an hour in stony silence, their sights adjusted, their fingers fondling their rifles, their eyes staring at the intrenchments of the enemy. The battalion had suffered heavy losses, and these losses had been hard to bear, for a soldier always reasons that men lost during a period of inaction are men badly lost.

The line now sounded like a great machine set to running frantically in the open air, the bright sunshine of a green field. To the prut of the magazine rifles was added the under-chorus of the clicking mechanism, steady and swift, as if the hand of one operator was controlling it all. It reminds one always of a loom, a great grand steel loom, clinking, clanking, plunking, plinking, to weave a woof of thin red threads, the cloth of death. By the men's shoulders under their eager hands dropped continually the yellow empty shells, spinning into the crushed grass blades to remain there and mark for the belated eye the line of a battalion's fight.

All impatience, all rebellious feeling, had passed out of the men as soon as they had been allowed to use their weapons against the enemy. They now were absorbed in this business of hitting something, and all the long training at the rifle ranges, all the pride of the marksman which had been so long alive in them, made them forget for the time everything but shooting. They were as deliberate and exact as so many watchmakers.

A new sense of safety was rightfully upon them. They knew that those mysterious men in the high far trenches in front were having the bullets sping in their faces with relentless and remarkable precision; they knew, in fact, that they were now doing the thing which they had been trained endlessly to do, and they knew they were doing it well. Nolan, for instance, was overjoyed. "Plug 'em," he said: "Plug 'em." He laid his face to his rifle as if it were his mistress. He was aiming under the shadow of a certain portico of a fortified house: there he could faintly see a long black line which he knew to be a loop-hole cut for riflemen, and he knew that every shot of his was going there under the portico, mayhap through the loop-hole to the brain of another man like himself. He loaded the awkward magazine of his rifle again and again. He was so intent that he did not know of new orders until he saw the men about him scrambling to their feet and running forward, crouching low as they ran.

He heard a shout. "Come on, boys! We can't be last! We're going up! We're going up." He sprang to his feet and, stooping, ran with the others. Something fine, soft, gentle, touched his heart as he ran. He had loved the regiment, the army, because the regiment, the army, was his life,—he had no other outlook; and now these men, his comrades, were performing his dream-scenes for him; they were doing as he had ordained in his visions. It is curious that in this charge he considered himself as rather unworthy. Although he himself was in the assault with the rest of them, it seemed to him that his comrades were dazzlingly courageous. His part, to his mind, was merely that of a man who was going along with the crowd.

He saw Grierson biting madly with his pincers at a barbed-wire fence. They were half-way up the beautiful sylvan slope; there was no enemy to be seen, and yet the landscape rained bullets. Somebody punched him violently in the stomach. He thought dully to lie down and rest, but instead he fell with a crash.

The sparse line of men in blue shirts and dirty slouch hats swept on up the hill. He decided to shut his eyes for a moment because he felt very dreamy and peaceful. It seemed only a minute before he heard a voice say, "There he is." Grierson and Watkins had come to look for him. He searched their faces at once and keenly, for he had a thought that the line might be driven down the hill and leave him in Spanish hands. But he saw that everything was secure, and he prepared no questions.

"Nolan," said Grierson clumsily, "do you know me?"

The man on the ground smiled softly. "Of course I know you, you chowder-faced monkey. Why wouldn't I know you?"

Watkins knelt beside him. "Where did they plug you, old boy?"

Nolan was somewhat dubious. "It ain't much. I don't think but it's somewheres there." He laid a finger on the pit of his stomach. They lifted his shirt, and then privately they exchanged a glance of horror.

"Does it hurt, Jimmie?" said Grierson, hoarsely.

"No," said Nolan, "it don't hurt any, but I feel sort of dead-to-the-world and numb all over. I don't think it's very bad."

"Oh, it's all right," said Watkins.

"What I need is a drink," said Nolan, grinning at them. "I'm chilly—lying on this damp ground."

"It ain't very damp, Jimmie," said Grierson.

"Well, it is damp," said Nolan, with sudden irritability. "I can feel it. I'm wet, I tell you—wet through—just from lying here."

They answered hastily. "Yes, that's so, Jimmie. It *is* damp. That's so."

"Just put your hand under my back and see how wet the ground is," he said.

"No," they answered. "That's all right, Jimmie. We know it's wet."

"Well, put your hand under and see," he cried, stubbornly.

"Oh, never mind, Jimmie."

"No," he said, in a temper. "See for yourself." Grierson seemed to be afraid of Nolan's agitation, and so he slipped a hand under the prostrate man, and presently withdrew it covered with blood. "Yes," he said, hiding his hand carefully from Nolan's eyes, "you were right, Jimmie."

"Of course I was," said Nolan, contentedly closing his eyes. "This hillside holds water like a swamp." After a moment he said, "Guess I ought to know. I'm flat here on it, and you fellers are standing up."

He did not know he was dying. He thought he was holding an argument on the condition of the turf.

## VI

"Cover his face," said Grierson, in a low and husky voice afterwards.

"What'll I cover it with?" said Watkins.

They looked at themselves. They stood in their shirts, trousers, leggings, shoes; they had nothing.

"Oh," said Grierson, "here's his hat." He brought it and laid it on the face of the dead man. They stood for a time. It was apparent that they thought it essential and decent to say or do something. Finally Watkins said in a broken voice, "Aw, it's a dam shame." They moved slowly off toward the firing line.

* * * *

In the blue gloom of evening, in one of the fever-tents, the two rows of still figures became hideous, charnel. The languid movement of a hand was surrounded with spectral mystery, and the occasional painful twisting of a body under a blanket was terrifying, as if dead men were moving in their graves under the sod. A heavy odour of sickness and medicine hung in the air.

"What regiment are you in?" said a feeble voice.

"Twenty-ninth Infantry," answered another voice.

"Twenty-ninth! Why, the man on the other side of me is in the Twenty-ninth."

"He is?... Hey, there, partner, are you in the Twenty-ninth?"

A third voice merely answered wearily. "Martin of C Company."

"What? Jack, is that you?"

"It's part of me.... Who are you?"

"Grierson, you fat-head. I thought you were wounded."

There was the noise of a man gulping a great drink of water, and at its conclusion Martin said, "I am."

"Well, what you doin' in the fever-place, then?"

Martin replied with drowsy impatience. "Got the fever too."

"Gee!" said Grierson.

Thereafter there was silence in the fever-tent, save for the noise made by a man over in a corner—a kind of man always found in an American crowd—a heroic, implacable comedian and patriot, of a humour that has bitterness and ferocity and love in it, and he was wringing from the situation a grim meaning by singing the "Star-Spangled Banner" with all the ardour which could be procured from his fever-stricken body.

"Billie," called Martin in a low voice, "where's Jimmy Nolan?"

"He's dead," said Grierson.

A triangle of raw gold light shone on a side of the tent. Somewhere in the valley an engine's bell was ringing, and it sounded of peace and home as if it hung on a cow's neck.

"And where's Ike Watkins?"

"Well, he ain't dead, but he got shot through the lungs. They say he ain't got much show."

Through the clouded odours of sickness and medicine rang the dauntless voice of the man in the corner.

# THE LONE CHARGE OF
# WILLIAM B. PERKINS

He could not distinguish between a five-inch quick-firing gun and a nickle-plated ice-pick, and so, naturally, he had been elected to fill the position of war-correspondent. The responsible party was the editor of the "Minnesota Herald." Perkins had no information of war, and no particular rapidity of mind for acquiring it, but he had that rank and fibrous quality of courage which springs from the thick soil of Western America.

It was morning in Guantanamo Bay. If the marines encamped on the hill had had time to turn their gaze seaward, they might have seen a small newspaper despatch-boat wending its way toward the entrance of the harbour over the blue, sunlit waters of the Caribbean. In the stern of this tug Perkins was seated upon some coal bags, while the breeze gently ruffled his greasy pajamas. He was staring at a brown line of entrenchments surmounted by a flag, which was Camp McCalla. In the harbour were anchored two or three grim, grey cruisers and a transport. As the tug steamed up the radiant channel, Perkins could see men moving on shore near the charred ruins of a village. Perkins was deeply moved; here already was more war than he had ever known in Minnesota. Presently he, clothed in the essential garments of a war-correspondent, was rowed to the sandy beach. Marines in yellow linen were handling an ammunition supply. They paid no attention to the visitor, being morose from the inconveniences of two days and nights of fighting. Perkins toiled up the zigzag path to the top of the hill, and looked with eager eyes at the trenches, the field-pieces, the funny little Colts, the flag, the grim marines lying wearily on their arms. And still more, he looked through the clear air over 1,000 yards of mysterious woods from which emanated at inopportune times repeated flocks of Mauser bullets.

Perkins was delighted. He was filled with admiration for these jaded and smoky men who lay so quietly in the trenches waiting for a resumption of guerilla enterprise. But he wished they would heed him. He wanted to talk about it. Save for sharp inquiring glances, no one acknowledged his existence.

Finally he approached two young lieutenants, and in his innocent Western way he asked them if they would like a drink. The effect on the two young lieutenants was immediate and astonishing. With one voice they answered, "Yes, we would." Perkins almost wept with joy at this amiable response, and he exclaimed that he would immediately board the tug and bring off a bottle of Scotch. This attracted the officers, and in a burst of confidence one explained that there had not been a drop in camp. Perkins lunged down the hill, and fled to his boat, where in his exuberance he engaged in a preliminary altercation with some whisky. Consequently he toiled again up the hill in the blasting sun with his enthusiasm in no ways abated. The parched officers were very gracious, and such was the state of mind of Perkins that he did not note properly how serious and solemn was his engagement with the whisky. And because of this fact, and because of his antecedents, there happened the lone charge of William B. Perkins.

Now, as Perkins went down the hill, something happened. A private in those high trenches found that a cartridge was clogged in his rifle. It then becomes necessary with most kinds of rifles to explode the cartridge. The private took the rifle to his captain, and explained the case. But it would not do in that camp to fire a rifle for mechanical purposes and without warning, because the eloquent sound would bring six hundred tired marines to tension and high expectancy. So the captain turned, and in a loud voice announced to the camp that he found it necessary to shoot into the air. The communication rang sharply from voice to voice. Then the captain raised the weapon and fired. Whereupon—and whereupon—a large line of guerillas lying in the bushes decided swiftly that their presence and position were discovered, and swiftly they volleyed.

In a moment the woods and the hills were alive with the crack and sputter of rifles. Men on the warships in the harbour heard the old familiar flut-flut-fluttery-fluttery-flut-flut-flut from the entrenchments. Incidentally the launch of the "Marblehead," commanded by one of our headlong American ensigns, streaked for the strategic woods like a galloping marine dragoon, peppering away with its blunderbuss in the bow.

Perkins had arrived at the foot of the hill, where began the arrangement of 150 marines that protected the short line of communication between the main body and the beach. These men had all swarmed into line behind fortifications improvised from the boxes of provisions. And to them were gathering naked men who had been bathing, naked men who arrayed themselves speedily in cartridge belts and rifles. The woods and the hills went flut-flut-flut-fluttery-fluttery-flut-fllllluttery-flut. Under the boughs of a beautiful tree lay five wounded men thinking vividly.

And now it befell Perkins to discover a Spaniard in the bush. The distance was some five hundred yards. In a loud voice he announced his perception. He also declared hoarsely, that if he only had a rifle, he would go and possess himself of this particular enemy. Immediately an amiable lad shot in the arm said: "Well, take mine." Perkins thus acquired a rifle and a clip of five cartridges.

"Come on!" he shouted. This part of the battalion was lying very tight, not yet being engaged, but not knowing when the business would swirl around to them.

To Perkins they replied with a roar. "Come back here, you damned fool. Do you want to get shot by your own crowd? Come back, damn it—!" As a detail, it might be mentioned that the fire from a part of the hill swept the journey upon which Perkins had started.

Now behold the solitary Perkins adrift in the storm of fighting, even as a champagne jacket of straw is lost in a great surf. He found it out quickly. Four seconds elapsed before he discovered that he was an almshouse idiot plunging through hot, crackling thickets on a June morning in Cuba. Sss-s-swing-sing-ing-pop went the lightning-swift metal grasshoppers over him and beside him. The beauties of rural Minnesota illuminated his conscience with the gold of lazy corn, with the sleeping green of meadows, with the cathedral gloom of pine forests. Sshsh-swing-pop! Perkins decided that if he cared to extract himself from a tangle of imbecility he must shoot. The entire situation was that he must shoot. It was necessary that he should shoot. Nothing would save him but shooting. It is a law that men thus decide when the waters of battle close over their minds. So with a prayer that the Americans would not hit him in the back nor the left side, and that the Spaniards would not hit him in the front, he knelt like a supplicant alone in the desert of chaparral, and emptied his magazine at his Spaniard before he discovered that his Spaniard was a bit of dried palm branch.

Then Perkins flurried like a fish. His reason for being was a Spaniard in the bush. When the Spaniard turned into a dried palm branch, he could no longer furnish himself with one adequate reason.

Then did he dream frantically of some anthracite hiding-place, some profound dungeon of peace where blind mules live placidly chewing the far-gathered hay.

"Sss-swing-win-pop! Prut-prut-prrrut!" Then a field-gun spoke. "*Boom*-ra-swow-ow-ow-ow-*pum*." Then a Colt automatic began to bark. "Crack-crk-crk-crk-crk-crk" endlessly. Raked, enfiladed, flanked, surrounded, and overwhelmed, what hope was there for William B. Perkins of the "Minnesota Herald?"

But war is a spirit. War provides for those that it loves. It provides sometimes death and sometimes a singular and incredible safety. There were few ways in which it was possible to preserve Perkins. One way was by means of a steam-boiler.

Perkins espied near him an old, rusty steam-boiler lying in the bushes. War only knows how it was there, but there it was, a temple shining resplendent with safety. With a moan of haste, Perkins flung himself through that hole which expressed the absence of the steam-pipe.

Then ensconced in his boiler, Perkins comfortably listened to the ring of a fight which seemed to be in the air above him. Sometimes bullets struck their strong, swift blow against the boiler's sides, but none entered to interfere with Perkins's rest.

Time passed. The fight, short anyhow, dwindled to prut … prut …prut-prut … prut. And when the silence came, Perkins might have been seen cautiously protruding from the boiler. Presently he strolled back toward the marine lines with his hat not able to fit his head for the new bumps of wisdom that were on it.

The marines, with an annoyed air, were settling down again when an apparitional figure came from the bushes. There was great excitement.

"It's that crazy man," they shouted, and as he drew near they gathered tumultuously about him and demanded to know how he had accomplished it.

Perkins made a gesture, the gesture of a man escaping from an unintentional mud-bath, the gesture of a man coming out of battle, and then he told them.

The incredulity was immediate and general. "Yes, you did! What? In an old boiler? An old boiler? Out in that brush? Well, we guess not." They did not believe him until two days later, when a patrol happened to find the rusty boiler, relic of some curious transaction in the ruin of the Cuban sugar industry. The patrol then marvelled at the truthfulness of war-correspondents until they were almost blind.

Soon after his adventure Perkins boarded the tug, wearing a countenance of poignant thoughtfulness.

# THE CLAN OF NO-NAME

Unwind my riddle.
Cruel as hawks the hours fly;
Wounded men seldom come home to die;
The hard waves see an arm flung high;
Scorn hits strong because of a lie;
Yet there exists a mystic tie.
Unwind my riddle.
She was out in the garden. Her mother came to her rapidly. "Margharita! Margharita, Mister Smith is here! Come!" Her mother was fat and commercially excited. Mister Smith was a matter of some importance to all Tampa people, and since he was really in love with Margharita he was distinctly of more importance to this particular household.

Palm trees tossed their sprays over the fence toward the rutted sand of the street. A little foolish fish-pond in the centre of the garden emitted a sound of red-fins flipping, flipping. "No, mamma," said the girl, "let Mr. Smith wait. I like the garden in the moonlight."

Her mother threw herself into that state of virtuous astonishment which is the weapon of her kind. "Margharita!"

The girl evidently considered herself to be a privileged belle, for she answered quite carelessly, "Oh, let him wait."

The mother threw abroad her arms with a semblance of great high-minded suffering and withdrew. Margharita walked alone in the moonlit garden. Also an electric light threw its shivering gleam over part of her parade.

There was peace for a time. Then suddenly through the faint brown palings was struck an envelope white and square. Margharita approached this envelope with an indifferent stride. She hummed a silly air, she bore herself casually, but there was something that made her grasp it hard, a peculiar muscular exhibition, not discernible to indifferent eyes. She did not clutch it, but she took it—simply took it in a way that meant everything, and, to measure it by vision, it was a picture of the most complete disregard.

She stood straight for a moment; then she drew from her bosom a photograph and thrust it through the palings. She walked rapidly into the house.

II

A man in garb of blue and white—something relating to what we call bed-ticking—was seated in a curious little cupola on the top of a Spanish blockhouse. The blockhouse sided a white military road that curved away from the man's sight into a blur of trees. On all sides of him were fields of tall grass, studded with palms and lined with fences of barbed wire. The sun beat aslant through the trees and the man sped his eyes deep into the dark tropical shadows that seemed velvet with coolness. These tranquil vistas resembled painted scenery in a theatre, and, moreover, a hot, heavy silence lay upon the land.

The soldier in the watching place leaned an unclean Mauser rifle in a corner, and, reaching down, took a glowing coal on a bit of palm bark handed up to him by a comrade. The men below were mainly asleep. The sergeant in command drowsed near the open door, the arm above his head, showing his long keen-angled chevrons attached carelessly with safety-pins. The sentry lit his cigarette and puffed languorously.

Suddenly he heard from the air around him the querulous, deadly-swift spit of rifle-bullets, and, an instant later, the poppety-pop of a small volley sounded in his face, close, as if it were fired only ten feet away. Involuntarily he threw back his head quickly as if he were protecting his nose from a falling tile. He screamed an alarm and fell into the blockhouse. In the gloom of it, men with their breaths coming sharply between their teeth, were tumbling wildly for positions at the loop-holes. The door had been slammed, but the sergeant lay just within, propped up as when he drowsed, but now with blood flowing steadily over the hand that he pressed flatly to his chest. His face was in stark yellow agony; he chokingly repeated: "Fuego! Por Dios, hombres!"

The men's ill-conditioned weapons were jammed through the loop-holes and they began to fire from all four sides of the blockhouse from the simple data, apparently, that the enemy were in the vicinity. The fumes of burnt powder grew stronger and stronger in the little square fortress. The rattling of the magazine locks was incessant, and the interior might have been that of a gloomy manufactory if it were not for the sergeant down under the feet of the men, coughing out: "Por Dios, hombres! Por Dios! Fuego!"

### III

A string of five Cubans, in linen that had turned earthy brown in colour, slid through the woods at a pace that was neither a walk nor a run. It was a kind of rack. In fact the whole manner of the men, as they thus moved, bore a rather comic resemblance to the American pacing horse. But they had come many miles since sun-up over mountainous and half-marked paths, and were plainly still fresh. The men were all practicos—guides. They made no sound in their swift travel, but moved their half-shod feet with the skill of cats. The woods lay around them in a deep silence, such as one might find at the bottom of a lake.

Suddenly the leading practico raised his hand. The others pulled up short and dropped the butts of their weapons calmly and noiselessly to the ground. The leader whistled a low note and immediately another practico appeared from the bushes. He moved close to the leader without a word, and then they spoke in whispers.

"There are twenty men and a sergeant in the blockhouse."

"And the road?"

"One company of cavalry passed to the east this morning at seven o'clock. They were escorting four carts. An hour later, one horseman rode swiftly to the westward. About noon, ten infantry soldiers with a corporal were taken from the big fort and put in the first blockhouse, to the east of the fort. There were already twelve men there. We saw a Spanish column moving off toward Mariel."

"No more?"

"No more."

"Good. But the cavalry?"

"It is all right. They were going a long march."

"The expedition is a half league behind. Go and tell the general."

The scout disappeared. The five other men lifted their guns and resumed their rapid and noiseless progress. A moment later no sound broke the stillness save the thump of a mango, as it dropped lazily from its tree to the grass. So strange had been the apparition of these men, their dress had been so allied in colour to the soil, their passing had so little disturbed the solemn rumination of the forest, and their going had been so like a spectral dissolution, that a witness could have wondered if he dreamed.

## IV

A small expedition had landed with arms from the United States, and had now come out of the hills and to the edge of a wood. Before them was a long-grassed rolling prairie marked with palms. A half-mile away was the military road, and they could see the top of a blockhouse. The insurgent scouts were moving somewhere off in the grass. The general sat comfortably under a tree, while his staff of three young officers stood about him chatting. Their linen clothing was notable from being distinctly whiter than those of the men who, one hundred and fifty in number, lay on the ground in a long brown fringe, ragged—indeed, bare in many places—but singularly reposeful, unworried, veteran-like.

The general, however, was thoughtful. He pulled continually at his little thin moustache. As far as the heavily patrolled and guarded military road was concerned, the insurgents had been in the habit of dashing across it in small bodies whenever they pleased, but to safely scoot over it with a valuable convoy of arms, was decidedly a more important thing. So the general awaited the return of his practicos with anxiety. The still pampas betrayed no sign of their existence.

The general gave some orders and an officer counted off twenty men to go with him, and delay any attempt of the troop of cavalry to return from the eastward. It was not an easy task, but it was a familiar task—checking the advance of a greatly superior force by a very hard fire from concealment. A few rifles had often bayed a strong column for sufficient length of time for all strategic purposes. The twenty men pulled themselves together tranquilly. They looked quite indifferent. Indeed, they had the supremely casual manner of old soldiers, hardened to battle as a condition of existence.

Thirty men were then told off, whose function it was to worry and rag at the blockhouse, and check any advance from the westward. A hundred men, carrying precious burdens—besides their own equipment—were to pass in as much of a rush as possible between these two wings, cross the road and skip for the hills, their retreat being covered by a combination of the two firing parties. It was a trick that needed both luck and neat arrangement. Spanish columns were for ever prowling through this province in all directions and at all times. Insurgent bands—the lightest of light infantry—were kept on the jump, even when they were not incommoded by fifty boxes, each one large enough for the coffin of a little man, and heavier than if the little man were in it; and fifty small but formidable boxes of ammunition.

The carriers stood to their boxes and the firing parties leaned on their rifles. The general arose and strolled to and fro, his hands behind him. Two of his staff were jesting at the third, a young man with a face less bronzed, and with very new accoutrements. On the strap of his cartouche were a gold star and a silver star, placed in a horizontal line, denoting that he was a second lieutenant. He seemed very happy; he laughed at all their jests, although his eye roved continually over the sunny grasslands, where was going to happen his first fight. One of his stars was bright, like his hopes, the other was pale, like death.

Two practicos came racking out of the grass. They spoke rapidly to the general; he turned and nodded to his officers. The two firing parties filed out and diverged toward their positions. The general watched them through his glasses. It was strange to note how soon they were dim to the unaided eye. The little patches of brown in the green grass did not look like men at all.

Practicos continually ambled up to the general. Finally he turned and made a sign to the bearers. The first twenty men in line picked up their boxes, and this movement rapidly spread to the tail of the line. The weighted procession moved painfully out upon the sunny prairie. The general, marching at the head of it, glanced continually back as if he were compelled to drag behind him some ponderous iron chain. Besides the obvious mental worry, his face bore an expression of intense physical strain, and he even bent his shoulders, unconsciously tugging at the chain to hurry it through this enemy-crowded valley.

<h1 style="text-align:center">V</h1>

The fight was opened by eight men who, snuggling in the grass, within three hundred yards of the blockhouse, suddenly blazed away at the bed-ticking figure in the cupola and at the open door where they could see vague outlines. Then they laughed and yelled insulting language, for they knew that as far as the Spaniards were concerned, the surprise was as much as having a diamond bracelet turn to soap. It was this volley that smote the sergeant and caused the man in the cupola to scream and tumble from his perch.

The eight men, as well as all other insurgents within fair range, had chosen good positions for lying close, and for a time they let the blockhouse rage, although the soldiers therein could occasionally hear, above the clamour of their weapons, shrill and almost wolfish calls, coming from men whose lips were laid against the ground. But it is not in the nature of them of Spanish blood, and armed with rifles, to long endure the sight of anything so tangible as an enemy's blockhouse without shooting at it—other conditions being partly favourable. Presently the steaming soldiers in the little fort could hear the sping and shiver of bullets striking the wood that guarded their bodies.

A perfectly white smoke floated up over each firing Cuban, the penalty of the Remington rifle, but about the blockhouse there was only the lightest gossamer of blue. The blockhouse stood always for some big, clumsy and rather incompetent animal, while the insurgents, scattered on two sides of it, were little enterprising creatures of another species, too wise to come too near, but joyously raging at its easiest flanks and drilling the lead into its sides in a way to make it fume, and spit and rave like the tom-cat when the glad, free-band fox-hound pups catch him in the lane.

The men, outlying in the grass, chuckled deliriously at the fury of the Spanish fire. They howled opprobrium to encourage the Spaniards to fire more ill-used, incapable bullets. Whenever an insurgent was about to fire, he ordinarily prefixed the affair with a speech. "Do you want something to eat? Yes? All right." Bang! "Eat that." The more common expressions of the incredibly foul Spanish tongue were trifles light as air in this badinage, which was shrieked out from the grass during the spin of bullets, and the dull rattle of the shooting.

But at some time there came a series of sounds from the east that began in a few disconnected pruts and ended as if an amateur was trying to play the long roll upon a muffled drum. Those of the insurgents in the blockhouse attacking party, who had neighbours in the grass, turned and looked at them seriously. They knew what the new sound meant. It meant that the twenty men who had gone to the eastward were now engaged. A column of some kind was approaching from that direction, and they knew by the clatter that it was a solemn occasion.

In the first place, they were now on the wrong side of the road. They were obliged to cross it to rejoin the main body, provided of course that the main body succeeded itself in crossing it. To accomplish this, the party at the blockhouse would have to move to the eastward, until out of sight or good range of the maddened little fort. But judging from the heaviness of the firing, the party of twenty who protected the east were almost sure to be driven immediately back. Hence travel in that direction would become exceedingly hazardous. Hence a man looked seriously at his neighbour. It might easily be that in a moment they were to become an isolated force and woefully on the wrong side of the road.

Any retreat to the westward was absurd, since primarily they would have to widely circle the blockhouse, and more than that, they could hear, even now in that direction, Spanish bugle calling to Spanish bugle, far and near, until one would think that every man in Cuba was a trumpeter, and had come forth to parade his talent.

## VI

The insurgent general stood in the middle of the road gnawing his lips. Occasionally, he stamped a foot and beat his hands passionately together. The carriers were streaming past him, patient, sweating fellows, bowed under their burdens, but they could not move fast enough for him when others of his men were engaged both to the east and to the west, and he, too, knew from the sound that those to the east were in a sore way. Moreover, he could hear that accursed bugling, bugling, bugling in the west.

He turned suddenly to the new lieutenant who stood behind him, pale and quiet. "Did you ever think a hundred men were so many?" he cried, incensed to the point of beating them. Then he said longingly: "Oh, for a half an hour! Or even twenty minutes!"

A practico racked violently up from the east. It is characteristic of these men that, although they take a certain roadster gait and hold it for ever, they cannot really run, sprint, race. "Captain Rodriguez is attacked by two hundred men, señor, and the cavalry is behind them. He wishes to know—"

The general was furious; he pointed. "Go! Tell Rodriguez to hold his place for twenty minutes, even if he leaves every man dead."

The practico shambled hastily off.

The last of the carriers were swarming across the road. The rifle-drumming in the east was swelling out and out, evidently coming slowly nearer. The general bit his nails. He wheeled suddenly upon the young lieutenant. "Go to Bas at the blockhouse. Tell him to hold the devil himself for ten minutes and then bring his men out of that place."

The long line of bearers was crawling like a dun worm toward the safety of the foot-hills. High bullets sang a faint song over the aide as he saluted. The bugles had in the west ceased, and that was more ominous than bugling. It meant that the Spanish troops were about to march, or perhaps that they had marched.

The young lieutenant ran along the road until he came to the bend which marked the range of sight from the blockhouse. He drew his machete, his stunning new machete, and hacked feverishly at the barbed wire fence which lined the north side of the road at that point. The first wire was obdurate, because it was too high for his stroke, but two more cut like candy, and he stepped over the remaining one, tearing his trousers in passing on the lively serpentine ends of the severed wires. Once out in the field and bullets seemed to know him and call for him and speak their wish to kill him. But he ran on, because it was his duty, and because he would be shamed before men if he did not do his duty, and because he was desolate out there all alone in the fields with death.

A man running in this manner from the rear was in immensely greater danger than those who lay snug and close. But he did not know it. He thought because he was five hundred—four hundred and fifty—four hundred yards away from the enemy and the others were only three hundred yards away that they were in far more peril. He ran to join them because of his opinion. He did not care to do it, but he thought that was what men of his kind would do in such a case. There was a standard and he must follow it, obey it, because it was a monarch, the Prince of Conduct.

A bewildered and alarmed face raised itself from the grass and a voice cried to him: "Drop, Manolo! Drop! Drop!" He recognised Bas and flung himself to the earth beside him.

"Why," he said panting, "what's the matter?"

"Matter?" said Bas. "You are one of the most desperate and careless officers I know. When I saw you coming I wouldn't have given a peseta for your life."

"Oh, no," said the young aide. Then he repeated his orders rapidly. But he was hugely delighted. He knew Bas well; Bas was a pupil of Maceo; Bas invariably led his men; he never was a mere spectator of their battle; he was known for it throughout the western end of the island. The new officer had early achieved a part of his ambition—to be called a brave man by established brave men.

"Well, if we get away from here quickly it will be better for us," said Bas, bitterly. "I've lost six men killed, and more wounded. Rodriguez can't hold his position there, and in a little time more than a thousand men will come from the other direction."

He hissed a low call, and later the young aide saw some of the men sneaking off with the wounded, lugging them on their backs as porters carry sacks. The fire from the blockhouse had become a-weary, and as the insurgent fire also slackened, Bas and the young lieutenant lay in the weeds listening to the approach of the eastern fight, which was sliding toward them like a door to shut them off.

Bas groaned. "I leave my dead. Look there." He swung his hand in a gesture and the lieutenant looking saw a corpse. He was not stricken as he expected; there was very little blood; it was a mere thing.

"Time to travel," said Bas suddenly. His imperative hissing brought his men near him; there were a few hurried questions and answers; then, characteristically, the men turned in the grass, lifted their rifles, and fired a last volley into the blockhouse, accompanying it with their shrill cries. Scrambling low to the ground, they were off in a winding line for safety. Breathing hard, the lieutenant stumbled his way forward. Behind him he could hear the men calling each to each: "Segue! Segue! Segue! Go on! Get out! Git!" Everybody understood that the peril of crossing the road was compounding from minute to minute.

## VII

When they reached the gap through which the expedition had passed, they fled out upon the road like scared wild-fowl tracking along a sea-beach. A cloud of blue figures far up this dignified shaded avenue, fired at once. The men already had begun to laugh as they shied one by one across the road. "Segue! Segue!" The hard part for the nerves had been the lack of information of the amount of danger. Now that they could see it, they accounted it all the more lightly for their previous anxiety.

Over in the other field, Bas and the young lieutenant found Rodriguez, his machete in one hand, his revolver in the other, smoky, dirty, sweating. He shrugged his shoulders when he saw them and pointed disconsolately to the brown thread of carriers moving toward the foot-hills. His own men were crouched in line just in front of him blazing like a prairie fire.

Now began the fight of a scant rear-guard to hold back the pressing Spaniards until the carriers could reach the top of the ridge, a mile away. This ridge by the way was more steep than any roof; it conformed, more, to the sides of a French war-ship. Trees grew vertically from it, however, and a man burdened only with his rifle usually pulled himself wheezingly up in a sort of ladder-climbing process, grabbing the slim trunks above him. How the loaded carriers were to conquer it in a hurry, no one knew. Rodriguez shrugged his shoulders as one who would say with philosophy, smiles, tears, courage: "Isn't this a mess!"

At an order, the men scattered back for four hundred yards with the rapidity and mystery of a handful of pebbles flung in the night. They left one behind who cried out, but it was now a game in which some were sure to be left behind to cry out.

The Spaniards deployed on the road and for twenty minutes remained there pouring into the field such a fire from their magazines as was hardly heard at Gettysburg. As a matter of truth the insurgents were at this time doing very little shooting, being chary of ammunition. But it is possible for the soldier to confuse himself with his own noise and undoubtedly the Spanish troops thought throughout their din that they were being fiercely engaged. Moreover, a firing-line—particularly at night or when opposed to a hidden foe—is nothing less than an emotional chord, a chord of a harp that sings because a puff of air arrives or when a bit of down touches it. This is always true of new troops or stupid troops and these troops were rather stupid troops. But, the way in which they mowed the verdure in the distance was a sight for a farmer.

Presently the insurgents slunk back to another position where they fired enough shots to stir again the Spaniards into an opinion that they were in a heavy fight. But such a misconception could only endure for a number of minutes. Presently it was plain that the Spaniards were about to advance and, moreover, word was brought to Rodriguez that a small band of guerillas were already making an attempt to worm around the right flank. Rodriguez cursed despairingly; he sent both Bas and the young lieutenant to that end of the line to hold the men to their work as long as possible.

In reality the men barely needed the presence of their officers. The kind of fighting left practically everything to the discretion of the individual and they arrived at concert of action mainly because of the equality of experience, in the wisdoms of bushwhacking.

The yells of the guerillas could plainly be heard and the insurgents answered in kind. The young lieutenant found desperate work on the right flank. The men were raving mad with it, babbling, tearful, almost frothing at the mouth. Two terrible bloody creatures passed him, creeping on all fours, and one in a whimper was calling upon God, his mother, and a saint. The guerillas, as effectually concealed as the insurgents, were driving their bullets low through the smoke at sight of a flame, a movement of the grass or sight of a patch of dirty brown coat. They were no column-o'-four soldiers; they were as slinky and snaky and quick as so many Indians. They were, moreover, native Cubans and because of their treachery to the one-star flag, they never by any chance received quarter if they fell into the hands of the insurgents. Nor, if the case was reversed, did they ever give quarter. It was life and life, death and death; there was no middle ground, no compromise. If a man's crowd was rapidly retreating and he was tumbled over by a slight hit, he should curse the sacred graves that the wound was not through the precise centre of his heart. The machete is a fine broad blade but it is not so nice as a drilled hole in the chest; no man wants his death-bed to be a shambles. The men fighting on the insurgents' right knew that if they fell they were lost.

On the extreme right, the young lieutenant found five men in a little saucer-like hollow. Two were dead, one was wounded and staring blankly at the sky and two were emptying hot rifles furiously. Some of the guerillas had snaked into positions only a hundred yards away.

The young man rolled in among the men in the saucer. He could hear the barking of the guerillas and the screams of the two insurgents. The rifles were popping and spitting in his face, it seemed, while the whole land was alive with a noise of rolling and drumming. Men could have gone drunken in all this flashing and flying and snarling and din, but at this time he was very deliberate. He knew that he was thrusting himself into a trap whose door, once closed, opened only when the black hand knocked and every part of him seemed to be in panic-stricken revolt. But something controlled him; something moved him inexorably in one direction; he perfectly understood but he was only sad, sad with a serene dignity, with the countenance of a mournful young prince. He was of a kind—that seemed to be it—and the men of his kind, on peak or plain, from the dark northern ice-fields to the hot wet jungles, through all wine and want, through all lies and unfamiliar truth, dark or light, the men of his kind were governed by their gods, and each man knew the law and yet could not give tongue to it, but it was the law and if the spirits of the men of his kind were all sitting in critical judgment upon him even then in the sky, he could not have bettered his conduct; he needs must obey the law and always with the law there is only one way. But from peak and plain, from dark northern ice-fields and hot wet jungles, through wine and want, through all lies and unfamiliar truth, dark or light, he heard breathed to him the approval and the benediction of his brethren.

He stooped and gently took a dead man's rifle and some cartridges. The battle was hurrying, hurrying, hurrying, but he was in no haste. His glance caught the staring eye of the wounded soldier, and he smiled at him quietly. The man—simple doomed peasant—was not of his kind, but the law on fidelity was clear.

He thrust a cartridge into the Remington and crept up beside the two unhurt men. Even as he did so, three or four bullets cut so close to him that all his flesh tingled. He fired carefully into the smoke. The guerillas were certainly not now more than fifty yards away.

He raised him coolly for his second shot, and almost instantly it was as if some giant had struck him in the chest with a beam. It whirled him in a great spasm back into the saucer. As he put his two hands to his breast, he could hear the guerillas screeching exultantly, every throat vomiting forth all the infamy of a language prolific in the phrasing of infamy.

One of the other men came rolling slowly down the slope, while his rifle followed him, and, striking another rifle, clanged out. Almost immediately the survivor howled and fled wildly. A whole volley missed him and then one or more shots caught him as a bird is caught on the wing.

The young lieutenant's body seemed galvanised from head to foot. He concluded that he was not hurt very badly, but when he tried to move he found that he could not lift his hands from his breast. He had turned to lead. He had had a plan of taking a photograph from his pocket and looking at it.

There was a stir in the grass at the edge of the saucer, and a man appeared there, looking where lay the four insurgents. His negro face was not an eminently

ferocious one in its lines, but now it was lit with an illimitable blood-greed. He and
the young lieutenant exchanged a singular glance; then he came stepping eagerly
down. The young lieutenant closed his eyes, for he did not want to see the flash of
the machete.

## VIII

The Spanish colonel was in a rage, and yet immensely proud; immensely proud,
and yet in a rage of disappointment. There had been a fight and the insurgents had
retreated leaving their dead, but still a valuable expedition had broken through his
lines and escaped to the mountains. As a matter of truth, he was not sure whether to
be wholly delighted or wholly angry, for well he knew that the importance lay not so
much in the truthful account of the action as it did in the heroic prose of the official
report, and in the fight itself lay material for a purple splendid poem. The insurgents
had run away; no one could deny it; it was plain even to whatever privates had fired
with their eyes shut. This was worth a loud blow and splutter. However, when all
was said and done, he could not help but reflect that if he had captured this expedition, he would have been a brigadier-general, if not more.

He was a short, heavy man with a beard, who walked in a manner common to
all elderly Spanish officers, and to many young ones; that is to say, he walked as if
his spine was a stick and a little longer than his body; as if he suffered from some
disease of the backbone, which allowed him but scant use of his legs. He toddled
along the road, gesticulating disdainfully and muttering: "Ca! Ca! Ca!"

He berated some soldiers for an immaterial thing, and as he approached the
men stepped precipitately back as if he were a fire-engine. They were most of them
young fellows, who displayed, when under orders, the manner of so many faithful dogs. At present, they were black, tongue-hanging, thirsty boys, bathed in the
nervous weariness of the after-battle time.

Whatever he may truly have been in character, the colonel closely resembled a
gluttonous and libidinous old pig, filled from head to foot with the pollution of a
sinful life. "Ca!" he snarled, as he toddled. "Ca! Ca!" The soldiers saluted as they
backed to the side of the road. The air was full of the odour of burnt rags. Over on
the prairie guerillas and regulars were rummaging the grass. A few unimportant
shots sounded from near the base of the hills.

A guerilla, glad with plunder, came to a Spanish captain. He held in his hand
a photograph. "Mira, señor. I took this from the body of an officer whom I killed
machete to machete."

The captain shot from the corner of his eye a cynical glance at the guerilla, a
glance which commented upon the last part of the statement. "M-m-m," he said.
He took the photograph and gazed with a slow faint smile, the smile of a man who
knows bloodshed and homes and love, at the face of a girl. He turned the photograph
presently, and on the back of it was written: "One lesson in English I will give
you—this: I love you, Margharita." The photograph had been taken in Tampa.

The officer was silent for a half-minute, while his face still wore the slow faint
smile. "Pobrecetto," he murmured finally, with a philosophic sigh, which was
brother to a shrug. Without deigning a word to the guerilla he thrust the photograph
in his pocket and walked away.

High over the green earth, in the dizzy blue heights, some great birds were
slowly circling with down-turned beaks.

# IX

Margharita was in the gardens. The blue electric rays shone through the plumes of the palm and shivered in feathery images on the walk. In the little foolish fishpond some stalwart fish was apparently bullying the others, for often there sounded a frantic splashing.

Her mother came to her rapidly. "Margharita! Mister Smith is here! Come!"

"Oh, is he?" cried the girl. She followed her mother to the house. She swept into the little parlor with a grand air, the egotism of a savage. Smith had heard the whirl of her skirts in the hall, and his heart, as usual, thumped hard enough to make him gasp. Every time he called, he would sit waiting with the dull fear in his breast that her mother would enter and indifferently announce that she had gone up to heaven or off to New York, with one of his dream-rivals, and he would never see her again in this wide world. And he would conjure up tricks to then escape from the house without any one observing his face break up into furrows. It was part of his love to believe in the absolute treachery of his adored one. So whenever he heard the whirl of her skirts in the hall he felt that he had again leased happiness from a dark fate.

She was rosily beaming and all in white. "Why, Mister Smith," she exclaimed, as if he was the last man in the world she expected to see.

"Good-evenin'," he said, shaking hands nervously. He was always awkward and unlike himself, at the beginning of one of these calls. It took him some time to get into form.

She posed her figure in operatic style on a chair before him, and immediately galloped off a mile of questions, information of herself, gossip and general outcries which left him no obligation, but to look beamingly intelligent and from time to time say: "Yes?" His personal joy, however, was to stare at her beauty.

When she stopped and wandered as if uncertain which way to talk, there was a minute of silence, which each of them had been educated to feel was very incorrect; very incorrect indeed. Polite people always babbled at each other like two brooks.

He knew that the responsibility was upon him, and, although his mind was mainly upon the form of the proposal of marriage which he intended to make later, it was necessary that he should maintain his reputation as a well-bred man by saying something at once. It flashed upon him to ask: "Won't you please play?" But the time for the piano ruse was not yet; it was too early. So he said the first thing that came into his head: "Too bad about young Manolo Prat being killed over there in Cuba, wasn't it?"

"Wasn't it a pity?" she answered.

"They say his mother is heart-broken," he continued. "They're afraid she's goin' to die."

"And wasn't it queer that we didn't hear about it for almost two months?"

"Well, it's no use tryin' to git quick news from there."

Presently they advanced to matters more personal, and she used upon him a series of star-like glances which rumpled him at once to squalid slavery. He gloated upon her, afraid, afraid, yet more avaricious than a thousand misers. She fully comprehended; she laughed and taunted him with her eyes. She impressed upon him that she was like a will-o'-the-wisp, beautiful beyond compare but impossible, almost impossible, at least very difficult; then again, suddenly, impossible—impossible— impossible. He was glum; he would never dare propose to this radiance; it was like asking to be pope.

A moment later, there chimed into the room something that he knew to be a more tender note. The girl became dreamy as she looked at him; her voice lowered to a delicious intimacy of tone. He leaned forward; he was about to outpour his bully-ragged soul in fine words, when—presto—she was the most casual person he had ever laid eyes upon, and was asking him about the route of the proposed trolley line.

But nothing short of a fire could stop him now. He grabbed her hand. "Margharita," he murmured gutturally, "I want you to marry me."

She glared at him in the most perfect lie of astonishment. "What do you say?"

He arose, and she thereupon arose also and fled back a step. He could only stammer out her name. And thus they stood, defying the principles of the dramatic art.

"I love you," he said at last.

"How—how do I know you really—truly love me?" she said, raising her eyes timorously to his face and this timorous glance, this one timorous glance, made him the superior person in an instant. He went forward as confident as a grenadier, and, taking both her hands, kissed her.

That night she took a stained photograph from her dressing-table and holding it over the candle burned it to nothing, her red lips meanwhile parted with the intentness of her occupation. On the back of the photograph was written: "One lesson in English I will give you—this: I love you."

For the word is clear only to the kind who on peak or plain, from dark northern ice-fields to the hot wet jungles, through all wine and want, through lies and unfamiliar truth, dark or light, are governed by the unknown gods, and though each man knows the law, no man may give tongue to it.

# GOD REST YE, MERRY GENTLEMEN

Little Nell, sometimes called the Blessed Damosel, was a war correspondent for the *New York Eclipse*, and at sea on the despatch boats he wore pajamas, and on shore he wore whatever fate allowed him, which clothing was in the main unsuitable to the climate. He had been cruising in the Caribbean on a small tug, awash always, habitable never, wildly looking for Cervera's fleet; although what he was going to do with four armoured cruisers and two destroyers in the event of his really finding them had not been explained by the managing editor. The cable instructions read:— "Take tug; go find Cervera's fleet." If his unfortunate nine-knot craft should happen to find these great twenty-knot ships, with their two spiteful and faster attendants, Little Nell had wondered how he was going to lose them again. He had marvelled, both publicly and in secret, on the uncompromising asininity of managing editors at odd moments, but he had wasted little time. The *Jefferson G. Johnson* was already coaled, so he passed the word to his skipper, bought some tinned meats, cigars, and beer, and soon the *Johnson* sailed on her mission, tooting her whistle in graceful farewell to some friends of hers in the bay.

So the *Johnson* crawled giddily to one wave-height after another, and fell, aslant, into one valley after another for a longer period than was good for the hearts of the men, because the *Johnson* was merely a harbour-tug, with no architectural intention of parading the high-seas, and the crew had never seen the decks all white water like a mere sunken reef. As for the cook, he blasphemed hopelessly hour in and hour out, meanwhile pursuing the equipment of his trade frantically from side to side of the galley. Little Nell dealt with a great deal of grumbling, but he knew it was not the real evil grumbling. It was merely the unhappy words of men who wished expression of comradeship for their wet, forlorn, half-starved lives, to which, they explained, they were not accustomed, and for which, they explained, they were not properly paid. Little Nell condoled and condoled without difficulty. He laid words of gentle sympathy before them, and smothered his own misery behind the face of a reporter of the *New York Eclipse*. But they tossed themselves in their cockleshell even as far as Martinique; they knew many races and many flags, but they did not find Cervera's fleet. If they had found that elusive squadron this timid story would never have been written; there would probably have been a lyric. The *Johnson* limped one morning into the Mole St. Nicholas, and there Little Nell received this despatch:—"Can't understand your inaction. What are you doing with the boat? Report immediately. Fleet transports already left Tampa. Expected destination near Santiago. Proceed there immediately. Place yourself under orders.—Rogers, *Eclipse*."

One day, steaming along the high, luminous blue coast of Santiago province, they fetched into view the fleets, a knot of masts and funnels, looking incredibly inshore, as if they were glued to the mountains. Then mast left mast, and funnel left funnel, slowly, slowly, and the shore remained still, but the fleets seemed to move out toward the eager *Johnson*. At the speed of nine knots an hour the scene separated into its parts. On an easily rolling sea, under a crystal sky, black-hulled transports—erstwhile packets—lay waiting, while grey cruisers and gunboats lay near shore, shelling the beach and some woods. From their grey sides came thin red flashes, belches of white smoke, and then over the waters sounded boom—boom—boom-boom.

The crew of the *Jefferson G. Johnson* forgave Little Nell all the suffering of a previous fortnight.

To the westward, about the mouth of Santiago harbour, sat a row of castellated grey battleships, their eyes turned another way, waiting.

The *Johnson* swung past a transport whose decks and rigging were aswarm with black figures, as if a tribe of bees had alighted upon a log. She swung past a cruiser indignant at being left out of the game, her deck thick with white-clothed tars watching the play of their luckier brethren. The cold blue, lifting seas tilted the big ships easily, slowly, and heaved the little ones in the usual sinful way, as if very little babes had surreptitiously mounted sixteen-hand trotting hunters. The *Johnson* leered and tumbled her way through a community of ships. The bombardment ceased, and some of the troopships edged in near the land. Soon boats black with men and towed by launches were almost lost to view in the scintillant mystery of light which appeared where the sea met the land. A disembarkation had begun. The *Johnson* sped on at her nine knots, and Little Nell chafed exceedingly, gloating upon the shore through his glasses, anon glancing irritably over the side to note the efforts of the excited tug. Then at last they were in a sort of a cove, with troopships, newspaper boats, and cruisers on all sides of them, and over the water came a great hum of human voices, punctuated frequently by the clang of engine-room gongs as the steamers manoeuvred to avoid jostling.

In reality it was the great moment—the moment for which men, ships, islands, and continents had been waiting for months; but somehow it did not look it. It was very calm; a certain strip of high, green, rocky shore was being rapidly populated from boat after boat; that was all. Like many preconceived moments, it refused to be supreme.

But nothing lessened Little Nell's frenzy. He knew that the army was landing— he could see it; and little did he care if the great moment did not look its part—it was his virtue as a correspondent to recognise the great moment in any disguise. The *Johnson* lowered a boat for him, and he dropped into it swiftly, forgetting everything. However, the mate, a bearded philanthropist, flung after him a mackintosh and a bottle of whisky. Little Nell's face was turned toward those other boats filled with men, all eyes upon the placid, gentle, noiseless shore. Little Nell saw many soldiers seated stiffly beside upright rifle barrels, their blue breasts crossed with white shelter tent and blanket-rolls. Launches screeched; jack-tars pushed or pulled with their boathooks; a beach was alive with working soldiers, some of them stark naked. Little Nell's boat touched the shore amid a babble of tongues, dominated at that time by a single stern voice, which was repeating, "Fall in, B Company!"

He took his mackintosh and his bottle of whisky and invaded Cuba. It was a trifle bewildering. Companies of those same men in blue and brown were being rapidly formed and marched off across a little open space—near a pool—near some palm trees—near a house—into the hills. At one side, a mulatto in dirty linen and an old straw hat was hospitably using a machete to cut open some green cocoanuts for a group of idle invaders. At the other side, up a bank, a blockhouse was burning furiously; while near it some railway sheds were smouldering, with a little Roger's engine standing amid the ruins, grey, almost white, with ashes until it resembled a ghost. Little Nell dodged the encrimsoned blockhouse, and proceeded where he saw a little village street lined with flimsy wooden cottages. Some ragged Cuban cavalrymen were tranquilly tending their horses in a shed which had not yet grown cold of the Spanish occupation. Three American soldiers were trying to explain to a Cuban that they wished to buy drinks. A native rode by, clubbing his pony, as always. The sky was blue; the sea talked with a gravelly accent at the feet of some rocks; upon its bosom the ships sat quiet as gulls. There was no mention, directly, of invasion—invasion for war—save in the roar of the flames at the blockhouse; but none even heeded this conflagration, excepting to note that it threw out a great heat. It was warm, very warm. It was really hard for Little Nell to keep from thinking of his own affairs: his debts, other misfortunes, loves, prospects of happiness. Nobody was in a flurry; the Cubans were not tearfully grateful; the American troops were visibly glad of being released from those ill transports, and the men often asked, with interest, "Where's the Spaniards?" And yet it must have been a great moment! It was a *great* moment!

It seemed made to prove that the emphatic time of history is not the emphatic time of the common man, who throughout the change of nations feels an itch on his shin, a pain in his head, hunger, thirst, a lack of sleep; the influence of his memory of past firesides, glasses of beer, girls, theatres, ideals, religions, parents, faces, hurts, joy.

Little Nell was hailed from a comfortable veranda, and, looking up, saw Walkley of the *Eclipse*, stretched in a yellow and green hammock, smoking his pipe with an air of having always lived in that house, in that village. "Oh, dear little Nell, how glad I am to see your angel face again! There! don't try to hide it; I can see it. Did you bring a corkscrew too? You're superseded as master of the slaves. Did you know it? And by Rogers, too! Rogers is a Sadducee, a cadaver and a pelican, appointed to the post of chief correspondent, no doubt, because of his rare gift of incapacity. Never mind."

"Where is he now?" asked Little Nell, taking seat on the steps.

"He is down interfering with the landing of the troops," answered Walkley, swinging a leg. "I hope you have the *Johnson* well stocked with food as well as with cigars, cigarettes and tobaccos, ales, wines and liquors. We shall need them. There is already famine in the house of Walkley. I have discovered that the system of transportation for our gallant soldiery does not strike in me the admiration which I have often felt when viewing the management of an ordinary bun-shop. A hunger, stifling, jammed together amid odours, and everybody irritable—ye gods, how irritable! And so I— Look! look!"

The *Jefferson G. Johnson*, well known to them at an incredible distance, could be seen striding the broad sea, the smoke belching from her funnel, headed for Jamaica. "The Army Lands in Cuba!" shrieked Walkley. "Shafter's Army Lands near Santiago! Special type! Half the front page! Oh, the Sadducee! The cadaver! The pelican!"

Little Nell was dumb with astonishment and fear. Walkley, however, was at least not dumb. "That's the pelican! That's Mr. Rogers making his first impression upon the situation. He has engraved himself upon us. We are tattooed with him. There will be a fight tomorrow, sure, and we will cover it even as you found Cervera's fleet. No food, no horses, no money. I am transport lame; you are sea-weak. We will never see our salaries again. Whereby Rogers is a fool."

"Anybody else here?" asked Little Nell wearily.

"Only young Point." Point was an artist on the *Eclipse*. "But he has nothing. Pity there wasn't an almshouse in this God-forsaken country. Here comes Point now." A sad-faced man came along carrying much luggage. "Hello, Point! lithographer *and* genius, have you food? Food. Well, then, you had better return yourself to Tampa by wire. You are no good here. Only one more little mouth to feed."

Point seated himself near Little Nell. "I haven't had anything to eat since day-break," he said gloomily, "and I don't care much, for I am simply dog-tired."

"Don' tell *me* you are dog-tired, my talented friend," cried Walkley from his hammock. "Think of me. And now what's to be done?"

They stared for a time disconsolately at where, over the rim of the sea, trailed black smoke from the *Johnson*. From the landing-place below and to the right came the howls of a man who was superintending the disembarkation of some mules. The burning blockhouse still rendered its hollow roar. Suddenly the men-crowded landing set up its cheer, and the steamers all whistled long and raucously. Tiny black figures were raising an American flag over a blockhouse on the top of a great hill.

"That's mighty fine Sunday stuff," said Little Nell. "Well, I'll go and get the order in which the regiments landed, and who was first ashore, and all that. Then I'll go and try to find General Lawton's headquarters. His division has got the advance, I think."

"And, lo! I will write a burning description of the raising of the flag," said Walkley. "While the brilliant Point buskies for food—and makes damn sure he gets it," he added fiercely.

Little Nell thereupon wandered over the face of the earth, threading out the story of the landing of the regiments. He only found about fifty men who had been the first American soldier to set foot on Cuba, and of these he took the most probable. The army was going forward in detail, as soon as the pieces were landed. There was a house something like a crude country tavern—the soldiers in it were looking over their rifles and talking. There was a well of water quite hot—more palm trees—an inscrutable background.

When he arrived again at Walkley's mansion he found the verandah crowded with correspondents in khaki, duck, dungaree and flannel. They wore riding-breeches, but that was mainly forethought. They could see now that fate intended them to walk. Some were writing copy, while Walkley discoursed from his hammock. Rhodes—doomed to be shot in action some days later—was trying to borrow a canteen from men who had one, and from men who had none. Young Point, wan, utterly worn out, was asleep on the floor. Walkley pointed to him. "That is how he appears after his foraging journey, during which he ran all Cuba through a sieve. Oh, yes; a can of corn and a half-bottle of lime juice."

"Say, does anybody know, the name of the commander of the 26th Infantry?"

"Who commands the first brigade of Kent's Division?"

"What was the name of the chap that raised the flag?"

"What time is it?"

And a woeful man was wandering here and there with a cold pipe, saying plaintively, "Who's got a match? Anybody here got a match?"

Little Nell's left boot hurt him at the heel, and so he removed it, taking great care and whistling through his teeth. The heated dust was upon them all, making everybody feel that bathing was unknown and shattering their tempers. Young Point developed a snore which brought grim sarcasm from all quarters. Always below, hummed the traffic of the landing-place.

When night came Little Nell thought best not to go to bed until late, because he recognised the mackintosh as but a feeble comfort. The evening was a glory. A breeze came from the sea, fanning spurts of flame out of the ashes and charred remains of the sheds, while overhead lay a splendid summer-night sky, aflash with great tranquil stars. In the streets of the village were two or three fires, frequently and suddenly reddening with their glare the figures of low-voiced men who moved here and there. The lights of the transports blinked on the murmuring plain in front of the village; and far to the westward Little Nell could sometimes note a subtle indication of a playing search-light, which alone marked the presence of the invisible battleships, half-mooned about the entrance of Santiago Harbour, waiting—waiting—waiting.

When Little Nell returned to the veranda he stumbled along a man-strewn place, until he came to the spot where he left his mackintosh; but he found it gone. His curses mingled then with those of the men upon whose bodies he had trodden. Two English correspondents, lying awake to smoke a last pipe, reared and looked at him lazily. "What's wrong, old chap?" murmured one. "Eh? Lost it, eh? Well, look here; come here and take a bit of my blanket. It's a jolly big one. Oh, no trouble at all, man. There you are. Got enough? Comfy? Good-night."

A sleepy voice arose in the darkness. "If this hammock breaks, I shall hit at least ten of those Indians down there. Never mind. This is war."

The men slept. Once the sound of three or four shots rang across the windy night, and one head uprose swiftly from the verandah, two eyes looked dazedly at nothing, and the head as swiftly sank. Again a sleepy voice was heard. "Usual thing! Nervous sentries!" The men slept. Before dawn a pulseless, penetrating chill came into the air, and the correspondents awakened, shivering, into a blue world. Some of the fires still smouldered. Walkley and Little Nell kicked vigorously into Point's framework. "Come on, brilliance! Wake up, talent! Don't be sodgering. It's too cold to sleep, but it's not too cold to hustle." Point sat up dolefully. Upon his face was a childish expression. "Where are we going to get breakfast?" he asked, sulking.

"There's no breakfast for you, you hound! Get up and hustle." Accordingly they hustled. With exceeding difficulty they learned that nothing emotional had happened during the night, save the killing of two Cubans who were so secure in ignorance that they could not understand the challenge of two American sentries. Then Walkley ran a gamut of commanding officers, and Little Nell pumped privates for their impressions of Cuba. When his indignation at the absence of breakfast allowed him, Point made sketches. At the full break of day the *Adolphus*, and *Eclipse* despatch boat, sent a boat ashore with Tailor and Shackles in it, and Walkley departed tearlessly for Jamaica, soon after he had bestowed upon his friends much tinned goods and blankets.

"Well, we've got our stuff off," said Little Nell. "Now Point and I must breakfast."

Shackles, for some reason, carried a great hunting-knife, and with it Little Nell opened a tin of beans.

"Fall to," he said amiably to Point.

There were some hard biscuits. Afterwards they—the four of them—marched off on the route of the troops. They were well loaded with luggage, particularly young Point, who had somehow made a great gathering of unnecessary things. Hills covered with verdure soon enclosed them. They heard that the army had advanced some nine miles with no fighting. Evidences of the rapid advance were here and there—coats, gauntlets, blanket rolls on the ground. Mule-trains came herding back along the narrow trail to the sound of a little tinkling bell. Cubans were appropriating the coats and blanket-rolls.

The four correspondents hurried onward. The surety of impending battle weighed upon them always, but there was a score of minor things more intimate. Little Nell's left heel had chafed until it must have been quite raw, and every moment he wished to take seat by the roadside and console himself from pain. Shackles and Point disliked each other extremely, and often they foolishly quarrelled over something, or nothing. The blanket-rolls and packages for the hand oppressed everybody. It was like being burned out of a boarding-house, and having to carry one's trunk eight miles to the nearest neighbour. Moreover, Point, since he had stupidly overloaded, with great wisdom placed various cameras and other trifles in the hands of his three less-burdened and more sensible friends. This made them fume and gnash, but in complete silence, since he was hideously youthful and innocent and unaware. They all wished to rebel, but none of them saw their way clear, because—they did not understand. But somehow it seemed a barbarous project—no one wanted to say anything—cursed him privately for a little ass, but—said nothing. For instance, Little Nell wished to remark, "Point, you are not a thoroughbred in a half of a way. You are an inconsiderate, thoughtless little swine." But, in truth, he said, "Point, when you started out you looked like a Christmas-tree. If we keep on robbing you of your bundles there soon won't be anything left for the children." Point asked dubiously, "What do you mean?" Little Nell merely laughed with deceptive good-nature.

They were always very thirsty. There was always a howl for the half-bottle of lime juice. Five or six drops from it were simply heavenly in the warm water from the canteens. Point seemed to try to keep the lime juice in his possession, in order that he might get more benefit of it. Before the war was ended the others found themselves declaring vehemently that they loathed Point, and yet when men asked them the reason they grew quite inarticulate. The reasons seemed then so small, so childish, as the reasons of a lot of women. And yet at the time his offences loomed enormous.

The surety of impending battle still weighed upon them. Then it came that Shackles turned seriously ill. Suddenly he dropped his own and much of Point's traps upon the trail, wriggled out of his blanket-roll, flung it away, and took seat heavily at the roadside. They saw with surprise that his face was pale as death, and yet streaming with sweat.

"Boys," he said in his ordinary voice, "I'm clean played out. I can't go another step. You fellows go on, and leave me to come as soon as I am able."

"Oh, no, that wouldn't do at all," said Little Nell and Tailor together.

Point moved over to a soft place, and dropped amid whatever traps he was himself carrying.

"Don't know whether it's ancestral or merely from the—sun—but I've got a stroke," said Shackles, and gently slumped over to a prostrate position before either Little Nell or Tailor could reach him.

Thereafter Shackles was parental; it was Little Nell and Tailor who were really suffering from a stroke, either ancestral or from the sun.

"Put my blanket-roll under my head, Nell, me son," he said gently. "There now! That is very nice. It is delicious. Why, I'm all right, only—only tired." He closed his eyes, and something like an easy slumber came over him. Once he opened his eyes. "Don't trouble about me," he remarked.

But the two fussed about him, nervous, worried, discussing this plan and that plan. It was Point who first made a business-like statement. Seated carelessly and indifferently upon his soft place, he finally blurted out:

"Say! Look here! Some of us have got to go on. We can't all stay here. Some of us have got to go on."

It was quite true; the *Eclipse* could take no account of strokes. In the end Point and Tailor went on, leaving Little Nell to bring on Shackles as soon as possible. The latter two spent many hours in the grass by the roadside. They made numerous abrupt acquaintances with passing staff officers, privates, muleteers, many stopping to inquire the wherefore of the death-faced figure on the ground. Favours were done often and often, by peer and peasant—small things, of no consequence, and yet warming.

It was dark when Shackles and Little Nell had come slowly to where they could hear the murmur of the army's bivouac.

"Shack," gasped Little Nell to the man leaning forlornly upon him, "I guess we'd better bunk down here where we stand."

"All right, old boy. Anything you say," replied Shackles, in the bass and hollow voice which arrives with such condition.

They crawled into some bushes, and distributed their belongings upon the ground. Little Nell spread out the blankets, and generally played housemaid. Then they lay down, supperless, being too weary to eat. The men slept.

At dawn Little Nell awakened and looked wildly for Shackles, whose empty blanket was pressed flat like a wet newspaper on the ground. But at nearly the same moment Shackles appeared, elate.

"Come on," he cried; "I've rustled an invitation for breakfast."

Little Nell came on with celerity.

"Where? Who?" he said.

"Oh! some officers," replied Shackles airily. If he had been ill the previous day, he showed it now only in some curious kind of deference he paid to Little Nell.

Shackles conducted his comrade, and soon they arrived at where a captain and his one subaltern arose courteously from where they were squatting near a fire of little sticks. They wore the wide white trouser-stripes of infantry officers, and upon the shoulders of their blue campaign shirts were the little marks of their rank; but otherwise there was little beyond their manners to render them different from the men who were busy with breakfast near them. The captain was old, grizzled—a common type of captain in the tiny American army—overjoyed at the active service, confident of his business, and yet breathing out in some way a note of pathos. The war was come too late. Age was grappling him, and honours were only for his widow and his children—merely a better life insurance policy. He had spent his life policing Indians with much labour, cold and heat, but with no glory for him nor his fellows. All he now could do was to die at the head of his men. If he had youthfully dreamed of a general's stars, they were now impossible to him, and he knew it. He was too old to leap so far; his sole honour was a new invitation to face death. And yet, with his ambitions lying half-strangled, he was going to take his men into any sort of holocaust, because his traditions were of gentlemen and soldiers, and because—he loved it for itself—the thing itself—the whirl, the unknown. If he had been degraded at that moment to be a pot-wrestler, no power could have starved him from going through the campaign as a spectator. Why, the army! It was in each drop of his blood.

The lieutenant was very young. Perhaps he had been hurried out of West Point at the last moment, upon a shortage of officers appearing. To him, all was opportunity. He was, in fact, in great luck. Instead of going off in 1898 to grill for an indefinite period on some God-forgotten heap of red-hot sand in New Mexico, he was here in Cuba, on real business, with his regiment. When the big engagement came he was sure to emerge from it either horizontally or at the head of a company, and what more could a boy ask? He was a very modest lad, and talked nothing of his frame of mind, but an expression of blissful contentment was ever upon his face. He really accounted himself the most fortunate boy of his time; and he felt almost certain that he would do well. It was necessary to do well. He would do well.

And yet in many ways these two were alike; the grizzled captain with his gently mournful countenance—"Too late"—and the elate young second lieutenant, his commission hardly dry. Here again it was the influence of the army. After all they were both children of the army.

It is possible to spring into the future here and chronicle what happened later. The captain, after thirty-five years of waiting for his chance, took his Mauser bullet through the brain at the foot of San Juan Hill in the very beginning of the battle, and the boy arrived on the crest panting, sweating, but unscratched, and not sure whether he commanded one company or a whole battalion. Thus fate dealt to the hosts of Shackles and Little Nell.

The breakfast was of canned tomatoes stewed with hard bread, more hard bread, and coffee. It was very good fare, almost royal. Shackles and Little Nell were absurdly grateful as they felt the hot bitter coffee tingle in them. But they departed joyfully before the sun was fairly up, and passed into Siboney. They never saw the captain again.

The beach at Siboney was furious with traffic, even as had been the beach at Daqueri. Launches shouted, jack-tars prodded with their boathooks, and load of men followed load of men. Straight, parade-like, on the shore stood a trumpeter playing familiar calls to the troop-horses who swam towards him eagerly through the salt seas. Crowding closely into the cove were transports of all sizes and ages. To the left and to the right of the little landing-beach green hills shot upward like the wings in a theatre. They were scarred here and there with blockhouses and rifle-pits. Up one hill a regiment was crawling, seemingly inch by inch. Shackles and Little Nell walked among palms and scrubby bushes, near pools, over spaces of sand holding little monuments of biscuit-boxes, ammunition-boxes, and supplies of all kinds. Some regiment was just collecting itself from the ships, and the men made great patches of blue on the brown sand.

Shackles asked a question of a man accidentally: "Where's that regiment going to?" He pointed to the force that was crawling up the hill. The man grinned, and said, "They're going to look for a fight!"

"Looking for a fight!" said Shackles and Little Nell together. They stared into each other's eyes. Then they set off for the foot of the hill. The hill was long and toilsome. Below them spread wider and wider a vista of ships quiet on a grey sea; a busy, black disembarkation-place; tall, still, green hills; a village of well separated cottages; palms; a bit of road; soldiers marching. They passed vacant Spanish trenches; little twelve-foot blockhouses. Soon they were on a fine upland near the sea. The path, under ordinary conditions, must have been a beautiful wooded way. It wound in the shade of thickets of fine trees, then through rank growths of bushes with revealed and fantastic roots, then through a grassy space which had all the beauty of a neglected orchard. But always from under their feet scuttled noisy land-crabs, demons to the nerves, which in some way possessed a semblance of moon-like faces upon their blue or red bodies, and these faces were turned with expressions of deepest horror upon Shackles and Little Nell as they sped to overtake the pugnacious regiment. The route was paved with coats, hats, tent and blanket rolls, ration-tins, haversacks—everything but ammunition belts, rifles and canteens.

They heard a dull noise of voices in front of them—men talking too loud for the etiquette of the forest—and presently they came upon two or three soldiers lying by the roadside, flame-faced, utterly spent from the hurried march in the heat. One man came limping back along the path. He looked to them anxiously for sympathy and comprehension. "Hurt m' knee. I swear I couldn't keep up with th' boys. I had to leave 'm. Wasn't that tough luck?" His collar rolled away from a red, muscular neck, and his bare forearms were better than stanchions. Yet he was almost baby-ishly tearful in his attempt to make the two correspondents feel that he had not turned back because he was afraid. They gave him scant courtesy, tinctured with one drop of sympathetic yet cynical understanding. Soon they overtook the hospital squad; men addressing chaste language to some pack-mules; a talkative sergeant; two amiable, cool-eyed young surgeons. Soon they were amid the rear troops of the dismounted volunteer cavalry regiment which was moving to attack. The men strode easily along, arguing one to another on ulterior matters. If they were going into battle, they either did not know it or they concealed it well. They were more like men going into a bar at one o'clock in the morning. Their laughter rang through the Cuban woods. And in the meantime, soft, mellow, sweet, sang the voice of the Cuban wood-dove, the Spanish guerilla calling to his mate—forest music; on the flanks, deep back on both flanks, the adorable wood-dove, singing only of love. Some of the advancing Americans said it was beautiful. It *was* beautiful. The Span-ish guerilla calling to his mate. What could be more beautiful?

Shackles and Little Nell rushed precariously through waist-high bushes until they reached the centre of the single-filed regiment. The firing then broke out in front. All the woods set up a hot sputtering; the bullets sped along the path and across it from both sides. The thickets presented nothing but dense masses of light green foliage, out of which these swift steel things were born supernaturally.

It was a volunteer regiment going into its first action, against an enemy of un-known force, in a country where the vegetation was thicker than fur on a cat. There might have been a dreadful mess; but in military matters the only way to deal with a situation of this kind is to take it frankly by the throat and squeeze it to death. Shackles and Little Nell felt the thrill of the orders. "Come ahead, men! Keep right ahead, men! Come on!" The volunteer cavalry regiment, with all the willingness in the world, went ahead into the angle of V-shaped Spanish formation.

It seemed that every leaf had turned into a soda-bottle and was popping its cork. Some of the explosions seemed to be against the men's very faces, others against the backs of their necks. "Now, men! Keep goin' ahead. Keep on goin'." The forward troops were already engaged. They, at least, had something at which to shoot. "Now, captain, if you're ready." "Stop that swearing there." "Got a match?" "Steady, now, men."

A gate appeared in a barbed-wire fence. Within were billowy fields of long grass, dotted with palms and luxuriant mango trees. It was Elysian—a place for lovers, fair as Eden in its radiance of sun, under its blue sky. One might have expected to see white-robed figures walking slowly in the shadows. A dead man, with a bloody face, lay twisted in a curious contortion at the waist. Someone was shot in the leg, his pins knocked cleanly from under him.

"Keep goin', men." The air roared, and the ground fled reelingly under their feet. Light, shadow, trees, grass. Bullets spat from every side. Once they were in a thicket, and the men, blanched and bewildered, turned one way, and then another, not knowing which way to turn. "Keep goin', men." Soon they were in the sunlight again. They could see the long scant line, which was being drained man by man—one might say drop by drop. The musketry rolled forth in great full measure from the magazine carbines. "Keep goin', men." "Christ, I'm shot!" "They're flankin' us, sir." "We're bein' fired into by our own crowd, sir." "Keep goin', men." A low ridge before them was a bottling establishment blowing up in detail. From the right—it seemed at that time to be the far right—they could hear steady, crashing volleys—the United States regulars in action.

Then suddenly—to use a phrase of the street—the whole bottom of the thing fell out. It was suddenly and mysteriously ended. The Spaniards had run away, and some of the regulars were chasing them. It was a victory.

When the wounded men dropped in the tall grass they quite disappeared, as if they had sunk in water. Little Nell and Shackles were walking along through the fields, disputing.

"Well, damn it, man!" cried Shackles, "we *must* get a list of the killed and wounded."

"That is not nearly so important," quoth little Nell, academically, "as to get the first account to New York of the first action of the army in Cuba."

They came upon Tailor, lying with a bared torso and a small red hole through his left lung. He was calm, but evidently out of temper. "Good God, Tailor!" they cried, dropping to their knees like two pagans; "are you hurt, old boy?"

"Hurt?" he said gently. "No, 'tis not so deep as a well nor so wide as a church-door, but 'tis enough, d'you see? You understand, do you? Idiots!"

Then he became very official. "Shackles, feel and see what's under my leg. It's a small stone, or a burr, or something. Don't be clumsy now! Be careful! Be careful!" Then he said, angrily, "Oh, you didn't find it at all. Damn it!"

In reality there was nothing there, and so Shackles could not have removed it. "Sorry, old boy," he said, meekly.

"Well, you may observe that I can't stay here more than a year," said Tailor, with some oratory, "and the hospital people have their own work in hand. It behoves you, Nell, to fly to Siboney, arrest a despatch boat, get a cot and some other things, and some minions to carry me. If I get once down to the base I'm all right, but if I stay here I'm dead. Meantime Shackles can stay here and try to look as if he liked it."

There was no disobeying the man. Lying there with a little red hole in his left lung, he dominated them through his helplessness, and through their fear that if they angered him he would move and—bleed.

"Well?" said Little Nell.

"Yes," said Shackles, nodding.

Little Nell departed.

"That blanket you lent me," Tailor called after him, "is back there somewhere with Point."

Little Nell noted that many of the men who were wandering among the wounded seemed so spent with the toil and excitement of their first action that they could hardly drag one leg after the other. He found himself suddenly in the same condition, His face, his neck, even his mouth, felt dry as sun-baked bricks, and his legs were foreign to him. But he swung desperately into his five-mile task. On the way he passed many things: bleeding men carried by comrades; others making their way grimly, with encrimsoned arms; then the little settlement of the hospital squad; men on the ground everywhere, many in the path; one young captain dying, with great gasps, his body pale blue, and glistening, like the inside of a rabbit's skin. But the voice of the Cuban wood-dove, soft, mellow, sweet, singing only of love, was no longer heard from the wealth of foliage.

Presently the hurrying correspondent met another regiment coming to assist—a line of a thousand men in single file through the jungle. "Well, how is it going, old man?" "How is it coming on?" "Are we doin' 'em?" Then, after an interval, came other regiments, moving out. He had to take to the bush to let these long lines pass him, and he was delayed, and had to flounder amid brambles. But at last, like a successful pilgrim, he arrived at the brow of the great hill overlooking Siboney. His practised eye scanned the fine broad brow of the sea with its clustering ships, but he saw thereon no *Eclipse*despatch boats. He zigzagged heavily down the hill, and arrived finally amid the dust and outcries of the base. He seemed to ask a thousand men if they had seen an *Eclipse* boat on the water, or an*Eclipse* correspondent on the shore. They all answered, "No."

He was like a poverty-stricken and unknown suppliant at a foreign Court. Even his plea got only ill-hearings. He had expected the news of the serious wounding of Tailor to appal the other correspondents, but they took it quite calmly. It was as if their sense of an impending great battle between two large armies had quite got them out of focus for these minor tragedies. Tailor was hurt—yes? They looked at Little Nell, dazed. How curious that Tailor should be almost the first—how*very* curious—yes. But, as far as arousing them to any enthusiasm of active pity, it seemed impossible. He was lying up there in the grass, was he? Too bad, too bad, too bad!

Little Nell went alone and lay down in the sand with his back against a rock. Tailor was prostrate up there in the grass. Never mind. Nothing was to be done. The whole situation was too colossal. Then into his zone came Walkley the invincible.

"Walkley!" yelled Little Nell. Walkley came quickly, and Little Nell lay weakly against his rock and talked. In thirty seconds Walkley understood everything, had hurled a drink of whisky into Little Nell, had admonished him to lie quiet, and had gone to organise and manipulate. When he returned he was a trifle dubious and backward. Behind him was a singular squad of volunteers from the *Adolphus*, carrying among them a wire-woven bed.

"Look here, Nell!" said Walkley, in bashful accents; "I've collected a battalion here which is willing to go bring Tailor; but—they say—you—can't you show them where he is?"

"Yes," said Little Nell, arising.

* * * *

When the party arrived at Siboney, and deposited Tailor in the best place, Walkley had found a house and stocked it with canned soups. Therein Shackles and Little Nell revelled for a time, and then rolled on the floor in their blankets. Little Nell tossed a great deal. "Oh, I'm so tired. Good God, I'm tired. I'm—tired."

In the morning a voice aroused them. It was a swollen, important, circus voice saying, "Where is Mr. Nell? I wish to see him immediately."

"Here I am, Rogers," cried Little Nell.

"Oh, Nell," said Rogers, "here's a despatch to me which I thought you had better read."

Little Nell took the despatch. It was: "Tell Nell can't understand his inaction; tell him come home first steamer from Port Antonio, Jamaica."

# THE REVENGE OF THE ADOLPHUS

## I

"Stand by."

Shackles had come down from the bridge of the *Adolphus* and flung this command at three fellow-correspondents who in the galley were busy with pencils trying to write something exciting and interesting from four days quiet cruising. They looked up casually. "What for?" They did not intend to arouse for nothing. Ever since Shackles had heard the men of the navy directing each other to stand by for this thing and that thing, he had used the two words as his pet phrase and was continually telling his friends to stand by. Sometimes its portentous and emphatic reiteration became highly exasperating and men were apt to retort sharply. "Well, I *am* standing by, ain't I?" On this occasion they detected that he was serious. "Well, what for?" they repeated. In his answer Shackles was reproachful as well as impressive. "Stand by? Stand by for a Spanish gunboat. A Spanish gunboat in chase! Stand by for *two* Spanish gunboats—*both* of them in chase!"

The others looked at him for a brief space and were almost certain that they saw truth written upon his countenance. Whereupon they tumbled out of the galley and galloped up to the bridge. The cook with a mere inkling of tragedy was now out on deck bawling, "What's the matter? What's the matter? What's the matter?" Aft, the grimy head of a stoker was thrust suddenly up through the deck, so to speak. The eyes flashed in a quick look astern and then the head vanished. The correspondents were scrambling on the bridge. "Where's my glasses, damn it? Here—let me take a look. Are they Spaniards, Captain? Are you sure?"

The skipper of the *Adolphus* was at the wheel. The pilot-house was so arranged that he could not see astern without hanging forth from one of the side windows, but apparently he had made early investigation. He did not reply at once. At sea, he never replied at once to questions. At the very first, Shackles had discovered the merits of this deliberate manner and had taken delight in it. He invariably detailed his talk with the captain to the other correspondents. "Look here. I've just been to see the skipper. I said 'I would like to put into Cape Haytien.' Then he took a little think. Finally he said: 'All right.' Then I said: 'I suppose we'll need to take on more coal there?' He took another little think. I said: 'Ever ran into that port before?' He took another little think. Finally he said: 'Yes.' I said 'Have a cigar?' He took another little think. See? There's where I fooled 'im—"

While the correspondents spun the hurried questions at him, the captain of the *Adolphus* stood with his brown hands on the wheel and his cold glance aligned straight over the bow of his ship.

"Are they Spanish gunboats, Captain? Are they, Captain?"

After a profound pause, he said: "Yes." The four correspondents hastily and in perfect time presented their backs to him and fastened their gaze on the pursuing foe. They saw a dull grey curve of sea going to the feet of the high green and blue coast-line of north-eastern Cuba, and on this sea were two miniature ships with clouds of iron-coloured smoke pouring from their funnels.

One of the correspondents strolled elaborately to the pilot-house. "Aw—Captain," he drawled, "do you think they can catch us?"

The captain's glance was still aligned over the bow of his ship. Ultimately he answered: "I don't know."

From the top of the little *Adolphus'* stack, thick dark smoke swept level for a few yards and then went rolling to leaward in great hot obscuring clouds. From time to time the grimy head was thrust through the deck, the eyes took the quick look astern and then the head vanished. The cook was trying to get somebody to listen to him. "Well, you know, damn it all, it won't be no fun to be ketched by them Spaniards. Be-Gawd, it won't. Look here, what do you think they'll do to us, hey? Say, I don't like this, you know. I'm damned if I do." The sea, cut by the hurried bow of the *Adolphus*, flung its waters astern in the formation of a wide angle and the lines of the angle ruffled and hissed as they fled, while the thumping screw tormented the water at the stern. The frame of the steamer underwent regular convulsions as in the strenuous sobbing of a child.

The mate was standing near the pilot-house. Without looking at him, the captain spoke his name. "Ed!"

"Yes, sir," cried the mate with alacrity.

The captain reflected for a moment. Then he said: "Are they gainin' on us?"

The mate took another anxious survey of the race. "No—o—yes, I think they are—a little."

After a pause the captain said: "Tell the chief to shake her up more."

The mate, glad of an occupation in these tense minutes, flew down to the engine-room door. "Skipper says shake 'er up more!" he bawled. The head of the chief engineer appeared, a grizzly head now wet with oil and sweat. "What?" he shouted angrily. It was as if he had been propelling the ship with his own arms. Now he was told that his best was not good enough. "What? shake 'er up more? Why she can't carry another pound, I tell you! Not another ounce! We—" Suddenly he ran forward and climbed to the bridge. "Captain," he cried in the loud harsh voice of one who lived usually amid the thunder of machinery, "she can't do it, sir! Be-Gawd, she can't! She's turning over now faster than she ever did in her life and we'll all blow to hell—"

The low-toned, impassive voice of the captain suddenly checked the chief's clamour. "I'll blow her up," he said, "but I won't git ketched if I kin help it." Even then the listening correspondents found a second in which to marvel that the captain had actually explained his point of view to another human being.

The engineer stood blank. Then suddenly he cried: "All right, sir!" He threw a hurried look of despair at the correspondents, the deck of the *Adolphus*, the pursuing enemy, Cuba, the sky and the sea; he vanished in the direction of his post.

A correspondent was suddenly regifted with the power of prolonged speech. "Well, you see, the game is up, damn it. See? We can't get out of it. The skipper will blow up the whole bunch before he'll let his ship be taken, and the Spaniards are gaining. Well, that's what comes from going to war in an eight-knot tub." He bitterly accused himself, the others, and the dark, sightless, indifferent world.

This certainty of coming evil affected each one differently. One was made garrulous; one kept absent-mindedly snapping his fingers and gazing at the sea; another stepped nervously to and fro, looking everywhere as if for employment for his mind. As for Shackles he was silent and smiling, but it was a new smile that caused the lines about his mouth to betray quivering weakness. And each man looked at the others to discover their degree of fear and did his best to conceal his own, holding his crackling nerves with all his strength.

As the *Adolphus* rushed on, the sun suddenly emerged from behind grey clouds and its rays dealt titanic blows so that in a few minutes the sea was a glowing blue plain with the golden shine dancing at the tips of the waves. The coast of Cuba glowed with light. The pursuers displayed detail after detail in the new atmosphere. The voice of the cook was heard in high vexation. "Am I to git dinner as usual? How do I know? Nobody tells me what to do? Am I to git dinner as usual?"

The mate answered ferociously. "Of course you are! What do you s'pose? Ain't you the cook, you damn fool?"

The cook retorted in a mutinous scream. "Well, how would I know? If this ship is goin' to blow up—"

## II

The captain called from the pilot-house. "Mr. Shackles! Oh, Mr. Shackles!" The correspondent moved hastily to a window. "What is it, Captain?" The skipper of the *Adolphus* raised a battered finger and pointed over the bows. "See 'er?" he asked, laconic but quietly jubilant. Another steamer was smoking at full speed over the sun-lit seas. A great billow of pure white was on her bows. "Great Scott!" cried Shackles. "Another Spaniard?"

"No," said the captain, "that there is a United States cruiser!"

"What?" Shackles was dumfounded into muscular paralysis. "No! Are you *sure*?"

The captain nodded. "Sure, take the glass. See her ensign? Two funnels, two masts with fighting tops. She ought to be the *Chancellorville*."

Shackles choked. "Well, I'm blowed!"

"Ed!" said the captain.

"Yessir!"

"Tell the chief there is no hurry."

Shackles suddenly bethought him of his companions. He dashed to them and was full of quick scorn of their gloomy faces. "Hi, brace up there! Are you blind? Can't you see her?"

"See what?"

"Why, the *Chancellorville*, you blind mice!" roared Shackles. "See 'er? See 'er? See 'er?"

The others sprang, saw, and collapsed. Shackles was a madman for the purpose of distributing the news. "Cook!" he shrieked. "Don't you see 'er, cook? Good Gawd, man, don't you see 'er?" He ran to the lower deck and howled his information everywhere. Suddenly the whole ship smiled. Men clapped each other on the shoulder and joyously shouted. The captain thrust his head from the pilot-house to look back at the Spanish ships. Then he looked at the American cruiser. "Now, we'll see," he said grimly and vindictively to the mate. "Guess somebody else will do some running," the mate chuckled.

The two gunboats were still headed hard for the *Adolphus* and she kept on her way. The American cruiser was coming swiftly. "It's the *Chancellorville*!" cried Shackles. "I know her! We'll see a fight at sea, my boys! A fight at sea!" The enthusiastic correspondents pranced in Indian revels.

The *Chancellorville*—2000 tons—18.6 knots—10 five-inch guns—came on tempestuously, sheering the water high with her sharp bow. From her funnels the smoke raced away in driven sheets. She loomed with extraordinary rapidity like a ship bulging and growing out of the sea. She swept by the *Adolphus* so close that one could have thrown a walnut on board. She was a glistening grey apparition with a blood-red water-line, with brown gun-muzzles and white-clothed motionless jack-tars; and in her rush she was silent, deadly silent. Probably there entered the mind of every man on board the*Adolphus* a feeling of almost idolatry for this living thing, stern but, to their thought, incomparably beautiful. They would have cheered but that each man seemed to feel that a cheer would be too puny a tribute.

It was at first as if she did not see the *Adolphus*. She was going to pass without heeding this little vagabond of the high-seas. But suddenly a megaphone gaped over the rail of her bridge and a voice was heard measuredly, calmly intoning. "Hello— there! Keep—well—to—the—north'ard—and—out of my—way—and I'll—go— in—and—see—what—those—people—want—" Then nothing was heard but the swirl of water. In a moment the *Adolphus* was looking at a high grey stern. On the quarter-deck, sailors were poised about the breach of the after-pivot-gun.

The correspondents were revelling. "Captain," yelled Shackles, "we can't miss this! We must see it!" But the skipper had already flung over the wheel. "Sure," he answered almost at once. "We can't miss it."

The cook was arrogantly, grossly triumphant. His voice rang along the deck. "There, now! How will the Spinachers like that? Now, it's our turn! We've been doin' the runnin' away but now we'll do the chasin'!" Apparently feeling some twinge of nerves from the former strain, he suddenly demanded: "Say, who's got any whisky? I'm near dead for a drink."

When the *Adolphus* came about, she laid her course for a position to the north-ward of a coming battle, but the situation suddenly became complicated. When the Spanish ships discovered the identity of the ship that was steaming toward them, they did not hesitate over their plan of action. With one accord they turned and ran for port. Laughter arose from the *Adolphus*. The captain broke his orders, and, instead of keeping to the northward, he headed in the wake of the impetuous*Chancellorville*. The correspondents crowded on the bow.

The Spaniards when their broadsides became visible were seen to be ships of no importance, mere little gunboats for work in the shallows back of the reefs, and it was certainly discreet to refuse encounter with the five-inch guns of the *Chancellorville*. But the joyful*Adolphus* took no account of this discretion. The pursuit of the Spaniards had been so ferocious that the quick change to heels-overhead flight filled that corner of the mind which is devoted to the spirit of revenge. It was this that moved Shackles to yell taunts futilely at the far-away ships. "Well, how do you like it, eh? How do you like it?" The*Adolphus* was drinking compensation for her previous agony.

The mountains of the shore now shadowed high into the sky and the square white houses of a town could be seen near a vague cleft which seemed to mark the entrance to a port. The gunboats were now near to it.

Suddenly white smoke streamed from the bow of the *Chancellorville*and developed swiftly into a great bulb which drifted in fragments down the wind. Presently the deep-throated boom of the gun came to the ears on board the *Adolphus*. The shot kicked up a high jet of water into the air astern of the last gunboat. The black smoke from the funnels of the cruiser made her look like a collier on fire, and in her desperation she tried many more long shots, but presently the*Adolphus*, murmuring disappointment, saw the *Chancellorville* sheer from the chase.

In time they came up with her and she was an indignant ship. Gloom and wrath was on the forecastle and wrath and gloom was on the quarter-deck. A sad voice from the bridge said: "Just missed 'em." Shackles gained permission to board the cruiser, and in the cabin, he talked to Lieutenant-Commander Surrey, tall, bald-headed and angry. "Shoals," said the captain of the *Chancellorville*. "I can't go any nearer and those gunboats could steam along a stone sidewalk if only it was wet." Then his bright eyes became brighter. "I tell you what! The *Chicken*, the *Holy Moses* and the *Mongolian* are on station off Nuevitas. If you will do me a favour—why, tomorrow I will give those people a game!"

### III

The *Chancellorville* lay all night watching off the port of the two gunboats and, soon after daylight, the lookout descried three smokes to the westward and they were later made out to be the *Chicken*, the *Holy Moses* and the *Adolphus*, the latter tagging hurriedly after the United States vessels.

The *Chicken* had been a harbour tug but she was now the U.S.S. *Chicken*, by your leave. She carried a six-pounder forward and a six-pounder aft and her main point was her conspicuous vulnerability. The *Holy Moses* had been the private yacht of a Philadelphia millionaire. She carried six six-pounders and her main point was the chaste beauty of the officer's quarters.

On the bridge of the *Chancellorville*, Lieutenant-Commander Surrey surveyed his squadron with considerable satisfaction. Presently he signalled to the lieutenant who commanded the *Holy Moses* and to the boatswain who commanded the *Chicken* to come aboard the flag-ship. This was all very well for the captain of the yacht, but it was not so easy for the captain of the tug-boat who had two heavy lifeboats swung fifteen feet above the water. He had been accustomed to talking with senior officers from his own pilot house through the intercession of the blessed megaphone. However he got a lifeboat overside and was pulled to the *Chancellorville* by three men—which cut his crew almost into halves.

In the cabin of the *Chancellorville*, Surrey disclosed to his two captains his desires concerning the Spanish gunboats and they were glad for being ordered down from the Nuevitas station where life was very dull. He also announced that there was a shore battery containing, he believed, four field guns—three-point-twos. His draught—he spoke of it as *his* draught—would enable him to go in close enough to engage the battery at moderate range, but he pointed out that the main parts of the attempt to destroy the Spanish gunboats must be left to the *Holy Moses* and the *Chicken*. His business, he thought, could only be to keep the air so singing about the ears of the battery that the men at the guns would be unable to take an interest in the dash of the smaller American craft into the bay.

The officers spoke in their turns. The captain of the *Chicken* announced that he saw no difficulties. The squadron would follow the senior officer in line ahead, the S. O. would engage the batteries as soon as possible, she would turn to starboard when the depth of water forced her to do so and the *Holy Moses* and the *Chicken* would run past her into the bay and fight the Spanish ships wherever they were to be found. The captain of the *Holy Moses* after some moments of dignified thought said that he had no suggestions to make that would better this plan.

Surrey pressed an electric bell; a marine orderly appeared; he was sent with a message. The message brought the navigating officer of the *Chancellorville* to the cabin and the four men nosed over a chart.

In the end Surrey declared that he had made up his mind and the juniors remained in expectant silence for three minutes while he stared at the bulkhead. Then he said that the plan of the *Chicken's* captain seemed to him correct in the main. He would make one change. It was that he should first steam in and engage the battery and the other vessels should remain in their present positions until he signalled them to run into the bay. If the squadron steamed ahead in line, the battery could, if it chose, divide its fire between the cruiser and the gunboats constituting the more important attack. He had no doubt, he said, that he could soon silence the battery by tumbling the earth-works on to the guns and driving away the men even if he did not succeed in hitting the pieces. Of course he had no doubt of being able to silence the battery in twenty minutes. Then he would signal for the *Holy Moses* and the *Chicken* to make their rush, and of course he would support them with his fire as much as conditions enabled him. He arose then indicating that the conference was at an end. In the few moments more that all four men remained in the cabin, the talk changed its character completely. It was now unofficial, and the sharp badinage concealed furtive affections, Academy friendships, the feelings of old-time ship-mates, hiding everything under a veil of jokes. "Well, good luck to you, old boy! Don't get that valuable packet of yours sunk under you. Think how it would weaken the navy. Would you mind buying me three pairs of pajamas in the town yonder? If your engines get disabled, tote her under your arm. You can do it. Good-bye, old man, don't forget to come out all right—"

When the captains of the *Holy Moses* and the *Chicken* emerged from the cabin, they strode the deck with a new step. They were proud men. The marine on duty above their boats looked at them curiously and with awe. He detected something which meant action, conflict.

The boats' crews saw it also. As they pulled their steady stroke, they studied fleetingly the face of the officer in the stern sheets. In both cases they perceived a glad man and yet a man filled with a profound consideration of the future.

IV

A bird-like whistle stirred the decks of the *Chancellorville*. It was followed by the hoarse bellowing of the boatswain's mate. As the cruiser turned her bow toward the shore, she happened to steam near the *Adolphus*. The usual calm voice hailed the despatch boat. "Keep—that—gauze under-shirt of yours—well—out of the—line of fire."

"Ay, ay, sir!"

The cruiser then moved slowly toward the shore, watched by every eye in the smaller American vessels. She was deliberate and steady, and this was reasonable even to the impatience of the other craft because the wooded shore was likely to suddenly develop new factors. Slowly she swung to starboard; smoke belched over her and the roar of a gun came along the water.

The battery was indicated by a long thin streak of yellow earth. The first shot went high, ploughing the chaparral on the hillside. The *Chancellorville* wore an air for a moment of being deep in meditation. She flung another shell, which landed squarely on the earth-work, making a great dun cloud. Before the smoke had settled, there was a crimson flash from the battery. To the watchers at sea, it was smaller than a needle. The shot made a geyser of crystal water, four hundred yards from the *Chancellorville*.

The cruiser, having made up her mind, suddenly went at the battery, hammer and tongs. She moved to and fro casually, but the thunder of her guns was gruff and angry. Sometimes she was quite hidden in her own smoke, but with exceeding regularity the earth of the battery spurted into the air. The Spanish shells, for the most part, went high and wide of the cruiser, jetting the water far away.

Once a Spanish gunner took a festive side-show chance at the waiting group of the three nondescripts. It went like a flash over the *Adolphus*, singing a wistful metallic note. Whereupon the *Adolphus* broke hurriedly for the open sea, and men on the *Holy Moses* and the *Chicken* laughed hoarsely and cruelly. The correspondents had been standing excitedly on top of the pilot-house, but at the passing of the shell, they promptly eliminated themselves by dropping with a thud to the deck below. The cook again was giving tongue. "Oh, say, this won't do! I'm damned if it will! We ain't no armoured cruiser, you know. If one of them shells hits us—well, we finish right there. 'Tain't like as if it was our *business*, foolin' 'round within the range of them guns. There's no sense in it. Them other fellows don't seem to mind it, but it's their *business*. If it's your *business*, you go ahead and do it, but if it ain't, you—look at that, would you!"

The *Chancellorville* had sent up a spread of flags, and the *Holy Moses* and the *Chicken* were steaming in.

V

They, on the *Chancellorville*, sometimes could see into the bay, and they perceived the enemy's gunboats moving out as if to give battle. Surrey feared that this impulse would not endure or that it was some mere pretence for the edification of the town's people and the garrison, so he hastily signalled the *Holy Moses* and the *Chicken* to go in. Thankful for small favours, they came on like charging bantams. The battery had ceased firing. As the two auxiliaries passed under the stern of the cruiser, the megaphone hailed them. "You—will—see—the—en—em—y—soon—as—you—round—the—point. A—fine—chance. Good—luck."

As a matter of fact, the Spanish gunboats had not been informed of the presence of the *Holy Moses* and the *Chicken* off the bar, and they were just blustering down the bay over the protective shoals to make it appear that they scorned the *Chancellorville*. But suddenly, from around the point, there burst into view a steam yacht, closely followed by a harbour tug. The gunboats took one swift look at this horrible sight and fled screaming.

Lieutenant Reigate, commanding the *Holy Moses*, had under his feet a craft that was capable of some speed, although before a solemn tribunal, one would have to admit that she conscientiously belied almost everything that the contractors had said of her, originally. Boatswain Pent, commanding the *Chicken*, was in possession of an utterly different kind. The *Holy Moses* was an antelope; the *Chicken* was a man who could carry a piano on his back. In this race Pent had the mortification of seeing his vessel outstripped badly.

The entrance of the two American craft had had a curious effect upon the shores of the bay. Apparently everyone had slept in the assurance that the *Chancellorville* could not cross the bar, and that the *Chancellorville* was the only hostile ship. Consequently, the appearance of the *Holy Moses* and the *Chicken*, created a curious and complete emotion. Reigate, on the bridge of the *Holy Moses*, laughed when he heard the bugles shrilling and saw through his glasses the wee figures of men running hither and thither on the shore. It was the panic of the china when the bull entered the shop. The whole bay was bright with sun. Every detail of the shore was plain. From a brown hut abeam of the *Holy Moses*, some little men ran out waving their arms and turning their tiny faces to look at the enemy. Directly ahead, some four miles, appeared the scattered white houses of a town with a wharf, and some schooners in front of it. The gunboats were making for the town. There was a stone fort on the hill overshadowing, but Reigate conjectured that there was no artillery in it.

There was a sense of something intimate and impudent in the minds of the Americans. It was like climbing over a wall and fighting a man in his own garden. It was not that they could be in any wise shaken in their resolve; it was simply that the overwhelmingly Spanish aspect of things made them feel like gruff intruders. Like many of the emotions of war-time, this emotion had nothing at all to do with war.

Reigate's only commissioned subordinate called up from the bow gun. "May I open fire, sir? I think I can fetch that last one."

"Yes." Immediately the six-pounder crashed, and in the air was the spinning-wire noise of the flying shot. It struck so close to the last gunboat that it appeared that the spray went aboard. The swift-handed men at the gun spoke of it. "Gave 'm a bath that time anyhow. First one they've ever had. Dry 'em off this time, Jim." The young ensign said: "Steady." And so the *Holy Moses* raced in, firing, until the whole town, fort, waterfront, and shipping were as plain as if they had been done on paper by a mechanical draftsman. The gunboats were trying to hide in the bosom of the town. One was frantically tying up to the wharf and the other was anchoring within a hundred yards of the shore. The Spanish infantry, of course, had dug trenches along the beach, and suddenly the air over the *Holy Moses* sung with bullets. The shore-line thrummed with musketry. Also some antique shells screamed.

<h2 style="text-align:center">VI</h2>

The *Chicken* was doing her best. Pent's posture at the wheel seemed to indicate that her best was about thirty-four knots. In his eagerness he was braced as if he alone was taking in a 10,000 ton battleship through Hell Gate.

But the *Chicken* was not too far in the rear and Pent could see clearly that he was to have no minor part to play. Some of the antique shells had struck the *Holy Moses* and he could see the escaped steam shooting up from her. She lay close inshore and was lashing out with four six-pounders as if this was the last opportunity she would have to fire them. She had made the Spanish gunboats very sick. A solitary gun on the one moored to the wharf was from time to time firing wildly; otherwise the gunboats were silent. But the beach in front of the town was a line of fire. The *Chicken* headed for the *Holy Moses* and, as soon as possible, the six-pounder in her bow began to crack at the gunboat moored to the wharf.

In the meantime, the *Chancellorville* prowled off the bar, listening to the firing, anxious, acutely anxious, and feeling her impotency in every inch of her smart steel frame. And in the meantime, the *Adolphus* squatted on the waves and brazenly waited for news. One could thoughtfully count the seconds and reckon that, in this second and that second, a man had died—if one chose. But no one did it. Undoubtedly, the spirit was that the flag should come away with honour, honour complete, perfect, leaving no loose unfinished end over which the Spaniards could erect a monument of satisfaction, glorification. The distant guns boomed to the ears of the silent blue-jackets at their stations on the cruiser.

The *Chicken* steamed up to the *Holy Moses* and took into her nostrils the odour of steam, gunpowder and burnt things. Rifle bullets simply steamed over them both. In the merest flash of time, Pent took into his remembrance the body of a dead quartermaster on the bridge of his consort. The two megaphones uplifted together, but Pent's eager voice cried out first. "Are you injured, sir?"

"No, not completely. My engines can get me out after—after we have sunk those gunboats." The voice had been utterly conventional but it changed to sharpness. "Go in and sink that gunboat at anchor."

As the *Chicken* rounded the *Holy Moses* and started inshore, a man called to him from the depths of finished disgust. "They're takin' to their boats, sir." Pent looked and saw the men of the anchored gunboat lower their boats and pull like mad for shore.

The *Chicken*, assisted by the *Holy Moses*, began a methodical killing of the anchored gunboat. The Spanish infantry on shore fired frenziedly at the *Chicken*. Pent, giving the wheel to a waiting sailor, stepped out to a point where he could see the men at the guns. One bullet spanged past him and into the pilot-house. He ducked his head into the window. "That hit you, Murry?" he inquired with interest.

"No, sir," cheerfully responded the man at the wheel.

Pent became very busy superintending the fire of his absurd battery. The anchored gunboat simply would not sink. It evinced that unnatural stubbornness which is sometimes displayed by inanimate objects. The gunboat at the wharf had sunk as if she had been scuttled but this riddled thing at anchor would not even take fire. Pent began to grow flurried—privately. He could not stay there for ever. Why didn't the damned gunboat admit its destruction. Why—

He was at the forward gun when one of his engine room force came to him and, after saluting, said serenely: "The men at the after-gun are all down, sir."

It was one of those curious lifts which an enlisted man, without in any way knowing it, can give his officer. The impudent tranquillity of the man at once set Pent to rights and the stoker departed admiring the extraordinary coolness of his captain.

The next few moments contained little but heat, an odour, applied mechanics and an expectation of death. Pent developed a fervid and amazed appreciation of the men, his men, men he knew very well, but strange men. What explained them? He was doing his best because he was captain of the *Chicken* and he lived or died by the*Chicken*. But what could move these men to watch his eye in bright anticipation of his orders and then obey them with enthusiastic rapidity? What caused them to speak of the action as some kind of a joke—particularly when they knew he could overhear them? What manner of men? And he anointed them secretly with his fullest affection.

Perhaps Pent did not think all this during the battle. Perhaps he thought it so soon after the battle that his full mind became confused as to the time. At any rate, it stands as an expression of his feeling.

The enemy had gotten a field-gun down to the shore and with it they began to throw three-inch shells at the *Chicken*. In this war it was usual that the down-trodden Spaniards in their ignorance should use smokeless powder while the Americans, by the power of the consistent everlasting three-ply, wire-woven, double back-action imbecility of a hay-seed government, used powder which on sea and on land cried their position to heaven, and, accordingly, good men got killed without reason. At first, Pent could not locate the field-gun at all, but as soon as he found it, he ran aft with one man and brought the after six-pounder again into action. He paid little heed to the old gun crew. One was lying on his face apparently dead; another was prone with a wound in the chest, while the third sat with his back to the deck-house holding a smitten arm. This last one called out huskily, "Give'm hell, sir."

The minutes of the battle were either days, years, or they were flashes of a second. Once Pent looking up was astonished to see three shell holes in the *Chicken's* funnel—made surreptitiously, so to speak…. "If we don't silence that field-gun, she'll sink us, boys."… The eyes of the man sitting with his back against the deck-house were looking from out his ghastly face at the new gun-crew. He spoke with the supreme laziness of a wounded man. "Give'm hell." … Pent felt a sudden twist of his shoulder. He was wounded—slightly…. The anchored gunboat was in flames.

# VII

Pent took his little blood-stained tow-boat out to the *Holy Moses*. The yacht was already under way for the bay entrance. As they were passing out of range the Spaniards heroically redoubled their fire—which is their custom. Pent, moving busily about the decks, stopped suddenly at the door of the engine-room. His face was set and his eyes were steely. He spoke to one of the engineers. "During the action I saw you firing at the enemy with a rifle. I told you once to stop, and then I saw you at it again. Pegging away with a rifle is no part of your business. I want you to understand that you are in trouble." The humbled man did not raise his eyes from the deck. Presently the *Holy Moses* displayed an anxiety for the *Chicken's* health.

"One killed and four wounded, sir."

"Have you enough men left to work your ship?"

After deliberation, Pent answered: "No, sir."

"Shall I send you assistance?"

"No, sir. I can get to sea all right."

As they neared the point they were edified by the sudden appearance of a serio-comic ally. The *Chancellorville* at last had been unable to stand the strain, and had sent in her launch with an ensign, five seamen and a number of marksmen marines. She swept hot-foot around the point, bent on terrible slaughter; the one-pounder of her bow presented a formidable appearance. The *Holy Moses* and the *Chicken* laughed until they brought indignation to the brow of the young ensign. But he forgot it when with some of his men he boarded the *Chicken* to do what was possible for the wounded. The nearest surgeon was aboard the *Chancellorville*. There was absolute silence on board the cruiser as the *Holy Moses* steamed up to report. The blue-jackets listened with all their ears. The commander of the yacht spoke slowly into his megaphone: "We have—destroyed—the two—gun-boats—sir." There was a burst of confused cheering on the forecastle of the *Chancellorville*, but an officer's cry quelled it.

"Very—good. Will—you—come aboard?"

Two correspondents were already on the deck of the cruiser. Before the last of the wounded were hoisted aboard the cruiser the *Adolphus* was on her way to Key West. When she arrived at that port of desolation Shackles fled to file the telegrams and the other correspondents fled to the hotel for clothes, good clothes, clean clothes; and food, good food, much food; and drink, much drink, any kind of drink.

Days afterward, when the officers of the noble squadron received the newspapers containing an account of their performance, they looked at each other somewhat dejectedly: "Heroic assault—grand daring of Boatswain Pent—superb accuracy of the *Holy Moses'* fire—gallant tars of the *Chicken*—their names should be remembered as long as America stands—terrible losses of the enemy—"

When the Secretary of the Navy ultimately read the report of Commander Surrey, S.O.P., he had to prick himself with a dagger in order to remember that anything at all out of the ordinary had occurred.

# THE SERGEANT'S PRIVATE MADHOUSE

The moonlight was almost steady blue flame and all this radiance was lavished out upon a still lifeless wilderness of stunted trees and cactus plants. The shadows lay upon the ground, pools of black and sharply outlined, resembling substances, fabrics, and not shadows at all. From afar came the sound of the sea coughing among the hollows in the coral rock.

The land was very empty; one could easily imagine that Cuba was a simple vast solitude; one could wonder at the moon taking all the trouble of this splendid illumination. There was no wind; nothing seemed to live.

But in a particular large group of shadows lay an outpost of some forty United States marines. If it had been possible to approach them from any direction without encountering one of their sentries, one could have gone stumbling among sleeping men and men who sat waiting, their blankets tented over their heads; one would have been in among them before one's mind could have decided whether they were men or devils. If a marine moved, he took the care and the time of one who walks across a death-chamber. The lieutenant in command reached for his watch and the nickel chain gave forth the faintest tinkling sound. He could see the glistening five or six pairs of eyes that slowly turned to regard him. His sergeant lay near him and he bent his face down to whisper. "Who's on post behind the big cactus plant?"

"Dryden," rejoined the sergeant just over his breath.

After a pause the lieutenant murmured: "He's got too many nerves. I shouldn't have put him there." The sergeant asked if he should crawl down and look into affairs at Dryden's post. The young officer nodded assent and the sergeant, softly cocking his rifle, went away on his hands and knees. The lieutenant with his back to a dwarf tree, sat watching the sergeant's progress for the few moments that he could see him moving from one shadow to another. Afterward, the officer waited to hear Dryden's quick but low-voiced challenge, but time passed and no sound came from the direction of the post behind the cactus bush.

The sergeant, as he came nearer and nearer to this cactus bush—a number of peculiarly dignified columns throwing shadows of inky darkness—had slowed his pace, for he did not wish to trifle with the feelings of the sentry, and he was expecting the stern hail and was ready with the immediate answer which turns away wrath. He was not made anxious by the fact that he could not yet see Dryden, for he knew that the man would be hidden in a way practised by sentry marines since the time when two men had been killed by a disease of excessive confidence on picket. Indeed, as the sergeant went still nearer, he became more and more angry. Dryden was evidently a most proper sentry.

Finally he arrived at a point where he could see Dryden seated in the shadow, staring into the bushes ahead of him, his rifle ready on his knee. The sergeant in his rage longed for the peaceful precincts of the Washington Marine Barracks where there would have been no situation to prevent the most complete non-commissioned oratory. He felt indecent in his capacity of a man able to creep up to the back of a G Company member on guard duty. Never mind; in the morning back at camp—

But, suddenly, he felt afraid. There was something wrong with Dryden. He remembered old tales of comrades creeping out to find a picket seated against a tree perhaps, upright enough but stone dead. The sergeant paused and gave the inscrutable back of the sentry a long stare. Dubious he again moved forward. At three paces, he hissed like a little snake. Dryden did not show a sign of hearing. At last, the sergeant was in a position from which he was able to reach out and touch Dryden on the arm. Whereupon was turned to him the face of a man livid with mad fright. The sergeant grabbed him by the wrist and with discreet fury shook him. "Here! Pull yourself together!"

Dryden paid no heed but turned his wild face from the newcomer to the ground in front. "Don't you see 'em, sergeant? Don't you see 'em?"

"Where?" whispered the sergeant.

"Ahead, and a little on the right flank. A reg'lar skirmish line. Don't you see 'em?"

"Naw," whispered the sergeant. Dryden began to shake. He began moving one hand from his head to his knee and from his knee to his head rapidly, in a way that is without explanation. "I don't dare fire," he wept. "If I do they'll see me, and oh, how they'll pepper me!"

The sergeant lying on his belly, understood one thing. Dryden had gone mad. Dryden was the March Hare. The old man gulped down his uproarious emotions as well as he was able and used the most simple device. "Go," he said, "and tell the lieutenant while I cover your post for you."

"No! They'd see me! They'd see me! And then they'd pepper me! O, how they'd pepper me!"

The sergeant was face to face with the biggest situation of his life. In the first place he knew that at night a large or small force of Spanish guerillas was never more than easy rifle range from any marine outpost, both sides maintaining a secrecy as absolute as possible in regard to their real position and strength. Everything was on a watch-spring foundation. A loud word might be paid for by a night-attack which would involve five hundred men who needed their earned sleep, not to speak of some of them who would need their lives. The slip of a foot and the rolling of a pint of gravel might go from consequence to consequence until various crews went to general quarters on their ships in the harbour, their batteries booming as the swift search-light flashes tore through the foliage. Men would get killed—notably the sergeant and Dryden—and outposts would be cut off and the whole night would be one pitiless turmoil. And so Sergeant George H. Peasley began to run his private madhouse behind the cactus-bush.

"Dryden," said the sergeant, "you do as I tell you and go tell the lieutenant."

"I don't dare move," shivered the man. "They'll see me if I move. They'll see me. They're almost up now. Let's hide—"

"Well, then you stay here a moment and I'll go and—"

Dryden turned upon him a look so tigerish that the old man felt his hair move. "Don't you stir," he hissed. "You want to give me away. You want them to see me. Don't you stir." The sergeant decided not to stir.

He became aware of the slow wheeling of eternity, its majestic incomprehensibility of movement. Seconds, minutes, were quaint little things, tangible as toys, and there were billions of them, all alike. "Dryden," he whispered at the end of a century in which, curiously, he had never joined the marine corps at all but had taken to another walk of life and prospered greatly in it. "Dryden, this is all foolishness." He thought of the expedient of smashing the man over the head with his rifle, but

Dryden was so supernaturally alert that there surely would issue some small scuffle and there could be not even the fraction of a scuffle. The sergeant relapsed into the contemplation of another century.

His patient had one fine virtue. He was in such terror of the phantom skirmish line that his voice never went above a whisper, whereas his delusion might have expressed itself in hyena yells and shots from his rifle. The sergeant, shuddering, had visions of how it might have been—the mad private leaping into the air and howling and shooting at his friends and making them the centre of the enemy's eager attention. This, to his mind, would have been conventional conduct for a maniac. The trembling victim of an idea was somewhat puzzling. The sergeant decided that from time to time he would reason with his patient. "Look here, Dryden, you don't see any real Spaniards. You've been drinking or—something. Now—"

But Dryden only glared him into silence. Dryden was inspired with such a profound contempt of him that it was become hatred. "Don't you stir!" And it was clear that if the sergeant did stir, the mad private would introduce calamity. "Now," said Peasley to himself, "if those guerillas *should* take a crack at us tonight, they'd find a lunatic asylum right in the front and it would be astonishing."

The silence of the night was broken by the quick low voice of a sentry to the left some distance. The breathless stillness brought an effect to the words as if they had been spoken in one's ear.

*"Halt—who's there—halt or I'll fire!"* Bang!

At the moment of sudden attack particularly at night, it is improbable that a man registers much detail of either thought or action. He may afterward say: "I was here." He may say: "I was there." "I did this." "I did that." But there remains a great incoherency because of the tumultuous thought which seethes through the head. "Is this defeat?" At night in a wilderness and against skilful foes half-seen, one does not trouble to ask if it is also Death. Defeat is Death, then, save for the miraculous. But the exaggerating magnifying first thought subsides in the ordered mind of the soldier and he knows, soon, what he is doing and how much of it. The sergeant's immediate impulse had been to squeeze close to the ground and listen—listen—above all else, listen. But the next moment he grabbed his private asylum by the scruff of its neck, jerked it to its feet and started to retreat upon the main outpost.

To the left, rifle-flashes were bursting from the shadows. To the rear, the lieutenant was giving some hoarse order or admonition. Through the air swept some Spanish bullets, very high, as if they had been fired at a man in a tree. The private asylum came on so hastily that the sergeant found he could remove his grip, and soon they were in the midst of the men of the outpost. Here there was no occasion for enlightening the lieutenant. In the first place such surprises required statement, question and answer. It is impossible to get a grossly original and fantastic idea through a man's head in less than one minute of rapid talk, and the sergeant knew the lieutenant could not spare the minute. He himself had no minutes to devote to anything but the business of the outpost. And the madman disappeared from his pen and he forgot about him.

It was a long night and the little fight was as long as the night. It was a heartbreaking work. The forty marines lay in an irregular oval. From all sides, the Mauser bullets sang low and hard. Their occupation was to prevent a rush, and to this end they potted carefully at the flash of a Mauser—save when they got excited for a moment, in which case their magazines rattled like a great Waterbury watch. Then they settled again to a systematic potting.

The enemy were not of the regular Spanish forces. They were of a corps of guerillas, native-born Cubans, who preferred the flag of Spain. They were all men who knew the craft of the woods and were all recruited from the district. They fought more like red Indians than any people but the red Indians themselves. Each seemed to possess an individuality, a fighting individuality, which is only found in the highest order of irregular soldiers. Personally they were as distinct as possible, but through equality of knowledge and experience, they arrived at concert of action. So long as they operated in the wilderness, they were formidable troops. It mattered little whether it was daylight or dark; they were mainly invisible. They had schooled from the Cubans insurgent to Spain. As the Cubans fought the Spanish troops, so would these particular Spanish troops fight the Americans. It was wisdom.

The marines thoroughly understood the game. They must lie close and fight until daylight when the guerillas promptly would go away. They had withstood other nights of this kind, and now their principal emotion was probably a sort of frantic annoyance.

Back at the main camp, whenever the roaring volleys lulled, the men in the trenches could hear their comrades of the outpost, and the guerillas pattering away interminably. The moonlight faded and left an equal darkness upon the wilderness. A man could barely see the comrade at his side. Sometimes guerillas crept so close that the flame from their rifles seemed to scorch the faces of the marines, and the reports sounded as if from two or three inches of their very noses. If a pause came, one could hear the guerillas gabbling to each other in a kind of drunken delirium. The lieutenant was praying that the ammunition would last. Everybody was praying for daybreak.

A black hour came finally, when the men were not fit to have their troubles increased. The enemy made a wild attack on one portion of the oval, which was held by about fifteen men. The remainder of the force was busy enough, and the fifteen were naturally left to their devices. Amid the whirl of it, a loud voice suddenly broke out in song:

"When shepherds guard their flocks by night,
All seated on the ground,
An angel of the Lord came down
And glory shone around."

"Who the hell is that?" demanded the lieutenant from a throat full of smoke. There was almost a full stop of the firing. The Americans were somewhat puzzled. Practical ones muttered that the fool should have a bayonet-hilt shoved down his throat. Others felt a thrill at the strangeness of the thing. Perhaps it was a sign!

"The minstrel boy to the war has gone,
In the ranks of death you'll find him,
His father's sword he has girded on
And his wild harp slung behind him."

This croak was as lugubrious as a coffin. "Who is it? Who is it?" snapped the lieutenant. "Stop him, somebody."

"It's Dryden, sir," said old Sergeant Peasley, as he felt around in the darkness for his madhouse. "I can't find him—yet."

"Please, O, please, O, do not let me fall;
You're—gurgh—ugh—"

The sergeant had pounced upon him.

This singing had had an effect upon the Spaniards. At first they had fired frenziedly at the voice, but they soon ceased, perhaps from sheer amazement. Both sides took a spell of meditation.

The sergeant was having some difficulty with his charge. "Here, you, grab 'im. Take 'im by the throat. Be quiet, you devil."

One of the fifteen men, who had been hard-pressed, called out, "We've only got about one clip a-piece, Lieutenant. If they come again—"

The lieutenant crawled to and fro among his men, taking clips of cartridges from those who had many. He came upon the sergeant and his madhouse. He felt Dryden's belt and found it simply stuffed with ammunition. He examined Dryden's rifle and found in it a full clip. The madhouse had not fired a shot. The lieutenant distributed these valuable prizes among the fifteen men. As the men gratefully took them, one said: "If they had come again hard enough, they would have had us, sir,—maybe."

But the Spaniards did not come again. At the first indication of daybreak, they fired their customary good-bye volley. The marines lay tight while the slow dawn crept over the land. Finally the lieutenant arose among them, and he was a bewildered man, but very angry. "Now where is that idiot, Sergeant?"

"Here he is, sir," said the old man cheerfully. He was seated on the ground beside the recumbent Dryden who, with an innocent smile on his face, was sound asleep.

"Wake him up," said the lieutenant briefly.

The sergeant shook the sleeper. "Here, Minstrel Boy, turn out. The lieutenant wants you."

Dryden climbed to his feet and saluted the officer with a dazed and childish air. "Yes, sir."

The lieutenant was obviously having difficulty in governing his feelings, but he managed to say with calmness, "You seem to be fond of singing, Dryden? Sergeant, see if he has any whisky on him."

"Sir?" said the madhouse stupefied. "Singing—fond of singing?"

Here the sergeant interposed gently, and he and the lieutenant held palaver apart from the others. The marines, hitching more comfortably their almost empty belts, spoke with grins of the madhouse. "Well, the Minstrel Boy made 'em clear out. They couldn't stand it. But—I wouldn't want to be in his boots. He'll see fireworks when the old man interviews him on the uses of grand opera in modern warfare. How do you think he managed to smuggle a bottle along without us finding it out?"

When the weary outpost was relieved and marched back to camp, the men could not rest until they had told a tale of the voice in the wilderness. In the meantime the sergeant took Dryden aboard a ship, and to those who took charge of the man, he defined him as "the most useful —— crazy man in the service of the United States."

# VIRTUE IN WAR

I

Gates had left the regular army in 1890, those parts of him which had not been frozen having been well fried. He took with him nothing but an oaken constitution and a knowledge of the plains and the best wishes of his fellow-officers. The Standard Oil Company differs from the United States Government in that it understands the value of the loyal and intelligent services of good men and is almost certain to reward them at the expense of incapable men. This curious practice emanates from no beneficent emotion of the Standard Oil Company, on whose feelings you could not make a scar with a hammer and chisel. It is simply that the Standard Oil Company knows more than the United States Government and makes use of virtue whenever virtue is to its advantage. In 1890 Gates really felt in his bones that, if he lived a rigorously correct life and several score of his class-mates and intimate friends died off, he would get command of a troop of horse by the time he was unfitted by age to be an active cavalry leader. He left the service of the United States and entered the service of the Standard Oil Company. In the course of time he knew that, if he lived a rigorously correct life, his position and income would develop strictly in parallel with the worth of his wisdom and experience, and he would not have to walk on the corpses of his friends.

But he was not happier. Part of his heart was in a barracks, and it was not enough to discourse of the old regiment over the port and cigars to ears which were polite enough to betray a languid ignorance. Finally came the year 1898, and Gates dropped the Standard Oil Company as if it were hot. He hit the steel trail to Washington and there fought the first serious action of the war. Like most Americans, he had a native State, and one morning he found himself major in a volunteer infantry regiment whose voice had a peculiar sharp twang to it which he could remember from childhood. The colonel welcomed the West Pointer with loud cries of joy; the lieutenant-colonel looked at him with the pebbly eye of distrust; and the senior major, having had up to this time the best battalion in the regiment, strongly disapproved of him. There were only two majors, so the lieutenant-colonel commanded the first battalion, which gave him an occupation. Lieutenant-colonels under the new rules do not always have occupations. Gates got the third battalion—four companies commanded by intelligent officers who could gauge the opinions of their men at two thousand yards and govern themselves accordingly. The battalion was immensely interested in the new major. It thought it ought to develop views about him. It thought it was its blankety-blank business to find out immediately if it liked him personally. In the company streets the talk was nothing else. Among the non-commissioned officers there were eleven old soldiers of the regular army, and they knew—and cared—that Gates had held commission in the "Sixteenth Cavalry"—as *Harper's Weekly* says. Over this fact they rejoiced and were glad, and they stood by to jump lively when he took command. He would know his work and he would know *their* work, and then in battle there would be killed only what men were absolutely necessary and the sick list would be comparatively free of fools.

The commander of the second battalion had been called by an Atlanta paper, "Major Rickets C. Carmony, the commander of the second battalion of the 307th

—, is when at home one of the biggest wholesale hardware dealers in his State. Last evening he had ice-cream, at his own expense, served out at the regular mess of the battalion, and after dinner the men gathered about his tent where three hearty cheers for the popular major were given." Carmony had bought twelve copies of this newspaper and mailed them home to his friends.

In Gates's battalion there were more kicks than ice-cream, and there was no ice-cream at all. Indignation ran high at the rapid manner in which he proceeded to make soldiers of them. Some of his officers hinted finally that the men wouldn't stand it. They were saying that they had enlisted to fight for their country—yes, but they weren't going to be bullied day in and day out by a perfect stranger. They were patriots, they were, and just as good men as ever stepped—just as good as Gates or anybody like him. But, gradually, despite itself, the battalion progressed. The men were not altogether conscious of it. They evolved rather blindly. Presently there were fights with Carmony's crowd as to which was the better battalion at drills, and at last there was no argument. It was generally admitted that Gates commanded the crack battalion. The men, believing that the beginning and the end of all soldiering was in these drills of precision, were somewhat reconciled to their major when they began to understand more of what he was trying to do for them, but they were still fiery untamed patriots of lofty pride and they resented his manner toward them. It was abrupt and sharp.

The time came when everybody knew that the Fifth Army Corps was the corps designated for the first active service in Cuba. The officers and men of the 307th observed with despair that their regiment was not in the Fifth Army Corps. The colonel was a strategist. He understood everything in a flash. Without a moment's hesitation he obtained leave and mounted the night express for Washington. There he drove Senators and Congressmen in span, tandem and four-in-hand. With the telegraph he stirred so deeply the governor, the people and the newspapers of his State that whenever on a quiet night the President put his head out of the White House he could hear the distant vast commonwealth humming with indignation. And as it is well known that the Chief Executive listens to the voice of the people, the 307th was transferred to the Fifth Army Corps. It was sent at once to Tampa, where it was brigaded with two dusty regiments of regulars, who looked at it calmly, and said nothing. The brigade commander happened to be no less a person than Gates's old colonel in the "Sixteenth Cavalry"—as Harper's Weekly says—and Gates was cheered. The old man's rather solemn look brightened when he saw Gates in the 307th. There was a great deal of battering and pounding and banging for the 307th at Tampa, but the men stood it more in wonder than in anger. The two regular regiments carried them along when they could, and when they couldn't waited impatiently for them to come up. Undoubtedly the regulars wished the volunteers were in garrison at Sitka, but they said practically nothing. They minded their own regiments. The colonel was an invaluable man in a telegraph office. When came the scramble for transports the colonel retired to a telegraph office and talked so ably to Washington that the authorities pushed a number of corps aside and made way for the 307th, as if on it depended everything. The regiment got one of the best transports, and after a series of delays and some starts, and an equal number of returns, they finally sailed for Cuba.

## II

Now Gates had a singular adventure on the second morning after his arrival at Atlanta to take his post as a major in the 307th.

He was in his tent, writing, when suddenly the flap was flung away and a tall young private stepped inside.

"Well, Maje," said the newcomer, genially, "how goes it?"

The major's head flashed up, but he spoke without heat.

"Come to attention and salute."

"Huh!" said the private.

"Come to attention and salute."

The private looked at him in resentful amazement, and then inquired:

"Ye ain't mad, are ye? Ain't nothin' to get huffy about, is there?"

"I— Come to attention and salute."

"Well," drawled the private, as he stared, "seein' as ye are so darn perticular, I don't care if I do—if it'll make yer meals set on yer stomick any better."

Drawing a long breath and grinning ironically, he lazily pulled his heels together and saluted with a flourish.

"There," he said, with a return to his earlier genial manner. "How's that suit ye, Maje?"

There was a silence which to an impartial observer would have seemed pregnant with dynamite and bloody death. Then the major cleared his throat and coldly said:

"And now, what is your business?"

"Who—me?" asked the private. "Oh, I just sorter dropped in." With a deeper meaning he added: "Sorter dropped in in a friendly way, thinkin' ye was mebbe a different kind of a feller from what ye be."

The inference was clearly marked.

It was now Gates's turn to stare, and stare he unfeignedly did.

"Go back to your quarters," he said at length.

The volunteer became very angry.

"Oh, ye needn't be so up-in-th'-air, need ye? Don't know's I'm dead anxious to inflict my company on yer since I've had a good look at ye. There may be men in this here battalion what's had just as much edjewcation as you have, and I'm damned if they ain't got better *manners*. Good-mornin'," he said, with dignity; and, passing out of the tent, he flung the flap back in place with an air of slamming it as if it had been a door. He made his way back to his company street, striding high. He was furious. He met a large crowd of his comrades.

"What's the matter, Lige?" asked one, who noted his temper.

"Oh, nothin'," answered Lige, with terrible feeling. "Nothin'. I jest been lookin' over the new major—that's all."

"What's he like?" asked another.

"Like?" cried Lige. "He's like nothin'. He ain't out'n the same kittle as us. No. Gawd made him all by himself—sep'rate. He's a speshul produc', he is, an' he won't have no truck with jest common—*men*, like you be."

He made a venomous gesture which included them all.

"Did he set on ye?" asked a soldier.

"Set on me? No," replied Lige, with contempt "I set on *him*. I sized 'im up in a minute. 'Oh, I don't know,' I says, as I was comin' out; 'guess you ain't the only man in the world,' I says."

For a time Lige Wigram was quite a hero. He endlessly repeated the tale of his adventure, and men admired him for so soon taking the conceit out of the new officer. Lige was proud to think of himself as a plain and simple patriot who had refused to endure any high-soaring nonsense.

But he came to believe that he had not disturbed the singular composure of the major, and this concreted his hatred. He hated Gates, not as a soldier sometimes hates an officer, a hatred half of fear. Lige hated as man to man. And he was enraged to see that so far from gaining any hatred in return, he seemed incapable of making Gates have any thought of him save as a unit in a body of three hundred men. Lige might just as well have gone and grimaced at the obelisk in Central Park.

When the battalion became the best in the regiment he had no part in the pride of the companies. He was sorry when men began to speak well of Gates. He was really a very consistent hater.

### III

The transport occupied by the 307th was commanded by some sort of a Scandinavian, who was afraid of the shadows of his own topmasts. He would have run his steamer away from a floating Gainsborough hat, and, in fact, he ran her away from less on some occasions. The officers, wishing to arrive with the other transports, sometimes remonstrated, and to them he talked of his owners. Every officer in the convoying warships loathed him, for in case any hostile vessel should appear they did not see how they were going to protect this rabbit, who would probably manage during a fight to be in about a hundred places on the broad, broad sea, and all of them offensive to the navy's plan. When he was not talking of his owners he was remarking to the officers of the regiment that a steamer really was not like a valise, and that he was unable to take his ship under his arm and climb trees with it. He further said that "them naval fellows" were not near so smart as they thought they were.

From an indigo sea arose the lonely shore of Cuba. Ultimately, the fleet was near Santiago, and most of the transports were bidden to wait a minute while the leaders found out their minds. The skipper, to whom the 307th were prisoners, waited for thirty hours half way between Jamaica and Cuba. He explained that the Spanish fleet might emerge from Santiago Harbour at any time, and he did not propose to be caught. His owners— Whereupon the colonel arose as one having nine hundred men at his back, and he passed up to the bridge and he spake with the captain. He explained indirectly that each individual of his nine hundred men had decided to be the first American soldier to land for this campaign, and that in order to accomplish the marvel it was necessary for the transport to be nearer than forty-five miles from the Cuban coast. If the skipper would only land the regiment the colonel would consent to his then taking his interesting old ship and going to hellwith it. And the skipper spake with the colonel. He pointed out that as far as he officially was concerned, the United States Government did not exist. He was responsible solely to his owners. The colonel pondered these sayings. He perceived that the skipper meant that he was running his ship as he deemed best, in consideration of the capital invested by his owners, and that he was not at all concerned with the feelings of a certain American military expedition to Cuba. He was a free son of the sea—he was a sovereign citizen of the republic of the waves. He was like Lige.

However, the skipper ultimately incurred the danger of taking his ship under the terrible guns of the *New York, Iowa,Oregon, Massachusetts, Indiana, Brooklyn,Texas* and a score of cruisers and gunboats. It was a brave act for the captain of a United States transport, and he was visibly nervous until he could again get to sea, where he offered praises that the accursed 307th was no longer sitting on his head. For almost a week he rambled at his cheerful will over the adjacent high seas, having in his hold a great quantity of military stores as successfully secreted as if they had been buried in a copper box in the cornerstone of a new public building in Boston.

He had had his master's certificate for twenty-one years, and those people couldn't tell a marlin-spike from the starboard side of the ship.

The 307th was landed in Cuba, but to their disgust they found that about ten thousand regulars were ahead of them. They got immediate orders to move out from the base on the road to Santiago. Gates was interested to note that the only delay was caused by the fact that many men of the other battalions strayed off sight-seeing. In time the long regiment wound slowly among hills that shut them from sight of the sea.

For the men to admire, there were palm-trees, little brown huts, passive, uninterested Cuban soldiers much worn from carrying American rations inside and outside. The weather was not oppressively warm, and the journey was said to be only about seven miles. There were no rumours save that there had been one short fight and the army had advanced to within sight of Santiago. Having a peculiar faculty for the derision of the romantic, the 307th began to laugh. Actually there was not *anything* in the world which turned out to be as books describe it. Here they had landed from the transport expecting to be at once flung into line of battle and sent on some kind of furious charge, and now they were trudging along a quiet trail lined with somnolent trees and grass. The whole business so far struck them as being a highly tedious burlesque.

After a time they came to where the camps of regular regiments marked the sides of the road—little villages of tents no higher than a man's waist. The colonel found his brigade commander and the 307th was sent off into a field of long grass, where the men grew suddenly solemn with the importance of getting their supper.

In the early evening some regulars told one of Gates's companies that at daybreak this division would move to an attack upon something.

"How d'you know?" said the company, deeply awed.

"Heard it."

"Well, what are we to attack?"

"Dunno."

The 307th was not at all afraid, but each man began to imagine the morrow. The regulars seemed to have as much interest in the morrow as they did in the last Christmas. It was none of their affair, apparently.

"Look here," said Lige Wigram, to a man in the 17th Regular Infantry, "whereabouts are we goin' ter-morrow an' who do we run up against—do ye know?"

The 17th soldier replied, truculently: "If I ketch th' — — — what stole my terbaccer, I'll whirl in an' break every — — bone in his body."

Gates's friends in the regular regiments asked him numerous questions as to the reliability of his organisation. Would the 307th stand the racket? They were certainly not contemptuous; they simply did not seem to consider it important whether the 307th would or whether it would not.

"Well," said Gates, "they won't run the length of a tent-peg if they can gain any idea of what they're fighting; they won't bunch if they've about six acres of open ground to move in; they won't get rattled at all if they see you fellows taking it easy, and they'll fight like the devil as long as they thoroughly, completely, absolutely, satisfactorily, exhaustively understand what the business is. They're lawyers. All excepting my battalion."

**IV**

Lige awakened into a world obscured by blue fog. Somebody was gently shaking him. "Git up; we're going to move." The regiment was buckling up itself. From the trail came the loud creak of a light battery moving ahead. The tones of all men were low; the faces of the officers were composed, serious. The regiment found itself moving along behind the battery before it had time to ask itself more than a hundred questions. The trail wound through a dense tall jungle, dark, heavy with dew.

The battle broke with a snap—far ahead. Presently Lige heard from the air above him a faint low note as if somebody were blowing softly in the mouth of a bottle. It was a stray bullet which had wandered a mile to tell him that war was before him. He nearly broke his neck looking upward. "Did ye hear that?" But the men were fretting to get out of this gloomy jungle. They wanted to see something. The faint rup-rup-rrrrup-rup on in the front told them that the fight had begun; death was abroad, and so the mystery of this wilderness excited them. This wilderness was portentously still and dark.

They passed the battery aligned on a hill above the trail, and they had not gone far when the gruff guns began to roar and they could hear the rocket-like swish of the flying shells. Presently everybody must have called out for the assistance of the 307th. Aides and couriers came flying back to them.

"Is this the 307th? Hurry up your men, please, Colonel. You're needed more every minute."

Oh, they were, were they? Then the regulars were not going to do *all* the fighting? The old 307th was bitterly proud or proudly bitter. They left their blanket rolls under the guard of God and pushed on, which is one of the reasons why the Cubans of that part of the country were, later, so well equipped. There began to appear fields, hot, golden-green in the sun. On some palm-dotted knolls before them they could see little lines of black dots—the American advance. A few men fell, struck down by other men who, perhaps half a mile away, were aiming at somebody else. The loss was wholly in Carmony's battalion, which immediately bunched and backed away, coming with a shock against Gates's advance company. This shock sent a tremor through all of Gates's battalion until men in the very last files cried out nervously, "Well, what in hell is up now?" There came an order to deploy and advance. An occasional hoarse yell from the regulars could be heard. The deploying made Gates's heart bleed for the colonel. The old man stood there directing the movement, straight, fearless, sombrely defiant of—everything. Carmony's four companies were like four herds. And all the time the bullets from no living man knows where kept pecking at them and pecking at them. Gates, the excellent Gates, the highly educated and strictly military Gates, grew rankly insubordinate. He knew that the regiment was suffering from nothing but the deadly range and oversweep of the modern rifle, of which many proud and confident nations know nothing save that they have killed savages with it, which is the least of all informations.

Gates rushed upon Carmony.

"— — it, man, if you can't get your people to deploy, for — sake give me a chance! I'm stuck in the woods!"

Carmony gave nothing, but Gates took all he could get and his battalion deployed and advanced like men. The old colonel almost burst into tears, and he cast one quick glance of gratitude at Gates, which the younger officer wore on his heart like a secret decoration.

There was a wild scramble up hill, down dale, through thorny thickets. Death smote them with a kind of slow rhythm, leisurely taking a man now here, now there, but the cat-spit sound of the bullets was always. A large number of the men of Carmony's battalion came on with Gates. They were willing to do anything,

anything. They had no real fault, unless it was that early conclusion that any brave high-minded youth was necessarily a good soldier immediately, from the beginning. In them had been born a swift feeling that the unpopular Gates knew everything, and they followed the trained soldier.

If they followed him, he certainly took them into it. As they swung heavily up one steep hill, like so many wind-blown horses, they came suddenly out into the real advance. Little blue groups of men were making frantic rushes forward and then flopping down on their bellies to fire volleys while other groups made rushes. Ahead they could see a heavy house-like fort which was inadequate to explain from whence came the myriad bullets. The remainder of the scene was landscape. Pale men, yellow men, blue men came out of this landscape quiet and sad-eyed with wounds. Often they were grimly facetious. There is nothing in the American regulars so amazing as his conduct when he is wounded—his apologetic limp, his deprecatory arm-sling, his embarrassed and ashamed shot-hole through the lungs. The men of the 307th looked at calm creatures who had divers punctures and they were made better. These men told them that it was only necessary to keep a-going. They of the 307th lay on their bellies, red, sweating and panting, and heeded the voice of the elder brother.

Gates walked back of his line, very white of face, but hard and stern past any-thing his men knew of him. After they had violently adjured him to lie down and he had given weak backs a cold, stiff touch, the 307th charged by rushes. The hatless colonel made frenzied speech, but the man of the time was Gates. The men seemed to feel that this was his business. Some of the regular officers said afterward that the advance of the 307th was very respectable indeed. They were rather surprised, they said. At least five of the crack regiments of the regular army were in this division, and the 307th could win no more than a feeling of kindly appreciation.

Yes, it was very good, very good indeed, but did you notice what was being done at the same moment by the 12th, the 17th, the 7th, the 8th, the 25th, the—

Gates felt that his charge was being a success. He was carrying out a successful function. Two captains fell bang on the grass and a lieutenant slumped quietly down with a death wound. Many men sprawled suddenly. Gates was keeping his men al-most even with the regulars, who were charging on his flanks. Suddenly he thought that he must have come close to the fort and that a Spaniard had tumbled a great stone block down upon his leg. Twelve hands reached out to help him, but he cried:

"No—damn your souls—go on—go on!"

He closed his eyes for a moment, and it really was only for a moment. When he opened them he found himself alone with Lige Wigram, who lay on the ground near him.

"Maje," said Lige, "yer a good man. I've been a-follerin' ye all day an' I want to say yer a good man."

The major turned a coldly scornful eye upon the private.

"Where are you wounded? Can you walk? Well, if you can, go to the rear and leave me alone. I'm bleeding to death, and you bother me."

Lige, despite the pain in his wounded shoulder, grew indignant.

"Well," he mumbled, "you and me have been on th' outs fer a long time, an' I only wanted to tell ye that what I seen of ye t'day has made me feel mighty differ-ent."

"Go to the rear—if you can walk," said the major.

"Now, Maje, look here. A little thing like that—"

"Go to the rear."

Lige gulped with sobs.

"Maje, I know I didn't understand ye at first, but ruther'n let a little thing like that come between us, I'd—I'd—"

"Go to the rear."

In this reiteration Lige discovered a resemblance to that first old offensive phrase, "Come to attention and salute." He pondered over the resemblance and he saw that nothing had changed. The man bleeding to death was the same man to whom he had once paid a friendly visit with unfriendly results. He thought now that he perceived a certain hopeless gulf, a gulf which is real or unreal, according to circumstances. Sometimes all men are equal; occasionally they are not. If Gates had ever criticised Lige's manipulation of a hay fork on the farm at home, Lige would have furiously disdained his hate or blame. He saw now that he must not openly approve the major's conduct in war. The major's pride was in his business, and his, Lige's congratulations, were beyond all enduring.

The place where they were lying suddenly fell under a new heavy rain of bullets. They sputtered about the men, making the noise of large grasshoppers.

"Major!" cried Lige. "Major Gates! It won't do for ye to be left here, sir. Ye'll be killed."

"But you can't help it, lad. You take care of yourself."

"I'm damned if I do," said the private, vehemently. "If I can't git*you* out, I'll stay and wait."

The officer gazed at his man with that same icy, contemptuous gaze.

"I'm—I'm a dead man anyhow. You go to the rear, do you hear?"

"No."

The dying major drew his revolver, cocked it and aimed it unsteadily at Lige's head.

"Will you obey orders?"

"No."

"One?"

"No."

"Two?"

"No."

Gates weakly dropped his revolver.

"Go to the devil, then. You're no soldier, but—" He tried to add something, "But—"

He heaved a long moan. "But—you—you—oh, I'm so-o-o tired."

V

After the battle, three correspondents happened to meet on the trail. They were hot, dusty, weary, hungry and thirsty, and they repaired to the shade of a mango tree and sprawled luxuriously. Among them they mustered twoscore friends who on that day had gone to the far shore of the hereafter, but their senses were no longer resonant. Shackles was babbling plaintively about mint-juleps, and the others were bidding him to have done.

"By-the-way," said one, at last, "it's too bad about poor old Gates of the 307th. He bled to death. His men were crazy. They were blubbering and cursing around there like wild people. It seems that when they got back there to look for him they found him just about gone, and another wounded man was trying to stop the flow with his hat! His hat, mind you. Poor old Gatesie!"

"Oh, no, Shackles!" said the third man of the party. "Oh, no, you're wrong. The best mint-juleps in the world are made right in New York, Philadelphia or Boston. That Kentucky idea is only a tradition."

A wounded man approached them. He had been shot through the shoulder and his shirt had been diagonally cut away, leaving much bare skin. Over the bullet's point of entry there was a kind of a white spider, shaped from pieces of adhesive plaster. Over the point of departure there was a bloody bulb of cotton strapped to the flesh by other pieces of adhesive plaster. His eyes were dreamy, wistful, sad. "Say, gents, have any of ye got a bottle?" he asked.

A correspondent raised himself suddenly and looked with bright eyes at the soldier.

"Well, you have got a nerve," he said grinning. "Have we got a bottle, eh! Who in hell do you think we are? If we had a bottle of good licker, do you suppose we could let the whole army drink out of it? You have too much faith in the generosity of men, my friend!"

The soldier stared, ox-like, and finally said, "Huh?"

"I say," continued the correspondent, somewhat more loudly, "that if we had had a bottle we would have probably finished it ourselves by this time."

"But," said the other, dazed, "I *meant* an empty bottle. I didn't mean no *full* bottle."

The correspondent was humorously irascible.

"An empty bottle! You must be crazy! Who ever heard of a man looking for an empty bottle? It isn't sense! I've seen a million men looking for full bottles, but you're the first man I ever saw who insisted on the bottle's being empty. What in the world do you want it for?"

"Well, ye see, mister," explained Lige, slowly, "our major he was killed this mornin' an' we're jes' goin' to bury him, an' I thought I'd jest take a look 'round an' see if I couldn't borry an empty bottle, an' then I'd take an' write his name an' reg'ment on a paper an' put it in th' bottle an' bury it with him, so's when they come fer to dig him up sometime an' take him home, there sure wouldn't be no mistake."

"Oh!"

# MARINES SIGNALLING UNDER FIRE AT GUANTANAMO

They were four Guantanamo marines, officially known for the time as signal-men, and it was their duty to lie in the trenches of Camp McCalla, that faced the water, and, by day, signal the *Marblehead* with a flag and, by night, signal the *Marblehead* with lanterns. It was my good fortune—at that time I considered it my bad fortune, indeed—to be with them on two of the nights when a wild storm of fighting was pealing about the hill; and, of all the actions of the war, none were so hard on the nerves, none strained courage so near the panic point, as those swift nights in Camp McCalla. With a thousand rifles rattling; with the field-guns booming in your ears; with the diabolic Colt automatics clacking; with the roar of the *Marblehead* coming from the bay, and, last, with Mauser bullets sneering always in the air a few inches over one's head, and with this enduring from dusk to dawn, it is extremely doubtful if any one who was there will be able to forget it easily. The noise; the impenetrable darkness; the knowledge from the sound of the bullets that the enemy was on three sides of the camp; the infrequent bloody stumbling and death of some man with whom, perhaps, one had messed two hours previous; the weariness of the body, and the more terrible weariness of the mind, at the endlessness of the thing, made it wonderful that at least some of the men did not come out of it with their nerves hopelessly in shreds.

But, as this interesting ceremony proceeded in the darkness, it was necessary for the signal squad to coolly take and send messages. Captain McCalla always participated in the defence of the camp by raking the woods on two of its sides with the guns of the *Marblehead*. Moreover, he was the senior officer present, and he wanted to know what was happening. All night long the crews of the ships in the bay would stare sleeplessly into the blackness toward the roaring hill.

The signal squad had an old cracker-box placed on top of the trench. When not signalling they hid the lanterns in this-box; but as soon as an order to send a message was received, it became necessary for one of the men to stand up and expose the lights. And then—oh, my eye—how the guerillas hidden in the gulf of night would turn loose at those yellow gleams!

Signalling in this way is done by letting one lantern remain stationary—on top of the cracker-box, in this case—and moving the other over to the left and right and so on in the regular gestures of the wig-wagging code. It is a very simple system of night communication, but one can see that it presents rare possibilities when used in front of an enemy who, a few hundred yards away, is overjoyed at sighting so definite a mark.

How, in the name of wonders, those four men at Camp McCalla were not riddled from head to foot and sent home more as repositories of Spanish ammunition than as marines is beyond all comprehension. To make a confession—when one of these men stood up to wave his lantern, I, lying in the trench, invariably rolled a little to the right or left, in order that, when he was shot, he would not fall on me. But the squad came off scathless, despite the best efforts of the most formidable corps in the Spanish army—the Escuadra de Guantanamo. That it was the most formidable corps in the Spanish army of occupation has been told me by many Spanish officers and also by General Menocal and other insurgent officers. General Menocal was Garcia's chief-of-staff when the latter was operating busily in Santiago province. The regiment was composed solely of *practicos*, or guides, who knew every shrub and tree on the ground over which they moved.

Whenever the adjutant, Lieutenant Draper, came plunging along through the darkness with an order—such as: "Ask the *Marblehead* to please shell the woods to the left"—my heart would come into my mouth, for I knew then that one of my pals was going to stand up behind the lanterns and have all Spain shoot at him.

The answer was always upon the instant:

"Yes, sir." Then the bullets began to snap, snap, snap, at his head while all the woods began to crackle like burning straw. I could lie near and watch the face of the signalman, illumed as it was by the yellow shine of lantern light, and the absence of excitement, fright, or any emotion at all on his countenance, was something to astonish all theories out of one's mind. The face was in every instance merely that of a man intent upon his business, the business of wig-wagging into the gulf of night where a light on the *Marblehead* was seen to move slowly.

These times on the hill resembled, in some days, those terrible scenes on the stage—scenes of intense gloom, blinding lightning, with a cloaked devil or assassin or other appropriate character muttering deeply amid the awful roll of the thunder-drums. It was theatric beyond words: one felt like a leaf in this booming chaos, this prolonged tragedy of the night. Amid it all one could see from time to time the yellow light on the face of a preoccupied signalman.

Possibly no man who was there ever before understood the true eloquence of the breaking of the day. We would lie staring into the east, fairly ravenous for the dawn. Utterly worn to rags, with our nerves standing on end like so many bristles, we lay and watched the east—the unspeakably obdurate and slow east. It was a wonder that the eyes of some of us did not turn to glass balls from the fixity of our gaze.

Then there would come into the sky a patch of faint blue light. It was like a piece of moonshine. Some would say it was the beginning of daybreak; others would declare it was nothing of the kind. Men would get very disgusted with each other in these low-toned arguments held in the trenches. For my part, this development in the eastern sky destroyed many of my ideas and theories concerning the dawning of the day; but then I had never before had occasion to give it such solemn attention.

This patch widened and whitened in about the speed of a man's accomplishment if he should be in the way of painting Madison Square Garden with a camel's hair brush. The guerillas always set out to whoop it up about this time, because they knew the occasion was approaching when it would be expedient for them to elope. I, at least, always grew furious with this wretched sunrise. I thought I could have walked around the world in the time required for the old thing to get up above the horizon.

One midnight, when an important message was to be sent to the *Marblehead*, Colonel Huntington came himself to the signal place with Adjutant Draper and Captain McCauley, the quartermaster. When the man stood up to signal, the colonel stood beside him. At sight of the lights, the Spaniards performed as usual. They drove enough bullets into that immediate vicinity to kill all the marines in the corps.

Lieutenant Draper was agitated for his chief. "Colonel, won't you step down, sir?"

"Why, I guess not," said the grey old veteran in his slow, sad, always-gentle way. "I am in no more danger than the man."

"But, sir—" began the adjutant.

"Oh, it's all right, Draper."

So the colonel and the private stood side to side and took the heavy fire without either moving a muscle.

Day was always obliged to come at last, punctuated by a final exchange of scattering shots. And the light shone on the marines, the dumb guns, the flag. Grimy yellow face looked into grimy yellow face, and grinned with weary satisfaction. Coffee!

Usually it was impossible for many of the men to sleep at once. It always took me, for instance, some hours to get my nerves combed down. But then it was great joy to lie in the trench with the four signalmen, and understand thoroughly that that night was fully over at last, and that, although the future might have in store other bad nights, that one could never escape from the prison-house which we call the past.

* * * *

At the wild little fight at Cusco there were some splendid exhibitions of wig-wagging under fire. Action began when an advanced detachment of marines under Lieutenant Lucas with the Cuban guides had reached the summit of a ridge overlooking a small valley where there was a house, a well, and a thicket of some kind of shrub with great broad, oily leaves. This thicket, which was perhaps an acre in extent, contained the guerillas. The valley was open to the sea. The distance from the top of the ridge to the thicket was barely two hundred yards.

The *Dolphin* had sailed up the coast in line with the marine advance, ready with her guns to assist in any action. Captain Elliott, who commanded the two hundred marines in this fight, suddenly called out for a signalman. He wanted a man to tell the *Dolphin* to open fire on the house and the thicket. It was a blazing, bitter hot day on top of the ridge with its shrivelled chaparral and its straight, tall cactus plants. The sky was bare and blue, and hurt like brass. In two minutes the prostrate marines were red and sweating like so many hull-buried stokers in the tropics.

Captain Elliott called out:

"Where's a signalman? Who's a signalman here?"

A red-headed "mick"—I think his name was Clancy—at any rate, it will do to call him Clancy—twisted his head from where he lay on his stomach pumping his Lee, and, saluting, said that he was a signalman.

There was no regulation flag with the expedition, so Clancy was obliged to tie his blue polka-dot neckerchief on the end of his rifle. It did not make a very good flag. At first Clancy moved a ways down the safe side of the ridge and wigwagged there very busily. But what with the flag being so poor for the purpose, and the background of ridge being so dark, those on the *Dolphin* did not see it. So Clancy had to return to the top of the ridge and outline himself and his flag against the sky.

The usual thing happened. As soon as the Spaniards caught sight of this silhouette, they let go like mad at it. To make things more comfortable for Clancy, the situation demanded that he face the sea and turn his back to the Spanish bullets. This was a hard game, mark you—to stand with the small of your back to volley firing. Clancy thought so. Everybody thought so. We all cleared out of his neighbourhood. If he wanted sole possession of any particular spot on that hill, he could have it for all we would interfere with him.

It cannot be denied that Clancy was in a hurry. I watched him. He was so occupied with the bullets that snarled close to his ears that he was obliged to repeat the letters of his message softly to himself. It seemed an intolerable time before the

*Dolphin* answered the little signal. Meanwhile, we gazed at him, marvelling every second that he had not yet pitched headlong. He swore at times.

Finally the *Dolphin* replied to his frantic gesticulation, and he delivered his message. As his part of the transaction was quite finished—whoop!—he dropped like a brick into the firing line and began to shoot; began to get "hunky" with all those people who had been plugging at him. The blue polka-dot neckerchief still fluttered from the barrel of his rifle. I am quite certain that he let it remain there until the end of the fight.

The shells of the *Dolphin* began to plough up the thicket, kicking the bushes, stones, and soil into the air as if somebody was blasting there.

Meanwhile, this force of two hundred marines and fifty Cubans and the force of—probably—six companies of Spanish guerillas were making such an awful din that the distant Camp McCalla was all alive with excitement. Colonel Huntington sent out strong parties to critical points on the road to facilitate, if necessary, a safe retreat, and also sent forty men under Lieutenant Magill to come up on the left flank of the two companies in action under Captain Elliott. Lieutenant Magill and his men had crowned a hill which covered entirely the flank of the fighting companies, but when the *Dolphin* opened fire, it happened that Magill was in the line of the shots. It became necessary to stop the *Dolphin* at once. Captain Elliott was not near Clancy at this time, and he called hurriedly for another signalman.

Sergeant Quick arose, and announced that he was a signalman. He produced from somewhere a blue polka-dot neckerchief as large as a quilt. He tied it on a long, crooked stick. Then he went to the top of the ridge, and turning his back to the Spanish fire, began to signal to the *Dolphin*. Again we gave a man sole possession of a particular part of the ridge. We didn't want it. He could have it and welcome. If the young sergeant had had the smallpox, the cholera, and the yellow fever, we could not have slid out with more celerity.

As men have said often, it seemed as if there was in this war a God of Battles who held His mighty hand before the Americans. As I looked at Sergeant Quick wig-wagging there against the sky, I would not have given a tin tobacco-tag for his life. Escape for him seemed impossible. It seemed absurd to hope that he would not be hit; I only hoped that he would be hit just a little, in the arm, the shoulder, or the leg.

I watched his face, and it was as grave and serene as that of a man writing in his own library. He was the very embodiment of tranquillity in occupation. He stood there amid the animal-like babble of the Cubans, the crack of rifles, and the whistling snarl of the bullets, and wig-wagged whatever he had to wig-wag without heeding anything but his business. There was not a single trace of nervousness or haste.

To say the least, a fight at close range is absorbing as a spectacle. No man wants to take his eyes from it until that time comes when he makes up his mind to run away. To deliberately stand up and turn your back to a battle is in itself hard work. To deliberately stand up and turn your back to a battle and hear immediate evidences of the boundless enthusiasm with which a large company of the enemy shoot at you from an adjacent thicket is, to my mind at least, a very great feat. One need not dwell upon the detail of keeping the mind carefully upon a slow spelling of an important code message.

I saw Quick betray only one sign of emotion. As he swung his clumsy flag to and fro, an end of it once caught on a cactus pillar, and he looked sharply over his shoulder to see what had it. He gave the flag an impatient jerk. He looked annoyed.

# THIS MAJESTIC LIE

In the twilight, a great crowd was streaming up the Prado in Havana. The people had been down to the shore to laugh and twiddle their fingers at the American blockading fleet—mere colourless shapes on the edge of the sea. Gorgeous challenges had been issued to the far-away ships by little children and women while the men laughed. Havana was happy, for it was known that the illustrious sailor Don Patricio de Montojo had with his fleet met the decaying ships of one Dewey and smitten them into stuffing for a baby's pillow. Of course the American sailors were drunk at the time, but the American sailors were always drunk. Newsboys galloped among the crowd crying *La Lucha* and*La Marina*. The papers said: "This is as we foretold. How could it be otherwise when the cowardly Yankees met our brave sailors?" But the tongues of the exuberant people ran more at large. One man said in a loud voice: "How unfortunate it is that we still have to buy meat in Havana when so much pork is floating in Manila Bay!" Amid the consequent laughter, another man retorted: "Oh, never mind! That pork in Manila is rotten. It always was rotten." Still another man said: "But, little friend, it would make good manure for our fields if only we had it." And still another man said: "Ah, wait until our soldiers get with the wives of the Americans and there will be many little Yankees to serve hot on our tables. The men of the *Maine* simply made our appetites good. Never mind the pork in Manila. There will be plenty." Women laughed; children laughed because their mothers laughed; everybody laughed. And—a word with you—these people were cackling and chuckling and insulting their own dead, their own dead men of Spain, for if the poor green corpses floated then in Manila Bay they were not American corpses.

The newsboys came charging with an extra. The inhabitants of Philadelphia had fled to the forests because of a Spanish bombardment and also Boston was besieged by the Apaches who had totally invested the town. The Apache artillery had proven singularly effective and an American garrison had been unable to face it. In Chicago millionaires were giving away their palaces for two or three loaves of bread. These despatches were from Madrid and every word was truth, but they added little to the enthusiasm because the crowd—God help mankind—was greatly occupied with visions of Yankee pork floating in Manila Bay. This will be thought to be embittered writing. Very well; the writer admits its untruthfulness in one particular. It is untruthful in that it fails to reproduce one-hundredth part of the grossness and indecency of popular expression in Havana up to the time when the people knew they were beaten.

There were no lights on the Prado or in other streets because of a military order. In the slow-moving crowd, there was a young man and an old woman. Suddenly the young man laughed a strange metallic laugh and spoke in English, not cautiously. "That's damned hard to listen to."

The woman spoke quickly. "Hush, you little idiot. Do you want to be walkin' across that grass-plot in Cabanas with your arms tied behind you?" Then she murmured sadly: "Johnnie, I wonder if that's true—what they say about Manila?"

"I don't know," said Johnnie, "but I think they're lying."

As they crossed the Plaza, they could see that the Café Tacon was crowded with Spanish officers in blue and white pajama uniforms. Wine and brandy was being wildly consumed in honour of the victory at Manila. "Let's hear what they say," said Johnnie to his companion, and they moved across the street and in under the *portales*. The owner of the Café Tacon was standing on a table making a speech amid cheers. He was advocating the crucifixion of such Americans as fell into Spanish hands and—it was all very sweet and white and tender, but above all, it was chivalrous, because it is well known that the Spaniards are a chivalrous people. It has been remarked both by the English newspapers and by the bulls that are bred for the red death. And secretly the corpses in Manila Bay mocked this jubilee; the mocking, mocking corpses in Manila Bay.

To be blunt, Johnnie was an American spy. Once he had been the manager of a sugar plantation in Pinar del Rio, and during the insurrection it had been his distinguished function to pay tribute of money, food and forage alike to Spanish columns and insurgent bands. He was performing this straddle with benefit to his crops and with mildew to his conscience when Spain and the United States agreed to skirmish, both in the name of honour. It then became a military necessity that he should change his base. Whatever of the province that was still alive was sorry to see him go for he had been a very dexterous man and food and wine had been in his house even when a man with a mango could gain the envy of an entire Spanish battalion. Without doubt he had been a mere trimmer, but it was because of his crop and he always wrote the word thus: C R O P. In those days a man of peace and commerce was in a position parallel to the watchmaker who essayed a task in the midst of a drunken brawl with oaths, bottles and bullets flying about his intent bowed head. So many of them—or all of them—were trimmers, and to any armed force they fervently said: "God assist you." And behold, the trimmers dwelt safely in a tumultuous land and without effort save that their little machines for trimming ran night and day. So many a plantation became covered with a maze of lies as if thick-webbing spiders had run from stalk to stalk in the cane. So sometimes a planter incurred an equal hatred from both sides and when in trouble there was no camp to which he could flee save, straight in air, the camp of the heavenly host.

If Johnnie had not had a crop, he would have been plainly on the side of the insurgents, but his crop staked him down to the soil at a point where the Spaniards could always be sure of finding him—him or his crop—it is the same thing. But when war came between Spain and the United States he could no longer be the cleverest trimmer in Pinar del Rio. And he retreated upon Key West losing much of his baggage train, not because of panic but because of wisdom. In Key West, he was no longer the manager of a big Cuban plantation; he was a little tan-faced refugee without much money. Mainly he listened; there was nought else to do. In the first place he was a young man of extremely slow speech and in the Key West Hotel tongues ran like pin-wheels. If he had projected his methodic way of thought and speech upon this hurricane, he would have been as effective as the man who tries to smoke against the gale. This truth did not impress him. Really, he was impressed with the fact that although he knew much of Cuba, he could not talk so rapidly and wisely of it as many war-correspondents who had not yet seen the island. Usually he brooded in silence over a bottle of beer and the loss of his crop. He received no sympathy, although there was a plentitude of tender souls. War's first step is to make expectation so high that all present things are fogged and darkened in a tense wonder of the future. None cared about the collapse of Johnnie's plantation when all were thinking of the probable collapse of cities and fleets.

In the meantime, battle-ships, monitors, cruisers, gunboats and torpedo craft arrived, departed, arrived, departed. Rumours sang about the ears of warships hurriedly coaling. Rumours sang about the ears of warships leisurely coming to anchor.

This happened and that happened and if the news arrived at Key West as a mouse, it was often enough cabled north as an elephant. The correspondents at Key West were perfectly capable of adjusting their perspective, but many of the editors in the United States were like deaf men at whom one has to roar. A few quiet words of information was not enough for them; one had to bawl into their ears a whirlwind tale of heroism, blood, death, victory—or defeat—at any rate, a tragedy. The papers should have sent playwrights to the first part of the war. Play-wrights are allowed to lower the curtain from time to time and say to the crowd: "Mark, ye, now! Three or four months are supposed to elapse. But the poor devils at Key West were obliged to keep the curtain up all the time." "This isn't a continuous performance." "Yes, it is; it's *got* to be a continuous performance. The welfare of the paper demands it. The people want news." Very well: continuous performance. It is strange how men of sense can go aslant at the bidding of other men of sense and combine to contribute to a general mess of exaggeration and bombast. But we did; and in the midst of the furor I remember the still figure of Johnnie, the planter, the ex-trimmer. He looked dazed.

This was in May.

We all liked him. From time to time some of us heard in his words the vibrant of a thoughtful experience. But it could not be well heard; it was only like the sound of a bell from under the floor. We were too busy with our own clatter. He was taciturn and competent while we solved the war in a babble of tongues. Soon we went about our peaceful paths saying ironically one to another: "War is hell." Meanwhile, managing editors fought us tooth and nail and we all were sent boxes of medals inscribed: "Incompetency." We became furious with ourselves. Why couldn't we send hair-raising despatches? Why couldn't we inflame the wires? All this we did. If a first-class armoured cruiser which had once been a tow-boat fired a six-pounder shot from her forward thirteen-inch gun turret, the world heard of it, you bet. We were not idle men. We had come to report the war and we did it. Our good names and our salaries depended upon it and we were urged by our managing-editors to remember that the American people were a collection of super-nervous idiots who would immediately have convulsions if we did not throw them some news—any news. It was not true, at all. The American people were anxious for things decisive to happen; they were not anxious to be lulled to satisfaction with a drug. But we lulled them. We told them this and we told them that, and I warrant you our screaming sounded like the noise of a lot of sea-birds settling for the night among the black crags.

In the meantime, Johnnie stared and meditated. In his unhurried, unstartled manner he was singularly like another man who was flying the pennant as commander-in-chief of the North Atlantic Squadron. Johnnie was a refugee; the admiral was an admiral. And yet they were much akin, these two. Their brother was the Strategy Board—the only capable political institution of the war. At Key West the naval officers spoke of their business and were devoted to it and were bound to succeed in it, but when the flag-ship was in port the only two people who were independent and sane were the admiral and Johnnie. The rest of us were lulling the public with drugs.

There was much discussion of the new batteries at Havana. Johnnie was a typical American. In Europe a typical American is a man with a hard eye, chin-whiskers and a habit of speaking through his nose. Johnnie was a young man of great energy, ready to accomplish a colossal thing for the basic reason that he was ignorant of its magnitude. In fact he attacked all obstacles in life in a spirit of contempt, seeing them smaller than they were until he had actually surmounted them—when he was likely to be immensely pleased with himself. Somewhere in him there was a sentimental tenderness, but it was like a light seen afar at night; it came, went, appeared again in a new place, flickered, flared, went out, left you in a void and angry. And if his sentimental tenderness was a light, the darkness in which it puzzled you was his irony of soul. This irony was directed first at himself; then at you; then at the nation and the flag; then at God. It was a midnight in which you searched for the little elusive, ashamed spark of tender sentiment. Sometimes, you thought this was all pretext, the manner and the way of fear of the wit of others; sometimes you thought he was a hardened savage; usually you did not think but waited in the cheerful certainty that in time the little flare of light would appear in the gloom.

Johnnie decided that he would go and spy upon the fortifications of Havana. If any one wished to know of those batteries it was the admiral of the squadron, but the admiral of the squadron knew much. I feel sure that he knew the size and position of every gun. To be sure, new guns might be mounted at any time, but they would not be big guns, and doubtless he lacked in his cabin less information than would be worth a man's life. Still, Johnnie decided to be a spy. He would go and look. We of the newspapers pinned him fast to the tail of our kite and he was taken to see the admiral. I judge that the admiral did not display much interest in the plan. But at any rate it seems that he touched Johnnie smartly enough with a brush to make him, officially, a spy. Then Johnnie bowed and left the cabin. There was no other machinery. If Johnnie was to end his life and leave a little book about it, no one cared—least of all, Johnnie and the admiral. When he came aboard the tug, he displayed his usual stalwart and rather selfish zest for fried eggs. It was all some kind of an ordinary matter. It was done every day. It was the business of packing pork, sewing shoes, binding hay. It was commonplace. No one could adjust it, get it in proportion, until—afterwards. On a dark night, they heaved him into a small boat and rowed him to the beach.

And one day he appeared at the door of a little lodging-house in Havana kept by Martha Clancy, born in Ireland, bred in New York, fifteen years married to a Spanish captain, and now a widow, keeping Cuban lodgers who had no money with which to pay her. She opened the door only a little way and looked down over her spectacles at him.

"Good-mornin' Martha," he said.

She looked a moment in silence. Then she made an indescribable gesture of weariness. "Come in," she said. He stepped inside. "And in God's name couldn't you keep your neck out of this rope? And so you had to come here, did you—to Havana? Upon my soul, Johnnie, my son, you are the biggest fool on two legs."

He moved past her into the court-yard and took his old chair at the table—between the winding stairway and the door—near the orange tree. "Why am I?" he demanded stoutly. She made no reply until she had taken seat in her rocking-chair and puffed several times upon a cigarette. Then through the smoke she said meditatively: "Everybody knows ye are a damned little mambi." Sometimes she spoke with an Irish accent.

He laughed. "I'm no more of a mambi than *you* are, anyhow."

"I'm no mambi. But your name is poison to half the Spaniards in Havana. That you know. And if you were once safe in Cayo Hueso, 'tis nobody but a born fool who would come blunderin' into Havana again. Have ye had your dinner?"

"What have you got?" he asked before committing himself.

She arose and spoke without confidence as she moved toward the cupboard. "There's some codfish salad."

"*What?*" said he.

"Codfish salad."

"*Codfish what?*"

"Codfish salad. Ain't it good enough for ye? Maybe this is Delmonico's—no? Maybe ye never heard that the Yankees have us blockaded, hey? Maybe ye think food can be picked in the streets here now, hey? I'll tell ye one thing, my son, if you stay here long you'll see the want of it and so you had best not throw it over your shoulder."

The spy settled determinedly in his chair and delivered himself his final decision. "That may all be true, but I'm *damned* if I eat codfish salad."

Old Martha was a picture of quaint despair. "You'll not?"

"No!"

"Then," she sighed piously, "may the Lord have mercy on ye, Johnnie, for you'll never do here. 'Tis not the time for you. You're due after the blockade. Will you do me the favour of translating why you won't eat codfish salad, you skinny little insurrecto?"

"Cod-fish salad!" he said with a deep sneer. "Who ever heard of it!"

Outside, on the jumbled pavement of the street, an occasional two-wheel cart passed with deafening thunder, making one think of the overturning of houses. Down from the pale sky over the patio came a heavy odour of Havana itself, a smell of old straw. The wild cries of vendors could be heard at intervals.

"You'll not?"

"No."

"And why not?"

"Cod-fish salad? Not by a blame sight!"

"Well—all right then. You are more of a pig-headed young imbecile than even I thought from seeing you come into Havana here where half the town knows you and the poorest Spaniard would give a gold piece to see you go into Cabanas and forget to come out. Did I tell you, my son Alfred is sick? Yes, poor little fellow, he lies up in the room you used to have. The fever. And did you see Woodham in Key West? Heaven save us, what quick time he made in getting out. I hear Figtree and Button are working in the cable office over there—no? And when is the war going to end? Are the Yankees going to try to take Havana? It will be a hard job, Johnnie? The Spaniards say it is impossible. Everybody is laughing at the Yankees. I hate to go into the street and hear them. Is General Lee going to lead the army? What's become of Springer? I see you've got a new pair of shoes."

In the evening there was a sudden loud knock at the outer door. Martha looked at Johnnie and Johnnie looked at Martha. He was still sitting in the patio, smoking. She took the lamp and set it on a table in the little parlour. This parlour connected the street-door with the patio, and so Johnnie would be protected from the sight of the people who knocked by the broad illuminated tract. Martha moved in pensive fashion upon the latch. "Who's there?" she asked casually.

"The police." There it was, an old melodramatic incident from the stage, from the romances. One could scarce believe it. It had all the dignity of a classic resurrection. "The police!" One sneers at its probability; it is too venerable. But so it happened.

"Who?" said Martha.

"The police!"

"What do you want here?"

"Open the door and we'll tell you."

Martha drew back the ordinary huge bolts of a Havana house and opened the door a trifle. "Tell me what you want and begone quickly," she said, "for my little boy is ill of the fever—"

She could see four or five dim figures, and now one of these suddenly placed a foot well within the door so that she might not close it. "We have come for Johnnie. We must search your house."

"Johnnie? Johnnie? Who is Johnnie?" said Martha in her best manner.

The police inspector grinned with the light upon his face. "Don't you know Señor Johnnie from Pinar del Rio?" he asked.

"Before the war—yes. But now—where is he—he must be in Key West?"

"He is in your house."

"He? In my house? Do me the favour to think that I have some intelligence. Would I be likely to be harbouring a Yankee in these times? You must think I have no more head than an Orden Publico. And I'll not have you search my house, for there is no one here save my son—who is maybe dying of the fever—and the doctor. The doctor is with him because now is the crisis, and any one little thing may kill or cure my boy, and you will do me the favour to consider what may happen if I allow five or six heavy-footed policemen to go tramping all over my house. You may think—"

"Stop it," said the chief police officer at last. He was laughing and weary and angry.

Martha checked her flow of Spanish. "There!" she thought, "I've done my best. He ought to fall in with it." But as the police entered she began on them again. "You will search the house whether I like it or no. Very well; but if anything happens to my boy? It is a nice way of conduct, anyhow—coming into the house of a widow at night and talking much about this Yankee and—"

"For God's sake, señora, hold your tongue. We—"

"Oh, yes, the señora can for God's sake very well hold her tongue, but that wouldn't assist you men into the street where you belong. Take care: if my sick boy suffers from this prowling! No, you'll find nothing in that wardrobe. And do you think he would be under the table? Don't overturn all that linen. Look you, when you go upstairs, tread lightly."

Leaving a man on guard at the street door and another in the patio, the chief policeman and the remainder of his men ascended to the gallery from which opened three sleeping-rooms. They were followed by Martha abjuring them to make no noise. The first room was empty; the second room was empty; as they approached the door of the third room, Martha whispered supplications. "Now, in the name of God, don't disturb my boy." The inspector motioned his men to pause and then he pushed open the door. Only one weak candle was burning in the room and its yellow light fell upon the bed whereon was stretched the figure of a little curly-headed boy in a white nightey. He was asleep, but his face was pink with fever and his lips were murmuring some half-coherent childish nonsense. At the head of the bed stood the motionless figure of a man. His back was to the door, but upon hearing a noise he held a solemn hand. There was an odour of medicine. Out on the balcony, Martha apparently was weeping.

The inspector hesitated for a moment; then he noiselessly entered the room and with his yellow cane prodded under the bed, in the cupboard and behind the window-curtains. Nothing came of it. He shrugged his shoulders and went out to the balcony. He was smiling sheepishly. Evidently he knew that he had been beaten. "Very good, Señora," he said. "You are clever; some day I shall be clever, too."

He shook his finger at her. He was threatening her but he affected to be playful. "Then—beware! Beware!"

Martha replied blandly, "My late husband, El Capitan Señor Don Patricio de Castellon y Valladolid was a cavalier of Spain and if he was alive tonight he would now be cutting the ears from the heads of you and your miserable men who smell frightfully of cognac."

"Por Dios!" muttered the inspector as followed by his band he made his way down the spiral staircase. "It is a tongue! One vast tongue!" At the street-door they made ironical bows; they departed; they were angry men.

Johnnie came down when he heard Martha bolting the door behind the police. She brought back the lamp to the table in the patio and stood beside it, thinking. Johnnie dropped into his old chair. The expression on the spy's face was curious; it pictured glee, anxiety, self-complacency; above all it pictured self-complacency. Martha said nothing; she was still by the lamp, musing.

The long silence was suddenly broken by a tremendous guffaw from Johnnie. "Did you ever see sich a lot of fools!" He leaned his head far back and roared victorious merriment.

Martha was almost dancing in her apprehension. "Hush! Be quiet, you little demon! Hush! Do me the favour to allow them to get to the corner before you bellow like a walrus. Be quiet."

The spy ceased his laughter and spoke in indignation. "Why?" he demanded. "Ain't I got a right to laugh?"

"Not with a noise like a cow fallin' into a cucumber-frame," she answered sharply. "Do me the favour—" Then she seemed overwhelmed with a sense of the general hopelessness of Johnnie's character. She began to wag her head. "Oh, but you are the boy for gettin' yourself into the tiger's cage without even so much as the thought of a pocket-knife in your thick head. You would be a genius of the first water if you only had a little sense. And now you're here, what are you going to do?"

He grinned at her. "I'm goin' to hold an inspection of the land and sea defences of the city of Havana."

Martha's spectacles dropped low on her nose and, looking over the rims of them in grave meditation, she said: "If you can't put up with codfish salad you had better make short work of your inspection of the land and sea defences of the city of Havana. You are likely to starve in the meantime. A man who is particular about his food has come to the wrong town if he is in Havana now."

"No, but—" asked Johnnie seriously. "Haven't you any bread?"

"*Bread!*"

"Well, coffee then? Coffee alone will do."

"*Coffee!*"

Johnnie arose deliberately and took his hat. Martha eyed him. "And where do you think you are goin'?" she asked cuttingly.

Still deliberate, Johnnie moved in the direction of the street-door. "I'm goin' where I can get something to eat."

Martha sank into a chair with a moan which was a finished opinion—almost a definition—of Johnnie's behaviour in life. "And where will you go?" she asked faintly.

"Oh, I don't know," he rejoined. "Some café. Guess I'll go to the Café Aguacate. They feed you well there. I remember—"

"*You* remember? *They* remember! They know you as well as if you were the sign over the door."

"Oh, they won't give me away," said Johnnie with stalwart confidence.

"Gi-give you away? Give you a-way?" stammered Martha.

The spy made no answer but went to the door, unbarred it and passed into the street. Martha caught her breath and ran after him and came face to face with him as he turned to shut the door. "Johnnie, if ye come back, bring a loaf of bread. I'm dyin' for one good honest bite in a slice of bread."

She heard his peculiar derisive laugh as she bolted the door. She returned to her chair in the patio. "Well, there," she said with affection, admiration and contempt. "There he goes! The most hard-headed little ignoramus in twenty nations! What does he care? Nothin'! And why is it? Pure bred-in-the-bone ignorance. Just because he can't stand codfish salad he goes out to a café! A café where they know him as if they had made him!… Well…. I won't see him again, probably…. But if he comes back, I hope he brings some bread. I'm near dead for it."

<h2 style="text-align:center">II</h2>

Johnnie strolled carelessly through dark narrow streets. Near every corner were two Orden Publicos—a kind of soldier-police—quiet in the shadow of some doorway, their Remingtons ready, their eyes shining. Johnnie walked past as if he owned them, and their eyes followed him with a sort of a lazy mechanical suspicion which was militant in none of its moods.

Johnnie was suffering from a desire to be splendidly imprudent. He wanted to make the situation gasp and thrill and tremble. From time to time he tried to conceive the idea of his being caught, but to save his eyes he could not imagine it. Such an event was impossible to his peculiar breed of fatalism which could not have conceded death until he had mouldered seven years.

He arrived at the Café Aguacate and found it much changed. The thick wooden shutters were up to keep light from shining into the street. Inside, there were only a few Spanish officers. Johnnie walked to the private rooms at the rear. He found an empty one and pressed the electric button. When he had passed through the main part of the café no one had noted him. The first to recognise him was the waiter who answered the bell. This worthy man turned to stone before the presence of Johnnie.

"Buenos noche, Francisco," said the spy, enjoying himself. "I have hunger. Bring me bread, butter, eggs and coffee." There was a silence; the waiter did not move; Johnnie smiled casually at him.

The man's throat moved; then like one suddenly re-endowed with life, he bolted from the room. After a long time, he returned with the proprietor of the place. In the wicked eye of the latter there gleamed the light of a plan. He did not respond to Johnnie's genial greeting, but at once proceeded to develop his position. "Johnnie," he said, "bread is very dear in Havana. It is very dear."

"Is it?" said Johnnie looking keenly at the speaker. He understood at once that here was some sort of an attack upon him.

"Yes," answered the proprietor of the Café Aguacate slowly and softly. "It is very dear. I think tonight one small bit of bread will cost you one centene—in advance." A centene approximates five dollars in gold.

The spy's face did not change. He appeared to reflect. "And how much for the butter?" he asked at last.

The proprietor gestured. "There is no butter. Do you think we can have everything with those Yankee pigs sitting out there on their ships?"

"And how much for the coffee?" asked Johnnie musingly.

Again the two men surveyed each other during a period of silence. Then the proprietor said gently, "I think your coffee will cost you about two centenes."

"And the eggs?"

"Eggs are very dear. I think eggs would cost you about three centenes for each one."

The new looked at the old; the North Atlantic looked at the Mediterranean; the wooden nutmeg looked at the olive. Johnnie slowly took six centenes from his pocket and laid them on the table. "That's for bread, coffee, and one egg. I don't think I could eat more than one egg tonight. I'm not so hungry as I was."

The proprietor held a perpendicular finger and tapped the table with it. "Oh, señor," he said politely, "I think you would like two eggs."

Johnnie saw the finger. He understood it. "Ye-e-es," he drawled. "I would like two eggs." He placed three more centenes on the table.

"And a little thing for the waiter? I am sure his services will be excellent, invaluable."

"Ye-e-es, for the waiter." Another centene was laid on the table.

The proprietor bowed and preceded the waiter out of the room. There was a mirror on the wall and, springing to his feet, the spy thrust his face close to the honest glass. "Well, I'm damned!" he ejaculated. "Is this me or is this the Honourable D. Hayseed Whiskers of Kansas? Who am I, anyhow? Five dollars in gold!… Say, these people are clever. They know their business, they do. Bread, coffee and two eggs and not even sure of getting it! Fifty dol— … Never mind; wait until the war is over. Fifty dollars gold!" He sat for a long time; nothing happened. "Eh," he said at last, "that's the game." As the front door of the café closed upon him, he heard the proprietor and one of the waiters burst into derisive laughter.

Martha was waiting for him. "And here ye are, safe back," she said with delight as she let him enter. "And did ye bring the bread? Did ye bring the bread?"

But she saw that he was raging like a lunatic. His face was red and swollen with temper; his eyes shot forth gleams. Presently he stood before her in the patio where the light fell on him. "Don't speak to me," he choked out waving his arms. "Don't speak to me! *Damn*your bread! I went to the Café Aguacate! Oh, yes, I went there! Of course, I did! And do you know what they did to me? No! Oh, they didn't do anything to me at all! Not a thing! Fifty dollars! Ten gold pieces!"

"May the saints guard us," cried Martha. "And what was that for?"

"Because they wanted them more than I did," snarled Johnnie. "Don't you see the game. I go into the Café Aguacate. The owner of the place says to himself, 'Hello! Here's that Yankee what they call Johnnie. He's got no right here in Havana. Guess I'll peach on him to the police. They'll put him in Cabanas as a spy.' Then he does a little more thinking, and finally he says, 'No; I guess I won't peach on him just this minute. First, I'll take a small flyer myself.' So in he comes and looks me right in the eye and says, 'Excuse me but it will be a centene for the bread, a centene for the coffee, and eggs are at three centenes each. Besides there will be a small matter of another gold-piece for the waiter.' I think this over. I think it over hard…. He's clever anyhow…. When this cruel war is over, I'll be after him…. I'm a nice secret agent of the United States government, I am. I come here to be too clever for all the Spanish police, and the first thing I do is get buncoed by a rotten, little thimble-rigger in a café. Oh, yes, I'm all right."

"May the saints guard us!" cried Martha again. "I'm old enough to be your mother, or maybe, your grandmother, and I've seen a lot; but it's many a year since I laid eyes on such a ign'rant and wrong-headed little, red Indian as ye are! Why didn't ye take my advice and stay here in the house with decency and comfort. But he must be all for doing everything high and mighty. The Café Aguacate, if ye please. No plain food for his highness. He turns up his nose at cod-fish sal—"

"Thunder and lightnin', are you going to ram that thing down my throat every two minutes, are you?" And in truth she could see that one more reference to that illustrious viand would break the back of Johnnie's gentle disposition as one breaks a twig on the knee. She shifted with Celtic ease. "Did ye bring the bread?" she asked.

He gazed at her for a moment and suddenly laughed. "I forgot to mention," he informed her impressively, "that they did not take the trouble to give me either the bread, the coffee or the eggs."

"The powers!" cried Martha.

"But it's all right. I stopped at a shop." From his pockets, he brought a small loaf, some kind of German sausage and a flask of Jamaica rum. "About all I could get. And they didn't want to sell them either. They expect presently they can exchange a box of sardines for a grand piano."

"'We are not blockaded by the Yankee warships; we are blockaded by our grocers,'" said Martha, quoting the epidemic Havana saying. But she did not delay long from the little loaf. She cut a slice from it and sat eagerly munching. Johnnie seemed more interested in the Jamaica rum. He looked up from his second glass, however, because he heard a peculiar sound. The old woman was weeping. "Hey, what's this?" he demanded in distress, but with the manner of a man who thinks gruffness is the only thing that will make people feel better and cease. "What's this anyhow? What are you cryin' for?"

"It's the bread," sobbed Martha. "It's the—the br-e-a-ddd."

"Huh? What's the matter with it?"

"It's so good, so g-good." The rain of tears did not prevent her from continuing her unusual report. "Oh, it's so good! This is the first in weeks. I didn't know bread could be so l-like heaven."

"Here," said Johnnie seriously. "Take a little mouthful of this rum. It will do you good."

"No; I only want the bub-bub-bread."

"Well, take the bread, too…. There you are. Now you feel better.…By Jove, when I think of that Café Aguacate man! Fifty dollars gold! And then not to get anything either. Say, after the war, I'm going there, and I'm just going to raze that place to the ground. You see! I'll make him think he can charge ME fifteen dollars for an egg…. And then not give me the egg."

III

Johnnie's subsequent activity in Havana could truthfully be related in part to a certain temporary price of eggs. It is interesting to note how close that famous event got to his eye so that, according to the law of perspective, it was as big as the Capitol of Washington, where centres the spirit of his nation. Around him, he felt a similar and ferocious expression of life which informed him too plainly that if he was caught, he was doomed. Neither the garrison nor the citizens of Havana would tolerate any nonsense in regard to him if he was caught. He would have the steel screw against his neck in short order. And what was the main thing to bear him up against the desire to run away before his work was done? A certain temporary price of eggs! It not only hid the Capitol at Washington; it obscured the dangers in Havana.

Something was learned of the Santa Clara battery, because one morning an old lady in black accompanied by a young man—evidently her son—visited a house which was to rent on the height, in rear of the battery. The portero was too lazy and sleepy to show them over the premises, but he granted them permission to investigate for themselves. They spent most of their time on the flat parapeted roof of the house. At length they came down and said that the place did not suit them. The portero went to sleep again.

Johnnie was never discouraged by the thought that his operations would be of small benefit to the admiral commanding the fleet in adjacent waters, and to the general commanding the army which was not going to attack Havana from the land side. At that time it was all the world's opinion that the army from Tampa would presently appear on the Cuban beach at some convenient point to the east or west of Havana. It turned out, of course, that the condition of the defences of Havana was of not the slightest military importance to the United States since the city was never attacked either by land or sea. But Johnnie could not foresee this. He continued to take his fancy risk, continued his majestic lie, with satisfaction, sometimes with delight, and with pride. And in the psychologic distance was old Martha dancing with fear and shouting: "Oh, Johnnie, me son, what a born fool ye are!"

Sometimes she would address him thus: "And when ye learn all this, how are ye goin' to get out with it?" She was contemptuous.

He would reply, as serious as a Cossack in his fatalism. "Oh, I'll get out some way."

His manœuvres in the vicinity of Regla and Guanabacoa were of a brilliant character. He haunted the sunny long grass in the manner of a jack-rabbit. Sometimes he slept under a palm, dreaming of the American advance fighting its way along the military road to the foot of Spanish defences. Even when awake, he often dreamed it and thought of the all-day crash and hot roar of an assault. Without consulting Washington, he had decided that Havana should be attacked from the south-east. An advance from the west could be contested right up to the bar of the Hotel Inglaterra, but when the first ridge in the south-east would be taken, the whole city with most of its defences would lie under the American siege guns. And the approach to this position was as reasonable as is any approach toward the muzzles of magazine rifles. Johnnie viewed the grassy fields always as a prospective battle-ground, and one can see him lying there, filling the landscape with visions of slow-crawling black infantry columns, galloping batteries of artillery, streaks of faint blue smoke marking the modern firing lines, clouds of dust, a vision of ten thousand tragedies. And his ears heard the noises.

But he was no idle shepherd boy with a head haunted by sombre and glorious fancies. On the contrary, he was much occupied with practical matters. Some months after the close of the war, he asked me: "Were you ever fired at from very near?" I explained some experiences which I had stupidly esteemed as having been rather near. "But did you ever have'm fire a volley on you from close—very close—say, thirty feet?"

Highly scandalised I answered, "No; in that case, I would not be the crowning feature of the Smithsonian Institute."

"Well," he said, "it's a funny effect. You feel as every hair on your head had been snatched out by the roots." Questioned further he said, "I walked right up on a Spanish outpost at daybreak once, and about twenty men let go at me. Thought I was a Cuban army, I suppose."

"What did you do?"

"I run."

"Did they hit you, at all?"

"Naw."

It had been arranged that some light ship of the squadron should rendezvous with him at a certain lonely spot on the coast on a certain day and hour and pick him up. He was to wave something white. His shirt was not white, but he waved it whenever he could see the signal-tops of a war-ship. It was a very tattered banner. After a ten-mile scramble through almost pathless thickets, he had very little on him which respectable men would call a shirt, and the less one says about his trousers the better. This naked savage, then, walked all day up and down a small bit of beach waving a brown rag. At night, he slept in the sand. At full daybreak he began to wave his rag; at noon he was waving his rag; at night-fall he donned his rag and strove to think of it as a shirt. Thus passed two days, and nothing had happened. Then he retraced a twenty-five mile way to the house of old Martha. At first she took him to be one of Havana's terrible beggars and cried, "And do you come here for alms? Look out, that I do not beg of you." The one unchanged thing was his laugh of pure mockery. When she heard it, she dragged him through the door. He paid no heed to her ejaculations but went straight to where he had hidden some gold. As he was untying a bit of string from the neck of a small bag, he said, "How is little Alfred?" "Recovered, thank Heaven." He handed Martha a piece of gold. "Take this and buy what you can on the corner. I'm hungry." Martha departed with expedition. Upon her return, she was beaming. She had foraged a thin chicken, a bunch of radishes and two bottles of wine. Johnnie had finished the radishes and one bottle of wine when the chicken was still a long way from the table. He called stoutly for more, and so Martha passed again into the street with another gold piece. She bought more radishes, more wine and some cheese. They had a grand feast, with Johnnie audibly wondering until a late hour why he had waved his rag in vain.

There was no end to his suspense, no end to his work. He knew everything. He was an animate guide-book. After he knew a thing once, he verified it in several different ways in order to make sure. He fitted himself for a useful career, like a young man in a college—with the difference that the shadow of the garote fell ever upon his way, and that he was occasionally shot at, and that he could not get enough to eat, and that his existence was apparently forgotten, and that he contracted the fever. But—

One cannot think of the terms in which to describe a futility so vast, so colossal. He had built a little boat, and the sea had receded and left him and his boat a thousand miles inland on the top of a mountain. The war-fate had left Havana out of its plan and thus isolated Johnnie and his several pounds of useful information. The war-fate left Havana to become the somewhat indignant victim of a peaceful occupation at the close of the conflict, and Johnnie's data were worth as much as a carpenter's lien on the north pole. He had suffered and laboured for about as complete a bit of absolute nothing as one could invent. If the company which owned the sugar plantation had not generously continued his salary during the war, he would not have been able to pay his expenses on the amount allowed him by the government, which, by the way, was a more complete bit of absolute nothing than one could possibly invent.

## IV

I met Johnnie in Havana in October, 1898. If I remember rightly the U.S.S. *Resolute* and the U.S.S. *Scorpion* were in the harbour, but beyond these two terrible engines of destruction there were not as yet any of the more stern signs of the American success. Many Americans were to be seen in the streets of Havana where they were not in any way molested. Among them was Johnnie in white duck and a straw hat, cool, complacent and with eyes rather more steady than ever. I addressed him upon the subject of his supreme failure, but I could not perturb his philosophy. In reply he simply asked me to dinner. "Come to the Café Aguacate at 7:30 tonight," he said. "I haven't been there in a long time. We shall see if they cook as well as ever." I turned up promptly and found Johnnie in a private room smoking a cigar in the presence of a waiter who was blue in the gills. "I've ordered the dinner," he said cheerfully. "Now I want to see if you won't be surprised how well they can do here in Havana." I was surprised. I was dumfounded. Rarely in the history of the world have two rational men sat down to such a dinner. It must have taxed the ability and endurance of the entire working force of the establishment to provide it. The variety of dishes was of course related to the markets of Havana, but the abundance and general profligacy was related only to Johnnie's imagination. Neither of us had an appetite. Our fancies fled in confusion before this puzzling luxury. I looked at Johnnie as if he were a native of Thibet. I had thought him to be a most simple man, and here I found him revelling in food like a fat, old senator of Rome's decadence. And if the dinner itself put me to open-eyed amazement, the names of the wines finished everything. Apparently Johnny had had but one standard, and that was the cost. If a wine had been very expensive, he had ordered it. I began to think him probably a maniac. At any rate, I was sure that we were both fools. Seeing my fixed stare, he spoke with affected languor: "I wish peacocks' brains and melted pearls were to be had here in Havana. We'd have 'em." Then he grinned. As a mere skirmisher I said, "In New York, we think we dine well; but really this, you know—well—Havana—"

Johnnie waved his hand pompously. "Oh, I know."

Directly after coffee, Johnnie excused himself for a moment and left the room. When he returned he said briskly, "Well, are you ready to go?" As soon as we were in a cab and safely out of hearing of the Café Aguacate, Johnnie lay back and laughed long and joyously.

But I was very serious. "Look here, Johnnie," I said to him solemnly, "when you invite me to dine with you, don't you ever do *that*again. And I'll tell you one thing—when you dine with me you will probably get the ordinary table d'hôte." I was an older man.

"Oh, that's all right," he cried. And then he too grew serious. "Well, as far as I am concerned—as far as I am concerned," he said, "the war is now over."

# WAR MEMORIES

"But to get the real thing!" cried Vernall, the war-correspondent. "It seems impossible! It is because war is neither magnificent nor squalid; it is simply life, and an expression of life can always evade us. We can never tell life, one to another, although sometimes we think we can."

When I climbed aboard the despatch-boat at Key West, the mate told me irritably that as soon as we crossed the bar, we would find ourselves monkey-climbing over heavy seas. It wasn't my fault, but he seemed to insinuate that it was all a result of my incapacity. There were four correspondents in the party. The leader of us came aboard with a huge bunch of bananas, which he hung like a chandelier in the centre of the tiny cabin. We made acquaintance over, around, and under this bunch of bananas, which really occupied the cabin as a soldier occupies a sentry box. But the bunch did not become really aggressive until we were well at sea. Then it began to spar. With the first roll of the ship, it launched its honest pounds at McCurdy and knocked him wildly through the door to the deck-rail, where he hung cursing hysterically. Without a moment's pause, it made for me. I flung myself head-first into my bunk and watched the demon sweep Brownlow into a corner and wedge his knee behind a sea-chest. Kary gave a shrill cry and fled. The bunch of bananas swung to and fro, silent, determined, ferocious, looking for more men. It had cleared a space for itself. My comrades looked in at the door, calling upon me to grab the thing and hold it. I pointed out to them the security and comfort of my position. They were angry. Finally the mate came and lashed the thing so that it could not prowl about the cabin and assault innocent war-correspondents. You see? War! A bunch of bananas rampant because the ship rolled.

In that early period of the war we were forced to continue our dreams. And we were all dreamers, envisioning the seas with death grapples, ship and ship. Even the navy grew cynical. Officers on the bridge lifted their megaphones and told you in resigned voices that they were out of ice, onions, and eggs. At other times, they would shoot quite casually at us with six-pounders. This industry usually progressed in the night, but it sometimes happened in the day. There was never any resentment on our side, although at moments there was some nervousness. They were impressively quick with their lanyards; our means of replying to signals were correspondingly slow. They gave you opportunity to say, "Heaven guard me!" Then they shot. But we recognised the propriety of it. Everything was correct save the war, which lagged and lagged and lagged. It did not play; it was not a gory giant; it was a bunch of bananas swung in the middle of the cabin.

Once we had the honour of being rammed at midnight by the U.S.S. *Machias*. In fact the exceeding industry of the naval commanders of the Cuban blockading fleet caused a certain liveliness to at times penetrate our mediocre existence. We were all greatly entertained over an immediate prospect of being either killed by rapid fire guns, cut in half by the ram or merely drowned, but even our great longing for diversion could not cause us to ever again go near the *Machias* on a dark night. We had sailed from Key West on a mission that had nothing to do with the coast of Cuba, and steaming due east and some thirty-five miles from the Cuban land, we did not think we were liable to an affair with any of the fierce American cruisers. Suddenly a familiar signal of red and white lights flashed like a brooch of jewels on the pall that covered the sea. It was far away and tiny, but we knew all about it. It was the electric question of an American war-ship and it demanded a swift answer in kind. The man behind the gun! What about the man in front of the gun? The war-ship signals vanished and the sea presented nothing but a smoky black stretch lit with the hissing white tops of the flying waves. A thin line of flame swept from a gun.

Thereafter followed one of those silences which had become so peculiarly instructive to the blockade-runner. Somewhere in the darkness we knew that a slate-coloured cruiser, red below the water-line and with a gold scroll on her bows, was flying over the waves toward us, while upon the dark decks the men stood at general quarters in silence about the long thin guns, and it was the law of life and death that we should make true answer in about the twelfth part of a second. Now I shall with regret disclose a certain dreadful secret of the despatch-boat service. Our signals, far from being electric, were two lanterns which we kept in a tub and covered with a tarpaulin. The tub was placed just forward of the pilot-house, and when we were accosted at night it was everybody's duty to scramble wildly for the tub and grab out the lanterns and wave them. It amounted to a slowness of speech. I remember a story of an army sentry who upon hearing a noise in his front one dark night called his usual sharp query. "Halt—who's there? Halt or I'll fire!" And getting no immediate response he fired even as he had said, killing a man with a hair-lip who unfortunately could not arrange his vocal machinery to reply in season. We were something like a boat with a hair-lip. And sometimes it was very trying to the nerves.... The pause was long. Then a voice spoke from the sea through a megaphone. It was faint but clear. "What ship is that?" No one hesitated over his answer in cases of this kind. Everybody was desirous of imparting fullest information. There was another pause. Then out of the darkness flew an American cruiser, silent as death, handled as ferociously as if the devil commanded her. Again the little voice hailed from the bridge. "What ship is that?" Evidently the reply to the first hail had been misunderstood or not heard. This time the voice rang with menace, menace of immediate and certain destruction, and the last word was intoned savagely and strangely across the windy darkness as if the officer would explain that the cruiser was after either fools or the common enemy. The yells in return did not stop her. She was hurling herself forward to ram us amidships, and the people on the little *Three Friends* looked at a tall swooping bow, and it was keener than any knife that has ever been made. As the cruiser lunged every man imagined the gallant and famous but frail *Three Friends* cut into two parts as neatly as if she had been cheese. But there was a sheer and a hard sheer to starboard, and down upon our quarter swung a monstrous thing larger than any ship in the world—the U.S.S. *Machias*. She had a freeboard of about three hundred feet and the top of her funnel was out of sight in the clouds like an Alp. I shouldn't wonder that at the top of that funnel there was a region of perpetual snow. And at a range which swiftly narrowed to nothing every gun in her port-battery swung deliberately into aim. It was closer, more deliciously intimate than a duel across a handkerchief. We all had an opportunity of looking miles down the muzzles of this festive artillery before came the collision. Then the *Machias* reeled her steel shoulder against the wooden side of the *Three Friends* and up went a roar as if a vast shingle roof had fallen. The poor little tug dipped as if she meant to pass under the war-ship, staggered and finally righted, trembling from head to foot. The cries of the splintered timbers ceased. The men on the tug gazed at each other with white faces shining faintly in the darkness. The *Machias* backed away even as the *Three Friends* drew slowly ahead, and again we were alone with the piping of the wind and the slash of the gale-driven water. Later, from some hidden part of the sea, the bullish eye of a searchlight looked at us and the widening white rays bathed us in the glare. There was another hail. "Hello there, *Three Friends*!" "Ay, ay, sir!" "Are you injured?" Our first mate had taken a lantern and was studying the side of the tug, and we held our breath for his answer. I was sure that he was going to say that we were sinking. Surely there could be no other ending to this terrific bloodthirsty assault. But the first mate said, "No, sir." Instantly the glare of the search-light was gone; the *Machias* was gone; the incident was closed.

I was dining once on board the flag-ship, the *New York*, armoured cruiser. It was the junior officers' mess, and when the coffee came, a young ensign went to the piano and began to bang out a popular tune. It was a cheerful scene, and it resembled only a cheerful scene. Suddenly we heard the whistle of the bos'n's mate, and directly above us, it seemed, a voice, hoarse as that of a sea-lion, bellowed a command: "Man the port battery." In a moment the table was vacant; the popular tune ceased in a jangle. On the quarter-deck assembled a group of officers—spectators. The quiet evening sea, lit with faint red lights, went peacefully to the feet of a verdant shore. One could hear the far-away measured tumbling of surf upon a reef. Only this sound pulsed in the air. The great grey cruiser was as still as the earth, the sea, and the sky. Then they let off a four-inch gun directly under my feet. I thought it turned me a back-somersault. That was the effect upon my mind. But it appears I did not move. The shell went carousing off to the Cuban shore, and from the vegetation there spirted a cloud of dust. Some of the officers on the quarter-deck laughed. Through their glasses they had seen a Spanish column of cavalry much agitated by the appearance of this shell among them. As far as I was concerned, there was nothing but the spirt of dust from the side of a long-suffering island. When I returned to my coffee I found that most of the young officers had also returned. Japanese boys were bringing liquors. The piano's clattering of the popular air was often interrupted by the boom of a four-inch gun. A bunch of bananas!

One day, our despatch-boat found the shores of Guantanamo Bay flowing past on either side. It was at nightfall and on the eastward point a small village was burning, and it happened that a fiery light was thrown upon some palm-trees so that it made them into enormous crimson feathers. The water was the colour of blue steel; the Cuban woods were sombre; high shivered the gory feathers. The last boatloads of the marine battalion were pulling for the beach. The marine officers gave me generous hospitality to the camp on the hill. That night there was an alarm and amid a stern calling of orders and a rushing of men, I wandered in search of some other man who had no occupation. It turned out to be the young assistant surgeon, Gibbs. We foregathered in the centre of a square of six companies of marines. There was no firing. We thought it rather comic. The next night there was an alarm; there was some firing; we lay on our bellies; it was no longer comic. On the third night the alarm came early; I went in search of Gibbs, but I soon gave over an active search for the more congenial occupation of lying flat and feeling the hot hiss of the bullets trying to cut my hair. For the moment I was no longer a cynic. I was a child who, in a fit of ignorance, had jumped into the vat of war. I heard somebody dying near me. He was dying hard. Hard. It took him a long time to die. He breathed as all noble machinery breathes when it is making its gallant strife against breaking, breaking. But he was going to break. He was going to break. It seemed to me, this breathing, the noise of a heroic pump which strives to subdue a mud which comes upon it in tons. The darkness was impenetrable. The man was lying in some depression within seven feet of me. Every wave, vibration, of his anguish beat upon my senses. He was long past groaning. There was only the bitter strife for air which pulsed out into the night in a clear penetrating whistle with intervals of terrible silence in which I held my own breath in the common unconscious aspiration to help. I thought this man would never die. I wanted him to die. Ultimately he died. At the moment the adjutant came bustling along erect amid the spitting bullets. I knew him by his voice. "Where's the doctor? There's some wounded men over there. Where's the doctor?" A man answered briskly: "Just died this minute, sir." It was as if he had said: "Just gone around the corner this minute, sir." Despite the horror of this night's business, the man's mind was somehow influenced by the coincidence of the adjutant's calling aloud for the doctor within a few seconds of the doctor's death. It—what shall I say? It interested him, this coincidence.

The day broke by inches, with an obvious and maddening reluctance. From some unfathomable source I procured an opinion that my friend was not dead at all—the wild and quivering darkness had caused me to misinterpret a few shouted words. At length the land brightened in a violent atmosphere, the perfect dawning of a tropic day, and in this light I saw a clump of men near me. At first I thought they were all dead. Then I thought they were all asleep. The truth was that a group of wan-faced, exhausted men had gone to sleep about Gibbs' body so closely and in such abandoned attitudes that one's eye could not pick the living from the dead until one saw that a certain head had beneath it a great dark pool.

In the afternoon a lot of men went bathing, and in the midst of this festivity firing was resumed. It was funny to see the men come scampering out of the water, grab at their rifles and go into action attired in nought but their cartridge-belts. The attack of the Spaniards had interrupted in some degree the services over the graves of Gibbs and some others. I remember Paine came ashore with a bottle of whisky which I took from him violently. My faithful shooting boots began to hurt me, and I went to the beach and poulticed my feet in wet clay, sitting on the little rickety pier near where the corrugated iron cable-station showed how the shells slivered through it. Some marines, desirous of mementoes, were poking with sticks in the smoking ruins of the hamlet. Down in the shallow water crabs were meandering among the weeds, and little fishes moved slowly in schools.

The next day we went shooting. It was exactly like quail shooting. I'll tell you. These guerillas who so cursed our lives had a well some five miles away, and it was the only water supply within about twelve miles of the marine camp. It was decided that it would be correct to go forth and destroy the well. Captain Elliott, of C company, was to take his men with Captain Spicer's company, D, out to the well, beat the enemy away and destroy everything. He was to start at the next daybreak. He asked me if I cared to go, and, of course, I accepted with glee; but all that night I was afraid. Bitterly afraid. The moon was very bright, shedding a magnificent radiance upon the trenches. I watched the men of C and D companies lying so tranquilly—some snoring, confound them—whereas I was certain that I could never sleep with the weight of a coming battle upon my mind, a battle in which the poor life of a war-correspondent might easily be taken by a careless enemy. But if I was frightened I was also very cold. It was a chill night and I wanted a heavy top-coat almost as much as I wanted a certificate of immunity from rifle bullets. These two feelings were of equal importance to my mind. They were twins. Elliott came and flung a tent-fly over Lieutenant Bannon and me as we lay on the ground back of the men. Then I was no longer cold, but I was still afraid, for tent-flies cannot mend a fear. In the morning I wished for some mild attack of disease, something that would incapacitate me for the business of going out gratuitously to be bombarded. But I was in an awkwardly healthy state, and so I must needs smile and look pleased with my prospects. We were to be guided by fifty Cubans, and I gave up all dreams of a postponement when I saw them shambling off in single file through the cactus. We followed presently. "Where you people goin' to?" "Don't know, Jim." "Well, good luck to you, boys." This was the world's lazy inquiry and conventional God-speed. Then the mysterious wilderness swallowed us.

The men were silent because they were ordered to be silent, but whatever faces I could observe were marked with a look of serious meditation. As they trudged slowly in single file they were reflecting upon—what? I don't know. But at length we came to ground more open. The sea appeared on our right, and we saw the gunboat *Dolphin*steaming along in a line parallel to ours. I was as glad to see her as if she had called out my name. The trail wound about the bases of some high bare spurs. If the Spaniards had occupied them I don't see how we could have gone further. But upon them were only the dove-voiced guerilla scouts calling back into the hills the news of our approach. The effect of sound is of course relative. I am sure I have never heard such a horrible sound as the beautiful cooing of the wood-dove when I was certain that it came from the yellow throat of a guerilla. Elliott sent Lieutenant Lucas with his platoon to ascend the hills and cover our advance by the trail. We halted and watched them climb, a long black streak of men in the vivid sunshine of the hillside. We did not know how tall were these hills until we saw Lucas and his men on top, and they were no larger than specks. We marched on until, at last, we heard—it seemed in the sky—the sputter of firing. This devil's dance was begun. The proper strategic movement to cover the crisis seemed to me to be to run away home and swear I had never started on this expedition. But Elliott yelled: "Now, men; straight up this hill." The men charged up against the cactus, and, because I cared for the opinion of others, I found myself tagging along close at Elliott's heels. I don't know how I got up that hill, but I think it was because I was afraid to be left behind. The immediate rear did not look safe. The crowd of strong young marines afforded the only spectacle of provisional security. So I tagged along at Elliott's heels. The hill was as steep as a Swiss roof. From it sprang out great pillars of cactus, and the human instinct was to assist one's self in the ascent by grasping cactus with one's hands. I remember the watch I had to keep upon this human instinct even when the sound of the bullets was attracting my nervous attention. However, the attractive thing to my sense at the time was the fact that every man of the marines was also climbing away like mad. It was one thing for Elliott, Spicer, Neville, Shaw and Bannon; it was another thing for me; but—what in the devil was it to the men? Not the same thing surely. It was perfectly easy for any marine to get overcome by the burning heat and, lying down, bequeath the work and the danger to his comrades. The fine thing about "the men" is that you can't explain them. I mean when you take them collectively. They do a thing, and afterward you find that they have done it because they have done it. However, when Elliott arrived at the top of the ridge, myself and many other men were with him. But there was no battle scene. Off on another ridge we could see Lucas' men and the Cubans peppering away into a valley. The bullets about our ears were really intended to lodge in them. We went over there.

I walked along the firing line and looked at the men. I kept somewhat on what I shall call the *lee* side of the ridge. Why? Because I was afraid of being shot. No other reason. Most of the men as they lay flat, shooting, looked contented, almost happy. They were pleased, these men, at the situation. I don't know. I cannot imagine. But they were pleased, at any rate. I wasn't pleased. I was picturing defeat. I was saying to myself:—"Now if the enemy should suddenly do so-and-so, or so-and-so, why—what would become of me?" During these first few moments I did not see the Spanish position because—I was afraid to look at it. Bullets were hissing and spitting over the crest of the ridge in such showers as to make observation to be a task for a brave man. No, now, look here, why the deuce should I have stuck my head up, eh? Why? Well, at any rate, I didn't until it seemed to be a far less thing than most of the men were doing as if they liked it. Then I saw nothing. At least it was only the bottom of a small valley. In this valley there was a thicket—a big thicket—and this thicket seemed to be crowded with a mysterious class of persons who were evidently trying to kill us. Our enemies? Yes—perhaps—I suppose so. Leave that to the people in the streets at home. They know and cry against the public enemy, but when men go into actual battle not one in a thousand concerns himself with an animus against the men who face him. The great desire is to beat them—beat them whoever they are as a matter, first, of personal safety, second, of personal glory. It is always safest to make the other chap quickly run away. And as he runs away, one feels, as one tries to hit him in the back and knock him sprawling, that he must be a very good and sensible fellow. But these people apparently did not mean to run away. They clung to their thicket and, amid the roar of the firing, one could sometimes hear their wild yells of insult and defiance. They were actually the most obstinate, headstrong, mulish people that you could ever imagine. The *Dolphin* was throwing shells into their immediate vicinity and the fire from the marines and Cubans was very rapid and heavy, but still those incomprehensible mortals remained in their thicket. The scene on the top of the ridge was very wild, but there was only one truly romantic figure. This was a Cuban officer who held in one hand a great glittering machete and in the other a cocked revolver. He posed like a statue of victory. Afterwards he confessed to me that he alone had been responsible for the winning of the fight. But outside of this splendid person it was simply a picture of men at work, men terribly hard at work, red-faced, sweating, gasping toilers. A Cuban negro soldier was shot though the heart and one man took the body on his back and another took it by its feet and trundled away toward the rear looking precisely like a wheelbarrow. A man in C company was shot through the ankle and he sat behind the line nursing his wound. Apparently he was pleased with it. It seemed to suit him. I don't know why. But beside him sat a comrade with a face drawn, solemn and responsible like that of a New England spinster at the bedside of a sick child.

The fight banged away with a roar like a forest fire. Suddenly a marine wriggled out of the firing line and came frantically to me. "Say, young feller, I'll give you five dollars for a drink of whisky." He tried to force into my hand a gold piece. "Go to the devil," said I, deeply scandalised. "Besides, I haven't got any whisky," "No, but look here," he beseeched me. "If I don't get a drink I'll die. And I'll give you five dollars for it. Honest, I will." I finally tried to escape from him by walking away, but he followed at my heels, importuning me with all the exasperating persistence of a professional beggar and trying to force this ghastly gold piece into my hand. I could not shake him off, and amid that clatter of furious fighting I found myself intensely embarrassed, and glancing fearfully this way and that way to make sure that people did not see me, the villain and his gold. In vain I assured him that if I had any whisky I should place it at his disposal. He could not be turned away. I thought of the European expedient in such a crisis—to jump in a cab. But unfortunately— In the meantime I had given up my occupation of tagging at Captain Elliott's heels, because his business required that he should go into places of great danger. But from time to time I was under his attention. Once he turned to me and said: "Mr. Vernall, will you go and satisfy yourself who those people are?" Some men had appeared on a hill about six hundred yards from our left flank. "Yes, sir," cried I with, I assure you, the finest alacrity and cheerfulness, and my tone proved to me that I had inherited histrionic abilities. This tone was of course a black lie, but I went off briskly and was as jaunty as a real soldier while all the time my heart was in my boots and I was cursing the day that saw me landed on the shores of the tragic isle. If the men on the distant hill had been guerillas, my future might have been seriously jeopardised, but I had not gone far toward them when I was able to recognise the uniforms of the marine corps. Whereupon I scampered back to the firing line and with the same alacrity and cheerfulness reported my information. I mention to you that I was afraid, because there were about me that day many men who did not seem to be afraid at all, men with quiet, composed faces who went about this business as if they proceeded from a sense of habit. They were not old soldiers; they were mainly recruits, but many of them betrayed all the emotion and merely the emotion that one sees in the face of a man earnestly at work.

I don't know how long the action lasted. I remember deciding in my own mind that the Spaniards stood forty minutes. This was a mere arbitrary decision based on nothing. But at any rate we finally arrived at the satisfactory moment when the enemy began to run away. I shall never forget how my courage increased. And then began the great bird shooting. From the far side of the thicket arose an easy slope covered with plum-coloured bush. The Spaniards broke in coveys of from six to fifteen men—or birds—and swarmed up this slope. The marines on our ridge then had some fine, open field shooting. No charge could be made because the shells from the *Dolphin* were helping the Spaniards to evacuate the thicket, so the marines had to be content with this extraordinary paraphrase of a kind of sport. It was strangely like the original. The shells from the *Dolphin* were the dogs; dogs who went in and stirred out the game. The marines were suddenly gentlemen in leggings, alive with the sharp instinct which marks the hunter. The Spaniards were the birds. Yes, they were the birds, but I doubt if they would sympathise with my metaphors.

We destroyed their camp, and when the tiled roof of a burning house fell with a crash it was so like the crash of a strong volley of musketry that we all turned with a start, fearing that we would have to fight again on that same day. And this struck me at least as being an impossible thing. They gave us water from the *Dolphin* and we filled our canteens. None of the men were particularly jubilant. They did not altogether appreciate their victory. They were occupied in being glad that the fight was over. I discovered to my amazement that we were on the summit of a hill so high that our released eyes seemed to sweep over half the world. The vast stretch of sea shimmering like fragile blue silk in the breeze, lost itself ultimately in an indefinite pink haze, while in the other direction, ridge after ridge, ridge after ridge, rolled brown and arid into the north. The battle had been fought high in the air—where the rain clouds might have been. That is why everybody's face was the colour of beetroot and men lay on the ground and only swore feebly when the cactus spurs sank into them.

Finally we started for camp. Leaving our wounded, our cactus pincushions, and our heat-prostrated men on board the *Dolphin*. I did not see that the men were elate or even grinning with satisfaction. They seemed only anxious to get to food and rest. And yet it was plain that Elliott and his men had performed a service that would prove invaluable to the security and comfort of the entire battalion. They had driven the guerillas to take a road along which they would have to proceed for fifteen miles before they could get as much water as would wet the point of a pin. And by the destruction of a well at the scene of the fight, Elliott made an arid zone almost twenty miles wide between the enemy and the base camp. In Cuba this is the best of protections. However, a cup of coffee! Time enough to think of a brilliant success after one had had a cup of coffee. The long line plodded wearily through the dusky jungle which was never again to be alive with ambushes.

It was dark when we stumbled into camp, and I was sad with an ungovernable sadness, because I was too tired to remember where I had left my kit. But some of my colleagues were waiting on the beach, and they put me on a despatch-boat to take my news to a Jamaica cable-station. The appearance of this despatch-boat struck me with wonder. It was reminiscent of something with which I had been familiar in early years. I looked with dull surprise at three men of the engine-room force, who sat aft on some bags of coal smoking their pipes and talking as if there had never been any battles fought anywhere. The sudden clang of the gong made me start and listen eagerly, as if I would be asking: "What was that?" The chunking of the screw affected me also, but I seemed to relate it to a former and pleasing experience. One of the correspondents on board immediately began to tell me of the chief engineer, who, he said, was a comic old character. I was taken to see this marvel, which presented itself as a gray-bearded man with an oil can, who had the cynical, malicious, egotistic eye of proclaimed and admired ignorance. I looked dazedly at the venerable impostor. What had he to do with battles—the humming click of the locks, the odour of burnt cotton, the bullets, the firing? My friend told the scoundrel that I was just returned from the afternoon's action. He said: "That so?" And looked at me with a smile, faintly, faintly derisive. You see? I had just come out of my life's most fiery time, and that old devil looked at me with that smile. What colossal conceit. The four-times-damned doddering old head-mechanic of a derelict junk shop. The whole trouble lay in the fact that I had not shouted out with mingled awe and joy as he stood there in his wisdom and experience, with all his ancient saws and home-made epigrams ready to fire.

My friend took me to the cabin. What a squalid hole! My heart sank. The reward after the labour should have been a great airy chamber, a gigantic four-poster, iced melons, grilled birds, wine, and the delighted attendance of my friends. When I had finished my cablegram, I retired to a little shelf of a berth, which reeked of oil, while the blankets had soaked recently with sea-water. The vessel heeled to leeward in spasmodic attempts to hurl me out, and I resisted with the last of my strength. The infamous pettiness of it all! I thought the night would never end. "But never mind," I said to myself at last, "tomorrow in Fort Antonio I shall have a great bath and fine raiment, and I shall dine grandly and there will be lager beer on ice. And there will be attendants to run when I touch a bell, and I shall catch every interested romantist in the town, and spin him the story of the fight at Cusco." We reached Fort Antonio and I fled from the cable office to the hotel. I procured the bath and, as I donned whatever fine raiment I had foraged, I called the boy and pompously told him of a dinner—a real dinner, with furbelows and complications, and yet with a basis of sincerity. He looked at me calf-like for a moment, and then he went away. After a long interval, the manager himself appeared and asked me some questions which led me to see that he thought I had attempted to undermine and disintegrate the intellect of the boy, by the elocution of Arabic incantations. Well, never mind. In the end, the manager of the hotel elicited from me that great cry, that cry which during the war, rang piteously from thousands of throats, that last grand cry of anguish and despair: "*Well, then, in the name of God, can I have a cold bottle of beer?*"

Well, you see to what war brings men? War is death, and a plague of the lack of small things, and toil. Nor did I catch my sentimentalists and pour forth my tale to them, and thrill, appal, and fascinate them. However, they did feel an interest in me, for I heard a lady at the hotel ask: "Who *is* that chap in the very dirty jack-boots?" So you see, that whereas you can be very much frightened upon going into action, you can also be greatly annoyed after you have come out.

Later, I fell into the hands of one of my closest friends, and he mercilessly outlined a scheme for landing to the west of Santiago and getting through the Spanish lines to some place from which we could view the Spanish squadron lying in the harbour. There was rumour that the *Viscaya* had escaped, he said, and it would be very nice to make sure of the truth. So we steamed to a point opposite a Cuban camp which my friend knew, and flung two crop-tailed Jamaica polo ponies into the sea. We followed in a small boat and were met on the beach by a small Cuban detachment who immediately caught our ponies and saddled them for us. I suppose we felt rather god-like. We were almost the first Americans they had seen and they looked at us with eyes of grateful affection. I don't suppose many men have the experience of being looked at with eyes of grateful affection. They guide us to a Cuban camp where, in a little palm-bark hut, a black-faced lieutenant-colonel was lolling in a hammock. I couldn't understand what was said, but at any rate he must have ordered his half-naked orderly to make coffee, for it was done. It was a dark syrup in smoky tin-cups, but it was better than the cold bottle of beer which I did not drink in Jamaica.

The Cuban camp was an expeditious affair of saplings and palm-bark tied with creepers. It could be burned to the ground in fifteen minutes and in ten reduplicated. The soldiers were in appearance an absolutely good-natured set of half-starved ragamuffins. Their breeches hung in threads about their black legs and their shirts were as nothing. They looked like a collection of real tropic savages at whom some philanthropist had flung a bundle of rags and some of the rags had stuck here and there. But their condition was now a habit. I doubt if they knew they were half-naked. Anyhow they didn't care. No more they should; the weather was warm. This lieutenant-colonel gave us an escort of five or six men and we went up into the mountains, lying flat on our Jamaica ponies while they went like rats up and down extraordinary trails. In the evening we reached the camp of a major who commanded the outposts. It was high, high in the hills. The stars were as big as cocoanuts. We lay in borrowed hammocks and watched the firelight gleam blood-red on the trees. I remember an utterly naked negro squatting, crimson, by the fire and cleaning an iron-pot. Some voices were singing an Afric wail of forsaken love and death. And at dawn we were to try to steal through the Spanish lines. I was very, very sorry.

In the cold dawn the situation was the same, but somehow courage seemed to be in the breaking day. I went off with the others quite cheerfully. We came to where the pickets stood behind bulwarks of stone in frameworks of saplings. They were peering across a narrow cloud-steeped gulch at a dull fire marking a Spanish post. There was some palaver and then, with fifteen men, we descended the side of this mountain, going down into the chill blue-and-grey clouds. We had left our horses with the Cuban pickets. We proceeded stealthily, for we were already within range of the Spanish pickets. At the bottom of the cañon it was still night. A brook, a regular salmon-stream, brawled over the rocks. There were grassy banks and most delightful trees. The whole valley was a sylvan fragrance. But—the guide waved his arm and scowled warningly, and in a moment we were off, threading thickets, climbing hills, crawling through fields on our hands and knees, sometimes sweeping like seventeen phantoms across a Spanish road. I was in a dream, but I kept my eye on the guide and halted to listen when he halted to listen and ambled onward when he ambled onward. Sometimes he turned and pantomimed as ably and fiercely as a man being stung by a thousand hornets. Then we knew that the situation was extremely delicate. We were now of course well inside the Spanish lines and we ascended a great hill which overlooked the harbour of Santiago. There, tranquilly at anchor, lay the *Oquendo*, the *Maria Theresa*, the *Christobal Colon*, the *Viscaya*, the *Pluton*, the *Furor*. The bay was white in the sun and the great blacked-hull armoured cruisers were impressive in a dignity massive yet graceful. We did not know that they were all doomed ships, soon to go out to a swift death. My friend drew maps and things while I devoted myself to complete rest, blinking lazily at the Spanish squadron. We did not know that we were the last Americans to view them alive and unhurt and at peace. Then we retraced our way, at the same noiseless canter. I did not understand my condition until I considered that we were well through the Spanish lines and practically out of danger. Then I discovered that I was a dead man. The nervous force having evaporated I was a mere corpse. My limbs were of dough and my spinal cord burned within me as if it were red-hot wire. But just at this time we were discovered by a Spanish patrol, and I ascertained that I was not dead at all. We ultimately reached the foot of the mother-mountain on whose shoulders were the Cuban pickets, and here I was so sure of safety that I could not resist the temptation to die again. I think I passed into eleven distinct stupors during the ascent of that mountain while the escort stood leaning on their Remingtons. We had done twenty-five miles at a sort of a man-gallop, never once using a beaten track, but always going promiscuously through the jungle and over the rocks. And many of the miles stood straight on end so that it was as hard to come down as it was to go up. But during my stupors, the escort *stood*, mind you, and chatted in low voices. For all the signs they showed, we might have been starting. And they had had nothing to eat but mangoes for over eight days. Previous to the eight days they had been living on mangoes and the carcase of a small lean pony. They were, in fact, of the stuff of Fenimore Cooper's Indians, only they made no preposterous orations. At the major's camp, my friend and I agreed that if our worthy escort would send down a representative with us to the coast, we would send back to them whatever we could spare from the stores of our despatch-boat. With one voice the escort answered that they themselves would go the additional four leagues, as in these starving times they did not care to trust a representative, thank you. "They can't do it; they'll peg out; there must be a limit," I said. "No," answered my friend. "They're all right; they'd run three times around the whole island for a mouthful of beer." So we saddled up and put off with our fifteen Cuban infantrymen wagging along tirelessly behind us. Sometimes, at the foot of a precipitous hill, a man asked permission to cling to my horse's tail, and then the Jamaica pony would snake him to the summit so swiftly that only his toes seemed to touch the rocks. And for this assistance the man was grateful. When we crowned the last great ridge we saw our squadron to the eastward spread in its patient semicircular about the mouth of the harbour. But as we wound towards the beach we saw a more dramatic thing—our own despatch-boat leaving the rendezvous and putting off to sea. Evidently we were late. Behind me were fifteen stomachs, empty. It was a frightful situation. My friend and I charged for the beach and those fifteen fools began to *run*.

It was no use. The despatch-boat went gaily away trailing black smoke behind her. We turned in distress wondering what we could say to that abused escort. If they massacred us, I felt that it would be merely a virtuous reply to fate and they should in no ways be blamed. There are some things which a man's feelings will not allow him to endure after a diet of mangoes and pony. However, we perceived to our amazement that they were not indignant at all. They simply smiled and made a gesture which expressed an habitual pessimism. It was a philosophy which denied the existence of everything but mangoes and pony. It was the Americans who refused to be comforted. I made a deep vow with myself that I would come as soon as possible and play a regular Santa Claus to that splendid escort. But—we put to sea in a dug-out with two black boys. The escort waved us a hearty good-bye from the shore and I never saw them again. I hope they are all on the police-force in the new Santiago.

In time we were rescued from the dug-out by our despatch-boat, and we relieved our feelings by over-rewarding the two black boys. In fact they reaped a harvest because of our emotion over our failure to fill the gallant stomachs of the escort. They were two rascals. We steamed to the flagship and were given permission to board her. Admiral Sampson is to me the most interesting personality of the war. I would not know how to sketch him for you even if I could pretend to sufficient material. Anyhow, imagine, first of all, a marble block of impassivity out of which is carved the figure of an old man. Endow this with life, and you've just begun. Then you must discard all your pictures of bluff, red-faced old gentlemen who roar against the gale, andunderstand that the quiet old man is a sailor and an admiral. This will be difficult; if I told you he was anything else it would be easy. He resembles other types; it is his distinction not to resemble the preconceived type of his standing. When first I met him I was impressed that he was immensely bored by the war and with the command of the North Atlantic Squadron. I perceived a manner where I thought I perceived a mood, a point of view. Later, he seemed so indifferent to small things which bore upon large things that I bowed to his apathy as a thing unprecedented, marvellous. Still I mistook a manner for a mood. Still I could not understand that this was the way of the man. I am not to blame, for my communication was slight and depended upon sufferance—upon, in fact, the traditional courtesy of the navy. But finally I saw that it was all manner, that hidden in his indifferent, even apathetic, manner, there was the alert, sure, fine mind of the best sea-captain that America has produced since—since Farragut? I don't know. I think—since Hull.

Men follow heartily when they are well led. They balk at trifles when a block-head cries go on. For my part, an impressive thing of the war is the absolute devotion to Admiral Sampson's person—no, to his judgment and wisdom—which was paid by his ship-commanders—Evans of the*Iowa*, Taylor of the *Oregon*, Higginson of the*Massachusetts*, Phillips of the *Texas*, and all the other captains—barring one. Once, afterward, they called upon him to avenge himself upon a rival—they were there and they would have to say—but he said no-o-o, he guessed it—wouldn't do—any—g-o-oo-o-d—to the—service.

Men feared him, but he never made threats; men tumbled heels over head to obey him, but he never gave a sharp order; men loved him, but he said no word, kindly or unkindly; men cheered for him and he said: "Who are they yelling for?" Men behaved badly to him and he said nothing. Men thought of glory and he considered the management of ships. All without a sound. A noiseless campaign—on his part. No bunting, no arches, no fireworks; nothing but the perfect management of a big fleet. That is a record for you. No trumpets, no cheers of the populace. Just plain, pure, unsauced accomplishment. But ultimately he will reap his reward in—in what? In text-books on sea-campaigns. No more. The people choose their own and they choose the kind they like. Who has a better right? Anyhow he is a great man. And when you are once started you can continue to be a great man without the help of bouquets and banquets. He don't need them—bless your heart.

The flag-ship's battle-hatches were down, and between decks it was insufferable despite the electric fans. I made my way somewhat forwards, past the smart orderly, past the companion, on to the den of the junior mess. Even there they were playing cards in somebody's cabin. "Hello, old man. Been ashore? How'd it look? It's your deal, Chick." There was nothing but steamy wet heat and the decent suppression of the consequent ill-tempers. The junior officers' quarters were no more comfortable than the admiral's cabin. I had expected it to be so because of my remembrance of their gay spirits. But they were not gay. They were sweltering. Hello, old man, had I been ashore? I fled to the deck, where other officers not on duty were smoking quiet cigars. The hospitality of the officers of the flag-ship is another charming memory of the war.

I rolled into my berth on the despatch-boat that night feeling a perfect wonder of the day. Was the figure that leaned over the card-game on the flag-ship, the figure with a whisky and soda in its hand and a cigar in its teeth—was it identical with the figure scrambling, afraid of its life, through Cuban jungle? Was it the figure of the situation of the fifteen pathetic hungry men? It was the same and it went to sleep, hard sleep. I don't know where we voyaged. I think it was Jamaica. But, at any rate, upon the morning of our return to the Cuban coast, we found the sea alive with transports—United States transports from Tampa, containing the Fifth Army Corps under Major-General Shafter. The rigging and the decks of these ships were black with men and everybody wanted to land first. I landed, ultimately, and immediately began to look for an acquaintance. The boats were banged by the waves against a little flimsy dock. I fell ashore somehow, but I did not at once find an acquaintance. I talked to a private in the 2d Massachusetts Volunteers who told me that he was going to write war correspondence for a Boston newspaper. This statement did not surprise me.

There was a straggly village, but I followed the troops who at this time seemed to be moving out by companies. I found three other correspondents and it was luncheon time. Somebody had two bottles of Bass, but it was so warm that it squirted out in foam. There was no firing; no noise of any kind. An old shed was full of soldiers loafing pleasantly in the shade. It was a hot, dusty, sleepy afternoon; bees hummed. We saw Major-General Lawton standing with his staff under a tree. He was smiling as if he would say: "Well, this will be better than chasing Apaches." His division had the advance, and so he had the right to be happy. A tall man with a grey moustache, light but very strong, an ideal cavalryman. He appealed to one all the more because of the vague rumours that his superiors—some of them—were going to take mighty good care that he shouldn't get much to do. It was rather sickening to hear such talk, but later we knew that most of it must have been mere lies.

Down by the landing-place a band of correspondents were making a sort of permanent camp. They worked like Trojans, carrying wall-tents, cots, and boxes of provisions. They asked me to join them, but I looked shrewdly at the sweat on their faces and backed away. The next day the army left this permanent camp eight miles to the rear. The day became tedious. I was glad when evening came. I sat by a camp-fire and listened to a soldier of the 8th Infantry who told me that he was the first enlisted man to land. I lay pretending to appreciate him, but in fact I considered him a great shameless liar. Less than a month ago, I learned that every word he said was gospel truth. I was much surprised. We went for breakfast to the camp of the 20th Infantry, where Captain Greene and his subaltern, Exton, gave us tomatoes stewed with hard bread and coffee. Later, I discovered Greene and Exton down at the beach good-naturedly dodging the waves which seemed to be trying to prevent them from washing the breakfast dishes. I felt tremendously ashamed because my cup and my plate were there, you know, and— Fate provides some men greased opportunities for making dizzy jackasses of themselves and I fell a victim to my flurry on this occasion. I was a blockhead. I walked away blushing. What? The battles? Yes, I saw something of all of them. I made up my mind that the next time I met Greene and Exton I'd say: "Look here; why didn't you tell me you had to wash your own dishes that morning so that I could have helped? I felt beastly when I saw you scrubbing there. And me walking around idly." But I never saw Captain Greene again. I think he is in the Philippines now fighting the Tagals. The next time I saw Exton—what? Yes, La Guasimas. That was the "rough rider fight." However, the next time I saw Exton I—what do you think? I forgot to speak about it. But if ever I meet Greene or Exton again—even if it should be twenty years—I am going to say, first thing: "Why—" What? Yes. Roosevelt's regiment and the First and Tenth Regular Cavalry. I'll say, first thing: "Say, why didn't you tell me you had to wash your own dishes, that morning, so that I could have helped?" My stupidity will be on my conscience until I die, if, before that, I do not meet either Greene or Exton. Oh, yes, you are howling for blood, but I tell you it is more emphatic that I lost my tooth-brush. Did I tell you that? Well, I lost it, you see, and I thought of it for ten hours at a stretch. Oh, yes—he? He was shot through the heart. But, look here, I contend that the French cable company buncoed us throughout the war. What? Him? My tooth-brush I never found, but he died of his wound in time. Most of the regular soldiers carried their tooth-brushes stuck in the bands of their hats. It made a quaint military decoration. I have had a line of a thousand men pass me in the jungle and not a hat lacking the simple emblem.

The first of July? All right. My Jamaica polo-pony was not present. He was still in the hills to the westward of Santiago, but the Cubans had promised to fetch him to me. But my kit was easy to carry. It had nothing superfluous in it but a pair of spurs which made me indignant every time I looked at them. Oh, but I must tell you about a man I met directly after the La Guasimas fight. Edward Marshall, a correspondent whom I had known with a degree of intimacy for seven years, was terribly hit in that fight and asked me if I would not go to Siboney—the base—and convey the news to his colleagues of the *New York Journal* and round up some assistance. I went to Siboney, and there was not a *Journal* man to be seen, although usually you judged from appearances that the *Journal* staff was about as large as the army. Presently I met two correspondents, strangers to me, but I questioned them, saying that Marshall was badly shot and wished for such succour as *Journal* men could bring from their despatch-boat. And one of these correspondents replied. He is the man I wanted to describe. I love him as a brother. He said: "Marshall? Marshall? Why, Marshall isn't in Cuba at all. He left for New York just before the expedition sailed from Tampa." I said: "Beg pardon, but I remarked that Marshall was shot in the fight this morning, and have you seen any *Journal* people?" After a pause, he said: "I am sure Marshall is not down here at all. He's in New York." I said: "Pardon me, but I remarked that Marshall was shot in the fight this morning, and have you seen any *Journal* people?" He said: "No; now look here, you must have gotten two chaps mixed somehow. Marshall isn't in Cuba at all. How could he be shot?" I said: "Pardon me, but I remarked that Marshall was shot in the fight this morning, and have you seen any *Journal* people?" He said: "But it can't really be Marshall, you know, for the simple reason that he's not down here." I clasped my hands to my temples, gave one piercing cry to heaven and fled from his presence. I couldn't go on with him. He excelled me at all points. I have faced death by bullets, fire, water, and disease, but to die thus—to wilfully batter myself against the ironclad opinion of this mummy—no, no, not that. In the meantime, it was admitted that a correspondent was shot, be his name Marshall, Bismarck, or Louis XIV. Now, supposing the name of this wounded correspondent had been Bishop Potter? Or Jane Austen? Or Bernhardt? Or Henri Georges Stephane Adolphe Opper de Blowitz? What effect—never mind.

We will proceed to July 1st. On that morning I marched with my kit—having everything essential save a tooth-brush—the entire army put me to shame, since there must have been at least fifteen thousand tooth-brushes in the invading force—I marched with my kit on the road to Santiago. It was a fine morning and everybody— the doomed and the immunes—how could we tell one from the other—everybody was in the highest spirits. We were enveloped in forest, but we could hear, from ahead, everybody peppering away at everybody. It was like the roll of many drums. This was Lawton over at El Caney. I reflected with complacency that Lawton's division did not concern me in a professional way. That was the affair of another man. My business was with Kent's division and Wheeler's division. We came to El Poso—a hill at nice artillery range from the Spanish defences. Here Grimes's battery was shooting a duel with one of the enemy's batteries. Scovel had established a little camp in the rear of the guns and a servant had made coffee. I invited Whigham to have coffee, and the servant added some hard biscuit and tinned tongue. I noted that Whigham was staring fixedly over my shoulder, and that he waved away the tinned tongue with some bitterness. It was a horse, a dead horse. Then a mule, which had been shot through the nose, wandered up and looked at Whigham. We ran away.

On top of the hill one had a fine view of the Spanish lines. We stared across almost a mile of jungle to ash-coloured trenches on the military crest of the ridge. A goodly distance back of this position were white buildings, all flying great red-cross flags. The jungle beneath us rattled with firing and the Spanish trenches crackled out regular volleys, but all this time there was nothing to indicate a tangible enemy. In truth, there was a man in a Panama hat strolling to and fro behind one of the Spanish trenches, gesticulating at times with a walking stick. A man in a Panama hat, walking with a stick! That was the strangest sight of my life—that symbol, that quaint figure of Mars. The battle, the thunderous row, was his possession. He was the master. He mystified us all with his infernal Panama hat and his wretched walking-stick. From near his feet came volleys and from near his side came roaring shells, but he stood there alone, visible, the one tangible thing. He was a Colossus, and he was half as high as a pin, this being. Always somebody would be saying: "Who *can* that fellow be?"

Later, the American guns shelled the trenches and a blockhouse near them, and Mars had vanished. It could not have been death. One cannot kill Mars. But there was one other figure, which arose to symbolic dignity. The balloon of our signal corps had swung over the tops of the jungle's trees toward the Spanish trenches. Whereat the balloon and the man in the Panama hat and with a walking stick— whereat these two waged tremendous battle.

Suddenly the conflict became a human thing. A little group of blue figures appeared on the green of the terrible hillside. It was some of our infantry. The attaché of a great empire was at my shoulder, and he turned to me and spoke with incredulity and scorn. "Why, they're trying to take the position," he cried, and I admitted meekly that I thought they were. "But they can't do it, you know," he protested vehemently. "It's impossible." And—good fellow that he was—he began to grieve and wail over a useless sacrifice of gallant men. "It's plucky, you know! By Gawd, it's plucky! But *they can't do it*!" He was profoundly moved; his voice was quite broken. "It will simply be a hell of a slaughter with no good coming out of it."

The trail was already crowded with stretcher-bearers and with wounded men who could walk. One had to stem a tide of mute agony. But I don't know that it was mute agony. I only know that it was mute. It was something in which the silence or, more likely, the reticence was an appalling and inexplicable fact. One's senses seemed to demand that these men should cry out. But you could really find wounded men who exhibited all the signs of a pleased and contented mood. When thinking of it now it seems strange beyond words. But at the time—I don't know—it did not attract one's wonder. A man with a hole in his arm or his shoulder, or even in the leg below the knee, was often whimsical, comic. "Well, this ain't exactly what I enlisted for, boys. If I'd been told about this in Tampa, I'd have resigned from th' army. Oh, yes, you can get the same thing if you keep on going. But I think the Spaniards may run out of ammunition in the course of a week or ten days." Then suddenly one would be confronted by the awful majesty of a man shot in the face. Particularly I remember one. He had a great dragoon moustache, and the blood streamed down his face to meet this moustache even as a torrent goes to meet the jammed log, and then swarmed out to the tips and fell in big slow drops. He looked steadily into my eyes; I was ashamed to return his glance. You understand? It is very curious—all that.

The two lines of battle were royally whacking away at each other, and there was no rest or peace in all that region. The modern bullet is a far-flying bird. It rakes the air with its hot spitting song at distances which, as a usual thing, place the whole landscape in the danger-zone. There was no direction from which they did not come. A chart of their courses over one's head would have resembled a spider's web. My friend Jimmie, the photographer, mounted to the firing line with me and we gallivanted as much as we dared. The "sense of the meeting" was curious. Most of the men seemed to have no idea of a grand historic performance, but they were grimly satisfied with themselves. "Well, begawd, we done it." Then they wanted to know about other parts of the line. "How are things looking, old man? Everything all right?" "Yes, everything is all right if you can hold this ridge." "Aw, hell," said the men, "we'll hold the ridge. Don't you worry about that, son."

It was Jimmie's first action, and, as we cautiously were making our way to the right of our lines, the crash of the Spanish fire became uproarious, and the air simply whistled. I heard a quavering voice near my shoulder, and, turning, I beheld Jimmie—Jimmie—with a face bloodless, white as paper. He looked at me with eyes opened extremely wide. "Say," he said, "this is pretty hot, ain't it?" I was delighted. I knew exactly what he meant. He wanted to have the situation defined. If I had told him that this was the occasion of some mere idle desultory firing and recommended that he wait until the real battle began, I think he would have gone in a bee-line for the rear. But I told him the truth. "Yes, Jimmie," I replied earnestly. "You can take it from me that this is patent, double-extra-what-for." And immediately he nodded. "All right." If this was a big action, then he was willing to pay in his fright as a rational price for the privilege of being present. But if this was only a penny affray, he considered the price exorbitant, and he would go away. He accepted my assurance with simple faith, and deported himself with kindly dignity as one moving amid great things. His face was still as pale as paper, but that counted for nothing. The main point was his perfect willingness to be frightened for reasons. I wonder where is Jimmie? I lent him the Jamaica polo-pony one day and it ran away with him and flung him off in the middle of a ford. He appeared to me afterward and made bitter speech concerning this horse which I had assured him was a gentle and pious animal. Then I never saw Jimmie again.

Then came the night of the first of July. A group of correspondents limped back to El Poso. It had been a day so long that the morning seemed as remote as a morning in the previous year. But I have forgotten to tell you about Reuben McNab. Many years ago, I went to school at a place called Claverack, in New York State, where there was a semi-military institution. Contemporaneous with me, as a student, was Reuben McNab, a long, lank boy, freckled, sandy-haired—an extraordinary boy in no way, and yet, I wager, a boy clearly marked in every recollection. Perhaps there is a good deal in that name. Reuben McNab. You can't fling that name carelessly over your shoulder and lose it. It follows you like the haunting memory of a sin. At any rate, Reuben McNab was identified intimately in my thought with the sunny irresponsible days at Claverack, when all the earth was a green field and all the sky was a rainless blue. Then I looked down into a miserable huddle at Bloody Bend, a huddle of hurt men, dying men, dead men. And there I saw Reuben McNab, a corporal in the 71st New York Volunteers, and with a hole through his lung. Also, several holes through his clothing. "Well, they got me," he said in greeting. Usually they said that. There were no long speeches. "Well, they got me." That was sufficient. The duty of the upright, unhurt, man is then difficult. I doubt if many of us learned how to speak to our own wounded. In the first place, one had to play that the wound was nothing; oh, a mere nothing; a casual interference with movement, perhaps, but nothing more; oh, really nothing more. In the second place, one had to show a comrade's appreciation of this sad plight. As a result I think most of us bungled and stammered in the presence of our wounded friends. That's curious, eh? "Well, they got me," said Reuben McNab. I had looked upon five hundred wounded men with stolidity, or with a conscious indifference which filled me with amazement. But the apparition of Reuben McNab, the schoolmate, lying there in the mud, with a hole through his lung, awed me into stutterings, set me trembling with a sense of terrible intimacy with this war which theretofore I could have believed was a dream—almost. Twenty shot men rolled their eyes and looked at me. Only one man paid no heed. He was dying; he had no time. The bullets hummed low over them all. Death, having already struck, still insisted upon raising a venomous crest. "If you're goin' by the hospital, step in and see me," said Reuben McNab. That was all.

At the correspondents' camp, at El Poso, there was hot coffee. It was very good. I have a vague sense of being very selfish over my blanket and rubber coat. I have a vague sense of spasmodic firing during my sleep; it rained, and then I awoke to hear that steady drumming of an infantry fire—something which was never to cease, it seemed. They were at it again. The trail from El Poso to the positions along San Juan ridge had become an exciting thoroughfare. Shots from large-bore rifles dropped in from almost every side. At this time the safest place was the extreme front. I remember in particular the one outcry I heard. A private in the 71st, without his rifle, had gone to a stream for some water, and was returning, being but a little in rear of me. Suddenly I heard this cry—"Oh, my God, come quick"—and I was conscious then to having heard the hateful zip of a close shot. He lay on the ground, wriggling. He was hit in the hip. Two men came quickly. Presently everybody seemed to be getting knocked down. They went over like men of wet felt, quietly, calmly, with no more complaint than so many automatons. It was only that lad—"Oh, my God, come quick." Otherwise, men seemed to consider that their hurts were not worthy of particular attention. A number of people got killed very courteously, tacitly absolving the rest of us from any care in the matter. A man fell; he turned blue; his face took on an expression of deep sorrow; and then his immediate friends worried about him, if he had friends. This was July 1. I crave the permission to leap back again to that date.

On the morning of July 2, I sat on San Juan hill and watched Lawton's division come up. I was absolutely sheltered, but still where I could look into the faces of men who were trotting up under fire. There wasn't a high heroic face among them. They were all men intent on business. That was all. It may seem to you that I am trying to make everything a squalor. That would be wrong. I feel that things were often sublime. But they were *differently* sublime. They were not of our shallow and preposterous fictions. They stood out in a simple, majestic commonplace. It was the behaviour of men on the street. It was the behaviour of men. In one way, each man was just pegging along at the heels of the man before him, who was pegging along at the heels of still another man, who was pegging along at the heels of still another man who— It was that in the flat and obvious way. In another way it was pageantry, the pageantry of the accomplishment of naked duty. One cannot speak of it—the spectacle of the common man serenely doing his work, his appointed work. It is the one thing in the universe which makes one fling expression to the winds and be satisfied to simply feel. Thus they moved at San Juan—the soldiers of the United States Regular Army. One pays them the tribute of the toast of silence.

Lying near one of the enemy's trenches was a red-headed Spanish corpse. I wonder how many hundreds were cognisant of this red-headed Spanish corpse? It arose to the dignity of a landmark. There were many corpses but only one with a red head. This red-head. He was always there. Each time I approached that part of the field I prayed that I might find that he had been buried. But he was always there—red-headed. His strong simple countenance was a malignant sneer at the system which was forever killing the credulous peasants in a sort of black night of politics, where the peasants merely followed whatever somebody had told them was lofty and good. But, nevertheless, the red-headed Spaniard was dead. He was irrevocably dead. And to what purpose? The honour of Spain? Surely the honour of Spain could have existed without the violent death of this poor red-headed peasant? Ah well, he was buried when the heavy firing ceased and men had time for such small things as funerals. The trench was turned over on top of him. It was a fine, honourable, soldierly fate—to be buried in a trench, the trench of the fight and the death. Sleep well, red-headed peasant. You came to another hemisphere to fight because—because you were told to, I suppose. Well, there you are, buried in your trench on San Juan hill. That is the end of it, your life has been taken—that is a flat, frank fact. And foreigners buried you expeditiously while speaking a strange tongue. Sleep well, red-headed mystery.

On the day before the destruction of Cervera's fleet, I steamed past our own squadron, doggedly lying in its usual semicircle, every nose pointing at the mouth of the harbour. I went to Jamaica, and on the placid evening of the next day I was again steaming past our own squadron, doggedly lying in its usual semicircle, every nose pointing at the mouth of the harbour. A megaphone-hail from the bridge of one of the yacht-gunboats came casually over the water. "Hello! hear the news?" "No; what was it?" "The Spanish fleet came out this morning." "Oh, of course, it did." "Honest, I mean." "Yes, I know; well, where are they now?" "Sunk." Was there ever such a preposterous statement? I was humiliated that my friend, the lieutenant on the yacht-gunboat, should have measured me as one likely to swallow this bad joke.

But it was all true; every word. I glanced back at our squadron, lying in its usual semicircle, every nose pointing at the mouth of the harbour. It would have been absurd to think that anything had happened. The squadron hadn't changed a button. There it sat without even a smile on the face of the tiger. And it had eaten four armoured cruisers and two torpedo-boat-destroyers while my back was turned for a moment. Courteously, but clearly, we announced across the waters that until despatch-boats came to be manned from the ranks of the celebrated horse-marines, the lieutenant's statement would probably remain unappreciated. He made a gesture, abandoning us to our scepticism. It infuriates an honourable and serious man to be taken for a liar or a joker at a time when he is supremely honourable and serious. However, when we went ashore, we found Siboney ringing with the news. It was true, then; that mishandled collection of sick ships had come out and taken the deadly thrashing which was rightfully the due of—I don't know—somebody in Spain—or perhaps nobody anywhere. One likes to wallop incapacity, but one has mingled emotions over the incapacity which is not so much personal as it is the development of centuries. This kind of incapacity cannot be centralised. You cannot hit the head which contains it all. This is the idea, I imagine, which moved the officers and men of our fleet. Almost immediately they began to speak of the Spanish Admiral as "poor old boy" with a lucid suggestion in their tones that his fate appealed to them as being undue hard, undue cruel. And yet the Spanish guns hit nothing. If a man shoots, he should hit something occasionally, and men say that from the time the Spanish ships broke clear of the harbour entrance until they were one by one overpowered, they were each a band of flame. Well, one can only mumble out that when a man shoots he should be required to hit something occasionally.

In truth, the greatest fact of the whole campaign on land and sea seems to be the fact that the Spaniards could only hit by chance, by a fluke. If he had been an able marksman, no man of our two unsupported divisions would have set foot on San Juan hill on July 1. They should have been blown to smithereens. The Spaniards had no immediate lack of ammunition, for they fired enough to kill the population of four big cities. I admit neither Velasquez nor Cervantes into this discussion, although they have appeared by authority as reasons for something which I do not clearly understand. Well, anyhow they couldn't hit anything. Velasquez? Yes. Cervantes? Yes. But the Spanish troops seemed only to try to make a very rapid fire. Thus we lost many men. We lost them because of the simple fury of the fire; never because the fire was well-directed, intelligent. But the Americans were called upon to be whipped because of Cervantes and Velasquez. It was impossible.

Out on the slopes of San Juan the dog-tents shone white. Some kind of negotiations were going forward, and men sat on their trousers and waited. It was all rather a blur of talks with officers, and a craving for good food and good water. Once Leighton and I decided to ride over to El Caney, into which town the civilian refugees from Santiago were pouring. The road from the beleaguered city to the out-lying village was a spectacle to make one moan. There were delicate gentle families on foot, the silly French boots of the girls twisting and turning in a sort of absolute paper futility; there were sons and grandsons carrying the venerable patriarch in his own armchair; there were exhausted mothers with babes who wailed; there were young dandies with their toilettes in decay; there were puzzled, guideless women who didn't know what had happened. The first sentence one heard was the murmurous "What a damn shame." We saw a godless young trooper of the Second Cavalry sharply halt a waggon. "Hold on a minute. You must carry this woman. She's fainted twice already." The virtuous driver of the U.S. Army waggon mildly answered: "But I'm full-up now." "You can make room for her," said the private of the Second Cavalry. A young, young man with a straight mouth. It was merely a plain bit of nothing—at—all but, thank God, thank God, he seemed to have not the slightest sense of excellence. He said: "If you've got any man in there who can walk at all, you put him out and let this woman get in." "But," answered the teamster, "I'm filled up with a lot of cripples and grandmothers." Thereupon they discussed the point fairly, and ultimately the woman was lifted into the waggon.

The vivid thing was the fact that these people did not visibly suffer. Somehow they were numb. There was not a tear. There was rarely a countenance which was not wondrously casual. There was no sign of fatalistic theory. It was simply that what was happening today had happened yesterday, as near as one could judge. I could fancy that these people had been thrown out of their homes every day. It was utterly, utterly casual. And they accepted the ministrations of our men in the same fashion. Everything was a matter of course. I had a filled canteen. I was frightfully conscious of this fact because a filled canteen was a pearl of price; it was a great thing. It was an enormous accident which led one to offer praises that he was luckier than ten thousand better men.

As Leighton and I rode along, we came to a tree under which a refugee family had halted. They were a man, his wife, two handsome daughters and a pimply son. It was plain that they were superior people, because the girls had dressed for the exodus and wore corsets which captivated their forms with a steel-ribbed vehemence only proper for wear on a sun-blistered road to a distant town. They asked us for water. Water was the gold of the moment. Leighton was almost maudlin in his generosity. I remember being angry with him. He lavished upon them his whole canteen and he received in return not even a glance of—what? Acknowledgment? No, they didn't even admit anything. Leighton wasn't a human being; he was some sort of a mountain spring. They accepted him on a basis of pure natural phenomena. His canteen was purely an occurrence. In the meantime the pimple-faced approached me. He asked for water and held out a pint cup. My response was immediate. I tilted my canteen and poured into his cup almost a pint of my treasure. He glanced into the cup and apparently he beheld there some innocent sediment for which he alone or his people were responsible. In the American camps the men were accustomed to a sediment. Well, he glanced at my poor cupful and then negligently poured it out on the ground and held up his cup for more. I gave him more; I gave him his cup full again, but there was something within me which made me swear him out completely. But he didn't understand a word. Afterward I watched if they were capable of being moved to help on their less able fellows on this miserable journey. Not they! Nor yet anybody else. Nobody cared for anybody save my young friend of the Second Cavalry, who rode seriously to and fro doing his best for people, who took him as a result of a strange upheaval.

The fight at El Caney had been furious. General Vera del Rey with somewhat less than 1000 men—the Spanish accounts say 520—had there made such a stand that only about 80 battered soldiers ever emerged from it. The attack cost Lawton about 400 men. The magazine rifle! But the town was now a vast parrot-cage of chattering refugees. If, on the road, they were silent, stolid and serene, in the town they found their tongues and set up such a cackle as one may seldom hear. Notably the women; it is they who invariably confuse the definition of situations, and one could wonder in amaze if this crowd of irresponsible, gabbling hens had already forgotten that this town was the deathbed, so to speak, of scores of gallant men whose blood was not yet dry; whose hands, of the hue of pale amber, stuck from the soil of the hasty burial. On the way to El Caney I had conjured a picture of the women of Santiago, proud in their pain, their despair, dealing glances of defiance, contempt, hatred at the invader; fiery ferocious ladies, so true to their vanquished and to their dead that they spurned the very existence of the low-bred churls who lacked both Velasquez and Cervantes. And instead, there was this mere noise, which reminded one alternately of a tea-party in Ireland, a village fête in the south of France, and the vacuous morning screech of a swarm of sea-gulls. "Good. There is Donna Maria. This will lower her high head. This will teach her better manners to her neighbours. She wasn't too grand to send her rascal of a servant to borrow a trifle of coffee of me in the morning, and then when I met her on the calle—por Dios, she was too blind to see me. But we are all equal here. No? Little Juan has a sore toe. Yes, Donna Maria; many thanks, many thanks. Juan, do me the favour to be quiet while Donna Maria is asking about your toe. Oh, Donna Maria, we were always poor, always. But you. My heart bleeds when I see how hard this is for you. The old cat! She gives me a head-shake."

Pushing through the throng in the plaza we came in sight of the door of the church, and here was a strange scene. The church had been turned into a hospital for Spanish wounded who had fallen into American hands. The interior of the church was too cave-like in its gloom for the eyes of the operating surgeons, so they had had the altar table carried to the doorway, where there was a bright light. Framed then in the black archway was the altar table with the figure of a man upon it. He was naked save for a breech-clout and so close, so clear was the ecclesiastic suggestion, that one's mind leaped to a phantasy that this thin, pale figure had just been torn down from a cross. The flash of the impression was like light, and for this instant it illumined all the dark recesses of one's remotest idea of sacrilege, ghastly and wanton. I bring this to you merely as an effect, an effect of mental light and shade, if you like; something done in thought similar to that which the French impressionists do in colour; something meaningless and at the same time overwhelming, crushing, monstrous. "Poor devil; I wonder if he'll pull through," said Leighton. An American surgeon and his assistants were intent over the prone figure. They wore white aprons. Something small and silvery flashed in the surgeon's hand. An assistant held the merciful sponge close to the man's nostrils, but he was writhing and moaning in some horrible dream of this artificial sleep. As the surgeon's instrument played, I fancied that the man dreamed that he was being gored by a bull. In his pleading, delirious babble occurred constantly the name of the Virgin, the Holy Mother. "Good morning," said the surgeon. He changed his knife to his left hand and gave me a wet palm. The tips of his fingers were wrinkled, shrunken, like those of a boy who has been in swimming too long. Now, in front of the door, there were three American sentries, and it was their business to—to do what? To keep this Spanish crowd from swarming over the operating table! It was perforce a public clinic. They would not be denied. The weaker women and the children jostled according to their might in the rear, while the stronger people, gaping in the front rank, cried out impatiently when the pushing disturbed their long stares. One burned with a sudden gift of public oratory. One wanted to say: "Oh, go away, go away, go away. Leave the man decently alone with his pain, you gogglers. This is not the national sport."

But within the church there was an audience of another kind. This was of the other wounded men awaiting their turn. They lay on their brown blankets in rows along the stone floor. Their eyes, too, were fastened upon the operating-table, but— that was different. Meek-eyed little yellow men lying on the floor awaiting their turns.

One afternoon I was seated with a correspondent friend, on the porch of one of the houses at Siboney. A vast man on horseback came riding along at a foot pace.

When he perceived my friend, he pulled up sharply. "Whoa! Where's that mule I lent you?" My friend arose and saluted. "I've got him all right, General, thank you," said my friend. The vast man shook his finger. "Don't you lose him now." "No, sir, I won't; thank you, sir." The vast man rode away. "Who the devil is that?" said I. My friend laughed. "That's General Shafter," said he.

I gave five dollars for the Bos'n—small, black, spry imp of Jamaica sin. When I first saw him he was the property of a fireman on the *Criton*. The fireman had found him—a little wharf rat—in Port Antonio. It was not the purchase of a slave; it was that the fireman believed that he had spent about five dollars on a lot of comic supplies for the Bos'n, including a little suit of sailor clothes. The Bos'n was an adroit and fantastic black gamin. His eyes were like white lights, and his teeth were a row of little piano keys; otherwise he was black. He had both been a jockey and a cabin-boy, and he had the manners of a gentleman. After he entered my service I don't think there was ever an occasion upon which he was useful, save when he told me quaint stories of Guatemala, in which country he seemed to have lived some portion of his infantile existence. Usually he ran funny errands like little foot-races, each about fifteen yards in length. At Siboney he slept under my hammock like a poodle, and I always expected that, through the breaking of a rope, I would some night descend and obliterate him. His incompetence was spectacular. When I wanted him to do a thing, the agony of supervision was worse than the agony of personal performance. It would have been easier to have gotten my own spurs or boots or blanket than to have the bother of this little incapable's service. But the good aspect was the humorous view. He was like a boy, a mouse, a scoundrel, and a devoted servitor. He was immensely popular. His name of Bos'n became a Siboney stock-word. Everybody knew it. It was a name like President McKinley, Admiral Sampson, General Shafter. The Bos'n became a figure. One day he approached me with four one-dollar notes in United States currency. He besought me to preserve them for him, and I pompously tucked them away in my riding breeches, with an air which meant that his funds were now as safe as if they were in a national bank. Still, I asked with some surprise, where he had reaped all this money. He frankly admitted at once that it had been given to him by the enthusiastic soldiery as a tribute to his charm of person and manner. This was not astonishing for Siboney, where money was meaningless. Money was not worth carrying—"packing." However, a soldier came to our house one morning, and asked, "Got any more tobacco to sell?" As befitted men in virtuous poverty, we replied with indignation. "What tobacco?" "Why, that tobacco what the little nigger is sellin' round."

I said, "Bos'n!" He said, "Yes, mawstah." Wounded men on bloody stretchers were being carried into the hospital next door. "Bos'n, you've been stealing my tobacco." His defence was as glorious as the defence of that forlorn hope in romantic history, which drew itself up and mutely died. He lied as desperately, as savagely, as hopelessly as ever man fought.

One day a delegation from the 33d Michigan came to me and said: "Are you the proprietor of the Bos'n?" I said: "Yes." And they said: "Well, would you please be so kind as to be so good as to give him to us?" A big battle was expected for the next day. "Why," I answered, "if you want him you can have him. But he's a thief, and I won't let him go save on his personal announcement." The big battle occurred the next day, and the Bos'n did not disappear in it; but he disappeared in my interest in the battle, even as a waif might disappear in a fog. My interest in the battle made the Bos'n dissolve before my eyes. Poor little rascal! I gave him up with pain. He was such an innocent villain. He knew no more of thievery than the whole of it.

Anyhow one was fond of him. He was a natural scoundrel. He was not an educated scoundrel. One cannot bear the educated scoundrel. He was ingenuous, simple, honest, abashed ruffianism.

I hope the 33d Michigan did not arrive home naked. I hope the Bos'n did not succeed in getting everything. If the Bos'n builds a palace in Detroit, I shall know where he got the money. He got it from the 33d Michigan. Poor little man. He was only eleven years old. He vanished. I had thought to preserve him as a relic, even as one preserves forgotten bayonets and fragments of shell. And now as to the pocket of my riding-breeches. It contained four dollars in United States currency. Bos'n! Hey, Bos'n, where are you? The morning was the morning of battle.

I was on San Juan Hill when Lieutenant Hobson and the men of the *Merrimac* were exchanged and brought into the American lines. Many of us knew that the exchange was about to be made, and gathered to see the famous party. Some of our Staff officers rode out with three Spanish officers—prisoners—these latter being blindfolded before they were taken through the American position. The army was majestically minding its business in the long line of trenches when its eye caught sight of this little procession. "What's that? What they goin' to do?" "They're goin' to exchange Hobson." Wherefore every man who was foot-free staked out a claim where he could get a good view of the liberated heroes, and two bands prepared to collaborate on "The Star Spangled Banner." There was a very long wait through the sunshiny afternoon. In our impatience, we imagined them—the Americans and Spaniards—dickering away out there under the big tree like so many peddlers. Once the massed bands, misled by a rumour, stiffened themselves into that dramatic and breathless moment when each man is ready to blow. But the rumour was exploded in the nick of time. We made ill jokes, saying one to another that the negotiations had found diplomacy to be a failure, and were playing freeze-out poker for the whole batch of prisoners.

But suddenly the moment came. Along the cut roadway, toward the crowded soldiers, rode three men, and it could be seen that the central one wore the undress uniform of an officer of the United States navy. Most of the soldiers were sprawled out on the grass, bored and wearied in the sunshine. However, they aroused at the old circus-parade, torch-light procession cry, "Here they come." Then the men of the regular army did a thing. They arose *en masse* and came to "Attention." Then the men of the regular army did another thing. They slowly lifted every weather-beaten hat and drooped it until it touched the knee. Then there was a magnificent silence, broken only by the measured hoof-beats of the little company's horses as they rode through the gap. It was solemn, funereal, this splendid silent welcome of a brave man by men who stood on a hill which they had earned out of blood and death—simply, honestly, with no sense of excellence, earned out of blood and death.

Then suddenly the whole scene went to rubbish. Before he reached the bottom of the hill, Hobson was bowing to right and left like another Boulanger, and, above the thunder of the massed bands, one could hear the venerable outbreak, "Mr. Hobson, I'd like to shake the hand of the man who—" But the real welcome was that welcome of silence. However, one could thrill again when the tail of the procession appeared—an army waggon containing the blue-jackets of the *Merrimac* adventure. I remember grinning heads stuck out from under the canvas cover of the waggon. And the army spoke to the navy. "Well, Jackie, how does it feel?" And the navy up and answered: "Great! Much obliged to you fellers for comin' here." "Say, Jackie, what did they arrest ye for anyhow? Stealin' a dawg?" The navy still grinned. Here was no rubbish. Here was the mere exchange of language between men.

Some of us fell in behind this small but royal procession and followed it to General Shafter's headquarters, some miles on the road to Siboney. I have a vague impression that I watched the meeting between Shafter and Hobson, but the impression ends there. However, I remember hearing a talk between them as to Hobson's men, and then the blue-jackets were called up to hear the congratulatory remarks of the general in command of the Fifth Army Corps. It was a scene in the fine shade of thickly-leaved trees. The general sat in his chair, his belly sticking ridiculously out before him as if he had adopted some form of artificial inflation. He looked like a joss. If the seamen had suddenly begun to burn a few sticks, most of the spectators would have exhibited no surprise. But the words he spoke were proper, clear, quiet, soldierly, the words of one man to others. The Jackies were comic. At the bidding of their officer they aligned themselves before the general, grinned with embarrassment one to the other, made funny attempts to correct the alignment, and—looked sheepish. They looked sheepish. They looked like bad little boys flagrantly caught. They had no sense of excellence. Here was no rubbish.

Very soon after this the end of the campaign came for me. I caught a fever. I am not sure to this day what kind of a fever it was. It was defined variously. I know, at any rate, that I first developed a languorous indifference to everything in the world. Then I developed a tendency to ride a horse even as a man lies on a cot. Then I—I am not sure—I think I grovelled and groaned about Siboney for several days. My colleagues, Scovel and George Rhea, found me and gave me of their best, but I didn't know whether London Bridge was falling down or whether there was a war with Spain. It was all the same. What of it? Nothing of it. Everything had happened, perhaps. But I cared not a jot. Life, death, dishonour—all were nothing to me. All I cared for was pickles. *Pickles* at any price! *Pickles!!*

If I had been the father of a hundred suffering daughters, I should have waved them all aside and remarked that they could be damned for all I cared. It was not a mood. One can defeat a mood. It was a physical situation. Sometimes one cannot defeat a physical situation. I heard the talk of Siboney and sometimes I answered, but I was as indifferent as the star-fish flung to die on the sands. The only fact in the universe was that my veins burned and boiled. Rhea finally staggered me down to the army-surgeon who had charge of the proceedings, and the army-surgeon looked me over with a keen healthy eye. Then he gave a permit that I should be sent home. The manipulation from the shore to the transport was something which was Rhea's affair. I am not sure whether we went in a boat or a balloon. I think it was a boat. Rhea pushed me on board and I swayed meekly and unsteadily toward the captain of the ship, a corpulent, well-conditioned, impickled person pacing noisily on the spar-deck. "Ahem, yes; well; all right. Have you got your own food? I hope, for Christ's sake, you don't expect us to feed you, do you?" Whereupon I went to the rail and weakly yelled at Rhea, but he was already afar. The captain was, meantime, remarking in bellows that, for Christ's sake, I couldn't expect him to feed me. I didn't expect to be fed. I didn't care to be fed. I wished for nothing on earth but some form of painless pause, oblivion. The insults of this old pie-stuffed scoundrel did not affect me then; they affect me now. I would like to tell him that, although I like collies, fox-terriers, and even screw-curled poodles, I do not like him. He was free to call me superfluous and throw me overboard, but he was not free to coarsely speak to a somewhat sick man. I—in fact I hate him—it is all wrong—I lose whatever ethics I possessed—but—I hate him, and I demand that you should imagine a milch cow endowed with a knowledge of navigation and in command of a ship—and perfectly capable of commanding a ship—oh, well, never mind.

I was crawling along the deck when somebody pounced violently upon me and thundered: "Who in hell are you, sir?" I said I was a correspondent. He asked me did I know that I had yellow fever. I said No. He yelled, "Well, by Gawd, you isolate yourself, sir." I said; "Where?" At this question he almost frothed at the mouth. I thought he was going to strike me. "Where?" he roared. "How in hell do I know, sir? I know as much about this ship as you do, sir. But you isolate yourself, sir." My clouded brain tried to comprehend these orders. This man was a doctor in the regular army, and it was necessary to obey him, so I bestirred myself to learn what he meant by these gorilla outcries. "All right, doctor; I'll isolate myself, but I wish you'd tell me where to go." And then he passed into such volcanic humour that I clung to the rail and gasped. "Isolate yourself, sir. Isolate yourself. That's all I've got to say, sir. I don't give a God damn where you go, but when you get there, stay there, sir." So I wandered away and ended up on the deck aft, with my head against the flagstaff and my limp body stretched on a little rug. I was not at all sorry for myself. I didn't care a tent-peg. And yet, as I look back upon it now, the situation was fairly exciting—a voyage of four or five days before me—no food—no friends—above all else, no friends—isolated on deck, and rather ill.

When I returned to the United States, I was able to move my feminine friends to tears by an account of this voyage, but, after all, it wasn't so bad. They kept me on my small reservation aft, but plenty of kindness loomed soon enough. At mess-time, they slid me a tin plate of something, usually stewed tomatoes and bread. Men are always good men. And, at any rate, most of the people were in worse condition than I—poor bandaged chaps looking sadly down at the waves. In a way, I knew the kind. First lieutenants at forty years of age, captains at fifty, majors at 102, lieutenant-colonels at 620, full colonels at 1000, and brigadiers at 9,768,295 plus. A man had to live two billion years to gain eminent rank in the regular army at that time. And, of course, they all had trembling wives at remote western posts waiting to hear the worst, the best, or the middle.

In rough weather, the officers made a sort of a common pool of all the sound legs and arms, and by dint of hanging hard to each other they managed to move from their deck chairs to their cabins and from their cabins again to their deck chairs. Thus they lived until the ship reached Hampton Roads. We slowed down opposite the curiously mingled hotels and batteries at Old Point Comfort, and at our mast-head we flew the yellow-flag, the grim ensign of the plague. Then we witnessed something which informed us that with all this ship-load of wounds and fevers and starvations we had forgotten the fourth element of war. We were flying the yellow flag, but a launch came and circled swiftly about us. There was a little woman in the launch, and she kept looking and looking and looking. Our ship was so high that she could see only those who rung at the rail, but she kept looking and looking and looking. It was plain enough—it was all plain enough—but my heart sank with the fear that she was not going to find him. But presently there was a commotion among some black dough-boys of the 24th Infantry, and two of them ran aft to Colonel Liscum, its gallant commander. Their faces were wreathed in darkey grins of delight. "Kunnel, ain't dat Mis' Liscum, Kunnel?" "What?" said the old man. He got up quickly and appeared at the rail, his arm in a sling. He cried, "Alice!" The little woman saw him, and instantly she covered up her face with her hands as if blinded with a flash of white fire. She made no outcry; it was all in this simply swift gesture, but we—we knew them. It told us. It told us the other part. And in a vision we all saw our own harbour-lights. That is to say those of us who had harbour-lights.

I was almost well, and had defeated the yellow-fever charge which had been brought against me, and so I was allowed ashore among the first. And now happened a strange thing. A hard campaign, full of wants and lacks and absences, brings a man speedily back to an appreciation of things long disregarded or forgotten. In camp, somewhere in the woods between Siboney and Santiago, I happened to think of ice-cream-soda. I had done very well without it for many years; in fact I think I loathe it; but I got to dreaming of ice-cream-soda, and I came near dying of longing for it. I couldn't get it out of my mind, try as I would to concentrate my thoughts upon the land crabs and mud with which I was surrounded. It certainly had been an institution of my childhood, but to have a ravenous longing for it in the year 1898 was about as illogical as to have a ravenous longing for kerosene. All I could do was to swear to myself that if I reached the United States again, I would immediately go to the nearest soda-water fountain and make it look like Spanish Fours. In a loud, firm voice, I would say, "Orange, please." And here is the strange thing: as soon as I was ashore I went to the nearest soda-water fountain, and in a loud, firm voice I said, "Orange, please." I remember one man who went mad that way over tinned peaches, and who wandered over the face of the earth saying plaintively, "Have you any peaches?"

Most of the wounded and sick had to be tabulated and marshalled in sections and thoroughly officialised, so that I was in time to take a position on the verandah of Chamberlain's Hotel and see my late shipmates taken to the hospital. The verandah was crowded with women in light, charming summer dresses, and with spruce officers from the Fortress. It was like a bank of flowers. It filled me with awe. All this luxury and refinement and gentle care and fragrance and colour seemed absolutely new. Then across the narrow street on the verandah of the hotel there was a similar bank of flowers. Two companies of volunteers dug a lane through the great crowd in the street and kept the way, and then through this lane there passed a curious procession. I had never known that they looked like that. Such a gang of dirty, ragged, emaciated, half-starved, bandaged cripples I had never seen. Naturally there were many men who couldn't walk, and some of these were loaded upon a big flat car which was in tow of a trolley-car. Then there were many stretchers, slow-moving. When that crowd began to pass the hotel the banks of flowers made a noise which could make one tremble. Perhaps it was a moan, perhaps it was a sob—but no, it was something beyond either a moan or a sob. Anyhow, the sound of women weeping was in it.—The sound of women weeping.

And how did these men of famous deeds appear when received thus by the people? Did they smirk and look as if they were bursting with the desire to tell everything which had happened? No they hung their heads like so many jail-birds. Most of them seemed to be suffering from something which was like stage-fright during the ordeal of this chance but supremely eloquent reception. No sense of excellence—that was it. Evidently they were willing to leave the clacking to all those natural born major-generals who after the war talked enough to make a great fall in the price of that commodity all over the world.

The episode was closed. And you can depend upon it that I have told you nothing at all, nothing at all, nothing at all.

# THE SECOND GENERATION

## I

Caspar Cadogan resolved to go to the tropic wars and do something. The air was blue and gold with the pomp of soldiering, and in every ear rang the music of military glory. Caspar's father was a United States Senator from the great State of Skowmulligan, where the war fever ran very high. Chill is the blood of many of the sons of millionaires, but Caspar took the fever and posted to Washington. His father had never denied him anything, and this time all that Caspar wanted was a little Captaincy in the Army—just a simple little Captaincy.

The old man had been entertaining a delegation of respectable bunco-steerers from Skowmulligan who had come to him on a matter which is none of the public's business.

Bottles of whisky and boxes of cigars were still on the table in the sumptuous private parlour. The Senator had said, "Well, gentlemen, I'll do what I can for you." By this sentence he meant whatever he meant.

Then he turned to his eager son. "Well, Caspar?" The youth poured out his modest desires. It was not altogether his fault. Life had taught him a generous faith in his own abilities. If any one had told him that he was simply an ordinary damned fool he would have opened his eyes wide at the person's lack of judgment. All his life people had admired him.

The Skowmulligan war-horse looked with quick disapproval into the eyes of his son. "Well, Caspar," he said slowly, "I am of the opinion that they've got all the golf experts and tennis champions and cotillion leaders and piano tuners and billiard markers that they really need as officers. Now, if you were a soldier—"

"I know," said the young man with a gesture, "but I'm not exactly a fool, I hope, and I think if I get a chance I can do something. I'd like to try. I would, indeed."

The Senator lit a cigar. He assumed an attitude of ponderous reflection. "Y— yes, but this country is full of young men who are not fools. Full of 'em."

Caspar fidgeted in the desire to answer that while he admitted the profusion of young men who were not fools, he felt that he himself possessed interesting and peculiar qualifications which would allow him to make his mark in any field of effort which he seriously challenged. But he did not make this graceful statement, for he sometimes detected something ironic in his father's temperament. The Skowmulligan war-horse had not thought of expressing an opinion of his own ability since the year 1865, when he was young, like Caspar.

"Well, well," said the Senator finally. "I'll see about it. I'll see about it." The young man was obliged to await the end of his father's characteristic method of thought. The war-horse never gave a quick answer, and if people tried to hurry him they seemed able to arouse only a feeling of irritation against making a decision at all. His mind moved like the wind, but practice had placed a Mexican bit in the mouth of his judgment. This old man of light quick thought had taught himself to move like an ox cart. Caspar said, "Yes, sir." He withdrew to his club, where, to the affectionate inquiries of some envious friends, he replied, "The old man is letting the idea soak."

The mind of the war-horse was decided far sooner than Caspar expected. In Washington a large number of well-bred handsome young men were receiving appointments as Lieutenants, as Captains, and occasionally as Majors. They were a strong, healthy, clean-eyed educated collection. They were a prime lot. A German Field-Marshal would have beamed with joy if he could have had them—to send to school. Anywhere in the world they would have made a grand show as material, but, intrinsically they were not Lieutenants, Captains and Majors. They were fine men, though manhood is only an essential part of a Lieutenant, a Captain or a Major. But at any rate, this arrangement had all the logic of going to sea in a bathing-machine.

The Senator found himself reasoning that Caspar was as good as any of them, and better than many. Presently he was bleating here and there that his boy should have a chance. "The boy's all right, I tell you, Henry. He's wild to go, and I don't see why they shouldn't give him a show. He's got plenty of nerve, and he's keen as a whiplash. I'm going to get him an appointment, and if you can do anything to help it along I wish you would."

Then he betook himself to the White House and the War Department and made a stir. People think that Administrations are always slavishly, abominably anxious to please the Machine. They are not; they wish the Machine sunk in red fire, for by the power of ten thousand past words, looks, gestures, writings, the Machine comes along and takes the Administration by the nose and twists it, and the Administration dare not even yell. The huge force which carries an election to success looks reproachfully at the Administration and says, "Give me a bun." That is a very small thing with which to reward a Colossus.

The Skowmulligan war-horse got his bun and took it to his hotel where Caspar was moodily reading war rumours. "Well, my boy, here you are." Caspar was a Captain and Commissary on the staff of Brigadier-General Reilly, commander of the Second Brigade of the First Division of the Thirtieth Army Corps.

"I had to work for it," said the Senator grimly. "They talked to me as if they thought you were some sort of empty-headed idiot. None of 'em seemed to know you personally. They just sort of took it for granted. Finally I got pretty hot in the collar." He paused a moment; his heavy, grooved face set hard; his blue eyes shone. He clapped a hand down upon the handle of his chair.

"Caspar, I've got you into this thing, and I believe you'll do all right, and I'm not saying this because I distrust either your sense or your grit. But I want you to understand you've *got to make a go of it*. I'm not going to talk any twaddle about your country and your country's flag. You understand all about that. But now you're a soldier, and there'll be this to do and that to do, and fighting to do, and you've got to do *every damned one of 'em* right up to the handle. I don't know how much of a shindy this thing is going to be, but any shindy is enough to show how much there is in a man. You've got your appointment, and that's all I can do for you; but I'll thrash you with my own hands if, when the Army gets back, the other fellows say my son is 'nothing but a good-looking dude.'"

He ceased, breathing heavily. Caspar looked bravely and frankly at his father, and answered in a voice which was not very tremulous. "I'll do my best. This is my chance. I'll do my best with it."

The Senator had a marvellous ability of transition from one manner to another. Suddenly he seemed very kind. "Well, that's all right, then. I guess you'll get along all right with Reilly. I know him well, and he'll see you through. I helped him along once. And now about this commissary business. As I understand it, a Commissary is a sort of caterer in a big way—that is, he looks out for a good many more things than a caterer has to bother his head about. Reilly's brigade has probably from two to three thousand men in it, and in regard to certain things you've got to look out for every man of 'em every day. I know perfectly well you couldn't successfully run a boarding-house in Ocean Grove. How are you going to manage for all these soldiers, hey? Thought about it?"

"No," said Caspar, injured. "I didn't want to be a Commissary. I wanted to be a Captain in the line."

"They wouldn't hear of it. They said you would have to take a staff appointment where people could look after you."

"Well, let them look after me," cried Caspar resentfully; "but when there's any fighting to be done I guess I won't necessarily be the last man."

"That's it," responded the Senator. "That's the spirit." They both thought that the problem of war would eliminate to an equation of actual battle.

Ultimately Caspar departed into the South to an encampment in salty grass under pine trees. Here lay an Army corps twenty thousand strong. Caspar passed into the dusty sunshine of it, and for many weeks he was lost to view.

## II

"Of course I don't know a blamed thing about it," said Caspar frankly and modestly to a circle of his fellow staff officers. He was referring to the duties of his office.

Their faces became expressionless; they looked at him with eyes in which he could fathom nothing. After a pause one politely said, "Don't you?" It was the inevitable two words of convention.

"Why," cried Caspar, "I didn't know what a commissary officer was until I *was* one. My old Guv'nor told me. He'd looked it up in a book somewhere, I suppose; but *I* didn't know."

"Didn't you?"

The young man's face glowed with sudden humour. "Do you know, the word was intimately associated in my mind with camels. Funny, eh? I think it came from reading that rhyme of Kipling's about the commissariat camel."

"Did it?"

"Yes. Funny, isn't it? Camels!"

The brigade was ultimately landed at Siboney as part of an army to attack Santiago. The scene at the landing sometimes resembled the inspiriting daily drama at the approach to the Brooklyn Bridge. There was a great bustle, during which the wise man kept his property gripped in his hands lest it might march off into the wilderness in the pocket of one of the striding regiments. Truthfully, Caspar should have had frantic occupation, but men saw him wandering bootlessly here and there crying, "Has any one seen my saddlebags? Why, if I lose them I'm ruined. I've got everything packed away in 'em. Everything!"

They looked at him gloomily and without attention. "No," they said. It was to intimate that they would not give a rip if he had lost his nose, his teeth and his self-respect. Reilly's brigade collected itself from the boats and went off, each regiment's soul burning with anger because some other regiment was in advance of it. Moving along through the scrub and under the palms, men talked mostly of things that did not pertain to the business in hand.

General Reilly finally planted his headquarters in some tall grass under a mango tree. "Where's Cadogan?" he said suddenly as he took off his hat and smoothed the wet grey hair from his brow. Nobody knew. "I saw him looking for his saddle-bags down at the landing," said an officer dubiously. "Bother him," said the General contemptuously. "Let him stay there."

Three venerable regimental commanders came, saluted stiffly and sat in the grass. There was a pow-wow, during which Reilly explained much that the Division Commander had told him. The venerable Colonels nodded; they understood. Everything was smooth and clear to their minds. But still, the Colonel of the Forty-fourth Regular Infantry murmured about the commissariat. His men—and then he launched forth in a sentiment concerning the privations of his men in which you were confronted with his feeling that his men—his men were the only creatures of importance in the universe, which feeling was entirely correct for him. Reilly grunted. He did what most commanders did. He set the competent line to doing the work of the incompetent part of the staff.

In time Caspar came trudging along the road merrily swinging his saddle-bags. "Well, General," he cried as he saluted, "I found 'em."

"Did you?" said Reilly. Later an officer rushed to him tragically: "General, Cadogan is off there in the bushes eatin' potted ham and crackers all by himself." The officer was sent back into the bushes for Caspar, and the General sent Caspar with an order. Then Reilly and the three venerable Colonels, grinning, partook of potted ham and crackers. "Tashe a' right," said Reilly, with his mouth full. "Dorsey, see if 'e got some'n else."

"Mush be selfish young pig," said one of the Colonels, with his mouth full. "Who's he, General?"

"Son—Sen'tor Cad'gan—ol' frien' mine—dash 'im."

Caspar wrote a letter:

"*Dear Father*: I am sitting under a tree using the flattest part of my canteen for a desk. Even as I write the division ahead of us is moving forward and we don't know what moment the storm of battle may break out. I don't know what the plans are. General Reilly knows, but he is so good as to give me very little of his confidence. In fact, I might be part of a forlorn hope from all to the contrary I've heard from him. I understood you to say in Washington that you at one time had been of some service to him, but if that is true I can assure you he has completely forgotten it. At times his manner to me is little short of being offensive, but of course I understand that it is only the way of a crusty old soldier who has been made boorish and bearish by a long life among the Indians. I dare say I shall manage it all right without a row.

"When you hear that we have captured Santiago, please send me by first steamer a box of provisions and clothing, particularly sardines, pickles, and light-weight underwear. The other men on the staff are nice quiet chaps, but they seem a bit crude. There has been no fighting yet save the skirmish by Young's brigade. Reilly was furious because we couldn't get in it. I met General Peel yesterday. He was very nice. He said he knew you well when he was in Congress. Young Jack May is on Peel's staff. I knew him well in college. We spent an hour talking over old times. Give my love to all at home."

The march was leisurely. Reilly and his staff strolled out to the head of the long, sinuous column and entered the sultry gloom of the forest. Some less fortunate regiments had to wait among the trees at the side of the trail, and as Reilly's brigade passed them, officer called to officer, classmate to classmate, and in these greetings rang a note of everything, from West Point to Alaska. They were going into an action in which they, the officers, would lose over a hundred in killed and wounded—officers alone—and these greetings, in which many nicknames occurred, were in many cases farewells such as one pictures being given with ostentation, solemnity, fervour. "There goes Gory Widgeon! Hello, Gory! Where you starting for? Hey, Gory!"

Caspar communed with himself and decided that he was not frightened. He was eager and alert; he thought that now his obligation to his country, or himself, was to be faced, and he was mad to prove to old Reilly and the others that after all he was a very capable soldier.

### III

Old Reilly was stumping along the line of his brigade and mumbling like a man with a mouthful of grass. The fire from the enemy's position was incredible in its swift fury, and Reilly's brigade was getting its share of a very bad ordeal. The old man's face was of the colour of a tomato, and in his rage he mouthed and sputtered strangely. As he pranced along his thin line, scornfully erect, voices arose from the grass beseeching him to take care of himself. At his heels scrambled a bugler with pallid skin and clenched teeth, a chalky, trembling youth, who kept his eye on old Reilly's back and followed it.

The old gentleman was quite mad. Apparently he thought the whole thing a dreadful mess, but now that his brigade was irrevocably in it he was full-tilting here and everywhere to establish some irreproachable, immaculate kind of behaviour on the part of every man jack in his brigade. The intentions of the three venerable Colonels were the same. They stood behind their lines, quiet, stern, courteous old fellows, admonishing their regiments to be very pretty in the face of such a hail of magazine-rifle and machine-gun fire as has never in this world been confronted save by beardless savages when the white man has found occasion to take his burden to some new place.

And the regiments were pretty. The men lay on their little stomachs and got peppered according to the law and said nothing, as the good blood pumped out into the grass, and even if a solitary rookie tried to get a decent reason to move to some haven of rational men, the cold voice of an officer made him look criminal with a shame that was a credit to his regimental education. Behind Reilly's command was a bullet-torn jungle through which it could not move as a brigade; ahead of it were Spanish trenches on hills. Reilly considered that he was in a fix no doubt, but he said this only to himself. Suddenly he saw on the right a little point of blue-shirted men already half-way up the hill. It was some pathetic fragment of the Sixth United States Infantry. Chagrined, shocked, horrified, Reilly bellowed to his bugler, and the chalked-faced youth unlocked his teeth and sounded the charge by rushes.

The men formed hastily and grimly, and rushed. Apparently there awaited them only the fate of respectable soldiers. But they went because—of the opinions of others, perhaps. They went because—no loud-mouthed lot of jail-birds such as the Twenty-Seventh Infantry could do anything that they could not do better. They went because Reilly ordered it. They went because they went.

And yet not a man of them to this day has made a public speech explaining precisely how he did the whole thing and detailing with what initiative and ability he comprehended and defeated a situation which he did not comprehend at all.

Reilly never saw the top of the hill. He was heroically striving to keep up with his men when a bullet ripped quietly through his left lung, and he fell back into the arms of the bugler, who received him as he would have received a Christmas present. The three venerable Colonels inherited the brigade in swift succession. The senior commanded for about fifty seconds, at the end of which he was mortally shot. Before they could get the news to the next in rank he, too, was shot. The junior

Colonel ultimately arrived with a lean and puffing little brigade at the top of the hill. The men lay down and fired volleys at whatever was practicable.

In and out of the ditch-like trenches lay the Spanish dead, lemon-faced corpses dressed in shabby blue and white ticking. Some were huddled down comfortably like sleeping children; one had died in the attitude of a man flung back in a dentist's chair; one sat in the trench with his chin sunk despondently to his breast; few preserved a record of the agitation of battle. With the greater number it was as if death had touched them so gently, so lightly, that they had not known of it. Death had come to them rather in the form of an opiate than of a bloody blow.

But the arrived men in the blue shirts had no thought of the sallow corpses. They were eagerly exchanging a hail of shots with the Spanish second line, whose ash-coloured entrenchments barred the way to a city white amid trees. In the pauses the men talked.

"We done the best. Old E Company got there. Why, one time the hull of B Company was *behind* us."

"Jones, he was the first man up. I saw 'im."

"Which Jones?"

"Did you see ol' Two-bars runnin' like a land-crab? Made good time, too. He hit only in the high places. He's all right."

"The Lootenant s all right, too. He was a good ten yards ahead of the best of us. I hated him at the post, but for this here active service there's none of 'em can touch him."

"This is mighty different from being at the post."

"Well, we done it, an' it wasn't b'cause *I* thought it could be done. When we started, I ses to m'self: 'Well, here goes a lot o' fools.'"

"'Tain't over yet."

"Oh, they'll never git us back from here. If they start to chase us back from here we'll pile 'em up so high the last ones can't climb over. We've come this far, an' we'll stay here. I ain't done pantin'."

"Anything is better than packin' through that jungle an' gettin' blistered from front, rear, an' both flanks. I'd rather tackle another hill than go trailin' in them woods, so thick you can't tell whether you are one man or a division of cav'lry."

"Where's that young kitchen-soldier, Cadogan, or whatever his name is. Ain't seen him today."

"Well, *I* seen him. He was right in with it. He got shot, too, about half up the hill, in the leg. I seen it. He's all right. Don't worry about him. He's all right."

"I seen 'im, too. He done his stunt. As soon as I can git this piece of barbed-wire entanglement out o' me throat I'll give 'm a cheer."

"He ain't shot at all b'cause there he stands, there. See 'im?"

Rearward, the grassy slope was populous with little groups of men searching for the wounded. Reilly's brigade began to dig with its bayonets and shovel with its meat-ration cans.

**IV**

Senator Cadogan paced to and fro in his private parlour and smoked small, brown weak cigars. These little wisps seemed utterly inadequate to console such a ponderous satrap.

It was the evening of the 1st of July, 1898, and the Senator was immensely excited, as could be seen from the superlatively calm way in which he called out to his private secretary, who was in an adjoining room. The voice was serene, gentle, affectionate, low.

"Baker, I wish you'd go over again to the War Department and see if they've heard anything about Caspar."

A very bright-eyed, hatchet-faced young man appeared in a doorway, pen still in hand. He was hiding a nettle-like irritation behind all the finished audacity of a smirk, sharp, lying, trustworthy young politician. "I've just got back from there, sir," he suggested.

The Skowmulligan war-horse lifted his eyes and looked for a short second into the eyes of his private secretary. It was not a glare or an eagle glance; it was something beyond the practice of an actor; it was simply meaning. The clever private secretary grabbed his hat and was at once enthusiastically away. "All right, sir," he cried. "I'll find out."

The War Department was ablaze with light, and messengers were running. With the assurance of a retainer of an old house Baker made his way through much small-calibre vociferation. There was rumour of a big victory; there was rumour of a big defeat. In the corridors various watchdogs arose from their armchairs and asked him of his business in tones of uncertainty which in no wise compared with their previous habitual deference to the private secretary of the war-horse of Skowmulligan.

Ultimately Baker arrived in a room where some kind of head clerk sat writing feverishly at a roll-top desk. Baker asked a question, and the head clerk mumbled profanely without lifting his head. Apparently he said: "How in the blankety-blank blazes do I know?"

The private secretary let his jaw fall. Surely some new spirit had come suddenly upon the heart of Washington—a spirit which Baker understood to be almost defiantly indifferent to the wishes of Senator Cadogan, a spirit which was not courteously oily. What could it mean? Baker's fox-like mind sprang wildly to a conception of overturned factions, changed friends, new combinations. The assurance which had come from experience of a broad political situation suddenly left him, and he would not have been amazed if some one had told him that Senator Cadogan now controlled only six votes in the State of Skowmulligan. "Well," he stammered in his bewilderment, "well—there isn't any news of the old man's son, hey?" Again the head clerk replied blasphemously.

Eventually Baker retreated in disorder from the presence of this head clerk, having learned that the latter did not give a damn if Caspar Cadogan were sailing through Hades on an ice yacht.

Baker stormed other and more formidable officials. In fact, he struck as high as he dared. They one and all flung him short, hard words, even as men pelt an annoying cur with pebbles. He emerged from the brilliant light, from the groups of men with anxious, puzzled faces, and as he walked back to the hotel he did not know if his name were Baker or Cholmondeley.

However, as he walked up the stairs to the Senator's rooms he contrived to concentrate his intellect upon a manner of speaking.

The war-horse was still pacing his parlour and smoking. He paused at Baker's entrance. "Well?"

"Mr. Cadogan," said the private secretary coolly, "they told me at the Department that they did not give a cuss whether your son was alive or dead."

The Senator looked at Baker and smiled gently. "What's that, my boy?" he asked in a soft and considerate voice.

"They said—" gulped Baker, with a certain tenacity. "They said that they didn't give a cuss whether your son was alive or dead."

There was a silence for the space of three seconds. Baker stood like an image; he had no machinery for balancing the issues of this kind of a situation, and he seemed to feel that if he stood as still as a stone frog he would escape the ravages of a terrible Senatorial wrath which was about to break forth in a hurricane speech which would snap off trees and sweep away barns.

"Well," drawled the Senator lazily, "who did you see, Baker?"

The private secretary resumed a certain usual manner of breathing. He told the names of the men whom he had seen.

"Ye—e—es," remarked the Senator. He took another little brown cigar and held it with a thumb and first finger, staring at it with the calm and steady scrutiny of a scientist investigating a new thing. "So they don't care whether Caspar is alive or dead, eh? Well … maybe they don't…. That's all right…. However … I think I'll just look in on 'em and state my views."

When the Senator had gone, the private secretary ran to the window and leaned afar out. Pennsylvania Avenue was gleaming silver blue in the light of many arc-lamps; the cable trains groaned along to the clangour of gongs; from the window, the walks presented a hardly diversified aspect of shirt-waists and straw hats. Sometimes a newsboy screeched.

Baker watched the tall, heavy figure of the Senator moving out to intercept a cable train. "Great Scott!" cried the private secretary to himself, "there'll be three distinct kinds of grand, plain practical fireworks. The old man is going for 'em. I wouldn't be in Lascum's boots. Ye gods, what a row there'll be."

In due time the Senator was closeted with some kind of deputy third-assistant battery-horse in the offices of the War Department. The official obviously had been told off to make a supreme effort to pacify Cadogan, and he certainly was acting according to his instructions. He was almost in tears; he spread out his hands in supplication, and his voice whined and wheedled.

"Why, really, you know, Senator, we can only beg you to look at the circumstances. Two scant divisions at the top of that hill; over a thousand men killed and wounded; the line so thin that any strong attack would smash our Army to flinders. The Spaniards have probably received reenforcements under Pando; Shafter seems to be too ill to be actively in command of our troops; Lawton can't get up with his division before tomorrow. We are actually expecting … no, I won't say expecting … but we would not be surprised … nobody in the department would be surprised if before daybreak we were compelled to give to the country the news of a disaster which would be the worst blow the National pride has ever suffered. Don't you see? Can't you see our position, Senator?"

The Senator, with a pale but composed face, contemplated the official with eyes that gleamed in a way not usual with the big, self-controlled politician.

"I'll tell you frankly, sir," continued the other. "I'll tell you frankly, that at this moment we don't know whether we are a-foot or a-horseback. Everything is in the air. We don't know whether we have won a glorious victory or simply got ourselves in a deuce of a fix."

The Senator coughed. "I suppose my boy is with the two divisions at the top of that hill? He's with Reilly."

"Yes; Reilly's brigade is up there."

"And when do you suppose the War Department can tell me if he is all right. I want to know."

"My dear Senator, frankly, I don't know. Again I beg you to think of our position. The Army is in a muddle; it's a General thinking that he must fall back, and yet not sure that he *can* fall back without losing the Army. Why, we're worrying about the lives of sixteen thousand men and the self-respect of the nation, Senator."

"I see," observed the Senator, nodding his head slowly. "And naturally the welfare of one man's son doesn't—how do they say it—doesn't cut any ice."

V

And in Cuba it rained. In a few days Reilly's brigade discovered that by their successful charge they had gained the inestimable privilege of sitting in a wet trench and slowly but surely starving to death. Men's tempers crumbled like dry bread. The soldiers who so cheerfully, quietly and decently had captured positions which the foreign experts had said were impregnable, now in turn underwent an attack which was furious as well as insidious. The heat of the sun alternated with rains which boomed and roared in their falling like mountain cataracts. It seemed as if men took the fever through sheer lack of other occupation. During the days of battle none had had time to get even a tropic headache, but no sooner was that brisk period over than men began to shiver and shudder by squads and platoons. Rations were scarce enough to make a little fat strip of bacon seem of the size of a corner lot, and coffee grains were pearls. There would have been godless quarreling over fragments if it were not that with these fevers came a great listlessness, so that men were almost content to die, if death required no exertion.

It was an occasion which distinctly separated the sheep from the goats. The goats were few enough, but their qualities glared out like crimson spots.

One morning Jameson and Ripley, two Captains in the Forty-fourth Foot, lay under a flimsy shelter of sticks and palm branches. Their dreamy, dull eyes contemplated the men in the trench which went to left and right. To them came Caspar Cadogan, moaning. "By Jove," he said, as he flung himself wearily on the ground, "I can't stand much more of this, you know. It's killing me." A bristly beard sprouted through the grime on his face; his eyelids were crimson; an indescribably dirty shirt fell away from his roughened neck; and at the same time various lines of evil and greed were deepened on his face, until he practically stood forth as a revelation, a confession. "I can't stand it. By Jove, I can't."

Stanford, a Lieutenant under Jameson, came stumbling along toward them. He was a lad of the class of '98 at West Point. It could be seen that he was flaming with fever. He rolled a calm eye at them. "Have you any water, sir?" he said to his Captain. Jameson got upon his feet and helped Stanford to lay his shaking length under the shelter. "No, boy," he answered gloomily. "Not a drop. You got any, Rip?"

"No," answered Ripley, looking with anxiety upon the young officer. "Not a drop."

"You, Cadogan?"

Here Caspar hesitated oddly for a second, and then in a tone of deep regret made answer, "No, Captain; not a mouthful."

Jameson moved off weakly. "You lay quietly, Stanford, and I'll see what I can rustle."

Presently Caspar felt that Ripley was steadily regarding him. He returned the look with one of half-guilty questioning.

"God forgive you, Cadogan," said Ripley, "but you are a damned beast. Your canteen is full of water."

Even then the apathy in their veins prevented the scene from becoming as sharp as the words sounded. Caspar sputtered like a child, and at length merely said: "No, it isn't." Stanford lifted his head to shoot a keen, proud glance at Caspar, and then turned away his face.

"You lie," said Ripley. "I can tell the sound of a full canteen as far as I can hear it."

"Well, if it is, I—I must have forgotten it."

"You lie; no man in this Army just now forgets whether his canteen is full or empty. Hand it over."

Fever is the physical counterpart of shame, and when a man has the one he accepts the other with an ease which would revolt his healthy self. However, Caspar made a desperate struggle to preserve the forms. He arose and taking the string from his shoulder, passed the canteen to Ripley. But after all there was a whine in his voice, and the assumption of dignity was really a farce. "I think I had better go, Captain. You can have the water if you want it, I'm sure. But—but I fail to see—I fail to see what reason you have for insulting me."

"Do you?" said Ripley stolidly. "That's all right."

Caspar stood for a terrible moment. He simply did not have the strength to turn his back on this—this affair. It seemed to him that he must stand forever and face it. But when he found the audacity to look again at Ripley he saw the latter was not at all concerned with the situation. Ripley, too, had the fever. The fever changes all laws of proportion. Caspar went away.

"Here, youngster; here is your drink."

Stanford made a weak gesture. "I wouldn't touch a drop from his blamed canteen if it was the last water in the world," he murmured in his high, boyish voice.

"Don't you be a young jackass," quoth Ripley tenderly.

The boy stole a glance at the canteen. He felt the propriety of arising and hurling it after Caspar, but—he, too, had the fever.

"Don't you be a young jackass," said Ripley again.

## VI

Senator Cadogan was happy. His son had returned from Cuba, and the 8:30 train that evening would bring him to the station nearest to the stone and red shingle villa which the Senator and his family occupied on the shores of Long Island Sound. The Senator's steam yacht lay some hundred yards from the beach. She had just returned from a trip to Montauk Point where the Senator had made a gallant attempt to gain his son from the transport on which he was coming from Cuba. He had fought a brave sea-fight with sundry petty little doctors and ship's officers who had raked him with broadsides, describing the laws of quarantine and had used inelegant speech to a United States Senator as he stood on the bridge of his own steam yacht. These men had grimly asked him to tell exactly how much better was Caspar than any other returning soldier.

But the Senator had not given them a long fight. In fact, the truth came to him quickly, and with almost a blush he had ordered the yacht back to her anchorage off the villa. As a matter of fact, the trip to Montauk Point had been undertaken largely from impulse. Long ago the Senator had decided that when his boy returned the greeting should have something Spartan in it. He would make a welcome such as most soldiers get. There should be no flowers and carriages when the other poor fellows got none. He should consider Caspar as a soldier. That was the way to treat a man. But in the end a sharp acid of anxiety had worked upon the iron old man, until he had ordered the yacht to take him out and make a fool of him. The result filled him with a chagrin which caused him to delegate to the mother and sisters the entire business of succouring Caspar at Montauk Point Camp. He had remained at home conducting the huge correspondence of an active National politician and waiting for this son whom he so loved and whom he so wished to be a man of a certain strong, taciturn, shrewd ideal. The recent yacht voyage he now looked upon as a kind of confession of his weakness, and he was resolved that no more signs should escape him.

But yet his boy had been down there against the enemy and among the fevers. There had been grave perils, and his boy must have faced them. And he could not prevent himself from dreaming through the poetry of fine actions in which visions his son's face shone out manly and generous. During these periods the people about him, accustomed as they were to his silence and calm in time of stress, considered that affairs in Skowmulligan might be most critical. In no other way could they account for this exaggerated phlegm.

On the night of Caspar's return he did not go to dinner, but had a tray sent to his library, where he remained writing. At last he heard the spin of the dog-cart's wheels on the gravel of the drive, and a moment later there penetrated to him the sound of joyful feminine cries. He lit another cigar; he knew that it was now his part to bide with dignity the moment when his son should shake off that other welcome and come to him. He could still hear them; in their exuberance they seemed to be capering like schoolchildren. He was impatient, but this impatience took the form of a polar stolidity.

Presently there were quick steps and a jubilant knock at his door. "Come in," he said.

In came Caspar, thin, yellow, and in soiled khaki. "They almost tore me to pieces," he cried, laughing. "They danced around like wild things." Then as they shook hands he dutifully said "How are you, sir?"

"How are you, my boy?" answered the Senator casually but kindly.

"Better than I might expect, sir," cried Caspar cheerfully. "We had a pretty hard time, you know."

"You look as if they'd given you a hard run," observed the father in a tone of slight interest.

Caspar was eager to tell. "Yes, sir," he said rapidly. "We did, indeed. Why, it was awful. We—any of us—were lucky to get out of it alive. It wasn't so much the Spaniards, you know. The Army took care of them all right. It was the fever and the—you know, we couldn't get anything to eat. And the mismanagement. Why, it was frightful."

"Yes, I've heard," said the Senator. A certain wistful look came into his eyes, but he did not allow it to become prominent. Indeed, he suppressed it. "And you, Caspar? I suppose you did your duty?"

Caspar answered with becoming modesty. "Well, I didn't do more than anybody else, I don't suppose, but—well, I got along all right, I guess."

"And this great charge up San Juan Hill?" asked, the father slowly. "Were you in that?"

"Well—yes; I was in it," replied the son.

The Senator brightened a trifle. "You were, eh? In the front of it? or just sort of going along?"

"Well—I don't know. I couldn't tell exactly. Sometimes I was in front of a lot of them, and sometimes I was—just sort of going along."

This time the Senator emphatically brightened. "That's all right, then. And of course—of course you performed your commissary duties correctly?"

The question seemed to make Caspar uncommunicative and sulky. "I did when there was anything to do," he answered. "But the whole thing was on the most unbusiness-like basis you can imagine. And they wouldn't tell you anything. Nobody would take time to instruct you in your duties, and of course if you didn't know a thing your superior officer would swoop down on you and ask you why in the deuce such and such a thing wasn't done in such and such a way. Of course I did the best I could."

The Senator's countenance had again become sombrely indifferent. "I see. But you weren't directly rebuked for incapacity, were you? No; of course you weren't. But—I mean—did any of your superior officers suggest that you were 'no good,' or anything of that sort? I mean—did you come off with a clean slate?"

Caspar took a small time to digest his father's meaning. "Oh, yes, sir," he cried at the end of his reflection. "The Commissary was in such a hopeless mess anyhow that nobody thought of doing anything but curse Washington."

"Of course," rejoined the Senator harshly. "But supposing that you had been a competent and well-trained commissary officer. What then?"

Again the son took time for consideration, and in the end deliberately replied "Well, if I had been a competent and well-trained Commissary I would have sat there and eaten up my heart and cursed Washington."

"Well, then, that's all right. And now about this charge up San Juan? Did any of the Generals speak to you afterward and say that you had done well? Didn't any of them see you?"

"Why, n—n—no, I don't suppose they did … any more than I did them. You see, this charge was a big thing and covered lots of ground, and I hardly saw anybody excepting a lot of the men."

"Well, but didn't any of the men see you? Weren't you ahead some of the time leading them on and waving your sword?"

Caspar burst into laughter. "Why, no. I had all I could do to scramble along and try to keep up. And I didn't want to go up at all."

"Why?" demanded the Senator.

"Because—because the Spaniards were shooting so much. And you could see men falling, and the bullets rushed around you in—by the bushel. And then at last it seemed that if we once drove them away from the top of the hill there would be less danger. So we all went up."

The Senator chuckled over this description. "And you didn't flinch at all?"

"Well," rejoined Caspar humorously, "I won't say I wasn't frightened."

"No, of course not. But then you did not let anybody know it?"

"Of course not."

"You understand, naturally, that I am bothering you with all these questions because I desire to hear how my only son behaved in the crisis. I don't want to worry you with it. But if you went through the San Juan charge with credit I'll have you made a Major."

"Well," said Caspar, "I wouldn't say I went through that charge with credit. I went through it all good enough, but the enlisted men around went through in the same way."

"But weren't you encouraging them and leading them on by your example?"

Caspar smirked. He began to see a point. "Well, sir," he said with a charming hesitation. "Aw—er—I—well, I dare say I was doing my share of it."

The perfect form of the reply delighted the father. He could not endure blatancy; his admiration was to be won only by a bashful hero. Now he beat his hand impulsively down upon the table. "That's what I wanted to know. That's it exactly. I'll have you made a Major next week. You've found your proper field at last. You stick to the Army, Caspar, and I'll back you up. That's the thing. In a few years it will be a great career. The United States is pretty sure to have an Army of about a hundred and fifty thousand men. And starting in when you did and with me to back you up—why, we'll make you a General in seven or eight years. That's the ticket. You stay in the Army." The Senator's cheek was flushed with enthusiasm, and he looked eagerly and confidently at his son.

But Caspar had pulled a long face. "The Army?" he said. "Stay in the Army?"

The Senator continued to outline quite rapturously his idea of the future. "The Army, evidently, is just the place for you. You know as well as I do that you have not been a howling success, exactly, in anything else which you have tried. But now the Army just suits you. It is the kind of career which especially suits you. Well, then, go in, and go at it hard. Go in to win. Go at it."

"But—" began Caspar.

The Senator interrupted swiftly. "Oh, don't worry about that part of it. I'll take care of all that. You won't get jailed in some Arizona adobe for the rest of your natural life. There won't be much more of that, anyhow; and besides, as I say, I'll look after all that end of it. The chance is splendid. A young, healthy and intelligent man, with the start you've already got, and with my backing, can do anything—anything! There will be a lot of active service—oh, yes, I'm sure of it—and everybody who—"

"But," said Caspar, wan, desperate, heroic, "father, I don't care to stay in the Army."

The Senator lifted his eyes and darkened. "What?" he said. "What's that?" He looked at Caspar.

The son became tightened and wizened like an old miser trying to withhold gold. He replied with a sort of idiot obstinacy, "I don't care to stay in the Army."

The Senator's jaw clinched down, and he was dangerous. But, after all, there was something mournful somewhere. "Why, what do you mean?" he asked gruffly.

"Why, I couldn't get along, you know. The—the—"

"The what?" demanded the father, suddenly uplifted with thunderous anger. "The what?"

Caspar's pain found a sort of outlet in mere irresponsible talk. "Well, you know—the other men, you know. I couldn't get along with them, you know. They're peculiar, somehow; odd; I didn't understand them, and they didn't understand me. We—we didn't hitch, somehow. They're a queer lot. They've got funny ideas. I don't know how to explain it exactly, but—somehow—I don't like 'em. That's all there is to it. They're good fellows enough, I know, but—"

"Oh, well, Caspar," interrupted the Senator. Then he seemed to weigh a great fact in his mind. "I guess—" He paused again in profound consideration. "I guess—" He lit a small, brown cigar. "I guess you are no damn good."

# THE BLACK RIDERS
# AND OTHER LINES

## I

*Black Riders came from the sea.*
*There was clang and clang of spear and shield,*
*And clash and clash of hoof and heel,*
*Wild shouts and the wave of hair*
*In the rush upon the wind:*
*Thus the ride of Sin.*

## II

*Three little birds in a row*
*Sat musing.*
*A man passed near that place.*
*Then did the little birds nudge each other.*
*They said, "He thinks he can sing."*
*They threw back their heads to laugh,*
*With quaint countenances*
*They regarded him.*
*They were very curious,*
*Those three little birds in a row.*

## III

*In the desert*
*I saw a creature, naked, bestial,*
*Who, squatting upon the ground,*
*Held his heart in his hands,*
*And ate of it.*
*I said, "Is it good, friend?"*
*"It is bitter—bitter," he answered;*
*"But I like it*
*Because it is bitter,*
*And because it is my heart."*

## IV

*Yes, I have a thousand tongues,*
*And nine and ninety-nine lie.*
*Though I strive to use the one,*
*It will make no melody at my will,*
*But is dead in my mouth.*

**V**

*Once there came a man*
*Who said,*
*"Range me all men of the world in rows."*
*And instantly*
*There was terrific clamor among the people*
*Against being ranged in rows.*
*There was a loud quarrel, world-wide.*
*It endured for ages;*
*And blood was shed*
*By those who would not stand in rows,*
*And by those who pined to stand in rows,*
*Eventually, the man went to death, weeping.*
*And those who staid in bloody scuffle*
*Knew not the great simplicity.*

**VI**

*God fashioned the ship of the world carefully*
*With the infinite skill of an All-Master*
*Made He the hull and the sails,*
*Held He the rudder*
*Ready for adjustment.*
*Erect stood He, scanning his work proudly.*
*Then—at fateful time—a Wrong called,*
*And God turned, heeding.*
*Lo, the ship, at this opportunity, slipped slyly,*
*Making cunning noiseless travel down the ways.*
*So that, forever rudderless, it went upon the seas*
*Going ridiculous voyages,*
*Making quaint progress,*
*Turning as with serious purpose*
*Before stupid winds.*
*And there were many in the sky*
*Who laughed at this thing.*

**VII**

*Mystic Shadow, bending near me,*
*Who art thou?*
*Whence come ye?*
*And—tell me—is it fair*
*Or is the truth bitter as eaten fire?*
*Tell me!*
*Fear not that I should quaver,*
*For I dare—I dare.*
*Then, tell me!*

**VIII**

*I looked here;*
*I looked there;*
*Nowhere could I see my love.*
*And—this time—*
*She was in my heart.*
*Truly, then, I have no complaint,*
*For though she be fair and fairer,*
*She is none so fair as she*
*In my heart.*

**IX**

*I stood upon a high place,*
*And saw, below, many devils*
*Running, leaping,*
*And carousing in sin.*
*One looked up, grinning,*
*And said, "Comrade! Brother!"*

**X**

*Should the wide world roll away,*
*Leaving black terror,*
*Limitless night,*
*Nor God, nor man, nor place to stand*
*Would be to me essential,*
*If thou and thy white arms were there,*
*And the fall to doom a long way.*

**XI**

*In a lonely place,*
*I encountered a sage*
*Who sat, all still,*
*Regarding a newspaper.*
*He accosted me:*
*"Sir, what is this?"*
*Then I saw that I was greater,*
*Aye, greater than this sage.*
*I answered him at once,*
*"Old, old man, it is the wisdom of the age."*
*The sage looked upon me with admiration.*

**XII**

*"and the sins of the fathers shall be*
*visited upon the heads of the children,*
*even unto the third and fourth*

*generation of them that hate me."*
*Well, then, I hate thee, Unrighteous Picture;*
*Wicked Image, I hate thee;*
*So, strike with thy vengeance*
*The heads of those little men*
*Who come blindly.*
*It will be a brave thing.*

## XIII

*If there is a witness to my little life,*
*To my tiny throes and struggles,*
*He sees a fool;*
*And it is not fine for gods to menace fools.*

## XIV

*There was crimson clash of war.*
*Lands turned black and bare;*
*Women wept;*
*Babes ran, wondering.*
*There came one who understood not these things.*
*He said, "Why is this?"*
*Whereupon a million strove to answer him.*
*There was such intricate clamor of tongues,*
*That still the reason was not.*

## XV

*"Tell brave deeds of war."*
*Then they recounted tales,—*
*"There were stern stands*
*"And bitter runs for glory."*
*Ah, I think there were braver deeds.*

## XVI

*Chanty, thou art a lie,*
*A toy of women,*
*A pleasure of certain men.*
*In the presence of justice,*
*Lo, the walls of the temple*
*Are visible*
*Through thy form of sudden shadows.*

## XVII

*There were many who went in huddled procession,*
*They knew not whither;*
*But, at any rate, success or calamity*

*Would attend all in equality.*
*There was one who sought a new road.*
*He went into direful thickets,*
*And ultimately he died thus, alone;*
*But they said he had courage.*

## XVIII

*In Heaven,*
*Some little blades of grass*
*Stood before God.*
*"What did you do?"*
*Then all save one of the little blades*
*Began eagerly to relate*
*The merits of their lives.*
*This one stayed a small way behind,*
*Ashamed.*
*Presently, God said,*
*"And what did you do?"*
*The little blade answered, "Oh, my Lord,*
*"Memory is bitter to me,*
*"For, if I did good deeds,*
*"I know not of them."*
*Then God, in all His splendor,*
*Arose from His throne.*
*"Oh, best little blade of grass!" He said.*

## XIX

*A god in wrath*
*Was beating a man;*
*He cuffed him loudly*
*With thunderous blows*
*That rang and rolled over the earth.*
*All people came running.*
*The man screamed and struggled,*
*And bit madly at the feet of the god.*
*The people cried,*
*"Ah, what a wicked man!"*
*And—*
*"Ah, what a redoubtable god!"*

## XX

*A learned man came to me once.*
*He said, "I know the way,—come."*
*And I was overjoyed at this.*
*Together we hastened.*

*Soon, too soon, were we*
*Where my eyes were useless,*
*And I knew not the ways of my feet*
*I clung to the hand of my friend;*
*But at last he cried, "I am lost."*

## XXI

*There was, before me,*
*Mile upon mile*
*Of snow, ice, burning sand.*
*And yet I could look beyond all this,*
*To a place of infinite beauty;*
*And I could see the loveliness of her*
*Who walked in the shade of the trees.*
*When I gazed,*
*All was lost*
*But this place of beauty and her.*
*When I gazed,*
*And in my gazing, desired,*
*Then came again*
*Mile upon mile,*
*Of snow, ice, burning sand.*

## XXII

*Once I saw Mountains angry,*
*And ranged in battle-front.*
*Against them stood a little man;*
*Aye, he was no bigger than my finger.*
*I laughed, and spoke to one near me,*
*"Will he prevail?"*
*"Surely," replied this other;*
*"His grandfathers beat them many times."*
*Then did I see much virtue in grandfathers,—*
*At least, for the little man*
*Who stood against the Mountains.*

## XXIII

*Places among the stars,*
*Soft gardens near the sun,*
*Keep your distant beauty;*
*Shed no beams upon my weak heart.*
*Since she is here*
*In a place of blackness,*
*Not your golden days*
*Nor your silver nights*

*Can call me to you.*
*Since she is here*
*In a place of blackness,*
*Here I stay and wait.*

## XXIV

*I saw a man pursuing the horizon;*
*Round and round they sped.*
*I was disturbed at this;*
*I accosted the man.*
*"It is futile," I said,*
*"You can never"—*
*"You lie," he cried,*
*And ran on.*

## XXV

*Behold, the grave of a wicked man,*
*And near it, a stern spirit.*
*There came a drooping maid with violets,*
*But the spirit grasped her arm.*
*"No flowers for him," he said.*
*The maid wept:*
*"Ah, I loved him."*
*But the spirit, grim and frowning:*
*"No flowers for him."*
*Now, this is it—*
*If the spirit was just,*
*Why did the maid weep?*

## XXVI

*There was set before me a mighty hill,*
*And long days I climbed*
*Through regions of snow.*
*When I had before me the summit-view,*
*It seemed that my labor*
*Had been to see gardens*
*Lying at impossible distances.*

## XXVII

*A youth in apparel that glittered*
*Went to walk in a grim forest.*
*There he met an assassin*
*Attired all in garb of old days;*
*He, scowling through the thickets,*
*And dagger poised quivering,*

*Rushed upon the youth.*
*"Sir," said this latter,*
*"I am enchanted, believe me,*
*"To die, thus,*
*"In this medieval fashion,*
*"According to the best legends;*
*"Ah, what joy!"*
*Then took he the wound, smiling,*
*And died, content.*

## XXVIII

*"Truth," said a traveller,*
*"Is a rock, a mighty fortress;*
*"Often have I been to it,*
*"Even to its highest tower,*
*"From whence the world looks black."*
*"Truth," said a traveller,*
*"Is a breath, a wind,*
*"A shadow, a phantom;*
*"Long have I pursued it,*
*"But never have I touched*
*"The hem of its garment."*
*And I believed the second traveller;*
*For truth was to me*
*A breath, a wind,*
*A shadow, a phantom,*
*And never had I touched*
*The hem of its garment.*

## XXIX

*Behold, from the land of the farther suns*
*I returned.*
*And I was in a reptile-swarming place,*
*Peopled, otherwise, with grimaces,*
*Shrouded above in black impenetrableness.*
*I shrank, loathing,*
*Sick with it.*
*And I said to him,*
*"What is this?"*
*He made answer slowly,*
*"Spirit, this is a world;*
*"This was your home."*

## XXX

*Supposing that I should have the courage*

*To let a red sword of virtue*
*Plunge into my heart,*
*Letting to the weeds of the ground*
*My sinful blood,*
*What can you offer me?*
*A gardened castle?*
*A flowery kingdom?*
*What? A hope?*
*Then hence with your red sword of virtue.*

## XXXI

*Many workmen*
*Built a huge ball of masonry*
*Upon a mountain-top.*
*Then they went to the valley below,*
*And turned to behold their work.*
*"It is grand," they said;*
*They loved the thing.*
*Of a sudden, it moved:*
*It came upon them swiftly;*
*It crushed them all to blood.*
*But some had opportunity to squeal.*

## XXXII

*Two or three angels*
*Came near to the earth.*
*They saw a fat church.*
*Little black streams of people*
*Came and went in continually.*
*And the angels were puzzled*
*To know why the people went thus,*
*And why they stayed so long within.*

## XXXIII

*There was one I met upon the road*
*Who looked at me with kind eyes.*
*He said, "Show me of your wares."*
*And this I did,*
*Holding forth one.*
*He said, "It is a sin."*
*Then held I forth another;*
*He said, "It is a sin."*
*Then held I forth another;*
*He said, "It is a sin."*
*And so to the end;*

*Always he said, "It is a sin."*
*And, finally, I cried out,*
*"But I have none other."*
*Then did he look at me*
*With kinder eyes.*
*"Poor soul!" he said.*

## XXXIV

*I stood upon a highway,*
*And, behold, there came*
*Many strange pedlers.*
*To me each one made gestures.*
*Holding forth little images, saying,*
*"This is my pattern of God.*
*"Now this is the God I prefer."*
*But I said, "Hence!*
*"Leave me with mine own,*
*"And take you yours away;*
*"I can't buy of your patterns of God,*
*"The little Gods you may rightly prefer."*

## XXXV

*A man saw a ball of gold in the sky;*
*He climbed for it,*
*And eventually he achieved it—*
*It was clay.*
*Now this is the strange part:*
*When the man went to the earth*
*And looked again,*
*Lo, there was the ball of gold.*
*Now this is the strange part:*
*It was a ball of gold.*
*Aye, by the Heavens, it was a ball of gold.*

## XXXVI

*I met a seer.*
*He held in his hands*
*The book of wisdom.*
*"Sir," I addressed him,*
*"Let me read."*
*"Child—" he began.*
*"Sir," I said,*
*"Think not that I am a child,*
*"For already I know much*
*"Of that which you hold.*

*"Aye, much."*
*He smiled.*
*Then he opened the book*
*And held it before me.—*
*Strange that I should have grown so suddenly blind.*

## XXXVII

*On the horizon the peaks assembled;*
*And as I looked,*
*The march of the mountains began.*
*As they marched, they sang,*
*"Aye! We come! We come!"*

## XXXVIII

*The ocean said to me once,*
*"Look!*
*"Yonder on the shore*
*"Is a woman, weeping.*
*"I have watched her.*
*"Go you and tell her this,—*
*"Her lover I have laid*
*"In cool green hall.*
*"There is wealth of golden sand*
*"And pillars, coral-red;*
*"Two white fish stand guard at his bier.*
*"Tell her this*
*"And more,—*
*"That the king of the seas*
*"Weeps too, old, helpless man.*
*"The bustling fates*
*"Heap his hands with corpses*
*"Until he stands like a child,*
*"With surplus of toys."*

## XXXIX

*The livid lightnings flashed in the clouds;*
*The leaden thunders crashed.*
*A worshipper raised his arm.*
*"Hearken! Hearken! The voice of God!"*
*"Not so," said a man.*
*"The voice of God whispers in the heart*
*"So softly*
*"That the soul pauses,*
*"Making no noise,*
*"And strives for these melodies,*

*"Distant, sighing, like faintest breath,*
*"And all the being is still to hear."*

### XL

*And you love me?*
*I love you.*
*You are, then, cold coward.*
*Aye; but, beloved,*
*When I strive to come to you,*
*Man's opinions, a thousand thickets,*
*My interwoven existence,*
*My life,*
*Caught in the stubble of the world*
*Like a tender veil,—*
*This stays me.*
*No strange move can I make*
*Without noise of tearing.*
*I dare not.*
*If love loves,*
*There is no world*
*Nor word.*
*All is lost*
*Save thought of love*
*And place to dream.*
*You love me?*
*I love you.*
*You are, then, cold coward.*
*Aye; but beloved—*

### XLI

*Love walked alone.*
*The rocks cut her tender feet,*
*And the brambles tore her fair limbs.*
*There came a companion to her,*
*But, alas, he was no help,*
*For his name was Heart's Pain.*

### XLII

*I walked in a desert.*
*And I cried,*
*"Ah, God, take me from this place!"*
*A voice said, "It is no desert."*
*I cried, "Well, but—*
*"The sand, the heat, the vacant horizon."*
*A voice said, "It is no desert."*

## XLIII

*There came whisperings in the winds*
*"Good bye! Good bye!"*
*Little voices called in the darkness:*
*"Good bye! Good bye!"*
*Then I stretched forth my arms.*
*"No—no—"*
*There came whisperings in the wind:*
*"Good bye! Good bye!"*
*Little voices called in the darkness:*
*"Good bye! Good bye!"*

## XLIV

*I was in the darkness;*
*I could not see my words*
*Nor the wishes of my heart.*
*Then suddenly there was a great light—*
*"Let me into the darkness again."*

## XLV

*Tradition, thou art for suckling children,*
*Thou art the enlivening milk for babes;*
*But no meat for men is in thee.*
*Then—*
*But, alas, we all are babes.*

## XLVI

*Many red devils ran from my heart*
*And out upon the page,*
*They were so tiny*
*The pen could mash them.*
*And many struggled in the ink.*
*It was strange*
*To write in this red muck*
*Of things from my heart.*

## XLVII

*"Think as I think," said a man,*
*"Or you are abominably wicked;*
*"You are a toad."*
*And after I had thought of it,*
*I said, "I will, then, be a toad."*

## XLVIII

*Once there was a man,—*

*Oh, so wise!*
*In all drink*
*He detected the bitter,*
*And in all touch*
*He found the sting.*
*At last he cried thus:*
*"There is nothing,—*
*"No life,*
*"No joy,*
*"No pain,—*
*"There is nothing save opinion,*
*"And opinion be damned."*

## XLIX

*I stood musing in a black world,*
*Not knowing where to direct my feet.*
*And I saw the quick stream of men*
*Pouring ceaselessly,*
*Filled with eager faces,*
*A torrent of desire.*
*I called to them,*
*"Where do you go? What do you see?"*
*A thousand voices called to me.*
*A thousand fingers pointed.*
*"Look! Look! There!"*
*I know not of it.*
*But, lo! in the far sky shone a radiance*
*Ineffable, divine,—*
*A vision painted upon a pall;*
*And sometimes it was,*
*And sometimes it was not.*
*I hesitated.*
*Then from the stream*
*Came roaring voices,*
*Impatient:*
*"Look! Look! There!"*
*So again I saw,*
*And leaped, unhesitant,*
*And struggled and fumed*
*With outspread clutching fingers.*
*The hard hills tore my flesh;*
*The ways bit my feet.*
*At last I looked again.*
*No radiance in the far sky,*
*Ineffable, divine;*
*No vision painted upon a pall;*

*And always my eyes ached for the light.*
*Then I cried in despair,*
*"I see nothing! Oh, where do I go?"*
*The torrent turned again its faces:*
*"Look! Look! There!"*
*And at the blindness of my spirit*
*They screamed,*
*"Fool! Fool! Fool!"*

## L

*You say you are holy,*
*And that*
*Because I have not seen you sin.*
*Aye, but there are those*
*Who see you sin, my friend.*

## LI

*A man went before a strange god,—*
*The god of many men, sadly wise.*
*And the deity thundered loudly,*
*Fat with rage, and puffing,*
*"Kneel, mortal, and cringe*
*"And grovel and do homage*
*"To my particularly sublime majesty."*
*The man fled.*
*Then the man went to another god,—*
*The god of his inner thoughts.*
*And this one looked at him*
*With soft eyes*
*Lit with infinite comprehension,*
*And said, "My poor child!"*

## LII

*Why do you strive for greatness, fool?*
*Go pluck a bough and wear it.*
*It is as sufficing.*
*My lord, there are certain barbarians*
*Who tilt their noses*
*As if the stars were flowers,*
*And thy servant is lost among their shoe-buckles.*
*Fain would I have mine eyes even with their eyes.*
*Fool, go pluck a bough and wear it.*

## LIII

I

*Blustering god,*
*Stamping across the sky*
*With loud swagger,*
*I fear you not.*
*No, though from your highest heaven*
*You plunge your spear at my heart,*
*I fear you not.*
*No, not if the blow*
*Is as the lightning blasting a tree,*
*I fear you not, puffing braggart.*

II

*If thou can see into my heart*
*That I fear thee not,*
*Thou wilt see why I fear thee not,*
*And why it is right.*
*So threaten not, thou, with thy bloody spears,*
*Else thy sublime ears shall hear curses.*

III

*Withal, there is one whom I fear;*
*I fear to see grief upon that face.*
*Perchance, Friend, he is not your god;*
*If so, spit upon him.*
*By it you will do no profanity.*
*But I—*
*Ah, sooner would I die*
*Than see tears in those eyes of my soul.*

## LIV

*"It was wrong to do this," said the angel.*
*"You should live like a flower,*
*"Holding malice like a puppy,*
*"Waging war like a lambkin."*
*"Not so," quoth the man*
*Who had no fear of spirits;*
*"It is only wrong for angels*
*"Who can live like the flowers,*
*"Holding malice like the puppies,*
*"Waging war like the lambkins."*

## LV

*A man toiled on a burning road,*
*Never resting.*
*Once he saw a fat, stupid ass*
*Grinning at him from a green place.*
*The man cried out in rage,*
*"Ah! Do not deride me, fool!*

*"I know you—*
*"All day stuffing your belly,*
*"Burying your heart*
*"In grass and tender sprouts:*
*"It will not suffice you."*
*But the ass only grinned at him from the green place.*

### LVI

*A man feared that he might find an assassin;*
*Another that he might find a victim.*
*One was more wise than the other.*

### LVII

*With eye and with gesture*
*You say you are holy.*
*I say you lie;*
*For I did see you*
*Draw away your coats*
*From the sin upon the hands*
*Of a little child.*
*Liar!*

### LVIII

*The sage lectured brilliantly.*
*Before him, two images:*
*"Now this one is a devil,*
*"And this one is me."*
*He turned away.*
*Then a cunning pupil*
*Changed the positions.*
*Turned the sage again:*
*"Now this one is a devil,*
*"And this one is me."*
*The pupils sat, all grinning,*
*And rejoiced in the game.*
*But the sage was a sage.*

### LIX

*Walking in the sky,*
*A man in strange black garb*
*Encountered a radiant form.*
*Then his steps were eager;*
*Bowed he devoutly.*
*"My Lord," said he.*
*But the spirit knew him not.*

# LX

*Upon the road of my life,*
*Passed me many fair creatures,*
*Clothed all in white, and radiant.*
*To one, finally, I made speech:*
*"Who art thou?"*
*But she, like the others,*
*Kept cowled her face,*
*And answered in haste, anxiously,*
*"I am Good Deed, forsooth;*
*"You have often seen me."*
*"Not uncowled," I made reply.*
*And with rash and strong hand,*
*Though she resisted,*
*I drew away the veil*
*And gazed at the features of Vanity*
*She, shamefaced, went on;*
*And after I had mused a time,*
*I said of myself,*
*"Fool!"*

# LXI

## I

*There was a man and a woman*
*Who sinned.*
*Then did the man heap the punishment*
*All upon the head of her,*
*And went away gayly.*

## II

*There was a man and a woman*
*Who sinned.*
*And the man stood with her.*
*As upon her head, so upon his,*
*Fell blow and blow,*
*And all people screaming, "Fool!"*
*He was a brave heart.*

## III

*He was a brave heart.*
*Would you speak with him, friend?*
*Well, he is dead,*
*And there went your opportunity.*
*Let it be your grief*
*That he is dead*
*And your opportunity gone;*
*For, in that, you were a coward.*

## LXII

*There was a man who lived a life of fire.*
*Even upon the fabric of time,*
*Where purple becomes orange*
*And orange purple,*
*This life glowed,*
*A dire red stain, indelible;*
*Yet when he was dead,*
*He saw that he had not lived.*

## LXIII

*There was a great cathedral.*
*To solemn songs,*
*A white procession*
*Moved toward the altar.*
*The chief man there*
*Was erect, and bore himself proudly.*
*Yet some could see him cringe,*
*As in a place of danger,*
*Throwing frightened glances into the air,*
*A-start at threatening faces of the past.*

## LXIV

*Friend, your white beard sweeps the ground,*
*Why do you stand, expectant?*
*Do you hope to see it*
*In one of your withered days?*
*With your old eyes*
*Do you hope to see*
*The triumphal march of Justice?*
*Do not wait, friend*
*Take your white beard*
*And your old eyes*
*To more tender lands.*

## LXV

*Once, I knew a fine song,*
*—It is true, believe me,—*
*It was all of birds,*
*And I held them in a basket;*
*When I opened the wicket,*
*Heavens! They all flew away.*
*I cried, "Come back, little thoughts!"*
*But they only laughed.*
*They flew on*

*Until they were as sand*
*Thrown between me and the sky.*

## LXVI

*If I should cast off this tattered coat,*
*And go free into the mighty sky;*
*If I should find nothing there*
*But a vast blue,*
*Echoless, ignorant,—*
*What then?*

## LXVII

*God lay dead in Heaven;*
*Angels sang the hymn of the end;*
*Purple winds went moaning,*
*Their wings drip-dripping*
*With blood*
*That fell upon the earth.*
*It, groaning thing,*
*Turned black and sank.*
*Then from the far caverns*
*Of dead sins*
*Came monsters, livid with desire.*
*They fought,*
*Wrangled over the world,*
*A morsel.*
*But of all sadness this was sad,—*
*A woman's arms tried to shield*
*The head of a sleeping man*
*From the jaws of the final beast.*

## LXVIII

*A spirit sped*
*Through spaces of night;*
*And as he sped, he called,*
*"God! God!"*
*He went through valleys*
*Of black death-slime,*
*Ever calling,*
*"God! God!"*
*Their echoes*
*From crevice and cavern*
*Mocked him:*
*"God! God! God!"*
*Fleetly into the plains of space*

He went, ever calling,
"God! God!"
Eventually, then, he screamed,
Mad in denial,
"Ah, there is no God!"
A swift hand,
A sword from the sky,
Smote him,
And he was dead.

# WHILOMVILLE STORIES

The following stories share the same setting and were published as "Whilomville Stories" (1900).

The Angel Child
Lynx-Hunting
The Lover and the Telltale
"Showin' Off"
Making an Orator
Shame
The Carriage-Lamps
The Knife
The Stove
The Trial, Execution, and Burial of Homer Phelps
The Fight
The City Urchin and the Chaste Villagers
A Little Pilgrimage

# THE ANGEL CHILD

I

Although Whilomville was in no sense a summer resort, the advent of the warm season meant much to it, for then came visitors from the city—people of considerable confidence—alighting upon their country cousins. Moreover, many citizens who could afford to do so escaped at this time to the sea-side. The town, with the commercial life quite taken out of it, drawled and drowsed through long months, during which nothing was worse than the white dust which arose behind every vehicle at blinding noon, and nothing was finer than the cool sheen of the hose sprays over the cropped lawns under the many maples in the twilight.

* * * *

One summer the Trescotts had a visitation. Mrs. Trescott owned a cousin who was a painter of high degree. I had almost said that he was of national reputation, but, come to think of it, it is better to say that almost everybody in the United States who knew about art and its travail knew about him. He had picked out a wife, and naturally, looking at him, one wondered how he had done it. She was quick, beautiful, imperious, while he was quiet, slow, and misty. She was a veritable queen of health, while he, apparently, was of a most brittle constitution. When he played tennis, particularly, he looked every minute as if he were going to break.

They lived in New York, in awesome apartments wherein Japan and Persia, and indeed all the world, confounded the observer. At the end was a cathedral-like studio. They had one child. Perhaps it would be better to say that they had one CHILD. It was a girl. When she came to Whilomville with her parents, it was patent that she had an inexhaustible store of white frocks, and that her voice was high and commanding. These things the town knew quickly. Other things it was doomed to discover by a process.

Her effect upon the children of the Trescott neighborhood was singular. They at first feared, then admired, then embraced. In two days she was a Begum. All day long her voice could be heard directing, drilling, and compelling those free-born children; and to say that they felt oppression would be wrong, for they really fought for records of loyal obedience.

All went well until one day was her birthday.

On the morning of this day she walked out into the Trescott garden and said to her father, confidently, "Papa, give me some money, because this is my birthday."

He looked dreamily up from his easel. "Your birthday?" he murmured. Her envisioned father was never energetic enough to be irritable unless some one broke through into that place where he lived with the desires of his life. But neither wife nor child ever heeded or even understood the temperamental values, and so some part of him had grown hardened to their inroads. "Money?" he said. "Here." He handed her a five-dollar bill. It was that he did not at all understand the nature of a five-dollar bill. He was deaf to it. He had it; he gave it; that was all.

She sallied forth to a waiting people—Jimmie Trescott, Dan Earl, Ella Earl, the Margate twins, the three Phelps children, and others. "I've got some pennies now," she cried, waving the bill, "and I am going to buy some candy." They were deeply stirred by this announcement. Most children are penniless three hundred days in the year, and to another possessing five pennies they pay deference. To little Cora waving a bright green note these children paid heathenish homage. In some disorder they thronged after her to a small shop on Bridge Street hill. First of all came ice-cream. Seated in the comic little back parlor, they clamored shrilly over plates of various flavors, and the shopkeeper marvelled that cream could vanish so quickly down throats that seemed wide open, always, for the making of excited screams.

These children represented the families of most excellent people. They were all born in whatever purple there was to be had in the vicinity of Whilomville. The Margate twins, for example, were out-and-out prize-winners. With their long golden curls and their countenances of similar vacuity, they shone upon the front bench of all Sunday-school functions, hand in hand, while their uplifted mother felt about her the envy of a hundred other parents, and less heavenly children scoffed from near the door.

Then there was little Dan Earl, probably the nicest boy in the world, gentle, fine-grained, obedient to the point where he obeyed anybody. Jimmie Trescott himself was, indeed, the only child who was at all versed in villany, but in these particular days he was on his very good behavior. As a matter of fact, he was in love. The beauty of his regal little cousin had stolen his manly heart.

Yes, they were all most excellent children, but, loosened upon this candy-shop with five dollars, they resembled, in a tiny way, drunken revelling soldiers within the walls of a stormed city. Upon the heels of ice-cream and cake came chocolate mice, butter-scotch, "everlastings," chocolate cigars, taffy-on-a-stick, taffy-on-a-slate-pencil, and many semi-transparent devices resembling lions, tigers, elephants, horses, cats, dogs, cows, sheep, tables, chairs, engines (both railway and for the fighting of fire), soldiers, fine ladies, odd-looking men, clocks, watches, revolvers, rabbits, and bedsteads. A cent was the price of a single wonder.

Some of the children, going quite daft, soon had thought to make fight over the spoils, but their queen ruled with an iron grip. Her first inspiration was to satisfy her own fancies, but as soon as that was done she mingled prodigality with a fine justice, dividing, balancing, bestowing, and sometimes taking away from somebody even that which he had.

It was an orgy. In thirty-five minutes those respectable children looked as if they had been dragged at the tail of a chariot. The sacred Margate twins, blinking and grunting, wished to take seat upon the floor, and even the most durable Jimmie Trescott found occasion to lean against the counter, wearing at the time a solemn and abstracted air, as if he expected something to happen to him shortly.

Of course their belief had been in an unlimited capacity, but they found there was an end. The shopkeeper handed the queen her change.

"Two seventy-three from five leaves two twenty-seven, Miss Cora," he said, looking upon her with admiration.

She turned swiftly to her clan. "O-oh!" she cried, in amazement. "Look how much I have left!" They gazed at the coins in her palm. They knew then that it was not their capacities which were endless; it was the five dollars.

The queen led the way to the street. "We must think up some way of spending more money," she said, frowning. They stood in silence, awaiting her further speech.

Suddenly she clapped her hands and screamed with delight. "Come on!" she cried. "I know what let's do." Now behold, she had discovered the red and white pole in front of the shop of one William Neeltje, a barber by trade.

It becomes necessary to say a few words concerning Neeltje. He was new to the town. He had come and opened a dusty little shop on dusty Bridge Street hill, and although the neighborhood knew from the courier winds that his diet was mainly cabbage, they were satisfied with that meagre data. Of course Riefsnyder came to investigate him for the local Barbers' Union, but he found in him only sweetness and light, with a willingness to charge any price at all for a shave or a haircut. In fact, the advent of Neeltje would have made barely a ripple upon the placid bosom of Whilomville if it were not that his name was Neeltje.

At first the people looked at his sign-board out of the eye corner, and wondered lazily why any one should bear the name of Neeltje; but as time went on, men spoke to other men, saying, "How do you pronounce the name of that barber up there on Bridge Street hill?" And then, before any could prevent it, the best minds of the town were splintering their lances against William Neeltje's sign-board. If a man had a mental superior, he guided him seductively to this name, and watched with glee his wrecking. The clergy of the town even entered the lists. There was one among them who had taken a collegiate prize in Syriac, as well as in several less opaque languages, and the other clergymen—at one of their weekly meetings—sought to betray him into this ambush. He pronounced the name correctly, but that mattered little, since none of them knew whether he did or did not; and so they took triumph according to their ignorance. Under these arduous circumstances it was certain that the town should look for a nickname, and at this time the nickname was in process of formation. So William Neeltje lived on with his secret, smiling foolishly towards the world.

"Come on," cried little Cora. "Let's all get our hair cut. That's what let's do. Let's all get our hair cut! Come on! Come on! Come on!" The others were carried off their feet by the fury of this assault. To get their hair cut! What joy! Little did they know if this were fun; they only knew that their small leader said it was fun. Chocolate-stained but confident, the band marched into William Neeltje's barber shop.

"We wish to get our hair cut," said little Cora, haughtily.

Neeltje, in his shirt-sleeves, stood looking at them with his half-idiot smile.

"Hurry, now!" commanded the queen. A dray-horse toiled step by step, step by step, up Bridge Street hill; a far woman's voice arose; there could be heard the ceaseless hammers of shingling carpenters; all was summer peace. "Come on, now. Who's goin' first? Come on, Ella; you go first. Gettin' our hair cut! Oh what fun!"

Little Ella Earl would not, however, be first in the chair. She was drawn towards it by a singular fascination, but at the same time she was afraid of it, and so she hung back, saying: "No! You go first! No! You go first!" The question was precipitated by the twins and one of the Phelps children. They made simultaneous rush for the chair, and screamed and kicked, each pair preventing the third child. The queen entered this mêlée, and decided in favor of the Phelps boy. He ascended the chair. Thereat an awed silence fell upon the band. And always William Neeltje smiled fatuously.

He tucked a cloth in the neck of the Phelps boy, and taking scissors, began to cut his hair. The group of children came closer and closer. Even the queen was deeply moved. "Does it hurt any?" she asked, in a wee voice.

"Naw," said the Phelps boy, with dignity. "Anyhow, I've had m' hair cut afore."

When he appeared to them looking very soldierly with his cropped little head, there was a tumult over the chair. The Margate twins howled; Jimmie Trescott was kicking them on the shins. It was a fight.

But the twins could not prevail, being the smallest of all the children. The queen herself took the chair, and ordered Neeltje as if he were a lady's-maid. To the floor there fell proud ringlets, blazing even there in their humiliation with a full fine bronze light. Then Jimmie Trescott, then Ella Earl (two long ash-colored plaits), then a Phelps girl, then another Phelps girl; and so on from head to head. The ceremony received unexpected check when the turn came to Dan Earl. This lad, usually docile to any rein, had suddenly grown mulishly obstinate. No, he would not, he would not. He himself did not seem to know why he refused to have his hair cut, but, despite the shrill derision of the company, he remained obdurate. Anyhow, the twins, long held in check, and now feverishly eager, were already struggling for the chair.

And so to the floor at last came the golden Margate curls, the heart treasure and glory of a mother, three aunts, and some feminine cousins.

All having been finished, the children, highly elate, thronged out into the street. They crowed and cackled with pride and joy, anon turning to scorn the cowardly Dan Earl.

Ella Earl was an exception. She had been pensive for some time, and now the shorn little maiden began vaguely to weep. In the door of his shop William Neeltje stood watching them, upon his face a grin of almost inhuman idiocy.

## II

It now becomes the duty of the unfortunate writer to exhibit these children to their fond parents. "Come on, Jimmie," cried little Cora, "let's go show mamma." And they hurried off, these happy children, to show mamma.

The Trescotts and their guests were assembled indolently awaiting the luncheon-bell. Jimmie and the angel child burst in upon them. "Oh, mamma," shrieked little Cora, "see how fine I am! I've had my hair cut! Isn't it splendid? And Jimmie too!"

The wretched mother took one sight, emitted one yell, and fell into a chair. Mrs. Trescott dropped a large lady's journal and made a nerveless mechanical clutch at it. The painter gripped the arms of his chair and leaned forward, staring until his eyes were like two little clock faces. Dr. Trescott did not move or speak.

To the children the next moments were chaotic. There was a loudly wailing mother, and a pale-faced, aghast mother; a stammering father, and a grim and terrible father. The angel child did not understand anything of it save the voice of calamity, and in a moment all her little imperialism went to the winds. She ran sobbing to her mother. "Oh, mamma! mamma! mamma!"

The desolate Jimmie heard out of this inexplicable situation a voice which he knew well, a sort of colonel's voice, and he obeyed like any good soldier. "Jimmie!"

He stepped three paces to the front. "Yes, sir."

"How did this—how did this happen?" said Trescott.

Now Jimmie could have explained how had happened anything which had happened, but he did not know what had happened, so he said, "I—I—nothin'."

"And, oh, look at her frock!" said Mrs. Trescott, brokenly.

The words turned the mind of the mother of the angel child. She looked up, her eyes blazing. "Frock!" she repeated. "Frock! What do I care for her frock? Frock!" she choked out again from the depths of her bitterness. Then she arose suddenly, and whirled tragically upon her husband. "Look!" she declaimed. "All—her lovely—hair—all her lovely hair—gone—gone!" The painter was apparently in a fit; his jaw was set, his eyes were glazed, his body was stiff and straight. "All gone—all—her lovely hair—all gone—my poor little darlin'—my—poor—little—darlin'!" And the angel child added her heart-broken voice to her mother's wail as they fled into each other's arms.

In the mean time Trescott was patiently unravelling some skeins of Jimmie's tangled intellect. "And then you went to this barber's on the hill. Yes. And where did you get the money? Yes. I see. And who besides you and Cora had their hair cut? The Margate twi—Oh, lord!"

Over at the Margate place old Eldridge Margate, the grandfather of the twins, was in the back garden picking pease and smoking ruminatively to himself. Suddenly he heard from the house great noises. Doors slammed, women rushed upstairs and down-stairs calling to each other in voices of agony. And then full and mellow upon the still air arose the roar of the twins in pain.

Old Eldridge stepped out of the pea-patch and moved towards the house, puzzled, staring, not yet having decided that it was his duty to rush forward. Then around the corner of the house shot his daughter Mollie, her face pale with horror.

"What's the matter?" he cried.

"Oh, father," she gasped, "the children! They—"

Then around the corner of the house came the twins, howling at the top of their power, their faces flowing with tears. They were still hand in hand, the ruling passion being strong even in this suffering. At sight of them old Eldridge took his pipe hastily out of his mouth. "Good God!" he said.

* * * *

And now what befell one William Neeltje, a barber by trade? And what was said by angry parents of the mother of such an angel child? And what was the fate of the angel child herself?

There was surely a tempest. With the exception of the Margate twins, the boys could well be eliminated from the affair. Of course it didn't matter if their hair was cut. Also the two little Phelps girls had had very short hair, anyhow, and their parents were not too greatly incensed. In the case of Ella Earl, it was mainly the pathos of the little girl's own grieving; but her mother played a most generous part, and called upon Mrs. Trescott, and condoled with the mother of the angel child over their equivalent losses. But the Margate contingent! They simply screeched.

Trescott, composed and cool-blooded, was in the middle of a giddy whirl. He was not going to allow the mobbing of his wife's cousins, nor was he going to pretend that the spoliation of the Margate twins was a virtuous and beautiful act. He was elected, gratuitously, to the position of a buffer.

But, curiously enough, the one who achieved the bulk of the misery was old Eldridge Margate, who had been picking pease at the time. The feminine Margates stormed his position as individuals, in pairs, in teams, and *en masse*. In two days they may have aged him seven years. He must destroy the utter Neeltje. He must midnightly massacre the angel child and her mother. He must dip his arms in blood to the elbows.

Trescott took the first opportunity to express to him his concern over the affair, but when the subject of the disaster was mentioned, old Eldridge, to the doctor's great surprise, actually chuckled long and deeply. "Oh, well, look-a-here," he said. "I never was so much in love with them there damn curls. The curls was purty— yes—but then I'd a darn sight rather see boys look more like boys than like two little wax figgers. An', ye know, the little cusses like it themselves. *They* never took no stock in all this washin' an' combin' an' fixin' an' goin' to church an' paradin' an' showin' off. They stood it because they were told to. That's all. Of course this here

Neel-te-gee, er whatever his name is, is a plumb dumb ijit, but I don't see what's to be done, now that the kids is full well cropped. I might go and burn his shop over his head, but that wouldn't bring no hair back onto the kids. They're even kicking on sashes now, and that's all right, 'cause what fer does a boy want a sash?"

Whereupon Trescott perceived that the old man wore his brains above his shoulders, and Trescott departed from him rejoicing greatly that it was only women who could not know that there was finality to most disasters, and that when a thing was fully done, no amount of door-slammings, rushing up-stairs and down-stairs, calls, lamentations, tears, could bring back a single hair to the heads of twins.

But the rains came and the winds blew in the most biblical way when a certain fact came to light in the Trescott household. Little Cora, corroborated by Jimmie, innocently remarked that five dollars had been given her by her father on her birthday, and with this money the evil had been wrought. Trescott had known it, but he—thoughtful man—had said nothing. For her part, the mother of the angel child had up to that moment never reflected that the consummation of the wickedness must have cost a small sum of money. But now it was all clear to her. He was the guilty one—he! "My angel child!"

The scene which ensued was inspiriting. A few days later, loungers at the railway station saw a lady leading a shorn and still undaunted lamb. Attached to them was a husband and father, who was plainly bewildered, but still more plainly vexed, as if he would be saying: "Damn 'em! Why can't they leave me alone?"

# LYNX-HUNTING

Jimmie lounged about the dining-room and watched his mother with large, serious eyes. Suddenly he said, "Ma—now—can I borrow pa's gun?"

She was overcome with the feminine horror which is able to mistake preliminary words for the full accomplishment of the dread thing. "Why, Jimmie!" she cried. "Of al-l wonders! Your father's gun! No indeed you can't!"

He was fairly well crushed, but he managed to mutter, sullenly, "Well, Willie Dalzel, he's got a gun." In reality his heart had previously been beating with such tumult—he had himself been so impressed with the daring and sin of his request—that he was glad that all was over now, and his mother could do very little further harm to his sensibilities. He had been influenced into the venture by the larger boys.

"Huh!" the Dalzel urchin had said; "your father's got a gun, hasn't he? Well, why don't you bring that?"

Puffing himself, Jimmie had replied, "Well, I can, if I want to." It was a black lie, but really the Dalzel boy was too outrageous with his eternal bill-posting about the gun which a beaming uncle had intrusted to him. Its possession made him superior in manfulness to most boys in the neighborhood—or at least they enviously conceded him such position—but he was so overbearing, and stuffed the fact of his treasure so relentlessly down their throats, that on this occasion the miserable Jimmie had lied as naturally as most animals swim.

Willie Dalzel had not been checkmated, for he had instantly retorted, "Why don't you get it, then?"

"Well, I can, if I want to."

"Well, get it, then!"

"Well, I can, if I want to."

Thereupon Jimmie had paced away with great airs of surety as far as the door of his home, where his manner changed to one of tremulous misgiving as it came upon him to address his mother in the dining-room. There had happened that which had happened.

When Jimmie returned to his two distinguished companions he was blown out with a singular pomposity. He spoke these noble words: "Oh, well, I guess I don't want to take the gun out today."

They had been watching him with gleaming ferret eyes, and they detected his falsity at once. They challenged him with shouted gibes, but it was not in the rules for the conduct of boys that one should admit anything whatsoever, and so Jimmie, backed into an ethical corner, lied as stupidly, as desperately, as hopelessly as ever lone savage fights when surrounded at last in his jungle.

Such accusations were never known to come to any point, for the reason that the number and kind of denials always equalled or exceeded the number of accusations, and no boy was ever brought really to book for these misdeeds.

In the end they went off together, Willie Dalzel with his gun being a trifle in advance and discoursing upon his various works. They passed along a maple-lined avenue, a highway common to boys bound for that free land of hills and woods in which they lived in some part their romance of the moment, whether it was of Indians, miners, smugglers, soldiers, or outlaws. The paths were their paths, and much was known to them of the secrets of the dark green hemlock thickets, the wastes of sweet-fern and huckleberry, the cliffs of gaunt bluestone with the sumach burning red at their feet. Each boy had, I am sure, a conviction that some day the wilderness was to give forth to him a marvellous secret. They felt that the hills and the forest knew much, and they heard a voice of it in the silence. It was vague, thrilling, fearful, and altogether fabulous. The grown folk seemed to regard these wastes merely as so much distance between one place and another place, or as a rabbit-cover, or as a district to be judged according to the value of the timber; but to the boys it spoke some great inspiring word, which they knew even as those who pace the shore know the enigmatic speech of the surf. In the mean time they lived there, in season, lives of ringing adventure—by dint of imagination.

The boys left the avenue, skirted hastily through some private grounds, climbed a fence, and entered the thickets. It happened that at school the previous day Willie Dalzel had been forced to read and acquire in some part a solemn description of a lynx. The meagre information thrust upon him had caused him grimaces of suffering, but now he said, suddenly, "I'm goin' to shoot a lynx."

The other boys admired this statement, but they were silent for a time. Finally Jimmie said, meekly, "What's a lynx?" He had endured his ignorance as long as he was able.

The Dalzel boy mocked him. "Why, don't you know what a lynx is? A lynx? Why, a lynx is a animal somethin' like a cat, an' it's got great big green eyes, and it sits on the limb of a tree an' jus' glares at you. It's a pretty bad animal, I tell you. Why, when I—"

"Huh!" said the third boy. "Where'd you ever see a lynx?"

"Oh, I've seen 'em—plenty of 'em. I bet you'd be scared if you seen one once."

Jimmie and the other boy each demanded, "How do you know I would?"

They penetrated deeper into the wood. They climbed a rocky zigzag path which led them at times where with their hands they could almost touch the tops of giant pines. The gray cliffs sprang sheer towards the sky. Willie Dalzel babbled about his impossible lynx, and they stalked the mountain-side like chamois-hunters, although no noise of bird or beast broke the stillness of the hills. Below them Whilomville was spread out somewhat like the cheap green and black lithograph of the time—"A Bird's-eye View of Whilomville, N. Y."

In the end the boys reached the top of the mountain and scouted off among wild and desolate ridges. They were burning with the desire to slay large animals. They thought continually of elephants, lions, tigers, crocodiles. They discoursed upon their immaculate conduct in case such monsters confronted them, and they all lied carefully about their courage.

The breeze was heavy with the smell of sweet-fern. The pines and hemlocks sighed as they waved their branches. In the hollows the leaves of the laurels were lacquered where the sunlight found them. No matter the weather, it would be impossible to long continue an expedition of this kind without a fire, and presently they built one, snapping down for fuel the brittle under-branches of the pines. About this fire they were willed to conduct a sort of play, the Dalzel boy taking the part of a bandit chief, and the other boys being his trusty lieutenants. They stalked to and fro, long-strided, stern yet devil-may-care, three terrible little figures.

Jimmie had an uncle who made game of him whenever he caught him in this kind of play, and often this uncle quoted derisively the following classic: "Once aboard the lugger, Bill, and the girl is mine. Now to burn the château and destroy all evidence of our crime. But, hark'e, Bill, no wiolence." Wheeling abruptly, he addressed these dramatic words to his comrades. They were impressed; they decided at once to be smugglers, and in the most ribald fashion they talked about carrying off young women.

At last they continued their march through the woods. The smuggling*motif* was now grafted fantastically upon the original lynx idea, which Willie Dalzel refused to abandon at any price.

Once they came upon an innocent bird who happened to be looking another way at the time. After a great deal of manœvering and big words, Willie Dalzel reared his fowling-piece and blew this poor thing into a mere rag of wet feathers, of which he was proud.

Afterwards the other big boy had a turn at another bird. Then it was plainly Jimmie's chance. The two others had, of course, some thought of cheating him out of this chance, but of a truth he was timid to explode such a thunderous weapon, and as soon as they detected this fear they simply overbore him, and made it clearly understood that if he refused to shoot he would lose his caste, his scalp-lock, his girdle, his honor.

They had reached the old death-colored snake-fence which marked the limits of the upper pasture of the Fleming farm. Under some hickory-trees the path ran parallel to the fence. Behold! a small priestly chipmonk came to a rail, and folding his hands on his abdomen, addressed them in his own tongue. It was Jimmie's shot. Adjured by the others, he took the gun. His face was stiff with apprehension. The Dalzel boy was giving forth fine words. "Go ahead. Aw, don't be afraid. It's nothin' to do. Why, I've done it a million times. Don't shut both your eyes, now. Jus' keep one open and shut the other one. He'll get away if you don't watch out. Now you're all right. Why don't you let'er go? Go ahead."

Jimmie, with his legs braced apart, was in the centre of the path. His back was greatly bent, owing to the mechanics of supporting the heavy gun. His companions were screeching in the rear. There was a wait.

Then he pulled trigger. To him there was a frightful roar, his cheek and his shoulder took a stunning blow, his face felt a hot flush of fire, and opening his two eyes, he found that he was still alive. He was not too dazed to instantly adopt a becoming egotism. It had been the first shot of his life.

But directly after the well-mannered celebration of this victory a certain cow, which had been grazing in the line of fire, was seen to break wildly across the pasture, bellowing and bucking. The three smugglers and lynx-hunters looked at each other out of blanched faces. Jimmie had hit the cow. The first evidence of his comprehension of this fact was in the celerity with which he returned the discharged gun to Willie Dalzel.

They turned to flee. The land was black, as if it had been overshadowed suddenly with thick storm-clouds, and even as they fled in their horror a gigantic Swedish farm-hand came from the heavens and fell upon them, shrieking in eerie triumph. In a twinkle they were clouted prostrate. The Swede was elate and ferocious in a foreign and fulsome way. He continued to beat them and yell.

From the ground they raised their dismal appeal. "Oh, please, mister, we didn't do it! He did it! I didn't do it! We didn't do it! We didn't mean to do it! Oh, please, mister!"

In these moments of childish terror little lads go half-blind, and it is possible that few moments of their after-life made them suffer as they did when the Swede flung them over the fence and marched them towards the farm- house. They begged like cowards on the scaffold, and each one was for himself. "Oh, please let me go, mister! I didn't do it, mister! He did it! Oh, p-l-ease let me go, mister!"

The boyish view belongs to boys alone, and if this tall and knotted laborer was needlessly without charity, none of the three lads questioned it. Usually when they were punished they decided that they deserved it, and the more they were punished the more they were convinced that they were criminals of a most subterranean type. As to the hitting of the cow being a pure accident, and therefore not of necessity a criminal matter, such reading never entered their heads. When things happened and they were caught, they commonly paid dire consequences, and they were accustomed to measure the probabilities of woe utterly by the damage done, and not in any way by the culpability. The shooting of the cow was plainly heinous, and undoubtedly their dungeons would be knee-deep in water.

"He did it, mister!" This was a general outcry. Jimmie used it as often as did the others. As for them, it is certain that they had no direct thought of betraying their comrade for their own salvation. They thought themselves guilty because they were caught; when boys were not caught they might possibly be innocent. But captured boys were guilty. When they cried out that Jimmie was the culprit, it was principally a simple expression of terror.

Old Henry Fleming, the owner of the farm, strode across the pasture towards them. He had in his hand a most cruel whip. This whip he flourished. At his approach the boys suffered the agonies of the fire regions. And yet anybody with half an eye could see that the whip in his hand was a mere accident, and that he was a kind old man—when he cared.

When he had come near he spoke crisply. "What you boys ben doin' to my cow?" The tone had deep threat in it. They all answered by saying that none of them had shot the cow. Their denials were tearful and clamorous, and they crawled knee by knee. The vision of it was like three martyrs being dragged towards the stake. Old Fleming stood there, grim, tight-lipped. After a time he said, "Which boy done it?"

There was some confusion, and then Jimmie spake. "I done it, mister."

Fleming looked at him. Then he asked, "Well, what did you shoot 'er fer?"

Jimmie thought, hesitated, decided, faltered, and then formulated this: "I thought she was a lynx."

Old Fleming and his Swede at once lay down in the grass and laughed themselves helpless.

# THE LOVER AND THE TELLTALE

When the angel child returned with her parents to New York, the fond heart of Jimmie Trescott felt its bruise greatly. For two days he simply moped, becoming a stranger to all former joys. When his old comrades yelled invitation, as they swept off on some interesting quest, he replied with mournful gestures of disillusion.

He thought often of writing to her, but of course the shame of it made him pause. Write a letter to a girl? The mere enormity of the idea caused him shudders. Persons of his quality never wrote letters to girls. Such was the occupation of mollycoddles and snivellers. He knew that if his acquaintances and friends found in him evidences of such weakness and general milkiness, they would fling themselves upon him like so many wolves, and bait him beyond the borders of sanity.

However, one day at school, in that time of the morning session when children of his age were allowed fifteen minutes of play in the school-grounds, he did not as usual rush forth ferociously to his games. Commonly he was of the worst hoodlums, preying upon his weaker brethren with all the cruel disregard of a grown man. On this particular morning he stayed in the school-room, and with his tongue stuck from the corner of his mouth, and his head twisting in a painful way, he wrote to little Cora, pouring out to her all the poetry of his hungry soul, as follows: "My dear Cora I love thee with all my hart oh come bac again, bac, bac gain for I love thee best of all oh come bac again When the spring come again we'l fly and we'l fly like a brid."

As for the last word, he knew under normal circumstances perfectly well how to spell "bird," but in this case he had transposed two of the letters through excitement, supreme agitation.

Nor had this letter been composed without fear and furtive glancing. There was always a number of children who, for the time, cared more for the quiet of the school-room than for the tempest of the play-ground, and there was always that dismal company who were being forcibly deprived of their recess—who were being "kept in." More than one curious eye was turned upon the desperate and lawless Jimmie Trescott suddenly taken to ways of peace, and as he felt these eyes he flushed guiltily, with felonious glances from side to side.

It happened that a certain vigilant little girl had a seat directly across the aisle from Jimmie's seat, and she had remained in the room during the intermission, because of her interest in some absurd domestic details concerning her desk. Parenthetically it might be stated that she was in the habit of imagining this desk to be a house, and at this time, with an important little frown, indicative of a proper matron, she was engaged in dramatizing her ideas of a household.

But this small Rose Goldege happened to be of a family which numbered few males. It was, in fact, one of those curious middle-class families that hold much of their ground, retain most of their position, after all their visible means of support have been dropped in the grave. It contained now only a collection of women who existed submissively, defiantly, securely, mysteriously, in a pretentious and often exasperating virtue. It was often too triumphantly clear that they were free of bad habits. However, bad habits is a term here used in a commoner meaning, because it is certainly true that the principal and indeed solitary joy which entered their lonely lives was the joy of talking wickedly and busily about their neighbors. It was all done without dream of its being of the vulgarity of the alleys. Indeed it was simply a constitutional but not incredible chastity and honesty expressing itself in its ordinary superior way of the whirling circles of life, and the vehemence of the criticism was not lessened by a further infusion of an acid of worldly defeat, worldly suffering, and worldly hopelessness.

Out of this family circle had sprung the typical little girl who discovered Jimmie Trescott agonizingly writing a letter to his sweetheart. Of course all the children were the most abandoned gossips, but she was peculiarly adapted to the purpose of making Jimmie miserable over this particular point. It was her life to sit of evenings about the stove and hearken to her mother and a lot of spinsters talk of many things. During these evenings she was never licensed to utter an opinion either one way or the other way. She was then simply a very little girl sitting open-eyed in the gloom, and listening to many things which she often interpreted wrongly. They on their part kept up a kind of a smug-faced pretence of concealing from her information in detail of the widespread crime, which pretence may have been more elaborately dangerous than no pretence at all. Thus all her home-teaching fitted her to recognize at once in Jimmie Trescott's manner that he was concealing something that would properly interest the world. She set up a scream. "Oh! Oh! Oh! Jimmie Trescott's writing to his girl! Oh! Oh!"

Jimmie cast a miserable glance upon her—a glance in which hatred mingled with despair. Through the open window he could hear the boisterous cries of his friends—his hoodlum friends—who would no more understand the utter poetry of his position than they would understand an ancient tribal sign-language. His face was set in a truer expression of horror than any of the romances describe upon the features of a man flung into a moat, a man shot in the breast with an arrow, a man cleft in the neck with a battle-axe. He was suppedaneous of the fullest power of childish pain. His one course was to rush upon her and attempt, by an impossible means of strangulation, to keep her important news from the public.

The teacher, a thoughtful young woman at her desk upon the platform, saw a little scuffle which informed her that two of her scholars were larking. She called out sharply. The command penetrated to the middle of an early world struggle. In Jimmie's age there was no particular scruple in the minds of the male sex against laying warrior hands upon their weaker sisters. But, of course, this voice from the throne hindered Jimmie in what might have been a berserk attack.

Even the little girl was retarded by the voice, but, without being unlawful, she managed soon to shy through the door and out upon the play-ground, yelling, "Oh, Jimmie Trescott's been writing to his girl!"

The unhappy Jimmie was following as closely as he was allowed by his knowledge of the decencies to be preserved under the eye of the teacher.

Jimmie himself was mainly responsible for the scene which ensued on the play-ground. It is possible that the little girl might have run, shrieking his infamy, without exciting more than a general but unmilitant interest. These barbarians were excited only by the actual appearance of human woe; in that event they cheered and danced. Jimmie made the strategic mistake of pursuing little Rose, and thus exposed his thin skin to the whole school. He had in his cowering mind a vision of a hundred children turning from their play under the maple-trees and speeding towards him over the gravel with sudden wild taunts. Upon him drove a yelping demoniac mob, to which his words were futile. He saw in this mob boys that he dimly knew, and his deadly enemies, and his retainers, and his most intimate friends. The virulence of his deadly enemy was no greater than the virulence of his intimate friend. From the outskirts the little informer could be heard still screaming the news, like a toy parrot with clock-work inside of it. It broke up all sorts of games, not so much because of the mere fact of the letter-writing, as because the children knew that some sufferer was at the last point, and, like little blood-fanged wolves, they thronged to the scene of his destruction. They galloped about him shrilly chanting insults. He turned from one to another, only to meet with howls. He was baited.

Then, in one instant, he changed all this with a blow. Bang! The most pitiless of the boys near him received a punch, fairly and skilfully, which made him bellow out like a walrus, and then Jimmie laid desperately into the whole world, striking out frenziedly in all directions. Boys who could handily whip him, and knew it, backed away from this onslaught. Here was intention—serious intention. They themselves were not in frenzy, and their cooler judgment respected Jimmie's efforts when he ran amuck. They saw that it really was none of their affair. In the mean time the wretched little girl who had caused the bloody riot was away, by the fence, weeping because boys were fighting.

Jimmie several times hit the wrong boy—that is to say, he several times hit a wrong boy hard enough to arouse also in him a spirit of strife. Jimmie wore a little shirt-waist. It was passing now rapidly into oblivion. He was sobbing, and there was one blood stain upon his cheek. The school-ground sounded like a pinetree when a hundred crows roost in it at night.

Then upon the situation there pealed a brazen bell. It was a bell that these children obeyed, even as older nations obey the formal law which is printed in calf-skin. It smote them into some sort of inaction; even Jimmie was influenced by its potency, although, as a finale, he kicked out lustily into the legs of an intimate friend who had been one of the foremost in the torture.

When they came to form into line for the march into the school-room it was curious that Jimmie had many admirers. It was not his prowess; it was the soul he had infused into his gymnastics; and he, still panting, looked about him with a stern and challenging glare.

And yet when the long tramping line had entered the school-room his status had again changed. The other children then began to regard him as a boy in disrepair, and boys in disrepair were always accosted ominously from the throne. Jimmie's march towards his seat was a feat. It was composed partly of a most slinking attempt to dodge the perception of the teacher and partly of pure braggadocio erected for the benefit of his observant fellow-men.

The teacher looked carefully down at him. "Jimmie Trescott," she said.

"Yes'm," he answered, with businesslike briskness, which really spelled out falsity in all its letters.

"Come up to the desk."

He rose amid the awe of the entire school-room. When he arrived she said,

"Jimmie, you've been fighting."

"Yes'm," he answered. This was not so much an admission of the fact as it was a concessional answer to anything she might say.

"Who have you been fighting?" she asked.

"I dunno', 'm."

Whereupon the empress blazed out in wrath. "You don't know who you've been fighting?"

Jimmie looked at her gloomily. "No, 'm."

She seemed about to disintegrate to mere flaming fagots of anger. "You don't know who you've been fighting?" she demanded, blazing. "Well, you stay in after school until you find out."

As he returned to his place all the children knew by his vanquished air that sorrow had fallen upon the house of Trescott. When he took his seat he saw gloating upon him the satanic black eyes of the little Goldege girl.

# "SHOWIN' OFF"

Jimmie Trescott's new velocipede had the largest front wheel of any velocipede in Whilomville. When it first arrived from New York he wished to sacrifice school, food, and sleep to it. Evidently he wished to become a sort of a perpetual velocipede-rider. But the powers of the family laid a number of judicious embargoes upon him, and he was prevented from becoming a fanatic. Of course this caused him to retain a fondness for the three-wheeled thing much longer than if he had been allowed to debauch himself for a span of days. But in the end it was an immaterial machine to him. For long periods he left it idle in the stable.

One day he loitered from school towards home by a very circuitous route. He was accompanied by only one of his retainers. The object of this détour was the wooing of a little girl in a red hood. He had been in love with her for some three weeks. His desk was near her desk in school, but he had never spoken to her. He had been afraid to take such a radical step. It was not customary to speak to girls. Even boys who had school-going sisters seldom addressed them during that part of a day which was devoted to education.

The reasons for this conduct were very plain. First, the more robust boys considered talking with girls an unmanly occupation; second, the greater part of the boys were afraid; third, they had no idea of what to say, because they esteemed the proper sentences should be supernaturally incisive and eloquent. In consequence, a small contingent of blue-eyed weaklings were the sole intimates of the frail sex, and for it they were boisterously and disdainfully called "girl-boys."

But this situation did not prevent serious and ardent wooing. For instance, Jimmie and the little girl who wore the red hood must have exchanged glances at least two hundred times in every school-hour, and this exchange of glances accomplished everything. In them the two children renewed their curious inarticulate vows.

Jimmie had developed a devotion to school which was the admiration of his father and mother. In the mornings he was so impatient to have it made known to him that no misfortune had befallen his romance during the night that he was actually detected at times feverishly listening for the "first bell." Dr. Trescott was exceedingly complacent of the change, and as for Mrs. Trescott, she had ecstatic visions of a white-haired Jimmie leading the nations in knowledge, comprehending all from bugs to comets. It was merely the doing of the little girl in the red hood.

When Jimmie made up his mind to follow his sweetheart home from school, the project seemed such an arbitrary and shameless innovation that he hastily lied to himself about it. No, he was not following Abbie. He was merely making his way homeward through the new and rather longer route of Bryant Street and Oakland Park. It had nothing at all to do with a girl. It was a mere eccentric notion.

"Come on," said Jimmie, gruffly, to his retainer. "Let's go home this way."

"What fer?" demanded the retainer.

"Oh, b'cause."

"Huh?"

"Oh, it's more fun—goin' this way."

The retainer was bored and loath, but that mattered very little. He did not know how to disobey his chief. Together they followed the trail of red-hooded Abbie and another small girl. These latter at once understood the object of the chase, and looking back giggling, they pretended to quicken their pace. But they were always looking back. Jimmie now began his courtship in earnest. The first thing to do was to prove his strength in battle. This was transacted by means of the retainer. He took that devoted boy and flung him heavily to the ground, meanwhile mouthing a preposterous ferocity.

The retainer accepted this behavior with a sort of bland resignation. After his overthrow he raised himself, coolly brushed some dust and dead leaves from his clothes, and then seemed to forget the incident.

"I can jump farther'n you can," said Jimmie, in a loud voice.

"I know it," responded the retainer, simply.

But this would not do. There must be a contest.

"Come on," shouted Jimmie, imperiously. "Let's see you jump."

The retainer selected a footing on the curb, balanced and calculated a moment, and jumped without enthusiasm. Jimmie's leap of course was longer.

"There!" he cried, blowing out his lips. "I beat you, didn't I? Easy. I beat you." He made a great hubbub, as if the affair was unprecedented.

"Yes," admitted the other, emotionless.

Later, Jimmie forced his retainer to run a race with him, held more jumping matches, flung him twice to earth, and generally behaved as if a retainer was indestructible. If the retainer had been in the plot, it is conceivable that he would have endured this treatment with mere whispered, half-laughing protests. But he was not in the plot at all, and so he became enigmatic. One cannot often sound the profound well in which lie the meanings of boyhood.

Following the two little girls, Jimmie eventually passed into that suburb of Whilomville which is called Oakland Park. At his heels came a badly battered retainer. Oakland Park was a somewhat strange country to the boys. They were dubious of the manners and customs, and of course they would have to meet the local chieftains, who might look askance upon this invasion.

Jimmie's girl departed into her home with a last backward glance that almost blinded the thrilling boy. On this pretext and that pretext, he kept his retainer in play before the house. He had hopes that she would emerge as soon as she had deposited her school-bag.

A boy came along the walk. Jimmie knew him at school. He was Tommie Semple, one of the weaklings who made friends with the fair sex. "Hello, Tom," said Jimmie. "You live round here?"

"Yeh," said Tom, with composed pride. At school he was afraid of Jimmie, but he did not evince any of this fear as he strolled well inside his own frontiers. Jimmie and his retainer had not expected this boy to display the manners of a minor chief, and they contemplated him attentively. There was a silence. Finally Jimmie said:

"I can put you down." He moved forward briskly. "Can't I?" he demanded.

The challenged boy backed away. "I know you can," he declared, frankly and promptly.

The little girl in the red hood had come out with a hoop. She looked at Jimmie with an air of insolent surprise in the fact that he still existed, and began to trundle her hoop off towards some other little girls who were shrilly playing near a nursemaid and a perambulator.

Jimmie adroitly shifted his position until he too was playing near the perambulator, pretentiously making mince-meat out of his retainer and Tommie Semple.

Of course little Abbie had defined the meaning of Jimmie's appearance in Oakland Park. Despite this nonchalance and grand air of accident, nothing could have been more plain. Whereupon she of course became insufferably vain in manner, and whenever Jimmie came near her she tossed her head and turned away her face, and daintily swished her skirts as if he were contagion itself. But Jimmie was happy. His soul was satisfied with the mere presence of the beloved object so long as he could feel that she furtively gazed upon him from time to time and noted his extraordinary prowess, which he was proving upon the persons of his retainer and Tommie Semple. And he was making an impression. There could be no doubt of it. He had many times caught her eye fixed admiringly upon him as he mauled the retainer. Indeed, all the little girls gave attention to his deeds, and he was the hero of the hour.

Presently a boy on a velocipede was seen to be tooling down towards them. "Who's this comin'?" said Jimmie, bluntly, to the Semple boy.

"That's Horace Glenn," said Tommie, "an' he's got a new velocipede, an' he can ride it like anything."

"Can you lick him?" asked Jimmie.

"I don't—I never fought with 'im," answered the other. He bravely tried to appear as a man of respectable achievement, but with Horace coming towards them the risk was too great. However, he added, "*Maybe* I could."

The advent of Horace on his new velocipede created a sensation which he haughtily accepted as a familiar thing. Only Jimmie and his retainer remained silent and impassive. Horace eyed the two invaders.

"Hello, Jimmie!"

"Hello, Horace!"

After the typical silence Jimmie said, pompously, "I got a velocipede."

"Have you?" asked Horace, anxiously. He did not wish anybody in the world but himself to possess a velocipede.

"Yes," sang Jimmie. "An' it's a bigger one than that, too! A good deal bigger! An' it's a better one, too!"

"Huh!" retorted Horace, sceptically.

"Ain't I, Clarence? Ain't I? Ain't I got one bigger'n that?"

The retainer answered with alacrity:

"Yes, he has! A good deal bigger! An' it's a dindy, too!"

This corroboration rather disconcerted Horace, but he continued to scoff at any statement that Jimmie also owned a velocipede. As for the contention that this supposed velocipede could be larger than his own, he simply wouldn't hear of it.

Jimmie had been a very gallant figure before the coming of Horace, but the new velocipede had relegated him to a squalid secondary position. So he affected to look with contempt upon it. Voluminously he bragged of the velocipede in the stable at home. He painted its virtues and beauty in loud and extravagant words, flaming words. And the retainer stood by, glibly endorsing everything.

The little company heeded him, and he passed on vociferously from extravagance to utter impossibility. Horace was very sick of it. His defence was reduced to a mere mechanical grumbling: "Don't believe you got one 'tall. Don't believe you got one 'tall."

Jimmie turned upon him suddenly. "How fast can you go? How fast can you go?" he demanded. "Let's see. I bet you can't go fast."

Horace lifted his spirits and answered with proper defiance. "Can't I?" he mocked. "Can't I?"

"No, you can't," said Jimmie. "You can't go fast."

Horace cried: "Well, you see me now! I'll show you! I'll show you if I can't go fast!" Taking a firm seat on his vermilion machine, he pedalled furiously up the walk, turned, and pedalled back again. "There, now!" he shouted, triumphantly. "Ain't that fast? There, now!" There was a low murmur of appreciation from the little girls. Jimmie saw with pain that even his divinity was smiling upon his rival. "There! Ain't that fast? Ain't that fast?" He strove to pin Jimmie down to an admission. He was exuberant with victory.

Notwithstanding a feeling of discomfiture, Jimmie did not lose a moment of time. "Why," he yelled, "that ain't goin' fast 'tall! That ain't goin' fast 'tall! Why, I can go almost *twice* as fast as that! Almost *twice* as fast! Can't I, Clarence?"

The royal retainer nodded solemnly at the wide-eyed group. "Course you can!"

"Why," spouted Jimmie, "you just ought to see me ride once! You just ought to see me! Why, I can go like the wind! Can't I, Clarence? And I can ride far, too—oh, awful far! Can't I, Clarence? Why, I wouldn't have that one! 'Tain't any good! You just ought to see mine once!"

The overwhelmed Horace attempted to reconstruct his battered glories. "I can ride right over the curb-stone—at some of the crossin's," he announced, brightly.

Jimmie's derision was a splendid sight. "'*Right over the curb-stone!*' Why, that wouldn't be *nothin'* for me to do! I've rode mine down Bridge Street hill. Yessir! Ain't I, Clarence? Why, it ain't nothin' to ride over a curb-stone—not for *me*! Is it, Clarence?"

"Down Bridge Street hill? You never!" said Horace, hopelessly.

"Well, didn't I, Clarence? Didn't I, now?"

The faithful retainer again nodded solemnly at the assemblage.

At last Horace, having fallen as low as was possible, began to display a spirit for climbing up again. "Oh, you can do wonders!" he said, laughing. "You can do wonders! I s'pose you could ride down that bank there?" he asked, with art. He had indicated a grassy terrace some six feet in height which bounded one side of the walk. At the bottom was a small ravine in which the reckless had flung ashes and tins. "I s'pose you could ride down that bank?"

All eyes now turned upon Jimmie to detect a sign of his weakening, but he instantly and sublimely arose to the occasion. "That bank?" he asked, scornfully. "Why, I've ridden down banks like that many a time. Ain't I, Clarence?"

This was too much for the company. A sound like the wind in the leaves arose; it was the song of incredulity and ridicule. "O—o—o—o—o!" And on the outskirts a little girl suddenly shrieked out, "Story-teller!"

Horace had certainly won a skirmish. He was gleeful. "Oh, you can do wonders!" he gurgled. "You can do wonders!" The neighborhood's superficial hostility to foreigners arose like magic under the influence of his sudden success, and Horace had the delight of seeing Jimmie persecuted in that manner known only to children and insects.

Jimmie called angrily to the boy on the velocipede, "If you'll lend me yours, I'll show you whether I can or not."

Horace turned his superior nose in the air. "Oh no! I don't ever lend it." Then he thought of a blow which would make Jimmie's humiliation complete. "Besides," he said, airily, "'tain't really anything hard to do. I could do it—easy—if I wanted to."

But his supposed adherents, instead of receiving this boast with cheers, looked upon him in a sudden blank silence. Jimmie and his retainer pounced like cats upon their advantage.

"Oh," they yelled, "you *could*, eh? Well, let's see you do it, then! Let's see you do it! Let's see you do it! Now!" In a moment the crew of little spectators were gibing at Horace.

The blow that would make Jimmie's humiliation complete! Instead, it had boomeranged Horace into the mud. He kept up a sullen muttering:

"'Tain't really anything! I could if I wanted to!"

"Dare you to!" screeched Jimmie and his partisans. "Dare you to! Dare you to! Dare you to!"

There were two things to be done—to make gallant effort or to retreat. Somewhat to their amazement, the children at last found Horace moving through their clamor to the edge of the bank. Sitting on the velocipede, he looked at the ravine, and then, with gloomy pride, at the other children. A hush came upon them, for it was seen that he was intending to make some kind of an ante-mortem statement.

"I—" he began. Then he vanished from the edge of the walk. The start had been unintentional—an accident.

The stupefied Jimmie saw the calamity through a haze. His first clear vision was when Horace, with a face as red as a red flag, arose bawling from his tangled velocipede. He and his retainer exchanged a glance of horror and fled the neighborhood. They did not look back until they had reached the top of the hill near the lake. They could see Horace walking slowly under the maples towards his home, pushing his shattered velocipede before him. His chin was thrown high, and the breeze bore them the sound of his howls.

# MAKING AN ORATOR

In the school at Whilomville it was the habit, when children had progressed to a certain class, to have them devote Friday afternoon to what was called elocution. This was in the piteously ignorant belief that orators were thus made. By process of school law, unfortunate boys and girls were dragged up to address their fellow-scholars in the literature of the mid-century. Probably the children who were most capable of expressing themselves, the children who were most sensitive to the power of speech, suffered the most wrong. Little blockheads who could learn eight lines of conventional poetry, and could get up and spin it rapidly at their classmates, did not undergo a single pang. The plan operated mainly to agonize many children permanently against arising to speak their thought to fellow-creatures.

Jimmie Trescott had an idea that by exhibition of undue ignorance he could escape from being promoted into the first class room which exacted such penalty from its inmates. He preferred to dwell in a less classic shade rather than venture into a domain where he was obliged to perform a certain duty which struck him as being worse than death. However, willy-nilly, he was somehow sent ahead into the place of torture.

Every Friday at least ten of the little children had to mount the stage beside the teacher's desk and babble something which none of them understood. This was to make them orators. If it had been ordered that they should croak like frogs, it would have advanced most of them just as far towards oratory.

Alphabetically Jimmie Trescott was near the end of the list of victims, but his time was none the less inevitable. "Tanner, Timmens, Trass, Trescott—" He saw his downfall approaching.

He was passive to the teacher while she drove into his mind the incomprehensible lines of "The Charge of the Light Brigade":

> *Half a league, half a league,*
> *Half a league onward—*

He had no conception of a league. If in the ordinary course of life somebody had told him that he was half a league from home, he might have been frightened that half a league was fifty miles; but he struggled manfully with the valley of death and a mystic six hundred, who were performing something there which was very fine, he had been told. He learned all the verses.

But as his own Friday afternoon approached he was moved to make known to his family that a dreadful disease was upon him, and was likely at any time to prevent him from going to his beloved school.

On the great Friday when the children of his initials were to speak their pieces Dr. Trescott was away from home, and the mother of the boy was alarmed beyond measure at Jimmie's curious illness, which caused him to lie on the rug in front of the fire and groan cavernously.

She bathed his feet in hot mustard water until they were lobster-red. She also placed a mustard plaster on his chest.

He announced that these remedies did him no good at all—no good at all. With an air of martyrdom he endured a perfect downpour of motherly attention all that day. Thus the first Friday was passed in safety.

With singular patience he sat before the fire in the dining-room and looked at picture-books, only complaining of pain when he suspected his mother of thinking that he was getting better.

The next day being Saturday and a holiday, he was miraculously delivered from the arms of disease, and went forth to play, a blatantly healthy boy.

He had no further attack until Thursday night of the next week, when he announced that he felt very, very poorly. The mother was already chronically alarmed over the condition of her son, but Dr. Trescott asked him questions which denoted some incredulity. On the third Friday Jimmie was dropped at the door of the school from the doctor's buggy. The other children, notably those who had already passed over the mountain of distress, looked at him with glee, seeing in him another lamb brought to butchery. Seated at his desk in the school-room, Jimmie sometimes remembered with dreadful distinctness every line of "The Charge of the Light Brigade," and at other times his mind was utterly empty of it. Geography, arithmetic, and spelling—usually great tasks—quite rolled off him. His mind was dwelling with terror upon the time when his name should be called and he was obliged to go up to the platform, turn, bow, and recite his message to his fellow-men.

Desperate expedients for delay came to him. If he could have engaged the services of a real pain, he would have been glad. But steadily, inexorably, the minutes marched on towards his great crisis, and all his plans for escape blended into a mere panic fear.

The maples outside were defeating the weakening rays of the afternoon sun, and in the shadowed school-room had come a stillness, in which, nevertheless, one could feel the complacence of the little pupils who had already passed through the flames. They were calmly prepared to recognize as a spectacle the torture of others.

Little Johnnie Tanner opened the ceremony. He stamped heavily up to the platform, and bowed in such a manner that he almost fell down. He blurted out that it would ill befit him to sit silent while the name of his fair Ireland was being reproached, and he appealed to the gallant soldier before him if every British battle-field was not sown with the bones of sons of the Emerald Isle. He was also heard to say that he had listened with deepening surprise and scorn to the insinuation of the honorable member from North Glenmorganshire that the loyalty of the Irish regiments in her Majesty's service could be questioned. To what purpose, then, he asked, had the blood of Irishmen flowed on a hundred fields? To what purpose had Irishmen gone to their death with bravery and devotion in every part of the world where the victorious flag of England had been carried? If the honorable member for North Glenmorganshire insisted upon construing a mere pothouse row between soldiers in Dublin into a grand treachery to the colors and to her Majesty's uniform, then it was time for Ireland to think bitterly of her dead sons, whose graves now marked every step of England's progress, and yet who could have their honors stripped from them so easily by the honorable member for North Glenmorganshire. Furthermore, the honorable member for North Glenmorganshire—

It is needless to say that little Johnnie Tanner's language made it exceedingly hot for the honorable member for North Glenmorganshire. But Johnnie was not angry. He was only in haste. He finished the honorable member for North Glenmorganshire in what might be called a gallop.

Susie Timmens then went to the platform, and with a face as pale as death whisperingly reiterated that she would be Queen of the May. The child represented there a perfect picture of unnecessary suffering. Her small lips were quite blue, and her eyes, opened wide, stared with a look of horror at nothing.

The phlegmatic Trass boy, with his moon face only expressing peasant parentage, calmly spoke some undeniably true words concerning destiny.

In his seat Jimmie Trescott was going half blind with fear of his approaching doom. He wished that the Trass boy would talk forever about destiny. If the schoolhouse had taken fire he thought that he would have felt simply relief. Anything was better. Death amid the flames was preferable to a recital of "The Charge of the Light Brigade."

But the Trass boy finished his remarks about destiny in a very short time. Jimmie heard the teacher call his name, and he felt the whole world look at him. He did not know how he made his way to the stage. Parts of him seemed to be of lead, and at the same time parts of him seemed to be light as air, detached. His face had gone as pale as had been the face of Susie Timmens. He was simply a child in torment; that is all there is to be said specifically about it; and to intelligent people the exhibition would have been not more edifying than a dog-fight.

He bowed precariously, choked, made an inarticulate sound, and then he suddenly said,

> *"Half a leg—"*

"*League*," said the teacher, coolly.

> *"Half a leg—"*

"*League*," said the teacher.

"*League*," repeated Jimmie, wildly.

> *"Half a league, half a league, half a league onward."*

He paused here and looked wretchedly at the teacher.

"Half a league," he muttered—"half a league—"

He seemed likely to keep continuing this phrase indefinitely, so after a time the teacher said, "Well, go on."

"Half a league," responded Jimmie.

The teacher had the opened book before her, and she read from it:

> *"'All in the valley of Death*
> *Rode the—'*

Go on," she concluded.

Jimmie said,

> *"All in the valley of Death*
> *Rode the—the—the—"*

He cast a glance of supreme appeal upon the teacher, and breathlessly whispered, "Rode the what?"

The young woman flushed with indignation to the roots of her hair.

> *"Rode the six hundred,"*

she snapped at him.

The class was arustle with delight at this cruel display. They were no better than a Roman populace in Nero's time.

Jimmie started off again:

> *"Half a leg—league, half a league, half a league onward.*
> *All in the valley of death rode the six hundred.*

"The Light Brigade," suggested the teacher, sharply.

"The Light Brigade," said Jimmie. He was about to die of the ignoble pain of his position.

As for Tennyson's lines, they had all gone grandly out of his mind, leaving it a whited wall.

The teacher's indignation was still rampant. She looked at the miserable wretch before her with an angry stare.

"You stay in after school and learn that all over again," she commanded. "And be prepared to speak it next Friday. I am astonished at you, Jimmie. Go to your seat."

If she had suddenly and magically made a spirit of him and left him free to soar high above all the travail of our earthly lives she could not have overjoyed him more. He fled back to his seat without hearing the low-toned gibes of his schoolmates. He gave no thought to the terrors of the next Friday. The evils of the day had been sufficient, and to a childish mind a week is a great space of time.

With the delightful inconsistency of his age he sat in blissful calm, and watched the sufferings of an unfortunate boy named Zimmerman, who was the next victim of education. Jimmie, of course, did not know that on this day there had been laid for him the foundation of a finished incapacity for public speaking which would be his until he died.

# SHAME

"Don't come in here botherin' me," said the cook, intolerantly. "What with your mother bein' away on a visit, an' your father comin' home soon to lunch, I have enough on my mind—and that without bein' bothered with *you*. The kitchen is no place for little boys, anyhow. Run away, and don't be interferin' with my work." She frowned and made a grand pretence of being deep in herculean labors; but Jimmie did not run away.

"Now—they're goin' to have a picnic," he said, half audibly.

"What?"

"Now—they're goin' to have a picnic."

"Who's goin' to have a picnic?" demanded the cook, loudly. Her accent could have led one to suppose that if the projectors did not turn out to be the proper parties, she immediately would forbid this picnic.

Jimmie looked at her with more hopefulness. After twenty minutes of futile skirmishing, he had at least succeeded in introducing the subject. To her question he answered, eagerly:

"Oh, everybody! Lots and lots of boys and girls. Everybody."

"Who's everybody?"

According to custom, Jimmie began to singsong through his nose in a quite indescribable fashion an enumeration of the prospective picnickers: "Willie Dalzel an' Dan Earl an' Ella Earl an' Wolcott Margate an' Reeves Margate an' Walter Phelps an' Homer Phelps an' Minnie Phelps an'—oh—lots more girls an'—everybody. An' their mothers an' big sisters too." Then he announced a new bit of information: "They're goin' to have a picnic."

"Well, let them," said the cook, blandly.

Jimmie fidgeted for a time in silence. At last he murmured, "I—now—I thought maybe you'd let me go."

The cook turned from her work with an air of irritation and amazement that Jimmie should still be in the kitchen. "Who's stoppin' you?" she asked, sharply. "I ain't stoppin' you, am I?"

"No," admitted Jimmie, in a low voice.

"Well, why don't you go, then? Nobody's stoppin' you."

"But," said Jimmie, "I—you—now—each fellow has got to take somethin' to eat with 'm."

"Oh ho!" cried the cook, triumphantly. "So that's it, is it? So that's what you've been shyin' round here fer, eh? Well, you may as well take yourself off without more words. What with your mother bein' away on a visit, an' your father comin' home soon to his lunch, I have enough on my mind—an' that without being bothered with *you*!"

Jimmie made no reply, but moved in grief towards the door. The cook continued: "Some people in this house seem to think there's 'bout a thousand cooks in this kitchen. Where I used to work b'fore, there was some reason in 'em. I ain't a horse. A picnic!"

Jimmie said nothing, but he loitered.

"Seems as if I had enough to do, without havin' *you* come round talkin' about picnics. Nobody ever seems to think of the work I have to do. Nobody ever seems to think of it. Then they come and talk to me about picnics! What do I care about picnics?"

Jimmie loitered.

"Where I used to work b'fore, there was some reason in 'em. I never heard tell of no picnics right on top of your mother bein' away on a visit an' your father comin' home soon to his lunch. It's all foolishness."

Little Jimmie leaned his head flat against the wall and began to weep. She stared at him scornfully. "Cryin', eh? Cryin'? What are you cryin' fer?"

"N-n-nothin'," sobbed Jimmie.

There was a silence, save for Jimmie's convulsive breathing. At length the cook said: "Stop that blubberin', now. Stop it! This kitchen ain't no place fer it. Stop it!… Very well! If you don't stop, I won't give you nothin' to go to the picnic with—there!"

For the moment he could not end his tears. "You never said," he sputtered— "you never said you'd give me anything."

"An' why would I?" she cried, angrily. "Why would I—with you in here a-cryin' an' a-blubberin' an' a-bleatin' round? Enough to drive a woman crazy! I don't see how you could expect me to! The idea!"

Suddenly Jimmie announced: "I've stopped cryin'. I ain't goin' to cry no more 'tall."

"Well, then," grumbled the cook—"well, then, stop it. I've got enough on my mind." It chanced that she was making for luncheon some salmon croquettes. A tin still half full of pinky prepared fish was beside her on the table. Still grumbling, she seized a loaf of bread and, wielding a knife, she cut from this loaf four slices, each of which was as big as a six-shilling novel. She profligately spread them with butter, and jabbing the point of her knife into the salmon-tin, she brought up bits of salmon, which she flung and flattened upon the bread. Then she crashed the pieces of bread together in pairs, much as one would clash cymbals. There was no doubt in her own mind but that she had created two sandwiches.

"There," she cried. "That'll do you all right. Lemme see. What'll I put 'em in? There—I've got it." She thrust the sandwiches into a small pail and jammed on the lid. Jimmie was ready for the picnic. "Oh, thank you, Mary!" he cried, joyfully, and in a moment he was off, running swiftly.

The picnickers had started nearly half an hour earlier, owing to his inability to quickly attack and subdue the cook, but he knew that the rendezvous was in the grove of tall, pillarlike hemlocks and pines that grew on a rocky knoll at the lake shore. His heart was very light as he sped, swinging his pail. But a few minutes previously his soul had been gloomed in despair; now he was happy. He was going to the picnic, where privilege of participation was to be bought by the contents of the little tin pail.

When he arrived in the outskirts of the grove he heard a merry clamor, and when he reached the top of the knoll he looked down the slope upon a scene which almost made his little breast burst with joy. They actually had two camp-fires! Two camp-fires! At one of them Mrs. Earl was making something—chocolate, no doubt—and at the other a young lady in white duck and a sailor hat was dropping eggs into boiling water. Other grown-up people had spread a white cloth and were laying upon it things from baskets. In the deep cool shadow of the trees the children scurried, laughing. Jimmie hastened forward to join his friends.

Homer Phelps caught first sight of him. "Ho!" he shouted; "here comes Jimmie Trescott! Come on, Jimmie; you be on our side!" The children had divided themselves into two bands for some purpose of play. The others of Homer Phelps's party loudly endorsed his plan. "Yes, Jimmie, you be on *our* side." Then arose the usual dispute. "Well, we got the weakest side."

"'Tain't any weaker'n ours."

Homer Phelps suddenly started, and looking hard, said, "What you got in the pail, Jim?"

Jimmie answered, somewhat uneasily, "Got m' lunch in it."

Instantly that brat of a Minnie Phelps simply tore down the sky with her shrieks of derision. "Got his *lunch* in it! In a *pail*!" She ran screaming to her mother. "Oh, mamma! Oh, mamma! Jimmie Trescott's got his picnic in a pail!"

Now there was nothing in the nature of this fact to particularly move the others—notably the boys, who were not competent to care if he had brought his luncheon in a coal-bin; but such is the instinct of childish society that they all immediately moved away from him. In a moment he had been made a social leper. All old intimacies were flung into the lake, so to speak. They dared not compromise themselves. At safe distances the boys shouted, scornfully: "Huh! Got his picnic in a pail!" Never again during that picnic did the little girls speak of him as Jimmie Trescott. His name now was Him.

His mind was dark with pain as he stood, the hangdog, kicking the gravel, and muttering as defiantly as he was able, "Well, I can have it in a pail if I want to." This statement of freedom was of no importance, and he knew it, but it was the only idea in his head.

He had been baited at school for being detected in writing a letter to little Cora, the angel child, and he had known how to defend himself, but this situation was in no way similar. This was a social affair, with grown people on all sides. It would be sweet to catch the Margate twins, for instance, and hammer them into a state of bleating respect for his pail; but that was a matter for the jungles of childhood, where grown folk seldom penetrated. He could only glower.

The amiable voice of Mrs. Earl suddenly called: "Come, children! Everything's ready!" They scampered away, glancing back for one last gloat at Jimmie standing there with his pail.

He did not know what to do. He knew that the grown folk expected him at the spread, but if he approached he would be greeted by a shameful chorus from the children—more especially from some of those damnable little girls. Still, luxuries beyond all dreaming were heaped on that cloth. One could not forget them. Perhaps if he crept up modestly, and was very gentle and very nice to the little girls, they would allow him peace. Of course it had been dreadful to come with a pail to such a grand picnic, but they might forgive him.

Oh no, they would not! He knew them better. And then suddenly he remembered with what delightful expectations he had raced to this grove, and self-pity overwhelmed him, and he thought he wanted to die and make every one feel sorry.

The young lady in white duck and a sailor hat looked at him, and then spoke to her sister, Mrs. Earl. "Who's that hovering in the distance, Emily?"

Mrs. Earl peered. "Why, it's Jimmie Trescott! Jimmie, come to the picnic! Why don't you come to the picnic, Jimmie?" He began to sidle towards the cloth.

But at Mrs. Earl's call there was another outburst from many of the children. "He's got his picnic in a pail! In a *pail*! Got it in a pail!"

Minnie Phelps was a shrill fiend. "Oh, mamma, he's got it in that pail! See! Isn't it funny? Isn't it dreadful funny?"

"What ghastly prigs children are, Emily!" said the young lady. "They are spoiling that boy's whole day, breaking his heart, the little cats! I think I'll go over and talk to him."

"Maybe you had better not," answered Mrs. Earl, dubiously. "Somehow these things arrange themselves. If you interfere, you are likely to prolong everything."

"Well, I'll try, at least," said the young lady.

At the second outburst against him Jimmie had crouched down by a tree, half hiding behind it, half pretending that he was not hiding behind it. He turned his sad gaze towards the lake. The bit of water seen through the shadows seemed perpendicular, a slate-colored wall. He heard a noise near him, and turning, he perceived the young lady looking down at him. In her hand she held plates. "May I sit near you?" she asked, coolly.

Jimmie could hardly believe his ears. After disposing herself and the plates upon the pine needles, she made brief explanation. "They're rather crowded, you see, over there. I don't like to be crowded at a picnic, so I thought I'd come here. I hope you don't mind."

Jimmie made haste to find his tongue. "Oh, I don't mind! I *like* to have you here." The ingenuous emphasis made it appear that the fact of his liking to have her there was in the nature of a law-dispelling phenomenon, but she did not smile.

"How large is that lake?" she asked.

Jimmie, falling into the snare, at once began to talk in the manner of a proprietor of the lake. "Oh, it's almost twenty miles long, an' in one place it's almost four miles wide! an' it's *deep* too—awful deep—an' it's got real steamboats on it, an'—oh— lots of other boats, an'—an'—an'—"

"Do you go out on it sometimes?"

"Oh, lots of times! My father's got a boat," he said, eying her to note the effect of his words.

She was correctly pleased and struck with wonder. "Oh, has he?" she cried, as if she never before had heard of a man owning a boat.

Jimmie continued: "Yes, an' it's a grea' big boat, too, with sails, real sails; an' sometimes he takes me out in her, too; an' once he took me fishin', an' we had sandwiches, plenty of 'em, an' my father he drank beer right out of the bottle—*right out of the bottle!*"

The young lady was properly overwhelmed by this amazing intelligence. Jimmie saw the impression he had created, and he enthusiastically resumed his narrative: "An' after, he let me throw the bottles in the water, and I throwed 'em 'way, 'way, 'way out. An' they sank, an'—never comed up," he concluded, dramatically.

His face was glorified; he had forgotten all about the pail; he was absorbed in this communion with a beautiful lady who was so interested in what he had to say.

She indicated one of the plates, and said, indifferently: "Perhaps you would like some of those sandwiches. I made them. Do you like olives? And there's a deviled egg. I made that also."

"Did you really?" said Jimmie, politely. His face gloomed for a moment because the pail was recalled to his mind, but he timidly possessed himself of a sandwich.

"Hope you are not going to scorn my deviled egg," said his goddess. "I am very proud of it." He did not; he scorned little that was on the plate.

Their gentle intimacy was ineffable to the boy. He thought he had a friend, a beautiful lady, who liked him more than she did anybody at the picnic, to say the least. This was proved by the fact that she had flung aside the luxuries of the spread cloth to sit with him, the exile. Thus early did he fall a victim to woman's wiles.

"Where do you live?" he asked, suddenly.

"Oh, a long way from here! In New York."

His next question was put very bluntly. "Are you married?"

"Oh no!" she answered, gravely.

Jimmie was silent for a time, during which he glanced shyly and furtively up at her face. It was evident that he was somewhat embarrassed. Finally he said, "When I grow up to be a man—"

"Oh, that is some time yet!" said the beautiful lady.

"But when I *do*, I—I should like to marry you."

"Well, I will remember it," she answered; "but don't talk of it now, because it's such a long time; and—I wouldn't wish you to consider yourself bound." She smiled at him.

He began to brag. "When I grow up to be a man, I'm goin' to have lots an' lots of money, an' I'm goin' to have a grea' big house, an' a horse an' a shot-gun, an' lots an' lots of books 'bout elephants an' tigers, an' lots an' lots of ice-cream an' pie an'—caramels." As before, she was impressed; he could see it. "An' I'm goin' to have lots an' lots of children—'bout three hundred, I guess—an' there won't none of 'em be girls. They'll all be boys—like me."

"Oh, my!" she said.

His garment of shame was gone from him. The pail was dead and well buried. It seemed to him that months elapsed as he dwelt in happiness near the beautiful lady and trumpeted his vanity.

At last there was a shout. "Come on! we're going home." The picnickers trooped out of the grove. The children wished to resume their jeering, for Jimmie still gripped his pail, but they were restrained by the circumstances. He was walking at the side of the beautiful lady.

During this journey he abandoned many of his habits. For instance, he never travelled without skipping gracefully from crack to crack between the stones, or without pretending that he was a train of cars, or without some mumming device of childhood. But now he behaved with dignity. He made no more noise than a little mouse. He escorted the beautiful lady to the gate of the Earl home, where he awkwardly, solemnly, and wistfully shook hands in good-by. He watched her go up the walk; the door clanged.

On his way home he dreamed. One of these dreams was fascinating. Supposing the beautiful lady was his teacher in school! Oh, my! wouldn't he be a good boy, sitting like a statuette all day long, and knowing every lesson to perfection, and—everything. And then supposing that a boy should sass her. Jimmie painted himself waylaying that boy on the homeward road, and the fate of the boy was a thing to make strong men cover their eyes with their hands. And she would like him more and more—more and more. And he—he would be a little god.

But as he was entering his father's grounds an appalling recollection came to him. He was returning with the bread-and-butter and the salmon untouched in the pail! He could imagine the cook, nine feet tall, waving her fist. "An' so that's what I took trouble for, is it? So's you could bring it back? So's you could bring it back?" He skulked towards the house like a marauding bushranger. When he neared the kitchen door he made a desperate rush past it, aiming to gain the stables and there secrete his guilt. He was nearing them, when a thunderous voice hailed him from the rear:

"Jimmie Trescott, where you goin' with that pail?"

It was the cook. He made no reply, but plunged into the shelter of the stables. He whirled the lid from the pail and dashed its contents beneath a heap of blankets. Then he stood panting, his eyes on the door. The cook did not pursue, but she was bawling:

"Jimmie Trescott, what you doin' with that pail?"

He came forth, swinging it. "Nothin'," he said, in virtuous protest.

"I know better," she said, sharply, as she relieved him of his curse.

In the morning Jimmie was playing near the stable, when he heard a shout from Peter Washington, who attended Dr. Trescott's horse:

"Jim! Oh, Jim!"

"What?"

"Come yah."

Jimmie went reluctantly to the door of the stable, and Peter Washington asked:

"Wut's dish yere fish an' brade doin' unner dese yer blankups?"

"I don't know. I didn't have nothin' to do with it," answered Jimmie, indignantly.

"Don' tell *me*!" cried Peter Washington, as he flung it all away—"don' tell *me*! When I fin' fish an' brade unner dese yer blankups, I don' go an' think dese yer ho'ses er yer pop's put 'em. I*know*. An' if I caitch enny more dish yer fish an' brade in dish yer stable, *I'll* tell yer pop."

# THE CARRIAGE-LAMPS

It was the fault of a small nickel-plated revolver, a most incompetent weapon, which, wherever one aimed, would fling the bullet as the devil willed, and no man, when about to use it, could tell exactly what was in store for the surrounding country. This treasure had been acquired by Jimmie Trescott after arduous bargaining with another small boy. Jimmie wended homeward, patting his hip pocket at every three paces.

Peter Washington, working in the carriage-house, looked out upon him with a shrewd eye. "Oh, Jim," he called, "wut you got in yer hind pocket?"

"Nothin'," said Jimmie, feeling carefully under his jacket to make sure that the revolver wouldn't fall out.

Peter chuckled. "S'more foolishness, I raikon. You gwine be hung one day, Jim, you keep up all dish yer nonsense."

Jimmie made no reply, but went into the back garden, where he hid the revolver in a box under a lilac-bush. Then he returned to the vicinity of Peter, and began to cruise to and fro in the offing, showing all the signals of one wishing to open treaty. "Pete," he said, "how much does a box of cartridges cost?"

Peter raised himself violently, holding in one hand a piece of harness, and in the other an old rag. "Ca'tridgers! *Ca'tridgers!*Lan'sake! wut the kid want with ca'tridgers? Knew it! Knew it! Come home er-holdin' on to his hind pocket like he got money in it. An' now he want ca'tridgers."

Jimmie, after viewing with dismay the excitement caused by his question, began to move warily out of the reach of a possible hostile movement.

"Ca'tridgers!" continued Peter, in scorn and horror. "Kid like you! No bigger'n er minute! Look yah, Jim, you done been swappin' round, an' you done got hol' of er pistol!" The charge was dramatic.

The wind was almost knocked out of Jimmie by this display of Peter's terrible miraculous power, and as he backed away his feeble denials were more convincing than a confession.

"I'll tell yer pop!" cried Peter, in virtuous grandeur. "I'll tell yer pop!"

In the distance Jimmie stood appalled. He knew not what to do. The dread adult wisdom of Peter Washington had laid bare the sin, and disgrace stared at Jimmie.

There was a whirl of wheels, and a high, lean trotting-mare spun Doctor Trescott's buggy towards Peter, who ran forward busily. As the doctor climbed out, Peter, holding the mare's head, began his denunciation:

"Docteh, I gwine tell on Jim. He come home er-holdin' on to his hind pocket, an' proud like he won a tuhkey-raffle, an' I sure know what he been up to, an' I done challenge him, an' he nev' say he didn't."

"Why, what do you mean?" said the doctor. "What's this, Jimmie?"

The boy came forward, glaring wrathfully at Peter. In fact, he suddenly was so filled with rage at Peter that he forgot all precautions. "It's about a pistol," he said, bluntly. "I've got a pistol. I swapped for it."

"I done tol' 'im his pop wouldn' stand no fiah-awms, an' him a kid like he is. I done tol' 'im. Lan' sake! he strut like he was a soldier! Come in yere proud, an' er-holdin' on to his hind pocket. He think he was Jesse James, I raikon. But I done tol' 'im his pop stan' no sech foolishness. First thing—*blam*—he shoot his haid off.

No, seh, he too tinety t' come in yere er-struttin' like he jest bought Main Street. I tol' 'im. I done tol' 'im—shawp. I don' wanter be loafin' round dis yer stable if Jim he gwine go shootin' round an' shootin' round—*blim—blam—blim—blam*! No, seh. I retiahs. I retiahs. It's all right if er grown man got er gun, but ain't no kids come foolishin' round *me* with fiah-awms. No, seh. I retiahs."

"Oh, be quiet, Peter!" said the doctor. "Where is this thing, Jimmie?"

The boy went sulkily to the box under the lilac-bush and returned with the revolver. "Here 'tis," he said, with a glare over his shoulder at Peter. The doctor looked at the silly weapon in critical contempt.

"It's not much of a thing, Jimmie, but I don't think you are quite old enough for it yet. I'll keep it for you in one of the drawers of my desk."

Peter Washington burst out proudly: "I done tol' 'im th' docteh wouldn' stan' no traffickin' round yere with fiah-awms. I done tol' 'im."

Jimmie and his father went together into the house, and as Peter unharnessed the mare he continued his comments on the boy and the revolver. He was not cast down by the absence of hearers. In fact, he usually talked better when there was no one to listen save the horses. But now his observations bore small resemblance to his earlier and public statements. Admiration and the keen family pride of a Southern negro who has been long in one place were now in his tone.

"That boy! He's er devil! When he get to be er man—wow! He'll jes take an' make things whirl round yere. Raikon we'll all take er back seat when he come erlong er-raisin' Cain."

He had unharnessed the mare, and with his back bent was pushing the buggy into the carriage-house.

"Er pistol! An' him no bigger than er minute!"

A small stone whizzed past Peter's head and clattered on the stable. He hastily dropped all occupation and struck a curious attitude. His right knee was almost up to his chin, and his arms were wreathed protectingly about his head. He had not looked in the direction from which the stone had come, but he had begun immediately to yell:

"You Jim! Quit! Quit, I tell yer, Jim! Watch out! You gwine break somethin', Jim!"

"Yah!" taunted the boy, as with the speed and ease of a light-cavalryman he manœuvred in the distance. "Yah! Told on me, did you! Told on me, hey! There! How do you like that?" The missiles resounded against the stable.

"Watch out, Jim! You gwine break something, Jim, I tell yer! Quit yer foolishness, Jim! Ow! Watch out, boy! I—"

There was a crash. With diabolic ingenuity, one of Jimmie's pebbles had entered the carriage-house and had landed among a row of carriage-lamps on a shelf, creating havoc which was apparently beyond all reason of physical law. It seemed to Jimmie that the racket of falling glass could have been heard in an adjacent county.

Peter was a prophet who after persecution was suffered to recall everything to the mind of the persecutor. "*There!* Knew it! Knew it!*Now* I raikon you'll quit. Hi! jes look ut dese yer lamps! Fer lan' sake! Oh, now yer pop jes break ev'ry bone in yer body!"

In the doorway of the kitchen the cook appeared with a startled face. Jimmie's father and mother came suddenly out on the front veranda. "What was that noise?" called the the doctor.

Peter went forward to explain. "Jim he was er-heavin' rocks at me, docteh, an' erlong come one rock an' go *blam* inter all th' lamps an' jes skitter 'em t' bits. I declayah—"

Jimmie, half blinded with emotion, was nevertheless aware of a lightning glance from his father, a glance which cowed and frightened him to the ends of his toes. He heard the steady but deadly tones of his father in a fury: "Go into the house and wait until I come."

Bowed in anguish, the boy moved across the lawn and up the steps. His mother was standing on the veranda still gazing towards the stable. He loitered in the faint hope that she might take some small pity on his state. But she could have heeded him no less if he had been invisible. He entered the house.

When the doctor returned from his investigation of the harm done by Jimmie's hand, Mrs. Trescott looked at him anxiously, for she knew that he was concealing some volcanic impulses. "Well?" she asked.

"It isn't the lamps," he said at first. He seated himself on the rail. "I don't know what we are going to do with that boy. It isn't so much the lamps as it is the other thing. He was throwing stones at Peter because Peter told me about the revolver. What are we going to do with him?"

"I'm sure I don't know," replied the mother. "We've tried almost everything. Of course much of it is pure animal spirits. Jimmie is not naturally vicious—"

"Oh, I know," interrupted the doctor, impatiently. "Do you suppose, when the stones were singing about Peter's ears, he cared whether they were flung by a boy who was naturally vicious or a boy who was not? The question might interest him afterward, but at the time he was mainly occupied in dodging these effects of pure animal spirits."

"Don't be too hard on the boy, Ned. There's lots of time yet. He's so young yet, and—I believe he gets most of his naughtiness from that wretched Dalzel boy. That Dalzel boy—well, he's simply awful!" Then, with true motherly instinct to shift blame from her own boy's shoulders, she proceeded to sketch the character of the Dalzel boy in lines that would have made that talented young vagabond stare. It was not admittedly her feeling that the doctor's attention should be diverted from the main issue and his indignation divided among the camps, but presently the doctor felt himself burn with wrath for the Dalzel boy.

"Why don't you keep Jimmie away from him?" he demanded. "Jimmie has no business consorting with abandoned little predestined jail-birds like him. If I catch him on the place I'll box his ears."

"It is simply impossible, unless we kept Jimmie shut up all the time," said Mrs. Trescott. "I can't watch him every minute of the day, and the moment my back is turned, he's off."

"I should think those Dalzel people would hire somebody to bring up their child for them," said the doctor. "They don't seem to know how to do it themselves."

Presently you would have thought from the talk that one Willie Dalzel had been throwing stones at Peter Washington because Peter Washington had told Doctor Trescott that Willie Dalzel had come into possession of a revolver.

In the mean time Jimmie had gone into the house to await the coming of his father. He was in a rebellious mood. He had not intended to destroy the carriage-lamps. He had been merely hurling stones at a creature whose perfidy deserved such action, and the hitting of the lamps had been merely another move of the great conspirator Fate to force one Jimmie Trescott into dark and troublous ways. The boy was beginning to find the world a bitter place. He couldn't win appreciation for a single virtue; he could only achieve quick, rigorous punishment for his misdemeanors. Everything was an enemy. Now there were those silly old lamps—what were they doing up on that shelf, anyhow? It would have been just as easy for them at the time to have been in some other place. But no; there they had been, like the crowd that is passing under the wall when the mason for the first time in twenty years lets fall a brick. Furthermore, the flight of that stone had been perfectly unreasonable. It had been a sort of freak in physical law. Jimmie understood that he might have thrown stones from the same fatal spot for an hour without hurting a single lamp. He was a victim—that was it. Fate had conspired with the detail of his environment to simply hound him into a grave or into a cell.

But who would understand? Who would understand? And here the boy turned his mental glance in every direction, and found nothing but what was to him the black of cruel ignorance. Very well; some day they would—

From somewhere out in the street he heard a peculiar whistle of two notes. It was the common signal of the boys in the neighborhood, and judging from the direction of the sound, it was apparently intended to summon him. He moved immediately to one of the windows of the sitting-room. It opened upon a part of the grounds remote from the stables and cut off from the veranda by a wing. He perceived Willie Dalzel loitering in the street. Jimmie whistled the signal after having pushed up the window-sash some inches. He saw the Dalzel boy turn and regard him, and then call several other boys. They stood in a group and gestured. These gestures plainly said: "Come out. We've got something on hand." Jimmie sadly shook his head.

But they did not go away. They held a long consultation. Presently Jimmie saw the intrepid Dalzel boy climb the fence and begin to creep among the shrubbery, in elaborate imitation of an Indian scout. In time he arrived under Jimmie's window, and raised his face to whisper: "Come on out! We're going on a bear-hunt."

A bear-hunt! Of course Jimmie knew that it would not be a real bear-hunt, but would be a sort of carouse of pretension and big talking and preposterous lying and valor, wherein each boy would strive to have himself called Kit Carson by the others. He was profoundly affected. However, the parental word was upon him, and he could not move. "No," he answered, "I can't. I've got to stay in."

"Are you a prisoner?" demanded the Dalzel boy, eagerly.

"No-o—yes—I s'pose I am."

The other lad became much excited, but he did not lose his wariness. "Don't you want to be rescued?"

"Why—no—I dun'no'," replied Jimmie, dubiously.

Willie Dalzel was indignant. "Why, of course you want to be rescued! We'll rescue you. I'll go and get my men." And thinking this a good sentence, he repeated, pompously, "I'll go and get my men." He began to crawl away, but when he was distant some ten paces he turned to say: "Keep up a stout heart. Remember that you have friends who will be faithful unto death. The time is not now far off when you will again view the blessed sunlight."

The poetry of these remarks filled Jimmie with ecstasy, and he watched eagerly for the coming of the friends who would be faithful unto death. They delayed some time, for the reason that Willie Dalzel was making a speech.

"Now, men," he said, "our comrade is a prisoner in yon—in yond—in that there fortress. We must to the rescue. Who volunteers to go with me?" He fixed them with a stern eye.

There was a silence, and then one of the smaller boys remarked,

"If Doc Trescott ketches us trackin' over his lawn—"

Willie Dalzel pounced upon the speaker and took him by the throat. The two presented a sort of a burlesque of the wood-cut on the cover of a dime novel which Willie had just been reading—*The Red Captain: A Tale of the Pirates of the Spanish Main*.

"You are a coward!" said Willie, through his clinched teeth.

"No, I ain't, Willie," piped the other, as best he could.

"I say you are," cried the great chieftain, indignantly. "Don't tell *me* I'm a liar." He relinquished his hold upon the coward and resumed his speech. "You know me, men. Many of you have been my followers for long years. You saw me slay Six-handed Dick with my own hand. You know I never falter. Our comrade is a prisoner in the cruel hands of our enemies. Aw, Pete Washington? He dassent. My pa says if Pete ever troubles me he'll brain 'im. Come on! To the rescue! Who will go with me to the rescue? Aw, come on! What are you afraid of?"

It was another instance of the power of eloquence upon the human mind. There was only one boy who was not thrilled by this oration, and he was a boy whose favorite reading had been of the road-agents and gun-fighters of the great West, and he thought the whole thing should be conducted in the Deadwood Dick manner. This talk of a "comrade" was silly; "pard" was the proper word. He resolved that he would make a show of being a pirate, and keep secret the fact that he really was Hold-up Harry, the Terror of the Sierras.

But the others were knit close in piratical bonds. One by one they climbed the fence at a point hidden from the house by tall shrubs. With many a low-breathed caution they went upon their perilous adventure.

Jimmie was grown tired of waiting for his friends who would be faithful unto death. Finally he decided that he would rescue himself. It would be a gross breach of rule, but he couldn't sit there all the rest of the day waiting for his faithful-unto-death friends. The window was only five feet from the ground. He softly raised the sash and threw one leg over the sill. But at the same time he perceived his friends snaking among the bushes. He withdrew his leg and waited, seeing that he was now to be rescued in an orthodox way. The brave pirates came nearer and nearer.

Jimmie heard a noise of a closing door, and turning, he saw his father in the room looking at him and the open window in angry surprise. Boys never faint, but Jimmie probably came as near to it as may the average boy.

"What's all this?" asked the doctor, staring. Involuntarily Jimmie glanced over his shoulder through the window. His father saw the creeping figures. "What are those boys doing?" he said, sharply, and he knit his brows.

"Nothin'."

"Nothing! Don't tell me that. Are they coming here to the window?"

"Y-e-s, sir."

"What for?"

"To—to see me."

"What about?"

"About—about nothin'."

"What about?"

Jimmie knew that he could conceal nothing.

He said, "They're comin' to—to—to rescue me." He began to whimper.

The doctor sat down heavily.

"What? To rescue you?" he gasped.

"Y-yes, sir."

The doctor's eyes began to twinkle. "Very well," he said presently. "I will sit here and observe this rescue. And on no account do you warn them that I am here. Understand?"

Of course Jimmie understood. He had been mad to warn his friends, but his father's mere presence had frightened him from doing it. He stood trembling at the window, while the doctor stretched in an easy-chair near at hand. They waited. The doctor could tell by his son's increasing agitation that the great moment was near. Suddenly he heard Willie Dalzel's voice hiss out a word: "S-s-silence!" Then the same voice addressed Jimmie at the window: "Good cheer, my comrade. The time is now at hand. I have come. Never did the Red Captain turn his back on a friend. One minute more and you will be free. Once aboard my gallant craft and you can bid defiance to your haughty enemies. Why don't you hurry up? What are you standin' there lookin' like a cow for?"

"I—er—now—you—" stammered Jimmie.

Here Hold-up Harry, the Terror of the Sierras, evidently concluded that Willie Dalzel had had enough of the premier part, so he said:

"Brace up, pard. Don't ye turn white-livered now, fer ye know that Hold-up Harry, the Terrar of the Sarahs, ain't the man ter—"

"Oh, stop it!" said Willie Dalzel. "He won't understand that, you know. He's a pirate. Now, Jimmie, come on. Be of light heart, my comrade. Soon you—"

"I 'low arter all this here long time in jail ye thought ye had no friends mebbe, but I tell ye Hold-up Harry, the Terrar of the Sarahs—"

"A boat is waitin'—"

"I have ready a trusty horse—"

Willie Dalzel could endure his rival no longer.

"Look here, Henry, you're spoilin' the whole thing. We're all pirates, don't you see, and you're a pirate too."

"I ain't a pirate. I'm Hold-up Harry, the Terrar of the Sarahs."

"You ain't, I say," said Willie, in despair. "You're spoilin' everything, you are. All right, now. You wait. I'll fix you for this, see if I don't! Oh, come on, Jimmie. A boat awaits us at the foot of the rocks. In one short hour you'll be free forever from your ex—exewable enemies, and their vile plots. Hasten, for the dawn approaches."

The suffering Jimmie looked at his father, and was surprised at what he saw. The doctor was doubled up like a man with the colic. He was breathing heavily. The boy turned again to his friends. "I—now—look here," he began, stumbling among the words. "You—I—I don't think I'll be rescued today."

The pirates were scandalized. "What?" they whispered, angrily. "Ain't you goin' to be rescued? Well, all right for you, Jimmie Trescott. That's a nice way to act, that is!" Their upturned eyes glowered at Jimmie.

Suddenly Doctor Trescott appeared at the window with Jimmie. "Oh, go home, boys!" he gasped, but they did not hear him. Upon the instant they had whirled and scampered away like deer. The first lad to reach the fence was the Red Captain, but Hold-up Harry, the Terror of the Sierras, was so close that there was little to choose between them.

Doctor Trescott lowered the window, and then spoke to his son in his usual quiet way. "Jimmie, I wish you would go and tell Peter to have the buggy ready at seven o'clock."

"Yes, sir," said Jimmie, and he swaggered out to the stables. "Pete, father wants the buggy ready at seven o'clock."

Peter paid no heed to this order, but with the tender sympathy of a true friend he inquired, "Hu't?"

"Hurt? Did what hurt?"

"Yer trouncin'."

"Trouncin'!" said Jimmie, contemptuously. "I didn't get any trouncin'."

"No?" said Peter. He gave Jimmie a quick shrewd glance, and saw that he was telling the truth. He began to mutter and mumble over his work. "Ump! Ump! Dese yer white folks act like they think er boy's made er glass. No trouncin'! Ump!" He was consumed with curiosity to learn why Jimmie had not felt a heavy parental hand, but he did not care to lower his dignity by asking questions about it. At last, however, he reached the limits of his endurance, and in a voice pretentiously careless he asked, "Didn' yer pop take on like mad er-bout dese yer cay'ge-lamps?"

"Carriage-lamps?" inquired Jimmie.

"Ump."

"No, he didn't say anything about carriage-lamps—not that I remember. Maybe he did, though. Lemme see.… No, he never mentioned 'em."

# THE KNIFE

## I

Si Bryant's place was on the shore of the lake, and his garden-patch, shielded from the north by a bold little promontory and a higher ridge inland, was accounted the most successful and surprising in all Whilomville township. One afternoon Si was working in the garden-patch, when Doctor Trescott's man, Peter Washington, came trudging slowly along the road, observing nature. He scanned the white man's fine agricultural results. "Take your eye off them there mellons, you rascal," said Si, placidly.

The negro's face widened in a grin of delight. "Well, Mist' Bryant, I raikon I ain't on'y make m'se'f covertous er-lookin' at dem yere mellums, sure 'nough. Dey suhtainly is grand."

"That's all right," responded Si, with affected bitterness of spirit. "That's all right. Just don't you admire 'em too much, that's all." Peter chuckled and chuckled. "Ma Lode! Mist' Bryant, y-y-you don' think I'm gwine come prowlin' in dish yer gawden?"

"No, I know you hain't," said Si, with solemnity. "B'cause, if you did, I'd shoot you so full of holes you couldn't tell yourself from a sponge."

"Um—no, seh! No, seh! I don' raikon you'll get chance at Pete, Mist' Bryant. No, seh. I'll take an' run 'long an' rob er bank 'fore I'll come foolishin' 'round *your* gawden, Mist' Bryant."

Bryant, gnarled and strong as an old tree, leaned on his hoe, and laughed a Yankee laugh. His mouth remained tightly closed, but the sinister lines which ran from the sides of his nose to the meetings of his lips developed to form a comic oval, and he emitted a series of grunts, while his eyes gleamed merrily and his shoulders shook. Pete, on the contrary, threw back his head and guffawed thunderously. The effete joke in regard to an American negro's fondness for watermelons was still an admirable pleasantry to them, and this was not the first time they had engaged in badinage over it. In fact, this venerable survival had formed between them a friendship of casual roadside quality.

Afterwards Peter went on up the road. He continued to chuckle until he was far away. He was going to pay a visit to old Alek Williams, a negro who lived with a large family in a hut clinging to the side of a mountain. The scattered colony of negroes which hovered near Whilomville was of interesting origin, being the result of some contrabands who had drifted as far north as Whilomville during the great civil war. The descendants of these adventurers were mainly conspicuous for their bewildering number, and the facility which they possessed for adding even to this number. Speaking, for example, of the Jacksons—one couldn't hurl a stone into the hills about Whilomville without having it land on the roof of a hut full of Jacksons. The town reaped little in labor from these curious suburbs. There were a few men who came in regularly to work in gardens, to drive teams, to care for horses, and there were a few women who came in to cook or to wash. These latter had usually drunken husbands. In the main the colony loafed in high spirits, and the industrious minority gained no direct honor from their fellows, unless they spent their earnings on raiment, in which case they were naturally treated with distinction. On the whole, the hardships of these people were the wind, the rain, the snow, and any other physical difficulties which they could cultivate. About twice a year the lady philanthropists of Whilomville went up against them, and came away poorer in goods but rich in complacence. After one of these attacks the colony would preserve a comic air of rectitude for two days, and then relapse again to the genial irresponsibility of a crew of monkeys.

Peter Washington was one of the industrious class who occupied a position of distinction, for he surely spent his money on personal decoration. On occasion he could dress better than the Mayor of Whilomville himself, or at least in more colors, which was the main thing to the minds of his admirers. His ideal had been the late gallant Henry Johnson, whose conquests in Watermelon Alley, as well as in the hill shanties, had proved him the equal if not the superior of any Pullman-car porter in the country. Perhaps Peter had too much Virginia laziness and humor in him to be a wholly adequate successor to the fastidious Henry Johnson, but, at any rate, he admired his memory so attentively as to be openly termed a dude by envious people.

On this afternoon he was going to call on old Alek Williams because Alek's eldest girl was just turned seventeen, and, to Peter's mind, was a triumph of beauty. He was not wearing his best clothes, because on his last visit Alek's half-breed hound Susie had taken occasion to forcefully extract a quite large and valuable part of the visitor's trousers. When Peter arrived at the end of the rocky field which contained old Alek's shanty he stooped and provided himself with several large stones, weighing them carefully in his hand, and finally continuing his journey with three stones of about eight ounces each. When he was near the house, three gaunt hounds, Rover and Carlo and Susie, came sweeping down upon him. His impression was that they were going to climb him as if he were a tree, but at the critical moment they swerved and went growling and snapping around him, their heads low, their eyes malignant. The afternoon caller waited until Susie presented her side to him, then he heaved one of his eight-ounce rocks. When it landed, her hollow ribs gave forth a drumlike sound, and she was knocked sprawling, her legs in the air. The other hounds at once fled in horror, and she followed as soon as she was able, yelping at the top of her lungs. The afternoon caller resumed his march.

At the wild expressions of Susie's anguish old Alek had flung open the door and come hastily into the sunshine. "Yah, you Suse, come erlong outa dat now. What fer you—Oh, how do, how do, Mist' Wash'ton—how do?"

"How do, Mist' Willums? I done foun' it necessa'y fer ter damnearkill dish yer dawg a yourn, Mist' Willums."

"Come in, come in, Mist' Wash'ton. Dawg no 'count, Mist' Wash'ton." Then he turned to address the unfortunate animal. "Hu't, did it? Hu't? 'Pears like you gwine dun some saince by time somebody brek yer back. 'Pears like I gwine club yer inter er frazzle 'fore you fin' out some saince. Gw'on 'way f'm yah!"

As the old man and his guest entered the shanty a body of black children spread out in crescent-shape formation and observed Peter with awe. Fat old Mrs. Williams greeted him turbulently, while the eldest girl, Mollie, lurked in a corner and giggled with finished imbecility, gazing at the visitor with eyes that were shy and bold by turns. She seemed at times absurdly over-confident, at times foolishly afraid; but her giggle consistently endured. It was a giggle on which an irascible but right-minded judge would have ordered her forthwith to be buried alive.

Amid a great deal of hospitable gabbling, Peter was conducted to the best chair out of the three that the house contained. Enthroned therein, he made himself charming in talk to the old people, who beamed upon him joyously. As for Mollie, he affected to be unaware of her existence. This may have been a method for entrapping the sentimental interest of that young gazelle, or it may be that the giggle had worked upon him.

He was absolutely fascinating to the old people. They could talk like rotary snow-ploughs, and he gave them every chance, while his face was illumined with appreciation. They pressed him to stay for supper, and he consented, after a glance at the pot on the stove which was too furtive to be noted.

During the meal old Alek recounted the high state of Judge Oglethorpe's kitchen-garden, which Alek said was due to his unremitting industry and fine intelligence. Alek was a gardener, whenever impending starvation forced him to cease temporarily from being a lily of the field.

"Mist' Bryant he suhtainly got er grand gawden," observed Peter.

"Dat so, dat so, Mist' Wash'ton," assented Alek. "He got fine gawden."

"Seems like I nev' *did* see sech mellums, big as er bar'l, layin' dere. I don't raikon an'body in dish yer county kin hol' it with Mist' Bryant when comes ter mellums."

"Dat so, Mist' Wash'ton."

They did not talk of watermelons until their heads held nothing else, as the phrase goes. But they talked of watermelons until, when Peter started for home that night over a lonely road, they held a certain dominant position in his mind. Alek had come with him as far as the fence, in order to protect him from a possible attack by the mongrels. There they had cheerfully parted, two honest men.

The night was dark, and heavy with moisture. Peter found it uncomfortable to walk rapidly. He merely loitered on the road. When opposite Si Bryant's place he paused and looked over the fence into the garden. He imagined he could see the form of a huge melon lying in dim stateliness not ten yards away. He looked at the Bryant house. Two windows, down-stairs, were lighted. The Bryants kept no dog, old Si's favorite child having once been bitten by a dog, and having since died, within that year, of pneumonia.

Peering over the fence, Peter fancied that if any low-minded night-prowler should happen to note the melon, he would not find it difficult to possess himself of it. This person would merely wait until the lights were out in the house, and the people presumably asleep. Then he would climb the fence, reach the melon in a few strides, sever the stem with his ready knife, and in a trice be back in the road with his prize. There need be no noise, and, after all, the house was some distance.

Selecting a smooth bit of turf, Peter took a seat by the road-side. From time to time he glanced at the lighted window.

## II

When Peter and Alek had said good-bye, the old man turned back in the rocky field and shaped a slow course towards that high dim light which marked the little window of his shanty. It would be incorrect to say that Alek could think of nothing but watermelons. But it was true that Si Bryant's watermelon-patch occupied a certain conspicuous position in his thoughts.

He sighed; he almost wished that he was again a conscienceless pickaninny, instead of being one of the most ornate, solemn, and look-at-me-sinner deacons that ever graced the handle of a collection-basket. At this time it made him quite sad to reflect upon his granite integrity. A weaker man might perhaps bow his moral head to the temptation, but for him such a fall was impossible. He was a prince of the church, and if he had been nine princes of the church he could not have been more proud. In fact, religion was to the old man a sort of personal dignity. And he was on Sundays so obtrusively good that you could see his sanctity through a door. He forced it on you until you would have felt its influence even in a forecastle.

It was clear in his mind that he must put watermelon thoughts from him, and after a moment he told himself, with much ostentation, that he had done so. But it was cooler under the sky than in the shanty, and as he was not sleepy, he decided to take a stroll down to Si Bryant's place and look at the melons from a pinnacle of spotless innocence. Reaching the road, he paused to listen. It would not do to let Peter hear him, because that graceless rapscallion would probably misunderstand him. But, assuring himself that Peter was well on his way, he set out, walking briskly until he was within four hundred yards of Bryant's place. Here he went to the side of the road, and walked thereafter on the damp, yielding turf. He made no sound.

He did not go on to that point in the main road which was directly opposite the water-melon-patch. He did not wish to have his ascetic contemplation disturbed by some chance wayfarer. He turned off along a short lane which led to Si Bryant's barn. Here he reached a place where he could see, over the fence, the faint shapes of the melons.

Alek was affected. The house was some distance away, there was no dog, and doubtless the Bryants would soon extinguish their lights and go to bed. Then some poor lost lamb of sin might come and scale the fence, reach a melon in a moment, sever the stem with his ready knife, and in a trice be back in the road with his prize. And this poor lost lamb of sin might even be a bishop, but no one would ever know it. Alek singled out with his eye a very large melon, and thought that the lamb would prove his judgment if he took that one.

He found a soft place in the grass, and arranged himself comfortably. He watched the lights in the windows.

### III

It seemed to Peter Washington that the Bryants absolutely consulted their own wishes in regard to the time for retiring; but at last he saw the lighted windows fade briskly from left to right, and after a moment a window on the second floor blazed out against the darkness. Si was going to bed. In five minutes this window abruptly vanished, and all the world was night.

Peter spent the ensuing quarter-hour in no mental debate. His mind was fixed. He was here, and the melon was there. He would have it. But an idea of being caught appalled him. He thought of his position. He was the beau of his community, honored right and left. He pictured the consternation of his friends and the cheers of his enemies if the hands of the redoubtable Si Bryant should grip him in his shame.

He arose, and going to the fence, listened. No sound broke the stillness, save the rhythmical incessant clicking of myriad insects, and the guttural chanting of the frogs in the reeds at the lake-side. Moved by sudden decision, he climbed the fence and crept silently and swiftly down upon the melon. His open knife was in his hand. There was the melon, cool, fair to see, as pompous in its fatness as the cook in a monastery.

Peter put out a hand to steady it while he cut the stem. But at the instant he was aware that a black form had dropped over the fence lining the lane in front of him and was coming stealthily towards him. In a palsy of terror he dropped flat upon the ground, not having strength enough to run away. The next moment he was looking into the amazed and agonized face of old Alek Williams.

There was a moment of loaded silence, and then Peter was overcome by a mad inspiration. He suddenly dropped his knife and leaped upon Alek. "I got che!" he hissed. "I got che! I got che!" The old man sank down as limp as rags. "I got che! I got che! Steal Mist' Bryant's mellums, hey?"

Alek, in a low voice, began to beg. "Oh, Mist' Peter Wash'ton, don' go fer ter be too ha'd on er ole man! I nev' come yere fer ter steal 'em. 'Deed I didn't, Mist' Wash'ton! I come yere jes fer ter *feel* 'em. Oh, please, Mist' Wash'ton—"

"Come erlong outa yere, you ol' rip," said Peter, "an' don' trumple on dese yer baids. I gwine put you wah you won' ketch col'."

Without difficulty he tumbled the whining Alek over the fence to the roadway, and followed him with sheriff-like expedition! He took him by the scruff. "Come erlong, deacon. I raikon I gwine put you wah you kin pray, deacon. Come erlong, deacon."

The emphasis and reiteration of his layman's title in the church produced a deadly effect upon Alek. He felt to his marrow the heinous crime into which this treacherous night had betrayed him. As Peter marched his prisoner up the road towards the mouth of the lane, he continued his remarks: "Come erlong, deacon. Nev' see er man so anxious like erbout er mellum-paitch, deacon. Seem like you jes must see 'em er-growin' an' *feel* 'em, deacon. Mist' Bryant he'll be s'prised, deacon, findin' out you come fer ter *feel* his mellums. Come erlong, deacon. Mist' Bryant he expectin' some ole rip like you come soon."

They had almost reached the lane when Alek's cur Susie, who had followed her master, approached in the silence which attends dangerous dogs; and seeing indications of what she took to be war, she appended herself swiftly but firmly to the calf of Peter's left leg. The mêlée was short, but spirited. Alek had no wish to have his dog complicate his already serious misfortunes, and went manfully to the defence of his captor. He procured a large stone, and by beating this with both hands down upon the resounding skull of the animal, he induced her to quit her grip. Breathing heavily, Peter dropped into the long grass at the road-side. He said nothing.

"Mist' Wash'ton," said Alek at last, in a quavering voice, "I raikon I gwine wait yere see what you gwine do ter me."

Whereupon Peter passed into a spasmodic state, in which he rolled to and fro and shook.

"Mist' Wash'ton, I hope dish yer dog ain't gone an' give you fitses?"

Peter sat up suddenly. "No, she ain't," he answered; "but she gin me er big skeer; an' fer yer 'sistance with er cobblestone, Mist' Willums, I tell you what I gwine do—I tell you what I gwine do." He waited an impressive moment. "I gwine 'lease you!"

Old Alek trembled like a little bush in a wind. "Mist' Wash'ton?"

Quoth Peter, deliberately, "I gwine 'lease you."

The old man was filled with a desire to negotiate this statement at once, but he felt the necessity of carrying off the event without an appearance of haste. "Yes, seh; thank 'e, seh; thank 'e, Mist' Wash'ton. I raikon I ramble home pressenly." He waited an interval, and then dubiously said, "Good-evenin', Mist' Wash'ton."

"Good-evenin', deacon. Don' come foolin' roun' *feelin'* no mellums, and I say troof. Good-evenin', deacon."

Alek took off his hat and made three profound bows. "Thank 'e, seh. Thank 'e, seh. Thank 'e, seh."

Peter underwent another severe spasm, but the old man walked off towards his home with a humble and contrite heart.

IV

The next morning Alek proceeded from his shanty under the complete but customary illusion that he was going to work. He trudged manfully along until he reached the vicinity of Si Bryant's place. Then, by stages, he relapsed into a slink. He was passing the garden-patch under full steam, when, at some distance ahead of him, he saw Si Bryant leaning casually on the garden fence.

"Good-mornin', Alek."

"Good-mawnin', Mist' Bryant," answered Alek, with a new deference. He was marching on, when he was halted by a word—"Alek!"

He stopped. "Yes, seh."

"I found a knife this mornin' in th' road," drawled Si, "an' I thought maybe it was yourn."

Improved in mind by this divergence from the direct line of attack, Alek stepped up easily to look at the knife. "No, seh," he said, scanning it as it lay in Si's palm, while the cold steel-blue eyes of the white man looked down into his stomach, "'tain't no knife er mine." But he knew the knife. He knew it as if it had been his mother. And at the same moment a spark flashed through his head and made wise his understanding. He knew everything. "'Tain't much of er knife, Mist' Bryant," he said, deprecatingly.

"'Tain't much of a knife, I know that," cried Si, in sudden heat, "but I found it this mornin' in my watermelon-patch—hear?"

"Watahmellum-paitch?" yelled Alek, not astounded.

"Yes, in my watermelon-patch," sneered Si, "an' I think you know something about it, too!"

"Me?" cried Alek. "Me?"

"Yes—you!" said Si, with icy ferocity. "Yes, damn you!" He had become convinced that Alek was not in any way guilty, but he was certain that the old man knew the owner of the knife, and so he pressed him at first on criminal lines. "Alek, you might as well own up now. You've been meddlin' with my watermelons!"

"Me?" cried Alek again. "Yah's *ma* knife. I done cah'e it foh yeahs."

Bryant changed his ways. "Look here, Alek," he said, confidentially: "I know you and you know me, and there ain't no use in any more skirmishin'. *I* know that *you* know whose knife that is. Now whose is it?"

This challenge was so formidable in character that Alek temporarily quailed and began to stammer. "Er—now—Mist' Bryant—you—you—frien' er mine—"

"I know I'm a friend of yours, but," said Bryant, inexorably, "who owns this knife?"

Alek gathered unto himself some remnants of dignity and spoke with reproach: "Mist' Bryant, dish yer knife ain' mine."

"No," said Bryant, "it ain't. But you know who it belongs to, an' I want you to tell me—quick."

"Well, Mist' Bryant," answered Alek, scratching his wool, "I won't say 's I *do* know who b'longs ter dish yer knife, an' I won't say 's I *don't*."

Bryant again laughed his Yankee laugh, but this time there was little humor in it. It was dangerous.

Alek, seeing that he had gotten himself into hot water by the fine diplomacy of his last sentence, immediately began to flounder and totally submerge himself. "No, Mist' Bryant," he repeated, "I won't say 's I *do* know who b'longs ter dish yer knife, an' I won't say 's I *don't*." And he began to parrot this fatal sentence again and again. It seemed wound about his tongue. He could not rid himself of it. Its very power to make trouble for him seemed to originate the mysterious Afric reason for its repetition.

"Is he a very close friend of yourn?" said Bryant, softly.

"F-frien'?" stuttered Alek. He appeared to weigh this question with much care. "Well, seems like he *was* er frien', an' then agin, it seems like he—"

"It seems like he *wasn't*?" asked Bryant.

"Yes, seh, jest so, jest so," cried Alek. "Sometimes it seems like he *wasn't*. Then agin—" He stopped for profound meditation.

The patience of the white man seemed inexhaustible. At length his low and oily voice broke the stillness. "Oh, well, of course if he's a friend of yourn, Alek! You know I wouldn't want to make no trouble for a friend of yourn."

"Yes, seh," cried the negro at once. "He's er frien' er mine. He is dat."

"Well, then, it seems as if about the only thing to do is for you to tell me his name so's I can send him his knife, and that's all there is to it."

Alek took off his hat, and in perplexity ran his hand over his wool. He studied the ground. But several times he raised his eyes to take a sly peep at the imperturbable visage of the white man. "Y—y—yes, Mist' Bryant. …I raikon dat's erbout all what kin be done. I gwine tell you who b'longs ter dish yer knife."

"Of course," said the smooth Bryant, "it ain't a very nice thing to have to do, but—"

"No, seh," cried Alek, brightly; "I'm gwine tell you, Mist' Bryant. I gwine tell you erbout dat knife. Mist' Bryant," he asked, solemnly, "does you know who b'longs ter dat knife?"

"No, I—"

"Well, I gwine tell. I gwine tell who, Mr Bryant—" The old man drew himself to a stately pose and held forth his arm. "I gwine tell who, Mist' Bryant, *dish yer knife b'longs ter Sam Jackson!*"

Bryant was startled into indignation. "Who in hell is Sam Jackson?" he growled.

"He's a nigger," said Alek, impressively, "and he wuks in er lumber-yawd up yere in Hoswego."

# THE STOVE

## I

"They'll bring her," said Mrs. Trescott, dubiously. Her cousin, the painter, the bewildered father of the angel child, had written to say that if they were asked, he and his wife would come to the Trescotts for the Christmas holidays. But he had not officially stated that the angel child would form part of the expedition. "But of course they'll bring her," said Mrs. Trescott to her husband.

The doctor assented. "Yes, they'll have to bring her. They wouldn't dare leave New York at her mercy."

"Well," sighed Mrs. Trescott, after a pause, "the neighbors will be pleased. When they see her they'll immediately lock up their children for safety."

"Anyhow," said Trescott, "the devastation of the Margate twins was complete. She can't do that particular thing again. I shall be interested to note what form her energy will take this time."

"Oh yes! that's it!" cried the wife. "You'll be *interested*. You've hit it exactly. You'll be interested to note what form her energy will take this time. And then, when the real crisis comes, you'll put on your hat and walk out of the house and leave *me* to straighten things out. This is not a scientific question; this is a practical matter."

"Well, as a practical man, I advocate chaining her out in the stable," answered the doctor.

When Jimmie Trescott was told that his old flame was again to appear, he remained calm. In fact, time had so mended his youthful heart that it was a regular apple of oblivion and peace. Her image in his thought was as the track of a bird on deep snow—it was an impression, but it did not concern the depths. However, he did what befitted his state. He went out and bragged in the street: "My cousin is comin' next week f'om New York." ..."My cousin is comin' tomorrow f'om New York."

"Girl or boy?" said the populace, bluntly; but, when enlightened, they speedily cried, "Oh, we remember *her*!" They were charmed, for they thought of her as an outlaw, and they surmised that she could lead them into a very ecstasy of sin. They thought of her as a brave bandit, because they had been whipped for various pranks into which she had led them. When Jimmie made his declaration, they fell into a state of pleased and shuddering expectancy.

Mrs. Trescott pronounced her point of view: "The child is a nice child, if only Caroline had some sense. But she hasn't. And Willis is like a wax figure. I don't see what can be done, unless—unless you simply go to Willis and put the whole thing right at him." Then, for purposes of indication, she improvised a speech: "Look here, Willis, you've got a little daughter, haven't you? But, confound it, man, she is not the only girl child ever brought into the sunlight. There are a lot of children. Children are an ordinary phenomenon. In China they drown girl babies. If you wish to submit to this frightful impostor and tyrant, that is all very well, but why in the name of humanity do you make us submit to it?"

Doctor Trescott laughed. "I wouldn't dare say it to him."

"Anyhow," said Mrs. Trescott, determinedly, "that is what you *should* say to him."

"It wouldn't do the slightest good. It would only make him very angry, and I would lay myself perfectly open to a suggestion that I had better attend to my own affairs with more rigor."

"Well, I suppose you are right," Mrs. Trescott again said.

"Why don't you speak to Caroline?" asked the doctor, humorously.

"Speak to Caroline! Why, I wouldn't for the *world*! She'd fly through the roof. She'd snap my head off! Speak to Caroline! You must be mad!"

One afternoon the doctor went to await his visitors on the platform of the railway station. He was thoughtfully smiling. For some quaint reason he was convinced that he was to be treated to a quick manifestation of little Cora's peculiar and interesting powers. And yet, when the train paused at the station, there appeared to him only a pretty little girl in a fur-lined hood, and with her nose reddening from the sudden cold, and—attended respectfully by her parents. He smiled again, reflecting that he had comically exaggerated the dangers of dear little Cora. It amused his philosophy to note that he had really been perturbed.

As the big sleigh sped homeward there was a sudden shrill outcry from the angel child: "Oh, mamma! mamma! They've forgotten my stove!"

"Hush, dear; hush!" said the mother. "It's all right."

"Oh, but, mamma, they've forgotten my stove!"

The doctor thrust his chin suddenly out of his top-coat collar. "Stove?" he said. "Stove? What stove?"

"Oh, just a toy of the child's," explained the mother. "She's grown so fond of it, she loves it so, that if we didn't take it everywhere with her she'd suffer dreadfully. So we always bring it."

"Oh!" said the doctor. He pictured a little tin trinket. But when the stove was really unmasked, it turned out to be an affair of cast iron, as big as a portmanteau, and, as the stage people say, practicable. There was some trouble that evening when came the hour of children's bedtime. Little Cora burst into a wild declaration that she could not retire for the night unless the stove was carried up-stairs and placed, at her bedside. While the mother was trying to dissuade the child, the Trescott's held their peace and gazed with awe. The incident closed when the lamb-eyed father gathered the stove in his arms and preceded the angel child to her chamber.

In the morning, Trescott was standing with his back to the dining room fire, awaiting breakfast, when he heard a noise of descending guests. Presently the door opened, and the party entered in regular order. First came the angel child, then the cooing mother, and last the great painter with his arm full of the stove. He deposited it gently in a corner, and sighed. Trescott wore a wide grin.

"What are you carting that thing all over the house for?" he said, brutally. "Why don't you put it some place where she can play with it, and leave it there?"

The mother rebuked him with a look. "Well, if it gives her pleasure, Ned?" she expostulated, softly. "If it makes the child happy to have the stove with her, why shouldn't she have it?"

"Just so," said the doctor, with calmness.

Jimmie's idea was the roaring fireplace in the cabin of the lone mountaineer. At first he was not able to admire a girl's stove built on well-known domestic lines. He eyed it and thought it was very pretty, but it did not move him immediately. But a certain respect grew to an interest, and he became the angel child's accomplice. And even if he had not had an interest grow upon him, he was certain to have been implicated sooner or later, because of the imperious way of little Cora, who made a serf of him in a few swift sentences. Together they carried the stove out into the desolate garden and squatted it in the snow. Jimmie's snug little muscles had been pitted against the sheer nervous vigor of this little golden-haired girl, and he had not won great honors. When the mind blazed inside the small body, the angel child was pure force. She began to speak: "Now, Jim, get some paper. Get some wood-little sticks at first. Now we want a match. You got a match? Well, go get a match. Get some more wood. Hurry up, now! No. *No!* I'll light it my own self. You get some more wood. There! Isn't that splendid? You get a whole lot of wood an' pile it up here by the stove. An' now what'll we cook? We must have somethin' to cook, you know, else it ain't like the real."

"Potatoes," said Jimmie, at once.

The day was clear, cold, bright. An icy wind sped from over the waters of the lake. A grown person would hardly have been abroad save on compulsion of a kind, and yet, when they were called to luncheon, the two little simpletons protested with great cries.

**II**

The ladies of Whilomville were somewhat given to the pagan habit of tea parties. When a tea party was to befall a certain house one could read it in the manner of the prospective hostess, who for some previous days would go about twitching this and twisting that, and dusting here and polishing there; the ordinary habits of the household began then to disagree with her, and her unfortunate husband and children fled to the lengths of their tethers. Then there was a hush. Then there was a tea party. On the fatal afternoon a small picked company of latent enemies would meet. There would be a fanfare of affectionate greetings, during which everybody would measure to an inch the importance of what everybody else was wearing. Those who wore old dresses would wish then that they had not come; and those who saw that, in the company, they were well clad, would be pleased or exalted, or filled with the joys of cruelty. Then they had tea, which was a habit and a delight with none of them, their usual beverage being coffee with milk.

Usually the party jerked horribly in the beginning, while the hostess strove and pulled and pushed to make its progress smooth. Then suddenly it would be off like the wind, eight, fifteen, or twenty-five tongues clattering, with a noise like a cotton-mill combined with the noise of a few penny whistles. Then the hostess had nothing to do but to look glad, and see that everybody had enough tea and cake. When the door was closed behind the last guest, the hostess would usually drop into a chair and say: "Thank Heaven! They're gone!" There would be no malice in this expression. It simply would be that, womanlike, she had flung herself headlong at the accomplishment of a pleasure which she could not even define, and at the end she felt only weariness.

The value and beauty, or oddity, of the tea-cups was another element which entered largely into the spirit of these terrible enterprises. The quality of the tea was an element which did not enter at all. Uniformly it was rather bad. But the cups! Some of the more ambitious people aspired to have cups each of a different pattern, possessing, in fact, the sole similarity that with their odd curves and dips of form they each resembled anything but a teacup. Others of the more ambitious aspired to a quite severe and godly "set," which, when viewed, appalled one with its austere and rigid family resemblances, and made one desire to ask the hostess if the teapot was not the father of all the little cups, and at the same time protesting gallantly that such a young and charming cream-jug surely could not be their mother.

But of course the serious part is that these collections so differed in style and the obvious amount paid for them that nobody could be happy. The poorer ones envied; the richer ones feared; the poorer ones continually striving to overtake the leaders; the leaders always with their heads turned back to hear overtaking footsteps. And none of these things here written did they know. Instead of seeing that they were very stupid, they thought they were very fine. And they gave and took heart-bruises—fierce, deep heart-bruises—under the clear impression that of such kind of rubbish was the kingdom of nice people. The characteristics of outsiders of course emerged in shreds from these tea parties, and it is doubtful if the characteristics of insiders escaped entirely. In fact, these tea parties were in the large way the result of a conspiracy of certain unenlightened people to make life still more uncomfortable.

Mrs. Trescott was in the circle of tea-fighters largely through a sort of artificial necessity—a necessity, in short, which she had herself created in a spirit of femininity.

When the painter and his family came for the holidays, Mrs. Trescott had for some time been feeling that it was her turn to give a tea party, and she was resolved upon it now that she was reinforced by the beautiful wife of the painter, whose charms would make all the other women feel badly. And Mrs. Trescott further resolved that the affair should be notable in more than one way. The painter's wife suggested that, as an innovation, they give the people good tea; but Mrs. Trescott shook her head; she was quite sure they would not like it.

It was an impressive gathering. A few came to see if they could not find out the faults of the painter's wife, and these, added to those who would have attended even without that attractive prospect, swelled the company to a number quite large for Whilomville. There were the usual preliminary jolts, and then suddenly the tea party was in full swing, and looked like an unprecedented success.

Mrs. Trescott exchanged a glance with the painter's wife. They felt proud and superior. This tea party was almost perfection.

### III

Jimmie and the angel child, after being oppressed by innumerable admonitions to behave correctly during the afternoon, succeeded in reaching the garden, where the stove awaited them. They were enjoying themselves grandly, when snow began to fall so heavily that it gradually dampened their ardor as well as extinguished the fire in the stove. They stood ruefully until the angel child devised the plan of carrying the stove into the stable, and there, safe from the storm, to continue the festivities. But they were met at the door of the stable by Peter Washington.

"What you 'bout, Jim?"

"Now—it's snowin' so hard, we thought we'd take the stove into the stable."

"An' have er fiah in it? No, seh! G'w'on 'way f'm heh!—g'w'on! Don' 'low no sech foolishin' round yer. No, seh!"

"Well, we ain't goin' to hurt your old stable, are we?" asked Jimmie, ironically.

"Dat you ain't, Jim! Not so long's I keep my two eyes right plumb squaah pinted at ol' Jim. No, seh!" Peter began to chuckle in derision.

The two vagabonds stood before him while he informed them of their iniquities as well as their absurdities, and further made clear his own masterly grasp of the spirit of their devices. Nothing affects children so much as rhetoric. It may not involve any definite presentation of common-sense, but if it is picturesque they surrender decently to its influence. Peter was by all means a rhetorician, and it was not long before the two children had dismally succumbed to him. They went away.

Depositing the stove in the snow, they straightened to look at each other. It did not enter either head to relinquish the idea of continuing the game. But the situation seemed invulnerable.

The angel child went on a scouting tour. Presently she returned, flying. "I know! Let's have it in the cellar! In the cellar! Oh, it'll be lovely!"

The outer door of the cellar was open, and they proceeded down some steps with their treasure. There was plenty of light; the cellar was high-walled, warm, and dry. They named it an ideal place. Two huge cylindrical furnaces were humming away, one at either end. Overhead the beams detonated with the different emotions which agitated the tea party.

Jimmie worked like a stoker, and soon there was a fine bright fire in the stove. The fuel was of small brittle sticks which did not make a great deal of smoke.

"Now what'll we cook?" cried little Cora. "What'll we cook, Jim? We must have something to cook, you know."

"Potatoes?" said Jimmie.

But the angel child made a scornful gesture. "No. I've cooked 'bout a million potatoes, I guess. Potatoes aren't nice any more."

Jimmie's mind was all said and done when the question of potatoes had been passed, and he looked weakly at his companion.

"Haven't you got any turnips in your house?" she inquired, contemptuously. "In *my* house we have *turnips*."

"Oh, turnips!" exclaimed Jimmie, immensely relieved to find that the honor of his family was safe. "Turnips? Oh, bushels an' bushels an' bushels! Out in the shed."

"Well, go an' get a whole lot," commanded the angel child. "Go an' get a whole lot. Grea' big ones. *We* always have grea' big ones."

Jimmie went to the shed and kicked gently at a company of turnips which the frost had amalgamated. He made three journeys to and from the cellar, carrying always the very largest types from his father's store. Four of them filled the oven of little Cora's stove. This fact did not please her, so they placed three rows of turnips on the hot top. Then the angel child, profoundly moved by an inspiration, suddenly cried out,

"Oh, Jimmie, let's play we're keepin' a hotel, an' have got to cook for 'bout a thousand people, an' those two furnaces will be the ovens, an' I'll be the chief cook—"

"No; I want to be chief cook some of the time," interrupted Jimmie.

"No; I'll be chief cook my own self. You must be my 'sistant. Now I'll prepare 'em—see? An' then you put 'em in the ovens. Get the shovel. We'll play that's the pan. I'll fix 'em, an' then you put 'em in the oven. Hold it still now."

Jim held the coal-shovel while little Cora, with a frown of importance, arranged turnips in rows upon it. She patted each one daintily, and then backed away to view it, with her head critically sideways.

"There!" she shouted at last. "That'll do, I guess. Put 'em in the oven."

Jimmie marched with his shovelful of turnips to one of the furnaces. The door was already open, and he slid the shovel in upon the red coals.

"Come on," cried little Cora. "I've got another batch nearly ready."

"But what am I goin' to do with these?" asked Jimmie. "There ain't only one shovel."

"Leave 'm in there," retorted the girl, passionately. "Leave 'm in there, an' then play you're comin' with another pan. 'Tain't right to stand there an' *hold* the pan, you goose."

So Jimmie expelled all his turnips from his shovel out upon the furnace fire, and returned obediently for another batch.

"These are puddings," yelled the angel child, gleefully. "Dozens an' dozens of puddings for the thousand people at our grea' big hotel."

**IV**

At the first alarm the painter had fled to the doctor's office, where he hid his face behind a book and pretended that he did not hear the noise of feminine revelling. When the doctor came from a round of calls, he too retreated upon the office, and the men consoled each other as well as they were able. Once Mrs. Trescott dashed in to say delightedly that her tea party was not only the success of the season, but it was probably the very nicest tea party that had ever been held in Whilomville. After vainly beseeching them to return with her, she dashed away again, her face bright with happiness.

The doctor and the painter remained for a long time in silence, Trescott tapping reflectively upon the window-pane. Finally he turned to the painter, and sniffing, said: "What is that, Willis? Don't you smell something?"

The painter also sniffed. "Why, yes! It's like—it's like turnips."

"Turnips? No; it can't be.

"Well, it's very much like it."

The puzzled doctor opened the door into the hall, and at first it appeared that he was going to give back two paces. A result of frizzling turnips, which was almost as tangible as mist, had blown in upon his face and made him gasp. "Good God! Willis, what can this be?" he cried.

"Whee!" said the painter. "It's awful, isn't it?"

The doctor made his way hurriedly to his wife, but before he could speak with her he had to endure the business of greeting a score of women. Then he whispered, "Out in the hall there's an awful—"

But at that moment it came to them on the wings of a sudden draught. The solemn odor of burning turnips rolled in like a sea-fog, and fell upon that dainty, perfumed tea party. It was almost a personality; if some unbidden and extremely odious guest had entered the room, the effect would have been much the same. The sprightly talk stopped with a jolt, and people looked at each other. Then a few brave and considerate persons made the usual attempt to talk away as if nothing had happened. They all looked at their hostess, who wore an air of stupefaction.

The odor of burning turnips grew and grew. To Trescott it seemed to make a noise. He thought he could hear the dull roar of this outrage. Under some circumstances he might have been able to take the situation from a point of view of comedy, but the agony of his wife was too acute, and, for him, too visible. She was saying: "Yes, we saw the play the last time we were in New York. I liked it very much. That scene in the second act—the gloomy church, you know, and all that—and the organ playing—and then when the four singing little girls came in—" But Trescott comprehended that she did not know if she was talking of a play or a parachute.

He had not been in the room twenty seconds before his brow suddenly flushed with an angry inspiration. He left the room hastily, leaving behind him an incoherent phrase of apology, and charged upon his office, where he found the painter somnolent.

"Willis!" he cried, sternly, "come with me. It's that damn kid of yours!"

The painter was immediately agitated. He always seemed to feel more than any one else in the world the peculiar ability of his child to create resounding excitement, but he seemed always to exhibit his feelings very late. He arose hastily, and hurried after Trescott to the top of the inside cellar stairway. Trescott motioned him to pause, and for an instant they listened.

"Hurry up, Jim," cried the busy little Cora. "Here's another whole batch of lovely puddings. Hurry up now, an' put 'em in the oven."

Trescott looked at the painter; the painter groaned. Then they appeared violently in the middle of the great kitchen of the hotel with a thousand people in it. "Jimmie, go up-stairs!" said Trescott, and then he turned to watch the painter deal with the angel child.

With some imitation of wrath, the painter stalked to his daughter's side and grasped her by the arm.

"Oh, papa! papa!" she screamed. "You're pinching me! You're pinching me! You're pinching me, papa!"

At first the painter had seemed resolved to keep his grip, but suddenly he let go her arm in a panic. "I've hurt her," he said, turning to Trescott.

Trescott had swiftly done much towards the obliteration of the hotel kitchen, but he looked up now and spoke, after a short period of reflection. "You've hurt her, have you? Well, hurt her again. Spank her!" he cried, enthusiastically. "Spank her, confound you, man! She needs it. Here's your chance. Spank her, and spank her good. Spank her!"

The painter naturally wavered over this incendiary proposition, but at last, in one supreme burst of daring, he shut his eyes and again grabbed his precious offspring.

The spanking was lamentably the work of a perfect bungler. It couldn't have hurt at all; but the angel child raised to heaven a loud, clear soprano howl that expressed the last word in even mediæval anguish. Soon the painter was aghast. "Stop it, darling! I didn't mean—I didn't mean to—to hurt you so much, you know." He danced nervously. Trescott sat on a box, and devilishly smiled.

But the pasture call of suffering motherhood came down to them, and a moment later a splendid apparition appeared on the cellar stairs. She understood the scene at a glance. "Willis! What have you been doing?"

Trescott sat on his box, the painter guiltily moved from foot to foot, and the angel child advanced to her mother with arms outstretched, making a piteous wail of amazed and pained pride that would have moved Peter the Great. Regardless of her frock, the panting mother knelt on the stone floor and took her child to her bosom, and looked, then, bitterly, scornfully, at the cowering father and husband.

The painter, for his part, at once looked reproachfully at Trescott, as if to say: "There! You see?"

Trescott arose and extended his hands in a quiet but magnificent gesture of despair and weariness. He seemed about to say something classic, and, quite instinctively, they waited. The stillness was deep, and the wait was longer than a moment. "Well," he said, "we can't live in the cellar. Let's go up-stairs."

# THE TRIAL, EXECUTION, AND BURIAL OF HOMER PHELPS

From time to time an enwearied pine bough let fall to the earth its load of melting snow, and the branch swung back glistening in the faint wintry sunlight. Down the gulch a brook clattered amid its ice with the sound of a perpetual breaking of glass. All the forest looked drenched and forlorn.

The sky-line was a ragged enclosure of gray cliffs and hemlocks and pines. If one had been miraculously set down in this gulch one could have imagined easily that the nearest human habitation was hundreds of miles away, if it were not for an old half-discernible wood-road that led towards the brook.

"Halt! Who's there?"

This low and gruff cry suddenly dispelled the stillness which lay upon the lonely gulch, but the hush which followed it seemed even more profound. The hush endured for some seconds, and then the voice of the challenger was again raised, this time with a distinctly querulous note in it.

"Halt! Who's there? Why don't you answer when I holler? Don't you know you're likely to get shot?"

A second voice answered, "Oh, you knew who I was easy enough."

"That don't make no diff'rence." One of the Margate twins stepped from a thicket and confronted Homer Phelps on the old wood-road. The majestic scowl of official wrath was upon the brow of Reeves Margate, a long stick was held in the hollow of his arm as one would hold a rifle, and he strode grimly to the other boy. "That don't make no diff'rence. You've got to answer when I holler, anyhow. Willie says so."

At the mention of the dread chieftain's name the Phelps boy daunted a trifle, but he still sulkily murmured, "Well, you knew it was me."

He started on his way through the snow, but the twin sturdily blocked the path. "You can't pass less'n you give the countersign."

"Huh?" said the Phelps boy. "Countersign?"

"Yes—countersign," sneered the twin, strong in his sense of virtue.

But the Phelps boy became very angry. "Can't I, hey? Can't I, hey? I'll show you whether I can or not! I'll show you, Reeves Margate!"

There was a short scuffle, and then arose the anguished clamor of the sentry: "Hey, fellers! Here's a man tryin' to run a-past the guard. Hey, fellers! Hey!"

There was a great noise in the adjacent underbrush. The voice of Willie could be heard exhorting his followers to charge swiftly and bravely. Then they appeared— Willie Dalzel, Jimmie Trescott, the other Margate twin, and Dan Earl. The chieftain's face was dark with wrath. "What's the matter? Can't you play it right? Ain't you got any sense?" he asked the Phelps boy.

The sentry was yelling out his grievance. "Now—he came along an' I hollered at 'im, an' he didn't pay no 'tention, an' when I ast 'im for the countersign, he wouldn't say nothin'. That ain't no way."

"Can't you play it right?" asked the chief again, with gloomy scorn.

"He knew it was me easy enough," said the Phelps boy.

"That ain't got nothin' to do with it," cried the chief, furiously. "That ain't got nothin' to do with it. If you're goin' to play, you've got to play it right. It ain't no fun if you go spoilin' the whole thing this way. Can't you play it right?"

"I forgot the countersign," lied the culprit, weakly.

Whereupon the remainder of the band yelled out, with one triumphant voice: "War to the knife! War to the knife! I remember it, Willie. Don't I, Willie?"

The leader was puzzled. Evidently he was trying to develop in his mind a plan for dealing correctly with this unusual incident. He felt, no doubt, that he must proceed according to the books, but unfortunately the books did not cover the point precisely. However, he finally said to Homer Phelps, "You are under arrest." Then with a stentorian voice he shouted, "Seize him!"

His loyal followers looked startled for a brief moment, but directly they began to move upon the Phelps boy. The latter clearly did not intend to be seized. He backed away, expostulating wildly. He even seemed somewhat frightened. "No, no; don't you touch me, I tell you; don't you dare touch me."

The others did not seem anxious to engage. They moved slowly, watching the desperate light in his eyes. The chieftain stood with folded arms, his face growing darker and darker with impatience. At length he burst out: "Oh, seize him, I tell you! Why don't you seize him? Grab him by the leg, Dannie! Hurry up, all of you! Seize him, I keep a-say-in'!"

Thus adjured, the Margate twins and Dan Earl made another pained effort, while Jimmie Trescott manœuvred to cut off a retreat. But, to tell the truth, there was a boyish law which held them back from laying hands of violence upon little Phelps under these conditions. Perhaps it was because they were only playing, whereas he was now undeniably serious. At any rate, they looked very sick of their occupation.

"Don't you dare!" snarled the Phelps boy, facing first one and then the other; he was almost in tears—"don't you dare touch me!"

The chieftain was now hopping with exasperation. "Oh, seize him, can't you? You're no good at all!" Then he loosed his wrath upon the Phelps boy: "Stand still, Homer, can't you? You've got to be seized, you know. That ain't the way. It ain't any fun if you keep a-dodgin' that way. Stand still, can't you! You've got to be seized."

"I don't *want* to be seized," retorted the Phelps boy, obstinate and bitter.

"But you've *got* to be seized!" yelled the maddened chief. "Don't you see? That's the way to play it."

The Phelps boy answered, promptly, "But I don't want to play that way."

"But that's the *right* way to play it. Don't you see? You've got to play it the right way. You've got to be seized, an' then we'll hold a trial on you, an'—an' all sorts of things."

But this prospect held no illusions for the Phelps boy. He continued doggedly to repeat, "I don't want to play that way!"

Of course in the end the chief stooped to beg and beseech this unreasonable lad. "Oh, come on, Homer! Don't be so mean. You're a-spoilin' everything. We won't hurt you any. Not the tintiest bit. It's all just playin'. What's the matter with you?"

The different tone of the leader made an immediate impression upon the other. He showed some signs of the beginning of weakness. "Well," he asked, "what you goin' to do?"

"Why, first we're goin' to put you in a dungeon, or tie you to a stake, or something like that—just pertend, you know," added the chief, hurriedly, "an' then we'll hold a trial, awful solemn, but there won't be anything what'll hurt you. Not a thing."

And so the game was readjusted. The Phelps boy was marched off between Dan Earl and a Margate twin. The party proceeded to their camp, which was hidden some hundred feet back in the thickets. There was a miserable little hut with a pine-bark roof, which so frankly and constantly leaked that existence in the open air was always preferable. At present it was noisily dripping melted snow into the black mouldy interior. In front of this hut a feeble fire was flickering through its unhappy career. Underfoot, the watery snow was of the color of lead.

The party having arrived at the camp, the chief leaned against a tree, and balancing on one foot, drew off a rubber boot. From this boot he emptied about a quart of snow. He squeezed his stocking, which had a hole from which protruded a lobster-red toe. He resumed his boot. "Bring up the prisoner," said he. They did it. "Guilty or not guilty?" he asked.

"Huh?" said the Phelps boy.

"Guilty or not guilty?" demanded the chief, peremptorily. "Guilty or not guilty? Don't you understand?"

Homer Phelps looked profoundly puzzled. "Guilty or not guilty?" he asked, slowly and weakly.

The chief made a swift gesture, and turned in despair to the others. "Oh, he don't do it right! He does it all wrong!" He again faced the prisoner with an air of making a last attempt, "Now look-a-here, Homer, when I say, 'Guilty or not guilty?' you want to up an' say, 'Not Guilty.' Don't you see?"

"Not guilty," said Homer, at once.

"No, no, no. Wait till I ask you. Now wait." He called out, pompously, "Pards, if this prisoner before us is guilty, what shall be his fate?"

All those well-trained little infants with one voice sung out, "*Death!*"

"Prisoner," continued the chief, "are you guilty or not guilty?"

"But look-a-here," argued Homer, "you said it wouldn't be nothin' that would hurt. I—"

"Thunder an' lightnin'!" roared the wretched chief. "Keep your mouth shut, can't ye? What in the mischief—"

But there was an interruption from Jimmie Trescott, who shouldered a twin aside and stepped to the front. "Here," he said, very contemptuously, "let me be the prisoner. I'll show 'im how to do it."

"All right, Jim," cried the chief, delighted; "you be the prisoner, then. Now all you fellers with guns stand there in a row! Get out of the way, Homer!" He cleared his throat, and addressed Jimmie. "Prisoner, are you guilty or not guilty?"

"Not guilty," answered Jimmie, firmly. Standing there before his judge—unarmed, slim, quiet, modest—he was ideal.

The chief beamed upon him, and looked aside to cast a triumphant and withering glance upon Homer Phelps. He said: "There! That's the way to do it."

The twins and Dan Earl also much admired Jimmie.

"That's all right so far, anyhow," said the satisfied chief. "An' now we'll—now we'll—we'll perceed with the execution."

"That ain't right," said the new prisoner, suddenly. "That ain't the next thing. You've got to have a trial first. You've got to fetch up a lot of people first who'll say I done it."

"That's so," said the chief. "I didn't think. Here, Reeves, you be first witness. Did the prisoner do it?"

The twin gulped for a moment in his anxiety to make the proper reply. He was at the point where the roads forked. Finally he hazarded, "Yes."

"There," said the chief, "that's one of 'em. Now, Dan, you be a witness. Did he do it?"

Dan Earl, having before him the twin's example, did not hesitate. "Yes," he said.

"Well, then, pards, what shall be his fate?"

Again came the ringing answer, "*Death*!"

With Jimmie in the principal rôle, this drama, hidden deep in the hemlock thicket neared a kind of perfection. "You must blind-fold me," cried the condemned lad, briskly, "an' then I'll go off an' stand, an' you must all get in a row an' shoot me."

The chief gave this plan his urbane countenance, and the twins and Dan Earl were greatly pleased. They blindfolded Jimmie under his careful directions. He waded a few paces into snow, and then turned and stood with quiet dignity, awaiting his fate. The chief marshalled the twins and Dan Earl in line with their sticks. He gave the necessary commands: "Load! Ready! Aim! Fire!" At the last command the firing party all together yelled, "Bang!"

Jimmie threw his hands high, tottered in agony for a moment, and then crashed full length into the snow—into, one would think, a serious case of pneumonia. It was beautiful.

He arose almost immediately and came back to them, wondrously pleased with himself. They acclaimed him joyously.

The chief was particularly grateful. He was always trying to bring off these little romantic affairs, and it seemed, after all, that the only boy who could ever really help him was Jimmie Trescott. "There," he said to the others, "that's the way it ought to be done."

They were touched to the heart by the whole thing, and they looked at Jimmie with big, smiling eyes. Jimmie, blown out like a balloon-fish with pride of his performance, swaggered to the fire and took seat on some wet hemlock boughs. "Fetch some more wood, one of you kids," he murmured, negligently. One of the twins came fortunately upon a small cedar-tree the lower branches of which were dead and dry. An armful of these branches flung upon the sick fire soon made a high, ruddy, warm blaze, which was like an illumination in honor of Jimmie's success.

The boys sprawled about the fire and talked the regular language of the game. "Waal, pards," remarked the chief, "it's many a night we've had together here in the Rockies among the b'ars an' the Indyuns, hey?"

"Yes, pard," replied Jimmie Trescott, "I reckon you're right. Our wild, free life is—there ain't nothin' to compare with our wild, free life."

Whereupon the two lads arose and magnificently shook hands, while the others watched them in an ecstasy. "I'll allus stick by ye, pard," said Jimmie, earnestly. "When yer in trouble, don't forget that Lightnin' Lou is at yer back."

"Thanky, pard," quoth Willie Dalzel, deeply affected. "I'll not forget it, pard. An' don't you forget, either, that Dead-shot Demon, the leader of the Red Raiders, never forgits a friend."

But Homer Phelps was having none of this great fun. Since his disgraceful refusal to be seized and executed he had been hovering unheeded on the outskirts of the band. He seemed very sorry; he cast a wistful eye at the romantic scene. He knew too well that if he went near at that particular time he would be certain to encounter a pitiless snubbing. So he vacillated modestly in the background.

At last the moment came when he dared venture near enough to the fire to gain some warmth, for he was now bitterly suffering with the cold. He sidled close to Willie Dalzel. No one heeded him. Eventually he looked at his chief, and with a bright face said,

"Now—if I was seized now to be executed, I could do it as well as Jimmie Trescott, I could."

The chief gave a crow of scorn, in which he was followed by the other'boys. "Ho!" he cried, "why didn't you do it, then? Why didn't you do it?" Homer Phelps felt upon him many pairs of disdainful eyes. He wagged his shoulders in misery.

"You're dead," said the chief, frankly. "That's what you are. We executed you, we did."

"When?" demanded the Phelps boy, with some spirit.

"Just a little while ago. Didn't we, fellers? Hey, fellers, didn't we?"

The trained chorus cried: "Yes, of course we did. You're dead, Homer. You can't play any more. You're dead."

"That wasn't me. It was Jimmie Trescott," he said, in a low and bitter voice, his eyes on the ground. He would have given the world if he could have retracted his mad refusals of the early part of the drama.

"No," said the chief, "it was you. We're playin' it was you, an' it *was* you. You're dead, you are." And seeing the cruel effect of his words, he did not refrain from administering some advice: "The next time, don't be such a chuckle-head."

Presently the camp imagined that it was attacked by Indians, and the boys dodged behind trees with their stick-rifles, shouting out, "Bang!" and encouraging each other to resist until the last. In the mean time the dead lad hovered near the fire, looking moodily at the gay and exciting scene. After the fight the gallant defenders returned one by one to the fire, where they grandly clasped hands, calling each other "old pard," and boasting of their deeds.

Parenthetically, one of the twins had an unfortunate inspiration. "I killed the Indy-un chief, fellers. Did you see me kill the Indy-un chief?"

But Willie Dalzel, his own chief, turned upon him wrathfully: "*You* didn't kill no chief. *I* killed 'im with me own hand."

"Oh!" said the twin, apologetically, at once. "It must have been some other Indy-un."

"Who's wounded?" cried Willie Dalzel. "Ain't anybody wounded?" The party professed themselves well and sound. The roving and inventive eye of the chief chanced upon Homer Phelps. "Ho! Here's a dead man! Come on, fellers, here's a dead man! We've got to bury him, you know." And at his bidding they pounced upon the dead Phelps lad. The unhappy boy saw clearly his road to rehabilitation, but mind and body revolted at the idea of burial, even as they had revolted at the thought of execution. "No!" he said, stubbornly. "No! I don't want to be buried! I don't want to be buried!"

"You've *got* to be buried!" yelled the chief, passionately. "'Tain't goin' to hurt ye, is it? Think you're made of glass? Come on, fellers, get the grave ready!"

They scattered hemlock boughs upon the snow in the form of a rectangle, and piled other boughs near at hand. The victim surveyed these preparations with a glassy eye. When all was ready, the chief turned determinedly to him: "Come on now, Homer. We've got to carry you to the grave. Get him by the legs, Jim!"

Little Phelps had now passed into that state which may be described as a curious and temporary childish fatalism. He still objected, but it was only feeble muttering, as if he did not know what he spoke. In some confusion they carried him to the rectangle of hemlock boughs and dropped him. Then they piled other boughs upon him until he was not to be seen. The chief stepped forward to make a short address, but before proceeding with it he thought it expedient, from certain indications, to speak to the grave itself. "Lie still, can't ye? Lie still until I get through." There was a faint movement of the boughs, and then a perfect silence.

The chief took off his hat. Those who watched him could see that his face was harrowed with emotion. "Pards," he began, brokenly—"pards, we've got one more debt to pay them murderin' red-skins. Bowie-knife Joe was a brave man an' a good pard, but—he's gone now—gone." He paused for a moment, overcome, and the stillness was only broken by the deep manly grief of Jimmie Trescott.

# THE FIGHT



The child life of the neighborhood was sometimes moved in its deeps at the sight of wagon-loads of furniture arriving in front of some house which, with closed blinds and barred doors, had been for a time a mystery, or even a fear. The boys often expressed this fear by stamping bravely and noisily on the porch of the house, and then suddenly darting away with screams of nervous laughter, as if they expected to be pursued by something uncanny. There was a group who held that the cellar of a vacant house was certainly the abode of robbers, smugglers, assassins, mysterious masked men in council about the dim rays of a candle, and possessing skulls, emblematic bloody daggers, and owls. Then, near the first of April, would come along a wagon-load of furniture, and children would assemble on the walk by the gate and make serious examination of everything that passed into the house, and taking no thought whatever of masked men.

One day it was announced in the neighborhood that a family was actually moving into the Hannigan house, next door to Dr. Trescott's. Jimmie was one of the first to be informed, and by the time some of his friends came dashing up he was versed in much.

"Any boys?" they demanded, eagerly.

"Yes," answered Jimmie, proudly. "One's a little feller, and one's most as big as me. I saw 'em, I did."

"Where are they?" asked Willie Dalzel, as if under the circumstances he could not take Jimmie's word, but must have the evidence of his senses.

"Oh, they're in there," said Jimmie, carelessly. It was evident he owned these new boys.

Willie Dalzel resented Jimmie's proprietary way.

"Ho!" he cried, scornfully. "Why don't they come out, then? Why don't they come out?"

"How d' I know?" said Jimmie.

"Well," retorted Willie Dalzel, "you seemed to know so thundering much about 'em."

At the moment a boy came strolling down the gravel walk which led from the front door to the gate. He was about the height and age of Jimmie Trescott, but he was thick through the chest and had fat legs. His face was round and rosy and plump, but his hair was curly black, and his brows were naturally darkling, so that he resembled both a pudding and a young bull.

He approached slowly the group of older inhabitants, and they had grown profoundly silent. They looked him over; he looked them over. They might have been savages observing the first white man, or white men observing the first savage. The silence held steady.

As he neared the gate the strange boy wandered off to the left in a definite way, which proved his instinct to make a circular voyage when in doubt. The motionless group stared at him. In time this unsmiling scrutiny worked upon him somewhat, and he leaned against the fence and fastidiously examined one shoe.

In the end Willie Dalzel authoritatively broke the stillness. "What's your name?" said he, gruffly.

"Johnnie Hedge 'tis," answered the new boy. Then came another great silence while Whilomville pondered this intelligence.

Again came the voice of authority—"Where'd you live b'fore?"

"Jersey City."

These two sentences completed the first section of the formal code. The second section concerned itself with the establishment of the new-comer's exact position in the neighborhood.

"I kin lick you," announced Willie Dalzel, and awaited the answer.

The Hedge boy had stared at Willie Dalzel, but he stared at him again. After a pause he said, "I know you kin."

"Well," demanded Willie, "kin *he* lick you?" And he indicated Jimmie Trescott with a sweep which announced plainly that Jimmie was the next in prowess.

Whereupon the new boy looked at Jimmie respectfully but carefully, and at length said, "I dun'no'."

This was the signal for an outburst of shrill screaming, and everybody pushed Jimmie forward. He knew what he had to say, and, as befitted the occasion, he said it fiercely: "Kin you lick me?"

The new boy also understood what he had to say, and, despite his unhappy and lonely state, he said it bravely: "Yes."

"Well," retorted Jimmie, bluntly, "come out and do it, then! Jest come out and do it!" And these words were greeted with cheers. These little rascals yelled that there should be a fight at once. They were in bliss over the prospect. "Go on, Jim! Make 'im come out. He said he could lick you. Aw-aw-aw! He said he could lick you!" There probably never was a fight among this class in Whilomville which was not the result of the goading and guying of two proud lads by a populace of urchins who simply wished to see a show.

Willie Dalzel was very busy. He turned first to the one and then to the other. "You said you could lick him. Well, why don't you come out and do it, then? You said you could lick him, didn't you?"

"Yes," answered the new boy, dogged and dubious.

Willie tried to drag Jimmie by the arm. "Aw, go on, Jimmie! You ain't afraid, are you?"

"No," said Jimmie.

The two victims opened wide eyes at each other. The fence separated them, and so it was impossible for them to immediately engage; but they seemed to understand that they were ultimately to be sacrificed to the ferocious aspirations of the other boys, and each scanned the other to learn something of his spirit. They were not angry at all. They were merely two little gladiators who were being clamorously told to hurt each other. Each displayed hesitation and doubt without displaying fear. They did not exactly understand what were their feelings, and they moodily kicked the ground and made low and sullen answers to Willie Dalzel, who worked like a circus-manager.

"Aw, go on, Jim! What's the matter with you? You ain't afraid, are you? Well, then, say something." This sentiment received more cheering from the abandoned little wretches who wished to be entertained, and in this cheering there could be heard notes of derision of Jimmie Trescott. The latter had a position to sustain; he was well known; he often bragged of his willingness and ability to thrash other boys; well, then, here was a boy of his size who said that he could not thrash him.

What was he going to do about it? The crowd made these arguments very clear, and repeated them again and again.

Finally Jimmie, driven to aggression, walked close to the fence and said to the new boy, "The first time I catch you out of your own yard I'll lam the head off'n you!" This was received with wild plaudits by the Whilomville urchins.

But the new boy stepped back from the fence. He was awed by Jimmie's formidable mien. But he managed to get out a semi-defiant sentence. "Maybe you will, and maybe you won't," said he.

However, his short retreat was taken as a practical victory for Jimmie, and the boys hooted him bitterly. He remained inside the fence, swinging one foot and scowling, while Jimmie was escorted off down the street amid acclamations. The new boy turned and walked back towards the house, his face gloomy, lined deep with discouragement, as if he felt that the new environment's antagonism and palpable cruelty were sure to prove too much for him.

## II

The mother of Johnnie Hedge was a widow, and the chief theory of her life was that her boy should be in school on the greatest possible number of days. He himself had no sympathy with this ambition, but she detected the truth of his diseases with an unerring eye, and he was required to be really ill before he could win the right to disregard the first bell, morning and noon. The chicken-pox and the mumps had given him vacations—vacations of misery, wherein he nearly died between pain and nursing. But bad colds in the head did nothing for him, and he was not able to invent a satisfactory hacking cough. His mother was not consistently a tartar. In most things he swayed her to his will. He was allowed to have more jam, pickles, and pie than most boys; she respected his profound loathing of Sunday-school; on summer evenings he could remain out-of-doors until 8.30; but in this matter of school she was inexorable. This single point in her character was of steel.

The Hedges arrived in Whilomville on a Saturday, and on the following Monday Johnnie wended his way to school with a note to the principal and his Jersey City school-books. He knew perfectly well that he would be told to buy new and different books, but in those days mothers always had an idea that old books would "do," and they invariably sent boys off to a new school with books which would not meet the selected and unchangeable views of the new administration. The old books never would "do." Then the boys brought them home to annoyed mothers and asked for ninety cents or sixty cents or eighty-five cents or some number of cents for another outfit. In the garret of every house holding a large family there was a collection of effete school-books, with mother rebellious because James could not inherit his books from Paul, who should properly be Peter's heir, while Peter should be a beneficiary under Henry's will.

But the matter of the books was not the measure of Johnnie Hedge's unhappiness. This whole business of changing schools was a complete torture. Alone he had to go among a new people, a new tribe, and he apprehended his serious time. There were only two fates for him. One meant victory. One meant a kind of serfdom in which he would subscribe to every word of some superior boy and support his every word. It was not anything like an English system of fagging, because boys invariably drifted into the figurative service of other boys whom they devotedly admired, and if they were obliged to subscribe to everything, it is true that they would have done so freely in any case. One means to suggest that Johnnie Hedge had to find his place. Willie Dalzel was a type of the little chieftain, and Willie was a master, but he was not a bully in a special physical sense. He did not drag little boys by the ears until they cried, nor make them tearfully fetch and carry for him. They fetched and carried, but it was because of their worship of his prowess and genius. And so all through the strata of boy life were chieftains and subchieftains and assistant subchieftains. There was no question of little Hedge being towed about by the nose; it was, as one has said, that he had to find his place in a new school. And this in itself was a problem which awed his boyish heart. He was a stranger cast away upon the moon. None knew him, understood him, felt for him. He would be surrounded for this initiative time by a horde of jackal creatures who might turn out in the end to be little boys like himself, but this last point his philosophy could not understand in its fulness.

He came to a white meeting-house sort of a place, in the squat tower of which a great bell was clanging impressively. He passed through an iron gate into a play-ground worn bare as the bed of a mountain brook by the endless runnings and scuf-flings of little children. There was still a half-hour before the final clangor in the squat tower, but the play-ground held a number of frolicsome imps. A loitering boy espied Johnnie Hedge, and he howled: "Oh! oh! Here's a new feller! Here's a new feller!" He advanced upon the strange arrival. "What's your name?" he demanded, belligerently, like a particularly offensive custom-house officer.

"Johnnie Hedge," responded the new-comer, shyly.

This name struck the other boy as being very comic. All new names strike boys as being comic. He laughed noisily.

"Oh, fellers, he says his name is Johnnie Hedge! Haw! haw! haw!"

The new boy felt that his name was the most disgraceful thing which had ever been attached to a human being.

"Johnnie Hedge! Haw! haw! What room you in?" said the other lad.

"I dun'no'," said Johnnie. In the mean time a small flock of interested vultures had gathered about him. The main thing was his absolute strangeness. He even would have welcomed the sight of his tormentors of Saturday; he had seen them before at least. These creatures were only so many incomprehensible problems. He diffidently began to make his way towards the main door of the school, and the other boys followed him. They demanded information.

"Are you through subtraction yet? We study jogerfre—did you, ever? You live here now? You goin' to school here now?"

To many questions he made answer as well as the clamor would permit, and at length he reached the main door and went quaking unto his new kings. As befitted them, the rabble stopped at the door. A teacher strolling along a corridor found a small boy holding in his hand a note. The boy palpably did not know what to do with the note, but the teacher knew, and took it. Thereafter this little boy was in harness.

A splendid lady in gorgeous robes gave him a seat at a double desk, at the end of which sat a hoodlum with grimy finger-nails, who eyed the inauguration with an extreme and personal curiosity. The other desks were gradually occupied by chil-dren, who first were told of the new boy, and then turned upon him a speculative and somewhat derisive eye. The school opened; little classes went forward to a position in front of the teacher's platform and tried to explain that they knew something. The new boy was not requisitioned a great deal; he was allowed to lie dormant until he became used to the scenes and until the teacher found, approximately, his mental position. In the mean time he suffered a shower of stares and whispers and giggles, as if he were a man-ape, whereas he was precisely like other children. From time to time he made funny and pathetic little overtures to other boys, but these overtures could not yet be received; he was not known; he was a foreigner. The village school was like a nation. It was tight. Its amiability or friendship must be won in certain ways.

At recess he hovered in the school-room around the weak lights of society and around the teacher, in the hope that somebody might be good to him, but none considered him save as some sort of a specimen. The teacher of course had a secondary interest in the fact that he was an additional one to a class of sixty-three.

At twelve o'clock, when the ordered files of boys and girls marched towards the door, he exhibited—to no eye—the tremblings of a coward in a charge. He exaggerated the lawlessness of the play-ground and the street.

But the reality was hard enough. A shout greeted him:

"Oh, here's the new feller! Here's the new feller!"

Small and utterly obscure boys teased him. He had a hard time of it to get to the gate. There never was any actual hurt, but everything was competent to smite the lad with shame. It was a curious, groundless shame, but nevertheless it was shame. He was a new-comer, and he definitely felt the disgrace of the fact. In the street he was seen and recognized by some lads who had formed part of the group of Saturday. They shouted:

"Oh, Jimmie! Jimmie! Here he is! Here's that new feller!"

Jimmie Trescott was going virtuously towards his luncheon when he heard these cries behind him. He pretended not to hear, and in this deception he was assisted by the fact that he was engaged at the time in a furious argument with a friend over the relative merits of two "Uncle Tom's Cabin" companies. It appeared that one company had only two bloodhounds, while the other had ten. On the other hand, the first company had two Topsys and two Uncle Toms, while the second had only one Topsy and one Uncle Tom.

But the shouting little boys were hard after him. Finally they were even pulling at his arms.

"Jimmie—"

"What?" he demanded, turning with a snarl. "What d'you want? Leggo my arm!"

"Here he is! Here's the new feller! Here's the new feller! Now!"

"I don't care if he is," said Jimmie, with grand impatience. He tilted his chin. "I don't care if he is."

Then they reviled him. "Thought you was goin' to lick him first time you caught him! Yah! You're a 'fraid-cat!" They began to sing "'Fraid-cat! 'Fraid-cat! 'Fraid-cat!" He expostulated hotly, turning from one to the other, but they would not listen. In the mean time the Hedge boy slunk on his way, looking with deep anxiety upon this attempt to send Jimmie against him. But Jimmie would have none of the plan.

### III

When the children met again on the play-ground, Jimmie was openly challenged with cowardice. He had made a big threat in the hearing of comrades, and when invited by them to take advantage of an opportunity, he had refused. They had been fairly sure of their amusement, and they were indignant. Jimmie was finally driven to declare that as soon as school was out for the day, he would thrash the Hedge boy.

When finally the children came rushing out of the iron gate, filled with the delights of freedom, a hundred boys surrounded Jimmie in high spirits, for he had said that he was determined. They waited for the lone lad from Jersey City. When he appeared, Jimmie wasted no time. He walked straight to him and said, "Did you say you kin lick me?"

Johnnie Hedge was cowed, shrinking, affrighted, and the roars of a hundred boys thundered in his ears, but again he knew what he had to say. "Yes," he gasped, in anguish.

"Then," said Jimmie, resolutely, "you've got to fight." There was a joyous clamor by the mob. The beleaguered lad looked this way and that way for succor, as Willie Dalzel and other officious youngsters policed an irregular circle in the crowd. He saw Jimmie facing him; there was no help for it; he dropped his books—the old books which would not "do."

Now it was the fashion among tiny Whilomville belligerents to fight much in the manner of little bear cubs. Two boys would rush upon each other, immediately grapple, and—the best boy having probably succeeded in getting the coveted "under hold"—there would presently be a crash to the earth of the inferior boy, and he would probably be mopped around in the dust, or the mud, or the snow, or whatever the material happened to be, until the engagement was over. Whatever havoc was dealt out to him was ordinarily the result of his wild endeavors to throw off his opponent and arise. Both infants wept during the fight, as a common thing, and if they wept very hard, the fight was a harder fight. The result was never very bloody, but the complete dishevelment of both victor and vanquished was extraordinary. As for the spectacle, it more resembled a collision of boys in a fog than it did the manly art of hammering another human being into speechless inability.

The fight began when Jimmie made a mad, bear-cub rush at the new boy, amid savage cries of encouragement. Willie Dalzel, for instance, almost howled his head off. Very timid boys on the outskirts of the throng felt their hearts leap to their throats. It was a time when certain natures were impressed that only man is vile.

But it appeared that bear-cub rushing was no part of the instruction received by boys in Jersey City. Boys in Jersey City were apparently schooled curiously. Upon the onslaught of Jimmie, the stranger had gone wild with rage—boylike. Some spark had touched his fighting-blood, and in a moment he was a cornered, desperate, fire-eyed little man. He began to swing his arms, to revolve them so swiftly that one might have considered him a small, working model of an extra-fine patented windmill which was caught in a gale. For a moment this defence surprised Jimmie more than it damaged him, but two moments later a small, knotty fist caught him squarely in the eye, and with a shriek he went down in defeat. He lay on the ground so stunned that he could not even cry; but if he had been able to cry, he would have cried over his prestige—or something—not over his eye.

There was a dreadful tumult. The boys cast glances of amazement and terror upon the victor, and thronged upon the beaten Jimmie Trescott. It was a moment of excitement so intense that one cannot say what happened. Never before had Whilomville seen such a thing—not the little tots. They were aghast, dumfounded, and they glanced often over their shoulders at the new boy, who stood alone, his clinched fists at his side, his face crimson, his lips still working with the fury of battle.

But there was another surprise for Whilom ville. It might have been seen that the little victor was silently debating against an impulse.

But the impulse won, for the lone lad from Jersey City suddenly wheeled, sprang like a demon, and struck another boy.

A curtain should be drawn before this deed. A knowledge of it is really too much for the heart to bear. The other boy was Willie Dalzel. The lone lad from Jersey City had smitten him full sore.

There is little to say of it. It must have been that a feeling worked gradually to the top of the little stranger's wrath that Jimmie Trescott had been a mere tool, that the front and centre of his persecutors had been Willie Dalzel, and being rendered temporarily lawless by his fighting-blood, he raised his hand and smote for revenge.

Willie Dalzel had been in the middle of a vandal's cry, which screeched out over the voices of everybody. The new boy's fist cut it in half, so to say. And then arose the howl of an amazed and terrorized walrus.

One wishes to draw a second curtain. Without discussion or inquiry or brief retort, Willie Dalzel ran away. He ran like a hare straight for home, this redoubtable chieftain. Following him at a heavy and slow pace ran the impassioned new boy. The scene was long remembered.

Willie Dalzel was no coward; he had been panic-stricken into running away from a new thing. He ran as a man might run from the sudden appearance of a vampire or a ghoul or a gorilla. This was no time for academics—he ran.

Jimmie slowly gathered himself and came to his feet. "Where's Willie?" said he, first of all. The crowd sniggered. "Where's Willie?" said Jimmie again.

"Why, he licked him *too*!" answered a boy suddenly.

"He did?" said Jimmie. He sat weakly down on the roadway. "He did?" After allowing a moment for the fact to sink into him, he looked up at the crowd with his one good eye and his one bunged eye, and smiled cheerfully.

# THE CITY URCHIN AND THE CHASTE VILLAGERS

After the brief encounters between the Hedge boy and Jimmie Trescott and the Hedge boy and Willie Dalzel, the neighborhood which contained the homes of the boys was, as far as child life is concerned, in a state resembling anarchy. This was owing to the signal overthrow and shameful retreat of the boy who had for several years led a certain little clan by the nose. The adherence of the little community did not go necessarily to the boy who could whip all the others, but it certainly could not go to a boy who had run away in a manner that made his shame patent to the whole world. Willie Dalzel found himself in a painful position. This tiny tribe which had followed him with such unwavering faith was now largely engaged in whistling and catcalling and hooting. He chased a number of them into the sanctity of their own yards, but from these coigns they continued to ridicule him.

But it must not be supposed that the fickle tribe went over in a body to the new light. They did nothing of the sort. They occupied themselves with avenging all which they had endured—gladly enough, too—for many months. As for the Hedge boy, he maintained a curious timid reserve, minding his own business with extreme care, and going to school with that deadly punctuality of which his mother was the genius. Jimmie Trescott suffered no adverse criticism from his fellows. He was entitled to be beaten by a boy who had made Willie Dalzel bellow like a bull-calf and run away. Indeed, he received some honors. He had confronted a very superior boy and received a bang in the eye which for a time was the wonder of the children, and he had not bellowed like a bull-calf. As a matter of fact, he was often invited to tell how it had felt, and this he did with some pride, claiming arrogantly that he had been superior to any particular pain.

Early in the episode he and the Hedge boy had patched up a treaty. Living next door to each other, they could not fail to have each other often in sight. One afternoon they wandered together in the strange indefinite diplomacy of boyhood. As they drew close the new boy suddenly said, "Napple?"

"Yes," said Jimmie, and the new boy bestowed upon him an apple. It was one of those green-coated winter-apples which lie for many months in safe and dry places, and can at any time be brought forth for the persecution of the unwary and inexperienced. An older age would have fled from this apple, but to the unguided youth of Jimmie Trescott it was a thing to be possessed and cherished. Wherefore this apple was the emblem of something more than a truce, despite the fact that it tasted like wet Indian meal; and Jimmie looked at the Hedge boy out of one good eye and one bunged eye. The long-drawn animosities of men have no place in the life of a boy. The boy's mind is flexible; he readjusts his position with an ease which is derived from the fact—simply—that he is not yet a man.

But there were other and more important matters. Johnnie Hedge's exploits had brought him into such prominence among the school-boys that it was necessary to settle a number of points once and for all. There was the usual number of boys in the school who were popularly known to be champions in their various classes. Among these Johnnie Hedge now had to thread his way, every boy taking it upon himself to feel anxious that Johnnie's exact position should be soon established. His fame as a fighter had gone forth to the world, but there were other boys who had fame as fighters, and the world was extremely anxious to know where to place the new-comer. Various heroes were urged to attempt this classification. Usually it was not accounted a matter of supreme importance, but in this boy life it was essential.

In all cases the heroes were backward enough. It was their followings who agitated the question. And so Johnnie Hedge was more or less beset.

He maintained his bashfulness. He backed away from altercation. It was plain that to bring matters to a point he must be forced into a quarrel. It was also plain that the proper person for the business was some boy who could whip Willie Dalzel, and these formidable warriors were distinctly averse to undertaking the new contract. It is a kind of a law in boy life that a quiet, decent, peace-loving lad is able to thrash a wide-mouthed talker. And so it had transpired that by a peculiar system of elimination most of the real chiefs were quiet, decent, peace-loving boys, and they had no desire to engage in a fight with a boy on the sole grounds that it was not known who could whip. Johnnie Hedge attended his affairs, they attended their affairs, and around them waged this discussion of relative merit. Jimmie Trescott took a prominent part in these arguments. He contended that Johnnie Hedge could thrash any boy in the world. He was certain of it, and to any one who opposed him he said, "You just get one of those smashes in the eye, and then you'll see." In the mean time there was a grand and impressive silence in the direction of Willie Dalzel. He had gathered remnants of his clan, but the main parts of his sovereignty were scattered to the winds. He was an enemy.

Owing to the circumspect behavior of the new boy, the commotions on the school grounds came to nothing. He was often asked, "Kin you lick him?" And he invariably replied, "I dun'no'." This idea of waging battle with the entire world appalled him.

A war for complete supremacy of the tribe which had been headed by Willie Dalzel was fought out in the country of the tribe. It came to pass that a certain half-dime blood-and-thunder pamphlet had a great vogue in the tribe at this particular time. This story relates the experience of a lad who began his career as cabin-boy on a pirate ship. Throughout the first fifteen chapters he was rope's-ended from one end of the ship to the other end, and very often he was felled to the deck by a heavy fist. He lived through enough hardships to have killed a battalion of Turkish soldiers, but in the end he rose upon them. Yes, he rose upon them. Hordes of pirates fell before his intrepid arm, and in the last chapters of the book he is seen jauntily careering on his own hook as one of the most gallous pirate captains that ever sailed the seas.

Naturally, when this tale was thoroughly understood by the tribe, they had to dramatize it, although it was a dramatization that would gain no royalties for the author. Now it was plain that the urchin who was cast for the cabin-boy's part would lead a life throughout the first fifteen chapters which would attract few actors. Willie Dalzel developed a scheme by which some small lad would play cabin-boy during this period of misfortune and abuse, and then, when the cabin-boy came to the part where he slew all his enemies and reached his zenith, that he, Willie Dalzel, should take the part.

This fugitive and disconnected rendering of a great play opened in Jimmie Trescott's back garden. The path between the two lines of gooseberry-bushes was elected unanimously to be the ship. Then Willie Dalzel insisted that Homer Phelps should be the cabin-boy. Homer tried the position for a time, and then elected that he would resign in favor of some other victim. There was no other applicant to succeed him, whereupon it became necessary to press some boy. Jimmie Trescott was a great actor, as is well known, but he steadfastly refused to engage for the part. Ultimately they seized upon little Dan Earl, whose disposition was so milky and docile that he would do whatever anybody asked of him. But Dan Earl made the one firm revolt of his life after trying existence as cabin-boy for some ten minutes. Willie Dalzel was in despair. Then he suddenly sighted the little brother of Johnnie Hedge, who had come into the garden, and in a poor-little-stranger sort of fashion was looking wistfully at the play. When he was invited to become the cabin-boy he accepted joyfully, thinking that it was his initiation into the tribe. Then they proceeded to give him the rope's end and to punch him with a realism which was not altogether painless. Directly he began to cry out. They exhorted him not to cry out, not to mind it, but still they continued to hurt him.

There was a commotion among the gooseberry-bushes, two branches were swept aside, and Johnnie Hedge walked down upon them. Every boy stopped in his tracks. Johnnie was boiling with rage.

"Who hurt him?" he said, ferociously. "Did *you*?" He had looked at Willie Dalzel.

Willie Dalzel began to mumble: "We was on'y playin'. Wasn't nothin' fer him to cry fer."

The new boy had at his command some big phrases, and he used them. "I am goin' to whip you within an inch of your life. I am goin' to tan the hide off'n you." And immediately there was a mixture—an infusion of two boys which looked as if it had been done by a chemist. The other children stood back, stricken with horror. But out of this whirl they presently perceived the figure of Willie Dalzel seated upon the chest of the Hedge boy.

"Got enough?" asked Willie, hoarsely.

"No," choked out the Hedge boy. Then there was another flapping and floundering, and finally another calm.

"Got enough?" asked Willie.

"No," said the Hedge boy. A sort of war-cloud again puzzled the sight of the observers. Both combatants were breathless, bloodless in their faces, and very weak.

"Got enough?" said Willie.

"No," said the Hedge boy. The carnage was again renewed. All the spectators were silent but Johnnie Hedge's little brother, who shrilly exhorted him to continue the struggle. But it was not plain that the Hedge boy needed any encouragement, for he was crying bitterly, and it has been explained that when a boy cried it was a bad time to hope for peace. He had managed to wriggle over upon his hands and knees. But Willie Dalzel was tenaciously gripping him from the back, and it seemed that his strength would spend itself in futility. The bear cub seemed to have the advantage of the working model of the windmill. They heaved, uttered strange words, wept, and the sun looked down upon them with steady, unwinking eye.

Peter Washington came out of the stable and observed this tragedy of the back garden. He stood transfixed for a moment, and then ran towards it, shouting: "Hi! What's all dish yere? Hi! Stopper dat, stopper dat, you two! For lan' sake, what's all dish yere?" He grabbed the struggling boys and pulled them apart. He was stormy and fine in his indignation. "For lan' sake! You two kids act like you gwine mad dogs. Stopper dat!" The whitened, tearful, soiled combatants, their clothing all awry, glared fiercely at each other as Peter stood between them, lecturing. They made several futile attempts to circumvent him and again come to battle. As he fended them off with his open hands he delivered his reproaches at Jimmie. "I's s'prised at *you*! I suhtainly is!"

"Why?" said Jimmie. "I ain't done nothin'. What have I done?"

"Y-y-you done 'courage dese yere kids ter scrap," said Peter, virtuously.

"Me?" cried Jimmie. "I ain't had nothin' to do with it."

"I raikon you ain't," retorted Peter, with heavy sarcasm. "I raikon you been er-prayin', ain't you?" Turning to Willie Dalzel, he said, "You jest take an' run erlong outer dish yere or I'll jest nachually take an' damnearkill you." Willie Dalzel went. To the new boy Peter said: "You look like you had some saince, but I raikon you don't know no more'n er rabbit. You jest take an' trot erlong off home, an' don' lemme caitch you round yere er-fightin' or I'll break yer back." The Hedge boy moved away with dignity, followed by his little brother. The latter, when he had placed a sufficient distance between himself and Peter, played his fingers at his nose and called out:

"Nig-ger-r-r! Nig-ger-r-r!"

Peter Washington's resentment poured out upon Jimmie.

"'Pears like you never would understan' you ain't reg'lar common trash. You take an' 'sociate with an'body what done come erlong."

"Aw, go on," retorted Jimmie, profanely. "Go soak your head, Pete."

The remaining boys retired to the street, whereupon they perceived Willie Dalzel in the distance. He ran to them.

"I licked him!" he shouted, exultantly. "I licked him! Didn't I, now?"

From the Whilomville point of view he was entitled to a favorable answer. They made it. "Yes," they said, "you did."

"I run in," cried Willie, "an' I grabbed 'im, an' afore he knew what it was I throwed 'im. An' then it was easy." He puffed out his chest and smiled like an English recruiting-sergeant. "An' now," said he, suddenly facing Jimmie Trescott, "whose side were you on?"

The question was direct and startling. Jimmie gave back two paces. "He licked you once," he explained, haltingly.

"He never saw the day when he could lick one side of me. I could lick him with my left hand tied behind me. Why, I could lick him when I was asleep." Willie Dalzel was magnificent.

A gate clicked, and Johnnie Hedge was seen to be strolling towards them.

"You said," he remarked, coldly, "you licked me, didn't you?"

Willie Dalzel stood his ground. "Yes," he said, stoutly.

"Well, you're a liar," said the Hedge boy.

"You're another," retorted Willie.

"No, I ain't, either, but *you're* a liar."

"You're another," retorted Willie.

"Don't you dare tell *me* I'm a liar, or I'll smack your mouth for you," said the Hedge boy.

"Well, I did, didn't I?" barked Willie. "An' whatche goin' to do about it?"

"I'm goin' to lam you," said the Hedge boy.

He approached to attack warily, and the other boys held their breaths. Willie Dalzel winced back a pace. "Hol' on a minute," he cried, raising his palm. "I'm not—"

But the comic windmill was again in motion, and between gasps from his exertions Johnnie Hedge remarked, "I'll show—you—whether—you kin—lick me—or not."

The first blows did not reach home on Willie, for he backed away with expedition, keeping up his futile cry, "Hol' on a minute." Soon enough a swinging fist landed on his cheek. It did not knock him down, but it hurt him a little and frightened him a great deal. He suddenly opened his mouth to an amazing and startling extent, tilted back his head, and howled, while his eyes, glittering with tears, were fixed upon this scowling butcher of a Johnnie Hedge. The latter was making slow and vicious circles, evidently intending to renew the massacre.

But the spectators really had been desolated and shocked by the terrible thing which had happened to Willie Dalzel. They now cried out: "No, no; don't hit 'im any more! Don't hit 'im any more!"

Jimmie Trescott, in a panic of bravery, yelled, "We'll all jump on you if you do."

The Hedge boy paused, at bay. He breathed angrily, and flashed his glance from lad to lad. They still protested: "No, no; don't hit 'im any more. Don't hit 'im no more."

"I'll hammer him until he can't stand up," said Johnnie, observing that they all feared him. "I'll fix him so he won't know hisself, an' if any of you kids bother with *me*—"

Suddenly he ceased, he trembled, he collapsed. The hand of one approaching from behind had laid hold upon his ear, and it was the hand of one whom he knew.

The other lads heard a loud, iron-filing voice say, "Caught ye at it again, ye brat, ye." They saw a dreadful woman with gray hair, with a sharp red nose, with bare arms, with spectacles of such magnifying quality that her eyes shone through them like two fierce white moons. She was Johnnie Hedge's mother. Still holding Johnnie by the ear, she swung out swiftly and dexterously, and succeeded in boxing the ears of two boys before the crowd regained its presence of mind and stampeded. Yes, the war for supremacy was over, and the question was never again disputed. The supreme power was Mrs. Hedge.

# A LITTLE PILGRIMAGE

One November it became clear to childish minds in certain parts of Whilomville that the Sunday-school of the Presbyterian church would not have for the children the usual tree on Christmas eve. The funds free for that ancient festival would be used for the relief of suffering among the victims of the Charleston earthquake.

The plan had been born in the generous head of the superintendent of the Sunday-school, and during one session he had made a strong plea that the children should forego the vain pleasures of a tree and, in glorious application of the Golden Rule, refuse a local use of the fund, and will that it be sent where dire pain might be alleviated. At the end of a tearfully eloquent speech the question was put fairly to a vote, and the children in a burst of virtuous abandon carried the question for Charleston. Many of the teachers had been careful to preserve a finely neutral attitude, but even if they had cautioned the children against being too impetuous they could not have checked the wild impulses.

But this was a long time before Christmas.

Very early, boys held important speech together. "Huh! you ain't goin' to have no Christmas tree at the Presbyterian Sunday-school."

Sullenly the victim answered, "No, we ain't."

"Huh!" scoffed the other denomination, "we are goin' to have the all-firedest biggest tree that you ever saw in the world."

The little Presbyterians were greatly downcast.

It happened that Jimmie Trescott had regularly attended the Presbyterian Sunday-school. The Trescotts were consistently undenominational, but they had sent their lad on Sundays to one of the places where they thought he would receive benefits. However, on one day in December, Jimmie appeared before his father and made a strong spiritual appeal to be forthwith attached to the Sunday-school of the Big Progressive church. Doctor Trescott mused this question considerably. "Well, Jim," he said, "why do you conclude that the Big Progressive Sunday-school is better for you than the Presbyterian Sunday-school?"

"Now—it's nicer," answered Jimmie, looking at his father with an anxious eye.

"How do you mean?"

"Why—now—some of the boys what go to the Presbyterian place, they ain't very nice," explained the flagrant Jimmie.

Trescott mused the question considerably once more. In the end he said: "Well, you may change if you wish, this one time, but you must not be changing to and fro. You decide now, and then you must abide by your decision."

"Yessir," said Jimmie, brightly. "Big Progressive."

"All right," said the father. "But remember what I've told you."

On the following Sunday morning Jimmie presented himself at the door of the basement of the Big Progressive church. He was conspicuously washed, notably raimented, prominently polished. And, incidentally, he was very uncomfortable because of all these virtues.

A number of acquaintances greeted him contemptuously. "Hello, Jimmie! What you doin' here? Thought you was a Presbyterian?"

Jimmie cast down his eyes and made no reply. He was too cowed by the change. However, Homer Phelps, who was a regular patron of the Big Progressive

Sunday-school, suddenly appeared and said, "Hello, Jim!" Jimmie seized upon him. Homer Phelps was amenable to Trescott laws, tribal if you like, but iron-bound, almost compulsory.

"Hello, Homer!" said Jimmie, and his manner was so good that Homer felt a great thrill in being able to show his superior a new condition of life.

"You ain't never come here afore, have you?" he demanded, with a new arrogance.

"No, I ain't," said Jimmie. Then they stared at each other and manœuvred.

"You don't know *my* teacher," said Homer.

"No, I don't know *her*" admitted Jimmie, but in a way which contended, modestly, that he knew countless other Sunday-school teachers.

"Better join our class," said Homer, sagely. "She wears spectacles; don't see very well. Sometimes we do almost what we like."

"All right," said Jimmie, glad to place himself in the hands of his friends. In due time they entered the Sunday-school room, where a man with benevolent whiskers stood on a platform and said, "We will now sing No. 33—'Pull for the Shore, Sailor, Pull for the Shore.'" And as the obedient throng burst into melody the man on the platform indicated the time with a fat, white, and graceful hand. He was an ideal Sunday-school superintendent—one who had never felt hunger or thirst or the wound of the challenge of dishonor; a man, indeed, with beautiful flat hands who waved them in greasy victorious beneficence over a crowd of children.

Jimmie, walking carefully on his toes, followed Homer Phelps. He felt that the kingly superintendent might cry out and blast him to ashes before he could reach a chair. It was a desperate journey. But at last he heard Homer muttering to a young lady, who looked at him through glasses which greatly magnified her eyes. "A new boy," she said, in an oily and deeply religious voice.

"Yes'm," said Jimmie, trembling. The five other boys of the class scanned him keenly and derided his condition.

"We will proceed to the lesson," said the young lady. Then she cried sternly, like a sergeant, "The seventh chapter of Jeremiah!"

There was a swift fluttering of leaflets. Then the name of Jeremiah, a wise man, towered over the feelings of these boys. Homer Phelps was doomed to read the fourth verse. He took a deep breath, he puffed out his lips, he gathered his strength for a great effort. His beginning was childishly explosive. He hurriedly said:

"*Trust ye not in lying words, saying The temple of the Lord, the temple of the Lord, the temple of the Lord, are these.*"

"Now," said the teacher, "Johnnie Scanlan, tell us what these words mean." The Scanlan boy shamefacedly muttered that he did not know. The teacher's countenance saddened. Her heart was in her work; she wanted to make a success of this Sunday-school class. "Perhaps Homer Phelps can tell us," she remarked.

Homer gulped; he looked at Jimmie. Through the great room hummed a steady hum. A little circle, very near, was being told about Daniel in the lion's den. They were deeply moved. At the moment they liked Sunday-school.

"Why—now—it means," said Homer, with a grand pomposity born of a sense of hopeless ignorance—"it means—why it means that they were in the wrong place."

"No," said the teacher, profoundly; "it means that we should be good, very good indeed. That is what it means. It means that we should love the Lord and be good. Love the Lord and be good. That is what it means."

The little boys suddenly had a sense of black wickedness as their teacher looked austerely upon them. They gazed at her with the wide-open eyes of simplicity. They were stirred again. This thing of being good—this great business of life—apparently it was always successful. They knew from the fairy tales. But it was difficult, wasn't it? It was said to be the most heart-breaking task to be generous, wasn't it? One had to pay the price of one's eyes in order to be pacific, didn't one? As for patience, it was tortured martyrdom to be patient, wasn't it? Sin was simple, wasn't it? But virtue was so difficult that it could only be practised by heavenly beings, wasn't it?

And the angels, the Sunday-school superintendent, and the teacher swam in the high visions of the little boys as beings so good that if a boy scratched his shin in the same room he was a profane and sentenced devil.

"And," said the teacher, "'The temple of the Lord'—what does that mean? I'll ask the new boy. What does that mean?"

"I dun'no'," said Jimmie, blankly.

But here the professional bright boy of the class suddenly awoke to his obligations. "Teacher," he cried, "it means church, same as this."

"Exactly," said the teacher, deeply satisfied with this reply. "You know your lesson well, Clarence. I am much pleased."

The other boys, instead of being envious, looked with admiration upon Clarence, while he adopted an air of being habituated to perform such feats every day of his life. Still, he was not much of a boy. He had the virtue of being able to walk on very high stilts, but when the season of stilts had passed he possessed no rank save this Sunday-school rank, this clever-little-Clarence business of knowing the Bible and the lesson better than the other boys. The other boys, sometimes looking at him meditatively, did not actually decide to thrash him as soon as he cleared the portals of the church, but they certainly decided to molest him in such ways as would re-establish their self-respect. Back of the superintendent's chair hung a lithograph of the martyrdom of St. Stephen.

Jimmie, feeling stiff and encased in his best clothes, waited for the ordeal to end. A bell pealed: the fat hand of the superintendent had tapped a bell. Slowly the rustling and murmuring dwindled to silence. The benevolent man faced the school. "I have to announce," he began, waving his body from side to side in the conventional bows of his kind, "that—" Bang went the bell. "Give me your attention, please, children. I have to announce that the Board has decided that this year there will be no Christmas tree, but the—"

Instantly the room buzzed with the subdued clamor of the children. Jimmie was speechless. He stood morosely during the singing of the closing hymn. He passed out into the street with the others, pushing no more than was required.

Speedily the whole idea left him. If he remembered Sunday-school at all, it was to remember that he did not like it.

# THE LITTLE REGIMENT

## I.

The fog made the clothes of the men of the column in the roadway seem of a luminous quality. It imparted to the heavy infantry overcoats a new colour, a kind of blue which was so pale that a regiment might have been merely a long, low shadow in the mist. However, a muttering, one part grumble, three parts joke, hovered in the air above the thick ranks, and blended in an undertoned roar, which was the voice of the column.

The town on the southern shore of the little river loomed spectrally, a faint etching upon the gray cloud-masses which were shifting with oily languor. A long row of guns upon the northern bank had been pitiless in their hatred, but a little battered belfry could be dimly seen still pointing with invincible resolution toward the heavens.

The enclouded air vibrated with noises made by hidden colossal things. The infantry tramplings, the heavy rumbling of the artillery, made the earth speak of gigantic preparation. Guns on distant heights thundered from time to time with sudden, nervous roar, as if unable to endure in silence a knowledge of hostile troops massing, other guns going to position. These sounds, near and remote, defined an immense battle-ground, described the tremendous width of the stage of the prospective drama. The voices of the guns, slightly casual, unexcited in their challenges and warnings, could not destroy the unutterable eloquence of the word in the air, a meaning of impending struggle which made the breath halt at the lips.

The column in the roadway was ankle-deep in mud. The men swore piously at the rain which drizzled upon them, compelling them to stand always very erect in fear of the drops that would sweep in under their coat-collars. The fog was as cold as wet cloths. The men stuffed their hands deep in their pockets, and huddled their muskets in their arms. The machinery of orders had rooted these soldiers deeply into the mud precisely as almighty nature roots mullein stalks.

They listened and speculated when a tumult of fighting came from the dim town across the river. When the noise lulled for a time they resumed their descriptions of the mud and graphically exaggerated the number of hours they had been kept waiting. The general commanding their division rode along the ranks, and they cheered admiringly, affectionately, crying out to him gleeful prophecies of the coming battle. Each man scanned him with a peculiarly keen personal interest, and afterward spoke of him with unquestioning devotion and confidence, narrating anecdotes which were mainly untrue.

When the jokers lifted the shrill voices which invariably belonged to them, flinging witticisms at their comrades, a loud laugh would sweep from rank to rank, and soldiers who had not heard would lean forward and demand repetition. When were borne past them some wounded men with gray and blood-smeared faces, and eyes that rolled in that helpless beseeching for assistance from the sky which comes with supreme pain, the soldiers in the mud watched intently, and from time to time asked of the bearers an account of the affair. Frequently they bragged of their corps, their division, their brigade, their regiment. Anon they referred to the mud and the cold drizzle. Upon this threshold of a wild scene of death they, in short, defied the proportion of events with that splendour of heedlessness which belongs only to veterans.

"Like a lot of wooden soldiers," swore Billie Dempster, moving his feet in the thick mass, and casting a vindictive glance indefinitely; "standing in the mud for a hundred years."

"Oh, shut up!" murmured his brother Dan. The manner of his words implied that this fraternal voice near him was an indescribable bore.

"Why should I shut up?" demanded Billie.

"Because you're a fool," cried Dan, taking no time to debate it; "the biggest fool in the regiment."

There was but one man between them, and he was habituated. These insults from brother to brother had swept across his chest, flown past his face, many times during two long campaigns. Upon this occasion he simply grinned first at one, then at the other.

The way of these brothers was not an unknown topic in regimental gossip. They had enlisted simultaneously, with each sneering loudly at the other for doing it. They left their little town, and went forward with the flag, exchanging protestations of undying suspicion. In the camp life they so openly despised each other that, when entertaining quarrels were lacking, their companions often contrived situations calculated to bring forth display of this fraternal dislike.

Both were large-limbed, strong young men, and often fought with friends in camp unless one was near to interfere with the other. This latter happened rather frequently, because Dan, preposterously willing for any manner of combat, had a very great horror of seeing Billie in a fight; and Billie, almost odiously ready himself, simply refused to see Dan stripped to his shirt and with his fists aloft. This sat queerly upon them, and made them the objects of plots.

When Dan jumped through a ring of eager soldiers and dragged forth his raving brother by the arm, a thing often predicted would almost come to pass. When Billie performed the same office for Dan, the prediction would again miss fulfilment by an inch. But indeed they never fought together, although they were perpetually upon the verge.

They expressed longing for such conflict. As a matter of truth, they had at one time made full arrangement for it, but even with the encouragement and interest of half of the regiment they somehow failed to achieve collision.

If Dan became a victim of police duty, no jeering was so destructive to the feelings as Billie's comment. If Billie got a call to appear at the headquarters, none would so genially prophesy his complete undoing as Dan. Small misfortunes to one were, in truth, invariably greeted with hilarity by the other, who seemed to see in them great re-enforcement of his opinion.

As soldiers, they expressed each for each a scorn intense and blasting. After a certain battle, Billie was promoted to corporal. When Dan was told of it, he seemed smitten dumb with astonishment and patriotic indignation. He stared in silence, while the dark blood rushed to Billie's forehead, and he shifted his weight from foot to foot. Dan at last found his tongue, and said: "Well, I'm durned!" If he had heard that an army mule had been appointed to the post of corps commander, his tone could not have had more derision in it. Afterward, he adopted a fervid insubordination, an almost religious reluctance to obey the new corporal's orders, which came near to developing the desired strife.

It is here finally to be recorded also that Dan, most ferociously profane in speech, very rarely swore in the presence of his brother; and that Billie, whose oaths came from his lips with the grace of falling pebbles, was seldom known to express himself in this manner when near his brother Dan.

At last the afternoon contained a suggestion of evening. Metallic cries rang suddenly from end to end of the column. They inspired at once a quick, business-like adjustment. The long thing stirred in the mud. The men had hushed, and were looking across the river. A moment later the shadowy mass of pale blue figures was moving steadily toward the stream. There could be heard from the town a clash of swift fighting and cheering. The noise of the shooting coming through the heavy air had its sharpness taken from it, and sounded in thuds.

There was a halt upon the bank above the pontoons. When the column went winding down the incline, and streamed out upon the bridge, the fog had faded to a great degree, and in the clearer dusk the guns on a distant ridge were enabled to perceive the crossing. The long whirling outcries of the shells came into the air above the men. An occasional solid shot struck the surface of the river, and dashed into view a sudden vertical jet. The distance was subtly illuminated by the lightning from the deep-booming guns. One by one the batteries on the northern shore aroused, the innumerable guns bellowing in angry oration at the distant ridge. The rolling thunder crashed and reverberated as a wild surf sounds on a still night, and to this music the column marched across the pontoons.

The waters of the grim river curled away in a smile from the ends of the great boats, and slid swiftly beneath the planking. The dark, riddled walls of the town up-reared before the troops, and from a region hidden by these hammered and tumbled houses came incessantly the yells and firings of a prolonged and close skirmish.

When Dan had called his brother a fool, his voice had been so decisive, so brightly assured, that many men had laughed, considering it to be great humour under the circumstances. The incident happened to rankle deep in Billie. It was not any strange thing that his brother had called him a fool. In fact, he often called him a fool with exactly the same amount of cheerful and prompt conviction, and before large audiences, too. Billie wondered in his own mind why he took such profound offence in this case; but, at any rate, as he slid down the bank and on to the bridge with his regiment, he was searching his knowledge for something that would pierce Dan's blithesome spirit. But he could contrive nothing at this time, and his impotency made the glance which he was once able to give his brother still more malignant.

The guns far and near were roaring a fearful and grand introduction for this column which was marching upon the stage of death. Billie felt it, but only in a numb way. His heart was cased in that curious dissonant metal which covers a man's emotions at such times. The terrible voices from the hills told him that in this wide conflict his life was an insignificant fact, and that his death would be an insignificant fact. They portended the whirlwind to which he would be as necessary as a but-terfly's waved wing. The solemnity, the sadness of it came near enough to make him wonder why he was neither solemn nor sad. When his mind vaguely adjusted events according to their importance to him, it appeared that the uppermost thing was the fact that upon the eve of battle, and before many comrades, his brother had called him a fool.

Dan was in a particularly happy mood. "Hurray! Look at 'em shoot," he said, when the long witches' croon of the shells came into the air. It enraged Billie when he felt the little thorn in him, and saw at the same time that his brother had com-pletely forgotten it.

The column went from the bridge into more mud. At this southern end there was a chaos of hoarse directions and commands. Darkness was coming upon the earth, and regiments were being hurried up the slippery bank. As Billie floundered in the black mud, amid the swearing, sliding crowd, he suddenly resolved that, in the absence of other means of hurting Dan, he would avoid looking at him, refrain from speaking to him, pay absolutely no heed to his existence; and this done skilfully would, he imagined, soon reduce his brother to a poignant sensitiveness.

At the top of the bank the column again halted and rearranged itself, as a man after a climb rearranges his clothing. Presently the great steel-backed brigade, an infinitely graceful thing in the rhythm and ease of its veteran movement, swung up a little narrow, slanting street.

Evening had come so swiftly that the fighting on the remote borders of the town was indicated by thin flashes of flame. Some building was on fire, and its reflection upon the clouds was an oval of delicate pink.

## II.

All demeanour of rural serenity had been wrenched violently from the little town by the guns and by the waves of men which had surged through it. The hand of war laid upon this village had in an instant changed it to a thing of remnants. It resembled the place of a monstrous shaking of the earth itself. The windows, now mere unsightly holes, made the tumbled and blackened dwellings seem skeletons. Doors lay splintered to fragments. Chimneys had flung their bricks everywhere. The artillery fire had not neglected the rows of gentle shade-trees which had lined the streets. Branches and heavy trunks cluttered the mud in drift-wood tangles, while a few shattered forms had contrived to remain dejectedly, mournfully upright. They expressed an innocence, a helplessness, which perforce created a pity for their happening into this cauldron of battle. Furthermore, there was under foot a vast collection of odd things reminiscent of the charge, the fight, the retreat. There were boxes and barrels filled with earth, behind which riflemen had lain snugly, and in these little trenches were the dead in blue with the dead in gray, the poses eloquent of the struggles for possession of the town until the history of the whole conflict was written plainly in the streets.

And yet the spirit of this little city, its quaint individuality, poised in the air above the ruins, defying the guns, the sweeping volleys; holding in contempt those avaricious blazes which had attacked many dwellings. The hard earthen sidewalks proclaimed the games that had been played there during long lazy days, in the careful shadows of the trees. "General Merchandise," in faint letters upon a long board, had to be read with a slanted glance, for the sign dangled by one end; but the porch of the old store was a palpable legend of wide-hatted men, smoking.

This subtle essence, this soul of the life that had been, brushed like invisible wings the thoughts of the men in the swift columns that came up from the river.

In the darkness a loud and endless humming arose from the great blue crowds bivouacked in the streets. From time to time a sharp spatter of firing from far picket lines entered this bass chorus. The smell from the smouldering ruins floated on the cold night breeze.

Dan, seated ruefully upon the doorstep of a shot-pierced house, was proclaiming the campaign badly managed. Orders had been issued forbidding camp-fires.

Suddenly he ceased his oration, and scanning the group of his comrades, said: "Where's Billie? Do you know?"

"Gone on picket."

"Get out! Has he?" said Dan. "No business to go on picket. Why don't some of them other corporals take their turn?"

A bearded private was smoking his pipe of confiscated tobacco, seated comfortably upon a horse-hair trunk which he had dragged from the house. He observed: "*Was* his turn."

"No such thing," cried Dan. He and the man on the horse-hair trunk held discussion in which Dan stoutly maintained that if his brother had been sent on picket it was an injustice. He ceased his argument when another soldier, upon whose arms could faintly be seen the two stripes of a corporal, entered the circle. "Humph," said Dan, "where you been?"

The corporal made no answer. Presently Dan said: "Billie, where you been?"

His brother did not seem to hear these inquiries. He glanced at the house which towered above them, and remarked casually to the man on the horse-hair trunk: "Funny, ain't it? After the pelting this town got, you'd think there wouldn't be one brick left on another."

"Oh," said Dan, glowering at his brother's back. "Getting mighty smart, ain't you?"

The absence of camp-fires allowed the evening to make apparent its quality of faint silver light in which the blue clothes of the throng became black, and the faces became white expanses, void of expression. There was considerable excitement a short distance from the group around the doorstep. A soldier had chanced upon a hoop-skirt, and arrayed in it he was performing a dance amid the applause of his companions. Billie and a greater part of the men immediately poured over there to witness the exhibition.

"What's the matter with Billie?" demanded Dan of the man upon the horse-hair trunk.

"How do I know?" rejoined the other in mild resentment. He arose and walked away. When he returned he said briefly, in a weather-wise tone, that it would rain during the night.

Dan took a seat upon one end of the horse-hair trunk. He was facing the crowd around the dancer, which in its hilarity swung this way and that way. At times he imagined that he could recognise his brother's face.

He and the man on the other end of the trunk thoughtfully talked of the army's position. To their minds, infantry and artillery were in a most precarious jumble in the streets of the town; but they did not grow nervous over it, for they were used to having the army appear in a precarious jumble to their minds. They had learned to accept such puzzling situations as a consequence of their position in the ranks, and were now usually in possession of a simple but perfectly immovable faith that somebody understood the jumble. Even if they had been convinced that the army was a headless monster, they would merely have nodded with the veteran's singular cynicism. It was none of their business as soldiers. Their duty was to grab sleep and food when occasion permitted, and cheerfully fight wherever their feet were planted until more orders came. This was a task sufficiently absorbing.

They spoke of other corps, and this talk being confidential, their voices dropped to tones of awe. "The Ninth"—"The First"—"The Fifth"—"The Sixth"—"The Third"—the simple numerals rang with eloquence, each having a meaning which was to float through many years as no intangible arithmetical mist, but as pregnant with individuality as the names of cities.

Of their own corps they spoke with a deep veneration, an idolatry, a supreme confidence which apparently would not blanch to see it match against everything.

It was as if their respect for other corps was due partly to a wonder that organizations not blessed with their own famous numeral could take such an interest in war.

They could prove that their division was the best in the corps, and that their brigade was the best in the division. And their regiment—it was plain that no fortune of life was equal to the chance which caused a man to be born, so to speak, into this command, the keystone of the defending arch.

At times Dan covered with insults the character of a vague, unnamed general to whose petulance and busy-body spirit he ascribed the order which made hot coffee impossible.

Dan said that victory was certain in the coming battle. The other man seemed rather dubious. He remarked upon the fortified line of hills, which had impressed him even from the other side of the river. "Shucks," said Dan. "Why, we—" He pictured a splendid overflowing of these hills by the sea of men in blue. During the period of this conversation Dan's glance searched the merry throng about the dancer. Above the babble of voices in the street a far-away thunder could sometimes be heard—evidently from the very edge of the horizon—the boom-boom of restless guns.

### III.

Ultimately the night deepened to the tone of black velvet. The outlines of the fireless camp were like the faint drawings upon ancient tapestry. The glint of a rifle, the shine of a button, might have been of threads of silver and gold sewn upon the fabric of the night. There was little presented to the vision, but to a sense more subtle there was discernible in the atmosphere something like a pulse; a mystic beating which would have told a stranger of the presence of a giant thing—the slumbering mass of regiments and batteries.

With fires forbidden, the floor of a dry old kitchen was thought to be a good exchange for the cold earth of December, even if a shell had exploded in it and knocked it so out of shape that when a man lay curled in his blanket his last waking thought was likely to be of the wall that bellied out above him as if strongly anxious to topple upon the score of soldiers.

Billie looked at the bricks ever about to descend in a shower upon his face, listened to the industrious pickets plying their rifles on the border of the town, imagined some measure of the din of the coming battle, thought of Dan and Dan's chagrin, and rolling over in his blanket went to sleep with satisfaction.

At an unknown hour he was aroused by the creaking of boards. Lifting himself upon his elbow, he saw a sergeant prowling among the sleeping forms. The sergeant carried a candle in an old brass candle-stick. He would have resembled some old farmer on an unusual midnight tour if it were not for the significance of his gleaming buttons and striped sleeves.

Billie blinked stupidly at the light until his mind returned from the journeys of slumber. The sergeant stooped among the unconscious soldiers, holding the candle close, and peering into each face.

"Hello, Haines," said Billie. "Relief?"

"Hello, Billie," said the sergeant. "Special duty."

"Dan got to go?"

"Jameson, Hunter, McCormack, D. Dempster. Yes. Where is he?"

"Over there by the winder," said Billie, gesturing. "What is it for, Haines?"

"You don't think I know, do you?" demanded the sergeant. He began to pipe sharply but cheerily at men upon the floor. "Come, Mac, get up here. Here's a special for you. Wake up, Jameson. Come along, Dannie, me boy."

Each man at once took this call to duty as a personal affront. They pulled themselves out of their blankets, rubbed their eyes, and swore at whoever was responsible. "Them's orders," cried the sergeant. "Come! Get out of here." An undetailed head with dishevelled hair thrust out from a blanket, and a sleepy voice said: "Shut up, Haines, and go home."

When the detail clanked out of the kitchen, all but one of the remaining men seemed to be again asleep. Billie, leaning on his elbow, was gazing into darkness. When the footsteps died to silence, he curled himself into his blanket.

At the first cool lavender lights of daybreak he aroused again, and scanned his recumbent companions. Seeing a wakeful one he asked: "Is Dan back yet?"

The man said: "Hain't seen 'im."

Billie put both hands behind his head, and scowled into the air. "Can't see the use of these cussed details in the night-time," he muttered in his most unreasonable tones. "Darn nuisances. Why can't they—" He grumbled at length and graphically.

When Dan entered with the squad, however, Billie was convincingly asleep.

<h2 style="text-align:center">IV.</h2>

The regiment trotted in double time along the street, and the colonel seemed to quarrel over the right of way with many artillery officers. Batteries were waiting in the mud, and the men of them, exasperated by the bustle of this ambitious infantry, shook their fists from saddle and caisson, exchanging all manner of taunts and jests. The slanted guns continued to look reflectively at the ground.

On the outskirts of the crumbled town a fringe of blue figures were firing into the fog. The regiment swung out into skirmish lines, and the fringe of blue figures departed, turning their backs and going joyfully around the flank.

The bullets began a low moan off toward a ridge which loomed faintly in the heavy mist. When the swift crescendo had reached its climax, the missiles zipped just overhead, as if piercing an invisible curtain. A battery on the hill was crashing with such tumult that it was as if the guns had quarrelled and had fallen pell-mell and snarling upon each other. The shells howled on their journey toward the town. From short range distance there came a spatter of musketry, sweeping along an invisible line and making faint sheets of orange light.

Some in the new skirmish lines were beginning to fire at various shadows discerned in the vapour, forms of men suddenly revealed by some humour of the laggard masses of clouds. The crackle of musketry began to dominate the purring of the hostile bullets. Dan, in the front rank, held his rifle poised, and looked into the fog keenly, coldly, with the air of a sportsman. His nerves were so steady that it was as if they had been drawn from his body, leaving him merely a muscular machine; but his numb heart was somehow beating to the pealing march of the fight.

The waving skirmish line went backward and forward, ran this way and that way. Men got lost in the fog, and men were found again. Once they got too close to the formidable ridge, and the thing burst out as if repulsing a general attack. Once another blue regiment was apprehended on the very edge of firing into them. Once a friendly battery began an elaborate and scientific process of extermination. Always as busy as brokers, the men slid here and there over the plain, fighting their foes, escaping from their friends, leaving a history of many movements in the wet yellow turf, cursing the atmosphere, blazing away every time they could identify the enemy.

In one mystic changing of the fog, as if the fingers of spirits were drawing aside these draperies, a small group of the gray skirmishers, silent, statuesque, were suddenly disclosed to Dan and those about him. So vivid and near were they that there was something uncanny in the revelation.

There might have been a second of mutual staring. Then each rifle in each group was at the shoulder. As Dan's glance flashed along the barrel of his weapon, the figure of a man suddenly loomed as if the musket had been a telescope. The short black beard, the slouch hat, the pose of the man as he sighted to shoot, made a quick picture in Dan's mind. The same moment, it would seem, he pulled his own trigger, and the man, smitten, lurched forward, while his exploding rifle made a slanting crimson streak in the air, and the slouch hat fell before the body. The billows of the fog, governed by singular impulses, rolled between.

"You got that feller sure enough," said a comrade to Dan. Dan looked at him absent-mindedly.

**V.**

When the next morning calmly displayed another fog, the men of the regiment exchanged eloquent comments; but they did not abuse it at length, because the streets of the town now contained enough galloping aides to make three troops of cavalry, and they knew that they had come to the verge of the great fight.

Dan conversed with the man who had once possessed a horse-hair trunk; but they did not mention the line of hills which had furnished them in more careless moments with an agreeable topic. They avoided it now as condemned men do the subject of death, and yet the thought of it stayed in their eyes as they looked at each other and talked gravely of other things.

The expectant regiment heaved a long sigh of relief when the sharp call: "Fall in," repeated indefinitely, arose in the streets. It was inevitable that a bloody battle was to be fought, and they wanted to get it off their minds. They were, however, doomed again to spend a long period planted firmly in the mud. They craned their necks, and wondered where some of the other regiments were going.

At last the mists rolled carelessly away. Nature made at this time all provisions to enable foes to see each other, and immediately the roar of guns resounded from every hill. The endless cracking of the skirmishers swelled to rolling crashes of musketry. Shells screamed with panther-like noises at the houses. Dan looked at the man of the horse-hair trunk, and the man said: "Well, here she comes!"

The tenor voices of younger officers and the deep and hoarse voices of the older ones rang in the streets. These cries pricked like spurs. The masses of men vibrated from the suddenness with which they were plunged into the situation of troops about to fight. That the orders were long-expected did not concern the emotion.

Simultaneous movement was imparted to all these thick bodies of men and horses that lay in the town. Regiment after regiment swung rapidly into the streets that faced the sinister ridge.

This exodus was theatrical. The little sober-hued village had been like the cloak which disguises the king of drama. It was now put aside, and an army, splendid thing of steel and blue, stood forth in the sunlight.

Even the soldiers in the heavy columns drew deep breaths at the sight, more majestic than they had dreamed. The heights of the enemy's position were crowded with men who resembled people come to witness some mighty pageant. But as the column moved steadily to their positions, the guns, matter-of-fact warriors, doubled their number, and shells burst with red thrilling tumult on the crowded plain. One came into the ranks of the regiment, and after the smoke and the wrath of it had faded, leaving motionless figures, everyone stormed according to the limits of his vocabulary, for veterans detest being killed when they are not busy.

The regiment sometimes looked sideways at its brigade companions composed of men who had never been in battle; but no frozen blood could withstand the heat of the splendour of this army before the eyes on the plain, these lines so long that the flanks were little streaks, this mass of men of one intention. The recruits carried themselves heedlessly. At the rear was an idle battery, and three artillery men in a foolish row on a caisson nudged each other and grinned at the recruits. "You'll catch it pretty soon," they called out. They were impersonally gleeful, as if they themselves were not also likely to catch it pretty soon. But with this picture of an army in their hearts, the new men perhaps felt the devotion which the drops may feel for the wave; they were of its power and glory; they smiled jauntily at the foolish row of gunners, and told them to go to blazes.

The column trotted across some little bridges, and spread quickly into lines of battle. Before them was a bit of plain, and back of the plain was the ridge. There was no time left for considerations. The men were staring at the plain, mightily wondering how it would feel to be out there, when a brigade in advance yelled and charged. The hill was all gray smoke and fire-points.

That fierce elation in the terrors of war, catching a man's heart and making it burn with such ardour that he becomes capable of dying, flashed in the faces of the men like coloured lights, and made them resemble leashed animals, eager, ferocious, daunting at nothing. The line was really in its first leap before the wild, hoarse crying of the orders.

The greed for close quarters which is the emotion of a bayonet charge, came then into the minds of the men and developed until it was a madness. The field, with its faded grass of a Southern winter, seemed to this fury miles in width.

High, slow-moving masses of smoke, with an odour of burning cotton, engulfed the line until the men might have been swimmers. Before them the ridge, the shore of this gray sea, was outlined, crossed, and re-crossed by sheets of flame. The howl of the battle arose to the noise of innumerable wind demons.

The line, galloping, scrambling, plunging like a herd of wounded horses, went over a field that was sown with corpses, the records of other charges.

Directly in front of the black-faced, whooping Dan, carousing in this onward sweep like a new kind of fiend, a wounded man appeared, raising his shattered body, and staring at this rush of men down upon him. It seemed to occur to him that he was to be trampled; he made a desperate, piteous effort to escape; then finally huddled in a waiting heap. Dan and the soldier near him widened the interval between them without looking down, without appearing to heed the wounded man. This little clump of blue seemed to reel past them as boulders reel past a train.

Bursting through a smoke-wave, the scampering, unformed bunches came upon the wreck of the brigade that had preceded them, a floundering mass stopped afar from the hill by the swirling volleys.

It was as if a necromancer had suddenly shown them a picture of the fate which awaited them; but the line with muscular spasm hurled itself over this wreckage and onward, until men were stumbling amid the relics of other assaults, the point where the fire from the ridge consumed.

The men, panting, perspiring, with crazed faces, tried to push against it; but it was as if they had come to a wall. The wave halted, shuddered in an agony from the quick struggle of its two desires, then toppled, and broke into a fragmentary thing which has no name.

Veterans could now at last be distinguished from recruits. The new regiments were instantly gone, lost, scattered, as if they never had been. But the sweeping failure of the charge, the battle, could not make the veterans forget their business. With a last throe, the band of maniacs drew itself up and blazed a volley at the hill, insignificant to those iron intrenchments, but nevertheless expressing that singular final despair which enables men coolly to defy the walls of a city of death.

After this episode the men renamed their command. They called it the Little Regiment.

## VI.

"I seen Dan shoot a feller yesterday. Yes sir. I'm sure it was him that done it. And maybe he thinks about that feller now, and wonders if *he* tumbled down just about the same way. Them things come up in a man's mind."

Bivouac fires upon the sidewalks, in the streets, in the yards, threw high their wavering reflections, which examined, like slim, red fingers, the dingy, scarred walls and the piles of tumbled brick. The droning of voices again arose from great blue crowds.

The odour of frying bacon, the fragrance from countless little coffee-pails floated among the ruins. The rifles, stacked in the shadows, emitted flashes of steely light. Wherever a a flag lay horizontally from one stack to another was the bed of an eagle which had led men into the mystic smoke.

The men about a particular fire were engaged in holding in check their jovial spirits. They moved whispering around the blaze, although they looked at it with a certain fine contentment, like labourers after a day's hard work.

There was one who sat apart. They did not address him save in tones suddenly changed. They did not regard him directly, but always in little sidelong glances.

At last a soldier from a distant fire came into this circle of light. He studied for a time the man who sat apart. Then he hesitatingly stepped closer, and said: "Got any news, Dan?"

"No," said Dan.

The new-comer shifted his feet. He looked at the fire, at the sky, at the other men, at Dan. His face expressed a curious despair; his tongue was plainly in rebellion. Finally, however, he contrived to say: "Well, there's some chance yet, Dan. Lots of the wounded are still lying out there, you know. There's some chance yet."

"Yes," said Dan.

The soldier shifted his feet again, and looked miserably into the air. After another struggle he said: "Well, there's some chance yet, Dan." He moved hastily away.

One of the men of the squad, perhaps encouraged by this example, now approached the still figure. "No news yet, hey?" he said, after coughing behind his hand.

"No," said Dan.

"Well," said the man, "I've been thinking of how he was fretting about you the night you went on special duty. You recollect? Well, sir, I was surprised. He couldn't say enough about it. I swan, I don't believe he slep' a wink after you left, but just lay awake cussing special duty and worrying. I was surprised. But there he lay cussing. He—"

Dan made a curious sound, as if a stone had wedged in his throat. He said: "Shut up, will you?"

Afterward the men would not allow this moody contemplation of the fire to be interrupted.

"Oh, let him alone, can't you?"

"Come away from there, Casey!"

"Say, can't you leave him be?"

They moved with reverence about the immovable figure, with its countenance of mask-like invulnerability.

## VII.

After the red round eye of the sun had stared long at the little plain and its burden, darkness, a sable mercy, came heavily upon it, and the wan hands of the dead were no longer seen in strange frozen gestures.

The heights in front of the plain shone with tiny camp-fires, and from the town in the rear, small shimmerings ascended from the blazes of the bivouac. The plain was a black expanse upon which, from time to time, dots of light, lanterns, floated slowly here and there. These fields were long steeped in grim mystery.

Suddenly, upon one dark spot, there was a resurrection. A strange thing had been groaning there, prostrate. Then it suddenly dragged itself to a sitting posture, and became a man.

The man stared stupidly for a moment at the lights on the hill, then turned and contemplated the faint colouring over the town. For some moments he remained thus, staring with dull eyes, his face unemotional, wooden.

Finally he looked around him at the corpses dimly to be seen. No change flashed into his face upon viewing these men. They seemed to suggest merely that his information concerning himself was not too complete. He ran his fingers over his arms and chest, bearing always the air of an idiot upon a bench at an almshouse door.

Finding no wound in his arms nor in his chest, he raised his hand to his head, and the fingers came away with some dark liquid upon them. Holding these fingers close to his eyes, he scanned them in the same stupid fashion, while his body gently swayed.

The soldier rolled his eyes again toward the town. When he arose, his clothing peeled from the frozen ground like wet paper. Hearing the sound of it, he seemed to see reason for deliberation. He paused and looked at the ground, then at his trousers, then at the ground.

Finally he went slowly off toward the faint reflection, holding his hands palm outward before him, and walking in the manner of a blind man.

## VIII.

The immovable Dan again sat unaddressed in the midst of comrades, who did not joke aloud. The dampness of the usual morning fog seemed to make the little camp-fires furious.

Suddenly a cry arose in the streets, a shout of amazement and delight. The men making breakfast at the fire looked up quickly. They broke forth in clamorous exclamation: "Well! Of all things! Dan! Dan! Look who's coming! Oh, Dan!"

Dan the silent raised his eyes and saw a man, with a bandage of the size of a helmet about his head, receiving a furious demonstration from the company. He was shaking hands, and explaining, and haranguing to a high degree.

Dan started. His face of bronze flushed to his temples. He seemed about to leap from the ground, but then suddenly he sank back, and resumed his impassive gazing.

The men were in a flurry. They looked from one to the other. "Dan! Look! See who's coming!" some cried again. "Dan! Look!"

He scowled at last, and moved his shoulders sullenly. "Well, don't I know it?"

But they could not be convinced that his eyes were in service. "Dan! Why can't you look? See who's coming!"

He made a gesture then of irritation and rage. "Curse it! Don't I know it?"

The man with a bandage of the size of a helmet moved forward, always shaking hands and explaining. At times his glance wandered to Dan, who saw with his eyes riveted.

After a series of shiftings, it occurred naturally that the man with the bandage was very near to the man who saw the flames. He paused, and there was a little silence. Finally he said: "Hello, Dan."

"Hello, Billie."

# THREE MIRACULOUS SOLDIERS.

## I.

The girl was in the front room on the second floor, peering through the blinds. It was the "best room." There was a very new rag carpet on the floor. The edges of it had been dyed with alternate stripes of red and green. Upon the wooden mantel there were two little puffy figures in clay—a shepherd and a shepherdess probably. A triangle of pink and white wool hung carefully over the edge of this shelf. Upon the bureau there was nothing at all save a spread newspaper, with edges folded to make it into a mat. The quilts and sheets had been removed from the bed and were stacked upon a chair. The pillows and the great feather mattress were muffled and tumbled until they resembled great dumplings. The picture of a man terribly leaden in complexion hung in an oval frame on one white wall and steadily confronted the bureau.

From between the slats of the blinds she had a view of the road as it wended across the meadow to the woods, and again where it reappeared crossing the hill, half a mile away. It lay yellow and warm in the summer sunshine. From the long grasses of the meadow came the rhythmic click of the insects. Occasional frogs in the hidden brook made a peculiar chug-chug sound, as if somebody throttled them. The leaves of the wood swung in gentle winds. Through the dark-green branches of the pines that grew in the front yard could be seen the mountains, far to the southeast, and inexpressibly blue.

Mary's eyes were fastened upon the little streak of road that appeared on the distant hill. Her face was flushed with excitement, and the hand which stretched in a strained pose on the sill trembled because of the nervous shaking of the wrist. The pines whisked their green needles with a soft, hissing sound against the house.

At last the girl turned from the window and went to the head of the stairs. "Well, I just know they're coming, anyhow," she cried argumentatively to the depths.

A voice from below called to her angrily: "They ain't. We've never seen one yet. They never come into this neighbourhood. You just come down here and 'tend to your work insteader watching for soldiers."

"Well, ma, I just know they're coming."

A voice retorted with the shrillness and mechanical violence of occasional housewives. The girl swished her skirts defiantly and returned to the window.

Upon the yellow streak of road that lay across the hillside there now was a handful of black dots—horsemen. A cloud of dust floated away. The girl flew to the head of the stairs and whirled down into the kitchen.

"They're coming! They're coming!"

It was as if she had cried "Fire!" Her mother had been peeling potatoes while seated comfortably at the table. She sprang to her feet. "No—it can't be—how you know it's them—where?" The stubby knife fell from her hand, and two or three curls of potato skin dropped from her apron to the floor.

The girl turned and dashed upstairs. Her mother followed, gasping for breath, and yet contriving to fill the air with questions, reproach, and remonstrance. The girl was already at the window, eagerly pointing. "There! There! See 'em! See 'em!"

Rushing to the window, the mother scanned for an instant the road on the hill. She crouched back with a groan. "It's them, sure as the world! It's them!" She waved her hands in despairing gestures.

The black dots vanished into the wood. The girl at the window was quivering and her eyes were shining like water when the sun flashes. "Hush! They're in the woods! They'll be here directly." She bent down and intently watched the green archway whence the road emerged. "Hush! I hear 'em coming," she swiftly whispered to her mother, for the elder woman had dropped dolefully upon the mattress and was sobbing. And indeed the girl could hear the quick, dull trample of horses. She stepped aside with sudden apprehension, but she bent her head forward in order to still scan the road.

"Here they are!"

There was something very theatrical in the sudden appearance of these men to the eyes of the girl. It was as if a scene had been shifted. The forest suddenly disclosed them—a dozen brown-faced troopers in blue—galloping.

"Oh, look!" breathed the girl. Her mouth was puckered into an expression of strange fascination as if she had expected to see the troopers change into demons and gloat at her. She was at last looking upon those curious beings who rode down from the North—those men of legend and colossal tale—they who were possessed of such marvellous hallucinations.

The little troop rode in silence. At its head was a youthful fellow with some dim yellow stripes upon his arm. In his right hand he held his carbine, slanting upward, with the stock resting upon his knee. He was absorbed in a scrutiny of the country before him.

At the heels of the sergeant the rest of the squad rode in thin column, with creak of leather and tinkle of steel and tin. The girl scanned the faces of the horsemen, seeming astonished vaguely to find them of the type she knew.

The lad at the head of the troop comprehended the house and its environments in two glances. He did not check the long, swinging stride of his horse. The troopers glanced for a moment like casual tourists, and then returned to their study of the region in front. The heavy thudding of the hoofs became a small noise. The dust, hanging in sheets, slowly sank.

The sobs of the woman on the bed took form in words which, while strong in their note of calamity, yet expressed a querulous mental reaching for some near thing to blame. "And it'll be lucky fer us if we ain't both butchered in our sleep—plundering and running off horses—old Santo's gone—you see if he ain't—plundering—"

"But, ma," said the girl, perplexed and terrified in the same moment, "they've gone."

"Oh, but they'll come back!" cried the mother, without pausing her wail. "They'll come back—trust them for that—running off horses. O John, John! why did you, why did you?" She suddenly lifted herself and sat rigid, staring at her daughter. "Mary," she said in tragic whisper, "the kitchen door isn't locked!" Already she was bended forward to listen, her mouth agape, her eyes fixed upon her daughter.

"Mother," faltered the girl.

Her mother again whispered, "The kitchen door isn't locked."

Motionless and mute they stared into each other's eyes.

At last the girl quavered, "We better—we better go and lock it." The mother nodded. Hanging arm in arm they stole across the floor toward the head of the stairs. A board of the floor creaked. They halted and exchanged a look of dumb agony.

At last they reached the head of the stairs. From the kitchen came the bass humming of the kettle and frequent sputterings and cracklings from the fire. These sounds were sinister. The mother and the girl stood incapable of movement. "There's somebody down there!" whispered the elder woman.

Finally, the girl made a gesture of resolution. She twisted her arm from her mother's hands and went two steps downward. She addressed the kitchen: "Who's there?" Her tone was intended to be dauntless. It rang so dramatically in the silence that a sudden new panic seized them as if the suspected presence in the kitchen had cried out to them. But the girl ventured again: "Is there anybody there?" No reply was made save by the kettle and the fire.

With a stealthy tread the girl continued her journey. As she neared the last step the fire crackled explosively and the girl screamed. But the mystic presence had not swept around the corner to grab her, so she dropped to a seat on the step and laughed. "It was—was only the—the fire," she said, stammering hysterically.

Then she arose with sudden fortitude and cried: "Why, there isn't anybody there! I know there isn't." She marched down into the kitchen. In her face was dread, as if she half expected to confront something, but the room was empty. She cried joyously: "There's nobody here! Come on down, ma." She ran to the kitchen door and locked it.

The mother came down to the kitchen. "Oh, dear, what a fright I've had! It's given me the sick headache. I know it has."

"Oh, ma," said the girl.

"I know it has—I know it. Oh, if your father was only here! He'd settle those Yankees mighty quick—he'd settle 'em! Two poor helpless women—"

"Why, ma, what makes you act so? The Yankees haven't—"

"Oh, they'll be back—they'll be back. Two poor helpless women! Your father and your uncle Asa and Bill off galavanting around and fighting when they ought to be protecting their home! That's the kind of men they are. Didn't I say to your father just before he left—"

"Ma," said the girl, coming suddenly from the window, "the barn door is open. I wonder if they took old Santo?"

"Oh, of course they have—of course—Mary, I don't see what we are going to do—I don't see what we are going to do."

The girl said, "Ma, I'm going to see if they took old Santo."

"Mary," cried the mother, "don't you dare!"

"But think of poor old Sant, ma."

"Never you mind old Santo. We're lucky to be safe ourselves, I tell you. Never mind old Santo. Don't you dare to go out there, Mary—Mary!"

The girl had unlocked the door and stepped out upon the porch. The mother cried in despair, "Mary!"

"Why, there isn't anybody out here," the girl called in response. She stood for a moment with a curious smile upon her face as of gleeful satisfaction at her daring.

The breeze was waving the boughs of the apple trees. A rooster with an air importantly courteous was conducting three hens upon a foraging tour. On the hillside at the rear of the gray old barn the red leaves of a creeper flamed amid the summer foliage. High in the sky clouds rolled toward the north. The girl swung impulsively from the little stoop and ran toward the barn.

The great door was open, and the carved peg which usually performed the office of a catch lay on the ground. The girl could not see into the barn because of the heavy shadows. She paused in a listening attitude and heard a horse munching placidly. She gave a cry of delight and sprang across the threshold. Then she suddenly shrank back and gasped. She had confronted three men in gray seated upon the floor with their legs stretched out and their backs against Santo's manger. Their dust-covered countenances were expanded in grins.

## II.

As Mary sprang backward and screamed, one of the calm men in gray, still grinning, announced, "I knowed you'd holler." Sitting there comfortably the three surveyed her with amusement.

Mary caught her breath, throwing her hand up to her throat. "Oh!" she said, "you—you frightened me!"

"We're sorry, lady, but couldn't help it no way," cheerfully responded another. "I knowed you'd holler when I seen you coming yere, but I raikoned we couldn't help it no way. We hain't a-troubling this yere barn, I don't guess. We been doing some mighty tall sleeping yere. We done woke when them Yanks loped past."

"Where did you come from? Did—did you escape from the—the Yankees?" The girl still stammered and trembled. The three soldiers laughed. "No, m'm. No, m'm. They never cotch us. We was in a muss down the road yere about two mile. And Bill yere they gin it to him in the arm, kehplunk. And they pasted me thar, too. Curious. And Sim yere, he didn't get nothing, but they chased us all quite a little piece, and we done lose track of our boys."

"Was it—was it those who passed here just now? Did they chase you?"

The men in gray laughed again. "What—them? No, indeedee! There was a mighty big swarm of Yanks and a mighty big swarm of our boys, too. What—that little passel? No, m'm."

She became calm enough to scan them more attentively. They were much begrimed and very dusty. Their gray clothes were tattered. Splashed mud had dried upon them in reddish spots. It appeared, too, that the men had not shaved in many days. In the hats there was a singular diversity. One soldier wore the little blue cap of the Northern infantry, with corps emblem and regimental number; one wore a great slouch hat with a wide hole in the crown; and the other wore no hat at all. The left sleeve of one man and the right sleeve of another had been slit and the arms were neatly bandaged with clean cloth. "These hain't no more than two little cuts," explained one. "We stopped up yere to Mis' Leavitts—she said her name was—and she bind them for us. Bill yere, he had the thirst come on him. And the fever too. We—"

"Did you ever see my father in the army?" asked Mary. "John Hinckson—his name is."

The three soldiers grinned again, but they replied kindly: "No, m'm. No, m'm, we hain't never. What is he—in the cavalry?"

"No," said the girl. "He and my uncle Asa and my cousin—his name is Bill Parker—they are all with Longstreet—they call him."

"Oh," said the soldiers. "Longstreet? Oh, they're a good smart ways from yere. 'Way off up nawtheast. There hain't nothing but cavalry down yere. They're in the infantry, probably."

"We haven't heard anything from them for days and days," said Mary.

"Oh, they're all right in the infantry," said one man, to be consoling. "The infantry don't do much fighting. They go bellering out in a big swarm and only a few of 'em get hurt. But if they was in the cavalry—the cavalry—"

Mary interrupted him without intention. "Are you hungry?" she asked.

The soldiers looked at each other, struck by some sudden and singular shame. They hung their heads. "No, m'm," replied one at last.

Santo, in his stall, was tranquilly chewing and chewing. Sometimes he looked benevolently over at them. He was an old horse and there was something about his eyes and his forelock which created the impression that he wore spectacles. Mary went and patted his nose. "Well, if you are hungry, I can get you something," she told the men. "Or you might come to the house."

"We wouldn't dast go to the house," said one. "That passel of Yanks was only a scouting crowd, most like. Just an advance. More coming, likely."

"Well, I can bring you something," cried the girl eagerly. "Won't you let me bring you something?"

"Well," said a soldier with embarrassment, "we hain't had much. If you could bring us a little snack-like—just a snack—we'd—"

Without waiting for him to cease, the girl turned toward the door. But before she had reached it she stopped abruptly. "Listen!" she whispered. Her form was bent forward, her head turned and lowered, her hand extended toward the men in a command for silence.

They could faintly hear the thudding of many hoofs, the clank of arms, and frequent calling voices.

"By cracky, it's the Yanks!" The soldiers scrambled to their feet and came toward the door. "I knowed that first crowd was only an advance."

The girl and the three men peered from the shadows of the barn. The view of the road was intersected by tree trunks and a little henhouse. However, they could see many horsemen streaming down the road. The horsemen were in blue. "Oh, hide—hide—hide!" cried the girl, with a sob in her voice.

"Wait a minute," whispered a gray soldier excitedly. "Maybe they're going along by. No, by thunder, they hain't! They're halting. Scoot, boys!"

They made a noiseless dash into the dark end of the barn. The girl, standing by the door, heard them break forth an instant later in clamorous whispers. "Where'll we hide? Where'll we hide? There hain't a place to hide!" The girl turned and glanced wildly about the barn. It seemed true. The stock of hay had grown low under Santo's endless munching, and from occasional levyings by passing troopers in gray. The poles of the mow were barely covered, save in one corner where there was a little bunch.

The girl espied the great feed box. She ran to it and lifted the lid. "Here! here!" she called. "Get in here."

They had been tearing noiselessly around the rear part of the barn. At her low call they came and plunged at the box. They did not all get in at the same moment without a good deal of a tangle. The wounded men gasped and muttered, but they at last were flopped down on the layer of feed which covered the bottom. Swiftly and softly the girl lowered the lid and then turned like a flash toward the door.

No one appeared there, so she went close to survey the situation. The troopers had dismounted and stood in silence by their horses. A gray-bearded man, whose red cheeks and nose shone vividly above the whiskers, was strolling about with two or three others. They wore double-breasted coats, and faded yellow sashes were wound under their black leather sword belts. The gray-bearded soldier was apparently giving orders, pointing here and there.

Mary tiptoed to the feed box. "They've all got off their horses," she said to it. A finger projected from a knothole near the top and said to her very plainly, "Come closer." She obeyed, and then a muffled voice could be heard: "Scoot for the house, lady, and if we don't see you again, why, much obliged for what you done."

"Good-bye," she said to the feed box.

She made two attempts to walk dauntlessly from the barn, but each time she faltered and failed just before she reached the point where she could have been seen by the blue-coated troopers. At last, however, she made a sort of a rush forward and went out into the bright sunshine.

The group of men in double-breasted coats wheeled in her direction at the instant. The gray-bearded officer forgot to lower his arm which had been stretched forth in giving an order.

She felt that her feet were touching the ground in a most unnatural manner. Her bearing, she believed, was suddenly grown awkward and ungainly. Upon her face she thought that this sentence was plainly written: "There are three men hidden in the feed box."

The gray-bearded soldier came toward her. She stopped; she seemed about to run away. But the soldier doffed his little blue cap and looked amiable. "You live here, I presume?" he said.

"Yes," she answered.

"Well, we are obliged to camp here for the night, and as we've got two wounded men with us I don't suppose you'd mind if we put them in the barn."

"In—in the barn?"

He became aware that she was agitated. He smiled assuringly. "You needn't be frightened. We won't hurt anything around here. You'll all be safe enough."

The girl balanced on one foot and swung the other to and fro in the grass. She was looking down at it. "But—but I don't think ma would like it if—if you took the barn."

The old officer laughed. "Wouldn't she?" said he. "That's so. Maybe she wouldn't." He reflected for a time and then decided cheerfully: "Well, we will have to go ask her, anyhow. Where is she? In the house?"

"Yes," replied the girl, "she's in the house. She—she'll be scared to death when she sees you!"

"Well, you go and ask her then," said the soldier, always wearing a benign smile. "You go ask her and then come and tell me."

When the girl pushed open the door and entered the kitchen, she found it empty. "Ma!" she called softly. There was no answer. The kettle still was humming its low song. The knife and the curl of potato skin lay on the floor.

She went to her mother's room and entered timidly. The new, lonely aspect of the house shook her nerves. Upon the bed was a confusion of coverings. "Ma!" called the girl, quaking in fear that her mother was not there to reply. But there was a sudden turmoil of the quilts, and her mother's head was thrust forth. "Mary!" she cried, in what seemed to be a supreme astonishment, "I thought—I thought—"

"Oh, ma," blurted the girl, "there's over a thousand Yankees in the yard, and I've hidden three of our men in the feed box!"

The elder woman, however, upon the appearance of her daughter had begun to thrash hysterically about on the bed and wail.

"Ma," the girl exclaimed, "and now they want to use the barn—and our men in the feed box! What shall I do, ma? What shall I do?"

Her mother did not seem to hear, so absorbed was she in her grievous flounderings and tears. "Ma!" appealed the girl. "Ma!"

For a moment Mary stood silently debating, her lips apart, her eyes fixed. Then she went to the kitchen window and peeked.

The old officer and the others were staring up the road. She went to another window in order to get a proper view of the road, and saw that they were gazing at a small body of horsemen approaching at a trot and raising much dust. Presently she recognised them as the squad that had passed the house earlier, for the young man with the dim yellow chevron still rode at their head. An unarmed horseman in gray was receiving their close attention.

As they came very near to the house she darted to the first window again. The gray-bearded officer was smiling a fine broad smile of satisfaction. "So you got him?" he called out. The young sergeant sprang from his horse and his brown hand moved in a salute. The girl could not hear his reply. She saw the unarmed horseman in gray stroking a very black mustache and looking about him coolly and with an interested air. He appeared so indifferent that she did not understand he was a prisoner until she heard the graybeard call out: "Well, put him in the barn. He'll be safe there, I guess." A party of troopers moved with the prisoner toward the barn.

The girl made a sudden gesture of horror, remembering the three men in the feed box.

### III.

The busy troopers in blue scurried about the long lines of stamping horses. Men crooked their backs and perspired in order to rub with cloths or bunches of grass these slim equine legs, upon whose splendid machinery they depended so greatly. The lips of the horses were still wet and frothy from the steel bars which had wrenched at their mouths all day. Over their backs and about their noses sped the talk of the men.

"Moind where yer plug is steppin', Finerty! Keep 'im aff me!"

"An ould elephant! He shtrides like a schoolhouse."

"Bill's little mar—she was plum beat when she come in with Crawford's crowd."

"Crawford's the hardest-ridin' cavalryman in the army. An he don't use up a horse, neither—much. They stay fresh when the others are most a-droppin'."

"Finerty, will yeh moind that cow a yours?"

Amid a bustle of gossip and banter, the horses retained their air of solemn rumination, twisting their lower jaws from side to side and sometimes rubbing noses dreamfully.

Over in front of the barn three troopers sat talking comfortably. Their carbines were leaned against the wall. At their side and outlined in the black of the open door stood a sentry, his weapon resting in the hollow of his arm. Four horses, saddled and accoutred, were conferring with their heads close together. The four bridle reins were flung over a post.

Upon the calm green of the land, typical in every way of peace, the hues of war brought thither by the troops shone strangely. Mary, gazing curiously, did not feel that she was contemplating a familiar scene. It was no longer the home acres. The new blue, steel, and faded yellow thoroughly dominated the old green and brown. She could hear the voices of the men, and it seemed from their tone that they had camped there for years. Everything with them was usual. They had taken possession of the landscape in such a way that even the old marks appeared strange and formidable to the girl.

Mary had intended to go and tell the commander in blue that her mother did not wish his men to use the barn at all, but she paused when she heard him speak to the sergeant. She thought she perceived then that it mattered little to him what her mother wished, and that an objection by her or by anybody would be futile. She saw the soldiers conduct the prisoner in gray into the barn, and for a long time she watched the three chatting guards and the pondering sentry. Upon her mind in desolate weight was the recollection of the three men in the feed box.

It seemed to her that in a case of this description it was her duty to be a heroine. In all the stories she had read when at boarding school in Pennsylvania, the girl characters, confronted with such difficulties, invariably did hair breadth things. True, they were usually bent upon rescuing and recovering their lovers, and neither the calm man in gray nor any of the three in the feed box was lover of hers, but then a real heroine would not pause over this minor question. Plainly a heroine would take measures to rescue the four men. If she did not at least make the attempt, she would be false to those carefully constructed ideals which were the accumulation of years of dreaming.

But the situation puzzled her. There was the barn with only one door, and with four armed troopers in front of this door, one of them with his back to the rest of the world, engaged, no doubt, in a steadfast contemplation of the calm man and, incidentally, of the feed box. She knew, too, that even if she should open the kitchen door, three heads and perhaps four would turn casually in her direction. Their ears were real ears.

Heroines, she knew, conducted these matters with infinite precision and despatch. They severed the hero's bonds, cried a dramatic sentence, and stood between him and his enemies until he had run far enough away. She saw well, however, that even should she achieve all things up to the point where she might take glorious stand between the escaping and the pursuers, those grim troopers in blue would not pause. They would run around her, make a circuit. One by one she saw the gorgeous contrivances and expedients of fiction fall before the plain, homely difficulties of this situation. They were of no service. Sadly, ruefully, she thought of the calm man and of the contents of the feed box.

The sum of her invention was that she could sally forth to the commander of the blue cavalry, and confessing to him that there were three of her friends and his enemies secreted in the feed box, pray him to let them depart unmolested. But she was beginning to believe the old graybeard to be a bear. It was hardly probable that he would give this plan his support. It was more probable that he and some of his men would at once descend upon the feed box and confiscate her three friends. The difficulty with her idea was that she could not learn its value without trying it, and then in case of failure it would be too late for remedies and other plans. She reflected that war made men very unreasonable.

All that she could do was to stand at the window and mournfully regard the barn. She admitted this to herself with a sense of deep humiliation. She was not, then, made of that fine stuff, that mental satin, which enabled some other beings to be of such mighty service to the distressed. She was defeated by a barn with one door, by four men with eight eyes and eight ears—trivialities that would not impede the real heroine.

The vivid white light of broad day began slowly to fade. Tones of gray came upon the fields, and the shadows were of lead. In this more sombre atmosphere the fires built by the troops down in the far end of the orchard grew more brilliant, becoming spots of crimson colour in the dark grove.

The girl heard a fretting voice from her mother's room. "Mary!" She hastily obeyed the call. She perceived that she had quite forgotten her mother's existence in this time of excitement.

The elder woman still lay upon the bed. Her face was flushed and perspiration stood amid new wrinkles upon her forehead. Weaving wild glances from side to side, she began to whimper. "Oh, I'm just sick—I'm just sick! Have those men gone yet? Have they gone?"

The girl smoothed a pillow carefully for her mother's head. "No, ma. They're here yet. But they haven't hurt anything—it doesn't seem. Will I get you something to eat?"

Her mother gestured her away with the impatience of the ill. "No—no—just don't bother me. My head is splitting, and you know very well that nothing can be done for me when I get one of these spells. It's trouble—that's what makes them. When are those men going? Look here, don't you go 'way. You stick close to the house now."

"I'll stay right here," said the girl. She sat in the gloom and listened to her mother's incessant moaning. When she attempted to move, her mother cried out at her. When she desired to ask if she might try to alleviate the pain, she was interrupted shortly. Somehow her sitting in passive silence within hearing of this illness seemed to contribute to her mother's relief. She assumed a posture of submission. Sometimes her mother projected questions concerning the local condition, and although she laboured to be graphic and at the same time soothing, unalarming, her form of reply was always displeasing to the sick woman, and brought forth ejaculations of angry impatience.

Eventually the woman slept in the manner of one worn from terrible labour. The girl went slowly and softly to the kitchen. When she looked from the window, she saw the four soldiers still at the barn door. In the west, the sky was yellow. Some tree trunks intersecting it appeared black as streaks of ink. Soldiers hovered in blue clouds about the bright splendour of the fires in the orchard. There were glimmers of steel.

The girl sat in the new gloom of the kitchen and watched. The soldiers lit a lantern and hung it in the barn. Its rays made the form of the sentry seem gigantic. Horses whinnied from the orchard. There was a low hum of human voices. Sometimes small detachments of troopers rode past the front of the house. The girl heard the abrupt calls of sentries. She fetched some food and ate it from her hand, standing by the window. She was so afraid that something would occur that she barely left her post for an instant.

A picture of the interior of the barn hung vividly in her mind. She recalled the knot-holes in the boards at the rear, but she admitted that the prisoners could not escape through them. She remembered some inadequacies of the roof, but these also counted for nothing. When confronting the problem, she felt her ambitions, her ideals tumbling headlong like cottages of straw.

Once she felt that she had decided to reconnoitre at any rate. It was night; the lantern at the barn and the camp fires made everything without their circle into masses of heavy mystic blackness. She took two steps toward the door. But there she paused. Innumerable possibilities of danger had assailed her mind. She returned to the window and stood wavering. At last, she went swiftly to the door, opened it, and slid noiselessly into the darkness.

For a moment she regarded the shadows. Down in the orchard the camp fires of the troops appeared precisely like a great painting, all in reds upon a black cloth. The voices of the troopers still hummed. The girl started slowly off in the opposite direction. Her eyes were fixed in a stare; she studied the darkness in front for a moment, before she ventured upon a forward step. Unconsciously, her throat was arranged for a sudden shrill scream. High in the tree branches she could hear the voice of the wind, a melody of the night, low and sad, the plaint of an endless, incommunicable sorrow. Her own distress, the plight of the men in gray—these near matters as well as all she had known or imagined of grief—everything was expressed in this soft mourning of the wind in the trees. At first she felt like weeping. This sound told her of human impotency and doom. Then later the trees and the wind breathed strength to her, sang of sacrifice, of dauntless effort, of hard carven faces that did not blanch when Duty came at midnight or at noon.

She turned often to scan the shadowy figures that moved from time to time in the light at the barn door. Once she trod upon a stick, and it flopped, crackling in the intolerable manner of all sticks. At this noise, however, the guards at the barn made no sign. Finally, she was where she could see the knot-holes in the rear of the structure gleaming like pieces of metal from the effect of the light within. Scarcely breathing in her excitement she glided close and applied an eye to a knothole. She had barely achieved one glance at the interior before she sprang back shuddering.

For the unconscious and cheerful sentry at the door was swearing away in flaming sentences, heaping one gorgeous oath upon another, making a conflagration of his description of his troop horse.

"Why," he was declaring to the calm prisoner in gray, "you ain't got a horse in your hull damn army that can run forty rod with that there little mar'!"

As in the outer darkness Mary cautiously returned to the knothole, the three guards in front suddenly called in low tones: "Shhh!"

"Quit, Pete; here comes the lieutenant." The sentry had apparently been about to resume his declamation, but at these warnings he suddenly posed in a soldierly manner.

A tall and lean officer with a smooth face entered the barn. The sentry saluted primly. The officer flashed a comprehensive glance about him. "Everything all right?"

"All right, sir."

This officer had eyes like the points of stilettos. The lines from his nose to the corners of his mouth were deep and gave him a slightly disagreeable aspect, but somewhere in his face there was a quality of singular thoughtfulness, as of the absorbed student dealing in generalities, which was utterly in opposition to the rapacious keenness of the eyes which saw everything.

Suddenly he lifted a long finger and pointed. "What's that?"

"That? That's a feed box, I suppose."

"What's in it?"

"I don't know. I—"

"You ought to know," said the officer sharply. He walked over to the feed box and flung up the lid. With a sweeping gesture, he reached down and scooped a handful of feed. "You ought to know what's in everything when you have prisoners in your care," he added, scowling.

During the time of this incident, the girl had nearly swooned. Her hands searched weakly over the boards for something to which to cling. With the pallor of the dying she had watched the downward sweep of the officer's arm, which after all had only brought forth a handful of feed. The result was a stupefaction of her mind. She was astonished out of her senses at this spectacle of three large men metamorphosed into a handful of feed.

**IV.**

It is perhaps a singular thing that this absence of the three men from the feed box at the time of the sharp lieutenant's investigation should terrify the girl more than it should joy her. That for which she had prayed had come to pass. Apparently the escape of these men in the face of every improbability had been granted her, but her dominating emotion was fright. The feed box was a mystic and terrible machine, like some dark magician's trap. She felt it almost possible that she should see the three weird men floating spectrally away through the air. She glanced with swift apprehension behind her, and when the dazzle from the lantern's light had left her eyes, saw only the dim hillside stretched in solemn silence.

The interior of the barn possessed for her another fascination because it was now uncanny. It contained that extraordinary feed box. When she peeped again at the knothole, the calm, gray prisoner was seated upon the feed box, thumping it with his dangling, careless heels as if it were in nowise his conception of a remarkable feed-box. The sentry also stood facing it. His carbine he held in the hollow of his arm. His legs were spread apart, and he mused. From without came the low mumble of the three other troopers. The sharp lieutenant had vanished.

The trembling yellow light of the lantern caused the figures of the men to cast monstrous wavering shadows. There were spaces of gloom which shrouded ordinary things in impressive garb. The roof presented an inscrutable blackness, save where small rifts in the shingles glowed phosphorescently. Frequently old Santo put down a thunderous hoof. The heels of the prisoner made a sound like the booming of a wild kind of drum. When the men moved their heads, their eyes shone with ghoulish whiteness, and their complexions were always waxen and unreal. And there was that profoundly strange feed box, imperturbable with its burden of fantastic mystery.

Suddenly from down near her feet the girl heard a crunching sound, a sort of a nibbling, as if some silent and very discreet terrier was at work upon the turf. She faltered back; here was no doubt another grotesque detail of this most unnatural episode. She did not run, because physically she was in the power of these events. Her feet chained her to the ground in submission to this march of terror after terror. As she stared at the spot from which this sound seemed to come, there floated through her mind a vague, sweet vision—a vision of her safe little room, in which at this hour she usually was sleeping.

The scratching continued faintly and with frequent pauses, as if the terrier was then listening. When the girl first removed her eyes from the knothole the scene appeared of one velvet blackness; then gradually objects loomed with a dim lustre. She could see now where the tops of the trees joined the sky and the form of the barn was before her dyed in heavy purple. She was ever about to shriek, but no sound came from her constricted throat. She gazed at the ground with the expression of countenance of one who watches the sinister-moving grass where a serpent approaches.

Dimly she saw a piece of sod wrenched free and drawn under the great foundation beam of the barn. Once she imagined that she saw human hands, not outlined at all, but sufficient in colour, form, or movement to make subtle suggestion.

Then suddenly a thought that illuminated the entire situation flashed in her mind like a light. The three men, late of the feed box, were beneath the floor of the barn and were now scraping their way under this beam. She did not consider for a moment how they could come there. They were marvellous creatures. The supernatural was to be expected of them. She no longer trembled, for she was possessed upon this instant of the most unchangeable species of conviction. The evidence before her amounted to no evidence at all, but nevertheless her opinion grew in an instant from an irresponsible acorn to a rooted and immovable tree. It was as if she was on a jury.

She stooped down hastily and scanned the ground. There she indeed saw a pair of hands hauling at the dirt where the sod had been displaced. Softly, in a whisper like a breath, she said, "Hey!"

The dim hands were drawn hastily under the barn. The girl reflected for a moment. Then she stooped and whispered: "Hey! It's me!"

After a time there was a resumption of the digging. The ghostly hands began once more their cautious mining. She waited. In hollow reverberations from the interior of the barn came the frequent sounds of old Santo's lazy movements. The sentry conversed with the prisoner.

At last the girl saw a head thrust slowly from under the beam. She perceived the face of one of the miraculous soldiers from the feed box. A pair of eyes glintered and wavered, then finally settled upon her, a pale statue of a girl. The eyes became lit with a kind of humorous greeting. An arm gestured at her.

Stooping, she breathed, "All right." The man drew himself silently back under the beam. A moment later the pair of hands resumed their cautious task. Ultimately the head and arms of the man were thrust strangely from the earth. He was lying on his back. The girl thought of the dirt in his hair. Wriggling slowly and pushing at the beam above him he forced his way out of the curious little passage. He twisted his body and raised himself upon his hands. He grinned at the girl and drew his feet carefully from under the beam. When he at last stood erect beside her, he at once began mechanically to brush the dirt from his clothes with his hands. In the barn the sentry and his prisoner were evidently engaged in an argument.

The girl and the first miraculous soldier signalled warily. It seemed that they feared that their arms would make noises in passing through the air. Their lips moved, conveying dim meanings.

In this sign language the girl described the situation in the barn. With guarded motions, she told him of the importance of absolute stillness. He nodded, and then in the same manner he told her of his two companions under the barn floor. He informed her again of their wounded state, and wagged his head to express his despair. He contorted his face, to tell how sore were their arms; and jabbed the air mournfully, to express their remote geographical position.

This signalling was interrupted by the sound of a body being dragged or dragging itself with slow, swishing sound under the barn. The sound was too loud for safety. They rushed to the hole and began to semaphore until a shaggy head appeared with rolling eyes and quick grin.

With frantic downward motions of their arms they suppressed this grin and with it the swishing noise. In dramatic pantomime they informed this head of the terrible consequences of so much noise. The head nodded, and painfully but with extreme care the second man pushed and pulled himself from the hole.

In a faint whisper the first man said, "Where's Sim?"

The second man made low reply. "He's right here." He motioned reassuringly toward the hole.

When the third head appeared, a soft smile of glee came upon each face, and the mute group exchanged expressive glances.

When they all stood together, free from this tragic barn, they breathed a long sigh that was contemporaneous with another smile and another exchange of glances.

One of the men tiptoed to a knothole and peered into the barn. The sentry was at that moment speaking. "Yes, we know 'em all. There isn't a house in this region that we don't know who is in it most of the time. We collar 'em once in a while—like we did you. Now, that house out yonder, we—"

The man suddenly left the knothole and returned to the others. Upon his face, dimly discerned, there was an indication that he had made an astonishing discovery. The others questioned him with their eyes, but he simply waved an arm to express his inability to speak at that spot. He led them back toward the hill, prowling carefully. At a safe distance from the barn he halted and as they grouped eagerly about him, he exploded in an intense undertone: "Why, that—that's Cap'n Sawyer they got in yonder."

"Cap'n Sawyer!" incredulously whispered the other men.

But the girl had something to ask. "How did you get out of that feed box?" He smiled. "Well, when you put us in there, we was just in a minute when we allowed it wasn't a mighty safe place, and we allowed we'd get out. And we did. We skedaddled 'round and 'round until it 'peared like we was going to get cotched, and then we flung ourselves down in the cow stalls where it's low-like—just dirt floor—and then we just naturally went a-whooping under the barn floor when the Yanks come. And we didn't know Cap'n Sawyer by his voice nohow. We heard 'im discoursing, and we allowed it was a mighty pert man, but we didn't know that it was him. No, m'm."

These three men, so recently from a situation of peril, seemed suddenly to have dropped all thought of it. They stood with sad faces looking at the barn. They seemed to be making no plans at all to reach a place of more complete safety. They were halted and stupefied by some unknown calamity.

"How do you raikon they cotch him, Sim?" one whispered mournfully.

"I don't know," replied another, in the same tone.

Another with a low snarl expressed in two words his opinion of the methods of Fate: "Oh, hell!"

The three men started then as if simultaneously stung and gazed at the young girl who stood silently near them. The man who had sworn began to make agitated apology: "Pardon, miss! 'Pon my soul I clean forgot you was by. 'Deed, and I wouldn't swear like that if I had knowed. 'Deed, I wouldn't."

The girl did not seem to hear him. She was staring at the barn. Suddenly she turned and whispered, "Who is he?"

"He's Cap'n Sawyer, m'm," they told her sorrowfully. "He's our own cap'n. He's been in command of us yere since a long time. He's got folks about yere. Raikon they cotch him while he was a-visiting."

She was still for a time and then, awed, she said, "Will they—will they hang him?"

"No, m'm. Oh, no, m'm. Don't raikon no such thing. No, m'm."

The group became absorbed in a contemplation of the barn. For a time no one moved nor spoke. At last the girl was aroused by slight sounds, and turning, she perceived that the three men who had so recently escaped from the barn were now advancing toward it.

**V.**

The girl, waiting in the darkness, expected to hear the sudden crash and uproar of a fight as soon as the three creeping men should reach the barn. She reflected in an agony upon the swift disaster that would befall any enterprise so desperate. She had an impulse to beg them to come away. The grass rustled in silken movements as she sped toward the barn.

When she arrived, however, she gazed about her bewildered. The men were gone. She searched with her eyes, trying to detect some moving thing, but she could see nothing.

Left alone again, she began to be afraid of the night. The great stretches of darkness could hide crawling dangers. From sheer desire to see a human, she was obliged to peep again at the knothole. The sentry had apparently wearied of talking. Instead, he was reflecting. The prisoner still sat on the feed box, moodily staring at the floor. The girl felt in one way that she was looking at a ghastly group in wax. She started when the old horse put down an echoing hoof. She wished the men would speak; their silence re-enforced the strange aspect. They might have been two dead men.

The girl felt impelled to look at the corner of the interior where were the cow stalls. There was no light there save the appearance of peculiar gray haze which marked the track of the dimming rays of the lantern. All else was sombre shadow. At last she saw something move there. It might have been as small as a rat, or it might have been a part of something as large as a man. At any rate, it proclaimed that something in that spot was alive. At one time she saw it plainly and at other times it vanished, because her fixture of gaze caused her occasionally to greatly tangle and blur those peculiar shadows and faint lights. At last, however, she perceived a human head. It was monstrously dishevelled and wild. It moved slowly forward until its glance could fall upon the prisoner and then upon the sentry. The wandering rays caused the eyes to glitter like silver. The girl's heart pounded so that she put her hand over it.

The sentry and the prisoner remained immovably waxen, and over in the gloom the head thrust from the floor watched them with its silver eyes.

Finally, the prisoner slipped from the feed box, and, raising his arms, yawned at great length. "Oh, well," he remarked, "you boys will get a good licking if you fool around here much longer. That's some satisfaction, anyhow, even if you did bag me. You'll get a good walloping." He reflected for a moment, and decided: "I'm sort of willing to be captured if you fellows only get a damned good licking for being so smart."

The sentry looked up and smiled a superior smile. "Licking, hey? Nixey!" He winked exasperatingly at the prisoner. "You fellows are not fast enough, my boy. Why didn't you lick us at —? and at —? and at——?" He named some of the great battles.

To this the captive officer blurted in angry astonishment, "Why, we did!"

The sentry winked again in profound irony. "Yes—I know you did. Of course. You whipped us, didn't you? Fine kind of whipping that was! Why, we—"

He suddenly ceased, smitten mute by a sound that broke the stillness of the night. It was the sharp crack of a distant shot that made wild echoes among the hills. It was instantly followed by the hoarse cry of a human voice, a far-away yell of warning, singing of surprise, peril, fear of death. A moment later there was a distant, fierce spattering of shots. The sentry and the prisoner stood facing each other, their lips apart, listening.

The orchard at that instant awoke to sudden tumult. There were the thud and scramble and scamper of feet, the mellow, swift clash of arms, men's voices in question, oath, command, hurried and unhurried, resolute and frantic. A horse sped along the road at a raging gallop. A loud voice shouted, "What is it, Ferguson?" Another voice yelled something incoherent. There was a sharp, discordant chorus of command. An uproarious volley suddenly rang from the orchard. The prisoner in gray moved from his intent, listening attitude. Instantly the eyes of the sentry blazed, and he said with a new and terrible sternness, "Stand where you are!"

The prisoner trembled in his excitement. Expressions of delight and triumph bubbled to his lips. "A surprise, by Gawd! Now—now, you'll see!"

The sentry stolidly swung his carbine to his shoulder. He sighted carefully along the barrel until it pointed at the prisoner's head, about at his nose. "Well, I've got you, anyhow. Remember that! Don't move!"

The prisoner could not keep his arms from nervously gesturing. "I won't; but—"

"And shut your mouth!"

The three comrades of the sentry flung themselves into view. "Pete—devil of a row!—can you—"

"I've got him," said the sentry calmly and without moving. It was as if the barrel of the carbine rested on piers of stone. The three comrades turned and plunged into the darkness.

In the orchard it seemed as if two gigantic animals were engaged in a mad, floundering encounter, snarling, howling in a whirling chaos of noise and motion. In the barn the prisoner and his guard faced each other in silence.

As for the girl at the knothole, the sky had fallen at the beginning of this clamour. She would not have been astonished to see the stars swinging from their abodes, and the vegetation, the barn, all blow away. It was the end of everything, the grand universal murder. When two of the three miraculous soldiers who formed the original feed-box corps emerged in detail from the hole under the beam and slid away into the darkness, she did no more than glance at them.

Suddenly she recollected the head with silver eyes. She started forward and again applied her eyes to the knothole. Even with the din resounding from the orchard, from up the road and down the road, from the heavens and from the deep earth, the central fascination was this mystic head. There, to her, was the dark god of the tragedy.

The prisoner in gray at this moment burst into a laugh that was no more than a hysterical gurgle. "Well, you can't hold that gun out forever! Pretty soon you'll have to lower it."

The sentry's voice sounded slightly muffled, for his cheek was pressed against the weapon. "I won't be tired for some time yet."

The girl saw the head slowly rise, the eyes fixed upon the sentry's face. A tall, black figure slunk across the cow stalls and vanished back of old Santo's quarters. She knew what was to come to pass. She knew this grim thing was upon a terrible mission, and that it would reappear again at the head of the little passage between Santo's stall and the wall, almost at the sentry's elbow; and yet when she saw a faint indication as of a form crouching there, a scream from an utterly new alarm almost escaped her.

The sentry's arms, after all, were not of granite. He moved restively. At last he spoke in his even, unchanging tone: "Well, I guess you'll have to climb into that feed box. Step back and lift the lid."

"Why, you don't mean—"

"Step back!"

The girl felt a cry of warning arising to her lips as she gazed at this sentry. She noted every detail of his facial expression. She saw, moreover, his mass of brown hair bunching disgracefully about his ears, his clear eyes lit now with a hard, cold light, his forehead puckered in a mighty scowl, the ring upon the third finger of the left hand. "Oh, they won't kill him! Surely they won't kill him!" The noise of the fight in the orchard was the loud music, the thunder and lightning, the rioting of the tempest which people love during the critical scene of a tragedy.

When the prisoner moved back in reluctant obedience, he faced for an instant the entrance of the little passage, and what he saw there must have been written swiftly, graphically in his eyes. And the sentry read it and knew then that he was upon the threshold of his death. In a fraction of time, certain information went from the grim thing in the passage to the prisoner, and from the prisoner to the sentry. But at that instant the black formidable figure arose, towered, and made its leap. A new shadow flashed across the floor when the blow was struck.

As for the girl at the knothole, when she returned to sense she found herself standing with clinched hands and screaming with her might.

As if her reason had again departed from her, she ran around the barn, in at the door, and flung herself sobbing beside the body of the soldier in blue.

The uproar of the fight became at last coherent, inasmuch as one party was giving shouts of supreme exultation. The firing no longer sounded in crashes; it was now expressed in spiteful crackles, the last words of the combat, spoken with feminine vindictiveness.

Presently there was a thud of flying feet. A grimy panting, red-faced mob of troopers in blue plunged into the barn, became instantly frozen to attitudes of amazement and rage, and then roared in one great chorus, "He's gone!"

The girl who knelt beside the body upon the floor turned toward them her lamenting eyes and cried: "He's not dead, is he? He can't be dead?"

They thronged forward. The sharp lieutenant who had been so particular about the feed box knelt by the side of the girl and laid his head against the chest of the prostrate soldier. "Why, no," he said, rising and looking at the man. "He's all right. Some of you boys throw some water on him."

"Are you sure?" demanded the girl, feverishly.

"Of course! He'll be better after awhile."

"Oh!" said she softly, and then looked down at the sentry. She started to arise, and the lieutenant reached down and hoisted rather awkwardly at her arm.

"Don't you worry about him. He's all right."

She turned her face with its curving lips and shining eyes once more toward the unconscious soldier upon the floor. The troopers made a lane to the door, the lieutenant bowed, the girl vanished.

"Queer," said a young officer. "Girl very clearly worst kind of rebel, and yet she falls to weeping and wailing like mad over one of her enemies. Be around in the morning with all sorts of doctoring—you see if she ain't. Queer."

The sharp lieutenant shrugged his shoulders. After reflection he shrugged his shoulders again. He said: "War changes many things; but it doesn't change everything, thank God!"

# A MYSTERY OF HEROISM

The dark uniforms of the men were so coated with dust from the incessant wrestling of the two armies that the regiment almost seemed a part of the clay bank which shielded them from the shells. On the top of the hill a battery was arguing in tremendous roars with some other guns, and to the eye of the infantry, the artillerymen, the guns, the caissons, the horses, were distinctly outlined upon the blue sky. When a piece was fired, a red streak as round as a log flashed low in the heavens, like a monstrous bolt of lightning. The men of the battery wore white duck trousers, which somehow emphasized their legs; and when they ran and crowded in little groups at the bidding of the shouting officers, it was more impressive than usual to the infantry.

Fred Collins, of A Company, was saying: "Thunder! I wisht I had a drink. Ain't there any water round here?" Then somebody yelled, "There goes th' bugler!"

As the eyes of half the regiment swept in one machinelike movement there was an instant's picture of a horse in a great convulsive leap of a death wound and a rider leaning back with a crooked arm and spread fingers before his face. On the ground was the crimson terror of an exploding shell, with fibres of flame that seemed like lances. A glittering bugle swung clear of the rider's back as fell headlong the horse and the man. In the air was an odour as from a conflagration.

Sometimes they of the infantry looked down at a fair little meadow which spread at their feet. Its long, green grass was rippling gently in a breeze. Beyond it was the gray form of a house half torn to pieces by shells and by the busy axes of soldiers who had pursued firewood. The line of an old fence was now dimly marked by long weeds and by an occasional post. A shell had blown the well-house to fragments. Little lines of gray smoke ribboning upward from some embers indicated the place where had stood the barn.

From beyond a curtain of green woods there came the sound of some stupendous scuffle, as if two animals of the size of islands were fighting. At a distance there were occasional appearances of swift-moving men, horses, batteries, flags, and, with the crashing of infantry volleys were heard, often, wild and frenzied cheers. In the midst of it all Smith and Ferguson, two privates of A Company, were engaged in a heated discussion, which involved the greatest questions of the national existence.

The battery on the hill presently engaged in a frightful duel. The white legs of the gunners scampered this way and that way, and the officers redoubled their shouts. The guns, with their demeanours of stolidity and courage, were typical of something infinitely self-possessed in this clamour of death that swirled around the hill.

One of a "swing" team was suddenly smitten quivering to the ground, and his maddened brethren dragged his torn body in their struggle to escape from this turmoil and danger. A young soldier astride one of the leaders swore and fumed in his saddle, and furiously jerked at the bridle. An officer screamed out an order so violently that his voice broke and ended the sentence in a falsetto shriek.

The leading company of the infantry regiment was somewhat exposed, and the colonel ordered it moved more fully under the shelter of the hill. There was the clank of steel against steel.

A lieutenant of the battery rode down and passed them, holding his right arm carefully in his left hand. And it was as if this arm was not at all a part of him, but belonged to another man. His sober and reflective charger went slowly. The officer's face was grimy and perspiring, and his uniform was tousled as if he had been in direct grapple with an enemy. He smiled grimly when the men stared at him. He turned his horse toward the meadow.

Collins, of A Company, said: "I wisht I had a drink. I bet there's water in that there ol' well yonder!"

"Yes; but how you goin' to git it?"

For the little meadow which intervened was now suffering a terrible onslaught of shells. Its green and beautiful calm had vanished utterly. Brown earth was being flung in monstrous handfuls. And there was a massacre of the young blades of grass. They were being torn, burned, obliterated. Some curious fortune of the battle had made this gentle little meadow the object of the red hate of the shells, and each one as it exploded seemed like an imprecation in the face of a maiden.

The wounded officer who was riding across this expanse said to himself, "Why, they couldn't shoot any harder if the whole army was massed here!"

A shell struck the gray ruins of the house, and as, after the roar, the shattered wall fell in fragments, there was a noise which resembled the flapping of shutters during a wild gale of winter. Indeed, the infantry paused in the shelter of the bank appeared as men standing upon a shore contemplating a madness of the sea. The angel of calamity had under its glance the battery upon the hill. Fewer white-legged men laboured about the guns. A shell had smitten one of the pieces, and after the flare, the smoke, the dust, the wrath of this blow were gone, it was possible to see white legs stretched horizontally upon the ground. And at that interval to the rear, where it is the business of battery horses to stand with their noses to the fight awaiting the command to drag their guns out of the destruction or into it or wheresoever these incomprehensible humans demanded with whip and spur—in this line of passive and dumb spectators, whose fluttering hearts yet would not let them forget the iron laws of man's control of them—in this rank of brute-soldiers there had been relentless and hideous carnage. From the ruck of bleeding and prostrate horses, the men of the infantry could see one animal raising its stricken body with its fore legs, and turning its nose with mystic and profound eloquence toward the sky.

Some comrades joked Collins about his thirst. "Well, if yeh want a drink so bad, why don't yeh go git it!"

"Well, I will in a minnet, if yeh don't shut up!"

A lieutenant of artillery floundered his horse straight down the hill with as great concern as if it were level ground. As he galloped past the colonel of the infantry, he threw up his hand in swift salute. "We've got to get out of that," he roared angrily. He was a black-bearded officer, and his eyes, which resembled beads, sparkled like those of an insane man. His jumping horse sped along the column of infantry.

The fat major, standing carelessly with his sword held horizontally behind him and with his legs far apart, looked after the receding horseman and laughed. "He wants to get back with orders pretty quick, or there'll be no batt'ry left," he observed.

The wise young captain of the second company hazarded to the lieutenant colonel that the enemy's infantry would probably soon attack the hill, and the lieutenant colonel snubbed him.

A private in one of the rear companies looked out over the meadow, and then turned to a companion and said, "Look there, Jim!" It was the wounded officer from the battery, who some time before had started to ride across the meadow, supporting his right arm carefully with his left hand. This man had encountered a shell apparently at a time when no one perceived him, and he could now be seen lying face downward with a stirruped foot stretched across the body of his dead horse. A leg of the charger extended slantingly upward precisely as stiff as a stake. Around this motionless pair the shells still howled.

There was a quarrel in A Company. Collins was shaking his fist in the faces of some laughing comrades. "Dern yeh! I ain't afraid t' go. If yeh say much, I will go!"

"Of course, yeh will! You'll run through that there medder, won't yeh?"

Collins said, in a terrible voice, "You see now!" At this ominous threat his comrades broke into renewed jeers.

Collins gave them a dark scowl and went to find his captain. The latter was conversing with the colonel of the regiment.

"Captain," said Collins, saluting and standing at attention—in those days all trousers bagged at the knees—"captain, I want t' get permission to go git some water from that there well over yonder!"

The colonel and the captain swung about simultaneously and stared across the meadow. The captain laughed. "You must be pretty thirsty, Collins?"

"Yes, sir, I am."

"Well—ah," said the captain. After a moment, he asked, "Can't you wait?"

"No, sir."

The colonel was watching Collins's face. "Look here, my lad," he said, in a pious sort of a voice—"look here, my lad"—Collins was not a lad—"don't you think that's taking pretty big risks for a little drink of water?"

"I dunno," said Collins uncomfortably. Some of the resentment toward his companions, which perhaps had forced him into this affair, was beginning to fade. "I dunno wether 'tis."

The colonel and the captain contemplated him for a time.

"Well," said the captain finally.

"Well," said the colonel, "if you want to go, why, go."

Collins saluted. "Much obliged t' yeh."

As he moved away the colonel called after him. "Take some of the other boys' canteens with you an' hurry back now."

"Yes, sir, I will."

The colonel and the captain looked at each other then, for it had suddenly occurred that they could not for the life of them tell whether Collins wanted to go or whether he did not.

They turned to regard Collins, and as they perceived him surrounded by gesticulating comrades, the colonel said: "Well, by thunder! I guess he's going."

Collins appeared as a man dreaming. In the midst of the questions, the advice, the warnings, all the excited talk of his company mates, he maintained a curious silence.

They were very busy in preparing him for his ordeal. When they inspected him carefully it was somewhat like the examination that grooms give a horse before a race; and they were amazed, staggered by the whole affair. Their astonishment found vent in strange repetitions.

"Are yeh sure a-goin'?" they demanded again and again.

"Certainly I am," cried Collins, at last furiously.

He strode sullenly away from them. He was swinging five or six canteens by their cords. It seemed that his cap would not remain firmly on his head, and often he reached and pulled it down over his brow.

There was a general movement in the compact column. The long animal-like thing moved slightly. Its four hundred eyes were turned upon the figure of Collins.

"Well, sir, if that ain't th' derndest thing! I never thought Fred Collins had the blood in him for that kind of business."

"What's he goin' to do, anyhow?"

"He's goin' to that well there after water."

"We ain't dyin' of thirst, are we? That's foolishness."

"Well, somebody put him up to it, an' he's doin' it."

"Say, he must be a desperate cuss."

When Collins faced the meadow and walked away from the regiment, he was vaguely conscious that a chasm, the deep valley of all prides, was suddenly between him and his comrades. It was provisional, but the provision was that he return as a victor. He had blindly been led by quaint emotions, and laid himself under an obligation to walk squarely up to the face of death.

But he was not sure that he wished to make a retraction, even if he could do so without shame. As a matter of truth, he was sure of very little. He was mainly surprised.

It seemed to him supernaturally strange that he had allowed his mind to maneuvre his body into such a situation. He understood that it might be called dramatically great.

However, he had no full appreciation of anything, excepting that he was actually conscious of being dazed. He could feel his dulled mind groping after the form and colour of this incident. He wondered why he did not feel some keen agony of fear cutting his sense like a knife. He wondered at this, because human expression had said loudly for centuries that men should feel afraid of certain things, and that all men who did not feel this fear were phenomena—heroes.

He was, then, a hero. He suffered that disappointment which we would all have if we discovered that we were ourselves capable of those deeds which we most admire in history and legend. This, then, was a hero. After all, heroes were not much.

No, it could not be true. He was not a hero. Heroes had no shames in their lives, and, as for him, he remembered borrowing fifteen dollars from a friend and promising to pay it back the next day, and then avoiding that friend for ten months. When at home his mother had aroused him for the early labour of his life on the farm, it had often been his fashion to be irritable, childish, diabolical; and his mother had died since he had come to the war.

He saw that, in this matter of the well, the canteens, the shells, he was an intruder in the land of fine deeds.

He was now about thirty paces from his comrades. The regiment had just turned its many faces toward him.

From the forest of terrific noises there suddenly emerged a little uneven line of men. They fired fiercely and rapidly at distant foliage on which appeared little puffs of white smoke. The spatter of skirmish firing was added to the thunder of the guns on the hill. The little line of men ran forward. A colour sergeant fell flat with his flag as if he had slipped on ice. There was hoarse cheering from this distant field.

Collins suddenly felt that two demon fingers were pressed into his ears. He could see nothing but flying arrows, flaming red. He lurched from the shock of this explosion, but he made a mad rush for the house, which he viewed as a man submerged to the neck in a boiling surf might view the shore. In the air, little pieces of shell howled and the earthquake explosions drove him insane with the menace of their roar. As he ran the canteens knocked together with a rhythmical tinkling.

As he neared the house, each detail of the scene became vivid to him. He was aware of some bricks of the vanished chimney lying on the sod. There was a door which hung by one hinge.

Rifle bullets called forth by the insistent skirmishers came from the far-off bank of foliage. They mingled with the shells and the pieces of shells until the air was torn in all directions by hootings, yells, howls. The sky was full of fiends who directed all their wild rage at his head.

When he came to the well, he flung himself face downward and peered into its darkness. There were furtive silver glintings some feet from the surface. He grabbed one of the canteens and, unfastening its cap, swung it down by the cord. The water flowed slowly in with an indolent gurgle.

And now as he lay with his face turned away he was suddenly smitten with the terror. It came upon his heart like the grasp of claws. All the power faded from his muscles. For an instant he was no more than a dead man.

The canteen filled with a maddening slowness, in the manner of all bottles. Presently he recovered his strength and addressed a screaming oath to it. He leaned over until it seemed as if he intended to try to push water into it with his hands. His eyes as he gazed down into the well shone like two pieces of metal and in their expression was a great appeal and a great curse. The stupid water derided him.

There was the blaring thunder of a shell. Crimson light shone through the swift-boiling smoke and made a pink reflection on part of the wall of the well. Collins jerked out his arm and canteen with the same motion that a man would use in withdrawing his head from a furnace.

He scrambled erect and glared and hesitated. On the ground near him lay the old well bucket, with a length of rusty chain. He lowered it swiftly into the well. The bucket struck the water and then, turning lazily over, sank. When, with hand reaching tremblingly over hand, he hauled it out, it knocked often against the walls of the well and spilled some of its contents.

In running with a filled bucket, a man can adopt but one kind of gait. So through this terrible field over which screamed practical angels of death Collins ran in the manner of a farmer chased out of a dairy by a bull.

His face went staring white with anticipation—anticipation of a blow that would whirl him around and down. He would fall as he had seen other men fall, the life knocked out of them so suddenly that their knees were no more quick to touch the ground than their heads. He saw the long blue line of the regiment, but his comrades were standing looking at him from the edge of an impossible star. He was aware of some deep wheel ruts and hoofprints in the sod beneath his feet.

The artillery officer who had fallen in this meadow had been making groans in the teeth of the tempest of sound. These futile cries, wrenched from him by his agony, were heard only by shells, bullets. When wild-eyed Collins came running, this officer raised himself. His face contorted and blanched from pain, he was about to utter some great beseeching cry. But suddenly his face straightened and he called: "Say, young man, give me a drink of water, will you?"

Collins had no room amid his emotions for surprise. He was mad from the threats of destruction.

"I can't!" he screamed, and in his reply was a full description of his quaking apprehension. His cap was gone and his hair was riotous. His clothes made it appear that he had been dragged over the ground by the heels. He ran on.

The officer's head sank down and one elbow crooked. His foot in its brass-bound stirrup still stretched over the body of his horse and the other leg was under the steed.

But Collins turned. He came dashing back. His face had now turned gray and in his eyes was all terror. "Here it is! here it is!"

The officer was as a man gone in drink. His arm bent like a twig. His head drooped as if his neck were of willow. He was sinking to the ground, to lie face downward.

Collins grabbed him by the shoulder. "Here it is. Here's your drink. Turn over. Turn over, man, for God's sake!"

With Collins hauling at his shoulder, the officer twisted his body and fell with his face turned toward that region where lived the unspeakable noises of the swirling missiles. There was the faintest shadow of a smile on his lips as he looked at Collins. He gave a sigh, a little primitive breath like that from a child.

Collins tried to hold the bucket steadily, but his shaking hands caused the water to splash all over the face of the dying man. Then he jerked it away and ran on.

The regiment gave him a welcoming roar. The grimed faces were wrinkled in laughter.

His captain waved the bucket away. "Give it to the men!"

The two genial, skylarking young lieutenants were the first to gain possession of it. They played over it in their fashion.

When one tried to drink the other teasingly knocked his elbow. "Don't, Billie! You'll make me spill it," said the one. The other laughed.

Suddenly there was an oath, the thud of wood on the ground, and a swift murmur of astonishment among the ranks. The two lieutenants glared at each other. The bucket lay on the ground empty.

# AN INDIANA CAMPAIGN

## I.

When the able-bodied citizens of the village formed a company and marched away to the war, Major Tom Boldin assumed in a manner the burden of the village cares. Everybody ran to him when they felt obliged to discuss their affairs. The sorrows of the town were dragged before him. His little bench at the sunny side of Migglesville tavern became a sort of an open court where people came to speak resentfully of their grievances. He accepted his position and struggled manfully under the load. It behooved him, as a man who had seen the sky red over the quaint, low cities of Mexico, and the compact Northern bayonets gleaming on the narrow roads.

One warm summer day the major sat asleep on his little bench. There was a lull in the tempest of discussion which usually enveloped him. His cane, by use of which he could make the most tremendous and impressive gestures, reposed beside him. His hat lay upon the bench, and his old bald head had swung far forward until his nose actually touched the first button of his waistcoat.

The sparrows wrangled desperately in the road, defying perspiration. Once a team went jangling and creaking past, raising a yellow blur of dust before the soft tones of the field and sky. In the long grass of the meadow across the road the insects chirped and clacked eternally.

Suddenly a frouzy-headed boy appeared in the roadway, his bare feet pattering rapidly. He was extremely excited. He gave a shrill whoop as he discovered the sleeping major and rushed toward him. He created a terrific panic among some chickens who had been scratching intently near the major's feet. They clamoured in an insanity of fear, and rushed hither and thither seeking a way of escape, whereas in reality all ways lay plainly open to them.

This tumult caused the major to arouse with a sudden little jump of amazement and apprehension. He rubbed his eyes and gazed about him. Meanwhile, some clever chicken had discovered a passage to safety and led the flock into the garden, where they squawked in sustained alarm.

Panting from his run and choked with terror, the little boy stood before the major, struggling with a tale that was ever upon the tip of his tongue.

"Major—now—major—"

The old man, roused from a delicious slumber, glared impatiently at the little boy. "Come, come! What's th' matter with yeh?" he demanded. "What's th' matter? Don't stand there shaking! Speak up!"

"Lots is th' matter!" the little boy shouted valiantly, with a courage born of the importance of his tale. "My ma's chickens 'uz all stole, an'—now—he's over in th' woods!"

"Who is? Who is over in the woods? Go ahead!"

"Now—th' rebel is!"

"What?" roared the major.

"Th' rebel!" cried the little boy, with the last of his breath.

The major pounced from his bench in tempestuous excitement. He seized the little boy by the collar and gave him a great jerk. "Where? Are yeh sure? Who saw 'im? How long ago? Where is he now? Did you see 'im?"

The little boy, frightened at the major's fury, began to sob. After a moment he managed to stammer: "He—now—he's in the woods. I saw 'im. He looks uglier'n anythin'."

The major released his hold upon the boy, and, pausing for a time, indulged in a glorious dream. Then he said: "By thunder! we'll ketch th' cuss. You wait here," he told the boy, "an' don't say a word t' anybody. Do yeh hear?"

The boy, still weeping, nodded, and the major hurriedly entered the inn. He took down from its pegs an awkward, smoothbore rifle and carefully examined the enormous percussion cap that was fitted over the nipple. Mistrusting the cap, he removed it and replaced it with a new one. He scrutinized the gun keenly, as if he could judge in this manner of the condition of the load. All his movements were deliberate and deadly.

When he arrived upon the porch of the tavern he beheld the yard filled with people. Peter Witheby, sooty-faced and grinning, was in the van. He looked at the major. "Well?" he said.

"Well?" returned the major, bridling.

"Well, what's 'che got?" said old Peter.

"'Got?' Got a rebel over in th' woods!" roared the major.

At this sentence the women and boys, who had gathered eagerly about him, gave vent to startled cries. The women had come from adjacent houses, but the little boys represented the entire village. They had miraculously heard the first whisper of rumour, and they performed wonders in getting to the spot. They clustered around the important figure of the major and gazed in silent awe. The women, however, burst forth. At the word "rebel," which represented to them all terrible things, they deluged the major with questions which were obviously unanswerable.

He shook them off with violent impatience. Meanwhile Peter Witheby was trying to force exasperating interrogations through the tumult to the major's ears. "What? No! Yes! How d' I know?" the maddened veteran snarled as he struggled with his friends. "No! Yes! What? How in thunder d' I know?" Upon the steps of the tavern the landlady sat, weeping forlornly.

At last the major burst through the crowd, and went to the roadway. There, as they all streamed after him, he turned and faced them. "Now, look a' here, I don't know any more about this than you do," he told them forcibly. "All that I know is that there's a rebel over in Smith's woods, an' all I know is that I'm agoin' after 'im."

"But hol' on a minnet," said old Peter. "How do yeh know he's a rebel?"

"I know he is!" cried the major. "Don't yeh think I know what a rebel is?"

Then, with a gesture of disdain at the babbling crowd, he marched determinedly away, his rifle held in the hollow of his arm. At this heroic moment a new clamour arose, half admiration, half dismay. Old Peter hobbled after the major, continually repeating, "Hol' on a minnet."

The little boy who had given the alarm was the centre of a throng of lads who gazed with envy and awe, discovering in him a new quality. He held forth to them eloquently. The women stared after the figure of the major and old Peter, his pursuer. Jerozel Bronson, a half-witted lad who comprehended nothing save an occasional genial word, leaned against the fence and grinned like a skull. The major and the pursuer passed out of view around the turn in the road where the great maples lazily shook the dust that lay on their leaves.

For a moment the little group of women listened intently as if they expected to hear a sudden shot and cries from the distance. They looked at each other, their lips a little ways apart. The trees sighed softly in the heat of the summer sun. The insects in the meadow continued their monotonous humming, and, somewhere, a hen had been stricken with fear and was cackling loudly.

Finally, Mrs. Goodwin said, "Well, I'm goin' up to th' turn a' th' road, anyhow." Mrs. Willets and Mrs. Joe Petersen, her particular friends, cried out at this temerity, but she said, "Well, I'm goin', anyhow."

She called Bronson. "Come on, Jerozel. You're a man, an' if he should chase us, why, you mus' pitch inteh 'im. Hey?"

Bronson always obeyed everybody. He grinned an assent, and went with her down the road.

A little boy attempted to follow them, but a shrill scream from his mother made him halt.

The remaining women stood motionless, their eyes fixed upon Mrs. Goodwin and Jerozel. Then at last one gave a laugh of triumph at her conquest of caution and fear, and cried, "Well, I'm goin' too!"

Another instantly said, "So am I." There began a general movement. Some of the little boys had already ventured a hundred feet away from the main body, and at this unanimous advance they spread out ahead in little groups. Some recounted terrible stories of rebel ferocity. Their eyes were large with excitement. The whole thing with its possible dangers had for them a delicious element. Johnnie Peterson, who could whip any boy present, explained what he would do in case the enemy should happen to pounce out at him.

The familiar scene suddenly assumed a new aspect. The field of corn which met the road upon the left was no longer a mere field of corn. It was a darkly mystic place whose recesses could contain all manner of dangers. The long green leaves, waving in the breeze, rustled from the passing of men. In the song of the insects there were now omens, threats.

There was a warning in the enamel blue of the sky, in the stretch of yellow road, in the very atmosphere. Above the tops of the corn loomed the distant foliage of Smith's woods, curtaining the silent action of a tragedy whose horrors they imagined.

The women and the little boys came to a halt, overwhelmed by the impressiveness of the landscape. They waited silently.

Mrs. Goodwin suddenly said, "I'm goin' back." The others, who all wished to return, cried at once disdainfully:

"Well, go back, if yeh want to!"

A cricket at the roadside exploded suddenly in his shrill song, and a woman who had been standing near shrieked in startled terror. An electric movement went through the group of women. They jumped and gave vent to sudden screams. With the fears still upon their agitated faces, they turned to berate the one who had shrieked. "My! what a goose you are, Sallie! Why, it took my breath away. Goodness sakes, don't holler like that again!"

## II.

"Hol' on a minnet!" Peter Witheby was crying to the major, as the latter, full of the importance and dignity of his position as protector of Migglesville, paced forward swiftly. The veteran already felt upon his brow a wreath formed of the flowers of gratitude, and as he strode he was absorbed in planning a calm and self-contained manner of wearing it. "Hol' on a minnet!" piped old Peter in the rear.

At last the major, aroused from his dream of triumph, turned about wrathfully. "Well, what?"

"Now, look a' here," said Peter. "What 'che goin' t' do?"

The major, with a gesture of supreme exasperation, wheeled again and went on. When he arrived at the cornfield he halted and waited for Peter. He had suddenly felt that indefinable menace in the landscape.

"Well?" demanded Peter, panting.

The major's eyes wavered a trifle. "Well," he repeated—"well, I'm goin' in there an' bring out that there rebel."

They both paused and studied the gently swaying masses of corn, and behind them the looming woods, sinister with possible secrets.

"Well," said old Peter.

The major moved uneasily and put his hand to his brow. Peter waited in obvious expectation.

The major crossed through the grass at the roadside and climbed the fence. He put both legs over the topmost rail and then sat perched there, facing the woods. Once he turned his head and asked, "What?"

"I hain't said anythin'," answered Peter.

The major clambered down from the fence and went slowly into the corn, his gun held in readiness. Peter stood in the road.

Presently the major returned and said, in a cautious whisper, "If yeh hear anythin', you come a-runnin', will yeh?"

"Well, I hain't got no gun nor nuthin'," said Peter, in the same low tone; "what good 'ud I do?"

"Well, yeh might come along with me an' watch," said the major. "Four eyes is better'n two."

"If I had a gun—" began Peter.

"Oh, yeh don't need no gun," interrupted the major, waving his hand. "All I'm afraid of is that I won't find 'im. My eyes ain't so good as they was."

"Well—"

"Come along," whispered the major. "Yeh hain't afraid, are yeh?"

"No, but—"

"Well, come along, then. What's th' matter with yeh?"

Peter climbed the fence. He paused on the top rail and took a prolonged stare at the inscrutable woods. When he joined the major in the cornfield he said, with a touch of anger:

"Well, you got the gun. Remember that. If he comes for me, I hain't got a blame thing!"

"Shucks!" answered the major. "He ain't agoin' t' come for yeh."

The two then began a wary journey through the corn. One by one the long aisles between the rows appeared. As they glanced along each of them it seemed as if some gruesome thing had just previously vacated it. Old Peter halted once and whispered: "Say, look a' here; supposin'—supposin'—"

"Supposin' what?" demanded the major.

"Supposin'—" said Peter. "Well, remember you got th' gun, an' I hain't got anythin'."

"Thunder!" said the major.

When they got to where the stalks were very short because of the shade cast by the trees of the wood, they halted again. The leaves were gently swishing in the breeze. Before them stretched the mystic green wall of the forest, and there seemed to be in it eyes which followed each of their movements.

Peter at last said, "I don't believe there's anybody in there."

"Yes, there is, too," said the major. "I'll bet anythin' he's in there."

"How d' yeh know?" asked Peter. "I'll bet he ain't within a mile o' here."

The major suddenly ejaculated, "Listen!"

They bent forward, scarce breathing, their mouths agape, their eyes glinting. Finally, the major turned his head. "Did yeh hear that?" he said hoarsely.

"No," said Peter, in a low voice. "What was it?"

The major listened for a moment. Then he turned again. "I thought I heered somebody holler!" he explained cautiously.

They both bent forward and listened once more. Peter in the intentness of his attitude lost his balance and was obliged to lift his foot hastily and with noise. "S-s-sh!" hissed the major.

After a minute Peter spoke quite loudly, "Oh, shucks! I don't believe yeh heered anythin'."

The major made a frantic downward gesture with his hand. "Shet up, will yeh!" he said, in an angry undertone.

Peter became silent for a moment, but presently he said again, "Oh, yeh didn't hear anythin'."

The major turned to glare at his companion in despair and wrath.

"What's th' matter with yeh? Can't yeh shet up?"

"Oh, this here ain't no use. If you're goin' in after 'im, why don't yeh go in after 'im?"

"Well, gimme time, can't yeh?" said the major, in a growl. And, as if to add more to this reproach, he climbed the fence that compassed the woods, looking resentfully back at his companion.

"Well," said Peter, when the major paused.

The major stepped down upon the thick carpet of brown leaves that stretched under the trees. He turned then to whisper, "You wait here, will yeh?" His face was red with determination.

"Well, hol' on a minnet!" said Peter. "You—I—we'd better—"

"No," said the major. "You wait here."

He went stealthily into the thickets. Peter watched him until he grew to be a vague, slow-moving shadow. From time to time he could hear the leaves crackle and twigs snap under the major's awkward tread. Peter, intent, breathless, waited for the peal of sudden tragedy. Finally, the woods grew silent in a solemn and impressive hush that caused Peter to feel the thumping of his heart. He began to look about him to make sure that nothing should spring upon him from the sombre shadows. He scrutinized this cool gloom before him, and at times he thought he could perceive the moving of swift silent shapes. He concluded that he had better go back and try to muster some assistance to the major.

As Peter came through the corn, the women in the road caught sight of the glittering figure and screamed. Many of them began to run. The little boys, with all their valour, scurried away in clouds. Mrs. Joe Peterson, however, cast a glance over her shoulders as she, with her skirts gathered up, was running as best she could. She instantly stopped and, in tones of deepest scorn, called out to the others, "Why, it's on'y Pete Witheby!" They came faltering back then, those who had been naturally swiftest in the race avoiding the eyes of those whose limbs had enabled them to flee a short distance.

Peter came rapidly, appreciating the glances of vivid interest in the eyes of the women. To their lightning-like questions, which hit all sides of the episode, he opposed a new tranquillity gained from his sudden ascent in importance. He made no answer to their clamour. When he had reached the top of the fence, he called out commandingly: "Here you, Johnnie, you and George, run an' git my gun! It's hangin' on th' pegs over th' bench in th' shop."

At this terrible sentence, a shuddering cry broke from the women. The boys named sped down the road, accompanied by a retinue of envious companions.

Peter swung his legs over the rail and faced the woods again. He twisted his head once to say: "Keep still, can't yeh? Quit scufflin' aroun'!" They could see by his manner that this was a supreme moment. The group became motionless and still. Later, Peter turned to say, "S-s-sh!" to a restless boy, and the air with which he said it smote them all with awe.

The little boys who had gone after the gun came pattering along hurriedly, the weapon borne in the midst of them. Each was anxious to share in the honour. The one who had been delegated to bring it was bullying and directing his comrades.

Peter said, "S-s-sh!" He took the gun and poised it in readiness to sweep the cornfield. He scowled at the boys and whispered angrily: "Why didn't yeh bring th' powder horn an' th' thing with th' bullets in? I told yeh t' bring 'em. I'll send somebody else next time."

"Yeh didn't tell us!" cried the two boys shrilly.

"S-s-sh! Quit yeh noise," said Peter, with a violent gesture.

However, this reproof enabled other boys to recover that peace of mind which they had lost when seeing their friends loaded with honours.

The women had cautiously approached the fence and, from time to time, whispered feverish questions; but Peter repulsed them savagely, with an air of being infinitely bothered by their interference in his intent watch. They were forced to listen again in silence to the weird and prophetic chanting of the insects and the mystic silken rustling of the corn.

At last the thud of hurrying feet in the soft soil of the field came to their ears. A dark form sped toward them. A wave of a mighty fear swept over the group, and the screams of the women came hoarsely from their choked throats. Peter swung madly from his perch, and turned to use the fence as a rampart.

But it was the major. His face was inflamed and his eyes were glaring. He clutched his rifle by the middle and swung it wildly. He was bounding at a great speed for his fat, short body.

"It's all right! it's all right!" he began to yell, some distance away. "It's all right! It's on'y ol' Milt' Jacoby!"

When he arrived at the top of the fence, he paused and mopped his brow.

"What?" they thundered, in an agony of sudden unreasoning disappointment.

Mrs. Joe Petersen, who was a distant connection of Milton Jacoby, thought to forestall any damage to her social position by saying at once disdainfully, "Drunk, I s'pose!"

"Yep," said the major, still on the fence, and mopped his brow. "Drunk as a fool. Thunder! I was surprised. I—I—thought it was a rebel, sure."

The thoughts of all these women wavered for a time. They were at a loss for precise expression of their emotion. At last, however, they hurled this superior sentence at the major:

"Well, yeh might have known."

# A GRAY SLEEVE

## I.

"It looks as if it might rain this afternoon," remarked the lieutenant of artillery.

"So it does," the infantry captain assented. He glanced casually at the sky. When his eyes had lowered to the green-shadowed landscape before him, he said fretfully: "I wish those fellows out yonder would quit pelting at us. They've been at it since noon."

At the edge of a grove of maples, across wide fields, there occasionally appeared little puffs of smoke of a dull hue in this gloom of sky which expressed an impending rain. The long wave of blue and steel in the field moved uneasily at the eternal barking of the far-away sharpshooters, and the men, leaning upon their rifles, stared at the grove of maples. Once a private turned to borrow some tobacco from a comrade in the rear rank, but, with his hand still stretched out, he continued to twist his head and glance at the distant trees. He was afraid the enemy would shoot him at a time when he was not looking.

Suddenly the artillery officer said, "See what's coming!"

Along the rear of the brigade of infantry a column of cavalry was sweeping at a hard gallop. A lieutenant, riding some yards to the right of the column, bawled furiously at the four troopers just at the rear of the colours. They had lost distance and made a little gap, but at the shouts of the lieutenant they urged their horses forward. The bugler, careering along behind the captain of the troop, fought and tugged like a wrestler to keep his frantic animal from bolting far ahead of the column.

On the springy turf the innumerable hoofs thundered in a swift storm of sound. In the brown faces of the troopers their eyes were set like bits of flashing steel.

The long line of the infantry regiments standing at ease underwent a sudden movement at the rush of the passing squadron. The foot soldiers turned their heads to gaze at the torrent of horses and men.

The yellow folds of the flag fluttered back in silken, shuddering waves as if it were a reluctant thing. Occasionally a giant spring of a charger would rear the firm and sturdy figure of a soldier suddenly head and shoulders above his comrades. Over the noise of the scudding hoofs could be heard the creaking of leather trappings, the jingle and clank of steel, and the tense, low-toned commands or appeals of the men to their horses. And the horses were mad with the headlong sweep of this movement. Powerful under jaws bent back and straightened so that the bits were clamped as rigidly as vices upon the teeth, and glistening necks arched in desperate resistance to the hands at the bridles. Swinging their heads in rage at the granite laws of their lives, which compelled even their angers and their ardours to chosen directions and chosen faces, their flight was as a flight of harnessed demons.

The captain's bay kept its pace at the head of the squadron with the lithe bounds of a thoroughbred, and this horse was proud as a chief at the roaring trample of his fellows behind him. The captain's glance was calmly upon the grove of maples whence the sharpshooters of the enemy had been picking at the blue line. He seemed to be reflecting. He stolidly rose and fell with the plunges of his horse in all the indifference of a deacon's figure seated plumply in church. And it occurred to many of the watching infantry to wonder why this officer could remain imperturbable and reflective when his squadron was thundering and swarming behind him like the rushing of a flood.

The column swung in a sabre-curve toward a break in a fence, and dashed into a roadway. Once a little plank bridge was encountered, and the sound of the hoofs upon it was like the long roll of many drums. An old captain in the infantry turned to his first lieutenant and made a remark which was a compound of bitter disparagement of cavalry in general and soldiery admiration of this particular troop.

Suddenly the bugle sounded, and the column halted with a jolting upheaval amid sharp, brief cries. A moment later the men had tumbled from their horses, and, carbines in hand, were running in a swarm toward the grove of maples. In the road one of every four of the troopers was standing with braced legs, and pulling and hauling at the bridles of four frenzied horses.

The captain was running awkwardly in his boots. He held his sabre low so that the point often threatened to catch in the turf. His yellow hair ruffled out from under his faded cap. "Go in hard now!" he roared, in a voice of hoarse fury. His face was violently red.

The troopers threw themselves upon the grove like wolves upon a great animal. Along the whole front of woods there was the dry, crackling of musketry, with bitter, swift flashes and smoke that writhed like stung phantoms. The troopers yelled shrilly and spanged bullets low into the foliage.

For a moment, when near the woods, the line almost halted. The men struggled and fought for a time like swimmers encountering a powerful current. Then with a supreme effort they went on again. They dashed madly at the grove, whose foliage from the high light of the field was as inscrutable as a wall.

Then suddenly each detail of the calm trees became apparent, and with a few more frantic leaps the men were in the cool gloom of the woods. There was a heavy odour as from burned paper. Wisps of gray smoke wound upward. The men halted and, grimy, perspiring, and puffing, they searched the recesses of the woods with eager, fierce glances. Figures could be seen flitting afar off. A dozen carbines rattled at them in an angry volley.

During this pause the captain strode along the line, his face lit with a broad smile of contentment. "When he sends this crowd to do anything, I guess he'll find we do it pretty sharp," he said to the grinning lieutenant.

"Say, they didn't stand that rush a minute, did they?" said the subaltern. Both officers were profoundly dusty in their uniforms, and their faces were soiled like those of two urchins.

Out in the grass behind them were three tumbled and silent forms.

Presently the line moved forward again. The men went from tree to tree like hunters stalking game. Some at the left of the line fired occasionally, and those at the right gazed curiously in that direction. The men still breathed heavily from their scramble across the field.

Of a sudden a trooper halted and said: "Hello! there's a house!" Every one paused. The men turned to look at their leader.

The captain stretched his neck and swung his head from side to side. "By George, it is a house!" he said.

Through the wealth of leaves there vaguely loomed the form of a large, white house. These troopers, brown-faced from many days of campaigning, each feature of them telling of their placid confidence and courage, were stopped abruptly by the appearance of this house. There was some subtle suggestion—some tale of an unknown thing—which watched them from they knew not what part of it.

A rail fence girded a wide lawn of tangled grass. Seven pines stood along a drive-way which led from two distant posts of a vanished gate. The blue-clothed troopers moved forward until they stood at the fence peering over it.

The captain put one hand on the top rail and seemed to be about to climb the fence, when suddenly he hesitated, and said in a low voice, "Watson, what do you think of it?"

The lieutenant stared at the house. "Derned if I know!" he replied.

The captain pondered. It happened that the whole company had turned a gaze of profound awe and doubt upon this edifice which confronted them. The men were very silent.

At last the captain swore and said: "We are certainly a pack of fools. Derned old deserted house halting a company of Union cavalry, and making us gape like babies!"

"Yes, but there's something—something—" insisted the subaltern in a half stammer.

"Well, if there's 'something—something' in there, I'll get it out," said the captain. "Send Sharpe clean around to the other side with about twelve men, so we will sure bag your 'something—something,' and I'll take a few of the boys and find out what's in the damned old thing!"

He chose the nearest eight men for his "storming party," as the lieutenant called it. After he had waited some minutes for the others to get into position, he said "Come ahead" to his eight men, and climbed the fence.

The brighter light of the tangled lawn made him suddenly feel tremendously apparent, and he wondered if there could be some mystic thing in the house which was regarding this approach. His men trudged silently at his back. They stared at the windows and lost themselves in deep speculations as to the probability of there being, perhaps, eyes behind the blinds—malignant eyes, piercing eyes.

Suddenly a corporal in the party gave vent to a startled exclamation, and half threw his carbine into position. The captain turned quickly, and the corporal said: "I saw an arm move the blinds. An arm with a gray sleeve!"

"Don't be a fool, Jones, now!" said the captain sharply.

"I swear t'—" began the corporal, but the captain silenced him.

When they arrived at the front of the house, the troopers paused, while the captain went softly up the front steps. He stood before the large front door and studied it. Some crickets chirped in the long grass, and the nearest pine could be heard in its endless sighs. One of the privates moved uneasily, and his foot crunched the gravel. Suddenly the captain swore angrily and kicked the door with a loud crash. It flew open.

## II.

The bright lights of the day flashed into the old house when the captain angrily kicked open the door. He was aware of a wide hallway carpeted with matting and extending deep into the dwelling. There was also an old walnut hatrack and a little marble-topped table with a vase and two books upon it. Farther back was a great, venerable fireplace containing dreary ashes.

But directly in front of the captain was a young girl. The flying open of the door had obviously been an utter astonishment to her, and she remained transfixed there in the middle of the floor, staring at the captain with wide eyes.

She was like a child caught at the time of a raid upon the cake. She wavered to and fro upon her feet, and held her hands behind her. There were two little points of terror in her eyes, as she gazed up at the young captain in dusty blue, with his reddish, bronze complexion, his yellow hair, his bright sabre held threateningly.

These two remained motionless and silent, simply staring at each other for some moments.

The captain felt his rage fade out of him and leave his mind limp. He had been violently angry, because this house had made him feel hesitant, wary. He did not like to be wary. He liked to feel confident, sure. So he had kicked the door open, and had been prepared to march in like a soldier of wrath.

But now he began, for one thing, to wonder if his uniform was so dusty and old in appearance. Moreover, he had a feeling that his face was covered with a compound of dust, grime, and perspiration. He took a step forward and said, "I didn't mean to frighten you." But his voice was coarse from his battle-howling. It seemed to him to have hempen fibres in it.

The girl's breath came in little, quick gasps, and she looked at him as she would have looked at a serpent.

"I didn't mean to frighten you," he said again.

The girl, still with her hands behind her, began to back away.

"Is there any one else in the house?" he went on, while slowly following her. "I don't wish to disturb you, but we had a fight with some rebel skirmishers in the woods, and I thought maybe some of them might have come in here. In fact, I was pretty sure of it. Are there any of them here?"

The girl looked at him and said, "No!" He wondered why extreme agitation made the eyes of some women so limpid and bright.

"Who is here besides yourself?"

By this time his pursuit had driven her to the end of the hall, and she remained there with her back to the wall and her hands still behind her. When she answered this question, she did not look at him but down at the floor. She cleared her voice and then said, "There is no one here."

"No one?"

She lifted her eyes to him in that appeal that the human being must make even to falling trees, crashing bowlders, the sea in a storm, and said, "No, no, there is no one here." He could plainly see her tremble.

Of a sudden he bethought him that she continually kept her hands behindher. As he recalled her air when first discovered, he remembered she appeared precisely as a child detected at one of the crimes of childhood. Moreover, she had always backed away from him. He thought now that she was concealing something which was an evidence of the presence of the enemy in the house.

"What are you holding behind you?" he said suddenly.

She gave a little quick moan, as if some grim hand had throttled her.

"What are you holding behind you?"

"Oh, nothing—please. I am not holding anything behind me; indeed I'm not."

"Very well. Hold your hands out in front of you, then."

"Oh, indeed, I'm not holding anything behind me. Indeed, I'm not."

"Well," he began. Then he paused, and remained for a moment dubious. Finally, he laughed. "Well, I shall have my men search the house, anyhow. I'm sorry to trouble you, but I feel sure that there is some one here whom we want." He turned to the corporal, who with the other men was gaping quietly in at the door, and said, "Jones, go through the house."

As for himself, he remained planted in front of the girl, for she evidently did not dare to move and allow him to see what she held so carefully behind her back. So she was his prisoner.

The men rummaged around on the ground floor of the house. Sometimes the captain called to them, "Try that closet," "Is there any cellar?" But they found no one, and at last they went trooping toward the stairs which led to the second floor.

But at this movement on the part of the men the girl uttered a cry—a cry of such fright and appeal that the men paused. "Oh, don't go up there! Please don't go up there!—ple—ease! There is no one there! Indeed—indeed there is not! Oh, ple—ease!"

"Go on, Jones," said the captain calmly.

The obedient corporal made a preliminary step, and the girl bounded toward the stairs with another cry.

As she passed him, the captain caught sight of that which she had concealed behind her back, and which she had forgotten in this supreme moment. It was a pistol.

She ran to the first step, and standing there, faced the men, one hand extended with perpendicular palm, and the other holding the pistol at her side. "Oh, please, don't go up there! Nobody is there—indeed, there is not! P-l-e-a-s-e!" Then suddenly she sank swiftly down upon the step, and, huddling forlornly, began to weep in the agony and with the convulsive tremors of an infant. The pistol fell from her fingers and rattled down to the floor.

The astonished troopers looked at their astonished captain. There was a short silence.

Finally, the captain stooped and picked up the pistol. It was a heavy weapon of the army pattern. He ascertained that it was empty.

He leaned toward the shaking girl, and said gently, "Will you tell me what you were going to do with this pistol?"

He had to repeat the question a number of times, but at last a muffled voice said, "Nothing."

"Nothing!" He insisted quietly upon a further answer. At the tender tones of the captain's voice, the phlegmatic corporal turned and winked gravely at the man next to him.

"Won't you tell me?"

The girl shook her head.

"Please tell me!"

The silent privates were moving their feet uneasily and wondering how long they were to wait.

The captain said, "Please won't you tell me?"

Then this girl's voice began in stricken tones half coherent, and amid violent sobbing: "It was grandpa's. He—he—he said he was going to shoot anybody who came in here—he didn't care if there were thousands of 'em. And—and I know he would, and I was afraid they'd kill him. And so—and—so I stole away his pistol— and I was going to hide it when you—you—you kicked open the door."

The men straightened up and looked at each other. The girl began to weep again.

The captain mopped his brow. He peered down at the girl. He mopped his brow again. Suddenly he said, "Ah, don't cry like that."

He moved restlessly and looked down at his boots. He mopped his brow again.

Then he gripped the corporal by the arm and dragged him some yards back from the others. "Jones," he said, in an intensely earnest voice, "will you tell me what in the devil I am going to do?"

The corporal's countenance became illuminated with satisfaction at being thus requested to advise his superior officer. He adopted an air of great thought, and finally said: "Well, of course, the feller with the gray sleeve must be upstairs, and we must get past the girl and up there somehow. Suppose I take her by the arm and lead her—"

"What!" interrupted the captain from between his clinched teeth. As he turned away from the corporal, he said fiercely over his shoulder, "You touch that girl and I'll split your skull!"

<h2 style="text-align:center">III.</h2>

The corporal looked after his captain with an expression of mingled amazement, grief, and philosophy. He seemed to be saying to himself that there unfortunately were times, after all, when one could not rely upon the most reliable of men. When he returned to the group he found the captain bending over the girl and saying, "Why is it that you don't want us to search upstairs?"

The girl's head was buried in her crossed arms. Locks of her hair had escaped from their fastenings and these fell upon her shoulder.

"Won't you tell me?"

The corporal here winked again at the man next to him.

"Because," the girl moaned—"because—there isn't anybody up there."

The captain at last said timidly, "Well, I'm afraid—I'm afraid we'll have to—"

The girl sprang to her feet again, and implored him with her hands. She looked deep into his eyes with her glance, which was at this time like that of the fawn when it says to the hunter, "Have mercy upon me!"

These two stood regarding each other. The captain's foot was on the bottom step, but he seemed to be shrinking. He wore an air of being deeply wretched and ashamed. There was a silence.

Suddenly the corporal said in a quick, low tone, "Look out, captain!"

All turned their eyes swiftly toward the head of the stairs. There had appeared there a youth in a gray uniform. He stood looking coolly down at them. No word was said by the troopers. The girl gave vent to a little wail of desolation, "O Harry!"

He began slowly to descend the stairs. His right arm was in a white sling, and there were some fresh blood stains upon the cloth. His face was rigid and deathly pale, but his eyes flashed like lights. The girl was again moaning in an utterly dreary fashion, as the youth came slowly down toward the silent men in blue.

Six steps from the bottom of the flight he halted and said, "I reckon it's me you're looking for."

The troopers had crowded forward a trifle and, posed in lithe, nervous attitudes, were watching him like cats. The captain remained unmoved. At the youth's question he merely nodded his head and said, "Yes."

The young man in gray looked down at the girl, and then, in the same even tone which now, however, seemed to vibrate with suppressed fury, he said, "And is that any reason why you should insult my sister?"

At this sentence, the girl intervened, desperately, between the young man in gray and the officer in blue. "Oh, don't, Harry, don't! He was good to me! He was good to me, Harry—indeed he was!"

The youth came on in his quiet, erect fashion until the girl could have touched either of the men with her hand, for the captain still remained with his foot upon the first step. She continually repeated: "O Harry! O Harry!"

The youth in gray maneuvred to glare into the captain's face, first over one shoulder of the girl and then over the other. In a voice that rang like metal, he said: "You are armed and unwounded, while I have no weapons and am wounded; but—"

The captain had stepped back and sheathed his sabre. The eyes of these two men were gleaming fire, but otherwise the captain's countenance was imperturbable. He said: "You are mistaken. You have no reason to—"

"You lie!"

All save the captain and the youth in gray started in an electric movement. These two words crackled in the air like shattered glass. There was a breathless silence.

The captain cleared his throat. His look at the youth contained a quality of singular and terrible ferocity, but he said in his stolid tone, "I don't suppose you mean what you say now."

Upon his arm he had felt the pressure of some unconscious little fingers. The girl was leaning against the wall as if she no longer knew how to keep her balance, but those fingers—he held his arm very still. She murmured: "O Harry, don't! He was good to me—indeed he was!"

The corporal had come forward until he in a measure confronted the youth in gray, for he saw those fingers upon the captain's arm, and he knew that sometimes very strong men were not able to move hand nor foot under such conditions.

The youth had suddenly seemed to become weak. He breathed heavily and clung to the rail. He was glaring at the captain, and apparently summoning all his will power to combat his weakness. The corporal addressed him with profound straightforwardness, "Don't you be a derned fool!" The youth turned toward him so fiercely that the corporal threw up a knee and an elbow like a boy who expects to be cuffed.

The girl pleaded with the captain. "You won't hurt him, will you? He don't know what he's saying. He's wounded, you know. Please don't mind him!"

"I won't touch him," said the captain, with rather extraordinary earnestness; "don't you worry about him at all. I won't touch him!"

Then he looked at her, and the girl suddenly withdrew her fingers from his arm.

The corporal contemplated the top of the stairs, and remarked without surprise, "There's another of 'em coming!"

An old man was clambering down the stairs with much speed. He waved a cane wildly. "Get out of my house, you thieves! Get out! I won't have you cross my threshold! Get out!" He mumbled and wagged his head in an old man's fury. It was plainly his intention to assault them.

And so it occurred that a young girl became engaged in protecting a stalwart captain, fully armed, and with eight grim troopers at his back, from the attack of an old man with a walking-stick!

A blush passed over the temples and brow of the captain, and he looked particularly savage and weary. Despite the girl's efforts, he suddenly faced the old man.

"Look here," he said distinctly, "we came in because we had been fighting in the woods yonder, and we concluded that some of the enemy were in this house, especially when we saw a gray sleeve at the window. But this young man is wounded, and I have nothing to say to him. I will even take it for granted that there are no others like him upstairs. We will go away, leaving your old house just as we found it! And we are no more thieves and rascals than you are!"

The old man simply roared: "I haven't got a cow nor a pig nor a chicken on the place! Your soldiers have stolen everything they could carry away. They have torn down half my fences for firewood. This afternoon some of your accursed bullets even broke my window panes!"

The girl had been faltering: "Grandpa! O grandpa!"

The captain looked at the girl. She returned his glance from the shadow of the old man's shoulder. After studying her face a moment, he said, "Well, we will go now." He strode toward the door and his men clanked docilely after him.

At this time there was the sound of harsh cries and rushing footsteps from without. The door flew open, and a whirlwind composed of blue-coated troopers came in with a swoop. It was headed by the lieutenant. "Oh, here you are!" he cried, catching his breath. "We thought—Oh, look at the girl!"

The captain said intensely, "Shut up, you fool!"

The men settled to a halt with a clash and a bang. There could be heard the dulled sound of many hoofs outside of the house.

"Did you order up the horses?" inquired the captain.

"Yes. We thought—"

"Well, then, let's get out of here," interrupted the captain morosely.

The men began to filter out into the open air. The youth in gray had been hanging dismally to the railing of the stairway. He now was climbing slowly up to the second floor. The old man was addressing himself directly to the serene corporal.

"Not a chicken on the place!" he cried.

"Well, I didn't take your chickens, did I?"

"No, maybe you didn't, but—"

The captain crossed the hall and stood before the girl in rather a culprit's fashion. "You are not angry at me, are you?" he asked timidly.

"No," she said. She hesitated a moment, and then suddenly held out her hand. "You were good to me—and I'm—much obliged."

The captain took her hand, and then he blushed, for he found himself unable to formulate a sentence that applied in any way to the situation.

She did not seem to heed that hand for a time.

He loosened his grasp presently, for he was ashamed to hold it so long without saying anything clever. At last, with an air of charging an intrenched brigade, he contrived to say, "I would rather do anything than frighten or trouble you."

His brow was warmly perspiring. He had a sense of being hideous in his dusty uniform and with his grimy face.

She said, "Oh, I'm so glad it was you instead of somebody who might have—might have hurt brother Harry and grandpa!"

He told her, "I wouldn't have hurt 'em for anything!"

There was a little silence.

"Well, good-bye!" he said at last.

"Good-bye!"

He walked toward the door past the old man, who was scolding at the vanishing figure of the corporal. The captain looked back. She had remained there watching him.

At the bugle's order, the troopers standing beside their horses swung briskly into the saddle. The lieutenant said to the first sergeant:

"Williams, did they ever meet before?"

"Hanged if I know!"

"Well, say—"

The captain saw a curtain move at one of the windows. He cantered from his position at the head of the column and steered his horse between two flower beds.

"Well, good-bye!"

The squadron trampled slowly past.

"Good-bye!"

They shook hands.

He evidently had something enormously important to say to her, but it seems that he could not manage it. He struggled heroically. The bay charger, with his great mystically solemn eyes, looked around the corner of his shoulder at the girl.

The captain studied a pine tree. The girl inspected the grass beneath the window. The captain said hoarsely, "I don't suppose—I don't suppose—I'll ever see you again!"

She looked at him affrightedly and shrank back from the window. He seemed to have woefully expected a reception of this kind for his question. He gave her instantly a glance of appeal.

She said, "Why, no, I don't suppose we will."

"Never?"

"Why, no, 'tain't possible. You—you are a—Yankee!"

"Oh, I know it, but—" Eventually he continued, "Well, some day, you know, when there's no more fighting, we might—" He observed that she had again withdrawn suddenly into the shadow, so he said, "Well, good-bye!"

When he held her fingers she bowed her head, and he saw a pink blush steal over the curves of her cheek and neck.

"Am I never going to see you again?"

She made no reply.

"Never?" he repeated.

After a long time, he bent over to hear a faint reply: "Sometimes—when there are no troops in the neighbourhood—grandpa don't mind if I—walk over as far as that old oak tree yonder—in the afternoons."

It appeared that the captain's grip was very strong, for she uttered an exclamation and looked at her fingers as if she expected to find them mere fragments. He rode away.

The bay horse leaped a flower bed. They were almost to the drive, when the girl uttered a panic-stricken cry.

The captain wheeled his horse violently and upon his return journey went straight through a flower bed.

The girl had clasped her hands. She beseeched him wildly with her eyes. "Oh, please, don't believe it! I never walk to the old oak tree. Indeed, I don't! I never—never—never walk there."

The bridle drooped on the bay charger's neck. The captain's figure seemed limp. With an expression of profound dejection and gloom he stared off at where the leaden sky met the dark green line of the woods. The long-impending rain began to fall with a mournful patter, drop and drop. There was a silence.

At last a low voice said, "Well—I might—sometimes I might—perhaps—but only once in a great while—I might walk to the old tree—in the afternoons."

# THE VETERAN

Out of the low window could be seen three hickory trees placed irregularly in a meadow that was resplendent in springtime green. Farther away, the old, dismal belfry of the village church loomed over the pines. A horse meditating in the shade of one of the hickories lazily swished his tail. The warm sunshine made an oblong of vivid yellow on the floor of the grocery.

"Could you see the whites of their eyes?" said the man who was seated on a soap box.

"Nothing of the kind," replied old Henry warmly. "Just a lot of flitting figures, and I let go at where they 'peared to be the thickest. Bang!"

"Mr. Fleming," said the grocer—his deferential voice expressed somehow the old man's exact social weight—"Mr. Fleming, you never was frightened much in them battles, was you?"

The veteran looked down and grinned. Observing his manner, the entire group tittered. "Well, I guess I was," he answered finally. "Pretty well scared, sometimes. Why, in my first battle I thought the sky was falling down. I thought the world was coming to an end. You bet I was scared."

Every one laughed. Perhaps it seemed strange and rather wonderful to them that a man should admit the thing, and in the tone of their laughter there was probably more admiration than if old Fleming had declared that he had always been a lion. Moreover, they knew that he had ranked as an orderly sergeant, and so their opinion of his heroism was fixed. None, to be sure, knew how an orderly sergeant ranked, but then it was understood to be somewhere just shy of a major general's stars. So, when old Henry admitted that he had been frightened, there was a laugh.

"The trouble was," said the old man, "I thought they were all shooting at me. Yes, sir, I thought every man in the other army was aiming at me in particular, and only me. And it seemed so darned unreasonable, you know. I wanted to explain to 'em what an almighty good fellow I was, because I thought then they might quit all trying to hit me. But I couldn't explain, and they kept on being unreasonable—blim!—blam!—bang! So I run!"

Two little triangles of wrinkles appeared at the corners of his eyes. Evidently he appreciated some comedy in this recital. Down near his feet, however, little Jim, his grandson, was visibly horror-stricken. His hands were clasped nervously, and his eyes were wide with astonishment at this terrible scandal, his most magnificent grandfather telling such a thing.

"That was at Chancellorsville. Of course, afterward I got kind of used to it. A man does. Lots of men, though, seem to feel all right from the start. I did, as soon as I 'got on to it,' as they say now; but at first I was pretty well flustered. Now, there was young Jim Conklin, old Si Conklin's son—that used to keep the tannery—you none of you recollect him—well, he went into it from the start just as if he was born to it. But with me it was different. I had to get used to it."

When little Jim walked with his grandfather he was in the habit of skipping along on the stone pavement in front of the three stores and the hotel of the town and betting that he could avoid the cracks. But upon this day he walked soberly, with his hand gripping two of his grandfather's fingers. Sometimes he kicked abstractedly at dandelions that curved over the walk. Any one could see that he was much troubled.

"There's Sickles's colt over in the medder, Jimmie," said the old man. "Don't you wish you owned one like him?"

"Um," said the boy, with a strange lack of interest. He continued his reflections. Then finally he ventured, "Grandpa—now—was that true what you was telling those men?"

"What?" asked the grandfather. "What was I telling them?"

"Oh, about your running."

"Why, yes, that was true enough, Jimmie. It was my first fight, and there was an awful lot of noise, you know."

Jimmie seemed dazed that this idol, of its own will, should so totter. His stout boyish idealism was injured.

Presently the grandfather said: "Sickles's colt is going for a drink. Don't you wish you owned Sickles's colt, Jimmie?"

The boy merely answered, "He ain't as nice as our'n." He lapsed then into another moody silence.

* * * *

One of the hired men, a Swede, desired to drive to the county seat for purposes of his own. The old man loaned a horse and an unwashed buggy. It appeared later that one of the purposes of the Swede was to get drunk.

After quelling some boisterous frolic of the farm hands and boys in the garret, the old man had that night gone peacefully to sleep, when he was aroused by clamouring at the kitchen door. He grabbed his trousers, and they waved out behind as he dashed forward. He could hear the voice of the Swede, screaming and blubbering. He pushed the wooden button, and, as the door flew open, the Swede, a maniac, stumbled inward, chattering, weeping, still screaming: "De barn fire! Fire! Fire! De barn fire! Fire! Fire! Fire!"

There was a swift and indescribable change in the old man. His face ceased instantly to be a face; it became a mask, a gray thing, with horror written about the mouth and eyes. He hoarsely shouted at the foot of the little rickety stairs, and immediately, it seemed, there came down an avalanche of men. No one knew that during this time the old lady had been standing in her night clothes at the bedroom door, yelling: "What's th' matter? What's th' matter? What's th' matter?"

When they dashed toward the barn it presented to their eyes its usual appearance, solemn, rather mystic in the black night. The Swede's lantern was overturned at a point some yards in front of the barn doors. It contained a wild little conflagration of its own, and even in their excitement some of those who ran felt a gentle secondary vibration of the thrifty part of their minds at sight of this overturned lantern. Under ordinary circumstances it would have been a calamity.

But the cattle in the barn were trampling, trampling, trampling, and above this noise could be heard a humming like the song of innumerable bees. The old man hurled aside the great doors, and a yellow flame leaped out at one corner and sped and wavered frantically up the old gray wall. It was glad, terrible, this single flame, like the wild banner of deadly and triumphant foes.

The motley crowd from the garret had come with all the pails of the farm. They flung themselves upon the well. It was a leisurely old machine, long dwelling in indolence. It was in the habit of giving out water with a sort of reluctance. The men stormed at it, cursed it; but it continued to allow the buckets to be filled only after the wheezy windlass had howled many protests at the mad-handed men.

With his opened knife in his hand old Fleming himself had gone headlong into the barn, where the stifling smoke swirled with the air currents, and where could be heard in its fulness the terrible chorus of the flames, laden with tones of hate and death, a hymn of wonderful ferocity.

He flung a blanket over an old mare's head, cut the halter close to the manger, led the mare to the door, and fairly kicked her out to safety. He returned with the same blanket, and rescued one of the work horses. He took five horses out, and then came out himself, with his clothes bravely on fire. He had no whiskers, and very little hair on his head. They soused five pailfuls of water on him. His eldest son made a clean miss with the sixth pailful, because the old man had turned and was running down the decline and around to the basement of the barn, where were the stanchions of the cows. Some one noticed at the time that he ran very lamely, as if one of the frenzied horses had smashed his hip.

The cows, with their heads held in the heavy stanchions, had thrown themselves, strangled themselves, tangled themselves: done everything which the ingenuity of their exuberant fear could suggest to them.

Here, as at the well, the same thing happened to every man save one. Their hands went mad. They became incapable of everything save the power to rush into dangerous situations.

The old man released the cow nearest the door, and she, blind drunk with terror, crashed into the Swede. The Swede had been running to and fro babbling. He carried an empty milk pail, to which he clung with an unconscious, fierce enthusiasm. He shrieked like one lost as he went under the cow's hoofs, and the milk pail, rolling across the floor, made a flash of silver in the gloom.

Old Fleming took a fork, beat off the cow, and dragged the paralyzed Swede to the open air. When they had rescued all the cows save one, which had so fastened herself that she could not be moved an inch, they returned to the front of the barn and stood sadly, breathing like men who had reached the final point of human effort.

Many people had come running. Some one had even gone to the church, and now, from the distance, rang the tocsin note of the old bell. There was a long flare of crimson on the sky, which made remote people speculate as to the whereabouts of the fire.

The long flames sang their drumming chorus in voices of the heaviest bass. The wind whirled clouds of smoke and cinders into the faces of the spectators. The form of the old barn was outlined in black amid these masses of orange-hued flames.

And then came this Swede again, crying as one who is the weapon of the sinister fates. "De colts! De colts! You have forgot de colts!"

Old Fleming staggered. It was true; they had forgotten the two colts in the box stalls at the back of the barn. "Boys," he said, "I must try to get 'em out." They clamoured about him then, afraid for him, afraid of what they should see. Then they talked wildly each to each. "Why, it's sure death!" "He would never get out!" "Why, it's suicide for a man to go in there!" Old Fleming stared absent-mindedly at the open doors. "The poor little things!" he said. He rushed into the barn.

When the roof fell in, a great funnel of smoke swarmed toward the sky, as if the old man's mighty spirit, released from its body—a little bottle—had swelled like the genie of fable. The smoke was tinted rose-hue from the flames, and perhaps the unutterable midnights of the universe will have no power to daunt the colour of this soul.

# THE MONSTER

## I

Little Jim was, for the time, engine Number 36, and he was making the run between Syracuse and Rochester. He was fourteen minutes behind time, and the throttle was wide open. In consequence, when he swung around the curve at the flower-bed, a wheel of his cart destroyed a peony. Number 36 slowed down at once and looked guiltily at his father, who was mowing the lawn. The doctor had his back to this accident, and he continued to pace slowly to and fro, pushing the mower.

Jim dropped the tongue of the cart. He looked at his father and at the broken flower. Finally he went to the peony and tried to stand it on its pins, resuscitated, but the spine of it was hurt, and it would only hang limply from his hand. Jim could do no reparation. He looked again towards his father.

He went on to the lawn, very slowly, and kicking wretchedly at the turf. Presently his father came along with the whirring machine, while the sweet, new grass blades spun from the knives. In a low voice, Jim said, "Pa!"

The doctor was shaving this lawn as if it were a priest's chin. All during the season he had worked at it in the coolness and peace of the evenings after supper. Even in the shadow of the cherry-trees the grass was strong and healthy. Jim raised his voice a trifle. "Pa!"

The doctor paused, and with the howl of the machine no longer occupying the sense, one could hear the robins in the cherry-trees arranging their affairs. Jim's hands were behind his back, and sometimes his fingers clasped and unclasped. Again he said, "Pa!" The child's fresh and rosy lip was lowered.

The doctor stared down at his son, thrusting his head forward and frowning attentively. "What is it, Jimmie?"

"Pa!" repeated the child at length. Then he raised his finger and pointed at the flowerbed. "There!"

"What?" said the doctor, frowning more. "What is it, Jim?"

After a period of silence, during which the child may have undergone a severe mental tumult, he raised his finger and repeated his former word—"There!" The father had respected this silence with perfect courtesy. Afterwards his glance carefully followed the direction indicated by the child's finger, but he could see nothing which explained to him. "I don't understand what you mean, Jimmie," he said.

It seemed that the importance of the whole thing had taken away the boy's vocabulary. He could only reiterate, "There!"

The doctor mused upon the situation, but he could make nothing of it. At last he said, "Come, show me."

Together they crossed the lawn towards the flower-bed. At some yards from the broken peony Jimmie began to lag. "There!" The word came almost breathlessly.

"Where?" said the doctor.

Jimmie kicked at the grass. "There!" he replied.

The doctor was obliged to go forward alone. After some trouble he found the subject of the incident, the broken flower. Turning then, he saw the child lurking at the rear and scanning his countenance.

The father reflected. After a time he said, "Jimmie, come here." With an infinite modesty of demeanor the child came forward. "Jimmie, how did this happen?"

The child answered, "Now—I was playin' train—and—now—I runned over it."

"You were doing what?"

"I was playin' train."

The father reflected again. "Well, Jimmie," he said, slowly, "I guess you had better not play train any more today. Do you think you had better?"

"No, sir," said Jimmie.

During the delivery of the judgment the child had not faced his father, and afterwards he went away, with his head lowered, shuffling his feet.

## II

It was apparent from Jimmie's manner that he felt some kind of desire to efface himself. He went down to the stable. Henry Johnson, the negro who cared for the doctor's horses, was sponging the buggy. He grinned fraternally when he saw Jimmie coming. These two were pals. In regard to almost everything in life they seemed to have minds precisely alike. Of course there were points of emphatic divergence. For instance, it was plain from Henry's talk that he was a very handsome negro, and he was known to be a light, a weight, and an eminence in the suburb of the town, where lived the larger number of the negroes, and obviously this glory was over Jimmie's horizon; but he vaguely appreciated it and paid deference to Henry for it mainly because Henry appreciated it and deferred to himself. However, on all points of conduct as related to the doctor, who was the moon, they were in complete but unexpressed understanding. Whenever Jimmie became the victim of an eclipse he went to the stable to solace himself with Henry's crimes. Henry, with the elasticity of his race, could usually provide a sin to place himself on a footing with the disgraced one. Perhaps he would remember that he had forgotten to put the hitching-strap in the back of the buggy on some recent occasion, and had been reprimanded by the doctor. Then these two would commune subtly and without words concerning their moon, holding themselves sympathetically as people who had committed similar treasons. On the other hand, Henry would sometimes choose to absolutely repudiate this idea, and when Jimmie appeared in his shame would bully him most virtuously, preaching with assurance the precepts of the doctor's creed, and pointing out to Jimmie all his abominations. Jimmie did not discover that this was odious in his comrade. He accepted it and lived in its shadow with humility, merely trying to conciliate the saintly Henry with acts of deference. Won by this attitude, Henry would sometimes allow the child to enjoy the felicity of squeezing the sponge over a buggy-wheel, even when Jimmie was still gory from unspeakable deeds.

Whenever Henry dwelt for a time in sackcloth, Jimmie did not patronize him at all. This was a justice of his age, his condition. He did not know. Besides, Henry could drive a horse, and Jimmie had a full sense of this sublimity. Henry personally conducted the moon during the splendid journeys through the country roads, where farms spread on all sides, with sheep, cows, and other marvels abounding.

"Hello, Jim!" said Henry, poising his sponge. Water was dripping from the buggy. Sometimes the horses in the stalls stamped thunderingly on the pine floor. There was an atmosphere of hay and of harness.

For a minute Jimmie refused to take an interest in anything. He was very downcast. He could not even feel the wonders of wagon washing. Henry, while at his work, narrowly observed him.

"Your pop done wallop yer, didn't he?" he said at last.

"No," said Jimmie, defensively; "he didn't."

After this casual remark Henry continued his labor, with a scowl of occupation. Presently he said: "I done tol' yer many's th' time not to go a-foolin' an' a-projjeckin' with them flowers. Yer pop don' like it nohow." As a matter of fact, Henry had never mentioned flowers to the boy.

Jimmie preserved a gloomy silence, so Henry began to use seductive wiles in this affair of washing a wagon. It was not until he began to spin a wheel on the tree, and the sprinkling water flew everywhere, that the boy was visibly moved. He had been seated on the sill of the carriage-house door, but at the beginning of this ceremony he arose and circled towards the buggy, with an interest that slowly consumed the remembrance of a late disgrace.

Johnson could then display all the dignity of a man whose duty it was to protect Jimmie from a splashing. "Look out, boy! look out! You done gwi' spile yer pants. I raikon your mommer don't 'low this foolishness, she know it. I ain't gwi' have you round yere spilin' yer pants, an' have Mis' Trescott light on me pressen'ly. 'Deed I ain't." He spoke with an air of great irritation, but he was not annoyed at all. This tone was merely a part of his importance. In reality he was always delighted to have the child there to witness the business of the stable. For one thing, Jimmie was invariably overcome with reverence when he was told how beautifully a harness was polished or a horse groomed. Henry explained each detail of this kind with unction, procuring great joy from the child's admiration.

### III

After Johnson had taken his supper in the kitchen, he went to his loft in the carriage house and dressed himself with much care. No belle of a court circle could bestow more mind on a toilet than did Johnson. On second thought, he was more like a priest arraying himself for some parade of the church. As he emerged from his room and sauntered down the carriage-drive, no one would have suspected him of ever having washed a buggy.

It was not altogether a matter of the lavender trousers, nor yet the straw hat with its bright silk band. The change was somewhere, far in the interior of Henry. But there was no cake-walk hyperbole in it. He was simply a quiet, well-bred gentleman of position, wealth, and other necessary achievements out for an evening stroll, and he had never washed a wagon in his life.

In the morning, when in his working-clothes, he had met a friend—"Hello, Pete!" "Hello, Henry!" Now, in his effulgence, he encountered this same friend. His bow was not at all haughty. If it expressed anything, it expressed consummate generosity—"Good-evenin', Misteh Washington." Pete, who was very dirty, being at work in a potato-patch, responded in a mixture of abasement and appreciation—Good-evenin', Misteh Johnsing."

The shimmering blue of the electric arc lamps was strong in the main street of the town. At numerous points it was conquered by the orange glare of the outnumbering gaslights in the windows of shops. Through this radiant lane moved a crowd, which culminated in a throng before the post-office, awaiting the distribution of the evening mails. Occasionally there came into it a shrill electric street-car, the motor singing like a cageful of grasshoppers, and possessing a great gong that clanged forth both warnings and simple noise. At the little theatre, which was a varnish and red plush miniature of one of the famous New York theatres, a company of strollers was to play "East Lynne." The young men of the town were mainly gathered at the corners, in distinctive groups, which expressed various shades and lines of chumship, and had little to do with any social gradations. There they discussed everything with critical insight, passing the whole town in review as it swarmed in the street. When the gongs of the electric cars ceased for a moment to harry the ears, there could be heard the sound of the feet of the leisurely crowd on the bluestone pavement, and it was like the peaceful evening lashing at the shore of a lake. At the foot of the hill, where two lines of maples sentinelled the way, an electric lamp glowed high among the embowering branches, and made most wonderful shadow-etchings on the road below it.

When Johnson appeared amid the throng a member of one of the profane groups at a corner instantly telegraphed news of this extraordinary arrival to his companions. They hailed him. "Hello, Henry! Going to walk for a cake tonight?"

"Ain't he smooth?"

"Why, you've got that cake right in your pocket, Henry!"

"Throw out your chest a little more."

Henry was not ruffled in any way by these quiet admonitions and compliments. In reply he laughed a supremely good-natured, chuckling laugh, which nevertheless expressed an underground complacency of superior metal.

Young Griscom, the lawyer, was just emerging from Reifsnyder's barber shop, rubbing his chin contentedly. On the steps he dropped his hand and looked with wide eyes into the crowd. Suddenly he bolted back into the shop. "Wow!" he cried to the parliament; "you ought to see the coon that's coming!"

Reifsnyder and his assistant instantly poised their razors high and turned towards the window. Two belathered heads reared from the chairs. The electric shine in the street caused an effect like water to them who looked through the glass from the yellow glamour of Reifsnyder's shop. In fact, the people without resembled the inhabitants of a great aquarium that here had a square pane in it. Presently into this frame swam the graceful form of Henry Johnson.

"Chee!" said Reifsnyder. He and his assistant with one accord threw their obligations to the winds, and leaving their lathered victims helpless, advanced to the window. "Ain't he a taisy?" said Reifsnyder, marvelling.

But the man in the first chair, with a grievance in his mind, had found a weapon. "Why, that's only Henry Johnson, you blamed idiots! Come on now, Reif, and shave me. What do you think I am—a mummy?"

Reifsnyder turned, in a great excitement. "I bait you any money that vas not Henry Johnson! Henry Johnson! Rats!" The scorn put into this last word made it an explosion. "That man was a Pullman-car porter or someding. How could that be Henry Johnson?" he demanded, turbulently. "You vas crazy."

The man in the first chair faced the barber in a storm of indignation. "Didn't I give him those lavender trousers?" he roared.

And young Griscom, who had remained attentively at the window, said: "Yes, I guess that was Henry. It looked like him."

"Oh, vell," said Reifsnyder, returning to his business, "if you think so! Oh, vell!" He implied that he was submitting for the sake of amiability.

Finally the man in the second chair, mumbling from a mouth made timid by adjacent lather, said: "That was Henry Johnson all right. Why, he always dresses like that when he wants to make a front! He's the biggest dude in town—anybody knows that."

"Chinger!" said Reifsnyder.

Henry was not at all oblivious of the wake of wondering ejaculation that streamed out behind him. On other occasions he had reaped this same joy, and he always had an eye for the demonstration. With a face beaming with happiness he turned away from the scene of his victories into a narrow side street, where the electric light still hung high, but only to exhibit a row of tumble-down houses leaning together like paralytics.

The saffron Miss Bella Farragut, in a calico frock, had been crouched on the front stoop, gossiping at long range, but she espied her approaching caller at a distance. She dashed around the corner of the house, galloping like a horse. Henry saw it all, but he preserved the polite demeanor of a guest when a waiter spills claret down his cuff. In this awkward situation he was simply perfect.

The duty of receiving Mr. Johnson fell upon Mrs. Farragut, because Bella, in another room, was scrambling wildly into her best gown. The fat old woman met him with a great ivory smile, sweeping back with the door, and bowing low. "Walk in, Misteh Johnson, walk in. How is you dis ebenin', Misteh Johnson—how is you?"

Henry's face showed like a reflector as he bowed and bowed, bending almost from his head to his ankles, "Good-evenin', Mis' Fa'gut; good-evenin'. How is you dis evenin'? Is all you' folks well, Mis' Fa'gut?"

After a great deal of kowtow, they were planted in two chairs opposite each other in the living-room. Here they exchanged the most tremendous civilities, until Miss Bella swept into the room, when there was more kowtow on all sides, and a smiling show of teeth that was like an illumination.

The cooking-stove was of course in this drawing-room, and on the fire was some kind of a long-winded stew. Mrs. Farragut was obliged to arise and attend to it from time to time. Also young Sim came in and went to bed on his pallet in the corner. But to all these domesticities the three maintained an absolute dumbness. They bowed and smiled and ignored and imitated until a late hour, and if they had been the occupants of the most gorgeous salon in the world they could not have been more like three monkeys.

After Henry had gone, Bella, who encouraged herself in the appropriation of phrases, said, "Oh, ma, isn't he divine?"

<h2 style="text-align:center">IV</h2>

A Saturday evening was a sign always for a larger crowd to parade the thoroughfare. In summer the band played until ten o'clock in the little park. Most of the young men of the town affected to be superior to this band, even to despise it; but in the still and fragrant evenings they invariably turned out in force, because the girls were sure to attend this concert, strolling slowly over the grass, linked closely in pairs, or preferably in threes, in the curious public dependence upon one another which was their inheritance. There was no particular social aspect to this gathering, save that group regarded group with interest, but mainly in silence. Perhaps one girl would nudge another girl and suddenly say, "Look! there goes Gertie Hodgson and her sister!" And they would appear to regard this as an event of importance.

On a particular evening a rather large company of young men were gathered on the sidewalk that edged the park. They remained thus beyond the borders of the festivities because of their dignity, which would not exactly allow them to appear in anything which was so much fun for the younger lads. These latter were careering madly through the crowd, precipitating minor accidents from time to time, but usually fleeing like mist swept by the wind before retribution could lay hands upon them.

The band played a waltz which involved a gift of prominence to the bass horn, and one of the young men on the sidewalk said that the music reminded him of the new engines on the hill pumping water into the reservoir. A similarity of this kind was not inconceivable, but the young man did not say it because he disliked the band's playing. He said it because it was fashionable to say that manner of thing concerning the band. However, over in the stand, Billie Harris, who played the snare-drum, was always surrounded by a throng of boys, who adored his every whack.

After the mails from New York and Rochester had been finally distributed, the crowd from the post-office added to the mass already in the park. The wind waved the leaves of the maples, and, high in the air, the blue-burning globes of the arc lamps caused the wonderful traceries of leaf shadows on the ground. When the light fell upon the upturned face of a girl, it caused it to glow with a wonderful pallor. A policeman came suddenly from the darkness and chased a gang of obstreperous little boys. They hooted him from a distance. The leader of the band had some of the mannerisms of the great musicians, and during a period of silence the crowd smiled when they saw him raise his hand to his brow, stroke it sentimentally, and glance upward with a look of poetic anguish. In the shivering light, which gave to the park an effect like a great vaulted hall, the throng swarmed, with a gentle murmur of dresses switching the turf, and with a steady hum of voices.

Suddenly, without preliminary bars, there arose from afar the great hoarse roar of a factory whistle. It raised and swelled to a sinister note, and then it sang on the night wind one long call that held the crowd in the park immovable, speechless. The band-master had been about to vehemently let fall his hand to start the band on a thundering career through a popular march, but, smitten by this giant voice from the night, his hand dropped slowly to his knee, and, his mouth agape, he looked at his men in silence. The cry died away to a wail and then to stillness. It released the muscles of the company of young men on the sidewalk, who had been like statues, posed eagerly, lithely, their ears turned. And then they wheeled upon each other simultaneously, and, in a single explosion, they shouted, "One!"

Again the sound swelled in the night and roared its long ominous cry, and as it died away the crowd of young men wheeled upon each other and, in chorus, yelled, "Two!"

There was a moment of breathless waiting. Then they bawled, "Second district!" In a flash the company of indolent and cynical young men had vanished like a snowball disrupted by dynamite.

V

Jake Rogers was the first man to reach the home of Tuscarora Hose Company Number Six. He had wrenched his key from his pocket as he tore down the street, and he jumped at the spring-lock like a demon. As the doors flew back before his hands he leaped and kicked the wedges from a pair of wheels, loosened a tongue from its clasp, and in the glare of the electric light which the town placed before each of its hose-houses the next comers beheld the spectacle of Jake Rogers bent like hickory in the manfulness of his pulling, and the heavy cart was moving slowly towards the doors. Four men joined him at the time, and as they swung with the cart out into the street, dark figures sped towards them from the ponderous shadows back of the electric lamps. Some set up the inevitable question, "What district?"

"Second," was replied to them in a compact howl. Tuscarora Hose Company Number Six swept on a perilous wheel into Niagara Avenue, and as the men, attached to the cart by the rope which had been paid out from the windlass under the tongue, pulled madly in their fervor and abandon, the gong under the axle clanged incitingly. And sometimes the same cry was heard, "What district?"

"Second."

On a grade Johnnie Thorpe fell, and exercising a singular muscular ability, rolled out in time from the track of the on-coming wheel, and arose, dishevelled and aggrieved, casting a look of mournful disenchantment upon the black crowd that poured after the machine. The cart seemed to be the apex of a dark wave that was whirling as if it had been a broken dam. Back of the lad were stretches of lawn, and in that direction front-doors were banged by men who hoarsely shouted out into the clamorous avenue, "What district?"

At one of these houses a woman came to the door bearing a lamp, shielding her face from its rays with her hands. Across the cropped grass the avenue represented to her a kind of black torrent, upon which, nevertheless, fled numerous miraculous figures upon bicycles. She did not know that the towering light at the corner was continuing its nightly whine.

Suddenly a little boy somersaulted around the corner of the house as if he had been projected down a flight of stairs by a catapultian boot. He halted himself in front of the house by dint of a rather extraordinary evolution with his legs. "Oh, ma," he gasped, "can I go? Can I, ma?"

She straightened with the coldness of the exterior mother-judgment, although the hand that held the lamp trembled slightly. "No, Willie; you had better come to bed."

Instantly he began to buck and fume like a mustang. "Oh, ma," he cried, contorting himself—"oh, ma, can't I go? Please, ma, can't I go? Can't I go, ma?"

"It's half-past nine now, Willie."

He ended by wailing out a compromise: "Well, just down to the corner, ma? Just down to the corner?"

From the avenue came the sound of rushing men who wildly shouted. Somebody had grappled the bell-rope in the Methodist church, and now over the town rang this solemn and terrible voice, speaking from the clouds. Moved from its peaceful business, this bell gained a new spirit in the portentous night, and it swung the heart to and fro, up and down, with each peal of it.

"Just down to the corner, ma?"

"Willie, it's half-past nine now."

## VI

The outlines of the house of Dr. Trescott had faded quietly into the evening, hiding a shape such as we call Queen Anne against the pall of the blackened sky. The neighborhood was at this time so quiet, and seemed so devoid of obstructions, that Hannigan's dog thought it a good opportunity to prowl in forbidden precincts, and so came and pawed Trescott's lawn, growling, and considering himself a formidable beast. Later, Peter Washington strolled past the house and whistled, but there was no dim light shining from Henry's loft, and presently Peter went his way. The rays from the street, creeping in silvery waves over the grass, caused the row of shrubs along the drive to throw a clear, bold shade.

A wisp of smoke came from one of the windows at the end of the house and drifted quietly into the branches of a cherry-tree. Its companions followed it in slowly increasing numbers, and finally there was a current controlled by invisible banks which poured into the fruit-laden boughs of the cherry-tree. It was no more to be noted than if a troop of dim and silent gray monkeys had been climbing a grapevine into the clouds.

After a moment the window brightened as if the four panes of it had been stained with blood, and a quick ear might have been led to imagine the fire-imps calling and calling, clan joining clan, gathering to the colors. From the street, however, the house maintained its dark quiet, insisting to a passer-by that it was the safe dwelling of people who chose to retire early to tranquil dreams. No one could have heard this low droning of the gathering clans.

Suddenly the panes of the red window tinkled and crashed to the ground, and at other windows there suddenly reared other flames, like bloody spectres at the apertures of a haunted house. This outbreak had been well planned, as if by professional revolutionists.

A man's voice suddenly shouted: "Fire! Fire! Fire!" Hannigan had flung his pipe frenziedly from him because his lungs demanded room. He tumbled down from his perch, swung over the fence, and ran shouting towards the front-door of the Trescotts'. Then he hammered on the door, using his fists as if they were mallets. Mrs. Trescott instantly came to one of the windows on the second floor. Afterwards she knew she had been about to say, "The doctor is not at home, but if you will leave your name, I will let him know as soon as he comes."

Hannigan's bawling was for a minute incoherent, but she understood that it was not about croup.

"What?" she said, raising the window swiftly.

"Your house is on fire! You're all ablaze! Move quick if—" His cries were resounding, in the street as if it were a cave of echoes. Many feet pattered swiftly on the stones. There was one man who ran with an almost fabulous speed. He wore lavender trousers. A straw hat with a bright silk band was held half crumpled in his hand.

As Henry reached the front-door, Hannigan had just broken the lock with a kick. A thick cloud of smoke poured over them, and Henry, ducking his head, rushed into it. From Hannigan's clamor he knew only one thing, but it turned him blue with horror. In the hall a lick of flame had found the cord that supported "Signing the Declaration." The engraving slumped suddenly down at one end, and then dropped to the floor, where it burst with the sound of a bomb. The fire was already roaring like a winter wind among the pines.

At the head of the stairs Mrs. Trescott was waving her arms as if they were two reeds.

"Jimmie! Save Jimmie!" she screamed in Henry's face. He plunged past her and disappeared, taking the long-familiar routes among these upper chambers, where he had once held office as a sort of second assistant house-maid.

Hannigan had followed him up the stairs, and grappled the arm of the maniacal woman there. His face was black with rage. "You must come down," he bellowed.

She would only scream at him in reply: "Jimmie! Jimmie! Save Jimmie!" But he dragged her forth while she babbled at him.

As they swung out into the open air a man ran across the lawn, and seizing a shutter, pulled it from its hinges and flung it far out upon the grass. Then he frantically attacked the other shutters one by one. It was a kind of temporary insanity.

"Here, you," howled Hannigan, "hold Mrs. Trescott—And stop—"

The news had been telegraphed by a twist of the wrist of a neighbor who had gone to the fire-box at the corner, and the time when Hannigan and his charge struggled out of the house was the time when the whistle roared its hoarse night call, smiting the crowd in the park, causing the leader of the band, who was about to order the first triumphal clang of a military march, to let his hand drop slowly to his knees.

**VII**

Henry pawed awkwardly through the smoke in the upper halls. He had attempted to guide himself by the walls, but they were too hot. The paper was crimpling, and he expected at any moment to have a flame burst from under his hands.

"Jimmie!"

He did not call very loud, as if in fear that the humming flames below would overhear him.

"Jimmie! Oh, Jimmie!"

Stumbling and panting, he speedily reached the entrance to Jimmie's room and flung open the door. The little chamber had no smoke in it at all. It was faintly illuminated by a beautiful rosy light reflected circuitously from the flames that were consuming the house. The boy had apparently just been aroused by the noise. He sat in his bed, his lips apart, his eyes wide, while upon his little white-robed figure played caressingly the light from the fire. As the door flew open he had before him this apparition of his pal, a terror-stricken negro, all tousled and with wool scorching, who leaped upon him and bore him up in a blanket as if the whole affair were a case of kidnapping by a dreadful robber chief. Without waiting to go through the usual short but complete process of wrinkling up his face, Jimmie let out a gorgeous bawl, which resembled the expression of a calf's deepest terror. As Johnson, bearing him, reeled into the smoke of the hall, he flung his arms about his neck and buried his face in the blanket. He called twice in muffled tones: "Mam-ma! Mam-ma!" When Johnson came to the top of the stairs with his burden, he took a quick step backward. Through the smoke that rolled to him he could see that the lower hall was all ablaze. He cried out then in a howl that resembled Jimmie's former achievement. His legs gained a frightful faculty of bending sideways. Swinging about precariously on these reedy legs, he made his way back slowly, back along the upper hall. From the way of him then, he had given up almost all idea of escaping from the burning house, and with it the desire. He was submitting, submitting because of his fathers, bending his mind in a most perfect slavery to this conflagration.

He now clutched Jimmie as unconsciously as when, running toward the house, he had clutched the hat with the bright silk band.

Suddenly he remembered a little private staircase which led from a bedroom to an apartment which the doctor had fitted up as a laboratory and work-house, where he used some of his leisure, and also hours when he might have been sleeping, in devoting himself to experiments which came in the way of his study and interest.

When Johnson recalled this stairway the submission to the blaze departed instantly. He had been perfectly familiar with it, but his confusion had destroyed the memory of it.

In his sudden momentary apathy there had been little that resembled fear, but now, as a way of safety came to him, the old frantic terror caught him. He was no longer creature to the flames, and he was afraid of the battle with them. It was a singular and swift set of alternations in which he feared twice without submission, and submitted once without fear.

"Jimmie!" he wailed, as he staggered on his way. He wished this little inanimate body at his breast to participate in his tremblings. But the child had lain limp and still during these headlong charges and countercharges, and no sign came from him.

Johnson passed through two rooms and came to the head of the stairs. As he opened the door great billows of smoke poured out, but gripping Jimmie closer, he plunged down through them. All manner of odors assailed him during this flight. They seemed to be alive with envy, hatred, and malice. At the entrance to the laboratory he confronted a strange spectacle. The room was like a garden in the region where might be burning flowers. Flames of violet, crimson, green, blue, orange, and purple were blooming everywhere. There was one blaze that was precisely the hue of a delicate coral. In another place was a mass that lay merely in phosphorescent inaction like a pile of emeralds. But all these marvels were to be seen dimly through clouds of heaving, turning, deadly smoke.

Johnson halted for a moment on the threshold. He cried out again in the negro wail that had in it the sadness of the swamps. Then he rushed across the room. An orange-colored flame leaped like a panther at the lavender trousers. This animal bit deeply into Johnson. There was an explosion at one side, and suddenly before him there reared a delicate, trembling sapphire shape like a fairy lady. With a quiet smile she blocked his path and doomed him and Jimmie. Johnson shrieked, and then ducked in the manner of his race in fights. He aimed to pass under the left guard of the sapphire lady. But she was swifter than eagles, and her talons caught in him as he plunged past her. Bowing his head as if his neck had been struck, Johnson lurched forward, twisting this way and that way. He fell on his back. The still form in the blanket flung from his arms, rolled to the edge of the floor and beneath the window.

Johnson had fallen with his head at the base of an old-fashioned desk. There was a row of jars upon the top of this desk. For the most part, they were silent amid this rioting, but there was one which seemed to hold a scintillant and writhing serpent.

Suddenly the glass splintered, and a ruby-red snakelike thing poured its thick length out upon the top of the old desk. It coiled and hesitated, and then began to swim a languorous way down the mahogany slant. At the angle it waved its sizzling molten head to and fro over the closed eyes of the man beneath it. Then, in a moment, with a mystic impulse, it moved again, and the red snake flowed directly down into Johnson's upturned face.

Afterwards the trail of this creature seemed to reek, and amid flames and low explosions drops like red-hot jewels pattered softly down it at leisurely intervals.

## VIII

Suddenly all roads led to Dr. Trescott's. The whole town flowed towards one point. Chippeway Hose Company Number One toiled desperately up Bridge Street Hill even as the Tuscaroras came in an impetuous sweep down Niagara Avenue. Meanwhile the machine of the hook-and-ladder experts from across the creek was spinning on its way. The chief of the fire department had been playing poker in the rear room of Whiteley's cigar-store, but at the first breath of the alarm he sprang through the door like a man escaping with the kitty.

In Whilomville, on these occasions, there was always a number of people who instantly turned their attention to the bells in the churches and school-houses. The bells not only emphasized the alarm, but it was the habit to send these sounds rolling across the sky in a stirring brazen uproar until the flames were practically vanquished. There was also a kind of rivalry as to which bell should be made to produce the greatest din. Even the Valley Church, four miles away among the farms, had heard the voices of its brethren, and immediately added a quaint little yelp.

Dr. Trescott had been driving homeward, slowly smoking a cigar, and feeling glad that this last case was now in complete obedience to him, like a wild animal that he had subdued, when he heard the long whistle, and chirped to his horse under the unlicensed but perfectly distinct impression that a fire had broken out in Oakhurst, a new and rather high-flying suburb of the town which was at least two miles from his own home. But in the second blast and in the ensuing silence he read the designation of his own district. He was then only a few blocks from his house. He took out the whip and laid it lightly on the mare. Surprised and frightened at this extraordinary action, she leaped forward, and as the reins straightened like steel bands, the doctor leaned backward a trifle. When the mare whirled him up to the closed gate he was wondering whose house could be afire. The man who had rung the signal-box yelled something at him, but he already knew. He left the mare to her will.

In front of his door was a maniacal woman in a wrapper. "Ned!" she screamed at sight of him. "Jimmie! Save Jimmie!"

Trescott had grown hard and chill. "Where?" he said. "Where?"

Mrs. Trescott's voice began to bubble. "Up—up—up—" She pointed at the second-story windows.

Hannigan was already shouting: "Don't go in that way! You can't go in that way!"

Trescott ran around the corner of the house and disappeared from them. He knew from the view he had taken of the main hall that it would be impossible to ascend from there. His hopes were fastened now to the stairway which led from the laboratory. The door which opened from this room out upon the lawn was fastened with a bolt and lock, but he kicked close to the lock and then close to the bolt. The door with a loud crash flew back. The doctor recoiled from the roll of smoke, and then bending low, he stepped into the garden of burning flowers. On the floor his stinging eyes could make out a form in a smouldering blanket near the window. Then, as he carried his son towards the door, he saw that the whole lawn seemed now alive with men and boys, the leaders in the great charge that the whole town was making. They seized him and his burden, and overpowered him in wet blankets and water.

But Hannigan was howling: "Johnson is in there yet! Henry Johnson is in there yet! He went in after the kid! Johnson is in there yet!"

These cries penetrated to the sleepy senses of Trescott, and he struggled with his captors, swearing, unknown to him and to them, all the deep blasphemies of his medical-student days. He rose to his feet and went again towards the door of the laboratory. They endeavored to restrain him, although they were much affrighted at him.

But a young man who was a brakeman on the railway, and lived in one of the rear streets near the Trescotts, had gone into the laboratory and brought forth a thing which he laid on the grass.

## IX

There were hoarse commands from in front of the house. "Turn on your water, Five!" "Let 'er go, One!" The gathering crowd swayed this way and that way. The flames, towering high, cast a wild red light on their faces. There came the clangor of a gong from along some adjacent street. The crowd exclaimed at it. "Here comes Number Three!" "That's Three a-comin'!" A panting and irregular mob dashed into view, dragging a hose-cart. A cry of exultation arose from the little boys. "Here's Three!" The lads welcomed Never-Die Hose Company Number Three as if it was composed of a chariot dragged by a band of gods. The perspiring citizens flung themselves into the fray. The boys danced in impish joy at the displays of prowess.

They acclaimed the approach of Number Two. They welcomed Number Four with cheers. They were so deeply moved by this whole affair that they bitterly guyed the late appearance of the hook and ladder company, whose heavy apparatus had almost stalled them on the Bridge Street hill. The lads hated and feared a fire, of course. They did not particularly want to have anybody's house burn, but still it was fine to see the gathering of the companies, and amid a great noise to watch their heroes perform all manner of prodigies.

They were divided into parties over the worth of different companies, and supported their creeds with no small violence. For instance, in that part of the little city where Number Four had its home it would be most daring for a boy to contend the superiority of any other company. Likewise, in another quarter, where a strange boy was asked which fire company was the best in Whilomville, he was expected to answer "Number One." Feuds, which the boys forgot and remembered according to chance or the importance of some recent event, existed all through the town.

They did not care much for John Shipley, the chief of the department. It was true that he went to a fire with the speed of a falling angel, but when there he invariably lapsed into a certain still mood, which was almost a preoccupation, moving leisurely around the burning structure and surveying it, putting meanwhile at a cigar. This quiet man, who even when life was in danger seldom raised his voice, was not much to their fancy. Now old Sykes Huntington, when he was chief, used to bellow continually like a bull and gesticulate in a sort of delirium. He was much finer as a spectacle than this Shipley, who viewed a fire with the same steadiness that he viewed a raise in a large jack-pot. The greater number of the boys could never understand why the members of these companies persisted in re-electing Shipley, although they often pretended to understand it, because "My father says" was a very formidable phrase in argument, and the fathers seemed almost unanimous in advocating Shipley.

At this time there was considerable discussion as to which company had gotten the first stream of water on the fire. Most of the boys claimed that Number Five owned that distinction, but there was a determined minority who contended for Number One. Boys who were the blood adherents of other companies were obliged to choose between the two on this occasion, and the talk waxed warm.

But a great rumor went among the crowds. It was told with hushed voices. Afterwards a reverent silence fell even upon the boys. Jimmie Trescott and Henry Johnson had been burned to death, and Dr. Trescott himself had been most savagely hurt. The crowd did not even feel the police pushing at them. They raised their eyes, shining now with awe, towards the high flames.

The man who had information was at his best. In low tones he described the whole affair. "That was the kid's room—in the corner there. He had measles or somethin', and this coon—Johnson—was a-settin' up with 'im, and Johnson got sleepy or somethin' and upset the lamp, and the doctor he was down in his office, and he came running up, and they all got burned together till they dragged 'em out."

Another man, always preserved for the deliverance of the final judgment, was saying: "Oh, they'll die sure. Burned to flinders. No chance. Hull lot of 'em. Anybody can see." The crowd concentrated its gaze still more closely upon these flags of fire which waved joyfully against the black sky. The bells of the town were clashing unceasingly.

A little procession moved across the lawn and towards the street. There were three cots, borne by twelve of the firemen. The police moved sternly, but it needed no effort of theirs to open a lane for this slow cortege. The men who bore the cots were well known to the crowd, but in this solemn parade during the ringing of the bells and the shouting, and with the red glare upon the sky, they seemed utterly foreign, and Whilomville paid them a deep respect. Each man in this stretcher party had gained a reflected majesty. They were footmen to death, and the crowd made subtle obeisance to this august dignity derived from three prospective graves. One woman turned away with a shriek at sight of the covered body on the first stretcher, and people faced her suddenly in silent and mournful indignation. Otherwise there was barely a sound as these twelve important men with measured tread carried their burdens through the throng.

The little boys no longer discussed the merits of the different fire companies. For the greater part they had been routed. Only the more courageous viewed closely the three figures veiled in yellow blankets.

## X

Old Judge Denning Hagenthorpe, who lived nearly opposite the Trescotts, had thrown his door wide open to receive the afflicted family. When it was publicly learned that the doctor and his son and the negro were still alive, it required a specially detailed policeman to prevent people from scaling the front porch and interviewing these sorely wounded. One old lady appeared with a miraculous poultice, and she quoted most damning Scripture to the officer when he said that she could not pass him. Throughout the night some lads old enough to be given privileges or to compel them from their mothers remained vigilantly upon the kerb in anticipation of a death or some such event. The reporter of the Morning Tribune rode thither on his bicycle every hour until three o'clock.

Six of the ten doctors in Whilomville attended at Judge Hagenthorpe's house.

Almost at once they were able to know that Trescott's burns were not vitally important. The child would possibly be scarred badly, but his life was undoubtedly safe. As for the negro Henry Johnson, he could not live. His body was frightfully seared, but more than that, he now had no face. His face had simply been burned away.

Trescott was always asking news of the two other patients. In the morning he seemed fresh and strong, so they told him that Johnson was doomed. They then saw him stir on the bed, and sprang quickly to see if the bandages needed readjusting. In the sudden glance he threw from one to another he impressed them as being both leonine and impracticable.

The morning paper announced the death of Henry Johnson. It contained a long interview with Edward J. Hannigan, in which the latter described in full the performance of Johnson at the fire. There was also an editorial built from all the best words in the vocabulary of the staff. The town halted in its accustomed road of thought, and turned a reverent attention to the memory of this hostler. In the breasts of many people was the regret that they had not known enough to give him a hand and a lift when he was alive, and they judged themselves stupid and ungenerous for this failure.

The name of Henry Johnson became suddenly the title of a saint to the little boys. The one who thought of it first could, by quoting it in an argument, at once overthrow his antagonist, whether it applied to the subject or whether it did not.

> *"Nigger, nigger, never die.*
> *Black face and shiny eye."*

Boys who had called this odious couplet in the rear of Johnson's march buried the fact at the bottom of their hearts.

Later in the day Miss Bella Farragut, of No. 7 Watermelon Alley, announced that she had been engaged to marry Mr. Henry Johnson.

## XI

The old judge had a cane with an ivory head. He could never think at his best until he was leaning slightly on this stick and smoothing the white top with slow movements of his hands. It was also to him a kind of narcotic. If by any chance he mislaid it, he grew at once very irritable, and was likely to speak sharply to his sister, whose mental incapacity he had patiently endured for thirty years in the old mansion on Ontario Street. She was not at all aware of her brother's opinion of her endowments, and so it might be said that the judge had successfully dissembled for more than a quarter of a century, only risking the truth at the times when his cane was lost.

On a particular day the judge sat in his armchair on the porch. The sunshine sprinkled through the lilac-bushes and poured great coins on the boards. The sparrows disputed in the trees that lined the pavements. The judge mused deeply, while his hands gently caressed the ivory head of his cane.

Finally he arose and entered the house, his brow still furrowed in a thoughtful frown. His stick thumped solemnly in regular beats. On the second floor he entered a room where Dr. Trescott was working about the bedside of Henry Johnson. The bandages on the negro's head allowed only one thing to appear, an eye, which unwinkingly stared at the judge. The later spoke to Trescott on the condition of the patient. Afterward he evidently had something further to say, but he seemed to be kept from it by the scrutiny of the unwinking eye, at which he furtively glanced from time to time.

When Jimmie Trescott was sufficiently recovered, his mother had taken him to pay a visit to his grandparents in Connecticut. The doctor had remained to take care of his patients, but as a matter of truth he spent most of his time at Judge Hagenthorpe's house, where lay Henry Johnson. Here he slept and ate almost every meal in the long nights and days of his vigil.

At dinner, and away from the magic of the unwinking eye, the judge said, suddenly, "Trescott, do you think it is—" As Trescott paused expectantly, the judge fingered his knife. He said, thoughtfully, "No one wants to advance such ideas, but somehow I think that that poor fellow ought to die."

There was in Trescott's face at once a look of recognition, as if in this tangent of the judge he saw an old problem. He merely sighed and answered, "Who knows?" The words were spoken in a deep tone that gave them an elusive kind of significance.

The judge retreated to the cold manner of the bench. "Perhaps we may not talk with propriety of this kind of action, but I am induced to say that you are performing a questionable charity in preserving this negro's life. As near as I can understand, he will hereafter be a monster, a perfect monster, and probably with an affected brain. No man can observe you as I have observed you and not know that it was a matter of conscience with you, but I am afraid, my friend, that it is one of the blunders of virtue." The judge had delivered his views with his habitual oratory. The last three words he spoke with a particular emphasis, as if the phrase was his discovery.

The doctor made a weary gesture. "He saved my boy's life."

"Yes," said the judge, swiftly—"yes, I know!"

"And what am I to do?" said Trescott, his eyes suddenly lighting like an outburst from smouldering peat. "What am I to do? He gave himself for—for Jimmie. What am I to do for him?"

The judge abased himself completely before these words. He lowered his eyes for a moment. He picked at his cucumbers.

Presently he braced himself straightly in his chair. "He will be your creation, you understand. He is purely your creation. Nature has very evidently given him up. He is dead. You are restoring him to life. You are making him, and he will be a monster, and with no mind.

"He will be what you like, judge," cried Trescott, in sudden, polite fury. "He will be anything, but, by God! he saved my boy."

The judge interrupted in a voice trembling with emotion: "Trescott! Trescott! Don't I know?"

Trescott had subsided to a sullen mood. "Yes, you know," he answered, acidly; "but you don't know all about your own boy being saved from death." This was a perfectly childish allusion to the judge's bachelorhood. Trescott knew that the remark was infantile, but he seemed to take desperate delight in it.

But it passed the judge completely. It was not his spot.

"I am puzzled," said he, in profound thought. "I don't know what to say."

Trescott had become repentant. "Don't think I don't appreciate what you say, judge. But—"

"Of course!" responded the judge, quickly. "Of course."

"It—" began Trescott.

"Of course," said the judge.

In silence they resumed their dinner.

"Well," said the judge, ultimately, "it is hard for a man to know what to do."

"It is," said the doctor, fervidly.

There was another silence. It was broken by the judge:

"Look here, Trescott; I don't want you to think—"

"No, certainly not," answered the doctor, earnestly.

"Well, I don't want you to think I would say anything to—It was only that I thought that I might be able to suggest to you that—perhaps—the affair was a little dubious."

With an appearance of suddenly disclosing his real mental perturbation, the doctor said: "Well, what would you do? Would you kill him?" he asked, abruptly and sternly.

"Trescott, you fool," said the old man, gently.

"Oh, well, I know, judge, but then—" He turned red, and spoke with new violence: "Say, he saved my boy—do you see? He saved my boy."

"You bet he did," cried the judge, with enthusiasm. "You bet he did." And they remained for a time gazing at each other, their faces illuminated with memories of a certain deed.

After another silence, the judge said, "It is hard for a man to know what to do."

## XII

Late one evening Trescott, returning from a professional call, paused his buggy at the Hagenthorpe gate. He tied the mare to the old tin-covered post, and entered the house. Ultimately he appeared with a companion—a man who walked slowly and carefully, as if he were learning. He was wrapped to the heels in an old-fashioned ulster. They entered the buggy and drove away.

After a silence only broken by the swift and musical humming of the wheels on the smooth road, Trescott spoke. "Henry," he said, "I've got you a home here with old Alek Williams. You will have everything you want to eat and a good place to sleep, and I hope you will get along there all right. I will pay all your expenses, and come to see you as often as I can. If you don't get along, I want you to let me know as soon as possible, and then we will do what we can to make it better."

The dark figure at the doctor's side answered with a cheerful laugh. "These buggy wheels don' look like I washed 'em yesterday, docteh," he said.

Trescott hesitated for a moment, and then went on insistently, "I am taking you to Alek Williams, Henry, and I—"

The figure chuckled again. "No, 'deed! No, seh! Alek Williams don' know a hoss! 'Deed he don't. He don' know a hoss from a pig." The laugh that followed was like the rattle of pebbles.

Trescott turned and looked sternly and coldly at the dim form in the gloom from the buggy-top. "Henry," he said, "I didn't say anything about horses. I was saying—"

"Hoss? Hoss?" said the quavering voice from these near shadows. "Hoss? 'Deed I don' know all erbout a boss! 'Deed I don't." There was a satirical chuckle.

At the end of three miles the mare slackened and the doctor leaned forward, peering, while holding tight reins. The wheels of the buggy bumped often over out-cropping bowlders. A window shone forth, a simple square of topaz on a great black hill-side. Four dogs charged the buggy with ferocity, and when it did not promptly retreat, they circled courageously around the flanks, baying. A door opened near the window in the hill-side, and a man came and stood on a beach of yellow light.

"Yah! yah! You Roveh! You Susie! Come yah! Come yah this minit!"

Trescott called across the dark sea of grass, "Hello, Alek!"

"Hello!"

"Come down here and show me where to drive."

The man plunged from the beach into the surf, and Trescott could then only trace his course by the fervid and polite ejaculations of a host who was somewhere approaching. Presently Williams took the mare by the head, and uttering cries of welcome and scolding the swarming dogs, led the equipage towards the lights. When they halted at the door and Trescott was climbing out, Williams cried, "Will she stand, docteh?"

"She'll stand all right, but you better hold her for a minute. Now, Henry." The doctor turned and held both arms to the dark figure. It crawled to him painfully like a man going down a ladder. Williams took the mare away to be tied to a little tree, and when he returned he found them awaiting him in the gloom beyond the rays from the door.

He burst out then like a siphon pressed by a nervous thumb. "Hennery! Hennery, ma ol' frien'. Well, if I ain' glade. If I ain' glade!"

Trescott had taken the silent shape by the arm and led it forward into the full revelation of the light. "Well, now, Alek, you can take Henry and put him to bed, and in the morning I will—"

Near the end of this sentence old Williams had come front to front with Johnson. He gasped for a second, and then yelled the yell of a man stabbed in the heart.

For a fraction of a moment Trescott seemed to be looking for epithets. Then he roared: "You old black chump! You old black—Shut up! Shut up! Do you hear?"

Williams obeyed instantly in the matter of his screams, but he continued in a lowered voice: "Ma Lode amassy! Who'd ever think? Ma Lode amassy!"

Trescott spoke again in the manner of a commander of a battalion. "Alek!"

The old negro again surrendered, but to himself he repeated in a whisper, "Ma Lode!" He was aghast and trembling.

As these three points of widening shadows approached the golden doorway a hale old negress appeared there, bowing. "Good-evenin', docteh! Good-evenin'! Come in! come in!" She had evidently just retired from a tempestuous struggle to place the room in order, but she was now bowing rapidly. She made the effort of a person swimming.

"Don't trouble yourself, Mary," said Trescott, entering. "I've brought Henry for you to take care of, and all you've got to do is to carry out what I tell you." Learning that he was not followed, he faced the door, and said, "Come in, Henry."

Johnson entered. "Whee!" shrieked Mrs. Williams. She almost achieved a back somersault. Six young members of the tribe of Williams made a simultaneous plunge for a position behind the stove, and formed a wailing heap.

## XIII

"You know very well that you and your family lived usually on less than three dollars a week, and now that Dr. Trescott pays you five dollars a week for Johnson's board, you live like millionaires. You haven't done a stroke of work since Johnson began to board with you—everybody knows that—and so what are you kicking about?"

The judge sat in his chair on the porch, fondling his cane, and gazing down at old Williams, who stood under the lilac-bushes. "Yes, I know, jedge," said the negro, wagging his head in a puzzled manner. "Tain't like as if I didn't 'preciate what the docteh done, but—but—well, yeh see, jedge," he added, gaining a new impetus, "it's—it's hard wuk. This ol' man nev' did wuk so hard. Lode, no."

"Don't talk such nonsense, Alek," spoke the judge, sharply. "You have never really worked in your life—anyhow, enough to support a family of sparrows, and now when you are in a more prosperous condition than ever before, you come around talking like an old fool."

The negro began to scratch his head. "Yeh see, jedge," he said at last, "my ol' 'ooman she cain't 'ceive no lady callahs, nohow."

"Hang lady callers'" said the judge, irascibly. "If you have flour in the barrel and meat in the pot, your wife can get along without receiving lady callers, can't she?"

"But they won't come ainyhow, jedge," replied Williams, with an air of still deeper stupefaction. "Noner ma wife's frien's ner noner ma frien's'll come near ma res'dence."

"Well, let them stay home if they are such silly people."

The old negro seemed to be seeking a way to elude this argument, but evidently finding none, he was about to shuffle meekly off. He halted, however. "Jedge," said he, "ma ol' 'ooman's near driv' abstracted."

"Your old woman is an idiot," responded the judge.

Williams came very close and peered solemnly through a branch of lilac. "Judge," he whispered, "the chillens."

"What about them?"

Dropping his voice to funereal depths, Williams said, "They—they cain't eat."

"Can't eat!" scoffed the judge, loudly. "Can't eat! You must think I am as big an old fool as you are. Can't eat—the little rascals! What's to prevent them from eating?"

In answer, Williams said, with mournful emphasis, "Hennery." Moved with a kind of satisfaction at his tragic use of the name, he remained staring at the judge for a sign of its effect.

The judge made a gesture of irritation. "Come, now, you old scoundrel, don't beat around the bush any more. What are you up to? What do you want? Speak out like a man, and don't give me any more of this tiresome rigamarole."

"I ain't er-beatin' round 'bout nuffin, jedge," replied Williams, indignantly. "No, seh; I say whatter got to say right out. 'Deed I do."

"Well, say it, then."

"Jedge," began the negro, taking off his hat and switching his knee with it, "Lode knows I'd do jes 'bout as much fer five dollehs er week as ainy cul'd man, but—but this yere business is awful, jedge. I raikon ain't been no sleep in—in my house sence docteh done fetch 'im."

"Well, what do you propose to do about it?"

Williams lifted his eyes from the ground and gazed off through the trees. "Raikon I got good appetite, an' sleep jes like er dog, but he—he's done broke me all up. 'Tain't no good, nohow. I wake up in the night; I hear 'im, mebbe, er-whimperin' an' er-whimperin', an' I sneak an' I sneak until I try th' do' to see if he locked in. An' he keep me er-puzzlin' an' er-quakin' all night long. Don't know how'll do in th' winter. Can't let 'im out where th' chillen is. He'll done freeze where he is now." Williams spoke these sentences as if he were talking to himself. After a silence of deep reflection he continued: "Folks go round sayin' he ain't Hennery Johnson at all. They say he's er devil!"

"What?" cried the judge.

"Yesseh," repeated Williams, in tones of injury, as if his veracity had been challenged. "Yesseh. I'm er-tellin' it to yeh straight, jedge. Plenty cul'd people folks up my way say it is a devil."

"Well, you don't think so yourself, do you?"

"No. 'Tain't no devil. It's Hennery Johnson."

"Well, then, what is the matter with you? You don't care what a lot of foolish people say. Go on 'tending to your business, and pay no attention to such idle nonsense."

"'Tis nonsense, jedge; but he *looks* like er devil."

"What do you care what he looks like?" demanded the judge.

"Ma rent is two dollehs and er half er month," said Williams, slowly.

"It might just as well be ten thousand dollars a month," responded the judge. "You never pay it, anyhow."

"Then, anoth' thing," continued Williams, in his reflective tone. "If he was all right in his haid I could stan' it; but, jedge, he's crazier 'n er loon. Then when he looks like er devil, an' done skears all ma frien's away, an' ma chillens cain't eat, an' ma ole 'ooman jes raisin' Cain all the time, an' ma rent two dollehs an' er half er month, an' him not right in his haid, it seems like five dollehs er week—"

The judge's stick came down sharply and suddenly upon the floor of the porch. "There," he said, "I thought that was what you were driving at."

Williams began swinging his head from side to side in the strange racial mannerism. "Now hol' on a minnet, jedge," he said, defensively. "'Tain't like as if I didn't 'preciate what the docteh done. 'Tain't that. Docteh Trescott is er kind man, an' 'tain't like as if I didn't 'preciate what he done; but—but—"

"But what? You are getting painful, Alek. Now tell me this: did you ever have five dollars a week regularly before in your life?"

Williams at once drew himself up with great dignity, but in the pause after that question he drooped gradually to another attitude. In the end he answered, heroically: "No, jedge, I ain't. An' 'tain't like as if I was er-sayin' five dollehs wasn't er lot er money for a man like me. But, jedge, what er man oughter git fer this kinder wuk is er salary. Yesseh, jedge," he repeated, with a great impressive gesture; "fer this kinder wuk er man oughter git er Salary." He laid a terrible emphasis upon the final word.

The judge laughed. "I know Dr. Trescott's mind concerning this affair, Alek; and if you are dissatisfied with your boarder, he is quite ready to move him to some other place; so, if you care to leave word with me that you are tired of the arrangement and wish it changed, he will come and take Johnson away."

Williams scratched his head again in deep perplexity. "Five dollehs is er big price fer bo'd, but 'tain't no big price fer the bo'd of er crazy man," he said, finally.

"What do you think you ought to get?" asked the judge.

"Well," answered Alek, in the manner of one deep in a balancing of the scales, "he looks like er devil, an' done skears e'rybody, an' ma chillens cain't eat, an' I cain't sleep, an' he ain't right in his haid, an'—"

"You told me all those things."

After scratching his wool, and beating his knee with his hat, and gazing off through the trees and down at the ground, Williams said, as he kicked nervously at the gravel, "Well, jedge, I think it is wuth—" He stuttered.

"Worth what?"

"Six dollehs," answered Williams, in a desperate outburst.

The judge lay back in his great arm-chair and went through all the motions of a man laughing heartily, but he made no sound save a slight cough. Williams had been watching him with apprehension.

"Well," said the judge, "do you call six dollars a salary?"

"No, seh," promptly responded Williams. "'Tain't a salary. No, 'deed! 'Tain't a salary." He looked with some anger upon the man who questioned his intelligence in this way.

"Well, supposing your children can't eat?"

"I—"

"And supposing he looks like a devil? And supposing all those things continue? Would you be satisfied with six dollars a week?"

Recollections seemed to throng in Williams's mind at these interrogations, and he answered dubiously. "Of co'se a man who ain't right in his haid, an' looks like er devil—But six dollehs—" After these two attempts at a sentence Williams suddenly appeared as an orator, with a great shiny palm waving in the air. "I tell yeh, jedge, six dollehs is six dollehs, but if I git six dollehs for bo'ding Hennery Johnson, I uhns it! I uhns it!"

"I don't doubt that you earn six dollars for every week's work you do," said the judge.

"Well, if I bo'd Hennery Johnson fer six dollehs er week, I uhns it! I uhns it!" cried Williams, wildly.


<h2 style="text-align:center">XIV</h2>

Reifsnyder's assistant had gone to his supper, and the owner of the shop was trying to placate four men who wished to be shaved at once. Reifsnyder was very garrulous—a fact which made him rather remarkable among barbers, who, as a class, are austerely speechless, having been taught silence by the hammering reiteration of a tradition. It is the customers who talk in the ordinary event.

As Reifsnyder waved his razor down the cheek of a man in the chair, he turned often to cool the impatience of the others with pleasant talk, which they did not particularly heed.

"Oh, he should have let him die," said Bainbridge, a railway engineer, finally replying to one of the barber's orations. "Shut up, Reif, and go on with your business!"

Instead, Reifsnyder paused shaving entirely, and turned to front the speaker. "Let him die?" he demanded. "How vas that? How can you let a man die?"

"By letting him die, you chump," said the engineer. The others laughed a little, and Reifsnyder turned at once to his work, sullenly, as a man overwhelmed by the derision of numbers.

"How vas that?" he grumbled later. "How can you let a man die when he vas done so much for you?"

"'When he vas done so much for you?'" repeated Bainbridge. "You better shave some people. How vas that? Maybe this ain't a barber shop?"

A man hitherto silent now said, "If I had been the doctor, I would have done the same thing."

"Of course," said Reifsnyder. "Any man vould do it. Any man that vas not like you, you—old—flint-hearted—fish." He had sought the final words with painful care, and he delivered the collection triumphantly at Bainbridge. The engineer laughed.

The man in the chair now lifted himself higher, while Reifsnyder began an elaborate ceremony of anointing and combing his hair. Now free to join comfortably in the talk, the man said: "They say he is the most terrible thing in the world. Young Johnnie Bernard—that drives the grocery wagon—saw him up at Alek Williams's shanty, and he says he couldn't eat anything for two days."

"Chee!" said Reifsnyder.

"Well, what makes him so terrible?" asked another.

"Because he hasn't got any face," replied the barber and the engineer in duct.

"Hasn't got any face!" repeated the man. "How can he do without any face?"

> *"He has no face in the front of his head.*
> *In the place where his face ought to grow."*

Bainbridge sang these lines pathetically as he arose and hung his hat on a hook. The man in the chair was about to abdicate in his favor. "Get a gait on you now," he said to Reifsnyder. "I go out at 7.31."

As the barber foamed the lather on the cheeks of the engineer he seemed to be thinking heavily. Then suddenly he burst out. "How would you like to be with no face?" he cried to the assemblage.

"Oh, if I had to have a face like yours—" answered one customer.

Bainbridge's voice came from a sea of lather. "You're kicking because if losing faces became popular, you'd have to go out of business."

"I don't think it will become so much popular," said Reifsnyder.

"Not if it's got to be taken off in the way his was taken off," said another man. "I'd rather keep mine, if you don't mind."

"I guess so!" cried the barber. "Just think!"

The shaving of Bainbridge had arrived at a time of comparative liberty for him. "I wonder what the doctor says to himself?" he observed. "He may be sorry he made him live."

"It was the only thing he could do," replied a man. The others seemed to agree with him.

"Supposing you were in his place," said one, "and Johnson had saved your kid. What would you do?"

"Certainly!"

"Of course! You would do anything on earth for him. You'd take all the trouble in the world for him. And spend your last dollar on him. Well, then?"

"I wonder how it feels to be without any face?" said Reifsnyder, musingly.

The man who had previously spoken, feeling that he had expressed himself well, repeated the whole thing. "You would do anything on earth for him. You'd take all the trouble in the world for him. And spend your last dollar on him. Well, then?"

"No, but look," said Reifsnyder; "supposing you don't got a face!"

<h1 style="text-align:center">XV</h1>

As soon as Williams was hidden from the view of the old judge he began to gesture and talk to himself. An elation had evidently penetrated to his vitals, and caused him to dilate as if he had been filled with gas. He snapped his fingers in the air, and whistled fragments of triumphal music. At times, in his progress towards his shanty, he indulged in a shuffling movement that was really a dance. It was to be learned from the intermediate monologue that he had emerged from his trials laurelled and proud. He was the unconquerable Alexander Williams. Nothing could exceed the bold self-reliance of his manner. His kingly stride, his heroic song, the derisive flourish of his hands—all betokened a man who had successfully defied the world.

On his way he saw Zeke Paterson coming to town. They hailed each other at a distance of fifty yards.

"How do, Broth' Paterson?"

"How do, Broth' Williams?"

They were both deacons.

"Is you' folks well, Broth' Paterson?"

"Middlin', middlin'. How's you' folks, Broth' Williams?"

Neither of them had slowed his pace in the smallest degree. They had simply begun this talk when a considerable space separated them, continued it as they passed, and added polite questions as they drifted steadily apart. Williams's mind seemed to be a balloon. He had been so inflated that he had not noticed that Paterson had definitely shied into the dry ditch as they came to the point of ordinary contact.

Afterwards, as he went a lonely way, he burst out again in song and pantomimic celebration of his estate. His feet moved in prancing steps.

When he came in sight of his cabin, the fields were bathed in a blue dusk, and the light in the window was pale. Cavorting and gesticulating, he gazed joyfully for some moments upon this light. Then suddenly another idea seemed to attack his mind, and he stopped, with an air of being suddenly dampened. In the end he approached his home as if it were the fortress of an enemy.

Some dogs disputed his advance for a loud moment, and then discovering their lord, slunk away embarrassed. His reproaches were addressed to them in muffled tones.

Arriving at the door, he pushed it open with the timidity of a new thief. He thrust his head cautiously sideways, and his eyes met the eyes of his wife, who sat by the table, the lamp-light defining a half of her face. "'Sh!" he said, uselessly. His glance travelled swiftly to the inner door which shielded the one bed-chamber. The pickaninnies, strewn upon the floor of the living-room, were softly snoring. After a hearty meal they had promptly dispersed themselves about the place and gone to sleep. "'Sh!" said Williams again to his motionless and silent wife. He had allowed only his head to appear. His wife, with one hand upon the edge of the table and the other at her knee, was regarding him with wide eyes and parted lips as if he were a spectre. She looked to be one who was living in terror, and even the familiar face at the door had thrilled her because it had come suddenly.

Williams broke the tense silence. "Is he all right?" he whispered, waving his eyes towards the inner door. Following his glance timorously, his wife nodded, and in a low tone answered:

"I raikon he's done gone t' sleep."

Williams then slunk noiselessly across his threshold.

He lifted a chair, and with infinite care placed it so that it faced the dreaded inner door. His wife moved slightly, so as to also squarely face it. A silence came upon them in which they seemed to be waiting for a calamity, pealing and deadly.

Williams finally coughed behind his hand. His wife started, and looked upon him in alarm. "Pears like he done gwine keep quiet ternight," he breathed. They continually pointed their speech and their looks at the inner door, paying it the homage due to a corpse or a phantom. Another long stillness followed this sentence. Their eyes shone white and wide. A wagon rattled down the distant road. From their chairs they looked at the window, and the effect of the light in the cabin was a presentation of an intensely black and solemn night. The old woman adopted the attitude used always in church at funerals. At times she seemed to be upon the point of breaking out in prayer.

"He mighty quiet ter-night," whispered Williams. "Was he good ter-day?" For answer his wife raised her eyes to the ceiling in the supplication of Job. Williams moved restlessly. Finally he tiptoed to the door. He knelt slowly and without a sound, and placed his ear near the key-hole. Hearing a noise behind him, he turned quickly. His wife was staring at him aghast. She stood in front of the stove, and her arms were spread out in the natural movement to protect all her sleeping ducklings.

But Williams arose without having touched the door. "I raikon he er-sleep," he said, fingering his wool. He debated with himself for some time. During this interval his wife remained, a great fat statue of a mother shielding her children.

It was plain that his mind was swept suddenly by a wave of temerity. With a sounding step he moved towards the door. His fingers were almost upon the knob when he swiftly ducked and dodged away, clapping his hands to the back of his head. It was as if the portal had threatened him. There was a little tumult near the stove, where Mrs. Williams's desperate retreat had involved her feet with the prostrate children.

After the panic Williams bore traces of a feeling of shame. He returned to the charge. He firmly grasped the knob with his left hand, and with his other hand turned the key in the lock. He pushed the door, and as it swung portentously open he sprang nimbly to one side like the fearful slave liberating the lion. Near the stove a group had formed, the terror stricken mother, with her arms stretched, and the aroused children clinging frenziedly to her skirts.

The light streamed after the swinging door, and disclosed a room six feet one way and six feet the other way. It was small enough to enable the radiance to lay it plain. Williams peered warily around the corner made by the door-post.

Suddenly he advanced, retired, and advanced again with a howl. His palsied family had expected him to spring backward, and at his howl they heaped themselves wondrously. But Williams simply stood in the little room emitting his howls before an open window. "He's gone! He's gone! He's gone!" His eye and his hand had speedily proved the fact. He had even thrown open a little cupboard.

Presently he came flying out. He grabbed his hat, and hurled the outer door back upon its hinges. Then he tumbled headlong into the night. He was yelling: "Docteh Trescott! Docteh Trescott!" He ran wildly through the fields, and galloped in the direction of town. He continued to call to Trescott, as if the latter was within easy hearing. It was as if Trescott was poised in the contemplative sky over the running negro, and could heed this reaching voice—"Docteh Trescott!"

In the cabin, Mrs. Williams, supported by relays from the battalion of children, stood quaking watch until the truth of daylight came as a reinforcement and made the arrogant, strutting, swashbuckler children, and a mother who proclaimed her illimitable courage.

<h1 style="text-align:center">XVI</h1>

Theresa Page was giving a party. It was the outcome of a long series of arguments addressed to her mother, which had been overheard in part by her father. He had at last said five words, "Oh, let her have it." The mother had then gladly capitulated.

Theresa had written nineteen invitations, and distributed them at recess to her schoolmates. Later her mother had composed five large cakes, and still later a vast amount of lemonade.

So the nine little girls and the ten little boys sat quite primly in the dining-room, while Theresa and her mother plied them with cake and lemonade, and also with ice-cream. This primness sat now quite strangely upon them. It was owing to the presence of Mrs. Page. Previously in the parlor alone with their games they had overturned a chair; the boys had let more or less of their hoodlum spirit shine forth. But when circumstances could be possibly magnified to warrant it, the girls made the boys victims of an insufferable pride, snubbing them mercilessly. So in the dining-room they resembled a class at Sunday-school, if it were not for the subterranean smiles, gestures, rebuffs, and poutings which stamped the affair as a children's party.

Two little girls of this subdued gathering were planted in a settle with their backs to the broad window. They were beaming lovingly upon each other with an effect of scorning the boys.

Hearing a noise behind her at the window, one little girl turned to face it. Instantly she screamed and sprang away, covering her face with her hands. "What was it? What was it?" cried every one in a roar. Some slight movement of the eyes of the weeping and shuddering child informed the company that she had been frightened by an appearance at the window. At once they all faced the imperturbable window, and for a moment there was a silence. An astute lad made an immediate census of the other lads. The prank of slipping out and looming spectrally at a window was too venerable. But the little boys were all present and astonished.

As they recovered their minds they uttered warlike cries, and through a side door sallied rapidly out against the terror. They vied with each other in daring.

None wished particularly to encounter a dragon in the darkness of the garden, but there could be no faltering when the fair ones in the dining-room were present. Calling to each other in stern voices, they went dragooning over the lawn, attacking the shadows with ferocity, but still with the caution of reasonable beings. They found, however, nothing new to the peace of the night. Of course there was a lad who told a great lie. He described a grim figure, bending low and slinking off along the fence. He gave a number of details, rendering his lie more splendid by a repetition of certain forms which he recalled from romances. For instance, he insisted that he had heard the creature emit a hollow laugh.

Inside the house the little girl who had raised the alarm was still shuddering and weeping. With the utmost difficulty was she brought to a state approximating calmness by Mrs. Page. Then she wanted to go home at once.

Page entered the house at this time. He had exiled himself until he concluded that this children's party was finished and gone. He was obliged to escort the little girl home because she screamed again when they opened the door and she saw the night.

She was not coherent even to her mother. Was it a man? She didn't know. It was simply a thing, a dreadful thing.

## XVII

In Watermelon Alley the Farraguts were spending their evening as usual on the little rickety porch. Sometimes they howled gossip to other people on other rickety porches. The thin wail of a baby arose from a near house. A man had a terrific altercation with his wife, to which the alley paid no attention at all.

There appeared suddenly before the Farraguts a monster making a low and sweeping bow. There was an instant's pause, and then occurred something that resembled the effect of an upheaval of the earth's surface. The old woman hurled herself backward with a dreadful cry. Young Sim had been perched gracefully on a railing. At sight of the monster he simply fell over it to the ground. He made no sound, his eyes stuck out, his nerveless hands tried to grapple the rail to prevent a tumble, and then he vanished. Bella, blubbering, and with her hair suddenly and mysteriously dishevelled, was crawling on her hands and knees fearsomely up the steps.

Standing before this wreck of a family gathering, the monster continued to bow. It even raised a deprecatory claw. "Doh' make no botheration 'bout me, Miss Fa'gut," it said, politely. "No, 'deed. I jes drap in ter ax if yer well this evenin', Miss Fa'gut. Don' make no botheration. No, 'deed. I gwine ax you to go to er daince with me, Miss Fa'gut. I ax you if I can have the magnifercent gratitude of you' company on that 'casion, Miss Fa'gut."

The girl cast a miserable glance behind her. She was still crawling away. On the ground beside the porch young Sim raised a strange bleat, which expressed both his fright and his lack of wind. Presently the monster, with a fashionable amble, ascended the steps after the girl.

She grovelled in a corner of the room as the creature took a chair. It seated itself very elegantly on the edge. It held an old cap in both hands. "Don' make no botheration, Miss Fa'gut. Don' make no botherations. No, 'deed. I jes drap in ter ax you if you won' do me the proud of acceptin' ma humble invitation to er daince, Miss Fa'gut."

She shielded her eyes with her arms and tried to crawl past it, but the genial monster blocked the way. "I jes drap in ter ax you 'bout er daince, Miss Fa'gut. I ax you if I kin have the magnifercent gratitude of you' company on that 'casion, Miss Fa'gut."

In a last outbreak of despair, the girl, shuddering and wailing, threw herself face downward on the floor, while the monster sat on the edge of the chair gabbling courteous invitations, and holding the old hat daintily to his stomach.

At the back of the house, Mrs. Farragut, who was of enormous weight, and who for eight years had done little more than sit in an armchair and describe her various ailments, had with speed and agility scaled a high board fence.

## XVIII

The black mass in the middle of Trescott's property was hardly allowed to cool before the builders were at work on another house. It had sprung upward at a fabulous rate. It was like a magical composition born of the ashes. The doctor's office was the first part to be completed, and he had already moved in his new books and instruments and medicines.

Trescott sat before his desk when the chief of police arrived. "Well, we found him," said the latter.

"Did you?" cried the doctor. "Where?"

"Shambling around the streets at daylight this morning. I'll be blamed if I can figure on where he passed the night."

"Where is he now?"

"Oh, we jugged him. I didn't know what else to do with him. That's what I want you to tell me. Of course we can't keep him. No charge could be made, you know."

"I'll come down and get him."

The official grinned retrospectively. "Must say he had a fine career while he was out. First thing he did was to break up a children's party at Page's. Then he went to Watermelon Alley. Whoo! He stampeded the whole outfit. Men, women, and children running pell-mell, and yelling. They say one old woman broke her leg, or something, shinning over a fence. Then he went right out on the main street, and an Irish girl threw a fit, and there was a sort of a riot. He began to run, and a big crowd chased him, firing rocks. But he gave them the slip somehow down there by the foundry and in the railroad yard. We looked for him all night, but couldn't find him."

"Was he hurt any? Did anybody hit him with a stone?"

"Guess there isn't much of him to hurt any more, is there? Guess he's been hurt up to the limit. No. They never touched him. Of course nobody really wanted to hit him, but you know how a crowd gets. It's like—it's like—"

"Yes, I know."

For a moment the chief of the police looked reflectively at the floor. Then he spoke hesitatingly. "You know Jake Winter's little girl was the one that he scared at the party. She is pretty sick, they say."

"Is she? Why, they didn't call me. I always attend the Winter family."

"No? Didn't they?" asked the chief, slowly. "Well—you know—Winter is—well, Winter has gone clean crazy over this business. He wanted—he wanted to have you arrested."

"Have me arrested? The idiot! What in the name of wonder could he have me arrested for?"

"Of course. He is a fool. I told him to keep his trap shut. But then you know how he'll go all over town yapping about the thing. I thought I'd better tip you."

"Oh, he is of no consequence; but then, of course, I'm obliged to you, Sam."

"That's all right. Well, you'll be down tonight and take him out, eh? You'll get a good welcome from the jailer. He don't like his job for a cent. He says you can have your man whenever you want him. He's got no use for him."

"But what is this business of Winter's about having me arrested?"

"Oh, it's a lot of chin about your having no right to allow this—this—this man to be at large. But I told him to tend to his own business. Only I thought I'd better let you know. And I might as well say right now, doctor, that there is a good deal of talk about this thing. If I were you, I'd come to the jail pretty late at night, because there is likely to be a crowd around the door, and I'd bring a—er—mask, or some kind of a veil, anyhow."

## XIX

Martha Goodwin was single, and well along into the thin years. She lived with her married sister in Whilomville. She performed nearly all the house-work in exchange for the privilege of existence. Every one tacitly recognized her labor as a form of penance for the early end of her betrothed, who had died of small-pox, which he had not caught from her.

But despite the strenuous and unceasing workaday of her life, she was a woman of great mind. She had adamantine opinions upon the situation in Armenia, the condition of women in China, the flirtation between Mrs. Minster of Niagara Avenue and young Griscom, the conflict in the Bible class of the Baptist Sunday-school, the duty of the United States towards the Cuban insurgents, and many other colossal matters. Her fullest experience of violence was gained on an occasion when she had seen a hound clubbed, but in the plan which she had made for the reform of the world she advocated drastic measures. For instance, she contended that all the Turks should be pushed into the sea and drowned, and that Mrs. Minster and young Griscom should be hanged side by side on twin gallows. In fact, this woman of peace, who had seen only peace, argued constantly for a creed of illimitable ferocity. She was invulnerable on these questions, because eventually she overrode all opponents with a sniff. This sniff was an active force. It was to her antagonists like a bang over the head, and none was known to recover from this expression of exalted contempt. It left them windless and conquered. They never again came forward as candidates for suppression. And Martha walked her kitchen with a stern brow, an invincible being like Napoleon.

Nevertheless her acquaintances, from the pain of their defeats, had been long in secret revolt. It was in no wise a conspiracy, because they did not care to state their open rebellion, but nevertheless it was understood that any woman who could not coincide with one of Martha's contentions was entitled to the support of others in the small circle. It amounted to an arrangement by which all were required to disbelieve any theory for which Martha fought. This, however, did not prevent them from speaking of her mind with profound respect.

Two people bore the brunt of her ability. Her sister Kate was visibly afraid of her, while Carrie Dungen sailed across from her kitchen to sit respectfully at Martha's feet and learn the business of the world. To be sure, afterwards, under another sun, she always laughed at Martha and pretended to deride her ideas, but in the presence of the sovereign she always remained silent or admiring. Kate, the sister, was of no consequence at all. Her principal delusion was that she did all the work in the up-stairs rooms of the house, while Martha did it down-stairs. The truth was seen only by the husband, who treated Martha with a kindness that was half banter, half deference. Martha herself had no suspicion that she was the only pillar of the domestic edifice. The situation was without definitions. Martha made definitions, but she devoted them entirely to the Armenians and Griscom and the Chinese and other subjects. Her dreams, which in early days had been of love of meadows and the shade of trees, of the face of a man, were now involved otherwise, and they were companioned in the kitchen curiously, Cuba, the hot-water kettle, Armenia, the washing of the dishes, and the whole thing being jumbled. In regard to social misdemeanors, she who was simply the mausoleum of a dead passion was probably the most savage critic in town. This unknown woman, hidden in a kitchen as in a well, was sure to have a considerable effect of the one kind or the other in the life of the town. Every time it moved a yard, she had personally contributed an inch. She could hammer so stoutly upon the door of a proposition that it would break from its hinges and fall upon her, but at any rate it moved. She was an engine, and the fact that she did not know that she was an engine contributed largely to the effect. One reason that she was formidable was that she did not even imagine that she was formidable. She remained a weak, innocent, and pig-headed creature, who alone would defy the universe if she thought the universe merited this proceeding.

One day Carrie Dungen came across from her kitchen with speed. She had a great deal of grist. "Oh," she cried, "Henry Johnson got away from where they was keeping him, and came to town last night, and scared everybody almost to death."

Martha was shining a dish-pan, polishing madly. No reasonable person could see cause for this operation, because the pan already glistened like silver. "Well!" she ejaculated. She imparted to the word a deep meaning. "This, my prophecy, has come to pass." It was a habit.

The overplus of information was choking Carrie. Before she could go on she was obliged to struggle for a moment. "And, oh, little Sadie Winter is awful sick, and they say Jake Winter was around this morning trying to get Doctor Trescott arrested. And poor old Mrs. Farragut sprained her ankle in trying to climb a fence. And there's a crowd around the jail all the time. They put Henry in jail because they didn't know what else to do with him, I guess. They say he is perfectly terrible."

Martha finally released the dish-pan and confronted the headlong speaker. "Well!" she said again, poising a great brown rag. Kate had heard the excited new-comer, and drifted down from the novel in her room. She was a shivery little woman. Her shoulder-blades seemed to be two panes of ice, for she was constantly shrugging and shrugging. "Serves him right if he was to lose all his patients," she said suddenly, in blood-thirsty tones. She snipped her words out as if her lips were scissors.

"Well, he's likely to," shouted Carrie Dungen. "Don't a lot of people say that they won't have him any more? If you're sick and nervous, Doctor Trescott would scare the life out of you, wouldn't he? He would me. I'd keep thinking."

Martha, stalking to and fro, sometimes surveyed the two other women with a contemplative frown.

**XX**

After the return from Connecticut, little Jimmie was at first much afraid of the monster who lived in the room over the carriage-house. He could not identify it in any way. Gradually, however, his fear dwindled under the influence of a weird fascination. He sidled into closer and closer relations with it.

One time the monster was seated on a box behind the stable basking in the rays of the afternoon sun. A heavy crepe veil was swathed about its head.

Little Jimmie and many companions came around the corner of the stable. They were all in what was popularly known as the baby class, and consequently escaped from school a half-hour before the other children. They halted abruptly at sight of the figure on the box. Jimmie waved his hand with the air of a proprietor.

"There he is," he said.

"O-o-o!" murmured all the little boys—"o-o-o!" They shrank back, and grouped according to courage or experience, as at the sound the monster slowly turned its head. Jimmie had remained in the van alone. "Don't be afraid! I won't let him hurt you," he said, delighted.

"Huh!" they replied, contemptuously. "We ain't afraid."

Jimmie seemed to reap all the joys of the owner and exhibitor of one of the world's marvels, while his audience remained at a distance—awed and entranced, fearful and envious.

One of them addressed Jimmie gloomily. "Bet you dassent walk right up to him." He was an older boy than Jimmie, and habitually oppressed him to a small degree. This new social elevation of the smaller lad probably seemed revolutionary to him.

"Huh!" said Jimmie, with deep scorn. "Dassent I? Dassent I, hey? Dassent I?"

The group was immensely excited. It turned its eyes upon the boy that Jimmie addressed. "No, you dassent," he said, stolidly, facing a moral defeat. He could see that Jimmie was resolved. "No, you dassent," he repeated, doggedly.

"Ho?" cried Jimmie. "You just watch!—you just watch!"

Amid a silence he turned and marched towards the monster. But possibly the palpable wariness of his companions had an effect upon him that weighed more than his previous experience, for suddenly, when near to the monster, he halted dubiously. But his playmates immediately uttered a derisive shout, and it seemed to force him forward. He went to the monster and laid his hand delicately on its shoulder. "Hello, Henry," he said, in a voice that trembled a trifle. The monster was crooning a weird line of negro melody that was scarcely more than a thread of sound, and it paid no heed to the boy.

Jimmie: strutted back to his companions. They acclaimed him and hooted his opponent. Amid this clamor the larger boy with difficulty preserved a dignified attitude.

"I dassent, dassent I?" said Jimmie to him.

"Now, you're so smart, let's see you do it!"

This challenge brought forth renewed taunts from the others. The larger boy puffed out his checks. "Well, I ain't afraid," he explained, sullenly. He had made a mistake in diplomacy, and now his small enemies were tumbling his prestige all about his ears. They crowed like roosters and bleated like lambs, and made many other noises which were supposed to bury him in ridicule and dishonor. "Well, I ain't afraid," he continued to explain through the din.

Jimmie, the hero of the mob, was pitiless. "You ain't afraid, hey?" he sneered. "If you ain't afraid, go do it, then."

"Well, I would if I wanted to," the other retorted. His eyes wore an expression of profound misery, but he preserved steadily other portions of a pot-valiant air. He suddenly faced one of his persecutors. "If you're so smart, why don't you go do it?" This persecutor sank promptly through the group to the rear. The incident gave the badgered one a breathing-spell, and for a moment even turned the derision in another direction. He took advantage of his interval. "I'll do it if anybody else will," he announced, swaggering to and fro.

Candidates for the adventure did not come forward. To defend themselves from this counter-charge, the other boys again set up their crowing and bleating. For a while they would hear nothing from him. Each time he opened his lips their chorus of noises made oratory impossible. But at last he was able to repeat that he would volunteer to dare as much in the affair as any other boy.

"Well, you go first," they shouted.

But Jimmie intervened to once more lead the populace against the large boy. "You're mighty brave, ain't you?" he said to him. "You dared me to do it, and I did—didn't I? Now who's afraid?" The others cheered this view loudly, and they instantly resumed the baiting of the large boy.

He shamefacedly scratched his left shin with his right foot. "Well, I ain't afraid." He cast an eye at the monster. "Well, I ain't afraid." With a glare of hatred at his squalling tormentors, he finally announced a grim intention. "Well, I'll do it, then, since you're so fresh. Now!"

The mob subsided as with a formidable countenance he turned towards the impassive figure on the box. The advance was also a regular progression from high daring to craven hesitation. At last, when some yards from the monster, the lad came to a full halt, as if he had encountered a stone wall. The observant little boys in the distance promptly hooted. Stung again by these cries, the lad sneaked two yards forward. He was crouched like a young cat ready for a backward spring. The crowd at the rear, beginning to respect this display, uttered some encouraging cries. Suddenly the lad gathered himself together, made a white and desperate rush forward, touched the monster's shoulder with a far-outstretched finger, and sped away, while his laughter rang out wild, shrill, and exultant.

The crowd of boys reverenced him at once, and began to throng into his camp, and look at him, and be his admirers. Jimmie was discomfited for a moment, but he and the larger boy, without agreement or word of any kind, seemed to recognize a truce, and they swiftly combined and began to parade before the others.

"Why, it's just as easy as nothing," puffed the larger boy. "Ain't it, Jim?"

"Course," blew Jimmie. "Why, it's as e-e-easy."

They were people of another class. If they had been decorated for courage on twelve battle-fields, they could not have made the other boys more ashamed of the situation.

Meanwhile they condescended to explain the emotions of the excursion, expressing unqualified contempt for any one who could hang back. "Why, it ain't nothin'. He won't do nothin' to you," they told the others, in tones of exasperation.

One of the very smallest boys in the party showed signs of a wistful desire to distinguish himself, and they turned their attention to him, pushing at his shoulders while he swung away from them, and hesitated dreamily. He was eventually induced to make furtive expedition, but it was only for a few yards. Then he paused, motionless, gazing with open mouth. The vociferous entreaties of Jimmie and the large boy had no power over him.

Mrs. Hannigan had come out on her back porch with a pail of water. From this coign she had a view of the secluded portion of the Trescott grounds that was behind the stable. She perceived the group of boys, and the monster on the box. She shaded her eyes with her hand to benefit her vision. She screeched then as if she was being murdered. "Eddie! Eddie! You come home this minute!"

Her son querulously demanded, "Aw, what for?"

"You come home this minute. Do you hear?"

The other boys seemed to think this visitation upon one of their number required them to preserve for a time the hang-dog air of a collection of culprits, and they remained in guilty silence until the little Hannigan, wrathfully protesting, was pushed through the door of his home. Mrs. Hannigan cast a piercing glance over the group, stared with a bitter face at the Trescott house, as if this new and handsome edifice was insulting her, and then followed her son.

There was wavering in the party. An inroad by one mother always caused them to carefully sweep the horizon to see if there were more coming. "This is my yard," said Jimmie, proudly. "We don't have to go home."

The monster on the box had turned its black crepe countenance towards the sky, and was waving its arms in time to a religious chant. "Look at him now," cried a little boy. They turned, and were transfixed by the solemnity and mystery of the indefinable gestures. The wail of the melody was mournful and slow. They drew back. It seemed to spellbind them with the power of a funeral. They were so absorbed that they did not hear the doctor's buggy drive up to the stable. Trescott got out, tied his horse, and approached the group. Jimmie saw him first, and at his look of dismay the others wheeled.

"What's all this, Jimmie?" asked Trescott, in surprise.

The lad advanced to the front of his companions, halted, and said nothing. Trescott's face gloomed slightly as he scanned the scene.

"What were you doing, Jimmie?"

"We was playin'," answered Jimmie, huskily.

"Playing at what?"

"Just playin'."

Trescott looked gravely at the other boys, and asked them to please go home. They proceeded to the street much in the manner of frustrated and revealed assassins. The crime of trespass on another boy's place was still a crime when they had only accepted the other boy's cordial invitation, and they were used to being sent out of all manner of gardens upon the sudden appearance of a father or a mother. Jimmie had wretchedly watched the departure of his companions. It involved the loss of his position as a lad who controlled the privileges of his father's grounds, but then he knew that in the beginning he had no right to ask so many boys to be his guests.

Once on the sidewalk, however, they speedily forgot their shame as trespassers, and the large boy launched forth in a description of his success in the late trial of courage. As they went rapidly up the street, the little boy who had made the furtive expedition cried out confidently from the rear, "Yes, and I went almost up to him, didn't I, Willie?"

The large boy crushed him in a few words. "Huh!" he scoffed. "You only went a little way. I went clear up to him."

The pace of the other boys was so manly that the tiny thing had to trot, and he remained at the rear, getting entangled in their legs in his attempts to reach the front rank and become of some importance, dodging this way and that way, and always piping out his little claim to glory.

## XXI

"By-the-way, Grace," said Trescott, looking into the dining-room from his office door, "I wish you would send Jimmie to me before school-time."

When Jimmie came, he advanced so quietly that Trescott did not at first note him. "Oh," he said, wheeling from a cabinet, "here you are, young man."

"Yes, sir."

Trescott dropped into his chair and tapped the desk with a thoughtful finger. "Jimmie, what were you doing in the back garden yesterday—you and the other boys—to Henry?"

"We weren't doing anything, pa."

Trescott looked sternly into the raised eyes of his son. "Are you sure you were not annoying him in any way? Now what were you doing, exactly?"

"Why, we—why, we—now—Willie Dalzel said I dassent go right up to him, and I did; and then he did; and then—the other boys were 'fraid; and then—you comed."

Trescott groaned deeply. His countenance was so clouded in sorrow that the lad, bewildered by the mystery of it, burst suddenly forth in dismal lamentations. "There, there. Don't cry, Jim," said Trescott, going round the desk. "Only—" He sat in a great leather reading-chair, and took the boy on his knee. "Only I want to explain to you—"

After Jimmie had gone to school, and as Trescott was about to start on his round of morning calls, a message arrived from Doctor Moser. It set forth that the latter's sister was dying in the old homestead, twenty miles away up the valley, and asked Trescott to care for his patients for the day at least. There was also in the envelope a little history of each case and of what had already been done. Trescott replied to the messenger that he would gladly assent to the arrangement.

He noted that the first name on Moser's list was Winter, but this did not seem to strike him as an important fact. When its turn came, he rang the Winter bell. "Good-morning, Mrs. Winter," he said, cheerfully, as the door was opened. "Doctor Moser has been obliged to leave town today, and he has asked me to come in his stead. How is the little girl this morning?"

Mrs. Winter had regarded him in stony surprise. At last she said: "Come in! I'll see my husband." She bolted into the house. Trescott entered the hall, and turned to the left into the sitting-room.

Presently Winter shuffled through the door. His eyes flashed towards Trescott. He did not betray any desire to advance far into the room. "What do you want?" he said.

"What do I want? What do I want?" repeated Trescott, lifting his head suddenly. He had heard an utterly new challenge in the night of the jungle.

"Yes, that's what I want to know," snapped Winter. "What do you want?"

Trescott was silent for a moment. He consulted Moser's memoranda. "I see that your little girl's case is a trifle serious," he remarked. "I would advise you to call a physician soon. I will leave you a copy of Dr. Moser's record to give to any one you may call." He paused to transcribe the record on a page of his note-book. Tearing out the leaf, he extended it to Winter as he moved towards the door. The latter shrunk against the wall. His head was hanging as he reached for the paper. This caused him to grasp air, and so Trescott simply let the paper flutter to the feet of the other man.

"Good-morning," said Trescott from the hall. This placid retreat seemed to suddenly arouse Winter to ferocity. It was as if he had then recalled all the truths which he had formulated to hurl at Trescott. So he followed him into the hall, and down the hall to the door, and through the door to the porch, barking in fiery rage from a respectful distance. As Trescott imperturbably turned the mare's head down the road, Winter stood on the porch, still yelping. He was like a little dog.

## XXII

"Have you heard the news?" cried Carrie Dungen as she sped towards Martha's kitchen. "Have you heard the news?" Her eyes were shining with delight.

"No," answered Martha's sister Kate, bending forward eagerly. "What was it? What was it?"

Carrie appeared triumphantly in the open door. "Oh, there's been an awful scene between Doctor Trescott and Jake Winter. I never thought that Jake Winter had any pluck at all, but this morning he told the doctor just what he thought of him."

"Well, what did he think of him?" asked Martha.

"Oh, he called him everything. Mrs. Howarth heard it through her front blinds. It was terrible, she says. It's all over town now. Everybody knows it."

"Didn't the doctor answer back?"

"No! Mrs. Howarth—she says he never said a word. He just walked down to his buggy and got in, and drove off as co-o-o-l. But Jake gave him jinks, by all accounts."

"But what did he say?" cried Kate, shrill and excited. She was evidently at some kind of a feast.

"Oh, he told him that Sadie had never been well since that night Henry Johnson frightened her at Theresa Page's party, and he held him responsible, and how dared he cross his threshold—and—and—and—"

"And what?" said Martha.

"Did he swear at him?" said Kate, in fearsome glee.

"No—not much. He did swear at him a little, but not more than a man does anyhow when he is real mad, Mrs. Howarth says."

"O-oh!" breathed Kate. "And did he call him any names?"

Martha, at her work, had been for a time in deep thought. She now interrupted the others. "It don't seem as if Sadie Winter had been sick since that time Henry Johnson got loose. She's been to school almost the whole time since then, hasn't she?"

They combined upon her in immediate indignation. "School? School? I should say not. Don't think for a moment. School!"

Martha wheeled from the sink. She held an iron spoon, and it seemed as if she was going to attack them. "Sadie Winter has passed here many a morning since then carrying her schoolbag. Where was she going? To a wedding?"

The others, long accustomed to a mental tyranny, speedily surrendered.

"Did she?" stammered Kate. "I never saw her."

Carrie Dungen made a weak gesture.

"If I had been Doctor Trescott," exclaimed Martha, loudly, "I'd have knocked that miserable Jake Winter's head off."

Kate and Carrie, exchanging glances, made an alliance in the air. "I don't see why you say that, Martha," replied Carrie, with considerable boldness, gaining support and sympathy from Kate's smile. "I don't see how anybody can be blamed for getting angry when their little girl gets almost scared to death and gets sick from it, and all that. Besides, everybody says—"

"Oh, I don't care what everybody says," said Martha.

"Well, you can't go against the whole town," answered Carrie, in sudden sharp defiance.

"No, Martha, you can't go against the whole town," piped Kate, following her leader rapidly.

"'The whole town,'" cried Martha. "I'd like to know what you call 'the whole town.' Do you call these silly people who are scared of Henry Johnson 'the whole town'?"

"Why, Martha," said Carrie, in a reasoning tone, "you talk as if you wouldn't be scared of him!"

"No more would I," retorted Martha.

"O-oh, Martha, how you talk!" said Kate. "Why, the idea! Everybody's afraid of him."

Carrie was grinning. "You've never seen him, have you?" she asked, seductively.

"No," admitted Martha.

"Well, then, how do you know that you wouldn't be scared?"

Martha confronted her. "Have you ever seen him? No? Well, then, how do you know you *would* be scared?"

The allied forces broke out in chorus: "But, Martha, everybody says so. Everybody says so."

"Everybody says what?"

"Everybody that's seen him say they were frightened almost to death. Tisn't only women, but it's men too. It's awful."

Martha wagged her head solemnly. "I'd try not to be afraid of him."

"But supposing you could not help it?" said Kate.

"Yes, and look here," cried Carrie. "I'll tell you another thing. The Hannigans are going to move out of the house next door."

"On account of him?" demanded Martha.

Carrie nodded. "Mrs. Hannigan says so herself."

"Well, of all things!" ejaculated Martha. "Going to move, eh? You don't say so! Where they going to move to?"

"Down on Orchard Avenue."

"Well, of all things! Nice house?"

"I don't know about that. I haven't heard. But there's lots of nice houses on Orchard."

"Yes, but they're all taken," said Kate. "There isn't a vacant house on Orchard Avenue."

"Oh yes, there is," said Martha. "The old Hampstead house is vacant."

"Oh, of course," said Kate. "But then I don't believe Mrs. Hannigan would like it there. I wonder where they can be going to move to?"

"I'm sure I don't know," sighed Martha. "It must be to some place we don't know about."

"Well." said Carrie Dungen, after a general reflective silence, "it's easy enough to find out, anyhow."

"Who knows—around here?" asked Kate.

"Why, Mrs. Smith, and there she is in her garden," said Carrie, jumping to her feet. As she dashed out of the door, Kate and Martha crowded at the window. Carrie's voice rang out from near the steps. "Mrs. Smith! Mrs. Smith! Do you know where the Hannigans are going to move to?"

## XXIII

The autumn smote the leaves, and the trees of Whilomville were panoplied in crimson and yellow. The winds grew stronger, and in the melancholy purple of the nights the home shine of a window became a finer thing. The little boys, watching the sear and sorrowful leaves drifting down from the maples, dreamed of the near time when they could heap bushels in the streets and burn them during the abrupt evenings.

Three men walked down the Niagara Avenue. As they approached Judge Hagenthorpe's house he came down his walk to meet them in the manner of one who has been waiting.

"Are you ready, judge?" one said.

"All ready," he answered.

The four then walked to Trescott's house. He received them in his office, where he had been reading. He seemed surprised at this visit of four very active and influential citizens, but he had nothing to say of it.

After they were all seated, Trescott looked expectantly from one face to another. There was a little silence. It was broken by John Twelve, the wholesale grocer, who was worth $400,000, and reported to be worth over a million.

"Well, doctor," he said, with a short laugh, "I suppose we might as well admit at once that we've come to interfere in something which is none of our business."

"Why, what is it?" asked Trescott, again looking from one face to another. He seemed to appeal particularly to Judge Hagenthorpe, but the old man had his chin lowered musingly to his cane, and would not look at him.

"It's about what nobody talks of—much," said Twelve. "It's about Henry Johnson."

Trescott squared himself in his chair. "Yes?" he said.

Having delivered himself of the title, Twelve seemed to become more easy. "Yes," he answered, blandly, "we wanted to talk to you about it."

"Yes?" said Trescott.

Twelve abruptly advanced on the main attack. "Now see here, Trescott, we like you, and we have come to talk right out about this business. It may be none of our affairs and all that, and as for me, I don't mind if you tell me so; but I am not going to keep quiet and see you ruin yourself. And that's how we all feel."

"I am not ruining myself," answered Trescott.

"No, maybe you are not exactly ruining yourself," said Twelve, slowly, "but you are doing yourself a great deal of harm. You have changed from being the leading doctor in town to about the last one. It is mainly because there are always a large number of people who are very thoughtless fools, of course, but then that doesn't change the condition."

A man who had not heretofore spoken said, solemnly, "It's the women."

"Well, what I want to say is this," resumed Twelve: "Even if there are a lot of fools in the world, we can't see any reason why you should ruin yourself by opposing them. You can't teach them anything, you know."

"I am not trying to teach them anything." Trescott smiled wearily. "I—It is a matter of—well—"

"And there are a good many of us that admire you for it immensely," interrupted Twelve; "but that isn't going to change the minds of all those ninnies."

"It's the women," stated the advocate of this view again.

"Well, what I want to say is this," said Twelve. "We want you to get out of this trouble and strike your old gait again. You are simply killing your practice through your infernal pigheadedness. Now this thing is out of the ordinary, but there must be ways to—to beat the game somehow, you see. So we've talked it over—about a dozen of us—and, as I say, if you want to tell us to mind our own business, why, go ahead; but we've talked it over, and we've come to the conclusion that the only way to do is to get Johnson a place somewhere off up the valley, and—"

Trescott wearily gestured. "You don't know, my friend. Everybody is so afraid of him, they can't even give him good care. Nobody can attend to him as I do myself."

"But I have a little no-good farm up beyond Clarence Mountain that I was going to give to Henry," cried Twelve, aggrieved. "And if you—and if you—if you—through your house burning down, or anything—why, all the boys were prepared to take him right off your hands, and—and—"

Trescott arose and went to the window. He turned his back upon them. They sat waiting in silence. When he returned he kept his face in the shadow. "No, John Twelve," he said, "it can't be done."

There was another stillness. Suddenly a man stirred on his chair.

"Well, then, a public institution—" he began.

"No," said Trescott; "public institutions are all very good, but he is not going to one."

In the background of the group old Judge Hagenthorpe was thoughtfully smoothing the polished ivory head of his cane.

### XXIV

Trescott loudly stamped the snow from his feet and shook the flakes from his shoulders. When he entered the house he went at once to the dining-room, and then to the sitting-room. Jimmie was there, reading painfully in a large book concerning giraffes and tigers and crocodiles.

"Where is your mother, Jimmie?" asked Trescott.

"I don't know, pa," answered the boy. "I think she is up-stairs."

Trescott went to the foot of the stairs and called, but there came no answer. Seeing that the door of the little drawing-room was open, he entered. The room was bathed in the half-light that came from the four dull panes of mica in the front of the great stove. As his eyes grew used to the shadows he saw his wife curled in an arm-chair. He went to her. "Why, Grace." he said, "didn't you hear me calling you?"

She made no answer, and as he bent over the chair he heard her trying to smother a sob in the cushion.

"Grace!" he cried. "You're crying!"

She raised her face. "I've got a headache, a dreadful headache, Ned."

"A headache?" he repeated, in surprise and incredulity.

He pulled a chair close to hers. Later, as he cast his eye over the zone of light shed by the dull red panes, he saw that a low table had been drawn close to the stove, and that it was burdened with many small cups and plates of uncut tea-cake. He remembered that the day was Wednesday, and that his wife received on Wednesdays.

"Who was here today, Gracie?" he asked.

From his shoulder there came a mumble, "Mrs. Twelve."

"Was she—um," he said. "Why—didn't Anna Hagenthorpe come over?"

The mumble from his shoulder continued, "She wasn't well enough."

Glancing down at the cups, Trescott mechanically counted them. There were fifteen of them. "There, there," he said. "Don't cry, Grace. Don't cry."

The wind was whining round the house, and the snow beat aslant upon the windows. Sometimes the coal in the stove settled with a crumbling sound, and the four panes of mica flashed a sudden new crimson. As he sat holding her head on his shoulder, Trescott found himself occasionally trying to count the cups. There were fifteen of them.

# THE BLUE HOTEL

## I

The Palace Hotel at Fort Romper was painted a light blue, a shade that is on the legs of a kind of heron, causing the bird to declare its position against any background. The Palace Hotel, then, was always screaming and howling in a way that made the dazzling winter landscape of Nebraska seem only a gray swampish hush. It stood alone on the prairie, and when the snow was falling the town two hundred yards away was not visible. But when the traveller alighted at the railway station he was obliged to pass the Palace Hotel before he could come upon the company of low clapboard houses which composed Fort Romper, and it was not to be thought that any traveller could pass the Palace Hotel without looking at it. Pat Scully, the proprietor, had proved himself a master of strategy when he chose his paints. It is true that on clear days, when the great trans-continental expresses, long lines of swaying Pullmans, swept through Fort Romper, passengers were overcome at the sight, and the cult that knows the brown-reds and the subdivisions of the dark greens of the East expressed shame, pity, horror, in a laugh. But to the citizens of this prairie town and to the people who would naturally stop there, Pat Scully had performed a feat. With this opulence and splendor, these creeds, classes, egotisms, that streamed through Romper on the rails day after day, they had no color in common.

As if the displayed delights of such a blue hotel were not sufficiently enticing, it was Scully's habit to go every morning and evening to meet the leisurely trains that stopped at Romper and work his seductions upon any man that he might see wavering, gripsack in hand.

One morning, when a snow-crusted engine dragged its long string of freight cars and its one passenger coach to the station, Scully performed the marvel of catching three men. One was a shaky and quick-eyed Swede, with a great shining cheap valise; one was a tall bronzed cowboy, who was on his way to a ranch near the Dakota line; one was a little silent man from the East, who didn't look it, and didn't announce it. Scully practically made them prisoners. He was so nimble and merry and kindly that each probably felt it would be the height of brutality to try to escape. They trudged off over the creaking board sidewalks in the wake of the eager little Irishman. He wore a heavy fur cap squeezed tightly down on his head. It caused his two red ears to stick out stiffly, as if they were made of tin.

At last, Scully, elaborately, with boisterous hospitality, conducted them through the portals of the blue hotel. The room which they entered was small. It seemed to be merely a proper temple for an enormous stove, which, in the centre, was humming with godlike violence. At various points on its surface the iron had become luminous and glowed yellow from the heat. Beside the stove Scully's son Johnnie was playing High-Five with an old farmer who had whiskers both gray and sandy. They were quarrelling. Frequently the old farmer turned his face towards a box of sawdust—colored brown from tobacco juice—that was behind the stove, and spat with an air of great impatience and irritation. With a loud flourish of words Scully destroyed the game of cards, and bustled his son up-stairs with part of the baggage of the new guests. He himself conducted them to three basins of the coldest water in the world. The cowboy and the Easterner burnished themselves fiery-red with this water, until it seemed to be some kind of a metal polish. The Swede, however, merely dipped his fingers gingerly and with trepidation. It was notable that throughout this series of small ceremonies the three travellers were made to feel that Scully was very benevolent. He was conferring great favors upon them. He handed the towel from one to the other with an air of philanthropic impulse.

Afterwards they went to the first room, and, sitting about the stove, listened to Scully's officious clamor at his daughters, who were preparing the mid-day meal. They reflected in the silence of experienced men who tread carefully amid new people. Nevertheless, the old farmer, stationary, invincible in his chair near the warmest part of the stove, turned his face from the sawdust box frequently and addressed a glowing commonplace to the strangers. Usually he was answered in short but adequate sentences by either the cowboy or the Easterner. The Swede said nothing. He seemed to be occupied in making furtive estimates of each man in the room. One might have thought that he had the sense of silly suspicion which comes to guilt. He resembled a badly frightened man.

Later, at dinner, he spoke a little, addressing his conversation entirely to Scully. He volunteered that he had come from New York, where for ten years he had worked as a tailor. These facts seemed to strike Scully as fascinating, and afterwards he volunteered that he had lived at Romper for fourteen years. The Swede asked about the crops and the price of labor. He seemed barely to listen to Scully's extended replies. His eyes continued to rove from man to man.

Finally, with a laugh and a wink, he said that some of these Western communities were very dangerous; and after his statement he straightened his legs under the table, tilted his head, and laughed again, loudly. It was plain that the demonstration had no meaning to the others. They looked at him wondering and in silence.

## II

As the men trooped heavily back into the front-room, the two little windows presented views of a turmoiling sea of snow. The huge arms of the wind were making attempts—mighty, circular, futile—to embrace the flakes as they sped. A gate-post like a still man with a blanched face stood aghast amid this profligate fury. In a hearty voice Scully announced the presence of a blizzard. The guests of the blue hotel, lighting their pipes, assented with grunts of lazy masculine contentment. No island of the sea could be exempt in the degree of this little room with its humming stove. Johnnie, son of Scully, in a tone which defined his opinion of his ability as a card-player, challenged the old farmer of both gray and sandy whiskers to a game of High-Five. The farmer agreed with a contemptuous and bitter scoff. They sat close to the stove, and squared their knees under a wide board. The cowboy and the Easterner watched the game with interest. The Swede remained near the window, aloof, but with a countenance that showed signs of an inexplicable excitement.

The play of Johnnie and the gray-beard was suddenly ended by another quarrel. The old man arose while casting a look of heated scorn at his adversary. He slowly buttoned his coat, and then stalked with fabulous dignity from the room. In the discreet silence of all other men the Swede laughed. His laughter rang somehow childish. Men by this time had begun to look at him askance, as if they wished to inquire what ailed him.

A new game was formed jocosely. The cowboy volunteered to become the partner of Johnnie, and they all then turned to ask the Swede to throw in his lot with the little Easterner. He asked some questions about the game, and, learning that it wore many names, and that he had played it when it was under an alias, he accepted the invitation. He strode towards the men nervously, as if he expected to be assaulted. Finally, seated, he gazed from face to face and laughed shrilly. This laugh was so strange that the Easterner looked up quickly, the cowboy sat intent and with his mouth open, and Johnnie paused, holding the cards with still fingers.

Afterwards there was a short silence. Then Johnnie said, "Well, let's get at it. Come on now!" They pulled their chairs forward until their knees were bunched under the board. They began to play, and their interest in the game caused the others to forget the manner of the Swede.

The cowboy was a board-whacker. Each time that he held superior cards he whanged them, one by one, with exceeding force, down upon the improvised table, and took the tricks with a glowing air of prowess and pride that sent thrills of indignation into the hearts of his opponents. A game with a board-whacker in it is sure to become intense. The countenances of the Easterner and the Swede were miserable whenever the cowboy thundered down his aces and kings, while Johnnie, his eyes gleaming with joy, chuckled and chuckled.

Because of the absorbing play none considered the strange ways of the Swede. They paid strict heed to the game. Finally, during a lull caused by a new deal, the Swede suddenly addressed Johnnie: "I suppose there have been a good many men killed in this room." The jaws of the others dropped and they looked at him.

"What in hell are you talking about?" said Johnnie.

The Swede laughed again his blatant laugh, full of a kind of false courage and defiance. "Oh, you know what I mean all right," he answered.

"I'm a liar if I do!" Johnnie protested. The card was halted, and the men stared at the Swede. Johnnie evidently felt that as the son of the proprietor he should make a direct inquiry. "Now, what might you be drivin' at, mister?" he asked. The Swede winked at him. It was a wink full of cunning. His fingers shook on the edge of the board. "Oh, maybe you think I have been to nowheres. Maybe you think I'm a tenderfoot?"

"I don't know nothin' about you," answered Johnnie, "and I don't give a damn where you've been. All I got to say is that I don't know what you're driving at. There hain't never been nobody killed in this room."

The cowboy, who had been steadily gazing at the Swede, then spoke: "What's wrong with you, mister?"

Apparently it seemed to the Swede that he was formidably menaced. He shivered and turned white near the corners of his mouth. He sent an appealing glance in the direction of the little Easterner. During these moments he did not forget to wear his air of advanced pot-valor. "They say they don't know what I mean," he remarked mockingly to the Easterner.

The latter answered after prolonged and cautious reflection. "I don't understand you," he said, impassively.

The Swede made a movement then which announced that he thought he had encountered treachery from the only quarter where he had expected sympathy, if not help. "Oh, I see you are all against me. I see—"

The cowboy was in a state of deep stupefaction. "Say." he cried, as he tumbled the deck violently down upon the board "—say, what are you gittin' at, hey?"

The Swede sprang up with the celerity of a man escaping from a snake on the floor. "I don't want to fight!" he shouted. "I don't want to fight!"

The cowboy stretched his long legs indolently and deliberately. His hands were in his pockets. He spat into the sawdust box. "Well, who the hell thought you did?" he inquired.

The Swede backed rapidly towards a corner of the room. His hands were out protectingly in front of his chest, but he was making an obvious struggle to control his fright. "Gentlemen," he quavered, "I suppose I am going to be killed before I can leave this house! I suppose I am going to be killed before I can leave this house!" In his eyes was the dying-swan look. Through the windows could be seen the snow turning blue in the shadow of dusk. The wind tore at the house and some loose thing beat regularly against the clap-boards like a spirit tapping.

A door opened, and Scully himself entered. He paused in surprise as he noted the tragic attitude of the Swede. Then he said, "What's the matter here?"

The Swede answered him swiftly and eagerly: "These men are going to kill me."

"Kill you!" ejaculated Scully. "Kill you! What are you talkin'?"

The Swede made the gesture of a martyr.

Scully wheeled sternly upon his son. "What is this, Johnnie?"

The lad had grown sullen. "Damned if I know," he answered. "I can't make no sense to it." He began to shuffle the cards, fluttering them together with an angry snap. "He says a good many men have been killed in this room, or something like that. And he says he's goin' to be killed here too. I don't know what ails him. He's crazy, I shouldn't wonder."

Scully then looked for explanation to the cowboy, but the cowboy simply shrugged his shoulders.

"Kill you?" said Scully again to the Swede. "Kill you? Man, you're off your nut."

"Oh, I know." burst out the Swede. "I know what will happen. Yes, I'm crazy—yes. Yes, of course, I'm crazy—yes. But I know one thing—" There was a sort of sweat of misery and terror upon his face. "I know I won't get out of here alive."

The cowboy drew a deep breath, as if his mind was passing into the last stages of dissolution. "Well, I'm dog-goned," he whispered to himself.

Scully wheeled suddenly and faced his son. "You've been troublin' this man!"

Johnnie's voice was loud with its burden of grievance. "Why, good Gawd, I ain't done nothin' to 'im."

The Swede broke in. "Gentlemen, do not disturb yourselves. I will leave this house. I will go away because"—he accused them dramatically with his glance—"because I do not want to be killed."

Scully was furious with his son. "Will you tell me what is the matter, you young divil? What's the matter, anyhow? Speak out!"

"Blame it!" cried Johnnie in despair, "don't I tell you I don't know. He—he says we want to kill him, and that's all I know. I can't tell what ails him."

The Swede continued to repeat: "Never mind, Mr. Scully; nevermind. I will leave this house. I will go away, because I do not wish to be killed. Yes, of course, I am crazy—yes. But I know one thing! I will go away. I will leave this house. Never mind, Mr. Scully; never mind. I will go away."

"You will not go 'way," said Scully. "You will not go 'way until I hear the reason of this business. If anybody has troubled you I will take care of him. This is my house. You are under my roof, and I will not allow any peaceable man to be troubled here." He cast a terrible eye upon Johnnie, the cowboy, and the Easterner.

"Never mind, Mr. Scully; never mind. I will go away. I do not wish to be killed." The Swede moved towards the door, which opened upon the stairs. It was evidently his intention to go at once for his baggage.

"No, no," shouted Scully peremptorily; but the white-faced man slid by him and disappeared. "Now," said Scully severely, "what does this mane?"

Johnnie and the cowboy cried together: "Why, we didn't do nothin' to 'im!"

Scully's eyes were cold. "No," he said, "you didn't?"

Johnnie swore a deep oath. "Why this is the wildest loon I ever see. We didn't do nothin' at all. We were jest sittin' here play in' cards, and he—"

The father suddenly spoke to the Easterner. "Mr. Blanc," he asked, "what has these boys been doin'?"

The Easterner reflected again. "I didn't see anything wrong at all," he said at last, slowly.

Scully began to howl. "But what does it mane?" He stared ferociously at his son. "I have a mind to lather you for this, me boy."

Johnnie was frantic. "Well, what have I done?" he bawled at his father.

### III

"I think you are tongue-tied," said Scully finally to his son, the cowboy, and the Easterner; and at the end of this scornful sentence he left the room.

Up-stairs the Swede was swiftly fastening the straps of his great valise. Once his back happened to be half turned towards the door, and, hearing a noise there, he wheeled and sprang up, uttering a loud cry. Scully's wrinkled visage showed grimly in the light of the small lamp he carried. This yellow effulgence, streaming upward, colored only his prominent features, and left his eyes, for instance, in mysterious shadow. He resembled a murderer.

"Man! man!" he exclaimed, "have you gone daffy?"

"Oh, no! Oh, no!" rejoined the other. "There are people in this world who know pretty nearly as much as you do—understand?"

For a moment they stood gazing at each other. Upon the Swede's deathly pale checks were two spots brightly crimson and sharply edged, as if they had been carefully painted. Scully placed the light on the table and sat himself on the edge of the bed. He spoke ruminatively. "By cracky, I never heard of such a thing in my life. It's a complete muddle. I can't, for the soul of me, think how you ever got this idea into your head." Presently he lifted his eyes and asked: "And did you sure think they were going to kill you?"

The Swede scanned the old man as if he wished to see into his mind. "I did," he said at last. He obviously suspected that this answer might precipitate an outbreak. As he pulled on a strap his whole arm shook, the elbow wavering like a bit of paper.

Scully banged his hand impressively on the foot-board of the bed. "Why, man, we're goin' to have a line of ilictric street-cars in this town next spring."

"'A line of electric street-cars,'" repeated the Swede, stupidly.

"And," said Scully, "there's a new railroad goin' to be built down from Broken Arm to here. Not to mintion the four churches and the smashin' big brick school-house. Then there's the big factory, too. Why, in two years Romper'll be a *metropolis.*"

Having finished the preparation of his baggage, the Swede straightened himself. "Mr. Scully," he said, with sudden hardihood, "how much do I owe you?"

"You don't owe me anythin'," said the old man, angrily.

"Yes, I do," retorted the Swede. He took seventy-five cents from his pocket and tendered it to Scully; but the latter snapped his fingers in disdainful refusal. However, it happened that they both stood gazing in a strange fashion at three silver pieces on the Swede's open palm.

"I'll not take your money," said Scully at last. "Not after what's been goin' on here." Then a plan seemed to strike him. "Here," he cried, picking up his lamp and moving towards the door. "Here! Come with me a minute."

"No," said the Swede, in overwhelming alarm.

"Yes," urged the old man. "Come on! I want you to come and see a picter—just across the hall—in my room."

The Swede must have concluded that his hour was come. His jaw dropped and his teeth showed like a dead man's. He ultimately followed Scully across the corridor, but he had the step of one hung in chains.

Scully flashed the light high on the wall of his own chamber. There was revealed a ridiculous photograph of a little girl. She was leaning against a balustrade of gorgeous decoration, and the formidable bang to her hair was prominent. The figure was as graceful as an upright sled-stake, and, withal, it was of the hue of lead. "There," said Scully, tenderly, "that's the picter of my little girl that died. Her name was Carrie. She had the purtiest hair you ever saw! I was that fond of her, she—"

Turning then, he saw that the Swede was not contemplating the picture at all, but, instead, was keeping keen watch on the gloom in the rear.

"Look, man!" cried Scully, heartily. "That's the picter of my little gal that died. Her name was Carrie. And then here's the picter of my oldest boy, Michael. He's a lawyer in Lincoln, an' doin' well. I gave that boy a grand eddycation, and I'm glad for it now. He's a fine boy. Look at 'im now. Ain't he bold as blazes, him there in Lincoln, an honored an' respicted gintleman. An honored an' respicted gintleman," concluded Scully with a flourish. And, so saying, he smote the Swede jovially on the back.

The Swede faintly smiled.

"Now," said the old man, "there's only one more thing." He dropped suddenly to the floor and thrust his head beneath the bed. The Swede could hear his muffled voice. "I'd keep it under me piller if it wasn't for that boy Johnnie. Then there's the old woman—Where is it now? I never put it twice in the same place. Ah, now come out with you!"

Presently he backed clumsily from under the bed, dragging with him an old coat rolled into a bundle. "I've fetched him," he muttered. Kneeling on the floor, he unrolled the coat and extracted from its heart a large yellow-brown whiskey bottle.

His first maneuver was to hold the bottle up to the light. Reassured, apparently, that nobody had been tampering with it, he thrust it with a generous movement towards the Swede.

The weak-kneed Swede was about to eagerly clutch this element of strength, but he suddenly jerked his hand away and cast a look of horror upon Scully.

"Drink," said the old man affectionately. He had risen to his feet, and now stood facing the Swede.

There was a silence. Then again Scully said: "Drink!"

The Swede laughed wildly. He grabbed the bottle, put it to his mouth, and as his lips curled absurdly around the opening and his throat worked, he kept his glance, burning with hatred, upon the old man's face.

**IV**

After the departure of Scully the three men, with the card-board still upon their knees, preserved for a long time an astounded silence. Then Johnnie said: "That's the dod-dangest Swede I ever see."

"He ain't no Swede," said the cowboy, scornfully.

"Well, what is he then?" cried Johnnie. "What is he then?"

"It's my opinion," replied the cowboy deliberately, "he's some kind of a Dutchman." It was a venerable custom of the country to entitle as Swedes all light-haired men who spoke with a heavy tongue. In consequence the idea of the cowboy was not without its daring. "Yes, sir," he repeated. "It's my opinion this feller is some kind of a Dutchman."

"Well, he says he's a Swede, anyhow," muttered Johnnie, sulkily. He turned to the Easterner: "What do you think, Mr. Blanc?"

"Oh, I don't know," replied the Easterner.

"Well, what do you think makes him act that way?" asked the cowboy.

"Why, he's frightened." The Easterner knocked his pipe against a rim of the stove. "He's clear frightened out of his boots."

"What at?" cried Johnnie and cowboy together.

The Easterner reflected over his answer.

"What at?" cried the others again.

"Oh, I don't know, but it seems to me this man has been reading dime-novels, and he thinks he's right out in the middle of it—the shootin' and stabbin' and all."

"But," said the cowboy, deeply scandalized, "this ain't Wyoming, ner none of them places. This is Nebrasker."

"Yes," added Johnnie, "an' why don't he wait till he gits *out West?*"

The travelled Easterner laughed. "It isn't different there even—not in these days. But he thinks he's right in the middle of hell."

Johnnie and the cowboy mused long.

"It's awful funny," remarked Johnnie at last.

"Yes," said the cowboy. "This is a queer game. I hope we don't git snowed in, because then we'd have to stand this here man bein' around with us all the time. That wouldn't be no good."

"I wish pop would throw him out," said Johnnie.

Presently they heard a loud stamping on the stairs, accompanied by ringing jokes in the voice of old Scully, and laughter, evidently from the Swede. The men around the stove stared vacantly at each other. "Gosh!" said the cowboy. The door flew open, and old Scully, flushed and anecdotal, came into the room. He was jabbering at the Swede, who followed him, laughing bravely. It was the entry of two roisterers from a banquet-hall.

"Come now," said Scully sharply to the three seated men, "move up and give us a chance at the stove." The cowboy and the Easterner obediently sidled their chairs to make room for the new-comers. Johnnie, however, simply arranged himself in a more indolent attitude, and then remained motionless.

"Come! Git over, there," said Scully.

"Plenty of room on the other side of the stove," said Johnnie.

"Do you think we want to sit in the draught?" roared the father.

But the Swede here interposed with a grandeur of confidence. "No, no. Let the boy sit where he likes," he cried in a bullying voice to the father.

"All right! All right!" said Scully, deferentially. The cowboy and the Easterner exchanged glances of wonder.

The five chairs were formed in a crescent about one side of the stove. The Swede began to talk; he talked arrogantly, profanely, angrily. Johnnie, the cowboy, and the Easterner maintained a morose silence, while old Scully appeared to be receptive and eager, breaking in constantly with sympathetic ejaculations.

Finally the Swede announced that he was thirsty. He moved in his chair, and said that he would go for a drink of water.

"I'll git it for you," cried Scully at once.

"No," said the Swede, contemptuously. "I'll get it for myself." He arose and stalked with the air of an owner off into the executive parts of the hotel.

As soon as the Swede was out of hearing Scully sprang to his feet and whispered intensely to the others: "Up-stairs he thought I was tryin' to poison 'im."

"Say," said Johnnie, "this makes me sick. Why don't you throw 'im out in the snow?"

"Why, he's all right now," declared Scully. "It was only that he was from the East, and he thought this was a tough place. That's all. He's all right now."

The cowboy looked with admiration upon the Easterner. "You were straight," he said. "You were on to that there Dutchman."

"Well," said Johnnie to his father, "he may be all right now, but I don't see it. Other time he was scared, but now he's too fresh."

Scully's speech was always a combination of Irish brogue and idiom, Western twang and idiom, and scraps of curiously formal diction taken from the story-books and newspapers. He now hurled a strange mass of language at the head of his son.

"What do I keep? What do I keep? What do I keep?" he demanded, in a voice of thunder. He slapped his knee impressively, to indicate that he himself was going to make reply, and that all should heed. "I keep a hotel," he shouted. "A hotel, do you mind? A guest under my roof has sacred privileges. He is to be intimidated by none. Not one word shall he hear that would prejudice him in favor of goin' away. I'll not have it. There's no place in this here town where they can say they iver took in a guest of mine because he was afraid to stay here." He wheeled suddenly upon the cowboy and the Easterner. "Am I right?"

"Yes, Mr. Scully," said the cowboy, "I think you're right."

"Yes, Mr. Scully," said the Easterner, "I think you're right."

V

At six-o'clock supper, the Swede fizzed like a fire-wheel. He sometimes seemed on the point of bursting into riotous song, and in all his madness he was encouraged by old Scully. The Easterner was incased in reserve; the cowboy sat in wide-mouthed amazement, forgetting to eat, while Johnnie wrathily demolished great plates of food. The daughters of the house, when they were obliged to replenish the biscuits, approached as warily as Indians, and, having succeeded in their purpose, fled with ill-concealed trepidation. The Swede domineered the whole feast, and he gave it the appearance of a cruel bacchanal. He seemed to have grown suddenly taller; he gazed, brutally disdainful, into every face. His voice rang through the room. Once when he jabbed out harpoon-fashion with his fork to pinion a biscuit, the weapon nearly impaled the hand of the Easterner which had been stretched quietly out for the same biscuit.

After supper, as the men filed towards the other room, the Swede smote Scully ruthlessly on the shoulder. "Well, old boy, that was a good, square meal." Johnnie looked hopefully at his father; he knew that shoulder was tender from an old fall; and, indeed, it appeared for a moment as if Scully was going to flame out over the matter, but in the end he smiled a sickly smile and remained silent. The others understood from his manner that he was admitting his responsibility for the Swede's new view-point.

Johnnie, however, addressed his parent in an aside. "Why don't you license somebody to kick you down-stairs?" Scully scowled darkly by way of reply.

When they were gathered about the stove, the Swede insisted on another game of High Five. Scully gently deprecated the plan at first, but the Swede turned a wolfish glare upon him. The old man subsided, and the Swede canvassed the others. In his tone there was always a great threat. The cowboy and the Easterner both remarked indifferently that they would play. Scully said that he would presently have to go to meet the 6.58 train, and so the Swede turned menacingly upon Johnnie. For a moment their glances crossed like blades, and then Johnnie smiled and said, "Yes, I'll play."

They formed a square, with the little board on their knees. The Easterner and the Swede were again partners. As the play went on, it was noticeable that the cowboy was not board-whacking as usual. Meanwhile, Scully, near the lamp, had put on his spectacles and, with an appearance curiously like an old priest, was reading a newspaper. In time he went out to meet the 6.58 train, and, despite his precautions, a gust of polar wind whirled into the room as he opened the door. Besides scattering the cards, it dulled the players to the marrow. The Swede cursed frightfully. When Scully returned, his entrance disturbed a cosey and friendly scene. The Swede again cursed. But presently they were once more intent, their heads bent forward and their hands moving swiftly. The Swede had adopted the fashion of board-whacking.

Scully took up his paper and for a long time remained immersed in matters which were extraordinarily remote from him. The lamp burned badly, and once he stopped to adjust the wick. The newspaper, as he turned from page to page, rustled with a slow and comfortable sound. Then suddenly he heard three terrible words: "You are cheatin'!"

Such scenes often prove that there can be little of dramatic import in environment. Any room can present a tragic front; any room can be comic. This little den was now hideous as a torture-chamber. The new faces of the men themselves had changed it upon the instant. The Swede held a huge fist in front of Johnnie's face, while the latter looked steadily over it into the blazing orbs of his accuser. The Easterner had grown pallid; the cowboy's jaw had dropped in that expression of bovine amazement which was one of his important mannerisms. After the three words, the first sound in the room was made by Scully's paper as it floated forgotten to his feet. His spectacles had also fallen from his nose, but by a clutch he had saved them in air. His hand, grasping the spectacles, now remained poised awkwardly and near his shoulder. He stared at the card-players.

Probably the silence was while a second elapsed. Then, if the floor had been suddenly twitched out from under the men they could not have moved quicker. The five had projected themselves headlong towards a common point. It happened that Johnnie, in rising to hurl himself upon the Swede, had stumbled slightly because of his curiously instinctive care for the cards and the board. The loss of the moment allowed time for the arrival of Scully, and also allowed the cowboy time to give the Swede a great push which sent him staggering back. The men found tongue together, and hoarse shouts of rage, appeal, or fear burst from every throat. The cowboy pushed and jostled feverishly at the Swede, and the Easterner and Scully clung wildly to Johnnie; but, through the smoky air, above the swaying bodies of the peace-compellers, the eyes of the two warriors ever sought each other in glances of challenge that were at once hot and steely.

Of course the board had been overturned, and now the whole company of cards was scattered over the floor, where the boots of the men trampled the fat and painted kings and queens as they gazed with their silly eyes at the war that was waging above them.

Scully's voice was dominating the yells. "Stop now? Stop, I say! Stop, now—"

Johnnie, as he struggled to burst through the rank formed by Scully and the Easterner, was crying, "Well, he says I cheated! He says I cheated! I won't allow no man to say I cheated! If he says I cheated, he's a little ——!"

The cowboy was telling the Swede, "Quit, now! Quit, d'ye hear—"

The screams of the Swede never ceased: "He did cheat! I saw him! I saw him—"

As for the Easterner, he was importuning in a voice that was not heeded: "Wait a moment, can't you? Oh, wait a moment. What's the good of a fight over a game of cards? Wait a moment—"

In this tumult no complete sentences were clear. "Cheat"—"Quit"—"He says"—these fragments pierced the uproar and rang out sharply. It was remarkable that, whereas Scully undoubtedly made the most noise, he was the least heard of any of the riotous band.

Then suddenly there was a great cessation. It was as if each man had paused for breath; and although the room was still lighted with the anger of men, it could be seen that there was no danger of immediate conflict, and at once Johnnie, shouldering his way forward, almost succeeded in confronting the Swede. "What did you say I cheated for? What did you say I cheated for? I don't cheat, and I won't let no man say I do!"

The Swede said, "I saw you! I saw you!"

"Well," cried Johnnie, "I'll fight any man what says I cheat!"

"No, you won't," said the cowboy. "Not here."

"Ah, be still, can't you?" said Scully, coming between them.

The quiet was sufficient to allow the Easterner's voice to be heard. He was repeating, "Oh, wait a moment, can't you? What's the good of a fight over a game of cards? Wait a moment!"

Johnnie, his red face appearing above his father's shoulder, hailed the Swede again. "Did you say I cheated?"

The Swede showed his teeth. "Yes."

"Then," said Johnnie, "we must fight."

"Yes, fight," roared the Swede. He was like a demoniac. "Yes, fight! I'll show you what kind of a man I am! I'll show you who you want to fight! Maybe you think I can't fight! Maybe you think I can't! I'll show you, you skin, you card-sharp! Yes, you cheated! You cheated! You cheated!"

"Well, let's go at it, then, mister," said Johnnie, coolly.

The cowboy's brow was beaded with sweat from his efforts in intercepting all sorts of raids. He turned in despair to Scully. "What are you goin' to do now?"

A change had come over the Celtic visage of the old man. He now seemed all eagerness; his eyes glowed.

"We'll let them fight," he answered, stalwartly. "I can't put up with it any longer. I've stood this damned Swede till I'm sick. We'll let them fight."

VI

The men prepared to go out-of-doors. The Easterner was so nervous that he had great difficulty in getting his arms into the sleeves of his new leather coat. As the cowboy drew his fur cap down over his cars his hands trembled. In fact, Johnnie and old Scully were the only ones who displayed no agitation. These preliminaries were conducted without words.

Scully threw open the door. "Well, come on," he said. Instantly a terrific wind caused the flame of the lamp to struggle at its wick, while a puff of black smoke sprang from the chimney-top. The stove was in mid-current of the blast, and its voice swelled to equal the roar of the storm. Some of the scarred and bedabbled cards were caught up from the floor and dashed helplessly against the farther wall. The men lowered their heads and plunged into the tempest as into a sea.

No snow was falling, but great whirls and clouds of flakes, swept up from the ground by the frantic winds, were streaming southward with the speed of bullets. The covered land was blue with the sheen of an unearthly satin, and there was no other hue save where, at the low, black railway station—which seemed incredibly distant—one light gleamed like a tiny jewel. As the men floundered into a thigh deep drift, it was known that the Swede was bawling out something. Scully went to him, put a hand on his shoulder and projected an ear. "What's that you say?" he shouted.

"I say," bawled the Swede again, "I won't stand much show against this gang. I know you'll all pitch on me."

Scully smote him reproachfully on the arm. "Tut, man!" he yelled. The wind tore the words from Scully's lips and scattered them far alee.

"You are all a gang of—" boomed the Swede, but the storm also seized the remainder of this sentence.

Immediately turning their backs upon the wind, the men had swung around a corner to the sheltered side of the hotel. It was the function of the little house to preserve here, amid this great devastation of snow, an irregular V-shape of heavily incrusted grass, which crackled beneath the feet. One could imagine the great drifts piled against the windward side. When the party reached the comparative peace of this spot it was found that the Swede was still bellowing.

"Oh, I know what kind of a thing this is! I know you'll all pitch on me. I can't lick you all!"

Scully turned upon him panther fashion. "You'll not have to whip all of us. You'll have to whip my son Johnnie. An' the man what troubles you durin' that time will have me to dale with."

The arrangements were swiftly made. The two men faced each other, obedient to the harsh commands of Scully, whose face, in the subtly luminous gloom, could be seen set in the austere impersonal lines that are pictured on the countenances of the Roman veterans. The Easterner's teeth were chattering, and he was hopping up and down like a mechanical toy. The cowboy stood rock-like.

The contestants had not stripped off any clothing. Each was in his ordinary attire. Their fists were up, and they eyed each other in a calm that had the elements of leonine cruelty in it.

During this pause, the Easterner's mind, like a film, took lasting impressions of three men—the iron-nerved master of the ceremony; the Swede, pale, motionless, terrible; and Johnnie, serene yet ferocious, brutish yet heroic. The entire prelude had in it a tragedy greater than the tragedy of action, and this aspect was accentuated by the long, mellow cry of the blizzard, as it sped the tumbling and wailing flakes into the black abyss of the south.

"Now!" said Scully.

The two combatants leaped forward and crashed together like bullocks. There was heard the cushioned sound of blows, and of a curse squeezing out from between the tight teeth of one.

As for the spectators, the Easterner's pent-up breath exploded from him with a pop of relief, absolute relief from the tension of the preliminaries. The cowboy bounded into the air with a yowl. Scully was immovable as from supreme amazement and fear at the fury of the fight which he himself had permitted and arranged.

For a time the encounter in the darkness was such a perplexity of flying arms that it presented no more detail than would a swiftly revolving wheel. Occasionally a face, as if illumined by a flash of light, would shine out, ghastly and marked with pink spots. A moment later, the men might have been known as shadows, if it were not for the involuntary utterance of oaths that came from them in whispers.

Suddenly a holocaust of warlike desire caught the cowboy, and he bolted forward with the speed of a broncho. "Go it, Johnnie! go it! Kill him! Kill him!"

Scully confronted him. "Kape back," he said; and by his glance the cowboy could tell that this man was Johnnie's father.

To the Easterner there was a monotony of unchangeable fighting that was an abomination. This confused mingling was eternal to his sense, which was concentrated in a longing for the end, the priceless end. Once the fighters lurched near him, and as he scrambled hastily backward he heard them breathe like men on the rack.

"Kill him, Johnnie! Kill him! Kill him! Kill him!" The cowboy's face was contorted like one of those agony masks in museums.

"Keep still," said Scully, icily.

Then there was a sudden loud grunt, incomplete, cut short, and Johnnie's body swung away from the Swede and fell with sickening heaviness to the grass. The cowboy was barely in time to prevent the mad Swede from flinging himself upon his prone adversary. "No, you don't," said the cowboy, interposing an arm. "Wait a second."

Scully was at his son's side. "Johnnie! Johnnie, me boy!" His voice had a quality of melancholy tenderness. "Johnnie! Can you go on with it?" He looked anxiously down into the bloody, pulpy face of his son.

There was a moment of silence, and then Johnnie answered in his ordinary voice, "Yes, I—it—yes."

Assisted by his father he struggled to his feet. "Wait a bit now till you git your wind," said the old man.

A few paces away the cowboy was lecturing the Swede. "No, you don't! Wait a second!"

The Easterner was plucking at Scully's sleeve. "Oh, this is enough," he pleaded. "This is enough! Let it go as it stands. This is enough!"

"Bill," said Scully, "git out of the road." The cowboy stepped aside. "Now." The combatants were actuated by a new caution as they advanced towards collision. They glared at each other, and then the Swede aimed a lightning blow that carried with it his entire weight. Johnnie was evidently half stupid from weakness, but he miraculously dodged, and his fist sent the over-balanced Swede sprawling.

The cowboy, Scully, and the Easterner burst into a cheer that was like a chorus of triumphant soldiery, but before its conclusion the Swede had scuffled agilely to his feet and come in berserk abandon at his foe. There was another perplexity of flying arms, and Johnnie's body again swung away and fell, even as a bundle might fall from a roof. The Swede instantly staggered to a little wind-waved tree and leaned upon it, breathing like an engine, while his savage and flame-lit eyes roamed from face to face as the men bent over Johnnie. There was a splendor of isolation in his situation at this time which the Easterner felt once when, lifting his eyes from the man on the ground, he beheld that mysterious and lonely figure, waiting.

"Arc you any good yet, Johnnie?" asked Scully in a broken voice.

The son gasped and opened his eyes languidly. After a moment he answered, "No—I ain't—any good—any—more." Then, from shame and bodily ill he began to weep, the tears furrowing down through the blood-stains on his face. "He was too—too—too heavy for me."

Scully straightened and addressed the waiting figure. "Stranger," he said, evenly, "it's all up with our side." Then his voice changed into that vibrant huskiness which is commonly the tone of the most simple and deadly announcements. "Johnnie is whipped."

Without replying, the victor moved off on the route to the front door of the hotel.

The cowboy was formulating new and un-spellable blasphemies. The Easterner was startled to find that they were out in a wind that seemed to come direct from the shadowed arctic floes. He heard again the wail of the snow as it was flung to its grave in the south. He knew now that all this time the cold had been sinking into him deeper and deeper, and he wondered that he had not perished. He felt indifferent to the condition of the vanquished man.

"Johnnie, can you walk?" asked Scully.

"Did I hurt—hurt him any?" asked the son.

"Can you walk, boy? Can you walk?"

Johnnie's voice was suddenly strong. There was a robust impatience in it. "I asked you whether I hurt him any!"

"Yes, yes, Johnnie," answered the cowboy, consolingly; "he's hurt a good deal."

They raised him from the ground, and as soon as he was on his feet he went tottering off, rebuffing all attempts at assistance. When the party rounded the corner they were fairly blinded by the pelting of the snow. It burned their faces like fire. The cowboy carried Johnnie through the drift to the door. As they entered some cards again rose from the floor and beat against the wall.

The Easterner rushed to the stove. He was so profoundly chilled that he almost dared to embrace the glowing iron. The Swede was not in the room. Johnnie sank into a chair, and, folding his arms on his knees, buried his face in them. Scully, warming one foot and then the other at a rim of the stove, muttered to himself with Celtic mournfulness. The cowboy had removed his fur cap, and with a dazed and rueful air he was running one hand through his tousled locks. From overhead they could hear the creaking of boards, as the Swede tramped here and there in his room.

The sad quiet was broken by the sudden flinging open of a door that led towards the kitchen. It was instantly followed by an inrush of women. They precipitated themselves upon Johnnie amid a chorus of lamentation. Before they carried their prey off to the kitchen, there to be bathed and harangued with that mixture of sympathy and abuse which is a feat of their sex, the mother straightened herself and fixed old Scully with an eye of stern reproach. "Shame be upon you, Patrick Scully!" she cried. "Your own son, too. Shame be upon you!"

"There, now! Be quiet, now!" said the old man, weakly.

"Shame be upon you, Patrick Scully!" The girls, rallying to this slogan, sniffed disdainfully in the direction of those trembling accomplices, the cowboy and the Easterner. Presently they bore Johnnie away, and left the three men to dismal reflection.

**VII**

"I'd like to fight this here Dutchman myself," said the cowboy, breaking a long silence.

Scully wagged his head sadly. "No, that wouldn't do. It wouldn't be right. It wouldn't be right."

"Well, why wouldn't it?" argued the cowboy. "I don't see no harm in it."

"No," answered Scully, with mournful heroism. "It wouldn't be right. It was Johnnie's fight, and now we mustn't whip the man just because he whipped Johnnie."

"Yes, that's true enough," said the cowboy; "but—he better not get fresh with me, because I couldn't stand no more of it."

"You'll not say a word to him," commanded Scully, and even then they heard the tread of the Swede on the stairs. His entrance was made theatric. He swept the door back with a bang and swaggered to the middle of the room. No one looked at him. "Well," he cried, insolently, at Scully, "I s'pose you'll tell me now how much I owe you?"

The old man remained stolid. "You don't owe me nothin'.'"

"Huh!" said the Swede, "huh! Don't owe 'im nothin'."

The cowboy addressed the Swede. "Stranger, I don't see how you come to be so gay around here."

Old Scully was instantly alert. "Stop!" he shouted, holding his hand forth, fingers upward. "Bill, you shut up!"

The cowboy spat carelessly into the sawdust box. "I didn't say a word, did I?" he asked.

"Mr. Scully," called the Swede, "how much do I owe you?" It was seen that he was attired for departure, and that he had his valise in his hand.

"You don't owe me nothin'," repeated Scully in his same imperturbable way.

"Huh!" said the Swede. "I guess you're right. I guess if it was any way at all, you'd owe me somethin'. That's what I guess." He turned to the cowboy. "'Kill him! Kill him! Kill him!'" he mimicked, and then guffawed victoriously. "'Kill him!'" He was convulsed with ironical humor.

But he might have been jeering the dead. The three men were immovable and silent, staring with glassy eyes at the stove.

The Swede opened the door and passed into the storm, giving one derisive glance backward at the still group.

As soon as the door was closed, Scully and the cowboy leaped to their feet and began to curse. They trampled to and fro, waving their arms and smashing into the air with their fists. "Oh, but that was a hard minute!" wailed Scully. "That was a hard minute! Him there leerin' and scoffin'! One bang at his nose was worth forty dollars to me that minute! How did you stand it, Bill?"

"How did I stand it?" cried the cowboy in a quivering voice. "How did I stand it? Oh!"

The old man burst into sudden brogue. "I'd loike to take that Swade," he wailed, "and hould 'im down on a shtone flure and bate 'im to a jelly wid a shtick!"

The cowboy groaned in sympathy. "I'd like to git him by the neck and ha-am-mer him "—he brought his hand down on a chair with a noise like a pistol-shot—"hammer that there Dutchman until he couldn't tell himself from a dead coyote!"

"I'd bate 'im until he—"

"I'd show *him* some things—"

And then together they raised a yearning, fanatic cry—"Oh-o-oh! if we only could—"

"Yes!"

"Yes!"

"And then I'd—"
"O-o-oh!"

## VIII

The Swede, tightly gripping his valise, tacked across the face of the storm as if he carried sails. He was following a line of little naked, gasping trees, which he knew must mark the way of the road. His face, fresh from the pounding of Johnnie's fists, felt more pleasure than pain in the wind and the driving snow. A number of square shapes loomed upon him finally, and he knew them as the houses of the main body of the town. He found a street and made travel along it, leaning heavily upon the wind whenever, at a corner, a terrific blast caught him.

He might have been in a deserted village. We picture the world as thick with conquering and elate humanity, but here, with the bugles of the tempest pealing, it was hard to imagine a peopled earth. One viewed the existence of man then as a marvel, and conceded a glamour of wonder to these lice which were caused to cling to a whirling, fire-smote, ice-locked, disease-stricken, space-lost bulb. The conceit of man was explained by this storm to be the very engine of life. One was a coxcomb not to die in it. However, the Swede found a saloon.

In front of it an indomitable red light was burning, and the snow-flakes were made blood color as they flew through the circumscribed territory of the lamp's shining. The Swede pushed open the door of the saloon and entered. A sanded expanse was before him, and at the end of it four men sat about a table drinking. Down one side of the room extended a radiant bar, and its guardian was leaning upon his elbows listening to the talk of the men at the table. The Swede dropped his valise upon the floor, and, smiling fraternally upon the barkeeper, said, "Gimme some whiskey, will you?" The man placed a bottle, a whiskey-glass, and a glass of ice-thick water upon the bar. The Swede poured himself an abnormal portion of whiskey and drank it in three gulps. "Pretty bad night," remarked the bartender, indifferently. He was making the pretension of blindness which is usually a distinction of his class; but it could have been seen that he was furtively studying the half-erased blood-stains on the face of the Swede. "Bad night," he said again.

"Oh, it's good enough for me," replied the Swede, hardily, as he poured himself some more whiskey. The barkeeper took his coin and maneuvered it through its reception by the highly nickelled cash-machine. A bell rang; a card labelled "20 cts." had appeared.

"No," continued the Swede, "this isn't too bad weather. It's good enough for me."

"So?" murmured the barkeeper, languidly.

The copious drams made the Swede's eyes swim, and he breathed a trifle heavier. "Yes, I like this weather. I like it. It suits me." It was apparently his design to impart a deep significance to these words.

"So?" murmured the bartender again. He turned to gaze dreamily at the scroll-like birds and bird-like scrolls which had been drawn with soap upon the mirrors back of the bar.

"Well, I guess I'll take another drink," said the Swede, presently. "Have something?"

"No, thanks; I'm not drinkin'," answered the bartender. Afterwards he asked, "How did you hurt your face?"

The Swede immediately began to boast loudly. "Why, in a fight. I thumped the soul out of a man down here at Scully's hotel."

The interest of the four men at the table was at last aroused.

"Who was it?" said one.

"Johnnie Scully," blustered the Swede. "Son of the man what runs it. He will be pretty near dead for some weeks, I can tell you. I made a nice thing of him, I did. He couldn't get up. They carried him in the house. Have a drink?"

Instantly the men in some subtle way incased themselves in reserve. "No, thanks," said one. The group was of curious formation. Two were prominent local business men; one was the district-attorney; and one was a professional gambler of the kind known as "square." But a scrutiny of the group would not have enabled an observer to pick the gambler from the men of more reputable pursuits. He was, in fact, a man so delicate in manner, when among people of fair class, and so judicious in his choice of victims, that in the strictly masculine part of the town's life he had come to be explicitly trusted and admired. People called him a thoroughbred. The fear and contempt with which his craft was regarded was undoubtedly the reason that his quiet dignity shone conspicuous above the quiet dignity of men who might be merely hatters, billiard markers, or grocery-clerks. Beyond an occasional unwary traveller, who came by rail, this gambler was supposed to prey solely upon reckless and senile farmers, who, when flush with good crops, drove into town in all the pride and confidence of an absolutely invulnerable stupidity. Hearing at times in circuitous fashion of the despoilment of such a farmer, the important men of Romper invariably laughed in contempt of the victim, and, if they thought of the wolf at all, it was with a kind of pride at the knowledge that he would never dare think of attacking their wisdom and courage. Besides, it was popular that this gambler had a real wife and two real children in a neat cottage in a suburb, where he led an exemplary home life; and when any one even suggested a discrepancy in his character, the crowd immediately vociferated descriptions of this virtuous family circle. Then men who led exemplary home lives, and men who did not lead exemplary home lives, all subsided in a bunch, remarking that there was nothing more to be said.

However, when a restriction was placed upon him—as, for instance, when a strong clique of members of the new Pollywog Club refused to permit him, even as a spectator, to appear in the rooms of the organization—the candor and gentleness with which he accepted the judgment disarmed many of his foes and made his friends more desperately partisan. He invariably distinguished between himself and a respectable Romper man so quickly and frankly that his manner actually appeared to be a continual broadcast compliment.

And one must not forget to declare the fundamental fact of his entire position in Romper. It is irrefutable that in all affairs outside of his business, in all matters that occur eternally and commonly between man and man, this thieving card-player was so generous, so just, so moral, that, in a contest, he could have put to flight the consciences of nine-tenths of the citizens of Romper.

And so it happened that he was seated in this saloon with the two prominent local merchants and the district-attorney.

The Swede continued to drink raw whiskey, meanwhile babbling at the barkeeper and trying to induce him to indulge in potations. "Come on. Have a drink. Come on. What—no? Well, have a little one, then. By gawd, I've whipped a man tonight, and I want to celebrate. I whipped him good, too. Gentlemen," the Swede cried to the men at the table, "have a drink?"

"Ssh!" said the barkeeper.

The group at the table, although furtively attentive, had been pretending to be deep in talk, but now a man lifted his eyes towards the Swede and said, shortly, "Thanks. We don't want any more."

At this reply the Swede ruffled out his chest like a rooster. "Well," he exploded, "it seems I can't get anybody to drink with me in this town. Seems so, don't it? Well!"

"Ssh!" said the barkeeper.

"Say," snarled the Swede, "don't you try to shut me up. I won't have it. I'm a gentleman, and I want people to drink with me. And I want 'em to drink with me now. *Now*—do you understand?" He rapped the bar with his knuckles.

Years of experience had calloused the bartender. He merely grew sulky. "I hear you," he answered.

"Well," cried the Swede, "listen hard then. See those men over there? Well, they're going to drink with me, and don't you forget it. Now you watch."

"Hi!" yelled the barkeeper, "this won't do!"

"Why won't it?" demanded the Swede. He stalked over to the table, and by chance laid his hand upon the shoulder of the gambler. "How about this?" he asked, wrathfully. "I asked you to drink with me."

The gambler simply twisted his head and spoke over his shoulder. "My friend, I don't know you."

"Oh, hell!" answered the Swede, "come and have a drink."

"Now, my boy," advised the gambler, kindly, "take your hand off my shoulder and go 'way and mind your own business." He was a little, slim man, and it seemed strange to hear him use this tone of heroic patronage to the burly Swede. The other men at the table said nothing.

"What! You won't drink with me, you little dude? I'll make you then! I'll make you!" The Swede had grasped the gambler frenziedly at the throat, and was dragging him from his chair. The other men sprang up. The barkeeper dashed around the corner of his bar. There was a great tumult, and then was seen a long blade in the hand of the gambler. It shot forward, and a human body, this citadel of virtue, wisdom, power, was pierced as easily as if it had been a melon. The Swede fell with a cry of supreme astonishment.

The prominent merchants and the district attorney must have at once tumbled out of the place backward. The bartender found himself hanging limply to the arm of a chair and gazing into the eyes of a murderer.

"Henry," said the latter, as he wiped his knife on one of the towels that hung beneath the bar-rail, "you tell 'em where to find me. I'll be home, waiting for 'em." Then he vanished. A moment afterwards the barkeeper was in the street dinning through the storm for help, and, moreover, companionship.

The corpse of the Swede, alone in the saloon, had its eyes fixed upon a dreadful legend that dwelt atop of the cash-machine: "This registers the amount of your purchase."


## IX


Months later, the cowboy was frying pork over the stove of a little ranch near the Dakota line, when there was a quick thud of hoofs outside, and presently the Easterner entered with the letters and the papers.

"Well," said the Easterner at once, "the chap that killed the Swede has got three years. Wasn't much, was it?"

"He has? Three years?" The cowboy poised his pan of pork, while he ruminated upon the news. "Three years. That ain't much."

"No. It was a light sentence," replied the Easterner as he unbuckled his spurs. "Seems there was a good deal of sympathy for him in Romper."

"If the bartender had been any good," observed the cowboy, thoughtfully, "he would have gone in and cracked that there Dutchman on the head with a bottle in the beginnin' of it and stopped all this here murderin'."

"Yes, a thousand things might have happened," said the Easterner, tartly.

The cowboy returned his pan of pork to the fire, but his philosophy continued. "It's funny, ain't it? If he hadn't said Johnnie was cheatin' he'd be alive this minute. He was an awful fool. Game played for fun, too. Not for money. I believe he was crazy."

"I feel sorry for that gambler," said the Easterner.

"Oh, so do I," said the cowboy. "He don't deserve none of it for killin' who he did."

"The Swede might not have been killed if everything had been square."

"Might not have been killed?" exclaimed the cowboy. "Everythin' square? Why, when he said that Johnnie was cheatin' and acted like such a jackass? And then in the saloon he fairly walked up to git hurt?" With these arguments the cowboy browbeat the Easterner and reduced him to rage.

"You're a fool!" cried the Easterner, viciously. "You're a bigger jackass than the Swede by a million majority. Now let me tell you one thing. Let me tell you something. Listen! Johnnie *was* cheating!"

"'Johnnie,'" said the cowboy, blankly. There was a minute of silence, and then he said, robustly, "Why, no. The game was only for fun."

"Fun or not," said the Easterner, "Johnnie was cheating. I saw him. I know it. I saw him. And I refused to stand up and be a man. I let the Swede fight it out alone. And you—you were simply puffing around the place and wanting to fight. And then old Scully himself! We are all in it! This poor gambler isn't even a noun. He is kind of an adverb. Every sin is the result of a collaboration. We, five of us, have collaborated in the murder of this Swede. Usually there are from a dozen to forty women really involved in every murder, but in this case it seems to be only five men—you, I, Johnnie, old Scully, and that fool of an unfortunate gambler came merely as a culmination, the apex of a human movement, and gets all the punishment."

The cowboy, injured and rebellious, cried out blindly into this fog of mysterious theory: "Well, I didn't do anythin', did I?"

# HIS NEW MITTENS

## I

Little Horace was walking home from school, brilliantly decorated by a pair of new red mittens. A number of boys were snowballing gleefully in a field. They hailed him. "Come on, Horace! We're having a battle."

Horace was sad. "No," he said, "I can't. I've got to go home." At noon his mother had admonished him: "Now, Horace, you come straight home as soon as school is out. Do you hear? And don't you get them nice new mittens all wet, either. Do you hear?" Also his aunt had said: "I declare, Emily, it's a shame the way you allow that child to ruin his things." She had meant mittens. To his mother, Horace had dutifully replied, "Yes'm." But he now loitered in the vicinity of the group of uproarious boys, who were yelling like hawks as the white balls flew.

Some of them immediately analyzed this extraordinary hesitancy. "Hah!" they paused to scoff, "afraid of your new mittens, ain't you?" Some smaller boys, who were not yet so wise in discerning motives, applauded this attack with unreasonable vehemence. "A-fray-ed of his mit-tens! A-fray-ed of his mit-tens." They sang these lines to cruel and monotonous music which is as old perhaps as American child-hood, and which it is the privilege of the emancipated adult to completely forget. "Afray-ed of his mit-tens!"

Horace cast a tortured glance towards his playmates, and then dropped his eyes to the snow at his feet. Presently he turned to the trunk of one of the great maple-trees that lined the curb. He made a pretence of closely examining the rough and virile bark. To his mind, this familiar street of Whilomville seemed to grow dark in the thick shadow of shame. The trees and the houses were now palled in purple.

"A-fray-ed of his mit-tens!" The terrible music had in it a meaning from the moonlit war-drums of chanting cannibals.

At last Horace, with supreme effort, raised his head. "'Tain't them I care about," he said, gruffly. "I've got to go home. That's all."

Whereupon each boy held his left forefinger as if it were a pencil and began to sharpen it derisively with his right forefinger. They came closer, and sang like a trained chorus, "A-fray-ed of his mittens!"

When he raised his voice to deny the charge it was simply lost in the screams of the mob. He was alone, fronting all the traditions of boyhood held before him by inexorable representatives. To such a low state had he fallen that one lad, a mere baby, outflanked him and then struck him in the cheek with a heavy snowball. The act was acclaimed with loud jeers. Horace turned to dart at his assailant, but there was an immediate demonstration on the other flank, and he found himself obliged to keep his face towards the hilarious crew of tormentors. The baby retreated in safety to the rear of the crowd, where he was received with fulsome compliments upon his daring. Horace retreated slowly up the walk. He continually tried to make them heed him, but the only sound was the chant, "A-fray-ed of his mit-tens!" In this desperate withdrawal the beset and haggard boy suffered more than is the common lot of man.

Being a boy himself, he did not understand boys at all. He had, of course, the dismal conviction that they were going to dog him to his grave. But near the corner of the field they suddenly seemed to forget all about it. Indeed, they possessed only the malevolence of so many flitter-headed sparrows. The interest had swung capriciously to some other matter. In a moment they were off in the field again, carousing amid the snow. Some authoritative boy had probably said, "Aw, come on!"

As the pursuit ceased, Horace ceased his retreat. He spent some time in what was evidently an attempt to adjust his self respect, and then began to wander furtively down towards the group. He, too, had undergone an important change. Perhaps his sharp agony was only as durable as the malevolence of the others. In this boyish life obedience to some unformulated creed of manners was enforced with capricious but merciless rigor. However, they were, after all, his comrades, his friends.

They did not heed his return. They were engaged in an altercation. It had evidently been planned that this battle was between Indians and soldiers. The smaller and weaker boys had been induced to appear as Indians in the initial skirmish, but they were now very sick of it, and were reluctantly but steadfastly, affirming their desire for a change of caste. The larger boys had all won great distinction, devastating Indians materially, and they wished the war to go on as planned. They explained vociferously that it was proper for the soldiers always to thrash the Indians. The little boys did not pretend to deny the truth of this argument; they confined themselves to the simple statement that, in that case, they wished to be soldiers. Each little boy willingly appealed to the others to remain Indians, but as for himself he reiterated his desire to enlist as a soldier. The larger boys were in despair over this dearth of enthusiasm in the small Indians. They alternately wheedled and bullied, but they could not persuade the little boys, who were really suffering dreadful humiliation rather than submit to another onslaught of soldiers. They were called all the baby names that had the power of stinging deep into their pride, but they remained firm.

Then a formidable lad, a leader of reputation, one who could whip many boys that wore long trousers, suddenly blew out his checks and shouted, "Well, all right then. I'll be an Indian myself. Now." The little boys greeted with cheers this addition to their wearied ranks, and seemed then content. But matters were not mended in the least, because all of the personal following of the formidable lad, with the addition of every outsider, spontaneously forsook the flag and declared themselves Indians. There were now no soldiers. The Indians had carried everything unanimously. The formidable lad used his influence, but his influence could not shake the loyalty of his friends, who refused to fight under any colors but his colors.

Plainly there was nothing for it but to coerce the little ones. The formidable lad again became a soldier, and then graciously permitted to join him all the real fighting strength of the crowd, leaving behind a most forlorn band of little Indians. Then the soldiers attacked the Indians, exhorting them to opposition at the same time.

The Indians at first adopted a policy of hurried surrender, but this had no success, as none of the surrenders were accepted. They then turned to flee, bawling out protests. The ferocious soldiers pursued them amid shouts. The battle widened, developing all manner of marvellous detail.

Horace had turned towards home several times, but, as a matter of fact, this scene held him in a spell. It was fascinating beyond anything which the grown man understands. He had always in the back of his head a sense of guilt, even a sense of impending punishment for disobedience, but they could not weigh with the delirium of this snow-battle.

## II

One of the raiding soldiers, espying Horace, called out in passing, "A-fray-ed of his mit-tens!" Horace flinched at this renewal, and the other lad paused to taunt him again. Horace scooped some snow, moulded it into a ball, and flung it at the other. "Ho!" cried the boy, "you're an Indian, are you? Hey, fellers, here's an Indian that ain't been killed yet." He and Horace engaged in a duel in which both were in such haste to mould snowballs that they had little time for aiming.

Horace once struck his opponent squarely in the chest. "Hey," he shouted, "you're dead. You can't fight any more, Pete. I killed you. You're dead."

The other boy flushed red, but he continued frantically to make ammunition. "You never touched me!" he retorted, glowering. "You never touched me! Where, now?" he added, defiantly. "Where did you hit me?"

"On the coat! Right on your breast! You can't fight any more! You're dead!"

"You never!"

"I did, too! Hey, fellers, ain't he dead? I hit 'im square!"

"He never!"

Nobody had seen the affair, but some of the boys took sides in absolute accordance with their friendship for one of the concerned parties. Horace's opponent went about contending, "He never touched me! He never came near me! He never came near me!"

The formidable leader now came forward and accosted Horace. "What was you? An Indian? Well, then, you're dead—that's all. He hit you. I saw him."

"Me?" shrieked Horace. "He never came within a mile of me—"

At that moment he heard his name called in a certain familiar tune of two notes, with the last note shrill and prolonged. He looked towards the sidewalk, and saw his mother standing there in her widow's weeds, with two brown paper parcels under her arm. A silence had fallen upon all the boys. Horace moved slowly towards his mother. She did not seem to note his approach; she was gazing austerely off through the naked branches of the maples where two crimson sunset bars lay on the deep blue sky.

At a distance of ten paces Horace made a desperate venture. "Oh, ma," he whined, "can't I stay out for a while?"

"No," she answered solemnly, "you come with me." Horace knew that profile; it was the inexorable profile. But he continued to plead, because it was not beyond his mind that a great show of suffering now might diminish his suffering later.

He did not dare to look back at his playmates. It was already a public scandal that he could not stay out as late as other boys, and he could imagine his standing now that he had been again dragged off by his mother in sight of the whole world. He was a profoundly miserable human being.

Aunt Martha opened the door for them. Light streamed about her straight skirt. "Oh," she said, "so you found him on the road, eh? Well, I declare! It was about time!"

Horace slunk into the kitchen. The stove, straddling out on its four iron legs, was gently humming. Aunt Martha had evidently just lighted the lamp, for she went to it and began to twist the wick experimentally.

"Now," said the mother, "let's see them mittens."

Horace's chin sank. The aspiration of the criminal, the passionate desire for an asylum from retribution, from justice, was aflame in his heart. "I—I—don't—don't know where they are." he gasped finally, as he passed his hand over his pockets.

"Horace," intoned his mother, "you are tellin' me a story!"

"'Tain't a story," he answered, just above his breath. He looked like a sheep-stealer.

His mother held him by the arm, and began to search his pockets. Almost at once she was able to bring forth a pair of very wet mittens. "Well, I declare!" cried Aunt Martha. The two women went close to the lamp, and minutely examined the mittens, turning them over and over. Afterwards, when Horace looked up, his mother's sad-lined, homely face was turned towards him. He burst into tears.

His mother drew a chair near the stove. "Just you sit there now, until I tell you to git off." He sidled meekly into the chair. His mother and his aunt went briskly about the business of preparing supper. They did not display a knowledge of his existence; they carried an effect of oblivion so far that they even did not speak to each other. Presently they went into the dining and living room; Horace could hear the dishes rattling. His Aunt Martha brought a plate of food, placed it on a chair near him, and went away without a word.

Horace instantly decided that he would not touch a morsel of the food. He had often used this ruse in dealing with his mother. He did not know why it brought her to terms, but certainly it sometimes did.

The mother looked up when the aunt returned to the other room. "Is he eatin' his supper?" she asked.

The maiden aunt, fortified in ignorance, gazed with pity and contempt upon this interest. "Well, now, Emily, how do I know?" she queried. "Was I goin' to stand over 'im? Of all the worryin' you do about that child! It's a shame the way you're bringin' up that child."

"Well, he ought to eat somethin'. It won't do fer him to go without eatin'," the mother retorted, weakly.

Aunt Martha, profoundly scorning the policy of concession which these words meant, uttered a long, contemptuous sigh.

## III

Alone in the kitchen, Horace stared with sombre eyes at the plate of food. For a long time he betrayed no sign of yielding. His mood was adamantine. He was resolved not to sell his vengeance for bread, cold ham, and a pickle, and yet it must be known that the sight of them affected him powerfully. The pickle in particular was notable for its seductive charm. He surveyed it darkly.

But at last, unable to longer endure his state, his attitude in the presence of the pickle, he put out an inquisitive finger and touched it, and it was cool and green and plump. Then a full conception of the cruel woe of his situation swept upon him suddenly, and his eyes filled with tears, which began to move down his cheeks. He sniffled. His heart was black with hatred. He painted in his mind scenes of deadly retribution. His mother would be taught that he was not one to endure persecution meekly, without raising an arm in his defence. And so his dreams were of a slaughter of feelings, and near the end of them his mother was pictured as coming, bowed with pain, to his feet. Weeping, she implored his charity. Would he forgive her? No; his once tender heart had been turned to stone by her injustice. He could not forgive her. She must pay the inexorable penalty.

The first item in this horrible plan was the refusal of the food. This he knew by experience would work havoc in his mother's heart. And so he grimly waited.

But suddenly it occurred to him that the first part of his revenge was in danger of failing. The thought struck him that his mother might not capitulate in the usual way. According to his recollection, the time was more than due when she should come in, worried, sadly affectionate, and ask him if he was ill. It had then been his custom to hint in a resigned voice that he was the victim of secret disease, but that he preferred to suffer in silence and alone. If she was obdurate in her anxiety, he always asked her in a gloomy, low voice to go away and leave him to suffer in silence and alone in the darkness without food. He had known this maneuvering to result even in pie.

But what was the meaning of the long pause and the stillness? Had his old and valued ruse betrayed him? As the truth sank into his mind, he supremely loathed life, the world, his mother. Her heart was beating back the besiegers; he was a defeated child.

He wept for a time before deciding upon the final stroke. He would run away. In a remote corner of the world he would become some sort of bloody-handed person driven to a life of crime by the barbarity of his mother. She should never know his fate. He would torture her for years with doubts and doubts, and drive her implacably to a repentant grave. Nor would Aunt Martha escape. Some day, a century hence, when his mother was dead, he would write to his Aunt Martha, and point out her part in the blighting of his life. For one blow against him now he would, in time, deal back a thousand—aye, ten thousand.

He arose and took his coat and cap. As he moved stealthily towards the door he cast a glance backward at the pickle. He was tempted to take it, but he knew that if he left the plate inviolate his mother would feel even worse.

A blue snow was falling. People, bowed forward, were moving briskly along the walks. The electric lamps hummed amid showers of flakes. As Horace emerged from the kitchen, a shrill squall drove the flakes around the corner of the house. He cowered away from it, and its violence illumined his mind vaguely in new directions. He deliberated upon a choice of remote corners of the globe. He found that he had no plans which were definite enough in a geographical way, but without much loss of time he decided upon California. He moved briskly as far as his mother's front gate on the road to California. He was off at last. His success was a trifle dreadful; his throat choked.

But at the gate he paused. He did not know if his journey to California would be shorter if he went down Niagara Avenue or off through Hogan Street. As the storm was very cold and the point was very important, he decided to withdraw for reflection to the wood-shed. He entered the dark shanty, and took seat upon the old chopping-block upon which he was supposed to perform for a few minutes every afternoon when he returned from school. The wind screamed and shouted at the loose boards, and there was a rift of snow on the floor to leeward of a crack.

Here the idea of starting for California on such a night departed from his mind, leaving him ruminating miserably upon his martyrdom. He saw nothing for it but to sleep all night in the wood-shed and start for California in the morning bright and early. Thinking of his bed, he kicked over the floor and found that the innumerable chips were all frozen tightly, bedded in ice.

Later he viewed with joy some signs of excitement in the house. The flare of a lamp moved rapidly from window to window. Then the kitchen door slammed loudly and a shawled figure sped towards the gate. At last he was making them feel his power. The shivering child's face was lit with saturnine glee as in the darkness of the wood-shed he gloated over the evidences of consternation in his home. The shawled figure had been his Aunt Martha dashing with the alarm to the neighbors.

The cold of the wood-shed was tormenting him. He endured only because of the terror he was causing. But then it occurred to him that, if they instituted a search for him, they would probably examine the wood-shed. He knew that it would not be manful to be caught so soon. He was not positive now that he was going to remain away forever, but at any rate he was bound to inflict some more damage before allowing himself to be captured. If he merely succeeded in making his mother angry, she would thrash him on sight. He must prolong the time in order to be safe. If he held out properly, he was sure of a welcome of love, even though he should drip with crimes.

Evidently the storm had increased, for when he went out it swung him violently with its rough and merciless strength. Panting, stung, half blinded with the driving flakes, he was now a waif, exiled, friendless, and poor. With a bursting heart, he thought of his home and his mother. To his forlorn vision they were as far away as heaven.

<h2 style="text-align:center">IV</h2>

Horace was undergoing changes of feeling so rapidly that he was merely moved hither and then thither like a kite. He was now aghast at the merciless ferocity of his mother. It was she who had thrust him into this wild storm, and she was perfectly indifferent to his fate, perfectly indifferent. The forlorn wanderer could no longer weep. The strong sobs caught at his throat, making his breath come in short, quick snuffles. All in him was conquered save the enigmatical childish ideal of form, manner. This principle still held out, and it was the only thing between him and submission. When he surrendered, he must surrender in a way that deferred to the undefined code. He longed simply to go to the kitchen and stumble in, but his unfathomable sense of fitness forbade him.

Presently he found himself at the head of Niagara Avenue, staring through the snow into the blazing windows of Stickney's butcher-shop. Stickney was the family butcher, not so much because of a superiority to other Whilomville butchers as because he lived next door and had been an intimate friend of the father of Horace. Rows of glowing pigs hung head downward back of the tables, which bore huge pieces of red beef. Clumps of attenuated turkeys were suspended here and there. Stickney, hale and smiling, was bantering with a woman in a cloak, who, with a monster basket on her arm, was dickering for eight cents' worth of some thing. Horace watched them through a crusted pane. When the woman came out and passed him, he went towards the door. He touched the latch with his finger, but withdrew again suddenly to the sidewalk. Inside Stickney was whistling cheerily and assorting his knives.

Finally Horace went desperately forward, opened the door, and entered the shop. His head hung low. Stickney stopped whistling. "Hello, young man," he cried, "what brings you here?"

Horace halted, but said nothing. He swung one foot to and fro over the saw-dust floor.

Stickney had placed his two fat hands palms downward and wide apart on the table, in the attitude of a butcher facing a customer, but now he straightened.

"Here," he said, "what's wrong? What's wrong, kid?"

"Nothin'," answered Horace, huskily. He labored for a moment with something in his throat, and afterwards added, "O'ny—I've—I've run away, and—"

"Run away!" shouted Stickney. "Run away from what? Who?"

"From—home," answered Horace. "I don't like it there any more. I—" He had arranged an oration to win the sympathy of the butcher; he had prepared a table setting forth the merits of his case in the most logical fashion, but it was as if the wind had been knocked out of his mind. "I've run away. I—"

Stickney reached an enormous hand over the array of beef, and firmly grappled the emigrant. Then he swung himself to Horace's side. His face was stretched with laughter, and he playfully shook his prisoner. "Come—come—come. What dashed nonsense is this? Run away, hey? Run away?" Whereupon the child's long-tried spirit found vent in howls.

"Come, come," said Stickney, busily. "Never mind now, never mind. You just come along with me. It'll be all right. I'll fix it. Never you mind."

Five minutes later the butcher, with a great ulster over his apron, was leading the boy homeward.

At the very threshold, Horace raised his last flag of pride. "No—no," he sobbed. "I don't want to. I don't want to go in there." He braced his foot against the step and made a very respectable resistance.

"Now, Horace," cried the butcher. He thrust open the door with a bang. "Hello there!" Across the dark kitchen the door to the living-room opened and Aunt Martha appeared. "You've found him!" she screamed.

"We've come to make a call," roared the butcher. At the entrance to the living-room a silence fell upon them all. Upon a couch Horace saw his mother lying limp, pale as death, her eyes gleaming with pain. There was an electric pause before she swung a waxen hand towards Horace. "My child," she murmured, tremulously. Whereupon the sinister person addressed, with a prolonged wail of grief and joy, ran to her with speed. "Mam-ma! Mam-ma! Oh, mam-ma!" She was not able to speak in a known tongue as she folded him in her weak arms.

Aunt Martha turned defiantly upon the butcher because her face betrayed her. She was crying. She made a gesture half military, half feminine. "Won't you have a glass of our root-beer, Mr. Stickney? We make it ourselves."

# WAR IS KIND

*Do not weep, maiden, for war is kind.*
*Because your lover threw wild hands toward the sky*
*And the affrighted steed ran on alone,*
*Do not weep.*
*War is kind.*

*Hoarse, booming drums of the regiment,*
*Little souls who thirst for fight,*
*These men were born to drill and die.*
*The unexplained glory flies above them,*
*Great is the battle-god, great, and his kingdom—;*
*A field where a thousand corpses lie.*

*Do not weep, babe, for war is kind.*
*Because your father tumbled in the yellow trenches,*
*Raged at his breast, gulped and died,*
*Do not weep.*
*War is kind.*

*Swift blazing flag of the regiment,*
*Eagle with crest of red and gold,*
*These men were born to drill and die.*
*Point for them the virtue of the slaughter,*
*Make plain to them the excellence of killing*
*And a field where a thousand corpses lie.*

*Mother whose heart hung humble as a button*
*On the bright splendid shroud of your son,*
*Do not weep.*
*War is kind.*

* * * *

*What says the sea, little shell?*
*"What says the sea?*
*"Long has our brother been silent to us,*
*"Kept his message for the ships,*
*"Awkward ships, stupid ships."*

*"The sea bids you mourn, O Pines,*
*"Sing low in the moonlight.*
*"He sends tale of the land of doom,*
*"Of place where endless falls*
*"A rain of women's tears,*

*"And men in grey robes—*
*"Men in grey robes—*
*"Chant the unknown pain."*

* * * *

*"What says the sea, little shell?*
*"What says the sea?*
*"Long has our brother been silent to us,*
*"Kept is message for the ships,*
*"Puny ships, silly ships."*

*"The sea bids you teach, O Pines,*
*"Sing low in the moonlight;*
*"Teach the gold of patience,*
*"Cry gospel of gentle hands,*
*"Cry a brotherhood of hearts.*
*"The sea bids you teach, O Pines."*

*"And where is the reward, little shell?*
*"What says the sea?*
*"Long has our brother been silent to us,*
*"Kept his message for the ships,*
*"Puny ships, silly ships."*

* * * *

*"No word says the sea, O Pines,*
*"No word says the sea.*
*"Long will your brother be silent to you,*
*"Keep his message for the ships,*
*"O puny ships, silly pines."*

*To the maiden*
*The sea was blue meadow,*
*Alive with little froth-people*
*Singing.*

*To the sailor, wrecked,*
*The sea was dead grey walls*
*Superlative in vacancy,*
*Upon which nevertheless at fateful time*
*Was written*
*The grim hatred of nature.*

* * * *

*A little ink more or less!*
*It surely can't matter?*
*Even the sky and the opulent sea,*

*The plains and the hills, aloof,*
*Hear the uproar of all these books.*
*But it is only a little ink more or less.*

*What?*
*You define me God with these trinkets?*
*Can my misery meal on an ordered walking*
*Of surpliced numskulls?*
*And a fanfare of lights?*
*Or even upon the measured pulpitings*
*Of the familiar false and true?*
*Is this God?*
*Where, then is hell?*
*Show me some bastard mushrooms*
*Sprung from a pollution of blood.*
*It is better.*

*Where is God?*

* * * *

*"Have you ever made a just man?"*
*"Oh, I have made three," answered God,*
*"But two of them are dead,*
*"And the third—*
*"Listen! Listen!*
*"And you will hear the thud of his defeat."*

* * * *

*I explain the silvered passing of a ship at night,*
*The sweep of each sad lost wave,*
*The dwindling boom of the steel thing's striving,*
*The little cry of a man to a man,*
*A shadow falling across the greyer night,*
*And the sinking of the small star;*

*Then the waste, the far waste of waters,*
*And the soft lashing of black waves*
*For long and in loneliness.*

*Remember, thou, O ship of love,*
*Thou leavest a far waste of waters,*
*And the soft lashing of black waves*
*For long and in loneliness.*

* * * *

*"I have heard the sunset song of the birches,*
*"A white melody in the silence,*

*"I have seen a quarrel of the pines.*
*"At nightfall*
*"The little grasses have rushed by me*
*"With the wind men.*
*"These things have I lived," quoth the maniac,*
*"Possessing only eyes and ears.*
*"But you—*
*"You don green spectacles before you look at roses."*

* * * *

*Fast rode the knight*
*With spurs, hot and reeking,*
*Ever waving an eager sword,*
*"To save my lady!"*
*Fast rode the knight,*
*And leaped from saddle to war.*
*Men of steel flickered and gleamed*
*Like riot of silver lights,*
*And the gold of the knight's good banner*
*Still waved on a castle wall.*

* * * *

*A horse,*
*Blowing, staggering, bloody thing,*
*Forgotten at foot of castle wall.*
*A horse*
*Dead at foot of castle wall.*

* * * *

*Forth went the candid man*
*And spoke freely to the wind—*
*When he looked about him he was in a far strange country.*

*Forth went the candid man*
*And spoke freely to the stars—*
*Yellow light tore sight from his eye.*

*"My good fool," said a learned bystander,*
*"Your operations are mad."*

*"You are too candid," cried the candid man.*
*And when his stick left the head of the learned bystander*
*It was two sticks.*

* * * *

*You tell me this is God?*
*I tell you this is a printed list,*

*A burning candle and an ass.*

* * * *

*On the desert*
*A silence from the moon's deepest valley.*
*Fire rays fall athwart the robes*
*Of hooded men, squat and dumb.*
*Before them, a woman*
*Moves to the blowing of shrill whistles*
*And distant thunder of drums,*
*While mystic things, sinuous, dull with terrible color,*
*Sleepily fondle her body*
*Or move at her will, swishing stealthily over the sand.*
*The snakes whisper softly;*
*The whispering, whispering snakes,*
*Dreaming and swaying and staring,*
*But always whispering, softly whispering.*
*The wind streams from the lone reaches*
*Of Arabia, solemn with night,*
*And the wild fire makes shimmer of blood*
*Over the robes of the hooded men*
*Squat and dumb.*

*Bands of moving bronze, emerald, yellow,*
*Circle the throat and arms of her,*
*And over the sands serpents move warily*
*Slow, menacing and submissive,*
*Swinging to the whistles and drums,*
*The whispering, whispering snakes,*
*Dreaming and swaying and staring,*
*But always whispering, softly whispering.*
*The dignity of the accursed;*
*The glory of slavery, despair, death,*
*Is in the dance of the whispering snakes.*

* * * *

*A newspaper is a collection of half-injustices*
*Which, bawled by boys from mile to mile,*
*Spreads its curious opinion*
*To a million merciful and sneering men,*
*While families cuddle the joys of the fireside*
*When spurred by tale of dire lone agony.*
*A newspaper is a court*
*Where every one is kindly and unfairly tried*
*By a squalor of honest men.*
*A newspaper is a market*

*Where wisdom sells its freedom*
*And melons are crowned by the crowd.*
*A newspaper is a game*
*Where his error scores the player victory*
*While another's skill wins death.*
*A newspaper is a symbol;*
*It is fetless life's chronical,*
*A collection of loud tales*
*Concentrating eternal stupidities,*
*That in remote ages lived unhaltered,*
*Roaming through a fenceless world.*

* * * *

*The wayfarer,*
*Perceiving the pathway to truth,*
*Was struck with astonishment.*
*It was thickly grown with weeds.*
*"Ha," he said,*
*"I see that none has passed here*
*"In a long time."*
*Later he saw that each weed*
*Was a singular knife.*
*"Well," he mumbled at last,*
*"Doubtless there are other roads."*

* * * *

*A slant of sun on dull brown walls,*
*A forgotten sky of bashful blue.*

*Toward God a mighty hymn,*
*A song of collisions and cries,*
*Rumbling wheels, hoof-beats, bells,*
*Welcomes, farewells, love-calls, final moans,*
*Voices of joy, idiocy, warning, despair,*
*The unknown appeals of brutes,*
*The chanting of flowers,*
*The screams of cut trees,*
*The senseless babble of hens and wise men—*
*A cluttered incoherency that says at the stars;*
*"O God, save us!"*

* * * *

*Once a man clambering to the housetops*
*Appealed to the heavens.*
*With a strong voice he called to the deaf spheres;*
*A warrior's shout he raised to the suns.*

*Lo, at last, there was a dot on the clouds,*
*And—at last and at last—*
*—God—the sky was filled with armies.*

* * * *

*There was a man with tongue of wood*
*Who essayed to sing,*
*And in truth it was lamentable.*
*But there was one who heard*
*The clip-clapper of this tongue of wood*
*And knew what the man*
*Wished to sing,*
*And with that the singer was content.*

* * * *

*The successful man has thrust himself*
*Through the water of the years,*
*Reeking wet with mistakes,—*
*Bloody mistakes;*
*Slimed with victories over the lesser,*
*A figure thankful on the shore of money.*
*Then, with the bones of fools*
*He buys silken banners*
*Limned with his triumphant face;*
*With the skins of wise men*
*He buys the trivial bows of all.*
*Flesh painted with marrow*
*Contributes a coverlet,*
*A coverlet for his contented slumber.*
*In guiltless ignorance, in ignorant guilt,*
*He delivered his secrets to the riven multitude.*

*"Thus I defended: Thus I wrought."*
*Complacent, smiling,*
*He stands heavily on the dead.*
*Erect on a pillar of skulls*
*He declaims his trampling of babes;*
*Smirking, fat, dripping,*
*He makes speech in guiltless ignorance,*
*Innocence.*

* * * *

*In the night*
*Grey heavy clouds muffled the valleys,*
*And the peaks looked toward God alone.*
*"O Master that movest the wind with a finger,*

*"Humble, idle, futile peaks are we.*
*"Grant that we may run swiftly across the world*
*"To huddle in worship at Thy feet."*

*In the morning*
*A noise of men at work came the clear blue miles,*
*And the little black cities were apparent.*
*"O Master that knowest the meaning of raindrops,*
*"Humble, idle, futile peaks are we.*
*"Give voice to us, we pray, O Lord,*
*"That we may sing Thy goodness to the sun."*

*In the evening*
*The far valleys were sprinkled with tiny lights.*
*"O Master,*
*"Thou that knowest the value of kings and birds,*
*"Thou hast made us humble, idle, futile peaks.*
*"Thous only needest eternal patience;*
*"We bow to Thy wisdom, O Lord—*
*"Humble, idle, futile peaks."*

*In the night*
*Grey heavy clouds muffles the valleys,*
*And the peaks looked toward God alone.*

* * * *

*The chatter of a death-demon from a tree-top.*

*Blood—blood and torn grass—*
*Had marked the rise of his agony—*
*This lone hunter.*
*The grey-green woods impassive*
*Had watched the threshing of his limbs.*

*A canoe with flashing paddle,*
*A girl with soft searching eyes,*
*A call: "John!"*

* * * *

*Come, arise, hunter!*
*Can you not hear?*

*The chatter of a death-demon from a tree-top.*

* * * *

*The impact of a dollar upon the heart*

Smiles warm red light,
Sweeping from the hearth rosily upon the white table,
With the hanging cool velvet shadows
Moving softly upon the door.

The impact of a million dollars
Is a crash of flunkys,
And yawning emblems of Persia
Cheeked against oak, France and a sabre,
The outcry of old beauty
Whored by pimping merchants
To submission before wine and chatter.
Silly rich peasants stamp the carpets of men,
Dead men who dreamed fragrance and light
Into their woof, their lives;
The rug of an honest bear
Under the feet of a cryptic slave
Who speaks always of baubles,
Forgetting state, multitude, work, and state,
Champing and mouthing of hats,
Making ratful squeak of hats,
Hats.

* * * *

A man said to the universe:
"Sir, I exist!"
"However," replied the universe,
"The fact has not created in me
"A sense of obligation."

* * * *

When the prophet, a complacent fat man,
Arrived at the mountain-top,
He cried: "Woe to my knowledge!
"I intended to see good white lands
"And bad black lands,
"But the scene is grey."

* * * *

There was a land where lived no violets.
A traveller at once demanded: "Why?"
The people told him:
"Once the violets of this place spoke thus:
"'Until some woman freely give her lover
"'To another woman
"'We will fight in bloody scuffle.'"

*Sadly the people added:*
*"There are no violets here."*

* * * *

*There was one I met upon the road*
*Who looked at me with kind eyes.*
*He said: "Show me of your wares."*
*And I did,*
*Holding forth one,*
*He said: "It is a sin."*
*Then I held forth another.*
*He said: "It is a sin."*
*Then I held forth another.*
*He said: "It is a sin."*
*And so to the end.*
*Always He said: "It is a sin."*
*At last, I cried out:*
*"But I have non other."*
*He looked at me*
*With kinder eyes.*
*"Poor soul," he said.*

* * * *

*Aye, workman, make me a dream,*
*A dream for my love.*
*Cunningly weave sunlight,*
*Breezes, and flowers.*
*Let it be of the cloth of meadows.*
*And—good workman—*
*And let there be a man walking thereon.*

* * * *

*Each small gleam was a voice,*
*A lantern voice—*
*In little songs of carmine, violet, green, gold.*
*A chorus of colors came over the water;*
*The wondrous leaf-shadow no longer wavered,*
*No pines crooned on the hills,*
*The blue night was elsewhere a silence,*
*When the chorus of colors came over the water,*
*Little songs of carmine, violet, green, gold.*

*Small glowing pebbles*
*Thrown on the dark plane of evening*
*Sing good ballads of God*
*And eternity, with soul's rest.*

*Little priests, little holy fathers,*
*None can doubt the truth of hour hymning.*
*When the marvellous chorus comes over the water,*
*Songs of carmine, violet, green, gold.*

*The trees in the garden rained flowers.*
*Children ran there joyously.*
*They gathered the flowers*
*Each to himself.*
*Now there were some*
*Who gathered great heaps—*
*Having opportunity and skill—*
*Until, behold, only chance blossoms*
*Remained for the feeble.*
*Then a little spindling tutor*
*Ran importantly to the father, crying:*
*"Pray, come hither!*
*"See this unjust thing in your garden!"*
*But when the father had surveyed,*
*He admonished the tutor:*
*"Not so, small sage!*
*"This thing is just.*
*"For, look you,*
*"Are not they who possess the flowers*
*"Stronger, bolder, shrewder*
*"Than they who have none?*
*"Why should the strong—*
*"The beautiful strong—*
*"Why should they not have the flowers?*

*Upon reflection, the tutor bowed to the ground.*
*"My lord," he said,*
*"The stars are displaced*
*"By this towering wisdom."*

# INTRIGUE

*Thou art my love,*
*And thou art the peace of sundown*
*When the blue shadows soothe,*
*And the grasses and the leaves sleep*
*To the song of the little brooks,*
*Woe is me.*

*Thou art my love,*
*And thou art a strorm*
*That breaks black in the sky,*
*And, sweeping headlong,*
*Drenches and cowers each tree,*
*And at the panting end*
*There is no sound*
*Save the melancholy cry of a single owl—*
*Woe is me!*

*Thou are my love,*
*And thou art a tinsel thing,*
*And I in my play*
*Broke thee easily,*
*And from the little fragments*
*Arose my long sorrow—*
*Woe is me.*

*Thou art my love,*
*And thou art a wary violet,*
*Drooping from sun-caresses,*
*Answering mine carelessly—*
*Woe is me.*

*Thou art my love,*
*And thou art the ashes of other men's love,*
*And I bury my face in these ashes,*
*And I love them—*
*Woe is me.*

*Thou art my love,*
*And thou art the beard*
*On another man's face—*
*Woe is me.*

*Thou art my love,*
*And thou art a temple,*

*And in this temple is an altar,*
*And on this altar is my heart—*
*Woe is me.*

*Thou art my love,*
*And thou art a wretch.*
*Let these sacred love-lies choke thee,*
*From I am come to where I know your lies as truth*
*And you truth as lies—*
*Woe is me.*

* * * *

*Thou art my love,*
*And thou art a priestess,*
*And in they hand is a bloody dagger,*
*And my doom comes to me surely—*
*Woe is me.*

*Thou art my love,*
*And thou art a skull with ruby eyes,*
*And I love thee—*
*Woe is me.*

*Thou art my love,*
*And I doubt thee.*
*And if peace came with thy murder*
*Then would I murder—*
*Woe is me.*

* * * *

*Thou art my love,*
*And thou art death,*
*Aye, thou art death*
*Black and yet black,*
*But I love thee,*
*I love thee—*
*Woe, welcome woe, to me.*

* * * *

*Love, forgive me if I wish you grief,*
*For in your grief*
*You huddle to my breast,*
*And for it*
*Would I pay the price of your grief.*

*You walk among men*
*And all men do not surrender,*

*And thus I understand*
*That love reaches his hand*
*In mercy to me.*

*He had your picture in his room,*
*A scurvy traitor picture,*
*And he smiled*
*—Merely a fat complacence of men who know fine women—*
*And thus I divided with him*
*A part of my love.*

*Fool, not to know that thy little shoe*
*Can make men weep!*
*—Some men weep.*
*I weep and I gnash,*
*And I love the little shoe,*
*The little, little shoe.*

*God give me medals,*
*God give me loud honors,*
*That I may strut before you, sweetheart,*
*And be worthy of—*
*The love I bear you.*
*Now let me crunch you*
*With full weight of affrighted love.*
*I doubted you*
*—I doubted you—*
*And in this short doubting*
*My love grew like a genie*
*For my further undoing.*

*Beware of my friends,*
*Be not in speech too civil,*
*For in all courtesy*
*My weak heart sees spectres,*
*Mists of desire*
*Arising from the lips of my chosen;*
*Be not civil.*

*The flower I gave thee once*
*Was incident to a stride,*
*A detail of a gesture,*
*But search those pale petals*
*And see engraven thereon*
*A record of my intention.*

* * * *

*Ah, God, the way your little finger moved,*
*As you thrust a bare arm backward*
*And made play with your hair*
*And a comb, a silly gilt comb*
*—Ah, God—that I should suffer*
*Because of the way a little finger moved.*

* * * *

*Once I saw thee idly rocking*
*—Idly rocking—*
*And chattering girlishly to other girls,*
*Bell-voiced, happy,*
*Careless with the stout heart of unscarred womanhood,*
*And life to thee was all light melody.*
*I thought of the great storms of love as I knew it,*
*Torn, miserable, and ashamed of my open sorrow,*
*I thought of the thunders that lived in my head,*
*And I wish to be an ogre,*
*And hale and haul my beloved to a castle,*
*And make her mourn with my mourning.*

*Tell me why, behind thee,*
*I see always the shadow of another lover?*
*Is it real,*
*Or is this the thrice damned memory of a better happiness?*
*Plague on him if he be dead,*
*Plague on him if he be alive—*
*A swinish numskull*
*To intrude his shade*
*Always between me and my peace!*

* * * *

*And yet I have seen thee happy with me.*
*I am no fool*
*To poll stupidly into iron.*
*I have heard your quick breaths*
*And seen your arms writhe toward me;*
*At those times*
*—God help us—*
*I was impelled to be a grand knight,*
*And swagger and snap my fingers,*
*And explain my mind finely.*
*Oh, lost sweetheart,*
*I would that I had not been a grand knight.*
*I said: "Sweetheart."*
*Thou said'st: "Sweetheart."*

*And we preserved an admirable mimicry*
*Without heeding the drip of the blood*
*From my heart.*

** * * **

*I heard thee laugh,*
*And in this merriment*
*I defined the measure of my pain;*
*I knew that I was alone,*
*Alone with love,*
*Poor shivering love,*
*And he, little sprite,*
*Came to watch with me,*
*And at midnight,*
*We were like two creatures by a dead camp-fire.*

** * * **

*I wonder if sometimes in the dusk,*
*When the brave lights that gild thy evenings*
*Have not yet been touched with flame,*
*I wonder if sometimes in the dusk*
*Thou rememberest a time,*
*A time when thou loved me*
*And our love was to thee thy all?*
*Is the memory rubbish now?*
*An old gown*
*Worn in an age of other fashions?*
*Woe is me, oh, lost one,*
*For that love is now to me*
*A supernal dream,*
*White, white, white with many suns.*

** * * **

*Love met me at noonday,*
*—Reckless imp,*
*To leave his shaded nights*
*And brave the glare,—*
*And I saw him then plainly*
*For a bungler,*
*A stupid, simpering, eyeless bungler,*
*Breaking the hearts of brave people*
*As the snivelling idiot-boy cracks his bowl,*
*And I cursed him,*
*Cursed him to and fro, back and forth,*
*Into all the silly mazes of his mind,*
*But in the end*

*He laughed and pointed to my breast,*
*Where a heart still beat for thee, beloved.*

* * * *

*I have seen thy face aflame*
*For love of me,*
*Thy fair arms go mad,*
*Thy lips tremble and mutter and rave.*
*And—surely—*
*This should leave a man content?*
*Thou lovest not me now,*
*But thou didst love me,*
*And in loving me once*
*Thou gavest me an eternal privilege,*
*For I can think of thee.*

# THE THIRD VIOLET

## CHAPTER I.

The engine bellowed its way up the slanting, winding valley. Grey crags, and trees with roots fastened cleverly to the steeps looked down at the struggles of the black monster.

When the train finally released its passengers they burst forth with the enthusiasm of escaping convicts. A great bustle ensued on the platform of the little mountain station. The idlers and philosophers from the village were present to examine the consignment of people from the city. These latter, loaded with bundles and children, thronged at the stage drivers. The stage drivers thronged at the people from the city.

Hawker, with his clothes case, his paint-box, his easel, climbed awkwardly down the steps of the car. The easel swung uncontrolled and knocked against the head of a little boy who was disembarking backward with fine caution. "Hello, little man," said Hawker, "did it hurt?" The child regarded him in silence and with sudden interest, as if Hawker had called his attention to a phenomenon. The young painter was politely waiting until the little boy should conclude his examination, but a voice behind him cried, "Roger, go on down!" A nursemaid was conducting a little girl where she would probably be struck by the other end of the easel. The boy resumed his cautious descent.

The stage drivers made such great noise as a collection that as individuals their identities were lost. With a highly important air, as a man proud of being so busy, the baggageman of the train was thundering trunks at the other employees on the platform. Hawker, prowling through the crowd, heard a voice near his shoulder say, "Do you know where is the stage for Hemlock Inn?" Hawker turned and found a young woman regarding him. A wave of astonishment whirled into his hair, and he turned his eyes quickly for fear that she would think that he had looked at her. He said, "Yes, certainly, I think I can find it." At the same time he was crying to himself: "Wouldn't I like to paint her, though! What a glance—oh, murder! The—the—the distance in her eyes!"

He went fiercely from one driver to another. That obdurate stage for Hemlock Inn must appear at once. Finally he perceived a man who grinned expectantly at him. "Oh," said Hawker, "you drive the stage for Hemlock Inn?" The man admitted it. Hawker said, "Here is the stage." The young woman smiled.

The driver inserted Hawker and his luggage far into the end of the vehicle. He sat there, crooked forward so that his eyes should see the first coming of the girl into the frame of light at the other end of the stage. Presently she appeared there. She was bringing the little boy, the little girl, the nursemaid, and another young woman, who was at once to be known as the mother of the two children. The girl indicated the stage with a small gesture of triumph. When they were all seated uncomfortably in the huge covered vehicle the little boy gave Hawker a glance of recognition. "It hurted then, but it's all right now," he informed him cheerfully.

"Did it?" replied Hawker. "I'm sorry."

"Oh, I didn't mind it much," continued the little boy, swinging his long, red-leather leggings bravely to and fro. "I don't cry when I'm hurt, anyhow." He cast a meaning look at his tiny sister, whose soft lips set defensively.

The driver climbed into his seat, and after a scrutiny of the group in the gloom of the stage he chirped to his horses. They began a slow and thoughtful trotting. Dust streamed out behind the vehicle. In front, the green hills were still and serene in the evening air. A beam of gold struck them aslant, and on the sky was lemon and pink information of the sun's sinking. The driver knew many people along the road, and from time to time he conversed with them in yells.

The two children were opposite Hawker. They sat very correctly mucilaged to their seats, but their large eyes were always upon Hawker, calmly valuing him.

"Do you think it nice to be in the country? I do," said the boy.

"I like it very well," answered Hawker.

"I shall go fishing, and hunting, and everything. Maybe I shall shoot a bears."

"I hope you may."

"Did you ever shoot a bears?"

"No."

"Well, I didn't, too, but maybe I will. Mister Hollanden, he said he'd look around for one. Where I live—"

"Roger," interrupted the mother from her seat at Hawker's side, "perhaps every one is not interested in your conversation." The boy seemed embarrassed at this interruption, for he leaned back in silence with an apologetic look at Hawker. Presently the stage began to climb the hills, and the two children were obliged to take grip upon the cushions for fear of being precipitated upon the nursemaid.

Fate had arranged it so that Hawker could not observe the girl with the—the—the distance in her eyes without leaning forward and discovering to her his interest. Secretly and impiously he wriggled in his seat, and as the bumping stage swung its passengers this way and that way, he obtained fleeting glances of a cheek, an arm, or a shoulder.

The driver's conversation tone to his passengers was also a yell. "Train was an hour late t'night," he said, addressing the interior. "It'll be nine o'clock before we git t' th' inn, an' it'll be perty dark travellin'."

Hawker waited decently, but at last he said, "Will it?"

"Yes. No moon." He turned to face Hawker, and roared, "You're ol' Jim Hawker's son, hain't yeh?"

"Yes."

"I thort I'd seen yeh b'fore. Live in the city now, don't yeh?"

"Yes."

"Want t' git off at th' cross-road?"

"Yes."

"Come up fer a little stay doorin' th' summer?"

"Yes."

"On'y charge yeh a quarter if yeh git off at cross-road. Useter charge 'em fifty cents, but I ses t' th' ol' man. 'Tain't no use. Gol dern 'em, they'll walk ruther'n put up fifty cents.' Yep. On'y a quarter."

In the shadows Hawker's expression seemed assassinlike. He glanced furtively down the stage. She was apparently deep in talk with the mother of the children.

## CHAPTER II.

When Hawker pushed at the old gate, it hesitated because of a broken hinge. A dog barked with loud ferocity and came headlong over the grass.

"Hello, Stanley, old man!" cried Hawker. The ardour for battle was instantly smitten from the dog, and his barking swallowed in a gurgle of delight. He was a large orange and white setter, and he partly expressed his emotion by twisting his body into a fantastic curve and then dancing over the ground with his head and his tail very near to each other. He gave vent to little sobs in a wild attempt to vocally describe his gladness. "Well, 'e was a dreat dod," said Hawker, and the setter, overwhelmed, contorted himself wonderfully.

There were lights in the kitchen, and at the first barking of the dog the door had been thrown open. Hawker saw his two sisters shading their eyes and peering down the yellow stream. Presently they shouted, "Here he is!" They flung themselves out and upon him. "Why, Will! why, Will!" they panted.

"We're awful glad to see you!" In a whirlwind of ejaculation and unanswerable interrogation they grappled the clothes case, the paint-box, the easel, and dragged him toward the house.

He saw his old mother seated in a rocking-chair by the table. She had laid aside her paper and was adjusting her glasses as she scanned the darkness. "Hello, mother!" cried Hawker, as he entered. His eyes were bright. The old mother reached her arms to his neck. She murmured soft and half-articulate words. Meanwhile the dog writhed from one to another. He raised his muzzle high to express his delight. He was always fully convinced that he was taking a principal part in this ceremony of welcome and that everybody was heeding him.

"Have you had your supper?" asked the old mother as soon as she recovered herself. The girls clamoured sentences at him. "Pa's out in the barn, Will. What made you so late? He said maybe he'd go up to the cross-roads to see if he could see the stage. Maybe he's gone. What made you so late? And, oh, we got a new buggy!"

The old mother repeated anxiously, "Have you had your supper?"

"No," said Hawker, "but—"

The three women sprang to their feet. "Well, we'll git you something right away." They bustled about the kitchen and dove from time to time into the cellar. They called to each other in happy voices.

Steps sounded on the line of stones that led from the door toward the barn, and a shout came from the darkness. "Well, William, home again, hey?" Hawker's grey father came stamping genially into the room. "I thought maybe you got lost. I was comin' to hunt you," he said, grinning, as they stood with gripped hands. "What made you so late?"

While Hawker confronted the supper the family sat about and contemplated him with shining eyes. His sisters noted his tie and propounded some questions concerning it. His mother watched to make sure that he should consume a notable quantity of the preserved cherries. "He used to be so fond of 'em when he was little," she said.

"Oh, Will," cried the younger sister, "do you remember Lil' Johnson? Yeh? She's married. Married las' June."

"Is the boy's room all ready, mother?" asked the father.

"We fixed it this mornin'," she said.

"And do you remember Jeff Decker?" shouted the elder sister. "Well, he's dead. Yep. Drowned, pickerel fishin'—poor feller!"

"Well, how are you gitting along, William?" asked the father. "Sell many pictures?"

"An occasional one."

"Saw your illustrations in the May number of Perkinson's." The old man paused for a moment, and then added, quite weakly, "Pretty good."

"How's everything about the place?"

"Oh, just about the same—'bout the same. The colt run away with me last week, but didn't break nothin', though. I was scared, because I had out the new buggy— we got a new buggy—but it didn't break nothin'. I'mgoin' to sell the oxen in the fall; I don't want to winter 'em. And then in the spring I'll get a good hoss team. I rented th' back five-acre to John Westfall. I had more'n I could handle with only one hired hand. Times is pickin' up a little, but not much—not much."

"And we got a new school-teacher," said one of the girls.

"Will, you never noticed my new rocker," said the old mother, pointing. "I set it right where I thought you'd see it, and you never took no notice. Ain't it nice? Father bought it at Monticello for my birthday. I thought you'd notice it first thing."

When Hawker had retired for the night, he raised a sash and sat by the window smoking. The odour of the woods and the fields came sweetly to his nostrils. The crickets chanted their hymn of the night. On the black brow of the mountain he could see two long rows of twinkling dots which marked the position of Hemlock Inn.

## CHAPTER III.

Hawker had a writing friend named Hollanden. In New York Hollanden had announced his resolution to spend the summer at Hemlock Inn. "I don't like to see the world progressing," he had said; "I shall go to Sullivan County for a time."

In the morning Hawker took his painting equipment, and after manœuvring in the fields until he had proved to himself that he had no desire to go toward the inn, he went toward it. The time was only nine o'clock, and he knew that he could not hope to see Hollanden before eleven, as it was only through rumour that Hollanden was aware that there was a sunrise and an early morning.

Hawker encamped in front of some fields of vivid yellow stubble on which trees made olive shadows, and which was overhung by a china-blue sky and sundry little white clouds. He fiddled away perfunctorily at it. A spectator would have believed, probably, that he was sketching the pines on the hill where shone the red porches of Hemlock Inn.

Finally, a white-flannel young man walked into the landscape. Hawker waved a brush. "Hi, Hollie, get out of the colour-scheme!"

At this cry the white-flannel young man looked down at his feet apprehensively. Finally he came forward grinning. "Why, hello, Hawker, old boy! Glad to find you here." He perched on a boulder and began to study Hawker's canvas and the vivid yellow stubble with the olive shadows. He wheeled his eyes from one to the other. "Say, Hawker," he said suddenly, "why don't you marry Miss Fanhall?"

Hawker had a brush in his mouth, but he took it quickly out, and said, "Marry Miss Fanhall? Who the devil is Miss Fanhall?"

Hollanden clasped both hands about his knee and looked thoughtfully away. "Oh, she's a girl."

"She is?" said Hawker.

"Yes. She came to the inn last night with her sister-in-law and a small tribe of young Fanhalls. There's six of them, I think."

"Two," said Hawker, "a boy and a girl."

"How do you—oh, you must have come up with them. Of course. Why, then you saw her."

"Was that her?" asked Hawker listlessly.

"Was that her?" cried Hollanden, with indignation. "Was that her?"

"Oh!" said Hawker.

Hollanden mused again. "She's got lots of money," he said. "Loads of it. And I think she would be fool enough to have sympathy for you in your work. They are a tremendously wealthy crowd, although they treat it simply. It would be a good thing for you. I believe—yes, I am sure she could be fool enough to have sympathy for you in your work. And now, if you weren't such a hopeless chump—"

"Oh, shut up, Hollie," said the painter.

For a time Hollanden did as he was bid, but at last he talked again. "Can't think why they came up here. Must be her sister-in-law's health. Something like that. She—"

"Great heavens," said Hawker, "you speak of nothing else!"

"Well, you saw her, didn't you?" demanded Hollanden. "What can you expect, then, from a man of my sense? You—you old stick—you—"

"It was quite dark," protested the painter.

"Quite dark," repeated Hollanden, in a wrathful voice. "What if it was?"

"Well, that is bound to make a difference in a man's opinion, you know."

"No, it isn't. It was light down at the railroad station, anyhow. If you had any sand—thunder, but I did get up early this morning! Say, do you play tennis?"

"After a fashion," said Hawker. "Why?"

"Oh, nothing," replied Hollanden sadly. "Only they are wearing me out at the game. I had to get up and play before breakfast this morning with the Worcester girls, and there is a lot more mad players who will be down on me before long. It's a terrible thing to be a tennis player."

"Why, you used to put yourself out so little for people," remarked Hawker.

"Yes, but up there"—Hollanden jerked his thumb in the direction of the inn—"they think I'm so amiable."

"Well, I'll come up and help you out."

"Do," Hollanden laughed; "you and Miss Fanhall can team it against the littlest Worcester girl and me." He regarded the landscape and meditated. Hawker struggled for a grip on the thought of the stubble.

"That colour of hair and eyes always knocks me kerplunk," observed Hollanden softly.

Hawker looked up irascibly. "What colour hair and eyes?" he demanded. "I believe you're crazy."

"What colour hair and eyes?" repeated Hollanden, with a savage gesture. "You've got no more appreciation than a post."

"They are good enough for me," muttered Hawker, turning again to his work. He scowled first at the canvas and then at the stubble. "Seems to me you had best take care of yourself, instead of planning for me," he said.

"Me!" cried Hollanden. "Me! Take care of myself! My boy, I've got a past of sorrow and gloom. I—"

"You're nothing but a kid," said Hawker, glaring at the other man.

"Oh, of course," said Hollanden, wagging his head with midnight wisdom. "Oh, of course."

"Well, Hollie," said Hawker, with sudden affability, "I didn't mean to be unpleasant, but then you are rather ridiculous, you know, sitting up there and howling about the colour of hair and eyes."

"I'm not ridiculous."

"Yes, you are, you know, Hollie."

The writer waved his hand despairingly. "And you rode in the train with her, and in the stage."

"I didn't see her in the train," said Hawker.

"Oh, then you saw her in the stage. Ha-ha, you old thief! I sat up here, and you sat down there and lied." He jumped from his perch and belaboured Hawker's shoulders.

"Stop that!" said the painter.

"Oh, you old thief, you lied to me! You lied— Hold on—bless my life, here she comes now!"

## CHAPTER IV.

One day Hollanden said: "There are forty-two people at Hemlock Inn, I think. Fifteen are middle-aged ladies of the most aggressive respectability. They have come here for no discernible purpose save to get where they can see people and be displeased at them. They sit in a large group on that porch and take measurements of character as importantly as if they constituted the jury of heaven. When I arrived at Hemlock Inn I at once cast my eye searchingly about me. Perceiving this assemblage, I cried, 'There they are!' Barely waiting to change my clothes, I made for this formidable body and endeavoured to conciliate it. Almost every day I sit down among them and lie like a machine. Privately I believe they should be hanged, but publicly I glisten with admiration. Do you know, there is one of 'em who I know has not moved from the inn in eight days, and this morning I said to her, 'These long walks in the clear mountain air are doing you a world of good.' And I keep continually saying, 'Your frankness is so charming!' Because of the great law of universal balance, I know that this illustrious corps will believe good of themselves with exactly the same readiness that they will believe ill of others. So I ply them with it. In consequence, the worst they ever say of me is, 'Isn't that Mr. Hollanden a peculiar man?' And you know, my boy, that's not so bad for a literary person." After some thought he added: "Good people, too. Good wives, good mothers, and everything of that kind, you know. But conservative, very conservative. Hate anything radical. Can not endure it. Were that way themselves once, you know. They hit the mark, too, sometimes. Such general volleyings can't fail to hit everything. May the devil fly away with them!"

Hawker regarded the group nervously, and at last propounded a great question: "Say, I wonder where they all are recruited? When you come to think that almost every summer hotel—"

"Certainly," said Hollanden, "almost every summer hotel. I've studied the question, and have nearly established the fact that almost every summer hotel is furnished with a full corps of—"

"To be sure," said Hawker; "and if you search for them in the winter, you can find barely a sign of them, until you examine the boarding houses, and then you observe—"

"Certainly," said Hollanden, "of course. By the way," he added, "you haven't got any obviously loose screws in your character, have you?"

"No," said Hawker, after consideration, "only general poverty—that's all."

"Of course, of course," said Hollanden. "But that's bad. They'll get on to you, sure. Particularly since you come up here to see Miss Fanhall so much."

Hawker glinted his eyes at his friend. "You've got a deuced open way of speaking," he observed.

"Deuced open, is it?" cried Hollanden. "It isn't near so open as your devotion to Miss Fanhall, which is as plain as a red petticoat hung on a hedge."

Hawker's face gloomed, and he said, "Well, it might be plain to you, you infernal cat, but that doesn't prove that all those old hens can see it."

"I tell you that if they look twice at you they can't fail to see it. And it's bad, too. Very bad. What's the matter with you? Haven't you ever been in love before?"

"None of your business," replied Hawker.

Hollanden thought upon this point for a time. "Well," he admitted finally, "that's true in a general way, but I hate to see you managing your affairs so stupidly."

Rage flamed into Hawker's face, and he cried passionately, "I tell you it is none of your business!" He suddenly confronted the other man.

Hollanden surveyed this outburst with a critical eye, and then slapped his knee with emphasis. "You certainly have got it—a million times worse than I thought. Why, you—you—you're heels over head."

"What if I am?" said Hawker, with a gesture of defiance and despair.

Hollanden saw a dramatic situation in the distance, and with a bright smile he studied it. "Say," he exclaimed, "suppose she should not go to the picnic tomorrow? She said this morning she did not know if she could go. Somebody was expected from New York, I think. Wouldn't it break you up, though! Eh?"

"You're so dev'lish clever!" said Hawker, with sullen irony.

Hollanden was still regarding the distant dramatic situation. "And rivals, too! The woods must be crowded with them. A girl like that, you know. And then all that money! Say, your rivals must number enough to make a brigade of militia. Imagine them swarming around! But then it doesn't matter so much," he went on cheerfully; "you've got a good play there. You must appreciate them to her—you understand?—appreciate them kindly, like a man in a watch-tower. You must laugh at them only about once a week, and then very tolerantly—you understand?—and kindly, and—and appreciatively."

"You're a colossal ass, Hollie!" said Hawker. "You—"

"Yes, yes, I know," replied the other peacefully; "a colossal ass. Of course." After looking into the distance again, he murmured: "I'm worried about that picnic. I wish I knew she was going. By heavens, as a matter of fact, she must be made to go!"

"What have you got to do with it?" cried the painter, in another sudden outburst.

"There! there!" said Hollanden, waving his hand. "You fool! Only a spectator, I assure you."

Hawker seemed overcome then with a deep dislike of himself. "Oh, well, you know, Hollie, this sort of thing—" He broke off and gazed at the trees. "This sort of thing— It—"

"How?" asked Hollanden.

"Confound you for a meddling, gabbling idiot!" cried Hawker suddenly.

Hollanden replied, "What did you do with that violet she dropped at the side of the tennis court yesterday?"

## CHAPTER V.

Mrs. Fanhall, with the two children, the Worcester girls, and Hollanden, clambered down the rocky path. Miss Fanhall and Hawker had remained on top of the ledge. Hollanden showed much zeal in conducting his contingent to the foot of the falls. Through the trees they could see the cataract, a great shimmering white thing, booming and thundering until all the leaves gently shuddered.

"I wonder where Miss Fanhall and Mr. Hawker have gone?" said the younger Miss Worcester. "I wonder where they've gone?"

"Millicent," said Hollander, looking at her fondly, "you always had such great thought for others."

"Well, I wonder where they've gone?"

At the foot of the falls, where the mist arose in silver clouds and the green water swept into the pool, Miss Worcester, the elder, seated on the moss, exclaimed, "Oh, Mr. Hollanden, what makes all literary men so peculiar?"

"And all that just because I said that I could have made better digestive organs than Providence, if it is true that he made mine," replied Hollanden, with reproach. "Here, Roger," he cried, as he dragged the child away from the brink, "don't fall in there, or you won't be the full-back at Yale in 1907, as you have planned. I'm sure I don't know how to answer you, Miss Worcester. I've inquired of innumerable literary men, and none of 'em know. I may say I have chased that problem for years. I might give you my personal history, and see if that would throw any light on the subject." He looked about him with chin high until his glance had noted the two vague figures at the top of the cliff. "I might give you my personal history—"

Mrs. Fanhall looked at him curiously, and the elder Worcester girl cried, "Oh, do!"

After another scanning of the figures at the top of the cliff, Hollanden established himself in an oratorical pose on a great weather-beaten stone. "Well—you must understand—I started my career—my career, you understand—with a determination to be a prophet, and, although I have ended in being an acrobat, a trained bear of the magazines, and a juggler of comic paragraphs, there was once carved upon my lips a smile which made many people detest me, for it hung before them like a banshee whenever they tried to be satisfied with themselves. I was informed from time to time that I was making no great holes in the universal plan, and I came to know that one person in every two thousand of the people I saw had heard of me, and that four out of five of these had forgotten it. And then one in every two of those who remembered that they had heard of me regarded the fact that I wrote as a great impertinence. I admitted these things, and in defence merely builded a maxim that stated that each wise man in this world is concealed amid some twenty thousand fools. If you have eyes for mathematics, this conclusion should interest you. Meanwhile I created a gigantic dignity, and when men saw this dignity and heard that I was a literary man they respected me. I concluded that the simple campaign of existence for me was to delude the populace, or as much of it as would look at me. I did. I do. And now I can make myself quite happy concocting sneers about it. Others may do as they please, but as for me," he concluded ferociously, "I shall never disclose to anybody that an acrobat, a trained bear of the magazines, a juggler of comic paragraphs, is not a priceless pearl of art and philosophy."

"I don't believe a word of it is true," said Miss Worcester.

"What do you expect of autobiography?" demanded Hollanden, with asperity.

"Well, anyhow, Hollie," exclaimed the younger sister, "you didn't explain a thing about how literary men came to be so peculiar, and that's what you started out to do, you know."

"Well," said Hollanden crossly, "you must never expect a man to do what he starts to do, Millicent. And besides," he went on, with the gleam of a sudden idea in his eyes, "literary men are not peculiar, anyhow."

The elder Worcester girl looked angrily at him. "Indeed? Not you, of course, but the others."

"They are all asses," said Hollanden genially.

The elder Worcester girl reflected. "I believe you try to make us think and then just tangle us up purposely!"

The younger Worcester girl reflected. "You are an absurd old thing, you know, Hollie!"

Hollanden climbed offendedly from the great weather-beaten stone. "Well, I shall go and see that the men have not spilled the luncheon while breaking their necks over these rocks. Would you like to have it spread here, Mrs. Fanhall? Never mind consulting the girls. I assure you I shall spend a great deal of energy and temper in bullying them into doing just as they please. Why, when I was in Brussels—"

"Oh, come now, Hollie, you never were in Brussels, you know," said the younger Worcester girl.

"What of that, Millicent?" demanded Hollanden. "This is autobiography."

"Well, I don't care, Hollie. You tell such whoppers."

With a gesture of despair he again started away; whereupon the Worcester girls shouted in chorus, "Oh, I say, Hollie, come back! Don't be angry. We didn't mean to tease you, Hollie—really, we didn't!"

"Well, if you didn't," said Hollanden, "why did you—"

The elder Worcester girl was gazing fixedly at the top of the cliff. "Oh, there they are! I wonder why they don't come down?"

## CHAPTER VI.

Stanley, the setter, walked to the edge of the precipice and, looking over at the falls, wagged his tail in friendly greeting. He was braced warily, so that if this howling white animal should reach up a hand for him he could flee in time.

The girl stared dreamily at the red-stained crags that projected from the pines of the hill across the stream. Hawker lazily aimed bits of moss at the oblivious dog and missed him.

"It must be fine to have something to think of beyond just living," said the girl to the crags.

"I suppose you mean art?" said Hawker.

"Yes, of course. It must be finer, at any rate, than the ordinary thing."

He mused for a time. "Yes. It is—it must be," he said. "But then—I'd rather just lie here."

The girl seemed aggrieved. "Oh, no, you wouldn't. You couldn't stop. It's dreadful to talk like that, isn't it? I always thought that painters were—"

"Of course. They should be. Maybe they are. I don't know. Sometimes I am. But not today."

"Well, I should think you ought to be so much more contented than just ordinary people. Now, I—"

"You!" he cried—"you are not 'just ordinary people.'"

"Well, but when I try to recall what I have thought about in my life, I can't remember, you know. That's what I mean."

"You shouldn't talk that way," he told her.

"But why do you insist that life should be so highly absorbing for me?"

"You have everything you wish for," he answered, in a voice of deep gloom.

"Certainly not. I am a woman."

"But—"

"A woman, to have everything she wishes for, would have to be Providence. There are some things that are not in the world."

"Well, what are they?" he asked of her.

"That's just it," she said, nodding her head, "no one knows. That's what makes the trouble."

"Well, you are very unreasonable."

"What?"

"You are very unreasonable. If I were you—an heiress—"

The girl flushed and turned upon him angrily.

"Well!" he glowered back at her. "You are, you know. You can't deny it."

She looked at the red-stained crags. At last she said, "You seemed really contemptuous."

"Well, I assure you that I do not feel contemptuous. On the contrary, I am filled with admiration. Thank Heaven, I am a man of the world. Whenever I meet heiresses I always have the deepest admiration." As he said this he wore a brave hangdog expression. The girl surveyed him coldly from his chin to his eyebrows. "You have a handsome audacity, too."

He lay back in the long grass and contemplated the clouds.

"You should have been a Chinese soldier of fortune," she said.

He threw another little clod at Stanley and struck him on the head.

"You are the most scientifically unbearable person in the world," she said.

Stanley came back to see his master and to assure himself that the clump on the head was not intended as a sign of serious displeasure. Hawker took the dog's long ears and tried to tie them into a knot.

"And I don't see why you so delight in making people detest you," she continued.

Having failed to make a knot of the dog's ears, Hawker leaned back and surveyed his failure admiringly. "Well, I don't," he said.

"You do."

"No, I don't."

"Yes, you do. You just say the most terrible things as if you positively enjoyed saying them."

"Well, what did I say, now? What did I say?"

"Why, you said that you always had the most extraordinary admiration for heiresses whenever you met them."

"Well, what's wrong with that sentiment?" he said. "You can't find fault with that!"

"It is utterly detestable."

"Not at all," he answered sullenly. "I consider it a tribute—a graceful tribute."

Miss Fanhall arose and went forward to the edge of the cliff. She became absorbed in the falls. Far below her a bough of a hemlock drooped to the water, and each swirling, mad wave caught it and made it nod—nod—nod. Her back was half turned toward Hawker.

After a time Stanley, the dog, discovered some ants scurrying in the moss, and he at once began to watch them and wag his tail.

"Isn't it curious," observed Hawker, "how an animal as large as a dog will sometimes be so entertained by the very smallest things?"

Stanley pawed gently at the moss, and then thrust his head forward to see what the ants did under the circumstances.

"In the hunting season," continued Hawker, having waited a moment, "this dog knows nothing on earth but his master and the partridges. He is lost to all other sound and movement. He moves through the woods like a steel machine. And when he scents the bird—ah, it is beautiful! Shouldn't you like to see him then?"

Some of the ants had perhaps made war-like motions, and Stanley was pretending that this was a reason for excitement. He reared aback, and made grumbling noises in his throat.

After another pause Hawker went on: "And now see the precious old fool! He is deeply interested in the movements of the little ants, and as childish and ridiculous over them as if they were highly important.—There, you old blockhead, let them alone!"

Stanley could not be induced to end his investigations, and he told his master that the ants were the most thrilling and dramatic animals of his experience.

"Oh, by the way," said Hawker at last, as his glance caught upon the crags across the river, "did you ever hear the legend of those rocks yonder? Over there where I am pointing? Where I'm pointing? Did you ever hear it? What? Yes? No? Well, I shall tell it to you." He settled comfortably in the long grass.

## CHAPTER VII.

"Once upon a time there was a beautiful Indian maiden, of course. And she was, of course, beloved by a youth from another tribe who was very handsome and stalwart and a mighty hunter, of course. But the maiden's father was, of course, a stern old chief, and when the question of his daughter's marriage came up, he, of course, declared that the maiden should be wedded only to a warrior of her tribe. And, of course, when the young man heard this he said that in such case he would, of course, fling himself headlong from that crag. The old chief was, of course, obdurate, and, of course, the youth did, of course, as he had said. And, of course, the maiden wept." After Hawker had waited for some time, he said with severity, "You seem to have no great appreciation of folklore."

The girl suddenly bent her head. "Listen," she said, "they're calling. Don't you hear Hollie's voice?"

They went to another place, and, looking down over the shimmering tree-tops, they saw Hollanden waving his arms. "It's luncheon," said Hawker. "Look how frantic he is!"

The path required that Hawker should assist the girl very often. His eyes shone at her whenever he held forth his hand to help her down a blessed steep place. She seemed rather pensive. The route to luncheon was very long. Suddenly he took a seat on an old tree, and said: "Oh, I don't know why it is, whenever I'm with you, I—I have no wits, nor good nature, nor anything. It's the worst luck!"

He had left her standing on a boulder, where she was provisionally helpless. "Hurry!" she said; "they're waiting for us."

Stanley, the setter, had been sliding down cautiously behind them. He now stood wagging his tail and waiting for the way to be cleared.

Hawker leaned his head on his hand and pondered dejectedly. "It's the worst luck!"

"Hurry!" she said; "they're waiting for us."

At luncheon the girl was for the most part silent. Hawker was superhumanly amiable. Somehow he gained the impression that they all quite fancied him, and it followed that being clever was very easy. Hollanden listened, and approved him with a benign countenance.

There was a little boat fastened to the willows at the edge of the black pool. After the spread, Hollanden navigated various parties around to where they could hear the great hollow roar of the falls beating against the sheer rocks. Stanley swam after sticks at the request of little Roger.

Once Hollanden succeeded in making the others so engrossed in being amused that Hawker and Miss Fanhall were left alone staring at the white bubbles that floated solemnly on the black water. After Hawker had stared at them a sufficient time, he said, "Well, you are an heiress, you know."

In return she chose to smile radiantly. Turning toward him, she said, "If you will be good now—always—perhaps I'll forgive you."

They drove home in the sombre shadows of the hills, with Stanley padding along under the wagon. The Worcester girls tried to induce Hollanden to sing, and in consequence there was quarrelling until the blinking lights of the inn appeared above them as if a great lantern hung there.

Hollanden conveyed his friend some distance on the way home from the inn to the farm. "Good time at the picnic?" said the writer.

"Yes."

"Picnics are mainly places where the jam gets on the dead leaves, and from thence to your trousers. But this was a good little picnic." He glanced at Hawker. "But you don't look as if you had such a swell time."

Hawker waved his hand tragically. "Yes—no—I don't know."

"What's wrong with you?" asked Hollanden.

"I tell you what it is, Hollie," said the painter darkly, "whenever I'm with that girl I'm such a blockhead. I'm not so stupid, Hollie. You know I'm not. But when I'm with her I can't be clever to save my life."

Hollanden pulled contentedly at his pipe. "Maybe she don't notice it."

"Notice it!" muttered Hawker, scornfully; "of course she notices it. In conversation with her, I tell you, I am as interesting as an iron dog." His voice changed as he cried, "I don't know why it is. I don't know why it is."

Blowing a huge cloud of smoke into the air, Hollanden studied it thoughtfully. "Hits some fellows that way," he said. "And, of course, it must be deuced annoying. Strange thing, but now, under those circumstances, I'm very glib. Very glib, I assure you."

"I don't care what you are," answered Hawker. "All those confounded affairs of yours—they were not—"

"No," said Hollanden, stolidly puffing, "of course not. I understand that. But, look here, Billie," he added, with sudden brightness, "maybe you are not a blockhead, after all. You are on the inside, you know, and you can't see from there. Besides, you can't tell what a woman will think. You can't tell what a woman will think."

"No," said Hawker, grimly, "and you suppose that is my only chance?"

"Oh, don't be such a chump!" said Hollanden, in a tone of vast exasperation.

They strode for some time in silence. The mystic pines swaying over the narrow road made talk sibilantly to the wind. Stanley, the setter, took it upon himself to discover some menacing presence in the woods. He walked on his toes and with his eyes glinting sideways. He swore half under his breath.

"And work, too," burst out Hawker, at last. "I came up here this season to work, and I haven't done a thing that ought not be shot at."

"Don't you find that your love sets fire to your genius?" asked Hollanden gravely.

"No, I'm hanged if I do."

Hollanden sighed then with an air of relief. "I was afraid that a popular impression was true," he said, "but it's all right. You would rather sit still and moon, wouldn't you?"

"Moon—blast you! I couldn't moon to save my life."

"Oh, well, I didn't mean moon exactly."

## CHAPTER VIII.

The blue night of the lake was embroidered with black tree forms. Silver drops sprinkled from the lifted oars. Somewhere in the gloom of the shore there was a dog, who from time to time raised his sad voice to the stars.

"But still, the life of the studios—" began the girl.

Hawker scoffed. "There were six of us. Mainly we smoked. Sometimes we played hearts and at other times poker—on credit, you know—credit. And when we had the materials and got something to do, we worked. Did you ever see these beautiful red and green designs that surround the common tomato can?"

"Yes."

"Well," he said proudly, "I have made them. Whenever you come upon tomatoes, remember that they might once have been encompassed in my design. When first I came back from Paris I began to paint, but nobody wanted me to paint. Later, I got into green corn and asparagus—"

"Truly?"

"Yes, indeed. It is true."

"But still, the life of the studios—"

"There were six of us. Fate ordained that only one in the crowd could have money at one time. The other five lived off him and despised themselves. We despised ourselves five times as long as we had admiration."

"And was this just because you had no money?"

"It was because we had no money in New York," said Hawker.

"Well, after a while something happened—"

"Oh, no, it didn't. Something impended always, but it never happened."

"In a case like that one's own people must be such a blessing. The sympathy—"

"One's own people!" said Hawker.

"Yes," she said, "one's own people and more intimate friends. The appreciation—"

"'The appreciation!'" said Hawker. "Yes, indeed!"

He seemed so ill-tempered that she became silent. The boat floated through the shadows of the trees and out to where the water was like a blue crystal. The dog on the shore thrashed about in the reeds and waded in the shallows, mourning his unhappy state in an occasional cry. Hawker stood up and sternly shouted. Thereafter silence was among the reeds. The moon slipped sharply through the little clouds.

The girl said, "I liked that last picture of yours."

"What?"

"At the last exhibition, you know, you had that one with the cows—and things— in the snow—and—and a haystack."

"Yes," he said, "of course. Did you like it, really? I thought it about my best. And you really remembered it? Oh," he cried, "Hollanden perhaps recalled it to you."

"Why, no," she said. "I remembered it, of course."

"Well, what made you remember it?" he demanded, as if he had cause to be indignant.

"Why—I just remembered it because—I liked it, and because—well, the people with me said—said it was about the best thing in the exhibit, and they talked about it a good deal. And then I remember that Hollie had spoken of you, and then I—I—"

"Never mind," he said. After a moment, he added, "The confounded picture was no good, anyhow!"

The girl started. "What makes you speak so of it? It was good. Of course, I don't know—I can't talk about pictures, but," she said in distress, "everybody said it was fine."

"It wasn't any good," he persisted, with dogged shakes of the head.

From off in the darkness they heard the sound of Hollanden's oars splashing in the water. Sometimes there was squealing by the Worcester girls, and at other times loud arguments on points of navigation.

"Oh," said the girl suddenly, "Mr. Oglethorpe is coming tomorrow!"

"Mr. Oglethorpe?" said Hawker. "Is he?"

"Yes." She gazed off at the water.

"He's an old friend of ours. He is always so good, and Roger and little Helen simply adore him. He was my brother's chum in college, and they were quite inseparable until Herbert's death. He always brings me violets. But I know you will like him."

"I shall expect to," said Hawker.

"I'm so glad he is coming. What time does that morning stage get here?"

"About eleven," said Hawker.

"He wrote that he would come then. I hope he won't disappoint us."

"Undoubtedly he will be here," said Hawker.

The wind swept from the ridge top, where some great bare pines stood in the moonlight. A loon called in its strange, unearthly note from the lakeshore. As Hawker turned the boat toward the dock, the flashing rays from the boat fell upon the head of the girl in the rear seat, and he rowed very slowly.

The girl was looking away somewhere with a mystic, shining glance. She leaned her chin in her hand. Hawker, facing her, merely paddled subconsciously. He seemed greatly impressed and expectant.

At last she spoke very slowly. "I wish I knew Mr. Oglethorpe was not going to disappoint us."

Hawker said, "Why, no, I imagine not."

"Well, he is a trifle uncertain in matters of time. The children—and all of us— shall be anxious. I know you will like him."

## CHAPTER IX.

"Eh?" said Hollanden. "Oglethorpe? Oglethorpe? Why, he's that friend of the Fanhalls! Yes, of course, I know him! Deuced good fellow, too! What about him?"

"Oh, nothing, only he's coming here tomorrow," answered Hawker. "What kind of a fellow did you say he was?"

"Deuced good fellow! What are you so— Say, by the nine mad blacksmiths of Donawhiroo, he's your rival! Why, of course! Glory, but I must be thick-headed tonight!"

Hawker said, "Where's your tobacco?"

"Yonder, in that jar. Got a pipe?"

"Yes. How do you know he's my rival?"

"Know it? Why, hasn't he been— Say, this is getting thrilling!" Hollanden sprang to his feet and, filling a pipe, flung himself into the chair and began to rock himself madly to and fro. He puffed clouds of smoke.

Hawker stood with his face in shadow. At last he said, in tones of deep weariness, "Well, I think I'd better be going home and turning in."

"Hold on!" Hollanden exclaimed, turning his eyes from a prolonged stare at the ceiling, "don't go yet! Why, man, this is just the time when—Say, who would ever think of Jem Oglethorpe's turning up to harrie you! Just at this time, too!"

"Oh," cried Hawker suddenly, filled with rage, "you remind me of an accursed duffer! Why can't you tell me something about the man, instead of sitting there and gibbering those crazy things at the ceiling?"

"By the piper—"

"Oh, shut up! Tell me something about Oglethorpe, can't you? I want to hear about him. Quit all that other business!"

"Why, Jem Oglethorpe, he—why, say, he's one of the best fellows going. If he were only an ass! If he were only an ass, now, you could feel easy in your mind. But he isn't. No, indeed. Why, blast him, there isn't a man that knows him who doesn't like Jem Oglethorpe! Excepting the chumps!"

The window of the little room was open, and the voices of the pines could be heard as they sang of their long sorrow. Hawker pulled a chair close and stared out into the darkness. The people on the porch of the inn were frequently calling, "Good-night! Good-night!"

Hawker said, "And of course he's got train loads of money?"

"You bet he has! He can pave streets with it. Lordie, but this is a situation!"

A heavy scowl settled upon Hawker's brow, and he kicked at the dressing case. "Say, Hollie, look here! Sometimes I think you regard me as a bug and like to see me wriggle. But—"

"Oh, don't be a fool!" said Hollanden, glaring through the smoke. "Under the circumstances, you are privileged to rave and ramp around like a wounded lunatic, but for heaven's sake don't swoop down on me like that! Especially when I'm— when I'm doing all I can for you."

"Doing all you can for me! Nobody asked you to. You talk as if I were an infant."

"There! That's right! Blaze up like a fire balloon just because I said that, will you? A man in your condition—why, confound you, you are an infant!"

Hawker seemed again overwhelmed in a great dislike of himself. "Oh, well, of course, Hollie, it—" He waved his hand. "A man feels like—like—"

"Certainly he does," said Hollanden. "That's all right, old man."

"And look now, Hollie, here's this Oglethorpe—"

"May the devil fly away with him!"

"Well, here he is, coming along when I thought maybe—after a while, you know—I might stand some show. And you are acquainted with him, so give me a line on him."

"Well, I should advise you to—"

"Blow your advice! I want to hear about Oglethorpe."

"Well, in the first place, he is a rattling good fellow, as I told you before, and this is what makes it so—"

"Oh, hang what it makes it! Go on."

"He is a rattling good fellow and he has stacks of money. Of course, in this case his having money doesn't affect the situation much. Miss Fanhall—"

"Say, can you keep to the thread of the story, you infernal literary man!"

"Well, he's popular. He don't talk money—ever. And if he's wicked, he's not sufficiently proud of it to be perpetually describing his sins. And then he is not so hideously brilliant, either. That's great credit to a man in these days. And then he— well, take it altogether, I should say Jem Oglethorpe was a smashing good fellow."

"I wonder how long he is going to stay?" murmured Hawker.

During this conversation his pipe had often died out. It was out at this time. He lit another match. Hollanden had watched the fingers of his friend as the match was scratched. "You're nervous, Billie," he said.

Hawker straightened in his chair. "No, I'm not."

"I saw your fingers tremble when you lit that match."

"Oh, you lie!"

Hollanden mused again. "He's popular with women, too," he said ultimately; "and often a woman will like a man and hunt his scalp just because she knows other women like him and want his scalp."

"Yes, but not—"

"Hold on! You were going to say that she was not like other women, weren't you?"

"Not exactly that, but—"

"Well, we will have all that understood."

After a period of silence Hawker said, "I must be going."

As the painter walked toward the door Hollanden cried to him: "Heavens! Of all pictures of a weary pilgrim!" His voice was very compassionate.

Hawker wheeled, and an oath spun through the smoke clouds.

## CHAPTER X.

"Where's Mr. Hawker this morning?" asked the younger Miss Worcester. "I thought he was coming up to play tennis?"

"I don't know. Confound him! I don't see why he didn't come," said Hollanden, looking across the shining valley. He frowned questioningly at the landscape. "I wonder where in the mischief he is?"

The Worcester girls began also to stare at the great gleaming stretch of green and gold. "Didn't he tell you he was coming?" they demanded.

"He didn't say a word about it," answered Hollanden. "I supposed, of course, he was coming. We will have to postpone the *mêlée*."

Later he met Miss Fanhall. "You look as if you were going for a walk?"

"I am," she said, swinging her parasol. "To meet the stage. Have you seen Mr. Hawker today?"

"No," he said. "He is not coming up this morning. He is in a great fret about that field of stubble, and I suppose he is down there sketching the life out of it. These artists—they take such a fiendish interest in their work. I dare say we won't see much of him until he has finished it. Where did you say you were going to walk?"

"To meet the stage."

"Oh, well, I won't have to play tennis for an hour, and if you insist—"

"Of course."

As they strolled slowly in the shade of the trees Hollanden began, "Isn't that Hawker an ill-bred old thing?"

"No, he is not." Then after a time she said, "Why?"

"Oh, he gets so absorbed in a beastly smudge of paint that I really suppose he cares nothing for anything else in the world. Men who are really artists—I don't believe they are capable of deep human affections. So much of them is occupied by art. There's not much left over, you see."

"I don't believe it at all," she exclaimed.

"You don't, eh?" cried Hollanden scornfully. "Well, let me tell you, young woman, there is a great deal of truth in it. Now, there's Hawker—as good a fellow as ever lived, too, in a way, and yet he's an artist. Why, look how he treats—look how he treats that poor setter dog!"

"Why, he's as kind to him as he can be," she declared.

"And I tell you he is not!" cried Hollanden.

"He is, Hollie. You—you are unspeakable when you get in these moods."

"There—that's just you in an argument. I'm not in a mood at all. Now, look—the dog loves him with simple, unquestioning devotion that fairly brings tears to one's eyes—"

"Yes," she said.

"And he—why, he's as cold and stern—"

"He isn't. He isn't, Holly. You are awf'ly unfair."

"No, I'm not. I am simply a liberal observer. And Hawker, with his people, too," he went on darkly; "you can't tell—you don't know anything about it—but I tell you that what I have seen proves my assertion that the artistic mind has no space left for the human affections. And as for the dog—"

"I thought you were his friend, Hollie?"

"Whose?"

"No, not the dog's. And yet you—really, Hollie, there is something unnatural in you. You are so stupidly keen in looking at people that you do not possess common loyalty to your friends. It is because you are a writer, I suppose. That has to explain so many things. Some of your traits are very disagreeable."

"There! there!" plaintively cried Hollanden. "This is only about the treatment of a dog, mind you. Goodness, what an oration!"

"It wasn't about the treatment of a dog. It was about your treatment of your friends."

"Well," he said sagely, "it only goes to show that there is nothing impersonal in the mind of a woman. I undertook to discuss broadly—

"Oh, Hollie!"

"At any rate, it was rather below you to do such scoffing at me."

"Well, I didn't mean—not all of it, Hollie."

"Well, I didn't mean what I said about the dog and all that, either."

"You didn't?" She turned toward him, large-eyed.

"No. Not a single word of it."

"Well, what did you say it for, then?" she demanded indignantly.

"I said it," answered Hollanden placidly, "just to tease you." He looked abstractedly up to the trees.

Presently she said slowly, "Just to tease me?"

At this time Hollanden wore an unmistakable air of having a desire to turn up his coat collar. "Oh, come now—" he began nervously.

"George Hollanden," said the voice at his shoulder, "you are not only disagreeable, but you are hopelessly ridiculous. I—I wish you would never speak to me again!"

"Oh, come now, Grace, don't—don't— Look! There's the stage coming, isn't it?"

"No, the stage is not coming. I wish—I wish you were at the bottom of the sea, George Hollanden. And—and Mr. Hawker, too. There!"

"Oh, bless my soul! And all about an infernal dog," wailed Hollanden. "Look! Honest, now, there's the stage. See it? See it?"

"It isn't there at all," she said.

Gradually he seemed to recover his courage. "What made you so tremendously angry? I don't see why."

After consideration, she said decisively, "Well, because."

"That's why I teased you," he rejoined.

"Well, because—because—"

"Go on," he told her finally. "You are doing very well." He waited patiently.

"Well," she said, "it is dreadful to defend somebody so—so excitedly, and then have it turned out just a tease. I don't know what he would think."

"Who would think?"

"Why—he."

"What could he think? Now, what could he think? Why," said Hollanden, waxing eloquent, "he couldn't under any circumstances think—think anything at all. Now, could he?"

She made no reply.

"Could he?"

She was apparently reflecting.

"Under any circumstances," persisted Hollanden, "he couldn't think anything at all. Now, could he?"

"No," she said.

"Well, why are you angry at me, then?"

## CHAPTER XI.

"John," said the old mother, from the profound mufflings of the pillow and quilts.

"What?" said the old man. He was tugging at his right boot, and his tone was very irascible.

"I think William's changed a good deal."

"Well, what if he has?" replied the father, in another burst of ill-temper. He was then tugging at his left boot.

"Yes, I'm afraid he's changed a good deal," said the muffled voice from the bed. "He's got a good many fine friends, now, John—folks what put on a good many airs; and he don't care for his home like he did."

"Oh, well, I don't guess he's changed very much," said the old man cheerfully. He was now free of both boots.

She raised herself on an elbow and looked out with a troubled face. "John, I think he likes that girl."

"What girl?" said he.

"What girl? Why, that awful handsome girl you see around—of course."

"Do you think he likes 'er?"

"I'm afraid so—I'm afraid so," murmured the mother mournfully.

"Oh, well," said the old man, without alarm, or grief, or pleasure in his tone.

He turned the lamp's wick very low and carried the lamp to the head of the stairs, where he perched it on the step. When he returned he said, "She's mighty good-look-in'!"

"Well, that ain't everything," she snapped. "How do we know she ain't proud, and selfish, and—everything?"

"How do you know she is?" returned the old man.

"And she may just be leading him on."

"Do him good, then," said he, with impregnable serenity. "Next time he'll know better."

"Well, I'm worried about it," she said, as she sank back on the pillow again. "I think William's changed a good deal. He don't seem to care about—us—like he did."

"Oh, go to sleep!" said the father drowsily.

She was silent for a time, and then she said, "John?"

"What?"

"Do you think I better speak to him about that girl?"

"No."

She grew silent again, but at last she demanded, "Why not?"

"'Cause it's none of your business. Go to sleep, will you?" And presently he did, but the old mother lay blinking wild-eyed into the darkness.

In the morning Hawker did not appear at the early breakfast, eaten when the blue glow of dawn shed its ghostly lights upon the valley. The old mother placed various dishes on the back part of the stove. At ten o'clock he came downstairs. His mother was sweeping busily in the parlour at the time, but she saw him and ran to the back part of the stove. She slid the various dishes on to the table. "Did you oversleep?" she asked.

"Yes. I don't feel very well this morning," he said. He pulled his chair close to the table and sat there staring.

She renewed her sweeping in the parlour. When she returned he sat still staring undeviatingly at nothing.

"Why don't you eat your breakfast?" she said anxiously.

"I tell you, mother, I don't feel very well this morning," he answered quite sharply.

"Well," she said meekly, "drink some coffee and you'll feel better."

Afterward he took his painting machinery and left the house. His younger sister was at the well. She looked at him with a little smile and a little sneer. "Going up to the inn this morning?" she said.

"I don't see how that concerns you, Mary?" he rejoined, with dignity.

"Oh, my!" she said airily.

"But since you are so interested, I don't mind telling you that I'm not going up to the inn this morning."

His sister fixed him with her eye. "She ain't mad at you, is she, Will?"

"I don't know what you mean, Mary." He glared hatefully at her and strode away.

Stanley saw him going through the fields and leaped a fence jubilantly in pursuit. In a wood the light sifted through the foliage and burned with a peculiar reddish lustre on the masses of dead leaves. He frowned at it for a while from different points. Presently he erected his easel and began to paint. After a a time he threw down his brush and swore. Stanley, who had been solemnly staring at the scene as if he too was sketching it, looked up in surprise.

In wandering aimlessly through the fields and the forest Hawker once found himself near the road to Hemlock Inn. He shied away from it quickly as if it were a great snake.

While most of the family were at supper, Mary, the younger sister, came charging breathlessly into the kitchen. "Ma—sister," she cried, "I know why—why Will didn't go to the inn today. There's another fellow come. Another fellow."

"Who? Where? What do you mean?" exclaimed her mother and her sister.

"Why, another fellow up at the inn," she shouted, triumphant in her information. "Another fellow come up on the stage this morning. And she went out driving with him this afternoon."

"Well," exclaimed her mother and her sister.

"Yep. And he's an awful good-looking fellow, too. And she—oh, my—she looked as if she thought the world and all of him."

"Well," exclaimed her mother and her sister again.

"Sho!" said the old man. "You wimen leave William alone and quit your gabbling."

The three women made a combined assault upon him. "Well, we ain't a-hurting him, are we, pa? You needn't be so snifty. I guess we ain't a-hurting him much."

"Well," said the old man. And to this argument he added, "Sho!"

They kept him out of the subsequent consultations.

## CHAPTER XII.

The next day, as little Roger was going toward the tennis court, a large orange and white setter ran effusively from around the corner of the inn and greeted him. Miss Fanhall, the Worcester girls, Hollanden, and Oglethorpe faced to the front like soldiers. Hollanden cried, "Why, Billie Hawker must be coming!" Hawker at that moment appeared, coming toward them with a smile which was not overconfident.

Little Roger went off to perform some festivities of his own on the brown carpet under a clump of pines. The dog, to join him, felt obliged to circle widely about the tennis court. He was much afraid of this tennis court, with its tiny round things that sometimes hit him. When near it he usually slunk along at a little sheep trot and with an eye of wariness upon it.

At her first opportunity the younger Worcester girl said, "You didn't come up yesterday, Mr. Hawker."

Hollanden seemed to think that Miss Fanhall turned her head as if she wished to hear the explanation of the painter's absence, so he engaged her in swift and fierce conversation.

"No," said Hawker. "I was resolved to finish a sketch of a stubble field which I began a good many days ago. You see, I was going to do such a great lot of work this summer, and I've done hardly a thing. I really ought to compel myself to do some, you know."

"There," said Hollanden, with a victorious nod, "just what I told you!"

"You didn't tell us anything of the kind," retorted the Worcester girls with one voice.

A middle-aged woman came upon the porch of the inn, and after scanning for a moment the group at the tennis court she hurriedly withdrew. Presently she appeared again, accompanied by five more middle-aged women. "You see," she said to the others, "it is as I said. He has come back."

The five surveyed the group at the tennis court, and then said: "So he has. I knew he would. Well, I declare! Did you ever?" Their voices were pitched at low keys and they moved with care, but their smiles were broad and full of a strange glee.

"I wonder how he feels," said one in subtle ecstasy.

Another laughed. "You know how you would feel, my dear, if you were him and saw yourself suddenly cut out by a man who was so hopelessly superior to you. Why, Oglethorpe's a thousand times better looking. And then think of his wealth and social position!"

One whispered dramatically, "They say he never came up here at all yesterday."

Another replied: "No more he did. That's what we've been talking about. Stayed down at the farm all day, poor fellow!"

"Do you really think she cares for Oglethorpe?"

"Care for him? Why, of course she does. Why, when they came up the path yesterday morning I never saw a girl's face so bright. I asked my husband how much of the Chambers Street Bank stock Oglethorpe owned, and he said that if Oglethorpe took his money out there wouldn't be enough left to buy a pie."

The youngest woman in the corps said: "Well, I don't care. I think it is too bad. I don't see anything so much in that Mr. Oglethorpe."

The others at once patronized her. "Oh, you don't, my dear? Well, let me tell you that bank stock waves in the air like a banner. You would see it if you were her."

"Well, she don't have to care for his money."

"Oh, no, of course she don't have to. But they are just the ones that do, my dear. They are just the ones that do."

"Well, it's a shame."

"Oh, of course it's a shame."

The woman who had assembled the corps said to one at her side: "Oh, the commonest kind of people, my dear, the commonest kind. The father is a regular farmer, you know. He drives oxen. Such language! You can really hear him miles away bellowing at those oxen. And the girls are shy, half-wild things—oh, you have no idea! I saw one of them yesterday when we were out driving. She dodged as we came along, for I suppose she was ashamed of her frock, poor child! And the mother— well, I wish you could see her! A little, old, dried-up thing. We saw her carrying a pail of water from the well, and, oh, she bent and staggered dreadfully, poor thing!"

"And the gate to their front yard, it has a broken hinge, you know. Of course, that's an awful bad sign. When people let their front gate hang on one hinge you know what that means."

After gazing again at the group at the court, the youngest member of the corps said, "Well, he's a good tennis player anyhow."

The others smiled indulgently. "Oh, yes, my dear, he's a good tennis player."

## CHAPTER XIII.

One day Hollanden said, in greeting, to Hawker, "Well, he's gone."

"Who?" asked Hawker.

"Why, Oglethorpe, of course. Who did you think I meant?"

"How did I know?" said Hawker angrily.

"Well," retorted Hollanden, "your chief interest was in his movements, I thought."

"Why, of course not, hang you! Why should I be interested in his movements?"

"Well, you weren't, then. Does that suit you?"

After a period of silence Hawker asked, "What did he—what made him go?"

"Who?"

"Why—Oglethorpe."

"How was I to know you meant him? Well, he went because some important business affairs in New York demanded it, he said; but he is coming back again in a week. They had rather a late interview on the porch last evening."

"Indeed," said Hawker stiffly.

"Yes, and he went away this morning looking particularly elated. Aren't you glad?"

"I don't see how it concerns me," said Hawker, with still greater stiffness.

In a walk to the lake that afternoon Hawker and Miss Fanhall found themselves side by side and silent. The girl contemplated the distant purple hills as if Hawker were not at her side and silent. Hawker frowned at the roadway. Stanley, the setter, scouted the fields in a genial gallop.

At last the girl turned to him. "Seems to me," she said, "seems to me you are dreadfully quiet this afternoon."

"I am thinking about my wretched field of stubble," he answered, still frowning.

Her parasol swung about until the girl was looking up at his inscrutable profile. "Is it, then, so important that you haven't time to talk to me?" she asked with an air of what might have been timidity.

A smile swept the scowl from his face. "No, indeed," he said, instantly; "nothing is so important as that."

She seemed aggrieved then. "Hum—you didn't look so," she told him.

"Well, I didn't mean to look any other way," he said contritely. "You know what a bear I am sometimes. Hollanden says it is a fixed scowl from trying to see uproarious pinks, yellows, and blues."

A little brook, a brawling, ruffianly little brook, swaggered from side to side down the glade, swirling in white leaps over the great dark rocks and shouting challenge to the hillsides. Hollanden and the Worcester girls had halted in a place of ferns and wet moss. Their voices could be heard quarrelling above the clamour of the stream. Stanley, the setter, had soused himself in a pool and then gone and rolled in the dust of the road. He blissfully lolled there, with his coat now resembling an old door mat.

"Don't you think Jem is a wonderfully good fellow?" said the girl to the painter.

"Why, yes, of course," said Hawker.

"Well, he is," she retorted, suddenly defensive.

"Of course," he repeated loudly.

She said, "Well, I don't think you like him as well as I like him."

"Certainly not," said Hawker.

"You don't?" She looked at him in a kind of astonishment.

"Certainly not," said Hawker again, and very irritably. "How in the wide world do you expect me to like him as well as you like him?"

"I don't mean as well," she explained.

"Oh!" said Hawker.

"But I mean you don't like him the way I do at all—the way I expected you to like him. I thought men of a certain pattern always fancied their kind of men wherever they met them, don't you know? And I was so sure you and Jem would be friends."

"Oh!" cried Hawker. Presently he added, "But he isn't my kind of a man at all."

"He is. Jem is one of the best fellows in the world."

Again Hawker cried "Oh!"

They paused and looked down at the brook. Stanley sprawled panting in the dust and watched them. Hawker leaned against a hemlock. He sighed and frowned, and then finally coughed with great resolution. "I suppose, of course, that I am unjust to him. I care for you myself, you understand, and so it becomes—"

He paused for a moment because he heard a rustling of her skirts as if she had moved suddenly. Then he continued: "And so it becomes difficult for me to be fair to him. I am not able to see him with a true eye." He bitterly addressed the trees on the opposite side of the glen. "Oh, I care for you, of course. You might have expected it." He turned from the trees and strode toward the roadway. The uninformed and disreputable Stanley arose and wagged his tail.

As if the girl had cried out at a calamity, Hawker said again, "Well, you might have expected it."

## CHAPTER XIV.

At the lake, Hollanden went pickerel fishing, lost his hook in a gaunt, gray stump, and earned much distinction by his skill in discovering words to express his emotion without resorting to the list ordinarily used in such cases. The younger Miss Worcester ruined a new pair of boots, and Stanley sat on the bank and howled the song of the forsaken. At the conclusion of the festivities Hollanden said, "Billie, you ought to take the boat back."

"Why had I? You borrowed it."

"Well, I borrowed it and it was a lot of trouble, and now you ought to take it back."

Ultimately Hawker said, "Oh, let's both go!"

On this journey Hawker made a long speech to his friend, and at the end of it he exclaimed: "And now do you think she cares so much for Oglethorpe? Why, she as good as told me that he was only a very great friend."

Hollanden wagged his head dubiously. "What a woman says doesn't amount to shucks. It's the way she says it—that's what counts. Besides," he cried in a brilliant afterthought, "she wouldn't tell you, anyhow, you fool!"

"You're an encouraging brute," said Hawker, with a rueful grin.

Later the Worcester girls seized upon Hollanden and piled him high with ferns and mosses. They dragged the long gray lichens from the chins of venerable pines, and ran with them to Hollanden, and dashed them into his arms. "Oh, hurry up, Hollie!" they cried, because with his great load he frequently fell behind them in the march. He once positively refused to carry these things another step. Some distance farther on the road he positively refused to carry this old truck another step. When almost to the inn he positively refused to carry this senseless rubbish another step. The Worcester girls had such vivid contempt for his expressed unwillingness that they neglected to tell him of any appreciation they might have had for his noble struggle.

As Hawker and Miss Fanhall proceeded slowly they heard a voice ringing through the foliage: "Whoa! Haw! Git-ap, blast you! Haw! Haw, drat your hides! Will you haw? Git-ap! Gee! Whoa!"

Hawker said, "The others are a good ways ahead. Hadn't we better hurry a little?"

The girl obediently mended her pace.

"Whoa! haw! git-ap!" shouted the voice in the distance. "Git over there, Red, git over! Gee! Git-ap!" And these cries pursued the man and the maid.

At last Hawker said, "That's my father."

"Where?" she asked, looking bewildered.

"Back there, driving those oxen."

The voice shouted: "Whoa! Git-ap! Gee! Red, git over there now, will you? I'll trim the shin off'n you in a minute. Whoa! Haw! Haw! Whoa! Git-ap!"

Hawker repeated, "Yes, that's my father."

"Oh, is it?" she said. "Let's wait for him."

"All right," said Hawker sullenly.

Presently a team of oxen waddled into view around the curve of the road. They swung their heads slowly from side to side, bent under the yoke, and looked out at the world with their great eyes, in which was a mystic note of their humble, submissive, toilsome lives. An old wagon creaked after them, and erect upon it was the tall and tattered figure of the farmer swinging his whip and yelling: "Whoa! Haw there! Git-ap!" The lash flicked and flew over the broad backs of the animals.

"Hello, father!" said Hawker.

"Whoa! Back! Whoa! Why, hello, William, what you doing here?"

"Oh, just taking a walk. Miss Fanhall, this is my father. Father—"

"How d' you do?" The old man balanced himself with care and then raised his straw hat from his head with a quick gesture and with what was perhaps a slightly apologetic air, as if he feared that he was rather over-doing the ceremonial part.

The girl later became very intent upon the oxen. "Aren't they nice old things?" she said, as she stood looking into the faces of the team. "But what makes their eyes so very sad?"

"I dunno," said the old man.

She was apparently unable to resist a desire to pat the nose of the nearest ox, and for that purpose she stretched forth a cautious hand. But the ox moved restlessly at the moment and the girl put her hand apprehensively behind herself and backed away. The old man on the wagon grinned. "They won't hurt you," he told her.

"They won't bite, will they?" she asked, casting a glance of inquiry at the old man and then turning her eyes again upon the fascinating animals.

"No," said the old man, still grinning, "just as gentle as kittens."

She approached them circuitously. "Sure?" she said.

"Sure," replied the old man. He climbed from the wagon and came to the heads of the oxen. With him as an ally, she finally succeeded in patting the nose of the nearest ox. "Aren't they solemn, kind old fellows? Don't you get to think a great deal of them?"

"Well, they're kind of aggravating beasts sometimes," he said. "But they're a good yoke—a good yoke. They can haul with anything in this region."

"It doesn't make them so terribly tired, does it?" she said hopefully. "They are such strong animals."

"No-o-o," he said. "I dunno. I never thought much about it."

With their heads close together they became so absorbed in their conversation that they seemed to forget the painter. He sat on a log and watched them.

Ultimately the girl said, "Won't you give us a ride?"

"Sure," said the old man. "Come on, and I'll help you up." He assisted her very painstakingly to the old board that usually served him as a seat, and he clambered to a place beside her. "Come on, William," he called. The painter climbed into the wagon and stood behind his father, putting his hand on the old man's shoulder to preserve his balance.

"Which is the near ox?" asked the girl with a serious frown.

"Git-ap! Haw! That one there," said the old man.

"And this one is the off ox?"

"Yep."

"Well, suppose you sat here where I do; would this one be the near ox and that one the off ox, then?"

"Nope. Be just same."

"Then the near ox isn't always the nearest one to a person, at all? That ox there is always the near ox?"

"Yep, always. 'Cause when you drive 'em a-foot you always walk on the left side."

"Well, I never knew that before."

After studying them in silence for a while, she said, "Do you think they are happy?"

"I dunno," said the old man. "I never thought." As the wagon creaked on they gravely discussed this problem, contemplating profoundly the backs of the animals. Hawker gazed in silence at the meditating two before him. Under the wagon Stanley, the setter, walked slowly, wagging his tail in placid contentment and ruminating upon his experiences.

At last the old man said cheerfully, "Shall I take you around by the inn?"

Hawker started and seemed to wince at the question. Perhaps he was about to interrupt, but the girl cried: "Oh, will you? Take us right to the door? Oh, that will be awfully good of you!"

"Why," began Hawker, "you don't want—you don't want to ride to the inn on an—on an ox wagon, do you?"

"Why, of course I do," she retorted, directing a withering glance at him.

"Well—" he protested.

"Let 'er be, William," interrupted the old man. "Let 'er do what she wants to. I guess everybody in th' world ain't even got an ox wagon to ride in. Have they?"

"No, indeed," she returned, while withering Hawker again.

"Gee! Gee! Whoa! Haw! Git-ap! Haw! Whoa! Back!"

After these two attacks Hawker became silent.

"Gee! Gee! Gee there, blast—s'cuse me. Gee! Whoa! Git-ap!"

All the boarders of the inn were upon its porches waiting for the dinner gong. There was a surge toward the railing as a middle-aged woman passed the word along her middle-aged friends that Miss Fanhall, accompanied by Mr. Hawker, had arrived on the ox cart of Mr. Hawker's father.

"Whoa! Ha! Git-ap!" said the old man in more subdued tones. "Whoa there, Red! Whoa, now! Wh-o-a!"

Hawker helped the girl to alight, and she paused for a moment conversing with the old man about the oxen. Then she ran smiling up the steps to meet the Worcester girls.

"Oh, such a lovely time! Those dear old oxen—you should have been with us!"

## CHAPTER XV.

"Oh, Miss Fanhall!"

"What is it, Mrs. Truscot?"

"That was a great prank of yours last night, my dear. We all enjoyed the joke so much."

"Prank?"

"Yes, your riding on the ox cart with that old farmer and that young Mr. What's-his-name, you know. We all thought it delicious. Ah, my dear, after all—don't be offended—if we had your people's wealth and position we might do that sort of unconventional thing, too; but, ah, my dear, we can't, we can't! Isn't the young painter a charming man?"

Out on the porch Hollanden was haranguing his friends. He heard a step and glanced over his shoulder to see who was about to interrupt him. He suddenly ceased his oration, and said, "Hello! what's the matter with Grace?" The heads turned promptly.

As the girl came toward them it could be seen that her cheeks were very pink and her eyes were flashing general wrath and defiance.

The Worcester girls burst into eager interrogation. "Oh, nothing!" she replied at first, but later she added in an undertone, "That wretched Mrs. Truscot—"

"What did she say?" whispered the younger Worcester girl.

"Why, she said—oh, nothing!"

Both Hollanden and Hawker were industriously reflecting.

Later in the morning Hawker said privately to the girl, "I know what Mrs. Truscot talked to you about."

She turned upon him belligerently. "You do?"

"Yes," he answered with meekness. "It was undoubtedly some reference to your ride upon the ox wagon."

She hesitated a moment, and then said, "Well?"

With still greater meekness he said, "I am very sorry."

"Are you, indeed?" she inquired loftily. "Sorry for what? Sorry that I rode upon your father's ox wagon, or sorry that Mrs. Truscot was rude to me about it?"

"Well, in some ways it was my fault."

"Was it? I suppose you intend to apologize for your father's owning an ox wagon, don't you?"

"No, but—"

"Well, I am going to ride in the ox wagon whenever I choose. Your father, I know, will always be glad to have me. And if it so shocks you, there is not the slightest necessity of your coming with us."

They glowered at each other, and he said, "You have twisted the question with the usual ability of your sex."

She pondered as if seeking some particularly destructive retort. She ended by saying bluntly, "Did you know that we were going home next week?"

A flush came suddenly to his face. "No. Going home? Who? You?"

"Why, of course." And then with an indolent air she continued, "I meant to have told you before this, but somehow it quite escaped me."

He stammered, "Are—are you, honestly?"

She nodded. "Why, of course. Can't stay here forever, you know."

They were then silent for a long time.

At last Hawker said, "Do you remember what I told you yesterday?"

"No. What was it?"

He cried indignantly, "You know very well what I told you!"

"I do not."

"No," he sneered, "of course not! You never take the trouble to remember such things. Of course not! Of course not!"

"You are a very ridiculous person," she vouchsafed, after eying him coldly.

He arose abruptly. "I believe I am. By heavens, I believe I am!" he cried in a fury.

She laughed. "You are more ridiculous now than I have yet seen you."

After a pause he said magnificently, "Well, Miss Fanhall, you will doubtless find Mr. Hollanden's conversation to have a much greater interest than that of such a ridiculous person."

Hollanden approached them with the blithesome step of an untroubled man. "Hello, you two people, why don't you—oh—ahem! Hold on, Billie, where are you going?"

"I—" began Hawker.

"Oh, Hollie," cried the girl impetuously, "do tell me how to do that slam thing, you know. I've tried it so often, but I don't believe I hold my racket right. And you do it so beautifully."

"Oh, that," said Hollanden. "It's not so very difficult. I'll show it to you. You don't want to know this minute, do you?"

"Yes," she answered.

"Well, come over to the court, then. Come ahead, Billie!"

"No," said Hawker, without looking at his friend, "I can't this morning, Hollie. I've got to go to work. Good-bye!" He comprehended them both in a swift bow and stalked away.

Hollanden turned quickly to the girl. "What was the matter with Billie? What was he grinding his teeth for? What was the matter with him?"

"Why, nothing—was there?" she asked in surprise.

"Why, he was grinding his teeth until he sounded like a stone crusher," said Hollanden in a severe tone. "What was the matter with him?"

"How should I know?" she retorted.

"You've been saying something to him."

"I! I didn't say a thing."

"Yes, you did."

"Hollie, don't be absurd."

Hollanden debated with himself for a time, and then observed, "Oh, well, I always said he was an ugly-tempered fellow—"

The girl flashed him a little glance.

"And now I am sure of it—as ugly-tempered a fellow as ever lived."

"I believe you," said the girl. Then she added: "All men are. I declare, I think you to be the most incomprehensible creatures. One never knows what to expect of you. And you explode and go into rages and make yourselves utterly detestable over the most trivial matters and at the most unexpected times. You are all mad, I think."

"I!" cried Hollanden wildly. "What in the mischief have I done?"

## CHAPTER XVI.

"Look here," said Hollanden, at length, "I thought you were so wonderfully anxious to learn that stroke?"

"Well, I am," she said.

"Come on, then." As they walked toward the tennis court he seemed to be plunged into mournful thought. In his eyes was a singular expression, which perhaps denoted the woe of the optimist pushed suddenly from its height. He sighed. "Oh, well, I suppose all women, even the best of them, are that way."

"What way?" she said.

"My dear child," he answered, in a benevolent manner, "you have disappointed me, because I have discovered that you resemble the rest of your sex."

"Ah!" she remarked, maintaining a noncommittal attitude.

"Yes," continued Hollanden, with a sad but kindly smile, "even you, Grace, were not above fooling with the affections of a poor country swain, until he don't know his ear from the tooth he had pulled two years ago."

She laughed. "He would be furious if he heard you call him a country swain."

"Who would?" said Hollanden.

"Why, the country swain, of course," she rejoined.

Hollanden seemed plunged in mournful reflection again. "Well, it's a shame, Grace, anyhow," he observed, wagging his head dolefully. "It's a howling, wicked shame."

"Hollie, you have no brains at all," she said, "despite your opinion."

"No," he replied ironically, "not a bit."

"Well, you haven't, you know, Hollie."

"At any rate," he said in an angry voice, "I have some comprehension and sympathy for the feelings of others."

"Have you?" she asked. "How do you mean, Hollie? Do you mean you have feeling for them in their various sorrows? Or do you mean that you understand their minds?"

Hollanden ponderously began, "There have been people who have not questioned my ability to—"

"Oh, then, you mean that you both feel for them in their sorrows and comprehend the machinery of their minds. Well, let me tell you that in regard to the last thing you are wrong. You know nothing of anyone's mind. You know less about human nature than anybody I have met."

Hollanden looked at her in artless astonishment. He said, "Now, I wonder what made you say that?" This interrogation did not seem to be addressed to her, but was evidently a statement to himself of a problem. He meditated for some moments. Eventually he said, "I suppose you mean that I do not understand you?"

"Why do you suppose I mean that?"

"That's what a person usually means when he—or she—charges another with not understanding the entire world."

"Well, at any rate, it is not what I mean at all," she said. "I mean that you habitually blunder about other people's affairs, in the belief, I imagine, that you are a great philanthropist, when you are only making an extraordinary exhibition of yourself."

"The dev—" began Hollanden. Afterward he said, "Now, I wonder what in blue thunder you mean this time?"

"Mean this time? My meaning is very plain, Hollie. I supposed the words were clear enough."

"Yes," he said thoughtfully, "your words were clear enough, but then you were of course referring back to some event, or series of events, in which I had the singular ill fortune to displease you. Maybe you don't know yourself, and spoke only from the emotion generated by the event, or series of events, in which, as I have said, I had the singular ill fortune to displease you."

"How awf'ly clever!" she said.

"But I can't recall the event, or series of events, at all," he continued, musing with a scholarly air and disregarding her mockery. "I can't remember a thing about it. To be sure, it might have been that time when—"

"I think it very stupid of you to hunt for a meaning when I believe I made everything so perfectly clear," she said wrathfully.

"Well, you yourself might not be aware of what you really meant," he answered sagely. "Women often do that sort of thing, you know. Women often speak from motives which, if brought face to face with them, they wouldn't be able to distinguish from any other thing which they had never before seen."

"Hollie, if there is a disgusting person in the world it is he who pretends to know so much concerning a woman's mind."

"Well, that's because they who know, or pretend to know, so much about a woman's mind are invariably satirical, you understand," said Hollanden cheerfully.

A dog ran frantically across the lawn, his nose high in the air and his countenance expressing vast perturbation and alarm. "Why, Billie forgot to whistle for his dog when he started for home," said Hollanden. "Come here, old man! Well, 'e was a nice dog!" The girl also gave invitation, but the setter would not heed them. He spun wildly about the lawn until he seemed to strike his master's trail, and then, with his nose near to the ground, went down the road at an eager gallop. They stood and watched him.

"Stanley's a nice dog," said Hollanden.

"Indeed he is!" replied the girl fervently.

Presently Hollanden remarked: "Well, don't let's fight any more, particularly since we can't decide what we're fighting about. I can't discover the reason, and you don't know it, so—"

"I do know it. I told you very plainly."

"Well, all right. Now, this is the way to work that slam: You give the ball a sort of a lift—see!—underhanded and with your arm crooked and stiff. Here, you smash this other ball into the net. Hi! Look out! If you hit it that way you'll knock it over the hotel. Let the ball drop nearer to the ground. Oh, heavens, not on the ground! Well, it's hard to do it from the serve, anyhow. I'll go over to the other court and bat you some easy ones."

Afterward, when they were going toward the inn, the girl suddenly began to laugh.

"What are you giggling at?" said Hollanden.

"I was thinking how furious he would be if he heard you call him a country swain," she rejoined.

"Who?" asked Hollanden.

## CHAPTER XVII.

Oglethorpe contended that the men who made the most money from books were the best authors. Hollanden contended that they were the worst. Oglethorpe said that such a question should be left to the people. Hollanden said that the people habitually made wrong decisions on questions that were left to them. "That is the most odiously aristocratic belief," said Oglethorpe.

"No," said Hollanden, "I like the people. But, considered generally, they are a collection of ingenious blockheads."

"But they read your books," said Oglethorpe, grinning.

"That is through a mistake," replied Hollanden.

As the discussion grew in size it incited the close attention of the Worcester girls, but Miss Fanhall did not seem to hear it. Hawker, too, was staring into the darkness with a gloomy and preoccupied air.

"Are you sorry that this is your last evening at Hemlock Inn?" said the painter at last, in a low tone.

"Why, yes—certainly," said the girl.

Under the sloping porch of the inn the vague orange light from the parlours drifted to the black wall of the night.

"I shall miss you," said the painter.

"Oh, I dare say," said the girl.

Hollanden was lecturing at length and wonderfully. In the mystic spaces of the night the pines could be heard in their weird monotone, as they softly smote branch and branch, as if moving in some solemn and sorrowful dance.

"This has been quite the most delightful summer of my experience," said the painter.

"I have found it very pleasant," said the girl.

From time to time Hawker glanced furtively at Oglethorpe, Hollanden, and the Worcester girl. This glance expressed no desire for their well-being.

"I shall miss you," he said to the girl again. His manner was rather desperate. She made no reply, and, after leaning toward her, he subsided with an air of defeat.

Eventually he remarked: "It will be very lonely here again. I dare say I shall return to New York myself in a few weeks."

"I hope you will call," she said.

"I shall be delighted," he answered stiffly, and with a dissatisfied look at her.

"Oh, Mr. Hawker," cried the younger Worcester girl, suddenly emerging from the cloud of argument which Hollanden and Oglethorpe kept in the air, "won't it be sad to lose Grace? Indeed, I don't know what we shall do. Sha'n't we miss her dreadfully?"

"Yes," said Hawker, "we shall of course miss her dreadfully."

"Yes, won't it be frightful?" said the elder Worcester girl. "I can't imagine what we will do without her. And Hollie is only going to spend ten more days. Oh, dear! mamma, I believe, will insist on staying the entire summer. It was papa's orders, you know, and I really think she is going to obey them. He said he wanted her to have one period of rest at any rate. She is such a busy woman in town, you know."

"Here," said Hollanden, wheeling to them suddenly, "you all look as if you were badgering Hawker, and he looks badgered. What are you saying to him?"

"Why," answered the younger Worcester girl, "we were only saying to him how lonely it would be without Grace."

"Oh!" said Hollanden.

As the evening grew old, the mother of the Worcester girls joined the group. This was a sign that the girls were not to long delay the vanishing time. She sat almost upon the edge of her chair, as if she expected to be called upon at any moment to arise and bow "Good-night," and she repaid Hollanden's eloquent attention with the placid and absent-minded smiles of the chaperon who waits.

Once the younger Worcester girl shrugged her shoulders and turned to say, "Mamma, you make me nervous!" Her mother merely smiled in a still more placid and absent-minded manner.

Oglethorpe arose to drag his chair nearer to the railing, and when he stood the Worcester mother moved and looked around expectantly, but Oglethorpe took seat again. Hawker kept an anxious eye upon her.

Presently Miss Fanhall arose.

"Why, you are not going in already, are you?" said Hawker and Hollanden and Oglethorpe. The Worcester mother moved toward the door followed by her daughters, who were protesting in muffled tones. Hollanden pitched violently upon Oglethorpe. "Well, at any rate—" he said. He picked the thread of a past argument with great agility.

Hawker said to the girl, "I—I—I shall miss you dreadfully."

She turned to look at him and smiled. "Shall you?" she said in a low voice.

"Yes," he said. Thereafter he stood before her awkwardly and in silence. She scrutinized the boards of the floor. Suddenly she drew a violet from a cluster of them upon her gown and thrust it out to him as she turned toward the approaching Oglethorpe.

"Good-night, Mr. Hawker," said the latter. "I am very glad to have met you, I'm sure. Hope to see you in town. Good-night."

He stood near when the girl said to Hawker: "Good-bye. You have given us such a charming summer. We shall be delighted to see you in town. You must come some time when the children can see you, too. Good-bye."

"Good-bye," replied Hawker, eagerly and feverishly, trying to interpret the inscrutable feminine face before him. "I shall come at my first opportunity."

"Good-bye."

"Good-bye."

Down at the farmhouse, in the black quiet of the night, a dog lay curled on the door-mat. Of a sudden the tail of this dog began to thump, thump, on the boards. It began as a lazy movement, but it passed into a state of gentle enthusiasm, and then into one of curiously loud and joyful celebration. At last the gate clicked. The dog uncurled, and went to the edge of the steps to greet his master. He gave adoring, tremulous welcome with his clear eyes shining in the darkness. "Well, Stan, old boy," said Hawker, stooping to stroke the dog's head. After his master had entered the house the dog went forward and sniffed at something that lay on the top step. Apparently it did not interest him greatly, for he returned in a moment to the door-mat.

But he was again obliged to uncurl himself, for his master came out of the house with a lighted lamp and made search of the door-mat, the steps, and the walk, swearing meanwhile in an undertone. The dog wagged his tail and sleepily watched this ceremony. When his master had again entered the house the dog went forward and sniffed at the top step, but the thing that had lain there was gone.

## CHAPTER XVIII.

It was evident at breakfast that Hawker's sisters had achieved information. "What's the matter with you this morning?" asked one. "You look as if you hadn't slep' well."

"There is nothing the matter with me," he rejoined, looking glumly at his plate.

"Well, you look kind of broke up."

"How I look is of no consequence. I tell you there is nothing the matter with me."

"Oh!" said his sister. She exchanged meaning glances with the other feminine members of the family. Presently the other sister observed, "I heard she was going home today."

"Who?" said Hawker, with a challenge in his tone.

"Why, that New York girl—Miss What's-her-name," replied the sister, with an undaunted smile.

"Did you, indeed? Well, perhaps she is."

"Oh, you don't know for sure, I s'pose."

Hawker arose from the table, and, taking his hat, went away.

"Mary!" said the mother, in the sepulchral tone of belated but conscientious reproof.

"Well, I don't care. He needn't be so grand. I didn't go to tease him. I don't care."

"Well, you ought to care," said the old man suddenly. "There's no sense in you wimen folks pestering the boy all the time. Let him alone with his own business, can't you?"

"Well, ain't we leaving him alone?"

"No, you ain't—'cept when he ain't here. I don't wonder the boy grabs his hat and skips out when you git to going."

"Well, what did we say to him now? Tell us what we said to him that was so dreadful."

"Aw, thunder an' lightnin'!" cried the old man with a sudden great snarl. They seemed to know by this ejaculation that he had emerged in an instant from that place where man endures, and they ended the discussion. The old man continued his breakfast.

During his walk that morning Hawker visited a certain cascade, a certain lake, and some roads, paths, groves, nooks. Later in the day he made a sketch, choosing an hour when the atmosphere was of a dark blue, like powder smoke in the shade of trees, and the western sky was burning in strips of red. He painted with a wild face, like a man who is killing.

After supper he and his father strolled under the apple boughs in the orchard and smoked. Once he gestured wearily. "Oh, I guess I'll go back to New York in a few days."

"Um," replied his father calmly. "All right, William."

Several days later Hawker accosted his father in the barnyard. "I suppose you think sometimes I don't care so much about you and the folks and the old place any more; but I do."

"Um," said the old man. "When you goin'?"

"Where?" asked Hawker, flushing.

"Back to New York."

"Why—I hadn't thought much about— Oh, next week, I guess."

"Well, do as you like, William. You know how glad me an' mother and the girls are to have you come home with us whenever you can come. You know that. But you must do as you think best, and if you ought to go back to New York now, William, why—do as you think best."

"Well, my work—" said Hawker.

From time to time the mother made wondering speech to the sisters. "How much nicer William is now! He's just as good as he can be. There for a while he was so cross and out of sorts. I don't see what could have come over him. But now he's just as good as he can be."

Hollanden told him, "Come up to the inn more, you fool."

"I was up there yesterday."

"Yesterday! What of that? I've seen the time when the farm couldn't hold you for two hours during the day."

"Go to blazes!"

"Millicent got a letter from Grace Fanhall the other day."

"That so?"

"Yes, she did. Grace wrote— Say, does that shadow look pure purple to you?"

"Certainly it does, or I wouldn't paint it so, duffer. What did she write?"

"Well, if that shadow is pure purple my eyes are liars. It looks a kind of slate colour to me. Lord! if what you fellows say in your pictures is true, the whole earth must be blazing and burning and glowing and—"

Hawker went into a rage. "Oh, you don't know anything about colour, Hollie. For heaven's sake, shut up, or I'll smash you with the easel."

"Well, I was going to tell you what Grace wrote in her letter. She said—"

"Go on."

"Gimme time, can't you? She said that town was stupid, and that she wished she was back at Hemlock Inn."

"Oh! Is that all?"

"Is that all? I wonder what you expected? Well, and she asked to be recalled to you."

"Yes? Thanks."

"And that's all. 'Gad, for such a devoted man as you were, your enthusiasm and interest is stupendous."

The father said to the mother, "Well, William's going back to New York next week."

"Is he? Why, he ain't said nothing to me about it."

"Well, he is, anyhow."

"I declare! What do you s'pose he's going back before September for, John?"

"How do I know?"

"Well, it's funny, John. I bet—I bet he's going back so's he can see that girl."

"He says it's his work."

## CHAPTER XIX.

Wrinkles had been peering into the little dry-goods box that acted as a cupboard. "There are only two eggs and half a loaf of bread left," he announced brutally.

"Heavens!" said Warwickson from where he lay smoking on the bed. He spoke in a dismal voice. This tone, it is said, had earned him his popular name of Great Grief.

From different points of the compass Wrinkles looked at the little cupboard with a tremendous scowl, as if he intended thus to frighten the eggs into becoming more than two, and the bread into becoming a loaf. "Plague take it!" he exclaimed.

"Oh, shut up, Wrinkles!" said Grief from the bed.

Wrinkles sat down with an air austere and virtuous. "Well, what are we going to do?" he demanded of the others.

Grief, after swearing, said: "There, that's right! Now you're happy. The holy office of the inquisition! Blast your buttons, Wrinkles, you always try to keep us from starving peacefully! It is two hours before dinner, anyhow, and—"

"Well, but what are you going to do?" persisted Wrinkles.

Pennoyer, with his head afar down, had been busily scratching at a pen-and-ink drawing. He looked up from his board to utter a plaintive optimism. "The Monthly Amazement will pay me tomorrow. They ought to. I've waited over three months now. I'm going down there tomorrow, and perhaps I'll get it."

His friends listened with airs of tolerance. "Oh, no doubt, Penny, old man." But at last Wrinkles giggled pityingly. Over on the bed Grief croaked deep down in his throat. Nothing was said for a long time thereafter.

The crash of the New York streets came faintly to this room.

Occasionally one could hear the tramp of feet in the intricate corridors of the begrimed building which squatted, slumbering, and old, between two exalted commercial structures which would have had to bend afar down to perceive it. The northward march of the city's progress had happened not to overturn this aged structure, and it huddled there, lost and forgotten, while the cloud-veering towers strode on.

Meanwhile the first shadows of dusk came in at the blurred windows of the room. Pennoyer threw down his pen and tossed his drawing over on the wonderful heap of stuff that hid the table. "It's too dark to work." He lit a pipe and walked about, stretching his shoulders like a man whose labour was valuable.

When the dusk came fully the youths grew apparently sad. The solemnity of the gloom seemed to make them ponder. "Light the gas, Wrinkles," said Grief fretfully.

The flood of orange light showed clearly the dull walls lined with sketches, the tousled bed in one corner, the masses of boxes and trunks in another, a little dead stove, and the wonderful table. Moreover, there were wine-coloured draperies flung in some places, and on a shelf, high up, there were plaster casts, with dust in the creases. A long stove-pipe wandered off in the wrong direction and then turned impulsively toward a hole in the wall. There were some elaborate cobwebs on the ceiling.

"Well, let's eat," said Grief.

"Eat," said Wrinkles, with a jeer; "I told you there was only two eggs and a little bread left. How are we going to eat?"

Again brought face to face with this problem, and at the hour for dinner, Pennoyer and Grief thought profoundly. "Thunder and turf!" Grief finally announced as the result of his deliberations.

"Well, if Billie Hawker was only home—" began Pennoyer.

"But he isn't," objected Wrinkles, "and that settles that."

Grief and Pennoyer thought more. Ultimately Grief said, "Oh, well, let's eat what we've got." The others at once agreed to this suggestion, as if it had been in their minds.

Later there came a quick step in the passage and a confident little thunder upon the door. Wrinkles arranging the tin pail on the gas stove, Pennoyer engaged in slicing the bread, and Great Grief affixing the rubber tube to the gas stove, yelled, "Come in!"

The door opened, and Miss Florinda O'Connor, the model, dashed into the room like a gale of obstreperous autumn leaves.

"Why, hello, Splutter!" they cried.

"Oh, boys, I've come to dine with you."

It was like a squall striking a fleet of yachts.

Grief spoke first. "Yes, you have?" he said incredulously.

"Why, certainly I have. What's the matter?"

They grinned. "Well, old lady," responded Grief, "you've hit us at the wrong time. We are, in fact, all out of everything. No dinner, to mention, and, what's more, we haven't got a sou."

"What? Again?" cried Florinda.

"Yes, again. You'd better dine home tonight."

"But I'll—I'll stake you," said the girl eagerly. "Oh, you poor old idiots! It's a shame! Say, I'll stake you."

"Certainly not," said Pennoyer sternly.

"What are you talking about, Splutter?" demanded Wrinkles in an angry voice.

"No, that won't go down," said Grief, in a resolute yet wistful tone.

Florinda divested herself of her hat, jacket, and gloves, and put them where she pleased. "Got coffee, haven't you? Well, I'm not going to stir a step. You're a fine lot of birds!" she added bitterly, "You've all pulled me out of a whole lot of scrape—oh, any number of times—and now you're broke, you go acting like a set of dudes."

Great Grief had fixed the coffee to boil on the gas stove, but he had to watch it closely, for the rubber tube was short, and a chair was balanced on a trunk, and two bundles of kindling was balanced on the chair, and the gas stove was balanced on the kindling. Coffee-making was here accounted a feat.

Pennoyer dropped a piece of bread to the floor. "There! I'll have to go shy one."

Wrinkles sat playing serenades on his guitar and staring with a frown at the table, as if he was applying some strange method of clearing it of its litter.

Florinda assaulted Great Grief. "Here, that's not the way to make coffee!"

"What ain't?"

"Why, the way you're making it. You want to take—" She explained some way to him which he couldn't understand.

"For heaven's sake, Wrinkles, tackle that table! Don't sit there like a music box," said Pennoyer, grappling the eggs and starting for the gas stove.

Later, as they sat around the board, Wrinkles said with satisfaction, "Well, the coffee's good, anyhow."

"'Tis good," said Florinda, "but it isn't made right. I'll show you how, Penny. You first—"

"Oh, dry up, Splutter," said Grief. "Here, take an egg."

"I don't like eggs," said Florinda.

"Take an egg," said the three hosts menacingly.

"I tell you I don't like eggs."

"Take—an—egg!" they said again.

"Oh, well," said Florinda, "I'll take one, then; but you needn't act like such a set of dudes—and, oh, maybe you didn't have much lunch. I had such a daisy lunch! Up at Pontiac's studio. He's got a lovely studio."

The three looked to be oppressed. Grief said sullenly, "I saw some of his things over in Stencil's gallery, and they're rotten."

"Yes—rotten," said Pennoyer.

"Rotten," said Grief.

"Oh, well," retorted Florinda, "if a man has a swell studio and dresses—oh, sort of like a Willie, you know, you fellows sit here like owls in a cave and say rotten—rotten—rotten. You're away off. Pontiac's landscapes—"

"Landscapes be blowed! Put any of his work alongside of Billie Hawker's and see how it looks."

"Oh, well, Billie Hawker's," said Florinda. "Oh, well."

At the mention of Hawker's name they had all turned to scan her face.

## CHAPTER XX.

"He wrote that he was coming home this week," said Pennoyer.

"Did he?" asked Florinda indifferently.

"Yes. Aren't you glad?"

They were still watching her face.

"Yes, of course I'm glad. Why shouldn't I be glad?" cried the girl with defiance. They grinned.

"Oh, certainly. Billie Hawker is a good fellow, Splutter. You have a particular right to be glad."

"You people make me tired," Florinda retorted. "Billie Hawker doesn't give a rap about me, and he never tried to make out that he did."

"No," said Grief. "But that isn't saying that you don't care a rap about Billie Hawker. Ah, Florinda!"

It seemed that the girl's throat suffered a slight contraction. "Well, and what if I do?" she demanded finally.

"Have a cigarette?" answered Grief.

Florinda took a cigarette, lit it, and, perching herself on a divan, which was secretly a coal box, she smoked fiercely.

"What if I do?" she again demanded. "It's better than liking one of you dubs, anyhow."

"Oh, Splutter, you poor little outspoken kid!" said Wrinkle in a sad voice.

Grief searched among the pipes until he found the best one. "Yes, Splutter, don't you know that when you are so frank you defy every law of your sex, and wild eyes will take your trail?"

"Oh, you talk through your hat," replied Florinda. "Billie don't care whether I like him or whether I don't. And if he should hear me now, he wouldn't be glad or give a hang, either way. I know that." The girl paused and looked at the row of plaster casts. "Still, you needn't be throwing it at me all the time."

"We didn't," said Wrinkles indignantly. "You threw it at yourself."

"Well," continued Florinda, "it's better than liking one of you dubs, anyhow. He makes money and—"

"There," said Grief, "now you've hit it! Bedad, you've reached a point in eulogy where if you move again you will have to go backward."

"Of course I don't care anything about a fellow's having money—"

"No, indeed you don't, Splutter," said Pennoyer.

"But then, you know what I mean. A fellow isn't a man and doesn't stand up straight unless he has some money. And Billie Hawker makes enough so that you feel that nobody could walk over him, don't you know? And there isn't anything jay about him, either. He's a thoroughbred, don't you know?"

After reflection, Pennoyer said, "It's pretty hard on the rest of us, Splutter."

"Well, of course I like him, but—but—"

"What?" said Pennoyer.

"I don't know," said Florinda.

Purple Sanderson lived in this room, but he usually dined out. At a certain time in his life, before he came to be a great artist, he had learned the gas-fitter's trade, and when his opinions were not identical with the opinions of the art managers of the greater number of New York publications he went to see a friend who was a plumber, and the opinions of this man he was thereafter said to respect. He frequented a very neat restaurant on Twenty-third Street. It was known that on Saturday nights Wrinkles, Grief, and Pennoyer frequently quarreled with him.

As Florinda ceased speaking Purple entered. "Hello, there, Splutter!" As he was neatly hanging up his coat, he said to the others, "Well, the rent will be due in four days."

"Will it?" asked Pennoyer, astounded.

"Certainly it will," responded Purple, with the air of a superior financial man.

"My soul!" said Wrinkles.

"Oh, shut up, Purple!" said Grief. "You make me weary, coming around here with your chin about rent. I was just getting happy."

"Well, how are we going to pay it? That's the point," said Sanderson.

Wrinkles sank deeper in his chair and played despondently on his guitar. Grief cast a look of rage at Sanderson, and then stared at the wall. Pennoyer said, "Well, we might borrow it from Billie Hawker."

Florinda laughed then.

"Oh," continued Pennoyer hastily, "if those Amazement people pay me when they said they would I'll have the money."

"So you will," said Grief. "You will have money to burn. Did the Amazement people ever pay you when they said they would? You are wonderfully important all of a sudden, it seems to me. You talk like an artist."

Wrinkles, too, smiled at Pennoyer. "The Eminent Magazine people wanted Penny to hire models and make a try for them, too. It would only cost him a stack of blues. By the time he has invested all his money he hasn't got, and the rent is three weeks overdue, he will be able to tell the landlord to wait seven months until the Monday morning after the day of publication. Go ahead, Penny."

After a period of silence, Sanderson, in an obstinate manner, said, "Well, what's to be done? The rent has got to be paid."

Wrinkles played more sad music. Grief frowned deeper. Pennoyer was evidently searching his mind for a plan.

Florinda took the cigarette from between her lips that she might grin with greater freedom.

"We might throw Purple out," said Grief, with an inspired air. "That would stop all this discussion."

"You!" said Sanderson furiously. "You can't keep serious a minute. If you didn't have us to take care of you, you wouldn't even know when they threw you out into the street."

"Wouldn't I?" said Grief.

"Well, look here," interposed Florinda, "I'm going home unless you can be more interesting. I am dead sorry about the rent, but I can't help it, and—"

"Here! Sit down! Hold on, Splutter!" they shouted. Grief turned to Sanderson: "Purple, you shut up!"

Florinda curled again on the divan and lit another cigarette. The talk waged about the names of other and more successful painters, whose work they usually pronounced "rotten."

## CHAPTER XXI.

Pennoyer, coming home one morning with two gigantic cakes to accompany the coffee at the breakfast in the den, saw a young man bounce from a horse car. He gave a shout. "Hello, there, Billie! Hello!"

"Hello, Penny!" said Hawker. "What are you doing out so early?" It was somewhat after nine o'clock.

"Out to get breakfast," said Pennoyer, waving the cakes. "Have a good time, old man?"

"Great."

"Do much work?"

"No. Not so much. How are all the people?"

"Oh, pretty good. Come in and see us eat breakfast," said Pennoyer, throwing open the door of the den. Wrinkles, in his shirt, was making coffee. Grief sat in a chair trying to loosen the grasp of sleep. "Why, Billie Hawker, b'ginger!" they cried.

"How's the wolf, boys? At the door yet?"

"'At the door yet?' He's halfway up the back stairs, and coming fast. He and the landlord will be here tomorrow. 'Mr. Landlord, allow me to present Mr. F. Wolf, of Hunger, N. J. Mr. Wolf—Mr. Landlord.'"

"Bad as that?" said Hawker.

"You bet it is! Easy Street is somewhere in heaven, for all we know. Have some breakfast?—coffee and cake, I mean."

"No, thanks, boys. Had breakfast."

Wrinkles added to the shirt, Grief aroused himself, and Pennoyer brought the coffee. Cheerfully throwing some drawings from the table to the floor, they thus made room for the breakfast, and grouped themselves with beaming smiles at the board.

"Well, Billie, come back to the old gang again, eh? How did the country seem? Do much work?"

"Not very much. A few things. How's everybody?"

"Splutter was in last night. Looking out of sight. Seemed glad to hear that you were coming back soon."

"Did she? Penny, did anybody call wanting me to do a ten-thousand-dollar portrait for them?"

"No. That frame-maker, though, was here with a bill. I told him——"

Afterward Hawker crossed the corridor and threw open the door of his own large studio. The great skylight, far above his head, shed its clear rays upon a scene which appeared to indicate that some one had very recently ceased work here and started for the country. A distant closet door was open, and the interior showed the effects of a sudden pillage.

There was an unfinished "Girl in Apple Orchard" upon the tall Dutch easel, and sketches and studies were thick upon the floor. Hawker took a pipe and filled it from his friend the tan and gold jar. He cast himself into a chair and, taking an envelope from his pocket, emptied two violets from it to the palm of his hand and stared long at them. Upon the walls of the studio various labours of his life, in heavy gilt frames, contemplated him and the violets.

At last Pennoyer burst impetuously in upon him. "Hi, Billie! come over and— What's the matter?"

Hawker had hastily placed the violets in the envelope and hurried it to his pocket. "Nothing," he answered.

"Why, I thought—" said Pennoyer, "I thought you looked rather rattled. Didn't you have—I thought I saw something in your hand."

"Nothing, I tell you!" cried Hawker.

"Er—oh, I beg your pardon," said Pennoyer. "Why, I was going to tell you that Splutter is over in our place, and she wants to see you."

"Wants to see me? What for?" demanded Hawker. "Why don't she come over here, then?"

"I'm sure I don't know," replied Pennoyer. "She sent me to call you."

"Well, do you think I'm going to— Oh, well, I suppose she wants to be unpleasant, and knows she loses a certain mental position if she comes over here, but if she meets me in your place she can be as infernally disagreeable as she— That's it, I'll bet."

When they entered the den Florinda was gazing from the window. Her back was toward the door.

At last she turned to them, holding herself very straight. "Well, Billie Hawker," she said grimly, "you don't seem very glad to see a fellow."

"Why, heavens, did you think I was going to turn somersaults in the air?"

"Well, you didn't come out when you heard me pass your door," said Florinda, with gloomy resentment.

Hawker appeared to be ruffled and vexed. "Oh, great Scott!" he said, making a gesture of despair.

Florinda returned to the window. In the ensuing conversation she took no part, save when there was an opportunity to harry some speech of Hawker's, which she did in short contemptuous sentences. Hawker made no reply save to glare in her direction. At last he said, "Well, I must go over and do some work." Florinda did not turn from the window. "Well, so-long, boys," said Hawker, "I'll see you later."

As the door slammed Pennoyer apologetically said, "Billie is a trifle off his feed this morning."

"What about?" asked Grief.

"I don't know; but when I went to call him he was sitting deep in his chair staring at some—" He looked at Florinda and became silent.

"Staring at what?" asked Florinda, turning then from the window.

Pennoyer seemed embarrassed. "Why, I don't know—nothing, I guess—I couldn't see very well. I was only fooling."

Florinda scanned his face suspiciously. "Staring at what?" she demanded imperatively.

"Nothing, I tell you!" shouted Pennoyer.

Florinda looked at him, and wavered and debated. Presently she said, softly: "Ah, go on, Penny. Tell me."

"It wasn't anything at all, I say!" cried Pennoyer stoutly. "I was only giving you a jolly. Sit down, Splutter, and hit a cigarette."

She obeyed, but she continued to cast the dubious eye at Pennoyer. Once she said to him privately: "Go on, Penny, tell me. I know it was something from the way you are acting."

"Oh, let up, Splutter, for heaven's sake!"

"Tell me," beseeched Florinda.

"No."

"Tell me."

"No."

"Pl-e-a-se tell me."

"No."

"Oh, go on."

"No."

"Ah, what makes you so mean, Penny? You know I'd tell you, if it was the other way about."

"But it's none of my business, Splutter. I can't tell you something which is Billie Hawker's private affair. If I did I would be a chump."

"But I'll never say you told me. Go on."

"No."

"Pl-e-a-se tell me."

"No."

## CHAPTER XXII.

When Florinda had gone, Grief said, "Well, what was it?" Wrinkles looked curiously from his drawing-board.

Pennoyer lit his pipe and held it at the side of his mouth in the manner of a deliberate man. At last he said, "It was two violets."

"You don't say!" ejaculated Wrinkles.

"Well, I'm hanged!" cried Grief. "Holding them in his hand and moping over them, eh?"

"Yes," responded Pennoyer. "Rather that way."

"Well, I'm hanged!" said both Grief and Wrinkles. They grinned in a pleased, urchin-like manner. "Say, who do you suppose she is? Somebody he met this summer, no doubt. Would you ever think old Billie would get into that sort of a thing? Well, I'll be gol-durned!"

Ultimately Wrinkles said, "Well, it's his own business." This was spoken in a tone of duty.

"Of course it's his own business," retorted Grief. "But who would ever think—" Again they grinned.

When Hawker entered the den some minutes later he might have noticed something unusual in the general demeanour. "Say, Grief, will you loan me your— What's up?" he asked.

For answer they grinned at each other, and then grinned at him.

"You look like a lot of Chessy cats," he told them.

They grinned on.

Apparently feeling unable to deal with these phenomena, he went at last to the door. "Well, this is a fine exhibition," he said, standing with his hand on the knob and regarding them. "Won election bets? Some good old auntie just died? Found something new to pawn? No? Well, I can't stand this. You resemble those fish they discover at deep sea. Good-bye!"

As he opened the door they cried out: "Hold on, Billie! Billie, look here! Say, who is she?"

"What?"

"Who is she?"

"Who is who?"

They laughed and nodded. "Why, you know. She. Don't you understand? She."

"You talk like a lot of crazy men," said Hawker. "I don't know what you mean."

"Oh, you don't, eh? You don't? Oh, no! How about those violets you were mop-ing over this morning? Eh, old man! Oh, no, you don't know what we mean! Oh, no! How about those violets, eh? How about 'em?"

Hawker, with flushed and wrathful face, looked at Pennoyer. "Penny—" But Grief and Wrinkles roared an interruption. "Oh, ho, Mr. Hawker! so it's true, is it? It's true. You are a nice bird, you are. Well, you old rascal! Durn your picture!"

Hawker, menacing them once with his eyes, went away. They sat cackling.

At noon, when he met Wrinkles in the corridor, he said: "Hey, Wrinkles, come here for a minute, will you? Say, old man, I—I—"

"What?" said Wrinkles.

"Well, you know, I—I—of course, every man is likely to make an accursed idiot of himself once in a while, and I—"

"And you what?" asked Wrinkles.

"Well, we are a kind of a band of hoodlums, you know, and I'm just enough idiot to feel that I don't care to hear—don't care to hear—well, her name used, you know."

"Bless your heart," replied Wrinkles, "we haven't used her name. We don't know her name. How could we use it?"

"Well, I know," said Hawker. "But you understand what I mean, Wrinkles."

"Yes, I understand what you mean," said Wrinkles, with dignity. "I don't sup-pose you are any worse of a stuff than common. Still, I didn't know that we were such outlaws."

"Of course, I have overdone the thing," responded Hawker hastily. "But—you ought to understand how I mean it, Wrinkles."

After Wrinkles had thought for a time, he said: "Well, I guess I do. All right. That goes."

Upon entering the den, Wrinkles said, "You fellows have got to quit guying Billie, do you hear?"

"We?" cried Grief. "We've got to quit? What do you do?"

"Well, I quit too."

Pennoyer said: "Ah, ha! Billie has been jumping on you."

"No, he didn't," maintained Wrinkles; "but he let me know it was—well, rather a—rather a—sacred subject." Wrinkles blushed when the others snickered.

In the afternoon, as Hawker was going slowly down the stairs, he was almost impaled upon the feather of a hat which, upon the head of a lithe and rather slight girl, charged up at him through the gloom.

"Hello, Splutter!" he cried. "You are in a hurry."

"That you, Billie?" said the girl, peering, for the hallways of this old building remained always in a dungeonlike darkness.

"Yes, it is. Where are you going at such a headlong gait?"

"Up to see the boys. I've got a bottle of wine and some—some pickles, you know. I'm going to make them let me dine with them tonight. Coming back, Billie?"

"Why, no, I don't expect to."

He moved then accidentally in front of the light that sifted through the dull, gray panes of a little window.

"Oh, cracky!" cried the girl; "how fine you are, Billie! Going to a coronation?"

"No," said Hawker, looking seriously over his collar and down at his clothes. "Fact is—er—well, I've got to make a call."

"A call—bless us! And are you really going to wear those gray gloves you're holding there, Billie? Say, wait until you get around the corner. They won't stand 'em on this street."

"Oh, well," said Hawker, depreciating the gloves—"oh, well."

The girl looked up at him. "Who you going to call on?"

"Oh," said Hawker, "a friend."

"Must be somebody most extraordinary, you look so dreadfully correct. Come back, Billie, won't you? Come back and dine with us."

"Why, I—I don't believe I can."

"Oh, come on! It's fun when we all dine together. Won't you, Billie?"

"Well, I—"

"Oh, don't be so stupid!" The girl stamped her foot and flashed her eyes at him angrily.

"Well, I'll see—I will if I can—I can't tell—" He left her rather precipitately.

Hawker eventually appeared at a certain austere house where he rang the bell with quite nervous fingers.

But she was not at home. As he went down the steps his eyes were as those of a man whose fortunes have tumbled upon him. As he walked down the street he wore in some subtle way the air of a man who has been grievously wronged. When he rounded the corner, his lips were set strangely, as if he were a man seeking revenge.

## CHAPTER XXIII.

"It's just right," said Grief.

"It isn't quite cool enough," said Wrinkles.

"Well, I guess I know the proper temperature for claret."

"Well, I guess you don't. If it was buttermilk, now, you would know, but you can't tell anything about claret."

Florinda ultimately decided the question. "It isn't quite cool enough," she said, laying her hand on the bottle. "Put it on the window ledge, Grief."

"Hum! Splutter, I thought you knew more than—"

"Oh, shut up!" interposed the busy Pennoyer from a remote corner. "Who is going after the potato salad? That's what I want to know. Who is going?"

"Wrinkles," said Grief.

"Grief," said Wrinkles.

"There," said Pennoyer, coming forward and scanning a late work with an eye of satisfaction. "There's the three glasses and the little tumbler; and then, Grief, you will have to drink out of a mug."

"I'll be double-dyed black if I will!" cried Grief. "I wouldn't drink claret out of a mug to save my soul from being pinched!"

"You duffer, you talk like a bloomin' British chump on whom the sun never sets! What do you want?"

"Well, there's enough without that—what's the matter with you? Three glasses and the little tumbler."

"Yes, but if Billie Hawker comes—"

"Well, let him drink out of the mug, then. He—"

"No, he won't," said Florinda suddenly. "I'll take the mug myself."

"All right, Splutter," rejoined Grief meekly. "I'll keep the mug. But, still, I don't see why Billie Hawker—"

"I shall take the mug," reiterated Florinda firmly.

"But I don't see why—"

"Let her alone, Grief," said Wrinkles. "She has decided that it is heroic. You can't move her now."

"Well, who is going for the potato salad?" cried Pennoyer again. "That's what I want to know."

"Wrinkles," said Grief.

"Grief," said Wrinkles.

"Do you know," remarked Florinda, raising her head from where she had been toiling over the *spaghetti*, "I don't care so much for Billie Hawker as I did once?" Her sleeves were rolled above the elbows of her wonderful arms, and she turned from the stove and poised a fork as if she had been smitten at her task with this inspiration.

There was a short silence, and then Wrinkles said politely, "No."

"No," continued Florinda, "I really don't believe I do." She suddenly started. "Listen! Isn't that him coming now?"

The dull trample of a step could be heard in some distant corridor, but it died slowly to silence.

"I thought that might be him," she said, turning to the *spaghetti* again.

"I hope the old Indian comes," said Pennoyer, "but I don't believe he will. Seems to me he must be going to see—"

"Who?" asked Florinda.

"Well, you know, Hollanden and he usually dine together when they are both in town."

Florinda looked at Pennoyer. "I know, Penny. You must have thought I was remarkably clever not to understand all your blundering. But I don't care so much. Really I don't."

"Of course not," assented Pennoyer.

"Really I don't."

"Of course not."

"Listen!" exclaimed Grief, who was near the door. "There he comes now." Somebody approached, whistling an air from "Traviata," which rang loud and clear, and low and muffled, as the whistler wound among the intricate hallways. This air was as much a part of Hawker as his coat. The *spaghetti* had arrived at a critical stage. Florinda gave it her complete attention.

When Hawker opened the door he ceased whistling and said gruffly, "Hello!"

"Just the man!" said Grief. "Go after the potato salad, will you, Billie? There's a good boy! Wrinkles has refused."

"He can't carry the salad with those gloves," interrupted Florinda, raising her eyes from her work and contemplating them with displeasure.

"Hang the gloves!" cried Hawker, dragging them from his hands and hurling them at the divan. "What's the matter with you, Splutter?"

Pennoyer said, "My, what a temper you are in, Billie!"

"I am," replied Hawker. "I feel like an Apache. Where do you get this accursed potato salad?"

"In Second Avenue. You know where. At the old place."

"No, I don't!" snapped Hawker.

"Why—"

"Here," said Florinda, "I'll go." She had already rolled down her sleeves and was arraying herself in her hat and jacket.

"No, you won't," said Hawker, filled with wrath. "I'll go myself."

"We can both go, Billie, if you are so bent," replied the girl in a conciliatory voice.

"Well, come on, then. What are you standing there for?"

When these two had departed, Wrinkles said: "Lordie! What's wrong with Billie?"

"He's been discussing art with some pot-boiler," said Grief, speaking as if this was the final condition of human misery.

"No, sir," said Pennoyer. "It's something connected with the now celebrated violets."

Out in the corridor Florinda said, "What—what makes you so ugly, Billie?"

"Why, I am not ugly, am I?"

"Yes, you are—ugly as anything."

Probably he saw a grievance in her eyes, for he said, "Well, I don't want to be ugly." His tone seemed tender. The halls were intensely dark, and the girl placed her hand on his arm. As they rounded a turn in the stairs a straying lock of her hair brushed against his temple. "Oh!" said Florinda, in a low voice.

"We'll get some more claret," observed Hawker musingly. "And some cognac for the coffee. And some cigarettes. Do you think of anything more, Splutter?"

As they came from the shop of the illustrious purveyors of potato salad in Second Avenue, Florinda cried anxiously, "Here, Billie, you let me carry that!"

"What infernal nonsense!" said Hawker, flushing. "Certainly not!"

"Well," protested Florinda, "it might soil your gloves somehow."

"In heaven's name, what if it does? Say, young woman, do you think I am one of these cholly boys?"

"No, Billie; but then, you know—"

"Well, if you don't take me for some kind of a Willie, give us peace on this blasted glove business!"

"I didn't mean—"

"Well, you've been intimating that I've got the only pair of gray gloves in the universe, but you are wrong. There are several pairs, and these need not be preserved as unique in history."

"They're not gray. They're—"

"They are gray! I suppose your distinguished ancestors in Ireland did not educate their families in the matter of gloves, and so you are not expected to—"

"Billie!"

"You are not expected to believe that people wear gloves only in cold weather, and then you expect to see mittens."

On the stairs, in the darkness, he suddenly exclaimed, "Here, look out, or you'll fall!" He reached for her arm, but she evaded him. Later he said again: "Look out, girl! What makes you stumble around so? Here, give me the bottle of wine. I can carry it all right. There—now can you manage?"

## CHAPTER XXIV.

"Penny," said Grief, looking across the table at his friend, "if a man thinks a heap of two violets, how much would he think of a thousand violets?"

"Two into a thousand goes five hundred times, you fool!" said Pennoyer. "I would answer your question if it were not upon a forbidden subject."

In the distance Wrinkles and Florinda were making Welsh rarebits.

"Hold your tongues!" said Hawker. "Barbarians!"

"Grief," said Pennoyer, "if a man loves a woman better than the whole universe, how much does he love the whole universe?"

"Gawd knows," said Grief piously. "Although it ill befits me to answer your question."

Wrinkles and Florinda came with the Welsh rarebits, very triumphant. "There," said Florinda, "soon as these are finished I must go home. It is after eleven o'clock.— Pour the ale, Grief."

At a later time, Purple Sanderson entered from the world. He hung up his hat and cast a look of proper financial dissatisfaction at the remnants of the feast. "Who has been—"

"Before you breathe, Purple, you graceless scum, let me tell you that we will stand no reference to the two violets here," said Pennoyer.

"What the—"

"Oh, that's all right, Purple," said Grief, "but you were going to say something about the two violets, right then. Weren't you, now, you old bat?"

Sanderson grinned expectantly. "What's the row?" said he.

"No row at all," they told him. "Just an agreement to keep you from chattering obstinately about the two violets."

"What two violets?"

"Have a rarebit, Purple," advised Wrinkles, "and never mind those maniacs."

"Well, what is this business about two violets?"

"Oh, it's just some dream. They gibber at anything."

"I think I know," said Florinda, nodding. "It is something that concerns Billie Hawker."

Grief and Pennoyer scoffed, and Wrinkles said: "You know nothing about it, Splutter. It doesn't concern Billie Hawker at all."

"Well, then, what is he looking sideways for?" cried Florinda.

Wrinkles reached for his guitar, and played a serenade, "The silver moon is shining—"

"Dry up!" said Pennoyer.

Then Florinda cried again, "What does he look sideways for?"

Pennoyer and Grief giggled at the imperturbable Hawker, who destroyed rarebit in silence.

"It's you, is it, Billie?" said Sanderson. "You are in this two-violet business?"

"I don't know what they're talking about," replied Hawker.

"Don't you, honestly?" asked Florinda.

"Well, only a little."

"There!" said Florinda, nodding again. "I knew he was in it."

"He isn't in it at all," said Pennoyer and Grief.

Later, when the cigarettes had become exhausted, Hawker volunteered to go after a further supply, and as he arose, a question seemed to come to the edge of Florinda's lips and pend there. The moment that the door was closed upon him she demanded, "What is that about the two violets?"

"Nothing at all," answered Pennoyer, apparently much aggrieved. He sat back with an air of being a fortress of reticence.

"Oh, go on—tell me! Penny, I think you are very mean.—Grief, you tell me!"

*"The silver moon is shining;*
*Oh, come, my love, to me!*
*My heart—"*

"Be still, Wrinkles, will you?—What was it, Grief? Oh, go ahead and tell me!"

"What do you want to know for?" cried Grief, vastly exasperated. "You've got more blamed curiosity— It isn't anything at all, I keep saying to you."

"Well, I know it is," said Florinda sullenly, "or you would tell me."

When Hawker brought the cigarettes, Florinda smoked one, and then announced, "Well, I must go now."

"Who is going to take you home, Splutter?"

"Oh, anyone," replied Florinda.

"I tell you what," said Grief, "we'll throw some poker hands, and the one who wins will have the distinguished honour of conveying Miss Splutter to her home and mother."

Pennoyer and Wrinkles speedily routed the dishes to one end of the table. Grief's fingers spun the halves of a pack of cards together with the pleased eagerness of a good player. The faces grew solemn with the gambling solemnity. "Now, you Indians," said Grief, dealing, "a draw, you understand, and then a show-down."

Florinda leaned forward in her chair until it was poised on two legs. The cards of Purple Sanderson and of Hawker were faced toward her. Sanderson was gravely regarding two pair—aces and queens. Hawker scanned a little pair of sevens. "They draw, don't they?" she said to Grief.

"Certainly," said Grief. "How many, Wrink?"

"Four," replied Wrinkles, plaintively.

"Gimme three," said Pennoyer.

"Gimme one," said Sanderson.

"Gimme three," said Hawker. When he picked up his hand again Florinda's chair was tilted perilously. She saw another seven added to the little pair. Sanderson's draw had not assisted him.

"Same to the dealer," said Grief. "What you got, Wrink?"

"Nothing," said Wrinkles, exhibiting it face upward on the table. "Good-bye, Florinda."

"Well, I've got two small pair," ventured Pennoyer hopefully. "Beat 'em?"

"No good," said Sanderson. "Two pair—aces up."

"No good," said Hawker. "Three sevens."

"Beats me," said Grief. "Billie, you are the fortunate man. Heaven guide you in Third Avenue!"

Florinda had gone to the window. "Who won?" she asked, wheeling about carelessly.

"Billie Hawker."

"What! Did he?" she said in surprise.

"Never mind, Splutter. I'll win sometime," said Pennoyer. "Me too," cried Grief. "Good night, old girl!" said Wrinkles. They crowded in the doorway. "Hold on to Billie. Remember the two steps going up," Pennoyer called intelligently into the Stygian blackness. "Can you see all right?"

Florinda lived in a flat with fire-escapes written all over the front of it. The street in front was being repaired. It had been said by imbecile residents of the vicinity that the paving was never allowed to remain down for a sufficient time to be invalided by the tramping millions, but that it was kept perpetually stacked in little mountains through the unceasing vigilance of a virtuous and heroic city government, which insisted that everything should be repaired. The alderman for the district had sometimes asked indignantly of his fellow-members why this street had not been repaired, and they, aroused, had at once ordered it to be repaired. Moreover, shop-keepers, whose stables were adjacent, placed trucks and other vehicles strategically in the darkness. Into this tangled midnight Hawker conducted Florinda. The great avenue behind them was no more than a level stream of yellow light, and the distant merry bells might have been boats floating down it. Grim loneliness hung over the uncouth shapes in the street which was being repaired.

"Billie," said the girl suddenly, "what makes you so mean to me?"

A peaceful citizen emerged from behind a pile of *débris*, but he might not have been a peaceful citizen, so the girl clung to Hawker.

"Why, I'm not mean to you, am I?"

"Yes," she answered. As they stood on the steps of the flat of innumerable fire-escapes she slowly turned and looked up at him. Her face was of a strange pallour in this darkness, and her eyes were as when the moon shines in a lake of the hills.

He returned her glance. "Florinda!" he cried, as if enlightened, and gulping suddenly at something in his throat. The girl studied the steps and moved from side to side, as do the guilty ones in country schoolhouses. Then she went slowly into the flat.

There was a little red lamp hanging on a pile of stones to warn people that the street was being repaired.

## CHAPTER XXV.

"I'll get my check from the Gamin on Saturday," said Grief. "They bought that string of comics."

"Well, then, we'll arrange the present funds to last until Saturday noon," said Wrinkles. "That gives us quite a lot. We can have a *table d'hôte* on Friday night."

However, the cashier of the Gamin office looked under his respectable brass wiring and said: "Very sorry, Mr.—er—Warwickson, but our pay-day is Monday. Come around any time after ten."

"Oh, it doesn't matter," said Grief.

When he plunged into the den his visage flamed with rage. "Don't get my check until Monday morning, any time after ten!" he yelled, and flung a portfolio of mottled green into the danger zone of the casts.

"Thunder!" said Pennoyer, sinking at once into a profound despair

"Monday morning, any time after ten," murmured Wrinkles, in astonishment and sorrow.

While Grief marched to and fro threatening the furniture, Pennoyer and Wrinkles allowed their under jaws to fall, and remained as men smitten between the eyes by the god of calamity.

"Singular thing!" muttered Pennoyer at last. "You get so frightfully hungry as soon as you learn that there are no more meals coming."

"Oh, well—" said Wrinkles. He took up his guitar.

> *Oh, some folks say dat a niggah won' steal,*
> *'Way down yondeh in d' cohn'-fiel';*
> *But Ah caught two in my cohn'-fiel',*
> *Way down yondeh in d' cohn'-fiel'.*

"Oh, let up!" said Grief, as if unwilling to be moved from his despair.

"Oh, let up!" said Pennoyer, as if he disliked the voice and the ballad.

In his studio, Hawker sat braced nervously forward on a little stool before his tall Dutch easel. Three sketches lay on the floor near him, and he glared at them constantly while painting at the large canvas on the easel.

He seemed engaged in some kind of a duel. His hair dishevelled, his eyes gleaming, he was in a deadly scuffle. In the sketches was the landscape of heavy blue, as if seen through powder-smoke, and all the skies burned red. There was in these notes a sinister quality of hopelessness, eloquent of a defeat, as if the scene represented the last hour on a field of disastrous battle. Hawker seemed attacking with this picture something fair and beautiful of his own life, a possession of his mind, and he did it fiercely, mercilessly, formidably. His arm moved with the energy of a strange wrath. He might have been thrusting with a sword.

There was a knock at the door. "Come in." Pennoyer entered sheepishly. "Well?" cried Hawker, with an echo of savagery in his voice. He turned from the canvas precisely as one might emerge from a fight. "Oh!" he said, perceiving Pennoyer. The glow in his eyes slowly changed. "What is it, Penny?"

"Billie," said Pennoyer, "Grief was to get his check today, but they put him off until Monday, and so, you know—er—well—"

"Oh!" said Hawker again.

When Pennoyer had gone Hawker sat motionless before his work. He stared at the canvas in a meditation so profound that it was probably unconscious of itself.

The light from above his head slanted more and more toward the east.

Once he arose and lighted a pipe. He returned to the easel and stood staring with his hands in his pockets. He moved like one in a sleep. Suddenly the gleam shot into his eyes again. He dropped to the stool and grabbed a brush. At the end of a certain long, tumultuous period he clinched his pipe more firmly in his teeth and puffed strongly. The thought might have occurred to him that it was not alight, for he looked at it with a vague, questioning glance. There came another knock at the door. "Go to the devil!" he shouted, without turning his head.

Hollanden crossed the corridor then to the den.

"Hi, there, Hollie! Hello, boy! Just the fellow we want to see. Come in—sit down—hit a pipe. Say, who was the girl Billie Hawker went mad over this summer?"

"Blazes!" said Hollanden, recovering slowly from this onslaught. "Who—what—how did you Indians find it out?"

"Oh, we tumbled!" they cried in delight, "we tumbled."

"There!" said Hollanden, reproaching himself. "And I thought you were such a lot of blockheads."

"Oh, we tumbled!" they cried again in their ecstasy. "But who is she? That's the point."

"Well, she was a girl."

"Yes, go on."

"A New York girl."

"Yes."

"A perfectly stunning New York girl."

"Yes. Go ahead."

"A perfectly stunning New York girl of a very wealthy and rather old-fashioned family."

"Well, I'll be shot! You don't mean it! She is practically seated on top of the Matterhorn. Poor old Billie!"

"Not at all," said Hollanden composedly.

It was a common habit of Purple Sanderson to call attention at night to the resemblance of the den to some little ward in a hospital. Upon this night, when Sanderson and Grief were buried in slumber, Pennoyer moved restlessly. "Wrink!" he called softly into the darkness in the direction of the divan which was secretly a coal-box.

"What?" said Wrinkles in a surly voice. His mind had evidently been caught at the threshold of sleep.

"Do you think Florinda cares much for Billie Hawker?"

Wrinkles fretted through some oaths. "How in thunder do I know?" The divan creaked as he turned his face to the wall.

"Well—" muttered Pennoyer.

## CHAPTER XXVI.

The harmony of summer sunlight on leaf and blade of green was not known to the two windows, which looked forth at an obviously endless building of brownstone about which there was the poetry of a prison. Inside, great folds of lace swept down in orderly cascades, as water trained to fall mathematically. The colossal chandelier, gleaming like a Siamese headdress, caught the subtle flashes from unknown places.

Hawker heard a step and the soft swishing of a woman's dress. He turned toward the door swiftly, with a certain dramatic impulsiveness. But when she entered the room he said, "How delighted I am to see you again!"

She had said, "Why, Mr. Hawker, it was so charming in you to come!"

It did not appear that Hawker's tongue could wag to his purpose. The girl seemed in her mind to be frantically shuffling her pack of social receipts and finding none of them made to meet this situation. Finally, Hawker said that he thought Hearts at War was a very good play.

"Did you?" she said in surprise. "I thought it much like the others."

"Well, so did I," he cried hastily—"the same figures moving around in the mud of modern confusion. I really didn't intend to say that I liked it. Fact is, meeting you rather moved me out of my mental track."

"Mental track?" she said. "I didn't know clever people had mental tracks. I thought it was a privilege of the theologians."

"Who told you I was clever?" he demanded.

"Why," she said, opening her eyes wider, "nobody."

Hawker smiled and looked upon her with gratitude. "Of course, nobody. There couldn't be such an idiot. I am sure you should be astonished to learn that I believed such an imbecile existed. But—"

"Oh!" she said.

"But I think you might have spoken less bluntly."

"Well," she said, after wavering for a time, "you are clever, aren't you?"

"Certainly," he answered reassuringly.

"Well, then?" she retorted, with triumph in her tone. And this interrogation was apparently to her the final victorious argument.

At his discomfiture Hawker grinned.

"You haven't asked news of Stanley," he said. "Why don't you ask news of Stanley?"

"Oh! and how was he?"

"The last I saw of him he stood down at the end of the pasture—the pasture, you know—wagging his tail in blissful anticipation of an invitation to come with me, and when it finally dawned upon him that he was not to receive it, he turned and went back toward the house 'like a man suddenly stricken with age,' as the story-tellers eloquently say. Poor old dog!"

"And you left him?" she said reproachfully. Then she asked, "Do you remember how he amused you playing with the ants at the falls?"

"No."

"Why, he did. He pawed at the moss, and you sat there laughing. I remember it distinctly."

"You remember distinctly? Why, I thought—well, your back was turned, you know. Your gaze was fixed upon something before you, and you were utterly lost to the rest of the world. You could not have known if Stanley pawed the moss and I laughed. So, you see, you are mistaken. As a matter of fact, I utterly deny that Stanley pawed the moss or that I laughed, or that any ants appeared at the falls at all."

"I have always said that you should have been a Chinese soldier of fortune," she observed musingly. "Your daring and ingenuity would be prized by the Chinese."

"There are innumerable tobacco jars in China," he said, measuring the advantages. "Moreover, there is no perspective. You don't have to walk two miles to see a friend. No. He is always there near you, so that you can't move a chair without hitting your distant friend. You—"

"Did Hollie remain as attentive as ever to the Worcester girls?"

"Yes, of course, as attentive as ever. He dragged me into all manner of tennis games—"

"Why, I thought you loved to play tennis?"

"Oh, well," said Hawker, "I did until you left."

"My sister has gone to the park with the children. I know she will be vexed when she finds that you have called."

Ultimately Hawker said, "Do you remember our ride behind my father's oxen?"

"No," she answered; "I had forgotten it completely. Did we ride behind your father's oxen?"

After a moment he said: "That remark would be prized by the Chinese. We did. And you most graciously professed to enjoy it, which earned my deep gratitude and admiration. For no one knows better than I," he added meekly, "that it is no great comfort or pleasure to ride behind my father's oxen."

She smiled retrospectively. "Do you remember how the people on the porch hurried to the railing?"

## CHAPTER XXVII.

Near the door the stout proprietress sat intrenched behind the cash-box in a Parisian manner. She looked with practical amiability at her guests, who dined noisily and with great fire, discussing momentous problems furiously, making wide, maniacal gestures through the cigarette smoke. Meanwhile the little handful of waiters ran to and fro wildly. Imperious and importunate cries rang at them from all directions. "Gustave! Adolphe!" Their faces expressed a settled despair. They answered calls, commands, oaths in a semi-distraction, fleeting among the tables as if pursued by some dodging animal. Their breaths came in gasps. If they had been convict labourers they could not have surveyed their positions with countenances of more unspeakable injury. Withal, they carried incredible masses of dishes and threaded their ways with skill. They served people with such speed and violence that it often resembled a personal assault. They struck two blows at a table and left there a knife and fork. Then came the viands in a volley. The clatter of this business was loud and bewilderingly rapid, like the gallop of a thousand horses.

In a remote corner a band of mandolins and guitars played the long, sweeping, mad melody of a Spanish waltz. It seemed to go tingling to the hearts of many of the diners. Their eyes glittered with enthusiasm, with abandon, with deviltry. They swung their heads from side to side in rhythmic movement. High in air curled the smoke from the innumerable cigarettes. The long, black claret bottles were in clusters upon the tables. At an end of the hall two men with maudlin grins sang the waltz uproariously, but always a trifle belated.

An unsteady person, leaning back in his chair to murmur swift compliments to a woman at another table, suddenly sprawled out upon the floor. He scrambled to his feet, and, turning to the escort of the woman, heatedly blamed him for the accident. They exchanged a series of tense, bitter insults, which spatted back and forth between them like pellets. People arose from their chairs and stretched their necks. The musicians stood in a body, their faces turned with expressions of keen excitement toward this quarrel, but their fingers still twinkling over their instruments, sending into the middle of this turmoil the passionate, mad, Spanish music. The proprietor of the place came in agitation and plunged headlong into the argument, where he thereafter appeared as a frantic creature harried to the point of insanity, for they buried him at once in long, vociferous threats, explanations, charges, every form of declamation known to their voices. The music, the noise of the galloping horses, the voices of the brawlers, gave the whole thing the quality of war.

There were two men in the *café* who seemed to be tranquil. Hollanden carefully stacked one lump of sugar upon another in the middle of his saucer and poured cognac over them. He touched a match to the cognac and the blue and yellow flames eddied in the saucer. "I wonder what those two fools are bellowing at?" he said, turning about irritably.

"Hanged if I know!" muttered Hawker in reply. "This place makes me weary, anyhow. Hear the blooming din!"

"What's the matter?" said Hollanden. "You used to say this was the one natural, the one truly Bohemian, resort in the city. You swore by it."

"Well, I don't like it so much any more."

"Ho!" cried Hollanden, "you're getting correct—that's it exactly. You will become one of these intensely— Look, Billie, the little one is going to punch him!"

"No, he isn't. They never do," said Hawker morosely. "Why did you bring me here tonight, Hollie?"

"I? I bring you? Good heavens, I came as a concession to you! What are you talking about?—Hi! the little one is going to punch him, sure!"

He gave the scene his undivided attention for a moment; then he turned again: "You will become correct. I know you will. I have been watching. You are about to achieve a respectability that will make a stone saint blush for himself. What's the matter with you? You act as if you thought falling in love with a girl was a most extraordinary circumstance.—I wish they would put those people out.—Of course I know that you—There! The little one has swiped at him at last!"

After a time he resumed his oration. "Of course, I know that you are not reformed in the matter of this uproar and this remarkable consumption of bad wine. It is not that. It is a fact that there are indications that some other citizen was fortunate enough to possess your napkin before you; and, moreover, you are sure that you would hate to be caught by your correct friends with any such *consommé* in front of you as we had tonight. You have got an eye suddenly for all kinds of gilt. You are in the way of becoming a most unbearable person.—Oh, look! the little one and the proprietor are having it now.—You are in the way of becoming a most unbearable person. Presently many of your friends will not be fine enough.—In heaven's name, why don't they throw him out? Are you going to howl and gesticulate there all night?"

"Well," said Hawker, "a man would be a fool if he did like this dinner."

"Certainly. But what an immaterial part in the glory of this joint is the dinner! Who cares about dinner? No one comes here to eat; that's what you always claimed.—Well, there, at last they are throwing him out. I hope he lands on his head.—Really, you know, Billie, it is such a fine thing being in love that one is sure to be detestable to the rest of the world, and that is the reason they created a proverb to the other effect. You want to look out."

"You talk like a blasted old granny!" said Hawker. "Haven't changed at all. This place is all right, only—"

"You are gone," interrupted Hollanden in a sad voice. "It is very plain—you are gone."

## CHAPTER XXVIII.

The proprietor of the place, having pushed to the street the little man, who may have been the most vehement, came again and resumed the discussion with the remainder of the men of war. Many of these had volunteered, and they were very enduring.

"Yes, you are gone," said Hollanden, with the sobriety of graves in his voice. "You are gone.—Hi!" he cried, "there is Lucian Pontiac.—Hi, Pontiac! Sit down here."

A man with a tangle of hair, and with that about his mouth which showed that he had spent many years in manufacturing a proper modesty with which to bear his greatness, came toward them, smiling.

"Hello, Pontiac!" said Hollanden. "Here's another great painter. Do you know Mr. Hawker?—Mr. William Hawker—Mr. Pontiac."

"Mr. Hawker—delighted," said Pontiac. "Although I have not known you personally, I can assure you that I have long been a great admirer of your abilities."

The proprietor of the place and the men of war had at length agreed to come to an amicable understanding. They drank liquors, while each firmly, but now silently, upheld his dignity.

"Charming place," said Pontiac. "So thoroughly Parisian in spirit. And from time to time, Mr. Hawker, I use one of your models. Must say she has the best arm and wrist in the universe. Stunning figure—stunning!"

"You mean Florinda?" said Hawker.

"Yes, that's the name. Very fine girl. Lunches with me from time to time and chatters so volubly. That's how I learned you posed her occasionally. If the models didn't gossip we would never know what painters were addicted to profanity. Now that old Thorndike—he told me you swore like a drill-sergeant if the model winked a finger at the critical time. Very fine girl, Florinda. And honest, too—honest as the devil. Very curious thing. Of course honesty among the girl models is very common, very common—quite universal thing, you know—but then it always strikes me as being very curious, very curious. I've been much attracted by your girl Florinda."

"My girl?" said Hawker.

"Well, she always speaks of you in a proprietary way, you know. And then she considers that she owes you some kind of obedience and allegiance and devotion. I remember last week I said to her: 'You can go now. Come again Friday.' But she said: 'I don't think I can come on Friday. Billie Hawker is home now, and he may want me then.' Said I: 'The devil take Billie Hawker! He hasn't engaged you for Friday, has he? Well, then, I engage you now.' But she shook her head. No, she couldn't come on Friday. Billie Hawker was home, and he might want her any day. 'Well, then,' said I, 'you have my permission to do as you please, since you are resolved upon it anyway. Go to your Billie Hawker.' Did you need her on Friday?"

"No," said Hawker.

"Well, then, the minx, I shall scold her. Stunning figure—stunning! It was only last week that old Charley Master said to me mournfully: 'There are no more good models. Great Scott! not a one.' 'You're 'way off, my boy,' I said; 'there is one good model,' and then I named your girl. I mean the girl who claims to be yours."

"Poor little beggar!" said Hollanden.

"Who?" said Pontiac.

"Florinda," answered Hollanden. "I suppose—"

Pontiac interrupted. "Oh, of course, it is too bad. Everything is too bad. My dear sir, nothing is so much to be regretted as the universe. But this Florinda is such a sturdy young soul! The world is against her, but, bless your heart, she is equal to the battle. She is strong in the manner of a little child. Why, you don't know her. She—"

"I know her very well."

"Well, perhaps you do, but for my part I think you don't appreciate her formidable character and stunning figure—stunning!"

"Damn it!" said Hawker to his coffee cup, which he had accidentally overturned.

"Well," resumed Pontiac, "she is a stunning model, and I think, Mr. Hawker, you are to be envied."

"Eh?" said Hawker.

"I wish I could inspire my models with such obedience and devotion. Then I would not be obliged to rail at them for being late, and have to badger them for not showing up at all. She has a beautiful figure—beautiful."

## CHAPTER XXIX.

When Hawker went again to the house of the great window he looked first at the colossal chandelier, and, perceiving that it had not moved, he smiled in a certain friendly and familiar way.

"It must be a fine thing," said the girl dreamily. "I always feel envious of that sort of life."

"What sort of life?"

"Why—I don't know exactly; but there must be a great deal of freedom about it. I went to a studio tea once, and—"

"A studio tea! Merciful heavens— Go on."

"Yes, a studio tea. Don't you like them? To be sure, we didn't know whether the man could paint very well, and I suppose you think it is an imposition for anyone who is not a great painter to give a tea."

"Go on."

"Well, he had the dearest little Japanese servants, and some of the cups came from Algiers, and some from Turkey, and some from— What's the matter?"

"Go on. I'm not interrupting you."

"Well, that's all; excepting that everything was charming in colour, and I thought what a lazy, beautiful life the man must lead, lounging in such a studio, smoking monogrammed cigarettes, and remarking how badly all the other men painted."

"Very fascinating. But—"

"Oh! you are going to ask if he could draw. I'm sure I don't know, but the tea that he gave was charming."

"I was on the verge of telling you something about artist life, but if you have seen a lot of draperies and drunk from a cup of Algiers, you know all about it."

"You, then, were going to make it something very terrible, and tell how young painters struggled, and all that."

"No, not exactly. But listen: I suppose there is an aristocracy who, whether they paint well or paint ill, certainly do give charming teas, as you say, and all other kinds of charming affairs too; but when I hear people talk as if that was the whole life, it makes my hair rise, you know, because I am sure that as they get to know me better and better they will see how I fall short of that kind of an existence, and I shall probably take a great tumble in their estimation. They might even conclude that I can not paint, which would be very unfair, because I can paint, you know."

"Well, proceed to arrange my point of view, so that you sha'n't tumble in my estimation when I discover that you don't lounge in a studio, smoke monogrammed cigarettes, and remark how badly the other men paint."

"That's it. That's precisely what I wish to do."

"Begin."

"Well, in the first place—"

"In the first place—what?"

"Well, I started to study when I was very poor, you understand. Look here! I'm telling you these things because I want you to know, somehow. It isn't that I'm not ashamed of it. Well, I began very poor, and I—as a matter of fact—I—well, I earned myself over half the money for my studying, and the other half I bullied and badgered and beat out of my poor old dad. I worked pretty hard in Paris, and I returned here expecting to become a great painter at once. I didn't, though. In fact, I had my worst moments then. It lasted for some years. Of course, the faith and endurance of my father were by this time worn to a shadow—this time, when I needed him the most. However, things got a little better and a little better, until I found that by working quite hard I could make what was to me a fair income. That's where I am now, too."

"Why are you so ashamed of this story?"

"The poverty."

"Poverty isn't anything to be ashamed of."

"Great heavens! Have you the temerity to get off that old nonsensical remark? Poverty is everything to be ashamed of. Did you ever see a person not ashamed of his poverty? Certainly not. Of course, when a man gets very rich he will brag so loudly of the poverty of his youth that one would never suppose that he was once ashamed of it. But he was."

"Well, anyhow, you shouldn't be ashamed of the story you have just told me."

"Why not? Do you refuse to allow me the great right of being like other men?"

"I think it was—brave, you know."

"Brave? Nonsense! Those things are not brave. Impression to that effect created by the men who have been through the mill for the greater glory of the men who have been through the mill."

"I don't like to hear you talk that way. It sounds wicked, you know."

"Well, it certainly wasn't heroic. I can remember distinctly that there was not one heroic moment."

"No, but it was—it was—"

"It was what?"

"Well, somehow I like it, you know."

## CHAPTER XXX.

"There's three of them," said Grief in a hoarse whisper.

"Four, I tell you!" said Wrinkles in a low, excited tone.

"Four," breathed Pennoyer with decision.

They held fierce pantomimic argument. From the corridor came sounds of rustling dresses and rapid feminine conversation.

Grief had kept his ear to the panel of the door. His hand was stretched back, warning the others to silence. Presently he turned his head and whispered, "Three."

"Four," whispered Pennoyer and Wrinkles.

"Hollie is there, too," whispered Grief. "Billie is unlocking the door. Now they're going in. Hear them cry out, 'Oh, isn't it lovely!' Jinks!" He began a noiseless dance about the room. "Jinks! Don't I wish I had a big studio and a little reputation! Wouldn't I have my swell friends come to see me, and wouldn't I entertain 'em!" He adopted a descriptive manner, and with his forefinger indicated various spaces of the wall. "Here is a little thing I did in Brittany. Peasant woman in sabots. This brown spot here is the peasant woman, and those two white things are the sabots. Peasant woman in sabots, don't you see? Women in Brittany, of course, all wear sabots, you understand. Convenience of the painters. I see you are looking at that little thing I did in Morocco. Ah, you admire it? Well, not so bad—not so bad. Arab smoking pipe, squatting in doorway. This long streak here is the pipe. Clever, you say? Oh, thanks! You are too kind. Well, all Arabs do that, you know. Sole occupation. Convenience of the painters. Now, this little thing here I did in Venice. Grand Canal, you know. Gondolier leaning on his oar. Convenience of the painters. Oh, yes, American subjects are well enough, but hard to find, you know—hard to find. Morocco, Venice, Brittany, Holland—all oblige with colour, you know—quaint form—all that. We are so hideously modern over here; and, besides, nobody has painted us much. How the devil can I paint America when nobody has done it before me? My dear sir, are you aware that that would be originality? Good heavens! we are not æsthetic, you understand. Oh, yes, some good mind comes along and understands a thing and does it, and after that it is æsthetic. Yes, of course, but then—well— Now, here is a little Holland thing of mine; it—"

The others had evidently not been heeding him. "Shut up!" said Wrinkles suddenly. "Listen!" Grief paused his harangue and they sat in silence, their lips apart, their eyes from time to time exchanging eloquent messages. A dulled melodious babble came from Hawker's studio.

At length Pennoyer murmured wistfully, "I would like to see her."

Wrinkles started noiselessly to his feet. "Well, I tell you she's a peach. I was going up the steps, you know, with a loaf of bread under my arm, when I chanced to look up the street and saw Billie and Hollanden coming with four of them."

"Three," said Grief.

"Four; and I tell you I scattered. One of the two with Billie was a peach—a peach."

"O, Lord!" groaned the others enviously. "Billie's in luck."

"How do you know?" said Wrinkles. "Billie is a blamed good fellow, but that doesn't say she will care for him—more likely that she won't."

They sat again in silence, grinning, and listening to the murmur of voices.

There came the sound of a step in the hallway. It ceased at a point opposite the door of Hawker's studio. Presently it was heard again. Florinda entered the den. "Hello!" she cried, "who is over in Billie's place? I was just going to knock—"

They motioned at her violently. "Sh!" they whispered. Their countenances were very impressive.

"What's the matter with you fellows?" asked Florinda in her ordinary tone; whereupon they made gestures of still greater wildness. "S-s-sh!"

Florinda lowered her voice properly. "Who is over there?"

"Some swells," they whispered.

Florinda bent her head. Presently she gave a little start. "Who is over there?" Her voice became a tone of deep awe. "She?"

Wrinkles and Grief exchanged a swift glance. Pennoyer said gruffly, "Who do you mean?"

"Why," said Florinda, "you know. She. The—the girl that Billie likes."

Pennoyer hesitated for a moment and then said wrathfully: "Of course she is! Who do you suppose?"

"Oh!" said Florinda. She took a seat upon the divan, which was privately a coal-box, and unbuttoned her jacket at the throat. "Is she—is she—very handsome, Wrink?"

Wrinkles replied stoutly, "No."

Grief said: "Let's make a sneak down the hall to the little unoccupied room at the front of the building and look from the window there. When they go out we can pipe 'em off."

"Come on!" they exclaimed, accepting this plan with glee.

Wrinkles opened the door and seemed about to glide away, when he suddenly turned and shook his head. "It's dead wrong," he said, ashamed.

"Oh, go on!" eagerly whispered the others. Presently they stole pattering down the corridor, grinning, exclaiming, and cautioning each other.

At the window Pennoyer said: "Now, for heaven's sake, don't let them see you!—Be careful, Grief, you'll tumble.—Don't lean on me that way, Wrink; think I'm a barn door? Here they come. Keep back. Don't let them see you."

"O-o-oh!" said Grief. "Talk about a peach! Well, I should say so."

Florinda's fingers tore at Wrinkle's coat sleeve. "Wrink, Wrink, is that her? Is that her? On the left of Billie? Is that her, Wrink?"

"What? Yes. Stop punching me! Yes, I tell you! That's her. Are you deaf?"

## CHAPTER XXXI.

In the evening Pennoyer conducted Florinda to the flat of many fire-escapes. After a period of silent tramping through the great golden avenue and the street that was being repaired, she said, "Penny, you are very good to me."

"Why?" said Pennoyer.

"Oh, because you are. You—you are very good to me, Penny."

"Well, I guess I'm not killing myself."

"There isn't many fellows like you."

"No?"

"No. There isn't many fellows like you, Penny. I tell you 'most everything, and you just listen, and don't argue with me and tell me I'm a fool, because you know that it—because you know that it can't be helped, anyhow."

"Oh, nonsense, you kid! Almost anybody would be glad to—"

"Penny, do you think she is very beautiful?" Florinda's voice had a singular quality of awe in it.

"Well," replied Pennoyer, "I don't know."

"Yes, you do, Penny. Go ahead and tell me."

"Well—"

"Go ahead."

"Well, she is rather handsome, you know."

"Yes," said Florinda, dejectedly, "I suppose she is." After a time she cleared her throat and remarked indifferently, "I suppose Billie cares a lot for her?"

"Oh, I imagine that he does—in a way."

"Why, of course he does," insisted Florinda. "What do you mean by 'in a way'? You know very well that Billie thinks his eyes of her."

"No, I don't."

"Yes, you do. You know you do. You are talking in that way just to brace me up. You know you are."

"No, I'm not."

"Penny," said Florinda thankfully, "what makes you so good to me?"

"Oh, I guess I'm not so astonishingly good to you. Don't be silly."

"But you are good to me, Penny. You don't make fun of me the way—the way the other boys would. You are just as good as you can be.—But you do think she is beautiful, don't you?"

"They wouldn't make fun of you," said Pennoyer.

"But do you think she is beautiful?"

"Look here, Splutter, let up on that, will you? You keep harping on one string all the time. Don't bother me!"

"But, honest now, Penny, you do think she is beautiful?"

"Well, then, confound it—no! no! no!"

"Oh, yes, you do, Penny. Go ahead now. Don't deny it just because you are talking to me. Own up, now, Penny. You do think she is beautiful?"

"Well," said Pennoyer, in a dull roar of irritation, "do you?"

Florinda walked in silence, her eyes upon the yellow flashes which lights sent to the pavement. In the end she said, "Yes."

"Yes, what?" asked Pennoyer sharply.

"Yes, she—yes, she is—beautiful."

"Well, then?" cried Pennoyer, abruptly closing the discussion.

Florinda announced something as a fact. "Billie thinks his eyes of her."

"How do you know he does?"

"Don't scold at me, Penny. You—you—"

"I'm not scolding at you. There! What a goose you are, Splutter! Don't, for heaven's sake, go to whimpering on the street! I didn't say anything to make you feel that way. Come, pull yourself together."

"I'm not whimpering."

"No, of course not; but then you look as if you were on the edge of it. What a little idiot!"

## CHAPTER XXXII.

When the snow fell upon the clashing life of the city, the exiled stones, beaten by myriad strange feet, were told of the dark, silent forests where the flakes swept through the hemlocks and swished softly against the boulders.

In his studio Hawker smoked a pipe, clasping his knee with thoughtful, interlocked fingers. He was gazing sourly at his finished picture. Once he started to his feet with a cry of vexation. Looking back over his shoulder, he swore an insult into the face of the picture. He paced to and fro, smoking belligerently and from time to time eying it. The helpless thing remained upon the easel, facing him.

Hollanden entered and stopped abruptly at sight of the great scowl. "What's wrong now?" he said.

Hawker gestured at the picture. "That dunce of a thing. It makes me tired. It isn't worth a hang. Blame it!"

"What?" Hollanden strode forward and stood before the painting with legs apart, in a properly critical manner. "What? Why, you said it was your best thing."

"Aw!" said Hawker, waving his arms, "it's no good! I abominate it! I didn't get what I wanted, I tell you. I didn't get what I wanted. That?" he shouted, pointing thrust-way at it—"that? It's vile! Aw! it makes me weary."

"You're in a nice state," said Hollanden, turning to take a critical view of the painter. "What has got into you now? I swear, you are more kinds of a chump!"

Hawker crooned dismally: "I can't paint! I can't paint for a damn! I'm no good. What in thunder was I invented for, anyhow, Hollie?"

"You're a fool," said Hollanden. "I hope to die if I ever saw such a complete idiot! You give me a pain. Just because she don't—"

"It isn't that. She has nothing to do with it, although I know well enough—I know well enough—"

"What?"

"I know well enough she doesn't care a hang for me. It isn't that. It is because— it is because I can't paint. Look at that thing over there! Remember the thought and energy I— Damn the thing!"

"Why, did you have a row with her?" asked Hollanden, perplexed. "I didn't know—"

"No, of course you didn't know," cried Hawker, sneering; "because I had no row. It isn't that, I tell you. But I know well enough"—he shook his fist vaguely—"that she don't care an old tomato can for me. Why should she?" he demanded with a curious defiance. "In the name of Heaven, why should she?"

"I don't know," said Hollanden; "I don't know, I'm sure. But, then, women have no social logic. This is the great blessing of the world. There is only one thing which is superior to the multiplicity of social forms, and that is a woman's mind—a young woman's mind. Oh, of course, sometimes they are logical, but let a woman be so once, and she will repent of it to the end of her days. The safety of the world's balance lies in woman's illogical mind. I think—"

"Go to blazes!" said Hawker. "I don't care what you think. I am sure of one thing, and that is that she doesn't care a hang for me!"

"I think," Hollanden continued, "that society is doing very well in its work of bravely lawing away at Nature; but there is one immovable thing—a woman's illogical mind. That is our safety. Thank Heaven, it—"

"Go to blazes!" said Hawker again.

## CHAPTER XXXIII.

As Hawker again entered the room of the great windows he glanced in sidelong bitterness at the chandelier. When he was seated he looked at it in open defiance and hatred.

Men in the street were shovelling at the snow. The noise of their instruments scraping on the stones came plainly to Hawker's ears in a harsh chorus, and this sound at this time was perhaps to him a *miserere*.

"I came to tell you," he began, "I came to tell you that perhaps I am going away."

"Going away!" she cried. "Where?"

"Well, I don't know—quite. You see, I am rather indefinite as yet. I thought of going for the winter somewhere in the Southern States. I am decided merely this much, you know—I am going somewhere. But I don't know where. 'Way off, anyhow."

"We shall be very sorry to lose you," she remarked. "We—"

"And I thought," he continued, "that I would come and say 'adios' now for fear that I might leave very suddenly. I do that sometimes. I'm afraid you will forget me very soon, but I want to tell you that—"

"Why," said the girl in some surprise, "you speak as if you were going away for all time. You surely do not mean to utterly desert New York?"

"I think you misunderstand me," he said. "I give this important air to my farewell to you because to me it is a very important event. Perhaps you recollect that once I told you that I cared for you. Well, I still care for you, and so I can only go away somewhere—some place 'way off—where—where— See?"

"New York is a very large place," she observed.

"Yes, New York is a very large— How good of you to remind me! But then you don't understand. You can't understand. I know I can find no place where I will cease to remember you, but then I can find some place where I can cease to remember in a way that I am myself. I shall never try to forget you. Those two violets, you know—one I found near the tennis court and the other you gave me, you remember—I shall take them with me."

"Here," said the girl, tugging at her gown for a moment—"Here! Here's a third one." She thrust a violet toward him.

"If you were not so serenely insolent," said Hawker, "I would think that you felt sorry for me. I don't wish you to feel sorry for me. And I don't wish to be melodramatic. I know it is all commonplace enough, and I didn't mean to act like a tenor. Please don't pity me."

"I don't," she replied. She gave the violet a little fling.

Hawker lifted his head suddenly and glowered at her. "No, you don't," he at last said slowly, "you don't. Moreover, there is no reason why you should take the trouble. But—"

He paused when the girl leaned and peered over the arm of her chair precisely in the manner of a child at the brink of a fountain. "There's my violet on the floor," she said. "You treated it quite contemptuously, didn't you?"

"Yes."

Together they stared at the violet. Finally he stooped and took it in his fingers. "I feel as if this third one was pelted at me, but I shall keep it. You are rather a cruel person, but, Heaven guard us! that only fastens a man's love the more upon a woman."

She laughed. "That is not a very good thing to tell a woman."

"No," he said gravely, "it is not, but then I fancy that somebody may have told you previously."

She stared at him, and then said, "I think you are revenged for my serene insolence."

"Great heavens, what an armour!" he cried. "I suppose, after all, I did feel a trifle like a tenor when I first came here, but you have chilled it all out of me. Let's talk upon indifferent topics." But he started abruptly to his feet. "No," he said, "let us not talk upon indifferent topics. I am not brave, I assure you, and it—it might be too much for me." He held out his hand. "Good-bye."

"You are going?"

"Yes, I am going. Really I didn't think how it would bore you for me to come around here and croak in this fashion."

"And you are not coming back for a long, long time?"

"Not for a long, long time." He mimicked her tone. "I have the three violets now, you know, and you must remember that I took the third one even when you flung it at my head. That will remind you how submissive I was in my devotion. When you recall the two others it will remind you of what a fool I was. Dare say you won't miss three violets."

"No," she said.

"Particularly the one you flung at my head. That violet was certainly freely—given."

"I didn't fling it at your head." She pondered for a time with her eyes upon the floor. Then she murmured, "No more freely—given than the one I gave you that night—that night at the inn."

"So very good of you to tell me so!"

Her eyes were still upon the floor.

"Do you know," said Hawker, "it is very hard to go away and leave an impression in your mind that I am a fool? That is very hard. Now, you do think I am a fool, don't you?"

She remained silent. Once she lifted her eyes and gave him a swift look with much indignation in it.

"Now you are enraged. Well, what have I done?"

It seemed that some tumult was in her mind, for she cried out to him at last in sudden tearfulness: "Oh, do go! Go! Please! I want you to go!"

Under this swift change Hawker appeared as a man struck from the sky. He sprang to his feet, took two steps forward, and spoke a word which was an explosion of delight and amazement. He said, "What?"

With heroic effort she slowly raised her eyes until, alight with anger, defiance, unhappiness, they met his eyes.

Later, she told him that he was perfectly ridiculous.

# THE KICKING TWELFTH

The Spitzbergen army was backed by tradition of centuries of victory. In its chronicles, occasional defeats were not printed in italics, but were likely to appear as glorious stands against overwhelming odds. A favourite way to dispose of them was frankly to attribute them to the blunders of the civilian heads of government. This was very good for the army, and probably no army had more self-confidence. When it was announced that an expeditionary force was to be sent to Rostina to chastise an impudent people, a hundred barrack squares filled with excited men, and a hundred sergeant-majors hurried silently through the groups, and succeeded in looking as if they were the repositories of the secrets of empire. Officers on leave sped joyfully back to their harness, and recruits were abused with unflagging devotion by every man, from colonels to privates of experience.

The Twelfth Regiment of the Line—the Kicking Twelfth—was consumed with a dread that it was not to be included in the expedition, and the regiment formed itself into an informal indignation meeting. Just as they had proved that a great outrage was about to be perpetrated, warning orders arrived to hold themselves in readiness for active service abroad—in Rostina. The barrack yard was in a flash transferred into a blue-and-buff pandemonium, and the official bugle itself hardly had power to quell the glad disturbance.

Thus it was that early in the spring the Kicking Twelfth—sixteen hundred men in service equipment—found itself crawling along a road in Rostina. They did not form part of the main force, but belonged to a column of four regiments of foot, two batteries of field guns, a battery of mountain howitzers, a regiment of horse, and a company of engineers. Nothing had happened. The long column had crawled without amusement of any kind through a broad green valley. Big white farm-houses dotted the slopes; but there was no sign of man or beast, and no smoke from the chimneys. The column was operating from its own base, and its general was expected to form a junction with the main body at a given point.

A squadron of the cavalry was fanned out ahead, scouting, and day by day the trudging infantry watched the blue uniforms of the horsemen as they came and went. Sometimes there would sound the faint thuds of a few shots, but the cavalry was unable to find anything to engage.

The Twelfth had no record of foreign service, and it could hardly be said that it had served as a unit in the great civil war, when His Majesty the King had whipped the Pretender. At that time the regiment had suffered from two opinions, so that it was impossible for either side to depend upon it. Many men had deserted to the standard of the Pretender, and a number of officers had drawn their swords for him. When the King, a thorough soldier, looked at the remnant, he saw that they lacked the spirit to be of great help to him in the tremendous battles which he was waging for his throne. And so this emaciated Twelfth was sent off to a corner of the kingdom to guard a dockyard, where some of the officers so plainly expressed their disapproval of this policy that the regiment received its steadfast name, the Kicking Twelfth.

At the time of which I am writing the Twelfth had a few veteran officers and well-bitten sergeants; but the body of the regiment was composed of men who had never heard a shot fired excepting on the rifle-range. But it was an experience for which they longed, and when the moment came for the corps' cry—"Kim up, the Kickers"—there was not likely to be a man who would not go tumbling after his leaders.

Young Timothy Lean was a second lieutenant in the first company of the third battalion, and just at this time he was pattering along at the flank of the men, keeping a fatherly lookout for boots that hurt and packs that sagged. He was extremely bored. The mere far-away sound of desultory shooting was not war as he had been led to believe it.

It did not appear that behind that freckled face and under that red hair there was a mind which dreamed of blood. He was not extremely anxious to kill somebody, but he was very fond of soldiering—it had been the career of his father and of his grandfather—and he understood that the profession of arms lost much of its point unless a man shot at people and had people shoot at him. Strolling in the sun through a practically deserted country might be a proper occupation for a divinity student on a vacation, but the soul of Timothy Lean was in revolt at it. Some times at night he would go morosely to the camp of the cavalry and hear the infant subalterns laughingly exaggerate the comedy side of the adventures which they had had out with small patrols far ahead. Lean would sit and listen in glum silence to these tales, and dislike the young officers—many of them old military school friends—for having had experience in modern warfare.

"Anyhow," he said savagely, "presently you'll be getting into a lot of trouble, and then the Foot will have to come along and pull you out. We always do. That's history."

"Oh, we can take care of ourselves," said the Cavalry, with good-natured understanding of his mood.

But the next day even Lean blessed the cavalry, for excited troopers came whirling back from the front, bending over their speeding horses, and shouting wildly and hoarsely for the infantry to clear the way. Men yelled at them from the roadside as courier followed courier, and from the distance ahead sounded in quick succession six booms from field guns. The information possessed by the couriers was no longer precious. Everybody knew what a battery meant when it spoke. The bugles cried out, and the long column jolted into a halt. Old Colonel Sponge went bouncing in his saddle back to see the general, and the regiment sat down in the grass by the roadside, and waited in silence. Presently the second squadron of the cavalry trotted off along the road in a cloud of dust, and in due time old Colonel Sponge came bouncing back, and palavered his three majors and his adjutant. Then there was more talk by the majors, and gradually through the correct channels spread information which in due time reached Timothy Lean.

The enemy, 5000 strong, occupied a pass at the head of the valley some four miles beyond. They had three batteries well posted. Their infantry was entrenched. The ground in their front was crossed and lined with many ditches and hedges; but the enemy's batteries were so posted that it was doubtful if a ditch would ever prove convenient as shelter for the Spitzbergen infantry.

There was a fair position for the Spitzbergen artillery 2300 yards from the enemy. The cavalry had succeeded in driving the enemy's skirmishers back upon the main body; but, of course, had only tried to worry them a little. The position was almost inaccessible on the enemy's right, owing to steep hills, which had been crowned by small parties of infantry. The enemy's left, although guarded by a much larger force, was approachable, and might be flanked. This was what the cavalry had to say, and it added briefly a report of two troopers killed and five wounded.

Whereupon Major-General Richie, commanding a force of 7500 men of His Majesty of Spitzbergen, set in motion, with a few simple words, the machinery which would launch his army at the enemy. The Twelfth understood the orders when they saw the smart young aide approaching old Colonel Sponge, and they rose as one man, apparently afraid that they would be late. There was a clank of accoutrements. Men shrugged their shoulders tighter against their packs, and thrusting their thumbs between their belts and their tunics, they wriggled into a closer fit with regard to the heavy ammunition equipment. It is curious to note that almost every man took off his cap, and looked contemplatively into it as if to read a maker's name. Then they replaced their caps with great care. There was little talking, and it was not observable that a single soldier handed a token or left a comrade with a message to be delivered in case he should be killed. They did not seem to think of being killed; they seemed absorbed in a desire to know what would happen, and how it would look when it was happening. Men glanced continually at their officers in a plain desire to be quick to understand the very first order that would be given; and officers looked gravely at their men, measuring them, feeling their temper, worrying about them.

A bugle called; there were sharp cries, and the Kicking Twelfth was off to battle.

The regiment had the right of line in the infantry brigade, and the men tramped noisily along the white road, every eye was strained ahead; but, after all, there was nothing to be seen but a dozen farms—in short, a country-side. It resembled the scenery in Spitzbergen; every man in the Kicking Twelfth had often confronted a dozen such farms with a composure which amounted to indifference. But still down the road came galloping troopers, who delivered information to Colonel Sponge and then galloped on. In time the Twelfth came to the top of a rise, and below them on the plain was the heavy black streak of a Spitzbergen squadron, and behind the squadron loomed the grey bare hill of the Rostina position.

There was a little of skirmish firing. The Twelfth reached a knoll, which the officers easily recognised as the place described by the cavalry as suitable for the Spitzbergen guns. The men swarmed up it in a peculiar formation. They resembled a crowd coming off a race track; but, nevertheless, there was no stray sheep. It was simply that the ground on which actual battles are fought is not like a chess board. And after them came swinging a six-gun battery, the guns wagging from side to side as the long line turned out of the road, and the drivers using their whips as the leading horses scrambled at the hill. The halted Twelfth lifted its voice and spoke amiably, but with point, to the battery.

"Go on, Guns! We'll take care of you. Don't be afraid. Give it to them!" The teams—lead, swing and wheel—struggled and slipped over the steep and uneven ground; and the gunners, as they clung to their springless positions, wore their usual and natural airs of unhappiness. They made no reply to the infantry. Once upon the top of the hill, however, these guns were unlimbered in a flash, and directly the infantry could hear the loud voice of an officer drawling out the time for fuses. A moment later the first 3·2 bellowed out, and there could be heard the swish and the snarl of a fleeting shell.

Colonel Sponge and a number of officers climbed to the battery's position; but the men of the regiment sat in the shelter of the hill, like so many blindfolded people, and wondered what they would have been able to see if they had been officers. Sometimes the shells of the enemy came sweeping over the top of the hill, and burst in great brown explosions in the fields to the rear. The men looked after them and laughed. To the rear could be seen also the mountain battery coming at a comic trot, with every man obviously in a deep rage with every mule. If a man can put in long service with a mule battery and come out of it with an amiable disposition, he should be presented with a medal weighing many ounces. After the mule battery came a long black winding thing, which was three regiments of Spitzbergen infantry; and at the backs of them and to the right was an inky square, which was the remaining Spitzbergen guns. General Richie and his staff clattered up the hill. The blindfolded Twelfth sat still. The inky square suddenly became a long racing line. The howitzers joined their little bark to the thunder of the guns on the hill, and the three regiments of infantry came on. The Twelfth sat still.

Of a sudden a bugle rang its warning, and the officers shouted. Some used the old cry, "Attention! Kim up, the Kickers!"—and the Twelfth knew that it had been told to go on. The majority of the men expected to see great things as soon as they rounded the shoulder of the hill; but there was nothing to be seen save a complicated plain and the grey knolls occupied by the enemy. Many company commanders in low voices worked at their men, and said things which do not appear in the written reports. They talked soothingly; they talked indignantly; and they talked always like fathers. And the men heard no sentences completely; they heard no specific direction, these wide-eyed men. They understood that there was being delivered some kind of exhortation to do as they had been taught, and they also understood that a superior intelligence was anxious over their behaviour and welfare.

There was a great deal of floundering through hedges, climbing of walls and jumping of ditches. Curiously original privates tried to find new and easier ways for themselves, instead of following the men in front of them. Officers had short fits of fury over these people. The more originality they possessed, the more likely they were to become separated from their companies. Colonel Sponge was making an exciting progress on a big charger. When the first song of the bullets came from above, the men wondered why he sat so high; the charger seemed as tall as the Eiffel Tower. But if he was high in the air, he had a fine view, and that supposedly is why people ascend the Eiffel Tower. Very often he had been a joke to them, but when they saw this fat, old gentleman so coolly treating the strange new missiles which hummed in the air, it struck them suddenly that they had wronged him seriously; and a man who could attain the command of a Spitzbergen regiment was entitled to general respect. And they gave him a sudden, quick affection—an affection that would make them follow him heartily, trustfully, grandly—this fat, old gentleman, seated on a too-big horse. In a flash his tousled grey head, his short, thick legs, even his paunch, had become specially and humorously endeared to them. And this is the way of soldiers.

But still the Twelfth had not yet come to the place where tumbling bodies begin their test of the very heart of a regiment. They backed through more hedges, jumped more ditches, slid over more walls. The Rostina artillery had seemed to be asleep; but suddenly the guns aroused like dogs from their kennels, and around the Twelfth there began a wild, swift screeching. There arose cries to hurry, to come on; and, as the rifle bullets began to plunge into them, the men saw the high, formidable hills of the enemy's right, and perfectly understood that they were doomed to storm them. The cheering thing was the sudden beginning of a tremendous uproar on the enemy's left.

Every man ran, hard, tense, breathless. When they reached the foot of the hills, they thought they had won the charge already, but they were electrified to see officers above them waving their swords and yelling with anger, surprise, and shame. With a long murmurous outcry the Twelfth began to climb the hill; and as they went and fell, they could hear frenzied shouts—"Kim up, the Kickers!" The pace was slow. It was like the rising of a tide; it was determined, almost relentless in its appearance, but it was slow. If a man fell there was a chance that he would land twenty yards below the point where he was hit. The Kickers crawled, their rifles in their left hands as they pulled and tugged themselves up with their right hands. Ever arose the shout, "Kim up, the Kickers!" Timothy Lean, his face flaming, his eyes wild, yelled it back as if he were delivering the gospel.

The Kickers came up. The enemy—they had been in small force, thinking the hills safe enough from attack—retreated quickly from this preposterous advance, and not a bayonet in the Twelfth saw blood; bayonets very seldom do.

The homing of this successful charge wore an unromantic aspect. About twenty windless men suddenly arrived, and threw themselves upon the crest of the hill, and breathed. And these twenty were joined by others, and still others, until almost 1100 men of the Twelfth lay upon the hilltop, while the regiment's track was marked by body after body, in groups and singly. The first officer—perchance the first man, one never can be certain—the first officer to gain the top of the hill was Timothy Lean, and such was the situation that he had the honour to receive his colonel with a bashful salute.

The regiment knew exactly what it had done; it did not have to wait to be told by the Spitzbergen newspapers. It had taken a formidable position with the loss of about five hundred men, and it knew it. It knew, too, that it was great glory for the Kicking Twelfth; and as the men lay rolling on their bellies, they expressed their joy in a wild cry—"Kim up, the Kickers!" For a moment there was nothing but joy, and then suddenly company commanders were besieged by men who wished to go down the path of the charge and look for their mates. The answers were without the quality of mercy; they were short, snapped, quick words, "No; you can't."

The attack on the enemy's left was sounding in great rolling crashes. The shells in their flight through the air made a noise as of red-hot iron plunged into water, and stray bullets nipped near the ears of the Kickers.

The Kickers looked and saw. The battle was below them. The enemy were indicated by a long, noisy line of gossamer smoke, although there could be seen a toy battery with tiny men employed at the guns. All over the field the shrapnel was bursting, making quick bulbs of white smoke. Far away, two regiments of Spitzbergen infantry were charging, and at the distance this charge looked like a casual stroll. It appeared that small black groups of men were walking meditatively toward the Rostina entrenchments.

There would have been orders given sooner to the Twelfth, but unfortunately Colonel Sponge arrived on top of the hill without a breath of wind in his body. He could not have given an order to save the regiment from being wiped off the earth. Finally he was able to gasp out something and point at the enemy. Timothy Lean ran along the line yelling to the men to sight at 800 yards; and like a slow and ponderous machine the regiment again went to work. The fire flanked a great part of the enemy's trenches.

It could be said that there were only two prominent points of view expressed by the men after their victorious arrival on the crest. One was defined in the exulting use of the corps' cry. The other was a grief-stricken murmur which is invariably heard after a fight—"My God, we're all cut to pieces!"

Colonel Sponge sat on the ground and impatiently waited for his wind to return. As soon as it did, he arose and cried out, "Form up, and we'll charge again! We will win this battle as soon as we can hit them!" The shouts of the officers sounded wild, like men yelling on ship-board in a gale. And the obedient Kickers arose for their task. It was running down hill this time. The mob of panting men poured over the stones.

But the enemy had not been blind to the great advantage gained by the Twelfth, and they now turned upon them a desperate fire of small arms. Men fell in every imaginable way, and their accoutrements rattled on the rocky ground. Some landed with a crash, floored by some tremendous blows; others dropped gently down like sacks of meal; with others, it would positively appear that some spirit had suddenly seized them by their ankles and jerked their legs from under them. Many officers were down, but Colonel Sponge, stuttering and blowing, was still upright. He was almost the last man in the charge, but not to his shame, rather to his stumpy legs. At one time it seemed that the assault would be lost. The effect of the fire was some-what as if a terrible cyclone were blowing in the men's faces. They wavered, lowering their heads and shouldering weakly, as if it were impossible to make headway against the wind of battle. It was the moment of despair, the moment of the heroism which comes to the chosen of the war-god.

The colonel's cry broke and screeched absolute hatred; other officers simply howled; and the men, silent, debased, seemed to tighten their muscles for one last effort. Again they pushed against this mysterious power of the air, and once more the regiment was charging. Timothy Lean, agile and strong, was well in advance; and afterwards he reflected that the men who had been nearest to him were an old grizzled sergeant who would have gone to hell for the honour of the regiment, and a pie-faced lad who had been obliged to lie about his age in order to get into the army.

There was no shock of meeting. The Twelfth came down on a corner of the trenches, and as soon as the enemy had ascertained that the Twelfth was certain to arrive, they scuttled out, running close to the earth and spending no time in glances backward. In these days it is not discreet to wait for a charge to come home. You observe the charge, you attempt to stop it, and if you find that you can't, it is better to retire immediately to some other place. The Rostina soldiers were not heroes, perhaps, but they were men of sense. A maddened and badly-frightened mob of Kickers came tumbling into the trench, and shot at the backs of fleeing men. And at that very moment the action was won, and won by the Kickers. The enemy's flank was entirely crippled, and, knowing this, he did not await further and more disastrous information. The Twelfth looked at themselves and knew that they had a record. They sat down and grinned patronisingly as they saw the batteries galloping to advance position to shell the retreat, and they really laughed as the cavalry swept tumultuously forward.

The Twelfth had no more concern with the battle. They had won it, and the subsequent proceedings were only amusing.

There was a call from the flank, and the men wearily adjusted themselves as General Richie, stern and grim as a Roman, looked with his straight glance at a hammered and thin and dirty line of figures, which was His Majesty's Twelfth Regiment of the Line. When opposite old Colonel Sponge, a podgy figure standing at attention, the general's face set in still more grim and stern lines. He took off his helmet. "Kim up, the Kickers!" said he. He replaced his helmet and rode off. Down the cheeks of the little fat colonel rolled tears. He stood like a stone for a long moment, and wheeled in supreme wrath upon his surprised adjutant. "Delahaye, you damned fool, don't stand there staring like a monkey! Go, tell young Lean I want to see him." The adjutant jumped as if he were on springs, and went after Lean. That young officer presented himself directly, his face covered with disgraceful smudges, and he had also torn his breeches. He had never seen the colonel in such a rage. "Lean, you young whelp! you—you're a good boy." And even as the general had turned away from the colonel, the colonel turned away from the lieutenant.

# THE SHRAPNEL OF THEIR FRIENDS

From over the knolls came the tiny sound of a cavalry bugle singing out the recall, and later, detached parties of His Majesty's 2nd Hussars came trotting back to where the Spitzbergen infantry sat complacently on the captured Rostina position. The horsemen were well pleased, and they told how they had ridden thrice through the helterskelter of the fleeing enemy. They had ultimately been checked by the great truth, and when a good enemy runs away in daylight he sooner or later finds a place where he fetches up with a jolt, and turns face the pursuit—notably if it is a cavalry pursuit. The Hussars had discreetly withdrawn, displaying no foolish pride of corps at that time.

There was a general admission that the Kicking Twelfth had taken the chief honours of the day, but the artillery added that if the guns had not shelled so accurately the Twelfth's charge could not have been made so successfully, and the three other regiments of infantry, of course, did not conceal their feelings, that their attack on the enemy's left had withdrawn many rifles that would have been pelting at the Twelfth. The cavalry simply said that but for them the victory would not have been complete.

Corps' prides met each other face to face at every step, but the Kickers smiled easily and indulgently. A few recruits bragged, but they bragged because they were recruits. The older men did not wish it to appear that they were surprised and rejoicing at the performance of the regiment. If they were congratulated they simply smirked, suggesting that the ability of the Twelfth had been long known to them, and that the charge had been a little thing, you know, just turned off in the way of an afternoon's work.

Major-General Richie encamped his troops on the position which they had from the enemy. Old Colonel Sponge of the Twelfth redistributed his officers, and the losses had been so great that Timothy Lean got command of a company. It was not much of a company. Fifty-three smudged and sweating men faced their new commander. The company had gone into action with a strength of eighty-six. The heart of Timothy Lean beat high with pride. He intended to be some day a general, and if he ever became a general, that moment of promotion was not equal in joy to the moment when he looked at his new possession of fifty-three vagabonds. He scanned the faces, and recognised with satisfaction one old sergeant and two bright young corporals. "Now," said he to himself, "I have here a snug little body of men with which I can do something." In him burned the usual fierce fire to make them the best company in the regiment. He had adopted them; they were his men. "I will do what I can for you," he said. "Do you the same for me."

The Twelfth bivouacked on the ridge. Little fires were built, and there appeared among the men innumerable blackened tin cups, which were so treasured that a faint suspicion in connection with the loss of one could bring on the grimmest of fights. Meantime certain of the privates silently readjusted their kits as their names were called out by the sergeants. These were the men condemned to picket duty after a hard day of marching and fighting. The dusk came slowly, and the colour of the countless fires, spotting the ridge and the plain, grew in the falling darkness. Far-away pickets fired at something.

One by one the men's heads were lowered to the earth until the ridge was marked by two long shadowy rows of men. Here and there an officer satmusing in his dark cloak with a ray of a weakening fire gleaming on his sword-hilt. From the plain there came at times the sound of battery horses moving restlessly at their tethers, and one could imagine he heard the throaty, grumbling curse of the drivers. The moon died swiftly through flying light clouds. Far-away pickets fired at something.

In the morning the infantry and guns breakfasted to the music of a racket between the cavalry and the enemy, which was taking place some miles up the valley.

The ambitious Hussars had apparently stirred some kind of a hornet's nest, and they were having a good fight with no officious friends near enough to interfere. The remainder of the army looked toward the fight musingly over the tops of tin cups. In time the column crawled lazily forward to see.

The Twelfth, as it crawled, saw a regiment deploy to the right, and saw a battery dash to take position. The cavalry jingled back grinning with pride and expecting to be greatly admired. Presently the Twelfth was bidden to take seat by the roadside and await its turn. Instantly the wise men—and there were more than three—came out of the east and announced that they had divined the whole plan. The Kicking Twelfth was to be held in reserve until the critical moment of the fight, and then they were to be sent forward to win a victory. In corroboration, they pointed to the fact that the general in command was sticking close to them, in order, they said, to give the word quickly at the proper moment. And in truth, on a small hill to the right, Major-General Richie sat on his horse and used his glasses, while back of him his staff and the orderlies bestrode their champing, dancing mounts.

It is always good to look hard at a general, and the Kickers were transfixed with interest. The wise men again came out of the east and told what was inside the Richie head, but even the wise men wondered what was inside the Richie head.

Suddenly an exciting thing happened. To the left and ahead was a pounding Spitzbergen battery, and a toy suddenly appeared on the slope behind the guns. The toy was a man with a flag—the flag was white save for a square of red in the centre. And this toy began to wig-wag wag-wig, and it spoke to General Richie under the authority of the captain of the battery. It said: "The 88th are being driven on my centre and right."

Now, when the Kicking Twelfth had left Spitzbergen there was an average of six signalmen in each company. A proportion of these signallers had been destroyed in the first engagement, but enough remained so that the Kicking Twelfth read, as a unit, the news of the 88th. The word ran quickly. "The 88th are being driven on my centre and right."

Richie rode to where Colonel Sponge sat aloft on his big horse, and a moment later a cry ran along the column: "Kim up, the Kickers." A large number of the men were already in the road, hitching and twisting at their belts and packs. The Kickers moved forward.

They deployed and passed in a straggling line through the battery, and to the left and right of it. The gunners called out to them carefully, telling them not to be afraid.

The scene before them was startling. They were facing a country cut up by many steep-sided ravines, and over the resultant hills were retreating little squads of the 88th. The Twelfth laughed in its exultation. The men could now tell by the volume of fire that the 88th were retreating for reasons which were not sufficiently expressed in the noise of the Rostina shooting. Held together by the bugle, the Kickers swarmed up the first hill and laid on the crest. Parties of the 88th went through their lines, and the Twelfth told them coarsely its several opinions. The sights were clicked up to 600 yards, and, with a crashing volley, the regiment entered its second battle.

A thousand yards away on the right the cavalry and a regiment of infantry were creeping onward. Sponge decided not to be backward, and the bugle told the Twelfth to go ahead once more. The Twelfth charged, followed by a rabble of rallied men of the 88th, who were crying aloud that it had been all a mistake.

A charge in these days is not a running match. Those splendid pictures of levelled bayonets, dashing at headlong pace towards the closed ranks of the enemy are absurd as soon as they are mistaken for the actuality of the present. In these days charges are likely to cover at least the half of a mile, and to go at the pace exhibited in the pictures a man would be obliged to have a little steam engine inside of him.

The charge of the Kicking Twelfth somewhat resembled the advance of a great crowd of beaters who, for some reason, passionately desired to start the game. Men stumbled; men fell; men swore; there were cries: "This way!" "Come this way!" "Don't go that way!" "You can't get up that way!" Over the rocks the Twelfth scrambled, red in the face, sweating and angry. Soldiers fell because they were struck by bullets, and because they had not an ounce of strength left in them. Colonel Sponge, with a face like a red cushion, was being dragged windless up the steeps by devoted and athletic men. Three of the older captains lay afar back, and swearing with their eyes because their tongues were temporarily out of service.

And yet-and-yet, the speed of the charge was slow. From the position of the battery, it looked as if the Kickers were taking a walk over some extremely difficult country.

The regiment ascended a superior height, and found trenches and dead men. They took seat with the dead, satisfied with this company until they could get their wind. For thirty minutes purple-faced stragglers rejoined from the rear. Colonel Sponge looked behind him, and saw that Richie, with his staff, had approached by another route, and had evidently been near enough to see the full extent of the Kickers' exertions. Presently Richie began to pick a way for his horse towards the captured position. He disappeared in a gully between two hills.

Now it came to pass that a Spitzbergen battery on the far right took occasion to mistake the identity of the Kicking Twelfth, and the captain of these guns, not having anything to occupy him in front, directed his six 3·2's upon the ridge where the tired Kickers lay side by side with the Rostina dead. A shrapnel came swinging over the Kickers, seething and fuming. It burst directly over the trenches, and the shrapnel, of course, scattered forward, hurting nobody. But a man screamed out to his officer: "By God, sir, that is one of our own batteries!" The whole line quivered with fright. Five more shells streaked overhead, and one flungits hail into the middle of the 3rd battalion's line, and the Kicking Twelfth shuddered to the very centre of its heart, and arose, like one man, and fled.

Colonel Sponge, fighting, frothing at the month, dealing blows with his fist right and left, found himself confronting a fury on horseback. Richie was as pale as death, and his eyes sent out sparks. "What does this conduct mean?" he flashed out between his fastened teeth.

Sponge could only gurgle: "The battery—the battery—the battery!"

"The battery?" cried Richie, in a voice which sounded like pistol shots. "Are you afraid of the guns you almost took yesterday? Go back there, you white-livered cowards! You swine! You dogs! Curs! Curs! Curs! Go back there!"

Most of the men halted and crouched under the lashing tongue of their maddened general. But one man found desperate speech, and yelled: "General, it is our own battery that is firing on us!"

Many say that the General's face tightened until it looked like a mask. The Kicking Twelfth retired to a comfortable place, where they were only under the fire of the Rostina artillery. The men saw a staff officer riding over the obstructions in a manner calculated to break his neck directly.

The Kickers were aggrieved, but the heart of the colonel was cut in twain. He even babbled to his major, talking like a man who is about to die of simple rage. "Did you hear what he said to me? Did you hear what he called us? *Did you hear what he called us?*"

The majors searched their minds for words to heal a deep wound.

The Twelfth received orders to go into camp upon the hill where they had been insulted. Old Sponge looked as if he were about to knock the aide out of the saddle, but he saluted, and took the regiment back to the temporary companionship of the Rostina dead.

Major-General Richie never apologised to Colonel Sponge. When you are a commanding officer you do not adopt the custom of apologising for the wrong done to your subordinates. You ride away; and they understand, and are confident of the restitution to honour. Richie never opened his stern, young lips to Sponge in reference to the scene near the hill of the Rostina dead, but in time there was a general order No. 20, which spoke definitely of the gallantry of His Majesty's 12th regiment of the line and its colonel. In the end Sponge was given a high decoration, because he had been badly used by Richie on that day. Richie knew that it is hard for men to withstand the shrapnel of their friends.

A few days later the Kickers, marching in column on the road, came upon their friend the battery, halted in a field; and they addressed the battery, and the captain of the battery blanched to the tips of his ears. But the men of the battery told the Kickers to go to the devil—frankly, freely, placidly, told the Kickers to go to the devil.

And this story proves that it is sometimes better to be a private.

# THE SURRENDER OF FORTY FORT

Immediately after the battle of 3rd July, my mother said, "We had best take the children and go into the Fort."

But my father replied, "I will not go. I will not leave my property. All that I have in the world is here, and if the savages destroy it they may as well destroy me also."

My mother said no other word. Our household was ever given to stern silence, and such was my training that it did not occur to me to reflect that if my father cared for his property it was not my property, and I was entitled to care somewhat for my life.

Colonel Denison was true to the word which he had passed to me at the Fort before the battle. He sent a messenger to my father, and this messenger stood in the middle of our living-room and spake with a clear, indifferent voice. "Colonel Denison bids me come here and say that John Bennet is a wicked man, and the blood of his own children will be upon his head." As usual, my father said nothing. After the messenger had gone, he remained silent for hours in his chair by the fire, and this stillness was so impressive to his family that even my mother walked on tip-toe as she went about her work. After this long time my father said, "Mary!"

Mother halted and looked at him. Father spoke slowly, and as if every word was wrested from him with violent pangs. "Mary, you take the girls and go to the Fort. I and Solomon and Andrew will go over the mountain to Stroudsberg."

Immediately my mother called us all to set about packing such things as could be taken to the Fort. And by nightfall we had seen them within its pallisade, and my father, myself, and my little brother Andrew, who was only eleven years old, were off over the hills on a long march to the Delaware settlements. Father and I had our rifles, but we seldom dared to fire them, because of the roving bands of Indians. We lived as well as we could on blackberries and raspberries. For the most part, poor little Andrew rode first on the back of my father and then on my back. He was a good little man, and only cried when he would wake in the dead of night very cold and very hungry. Then my father would wrap him in an old grey coat that was so famous in the Wyoming country that there was not even an Indian who did not know of it. But this act he did without any direct display of tenderness, for the fear, I suppose, that he would weaken little Andrew's growing manhood. Now, in these days of safety, and even luxury, I often marvel at the iron spirit of the people of my young days. My father, without his coat and no doubt very cold, would then sometimes begin to pray to his God in the wilderness, but in low voice, because of the Indians. It was July, but even July nights are cold in the pine mountains, breathing a chill which goes straight to the bones.

But it is not my intention to give in this section the ordinary adventures of the masculine part of my family. As a matter of fact, my mother and the girls were undergoing in Forty Fort trials which made as nothing the happenings on our journey, which ended in safety.

My mother and her small flock were no sooner established in the crude quarters within the pallisade than negotiations were opened between Colonel Denison and Colonel Zebulon Butler on the American side, and "Indian Butler" on the British side, for the capitulation of the Fort with such arms and military stores as it contained, the lives of the settlers to be strictly preserved. But "Indian Butler" did not seem to feel free to promise safety for the lives of the Continental Butler and the pathetic little fragment of the regular troops. These men always fought so well against the Indians that whenever the Indians could get them at their mercy there was small chances of anything but a massacre. So every regular left before the surrender; and I fancy that Colonel Zebulon Butler considered himself a much-abused man, for if we had left ourselves entirely under his direction there is no doubt but what we could have saved the valley. He had taken us out on 3rd July because our militia officers had almost threatened him. In the end he had said, "Very well, I can go as far as any of you." I was always on Butler's side of the argument, but owing to the singular arrangement of circumstances, my opinion at the age of sixteen counted upon neither the one side nor the other.

The Fort was left in charge of Colonel Denison. He had stipulated before the surrender that no Indians should be allowed to enter the stockade and molest these poor families of women whose fathers and brothers were either dead or fled over the mountains, unless their physical debility had been such that they were able neither to get killed in the battle nor to take the long trail to the Delaware. Of course, this excepts those men who were with Washington.

For several days the Indians, obedient to the British officers, kept out of the Fort, but soon they began to enter in small bands and went sniffing and poking in every corner to find plunder. Our people had hidden everything as well as they were able, and for a period little was stolen. My mother told me that the first thing of importance to go was Colonel Denison's hunting shirt, made of "fine forty" linen. It had a double cape, and was fringed about the cape and about the wristbands. Colonel Denison at the time was in my mother's cabin. An Indian entered, and, rolling a thieving eye about the place, sighted first of all the remarkable shirt which Colonel Denison was wearing. He seized the shirt and began to tug, while the Colonel backed away, tugging and protesting at the same time. The women folk saw at once that the Colonel would be tomahawked if he did not give up his shirt, and they begged him to do it. He finally elected not to be tomahawked, and came out of his shirt. While my mother unbuttoned the wristbands, the Colonel cleverly dropped into the lap of a certain Polly Thornton a large packet of Continental bills, and his money was thus saved for the settlers.

Colonel Denison had several stormy interviews with "Indian Butler," and the British commander finally ended in frankly declaring that he could do nothing with the Indians at all. They were beyond control, and the defenceless people in the Fort would have to take the consequence. I do not mean that Colonel Denison was trying to recover his shirt; I mean that he was objecting to a situation which was now almost unendurable. I wish to record also that the Colonel lost a large beaver hat. In both cases he willed to be tomahawked and killed rather than suffer the indignity, but mother prevailed over him. I must confess to this discreet age that my mother engaged in fisticuffs with a squaw. This squaw came into the cabin, and, without preliminary discussion, attempted to drag from my mother the petticoat she was wearing. My mother forgot the fine advice she had given to Colonel Denison. She proceeded to beat the squaw out of the cabin, and although the squaw appealed to some warriors who were standing without the warriors only laughed, and my mother kept her petticoat.

The Indians took the feather beds of the people, and, ripping them open, flung the feathers broadcast. Then they stuffed these sacks full of plunder, and flung them across the backs of such of the settlers' horses as they had been able to find. In the old days my mother had had a side saddle, of which she was very proud when she rode to meeting on it. She had also a brilliant scarlet cloak, which every lady had in those days, and which I can remember as one of the admirations of my childhood. One day my mother had the satisfaction of seeing a squaw ride off from the Fort with this prize saddle reversed on a small nag, and with the proud squaw thus mounted wearing the scarlet cloak, also reversed. My sister Martha told me afterwards that they laughed, even in their misfortunes. A little later they had the satisfaction of seeing the smoke from our house and barn arising over the tops of the trees.

When the Indians first began their pillaging, an old Mr. Sutton, who occupied a cabin near my mother's cabin, anticipated them by donning all his best clothes. He had had a theory that the Americans would be free to retain the clothes that they wore. And his best happened to be a suit of Quaker grey, from beaver to boots, in which he had been married. Not long afterwards my mother and my sisters saw passing the door an Indian arrayed in Quaker grey, from beaver to boots. The only odd thing which impressed them was that the Indian had appended to the dress a long string of Yankee scalps. Sutton was a good Quaker, and if he had been wearing the suit there would have been no string of scalps.

They were, in fact, badgered, insulted, robbed by the Indians so openly that the British officers would not come into the Fort at all. They stayed in their camp, affecting to be ignorant of what was happening. It was about all they could do. The Indians had only one idea of war, and it was impossible to reason with them when they were flushed with victory and stolen rum.

The hand of fate fell heavily upon one rogue whose ambition it was to drink everything that the Fort contained. One day he inadvertently came upon a bottle of spirits of camphor, and in a few hours he was dead.

But it was known that General Washington contemplated sending a strong expedition into the valley, to clear it of the invaders and thrash them. Soon there were no enemies in the country save small roving parties of Indians, who prevented work in the fields and burned whatever cabins that earlier torches had missed.

The first large party to come into the valley was composed mainly of Captain Spaulding's company of regulars, and at its head rode Colonel Zebulon Butler. My father, myself, and little Andrew returned with this party to set to work immediately to build out of nothing a prosperity similar to that which had vanished in the smoke.

# "OL' BENNET" AND THE INDIANS

My father was so well known of the Indians that, as I was saying, his old grey coat was a sign through the northern country. I know of no reason for this save that he was honest and obstreperously minded his own affairs, and could fling a tomahawk better than the best Indian. I will not declare upon how hard it is for a man to be honest and to mind his own affairs, but I fully know that it is hard to throw a tomahawk as my father threw it, straighter than a bullet from a duelling pistol. He had always dealt fairly with the Indians, and I cannot tell why they paled him so bitterly, unless it was that when an Indian went foolishly drunk my father would deplore it with his foot, if it so happened that the drunkenness was done in our cabin. It is true to say that when the war came, a singular large number of kicked Indians journeyed from the Canadas to re-visit with torch and knife the scenes of the kicking.

If people had thoroughly known my father he would have had no enemies. He was the best of men. He had a code of behaviour for himself, and for the whole world as well. If people wished his good opinion they only had to do exactly as he did, and to have his views. I remember that once my sister Martha made me a waistcoat of rabbits' skins, and generally it was considered a great ornament. But one day my father espied me in it, and commanded me to remove it for ever. Its appearance was indecent, he said, and such a garment tainted the soul of him who wore it. In the ensuing fortnight a poor pedlar arrived from the Delaware, who had suffered great misfortunes in the snows. My father fed him and warmed him, and when he gratefully departed, gave him the rabbits' skin waistcoat, and the poor man went off clothed indecently in a garment that would taint his soul. Afterwards, in a daring mood, I asked my father why he had so cursed this pedlar, and he recommended that I should study my Bible more closely, and there read that my own devious ways should be mended before I sought to judge the enlightened acts of my elders. He set me to ploughing the upper twelve acres, and I was hardly allowed to loose my grip of the plough handles until every furrow was drawn.

The Indians called my father "Ol' Bennet," and he was known broadcast as a man whose doom was sealed when the redskins caught him. As I have said, the feeling is inexplicable to me. But Indians who had been ill-used and maltreated by downright ruffians, against whom revenge could with a kind of propriety be direct-ed—many of these Indians avowedly gave up a genuine wrong in order to direct a fuller attention to the getting of my father's scalp. This most unfair disposition of the Indians was a great, deep anxiety to all of us up to the time when General Sullivan and his avenging army marched through the valley and swept our tormentors afar.

And yet great calamities could happen in our valley even after the coming and passing of General Sullivan. We were partly mistaken in our gladness. The British force of Loyalists and Indians met Sullivan in one battle, and finding themselves over-matched and beaten, they scattered in all directions. The Loyalists, for the most part, went home, but the Indians cleverly broke up into small bands, and General Sullivan's army had no sooner marched beyond the Wyoming Valley than some of these small bands were back into the valley plundering outlying cabins and shooting people from the thickets and woods that bordered the fields.

General Sullivan had left a garrison at Wilkesbarre, and at this time we lived in its strong shadow. It was too formidable for the Indians to attack, and it could protect all who valued protection enough to remain under its wings, but it could do little against the flying small bands. My father chafed in the shelter of the garrison. His best lands lay beyond Forty Fort, and he wanted to be at his ploughing. He made several brief references to his ploughing that led us to believe that his ploughing was the fundamental principle of life. None of us saw any means of contending him. My sister Martha began to weep, but it no more mattered than if she had began to laugh. My mother said nothing. Aye, my wonderful mother said nothing. My father said he would go plough some of the land above Forty Fort. Immediately this was with us some sort of a law. It was like a rain, or a wind, or a drought.

He went, of course. My young brother Andrew went with him, and he took the new span of oxen and a horse. They began to plough a meadow which lay in a bend of the river above Forty Fort. Andrew rode the horse hitched ahead of the oxen. At a certain thicket the horse shied so that little Andrew was almost thrown down. My father seemed to have begun a period of apprehension at this time, but it was of no service. Four Indians suddenly appeared out of the thicket. Swiftly, and in silence, they pounced with tomahawk, rifle, and knife upon my father and my brother, and in a moment they were captives of the redskins—that fate whose very phrasing was a thrill to the heart of every colonist. It spelled death, or that horrible simple absence, vacancy, mystery, which is harder than death.

As for us, he had told my mother that if he and Andrew were not returned at sundown she might construe a calamity. So at sundown we gave the news to the Fort, and directly we heard the alarm gun booming out across the dusk like a salute to the death of my father, a solemn, final declaration. At the sound of this gun my sisters all began newly to weep. It simply defined our misfortune. In the morning a party was sent out, which came upon the deserted plough, the oxen calmly munching, and the horse still excited and affrighted. The soldiers found the trail of four Indians. They followed the trail some distance over the mountains, but the redskins with their captives had a long start, and pursuit was but useless. The result of this expedition was that we knew at least that father and Andrew had not been massacred immediately. But in those days this was a most meagre consolation. It was better to wish them well dead.

My father and Andrew were hurried over the hills at a terrible pace by the four Indians. Andrew told me afterwards that he could think sometimes that he was dreaming of being carried off by goblins. The redskins said no word, and their mocassined feet made no sound. They were like evil spirits. But it was as he caught glimpses of father's pale face, every wrinkle in it deepened and hardened, that Andrew saw everything in its light. And Andrew was but thirteen years old. It is a tender age at which to be burned at the stake.

In time the party came upon two more Indians, who had as a prisoner a man named Lebbeus Hammond. He had left Wilkesbarre in search of a strayed horse. He was riding the animal back to the Fort when the Indians caught him. He and my father knew each other well, and their greeting was like them.

"What! Hammond! You here?"

"Yes, I'm here."

As the march was resumed, the principal Indian bestrode Hammond's horse, but the horse was very high-nerved and scared, and the bridle was only a temporary one made from hickory withes. There was no saddle. And so finally the principal Indian came off with a crash, alighting with exceeding severity upon his head. When he got upon his feet he was in such a rage that the three captives thought to see him dash his tomahawk into the skull of the trembling horse, and, indeed, his arm was raised for the blow, but suddenly he thought better of it. He had been touched by a real point of Indian inspiration. The party was passing a swamp at the time, so he mired the horse almost up to its eyes, and left it to the long death.

I had said that my father was well known of the Indians, and yet I have to announce that none of his six captors knew him. To them he was a complete stranger, for upon camping the first night they left my father unbound. If they had had any idea that he was "Ol' Bennet" they would never have left him unbound. He suggested to Hammond that they try to escape that night, but Hammond seemed not to care to try it yet.

In time they met a party of over forty Indians, commanded by a Loyalist. In that band there were many who knew my father. They cried out with rejoicing when they perceived him. "Ha!" they shouted, "Ol' Bennet!" They danced about him, making gestures expressive of the torture. Later in the day my father accidentally pulled a button from his coat, and an Indian took it from him.

My father asked to be allowed to have it again, for he was a very careful man, and in those days all good husbands were trained to bring home the loose buttons. The Indians laughed, and explained that a man who was to die at Wyallusing—one day's march—need not be particular about a button.

The three prisoners were now sent off in care of seven Indians, while the Loyalist took the remainder of his men down the valley to further harass the settlers. The seven Indians were now very careful of my father, allowing him scarce a wink. Their tomahawks came up at the slightest sign. At the camp that night they bade the prisoners lie down, and then placed poles across them. An Indian lay upon either end of these poles. My father managed, however, to let Hammond know that he was determined to make an attempt to escape. There was only one night between him and the stake, and he was resolved to make what use he could of it. Hammond seems to have been dubious from the start, but the men of that time were not daunted by broad risks. In his opinion the rising would be a failure, but this did not prevent him from agreeing to rise with his friend. My brother Andrew was not considered at all. No one asked him if he wanted to rise against the Indians. He was only a boy, and supposed to obey his elders. So, as none asked his views, he kept them to himself; but I wager you he listened, all ears, to the furtive consultations, consultations which were mere casual phrases at times, and at other times swift, brief sentences shot out in a whisper.

The band of seven Indians relaxed in vigilance as they approached their own country, and on the last night from Wyallusing the Indian part of the camp seemed much inclined to take deep slumber after the long and rapid journey. The prisoners were held to the ground by poles as on the previous night, and then the Indians pulled their blankets over their heads and passed into heavy sleep. One old warrior sat by the fire as guard, but he seems to have been a singularly inefficient man, for he was continuously drowsing, and if the captives could have got rid of the poles across their chests and legs they would have made their flight sooner.

The camp was on a mountain side amid a forest of lofty pines. The night was very cold, and the blasts of wind swept down upon the crackling, resinous fire. A few stars peeped through the feathery pine branches. Deep in some gulch could be heard the roar of a mountain stream. At one o'clock in the morning three of the Indians arose, and, releasing the prisoners, commanded them to mend the fire. The prisoners brought dead pine branches; the ancient warrior on watch sleepily picked away with his knife at the deer's head which he had roasted; the other Indians retired again to their blankets, perhaps each depending upon the other for the exercise of precautions. It was a tremendously slack business; the Indians were feeling security because they knew that the prisoners were too wise to try to run away.

The warrior on watch mumbled placidly to himself as he picked at the deer's head. Then he drowsed again, just the short nap of a man who had been up too long. My father stepped quickly to a spear, and backed away from the Indian; then he drove it straight through his chest. The Indian raised himself spasmodically, and then collapsed into that camp fire which the captives had made burn so brilliantly, and as he fell he screamed. Instantly his blanket, his hair, he himself began to burn, and over him was my father tugging frantically to get the spear out again.

My father did not recover the spear. It had so gone through the old warrior that it could not readily be withdrawn, and my father left it.

The scream of the watchman instantly aroused the other warriors, who, as they scrambled in their blankets, found over them a terrible white-lipped creature with an axe—an axe, the most appallingly brutal of weapons. Hammond buried his weapon in the head of the leader of the Indians even as the man gave out his first great cry. The second blowmissed an agile warrior's head, but caught him in the nape of the neck, and he swung, to bury his face in the red-hot ashes at the edge of the fire.

Meanwhile my brother Andrew had been gallantly snapping empty guns. In fact he snapped three empty guns at the Indians, who were in the purest panic. He did not snap the fourth gun, but took it by the barrel, and, seeing a warrior rush past him, he cracked his skull with the clubbed weapon. He told me, however, that his snapping of the empty guns was very effective, because it made the Indians jump and dodge.

Well, this slaughter continued in the red glare of the fire on the lonely mountain side until two shrieking creatures ran off through the trees, but even then my father hurled a tomahawk with all his strength. It struck one of the fleeing Indians on the shoulder. His blanket dropped from him, and he ran on practically naked.

The three whites looked at each other, breathing deeply. Their work was plain to them in the five dead and dying Indians underfoot. They hastily gathered weapons and mocassins, and in six minutes from the time when my father had hurled the spear through the Indian sentinel they had started to make their way back to the settlements, leaving the camp fire to burn out its short career alone amid the dead.

# THE BATTLE OF FORTY FORT

The Congress, sitting at Philadelphia, had voted our Wyoming country two companies of infantry for its protection against the Indians, with the single provision that we raise the men and arm them ourselves. This was not too brave a gift, but no one could blame the poor Congress, and indeed one could wonder that they found occasion to think of us at all, since at the time every gentleman of them had his coat-tails gathered high in his hands in readiness for flight to Baltimore. But our two companies of foot were no sooner drilled, equipped, and in readiness to defend the colony when they were ordered off down to the Jerseys to join General Washington. So it can be seen what service Congress did us in the way of protection. Thus the Wyoming Valley, sixty miles deep in the wilderness, held its log-houses full of little besides mothers, maids, and children. To the clamour against this situation the badgered Congress could only reply by the issue of another generous order, directing that one full company of foot be raised in the town of Westmoreland for the defence of said town, and that the said company find their own arms, ammunition, and blankets. Even people with our sense of humour could not laugh at this joke.

When the first two companies were forming, I had thought to join one, but my father forbade me, saying that I was too young, although I was full sixteen, tall, and very strong. So it turned out that I was not off fighting with Washington's army when Butler with his rangers and Indians raided Wyoming. Perhaps I was in the better place to do my duty, if I could.

When wandering Indians visited the settlements, their drunkenness and insolence were extreme, but the few white men remained calm, and often enough pretended oblivion to insults which, because of their wives and families, they dared not attempt to avenge. In my own family, my father's imperturbability was scarce superior to my mother's coolness, and such was our faith in them that we twelve children also seemed to be fearless. Neighbour after neighbour came to my father in despair of the defenceless condition of the valley, declaring that they were about to leave everything and flee over the mountains to Stroudsberg. My father always wished them God-speed and said no more. If they urged him to fly also, he usually walked away from them.

Finally there came a time when all the Indians vanished. We rather would have had them tipsy and impudent in the settlements; we knew what their disappearance portended. It was the serious sign. Too soon the news came that "Indian Butler" was on his way.

The valley was vastly excited. People with their smaller possessions flocked into the block-houses, and militia officers rode everywhere to rally every man. A small force of Continentals—regulars of the line—had joined our people, and the little army was now under the command of a Continental officer, Major Zebulon Butler.

I had thought that with all this hubbub of an impending life and death struggle in the valley that my father would allow the work of our farm to slacken. But in this I was notably mistaken. The milking and the feeding and the work in the fields went on as if there never had been an Indian south of the Canadas. My mother and my sisters continued to cook, to wash, to churn, to spin, to dye, to mend, to make soap, to make maple sugar. Just before the break of each day, my younger brother Andrew and myself tumbled out for some eighteen hours' work, and woe to us if we departed the length of a dog's tail from the laws which our father had laid down. It was a life with which I was familiar, but it did seem to me that with the Indians almost upon us he might have allowed me, at least, to go to the Fort and see our men drilling.

But one morning we aroused as usual at his call at the foot of the ladder, and, dressing more quickly than Andrew, I climbed down from the loft to find my father seated by a blazing fire reading by its light in his Bible.

"Son," said he.

"Yes, father?"

"Go and fight."

Without a word more I made hasty preparation. It was the first time in my life that I had a feeling that my father would change his mind. So strong was this fear that I did not even risk a good-bye to my mother and sisters. At the end of the clearing I looked back. The door of the house was open, and in the blazing light of the fire I saw my father seated as I had left him.

At Forty Fort I found between three and four hundred under arms, while the stockade itself was crowded with old men, and women and children. Many of my acquaintances welcomed me; indeed, I seemed to know everybody save a number of the Continental officers. Colonel Zebulon Butler was in chief command, while directly under him was Colonel Denison, a man of the valley, and much respected. Colonel Denison asked news of my father, whose temper he well knew. He said to me—"If God spares Nathan Denison I shall tell that obstinate old fool my true opinion of him. He will get himself and all his family butchered and scalped."

I joined Captain Bidlack's company for the reason that a number of my friends were in it. Every morning we were paraded and drilled in the open ground before the Fort, and I learned to present arms and to keep my heels together, although to this day I have never been able to see any point to these accomplishments, and there was very little of the presenting of arms or of the keeping together of heels in the battle which followed these drills. I may say truly that I would now be much more grateful to Captain Bidlack if he had taught us to run like a wild horse.

There was considerable friction between the officers of our militia and the Continental officers. I believe the Continental officers had stated themselves as being in favour of a cautious policy, whereas the men of the valley were almost unanimous in their desire to meet "Indian Butler" more than half way. They knew the country, they said, and they knew the Indians, and they deduced that the proper plan was to march forth and attack the British force near the head of the valley. Some of the more hot-headed ones rather openly taunted the Continentals, but these veterans of Washington's army remained silent and composed amid more or less wildness of talk. My own concealed opinions were that, although our people were brave and determined, they had much better allow the Continental officers to manage the valley's affairs.

At the end of June, we heard the news that Colonel John Butler, with some four hundred British and Colonial troops, which he called the Rangers, and with about five hundred Indians, had entered the valley at its head and taken Fort Wintermoot after an opposition of a perfunctory character. I could present arms very well, but I do not think that I could yet keep my heels together. But "Indian Butler" was marching upon us, and even Captain Bidlack refrained from being annoyed at my refractory heels.

The officers held councils of war, but in truth both fort and camp rang with a discussion in which everybody joined with great vigour and endurance. I may except the Continental officers, who told us what they thought we should do, and then, declaring that there was no more to be said, remained in a silence which I thought was rather grim. The result was that on the 3rd of July our force of about 300 men marched away, amid the roll of drums and the proud career of flags, to meet "Indian Butler" and his two kinds of savages. There yet remains with me a vivid recollection of a close row of faces above the stockade of Forty Fort which viewed our departure with that profound anxiety which only an imminent danger of murder and scalping can produce. I myself was never particularly afraid of the Indians, for to my mind the great and almost the only military virtue of the Indians was that they were silent men in the woods. If they were met squarely on terms approaching equality, they could always be whipped. But it was another matter to a fort filled with women and children and cripples, to whom the coming of the Indians spelled pillage, arson, and massacre. The British sent against us in those days some curious upholders of the honour of the King, and although Indian Butler, who usually led them, afterwards contended that everything was performed with decency and care for the rules, we always found that such of our dead whose bodies we recovered invariably lacked hair on the tops of their heads, and if worse wasn't done to them we wouldn't even use the word mutilate.

Colonel Zebulon Butler rode along the column when we halted once for water. I looked at him eagerly, hoping to read in his face some sign of his opinions. But on the soldierly mask I could read nothing, although I am certain now that he felt that the fools among us were going to get us well beaten. But there was no vacillation in the direction of our march. We went straight until we could hear through the woods the infrequent shots of our leading party at retreating Indian scouts.

Our Colonel Butler then sent forward four of his best officers, who reconnoitered the ground in the enemy's front like so many engineers marking the place for a bastion. Then each of the six companies were told their place in the line. We of Captain Bidlack's company were on the extreme right. Then we formed in line and marched into battle, with me burning with the high resolve to kill Indian Butler and bear his sword into Forty Fort, while at the same time I was much shaken that one of Indian Butler's Indians might interfere with the noble plan. We moved stealthily among the pine trees, and I could not forbear looking constantly to right and left to make certain that everybody was of the same mind about this advance. With our Captain Bidlack was Captain Durkee of the regulars. He was also a valley man, and it seemed that every time I looked behind me I met the calm eye of this officer, and I came to refrain from looking behind me.

Still, I was very anxious to shoot Indians, and if I had doubted my ability in this direction I would have done myself a great injustice, for I could drive a nail to the head with a rifle ball at respectable range. I contend that I was not at all afraid of the enemy, but I much feared that certain of my comrades would change their minds about the expediency of battle on the 3rd July, 1778.

But our company was as steady and straight as a fence. I do not know who first saw dodging figures in the shadows of the trees in our front. The first fire we received, however, was from our flank, where some hidden Indians were yelling and firing, firing and yelling. We did not mind the war-whoops. We had heard too many drunken Indians in the settlements before the war. They wounded the lieutenant of the company next to ours, and a moment later they killed Captain Durkee. But we were steadily advancing and firing regular volleys into the shifting frieze of figures before us. The Indians gave their cries as if the imps of Hades had given tongue to their emotions. They fell back before us so rapidly and so cleverly that one had to watch his chance as the Indians sped from tree to tree. I had a sudden burst of rapture that they were beaten, and this was accentuated when I stepped over the body of an Indian whose forehead had a hole in it as squarely in the middle as if the location had been previously surveyed. In short, we were doing extremely well.

Soon we began to see the slower figures of white men through the trees, and it is only honest to say that they were easier to shoot. I myself caught sight of a fine officer in a uniform that seemed of green and buff. His sword-belt was fastened by a great shining brass plate, and, no longer feeling the elegancies of marksmanship, I fired at the brass plate. Such was the conformation of the ground between us that he disappeared as if he had sunk in the sea. We, all of us, were loading behind the trees and then charging ahead with fullest confidence.

But suddenly from our own left came wild cries from our men, while at the same time the yells of Indians redoubled in that direction. Our rush checked itself instinctively. The cries rolled toward us. Once I heard a word that sounded like "Quarte." Then, to be truthful, our line wavered. I heard Captain Bidlack give an angry and despairing shout, and I think he was killed before he finished it.

In a word, our left wing had gone to pieces. It was in complete rout. I know not the truth of the matter; but it seems that Colonel Denison had given an order which was misinterpreted for the order to retreat. At any rate, there can be no doubt of how fast the left wing ran away.

We ran away too. The company on our immediate left was the company of regulars, and I remember some red-faced and powder-stained men bellowing at me contemptuously. That company stayed, and, for the most part, died. I don't know what they mustered when we left the Fort, but from the battle eleven worn and ragged men emerged. In my running was wisdom. The country was suddenly full of fleet Indians, upon us with the tomahawk. Behind me as I ran I could hear the screams of men cleaved to the earth. I think the first things that most of us discarded were our rifles. Afterward, upon serious reflection, I could not recall where I gave my rifle to the grass.

I ran for the river. I saw some of our own men running ahead of me and I envied them. My point of contact with the river was the top of a high bank. But I did not hesitate to leap for the water with all my ounces of muscle. I struck out strongly for the other shore. I expected to be shot in the water. Up stream, and down stream, I could hear the crack of rifles, but none of the enemy seemed to be paying direct heed to me. I swam so well that I was soon able to put my feet on the slippery round stones and wade. When I reached a certain sandy beach, I lay down and puffed and blew my exhaustion. I watched the scene on the river. Indians appeared in groups on the opposite bank, firing at various heads of my comrades, who, like me, had chosen the Susquehanna as their refuge. I saw more than one hand fling up and the head turn sideways and sink.

I set out for home. I set out for home in that perfect spirit of dependence which I had always felt toward my father and my mother. When I arrived I found nobody in the living room but my father seated in his great chair and reading his Bible, even as I had left him.

The whole shame of the business came upon me suddenly. "Father," I choked out, "we have been beaten."

"Aye," said he, "I expected it."

# STORIES TOLD BY AN ARTIST IN NEW YORK

### *A Tale about How "Great Grief" got His Holiday Dinner.*

Wrinkles had been peering into the little dry-goods box that acted as a cupboard.

"There are only two eggs and a half of a loaf of bread left," he announced brutally.

"Heavens!" said Warwickson, from where he lay smoking on the bed. He spoke in his usual dismal voice. By it he had earned his popular name of Great Grief.

Wrinkles was a thrifty soul. A sight of an almost bare cupboard maddened him. Even when he was not hungry, the ghosts of his careful ancestors caused him to rebel against it. He sat down with a virtuous air. "Well, what are we going to do?" he demanded of the others. It is good to be the thrifty man in a crowd of unsuccessful artists, for then you can keep the others from starving peacefully. "What are we going to do?"

"Oh, shut up, Wrinkles," said Grief from the bed. "You make me think."

Little Pennoyer, with head bended afar down, had been busily scratching away at a pen and ink drawing. He looked up from his board to utter his plaintive optimism.

"The *Monthly Amazement* may pay me tomorrow. They ought to. I've waited over three months now. I'm going down there tomorrow, and perhaps I'll get it."

His friends listened to him tolerantly, but at last Wrinkles could not omit a scornful giggle. He was such an old man, almost twenty-eight, and he had seen so many little boys be brave. "Oh, no doubt, Penny, old man." Over on the bed Grief croaked deep down in his throat. Nothing was said for a long time thereafter.

The crash of the New York streets came faintly. Occasionally one could hear the tramp of feet in the intricate corridors of this begrimed building that squatted, slumbering and aged, between two exalted commercial structures that would have had to bend afar down to perceive it. The light snow beat pattering into the window corners, and made vague and grey the vista of chimneys and roofs. Often the wind scurried swiftly and raised a long cry.

Great Grief leaned upon his elbow. "See to the fire, will you, Wrinkles?"

Wrinkles pulled the coal-box out from under the bed and threw open the stove door preparatory to shovelling some fuel. A red glare plunged in the first faint shadow of dusk. Little Pennoyer threw down his pen and tossed his drawing over on the wonderful heap of stuff that hid the table. "It's too dark to work." He lit his pipe and walked about, stretching his shoulders like a man whose labour was valuable.

When dusk came it saddened these youths. The solemnity of darkness always caused them to ponder. "Light the gas, Wrinkles," said Grief.

The flood of orange light showed clearly the dull walls lined with scratches, the tousled bed in one corner, the mass of boxes and trunks in another, the little fierce stove, and the wonderful table. Moreover, there were some wine-coloured draperies flung in some places, and on a shelf, high up, there was a plaster cast dark with dust in the creases. A long stove-pipe wandered off in the wrong direction, and then twined impulsively toward a hole in the wall. There were some extensive cobwebs on the ceilings.

"Well, let's eat," said Grief.

Later, there came a sad knock at the door. Wrinkles, arranging a tin pail on the stove, little Pennoyer busy at slicing the bread, and Great Grief affixing the rubber tube to the gas stove, yelled: "Come in!"

The door opened and Corinson entered dejectedly. His overcoat was very new. Wrinkles flashed an envious glance at it, but almost immediately he cried: "Hello, Corrie, old boy!"

Corinson sat down and felt around among the pipes until he found a good one. Great Grief had fixed the coffee to boil on the gas stove, but he had to watch it closely, for the rubber tube was short, and a chair was balanced on a trunk, and then the gas stove was balanced on the chair. Coffee making was a feat.

"Well," said Grief, with his back turned, "how goes it, Corrie? How's Art, hey?" He fastened a terrible emphasis upon the word.

"Crayon portraits," said Corinson.

"What?" They turned towards him with one movement, as if from a lever connection. Little Pennoyer dropped his knife.

"Crayon portraits," repeated Corinson. He smoked away in profound cynicism. "Fifteen dollars a week or more this time of year, you know." He smiled at them like a man of courage.

Little Pennoyer picked up his knife again. "Well, I'll be blowed," said Wrinkles. Feeling it incumbent upon him to think, he dropped into a chair and began to play serenades on his guitar and watch to see when the water for the eggs would boil. It was a habitual pose.

Great Grief, however, seemed to observe something bitter in the affair. "When did you discover that you couldn't draw?" he said stiffly.

"I haven't discovered it yet," replied Corinson, with a serene air. "I merely discovered that I would rather eat."

"Oh!" said Grief.

"Hand me the eggs, Grief," said Wrinkles. "The water's boiling."

Little Pennoyer burst into the conversation. "We'd ask you to dinner, Corrie, but there's only three of us and there's two eggs. I dropped a piece of bread on the floor, too. I'd shy one."

"That's all right, Penny," said the other; "don't trouble yourself. You artists should never be hospitable. I'm going anyway. I've got to make a call. Well, good night, boys. I've got to make a call. Drop in and see me."

When the door closed upon him, Grief said: "The coffee's done; I hate that fellow. That overcoat cost thirty dollars, if it cost a red. His egotism is so tranquil. It isn't like yours, Wrinkles. He—"

The door opened again and Corinson thrust in his head. "Say, you fellows, you know it's Thanksgiving tomorrow?"

"Well, what of it?" demanded Grief.

Little Pennoyer said: "Yes, I know it is, Corrie, I thought of it this morning."

"Well, come out and have a table d'hote with me tomorrow night. I'll blow you off in good style."

While Wrinkles played an exuberant air on his guitar, little Pennoyer did part of a ballet. They cried ecstatically: "Will we? Well, I guess yes?"

When they were alone again, Grief said: "I'm not going, anyhow. I hate that fellow."

"Oh, fiddle," said Wrinkles. "You're an infernal crank. And besides, where's your dinner coming from tomorrow night if you don't go? Tell me that."

Little Pennoyer said: "Yes, that's so, Grief. Where's your dinner coming from if you don't go?"

Grief said: "Well, I hate him, anyhow."

* * * *

### As to Payment of the Rent.

Little Pennoyer's four dollars could not last for ever. When he received it he and Wrinkles and Great Grief went to a table d'hote. Afterwards little Pennoyer discovered that only two dollars and a half remained. A small magazine away down town had accepted one out of the six drawings that he had taken them, and later had given him four dollars for it. Penny was so disheartened when he saw that his money was not going to last for ever, that even with two dollars and a half in his pockets, he felt much worse than when he was penniless, for at that time he anticipated twenty-four. Wrinkles lectured upon "Finance."

Great Grief said nothing, for it was established that when he received six dollar cheques from comic weeklies he dreamed of renting studios at seventy-five dollars per month, and was likely to go out and buy five dollars' worth of second-hand curtains and plaster casts.

When he had money Penny always hated the cluttered den in the old building. He desired to go out and breathe boastfully like a man. But he obeyed Wrinkles, the elder and the wise, and if you had visited that room about ten o'clock of a morning or about seven of an evening you would have thought that rye bread, frankfurters, and potato salad from Second Avenue were the only foods in the world.

Purple Sanderson lived there too, but then he really ate. He had learned parts of the gasfitter's trade before he came to be such a great artist, and when his opinions disagreed with that of every art manager in New York, he went to see a plumber, a friend of his, for whose opinion he had a great respect. In consequence, he frequented a very great restaurant on Twenty-third Street, and sometimes on Saturday nights he openly scorned his companions.

Purple was a good fellow, Grief said, but one of his singularly bad traits was that he always remembered everything. One night, not long after little Pennoyer's great discovery, Purple came in, and as he was neatly hanging up his coat, said: "Well, the rent will be due in four days."

"Will it?" demanded Penny, astounded. Penny was always astounded when the rent came due. It seemed to him the most extraordinary occurrence.

"Certainly it will," said Purple, with the irritated air of a superior financial man.

"My soul!" said Wrinkles.

Great Grief lay on the bed smoking a pipe and waiting for fame. "Oh, go home, Purple. You resent something. It wasn't me, it was the calendar."

"Try and be serious a moment, Grief."

"You're a fool, Purple."

Penny spoke from where he was at work. "Well, if those *Amazement Magazine* people pay me when they said they would I'll have money then."

"So you will, dear," said Grief, satirically. "You'll have money to burn. Did the *Amazement* people ever pay you when they said they would? You're wonderfully important all of a sudden, it seems to me. You talk like an artist."

Wrinkles, too, smiled at little Pennoyer. "The *Established Magazine*people wanted Penny to hire models and make a try for them too. It will only cost him a big blue chip. By the time he has invested all the money he hasn't got and the rent is two weeks' overdue, he will be able to tell the landlord to wait seven months until the Monday morning after the publication. Go ahead, Penny."

It was the habit to make game of little Pennoyer. He was always having gorgeous opportunities, with no opportunity to take advantage of his opportunities.

Penny smiled at them, his tiny, tiny smile of courage.

"You're a confident little cuss," observed Grief, irrelevantly.

"Well, the world has no objection to your being confident also, Grief," said Purple.

"Hasn't it?" said Grief. "Well, I want to know."

Wrinkles could not be light-spirited long. He was obliged to despair when occasion offered. At last he sank down in a chair and seized his guitar.

"Well, what's to be done?" he said. He began to play mournfully.

"Throw Purple out," mumbled Grief from the bed.

"Are you fairly certain that you will have money then, Penny?" asked Purple.

Little Pennoyer looked apprehensive. "Well, I don't know," he said.

And then began that memorable discussion, great in four minds. The tobacco was of the "Long John" brand. It smelled like burning mummies.

## A Dinner on Sunday Evening.

Once Purple Sanderson went to his home in St. Lawrence county to enjoy some country air, and, incidentally, to explain his life failure to his people. Previously, Great Grief had given him odds that he would return sooner than he had planned, and everybody said that Grief had a good bet. It is not a glorious pastime, this explaining of life failures.

Later, Great Grief and Wrinkles went to Haverstraw to visit Grief's cousin and sketch. Little Pennoyer was disheartened, for it is bad to be imprisoned in brick and dust and cobbles when your ear can hear in the distance the harmony of the summer sunlight upon leaf and blade of green. Besides, he did not hear Wrinkles and Grief discoursing and quarrelling in the den, and Purple coming in at six o'clock with contempt.

On Friday afternoon he discovered that he only had fifty cents to last until Saturday morning, when he was to get his cheque from the *Gamin*. He was an artful little man by this time, however, and it is as true as the sky that when he walked toward the *Gamin* office on Saturday he had twenty cents remaining.

The cashier nodded his regrets, "Very sorry, Mr.—er—Pennoyer, but our payday, you know, is on Monday. Come around any time after ten."

"Oh, it don't matter," said Penny. As he walked along on his return he reflected deeply how he could invest his twenty cents in food to last until Monday morning any time after ten. He bought two coffee cakes in a third avenue bakery. They were very beautiful. Each had a hole in the centre, and a handsome scallop all around the edges.

Penny took great care of those cakes. At odd times he would rise from his work and go to see that no escape had been made. On Sunday he got up at noon and compressed breakfast and noon into one meal. Afterwards he had almost three-quarters of a cake still left to him. He congratulated himself that with strategy he could make it endure until Monday morning any time after ten.

At three in the afternoon there came a faint-hearted knock. "Come in," said Penny. The door opened and old Tim Connegan, who was trying to be a model, looked in apprehensively. "I beg pardon, sir," he said at once.

"Come in, Tim, you old thief," said Penny. Tim entered slowly and bashfully. "Sit down," said Penny. Tim sat down and began to rub his knees, for rheumatism had a mighty hold upon him.

Penny lit his pipe and crossed his legs. "Well, how goes it?"

Tim moved his square jaw upward and flashed Penny a little glance.

"Bad?" said Penny.

The old man raised his hand impressively. "I've been to every studio in the hull city, and I never see such absences in my life. What with the seashore and the mountains, and this and that resort, I think all the models will be starved by fall. I found one man in up on Fifty-seventh Street. He ses to me: 'Come around Tuesday—I may want yez and I may not.' That was last week. You know, I live down on the Bowery, Mr. Pennoyer, and when I got up there on Tuesday, he ses: 'Confound you, are you here again?' ses he. I went and sat down in the park, for I was too tired for the walk back. And there you are, Mr. Pennoyer. What with trampin' around to look for men that are thousand miles away, I'm near dead."

"It's hard," said Penny.

"It is, sir. I hope they'll come back soon. The summer is the death of us all, sir; it is. Sure, I never know where my next meal is coming until I get it. That's true."

"Had anything today?"

"Yes, sir, a little."

"How much?"

"Well, sir, a lady gave me a cup of coffee this morning. It was good, too, I'm telling you."

Penny went to his cupboard. When he returned, he said: "Here's some cake."

Tim thrust forward his hands, palms erect. "Oh, now, Mr. Pennoyer, I couldn't. You—"

"Go ahead. What's the odds?"

"Oh, now."

"Go ahead, you old bat."

Penny smoked.

When Tim was going out, he turned to grow eloquent again. "Well, I can't tell you how much I'm obliged to you, Mr. Pennoyer. You—"

"Don't mention it, old man."

Penny smoked.

# THE SILVER PAGEANT

"It's rotten," said Grief.

"Oh, it's fair, old man. Still, I would not call it a great contribution to American art," said Wrinkles.

"You've got a good thing, Gaunt, if you go at it right," said little Pennoyer.

These were all volunteer orations. The boys had come in one by one and spoken their opinions. Gaunt listened to them no more than if they had been so many match-peddlers. He never heard anything close at hand, and he never saw anything except-ing that which transpired across a mystic wide sea. The shadow of his thoughts was in his eyes, a little grey mist, and, when what you said to him had passed out of your mind, he asked: "Wha—a—at?" It was understood that Gaunt was very good to tolerate the presence of the universe, which was noisy and interested in itself. All the younger men, moved by an instinct of faith, declared that he would one day be a great artist if he would only move faster than a pyramid. In the meantime he did not hear their voices. Occasionally when he saw a man take vivid pleasure in life, he faintly evinced an admiration. It seemed to strike him as a feat. As for him, he was watching that silver pageant across a sea.

When he came from Paris to New York somebody told him that he must make his living. He went to see some book publishers, and talked to them in his manner— as if he had just been stunned. At last one of them gave him drawings to do, and it did not surprise him. It was merely as if rain had come down.

Great Grief went to see him in his studio, and returned to the den to say: "Gaunt is working in his sleep. Somebody ought to set fire to him."

It was then that the others went over and smoked, and gave their opinions of a drawing. Wrinkles said: "Are you really looking at it, Gaunt? I don't think you've seen it yet, Gaunt?"

"What?"

"Why don't you look at it?"

When Wrinkles departed, the model, who was resting at that time, followed him into the hall and waved his arms in rage. "That feller's crazy. Yeh ought t' see—" and he recited lists of all the wrongs that can come to models.

It was a superstitious little band over in the den. They talked often of Gaunt. "He's got pictures in his eyes," said Wrinkles. They had expected genius to blindly stumble at the perface and ceremonies of the world, and each new flounder by Gaunt made a stir in the den. It awed them, and they waited.

At last one morning Gaunt burst into the room. They were all as dead men.

"I'm going to paint a picture." The mist in his eyes was pierced by a Coverian gleam. His gestures were wild and extravagant. Grief stretched out smoking on the bed, Wrinkles and little Pennoyer working at their drawing-boards tilted against the table—were suddenly frozen. If bronze statues had come and danced heavily before them, they could not have been thrilled further.

Gaunt tried to tell them of something, but it became knotted in his throat, and then suddenly he dashed out again.

Later they went earnestly over to Gaunt's studio. Perhaps he would tell them of what he saw across the sea.

He lay dead upon the floor. There was a little grey mist before his eyes.

When they finally arrived home that night they took a long time to undress for bed, and then came the moment when they waited for some one to put out the gas. Grief said at last, with the air of a man whose brain is desperately driven: "I wonder—I—what do you suppose he was going to paint?"

Wrinkles reached and turned out the gas, and from the sudden profound darkness, he said: "There is a mistake. He couldn't have had pictures in his eyes."

# A STREET SCENE IN NEW YORK

The man and the boy conversed in Italian, mumbling the soft syllables and making little, quick egotistical gestures. Suddenly the man glared and wavered on his limbs for a moment as if some blinding light had flashed before his vision; then he swayed like a drunken man and fell. The boy grasped his arm convulsively, and made an attempt to support his companion so that the body slid to the side-walk with an easy motion like a corpse sinking into the sea. The boy screamed.

Instantly people from all directions turned their gaze upon that figure prone upon the side-walk. In a moment there was a dodging, peering, pushing crowd about the man. A volley of questions, replies, speculations flew to and fro among all the bobbing heads.

"What's th' matter? what's th' matter?"

"Oh, a jag, I guess!"

"Aw, he's got a fit!"

"What's th' matter? what's th' matter?"

Two streams of people coming from different directions met at this point to form a great crowd. Others came from across the street.

Down under their feet, almost lost under this mass of people, lay a man, hidden in the shadows caused by their forms, which, in fact, barely allowed a particle of light to pass between them. Those in the foremost rank bended down eagerly, anxious to see everything. Others behind them crowded savagely like starving men fighting for bread. Always, the question could be heard flying in the air. "What's th' matter." Some, near to the body, and perhaps feeling the danger of being forced over upon it, twisted their heads and protested violently to those unheeding ones who were scuffling in the rear: "Say, quit yer shovin', can't yeh? What do yeh want, anyhow? Quit!"

Somebody back in the throng suddenly said: "Say, young feller, cheese that pushin'! I ain't no peach!"

Another voice said: "Well, dat's all right—"

The boy who had been with the Italian was standing helplessly, a frightened look in his eyes, and holding the man's hand. Sometimes he looked about him dumbly, with indefinite hope, as if he expected sudden assistance to come from the clouds. The men about him frequently jostled him until he was obliged to put his hand upon the breast of the body to maintain his balance. Those nearest the man upon the sidewalk at first saw his body go through a singular contortion. It was as if an invisible hand had reached up from the earth and had seized him by the hair. He seemed dragged slowly, pitilessly backward, while his body stiffened convulsively, his hands clenched, and his arms swung rigidly upward. Through his pallid, half-closed lids one could see the steel-coloured, assassin-like gleam of his eye, that shone with a mystic light as a corpse might glare at those live ones who seemed about to trample it under foot. As for the men near, they hung back, appearing as if they expected it might spring erect and grab them. Their eyes, however, were held in a spell of fascination. They scarce seemed to breathe. They were contemplating a depth into which a human being had sunk, and the marvel of this mystery of life or death held them chained. Occasionally from the rear a man came thrusting his way impetuously, satisfied that there was a horror to be seen, and apparently insane to get a view of it.More self-contained men swore at these persons when they tread upon their toes.

The street cars jingled past this scene in endless parade. Occasionally, down where the elevated road crossed the street, one could hear sometimes a thunder, suddenly begun and suddenly ended. Over the heads of the crowd hung an immovable canvas sign: "Regular Dinner twenty cents."

The body on the pave seemed like a bit of debris sunk in this human ocean.

But after the first spasm of curiosity had passed away, there were those in the crowd who began to bethink themselves of some way to help. A voice called out: "Rub his wrists." The boy and a man on the other side of the body began to rub the wrists and slap the palms of the man. A tall German suddenly appeared, and resolutely began to push the crowd back. "Get back there—get back," he repeated continually while he pushed at them. He seemed to have authority; the crowd obeyed him. He and another man knelt down by the man in the darkness and loosened his shirt at the throat. Once they struck a match and held it close to the man's face. This livid visage suddenly appearing under their feet in the light of the match's yellow glare, made the crowd shudder. Half articulate exclamations could be heard. There were men who nearly created a riot in the madness of their desire to see the thing.

Meanwhile others had been questioning the boy. "What's his name? Where does he live?"

Then a policeman appeared. The first part of this little drama had gone on without his assistance, but now he came, striding swiftly, his helmet towering over the crowd and shading that impenetrable police face. He charged the crowd as if he were a squadron of Irish Lancers. The people fairly withered before this onslaught. Occasionally he shouted: "Come, make way there. Come, now!" He was evidently a man whose life was half-pestered out of him by people who were sufficiently unreasonable and stupid as to insist on walking in the streets. He felt the rage toward them that a placid cow feels toward the flies that hover in clouds and disturb its repose. When he arrived at the centre of the crowd he first said, threateningly: "What's th' matter here?" And then when he saw that human bit of wreckage at the bottom of the sea of men, he said to it: "Come, git up out that! Git out a here!"

Whereupon hands were raised in the crowd and a volley of decorated information was blazed at the officer.

"Ah, he's got a fit, can't yeh see?"

"He's got a fit!"

"What th'ell yeh doin'? Leave 'im be!"

The policeman menaced with a glance the crowd from whose safe precincts the defiant voices had emerged.

A doctor had come. He and the policeman bended down at the man's side. Occasionally the officer reared up to create room. The crowd fell away before his admonitions, his threats, his sarcastic questions, and before the sweep of those two huge buckskin gloves.

At last the peering ones saw the man on the side-walk begin to breathe heavily, strainedly, as if he had just come to the surface from some deep water. He uttered a low cry in his foreign way. It was like a baby's squeal or the side wail of a little storm-tossed kitten. As this cry went forth to all those eager ears the jostling, crowding recommenced again furiously, until the doctor was obliged to yell warningly a dozen times. The policeman had gone to send the ambulance call.

Then a man struck another match, and in its meagre light the doctor felt the skull of the prostrate man carefully to discover if any wound had been caused by his fall to the stone side-walk. The crowd pressed and crushed again. It was as if they fully expected to see blood by the light of the match, and the desire made them appear almost insane. The policeman returned and fought with them. The doctor looked up occasionally to scold and demand room.

At last, out of the faint haze of light far up the street, there came the sound of a gong beating rapidly. A monstrous truck loaded to the sky with barrels scurried to one side with marvellous agility. And then the black waggon, with its gleam of gold lettering and bright brass gong, clattered into view, the horse galloping. A young man, as imperturbable almost as if he were at a picnic, sat upon the rear seat. When they picked up the limp body, from which came little moans and howls, the crowd almost turned into a mob. When the ambulance started on its banging and clanging return, they stood and gazed until it was quite out of sight. Some resumed their way with an air of relief. Others still continued to stare after the vanished ambulance and its burden as if they had been cheated, as if the curtain had been rung down on a tragedy that was but half completed; and this impenetrable blanket intervening between a sufferer and their curiosity seemed to make them feel an injustice.

# MINETTA LANE, NEW YORK.

**Its Worst Days have Now Passed Away. But its Inhabitants Still
Include Many whose Deeds are Evil.
The Celebrated Resort of Mammy Ross.**

Minetta Lane is a small and becobbled valley between hills and dingy brick. At night the street lamps, burning dimly, cause the shadows to be important, and in the gloom one sees groups of quietly conversant negroes, with occasionally the gleam of a passing growler. Everything is vaguely outlined and of uncertain identity, unless, indeed, it be the flashing buttons and shield of the policeman on his coast. The Sixth Avenue horse-cars jingle past one end of the lane, and a block eastward the little thoroughfare ends in the darkness of M'Dougall Street.

One wonders how such an insignificant alley could get such an assuredly large reputation, but, as a matter of fact, Minetta Lane and Minetta Street, which leads from it southward to Bleecker Street, were, until a few years ago, two of the most enthusiastically murderous thoroughfares in New York. Bleecker Street, M'Dougall Street, and nearly all the streets thereabouts were most unmistakably bad; the other streets went away and hid. To gain a reputation in Minetta Lane in those days a man was obliged to commit a number of furious crimes, and no celebrity was more important than the man who had a good honest killing to his credit. The inhabitants, for the most part, were negroes, and they represented the very worst element of their race. The razor habit clung to them with the tenacity of an epidemic, and every night the uneven cobbles felt blood. Minetta Lane was not a public thoroughfare at this period. It was a street set apart, a refuge for criminals. Thieves came here preferably with their gains, and almost any day peculiar sentences passed among the inhabitants. "Big Jim turned a thousand last night." "No-Toe's made another haul." And the worshipful citizens would make haste to be present at the consequent revel.

As has been said, Minetta Lane was then no thoroughfare. A peaceable citizen chose to make a circuit rather than venture through this place, that swarmed with the most dangerous people in the city. Indeed, the thieves of the district used to say: "Once get in the lane and you're all right." Even a policeman in chase of a criminal would probably shy away instead of pursuing him into the lane. The odds were too great against a lone officer.

Sailors, and any men who might appear to have money about them, were welcomed with all proper ceremony at the terrible dens of the lane. At departure they were fortunate if they still retained their teeth. It was the custom to leave very little else to them. There was every facility for the capture of coin, from trap-doors to plain ordinary knock-out drops.

And yet Minetta Lane is built on the grave of Minetta Brook, where, in olden times, lovers walked under the willows on the bank, and Minetta Lane, in later times, was the home of many of the best families of the town.

A negro named Bloodthirsty was perhaps the most luminous figure of Minetta Lane's aggregation of desperadoes. Bloodthirsty supposedly is alive now, but he has vanished from the lane. The police want him for murder. Bloodthirsty is a large negro, and very hideous. He has a rolling eye that shows white at the wrong time, and his neck, under the jaw, is dreadfully scarred and pitted.

Bloodthirsty was particularly eloquent when drunk, and in the wildness of a spree he would rave so graphically about gore that even the habitated wool of old timers would stand straight.

Bloodthirsty meant most of it, too. That is why his orations were impressive. His remarks were usually followed by the wide, lightning sweep of his razor. None cared to exchange epithets with Bloodthirsty. A man in a boiler iron suit would walk down to City Hall and look at the clock before he would ask the time of day from the single-minded and ingenuous Bloodthirsty.

After Bloodthirsty, in combative importance, came No-Toe Charley. Singularly enough, Charley was called No-Toe Charley because he did not have a toe on his feet. Charley was a small negro, and his manner of amusement befitting a smaller man. Charley was more wise, more sly, more round-about than the other man. The path of his crimes was like a corkscrew in architecture, and his method led him to make many tunnels. With all his cleverness, however, No-Toe was finally induced to pay a visit to the gentlemen in the grim, grey building up the river—Sing Sing.

Black-Cat was another famous bandit who made the land his home. Black-Cat is dead. Jube Tyler has been sent to prison, and after mentioning the recent disappearance of Old Man Spriggs it may be said that the lane is now destitute of the men who once crowned it with a glory of crime. It is hardly essential to mention Guinea Johnson.

Guinea is not a great figure. Guinea is just an ordinary little crook. Sometimes Guinea pays a visit to his friends, the other little crooks who make homes in the lane, but he himself does not live there, and with him out of it there is now no one whose industry's unlawfulness has yet earned him the dignity of a nickname. Indeed, it is difficult to find people now who remember the old gorgeous days, although it is but two years since the lane shone with sin like a new head-light. But after a search the reporter found three.

Mammy Ross is one of the last relics of the days of slaughter still living there. Her weird history also reaches back to the blossoming of the first members of the Whyo gang in the Old Sixth Ward, and her mind is stored with bloody memories. She at one time kept a sailors' boarding-house near the Tombs prison, and the accounts of all the festive crimes of that neighbourhood in ancient years roll easily from her tongue. They killed a sailor man every day, and pedestrians went about the streets wearing stoves for fear of the handy knives. At the present day the route to Mammy's home is up a flight of grimy stairs that are pasted on the outside of an old and tottering frame house. Then there is a hall blacker than a wolf's throat, and this hall leads to a little kitchen where Mammy usually sits groaning by the fire. She is, of course, very old, and she is also very fat. She seems always to be in great pain. She says she is suffering from "de very las' dregs of de yaller fever."

During the first part of a reporter's recent visit, old Mammy seemed most dolefully oppressed by her various diseases. Her great body shook and her teeth clicked spasmodically during her long and painful respirations. From time to time she reached her trembling hand and drew a shawl closer about her shoulders. She presented as true a picture of a person undergoing steady, unchangeable, chronic pain as a patent medicine firm could wish to discover for miraculous purposes. She breathed like a fish thrown out on the bank, and her old head continually quivered in the nervous tremors of the extremely aged and debilitated person. Meanwhile her daughter hung over the stove and placidly cooked sausages.

Appeals were made to the old woman's memory. Various personages who had been sublime figures of crime in the long-gone days were mentioned to her, and presently her eyes began to brighten. Her head no longer quivered. She seemed to lose for a period her sense of pain in the gentle excitement caused by the invocation of the spirits of her memory.

It appears that she had had a historic quarrel with Apple Mag. She first recited the prowess of Apple Mag; how this emphatic lady used to argue with paving stones, carving knives, and bricks. Then she told of the quarrel; what Mag said; what she said. It seems that they cited each other as spectacles of sin and corruption in more fully explanatory terms than are commonly known to be possible. But it was one of Mammy's most gorgeous recollections, and, as she told it, a smile widened over her face.

Finally she explained her celebrated retort to one of the most illustrious thugs that had blessed the city in bygone days. "Ah says to 'im, ah says: 'You—you'll die in yer boots like Gallopin' Thompson—dat's what you'll do. You des min' dat', honey. Ah got o'ny one chile, an' he ain't nuthin' but er cripple; but le'me tel' you, man, dat boy'll live t' pick de feathers f'm de goose dat'll eat de grass dat grows over your grave, man.' Dat's what I tol' 'm. But—law sake—how I know dat in less'n three day, dat man be lying in de gutter wif a knife stickin' out'n his back. Lawd, no, I sholy never s'pected noting like dat."

These reminiscences, at once maimed and reconstructed, have been treasured by old Mammy as carefully, as tenderly, as if they were the various little tokens of an early love. She applies the same black-handed sentiment to them, and, as she sits groaning by the fire, it is plainly to be seen that there is only one food for her ancient brain, and that is the recollection of the beautiful fights and murders of the past.

On the other side of the lane, but near Mammy's house, Pop Babcock keeps a restaurant. Pop says it is a restaurant, and so it must be one; but you could pass there ninety times each day and never know you were passing a restaurant. There is one obscure little window in the basement, and if you went close and peered in you might, after a time, be able to make out a small, dusty sign, lying amid jars on a dusty shelf. This sign reads: "Oysters in every style." If you are of a gambling turn of mind, you will probably stand out in the street and bet yourself black in the face that there isn't an oyster within a hundred yards. But Pop Babcock made that sign, and Pop Babcock could not tell an untruth. Pop is a model of all the virtues which an inventive fate has made for us. He says so.

As far as goes the management of Pop's restaurant, it differs from Sherry's. In the first place, the door is always kept locked. The wardmen of the Fifteenth precinct have a way of prowling through the restaurant almost every night, and Pop keeps the door locked in order to keep out the objectionable people that cause the wardmen's visits. He says so. The cooking stove is located in the main room of the restaurant, and it is placed in such a strategic manner that it occupies about all the space that is not already occupied by a table, a bench, and two chairs. The table will, on a pinch, furnish room for the plates of two people if they are willing to crowd. Pop says he is the best cook in the world.

When questioned concerning the present condition of the lane, Pop said: "Quiet! Quiet! Lo'd save us, maybe it ain't. Quiet! Quiet!" His emphasis was arranged crescendo, until the last word was really a vocal explosion. "Why, dish er' lane ain't nohow like what it uster be—no, indeed it ain't. No, sir. 'Deed it ain't. Why, I kin remember when dey was a-cuttin' an' a-slashin' long yere all night. 'Deed dey wos. My-my, dem times was different. Dat der Kent, he kep' de place at Green Gate cou't down yer ol' Mammy's—an' he was a hard baby—'deed he was—an' ol' Black-Cat an' ol' Bloodthirsty, dey was a-comin' round yere a-cuttin', an' a-slashin', an' a-cuttin', an' a-slashin'. Didn't dar' say boo to a goose in dose days, dat you didn't, less'n you lookin' fer a scrap. No, sir." Then he gave information concerning his own prowess at that time. Pop is about as tall as a picket of an undersized fence. "But dey didn't have nothin' ter say ter me. No, sir, 'deed dey didn't. I would lay down fer none of 'em. No, sir. Dey knew my gait, 'deed dey did. Man, man, many's de time I buck up agin 'em."

At this time Pop had three customers in his place, one asleep on the bench, one asleep on two chairs, and one asleep on the floor behind the stove.

But there is one who lends dignity of the real bevel-edged type to Minetta Lane, and that man is Hank Anderson. Hank, of course, does not live in the lane, but the shadows of his social perfections fall upon it as refreshingly as a morning dew.

Hank gave a dance twice in each week at a hall hard by in M'Dougall Street, and the dusky aristocracy of the neighbourhood know their guiding beacon. Moreover, Hank holds an annual ball in Forty-fourth Street. Also, he gives a picnic each year to the Montezuma Club, when he again appears as a guiding beacon. This picnic is usually held on a barge, and the excursion is a very joyous one. Some years ago it required the entire reserve squad of an up-town police precinct to properly control the enthusiasm of the gay picnickers, but that was an exceptional exuberance, and no measure of Hank's ability for management.

He is really a great manager. He was Boss Tweed's body-servant in the days when Tweed was a political prince, and any one who saw Bill Tweed through a spy-glass learned the science of leading, pulling, driving, and hauling men in a way to keep the men ignorant of it. Hank imbibed from this fount of knowledge, and he applied his information in Thompson Street. Thompson Street salaamed. Presently he bore a proud title: "The Mayor of Thompson Street." Dignities from the principal political organisations of the city adorned his brow, and he speedily became illustrious.

Hank knew the lane well in its direful days. As for the inhabitants, he kept clear of them, and yet in touch with them, according to a method that he might have learned in the Sixth ward. The Sixth ward was a good place in which to learn that trick. Anderson can tell many strange tales and good of the lane, and he tells them in the graphic way of his class. "Why, they could steal your shirt without moving a wrinkle on it."

The killing of Joe Carey was the last murder that happened in the Minettas. Carey had what might be called a mixed-ale difference with a man named Kenny. They went out to the middle of Minetta Street to affably fight it out and determine the justice of the question.

In the scrimmage Kenny drew a knife, thrust quickly, and Carey fell. Kenny had not gone a hundred feet before he ran into the arms of a policeman.

There is probably no street in New York where the police keep closer watch than they do in Minetta Lane. There was a time when the inhabitants had a profound and reasonable contempt for the public guardians, but they have it no longer apparently. Any citizen can walk through there at any time in perfect safety, unless, perhaps, he should happen to get too frivolous. To be strictly accurate, the change began under the reign of police Captain Chapman. Under Captain Groo, a commander of the Fifteenth precinct, the lane donned a complete new garb. Its denizens brag now of its peace, precisely as they once bragged of its war. It is no more a bloody lane. The song of the razor is seldom heard. There are still toughs and semi-toughs galore in it, but they can't get a chance with the copper looking the other way. Groo got the poor lane by the throat. If a man should insist upon becoming a victim of the badger game, he could probably succeed, upon search in Minetta Lane, as indeed, he could on any of the great avenues, but then Minetta Lane is not supposed to be a pearly street of Paradise.

In the meantime the Italians have begun to dispute the possession of the lane with the negroes. Green Gate Court is filled with them now, and a row of houses near the M'Dougall Street corner is occupied entirely by Italian families. None of them seem to be over fond of the old Mulberry Bend fashion of life, and there are no cutting affrays among them worth mentioning. It is the original negro element that makes the trouble when there is trouble.

But they are happy in this condition are these people. The most extraordinary quality of the negro is his enormous capacity for happiness under most adverse circumstances. Minetta Lane is a place of poverty and sin, but these influences cannot destroy the broad smile of the negro—a vain and simple child, but happy. They all smile here, the most evil as well as the poorest. Knowing the negro, one always expects laughter from him, be he ever so poor, but it was a new experience to see a broad grin on the face of the devil. Even old Pop Babcock had a laugh as fine and mellow as would be the sound of falling glass, broken saints from high windows, in the silence of some great cathedral's hollow.

# THE ROOF GARDENS AND GARDENERS OF NEW YORK.

## A Phase of New York Life as Seen by a Close Observer.

When the hot weather comes the roof gardens burst into full bloom, and if an inhabitant of Chicago should take flight on his wings over this city, he would observe six or eight flashing spots in the darkness, spots as radiant as crowns. These are the roof gardens, and if a giant had flung a handful of monstrous golden coins upon the sombre-shadowed city he could not have benefited the metropolis more, although he would not have given the same opportunity to various commercial aspirants to charge a price and a half for everything. There are two classes of men—reporters and central office detectives—who do not mind these prices because they are very prodigal of their money.

Now is the time of the girl with the copper voice, the Irishman with circular whiskers, and the minstrel who had a reputation in 1833. To the street the noise of the band comes down on the wind in fitful gusts, and at the brilliantly illuminated rail there is suggestion of many straw hats.

One of the main features of the roof garden is the waiter, who stands directly in front of you whenever anything interesting transpires on the stage. This waiter is three hundred feet high and seventy-two feet wide. His finger can block your view of the golden-haired *soubrette*, and when he waves his arm the stage disappears as if by a miracle. What particularly fascinates you is his lack of self-appreciation. He doesn't know that his length over all is three hundred feet, and that his beam is seventy-two feet. He only knows that while the golden-haired *soubrette* is singing her first verse he is depositing beer on the table before some thirsty New Yorkers. He only knows that during the third verse the thirsty New Yorkers object to the roof-garden prices. He does not know that behind him are some fifty citizens who ordinarily would not give three whoops to see the golden-haired *soubrette*, but who, under these particular circumstances, are kept from swift assassination by sheer force of the human will. He gives an impressive exhibition of a man who is regardless of consequences, oblivious to everything save his task, which is to provide beer. Some day there may be a wholesale massacre of roof-garden waiters, but they will die with astonished faces and with questions on their lips. Skulls so steadfastly opaque defy axes, or any of the other methods which the populace occasionally use to cure colossal stupidity.

Between numbers on an ordinary roof-garden programme, the orchestra sometimes plays what the more enlightened and wary citizens of the town call a "beer overture." But, for reasons which no civil service commission could give, the waiter does not choose this time to serve the thirsty. No; he waits until the golden-haired *soubrette* appears, he waits until the haggard audience has goaded itself into some interest in the proceedings. Then he gets under way. Then he comes forth and blots out the stage. In case of war, all roof-garden waiters should be recruited in a special regiment and sent out in advance of everything. There is a peculiar quality of bullet-proofness about them which would turn a projectile pale.

If you have strategy enough in your soul you may gain furtive glimpses of the stage, despite the efforts of the waiters, and then, with something to engage the attention when the attention grows weary of the mystic wind, the flashing yellow lights, the music, and the undertone of the far street's roar, you should be happy.

Far up into the night there is a wildness, a temper to the air which suggests tossing tree boughs and the swift rustle of grass. The New Yorker, whose business will not allow him to go out to nature, perhaps, appreciates these little opportunities to go up to nature, although doubtless he thinks he goes to see the show.

One season two new roof gardens have opened. The one at the top of Grand Central Palace is large enough for a regimental drill room. The band is imprisoned still higher in a turreted affair, and a person who prefers gentle and unobtrusive amusement can gain deep pleasure and satisfaction from watching the leader of this band gesticulating upon the heavens. His figure is silhouetted beautifully against the sky, and every gesture in which he wrings noise from his band is interestingly accentuated.

The other new roof garden was Oscar Hammerstein's Olympia, which blazes on Broadway.

Oscar originally made a great reputation for getting out injunctions. All court judges in New York worked overtime when Oscar was in this business. He enjoined everybody in sight. He had a special machine made—"Drop a nickel in the judge and get an injunction." Then he sent a man to Washington for twenty-two thousand dollars' worth of nickels. In Harlem, where he then lived, it rained orders of the court every day at twelve o'clock. The street-cleaning commission was obliged to enlist a special force to deal with Oscar's injunctions. Citizens meeting on the street never said: "Good morning, how do you feel today?" They always said: "Good morning, have you been enjoined yet today?" When a man perhaps wished to enter a little game of draw, the universal form was changed when he sent a note to his wife: "Dear Louise, I have received an order of the court restraining me from coming home to dinner tonight. Yours, George."

But Oscar changed. He smashed his machine, girded himself, and resolved to provide the public with amusement. And now we see this great mind applying itself to a roof garden with the same unflagging industry and boundless energy which had previously expressed itself in injunctions. The Olympia, his new roof garden, is a feat. It has an exuberance which reminds one of the Union Depot train-shed of some western city. The steel arches of the roof make a wide and splendid sweep, and over in the corner there are real swans swimming in real water. The whole structure glares like a conflagration with the countless electric lights. Oscar has caused the execution of decorative paintings upon the walls. If he had caused the execution of the decorative painters he would have done better; but a man who has devoted the greater part of his life to the propagation of injunctions is not supposed to understand that wall decoration which appears to have been done with a nozzle is worse than none. But if carpers say that Oscar failed in his landscapes, none can say that he failed in his measurements of the popular mind. The people come in swarms to the Olympia. Two elevators are busy at conveying them to where the cool and steady night-wind insults the straw hat; and the scene here during the popular part of the evening is perhaps more gaudy and dazzling than any other in New York.

The bicycle has attained an economic position of vast importance. The roof garden ought to attain such a position, and it doubtless will soon—as we give it the opportunity it desires.

The Arab or the Moor probably invented the roof garden in some long-gone centuries, and they are at this day inveterate roof gardeners. The American, surprisingly belated—for him, has but recently seized upon the idea, and its development here has been only partial. The possibilities of the roof garden are still unknown.

Here is a vast city in which thousands of people in summer half stifle, cry out continually for air, fresher air. Just above their heads is what might be called a county of unoccupied land. It is not ridiculously small when compared with the area of New York county itself. But it is as lonely as a desert, this region of roofs. It is as untrodden as the corners of Arizona. Unless a man be a roof gardener, he knows practically nothing of this land.

Down in the slums necessity forces a solution of problems. It drives the people to the roofs. An evening upon a tenement roof with the great golden march of the stars across the sky, and Johnnie gone for a pail of beer, is not so bad if you have never seen the mountains nor heard, to your heart, the slow, sad song of the pines.

# IN THE BROADWAY CARS.

## Panorama of a Day from the Down-town Rush of the Morning to the Uninterrupted Whirr of the Cable at Night—The Man, and the Woman, and the Conductor.

The cable cars come down Broadway as the waters come down at Lodore. Years ago Father Knickerbocker had convulsions when it was proposed to lay impious rails on his sacred thoroughfare. At the present day the cars, by force of column and numbers, almost dominate the great street, and the eye of even an old New Yorker is held by these long yellow monsters which prowl intently up and down, up and down, in a mystic search.

In the grey of the morning they come out of the up-town, bearing janitors, porters, all that class which carries the keys to set alive the great down-town. Later, they shower clerks. Later still, they shower more clerks. And the thermometer which is attached to a conductor's temper is steadily rising, rising, and the blissful time arrives when everybody hangs to a strap and stands on his neighbour's toes. Ten o'clock comes, and the Broadway cars, as well as elevated cars, horse cars, and ferryboats innumerable, heave sighs of relief. They have filled lower New York with a vast army of men who will chase to and fro and amuse themselves until almost nightfall.

The cable car's pulse drops to normal. But the conductor's pulse begins now to beat in split seconds. He has come to the crisis in his day's agony. He is now to be overwhelmed with feminine shoppers. They all are going to give him two-dollar bills to change. They all are going to threaten to report him. He passes his hand across his brow and curses his beard from black to grey and from grey to black.

Men and women have different ways of hailing a car. A man—if he is not an old choleric gentleman, who owns not this road but some other road—throws up a timid finger, and appears to believe that the King of Abyssinia is careering past on his war-chariot, and only his opinion of other people's Americanism keeps him from deep salaams. The gripman usually jerks his thumb over his shoulder and indicates the next car, which is three miles away. Then the man catches the last platform, goes into the car, climbs upon some one's toes, opens his morning paper, and is happy.

When a woman hails a car there is no question of its being the King of Abyssinia's war-chariot. She has bought the car for three dollars and ninety-eight cents. The conductor owes his position to her, and the gripman's mother does her laundry. No captain in the Royal Horse Artillery ever stops his battery from going through a stone house in a way to equal her manner of bringing that car back on its haunches. Then she walks leisurely forward, and after scanning the step to see if there is any mud upon it, and opening her pocket-book to make sure of a two-dollar bill, she says: "Do you give transfers down Twenty-eighth Street?"

Some time the conductor breaks the bell strap when he pulls it under these conditions. Then, as the car goes on, he goes and bullies some person who had nothing to do with the affair.

The car sweeps on its diagonal path through the Tenderloin with its hotels, its theatres, its flower shops, its 10,000,000 actors who played with Booth and Barret. It passes Madison Square and enters the gorge made by the towering walls of great shops. It sweeps around the double curve at Union Square and Fourteenth Street, and a life insurance agent falls in a fit as the car dashes over the crossing, narrowly missing three old ladies, two old gentlemen, a newly-married couple, a sandwich man, a newsboy, and a dog. At Grace Church the conductor has an altercation with a brave and reckless passenger who beards him in his own car, and at Canal Street he takes dire vengeance by tumbling a drunken man on to the pavement. Meanwhile, the gripman has become involved with countless truck drivers, and inch by inch, foot by foot, he fights his way to City Hall Park. On past the Post Office the car goes, with the gripman getting advice, admonition, personal comment, an invitation to fight from the drivers, until Battery Park appears at the foot of the slope, and as the car goes sedately around the curve the burnished shield of the bay shines through the trees.

It is a great ride, full of exciting actions. Those inexperienced persons who have been merely chased by Indians know little of the dramatic quality which life may hold for them. These jungle of men and vehicles, these cañons of streets, these lofty mountains of iron and cut stone—a ride through them affords plenty of excitement. And no lone panther's howl is more serious in intention than the howl of the truck driver when the cable car bumps one of his rear wheels.

Owing to a strange humour of the gods that make our comfort, sailor hats with wide brims come into vogue whenever we are all engaged in hanging to cable-car straps. There is only one more serious combination known to science, but a trial of it is at this day impossible. If a troupe of Elizabethan courtiers in large ruffs should board a cable car, the complication would be a very awesome one, and the profanity would be in old English, but very inspiring. However, the combination of wide-brimmed hats and crowded cable cars is tremendous in its power to cause misery to the patient New York public.

Suppose you are in a cable car, clutching for life and family a creaking strap from overhead. At your shoulder is a little dude in a very wide-brimmed straw hat with a red band. If you were in your senses you would recognise this flaming band as an omen of blood. But you are not in your senses; you are in a Broadway cable car. You are not supposed to have any senses. From the forward end you hear the gripman uttering shrill whoops and running over citizens. Suddenly the car comes to a curve. Making a swift running start, it turns three hand-springs, throws a cart wheel for luck, bounds into the air, hurls six passengers over the nearest building, and comes down a-straddle of the track. That is the way in which we turn curves in New York.

Meanwhile, during the car's gamboling, the corrugated rim of the dude's hat has swept naturally across your neck, and has left nothing for your head to do but to quit your shoulders. As the car roars your head falls into the waiting arms of the proper authorities. The dude is dead; everything is dead. The interior of the car resembles the scene of the battle of Wounded Knee, but this gives you small satisfaction.

There was once a person possessing a fund of uncanny humour who greatly desired to import from past ages a corps of knights in full armour. He then purposed to pack the warriors into a cable car and send them around a curve. He thought that he could gain much pleasure by standing near and listening to the wild clash of steel upon steel—the tumult of mailed heads striking together, the bitter grind of armoured legs bending the wrong way. He thought that this would teach them that war is grim.

Towards evening, when the tides of travel set northward, it is curious to see how the gripman and conductor reverse their tempers. Their dispositions flop over like patent signals. During the down-trip they had in mind always the advantages of being at Battery Park. A perpetual picture of the blessings of Battery Park was before them, and every delay made them fume—made this picture all the more alluring. Now the delights of up-town appear to them. They have reversed the signs on the cars; they have reversed their aspirations. Battery Park has been gained and forgotten. There is a new goal. Here is a perpetual illustration which the philosophers of New York may use.

In the Tenderloin, the place of theatres, and of the restaurant where gayer New York does her dining, the cable cars in the evening carry a stratum of society which looks like a new one, but it is of the familiar strata in other clothes. It is just as good as a new stratum, however, for in evening dress the average man feels that he has gone up three pegs in the social scale, and there is considerable evening dress about a Broadway car in the evening. A car with its electric lamp resembles a brilliantly-lighted salon, and the atmosphere grows just a trifle strained. People sit more rigidly, and glance sidewise, perhaps, as if each was positive of possessing social value, but was doubtful of all others. The conductor says: "Ah, gwan. Git off th' earth." But this is to a man at Canal Street. That shows his versatility. He stands on the platform and beams in a modest and polite manner into the car. He notes a lifted finger and grabs swiftly for the bell strap. He reaches down to help a woman aboard. Perhaps his demeanour is a reflection of the manner of the people in the car. No one is in a mad New York hurry; no one is fretting and muttering; no one is perched upon his neighbour's toes. Moreover, the Tenderloin is a glory at night. Broadway of late years has fallen heir to countless signs illuminated with red, blue, green, and gold electric lamps, and the people certainly fly to these as the moths go to a candle. And perhaps the gods have allowed this opportunity to observe and study the best-dressed crowds in the world to operate upon the conductor until his mood is to treat us with care and mildness.

Late at night, after the diners and theatre-goers have been lost in Harlem, various inebriate persons may perchance emerge from the darker regions of Sixth Avenue and swing their arms solemnly at the gripman. If the Broadway cars run for the next 7000 years this will be the only time when one New Yorker will address another in public without an excuse sent direct from heaven. In these cars late at night it is not impossible that some fearless drunkard will attempt to inaugurate a general conversation. He is quite willing to devote his ability to the affair. He tells of the fun he thinks he has had; describes his feelings; recounts stories of his dim past. None reply, although all listen with every ear. The rake probably ends by borrowing a match, lighting a cigar, and entering into a wrangle with the conductor with an *abandon*, a ferocity, and a courage that do not come to us when we are sober.

In the meantime the figures on the street grow fewer and fewer. Strolling policemen test the locks of the great dark-fronted stores. Nighthawk cabs whirl by the cars on their mysterious errands. Finally the cars themselves depart in the way of the citizen, and for the few hours before dawn a new sound comes into the still thoroughfare—the cable whirring in its channel underground.

# THE ASSASSIN IN MODERN BATTLES

### The Torpedo Boat Destroyers that "Perform in the Darkness. An Act which Is more Peculiarly Murderous than most Things in War."

In the past century the gallant aristocracy of London liked to travel down the south bank of the Thames to Greenwich Hospital, where venerable pensioners of the crown were ready to hire telescopes at a penny each, and with these telescopes the lords and ladies were able to view at a better advantage the dried and enchained corpses of pirates hanging from the gibbets on the Isle of Dogs. In those times the dismal marsh was inhabited solely by the clanking figures whose feet moved in the wind like rather poorly-constructed weather cocks.

But even the Isle of Dogs could not escape the appetite of an expanding London. Thousands of souls now live on it, and it has changed its character from that of a place of execution, with mist, wet with fever, coiling forever from the mire and wandering among the black gibbets, to that of an ordinary, squalid, nauseating slum of London, whose streets bear a faint resemblance to that part of Avenue A which lies directly above Sixtieth Street in New York.

Down near the water front one finds a long brick building, three-storeyed and signless, which shuts off all view of the river. The windows, as well as the bricks, are very dirty, and you see no sign of life, unless some smudged workman dodges in through a little door. The place might be a factory for the making of lamps or stair rods, or any ordinary commercial thing. As a matter of fact, the building fronts the shipyard of Yarrow, the builder of torpedo boats, the maker of knives for the nations, the man who provides everybody with a certain kind of efficient weapon. One then remembers that if Russia fights England, Yarrow meets Yarrow; if Germany fights France, Yarrow meets Yarrow; if Chili fights Argentina, Yarrow meets Yarrow.

Besides the above-mentioned countries Yarrow has built torpedo boats for Italy, Austria, Holland, Japan, China, Ecuador, Brazil, Costa Rica, and Spain. There is a keeper of a great shop in London who is known as the Universal Provider. If a general conflagration of war should break out in the world, Yarrow would be known as one of the Universal Warriors, for it would practically be a battle between Yarrow, Armstrong, Krupp, and a few other firms. This is what makes interesting the dinginess of the cantonment on the Isle of Dogs.

The great Yarrow forte is to build speedy steamers of a tonnage of not more than 240 tons. This practically includes only yachts, launches, tugs, torpedo boat destroyers, torpedo boats, and of late shallow-draught gunboats for service on the Nile, Congo, and Niger. Some of the gunboats that shelled the dervishes from the banks of the Nile below Khartoum were built by Yarrow. Yarrow is always in action somewhere. Even if the firm's boats do not appear in every coming sea combat, the ideas of the firm will, for many nations, notably France and Germany, have bought specimens of the best models of Yarrow construction in order to reduplicate and reduplicate them in their own yards.

When the great fever to possess torpedo boats came upon the Powers of Europe, England was at first left far in the rear. Either Germany or France today has in her fleet more torpedo boats than has England. The British tar is a hard man to oust out of a habit. He had a habit of thinking that his battleships and cruisers were the final thing in naval construction. He scoffed at the advent of the torpedo boat. He did not scoff intelligently but because, mainly, he hated to be forced to change his ways.

You will usually find an Englishman balking and kicking at innovation up to the last moment. It takes him some years to get an idea into his head, and when finally it is inserted, he not only respects it, he reveres it. The Londoners have a fire brigade which would interest the ghost of a Babylonian, as an example of how much the method of extinguishing fires could degenerate in two thousand years, and in 1897, when a terrible fire devastated a part of the city, some voices were raised challenging the efficiency of the fire brigade. But that part of the London County Council which corresponds to fire commissioners in United States laid their hands upon their hearts and solemnly assured the public that they had investigated the matter, and had found the London fire brigade to be as good as any in the world. There were some isolated cases of dissent, but the great English public as a whole placidly accepted these assurances concerning the activity of the honoured corps.

For a long time England blundered in the same way over the matter of torpedo boats. They were authoritatively informed that there was nothing in all the talk about torpedo boats. Then came a great popular uproar, in which people tumbled over each other to get to the doors of the Admiralty and howl about torpedo boats. It was an awakening as unreasonable as had been the previous indifference and contempt. Then England began to build. She has never overtaken France or Germany in the number of torpedo boats, but she now heads the world with her collection of that marvel of marine architecture—the torpedo boat destroyer. She has about sixty-five of these vessels now in commission, and has about as many more in course of building.

People ordinarily have a false idea of the appearance of a destroyer. The common type is longer than an ordinary gunboat—a long, low, graceful thing, flying through the water at fabulous speed, with a great curve of water some yards back of the bow, and smoke flying horizontally from the three or four stacks.

Bushing this way and that way, circling, dodging, turning, they are like demons.

The best kind of modern destroyer has a length of 220 feet, with a beam of 26½ feet. The horse-power is about 6500, driving the boat at a speed of thirty-one knots or more. The engines are triple-expansion, with water tube boilers. They carry from 70 to 100 tons of coal, and at a speed of eight or nine knots can keep the sea for a week; so they are independent of coaling in a voyage of between 1300 and 1500 miles. They carry a crew of three or four officers, and about forty men.

They are armed usually with one twelve-pounder gun, and from three to five six-pounder guns, besides their equipment of torpedoes. Their hulls and top hamper are painted olive, buff, or preferably slate, in order to make them hard to find with the eye at sea.

Their principal functions, theoretically, are to discover and kill the enemy's torpedo boats, guard and scout for the main squadron, and perform messenger service. However, they are also torpedo boats of a most formidable kind, and in action will be found carrying out the torpedo boat idea in an expanded form. Four destroyers of this type building at the Yarrow yards were for Japan (1898).

The modern European ideal of a torpedo boat is a craft 152 feet long, with a beam of 15¼ feet. When the boat is fully loaded a speed of 24 knots is derived from her 2000 horse-power engines. The destroyers are twin screw, whereas the torpedo boats are commonly propelled by a single screw. The speed of twenty knots is for a run of three hours. These boats are not designed to keep at sea for any great length of time, and cannot raid toward a distant coast without the constant attendance of a cruiser to keep them in coal and provisions. Primarily they are for defence. Even with destroyers, England, in lately reinforcing her foreign stations, has seen fit to send cruisers in order to provide help for them in stormy weather.

Some years ago it was thought the proper thing to equip torpedo craft with rudders, which would enable them to turn in their own length when running at full speed. Yarrow found this to result in too much broken steering gear, and the firm's boats now have smaller rudders, which enable them to turn in a larger circle.

At one time a torpedo boat steaming at her best gait always carried a great bone in her teeth. During manœuvres the watch on the deck of a battleship often discovered the approach of the little enemy by the great white wave which the boat rolled at her bows during her headlong rush. This was mainly because the old-fashioned boats carried two torpedo tubes set in the bows, and the bows were consequently bluff.

The modern boat carries the great part of her armament amidships and astern on swivels, and her bow is like a dagger. With no more bow-waves, and with these phantom colours of buff, olive, bottle-green, or slate, the principal foe to a safe attack at night is bad firing in the stoke-room, which might cause flames to leap out of the stacks.

A captain of an English battleship recently remarked: "See those five destroyers lying there? Well, if they should attack me I would sink four of them, but the fifth one would sink me."

This was repeated to Yarrow's manager, who said: "He wouldn't sink four of them if the attack were at night and the boats were shrewdly and courageously handled." Anyhow, the captain's remark goes to show the wholesome respect which the great battleship has for these little fliers.

The Yarrow people say there is no sense in a torpedo flotilla attack on anything save vessels. A modern fortification is never built near enough to the water for a torpedo explosion to injure it, and, although some old stone flush-with-the-water castle might be badly crumpled, it would harm nobody in particular, even if the assault were wholly successful.

Of course, if a torpedo boat could get a chance at piers and dock gates they would make a disturbance, but the chance is extremely remote if the defenders have ordinary vigilance and some rapid fire guns. In harbour defence the searchlight would naturally play a most important part, whereas at sea experts are beginning to doubt its use as an auxiliary to the rapid fire guns against torpedo boats. About half the time it does little more than betray the position of the ship. On the other hand, a port cannot conceal its position anyhow, and searchlights would be invaluable for sweeping the narrow channels.

There could be only one direction from which the assault could come, and all the odds would be in favour of the guns on shore. A torpedo boat commander knows this perfectly. What he wants is a ship off at sea with a nervous crew staring into the encircling darkness from any point in which the terror might be coming.

Hi, then, for a grand, bold, silent rush and the assassin-like stab.

In stormy weather life on board a torpedo boat is not amusing. They tumble about like bucking bronchos, especially if they are going at anything like speed. Everything is battened down as if it were soldered, and the watch below feel that they are living in a football, which is being kicked every way at once.

And finally, while Yarrow and other great builders can make torpedo craft which are wonders of speed and manœuvring power, they cannot make that high spirit of daring and hardihood which is essential to a success.

That must exist in the mind of some young lieutenant who, knowing well that if he is detected, a shot or so from a rapid fire gun will cripple him if it does not sink him absolutely, nevertheless goes creeping off to sea to find a huge antagonist and perform stealthily in the darkness an act which is more peculiarly murderous than most things in war.

If a torpedo boat is caught within range in daylight, the fighting is all over before it begins. Any common little gunboat can dispose of it in a moment if the gunnery is not too Chinese.

# IRISH NOTES

## I.—AN OLD MAN GOES WOOING.

The melancholy fisherman made his way through a street that was mainly as dark as a tunnel. Sometimes an open door threw a rectangle of light upon the pavement, and within the cottages were scenes of working women and men, who comfortably smoked and talked. From them came the sounds of laughter and the babble of children. Each time the old man passed through one of the radiant zones the light etched his face in profile with touches flaming and sombre until there was a resemblance to a stern and mournful Dante portrait.

Once a whistling lad came through the darkness. He peered intently for purposes of recognition. "Good avenin', Mickey," he cried cheerfully. The old man responded with a groan, which intimated that the lamentable reckless optimism of the youth had forced from him an expression of an emotion that he had been enduring in saintly patience and silence. He continued his pilgrimage toward the kitchen of the village inn.

The kitchen is a great and worthy place. The long range with its lurid heat continually emits the fragrance of broiling fish, roasting mutton, joints, and fowl. The high black ceiling is ornamented with hams and flitches of bacon. There is a long, dark bench against one wall, and it is fronted by a dark table, handy for glasses of stout. On an old mahogany dresser rows of plates face the distant range, and reflect the red shine of the peat. Smoke which has in it the odour of an American forest fire eddies through the air. The great stones of the floor are scarred by the black mud from the inn yard. And here the gossip of a country-side goes on amid the sizzle of broiling fish and the loud protesting splutter of joints taken from the oven.

When the old man reached the door of this paradise, he stopped for a moment with his finger on the latch. He sighed deeply; evidently he was undergoing some lachrymose reflection. For somewhere overhead in the inn he could hear the wild clamour of dining pig-buyers, men who were come for the pig fair to be held on the morrow. Evidently in the little parlour of the inn these men were dining amid an uproar of shouted jests and laughter. The revelry sounded like the fighting of two mobs amid a rain of missiles and crash of shop windows. The old man raised his hand as if, unseen there in the darkness, he was going to solemnly damn the dinner of the pig-buyers.

Within the kitchen Nora, tall, strong, intrepid, approached the fiery stove in the manner of a boxer. Her left arm was held high to guard her face, which was already crimson from the blaze. With a flourish of her apron she achieved a great brown humming joint from the oven, and, emerging a glowing and triumphant figure from the steam and smoke and rapid play of heat, she slid the pan upon the table, even as she saw the old man standing within the room and lugubriously cleaning the mud from his boots. "Tis you, Mickey?" she said.

He made no reply until he had found his way to the long bench. "It is," he said then. It was clear that in the girl's opinion he had gained some kind of strategic advantage. The sanctity of her kitchen was successfully violated, but the old man betrayed no elation. Lifting one knee and placing it over the other, he grunted in the blissful weariness of a venerable labourer returned to his own fireside. He coughed dismally. "Ah, 'tis no good a man gits from fishin' these days. I moind the toimes whin they would be hoppin' up clear o' the wather, there was that little room fur thim. I would be likin' a bottle o' stout."

"Niver fear you, Mickey," answered the girl. Swinging here and there in the glare of the fire, Nora, with her towering figure and bare brawny arms, was like a feminine blacksmith at a forge. The old man, pallid, emaciated, watched her from the shadows at the other side of the room. The lines from the sides of his nose to the corners of his mouth sank low to an expression of despair deeper than any moans. He should have been painted upon the door of a tomb with wringing willows arched above him and men in grey robes slowly booming the drums of death. Finally he spoke. "I would be likin' a bottle o' stout, Nora, me girrl," he said.

"Niver fear you, Mickey," again she replied with cheerful obstinacy. She was admiring her famous roast, which now sat in its platter on the rack over the range. There was a lull in her tumultuous duties. The old man coughed and moved his foot with a scraping sound on the stones. The noise of dining pig-buyers, now heard through doors and winding corridors of the inn, was a roll of far-away storm.

A woman in a dark dress entered the kitchen and keenly examined the roast and Nora's other feats. "Mickey here would be wantin' a bottle o' stout," said the girl to her mistress. The woman turned towards the spectral figure in the gloom, and regarded it quietly with a clear eye. "Have yez the money, Mickey?" repeated the woman of the house.

Profoundly embittered, he replied in short terms, "I have."

"There now," cried Nora, in astonishment and admiration. Poising a large iron spoon, she was motionless, staring with open mouth at the old man. He searched his pockets slowly during a complete silence in the kitchen. He brought forth two coppers and laid them sadly, reproachfully, and yet defiantly on the table.

"There now," cried Nora, stupefied.

They brought him a bottle of the black brew, and Nora poured it out for him with her own red hand, which looked to be as broad as his chest. A collar of brown foam curled at the top of the glass. With measured moments the old man filled a short pipe. There came a sudden howl from another part of the inn. One of the pig-buyers was at the head of the stairs bawling for the mistress. The two women hurriedly freighted themselves with the roast and the vegetables, and sprang with them to placate the pig-buyers. Alone, the old man studied the gleam of the fire on the floor. It faded and brightened in the way of lightning at the horizon's edge.

When Nora returned, the strapping grenadier of a girl was blushing and giggling. The pig-buyers had been humorous. "I moind the toime—" began the man sorrow-fully. "I moind the toime whin yea was a wee bit of a girrl, Nora, an' wouldn't be havin' words wid min loike thim buyers."

"I moind the toime whin yea could attind to your own affairs, ye ould skileton," said the girl promptly. He made a gesture, which may have expressed his stirring grief at the levity of the new generation, and then lapsed into another stillness.

The girl, a giantess, carrying, lifting, pushing, an incarnation of dauntless labour, changing the look of the whole kitchen with a moment's manipulation of her great arms, did not heed the old man for a long time. When she finally glanced toward him, she saw that he was sunk forward with his grey face on his arms. A growl of heavy breathing ascended. He was asleep.

She marched to him and put both hands to his collar. Despite his feeble and dreamy protestations, she dragged him out from behind the table and across the floor. She opened the door and thrust him into the night.

## II.—BALLYDEHOB

The illimitable inventive incapacity of the excursion companies has made many circular paths throughout Ireland, and on these well-pounded roads the guardians of the touring public may be seen drilling the little travellers in squads. To rise in rebellion, to face the superior clerk in his bureau, to endure his smile of pity and derision, and finally to wring freedom from him, is as difficult in some parts of Ireland as it is in all parts of Switzerland. To see the tourists chained in gangs and taken to see the Lakes of Killarney is a sad spectacle, because these people believe that they are learning Ireland, even as men believe that they are studying America when they contemplate the Niagara Falls.

But afterwards, if one escapes, one can go forth, unguided, untaught and alone, and look at Ireland. The joys of the pig-market, the delirium of a little tap-room filled with brogue, the fierce excitement of viewing the Royal Irish Constabulary fishing for trout, the whole quaint and primitive machinery of the peasant life—its melancholy, its sunshine, its humour—all this is then the property of the man who breaks like a Texan steer out of the pens and corrals of the tourist agencies. For what syndicate of maiden ladies—it is these who masquerade as tourist agencies—what syndicate of maiden ladies knows of the existence, for instance, of Ballydehob?

One has a sense of disclosure at writing the name of Ballydehob. It was really a valuable secret. There is in Ballydehob not one thing that is commonly pointed out to the stranger as a thing worthy of a half-tone reproduction in a book. There is no cascade, no peak, no lake, no guide with a fund of useless information, no gamins practised in the seduction of tourists. It is not an exhibit, an entry for a prize, like a heap of melons or cow. It is simply an Irish village wherein live some three hundred Irish and four constables.

If one or two prayer-towers spindled above Ballydehob it would be a perfect Turkish village. The red tiles and red bricks of England do not appear at all. The houses are low, with soiled white walls. The doors open abruptly upon dark old rooms. Here and there in the street is some crude cobbling done with round stones taken from the bed of a brook. At times there is a great deal of mud. Chickens deprecate warily about the doorsteps, and intent pigs emerge for plunder from the alleys. It is unavoidable to admit that many people would consider Ballydehob quite too grimy.

Nobody lives here that has money. The average English tradesman with his back-breaking respect for this class, his reflex contempt for that class, his reverence for the tin gods, could here be a commercial lord and bully the people in one or two ways, until they were thrown back upon the defence which is always near them, the ability to cut his skin into strips with a wit that would be a foreign tongue to him. For amid his wrongs and his rights and his failures—his colossal failures—the Irishman retains this delicate blade for his enemies, for his friends, for himself, the ancestral dagger of fast sharp speaking from fast sharp seeing—an inheritance which could move the world. And the Royal Irish Constabulary fished for trout in the adjacent streams.

Mrs. Kearney keeps the hotel. In Ireland male innkeepers die young. Apparently they succumb to conviviality when it is presented to them in the guise of a business duty. Naturally honest, temperate men, their consciences are lulled to false security by this idea of hard drinking being necessary to the successful keeping of a public-house. It is very terrible.

But they invariably leave behind them capable widows, women who do not recognise conviviality as a business obligation. And so all through Ireland one finds these brisk widows keeping hotels with a precision that is almost military.

In Kearney's there is always a wonderful collection of old women, bent figures shrouded in shawls who reach up scrawny fingers to take their little purchases from Mary Agnes, who presides sometimes at the bar, but more often at the shop that fronts it in the same room. In the gloom of a late afternoon these old women are as mystic as the swinging, chanting witches on a dark stage when the thunder-drum rolls and the lightning flashes by schedule. When a grey rain sweeps through the narrow street of Ballydehob, and makes heavy shadows in Kearney's tap-room, these old creatures, with their high mournful voices, and the mystery of their shawls, their moans and aged mutterings when they are obliged to take a step, raise the dead superstitions from the bottom of a man's mind.

"My boy," remarked my London friend cheerfully, "these might have furnished sons to be Aldermen or Congressmen in the great city of New York."

"Aldermen or Congressmen of the great city of New York always take care of their mothers," I answered meekly.

On a barrel, over in a corner, sat a yellow-bearded Irish farmer in tattered clothes who wished to exchange views on the Armenian massacres. He had much information and a number of theories in regard to them. He also advanced the opinion that the chief political aim of Russia at present is in the direction of China, and that it behoved other Powers to keep an eye on her. He thought the revolutionists in Cuba would never accept autonomy at the hands of Spain. His pipe glowed comfortably from his corner; waving the tuppenny glass of stout in the air, he discoursed on the business of the remote ends of the earth with the glibness of a fourth secretary of Legation. Here was a little farmer, digging betimes in a forlorn patch of wet ground, a man to whom a sudden two shillings would appear as a miracle, a ragged, un-kempt peasant, whose mind roamed the world like the soul of a lost diplomat. This unschooled man believed that the earth was a sphere inhabited by men that are alike in the essentials, different in the manners, the little manners, which are accounted of such great importance by the emaciated. He was to a degree capable of knowing that he lived on a sphere and not on the apex of a triangle.

And yet, when the talk had turned another corner, he confidently assured the assembled company that a hair from a horse's tail when thrown in a brook would turn shortly to an eel.

## III.—THE ROYAL IRISH CONSTABULARY

The newspapers called it a Veritable Arsenal. There was a description of how the sergeant of Constabulary had bent an ear to receive whispered information of the concealed arms, and had then marched his men swiftly and by night to surround a certain house. The search elicited a double-barrelled breech-loading shot-gun, some empty shells, powder, shot, and a loading machine. The point of it was that some of the Irish papers called it a Veritable Arsenal, and appeared to congratulate the Government upon having strangled another unhappy rebellion in its nest. They floundered and misnamed and mis-reasoned, and made a spectacle of the great modern craft of journalism, until the affair of this poor poacher was too absurd to be pitiable, and Englishmen over their coffee next morning must have almost believed that the prompt action of the Constabulary had quelled a rising. Thus it is that the Irish fight the Irish.

One cannot look Ireland straight in the face without seeing a great many constables. The country is dotted with little garrisons. It must have been said a thousand times that there is an absolute military occupation. The fact is too plain.

The constable himself becomes a figure interesting in its isolation. He has in most cases a social position which is somewhat analogous to that of a Turk in Thessaly. But then, in the same way, the Turk has the Turkish army. He can have battalions as companions and make the acquaintance of brigades. The constable has the Constabulary, it is true; but to be cooped with three or four others in a small white-washed iron-bound house on some bleak country side is not an exact parallel to the Thessalian situation. It looks to be a life that is infinitely lonely, ascetic, and barren. Two keepers of a lighthouse at a bitter end of land in a remote sea will, if they are properly let alone, make a murder in time. Five constables imprisoned 'mid a folk that will not turn a face toward them, five constables planted in a populated silence, may develop an acute and vivid economy, dwell in scowling dislike. A religious asylum in a snow-buried mountain pass will breed conspiring monks. A separated people will beget an egotism that is almost titanic. A world floating distinctly in space will call itself the only world. The progression is perfect.

But the constables take the second degree. They are next to the lighthouse keepers. The national custom of meeting stranger and friend alike on the road with a cheery greeting like "God save you" is too kindly and human a habit not to be missed. But all through the South of Ireland one sees the peasant turn his eyes pretentiously to the side of the road at the passing of the constable. It seemed to be generally understood that to note the presence of a constable was to make a conventional error. None looked, nodded, or gave sign. There was a line drawn so sternly that it reared like a fence. Of course, any police force in any part of the world can gather at its heels a riff-raff of people, fawning always on a hand licensed to strike that would be larger than the army of the Potomac, but of these one ordinarily sees little. The mass of the Irish strictly obey the stern tenet. One hears often of the ostracism or other punishment that befell some girl who was caught flirting with a constable.

Naturally the constable retreats to his pride. He is commonly a soldierly-looking chap, straight, lean, long-strided, well set-up. His little saucer of a forage cap sits obediently on his ear, as it does for the British soldier. He swings a little cane. He takes his medicine with a calm and hard face, and evidently stares full into every eye. But it is singular to find in the situation of the Royal Irish Constabulary the quality of pathos.

It is not known if these places in the South of Ireland are called disturbed districts. Over them hangs the peace of Surrey, but the word disturbance has an elastic arrangement by which it can be made to cover anything. All of the villages visited garrisoned from four to ten men. They lived comfortably in their white houses, strolled in pairs over the country roads, picked blackberries, and fished for trout. If at some time there came a crisis, one man was more than enough to surround it. The remaining nine add dignity to the scene. The crisis chiefly consisted of occasional drunken men who were unable to understand the local geography on Saturday nights.

The note continually struck was that each group of constables lived on a little social island, and there was no boat to take them off. There has been no such marooning since the days of the pirates. The sequestration must be complete when a man with a dinky little cap on his ear is not allowed to talk to the girls.

But they fish for trout. Isaac Walton is the father of the Royal Irish Constabulary. They could be seen on any fine day whipping the streams from source to mouth. There was one venerable sergeant who made a rod less than a yard long. With a line of about the same length attached to this rod, he hunted the gorse-hung banks of the little streams in the hills. An eight-inch ribbon of water lined with masses of heather and gorse will be accounted contemptible by a fisherman with an ordinary rod. But it was the pleasure of the sergeant to lay on his stomach at the side of such a stream and carefully, inch by inch, scout his hook through the pools. He probably caught more trout than any three men in county Cork. He fished more than any twelve men in the county Cork. Some people had never seen him in any other posture but that of crowding forward on his stomach to peer into a pool. They did not believe the rumour that he sometimes stood or walked like a human.

## IV.—A FISHING VILLAGE

The brook curved down over the rocks, innocent and white, until it faced a little strand of smooth gravel and flat stones. It turned then to the left, and thereafter its guilty current was tinged with the pink of diluted blood. Boulders standing neck-deep in the water were rimmed with red; they wore bloody collars whose tops marked the supreme instant of some tragic movement of the stream. In the pale green shallows of the bay's edge, the outward flow from the criminal little brook was as eloquently marked as if a long crimson carpet had been laid upon the waters. The scene of the carnage was the strand of smooth gravel and flat stones, and the fruit of the carnage was cleaned mackerel.

Far to the south, where the slate of the sea and the grey of the sky wove together, could be seen Fastnet Rock, a mere button on the moving, shimmering cloth, while a liner, no larger than a needle, spun a thread of smoke aslant. The gulls swept screaming along the dull line of the other shore of roaring Water Bay, and near the mouth of the brook circled among the fishing boats that lay at anchor, their brown, leathery sails idle and straight. The wheeling, shrieking tumultuous birds stared with their hideous unblinking eyes at the Capers—men from Cape Clear—who prowled to and fro on the decks amid shouts and the creak of the tackle. Shoreward, a little shrivelled man, overcome by a profound melancholy, fished hopelessly from the end of the pier. Back of him, on a hillside, sat a white village, nestled among more trees than is common in this part of Southern Ireland.

A dinghy sculled by a youth in a blue jersey wobbled rapidly past the pier-head and stopped at the foot of the moss-green, dank, stone steps, where the waves were making slow but regular leaps to mount higher, and then falling back gurgling, choking, and waving the long, dark seaweeds. The melancholy fisherman walked over to the top of the steps. The young man was fastening the painter of his boat in an iron ring. In the dinghy were three round baskets heaped high with mackerel. They glittered like masses of new silver coin at times, and then other lights of faint carmine and peacock blue would chase across the sides of the fish in a radiance that was finer than silver.

The melancholy fisherman looked at this wealth. He shook his head mournfully. "Ah, now, Denny. This would not be a very good kill."

The young man snorted indignantly at his fellow-townsman. "This will be th' bist kill th' year, Mickey. Go along now."

The melancholy old man became immersed in deeper gloom. "Shure I have been in th' way of seein' miny a grand day whin th' fish was runnin' sthrong in these wathers, but there will be no more big kills here. No more. No more." At the last his voice was only a dismal croak.

"Come along outa that now, Mickey," cried the youth impatiently. "Come away wid you."

"All gone now. A-ll go-o-ne now!" The old man wagged his grey head, and, standing over the baskets of fishes, groaned as Mordecai groaned for his people.

"'Tis you would be cryin' out, Mickey, whativer," said the youth with scorn. He was giving his basket into the hands of five incompetent but jovial little boys to carry to a waiting donkey cart.

"An' why should I not?" said the old man sternly. "Me—in want—"

As the youth swung his boat swiftly out toward an anchored smack, he made answer in a softer tone. "Shure, if yez got for th' askin', 'tis you, Mickey, that would niver be in want." The melancholy old man returned to his line. And the only moral in this incident is that the young man is the type that America procures from Ireland, and the old man is one of the home types, bent, pallid, hungry, disheartened, with a vision that magnifies with a microscope glance any fly-wing of misfortune, and heroically and conscientiously invents disasters for the future. Usually the thing that remains to one of this type is a sympathy as quick and acute for others as is his pity for himself.

The donkey with his cart-load of gleaming fish, and escorted by the whooping and laughing boys, galloped along the quay and up a street of the village until he was turned off at the gravelly strand, at the point where the colour of the brook was changing. Here twenty people of both sexes and all ages were preparing the fish for market. The mackerel, beautiful as fire-etched salvers, first were passed to a long table, around which worked as many women as could have elbow room. Each one could clean a fish with two motions of the knife. Then the washers, men who stood over the troughs filled with running water from the brook, soused the fish until the outlet became a sinister element that in an instant changed the brook from a happy thing of gorse and heather of the hills to an evil stream, sullen and reddened. After being washed, the fish were carried to a group of girls with knives, who made the cuts that enabled each fish to flatten out in the manner known of the breakfast table. And after the girls came the men and boys, who rubbed each fish thoroughly with great handfuls of coarse salt, which was whiter than snow, and shone in the daylight from a multitude of gleaming points, diamond-like. Last came the packers, drilled in the art of getting neither too few nor too many mackerel into a barrel, sprinkling constantly prodigal layers of brilliant salt. There were many intermediate corps of boys and girls carrying fish from point to point, and sometimes building them in stacks convenient to the hands of the more important labourers.

A vast tree hung its branches over the place. The leaves made a shadow that was religious in its effect, as if the spot was a chapel consecrated to labour. There was a hush upon the devotees. The women at the large table worked intently, steadfastly, with bowed heads. Their old petticoats were tucked high, showing the coarse brogans which they wore—and the visible ankles were proportioned to the brogans as the diameter of a straw is to that of a half-crown. The national red under-petticoat was a fundamental part of the scene.

Just over the wall, in the sloping street, could be seen the bejerseyed Capers, brawny, and with shocks of yellow beard. They paced slowly to and fro amid the geese and children. They, too, spoke little, even to each other; they smoked short pipes in saturnine dignity and silence. It was the fish. They who go with nets upon the reeling sea grow still with the mystery and solemnity of the trade. It was Brittany;

the first respectable catch of the year had changed this garrulous Irish hamlet into a hamlet of Brittany.

The Capers were waiting for high tide. It had seemed for a long time that, for the south of Ireland, the mackerel had fled in company with potato; but here, at any rate, was a temporary success, and the occasion was momentous. A strolling Caper took his pipe and pointed with the stem out upon the bay. There was little wind, but an ambitious skipper had raised his anchor, and the craft, her strained brown sails idly swinging, was drifting away on the first oily turn of the tide.

On the top of the pier the figure of the melancholy old man was portrayed upon the polished water. He was still dangling his line hopelessly. He gazed down into the misty water. Once he stirred and murmured: "Bad luck to thim." Otherwise he seemed to remain motionless for hours. One by one the fishing-boats floated away. The brook changed its colour, and in the dusk showed a tumble of pearly white among the rocks.

A cold night wind, sweeping transversely across the pier, awakened perhaps the rheumatism in the old man's bones. He arose and, mumbling and grumbling, began to wind his line. The waves were lashing the stones. He moved off towards the intense darkness of the village streets.

# THE SQUIRE'S MADNESS

Linton was in his study remote from the interference of domestic sounds. He was writing verses. He was not a poet in the strict sense of the word, because he had eight hundred a year and a manor-house in Sussex. But he was devoted, at any rate, and no happiness was for him equal to the happiness of an imprisonment in this lonely study. His place had been a semi-fortified house in the good days when every gentleman was either abroad with a bared sword hunting his neighbours or behind oak-and-iron doors and three-feet walls while his neighbours hunted him. But in the life of Linton it may be said that the only part of the house which remained true to the idea of fortification was the study, which was free only to Linton's wife and certain terriers. The necessary appearance from time to time of a servant always grated upon Linton as much as if from time to time somebody had in the most well-bred way flung a brick through the little panes of his window.

This window looked forth upon a wide valley of hop-fields and sheep-pastures, dipping and rising this way and that way, but always a valley until it reached a high far away ridge upon which stood the upright figure of a windmill, usually making rapid gestures as if it were an excited sentry warning the old grey house of coming danger. A little to the right, on a knoll, red chimneys and parts of red-tiled roofs appeared among trees, and the venerable square tower of the village church rose above them.

For ten years Linton had left vacant Oldrestham Hall, and when at last it became known that he and his wife were to return from an incomprehensible wandering, the village, which for four centuries had turned a feudal eye toward the Hall, was wrung with a prospect of change, a proper change. The great family pew in Oldrestham church would be occupied each Sunday morning by a fat, happy-faced, utterly squire-looking man, who would be dutifully at his post when the parish was stirred by a subscription list. Then, for the first time in many years, the hunters would ride in the early morning merrily out through the park, and there would be also shooting parties, and in the summer groups of charming ladies would be seen walking the terrace, laughing on the lawns and in the rose gardens. The village expected to have the perfectly legal and fascinating privilege of discussing the performances of its own gentry.

The first intimation of calamity was in the news that Linton had rented all the shooting. This prepared the people for the blow, and it fell when they sighted the master of Oldrestham Hall. The older villagers remembered then that there had been nothing in the youthful Linton to promise a fat, happy-faced, dignified, hunting, shooting over-lord, but still they could not but resent the appearance of the new squire. There was no conceivable reason for his looking like a gaunt ascetic, who would surprise nobody if he borrowed a sixpence from the first yokel he met in the lanes.

Linton was in truth three inches more than six feet in height, but he had bowed himself to five feet eleven inches. His hair shocked out in front like hay, and under it were two spectacled eyes which never seemed to regard anything with particular attention. His face was pale and full of hollows, and the mouth apparently had no expression save a chronic pout of the under-lip. His hands were large and raw boned but uncannily white. His whole bent body was thin as that of a man from a long sick-bed, and all was finished by two feet which for size could not be matched in the county.

He was very awkward, but apparently it was not so much a physical characteristic as it was a mental inability to consider where he was going or what he was doing. For instance, when passing through a gate it was not uncommon for him to knock his side viciously against one of the posts. This was because he dreamed almost always, and if there had beenforty gates in a row he would not then have noted them more than he did the one. As far as the villagers and farmers were concerned he never came out of this manner save in wide-apart cases, when he had forced upon him either some great exhibition of stupidity or some faint indication of double-dealing, and then this smouldering man flared out encrimsoning his immediate surrounding with a brief fire of ancestral anger. But the lapse back to indifference was more surprising. It was far quicker than the flare in the beginning. His feeling was suddenly ashes at the moment when one was certain it would lick the sky.

Some of the villagers asserted that he was mad. They argued it long in the manner of their kind, repeating, repeating, and repeating, and when an opinion confusingly rational appeared they merely shook their heads in pig-like obstinacy. Anyhow, it was historically clear that no such squire had before been in the line of Lintons of Oldrestham Hall, and the present incumbent was a shock.

The servants at the Hall—notably those who lived in the country-side—came in for a lot of questioning, and none were found too backward in explaining many things which they themselves did not understand. The household was most irregular. They all confessed that it was really so uncustomary that they did not know but what they would have to give notice. The master was probably the most extraordinary man in the whole world. The butler said that Linton would drink beer with his meals day in and day out like any carrier resting at a pot-house. It didn't matter even if the meal were dinner. Then suddenly he would change his tastes to the most valuable wines, and in ten days would make the wine-cellar look as if it had been wrecked at sea. What was to be done with a gentleman of that kind? The butler said for his part he wanted a master with habits, and he protested that Linton did not have a habit to his name, at least, none that could properly be called a habit.

Barring the cook, the entire establishment agreed categorically with the butler. The cook didn't agree because she was a very good cook indeed, which she thought entitled her to be extremely aloof from the other servants' hall opinions.

As for the squire's lady, they described her as being not much different from the master. At least she gave support to his most unusual manner of life, and evidently believed that whatever he chose to do was quite correct.

Linton had written—

> *"The garlands of her hair are snakes,*
> *Black and bitter are her hating eyes,*
> *A cry the windy death-hall makes,*
> *O, love, deliver us.*
> *The flung cup rolls to her sandal's tip,*
> *His arm—"*

Whereupon his thought fumed over the next two lines, coursing like greyhounds, after a fugitive vision of a writhening lover with the foam of poison on his lips dying at the feet of the woman. Linton arose, lit a cigarette, placed it on the window ledge, took another cigarette, looked blindly for the matches, thrust a spiral of paper into the flame of the log fire, lit the second cigarette, placed it toppling on a book and began a search among his pipes for one that would draw well. He gazed at his pictures, at the books on the shelves, out at the green spread of country-side, all without taking mental note. At the window ledge he came upon the first cigarette, and in a matter of fact way he returned it to his lips, having forgotten that he had forgotten it.

There was a sound of steps on the stone floor of the quaint little passage that led down to his study, and turning from the window he saw that his wife had entered the room and was looking at him strangely.

"Jack," she said in a low voice, "what is the matter?"

His eyes were burning out from under his shock of hair with a fierceness that belied his feeling of simple surprise. "Nothing is the matter," he answered. "Why do you ask?"

She seemed immensely concerned, but she was visibly endeavouring to hide her concern as well as to abate it.

"I—I thought you acted queerly."

He answered: "Why no. I'm not acting queerly. On the contrary," he added smiling, "I'm in one of my most rational moods."

Her look of alarm did not subside. She continued to regard him with the same stare. She was silent for a time and did not move. His own thoughts had quite returned to a contemplation of a poisoned lover, and he did not note the manner of his wife. Suddenly she came to him, and laying a hand on his arm said, "Jack, you are ill?"

"Why no, dear," he said with a first impatience, "I'm not ill at all. I never felt better in my life." And his mind beleaguered by this pointless talk strove to break through to its old contemplation of the poisoned lover. "Hear what I have written." Then he read—

> *"The garlands of her hair are snakes,*
> *Black and bitter are her hating eyes,*
> *A cry the windy death-hall makes,*
> *O, love, deliver us.*
> *The flung cup rolls to her sandal's tip,*
> *His arm—"*

Linton said: "I can't seem to get the lines to describe the man who is dying of the poison on the floor before her. Really I'm having a time with it. What a bore. Sometimes I can write like mad and other times I don't seem to have an intelligent idea in my head."

He felt his wife's hand tighten on his arm and he looked into her face. It was so alight with horror that it brought him sharply out of his dreams. "Jack," she repeated tremulously, "you are ill."

He opened his eyes in wonder. "Ill! ill? No; not in the least!"

"Yes, you are ill. I can see it in your eyes. You—act so strangely."

"Act strangely? Why, my dear, what have I done? I feel quite well. Indeed, I was never more fit in my life."

As he spoke he threw himself into a large wing chair and looked up at his wife, who stood gazing at him from the other side of the black oak table upon which Linton wrote his verses.

"Jack, dear," she almost whispered, "I have noticed it for days," and she leaned across the table to look more intently into his face. "Yes, your eyes grow more fixed every day—you—you—your head, does it ache, dear?"

Linton arose from his chair and came around the big table toward his wife. As he approached her, an expression akin to terror crossed her face and she drew back as in fear, holding out both hands to ward him off.

He had been smiling in the manner of a man reassuring a frightened child, but at her shrinking from his outstretched hand he stopped in amazement. "Why, Grace, what is it? tell me."

She was glaring at him, her eyes wide with misery. Linton moved his left hand across his face, unconsciously trying to brush from it that which alarmed her.

"Oh, Jack, you must see some one; I am wretched about you. You are ill!"

"Why, my dear wife," he said, "I am quite, quite well; I am anxious to finish these verses but words won't come somehow, the man dying—"

"Yes, that is it, you cannot remember, you see that you cannot remember. You must see a doctor. We will go up to town at once," she answered quickly.

"'Tis true," he thought, "that my memory is not as good as it used to be. I cannot remember dates, and words won't fit in somehow. Perhaps I don't take enough exercise, dear; is that what worries you?" he asked.

"Yes, yes, dear, you do not go out enough," said his wife. "You cling to this room as the ivy clings to the walls—but we must go to London, you *must* see some one; promise me that you will go, that you will go immediately."

Again Linton saw his wife look at him as one looks at a creature of pity. The faint lines from her nose to the corners of her mouth deepened as if she were in physical pain; her eyes, open to their fullest extent, had in them the expression of a mother watching her dying babe. What was this strange wall that had suddenly raised itself between them? Was he ill? No; he never was in better health in his life. He found himself vainly searching for aches in his bones. Again he brushed away this thing which seemed to be upon his face. There must be something on my face, he thought, else why does she look at me with such hopeless despair in her eyes; these kindly eyes that had hitherto been so responsive to each glance of his own. *Why* did she think that he was ill? She who knew well his every mood. *Was he mad?* Did this thing of the poisoned cup that rolled to her sandal's tip—and her eyes, her hating eyes, mean that his—no, it could not be. He fumbled among the papers on the table for a cigarette. He could not find one. He walked to the huge fireplace and peered near-sightedly at the ashes on the hearth.

"What, what do you want, Jack? Be careful! The fire!" cried his wife.

"Why, I want a cigarette," he said.

She started, as if he had spoken roughly to her. "I will get you some, wait, sit quietly, I will bring you some," she replied as she hastened through the small passage-way up the stone steps that led from his study.

Linton stood with his back still bent, in the posture of a man picking something from the ground. He did not turn from the fireplace until the echo of his wife's footfall on the stone floors had died away. Then he straightened himself and said, "Well, I'm damned!" And Linton was not a man who swore.

* * * *

A month later the Squire and his wife were on their way to London to consult the great brain specialist, Doctor Redmond. Linton now believed that "something" was wrong with him. His wife's anxiety, which she could no longer conceal, forced him to this conclusion; "something" was wrong. Until these few last weeks Linton's wife had managed her household with the care and wisdom of a Chatelaine of mediæval times. Each day was planned for certain duties in house or village. She had theories as to the management and education of the village children, and this work occupied much of her time. She was the antithesis of her husband. He, a weaver of dream-stories, she of that type of woman who has ideas of the emancipation of women and who believe the problem could be solved by training the minds of the next generation of mothers. Linton was not interested in these questions, but he would smile indulgently at his wife as she talked of the equality of mind of the sexes and the public part in the world's history which would be played by the women of the future.

There was no talk of this kind now. The household management fell into the hands of servants. Night and day his wife watched Linton. He would awaken in the night to find her face close to his own, her eyes burning with feverish anxiety.

"What is it, Grace?" he would cry, "have I said anything? What is the reason you watch me in this fashion, dear?"

And she would sob, "Jack, you are ill, dear, you are ill; we must go to town, we must, indeed."

Then he would soothe her with fond words and promise that he would go to London.

This present journey was the outcome of those weeks of watching and fear in Linton's wife's mind.

* * * *

Linton's wife was trembling violently as he helped her down from the cab in front of Doctor Redmond's door. They had made an appointment, so that they were sure of little delay before the portentous interview.

A small page in blue livery opened the door and ushered them into a waiting-room. Mrs. Linton dropped heavily into a chair, looking with a frightened air from side to side and biting her under lip nervously. She was moaning half under her breath, "Oh, Jack, you are ill, you are ill."

A short stout man with clean-shaven face and scanty black hair entered the room. His nose was huge and misshapen and his mouth was a straight firm line. Overhanging black brows tried in vain to shadow the piercing dark eyes, that darted questioning looks at every one, seeming to search for hidden thoughts as a flashlight from the conning tower of a ship searches for the enemy in time of war.

He advanced toward Mrs. Linton with outstretched hand. "Mrs. Linton?" he said. "Ah!"

She almost jumped from her chair as he came near her, crying, "Oh, doctor, my husband is ill, very ill, very ill!"

Again Doctor Redmond with his eyes fixed upon her face ejaculated, "Ah!" Turning to Linton he said, "Please wait here, Squire; I will first talk to your wife. Will you step into my study, madam?" he said to Mrs. Linton, bowing courteously.

Linton's wife ran into the room which the doctor pointed toward as his study.

Linton waited. He moved softly about the room looking at the photographs of Greek ruins which adorned the walls. He stopped finally before a large picture of the Gate of Hadrian. He travelled once more into his dream country. His fancy painted in the figures of men and women who had passed through that gate. He had forgotten his fear of the blotting out of his mind that could conjure these glowing colours. He had forgotten himself.

From this dream he was recalled to the present by a hand being placed gently upon his arm. He half turned and saw the doctor regarding him with sympathetic eyes.

"Come, my dear sir, come into my study," said the doctor. "I have asked your wife to await us here." Linton then turned fully toward the centre of the room and found that his wife was seated quietly by a table. Doctor Redmond bowed low to Mrs. Linton as he passed her, and Linton waved his hand, smiled, and said, "Only a moment, dear." She did not reply. The door closed behind them.

"Be seated, my dear sir," said the doctor, drawing forward a chair, "be seated. I want to say something to you, but you must drink this first." He handed Linton a small glass of brandy.

Linton sat down, took the glass mechanically, and gulped the brandy in one great swallow. The doctor stood by the mantel and said slowly, "I rejoice to say to you, sir, that I have never met a man more sound mentally than yourself"—

Linton half started from his chair.

"Stop!" said the doctor, "I have not yet finished—but it is my painful duty to tell you the truth—It is your *wife* who is Mad! *Mad as a Hatter*!"

# HOW THE DONKEY
# LIFTED THE HILLS

Many people suppose that the donkey is lazy. This is a great mistake. It is his pride.

Years ago, there was nobody quite so fine as the donkey. He was a great swell in those times. No one could express an opinion of anything without the donkey showing where he was in it. No one could mention the name of an important personage without the donkey declaring how well he knew him.

The donkey was, above all things, a proud and aristocratic beast.

One day a party of animals were discussing one thing and another, until finally the conversation drifted around to mythology.

"I have always admired that giant, Atlas," observed the ox in the course of the conversation. "It was amazing how he could carry things."

"Oh, yes, Atlas," said the donkey, "I knew him very well. I once met a man and we got talking of Atlas. I expressed my admiration for the giant and my desire to meet him some day, if possible. Whereupon the man said there was nothing quite so easy. He was sure that his dear friend, Atlas, would be happy to meet so charming a donkey. Was I at leisure next Monday? Well, then, could I dine with him upon that date? So, you see, it was all arranged. I found Atlas to be a very pleasant fellow."

"It has always been a wonder to me how he could have carried the earth on his back," said the horse.

"Oh, my dear sir, nothing is more simple," cried the donkey. "One has only to make up one's mind to it, and then—do it. That is all. I am quite sure that if I wished I could carry a range of mountains upon my back."

All the others said, "Oh, my!"

"Yes, I could," asserted the donkey, stoutly. "It is merely a question of making up one's mind. I will bet."

"I will wager also," said the horse. "I will wager my ears that you can't carry a range of mountains upon your back."

"Done," cried the donkey.

Forthwith the party of animals set out for the mountains. Suddenly, however, the donkey paused and said, "Oh, but look here. Who will place this range of mountains upon my back? Surely I can not be expected to do the loading also."

Here was a great question. The party consulted. At length the ox said, "We will have to ask some men to shovel the mountain upon the donkey's back."

Most of the others clapped their hoofs or their paws and cried, "Ah, that is the thing."

The horse, however, shook his head doubtfully. "I don't know about these men. They are very sly. They will introduce some deviltry into the affair."

"Why, how silly," said the donkey. "Apparently you do not understand men. They are the most gentle, guileless creatures."

"Well," retorted the horse, "I will doubtless be able to escape since I am not to be encumbered with any mountains. Proceed."

The donkey smiled in derision at these observations by the horse.

Presently they came upon some men who were labouring away like mad, digging ditches, felling trees, gathering fruits, carrying water, building huts.

"Look at these men, would you," said the horse. "Can you trust them after this exhibition of their depravity? See how each one selfishly—"

The donkey interrupted with a loud laugh.

"What nonsense!"

And then he cried out to the men, "Ho, my friends, will you please come and shovel a range of mountains upon my back?"

"What?"

"Will you please come and shovel a range of mountains upon my back?"

The men were silent for a time. Then they went apart and debated. They gesticulated a great deal.

Some apparently said one thing and some another. At last they paused and one of their number came forward.

"Why do you wish a range of mountains shovelled upon your back?"

"It is a wager," cried the donkey.

The men consulted again. And as the discussion became older, their heads went closer and closer together, until they merely whispered, and did not gesticulate at all. Ultimately they cried, "Yes, certainly we will shovel a range of mountains upon your back for you."

"Ah, thanks," said the donkey.

"Here is surely some deviltry," said the horse behind his hoof to the ox.

The entire party proceeded then to the mountains. The donkey drew a long breath and braced his legs.

"Are you ready?" asked the men.

"All ready," cried the donkey.

The men began to shovel.

The dirt and stones flew over the donkey's back in showers. It was not long before his legs were hidden. Presently only his neck and head remained in view. Then at last this wise donkey vanished. There had been made no great effect upon the range of mountains. They still towered toward the sky.

The watching crowd saw a heap of dirt and stones make a little movement and then was heard a muffled cry. "Enough! Enough! It was not two ranges of mountains! It is not fair! It is not fair!"

But the men only laughed as they shovelled on.

"Enough! Enough! Oh, woe is me—thirty snow-capped peaks upon my little back. Ah, these false, false men! Oh, virtuous, wise, and holy men, desist."

The men again laughed. They were as busy as fiends with their shovels.

"Ah, brutal, cowardly, accursed men; ah, good, gentle, and holy men, please remove some of those damnable peaks. I will adore your beautiful shovels forever. I will be slave to the beckoning of your little fingers. I will no longer be my own donkey—I will be your donkey."

The men burst into a triumphant shout and ceased shovelling.

"Swear it, mountain-carrier."

"I swear! I swear! I swear!"

The other animals scampered away then, for these men in their plots and plans were very terrible. "Poor old foolish fellow," cried the horse; "he may keep his ears. He will need them to hear and count the blows that are now to fall upon him."

The men unearthed the donkey. They beat him with their shovels. "Ho, come on, slave." Encrusted with earth, yellow-eyed from fright, the donkey limped toward his prison. His ears hung down like leaves of the plantain during the great rain.

So, now, when you see a donkey with a church, a palace, and three villages upon his back, and he goes with infinite slowness, moving but one leg at a time, do not think him lazy. It is his pride.

# A MAN BY THE NAME OF MUD

Deep in a leather chair, the Kid sat looking out at where the rain slanted before the dull brown houses and hammered swiftly upon an occasional lonely cab. The happy crackle from the great and glittering fireplace behind him had evidently no meaning of content for him. He appeared morose and unapproachable, and when a man appears morose and unapproachable it is a fine chance for his intimate friends. Three or four of them discovered his mood, and so hastened to be obnoxious.

"What's wrong, Kid? Lost your thirst?"

"He can never be happy again. He has lost his thirst."

"That's right, Kid. When you quarrel with a man who can whip you, resort to sarcastic reflection and distance."

They cackled away persistently, but the Kid was mute and continued to stare gloomily at the street.

Once a man who had been writing letters looked up and said, "I saw your friend at the Comique the other night." He waited a moment and then added, "In back."

The Kid wheeled about in his chair at this information, and all the others saw then that it was important. One man said with deep intelligence, "Ho, ho, a woman, hey? A woman's come between the two Kids. A woman. Great, eh?" The Kid launched a glare of scorn across the room, and then turned again to a contemplation of the rain. His friends continued to do all in their power to worry him, but they fell ultimately before his impregnable silence.

As it happened, he had not been brooding upon his friend's mysterious absence at all. He had been concerned with himself. Once in a while he seemed to perceive certain futilities and lapsed them immediately into a state of voiceless dejection. These moods were not frequent.

An unexplained thing in his mind, however, was greatly enlightened by the words of the gossip. He turned then from his harrowing scrutiny of the amount of pleasure he achieved from living, and settled into a comfortable reflection upon the state of his comrade, the other Kid.

Perhaps it could be indicated in this fashion: "Went to Comique, I suppose. Saw girl. Secondary part, probably. Thought her rather natural. Went to Comique again. Went again. One time happened to meet omnipotent and good-natured friend. Broached subject to him with great caution. Friend said—'Why, certainly, my boy, come round tonight, and I'll take you in back. Remember, it's against all rules, but I think that in your case, etc.' Kid went. Chorus girls winked same old wink. 'Here's another dude on the prowl.' Kid aware of this, swearing under his breath and looking very stiff. Meets girl. Knew beforehand that the footlights might have sold him, but finds her very charming. Does not say single thing to her which she naturally expected to hear. Makes no reference to her beauty nor her voice—if she has any. Perhaps takes it for granted that she knows. Girl don't exactly love this attitude, but then feels admiration, because after all she can't tell whether he thinks her nice or whether he don't. New scheme this. Worked by occasional guys in Rome and Egypt, but still, new scheme. Kid goes away. Girl thinks. Later, nails omnipotent and good-natured friend. 'Who was that you brought back?' 'Oh, him? Why, he—' Describes the Kid's wealth, feats, and virtues—virtues of disposition. Girl propounds clever question—'Why did he wish to meet me?' Omnipotent person says, 'Damned if I know.'"

Later, Kid asks girl to supper. Not wildly anxious, but very evident that he asks her because he likes her. Girl accepts; goes to supper. Kid very good comrade and kind. Girl begins to think that here at last is a man who understands her. Details ambitions—long, wonderful ambitions. Explains her points of superiority over the other girls of stage. Says their lives disgust her. She wants to work and study and make something of herself. Kid smokes vast number of cigarettes. Displays and feels deep sympathy. Recalls, but faintly, that he has heard it on previous occasions. They have an awfully good time. Part at last in front of apartment house. "Good-night, old chap." "Good-night." Squeeze hands hard. Kid has no information at all about kissing her good-night, but don't even try. Noble youth. Wise youth. Kid goes home and smokes. Feels strong desire to kill people who say intolerable things of the girl in rows. "Narrow, mean, stupid, ignorant, damnable people." Contemplates the broad, fine liberality of his experienced mind.

Kid and girl become very chumy. Kid like a brother. Listens to her troubles. Takes her out to supper regularly and regularly. Chorus girls now tacitly recognise him as the main guy. Sometimes, may be, girl's mother sick. Can't go to supper. Kid always very noble. Understands perfectly the probabilities of there being others. Lays for 'em, but makes no discoveries. Begins to wonder whether he is a winner or whether she is a girl of marvellous cleverness. Can't tell. Maintains himself with dignity, however. Only occasionally inveighs against the men who prey upon the girls of the stage. Still noble.

Time goes on. Kid grows less noble. Perhaps decides not to be noble at all, or as little as he can. Still inveighs against the men who prey upon the girls of the stage. Thinks the girl stunning. Wants to be dead sure there are no others. Once suspects it, and immediately makes the colossal mistake of his life. Takes the girl to task. Girl won't stand it for a minute. Harangues him. Kid surrenders and pleads with her—pleads with her. Kid's name is mud.

# A POKER GAME

Usually a poker game is a picture of peace. There is no drama so low-voiced and serene and monotonous. If an amateur loser does not softly curse, there is no orchestral support. Here is one of the most exciting and absorbing occupations known to intelligent American manhood; here a year's reflection is compressed into a moment of thought; here the nerves may stand on end and scream to themselves, but a tranquillity as from heaven is only interrupted by the click of chips. The higher the stakes the more quiet the scene; this is a law that applies everywhere save on the stage.

And yet sometimes in a poker game things happen. Everybody remembers the celebrated corner on bay rum that was triumphantly consummated by Robert F. Cinch, of Chicago, assisted by the United States Courts and whatever other federal power he needed. Robert F. Cinch enjoyed his victory four months. Then he died, and young Bobbie Cinch came to New York in order to more clearly demonstrate that there was a good deal of fun in twenty-two million dollars.

Old Henry Spuytendyvil owns all the real estate in New York save that previously appropriated by the hospitals and Central Park. He had been a friend of Bob's father. When Bob appeared in New York, Spuytendyvil entertained him correctly. It came to pass that they just naturally played poker.

One night they were having a small game in an up-town hotel. There were five of them, including two lawyers and a politician. The stakes depended on the ability of the individual fortune.

Bobbie Cinch had won rather heavily. He was as generous as sunshine, and when luck chases a generous man it chases him hard, even though he cannot bet with all the skill of his opponents.

Old Spuytendyvil had lost a considerable amount. One of the lawyers from time to time smiled quietly, because he knew Spuytendyvil well, and he knew that anything with the name of loss attached to it sliced the old man's heart into sections.

At midnight Archie Bracketts, the actor, came into the room. "How you holding 'em, Bob?" said he.

"Pretty well," said Bob.

"Having any luck, Mr. Spuytendyvil?"

"Blooming bad," grunted the old man.

Bracketts laughed and put his foot on the round of Spuytendyvil's chair. "There," said he, "I'll queer your luck for you." Spuytendyvil sat at the end of the table. "Bobbie," said the actor, presently, as young Cinch won another pot, "I guess I better knock your luck." So he took his foot from the old man's chair and placed it on Bob's chair. The lad grinned good-naturedly and said he didn't care.

Bracketts was in a position to scan both of the hands. It was Bob's ante, and old Spuytendyvil threw in a red chip. Everybody passed out up to Bobbie. He filled in the pot and drew a card.

Spuytendyvil drew a card. Bracketts, looking over his shoulder, saw him holding the ten, nine, eight, and seven of diamonds. Theatrically speaking, straight flushes are as frequent as berries on a juniper tree, but as a matter of truth the reason that straight flushes are so admired is because they are not as common as berries on a juniper tree. Bracketts stared; drew a cigar slowly from his pocket, and placing it between his teeth forgot its existence.

Bobbie was the only other stayer. Bracketts flashed an eye for the lad's hand and saw the nine, eight, six, and five of hearts. Now, there are but six hundred and forty-five emotions possible to the human mind, and Bracketts immediately had them all. Under the impression that he had finished his cigar, he took it from his mouth and tossed it toward the grate without turning his eyes to follow its flight.

There happened to be a complete silence around the green-clothed table. Spuytendyvil was studying his hand with a kind of contemptuous smile, but in his eyes there perhaps was to be seen a cold, stern light expressing something sinister and relentless.

Young Bob sat as he had sat. As the pause grew longer, he looked up once inquiringly at Spuytendyvil.

The old man reached for a white chip. "Well, mine are worth about that much," said he, tossing it into the pot. Thereupon he leaned back comfortably in his chair and renewed his stare at the five straight diamond. Young Bob extended his hand leisurely toward his stack. It occurred to Bracketts that he was smoking, but he found no cigar in his mouth.

The lad fingered his chips and looked pensively at his hand. The silence of those moments oppressed Bracketts like the smoke from a conflagration.

Bobbie Cinch continued for some moments to coolly observe his cards. At last he breathed a little sigh and said, "Well, Mr. Spuytendyvil, I can't play a sure thing against you." He threw in a white chip. "I'll just call you. I've got a straight flush." He faced down his cards.

Old Spuytendyvil's fear, horror, and rage could only be equalled in volume to a small explosion of gasolene. He dashed his cards upon the table. "There!" he shouted, glaring frightfully at Bobbie. "I've got a straight flush, too! And mine is Jack high!"

Bobbie was at first paralysed with amazement, but in a moment he recovered, and apparently observing something amusing in the situation he grinned.

Archie Bracketts, having burst his bond of silence, yelled for joy and relief. He smote Bobbie on the shoulder. "Bob, my boy," he cried exuberantly, "you're no gambler, but you're a mighty good fellow, and if you hadn't been you would be losing a good many dollars this minute."

Old Spuytendyvil glowered at Bracketts. "Stop making such an infernal din, will you, Archie," he said morosely. His throat seemed filled with pounded glass. "Pass the whisky."

# A SELF-MADE MAN

### An Example of Success that Any One can Follow.

Tom had a hole in his shoe. It was very round and very uncomfortable, particularly when he went on wet pavements. Rainy days made him feel that he was walking on frozen dollars, although he had only to think for a moment to discover he was not.

He used up almost two packs of playing cards by means of putting four cards at a time inside his shoe as a sort of temporary sole, which usually lasted about half a day. Once he put in four aces for luck. He went down town that morning and got refused work. He thought it wasn't a very extraordinary performance for a young man of ability, and he was not sorry that night to find his packs were entirely out of aces.

One day Tom was strolling down Broadway. He was in pursuit of work, although his pace was slow. He had found that he must take the matter coolly. So he puffed tenderly at a cigarette and walked as if he owned stock. He imitated success so successfully, that if it wasn't for the constant reminder (king, queen, deuce, and tray) in his shoe, he would have gone into a store and bought something.

He had borrowed five cents that morning off his landlady, for his mouth craved tobacco. Although he owed her much for board, she had unlimited confidence in him, because his stock of self-assurance was very large indeed. And as it increased in a proper ratio with the amount of his bills, his relations with her seemed on a firm basis. So he strolled along and smoked with his confidence in fortune in nowise impaired by his financial condition.

Of a sudden he perceived on old man seated upon a railing and smoking a clay pipe.

He stopped to look, because he wasn't in a hurry, and because it was an unusual thing on Broadway to see old men seated upon railings and smoking clay pipes.

And to his surprise the old man regarded him very intently in return. He stared, with a wistful expression, into Tom's face, and he clasped his hands in trembling excitement.

Tom was filled with astonishment at the old man's strange demeanour. He stood puffing at his cigarette, and tried to understand matters. Failing, he threw his cigarette away, took a fresh one from his pocket, and approached the old man.

"Got a match?" he inquired, pleasantly.

The old man, much agitated, nearly fell from the railing as he leaned dangerously forward.

"Sonny, can you read?" he demanded in a quavering voice.

"Certainly, I can," said Tom, encouragingly. He waived the affair of the match.

The old man fumbled in his pocket. "You look honest, sonny. I've been looking for an honest feller fur a'most a week. I've set on this railing fur six days," he cried, plaintively.

He drew forth a letter and handed it to Tom. "Read it fur me, sonny, read it," he said, coaxingly.

Tom took the letter and leaned back against the railings. As he opened it and prepared to read, the old man wriggled like a child at a forbidden feast.

Thundering trucks made frequent interruptions, and seven men in a hurry jogged Tom's elbow, but he succeeded in reading what follows:—

Office of Ketchum R. Jones, Attorney-at-Law,
Tin Can, Nevada, May 19, 18—.
Rufus Wilkins, Esq.

Dear Sir,—I have as yet received no acknowledgment of the draft from the sale of the north section lots, which I forwarded to you on 25th June. I would request an immediate reply concerning it.

Since my last I have sold the three corner lots at five thousand each. The city grew so rapidly in that direction that they were surrounded by brick stores almost before you would know it. I have also sold for four thousand dollars the ten acres of out-laying sage bush, which you once foolishly tried to give away. Mr. Simpson, of Boston, bought the tract. He is very shrewd, no doubt, but he hasn't been in the west long. Still, I think if he holds it for about a thousand years, he may come out all right.

I worked him with the projected-horse-car-line gag.

Inform me of the address of your New York attorneys, and I will send on the papers. Pray do not neglect to write me concerning the draft sent on 25th June.

In conclusion, I might say that if you have any eastern friends who are after good western investments inform them of the glorious future of Tin Can. We now have three railroads, a bank, an electric light plant, a projected horse-car line, and an art society. Also, a saw manufactory, a patent car-wheel mill, and a Methodist Church. Tin Can is marching forward to take her proud stand as the metropolis of the west. The rose-hued future holds no glories to which Tin Can does not—

Tom stopped abruptly. "I guess the important part of the letter came first," he said.

"Yes," cried the old man, "I've heard enough. It is just as I thought. George has robbed his dad."

The old man's frail body quivered with grief. Two tears trickled slowly down the furrows of his face.

"Come, come, now," said Tom, patting him tenderly on the back. "Brace up, old feller. What you want to do is to get a lawyer and go put the screws on George."

"Is it really?" asked the old man, eagerly.

"Certainly, it is," said Tom.

"All right," cried the old man, with enthusiasm. "Tell me where to get one." He slid down from the railing and prepared to start off.

Tom reflected. "Well," he said, finally, "I might do for one myself."

"What," shouted the old man in a voice of admiration, "are you a lawyer as well as a reader?"

"Well," said Tom again, "I might appear to advantage as one. All you need is a big front," he added, slowly. He was a profane young man.

The old man seized him by the arm. "Come on, then," he cried, "and we'll go put the screws on George."

Tom permitted himself to be dragged by the weak arms of his companion around a corner and along a side street. As they proceeded, he was internally bracing himself for a struggle, and putting large bales of self-assurance around where they would be likely to obstruct the advance of discovery and defeat.

By the time they reached a brown-stone house, hidden away in a street of shops and warehouses, his mental balance was so admirable that he seemed to be in possession of enough information and brains to ruin half of the city, and he was no more concerned about the king, queen, deuce, and tray than if they had been discards that didn't fit his draw. He infused so much confidence and courage into his companion, that the old man went along the street, breathing war, like a decrepit hound on the scent of new blood.

He ambled up the steps of the brown-stone house as if he were charging earthworks. He unlocked the door and they passed along a dark hallway. In a rear room they found a man seated at table engaged with a very late breakfast. He had a diamond in his shirt front and a bit of egg on his cuff.

"George," said the old man in a fierce voice that came from his aged throat with a sound like the crackle of burning twigs, "here's my lawyer, Mr. er—ah—Smith, and we want to know what you did with the draft that was sent on 25th June."

The old man delivered the words as if each one was a musket shot. George's coffee spilled softly upon the tablecover, and his fingers worked convulsively upon a slice of bread. He turned a white, astonished face toward the old man and the intrepid Thomas.

The latter, straight and tall, with a highly legal air, stood at the old man's side. His glowing eyes were fixed upon the face of the man at the table. They seemed like two little detective cameras taking pictures of the other man's thoughts.

"Father, what d-do you mean," faltered George, totally unable to withstand the two cameras and the highly legal air.

"What do I mean?" said the old man with a feeble roar as from an ancient lion. "I mean that draft—that's what I mean. Give it up or we'll—we'll"—he paused to gain courage by a glance at the formidable figure at his side—"we'll put the screws on you."

"Well, I was—I was only borrowin' it for 'bout a month," said George.

"Ah," said Tom.

George started, glared at Tom, and then began to shiver like an animal with a broken back. There were a few moments of silence. The old man was fumbling about in his mind for more imprecations. George was wilting and turning limp before the glittering orbs of the valiant attorney. The latter, content with the exalted advantage he had gained by the use of the expression "Ah," spoke no more, but continued to stare.

"Well," said George, finally, in a weak voice, "I s'pose I can give you a cheque for it, 'though I was only borrowin' it for 'bout a month. I don't think you have treated me fairly, father, with your lawyers and your threats, and all that. But I'll give you the cheque."

The old man turned to his attorney. "Well?" he asked.

Tom looked at the son and held an impressive debate with himself. "I think we may accept the cheque," he said coldly after a time.

George arose and tottered across the room. He drew a cheque that made the attorney's heart come privately into his mouth. As he and his client passed triumphantly out, he turned a last highly legal glare upon George that reduced that individual to a mere paste.

On the side-walk the old man went into a spasm of delight and called his attorney all the admiring and endearing names there were to be had.

"Lord, how you settled him," he cried ecstatically.

They walked slowly back toward Broadway. "The scoundrel," murmured the old man. "I'll never see 'im again. I'll desert 'im. I'll find a nice quiet boarding-place and—"

"That's all right," said Tom. "I know one. I'll take you right up," which he did.

He came near being happy ever after. The old man lived at advanced rates in the front room at Tom's boarding-house. And the latter basked in the proprietress' smiles, which had a commercial value, and were a great improvement on many we see.

The old man, with his quantities of sage bush, thought Thomas owned all the virtues mentioned in high-class literature, and his opinion, too, was of commercial value. Also, he knew a man who knew another man who received an impetus which made him engage Thomas on terms that were highly satisfactory. Then it was that the latter learned he had not succeeded sooner because he did not know a man who knew another man.

So it came to pass that Tom grew to be Thomas G. Somebody. He achieved that position in life from which he could hold out for good wines when he went to poor restaurants. His name became entangled with the name of Wilkins in the ownership of vast and valuable tracts of sage bush in Tin Can, Nevada.

At the present day he is so great that he lunches frugally at high prices. His fame has spread through the land as a man who carved his way to fortune with no help but his undaunted pluck, his tireless energy, and his sterling integrity.

Newspapers apply to him now, and he writes long signed articles to struggling young men, in which he gives the best possible advice as to how to become wealthy. In these articles, he, in a burst of glorification, cites the king, queen, deuce, and tray, the four aces, and all that. He alludes tenderly to the nickel he borrowed and spent for cigarettes as the foundation of his fortune.

"To succeed in life," he writes, "the youth of America have only to see an old man seated upon a railing and smoking a clay pipe. Then go up and ask him for a match."

# A TALE OF MERE CHANCE

**Being an Account of the Pursuit of the Tiles, the
Statement of the Clock, and the Grip of a Coat of
Orange Spots, together with some Criticism of a
Detective said to be Carved from an Old Table-leg.**

Yes, my friend, I killed the man, but I would not have been detected in it were it
not for some very extraordinary circumstances. I had long considered this deed, but
I am a delicate and sensitive person, you understand, and I hesitated over it as the
diver hesitates on the brink of a dark and icy mountain pool. A thought of the shock
of the contact holds one back.

As I was passing his house one morning, I said to myself, "Well, at any rate, if
she loves him, it will not be for long." And after that decision I was not myself, but
a sort of a machine.

I rang the bell and the servants admitted me to the drawing-room. I waited there
while the old tall clock placidly ticked its speech of time. The rigid and austere
chairs remained in possession of their singular imperturbability, although, of course,
they were aware of my purpose, but the little white tiles of the floor whispered one
to another and looked at me. Presently he entered the room, and I, drawing my
revolver, shot him. He screamed—you know that scream—mostly amazement—
and as he fell forward his blood was upon the little white tiles. They huddled and
covered their eyes from this rain. It seemed to me that the old clock stopped ticking
as a man may gasp in the middle of a sentence, and a chair threw itself in my way
as I sprang toward the door.

A moment later, I was walking down the street, tranquil, you understand, and
I said to myself, "It is done. Long years from this day I will say to her that it was
I who killed him. After time has eaten the conscience of the thing, she will admire
my courage."

I was elated that the affair had gone off so smoothly, and I felt like returning
home and taking a long, full sleep, like a tired working man. When people passed
me, I contemplated their stupidity with a sense of satisfaction.

But those accursed little white tiles.

I heard a shrill crying and chattering behind me, and, looking back, I saw them,
blood-stained and impassioned, raising their little hands and screaming "Murder! It
was he!" I have said that they had little hands. I am not sure of it, but they had some
means of indicating me as unerringly as pointing fingers. As for their movement,
they swept along as easily as dry, light leaves are carried by the wind. Always they
were shrilly piping their song of my guilt.

My friend, may it never be your fortune to be pursued by a crowd of little blood-
stained tiles. I used a thousand means to be free from the clash-clash of these tiny
feet. I ran through the world at my best speed, but it was no better than that of an ox,
while they, my pursuers, were always fresh, eager, relentless.

I am an ingenious person, and I used every trick that a desperate, fertile man
can invent. Hundreds of times I had almost evaded them when some smouldering,
neglected spark would blaze up and discover me.

I felt that the eye of conviction would have no terrors for me, but the eyes of suspicion which I saw in city after city, on road after road, drove me to the verge of going forward and saying, "Yes, I have murdered."

People would see the following, clamorous troops of blood-stained tiles, and give me piercing glances, so that these swords played continually at my heart. But we are a decorous race, thank God. It is very vulgar to apprehend murderers on the public streets. We have learned correct manners from the English. Besides, who can be sure of the meaning of clamouring tiles? It might be merely a trick in politics.

Detectives? What are detectives? Oh, yes, I have read of them and their deeds, when I come to think of it. The prehistoric races must have been remarkable. I have never been able to understand how the detective navigated in stone boats. Still, specimens of their pottery excavated in Taumalipas show a remarkable knowledge of mechanics. I remember the little hydraulic—what's that? Well, what you say may be true, my friend, but I think you dream.

The little stained tiles. My friend, I stopped in an inn at the ends of the earth, and in the morning they were there flying like little birds and pecking at my window.

I should have escaped. Heavens, I should have escaped. What was more simple? I murdered and then walked into the world, which is wide and intricate.

Do you know that my own clock assisted in the hunting of me? They asked what time I left my home that morning, and it replied at once, "Half-after eight." The watch of a man I had chanced to pass near the house of the crime told the people "Seven minutes after nine." And, of course, the tall, old clock in the drawing-room went about day after day repeating, "Eighteen minutes after nine."

Do you say that the man who caught me was very clever? My friend, I have lived long, and he was the most incredible blockhead of my experience. An enslaved, dust-eating Mexican vaquero wouldn't hitch his pony to such a man. Do you think he deserves credit for my capture? If he had been as pervading as the atmosphere, he would never have caught me. If he was a detective, as you say, I could carve a better one from an old table-leg. But the tiles. That is another matter. At night I think they flew in long high flock, like pigeons. In the day, little mad things, they murmured on my trail like frothy-mouthed weasels.

I see that you note these great, round, vividly orange spots on my coat. Of course, even if the detective were really carved from an old table-leg, he could hardly fail to apprehend a man thus badged. As sores come upon one in the plague so came these spots upon my coat. When I discovered them, I made effort to free myself of this coat. I tore, tugged, wrenched at it, but around my shoulders it was like a grip of a dead man's arms. Do you know that I have plunged into a thousand lakes? I have smeared this coat with a thousand paints. But day and night the spots burn like lights. I might walk from this jail today if I could rid myself of this coat, but it clings—clings—clings.

At any rate, the person you call a detective was not so clever to discover a man in a coat of spotted orange, followed by shrieking, blood-stained tiles. Yes, that noise from the corridor is most peculiar. But they are always there, muttering and watching, clashing and jostling. It sounds as if the dishes of Hades were being washed. Yet I have become used to it. Once, indeed, in the night, I cried out to them, "In God's name, go away, little blood-stained tiles." But they doggedly answered, "It is the law."

# AT CLANCY'S WAKE

Scene—Room in the house of the lamented Clancy. The curtains are pulled down. A perfume of old roses and whisky hangs in the air. A weeping woman in black it seated at a table in the centre. A group of wide-eyed children are sobbing in a corner. Down the side of the room is a row of mourning friends of the family. Through an open door can be seen, half hidden in shadows, the silver and black of a coffin.

WIDOW—Oh, wirra, wirra, wirra!

CHILDREN—B-b boo-hoo-hoo!

FRIENDS (*conversing in low tones*)—Yis, Moike Clancy was a foine mahn, sure! None betther! No, I don't t'ink so. Did he? Sure, all th' elictions! He was th' bist in the warrud! He licked 'im widin an inch of his loife, aisy, an' th' other wan a big, shtrappin' buck of a mahn, an' him jes' free of th' pneumonia! Yis, he did! They carried th' warrud by six hunder! Yis, he was a foine mahn. None betther. Gawd sav' 'im!

> (*Enter MR. SLICK, of the "Daily Blanket," shown in by a maid-servant, whose hair has become disarranged through much tear-shedding. He is attired in a suit of grey check, and wears a red rose in his buttonhole.*)

MR. SLICK—Good afternoon, Mrs. Clancy. This is a sad misfortune for you, isn't it?

WIDOW—Oh, indade, indade, young mahn, me poor heart is bruk.

MR. SLICK—Very sad, Mrs. Clancy. A great misfortune, I'm sure. Now, Mrs. Clancy, I've called to—

WIDOW—Little did I t'ink, young mahn, win they brought poor Moike in that it was th' lasht!

MR. SLICK (*with conviction*)—True! True! Very true, indeed. It was a great grief to you, Mrs. Clancy. I've called this morning, Mrs. Clancy, to see if I could get from you a short obituary notice for the Blanket if you could—

WIDOW—An' his hid was done up in a rag, an' he was cursin' frightful. A damned Oytalian lit fall th' hod as Moike was walkin' pasht as dacint as you plaze. Win they carried 'im in, him all bloody, an' ravin' tur'ble 'bout Oytalians, me heart was near bruk, but I niver tawt—I niver tawt—I—I niver—(*Breaks forth into a long, forlorn cry. The children join in, and the chorus echoes wailfully through the rooms.*)

MR. SLICK (*as the yell, in a measure, ceases*)—Yes, indeed, a sad, sad affair. A terrible misfortune. Now, Mrs. Clancy—

WIDOW (*turning suddenly*)—Mary Ann. Where's thot lazy divil of a Mary Ann? (*As the servant appears.*) Mary Ann, bring th' bottle! Give th' gintlemin a dhrink!... Here's to Hiven savin' yez, young mahn. (*Drinks.*)

MR. SLICK (*drinks*)—A noble whisky, Mrs. Clancy. Many thanks. Now, Mrs. Clancy—

WIDOW—Take anodder wan! Take anodder wan! (*Fills his glass.*)

MR. SLICK (*impatiently*)—Yes, certainly, Mrs. Clancy, certainly. (*He drinks.*) Now, could you tell me, Mrs. Clancy, where your late husband was—

WIDOW—Who—Moike? Oh, young mahn, yez can just say thot he was the foinest mahn livin' an' breathin', an' niver a wan in th' warrud was betther. Oh, but he had th' tindther heart for 'is fambly, he did. Don't I remimber win he clipped little Patsey wid th' bottle, an' didn't he buy th' big rockin'-horse th' minit he got sober? Sure he did. Pass th' bottle, Mary Ann! (*Pours a beer-glass about half-full for her guest.*)

MR. SLICK (*taking a seat*)—True, Mr. Clancy was a fine man, Mrs. Clancy—a very fine man. Now, I—

WIDOW (*plaintively*)—An' don't yez loike th' rum? Dhrink th' rum, mahn! It was me own Moike's fav'rite bran'. Well I remimber win he fotched it home, an' half th' demijohn gone a'ready, an' him a-cursin' up th' stairs as dhrunk as Gawd plazed. It was a—Dhrink th' rum, young mahn, dhrink th' rum! If he cud see yez now, Moike Clancy wud git up from 'is—

MR. SLICK (*desperately*)—Very well, very well, Mrs. Clancy. Here's your good health. Now, can you tell me, Mrs. Clancy, when was Mr. Clancy born?

WIDOW—Win was he borrun. Sure, divil a bit do I care win he was borrun. He was th' good mahn to me an' his childher; an' Gawd knows I don't care win he was borrun. Mary Ann, pass th' bottle! Wud yez kape th' gintlemin starvin' for a dhrink here in Moike Clancy's own house? Gawd save yez.

(*When the bottle appears she pours a huge quantity out for her guest.*)

MR. SLICK—Well, then, Mrs. Clancy, where was he born?

WIDOW (*staring*)—In Oirland, mahn, in Oirland! Where did yez t'ink? (*Then, in sudden, wheedling tones.*) An' ain't yez goin' to dhrink th' rum? Are yez goin' to shirk th' good whisky what was th' pride of Moike's life, an' him gettin' full on it an' breakin' th' furnitir t'ree nights a week hard-runnin'? Shame an yez, an' Gawd save yer soul. Dhrink it oop now, there's a dear, dhrink it oop now, an' say: "Moike Clancy, be all th' powers in th' shky, Hiven sind yez rist!"

MR. SLICK—(*to himself*)—Holy smoke! (*He drinks, then regards the glass for a long time.*) ... Well, now, Mrs. Clancy, give me your attention for a moment, please. When did—

WIDOW—An' oh, but he was a power in th' warrud! Divil a mahn cud vote right widout Moike Clancy at 'is elbow. An' in th' calkus, sure didn't Mulrooney git th' nominashun jes' by raison of Moike's atthackin' th' opposashun wid th' shtovepoker. Mulrooney got it as aisy as dhirt, wid Moike rowlin' under th' tayble wid th' other candeedate. He was a good sit'zen, was Moike—divil a wan betther.

MR. SLICK spends some minutes in collecting his faculties.

MR. SLICK (*after he decides that he has them collected*)—Yes, yes, Mrs. Clancy, your husband's h-highly successful pol-pol-political career was w-well known to the public; but what I want to know is—what I want to know—(*Pauses to consider.*)

WIDOW (*finally*)—Pass th' glasses, Mary Ann, yez lazy divil; give th' gintlemin a dhrink! Here (*tendering him a glass*), take anodder wan to Moike Clancy, an' Gawd save yez for yer koindness to a poor widee woman!

MR. SLICK (*after solemnly regarding the glass*)—Certainly, I—I'll take a drink. Certainly, M—Mish Clanshy. Yes, certainly, Mish Clanshy. Now, Mish Clanshy, w-w-wash was Mr. Clanshy's n-name before he married you, Mish Clanshy?

WIDOW (*astonished*)—Why, divil a bit else but Clancy.

MR. SLICK (*after reflection*)—Well, but I mean—I mean, Mish Clanshy, I mean—what was date of birth? Did marry you 'fore then, or d-did marry you when 'e was born in N' York, Mish Clanshy?

WIDOW—Phwat th' divil—

MR. SLICK (*with dignity*)—Ansher my queshuns, pleash, Mish Clanshy. Did 'e bring chil'en withum f'm Irelan', or was you, after married in N' York, mother those chil'en 'e brought f'm Irelan'?

WIDOW—Be th' powers above, I—

MR. SLICK (*with gentle patience*)—I don't shink y' unnerstan' m' queshuns, Mish Clanshy. What I wanna fin' out is, what was 'e born in N' York for when he, before zat, came f'm Irelan'? Dash what puzzels me. I-I'm completely puzzled. An' alsho, I wanna fin' out—I wanna fin' out, if poshble—zat is, if it's poshble shing, I wanna fin' out—I wanna fin' out—if poshble—I wanna-shay, who the blazesh is dead here, anyhow?

# THE VOICE OF THE MOUNTAIN

The old man Popocatepetl was seated on a high rock with his white mantle about his shoulders. He looked at the sky, he looked at the sea, he looked at the land—nowhere could he see any food. And he was very hungry, too.

Who can understand the agony of a creature whose stomach is as large as a thousand churches, when this same stomach is as empty as a broken water jar?

He looked longingly at some island in the sea. "Ah, those flat cakes! If I had them." He stared at storm-clouds in the sky. "Ah, what a drink is there." But the King of Everything, you know, had forbidden the old man Popocatepetl to move at all, because he feared that every footprint would make a great hole in the land. So the old fellow was obliged to sit still and wait for his food to come within reach. Any one who has tried this plan knows what intervals lie between meals.

Once his friend, the little eagle, flew near, and Popocatepetl called to him. "Ho, tiny bird, come and consider with me as to how I shall be fed."

The little eagle came and spread his legs apart and considered manfully, but he could do nothing with the situation. "You see," he said, "this is no ordinary hunger which one goat will suffice—"

Popocatepetl groaned an assent.

"—but it is an enormous affair," continued the little eagle, "which requires something like a dozen stars. I don't see what can be done unless we get that little creature of the earth—that little animal with two arms, two legs, one head, and a very brave air, to invent something. He is said to be very wise."

"Who claims it for him?" asked Popocatepetl.

"He claims it for himself," responded the eagle.

"Well, summon him. Let us see. He is doubtless a kind little animal, and when he sees my distress he will invent something."

"Good!" The eagle flew until he discovered one of these small creatures. "Oh, tiny animal, the great chief Popocatepetl summons you!"

"Does he, indeed!"

"Popocatepetl, the great chief," said the eagle again, thinking that the little animal had not heard rightly.

"Well, and why does he summon me?"

"Because he is in distress, and he needs your assistance."

The little animal reflected for a time, and then said, "I will go."

When Popocatepetl perceived the little animal and the eagle he stretched forth his great, solemn arms. "Oh, blessed little animal with two arms, two legs, a head, and a very brave air, help me in my agony. Behold I, Popocatepetl, who saw the King of Everything fashioning the stars, I, who knew the sun in his childhood, I, Popocatepetl, appeal to you, little animal. I am hungry."

After a while the little animal asked: "How much will you pay?"

"Pay?" said Popocatepetl.

"Pay?" said the eagle.

"Assuredly," quoth the little animal, "pay!"

"But," demanded Popocatepetl, "were you never hungry? I tell you I am hungry, and is your first word then 'pay'?"

The little animal turned coldly away. "Oh, Popocatepetl, how much wisdom has flown past you since you saw the King of Everything fashioning the stars and since you knew the sun in his childhood? I said pay, and, moreover, your distress measures my price. It is our law. Yet it is true that we did not see the King of Everything fashioning the stars. Nor did we know the sun in his childhood."

Then did Popocatepetl roar and shake in his rage. "Oh, louse—louse—louse! Let us bargain then! How much for your blood?" Over the little animal hung death.

But he instantly bowed himself and prayed: "Popocatepetl, the great, you who saw the King of Everything fashioning the stars, and who knew the sun in his childhood, forgive this poor little animal. Your sacred hunger shall be my care. I am your servant."

"It is well," said Popocatepetl at once, for his spirit was ever kindly. "And now, what will you do?"

The little animal put his hand upon his chin and reflected. "Well, it seems you are hungry, and the King of Everything has forbidden you to go for food in fear that your monstrous feet will riddle the earth with holes. What you need is a pair of wings."

"A pair of wings!" cried Popocatepetl delightedly.

"A pair of wings!" screamed the eagle in joy.

"How very simple, after all."

"And yet how wise!"

"But," said Popocatepetl, after the first outburst, "who can make me these wings?"

The little animal replied: "I and my kind are great, because at times we can make one mind control a hundred thousand bodies. This is the secret of our performance. It will be nothing for us to make wings for even you, great Popocatepetl. I and my kind will come"—continued the crafty, little animal—"we will come and dwell on this beautiful plain that stretches from the sea to the sea, and we will make wings for you."

Popocatepetl wished to embrace the little animal. "Oh, glorious! Oh, best of little brutes! Run! run! run! Summon your kind, dwell in the plain and make me wings. Ah, when once Popocatepetl can soar on his wings from star to star, then, indeed—"

* * * *

Poor old stupid Popocatepetl! The little animal summoned his kind, they dwelt on the plains, they made this and they made that, but they made no wings for Popocatepetl.

And sometimes when the thunderous voice of the old peak rolls and rolls, if you know that tongue, you can hear him say: "Oh, traitor! Traitor! Traitor! Where are my wings? My wings, traitor! I am hungry! Where are my wings?"

But the little animal merely places his finger beside his nose and winks.

"Your wings, indeed, fool! Sit still and howl for them! Old idiot!"

# WHY DID THE YOUNG CLERK SWEAR?

## *OR, THE UNSATISFACTORY FRENCH.*

All was silent in the little gent's furnishing store. A lonely clerk with a blonde moustache and a red necktie raised a languid hand to his brow and brushed back a dangling lock. He yawned and gazed gloomily at the blurred panes of the windows.

Without, the wind and rain came swirling round the brick buildings and went sweeping over the streets. A horse-car rumbled stolidly by. In the mud on the pavements, a few pedestrians struggled with excited umbrellas.

"The deuce!" remarked the clerk. "I'd give ten dollars if somebody would come in and buy something, if 'twere only cotton socks."

He waited amid the shadows of the grey afternoon. No customers came. He heaved a long sigh and sat down on a high stool. From beneath a stack of unlaundried shirts he drew a French novel with a picture on the cover. He yawned again, glanced lazily toward the street, and settled himself as comfortable as the gods would let him upon the high stool.

He opened the book and began to read. Soon it could have been noticed that his blonde moustache took on a curl of enthusiasm, and the refractory locks on his brow showed symptoms of soft agitation.

"Silvere did not see the young girl for some days," read the clerk. "He was miserable. He seemed always to inhale that subtle perfume from her hair. At night he saw her eyes in the stars.

"His dreams were troubled. He watched the house. Heloise did not appear. One day he met Vibert. Vibert wore a black frock-coat. There were wine-stains on the right breast. His collar was soiled. He had not shaved.

"Silvere burst into tears. 'I love her! I love her! I shall die!' Vibert laughed scornfully. His necktie was second-hand. Idiotic, this boy in love. Fool! Simpleton! But at last he pitied him. She goes to the music-teacher's every morning. Silly Silvere embraced him.

"The next day Silvere waited at the street corner. A vendor was selling chestnuts. Two gamins were fighting in an alley. A woman was scrubbing some steps. This great Paris throbbed with life.

"Heloise came. She did not perceive Silvere. She passed with a happy smile on her face. She looked fresh, fair, innocent. Silvere felt himself swooning. 'Ah, my God!'

"She crossed the street. The young man received a shock that sent the warm blood to his brain. It had been raining. There was mud. With one slender hand Heloise lifted her skirts. Silvere leaning forward, saw her—"

A young man in a wet mackintosh came into the little gent's furnishing store.

"Ah, beg pardon," said he to the clerk, "but do you have an agency for a steam laundry here? I have been patronising a Chinaman down th' avenue for some time, but he—what? No? You have none here? Well, why don't you start one, anyhow?

It'd be a good thing in this neighbourhood. I live just round the corner, and it'd be a great thing for me. I know lots of people who would—what? Oh, you don't? Oh!"

As the young man in the wet mackintosh retreated, the clerk with a blonde moustache made a hungry grab at the novel. He continued to read: "Handkerchief fall in a puddle. Silvere sprang forward. He picked up the handkerchief. Their eyes met. As he returned the handkerchief, their hands touched. The young girl smiled. Silvere was in ecstacies. 'Ah, my God!'

"A baker opposite was quarrelling over two sous with an old woman.

"A grey-haired veteran with a medal upon his breast and a butcher's boy were watching a dog-fight. The smell of dead animals came from adjacentslaughter-houses. The letters on the sign over the tinsmith's shop on the corner shone redly like great clots of blood. It was hell on roller skates."

Here the clerk skipped some seventeen chapters descriptive of a number of intricate money transactions, the moles on the neck of a Parisian dressmaker, the process of making brandy, the milk-leg of Silvere's aunt, life in the coal-pits, and scenes in the Chamber of Deputies. In these chapters the reputation of the architect of Charlemagne's palace was vindicated, and it was explained why Heloise's grandmother didn't keep her stockings pulled up.

Then he proceeded: "Heloise went to the country. The next day Silvere followed. They met in the fields. The young girl had donned the garb of the peasants. She blushed. She looked fresh, fair, innocent. Silvere felt faint with rapture. 'Ah, my God!'

"She had been running. Out of breath, she sank down in the hay. She held out her hand. 'I am so glad to see you.' Silvere was enchanted at this vision. He bended toward her. Suddenly he burst into tears. 'I love you! I love you! I love you!' he stammered.

"A row of red and white shirts hung on a line some distance away. The third shirt from the left had a button off the neck. A cat on the rear steps of a cottage near the shirt was drinking milk from a platter. The north-east portion of the platter had a crack in it.

"'Heloise!' Silvere was murmuring hoarsely. He leaned toward her until his warm breath moved the curls on her neck. 'Heloise!' murmured Jean."

"Young man," said an elderly gentleman with a dripping umbrella to the clerk with a blonde moustache, "have you any night-shirts open front and back? Eh? Night-shirts open front and back, I said. D'you hear, eh? *Night-shirts open front and back.* Well, then, why didn't you say so? It would pay you to be a trifle more polite, young man. When you get as old as I am, you will find out that it pays to—what? I didn't see you adding any column of figures. In that case I am sorry. You have no night-shirts open front and back, eh? Well, good-day."

As the elderly gentleman vanished, the clerk with a blonde moustache grasped the novel like some famished animal. He read on: "A peasant stood before the two children. He wrung his hands. 'Have you seen a stray cow?' 'No,' cried the children in the same breath. The peasant wept. He wrung his hands. It was a supreme moment.

"'She loves me!' cried Silvere to himself, as he changed his clothes for dinner.

"It was evening. The children sat by the fire-place. Heloise wore a gown of clinging white. She looked fresh, fair, innocent. Silvere was in raptures. 'Ah, my God!'

"Old Jean, the peasant, saw nothing. He was mending harness. The fire crackled in the fire-place. The children loved each other. Through the open door to the kitchen came the sound of old Marie shrilly cursing the geese who wished to enter. In front of the window two pigs were quarrelling over a vegetable. Cattle were lowing in a distant field. A hay-waggon creaked slowly past. Thirty-two chickens were asleep in the branches of a tree. This subtle atmosphere had a mighty effect upon Heloise. It was beating down her self-control. She felt herself going. She was choking.

"The young girl made an effort. She stood up. 'Good-night, I must go.' Silvere took her hand. 'Heloise,' he murmured. Outside the two pigs were fighting.

"A warm blush overspread the young girl's face. She turned wet eyes toward her lover. She looked fresh, fair, innocent. Silvere was maddened. 'Ah, my God!'

"Suddenly the young girl began to tremble. She tried vainly to withdraw her hand. But her knee—"

"I wish to get my husband some shirts," said a shopping-woman with six bundles. The clerk with a blonde moustache made a private gesture of despair, and rapidly spread a score of different-patterned shirts upon the counter. "He's very particular about his shirts," said the shopping-woman. "Oh, I don't think any of these will do. Don't you keep the Invincible brand? He only wears that kind. He says they fit him better. And he's very particular about his shirts. What? You don't keep them? No? Well, how much do you think they would come at?" "Haven't the slightest idea." "Well, I suppose I must go somewhere else, then. Um, good-day."

The clerk with the blonde moustache was about to make further private gestures of despair, when the shopping-woman with six bundles turned and went out. His fingers instantly closed nervously over the book. He drew it from its hiding-place, and opened it at the place where he had ceased. His hungry eyes seemed to eat the words upon the page. He continued: "—struck cruelly against a chair. It seemed to awaken her. She started. She burst from the young man's arms. Outside the two pigs were grunting amiably.

"Silvere took his candle. He went toward his room. He was in despair. 'Ah, my God!'

"He met the young girl on the stairs. He took her hand. Tears were raining down his face. 'Heloise!' he murmured.

"The young girl shivered. As Silvere put his arms about her, she faintly resisted. This embrace seemed to sap her life. She wished to die. Her thoughts flew back to the old well and the broken hayrakes at Plassans.

"The young girl looked fresh, fair, innocent 'Heloise!' murmured Silvere. The children exchanged a long, clinging kiss. It seemed to unite their souls.

"The young girl was swooning. Her head sank on the young man's shoulder. There was nothing in space except these warm kisses on her neck. Silvere enfolded her. 'Ah, my God!'"

"Say, young fellow," said a youth with a tilted cigar to the clerk with a blonde moustache, "where th'll is Billie Carcart's joint round here? Know?"

"Next corner," said the clerk fiercely.

"Oh, th'll," said the youth, "yehs needn't git gay. See! When a feller asts a civil question yehs needn't git gay. See! Th'll!"

The youth stood and looked aggressive for a moment. Then he went away.

The clerk seemed almost to leap upon the book. His feverish fingers twirled the pages. When he found his place he glued his eyes to it. He read:

"Then a great flash of lightning illumined the hall-way. It threw livid hues over a row of flowerpots in the window-seat. Thunder shook the house to its foundation. From the kitchen arose the voice of old Marie in prayer.

"Heloise screamed. She wrenched herself from the young man's arms. She sprang inside her room. She locked the door. She flung herself face downward on the bed. She burst into tears. She looked fresh, fair, innocent.

"The rain pattering upon the thatched roof sounded in the stillness like the footsteps of spirits. In the sky toward Paris there shone a crimson light.

"The chickens had all fallen from the tree. They stood, sadly, in a puddle. The two pigs were asleep under the porch.

"Upstairs, in the hall-way, Silvers was furious."

The clerk with a blonde moustache gave here a wild scream of disappointment. He madly hurled the novel with the picture on the cover from him. He stood up and said: "Damn!"

# THE VICTORY OF THE MOON

The Strong Man of the Hills lost his wife. Immediately he went abroad, calling aloud. The people all crouched afar in the dark of their huts, and cried to him when he was yet a long distance away: "No, no, great chief, we have not even seen the imprint of your wife's sandal in the sand. If we had seen it, you would have found us bowed down in worship before the marks of her ten glorious brown toes, for we are but poor devils of Indians, and the grandeur of the sun rays on her hair would have turned our eyes to dust."

"Her toes are not brown. They are pink," said the Strong Man from the Hills. "Therefore do I believe that you speak the truth when you say you have not seen her, good little men of the valley. In this matter of her great loveliness, however, you speak a little too strongly. As she is no longer among my possessions, I have no mind to hear her praised. Whereabouts is the best man of you?"

None of them had stomach for this honour at the time. They surmised that the Strong Man of the Hills had some plan for combat, and they knew that the best of them would have in this encounter only the strength of the meat in the grip of the fire. "Great King," they said, in one voice, "there is no best man here."

"How is this?" roared the Strong Man. "There must be one who excels. It is a law. Let him step forward then."

But they solemnly shook their heads. "There is no best man here."

The Strong Man turned upon them so furiously that many fell to the ground. "There must be one. Let him step forward." Shivering, they huddled together and tried, in their fear, to thrust each other toward the Strong Man.

At this time a young philosopher approached the throng slowly. The philosophers of that age were all young men in the full heat of life. The old greybeards were, for the most part, very stupid, and were so accounted.

"Strong Man from the Hills," said the young philosopher, "go to yonder brook and bathe. Then come and eat of this fruit. Then gaze for a time at the blue sky and the green earth. Afterward I have something to say to you."

"You are not so wise that I am obliged to bathe before listening to you?" demanded the Strong Man, insolently.

"No," said the young philosopher. All the people thought this reply very strange.

"Why, then, must I bathe and eat of fruit and gaze at the earth and the sky?"

"Because they are pleasant things to do."

"Have I, do you think, any thirst at this time for pleasant things?"

"Bathe, eat, gaze," said the young philosopher with a gesture.

The Strong Man did, indeed, whirl his bronzed and terrible limbs in the silver water. Then he lay in the shadow of a tree and ate the cool fruit and gazed at the sky and the earth. "This is a fine comfort," he said. After a time he suddenly struck his forehead with his finger. "By the way, did I tell you that my wife had fled from me?"

"I know it," said the young philosopher.

Later the Strong Man slept peacefully. The young philosopher smiled.

But in the night the little men of the valley came clamouring: "Oh, Strong Man of the Hills, the moon derides you!"

The philosopher went to them in the darkness. "Be still, little people. It is nothing. The derision of the moon is nothing."

But the little men of the valley would not cease their uproar. "Oh, Strong Man! Strong Man, awake! Awake! The moon derides you!"

Then the Strong Man aroused and shook his locks away from his eyes. "What is it, good little men of the valley?"

"Oh, Strong Man, the moon derides you! Oh, Strong Man!"

The Strong Man looked, and there, indeed, was the moon laughing down at him. He sprang to his feet and roared. "Ah, old, fat, lump of moon, you laugh! Have you seen my wife?"

The moon said no word, but merely smiled in a way that was like a flash of silver bars.

"Well, then, moon, take this home to her," thundered the Strong Man, and he hurled his spear.

The moon clapped both hands to its eye, and cried: "Oh! Oh!"

The little people of the valley cried: "Oh, this is terrible, Strong Man! He has smitten our sacred moon in the eye!"

The young philosopher cried nothing at all.

The Strong Man threw his coat of crimson feathers upon the ground. He took his knife and felt its edge. "Look you, philosopher," he said. "I have lost my wife, and the bath, the meal of fruit in the shade, the sight of sky and earth are still good to me, but when this false moon derides me, there must be a killing."

"I understand you," said the young philosopher.

The Strong Man ran off into the night. The little men of the valley clapped their hands in ecstacy and terror. "Ah! ah! what a battle will there be!"

The Strong Man went into his own hills and gathered there many great rocks and trunks of trees. It was strange to see him erect upon a peak of the mountains and hurling these things at the moon. He kept the air full of them.

"Fat moon, come closer," he shouted. "Come closer, and let it be my knife against your knife. Oh, to think that we are obliged to tolerate such an old, fat, stupid, lazy, good-for-nothing moon. You are ugly as death, while I—Oh, moon, you stole my beloved, and it was nothing, but when you stole my beloved and laughed at me, it became another matter. And yet you are so ugly, so fat, so stupid, so lazy, so good-for-nothing. Ah, I shall go mad! Come closer, moon, and let me examine your round, grey skull with this club."

And he always kept the air full of great missiles.

The moon merely laughed, and said: "Why should I come closer?"

Wildly did the Strong Man pile rock upon rock. He builded him a tower that was the father of all towers. It made the mountains to appear to be babes. Upon the summit of it he swung his great club and flourished his knife.

The little men in the valley far below beheld a great storm, and at the end of it they said: "Look, the moon is dead." The cry went to and fro on the earth: "The moon is dead!"

The Strong Man went to the home of the moon. She, the sought one, lay upon a cloud, and her little foot dangled over the side of it. The Strong Man took this little foot in his two hands and kissed it. "Ah, beloved!" he moaned, "I would rather this little foot was upon my dead neck than that moon should ever have the privilege of seeing it."

She leaned over the edge of the cloud and gazed at him. "How dusty you are. Why do you puff so? Veritably, you are an ordinary person. Why did I ever find you interesting?"

The Strong Man flung his knife into the air and turned back toward the earth. "If the young philosopher had been at my elbow," he reflected, bitterly, "I would doubtless have gone at the matter in another way. What does my strength avail me in this contest?"

The battered moon, limping homeward, replied to the Strong Man from the Hills: "Aye, surely. My weakness is in this thing as strong as your strength. I am victor with ugliness, my age, my stoutness, my laziness, my good-for-nothingness. Woman is woman. Men are equal in everything save good fortune. I envy you not."

# ACTIVE SERVICE

## CHAPTER I

Marjory walked pensively along the hall. In the cool shadows made by the palms on the window ledge, her face wore the expression of thoughtful melancholy expected on the faces of the devotees who pace in cloistered gloom. She halted before a door at the end of the hall and laid her hand on the knob. She stood hesitating, her head bowed. It was evident that this mission was to require great fortitude.

At last she opened the door.

"Father," she began at once. There was disclosed an elderly, narrow-faced man seated at a large table and surrounded by manuscripts and books. The sunlight flowing through curtains of Turkey red fell sanguinely upon the bust of dead-eyed Pericles on the mantle. A little clock was ticking, hidden somewhere among the countless leaves of writing, the maps and broad heavy tomes that swarmed upon the table.

Her father looked up quickly with an ogreish scowl.

"Go away!" he cried in a rage. "Go away. Go away. Get out!" He seemed on the point of arising to eject the visitor. It was plain to her that he had been interrupted in the writing of one of his sentences, ponderous, solemn and endless, in which wandered multitudes of homeless and friendless prepositions, adjectives looking for a parent, and quarrelling nouns, sentences which no longer symbolized the language-form of thought but which had about them a quaint aroma from the dens of long-dead scholars. "Get out," snarled the professor.

Father," faltered the girl. Either because his formulated thought was now completely knocked out of his mind by his own emphasis in defending it, or because he detected something of portent in her expression, his manner suddenly changed, and with a petulant glance at his writing he laid down his pen and sank back in his chair to listen. "Well, what is it, my child?"

The girl took a chair near the window and gazed out upon the snow-stricken campus, where at the moment a group of students returning from a class room were festively hurling snowballs.

"I've got something important to tell you, father," said she, "but I don't quite know how to say it."

"Something important?" repeated the professor. He was not habitually interested in the affairs of his family, but this proclamation that something important could be connected with them, filled his mind with a capricious interest. "Well, what is it, Marjory?"

She replied calmly: "Rufus Coleman wants to marry me."

"What?" demanded the professor loudly. "Rufus Coleman. What do you mean?"

The girl glanced furtively at him. She did not seem to be able to frame a suitable sentence.

As for the professor, he had, like all men both thoughtless and thoughtful, told himself that one day his daughter would come to him with a tale of this kind. He had never forgotten that the little girl was to be a woman, and he had never forgotten that this tall, lithe creature, the present Marjory, *was* a woman. He had been entranced and confident, or entranced and apprehensive, according to the time. A man focused

upon astronomy, the pig market, or social progression may nevertheless have a secondary mind which hovers like a spirit over his dahlia tubers and dreams upon the
mystery of their slow and tender revelations. The professor's secondary mind had
dwelt always with his daughter and watched with a faith and delight the changing to
a woman of a certain fat and mumbling babe. However, he now saw this machine,
this self-sustaining, self-operative love, which had run with the ease of a clock, suddenly crumble to ashes and leave the mind of a great scholar staring at a calamity.

"Rufus Coleman," he repeated, stunned. Here was his daughter, very obviously
desirous of marrying Rufus Coleman. "Marjory," he cried in amazement and fear,
"what possesses, you? *Marry* Rufus Colman?"

The girl seemed to feel a strong sense of relief at his prompt recognition of a
fact. Being freed from the necessity of making a flat declaration, she simply hung
her head and blushed impressively. A hush fell upon them. The professor stared long
at his daughter. The shadow of unhappiness deepened upon his face.

"Marjory, Marjory," he murmured at last. He had tramped heroically upon his
panic and devoted his strength to bringing thought into some kind of attitude toward
this terrible fact. "I am—I am surprised," he began. Fixing her then with a stern eye,
he asked: "Why do you wish to marry *this* man? You, with your opportunities of
meeting persons of intelligence. And you want to marry—" His voice grew tragic.
"You want to marry the Sunday editor of the *New York Eclipse*."

"It is not so very terrible, is it?" said Marjory sullenly.

"Wait a moment; don't talk," cried the professor. He arose and walked nervously
to and fro, his hands flying in the air. He was very red behind the ears as when in
the classroom some student offended him. "A gambler, a sporter of fine clothes, an
expert on champagne, a polite loafer, a witness knave who edits the Sunday edition
of a great outrage upon our sensibilities. You want to marry *him*, this man? Marjory,
you are insane. This fraud who asserts that his work is intelligent, this fool comes
here to my house and—"

He became aware that his daughter was regarding him coldly.

"I thought we had best have all this part of it over at once," she remarked.

He confronted her in a new kind of surprise. The little keen-eyed professor was
at this time imperial, on the verge of a majestic outburst.

"Be still," he said. "Don't be clever with your father. Don't be a dodger. Or, if
you are, don't speak of it to me. I suppose this fine young man expects to see me
personally?"

"He was coming tomorrow," replied Marjory. She began to weep. "He was coming tomorrow."

"Um," said the professor. He continued his pacing while Marjory wept with her
head bowed to the arm of the chair. His brow made the three dark vertical crevices
well known to his students. Sometimes he glowered murderously at the photographs
of ancient temples which adorned the walls.

"My poor child," he said once, as he paused near her, "to think I never knew you
were a fool. I have been deluding myself. It has been my fault as much as it has been
yours. I will not readily forgive myself."

The girl raised her face and looked at him. Finally, resolved to disregard the
dishevelment wrought by tears, she presented a desperate front with her wet eyes
and flushed cheeks. Her hair was disarrayed.

"I don't see why you can call me a fool," she said.

The pause before this sentence had been so portentous of a wild and rebellious
speech that the professor almost laughed now. But still the father for the first time

knew that he was being undauntedly faced by his child in his own library, in the presence of 372 pages of the book that was to be his masterpiece. At the back of his mind he felt a great awe, as if his own youthful spirit had come from the past and challenged him with a glance. For a moment he was almost a defeated man. He dropped into a chair.

"Does your mother know of this?" he asked mournfully.

"Yes," replied the girl. "She knows. She has been trying to make me give up Rufus."

"Rufus," cried the professor rejuvenated by anger.

"Well, his name *is* Rufus," said the girl.

"But please don't call him so before me," said the father with icy dignity. "I do not recognize him as being named Rufus. That is a contention of yours which does not arouse my interest. I know him very well as a gambler and a drunkard, and if incidentally he is named Rufus, I fail to see any importance to it."

"He is not a gambler and he is not a drunkard," she said.

"Um. He drinks heavily—that is well known. He gambles. He plays cards for money—more than he possesses—at least he did when he was in college."

"You said you liked him when he was in college."

"So I did. So I did," answered the professor sharply. "I often find myself liking that kind of a boy in college. Don't I know them—those lads with their beer and their poker games in the dead of the night with a towel hung over the keyhole. Their habits are often vicious enough, but something remains in them through it all and they may go away and do great things. This happens. We know it. It happens with confusing insistence. It destroys theories. There—there isn't much to say about it. And sometimes we like this kind of a boy better than we do the—the others. For my part, I know of many a pure, pious, and fine-minded student that I have positively loathed from a personal point-of-view. But," he added, "this Rufus Coleman, his life in college and his life since, go to prove how often we get off the track. There is no gauge of collegiate conduct whatever, until we can get evidence of the man's work in the world. Your precious scoundrel's evidence is now all in, and he is a failure, or worse."

"You are not habitually so fierce in judging people," said the girl.

"I would be if they all wanted to marry my daughter," rejoined the professor. "Rather than let that man make love to you—or even be within a short railway journey of you—I'll cart you off to Europe this winter and keep you there until you forget. If you persist in this silly fancy, I shall at once become medieval."

Marjory had evidently recovered much of her composure.

"Yes, father, new climates are always supposed to cure one," she remarked with a kind of lightness.

"It isn't so much the old expedient," said the professor musingly, "as it is that I would be afraid to leave you here with no protection against that drinking gambler and gambling drunkard."

"Father, I have to ask you not to use such terms in speaking of the man that I shall marry."

There was a silence. To all intents, the professor remained unmoved. He smote the tips of his fingers thoughtfully together. "Ye-es," he observed. "That sounds reasonable from your standpoint."

His eyes studied her face in a long and steady glance. He arose and went into the hall. When he returned, he wore his hat and great coat. He took a book and some papers from the table and went away.

Marjory walked slowly through the halls and up to her room. From a window she could see her father making his way across the campus laboriously against the wind and whirling snow. She watched him, this little black figure, bent forward, patient, steadfast. It was an inferior fact that her father was one of the famous scholars of the generation. To her, he was now a little old man facing the wintry winds. Recollecting herself and Rufus Coleman, she began to weep again, wailing amid the ruins of her tumbled hopes. Her skies had turned to paper and her trees were mere bits of green sponge. But amid all this woe appeared the little black image of her father making his way against the storm.

## CHAPTER II.

In a high-walled corridor of one of the college buildings, a crowd of students waited amid jostlings and a loud buzz of talk. Suddenly a huge pair of doors flew open and a wedge of young men inserted itself boisterously and deeply into the throng. There was a great scuffle attended by a general banging of books upon heads. The two lower classes engaged in Herculean play while members of the two higher classes, standing aloof, devoted themselves strictly to the encouragement of whichever party for a moment lost ground or heart. This was in order to prolong the conflict.

The combat, waged in the desperation of proudest youth, waxed hot and hotter. The wedge had been instantly smitten into a kind of block of men. It had crumpled into an irregular square and on three sides it was now assailed with remarkable ferocity.

It was a matter of wall meets wall in terrific rushes, during which lads could feel their very hearts leaving them in the compress of friends and foes. They on the outskirts upheld the honor of their classes by squeezing into paper thickness the lungs of those of their fellows who formed the center of the melée

In some way it resembled a panic at a theatre.

The first lance-like attack of the Sophomores had been formidable, but the Freshmen outnumbering their enemies and smarting from continual Sophomoric oppression, had swarmed to the front like drilled collegians and given the arrogant foe the first serious check of the year. Therefore the tall Gothic windows which lined one side of the corridor looked down upon as incomprehensible and enjoyable a tumult as could mark the steps of advanced education. The Seniors and juniors cheered themselves ill. Long freed from the joy of such meetings, their only means for this kind of recreation was to involve the lower classes, and they had never seen the victims fall to with such vigor and courage. Bits of printed leaves, torn notebooks, dismantled collars and cravats, all floated to the floor beneath the feet of the warring hordes. There were no blows; it was a battle of pressure. It was a deadly pushing where the leaders on either side often suffered the most cruel and sickening agony caught thus between phalanxes of shoulders with friend as well as foe contributing to the pain.

Charge after charge of Freshmen beat upon the now compact and organized Sophomores. Then, finally, the rock began to give slow way. A roar came from the Freshmen and they hurled themselves in a frenzy upon their betters.

To be under the gaze of the juniors and Seniors is to be in sight of all men, and so the Sophomores at this important moment labored with the desperation of the half-doomed to stem the terrible Freshmen.

In the kind of game, it was the time when bad tempers came strongly to the front, and in many Sophomores' minds a thought arose of the incomparable insolence of the Freshmen. A blow was struck; an infuriated Sophomore had swung an arm high and smote a Freshman.

Although it had seemed that no greater noise could be made by the given numbers, the din that succeeded this manifestation surpassed everything. The Juniors and Seniors immediately set up an angry howl. These veteran classes projected themselves into the middle of the fight, buffeting everybody with small thought as to merit. This method of bringing peace was as militant as a landslide, but they had much trouble before they could separate the central clump of antagonists into its parts. A score of Freshmen had cried out: "It was Coke. Coke punched him. Coke." A dozen of them were tempestuously endeavoring to register their protest against fisticuffs by means of an introduction of more fisticuffs.

The upper classmen were swift, harsh and hard. "Come, now, Freshies, quit it. Get back, get back, d'y'hear?" With a wrench of muscles they forced themselves in front of Coke, who was being blindly defended by his classmates from intensely earnest attacks by outraged Freshmen.

These meetings between the lower classes at the door of a recitation room were accounted quite comfortable and idle affairs, and a blow delivered openly and in hatred fractured a sharply defined rule of conduct. The corridor was in a hubbub. Many Seniors and Juniors, bursting from old and iron discipline, wildly clamored that some Freshman should be given the privilege of a single encounter with Coke. The Freshmen themselves were frantic. They besieged the tight and dauntless circle of men that encompassed Coke. None dared confront the Seniors openly, but by headlong rushes at auspicious moments they tried to come to quarters with the rings of dark-browed Sophomores. It was no longer a festival, a game; it was a riot. Coke, wild-eyed, pallid with fury, a ribbon of blood on his chin, swayed in the middle of the mob of his classmates, comrades who waived the ethics of the blow under the circumstance of being obliged as a corps to stand against the scorn of the whole college, as well as against the tremendous assaults of the Freshmen. Shamed by their own man, but knowing full well the right time and the wrong time for a palaver of regret and disavowal, this battalion struggled in the desperation of despair. Once they were upon the verge of making unholy campaign against the interfering Seniors. This fiery impertinence was the measure of their state.

It was a critical moment in the play of the college. Four or five defeats from the Sophomores during the fall had taught the Freshmen much. They had learned the comparative measurements, and they knew now that their prowess was ripe to enable them to amply revenge what was, according to their standards, an execrable deed by a man who had not the virtue to play the rough game, but was obliged to resort to uncommon methods. In short, the Freshmen were almost out of control, and the Sophomores debased but defiant, were quite out of control. The Senior and Junior classes which, in American colleges dictate in these affrays, found their dignity toppling, and in consequence there was a sudden oncome of the entire force of upper classmen football players naturally in advance. All distinctions were dissolved at once in a general fracas. The stiff and still Gothic windows surveyed a scene of dire carnage.

Suddenly a voice rang brazenly through the tumult. It was not loud, but it was different. "Gentlemen! Gentlemen!"

Instantly there was a remarkable number of haltings, abrupt replacements, quick changes. Prof. Wainwright stood at the door of his recitation room, looking into the eyes of each member of the mob of three hundred. "Ssh!" said the mob. "Ssh! Quit! Stop! It's the Ambassador! Stop!" He had once been minister to Austro-Hungary, and forever now to the students of the college his name was Ambassador. He stepped into the corridor, and they cleared for him a little respectful zone of floor. He looked about him coldly.

"It seems quite a general dishevelment. The Sophomores display an energy in the halls which I do not detect in the class room." A feeble murmur of appreciation arose from the outskirts of the throng. While he had been speaking several remote groups of battling men had been violently signaled and suppressed by other students. The professor gazed into terraces of faces that were still inflamed. "I needn't say that I am surprised," he remarked in the accepted rhetoric of his kind. He added musingly: "There seems to be a great deal of torn linen. Who is the young gentleman with blood on his chin?"

The throng moved restlessly. A manful silence, such as might be in the tombs of stern and honorable knights, fell upon the shadowed corridor. The subdued rustling had fainted to nothing. Then out of the crowd Coke, pale and desperate, delivered himself.

"Oh, Mr. Coke," said the professor, "I would be glad if you would tell the gentlemen they may retire to their dormitories." He waited while the students passed out to the campus.

The professor returned to his room for some books, and then began his own march across the snowy campus. The wind twisted his coattails fantastically, and he was obliged to keep one hand firmly on the top of his hat. When he arrived home he met his wife in the hall. "Look here, Mary," he cried. She followed him into the library. "Look here," he said. "What is this all about? Marjory tells me she wants to marry Rufus Coleman."

Mrs. Wainwright was a fat woman who was said to pride herself upon being very wise and if necessary, sly. In addition she laughed continually in an inexplicably personal way, which apparently made everybody who heard her feel offended. Mrs. Wainwright laughed.

"Well," said the professor, bristling, "what do you mean by that?"

"Oh, Harris," she replied. "Oh, Harris."

The professor straightened in his chair. "I do not see any illumination in those remarks, Mary. I understand from Marjory's manner that she is bent upon marrying Rufus Coleman. She said you knew of it."

"Why, of course I knew. It was as plain—"

"Plain!" scoffed the professor. "Plain!"

Why, of course," she cried. "I knew it all along."

There was nothing in her tone which proved that she admired the event itself. She was evidently carried away by the triumph of her penetration.

"I knew it all along," she added, nodding.

The professor looked at her affectionately. "You knew it all along, then, Mary? Why didn't you tell me, dear?"

"Because you ought to have known it," she answered blatantly.

The professor was glaring. Finally he spoke in tones of grim reproach. "Mary, whenever you happen to know anything, dear, it seems only a matter of partial recompense that you should tell me."

The wife had been taught in a terrible school that she should never invent any inexpensive retorts concerning bookworms and so she yawed at once. "Really, Harris. Really, I didn't suppose the affair was serious. You could have knocked me down with a feather. Of course he has been here very often, but then Marjory gets a great deal of attention. A great deal of attention." The professor had been thinking.

"Rather than let my girl marry that scalawag, I'll take you and her to Greece this winter with the class. Separation. It is a sure cure that has the sanction of antiquity."

"Well," said Mrs. Wainwright, "you know best, Harris. You know best." It was a common remark with her, and it probably meant either approbation or disapprobation if it did not mean simple discretion.

## CHAPTER III.

THERE had been a babe with no arms born in one of the western counties of Massachusetts. In place of upper limbs the child had growing from its chest a pair of fin-like hands, mere bits of skin-covered bone. Furthermore, it had only one eye. This phenomenon lived four days, but the news of the birth had travelled up this country road and through that village until it reached the ears of the editor of the *Michaelstown Tribune*. He was also a correspondent of the *New York Eclipse*. On the third day he appeared at the home of the parents accompanied by a photographer. While the latter arranged his, instrument, the correspondent talked to the father and mother, two cow-eyed and yellow-faced people who seemed to suffer a primitive fright of the strangers. Afterwards as the correspondent and the photographer were climbing into their buggy, the mother crept furtively down to the gate and asked, in a foreigner's dialect, if they would send her a copy of the photograph. The correspondent carelessly indulgent, promised it. As the buggy swung away, the father came from behind an apple tree, and the two semi-humans watched it with its burden of glorious strangers until it rumbled across the bridge and disappeared. The correspondent was elate; he told the photographer that the *Eclipse* would probably pay fifty dollars for the article and the photograph.

The office of the *New York Eclipse* was at the top of the immense building on Broadway. It was a sheer mountain to the heights of which the interminable thunder of the streets arose faintly. The Hudson was a broad path of silver in the distance. Its edge was marked by the tracery of sailing ships' rigging and by the huge and many-colored stacks of ocean liners. At the foot of the cliff lay City Hall Park. It seemed no larger than a quilt. The grey walks patterned the snow-covering into triangles and ovals and upon them many tiny people scurried here and there, without sound, like a fish at the bottom of a pool. It was only the vehicles that sent high, unmistakable, the deep bass of their movement. And yet after listening one seemed to hear a singular murmurous note, a pulsation, as if the crowd made noise by its mere living, a mellow hum of the eternal strife. Then suddenly out of the deeps might ring a human voice, a newsboy shout perhaps, the cry of a faraway jackal at night.

From the level of the ordinary roofs, combined in many plateaus, dotted with short iron chimneys from which curled wisps of steam, arose other mountains like the *Eclipse* Building. They were great peaks, ornate, glittering with paint or polish. Northward they subsided to sun-crowned ranges.

From some of the windows of the *Eclipse* office dropped the walls of a terrible chasm in the darkness of which could be seen vague struggling figures. Looking down into this appalling crevice one discovered only the tops of hats and knees which in spasmodic jerks seemed to touch the rims of the hats. The scene represented some weird fight or dance or carouse. It was not an exhibition of men hurrying along a narrow street.

It was good to turn one's eyes from that place to the vista of the city's splendid reaches, with spire and spar shining in the clear atmosphere and the marvel of the Jersey shore, pearl-misted or brilliant with detail. From this height the sweep of a snowstorm was defined and majestic. Even a slight summer shower, with swords of lurid yellow sunlight piercing its edges as if warriors were contesting every foot of its advance, was from the *Eclipse* office something so inspiring that the chance pilgrim felt a sense of exultation as if from this peak he was surveying the worldwide war of the elements and life. The staff of the *Eclipse* usually worked without coats and amid the smoke from pipes.

To one of the editorial chambers came a photograph and an article from Michaelstown, Massachusetts. A boy placed the packet and many others upon the desk of a young man who was standing before a window and thoughtfully drumming upon the pane. He turned at the thudding of the packets upon his desk. "Blast you," he remarked amiably. "Oh, I guess it won't hurt you to work," answered the boy, grinning with a comrade's insolence. Baker, an assistant editor for the Sunday paper, took scat at his desk and began the task of examining the packets. His face could not display any particular interest because he had been at the same work for nearly a fortnight.

The first long envelope he opened was from a woman. There was a neat little manuscript accompanied by a letter which explained that the writer was a widow who was trying to make her living by her pen and who, further, hoped that the generosity of the editor of the *Eclipse* would lead him to give her article the opportunity which she was sure it deserved. She hoped that the editor would pay her as well as possible for it, as she needed the money greatly. She added that her brother was a reporter on the Little Rock Sentinel and he had declared that her literary style was excellent. Baker really did not read this note. His vast experience of a fortnight had enabled him to detect its kind in two glances. He unfolded the manuscript, looked at it woodenly and then tossed it with the letter to the top of his desk, where it lay with the other corpses. None could think of widows in Arkansas, ambitious from the praise of the reporter on the Little Rock Sentinel, waiting for a crown of literary glory and money. In the next envelope a man using the notepaper of a Boston journal begged to know if the accompanying article would be acceptable; if not it was to be kindly returned in the enclosed stamped envelope. It was a humorous essay on trolley cars. Adventuring through the odd scraps that were come to the great mill, Baker paused occasionally to relight his pipe.

As he went through envelope after envelope, the desks about him gradually were occupied by young men who entered from the hall with their faces still red from the cold of the streets. For the most part they bore the unmistakable stamp of the American college. They had that confident poise which is easily brought from the athletic field. Moreover, their clothes were quite in the way of being of the newest fashion. There was an air of precision about their cravats and linen. But on the other hand there might be with them some indifferent westerner who was obliged to resort to irregular means and harangue startled shopkeepers in order to provide himself with collars of a strange kind. He was usually very quick and brave of eye and noted for his inability to perceive a distinction between his own habit and the habit of others, his western character preserving itself inviolate amid a confusion of manners.

The men, coming one and one, or two and two, flung badinage to all corners of the room. Afterward, as they wheeled from time to time in their chairs, they bitterly insulted each other with the utmost good-nature, taking unerring aim at faults and riddling personalities with the quaint and cynical humor of a newspaper office. Throughout this banter, it was strange to note how infrequently the men smiled, particularly when directly engaged in an encounter.

A wide door opened into another apartment where were many little slanted tables, each under an electric globe with a green shade. Here a curly-headed scoundrel with a corncob pipe was hurling paper balls the size of apples at the head of an industrious man who, under these difficulties, was trying to draw a picture of an awful wreck with ghastly-faced sailors frozen in the rigging. Near this pair a lady was challenging a German artist who resembled Napoleon III. with having been publicly drunk at a music hall on the previous night. Next to the great gloomy corridor of this sixteenth floor was a little office presided over by an austere boy, and here waited in enforced patience a little dismal band of people who wanted to see the Sunday editor.

Baker took a manuscript and after glancing about the room, walked over to a man at another desk.

"Here is something that. I think might do," he said.

The man at the desk read the first two pages.

"But where is the photograph?" he asked then. "There should be a photograph with this thing."

"Oh, I forgot," said Baker. He brought from his desk a photograph of the babe that had been born lacking arms and one eye. Baker's superior braced a knee against his desk and settled back to a judicial attitude. He took the photograph and looked at it impassively. "Yes," he said, after a time, "that's a pretty good thing. You better show that to Coleman when he comes in."

In the little office where the dismal band waited, there had been a sharp hopeful stir when Rufus Coleman, the Sunday editor, passed rapidly from door to door and vanished within the holy precincts. It had evidently been in the minds of some to accost him then, but his eyes did not turn once in their direction. It was as if he had not seen them. Many experiences had taught him that the proper manner of passing through this office was at a blind gallop.

The dismal band turned then upon the austere office boy. Some demanded with terrible dignity that he should take in their cards at once. Others sought to ingratiate themselves by smiles of tender friendliness. He for his part employed what we would have called his knowledge of men and women upon the group, and in consequence blundered and bungled vividly, freezing with a glance an annoyed and importunate Arctic explorer who was come to talk of illustrations for an article that had been lavishly paid for in advance. The hero might have thought he was again in the northern seas. At the next moment the boy was treating almost courteously a German from the cast side who wanted the *Eclipse* to print a grand full page advertising description of his invention, a gun which was supposed to have a range of forty miles and to be able to penetrate anything with equanimity and joy. The gun, as a matter of fact, had once been induced to go off when it had hurled itself passionately upon its back, incidentally breaking its inventor's leg. The projectile had wandered some four hundred yards seaward, where it dug a hole in the water which was really a menace to navigation. Since then there had been nothing tangible save the inventor, in splints and out of splints, as the fortunes of science decreed. In short, this office boy mixed his business in the perfect manner of an underdone lad dealing with matters too large for him, and throughout he displayed the pride and assurance of a god.

As Coleman crossed the large office his face still wore the stern expression which he invariably used to carry him unmolested through the ranks of the dismal band. As he was removing his London overcoat he addressed the imperturbable back of one of his staff, who had a desk against the opposite wall. "Has Haskins sent in that drawing of the mine accident yet?"

The man did not lift his head from his work, but he answered at once:

"No; not yet."

Coleman was laying his hat on a chair.

"Well, why hasn't he?" he demanded. He glanced toward the door of the room in which the curly-headed scoundrel with the corncob pipe was still hurling paper balls at the man who was trying to invent the postures of dead mariners frozen in the rigging. The office boy came timidly from his post and informed Coleman of the waiting people. "All right," said the editor. He dropped into his chair and began to finger his letters, which had been neatly opened and placed in a little stack by a boy. Baker came in with the photograph of the miserable babe.

It was publicly believed that the Sunday staff of the *Eclipse* must have a kind of aesthetic delight in pictures of this kind, but Coleman's face betrayed no emotion as he looked at this specimen. He lit a fresh cigar, tilted his chair and surveyed it with a cold and stony stare. "Yes, that's all right," he said slowly. There seemed to be no affectionate relation between him and this picture. Evidently he was weighing its value as a morsel to be flung to a ravenous public, whose wolflike appetite, could only satisfy itself upon mental entrails, abominations. As for himself, he seemed to be remote, exterior. It was a matter of the *Eclipse* business.

Suddenly Coleman became executive. "Better give it to Schooner and tell him to make a half-page—or, no, send him in here and I'll tell him my idea. How's the article? Any good? Well, give it to Smith to rewrite."

An artist came from the other room and presented for inspection his drawing of the seamen dead in the rigging of the wreck, a company of grizzly and horrible figures, bony-fingered, shrunken and with awful eyes. "Hum," said Coleman, after a prolonged study, "that's all right. That's good, Jimmie. But you'd better work 'em up around the eyes a little more." The office boy was deploying in the distance, waiting for the correct moment to present some cards and names.

The artist was cheerfully taking away his corpses when Coleman hailed him. "Oh, Jim, let me see that thing again, will you? Now, how about this spar? This don't look right to me."

"It looks right to me," replied the artist, sulkily.

"But, see. It's going to take up half a page. Can't you change it somehow"

How am I going to change it?" said the other, glowering at Coleman. "That's the way it ought to be. How am I going to change it? That's the way it ought to be."

"No, it isn't at all," said Coleman. "You've got a spar sticking out of the main body of the drawing in a way that will spoil the look of the whole page."

The artist was a man of remarkable popular reputation and he was very stubborn and conceited of it, constantly making himself unbearable with covert, threats that if he was not delicately placated at all points, he would freight his genius over to the office of the great opposition journal.

"That's the way it ought to be," he repeated, in a tone at once sullen and superior. "The spar is all right. I can't rig spars on ships just to suit you."

"And I can't give up the whole paper to your accursed spars, either," said Coleman, with animation. "Don't you see you use about a third of a page with this spar sticking off into space? Now, you were always so clever, Jimmie, in adapting yourself to the page. Can't you shorten it, or cut it off, or something? Or, break it—that's the thing. Make it a broken spar dangling down. See?"

"Yes, I s'pose I could do that," said the artist, mollified by a thought of the ease with which he could make the change, and mollified, too, by the brazen tribute to a part of his cleverness.

"Well, do it, then," said the Sunday editor, turning abruptly away. The artist, with head high, walked majestically back to the other room. Whereat the curly-headed one immediately resumed the rain of paper balls upon him. The office boy came timidly to Coleman and suggested the presence of the people in the outer office.

"Let them wait until I read my mail," said Coleman. He shuffled the pack of letters indifferently through his hands. Suddenly he came upon a little grey envelope. He opened it at once and scanned its contents with the speed of his craft. Afterward he laid it down before him on the desk and surveyed it with a cool and musing smile. "So?" he remarked. "That's the case, is it?"

He presently swung around in his chair, and for a time held the entire attention of the men at the various desks. He outlined to them again their various parts in the composition of the next great Sunday edition. In a few brisk sentences he set a complex machine in proper motion. His men no longer thrilled with admiration at the precision with which he grasped each obligation of the campaign toward a successful edition. They had grown to accept it as they accepted his hat or his London clothes. At this time his face was lit with something of the self-contained enthusiasm of a general. Immediately afterward he arose and reached for his coat and hat.

The office boy, coming circuitously forward, presented him with some cards and also with a scrap of paper upon which was scrawled a long and semi-coherent word.

"What are these?" grumbled Coleman.

"They are waiting outside," answered the boy, with trepidation. It was part of the law that the lion of the anteroom should cringe like a cold monkey, more or less, as soon as he was out of his private jungle. "Oh, Tallerman," cried the Sunday editor, "here's this Arctic man come to arrange about his illustration. I wish you'd go and talk it over with him." By chance he picked up the scrap of paper with its cryptic word. "Oh," he said, scowling at the office boy. "Pity you can't remember that fellow. If you can't remember faces any better than that you should be a detective. Get out now and tell him to go to the devil." The wilted slave turned at once, but Coleman hailed him. "Hold on. Come to think of it, I will see this idiot. Send him in," he commanded, grimly.

Coleman lapsed into a dream over the sheet of grey note paper. Presently, a middle-aged man, a palpable German, came hesitatingly into the room and bunted among the desks as unmanageably as a tempest-tossed scow. Finally he was impatiently towed in the right direction. He came and stood at Coleman's elbow and waited nervously for the engrossed man to raise his eyes. It was plain that this interview meant important things to him. Somehow on his commonplace countenance was to be found the expression of a dreamer, a fashioner of great and absurd projects, a fine, tender fool. He cast hopeful and reverent glances at the man who was deeply contemplative of the grey note. He evidently believed himself on the threshold of a triumph of some kind, and he awaited his fruition with a joy that was only made sharper by the usual human suspicion of coming events.

Coleman glanced up at last and saw his visitor.

"Oh, it's you, is it?" he remarked icily, bending upon the German the stare of a tyrant. "So you've come again, have you?" He wheeled in his chair until he could fully display a contemptuous, merciless smile. "Now, Mr. What's-your-name, you've called here to see me about twenty times already and at last I am going to say something definite about your invention."

His listener's face, which had worn for a moment a look of fright and bewilderment, gladdened swiftly to a gratitude that seemed the edge of an outburst of tears.

"Yes," continued Coleman, "I am going to say something definite. I am going to say that it is the most imbecile bit of nonsense that has come within the range of my large newspaper experience. It is simply the aberration of a rather remarkable lunatic. It is no good; it is not worth the price of a cheese sandwich. I understand that its one feat has been to break your leg; if it ever goes off again, persuade it to break your neck. And now I want you to take this nursery rhyme of yours and get out. And don't ever come here again. Do You understand? You understand, do you?" He arose and bowed in courteous dismissal.

The German was regarding him with the surprise and horror of a youth shot mortally. He could not find his tongue for a moment. Ultimately he gasped: "But, Mister Editor "—Coleman interrupted him tigerishly. "You heard what I said? Get out." The man bowed his head and went slowly toward the door.

Coleman placed the little grey note in his breast pocket. He took his hat and top coat, and evading the dismal band by a shameless maneuver, passed through the halls to the entrance to the elevator shaft. He heard a movement behind him and saw that the German was also waiting for the elevator. Standing in the gloom of the corridor, Coleman felt the mournful owlish eyes of the German resting upon him. He took a case from his pocket and elaborately lit a cigarette. Suddenly there was a flash of light and a cage of bronze, gilt and steel dropped, magically from above.

Coleman yelled: "Down!"

A door flew open. Coleman, followed by the German, stepped upon the elevator.

"Well, Johnnie," he said cheerfully to the lad who operated this machine, "is business good?"

"Yes, sir, pretty good," answered the boy, grinning. The little cage sank swiftly; floor after floor seemed to be rising with marvelous speed; the whole building was winging straight into the sky. There were soaring lights, figures and the opalescent glow of ground glass doors marked with black inscriptions. Other lifts were springing heavenward. All the lofty corridors rang with cries. "Up!" "Down!" "Down!" "Up!" The boy's hand grasped a lever and his machine obeyed his lightest movement with sometimes an unbalancing swiftness.

Coleman discoursed briskly to the youthful attendant. Once he turned and regarded with a quick stare of insolent annoyance the despairing countenance of the German whose eyes had never left him. When the elevator arrived at the ground floor, Coleman departed with the outraged air of a man who for a time had been compelled to occupy a cell in company with a harmless specter.

He walked quickly away. Opposite a corner of the City Hall he was impelled to look behind him. Through the hordes of people with cable cars marching like panoplied elephants, he was able to distinguish the German, motionless and gazing after him. Coleman laughed. "That's a comic old boy," he said, to himself.

In the grill-room of a Broadway hotel he was obliged to wait some minutes for the fulfillment of his orders and he spent the time in reading and studying the little grey note. When his luncheon was served he ate with an expression of morose dignity.


## CHAPTER IV.

MARJORY paused again at her father's door. After hesitating in the original way she entered the library. Her father almost represented an emblematic figure, seated upon a column of books.

"Well," he cried. Then, seeing it was Marjory, he changed his tone. "Ah, under the circumstances, my dear, I admit your privilege of interrupting me at any hour of the day. You have important business with me." His manner was satanically indulgent.

The girl fingered a book. She turned the leaves in absolute semblance of a person reading. "Rufus Coleman called."

"Indeed," said the professor.

"And I've come to you, father, before seeing him."

The professor was silent for a time. "Well, Marjory," he said at last, "what do you want me to say?" He spoke very deliberately. "I am sure this is a singular situation. Here appears the man I formally forbid you to marry. I am sure I do not know what I am to say."

"I wish to see him," said the girl.

"You wish to see him?" enquired the professor. "You wish to see him. Marjory, I may as well tell you now that with all the books and plays I've read, I really don't know how the obdurate father should conduct himself. He is always pictured as an exceedingly dense gentleman with white whiskers, who does all the unintelligent things in the plot. You and I are going to play no drama, are we, Marjory? I admit that I have white whiskers, and I am an obdurate father. I am, as you well may say, a very obdurate father. You are not to marry Rufus Coleman. You understand the rest of the matter. He is here; you want to see him. What will you say to him when you see him?"

"I will say that you refuse to let me marry him, father and—" She hesitated a moment before she lifted her eyes fully and formidably to her father's face. "And that I shall marry him anyhow."

The professor did not cavort when this statement came from his daughter. He nodded and then passed into a period of reflection. Finally he asked: "But when? That is the point. When?"

The girl made a sad gesture. "I don't know. I don't know. Perhaps when you come to know Rufus better—"

"Know him better. Know that rapscallion better? Why, I know him much better than he knows himself. I know him too well. Do you think I am talking offhand about this affair? Do you think I am talking without proper information?"

Marjory made no reply.

"Well," said the professor, "you may see Coleman on condition that you inform him at once that I forbid your marriage to him. I don't understand at all how to manage these situations. I don't know what to do. I suppose I should go myself and— No, you can't see him, Marjory."

Still the girl made no reply. Her head sank forward and she breathed a trifle heavily. "Marjory," cried the professor, it is impossible that you should think so much of this man." He arose and went to his daughter. "Marjory, many wise children have been guided by foolish fathers, but we both suspect that no foolish child has ever been guided by a wise father. Let us change it. I present myself to you as a wise father. Follow my wishes in this affair and you will be at least happier than if you marry this wretched Coleman."

She answered: "He is waiting for me."

The professor turned abruptly from her and dropped into his chair at the table. He resumed a grip on his pen. "Go," he said, wearily. "Go. But if you have a remnant of sense, remember what I have said to you. Go." He waved his hand in a dismissal that was slightly scornful. "I hoped you would have a minor conception of what you were doing. It seems a pity." Drooping in tears, the girl slowly left the room.

Coleman had an idea that he had occupied the chair for several months. He gazed about at the pictures and the odds and ends of a drawing-room in an attempt to take an interest in them. The great garlanded paper shade over the piano lamp consoled his impatience in a mild degree because he knew that Marjory had made it. He noted the clusters of cloth violets which she had pinned upon the yellow paper and he dreamed over the fact. He was able to endow this shade with certain qualities of sentiment that caused his stare to become almost a part of an intimacy, a communion. He looked as if he could have unburdened his soul to this shade over the piano lamp.

Upon the appearance of Marjory he sprang up and came forward rapidly. "Dearest," he murmured, stretching out both hands.

She gave him one set of fingers with chilling convention. She said something which he understood to be, "Good-afternoon."

He started as if the woman before him had suddenly drawn a knife.

"Marjory," he cried, "what is the matter?"

They walked together toward a window. The girl looked at him in polite enquiry.

"Why?" she said. "Do I seem strange?"

There was a moment's silence while he gazed into her eyes, eyes full of innocence and tranquility. At last she tapped her foot upon the floor in expression of mild impatience.

"People do not like to be asked what is the matter when there is nothing the matter. What do you mean?"

Coleman's face had gradually hardened. "Well, what is wrong?" he demanded, abruptly. "What has happened? What is it, Marjory?"

She raised her glance in a perfect reality of wonder.

"What is wrong? What has happened? How absurd! Why nothing, of course." She gazed out of the window. "Look," she added, brightly, the students are rolling somebody in a drift. "Oh, the poor Man!"

Coleman, now wearing a bewildered air, made some pretense of being occupied with the scene.

"Yes," he said, ironically. "Very interesting, indeed."

"Oh," said Marjory, suddenly, "I forgot to tell you. Father is going to take mother and me to Greece this winter with him and the class."

Coleman replied at once. "Ah, indeed? That will be jolly."

"Yes. Won't it be charming?"

"I don't doubt it," he replied.

His composure may have displeased her, for she glanced at him furtively and in a way that denoted surprise, perhaps.

"Oh, of course," she said, in a glad voice. "It will be more fun. We expect to nave a fine time. There is such a nice lot of boys going. Sometimes father chooses these dreadfully studious ones. But this time he acts as if he knew precisely how to make up a party."

He reached for her hand and grasped it vise-like.

"Marjory," he breathed, passionately, "don't treat me so. Don't treat me—"

She wrenched her hand from him in regal indignation.

"One or two rings make it uncomfortable for the hand that is grasped by an angry gentleman." She held her fingers and gazed as if she expected to find them mere debris. "I am sorry that you are not interested in the students rolling that man in the snow. It is the greatest scene our quiet life can afford."

He was regarding her as a judge faces a lying culprit.

"I know," he said, after a pause. "Somebody has been telling you some stories. You have been hearing something about me."

"Some stories?" she enquired. "Some stories about you? What do you mean? Do you mean that I remember stories I may happen to hear about people?"

There was another pause and then Coleman's face flared red. He beat his hand violently upon a table.

"Good God, Marjory! Don't make a fool of me. Don't make this kind of a fool of me, at any rate. Tell me what you mean. Explain—"

She laughed at him.

"Explain? Really, your vocabulary is getting extensive, but it is dreadfully awkward to ask people to explain when there is nothing to explain."

He glanced at her, "I know as well as you do that your father is taking you to Greece in order to get rid of me."

"And do people have to go to Greece in order to get rid of you?" she asked, civilly. "I think you are getting excited."

"Marjory," he began, stormily.

She raised her hand.

"Hush," she said, "there is somebody coming."

A bell had rung. A maid entered the room.

"Mr. Coke," she said. Marjory nodded. In the interval of waiting, Coleman gave the girl a glance that mingled despair with rage and pride. Then Coke burst with half-tamed rapture into the room.

"Oh, Miss Wainwright," he almost shouted, "I can't tell you how glad I am. I just heard today you were going. Imagine it. It will be more—oh, how are you Coleman, how are you?"

Marjory welcomed the newcomer with a cordiality that might not have thrilled Coleman with pleasure. They took chairs that formed a triangle and one side of it vibrated with talk. Coke and Marjory engaged in a tumultuous conversation concerning the prospective trip to Greece. The Sunday editor, as remote as if the apex of his angle was the top of a hill, could only study the girl's clear profile. The youthful voices of the two others rang like bells. He did not scowl at Coke; he merely looked at him as if be gently disdained his mental caliber. In fact all the talk seemed to tire him; it was childish; as for him, he apparently found this babble almost insupportable.

"And, just think of the camel rides we'll have," cried Coke.

"Camel rides," repeated Coleman, dejectedly. "My dear Coke."

Finally he arose like an old man climbing from a sick bed. "Well, I am afraid I must go, Miss Wainwright." Then he said affectionately to Coke: "Good-bye, old boy. I hope you will have a good time."

Marjory walked with him to the door. He shook her hand in a friendly fashion. "Good-bye, Marjory,' he said. "Perhaps it may happen that I shan't see you again before you start for Greece and so I had best bid you God-speed—or whatever the term is now. You will have a charming time; Greece must be a delightful place. Really, I envy you, Marjory. And now my dear child—" His voice grew brotherly, filled with the patronage of generous fraternal love— "although I may never see you again let me wish you fifty as happy years as this last one has been for me." He smiled frankly into her eyes; then dropping her hand, he went away.

Coke renewed his tempest of talk as Marjory turned toward him. But after a series of splendid eruptions, whose red fire illumined all of ancient and modem Greece, he too went away.

The professor was in his library apparently absorbed in a book when a tottering pale-faced woman appeared to him and, in her course toward a couch in a corner of the room, described almost a semi-circle.

She flung herself face downward. A thick strand of hair swept over her shoulder. "Oh, my heart is broken! My heart is broken!"

The professor arose, grizzled and thrice-old with pain. He went to the couch, but he found himself a handless, fetless man.

"My poor child," he said. "My poor child." He remained listening stupidly to her convulsive sobbing. A ghastly kind of solemnity came upon the room.

Suddenly the girl lifted herself and swept the strand of hair away from her face. She looked at the professor with the wide-open dilated eyes of one who still sleeps.

"Father," she said in a hollow voice, "he don't love me. He don't love me. He don't love me at all. You were right, father." She began to laugh.

"Marjory," said the professor, trembling. "Be quiet, child. Be quiet."

"But," she said, "I thought he loved me—I was sure of it. But it don't—don't matter. I—I can't get over it. Women—women, the—but it don't matter."

"Marjory," said the professor. "Marjory, my poor daughter."

She did not heed his appeal, but continued in a dull whisper. "He was playing with me. He was—was—was flirting with me. He didn't care when I told him—I told him—I was going—going away." She turned her face wildly to the cushions again. Her young shoulders shook as if they might break. "Women—women—they always—"

## CHAPTER V.

By a strange mishap of management the train which bore Coleman back toward New York was fetched into an obscure side-track of some lonely region and there compelled to bide a change of fate. The engine wheezed and sneezed like a paused fat man. The lamps in the cars pervaded a stuffy odor of smoke and oil. Coleman examined his case and found only one cigar. Important brakemen proceeded rapidly along the aisles, and when they swung open the doors, a polar wind circled the legs of the passengers.

"Well, now, what is all this for?" demanded Coleman, furiously. "I want to get back to New York."

The conductor replied with sarcasm, "Maybe you think I'm stuck on it. I ain't running the road. I'm running this train, and I run it according to orders."

Amid the dismal comforts of the waiting cars, Coleman felt all the profound misery of the rebuffed true lover. He had been sentenced, he thought, to a penal servitude of the heart, as he watched the dusky, vague ribbons of smoke come from the lamps and felt to his knees the cold winds from the brakemen's busy flights. When the train started with a whistle and a jolt, he was elate as if in his abjection his beloved's hand had reached to him from the clouds.

When he had arrived in New York, a cab rattled him to an uptown hotel with speed. In the restaurant he first ordered a large bottle of champagne. The last of the wine he finished in somber mood like an unbroken and defiant man who chews the straw that litters his prison house. During his dinner he was continually sending out messenger boys. He was arranging a poker party. Through a window he watched the beautiful moving life of upper Broadway at night, with its crowds and clanging cable cars and its electric signs, mammoth and glittering, like the jewels of a giant-ess.

Word was brought to him that the poker players were arriving. He arose joyfully, leaving his cheese. In the broad hall, occupied mainly by miscellaneous people and actors, all deep in leather chairs, he found some of his friends waiting. They trooped up stairs to Coleman's rooms, where as a preliminary, Coleman began to hurl books and papers from the table to the floor. A boy came with drinks. Most of the men, in order to prepare for the game, removed their coats and cuffs and drew up the sleeves of their shirts. The electric globes shed a blinding light upon the table. The sound of clinking chips arose; the elected banker spun the cards, careless and dexterous.

Later, during a pause of dealing, Coleman said: "Billie, what kind of a lad is that young Coke up up at Washurst?"

He addressed an old college friend.

"Oh, you mean the Sophomore Coke?" asked the friend. "Seems a decent sort of a fellow. I don't know. Why?"

"Well, who is he? Where does he come from? What do you know about him?"

"He's one of those Ohio Cokes—regular thing— father millionaire—used to be a barber—good old boy—why?"

"Nothin'," said Coleman, looking at his cards. "I know the lad. I thought he was a good deal of an ass. I wondered who his people were."

"Oh, his people are all right—in one way. Father owns rolling mills. Do you raise it, Henry? Well, in order to make vice abhorrent to the young, I'm obliged to raise back."

"I'll see it," observed Coleman, slowly pushing forward two blue chips. Afterward he reached behind him and took another glass of wine.

To the others Coleman seemed to have something bitter upon his mind. He played poker quietly, steadfastly, and, without change of eye, following the mathematical religion of the game. Outside of the play he was savage, almost insupportable.

"What's the matter with you, Rufus?" said his old college friend. "Lost your job? Girl gone back on you? You're a hell of a host. We don't get anything but insults and drinks."

* * * *

Late at night Coleman began to lose steadily. In the meantime he drank glass after glass of wine. Finally he made reckless bets on a mediocre hand and an opponent followed him thoughtfully bet by bet, undaunted, calm, absolutely without emotion. Coleman lost; he hurled down his cards. "Nobody but a damned fool would have seen that last raise on anything less than a full hand."

"Steady. Come off. What's wrong with you, Rufus?" cried his guests.

"You're not drunk, are you?" said his old college friend, puritanically.

"Drunk?" repeated Coleman.

"Oh, say," cried a man, "let's play cards. What's all this gabbling?"

It was when a grey, dirty light of dawn evaded the thick curtains and fought on the floor with the feeble electric glow that Coleman, in the midst of play, lurched his chest heavily upon the table. Some chips rattled to the floor. "I'll call you," he murmured, sleepily.

"Well," replied a man, sternly, "three kings."

The other players with difficulty extracted five cards from beneath Coleman's pillowed head. "Not a pair! Come, come, this won't do. Oh, let's stop playing. This is the rottenest game I ever sat in. Let's go home. Why don't you put him to bed, Billie?"

When Coleman awoke next morning, he looked back upon the poker game as something that had transpired in previous years. He dressed and went down to the grill-room. For his breakfast he ordered some eggs on toast and a pint of champagne. A privilege of liberty belonged to a certain Irish waiter, and this waiter looked at him, grinning. "Maybe you had a pretty lively time last night, Mr. Coleman?"

"Yes, Pat," answered Coleman, "I did. It was all because of an unrequited affection, Patrick." The man stood near, a napkin over his arm. Coleman went on impressively. "The ways of the modern lover are strange. Now, I, Patrick, am a modern lover, and when, yesterday, the dagger of disappointment was driven deep into my heart, I immediately played poker as hard as I could and incidentally got loaded. This is the modern point of view. I understand on good authority that in old times lovers used to languish. That is probably a lie, but at any rate we do not, in these times, languish to any great extent. We get drunk. Do you understand, Patrick?" The waiter was used to a harangue at Coleman's breakfast time. He placed his hand over his mouth and giggled. "Yessir."

"Of course," continued Coleman, thoughtfully. "It might be pointed out by uneducated persons that it is difficult to maintain a high standard of drunkenness for the adequate length of time, but in the series of experiments which I am about to make I am sure I can easily prove them to be in the wrong."

"I am sure, sir," said the waiter, "the young ladies would not like to be hearing you talk this way."

"Yes; no doubt, no doubt. The young ladies have still quite medieval ideas. They don't understand. They still prefer lovers to languish."

"At any rate, sir, I don't see that your heart is sure enough broken. You seem to take it very easy."

"Broken!" cried Coleman. "Easy? Man, my heart is in fragments. Bring me another small bottle."

## CHAPTER VI.

Six weeks later, Coleman went to the office of the proprietor of the *Eclipse*. Coleman was one of those smooth-shaven old-young men who wear upon some occasions a singular air of temperance and purity. At these times, his features lost their quality of worldly shrewdness and endless suspicion and bloomed as the face of some innocent boy. It then would be hard to tell that he had ever encountered even such a crime as a lie or a cigarette. As he walked into the proprietor's office he was a perfect semblance of a fine, inexperienced youth. People usually concluded this change was due to a Turkish bath or some other expedient of recuperation, but it was due probably to the power of a physical characteristic.

"Boss in?" said Coleman.

"Yeh," said the secretary, jerking his thumb toward an inner door. In his private office, Sturgeon sat on the edge of the table dangling one leg and dreamily surveying the wall. As Coleman entered he looked up quickly. "Rufus," he cried, "you're just the man I wanted to see. I've got a scheme. A great scheme." He slid from the table and began to pace briskly to and fro, his hands deep in his trousers' pockets, his chin sunk in his collar, his light blue eyes afire with interest. "Now listen. This is immense. The *Eclipse* enlists a battalion of men to go to Cuba and fight the Spaniards under its own flag—the *Eclipse* flag. Collect trained officers from here and there—enlist every young devil we see—drill 'em—best rifles—loads of ammunition—provisions—staff of doctors and nurses—a couple of dynamite guns—everything complete best in the world. Now, isn't that great? What's the matter with that now? Eh? Eh? Isn't that great? It's great, isn't it? Eh? Why, my boy, we'll free—"

Coleman did not seem to ignite. "I have been arrested four or five times already on fool matters connected with the newspaper business," he observed, gloomily, "but I've never yet been hung. I think your scheme is a beauty."

Sturgeon paused in astonishment. "Why, what happens to be the matter with you? What are you kicking about?"

Coleman made a slow gesture. "I'm tired," he answered. "I need a vacation."

"Vacation!" cried Sturgeon. "Why don't you take one then?"

"That's what I've come to see you about. I've had a pretty heavy strain on me for three years now, and I want to get a little rest."

"Well, who in thunder has been keeping you from it? It hasn't been me."

"I know it hasn't been you, but, of course, I wanted the paper to go and I wanted to have my share in its success, but now that everything is all right I think I might go away for a time if you don't mind."

"Mind!" exclaimed Sturgeon falling into his chair and reaching for his check book. "Where do you want to go? How long do you want to be gone? How much money do you want?"

"I don't want very much. And as for where I want to go, I thought I might like to go to Greece for a while."

Sturgeon had been writing a check. He poised his pen in the air and began to laugh. "That's a queer place to go for a rest. Why, the biggest war of modern times— a war that may involve all Europe—is likely to start there at any moment. You are not likely to get any rest in Greece."

"I know that," answered Coleman. "I know there is likely to be a war there. But I think that is exactly what would rest me. I would like to report the war."

"You are a queer bird," answered Sturgeon deeply fascinated with this new idea. He had apparently forgotten his vision of a Cuban volunteer battalion. "War correspondence is about the most original medium for a rest I ever heard of."

"Oh, it may seem funny, but really, any change will be good for me now. I've been whacking at this old Sunday edition until I'm sick of it, and sometimes I wish the *Eclipse* was in hell."

That's all right," laughed the proprietor of the *Eclipse*. "But I still don't see how you are going to get any vacation out of a war that will upset the whole of Europe. But that's your affair. If you want to become the chief correspondent in the field in case of any such war, why, of course, I would be glad to have you. I couldn't get anybody better. But I don't see where your vacation comes in."

"I'll take care of that," answered Coleman. "When I take a vacation I want to take it my own way, and I think this will be a vacation because it will be different—don't you see—different?"

"No, I don't see any sense in it, but if you think that is the way that suits you, why, go ahead. How much money do you want?"

"I don't want much, just enough to see me through nicely."

Sturgeon scribbled on his check book and then ripped a check from it. "Here's a thousand dollars. Will that do you to start with?"

"That's plenty."

"When do you want to start?"

"Tomorrow."

"Oh," said Sturgeon. "You're in a hurry." This impetuous manner of exit from business seemed to appeal to him. "Tomorrow," he repeated smiling. In reality he was some kind of a poet using his millions romantically, spending wildly on a sentiment that might be with beauty or without beauty, according to the momentary vacillation. The vaguely-defined desperation in Coleman's last announcement appeared to delight him. He grinned and placed the points of his fingers together stretching out his legs in a careful attitude of indifference which might even mean disapproval. "Tomorrow," he murmured teasingly.

"By jiminy," exclaimed Coleman, ignoring the other man's mood, "I'm sick of the whole business. I've got out a Sunday paper once a week for three years and I feel absolutely incapable of getting out another edition. It would be all right if we were running on ordinary lines, but when each issue is more or less of an attempt to beat the previous issue, it becomes rather wearing, you know. If I can't get a vacation now I take one later in a lunatic asylum."

"Why, I'm not objecting to your having a vacation. I'm simply marveling at the kind of vacation you want to take. And 'tomorrow,' too, eh?"

"Well, it suits me," muttered Coleman, sulkily.

"Well, if it suits you, that's enough. Here's your check. Clear out now and don't let me see you again until you are thoroughly rested, even if it takes a year."

He arose and stood smiling. He was mightily pleased with himself. He liked to perform in this way. He was almost seraphic as he thrust the check for a thousand dollars toward Coleman.

Then his manner changed abruptly. "Hold on a minute. I must think a little about this thing if you are going to manage the correspondence. Of course it will be a long and bloody war."

"You bet."

"The big chance is that all Europe will be dragged into it. Of course then you would have to come out of Greece and take up a better position—say, Vienna."

"No, I wouldn't care to do that," said Coleman positively. "I just want to take care of the Greek end of it."

"It will be an idiotic way to take a vacation," observed Sturgeon.

"Well, it suits me," muttered Coleman again. "I tell you what it is—" he added suddenly. "I've got some private reasons—see?"

Sturgeon was radiant with joy. "Private reasons." He was charmed by the somber pain in Coleman's eyes and his own ability to eject it. "Good. Go now and be blowed. I will cable final instruction to meet you in London. As soon as you get to Greece, cable me an account of the situation there and we will arrange our plans." He began to laugh. "Private reasons. Come out to dinner with me."

"I can't very well," said Coleman. "If I go tomorrow, I've got to pack—"

But here the real tyrant appeared, emerging suddenly from behind the curtain of sentiment, appearing like a red devil in a pantomime.

"You can't?" snapped Sturgeon. "Nonsense—"

## CHAPTER VII.

Sweeping out from between two remote, half-submerged dunes on which stood slender sentry lighthouses, the steamer began to roll with a gentle insinuating motion. Passengers in their staterooms saw at rhythmical intervals the spray racing fleetly past the portholes. The waves grappled hurriedly at the sides of the great flying steamer and boiled discomfited astern in a turmoil of green and white. From the tops of the enormous funnels streamed level masses of smoke which were immediately torn to nothing by the headlong wind. Meanwhile as the steamer rushed into the northeast, men in caps and ulsters comfortably paraded the decks and stewards arranged deck chairs for the reception of various women who were coming from their cabins with rugs.

In the smoking room, old voyagers were settling down comfortably while new voyagers were regarding them with a diffident respect. Among the passengers Coleman found a number of people whom he knew, including a wholesale wine merchant, a Chicago railway magnate and a New York millionaire. They lived practically in the smoking room. Necessity drove them from time to time to the salon, or to their berths. Once indeed the millionaire was absent, from the group while penning a short note to his wife.

When the Irish coast was sighted Coleman came on deck to look at it. A tall young woman immediately halted in her walk until he had stepped up to her. "Well, of all ungallant men, Rufus Coleman, you are the star," she cried laughing and held out her hand.

"Awfully sorry, I'm sure," he murmured. "Been playing poker in the smoking room all voyage. Didn't have a look at the passenger list until just now. Why didn't you send me word?" These lies were told so modestly and sincerely that when the girl flashed her, brilliant eyes full upon their author there was a mix of admiration in the indignation.

"Send you a card? I don't believe you can read, else you would have known I was to sail on this steamer. If I hadn't been ill until today you would have seen me in the salon. I open at the Folly Theatre next week. Dear ol' Lunnon, y' know."

"Of course, I knew you were going," said Coleman. "But I thought you were to go later. What do you open in?"

"Fly by Night. Come walk along with me. See those two old ladies? They've been watching for me like hawks ever since we left New York. They expected me to flirt with every man on board. But I've fooled them. I've been just as g-o-o-d. I had to be."

As the pair moved toward the stern, enormous and radiant green waves were crashing futilely after the steamer. Ireland showed a dreary coast line to the north. A wretched man who had crossed the Atlantic eighty-four times was declaiming to a group of novices. A venerable banker, bundled in rugs, was asleep in his deck chair.

"Well, Nora," said Coleman, "I hope you make a hit in London. You deserve it if anybody does. You've worked hard."

"Worked hard," cried the girl. "I should think so. Eight years ago I was in the rear row. Now I have the centre of the stage whenever I want it. I made Chalmers cut out that great scene in the second act between the queen and Rodolfo. The idea! Did he think I would stand that? And just because he was in love with Clara Trotwood, too."

Coleman was dreamy. "Remember when I was dramatic man for the Gazette and wrote the first notice?"

"Indeed, I do," answered the girl affectionately. "Indeed, I do, Rufus. Ah, that was a great lift. I believe that was the first thing that had an effect on old Oliver. Before that, he never would believe that I was any good. Give me your arm, Rufus. Let's parade before the two old women." Coleman glanced at her keenly. Her voice had trembled slightly. Her eyes were lustrous as if she were about to weep.

"Good heavens," he said. "You are the same old Nora Black. I thought you would be proud and 'aughty by this time."

"Not to my friends," she murmured. "Not to my friends. I'm always the same and I never forget. Rufus."

"Never forget what?" asked Coleman.

"If anybody does me a favor I never forget it as long as I live," she answered fervently.

"Oh, you mustn't be so sentimental, Nora. You remember that play you bought from little Ben Whipple, just because he had once sent you some flowers in the old days when you were poor and happened to bed sick. A sense of gratitude cost you over eight thousand dollars that time, didn't it?" Coleman laughed heartily.

"Oh, it wasn't the flowers at all," she interrupted seriously. "Of course Ben was always a nice boy, but then his play was worth a thousand dollars. That's all I gave him. I lost some more in trying to make it go. But it was too good. That was what was the matter. It was altogether too good for the public. I felt awfully sorry for poor little Ben."

"Too good?" sneered Coleman. "Too good? Too indifferently bad, you mean. My dear girl, you mustn't imagine that you know a good play. You don't, at all."

She paused abruptly and faced him. This regal, creature was looking at him so sternly that Coleman felt awed for a moment as if he, were in the presence of a great mind. "Do you mean to say that I'm not an artist?" she asked.

Coleman remained cool. "I've never been decorated for informing people of their own affairs," he observed, "but I should say that you were about as much of an artist as I am."

Frowning slightly, she reflected upon this reply. Then, of a sudden, she laughed. "There is no use in being angry with you, Rufus. You always were a hopeless scamp. But," she added, childishly wistful, "have you ever seen Fly by Night? Don't you think my dance in the second act is artistic?"

"No," said Coleman, "I haven't seen Fly by Night yet, but of course I know that you are the most beautiful dancer on the stage. Everybody knows that."

It seemed that her hand tightened on his arm. Her face was radiant.

"There," she exclaimed. "Now you are forgiven. You are a nice boy, Rufus— sometimes."

When Miss Black went to her cabin, Coleman strolled into the smoking room. Every man there covertly or openly surveyed him. He dropped lazily into a chair at a table where the wine merchant, the Chicago railway king and the New York millionaire were playing cards. They made a noble pretense of not being aware of him. On the oil cloth top of the table the cards were snapped down, turn by turn.

Finally the wine merchant, without lifting his head to address a particular person, said: "New conquest."

Hailing a steward Coleman asked for a brandy and soda.

The millionaire said: "He's a sly cuss, anyhow." The railway man grinned. After an elaborate silence the wine merchant asked: "Know Miss Black long, Rufus?"

Coleman looked scornfully at his friends. "What's wrong with you there, fellows, anyhow?"

The Chicago man answered airily. "Oh, nothin'. Nothin' whatever."

At dinner in the crowded salon, Coleman was aware that more than one passenger glanced first at Nora Black and then at him, as if connecting them in some train of thought, moved to it by the narrow horizon of shipboard and by a sense of the mystery that surrounds the lives of the beauties of the stage. Near the captain's right hand sat the glowing and splendid Nora, exhibiting under the gaze of the persistent eyes of many meanings, a practiced and profound composure that to the populace was terrifying dignity.

Strolling toward the smoking room after dinner, Coleman met the New York millionaire, who seemed agitated. He took Coleman fraternally by the arm. "Say, old man, introduce me, won't you? I'm crazy to know her."

"Do you mean Miss Black?" asked Coleman.

"Why, I don't know that I have a right. Of course, you know, she hasn't been meeting anybody aboard. I'll ask her, though—certainly."

"Thanks, old man, thanks. I'd be tickled to death. Come along and have a drink. When will you ask her?"

"Why, I don't know when I'll see her. Tomorrow, I suppose—"

They had not been long in the smoking room, however, when the deck steward came with a card to Coleman. Upon it was written: "Come for' a stroll?" Everybody, saw Coleman read this card and then look up and whisper to the deck steward. The deck steward bent his head and whispered discreetly in reply. There was an abrupt pause in the hum of conversation. The interest was acute.

Coleman leaned carelessly back in his chair, puffing at his cigar. He mingled calmly in a discussion of the comparative merits of certain trans-Atlantic lines. After a time he threw away his cigar and arose. Men nodded. "Didn't I tell you?" His studiously languid exit was made dramatic by the eagle-eyed attention of the smoking room.

On deck he found Nora pacing to and fro. "You didn't hurry yourself," she said, as he joined her. The lights of Queenstown were twinkling. A warm wind, wet with the moisture of rain-stricken sod, was coming from the land.

"Why," said Coleman, "we've got all these duffers very much excited."

"Well what do you care?" asked the girl. "You don't, care do you?"

"No, I don't care. Only it's rather absurd to be watched all the time." He said this precisely as if he abhorred being watched in this case. "Oh by the way," he added. Then he paused for a moment. "Aw—a friend of mine—not a bad fellow—he asked me for an introduction. Of course, I told him I'd ask you."

She made a contemptuous gesture. "Oh, another Willie. Tell him no. Tell him to go home to his family. Tell him to run away."

"He isn't a bad fellow. He—" said Coleman diffidently, "he would probably be at the theatre every night in a box."

"yes, and get drunk and throw a wine bottle on the stage instead of a bouquet. No," she declared positively, "I won't see him."

Coleman did not seem to be oppressed by this ultimatum. "Oh, all right. I promised him—that was all."

"Besides, are you in a great hurry to get rid of me?"

"Rid of you? Nonsense."

They walked in the shadow. "How long are you going to be in London, Rufus?" asked Nora softly.

"Who? I? Oh, I'm going right off to Greece. First train. There's going to be a war, you know."

"A war? Why, who is going to fight? The Greeks and the—the—the what?"

"The Turks. I'm going right over there."

"Why, that's dreadful, Rufus," said the girl, mournful and shocked. "You might get hurt or something." Presently she asked: "And aren't you going to be in London any time at all?"

"Oh," he answered, puffing out his lips, "I may stop in London for three or four days on my way home. I'm not sure of it."

"And when will that be?"

"Oh, I can't tell. It may be in three or four months, or it may be a year from now. When the war stops."

There was a long silence as the walked up and down the swaying deck.

"Do you know," said Nora at last, "I like you, Rufus Coleman. I don't know any good reason for it either, unless it is because you are such a brute. Now, when I was asking you if you were to be in London you were perfectly detestable. You know I was anxious."

"I—detestable?" cried Coleman, feigning amazement. "Why, what did I say?"

"It isn't so much what you said—" began Nora slowly. Then she suddenly changed her manner. "Oh, well, don't let's talk about it any more. It's too foolish. Only—you are a disagreeable person sometimes."

In the morning, as the vessel steamed up the Irish channel, Coleman was on deck, keeping furtive watch on the cabin stairs. After two hours of waiting, he scribbled a message on a card and sent it below. He received an answer that Miss Black had a headache, and felt too ill to come on deck. He went to the smoking room. The three card-players glanced up, grinning. "What's the matter?" asked the wine merchant. "You look angry." As a matter of fact, Coleman had purposely wreathed his features in a pleasant and satisfied expression, so he was for a moment furious at the wine merchant.

"Confound the girl," he thought to himself. "She has succeeded in making all these beggars laugh at me." He mused that if he had another chance he would show her how disagreeable or detestable or scampish he was under some circumstances. He reflected ruefully that the complacence with which he had accepted the comradeship of the belle of the voyage might have been somewhat overdone. Perhaps he had got a little out of proportion. He was annoyed at the stares of the other men in the smoking room, who seemed now to be reading his discomfiture. As for Nora Black he thought of her wistfully and angrily as a superb woman whose company was honor and joy, a payment for any sacrifices.

"What's the matter?" persisted the wine merchant. "You look grumpy."

Coleman laughed. "Do I?"

* * * *

At Liverpool, as the steamer was being slowly warped to the landing stage by some tugs, the passengers crowded the deck with their handbags. Adieus were falling as dead leaves fall from a great tree. The stewards were handling small hills of luggage marked with flaming red labels. The ship was firmly against the dock before Miss Black came from her cabin. Coleman was at the time gazing shoreward, but his three particular friends instantly nudged him. "What? There she is? Oh, Miss Black?" He composedly walked toward her. It was impossible to tell whether she saw him coming or whether it was accident, but at any rate she suddenly turned and moved toward the stern of the ship. Ten watchful gossips had noted Coleman's travel in her direction and more than half the passengers noted his defeat. He wheeled casually and returned to his three friends. They were colic-stricken with a coarse and yet silent merriment. Coleman was glad that the voyage was over.

After the polite business of an English custom house, the travelers passed out to the waiting train. A nimble little theatrical agent of some kind, sent from London, dashed forward to receive Miss Black. He had a first-class compartment engaged for her and he bundled her and her maid into it in an exuberance of enthusiasm and admiration. Coleman passing moodily along the line of coaches heard Nora's voice hailing him.

"Rufus." There she was, framed in a carriage window, beautiful and smiling brightly. Every nearby person turned to contemplate this vision.

"Oh," said Coleman advancing, "I thought I was not going to get a chance to say good-bye to you." He held out his hand. "Good-bye."

She pouted. "Why, there's plenty of room in this compartment." Seeing that some forty people were transfixed in observation of her, she moved a short way back. "Come on in this compartment, Rufus," she said.

"Thanks. I prefer to smoke," said Coleman. He went off abruptly.

On the way to London, he brooded in his corner on the two divergent emotions he had experienced when refusing her invitation. At Euston Station in London, he was directing a porter, who had his luggage, when he heard Nora speak at his shoulder. "Well, Rufus, you sulky boy," she said, "I shall be at the Cecil. If you have time, come and see me."

"Thanks, I'm sure, my dear Nora," answered Coleman effusively. "But honestly, I'm off for Greece."

A brougham was drawn up near them and the nimble little agent was waiting. The maid was directing the establishment of a mass of luggage on and in a four-wheeler cab. "Well, put me into my carriage, anyhow," said Nora. "You will have time for that."

Afterward she addressed him from the dark interior.

"Now, Rufus, you must come to see me the minute you strike London again." She hesitated a moment and then smiling gorgeously upon him, she said: "Brute!"

## CHAPTER VIII.

As soon as Coleman had planted his belongings in a hotel he was bowled in a hansom briskly along the smoky Strand, through a dark city whose walls dripped like the walls of a cave and whose passages were only illuminated by flaring yellow and red signs.

Walkley the London correspondent of the *Eclipse*, whirled from his chair with a shout of joy and relief at sight of Coleman. "Cables," he cried. "Nothin' but cables! All the people in New York are writing cables to you. The wires groan with them. And we groan with them too. They come in here in bales. However, there is no reason why you should read them all. Many are similar in words and many more are similar in spirit. The sense of the whole thing is that you get to Greece quickly, taking with you immense sums of money and enormous powers over nations."

"Well, when does the row begin?"

"The most astute journalists in Europe have been predicting a general European smash-up every year since 1878," said Walkley, "and the prophets weep. The English are the only people who can pull off wars on schedule time, and they have to do it in odd corners of the globe. I fear the war business is getting tuckered. There is sorrow in the lodges of the lone wolves, the war correspondents. However, my boy, don't bury your face in your blanket. This Greek business looks very promising, very promising." He then began to proclaim trains and connections. "Dover, Calais, Paris, Brindisi, Corfu, Patras, Athens. That is your game. You are supposed to sky-rocket yourself over that route in the shortest possible time, but you would gain no time by starting before tomorrow, so you can cool your heels here in London until then. I wish I was going along."

Coleman returned to his hotel, a knight impatient and savage at being kept for a time out of the saddle. He went for a late supper to the grill room and as he was seated there alone, a party of four or five people came to occupy the table directly behind him. They talked a great deal even before they arrayed themselves at the table, and he at once recognized the voice of Nora Black. She was queening it, apparently, over a little band of awed masculine worshippers.

Either by accident or for some curious reason, she took a chair back to back with Coleman's chair. Her sleeve of fragrant stuff almost touched his shoulder and he felt appealing to him seductively a perfume of orris root and violet. He was drinking bottled stout with his chop; be sat with a face of wood.

"Oh, the little lord?" Nora was crying to some slave. "Now, do you know, he won't do at all. He is too awfully charming. He sits and ruminates for fifteen minutes and then he pays me a lovely compliment. Then he ruminates for another fifteen minutes and cooks up another fine thing. It is too tiresome. Do you know what kind of man. I like?" she asked softly and confidentially. And here she sank back in her chair until. Coleman knew from the tingle that her head was but a few inches from his head. Her, sleeve touched him. He turned more wooden under the spell of the orris root and violet. Her courtiers thought it all a graceful pose, but Coleman believed otherwise. Her voice sank to the liquid, siren note of a succubus. "Do you know what kind of a man I like? Really like? I like a man that a woman can't bend in a thousand different ways in five minutes. He must have some steel in him. He obliges me to admire him the most when he remains stolid; stolid to me lures. Ah, that is the only kind of a man who cap ever break a heart among us women of the world. His stolidity is not real; no; it is mere art, but it is a highly finished art and often enough we can't cut through it. Really we can't. And, then we may actually come to—er—care for the man. Really we may. Isn't it funny?"

Alt the end Coleman arose and strolled out of the room, smoking a cigarette. He did not betray, a sign. Before the door clashed softly behind him, Nora laughed a little defiantly, perhaps a little loudly. It made every man in the grill-room perk up his ears. As for her courtiers, they were entranced. In her description of the conquering man, she had easily contrived that each one of them wondered if she might not mean him. Each man was perfectly sure that he had plenty of steel in his composition and that seemed to be a main point.

Coleman delayed for a time in the smoking room and then went to his own quarters. In reality he was Somewhat puzzled in his mind by a projection of the beauties of Nora Black upon his desire for Greece and Marjory, His thoughts formed a duality. Once he was on the point of sending his card to Nora Black's parlor, inasmuch as Greece was very distant and he could not start until the morrow. But he suspected that he was holding the interest of the actress because of his recent appearance of impregnable serenity in the presence of her fascinations. If he now sent his card, it was a form of surrender and he knew her to be one to take a merciless advantage. He would not make this tactical mistake. On the contrary he would go to bed and think of war,

In reality he found it easy to fasten his mind upon the prospective war. He regarded himself cynically in most affairs, but he could not be cynical of war, because he had seen none of it. His rejuvenated imagination began to thrill to the roll of battle, through his thought passing all the lightning in the pictures of Detaille, de Neuville and Morot; lashed battery horse roaring over bridges; grand cuirassiers dashing headlong against stolid invincible red-faced lines of German infantry; furious and bloody grapplings in the streets of little villages of northeastern France. There was one thing at least of which he could still feel the spirit of a debutante. In this matter of war he was not, too, unlike a young girl embarking upon her first season of opera. Walkely, the next morning, saw this mood sitting quaintly upon

Coleman and cackled with astonishment and glee. Coleman's usual manner did not return until he detected Walkely's appreciation of his state and then he snubbed him according to the ritual of the Sunday editor of the *New York Eclipse*. Parenthetically, it might be said that if Coleman now recalled Nora Black to his mind at all, it was only to think of her for a moment with ironical complacence. He had beaten her.

When the train drew out of the station, Coleman felt himself thrill. Was ever fate less perverse? War and love—war and Marjory—were in conjunction both in Greece—and he could tilt with one lance at both gods. It was a great fine game to play and no man was ever so blessed in vacations. He was smiling continually to himself and sometimes actually on the point of talking aloud. This was despite the presence in the compartment of two fellow passengers who preserved in their uncomfortably rigid, icy and uncompromising manners many of the more or less ridiculous traditions of the English first class carriage. Coleman's fine humor betrayed him once into addressing one of these passengers and the man responded simply with a wide look of incredulity, as if he discovered that he was travelling in the same compartment with a zebu. It turned Coleman suddenly to evil temper and he wanted to ask the man questions concerning his education and his present mental condition: and so until the train arrived at Dover, his ballooning soul was in danger of collapsing. On the packet crossing the channel, too, he almost returned to the usual Rufus Coleman since all the world was seasick and he could not get a cabin in which to hide himself from it. However he reaped much consolation by ordering a bottle of champagne and drinking it in sight of the people, which made them still more seasick. From Calais to Brindisi really nothing met his disapproval save the speed of the train, the conduct of some of the passengers, the quality of the food served, the manners of the guards, the temperature of the carriages, the prices charged and the length of the journey.

In time he passed as in a vision from wretched Brindisi to charming Corfu, from Corfu to the little war-bitten city of Patras and from Patras by rail at the speed of an ox-cart to Athens.

With a smile of grim content and surrounded in his carriage with all his beautiful brown luggage, he swept through the dusty streets of the Greek capital. Even as the vehicle arrived in a great terraced square in front of the yellow palace, Greek recruits in garments representing many trades and many characters were marching up cheering for Greece and the king. Officers stood upon the little iron chairs in front of the cafes; all the urchins came running and shouting; ladies waved their handkerchiefs from the balconies; the whole city was vivified with a leaping and joyous enthusiasm. The Athenians—as dragomen or otherwise—had preserved an ardor for their glorious traditions, and it was as if that in the white dust which lifted from the plaza and floated across the old-ivory face of the palace, there were the souls of the capable soldiers of the past. Coleman was almost intoxicated with it. It seemed to celebrate his own reasons, his reasons of love and ambition to conquer in love.

When the carriage arrived in front of the Hotel D'Angleterre, Coleman found the servants of the place with more than one eye upon the scene in the plaza, but they soon paid heed to the arrival of a gentleman with such an amount of beautiful leather luggage, all marked boldly with the initials "R. C." Coleman let them lead him and follow him and conduct him and use bad English upon him without noting either their words, their salaams or their work. His mind had quickly fixed upon the fact that here was the probable headquarters of the Wainwright party and, with the rush of his western race fleeting through his veins, he felt that he would choke and die if he did not learn of the Wainwrights in the first two minutes. It was a tragic venture to attempt to make the Levantine mind understand something off the course, that the new arrival's first thought was to establish a knowledge of the whereabouts of some of his friends rather than to swarm helter-skelter into that part of the hotel for which he was willing to pay rent. In fact he failed to thus impress them; failed in dark wrath, but, nevertheless, failed. At last he was simply forced to concede the travel of files of men up the broad, red-carpeted staircase, each man being loaded with Coleman's luggage. The men in the hotel-bureau were then able to comprehend that the foreign gentleman might have something else on his mind. They raised their eyebrows languidly when he spoke of the Wainwright party in gentle surprise that he had not yet learned that they were gone some time. They were departed on some excursion. Where? Oh, really—it was almost laughable, indeed—they didn't know. Were they sure? Why, yes—it was almost laughable, indeed—they were quite sure. Where could the gentleman find out about them? Well, they—as they had explained—did not know, but—it was possible—the American minister might know. Where was he to be found? Oh, that was very simple. It was well known that the American minister had apartments in the hotel. Was he in? Ah, that they could not say. So Coleman, rejoicing at his final emancipation and with the grime of travel still upon him, burst in somewhat violently upon the secretary of the Hon. Thomas M. Gordner of Nebraska, the United States minister to Greece. From his desk the secretary arose from behind an accidental bulwark of books and governmental pamphlets. "Yes, certainly. Mr. Gordner is in. If you would give me your card—"

Directly. Coleman was introduced into another room where a quiet man who was rolling a cigarette looked him frankly but carefully in the eye. "The Wainwrights" asked the minister immediately after the question. "Why, I myself am immensely concerned about them at present. I'm afraid they've gotten themselves into trouble.'

"Really?" said Coleman.

"Yes. That little professor is rather—stubborn; Isn't he? He wanted to make an expedition to Nikopolis and I explained to him all the possibilities of war and begged him to at least not take his wife and daughter with him."

"Daughter," murmured Coleman, as if in his sleep.

"But that little old man had a head like a stone and only laughed at me. Of course those villainous young students were only too delighted at a prospect of war, but it was a stupid and absurd thing for the man to take his wife and daughter there. They are up there now. I can't get a word from them or get a word to them."

Coleman had been choking. "Where is Nikopolis?" he asked.

The minister gazed suddenly in comprehension of the man before him. "Nikopolis is in Turkey," he answered gently.

Turkey at that time was believed to be a country of delay, corruption, turbulence and massacre. It meant everything. More than a half of the Christians of the world shuddered at the name of Turkey. Coleman's lips tightened and perhaps blanched, and his chin moved out strangely, once, twice, thrice. "How can I get to Nikopolis?" he said.

The minister smiled. "It would take you the better part of four days if you could get there, but as a matter of fact you can't get there at the present time. A Greek army and a Turkish army are looking at each other from the sides of the river at Arta—the river is there the frontier—and Nikopolis happens to be on the wrong side. You can't reach them. The forces at Arta will fight within three days. I know it. Of course I've notified our legation at Constantinople, but, with Turkish methods of communication, Nikopolis is about as far from Constantinople as New York is from Peking."

Coleman arose. "They've run themselves into a nice mess," he said crossly. "Well, I'm a thousand times obliged to you, I'm sure."

The minister opened his eyes a trifle. You are not going to try to reach them, are you?"

"Yes," answered Coleman, abstractedly. "I'm going to have a try at it. Friends of mine, you know—"

At the bureau of the hotel, the correspondent found several cables awaiting him from the alert office of the *New York Eclipse*. One of them read: "State Department gives out bad plight of Wainwright party lost somewhere; find them. *Eclipse*." When Coleman perused the message he began to smile with seraphic bliss. Could fate have ever been less perverse.

Whereupon he whirled himself in Athens. And it was to the considerable astonishment of some Athenians. He discovered and instantly subsidized a young Englishman who, during his absence at the front, would act as correspondent for the *Eclipse* at the capital. He took unto himself a dragoman and then bought three horses and hired a groom at a speed that caused a little crowd at the horse dealer's place to come out upon the pavement and watch this surprising young man ride back toward his hotel. He had already driven his dragoman into a curious state of Oriental bewilderment and panic in which he could only lumber hastily and helplessly here and there, with his face in the meantime marked with agony. Coleman's own field equipment had been ordered by cable from New York to London, but it was necessary to buy much tinned meats, chocolate, coffee, candles, patent food, brandy, tobaccos, medicine and other things.

He went to bed that night feeling more placid. The train back to Patras was to start in the early morning, and he felt the satisfaction of a man who is at last about to start on his own great quest. Before he dropped off to slumber, he heard crowds cheering exultantly in the streets, and the cheering moved him as it had done in the morning. He felt that the celebration of the people was really an accompaniment to his primal reason, a reason of love and ambition to conquer in love—even as in the theatre, the music accompanies the heroin his progress. He arose once during the night to study a map of the Balkan peninsula and get nailed into his mind the exact position of Nikopolis. It was important.

## CHAPTER IX.

COLEMAN'S dragoman aroused him in the blue before dawn. The correspondent arrayed himself in one of his new khaki suits—riding breeches and a tunic well marked with buttoned pockets—and accompanied by some of his beautiful brown luggage, they departed for the station.

The ride to Patras is a terror under ordinary circumstances. It begins in the early morning and ends in the twilight. To Coleman, having just come from Patras to Athens, this journey from Athens to Patras had all the exasperating elements of a forced recantation. Moreover, he had not come prepared to view with awe the ancient city of Corinth nor to view with admiration the limpid beauties of the gulf of that name with its olive grove shore. He was not stirred by Parnassus, a far-away snow-field high on the black shoulders of the mountains across the gulf. No; he wished to go to Nikopolis. He passed over the graves of an ancient race the gleam of whose mighty minds shot, hardly dimmed, through the clouding ages. No; he wished to go to Nikopolis. The train went at a snail's pace, and if Coleman bad an interest it was in the people who lined the route and cheered the soldiers on the train. In Coleman s compartment there was a greasy person who spoke a little English. He explained that he was a poet, a poet who now wrote of nothing but war. When a man is in pursuit of his love and success is known to be at least remote, it often relieves his strain if he is deeply bored from time to time.

The train was really obliged to arrive finally at Patras even if it was a tortoise, and when this happened, a hotel runner appeared, who lied for the benefit of the hotel in saying that there was no boat over to Mesalonghi that night. When, all too late, Coleman discovered the truth of the matter his wretched dragoman came in for a period of infamy and suffering. However, while strolling in the plaza at Patras, amid newsboys from every side, by rumor and truth, Coleman learned things to his advantage. A Greek fleet was bombarding Prevasa. Prevasa was near Nikopolis. The opposing armies at Arta were engaged, principally in an artillery duel. Arta was on the road from Nikopolis into Greece. Hearing this news in the sunlit square made him betray no weakness, but in the darkness of his room at the hotel, he seemed to behold Marjory encircled by insurmountable walls of flame. He could look out of his window into the black night of the north and feel every ounce of a hideous circumstance. It appalled him; here was no power of calling up a score of reporters and sending them scampering to accomplish everything. He even might as well have been without a tongue as far as it could serve him in goodly speech. He was alone, confronting the black ominous Turkish north behind which were the deadly flames; behind the flames was Marjory. It worked upon him until he felt obliged to call in his dragoman, and then, seated upon the edge of his bed and waving his pipe eloquently, he described the plight of some very dear friends who were cut off at Nikopolis in Epirus. Some of his talk was almost wistful in its wish for sympathy from his servant, but at the end he bade the dragoman understand that be, Coleman, was going to their rescue, and he defiantly asked the hireling if he was prepared to go with him. But he did not know the Greek nature. In two minutes the dragoman was weeping tears of enthusiasm, and, for these tears, Coleman was over-grateful, because he had not been told that any of the more crude forms of sentiment arouse the common Greek to the highest pitch, but sometimes, when it comes to what the Americans call a "show down," when he gets backed toward his last corner with a solitary privilege of dying for these sentiments, perhaps he does not always exhibit those talents which are supposed to be possessed by the bulldog. He often then, goes into the cafes and take's it out in oration, like any common Parisian.

In the morning A steamer carried them across the strait and landed them near Mesalonghi at the foot of the railroad that leads to Agrinion. At Agrinion Coleman at last began to feel that he was nearing his goal. There were plenty of soldiers in the town, who received with delight and applause this gentleman in the distinguished-looking khaki clothes with his revolver and his field glasses and his canteen and; his dragoman. The dragoman lied, of course, and vociferated that the gentleman in the distinguished-looking khaki clothes was an English soldier of reputation, who had, naturally, come to help the cross in its fight against, the crescent. He also said that his master had three superb horses coming from Athens in charge of a groom, and was undoubtedly going to join the cavalry. Whereupon the soldiers wished to embrace and kiss the gentleman in the distinguished-looking khaki clothes.

There was more or less of a scuffle. Coleman would have taken to kicking and punching, but he found that by a series of elusive movements he could dodge the demonstrations of affection without losing his popularity. Escorted by the soldiers, citizens, children and dogs, he went to the diligence which was to take him and others the next stage of the journey. As the diligence proceeded, Coleman's mind suffered another little inroad of ill-fate as to the success of his expedition. In the first place it appeared foolish to expect that this diligence would ever arrive anywhere. Moreover, the accommodations were about equal to what one would endure if one undertook to sleep for a night in a tree.

Then there was a devil-dog, a little black-and-tan terrier in a blanket gorgeous and belled, whose duty it was to stand on the top of the coach and bark incessantly to keep the driver fully aroused to the enormity of his occupation. To have this cur silenced either by strangulation or ordinary clubbing, Coleman struggled with his dragoman as Jacob struggled with the angel, but in the first place, the dragoman was a Greek whose tongue could go quite drunk, a Greek who became a slave to the heralding and establishment of one certain fact, or lie, and now he was engaged in describing to every village and to all the country side the prowess of the gentleman in the distinguished-looking khaki clothes. It was the general absurdity of this advance to the frontier and the fighting, to the crucial place where he was resolved to make an attempt to rescue his sweetheart; it was this ridiculous aspect that caused to come to Coleman a premonition of failure. No knight ever went out to recover a lost love in such a diligence and with such a devil-dog, tinkling his little bells and yelping insanely to keep the driver awake.

After nightfall, they arrived at a town on the southern coast of the Gulf of Arta and the goaded dragoman was-thrust forth from the little inn into the street to find the first possible means of getting on to Arta. He returned at last to tremulously say that there was no single chance of starting for Arta that night. Where upon he was again thrust into the street with orders, strict orders. In due time, Coleman spread his rugs upon the floor of his little room and thought himself almost asleep, when the dragoman entered with a really intelligent man who, for some reason, had agreed to consort with him in the business of getting the stranger off to Arta. They announced that there was a brigantine about to sail with a load of soldiers for a little port near Arta, and if Coleman hurried he could catch it, permission from an officer having already been obtained. He was up at once, and the dragoman and the unaccountably intelligent person hastily gathered his chattels. Stepping out into a black street and moving to the edge of black water and embarking in a black boat filled with soldiers whose rifles dimly shone, was as impressive to Coleman as if, really, it had been the first start. He had endured many starts, it was true, but the latest one always touched him as being conclusive.

There were no lights on the brigantine and the men swung precariously up her sides to the deck which was already occupied by a babbling multitude. The dragoman judiciously found a place for his master where during the night the latter had to move quickly every time the tiller was shifted to starboard.

The craft raised her shadowy sails and swung slowly off into the deep gloom. Forward, some of the soldiers began to sing weird minor melodies. Coleman, enveloped in his rugs, smoked three or four cigars. He was content and miserable, lying there, hearing these melodies which defined to him his own affairs.

At dawn they were at the little port. First, in the carmine and grey tints from a sleepy sun, they could see little mobs of soldiers working amid boxes of stores. And then from the back in some dun and green hills sounded a deep-throated thunder of artillery An officer gave Coleman and his dragoman positions in one of the first boats, but of course it could not be done without an almost endless amount of palaver. Eventually they landed with their traps. Coleman felt through the sole of his boot his foot upon the shore. He was within striking distance.

But here it was smitten into the head of Coleman's servant to turn into the most inefficient dragoman, probably in the entire East. Coleman discerned it immediately, before any blunder could tell him. He at first thought that it was the voices of the guns which had made a chilly inside for the man, but when he reflected upon the incompetency, or childish courier's falsity, at Patras and his discernible lack of sense from Agrinion onward, he felt that the fault was elemental in his nature. It was a mere basic inability to front novel situations which was somehow in the dragoman; he retreated from everything difficult in a smoke of gibberish and gesticulation. Coleman glared at him with the hatred that sometimes ensues when breed meets breed, but he saw that this man was indeed a golden link in his possible success. This man connected him with Greece and its language. If he destroyed him he delayed what was now his main desire in life. However, this truth did not prevent him from addressing the man in elegant speech.

The two little men who were induced to carry Coleman's luggage as far as the Greek camp were really procured by the correspondent himself, who pantomimed vigorously and with unmistakable vividness. Followed by his dragoman and the two little men, he strode off along a road which led straight as a stick to where the guns were at intervals booming. Meanwhile the dragoman and the two little men talked, talked, talked.

Coleman was silent, puffing his cigar and reflecting upon the odd things which happen to chivalry in the modern age.

He knew of many men who would have been astonished if they could have seen into his mind at that time, and he knew of many more men who would have laughed if they had the same privilege of sight. He made no attempt to conceal from himself that the whole thing was romantic, romantic despite the little tinkling dog, the decrepit diligence, the palavering natives, the super-idiotic dragoman. It was fine. It was from another age and even the actors could not deface the purity of the picture. However it was true that upon the brigantine the previous night he had unaccountably wetted all his available matches. This was momentous, important, cruel truth, but Coleman, after all, was taking as well as he could a solemn and knightly joy of this adventure, and there were as many portraits of his lady envisioning before him as ever held the heart of an armor-encased young gentleman of medieval poetry. If he had been travelling in this region as an ordinary tourist, he would have been apparent mainly for his lofty impatience over trifles, but now there was in him a positive assertion of direction which was undoubtedly one of the reasons for the despair of the accomplished dragoman.

Before them the country slowly opened and opened, the straight white road always piercing it like a lance-shaft. Soon they could see black masses of men marking the green knolls. The artillery thundered loudly and now vibrated augustly through the air. Coleman quickened his pace, to the despair of the little men carrying the traps. They finally came up with one of these black bodies of men and found it to be composed of a considerable number of soldiers who were idly watching some hospital people bury a dead Turk. The dragoman at once dashed forward to peer through the throng and see the face of the corpse. Then he came and supplicated Coleman as if he were hawking him to look at a relic and Coleman moved by a strong, mysterious impulse, went forward to look at the poor little clay-colored body. At that moment a snake ran out from a tuft of grass at his feet and wriggled wildly over the sod. The dragoman shrieked, of course, but one of the soldiers put his heel upon the head of the reptile and it flung itself into the agonizing knot of death. Then the whole crowd powwowed, turning from the dead man to the dead snake. Coleman signaled his contingent and proceeded along the road.

This incident, this paragraph, had seemed a strange introduction to war. The snake, the dead man, the entire sketch, made him shudder of itself, but more than anything he felt an uncanny symbolism. It was no doubt a mere occurrence; nothing but an occurrence; but inasmuch as all the detail of this daily life associated itself with Marjory, he felt a different horror. He had thought of the little devil-dog and Marjory in an interwoven way. Supposing Marjory had been riding in the diligence with the devil-dog a-top? What would she have said? Of her fund of expressions, a fund uncountable, which would she have innocently projected against the background of the Greek hills? Would it have smitten her nerves badly or would she have laughed? And supposing Marjory could have seen him in his new khaki clothes cursing his dragoman as he listened to the devil-dog?

And now he interwove his memory of Marjory with a dead man and with a snake in the throes of the end of life. They crossed, intersected, tangled, these two thoughts. He perceived it clearly; the incongruity of it. He academically reflected upon the mysteries of the human mind, this homeless machine which lives here and then there and often lives in two or three opposing places at the same instant. He decided that the incident of the snake and the dead man had no more meaning than the greater number of the things which happen to us in our daily lives. Nevertheless it bore upon him.

On a spread of plain they saw a force drawn up in a long line. It was a flagrant inky streak on the verdant prairie. From somewhere near it sounded the timed reverberations of guns. The brisk walk of the next ten minutes was actually exciting to Coleman. He could not but reflect that those guns were being fired with serious purpose at certain human bodies much like his own.

As they drew nearer they saw that the inky streak was composed of cavalry, the troopers standing at their bridles. The sunlight flicked, upon their bright weapons. Now the dragoman developed in one of his extraordinary directions. He announced forsooth that an intimate friend was a captain of cavalry in this command. Coleman at first thought that this was some kind of mysterious lie, but when he arrived where they could hear the stamping of hoofs, the clank of weapons, and the murmur of men, behold, a most dashing young officer gave a shout of joy and he and the dragoman hurled themselves into a mad embrace. After this first ecstasy was over, the dragoman bethought him of his employer, and looking toward Coleman hastily explained him to the officer. The latter, it appeared, was very affable indeed. Much had happened. The Greeks and the Turks had been fighting over a shallow part of the river nearly opposite this point and the Greeks had driven back the Turks and succeeded in throwing a bridge of casks and planking across the stream. It was now the duty and the delight of this force of cavalry to cross the bridge and, passing, the little force of covering Greek infantry, to proceed into Turkey until they came in touch with the enemy.

Coleman's eyes dilated. Was ever fate less perverse? Partly in wretched French to the officer and partly in idiomatic English to the dragoman, he proclaimed his fiery desire to accompany the expedition. The officer immediately beamed upon him. In fact, he was delighted. The dragoman had naturally told him many falsehoods concerning Coleman, incidentally referring to himself more as a philanthropic guardian and, valuable friend of the correspondent than as, a plain, unvarnished dragoman with an exceedingly good eye for the financial possibilities of his position.

Coleman wanted to ask his servant if there was any chance of the scout taking them near Nikopolis, but he delayed being informed upon this point until such time as he could find out, secretly, for himself. To ask the dragoman would be mere stupid questioning which would surely make the animal shy. He tried to be content that fate had given him this early opportunity of dealing with a Medieval situation with some show of proper form; that is to say, armed, on horseback, and in danger. Then he could feel that to the gods of the game he was not laughable, as when he rode to rescue his love in a diligence with a devil-dog yelping atop.

With some flourish, the young captain presented him to the major who commanded the cavalry. This officer stood with his legs wide apart, eating the rind of a fresh lemon and talking betimes to some of his officers. The major also beamed upon Coleman when the captain explained that the gentleman in the distinguished-looking khaki clothes wished to accompany the expedition. He at once said that he would provide two troop horses for Coleman and the dragoman. Coleman thanked fate for his behavior and his satisfaction was not without a vestige of surprise. At that time he judged it to be a remarkable amiability of individuals, but in later years he came to believe in certain laws which he deemed existent solely for the benefit of war correspondents. In the minds of governments, war offices and generals they have no function save one of disturbance, but Coleman deemed it proven that the common men, and many uncommon men, when they go away to the fighting ground, out of the sight, out of the hearing of the world known to them, and are eager to perform feats of war in this new place, they feel an absolute longing for a spectator. It is indeed the veritable coronation of this world. There is not too much vanity of the street in this desire of men to have some disinterested fellows perceive their deeds. It is merely that a man doing his best in the middle of a sea of war, longs to have people see him doing his best. This feeling is often notably serious if, in peace, a man has done his worst, or part of his worst. Coleman believed that, above everybody, young, proud and brave subalterns had this itch, but it existed, truly enough, from lieutenants to colonels. None wanted to conceal from his left hand that his right hand was performing a manly and valiant thing, although there might be times when an application of the principle would be immensely convenient. The war correspondent arises, then, to become a sort of a cheap telescope for the people at home; further still, there have been fights where the eyes of a solitary man were the eyes of the world; one spectator, whose business it was to transfer, according to his ability, his visual impressions to other minds.

Coleman and his servant were conducted to two saddled troop horses, and beside them, waited decently in the rear of the ranks. The uniform of the troopers was of plain, dark green cloth and they were well and sensibly equipped. The mounts, however, had in no way been picked; there were little horses and big horses, fat horses and thin horses. They looked the result of a wild conscription. Coleman noted the faces of the troopers, and they were calm enough save when a man betrayed himself by perhaps a disproportionate angry jerk at the bridle of his restive horse.

The major, artistically drooping his cloak from his left shoulder and tenderly and musingly fingering his long yellow moustache, rode slowly to the middle of the line and wheeled his horse to face his men. A bugle called attention, and then he addressed them in a loud and rapid speech, which did not seem to have an end. Coleman imagined that the major was paying tribute to the Greek tradition of the power of oratory. Again the trumpet rang out, and this parade front swung off into column formation. Then Coleman and the dragoman trotted at the tail of the squadron, restraining with difficulty their horses, who could not understand their new places in the procession, and worked feverishly to regain what they considered their positions in life.

The column jangled musically over the sod, passing between two hills on one of which a Greek light battery was posted. Its men climbed to the tops of their entrenchments to witness the going of the cavalry. Then the column curved along over ditch and through hedge to the shallows of the river. Across this narrow stream was Turkey. Turkey, however, presented nothing to the eye but a muddy bank with fringes of trees back of it. It seemed to be a great plain with sparse collections of foliage marking it, whereas the Greek side, presented in the main a vista of high, gaunt rocks. Perhaps one of the first effects of war upon the mind, is a new recognition and fear of the circumscribed ability of the eye, making all landscape seem inscrutable. The cavalry drew up in platoon formation on their own bank of the stream and waited. If Coleman had known anything of war, he would have known, from appearances, that there was nothing in the immediate vicinity to, cause heart-jumping, but as a matter of truth he was deeply moved and wondered what was hidden, what was veiled by those trees. Moreover, the squadrons resembled art old picture of a body of horse awaiting Napoleon's order to charge. In the, meantime his mount fumed at the bit, plunging to get back to the ranks. The sky was, without a cloud, and the sun rays swept down upon them. Sometimes Coleman was on the verge of addressing the dragoman, according to his anxiety, but in the end he simply told him to go to the river and fill the canteens.

At last an order came, and the first troop moved with muffled tumult across the bridge. Coleman and his dragoman followed the last troop. The horses scrambled up the muddy bank much as if they were merely breaking out of a pasture, but probably all the men felt a sudden tightening of their muscles. Coleman, in his excitement, felt, more than he saw, glossy horse flanks, green-clothed men chomping in their saddles, banging sabers and canteens, and carbines slanted in line.

There were some Greek infantry in a trench. They were heavily overcoated, despite the heat, and some were engaged in eating loaves of round, thick bread. They called out lustily as the cavalry passed them. The troopers smiled slowly, somewhat proudly in response.

Presently there was another halt and Coleman saw the major trotting busily here and there, while troop commanders rode out to meet him. Spreading groups of scouts and flankers moved off and disappeared. Their dashing young officer friend cantered past them with his troop at his heels. He waved a joyful good-bye. It was the doings of cavalry in actual service, horsemen fanning out in all forward directions. There were two troops held in reserve, and as they jangled ahead at a foot pace, Coleman and his dragoman followed them.

The dragoman was now moved to erect many reasons for an immediate return. It was plain that he had no stomach at all for this business, and that he wished himself safely back on the other side of the river. Coleman looked at him askance. When these men talked together Coleman might as well have been a polar bear for all he understood of it. When he saw the trepidation of his dragoman, he did not know what it foreboded. In this situation it was not for him to say that the dragoman's fears were founded on nothing. And ever the dragoman raised his reasons for a retreat. Coleman spoke to himself. "I am just a trifle rattled," he said to his heart, and after he had communed for a time upon the duty of steadiness, he addressed the dragoman in cool language. "Now, my persuasive friend, just quit all that, because business is business, and it may be rather annoying business, but you will have to go through with it." Long afterward, when ruminating over the feelings of that morning, he saw with some astonishment that there was not a single thing within sound or sight to cause a rational being any quaking. He was simply riding with some soldiers over a vast tree-dotted prairie.

Presently the commanding officer turned in his saddle and told the dragoman that he was going to ride forward with his orderly to where he could see the flanking parties and the scouts, and courteously, with the manner of a gentleman entertaining two guests, he asked if the civilians cared to accompany him. The dragoman would not have passed this question correctly on to Coleman if he had thought he could have avoided it, but, with both men regarding him, he considered that a lie probably meant instant detection. He spoke almost the truth, contenting himself with merely communicating to Coleman in a subtle way his sense that a ride forward with the commanding officer and his orderly would be depressing and dangerous occupation. But Coleman immediately accepted the invitation mainly because it was the invitation of the major, and in war it is a brave man who can refuse the invitation of a commanding officer. The little party of four trotted away from the reserves, curving in single file about the water-holes. In time they arrived at where the plain lacked trees and was one great green lake of grass; grass and scrubs. On this expanse they could see the Greek horsemen riding, mainly appearing as little black dots. Far to the left there was a squad said to be composed of only twenty troopers, but in the distance their black mass seemed to be a regiment.

As the officer and his guests advanced they came in view of what one may call the shore of the plain. The rise of ground was heavily clad with trees, and over the tops of them appeared the cupola and part of the walls of a large white house, and there were glimpses of huts near it as if a village was marked. The black specks seemed to be almost to it. The major galloped forward and the others followed at his pace. The house grew larger and larger and they came nearly to the advance scouts who they could now see were not quite close to the village. There had been a deception of the eye precisely as occurs at sea. Herds of unguarded sheep drifted over the plain and little ownerless horses, still cruelly hobbled, leaped painfully away, frightened, as if they understood that an anarchy had come upon them. The party rode until they were very nearly up with the scouts, and then from low down at the very edge of the plain there came a long rattling noise which endured as if some kind of grinding machine had been put in motion. Smoke arose, faintly marking the position of an entrenchment. Sometimes a swift spitting could be heard from the air over the party.

It was Coleman's fortune to think at first that the Turks were not firing in his direction, but as soon as he heard the weird voices in the air he knew that war was upon him. But it was plain that the range was almost excessive, plain even to his ignorance. The major looked at him and laughed; he found no difficulty in smiling in response. If this was war, it could be withstood somehow. He could not at this time understand what a mere trifle was the present incident. He felt upon his cheek a little breeze which was moving the grass-blades. He had tied his canteen in a wrong place on the saddle and every time the horse moved quickly the canteen banged the correspondent, to his annoyance and distress, forcibly on the knee. He had forgotten about his dragoman, but happening to look upon that faithful servitor, he saw him gone white with horror. A bullet at that moment twanged near his head and the slave to fear ducked in a spasm. Coleman called the orderly's attention and they both laughed discreetly. They made no pretension of being heroes, but they saw plainly that they were better than this man. Coleman said to him: "How far is it now to Nikopolis?" The dragoman replied only, with a look of agonized impatience.

But of course there was no going to Nikopolis that day. The officer had advanced his men as far as was intended by his superiors, and presently they were all recalled and trotted back to the bridge. They crossed it to their old camp.

An important part of Coleman's traps was back with his Athenian horses and their groom, but with his present equipment he could at least lie smoking on his blankets and watch the dragoman prepare food. But he reflected that for that day he had only attained the simple discovery that the approach to Nikopolis was surrounded with difficulties.

## CHAPTER X.

The same afternoon Coleman and the dragoman rode up to Arta on their borrowed troop horses. The correspondent first went to the telegraph office and found there the usual number of despairing clerks. They were outraged when they found he was going to send messages and thought it preposterous that he insisted upon learning if there were any in the office for him. They had trouble enough with endless official communications without being hounded about private affairs by a confident young man in khaki. But Coleman at last unearthed six cablegrams which collective said that the *Eclipse* wondered why they did not hear from him, that Walkley had been relieved from duty in London and sent to join the army of the crown prince, that young Point, the artist, had been shipped to Greece, that if he, Coleman, succeeded in finding the Wainwright party the paper was prepared to make a tremendous uproar of a celebration over it and, finally, the paper wondered twice more why they did not hear from him.

When Coleman went forth to enquire if anybody knew of the whereabouts of the Wainwright party he thought first of his fellow correspondents. He found most of them in a cafe where was to be had about the only food in the soldier-laden town. It was a slothful den where even an ordinary boiled egg could be made unpalatable. Such a common matter as the salt men watched with greed and suspicion as if they were always about to grab it from each other. The proprietor, in a dirty shirt, could always be heard whining, evidently telling the world that he was being abused, but he had spirit enough remaining to charge three prices for everything with an almost Jewish fluency.

The correspondents consoled themselves largely upon black bread and the native wines. Also there were certain little oiled fishes, and some green odds and ends for salads. The correspondents were practically all Englishmen. Some of them were veterans of journalism in the Sudan, in India, in South Africa; and there were others who knew as much of war as they could learn by sitting at a desk and editing the London stock reports. Some were on their own hook; some had horses and dragomen and some had neither the one nor the other; many knew how to write and a few had it yet to learn. The thing in common was a spirit of adventure which found pleasure in the extraordinary business of seeing how men kill each other.

They were talking of an artillery duel which had been fought the previous day between the Greek batteries above the town and the Turkish batteries across the river. Coleman took seat at one of the long tables, and the astute dragoman got somebody in the street to hold the horses in order that he might be present at any feasting.

One of the experienced correspondents was remarking that the fire of the Greek batteries in the engagement had been the finest artillery practice of the century. He spoke a little loudly, perhaps, in the wistful hope that some of the Greek officers would understand enough English to follow his meaning, for it is always good for a correspondent to admire the prowess on his own side of the battlefield. After a time Coleman spoke in a lull, and describing the supposed misfortunes of the Wainwright party, asked if anyone had news of them. The correspondents were surprised; they had none of them heard even of the existence of a Wainwright party. Also none of them seemed to care exceedingly. The conversation soon changed to a discussion of the probable result of the general Greek advance announced for the morrow.

Coleman silently commented that this remarkable appearance of indifference to the mishap of the Wainwrights, a little party, a single group, was a better definition of a real condition of war than that bit of long-range musketry of the morning. He took a certain dispatch out of his pocket and again read it. "Find Wainwright party at all hazards; much talk here; success means red fire by ton. *Eclipse.*" It was an important matter. He could imagine how the American people, vibrating for years to stories of the cruelty of the Turk, would tremble—indeed, was now trembling— while the newspapers howled out the dire possibilities. He saw all the kinds of people, from those who would read the Wainwright chapters from day to day as a sort of sensational novel, to those who would work up a gentle sympathy for the woe of others around the table in the evenings. He saw bar keepers and policemen taking a high gallery thrill out of this kind of romance. He saw even the emotion among American colleges over the tragedy of a professor and some students. It certainly was a big affair. Marjory of course was everything in one way, but that, to the world, was not a big affair. It was the romance of the Wainwright party in its simplicity that to the American world was arousing great sensation; one that in the old days would have made his heart leap like a colt.

Still, when batteries had fought each other savagely, and horse, foot and guns were now about to make a general advance, it was difficult, he could see, to stir men to think and feel out of the present zone of action; to adopt for a time in fact the thoughts and feelings of the other side of the world. It made Coleman dejected as he saw clearly that the task was wholly on his own shoulders.

Of course they were men who when at home manifested the most gentle and wide-reaching feelings; most of them could not by any possibility have slapped a kitten merely for the prank and yet all of them who had seen an unknown man shot through the head in battle had little more to think of it than if the man had been a rag-baby. Tender they might be; poets they might be; but they were all horned with a provisional, temporary, but absolutely essential callous which was formed by their existence amid war with its quality of making them always think of the sights and sounds concealed in their own direct future.

They had been simply polite. "Yes?" said one to Coleman. "How many people in the party? Are they all Americans? Oh, I suppose it will be quite right. Your minister in Constantinople will arrange that easily. Where did you say? At Nikopolis? Well, we conclude that the Turks will make no stand between here and Pentepigadia. In that case your Nikopolis will be uncovered unless the garrison at Prevasa intervenes. That garrison at Prevasa, by the way, may make a deal of trouble. Remember Plevna."

"Exactly how far is it to Nikopolis?" asked Coleman.

"Oh, I think it is about thirty kilometers," replied the others. "There is a good military road as soon as you cross the Louros river. I've got the map of the Austrian general staff. Would you like to look at it?"

Coleman studied the map, speeding with his eye rapidly to and fro between Arta and Nikopolis. To him it was merely a brown lithograph of mystery, but he could study the distances.

He had received a cordial invitation from the commander of the cavalry to go with him for another ride into Turkey, and he inclined to believe that his project would be furthered if he stuck close to the cavalry. So he rode back to the cavalry camp and went peacefully to sleep on the sod. He awoke in the morning with chattering teeth to find his dragoman saying that the major had unaccountably withdrawn his loan of the two troop horses. Coleman of course immediately said to himself that the dragoman was lying again in order to prevent another expedition into ominous Turkey, but after all if the commander, of the cavalry had suddenly turned the light of his favor from the correspondent it was only a proceeding consistent with the nature which Coleman now thought he was beginning to discern a nature which can never think twice in the same place, a gaseous mind which drifts, dissolves, combines, vanishes with the ability of an aerial thing until the man of the north feels that when he clutches it with full knowledge of his senses he is only the victim of his ardent imagination. It is the difference in standards, in creeds, which is the more luminous when men call out that they are all alike.

So Coleman and his dragoman loaded their traps and moved out to again invade Turkey. It was not yet clear daylight, but they felt that they might well start early since they were no longer mounted men.

On the way to the bridge, the dragoman, although he was curiously in love with his forty francs a day and his opportunities, ventured a stout protest, based apparently upon the fact that after all this foreigner, four days out from Athens was somewhat at his mercy. "Meester Coleman," he said, stopping suddenly, "I think we make no good if we go there. Much better we wait Arta for our horse. Much better. I think this no good. There is coming one big fight and I think much better we go stay Arta. Much better."

"Oh, come off," said Coleman. And in clear language he began to labor with the man. "Look here, now, if you think you are engaged in steering a bunch of wooden-headed guys about the Acropolis, my dear partner of my joys and sorrows, you are extremely mistaken. As a matter of fact you are now the dragoman of a war correspondent and you were engaged and are paid to be one. It becomes necessary that you make good. Make good, do you understand? I'm not out here to be buncoed by this sort of game." He continued indefinitely in this strain and at intervals he asked sharply Do you understand?

Perhaps the dragoman was dumbfounded that the laconic Coleman could on occasion talk so much, or perhaps he understood everything and was impressed by the argumentative power. At any rate he suddenly wilted. He made a gesture which was a protestation of martyrdom and picking up his burden proceeded on his way.

When they reached the bridge, they saw strong columns of Greek infantry, dead black in the dim light, crossing the stream and slowly deploying on the other shore. It was a bracing sight to the dragoman, who then went into one of his absurd babbling moods, in which he would have talked the head off any man who was not born in a country laved by the childish Mediterranean. Coleman could not understand what he said to the soldiers as they passed, but it was evidently all grandiose nonsense.

Two light batteries had precariously crossed the rickety bridge during the night, and now this force of several thousand infantry, with the two batteries, was moving out over the territory which the cavalry had reconnoitered on the previous day. The ground being familiar to Coleman, he no longer knew a tremor, and, regarding his dragoman, he saw that that invaluable servitor was also in better form. They marched until they found one of the light batteries unlimbered and aligned on the lake of grass about a mile from where parts of the white house appeared above the treetops. Here the dragoman talked with the captain of artillery, a tiny man on an immense horse, who for some unknown reason told him that this force was going to raid into Turkey and try to swing around the opposing army's right flank. He announced, as he showed his teeth in a smile, that it would be very, very dangerous work. The dragoman precipitated himself upon Coleman.

"This is much danger. The captain he tell me the troops go now in back of the Turks. It will be much danger. I think much better we go Arta wait for horse. Much better." Coleman, although be believed he despised the dragoman, could not help but be influenced by his fears. They were, so to speak, in a room with one window, and only the dragoman looked forth from the window, so if he said that what he saw outside frightened him, Coleman was perforce frightened also in a measure. But when the correspondent raised his eyes he saw the captain of the battery looking at him, his teeth still showing in a smile, as if his information, whether true or false, had been given to convince the foreigner that the Greeks were a very superior and brave people, notably one little officer of artillery. He had apparently assumed that Coleman would balk from venturing with such a force upon an excursion to trifle with the rear of a hard fighting Ottoman army. He exceedingly disliked that man, sitting up there on his tall horse and grinning like a cruel little ape with a secret. In truth, Coleman was taken back at the outlook, but he could no more refrain from instantly accepting this half-concealed challenge than he could have refrained from resenting an ordinary form of insult. His mind was not at peace, but the small vanities are very large. He was perfectly aware that he was, being misled into the thing by an odd pride, but anyhow, it easily might turn out to be a stroke upon the doors of Nikopolis. He nodded and smiled at the officer in grateful acknowledgment of his service.

The infantry was moving steadily a-field. Black blocks of men were trailing in column slowly over the plain. They were not unlike the backs of dominoes on a green baize table; they were so vivid, so startling. The correspondent and his servant followed them. Eventually they overtook two companies in command of a captain, who seemed immensely glad to have the strangers with him. As they marched, the captain spoke through the dragoman upon the virtues of his men, announcing with other news the fact that his first sergeant was the bravest man in the world.

A number of columns were moving across the plain parallel to their line of march, and the whole force seemed to have orders to halt when they reached a long ditch about four hundred yards from where the shore of the plain arose to the luxuriant groves with the cupola of the big white house sticking above them. The soldiers lay along the ditch, and the bravest man in the world spread his blanket on the ground for the captain, Coleman and himself. During a long pause Coleman tried to elucidate the question of why the Greek soldiers wore heavy overcoats, even in the bitter heat of midday, but he could only learn that the dews, when they came, were very destructive to the lungs, Further, he convinced himself anew that talking through an interpreter to the minds of other men was as satisfactory as looking at landscape through a stained glass window.

After a time there was, in front, a stir near where a curious hedge of dry brambles seemed to outline some sort of a garden patch. Many of the soldiers exclaimed and raised their guns. But there seemed to come a general understanding to the line that it was wrong to fire. Then presently into the open came a dirty brown figure, and Coleman could see through his glasses that its head was crowned with a dirty fez which had once been white. This indicated that the figure was that of one of the Christian peasants of Epirus. Obedient to the captain, the sergeant arose and waved invitation.

The peasant wavered, changed his mind, was obviously terror-stricken, regained confidence and then began to advance circuitously toward the Greek lines. When he arrived within hailing distance, the captain, the sergeant, Coleman's dragoman and many of the soldiers yelled human messages, and a moment later he was seen to be a poor, yellow-faced stripling with a body which seemed to have been first twisted by an ill-birth and afterward maimed by either labor or oppression, these being often identical in their effects.

His reception of the Greek soldiery was no less fervid than their welcome of him to their protection. He threw his grimy fez in the air and croaked out cheers, while tears wet his cheeks. When he had come upon the right side of the ditch he ran capering among them and the captain, the sergeant, the dragoman and a number of soldiers received wild embraces and kisses. He made a dash at Coleman, but Coleman was now wary in the game, and retired dexterously behind different groups with a finished appearance of not noting that the young man wished to greet him.

Behind the hedge of dry brambles there were more indications of life, and the peasant stood up and made beseeching gestures. Soon a whole flock of miserable people had come out to the Greeks, men, women and children, in crude and comic smocks, prancing here and there, uproariously embracing and kissing their deliverers. An old, tearful, toothless hag flung herself rapturously into the arms of the captain, and Coleman's brick-and-iron soul was moved to admiration at the way in which the officer administered a chaste salute upon the furrowed cheek. The dragoman told the correspondent that the Turks had run away from the village on up a valley toward Jannina. Everybody was proud and happy. A major of infantry came from the rear at this time and asked the captain in sharp tones who were the two strangers in civilian attire. When the captain had answered correctly the major was immediately mollified, and had it announced to the correspondent that his battalion was going to move immediately into the village, and that he would be delighted to have his company.

The major strode at the head of his men with the group of villagers singing and dancing about him and looking upon him as if he were a god. Coleman and the dragoman, at the officer's request, marched one on either side of him, and in this manner they entered the village. From all sorts of hedges and thickets, people came creeping out to pass into a delirium of joy. The major borrowed three little pack horses with rope-bridles, and thus mounted and followed by the clanking column, they rode on in triumph.

It was probably more of a true festival than most men experience even in the longest life time. The major with his Greek instinct of drama was a splendid personification of poetic quality; in fact he was himself almost a lyric. From time to time he glanced back at Coleman with eyes half dimmed with appreciation. The people gathered flowers, great blossoms of purple and corn color. They sprinkled them over the three horsemen and flung them deliriously under the feet of the little nags. Being now mounted Coleman had no difficulty in avoiding the embraces of the peasants, but he felt to the tips of his toes an abandonment to a kind of pleasure with which he was not at all familiar. Riding thus amid cries of thanksgiving addressed at him equally with the others, he felt a burning virtue and quite lost his old self in an illusion of noble benignity. And there continued the fragrant hail of blossoms.

Miserable little huts straggled along the sides of the village street as if they were following at the heels of the great white house. The column proceeded northward, announcing laughingly to the glad villagers that they would never see another Turk. Before them on the road was here and there a fez from the head of a fled Turkish soldier and they lay like drops of blood from some wounded leviathan. Ultimately it grew cloudy. It even rained slightly. In the misty downfall the column of soldiers in blue was dim as if it were merely a long trail of low-hung smoke.

They came to the ruins of a church and there the major halted his battalion. Coleman worried at his dragoman to learn if the halt was only temporary. It was a long time before there was answer from the major, for he had drawn up his men in platoons and was addressing them in a speech as interminable as any that Coleman had heard in Greece. The officer waved his arms and roared out evidently the glories of patriotism and soldierly honor, the glories of their ancient people, and he may have included any subject in this wonderful speech, for the reason that he had plenty of time in which to do it. It was impossible to tell whether the oration was a good one or bad one, because the men stood in their loose platoons without discernible feelings as if to them this appeared merely as one of the inevitable consequences of a campaign, an established rule of warfare. Coleman ate black bread and chocolate tablets while the dragoman hovered near the major with the intention of pouncing upon him for information as soon as his lungs yielded to the strain upon them.

The dragoman at last returned with a very long verbal treatise from the major, who apparently had not been as exhausted after his speech to the men as one would think. The major had said that he had been ordered to halt here to form a junction with some of the troops coming direct from Arta, and that he expected that in the morning the army would be divided and one wing would chase the retreating Turks on toward Jannina, while the other wing would advance upon Prevasa because the enemy had a garrison there which had not retreated an inch, and, although it was cut off, it was necessary to send either a force to hold it in its place or a larger force to go through with the business of capturing it. Else there would be left in the rear of the left flank of a Greek advance upon Jannina a body of the enemy which at any moment might become active. The major said that his battalion would probably form part of the force to advance upon Prevasa. Nikopolis was on the road to Prevasa and only three miles away from it.

## CHAPTER XI.

Coleman spent a long afternoon in the drizzle Enveloped in his macintosh he sat on a boulder in the lee of one of the old walls and moodily smoked cigars and listened to the ceaseless clatter of tongues. A ray of light penetrated the mind of the dragoman and he labored assiduously with wet fuel until he had accomplished a tin mug of coffee. Bits of cinder floated in it, but Coleman rejoiced and was kind to the dragoman.

The night was of cruel monotony. Afflicted by the wind and the darkness, the correspondent sat with nerves keyed high waiting to hear the pickets open fire on a night attack. He was so unaccountably sure that there would be a tumult and panic of this kind at some time of the night that he prevented himself from getting a reasonable amount of rest. He could hear the soldiers breathing in sleep all about him. He wished to arouse them from this slumber which, to his ignorance, seemed stupid. The quality of mysterious menace in the great gloom and the silence would have caused him to pray if prayer would have transported him magically to New York and made him a young man with no coat playing billiards at his club.

The chill dawn came at last and with a fine elation which ever follows a dismal night in war; an elation which bounds in the bosom as soon as day has knocked the shackles from a trembling mind. Although Coleman had slept but a short time he was now as fresh as a total abstainer coming from the bath. He heard the creak of battery wheels; he saw crawling bodies of infantry moving in the dim light like ghostly processions. He felt a tremendous virility come with this new hope in the daylight. He again took satisfaction in his sentimental journey. It was a shining affair. He was on active service, an active service of the heart, and he' felt that he was a strong man ready to conquer difficulty even as the olden heroes conquered difficulty. He imagined himself in a way like them. He, too, had come out to fight for love with giants, dragons and witches. He had never known that he could be so pleased with that kind of a parallel.

The dragoman announced that the major had suddenly lent their horses to some other people, and after cursing this versatility of interest, he summoned his henchmen and they moved out on foot, following the sound of the creaking wheels. They came in time to a bridge, and on the side of this bridge was a hard military road which sprang away in two directions, north and west. Some troops were creeping out the westward way and the dragoman pointing at them said: "They going Prevasa. That is road to Nikopolis."

Coleman grinned from ear to car and slapped his dragoman violently on the shoulder. For a moment he intended to hand the man a reward, but he changed his mind.

Their traps were in the way of being heavy, but they minded little since the dragoman was now a victim of the influence of Coleman's enthusiasm. The road wound along the base of the mountain range, sheering around the abutments in wide white curves and then circling into glens where immense trees spread their shade over it. Some of the great trunks were oppressed with vines green as garlands, and these vines even ran like verdant foam over the rocks. Streams of translucent water showered down from the hills, and made pools in which every pebble, every leaf of a water plant shone with magic luster, and if the bottom of a pool was only of clay, the clay glowed with sapphire light. The day was fair. The country was part of that land which turned the minds of its ancient poets toward a more tender dreaming, so that indeed their nymphs would die, one is sure, in the cold mythology of the north with its storms amid the gloom of pine forests. It was all wine to Coleman's spirit. It enlivened him to think of success with absolute surety. To be sure one of his boots began soon to rasp his toes, but he gave it no share of his attention. They passed at a much faster pace than the troops, and everywhere they met laughter and confidence and the cry. "On to Prevasa!"

At midday they were at the heels of the advance battalion, among its stragglers, taking its white dust into their throats and eyes. The dragoman was waning and he made a number of attempts to stay Coleman, but no one could have had influence upon Coleman's steady rush with his eyes always straight to the front as if thus to symbolize his steadiness of purpose. Rivulets of sweat marked the dust on his face, and two of his toes were now paining as if they were being burned off. He was obliged to concede a privilege of limping, but he would not stop.

At nightfall they halted with the outpost battalion of the infantry. All the cavalry had in the meantime come up and they saw their old friends. There was a village from which the Christian peasants came and cheered like a trained chorus. Soldiers were driving a great flock of fat sheep into a corral. They had belonged to a Turkish bey and they bleated as if they knew that they were now mere spoils of war. Coleman lay on the steps of the bey's house smoking with his head on his blanket roll. Camp fires glowed off in the fields. He was now about four miles from Nikopolis.

Within the house, the commander of the cavalry was writing dispatches. Officers clanked up and down the stairs. The dashing young captain came and said that there would be a general assault on Prevasa at the dawn of the next day. Afterward the dragoman descended upon the village and in some way wrenched a little grey horse from an inhabitant. Its pack saddle was on its back and it would very handily carry the traps. In this matter the dragoman did not consider his master; he considered his own sore back.

Coleman ate more bread and chocolate tablets and also some tinned sardines. He was content with the day's work. He did not see how he could have improved it. There was only one route by which the Wainwright party could avoid him, and that was by going to Prevasa and thence taking ship. But since Prevasa was blockaded by a Greek fleet, he conceived that event to be impossible. Hence, he had them hedged on this peninsula and they must be either at Nikopolis or Prevasa. He would probably know all early in the morning. He reflected that he was too tired to care if there might be a night attack and then wrapped in his blankets he went peacefully to sleep in the grass under a big tree with the crooning of some soldiers around their fire blending into his slumber.

And now, although the dragoman had performed a number of feats of incapacity, he achieved during the one hour of Coleman's sleeping a blunder which for real finish was simply a perfection of art. When Coleman, much later, extracted the full story, it appeared that ringing events happened during that single hour of sleep. Ten minutes after he had lain down for a night of oblivion, the battalion of infantry, which had advanced a little beyond the village, was recalled and began a hurried night march back on the way it had so festively come. It was significant enough to appeal to almost any mind, but the dragoman was able to not understand it. He remained jabbering to some acquaintances among the troopers. Coleman had been asleep his hour when the dashing young captain perceived the dragoman, and completely horrified by his presence at that place, ran to him and whispered to him swiftly that the game was to flee, flee, flee. The wing of the army which had advanced northward upon Jannina had already been tumbled back by the Turks and all the other wing had been recalled to the Louros river and there was now nothing practically between him and his sleeping master and the enemy but a cavalry picket. The cavalry was immediately going to make a forced march to the rear. The stricken dragoman could even then see troopers getting into their saddles. He, rushed to, the, tree, and in a panic simply bundled Coleman upon his feet before he was awake. He stuttered out his tale, and the dazed, correspondent heard it punctuated by the steady trample of the retiring cavalry. The dragoman saw a man's face then turn in a flash from an expression of luxurious drowsiness to an expression of utter malignancy. However, he was in too much of a hurry to be afraid of it; he ran off to the little grey horse and frenziedly but skillfully began to bind the traps upon the packsaddle. He appeared in a moment tugging at the halter. He could only say: "Come! Come! Come! Queek! Queek!" They slid hurriedly down a bank to the road and started to do again that which they had accomplished with considerable expenditure of physical power during the day. The hoof beats of the cavalry had already died away and the mountains shadowed them in lonely silence. They were the rear guard after the rear guard.

The dragoman muttered hastily his last dire rumors. Five hundred Circassian cavalry were coming. The mountains were now infested with the dread Albanian irregulars, Coleman had thought in his daylight tramp that he had appreciated the noble distances, but he found that he knew nothing of their nobility until he tried this night stumbling. And the hoofs of the little horse made on the hard road more noise than could be made by men beating with hammers upon brazen cylinders.

The correspondent glanced continually up at the crags. From the other side he could sometimes hear the metallic clink of water deep down in a glen. For the first time in his life he seriously opened the flap of his holster and let his fingers remain on the handle of his revolver. From just in front of him he could hear the chattering of the dragoman's teeth which no attempt at more coolness could seem to prevent. In the meantime the casual manner of the little grey horse struck Coleman with maddening vividness. If the blank darkness was simply filled with ferocious Albanians, the horse did not care a button; he leisurely put his feet down with a resounding ring. Coleman whispered hastily to the dragoman. "If they rush us, jump down the bank, no matter how deep it is. That's our only chance. And try to keep together."

All they saw of the universe was, in front of them, a place faintly luminous near their feet, but fading in six yards to the darkness of a dungeon. This represented the bright white road of the day time. It had no end. Coleman had thought that he could tell from the very feel of the air some of the landmarks of his daytime journey, but he had now no sense of location at all. He would not have denied that he was squirming on his belly like a worm through black mud. They went on and on. Visions of his past were sweeping through Coleman's mind precisely as they are said to sweep through the mind of a drowning person. But he had no regret for any bad deeds; he regretted merely distant hours of peace and protection. He was no longer a hero going to rescue his love. He was a slave making a gasping attempt to escape from the most incredible tyranny of circumstances. He half vowed to himself that if the God whom he had in no wise heeded, would permit him to crawl out of this slavery he would never again venture a yard toward a danger any greater than may be incurred from the police of a most proper metropolis. If his juvenile and uplifting thoughts of other days had reproached him he would simply have repeated and repeated: "Adventure be damned."

It became known to them that the horse had to be led. The debased creature was asserting its right to do as it had been trained, to follow its customs; it was asserting this right during a situation which required conduct superior to all training and custom. It was so grossly conventional that Coleman would have understood that demoniac form of anger which sometimes leads men to jab knives into warm bodies. Coleman from cowardice tried to induce the dragoman to go ahead leading the horse, and the dragoman from cowardice tried to induce Coleman to go ahead leading the horse. Coleman of course had to succumb. The dragoman was only good to walk behind and tearfully whisper maledictions as he prodded the flanks of their tranquil beast.

In the absolute black of the frequent forests, Coleman could not see his feet and he often felt like a man walking forward to fall at any moment down a thousand yards of chasm. He heard whispers; he saw skulking figures, and these frights turned out to be the voice of a little trickle of water or the effects of wind among the leaves, but they were replaced by the same terrors in slightly different forms.

Then the poignant thing interpolated. A volley crashed ahead of them some half of a mile away and another volley answered from a still nearer point. Swishing noises which the correspondent had heard in the air he now know to have been from the passing of bullets. He and the dragoman came stock still. They heard three other volleys sounding with the abrupt clamor of a hail of little stones upon a hollow surface. Coleman and the dragoman came close together and looked into the whites of each other's eyes. The ghastly horse at that moment stretched down his neck and began placidly to pluck the grass at the roadside. The two men were equally blank with fear and each seemed to seek in the other some newly rampant manhood upon which he could lean at this time. Behind them were the Turks. In front of them was a fight in the darkness. In front it was mathematic to suppose in fact were also the Turks. They were barred; enclosed; cut off. The end was come.

Even at that moment they heard from behind them the sound of slow, stealthy footsteps. They both wheeled instantly, choking with this additional terror. Coleman saw the dragoman move swiftly to the side of the road, ready to jump into whatever abyss happened to be there. Coleman still gripped the halter as if it were in truth a straw. The stealthy footsteps were much nearer. Then it was that an insanity came upon him as if fear had flamed up within him until it gave him all the magnificent desperation of a madman. He jerked the grey horse broadside to the approaching mystery, and grabbing out his revolver aimed it from the top of his improvised bulwark. He hailed the darkness.

"Halt. Who's there?" He had expected his voice to sound like a groan, but instead it happened to sound clear, stern, commanding, like the voice of a young sentry at an encampment of volunteers. He did not seem to have any privilege of selection as to the words. They were born of themselves.

He waited then, blanched and hopeless, for death to wing out of the darkness and strike him down. He heard a voice. The voice said: "Do you speak English?" For one or two seconds he could not even understand English, and then the great fact swelled up and within him. This voice with all its new quavers was still undoubtedly the voice of Prof. Harrison B. Wainwright of Washurst College

## CHAPTER XII.

A CHANGE flashed over Coleman as if it had come from an electric storage. He had known the professor long, but he had never before heard a quaver in his voice, and it was this little quaver that seemed to impel him to supreme disregard of the dangers which he looked upon as being the final dangers. His own voice had not quavered.

When he spoke, he spoke in a low tone, it was the voice of the master of the situation. He could hear his dupes fluttering there in the darkness. "Yes," he said, "I speak English. There is some danger. Stay where you are and make no noise." He was as cool as an iced drink. To be sure the circumstances had in no wise changed as to his personal danger, but beyond the important fact that there were now others to endure it with him, he seemed able to forget it in a strange, unauthorized sense of victory. It came from the professor's quavers.

Meanwhile he had forgotten the dragoman, but he recalled him in time to bid him wait. Then, as well concealed as a monk hiding in his cowl, he tiptoed back into a group of people who knew him intimately.

He discerned two women mounted on little horses and about them were dim men. He could hear them breathing hard. "It is all right" he began smoothly. "You only need to be very careful—"

Suddenly out of the blackness projected a half phosphorescent face. It was the face of the little professor. He stammered. "We—we—do you really speak English?"

Coleman in his feeling of superb triumph could almost have laughed. His nerves were as steady as hemp, but he was in haste and his haste allowed him to administer rebuke to his old professor.

"Didn't you hear me?" he hissed through his tightening lips. "They are fighting just ahead of us on the road and if you want to save yourselves don't waste time."

Another face loomed faintly like a mask painted in dark grey. It belonged to Coke, and it was a mask figured in profound stupefaction. The lips opened and tensely breathed out the name: "Coleman." Instantly the correspondent felt about him that kind of a tumult which tries to suppress itself. He knew that it was the most theatric moment of his life. He glanced quickly toward the two figures on horseback. He believed that one was making foolish gesticulation while the other sat rigid and silent. This latter one he knew to be Marjory. He was content that she did not move. Only a woman who was glad he had come but did not care for him would have moved. This applied directly to what he thought he knew of Marjory's nature.

There was confusion among the students, but Coleman suppressed it as in such situation might a centurion. "S-s-steady!" He seized the arm of the professor and drew him forcibly close. "The condition is this," he whispered rapidly. "We are in a fix with this fight on up the road. I was sent after you, but I can't get you into the Greek lines tonight. Mrs. Wainwright and Marjory must dismount and I and my man will take the horses on and hide them. All the rest of you must go up about a hundred feet into the woods and hide. When I come back, I'll hail you and you answer low." The professor was like pulp in his grasp. He choked out the word "Coleman" in agony and wonder, but he obeyed with a palpable gratitude. Coleman sprang to the side of the shadowy figure of Marjory. "Come," he said authoritatively. She laid in his palm a little icy cold hand and dropped from her horse. He had an impulse to cling to the small fingers, but he loosened them immediately, imparting to his manner, as well as the darkness permitted him, a kind of casual politeness as if he were too intent upon the business in hand. He bunched the crowd and pushed them into the wood. Then he and the dragoman took the horses a hundred yards onward and tethered them. No one would care if they were stolen; the great point was to get them where their noise would have no power of revealing the whole party. There had been no further firing.

After he had tied the little grey horse to a tree he unroped his luggage and carried the most of it back to the point where the others had left the road. He called out cautiously and received a sibilant answer. He and the dragoman bunted among the trees until they came to where a forlorn company was seated awaiting them lifting their faces like frogs out of a pond. His first question did not give them any assurance. He said at once: "Are any of you armed?" Unanimously they lowly breathed: "No." He searched them out one by one and finally sank down by the professor. He kept sort of a hypnotic handcuff upon the dragoman, because he foresaw that this man was really going to be the key to the best means of escape. To a large neutral party wandering between hostile lines there was technically no danger, but actually there was a great deal. Both armies had too many irregulars, lawless hillsmen come out to fight in their own way, and if they were encountered in the dead of night on such hazardous ground the Greek hillsmen with their white cross on a blue field would be precisely as dangerous as the blood-hungry Albanians. Coleman knew that the rational way was to reach the Greek lines, and he had no intention of reaching the Greek lines without a tongue, and the only tongue was in the mouth of the dragoman. He was correct in thinking that the professor's deep knowledge of the ancient language would give him small clue to the speech of the modern Greek.

As he settled himself by the professor the band of students, eight in number pushed their faces close.

He did not see any reason for speaking. There were thirty seconds of deep silence in which he felt that all were bending to hearken to his words of counsel The professor huskily broke the stillness. Well—what are we to do now?"

Coleman was decisive, indeed absolute. "We'll stay here until daylight unless you care to get shot."

"All right," answered the professor. He turned and made a useless remark to his flock. "Stay here."

Coleman asked civilly, "Have you had anything to eat? Have you got anything to wrap around you?"

"We have absolutely nothing," answered the professor. "Our servants ran away and—and then we left everything behind us—and I've never been in such a position in my life."

Coleman moved softly in the darkness and unbuckled some of his traps. On his knee he broke the hard cakes of bread and with his fingers he broke the little tablets of chocolate. These he distributed to his people. And at this time he felt fully the appreciation of the conduct of the eight American college students They had not yet said a word—with the exception of the bewildered exclamation from Coke. They all knew him well. In any circumstance of life which as far as he truly believed, they had yet encountered, they would have been privileged to accost him in every form of their remarkable vocabulary. They were as new to this game as, would have been eight newly-caught Apache Indians if such were set to run the elevators in the Tract Society Building. He could see their eyes gazing at him anxiously and he could hear their deep-drawn breaths. But they said no word. He knew that they were looking upon him as their leader, almost as their savior, and he knew also that they were going to follow him without a murmur in the conviction that he knew ten-fold more than they knew. It occurred to him that his position was ludicrously false, but, anyhow, he was glad. Surely it would be a very easy thing to lead them to safety in the morning and he foresaw the credit which would come to him. He concluded that it was beneath his dignity as preserver to vouchsafe them many words. His business was to be the cold, masterful, enigmatic man. It might be said that these reflections were only half-thoughts in his mind. Meanwhile a section of his intellect was flying hither and thither, speculating upon the Circassian cavalry and the Albanian guerillas and even the Greek outposts.

He unbuckled his blanket roll and taking one blanket placed it about the shoulders of the shadow which was Mrs. Wainwright.

The shadow protested incoherently, but he muttered, "Oh that's all right." Then he took his other blanket and went to the shadow which was Marjory.

It was something like putting a wrap about the shoulders of a statue. He was base enough to linger in the hopes that he could detect some slight trembling but as far as he knew she was of stone. His macintosh he folded around the body of the professor amid quite senile protest, so senile that the professor seemed suddenly proven to him as an old, old man, a fact which had never occurred to Washurst or her children. Then he went to the dragoman and pre-empted half of his blankets. The dragoman grunted in protest, but Coleman did not relent. It would not do to have this dragoman develop a luxurious temperament when eight American college students were, without speech, shivering in the cold night.

Coleman really begun to ruminate upon his glory, but he found that he could not do this well without Smoking, so he crept away some distance from this fireless, encampment, and bending his face to the ground at the foot of a tree he struck a match and lit a cigar. His return to the others would have been somewhat in the manner of coolness as displayed on the stage if he had not been prevented by the necessity of making no noise. He saw regarding him as before the dimly visible eyes of the eight students and Marjory and her father and mother. Then he whispered the conventional words. "Go to sleep if you can. You'll need your strength in the morning. I and this man here will keep watch."

Three of the college students of course crawled up to him and each said: "I'll keep watch, old man."

"No. We'll keep watch. You people try to sleep."

He deemed that it might be better to yield the dragoman his blanket, and so he got up and leaned against a tree, holding his hand to cover the brilliant point of his cigar. He knew perfectly well that none of them could sleep. But he stood there somewhat like a sentry without the attitude, but with all the effect of responsibility.

He had no doubt but what escape to civilization would be easy, but anyhow his heroism should be preserved. He was the rescuer. His thoughts of Marjory were somewhat in a puzzle. The meeting had placed him in such a position that he had expected a lot of condescension on his own part. Instead she had exhibited about as much recognition of him as would a stone fountain on his grandfather's place in Connecticut. This in his opinion was not the way to greet the knight who had come to the rescue of his lady. He had not expected it so to happen. In fact from Athens to this place he had engaged himself with imagery of possible meetings. He was vexed, certainly, but, far beyond that, he knew a deeper admiration for this girl. To him she represented the sex, and so the sex as embodied in her seemed a mystery to be feared. He wondered if safety came on the morrow he would not surrender to this feminine invulnerability. She had not done anything that he had expected of her and so inasmuch as he loved her he loved her more. It was bewitching. He half considered himself a fool. But at any rate he thought resentfully she should be thankful to him for having rendered her a great service. However, when he came to consider this proposition he knew that on a basis of absolute manly endeavor he had rendered her little or no service.

The night was long.

## CHAPTER XIII.

COLEMAN suddenly found himself looking upon his pallid dragoman. He saw that he had been asleep crouched at the foot of the tree. Without any exchange of speech at all he knew there had been alarming noises. Then shots sounded from nearby. Some were from rifles aimed in that direction and some were from rifles opposed to them. This was distinguishable to the experienced man, but all that Coleman knew was that the conditions of danger were now triplicated. Unconsciously he stretched his hands in supplication over his charges. "Don't move! Don't move! And keep close to the ground!" All heeded him but Marjory. She still sat straight. He himself was on his feet, but he now knew the sound of bullets, and he knew that no bullets had spun through the trees. He could not see her distinctly, but it was known to him in some way that she was mutinous. He leaned toward her and spoke as harshly as possible. "Marjory, get down!" She wavered for a moment as if resolved to defy him. As he turned again to peer in the direction of the firing it went through his mind that she must love him very much indeed. He was assured of it. It must have been some small outpour between nervous pickets and eager hillsmen, for it ended in a moment. The party waited in abasement for what seemed to them a time, and the blue dawn began, to laggardly shift the night as they waited. The dawn itself seemed prodigiously long in arriving at anything like discernible landscape. When this was consummated, Coleman, in somewhat the manner of the father of a church, dealt bits of chocolate out to the others. He had already taken the precaution to confer with the dragoman, so he said: "Well, come ahead. We'll make a try for it." They arose at his bidding and followed him to the road. It was the same broad, white road, only that the white was in the dawning something like the grey of a veil. It took some courage to venture upon this thoroughfare, but Coleman stepped out—after looking quickly in both directions. The party tramped to where the horses had been left, and there they were found without change of a rope. Coleman rejoiced to see that his dragoman now followed him in the way of a good lieutenant. They both dashed in among the trees and had the horses out into the road in a twinkle. When Coleman turned to direct that utterly subservient, group he knew that his face was drawn from hardship and anxiety, but he saw everywhere the same style of face with the exception of the face of Marjory, who looked simply of lovely marble. He noted with a curious satisfaction, as if the thing was a tribute to himself, that his macintosh was over the professor's shoulder, that Marjory and her mother were each carrying a blanket, and that, the corps of students had dutifully brought all the traps which his dragoman had forgotten. It was grand.

He addressed them to say: "Now, approaching outposts is very dangerous business at this time in the morning. So my man, who can talk both Greek and Turkish, will go ahead forty yards, and I will follow somewhere between him and you. Try not to crowd forward."

He directed the ladies upon their horses and placed the professor upon the little grey nag. Then they took up their line of march. The dragoman had looked somewhat dubiously upon this plan of having him go forty yards in advance, but he had the utmost confidence in this new Coleman, whom yesterday he had not known. Besides, he himself was a very gallant man indeed, and it befitted him to take the post of danger before the eyes of all these foreigners. In his new position he was as proud and unreasonable as a rooster. He was continually turning his head to scowl back at them, when only the clank of hoofs was sounding. An impenetrable mist lay on the valley and the hilltops were shrouded. As for the people, they were like mice. Coleman paid no attention to the Wainwright party, but walked steadily along near the dragoman.

Perhaps the whole thing was a trifle absurd, but to a great percentage, of the party it was terrible. For instance, those eight boys, fresh from a school, could in no wise gauge the dimensions. And if this was true of the students, it was more distinctly true of Marjory and her mother. As for the professor, he seemed Weighted to the earth by his love and his responsibility.

Suddenly the dragoman wheeled and made demoniac signs. Coleman half-turned to survey the main body, and then paid his attention swiftly to the front. The white road sped to the top of a hill where it seemed to make a rotund swing into oblivion. The top of the curve was framed in foliage, and therein was a horseman. He had his carbine slanted on his thigh, and his bridle-reins taut. Upon sight of them he immediately wheeled and galloped down the other slope and vanished.

The dragoman was throwing wild gestures into the air. As Coleman looked back at the Wainwright party he saw plainly that to an ordinary eye they might easily appear as a strong advance of troops. The peculiar light would emphasize such theory. The dragoman ran to him jubilantly, but he contained now a form of intelligence which caused him to whisper; "That was one Greek. That was one Greek—what do you call—sentree?"

Coleman addressed the others. He said: "It's all right. Come ahead. That was a Greek picket. There is only one trouble now, and that is to approach them easy—do you see—easy."

His obedient charges came forward at his word. When they arrived at the top of this rise they saw nothing. Coleman was very uncertain. He was not sure that this picket had not carried with him a general alarm, and in that case there would soon occur a certain amount of shooting. However, as far as he understood the business, there was no way but forward. Inasmuch as he did not indicate to the Wainwright party that he wished them to do differently, they followed on doggedly after him and the dragoman. He knew now that the dragoman's heart had for the tenth time turned to dog-biscuit, so he kept abreast of him. And soon together they walked into a cavalry outpost, commanded by no less a person than the dashing young captain, who came laughing out to meet them.

Suddenly losing all color of war, the condition was now such as might occur in a drawing room. Coleman felt the importance of establishing highly conventional relations between the captain and the Wainwright party. To compass this, he first seized his dragoman, and the dragoman, enlightened immediately, spun a series of lies which must have led the captain to believe that the entire heart of the American republic had been taken out of that western continent and transported to Greece.

Coleman was proud of the captain. The latter immediately went and bowed in the manner of the French school and asked everybody to have a cup of coffee, although acceptation would have proved his ruin and disgrace. Coleman refused in the name of courtesy. He called his party forward, and now they proceeded merely as one crowd. Marjory had dismounted in the meantime.

The moment was come. Coleman felt it. The first rush was from the students. Immediately he was buried in a thrashing mob of them. "Good boy! Good boy! Great man! Oh, isn't he a peach? How did he do it? He came in strong at the finish! Good boy, Coleman!" Through this mist of glowing youthful congratulation he saw the professor standing at the outskirts with direct formal thanks already moving on his lips, while near him his wife wept joyfully. Marjory was evidently enduring some inscrutable emotion.

After all, it did penetrate his mind that it was indecent to accept all this wild gratitude, but there was built within him no intention of positively declaring himself lacking in all credit, or at least, lacking in all credit in the way their praises defined it. In truth he had assisted them, but he had been at the time largely engaged in assisting himself, and their coming had been more of a boon to his loneliness than an addition to his care. However, he soon had no difficulty in making his conscience appropriate every line in these hymns sung in his honor. The students, curiously wise of men, thought his conduct quite perfect.

"Oh, say, come off!" he protested. "Why, I didn't do anything. You fellows are crazy. You would have gotten in all right by yourselves. Don't act like asses—"

As soon as the professor had opportunity he came to Coleman. He was a changed little man, and his extraordinary bewilderment showed in his face. It was the disillusion and amazement of a stubborn mind that had gone implacably in its one direction and found in the end that the direction was all wrong, and that really a certain mental machine had not been infallible. Coleman remembered what the American minister in Athens had described of his protests against the starting of the professor's party on this journey, and of the complete refusal of the professor to recognize any value in the advice. And here now was the consequent defeat. It was mirrored in the professor's astonished eyes.

Coleman went directly to his dazed old teacher.

"Well, you're out of it now, professor," he said warmly. "I congratulate you on your escape, sir."

The professor looked at him, helpless to express himself, but the correspondent was at that time suddenly enveloped in the hysterical gratitude of Mrs. Wainwright, who hurled herself upon him with extravagant manifestations. Coleman played his part with skill. To both the professor and Mrs. Wainwright his manner was a combination of modestly filial affection and a pretentious disavowal of his having done anything at all. It seemed to charm everybody but Marjory. It irritated him to see that she was apparently incapable of acknowledging that he was a grand man.

He was actually compelled to go to her and offer congratulations upon her escape, as he had congratulated the professor. If his manner to her parents had been filial, his manner to her was parental. "Well, Marjory," he said kindly, "you have been in considerable danger. I suppose you're glad to be through with it." She at that time made no reply, but by her casual turn he knew that he was expected to walk along by her side. The others knew it, too, and the rest of the party left them free to walk side by side in the rear.

"This is a beautiful country hereabouts if one gets a good chance to see it," he remarked. Then he added: "But I suppose you had a view of it when you were going out to Nikopolis?"

She answered in muffled tones. "Yes, we thought it very beautiful."

Did you note those streams from the mountains? That seemed to me the purest water I'd ever seen, but I bet it would make one ill to drink it. There is, you know, a prominent German chemist who has almost proven that really pure water is practical poison to the human stomach."

"Yes?" she said.

There was a period of silence, during which he was perfectly comfortable because he knew that she was ill at ease. If the silence was awkward, she was suffering from it. As for himself, he had no inclination to break it. His position was, as far as the entire Wainwright party was concerned, a place where he could afford to wait. She turned to him at last. "Of course, I know how much you have done for us, and I want you to feel that we all appreciate it deeply-deeply." There was discernible to the ear a certain note of desperation.

"Oh, not at all," he said generously. "Not at all. I didn't do anything. It was quite an accident. Don't let that trouble you for a moment."

"Well, of course you would say that," she said more steadily. "But I—we—we know how good and how—brave it was in you to come for us, and I—we must never forget it."

As a matter of fact," replied Coleman, with an appearance of ingenuous candor, "I was sent out here by the *Eclipse* to find you people, and of course I worked rather hard to reach you, but the final meeting was purely accidental and does not redound to my credit in the least."

As he had anticipated, Marjory shot him a little glance of disbelief. "Of course you would say that," she repeated with gloomy but flattering conviction.

"Oh, if I had been a great hero," he said smiling, "no doubt I would have kept up this same manner which now sets so well upon me, but I am telling you the truth when I say that I had no part in your rescue at all."

She became slightly indignant. "Oh, if you care to tell us constantly that you were of no service to us, I don't see what we can do but continue to declare that you were."

Suddenly he felt vulgar. He spoke to her this time with real meaning. "I beg of you never to mention it again. That will be the best way."

But to this she would not accede. "No, we will often want to speak of it."

He replied "How do you like Greece? Don't you think that some of these ruins are rather out of shape in the popular mind? Now, for my part, I would rather look at a good strong finish at a horserace than to see ten thousand Parthenons in a bunch."

She was immediately in the position of defending him from himself. "You would rather see no such thing. You shouldn't talk in that utterly trivial way. I like the Parthenon, of course, but I can't think of it now because my head is too full of my escape from where I was so—so frightened."

Coleman grinned. "Were you really frightened?"

"Naturally," she answered. "I suppose I was more frightened for mother and father, but I was frightened enough for myself. It was not—not a nice thing."

"No, it wasn't," said Coleman. "I could hardly believe my senses, when the minister at Athens told me that, you all had ventured into such a trap, and there is no doubt but what you can be glad that you are well out of it."

She seemed to have some struggle with herself and then she deliberately said: "Thanks to you."

Coleman embarked on what he intended to make a series of high-minded protests. "Not at all—" but at that moment the dragoman whirled back from the vanguard with a great collection of the difficulties which had been gathering upon him. Coleman was obliged to resign Marjory and again take up the active leadership. He disposed of the dragoman's difficulties mainly by declaring that they were not difficulties at all. He had learned that this was the way to deal with dragomen. The fog had already lifted from the valley and, as they passed along the wooded mountainside the fragrance of leaves and earth came to them. Ahead, along the hooded road, they could see the blue clad figures of Greek infantrymen. Finally they passed an encampment of a battalion whose line was at a right angle to the highway. A hundred yards in advance was the bridge across the Louros river. And there a battery of artillery was encamped. The dragoman became involved in all sorts of discussions with other Greeks, but Coleman stuck to his elbow and stifled all aimless oration. The Wainwright party waited for them in the rear in an observant but patient group.

Across a plain, the hills directly behind Arta loomed up showing the straight yellow scar of a modern entrenchment. To the north of Arta were some grey mountains with a dimly marked road winding to the summit. On one side of this road were two shadows. It took a moment for the eye to find these shadows, but when this was accomplished it was plain that they were men. The captain of the battery explained to the dragoman that he did not know that they were not also Turks. In which case the road to Arta was a dangerous path. It was no good news to Coleman. He waited a moment in order to gain composure and then walked back to the Wainwright party. They must have known at once from his peculiar gravity that all was not well. Five of the students and the professor immediately asked: "What is it?"

He had at first some old-fashioned idea of concealing the ill tidings from the ladies, but he perceived what flagrant nonsense this would be in circumstances in which all were fairly likely to incur equal dangers, and at any rate he did not see his way clear to allow their imagination to run riot over a situation which might not turn out to be too bad.

He said slowly: "You see those mountains over there? Well, troops have been seen there and the captain of this battery thinks they are Turks. If they are Turks the road to Arta is distinctly—er—unsafe."

This new blow first affected the Wainwright party as being too much to endure. They thought they had gone through enough. This was a general sentiment. Afterward the emotion took color according to the individual character. One student laughed and said: "Well, I see our finish."

Another student piped out: "How do they know they are Turks? What makes them think they are Turks"

Another student expressed himself with a sigh. "This is a long way from the Bowery."

The professor said nothing but looked annihilated; Mrs. Wainwright wept profoundly; Marjory looked expectantly toward Coleman.

As for the correspondent, he was adamant and reliable and stern, for he had not the slightest idea that those men on the distant hill were Turks at all.

## CHAPTER XIV.

"Oh," said a student, "this game ought to quit. I feel like thirty cents. We didn't come out here to be pursued about the country by these Turks. Why don't they stop it?"

Coleman was remarking: "Really, the only sensible thing to do now is to have breakfast. There is no use in worrying ourselves silly over this thing until we've got to."

They spread the blankets on the ground and sat about a feast of bread, watercress, and tinned beef. Coleman was the real host, but he contrived to make the professor appear as that honorable person. They ate, casting their eyes from time to time at the distant mountain with its two shadows. People began to fly down the road from Jannina, peasants hurriedly driving little flocks, women and children on donkeys and little horses which they clubbed unceasingly. One man rode at a gallop, shrieking and flailing his arms in the air. They were all Christian peasants of Turkey, but they were in flight now because they did not wish to be at home if the Turk was going to return and reap revenge for his mortification.

The Wainwright party looked at Coleman in abrupt questioning.

"Oh, it's all right," he said, easily. "They are always taking on that way."

Suddenly the dragoman gave a shout and dashed up the road to the scene of a melée where a little rat-faced groom was vociferously defending three horses from some Greek officers, who as vociferously were stating their right to requisition them. Coleman ran after his dragoman. There was a sickening pow-wow, but in the end Coleman, straight and easy in the saddle, came cantering back on a superb open-mouthed snorting bay horse. He did not mind if the half-wild animal plunged crazily. It was part of his role.

"They were trying to steal my horses," he explained. He leaped to the ground, and holding the horse by the bridle, he addressed his admiring companions. "The groom—the man who has charge of the horses—says that he thinks that the people on the mountainside are Turks, but I don't see how that is possible. You see—" he pointed wisely—"that road leads directly south to Arta, and it is hardly possible that the Greek army would come over here and leave that approach to Arta utterly unguarded. It would be too foolish. They must have left some men to cover it, and that is certainly what those troops are. If you are all ready and willing, I don't see anything to do but make a good, stout-hearted dash for Arta. It would be no more dangerous than to sit here."

The professor was at last able to make his formal speech.

"Mr. Coleman," he said distinctly, "we place ourselves entirely in your hands." It was somehow pitiful. This man who, for years and years had reigned in a little college town almost as a monarch, passing judgment with the air of one who words the law, dealing criticism upon the universe as one to whom all things are plain, publicly disdaining defeat as one to whom all things are easy—this man was now veritably appealing to Coleman to save his wife, his daughter and himself, and really declared himself dependent for safety upon the ingenuity and courage of the correspondent.

The attitude of the students was utterly indifferent. They did not consider themselves helpless at all; they were evidently quite ready to withstand anything, but they looked frankly up to Coleman as their intelligent leader. If they suffered any, their only expression of it was in the simple grim slang of their period.

"I wish I was at Coney Island."

"This is not so bad as trigonometry, but it's worse than playing billiards for the beers."

And Coke said privately to Coleman: "Say, what in hell are these two damn peoples fighting for, anyhow?"

When he saw that all opinions were in favor of following him loyally, Coleman was impelled to feel a responsibility. He was now no errant rescuer, but a properly elected leader of fellow beings in distress. While one of the students held his horse, he took the dragoman for another consultation with the captain of the battery. The officer was sitting on a large stone, with his eyes fixed into his field glasses. When again questioned he could give no satisfaction as to the identity of the troops on the distant mountain. He merely shrugged his shoulders and said that if they were Greeks it was very good, but if they were Turks it was very bad. He seemed more occupied in trying to impress the correspondent that it was a matter of soldierly indifference to himself. Coleman, after loathing him sufficiently in silence, returned to the others and said: "Well, we'll chance it."

They looked to him to arrange the caravan. Speaking to the men of the party he said: "Of course, any one of you is welcome to my horse if you can ride it, but—if you're not too tired—I think I had myself better ride, so that I can go ahead at times."

His manner was so fine as he said this that the students seemed fairly to worship him. Of course it had been most improbable that any of them could have ridden that volcanic animal even if one of them had tried it.

He saw Mrs. Wainwright and Marjory upon the backs of their two little natives, and hoisted the professor into the saddle of the groom's horse, leaving instructions with the servant to lead the animal always and carefully. He and the dragoman then mounted at the head of the procession, and amid curious questionings from the soldiery they crossed the bridge and started on the trail to Arta. The rear was brought up by the little grey horse with the luggage, led by one student and flogged by another.

Coleman, checking with difficulty the battling disposition of his horse, was very uneasy in his mind because the last words of the captain of the battery had made him feel that perhaps on this ride he would be placed in a position where only the best courage would count, and he did not see his way clear to feeling very confident about his conduct in such a case. Looking back upon the caravan, he saw it as a most unwieldy thing, not even capable of running away. He hurried it with sudden, sharp contemptuous phrases.

On the march there incidentally flashed upon him a new truth. More than half of that student band were deeply in love with Marjory. Of course, when he had been distant from her he had had an eternal jealous reflection to that effect. It was natural that he should have thought of the intimate camping relations between Marjory and these young students with a great deal of bitterness, grinding his teeth when picturing their opportunities to make Marjory fall in love with some one of them. He had raged particularly about Coke, whose father had millions of dollars. But he had forgotten all these jealousies in the general splendour of his exploits. Now, when he saw the truth, it seemed to bring him back to his common life and he saw himself suddenly as not being frantically superior in any way to those other young men. The more closely he looked at this last fact, the more convinced he was of its truth. He seemed to see that he had been improperly elated over his services to the Wainwrights, and that, in the end, the girl might fancy a man because the man had done her no service at all. He saw his proud position lower itself to be a pawn in the game. Looking back over the students, he wondered which one Marjory might love. This hideous Nikopolis had given eight men chance to win her. His scorn and his malice quite centered upon Coke, for he could never forget that the man's father had millions of dollars. The unfortunate Coke chose that moment to address him querulously: "Look here, Coleman, can't you tell us how far it is to Arta?"

"Coke," said Coleman, "I don't suppose you take me for a tourist agency, but if you can only try to distinguish between me and a map with the scale of miles printed in the lower left-hand corner, you will not contribute so much to the sufferings of the party which you now adorn."

The students within hearing guffawed and Coke retired, in confusion.

The march was not rapid. Coleman almost wore out his arms holding in check his impetuous horse. Often the caravan floundered through mud, while at the same time a hot, yellow dust came from the north.

They were perhaps half way to Arta when Coleman decided that a rest and luncheon were the things to be considered. He halted his troop then in the shade of some great trees, and privately he bade his dragoman prepare the best feast which could come out of those saddlebags fresh from Athens. The result was rather gorgeous in the eyes of the poor wanderers. First of all there were three knives, three forks, three spoons, three tin cups and three tin plates, which the entire party of twelve used on a most amiable socialistic principle. There were crisp, salty biscuits and olives, for which they speared in the bottle. There was potted turkey, and potted ham, and potted tongue, all tasting precisely alike. There were sardines and the ordinary tinned beef, disguised sometimes with onions, carrots and potatoes. Out of the saddlebags came pepper and salt and even mustard. The dragoman made coffee over a little fire of sticks that blazed with a white light. The whole thing was prodigal, but any philanthropist would have approved of it if he could have seen the way in which the eight students laid into the spread. When there came a polite remonstrance—notably from Mrs. Wainwright—Coleman merely pointed to a large bundle strapped back of the groom's saddle. During the coffee he was considering how best to get the students one by one out of the sight of the Wainwrights where he could give them good drinks of whisky.

There was an agitation on the road toward Arta. Some people were coming on horses. He paid small heed until he heard a thump of pausing hoofs near him, and a musical voice say: "Rufus!"

He looked up quickly, and then all present saw his eyes really bulge. There on a fat and glossy horse sat Nora Black, dressed in probably one of the most correct riding habits which had ever been seen in the East. She was smiling a radiant smile, which held the eight students simply spellbound. They would have recognized her if it had not been for this apparitional coming in the wilds of southeastern Europe. Behind her were her people—some servants and an old lady on a very little pony.

"Well, Rufus?" she said.

Coleman made the mistake of hesitating. For a fraction of a moment he had acted as if he were embarrassed, and was only going to nod and say: "How d'ya do?"

He arose and came forward too late. She was looking at him with a menacing glance which meant difficulties for him if he was not skilful. Keen as an eagle, she swept her glance over the face and figure of Marjory. Without further introduction, the girls seemed to understand that they were enemies.

Despite his feeling of awkwardness, Coleman's mind was mainly occupied by pure astonishment. "Nora Black?" he said, as if even then he could not believe his senses. "How in the world did you get down here?

She was not too amiable, evidently, over his reception, and she seemed to know perfectly that it was in her power to make him feel extremely unpleasant. "Oh, it's not so far," she answered. "I don't see where you come in to ask me what I'm doing here. What are you doing here?" She lifted her eyes and shot the half of a glance at Marjory. Into her last question she had interjected a spirit of ownership in which he saw future woe. It turned him cowardly. "Why, you know I was sent up here by the paper to rescue the Wainwright party, and I've got them. I'm taking them to Arta. But why are you here?"

"I am here," she said, giving him the most defiant of glances, "principally to look for you."

Even the horse she rode betrayed an intention of abiding upon that spot forever. She had made her communication with Coleman appear to the Wainwright party as a sort of tender reunion.

Coleman looked at her with a steely eye. "Nora, you can certainly be a devil when you choose."

"Why don't you present me to your friends? Miss Nora Black, special correspondent of the *New York Daylight*, if you please. I belong to your opposition. I am your rival, Rufus, and I draw a bigger salary—see? Funny looking gang, that. Who is the old Johnnie in the white wig?"

"Er—where you goin'—you can't—" blundered Coleman miserably "Aw—the army is in retreat and you must go back, too—don't you see?"

"Is it?" she asked. After a pause she added coolly: "Then I shall go back to Arta with you and your precious Wainwrights."

## CHAPTER XV.

GIVING Coleman another glance of subtle menace Nora repeated: "Why don't you present me to your friends?" Coleman had been swiftly searching the whole world for a way clear of this unhappiness, but he knew at last that he could only die at his guns. "Why, certainly," he said quickly, "if you wish it." He sauntered easily back to the luncheon blanket. "This is Miss Black of the New York Daylight and she says that those people on the mountain are Greeks." The students were gaping at him, and Marjory and her father sat in the same silence. But to the relief of Coleman and to the high edification of the students, Mrs. Wainwright cried out: "Why, is she an American woman?" And seeing Coleman's nod of assent she rustled to her feet and advanced hastily upon the complacent horsewoman. "I'm delighted to see you. Who would think of seeing an American woman way over here. Have you been here long? Are you going on further? Oh, we've had such a dreadful time." Coleman remained long enough to hear Nora say: "Thank you very much, but I shan't dismount. I am going to ride back to Arta presently."

Then he heard Mrs. Wainwright cry: "Oh, are you indeed? Why we, too, are going at once to Arta. We can all go together." Coleman fled then to the bosom of the students, who all looked at him with eyes of cynical penetration. He cast a glance at Marjory more than fearing a glare which denoted an implacable resolution never to forgive this thing. On the contrary he had never seen her so content and serene.

"You have allowed your coffee to get chilled," she said considerately. "Won't you have the man warm you some more?"

"Thanks, no," he answered with gratitude.

Nora, changing her mind, had dismounted and was coming with Mrs. Wainwright. That worthy lady had long had a fund of information and anecdote the sound of which neither her husband nor her daughter would endure for a moment. Of course the rascally students were out of the question. Here, then, was really the first ear amiably and cheerfully open, and she was talking at what the students called her "thirty knot gait."

"Lost everything. Absolutely everything. Neither of us have even a brush and comb, or a cake of soap, or enough hairpins to hold up our hair. I'm going to take Marjory's away from her and let her braid her hair down her back. You can imagine how dreadful it is—"

From time to time the cool voice of Nora sounded without effort through this clamor. "Oh, it will be no trouble at all. I have more than enough of everything. We can divide very nicely."

Coleman broke somewhat imperiously into this feminine chat. "Well, we must be moving, you know, "and his voice started the men into activity. When the traps were all packed again on the horse Coleman looked back surprised to see the three women engaged in the most friendly discussion. The combined parties now made a very respectable squadron. Coleman rode off at its head without glancing behind at all. He knew that they were following from the soft pounding of the horses hoofs on the sod and from the mellow hum of human voices.

For a long time he did not think to look upon himself as anything but a man much injured by circumstances. Among his friends he could count numbers who had lived long lives without having this peculiar class of misfortune come to them. In fact it was so unusual a misfortune that men of the world had not found it necessary to pass from mind to mind a perfect formula for dealing with it. But he soon began to consider himself an extraordinarily lucky person inasmuch as Nora Black had come upon him with her saddle bags packed with inflammable substances, so to speak, and there had been as yet only enough fire to boil coffee for luncheon. He laughed tenderly when he thought of the innocence of Mrs. Wainwright, but his face and back flushed with heat when lie thought of the canniness of the eight American college students.

He heard a horse cantering up on his left side and looking he saw Nora Black. She was beaming with satisfaction and good nature. "Well, Rufus," she cried flippantly, "how goes it with the gallant rescuer? You've made a hit, my boy. You are the success of the season."

Coleman reflected upon the probable result of a direct appeal to Nora. He knew of course that such appeals were usually idle, but he did not consider Nora an ordinary person. His decision was to venture it. He drew his horse close to hers. "Nora," he said, "do you know that you are raising the very devil?"

She lifted her finely penciled eyebrows and looked at him with the baby-stare. "How?" she enquired.

"You know well enough," he gritted out wrathfully.

"Raising the very devil?" she asked. "How do you mean?" She was palpably interested for his answer. She waited for his reply for an interval, and then she asked him outright. "Rufus Coleman do you mean that I am not a respectable woman?"

In reality he had meant nothing of the kind, but this direct throttling of a great question stupefied him utterly, for he saw now that she' would probably never understand him in the least and that she would at any rate always pretend not to understand him and that the more he said the more harm he manufactured. She studied him over carefully and then wheeled her horse towards the rear with some parting remarks. "I suppose you should attend more strictly to your own affairs, Rufus. Instead of raising the devil I am lending hairpins. I have seen you insult people, but I have never seen you insult anyone quite for the whim of the thing. Go soak your head."

Not considering it advisable to then indulge in such immersion Coleman rode moodily onward. The hot dust continued to sting the cheeks of the travelers and in some places great clouds of dead leaves roared in circles about them. All of the Wainwright party were utterly fagged. Coleman felt his skin crackle and his throat seemed to be coated with the white dust. He worried his dragoman as to the distance to Arta until the dragoman lied to the point where he always declared that Arta was only off some hundreds of yards.

At their places in the procession, Mrs. Wainwright and Marjory were animatedly talking to Nora and the old lady on the little pony. They had at first suffered great amazement at the voluntary presence of the old lady, but she was there really because she knew no better. Her colossal ignorance took the form, mainly, of a most obstreperous patriotism, and indeed she always acted in a foreign country as if she were the special commissioner of the President, or perhaps as a special commissioner could not act at all. She was very aggressive, and when any of the travelling arrangements in Europe did not suit her ideas, she was wont to shrilly exclaim: "Well! New York is good enough for me."

Nora, morbidly afraid that her expense bill to the *Daylight* would not be large enough, had dragged her bodily off to Greece as her companion, friend, and protection. At Arta they had heard of the grand success of the Greek army. The Turks had not stood for a moment before that gallant and terrible advance; no; they had scampered howling with fear into the north. Jannina would fall—well, Jannina would fall as soon as the Greeks arrived. There was no doubt of it. The correspondent and her friend, deluded and hurried by the light-hearted confidence of the Greeks in Arta, had hastened out then on a regular tourist's excursion to see Jannina after its capture.

Nora concealed from her friend the fact that the editor of the *Daylight* particularly wished her to see a battle so that she might write an article on actual warfare from a woman's point of view. With her name as a queen of comic opera, such an article from her pen would be a burning, sensation.

Coleman had been the first to point out to Nora that instead of going on a picnic to Jannina, she had better run back to Arta. When the old lady heard that they had not been entirely safe, she was furious with Nora.

"The idea!" she exclaimed to Mrs. Wainwright. "They might have caught us! They might have caught us!"

"Well," said Mrs. Wainwright. "I verily believe they *would* have caught us if it had not been for Mr. Coleman."

"Is he the gentleman on the fine horse?"

"Yes; that's him. Oh, he has been simply *splendid*. I confess I was a little bit—er—surprised. He was in college under my husband. I don't know that we thought very great things of him, but if ever a man won golden opinions he has done so from us."

"Oh, that must be the Coleman who is such a great friend of Nora's."

"Yes?" said Mrs. Wainwright insidiously. "Is he? I didn't know. Of course he knows so many people." Her mind had been suddenly illumined by the old lady and she thought extravagantly of the arrival of Nora upon the scene. She remained all sweetness to the old lady. "Did you know he was here? Did you expect to meet him? I seemed such a delightful coincidence." In truth she was being subterraneously clever.

"Oh, no; I don't think so. I didn't hear Nora mention it. Of course she would have told me. You know, our coming to Greece was such a surprise. Nora had an engagement in London at the Folly Theatre in Fly by Night, but the manager was insufferable, oh, insufferable. So, of course, Nora wouldn't stand it a minute, and then these newspaper people came along and asked her to go to Greece for them and she accepted. I am sure I never expected to find us—aw—fleeing from the Turks or I shouldn't have Come."

"Mrs. Wainwright was gasping. "You don't mean that she is—she is Nora Black, the actress."

"Of course she is," said the old lady jubilantly.

"Why, how strange," choked Mrs. Wainwright. Nothing she knew of Nora could account for her stupefaction and grief. What happened glaringly to her was the duplicity of man. Coleman was a ribald deceiver. He must have known and yet he had pretended throughout that the meeting was a pure accident She turned with a nervous impulse to sympathize with her daughter, but despite the lovely tranquility of the girl's face there was something about her which forbade the mother to meddle. Anyhow Mrs. Wainwright was sorry that she had told nice things of Coleman's behavior, so she said to the old lady: "Young men of these times get a false age so quickly. We have always thought it a great pity, about Mr. Coleman."

"Why, how so?" asked the old lady.

"Oh, really nothing. Only, to us he seemed rather—er—prematurely experienced or something of that kind. The old lady did not catch the meaning of the phrase. She seemed surprised. "Why, I've never seen any full-grown person in this world who got experience any too quick for his own good."

At the tail of the procession there was talk between the two students who had in charge the little grey horse—one to lead and one to flog. "Billie," said one, "it now becomes necessary to lose this hobby into the hands of some of the other fellows. Whereby we will gain opportunity to pay homage to the great Nora. Why, you egregious thick-head, this is the chance of a lifetime. I'm damned if I'm going to tow this beast of burden much further."

"You wouldn't stand a show," said Billie pessimistically. "Look at Coleman."

"That's all right. Do you mean to say that you prefer to continue towing pack horses in the presence of this queen of song and the dance just because you think Coleman can throw out his chest a little more than you. Not so. Think of your bright and sparkling youth. There's Coke and Pete Tounley near Marjory. We'll call 'em." Whereupon he set up a cry. "Say, you people, we're not getting a, salary for this. Supposin' you try for a time. It'll do you good." When the two addressed bad halted to await the arrival of the little grey horse, they took on glum expressions. "You look like poisoned pups," said the student who led the horse. "Too strong for light work. Grab onto the halter, now, Peter, and tow. We are going ahead to talk to Nora Black."

"Good time you'll have," answered Peter Tounley.

"Coleman is cuttin' up scandalous. You won't stand a show."

"What do you think of him?" said Coke. "Seems curious, all 'round. Do you suppose he knew she would show up? It was nervy to—"

"Nervy to what?" asked Billie.

"Well," said Coke, "seems to me he is playing both ends against the middle. I don't know anything about Nora Black, but——"

The three other students expressed themselves with conviction and in chorus. "Coleman's all right."

"Well, anyhow," continued Coke, "I don't see my way free to admiring him introducing Nora Black to the Wainwrights."

"He didn't," said the others, still in chorus.

"Queer game," said Peter Tounley. "He seems to know her pretty well."

"Pretty damn well," said Billie.

"Anyhow he's a brick," said Peter Tounley. "We mustn't forget that. Lo, I begin to feel that our Rufus is a fly guy of many different kinds. Any play that he is in commands my respect. He won't be hit by a chimney in the daytime, for unto him has come much wisdom, I don't think I'll worry."

"Is he stuck on Nora Black, do you know?" asked Billie.

"One thing is plain," replied Coke. "She has got him somehow by the short hair and she intends him to holler murder. Anybody can see that."

"Well, he won't holler murder," said one of them with conviction. "I'll bet you he won't. He'll hammer the war-post and beat the tom-tom until he drops, but he won't holler murder."

"Old Mother Wainwright will be in his wool presently," quoth Peter Tounley musingly, "I could see it coming in her eye. Somebody has given his snap away, or something."

"Aw, he had no snap," said Billie. "Couldn't you see how rattled he was? He would have had a fit if dear Nora hadn't turned up."

"Of course," the others assented. "He was rattled."

"Looks queer. And nasty," said Coke.

"Nora herself had an axe ready for him."

They began to laugh. "If she had had an umbrella she would have basted him over the head with it. Oh, my! He was green."

"Nevertheless," said Peter Tounley, "I refuse to worry over our Rufus. When he can't take care of himself the rest of us want to hunt cover. He is a fly guy——"

Coleman in the meantime had become aware that the light of Mrs. Wainwright's countenance was turned from him. The party stopped at a well, and when he offered her a drink from his cup he thought she accepted it with scant thanks. Marjory was still gracious, always gracious, but this did not reassure him, because he felt there was much unfathomable deception in it. When he turned to seek consolation in the manner of the professor he found him as before, stunned with surprise, and the only idea he had was to be as tractable as a child.

When he returned to the head of the column, Nora again cantered forward to join him. "Well, me gay Lochinvar," she cried, "and has your disposition improved?"

"You are very fresh," he said.

She laughed loud enough to be heard the full length of the caravan. It was a beautiful laugh, but full of insolence and confidence. He flashed his eyes malignantly upon her, but then she only laughed more. She could see that he wished to strangle her. "What a disposition!" she said. "What a disposition! You are not nearly so nice as your friends. Now, they are charming, but you—Rufus, I wish you would get that temper mended. Dear Rufus, do it to please me. You know you like to please me. Don't you now, dear?" He finally laughed. "Confound you, Nora. I would like to kill you."

But at his laugh she was all sunshine. It was as if she had been trying to taunt him into good humor with her. "Aw, now, Rufus, don't be angry. I'll be good, Rufus. Really, I will. Listen. I want to tell you something. Do you know what I did? Well, you know, I never was cut out for this business, and, back there, when you told me about the Turks being near and all that sort of thing, I was frightened almost to death. Really, I was. So, when nobody was looking, I sneaked two or three little drinks out of my flask. Two or three little drinks—"

## CHAPTER XVI.

"GOOD God!" said Coleman. "You don't Mean—"

Nora smiled rosily at him. "Oh, I'm all right," she answered. "Don't worry about your Aunt Nora, my precious boy. Not for a minute."

Coleman was horrified. "But you are not going to—you are not going to—"

"Not at all, me son. Not at all," she answered.

I'm not going to prance. I'm going to be as nice as pie, and just ride quietly along here with dear little Rufus. Only—you know what I can do when I get started, so you had better be a very good boy. I might take it into my head to say some things, you know."

Bound hand and foot at his stake, he could not even chant his defiant torture song. It might precipitate— in fact, he was sure it would precipitate the grand smash. But to the very core of his soul, he for the time hated Nora Black. He did not dare to remind her that he would revenge himself; he dared only to dream of this revenge, but it fairly made his thoughts flame, and deep in his throat he was swearing an inflexible persecution of Nora Black. The old expression of his sex came to him, "Oh, if she were only a man!" she had been a man, he would have fallen upon her tooth and nail. Her motives for all this impressed him not at all; she was simply a witch who bound him helpless with the power of her femininity, and made him eat cinders. He was so sure that his face betrayed him that he did not dare let her see it. "Well, what are you going to do about it?" he asked, over his shoulder.

"O-o-oh," she drawled, impudently. "Nothing."

He could see that she was determined not to be confessed. "I may do this or I may do that. It all depends upon your behavior, my dear Rufus."

As they rode on, he deliberated as to the best means of dealing with this condition. Suddenly he resolved to go with the whole tale direct to Marjory, and to this end he half wheeled his horse. He would reiterate that he loved her and then explain—explain! He groaned when he came to the word, and ceased formulation.

The cavalcade reached at last the bank of the Aracthus river, with its lemon groves and lush grass. A battery wheeled before them over the ancient bridge—a flight of short, broad cobbled steps up as far as the centre of the stream and a similar flight down to the other bank. The returning aplomb of the travelers was well illustrated by the professor, who, upon sighting this bridge, murmured: "Byzantine."

This was the first indication that he had still within him a power to resume the normal.

The steep and narrow street was crowded with soldiers; the smoky little coffee shops were a-babble with people discussing the news from the front. None seemed to heed the remarkable procession that wended its way to the cable office. Here Coleman resolutely took precedence. He knew that there was no good in expecting intelligence out of the chaotic clerks, but he managed to get upon the wires this message:

"*Eclipse*, New York: Got Wainwright party; all well. Coleman." The students had struggled to send messages to their people in America, but they had only succeeded in deepening the tragic boredom of the clerks.

When Coleman returned to the street he thought that he had seldom looked upon a more moving spectacle than the Wainwright party presented at that moment. Most of the students were seated in a row, dejectedly, upon the curb. The professor and Mrs. Wainwright looked like two old pictures, which, after an existence in a considerate gloom, had been brought out in their tawdriness to the clear light. Hot white dust covered everybody, and from out the grimy faces the eyes blinked, red-fringed with sleeplessness. Desolation sat upon all, save Marjory. She possessed some marvelous power of looking always fresh. This quality had indeed impressed the old lady on the little pony until she had said to Nora Black: "That girl would look well anywhere." Nora Black had not been amiable in her reply.

Coleman called the professor and the dragoman for a durbar. The dragoman said: "Well, I can get one carriage, and we can go immediate-lee."

"Carriage be blowed!" said Coleman. "What these people need is rest, sleep. You must find a place at once. These people can't remain in the street." He spoke in anger, as if he had previously told the dragoman and the latter had been inattentive. The man immediately departed.

Coleman remarked that there was no course but to remain in the street until his dragoman had found them a habitation. It was a mournful waiting. The students sat on the curb. Once they whispered to Coleman, suggesting a drink, but he told them that he knew only one cafe, the entrance of which would be in plain sight of the rest of the party. The ladies talked together in a group of four. Nora Black was bursting with the fact that her servant had hired rooms in Arta on their outcoming journey, and she wished Mrs. Wainwright and Marjory to come to them, at least for a time, but she dared not risk a refusal, and she felt something in Mrs. Wainwright's manner which led her to be certain that such would be the answer to her invitation. Coleman and the professor strolled slowly up and down the walk.

"Well, my work is over, sir," said Coleman. "My paper told me to find you, and, through no virtue of my own, I found you. I am very glad of it. I don't know of anything in my life that has given me greater pleasure."

The professor was himself again in so far as he had lost all manner of dependence. But still he could not yet be bumptious. "Mr. Coleman," he said, "I am placed under lifelong obligation to you. I am not thinking of myself so much…. My wife and daughter—" His gratitude was so genuine that he could not finish its expression.

"Oh, don't speak of it," said Coleman. "I really didn't do anything at all."

The dragoman finally returned and led them all to a house which he had rented for gold. In the great, bare, upper chamber the students dropped wearily to the floor, while the woman of the house took the Wainwrights to a more secluded apartment. As the door closed on them, Coleman turned like a flash.

"Have a drink," he said. The students arose around him like the wave of a flood. "You bet." In the absence of changes of clothing, ordinary food, the possibility of a bath, and in the presence of great weariness and dust, Coleman's whisky seemed to them a glistening luxury. Afterward they laid down as if to sleep, but in reality they were too dirty and too fagged to sleep. They simply lay murmuring Peter Tounley even developed a small fever.

It was at this time that Coleman suddenly discovered his acute interest in the progressive troubles of his affair of the heart had placed the business of his newspaper in the rear of his mind. The greater part of the next hour he spent in getting off to

New York that dispatch which created so much excitement for him later. Afterward he was free to reflect moodily upon the ability of Nora Black to distress him. She, with her retinue, had disappeared toward her own rooms. At dusk he went into the street, and was edified to see Nora's dragoman dodging along in his wake. He thought that this was simply another manifestation of Nora's interest in his movements, and so he turned a corner, and there pausing, waited until the dragoman spun around directly into his arms. But it seemed that the man had a note to deliver, and this was only his Oriental way of doing it.

The note read: "Come and dine with me tonight." It was, not a request. It was peremptory. "All right," he said, scowling at the man.

He did not go at once, for he wished to reflect for a time and find if he could not evolve some weapons of his own. It seemed to him that all the others were liberally supplied with weapons.

A clear, cold night had come upon the earth when he signified to the lurking dragoman that he was in readiness to depart with him to Nora's abode. They passed finally into a dark courtyard, up a winding staircase, across an embowered balcony, and Coleman entered alone a room where there were lights.

His, feet were scarcely over the threshold before he had concluded that the tigress was now going to try some velvet purring. He noted that the arts of the stage had not been thought too cheaply obvious for use. Nora sat facing the door. A bit of yellow silk had been twisted about the crude shape of the lamp, and it made the play of light, amber-like, shadowy and yet perfectly clear, the light which women love. She was arrayed in a puzzling gown of that kind of Grecian silk which is so docile that one can pull yards of it through a ring. It was of the color of new straw. Her chin was leaned pensively upon her palm and the light fell on a pearly rounded forearm. She was looking at him with a pair of famous eyes, azure, perhaps—certainly purple at times—and it may be, black at odd moments—a pair of eyes that had made many an honest man's heart jump if he thought they were looking at him. It was a vision, yes, but Coleman's cynical knowledge of drama overpowered his sense of its beauty. He broke out brutally, in the phrases of the American street. "Your dragoman is a rubberneck. If he keeps darking me I will simply have to kick the stuffing out of him."

She was alone in the room. Her old lady had been instructed to have a headache and send apologies. She was not disturbed by Coleman's words. "Sit down, Rufus, and have a cigarette, and don't be cross, because I won't stand it."

He obeyed her glumly. She had placed his chair where not a charm of her could be lost upon an observant man. Evidently she did not purpose to allow him to irritate her away from her original plan. Purring was now her method, and none of his insolence could achieve a growl from the tigress. She arose, saying softly: "You look tired, almost ill, poor boy. I will give you some brandy. I have almost everything that I could think to make those Daylight people buy." With a sweep of her hand she indicated the astonishing opulence of the possessions in different parts of the room.

As she stood over him with the brandy there came through the smoke of his cigarette the perfume of orris-root and violet.

A servant began to arrange the little cold dinner on a camp table, and Coleman saw with an enthusiasm which he could not fully master, four quart bottles of a notable brand of champagne placed in a rank on the floor.

At dinner Nora was sisterly. She watched him, waited upon him, treated him to an affectionate intimacy for which he knew a thousand men who would have hated him. The champagne was cold.

Slowly he melted. By the time that the boy came with little cups of Turkish coffee he was at least amiable. Nora talked dreamily. "The dragoman says this room used to be part of the harem long ago." She shot him a watchful glance, as if she had expected the fact to affect him. "Seems curious, doesn't it? A harem. Fancy that." He smoked one cigar and then discarded tobacco, for the perfume of orris-root and violet was making him meditate. Nora talked on in a low voice. She knew that, through half-closed lids, he was looking at her in steady speculation. She knew that she was conquering, but no movement of hers betrayed an elation. With the most exquisite art she aided his contemplation, baring to him, for instance, the glories of a statuesque neck, doing it all with the manner of a splendid and fabulous virgin who knew not that there was such a thing as shame. Her stockings were of black silk.

Coleman presently answered her only in monosyllable, making small distinction between yes and no. He simply sat watching her with eyes in which there were two little covetous steel-colored flames.

He was thinking, "To go to the devil—to go to the devil—to go to the devil with this girl is not a bad fate—not a bad fate—not a bad fate."

## CHAPTER XVII.

"Come out on the balcony," cooed Nora. "There are some funny old storks on top of some chimneys near here and they clatter like mad all day and night."

They moved together out to the balcony, but Nora retreated with a little cry when she felt the coldness of the night. She said that she would get a cloak. Coleman was not unlike a man in a dream. He walked to the rail of the balcony where a great vine climbed toward the roof. He noted that it was dotted with blossoms, which in the deep purple of the Oriental night were colored in strange shades of maroon. This truth penetrated his abstraction until when Nora came she found him staring at them as if their color was a revelation which affected him vitally. She moved to his side without sound and he first knew of her presence from the damning fragrance. She spoke just above her breath. "It's a beautiful evening."

"Yes," he answered. She was at his shoulder. If he moved two inches he must come in contact. They remained in silence leaning upon the rail. Finally he began to mutter some commonplaces which meant nothing particularly, but into his tone as he mouthed them was the note of a forlorn and passionate lover. Then as if by accident he traversed the two inches and his shoulder was against the soft and yet firm shoulder of Nora Black. There was something in his throat at this time which changed his voice into a mere choking noise. She did not move. He could see her eyes glowing innocently out of the pallor which the darkness gave to her face. If he was touching her, she did not seem to know it.

"I am awfully tired," said Coleman, thickly. "I think I will go home and turn in."

"You must be, poor boy," said Nora tenderly.

"Wouldn't you like a little more of that champagne?"

"Well, I don't mind another glass."

She left him again and his galloping thought pounded to the old refrain. "To go to the devil—to go to the devil—to go to the devil with this girl is not a bad fate— not a bad fate—not a bad fate." When she returned he drank his glass of champagne. Then he mumbled: "You must be cold. Let me put your cape around you better. It won't do to catch cold here, you know."

She made a sweet pretence of rendering herself to his care. "Oh, thanks… I am not really cold.… There that's better."

Of course all his manipulation of the cloak had been a fervid caress, and although her acting up to this point had remained in the role of the splendid and fabulous virgin she now turned her liquid eyes to his with a look that expressed knowledge, triumph and delight. She was sure of her victory. And she said: "Sweetheart…don't you think I am as nice as Marjory?"

The impulse had been airily confident. It was as if the silken cords had been parted by the sweep of a sword. Coleman's face had instantly stiffened and he looked like a man suddenly recalled to the ways of light. It may easily have been that in a moment he would have lapsed again to his luxurious dreaming. But in his face the girl had read a fatal character to her blunder and her resentment against him took precedence of any other emotion.

She wheeled abruptly from him and said with great contempt: "Rufus, you had better go home. You're tired and sleepy, and more or less drunk."

He knew that the grand tumble of all their little embowered incident could be neither stayed or mended.

"Yes," he answered, sulkily, "I think so too."

They shook hands huffily and he went away.

* * * *

When he arrived among the students he found that they had appropriated everything of his which would conduce to their comfort. He was furious over it. But to his bitter speeches they replied in jibes.

"Rufus is himself again. Admire his angelic disposition. See him smile. Gentle soul."

A sleepy voice said from a comer: "I know what pinches him."

"What?" asked several.

"He's been to see Nora and she flung him out bodily."

"Yes?" sneered Coleman. "At times I seem to see in you, Coke, the fermentation of some primeval form of sensation, as if it were possible for you to develop a mind in two or three thousand years, and then at other times you appear much as you are now."

* * * *

As soon as they had well measured Coleman's temper, all of the students save Coke kept their mouths tightly closed. Coke either did not understand or his mood was too vindictive for silence.

"Well, I know you got a throw-down all right," he muttered.

"And how would you know when I got a throw down? You pimply, milk-fed Sophomore."

The others perked up their ears in mirthful appreciation of this language.

"Of course," continued Coleman, "no one would protest against your continued existence, Coke, unless you insist on recalling yourself violently to people's attention in this way. The mere fact of your living would not usually be offensive to people if you weren't eternally turning a sort of calcium light on your prehensile attributes." Coke was suddenly angry, angry much like a peasant, and his anger first evinced itself in a mere sputtering and spluttering. Finally he got out a rather long speech, full of grumbling noises, but he was understood by all to declare that his prehensile attributes had not led him to cart a notorious woman about the world with him. When they quickly looked at Coleman they saw that he was livid. "You—"

But, of course, there immediately arose all sorts of protesting cries from the seven non-combatants. Coleman, as he took two strides toward Coke's corner, looked fully able to break him across his knee, but for this Coke did not seem to care at all. He was on his feet with a challenge in his eye. Upon each cheek burned a sudden hectic spot. The others were clamoring, "Oh, say, this won't do. Quit it. Oh, we mustn't have a fight. He didn't mean it, Coleman." Peter Tounley pressed Coke to the wall saying: "You damned young jackass, be quiet."

They were in the midst of these festivities when a door opened and disclosed the professor. He might have been coming into the middle of a row in one of the corridors of the college at home only this time he carried a candle. His speech, however, was a Washurst speech: "Gentlemen, gentlemen, what does this mean?" All seemed to expect Coleman to make the answer. He was suddenly very cool. "Nothing, professor," he said, "only that this—only that Coke has insulted me. I suppose that it was only the irresponsibility of a boy, and I beg that you will not trouble over it."

"Mr. Coke," said the professor, indignantly, "what have you to say to this?" Evidently he could not clearly see Coke, and he peered around his candle at where the virtuous Peter Tounley was expostulating with the young man. The figures of all the excited group moving in the candle light caused vast and uncouth shadows to have conflicts in the end of the room.

Peter Tounley's task was not light, and beyond that he had the conviction that his struggle with Coke was making him also to appear as a rowdy. This conviction was proven to be true by a sudden thunder from the old professor, "Mr. Tounley, desist!"

In wrath he desisted and Coke flung himself forward. He paid less attention to the professor than if the latter had been a jackrabbit. "You say I insulted you? he shouted crazily in Coleman's face.

"Well…I meant to, do you see?"

Coleman was glacial and lofty beyond everything. "I am glad to have you admit the truth of what I have said."

Coke was, still suffocating with his peasant rage, which would not allow him to meet the clear, calm expressions of Coleman. "Yes…I insulted you…. I insulted you because what I said was correct…my prehensile attributes…yes but I have never—"

He was interrupted by a chorus from the other students. "Oh, no, that won't do. Don't say that. Don't repeat that, Coke."

Coleman remembered the weak bewilderment of the little professor in hours that had not long passed, and it was with something of an impersonal satisfaction that he said to himself: "The old boy's got his war-paint on again." The professor had stepped sharply up to Coke and looked at him with eyes that seemed to throw out flame and heat. There was a moment's pause, and then the old scholar spoke, biting his words as if they were each a short section of steel wire. "Mr. Coke, your behavior will end your college career abruptly and in gloom, I promise you. You have been drinking."

Coke, his head simply floating in a sea of universal defiance, at once blurted out: "Yes, sir."

"You have been drinking?" cried the professor, ferociously. "Retire to your—retire to your—retire—" And then in a voice of thunder he shouted: "Retire."

Whereupon seven hoodlum students waited a decent moment, then shrieked with laughter. But the old professor would have none of their nonsense. He quelled them all with force and finish.

Coleman now spoke a few words.

"Professor, I can't tell you how sorry I am that I should be concerned in any such riot as this, and since we are doomed to be bound so closely into each other's society, I offer myself without reservation as being willing to repair the damage as well as may be done. I don't see how I can forget at once that Coke's conduct was insolently unwarranted, but if he has anything to say of a nature that might heal the breach, I would be willing to meet him in the openest manner."

As he made these remarks, Coleman's dignity was something grand, and, moreover, there was now upon his face that curious look of temperance and purity which had been noted in New York as a singular physical characteristic. If he was guilty of anything in this affair at all—in fact, if he had ever at any time been guilty of anything—no mark had come to stain that bloom of innocence.

The professor nodded in the fullest appreciation and sympathy. "Of course—really, there is no other sleeping place. I suppose it would be better—" Then he again attacked Coke. "Young man, you have chosen an unfortunate moment to fill us with a suspicion that you may not be a gentleman. For the time there is nothing to be done with you." He addressed the other students. "There is nothing for me to do, young gentleman, but to leave Mr. Coke in your care. Good-night, sirs. Good-night, Coleman."

He left the room with his candle.

When Coke was bade to "Retire," he had, of course, simply retreated fuming to a corner of the room where he remained looking with yellow eyes like an animal from a cave. When the others were able to see through the haze of mental confusion, they found that Coleman was with deliberation taking off his boots. Afterward, when he removed his waist-coat, he took great care to wind his large gold watch.

The students, much subdued, lay again in their places, and when there was any talking it was of an extremely local nature, referring principally to the floor as being unsuitable for beds, and also referring from time to time to a real or an alleged selfishness on the part of some one of the recumbent men. Soon there was only the sound of heavy breathing.

* * * *

When the professor had returned to what he called the Wainwright part of the house, he was greeted instantly with the question: "What was it?" His wife and daughter were up in alarm. "What was it?" they repeated wildly.

He was peevish. "Oh, nothing, nothing. But that young Coke is a regular ruffian. He had gotten himself into some tremendous uproar with Coleman. When I arrived, he seemed actually trying to assault him. Revolting! He had been drinking. Coleman's behavior, I must say, was splendid. Recognized at once the delicacy of my position—he not being a student. If I had found him in the wrong it would have been simpler than finding him in the right. Confound that rascal of a Coke."

Then, as he began a partial disrobing, he treated them to grunted scrap of information. "Coke was quite insane. I feared that I couldn't control him…Coleman was like ice—and as much as I have seen to admire in him during the last few days, this quiet beat it all. If he had not recognized my helplessness as far as he was concerned, the whole thing might have been a most miserable business. He is a very fine young man."

The dissenting voice to this last tribute was the voice of Mrs. Wainwright. She said: "Well, Coleman drinks, too—everybody knows that."

"I know," responded the professor, rather bashfully, but I am confident that he had not touched a drop."

Marjory said nothing.

The earlier artillery battles had frightened most of the furniture out of the houses of Arta, and there was left in this room only a few old red cushions, and the Wainwrights were camping upon the floor. Marjory was wrapped in Coleman's macintosh, and while the professor and his wife maintained some low talk of the recent incident, she in silence had turned her cheek into the yellow velvet collar of the coat. She felt something against her bosom, and putting her hand carefully into the top pocket of the coat, she found three cigars. These she took in the darkness and laid aside, telling herself to remember their position in the morning. She had no doubt that Coleman would rejoice over them before he could get back to Athens, where there were other good cigars.

## CHAPTER XVIII.

The ladies of the Wainwright party had not complained at all when deprived of even such civilized advantages as a shelter and a knife and fork and soap and water, but Mrs. Wainwright complained bitterly amid the half-civilization of Arta. She could see here no excuse for the absence of several hundred things which she had always regarded as essential to life.

She began at 8.30 A. M. to make both the professor and Marjory woeful with an endless dissertation upon the beds in the hotel at Athens. Of course she had not regarded them at the time as being exceptional beds—that was quite true—but then one really never knew what one was really missing until one really missed it.... She would never have thought that she would come to consider those Athenian beds as excellent, but experience is a great teacher—makes one reflect upon the people who year in and year out have no beds at all, poor things. Well, it made one glad if one did have a good bed, even if it was at the time on the other side of the world. If she ever reached it she did not know what could ever induce her to leave it again. She would never be induced—

"'Induced!'" snarled the professor. The word represented to him a practiced feminine misusage of truth, and at such his white warlock always arose. "'Induced!' Out of four American women I have seen lately, you seem to be the only one who would say that you had endured this thing because you had been 'induced' by others to come over here. How absurd!"

Mrs. Wainwright fixed her husband with a steely eye. She saw opportunity for a shattering retort. "You don't mean, Harrison, to include Marjory and I in the same breath with those two women?"

The professor saw no danger ahead for himself. He merely answered: "I had no thought either way. It did not seem important."

"Well, it is important," snapped Mrs. Wainwright.

"Do you know that you are speaking in the same breath of Marjory and Nora Black, the actress?"

"No," said the professor. "Is that so?" He was astonished, but he was not aghast at all. "Do you mean to say that is Nora Black, the comic opera star?"

"That's exactly who she is," said Mrs. Wainwright, dramatically. "And I consider that—I consider that Rufus Coleman has done no less than—misled us."

This last declaration seemed to have no effect upon the professor's pure astonishment, but Marjory looked at her mother suddenly. However, she said no word, exhibiting again that strange and, inscrutable countenance which masked even the tiniest of her maidenly emotions.

Mrs. Wainwright was triumphant, and she immediately set about celebrating her victory. "Men never see those things," she said to her husband. "Men never see those things. You would have gone on forever without finding out that your—your—hospitality was, being abused by that Rufus Coleman."

The professor woke up." Hospitality?" he said, indignantly. "Hospitality? I have not had any hospitality to be abused. Why don't you talk sense? It is not that, but—it might—" He hesitated and then spoke slowly. "It might be very awkward. Of course one never knows anything definite about such people, but I suppose— Anyhow, it was strange in Coleman to allow her to meet us."

"It Was all a pre-arranged plan," announced the triumphant Mrs. Wainwright. "She came here on purpose to meet Rufus Coleman, and he knew it, and I should not wonder if they had not the exact spot picked out where they were going to meet."

"I can hardly believe that," said the professor, in distress. "I can, hardly believe that. It does, not seem to me that Coleman—"

"Oh yes. Your dear Rufus Coleman," cried Mrs. Wainwright. "You think he is very fine now. But I can remember when you didn't think—"

And the parents turned together an abashed look at their daughter. The professor actually flushed with shame. It seemed to him that he had just committed an atrocity upon the heart of his child. The instinct of each of them was to go to her and console her in their arms. She noted it immediately, and seemed to fear it. She spoke in a clear and even voice. "I don't think, father, that you should distress me by supposing that I am concerned at all if Mr. Coleman cares to get Nora Black over here."

"Not at all," stuttered the professor. "I—"

Mrs. Wainwright's consternation turned suddenly to, anger. "He is a scapegrace. A rascal. A— a—"

"Oh," said Marjory, coolly, "I don't see why it isn't his own affair. He didn't re-ally present her to you, mother, you remember? She seemed quite to force her way at first, and then you—you did the rest. It should be very easy to avoid her, now that we are out of the wilderness. And then it becomes a private matter of Mr. Coleman's. For my part, I rather liked her. I don't see such a dreadful calamity."

"Marjory!" screamed her mother. "How dreadful. Liked her! Don't let me hear you say such shocking things."

"I fail to see anything shocking," answered Marjory, stolidly.

The professor was looking helplessly from his daughter to his wife, and from his wife to his daughter, like a man who was convinced that his troubles would never end. This new catastrophe created a different kind of difficulty, but he considered that the difficulties were as robust as had been the preceding ones. He put on his hat and went out of the room. He felt an impossibility of saying anything to Coleman, but he felt that he must look upon him. He must look upon this man and try to know from his manner the measure of guilt. And incidentally he longed for the machinery of a finished society which prevents its parts from clashing, prevents it with its great series of I law upon law, easily operative but relentless. Here he felt as a man flung into the jungle with his wife and daughter, where they could become the victims of any sort of savagery. His thought referred once more to what he considered the invaluable services of Coleman, and as he observed them in conjunction with the present accusation, he was simply dazed. It was then possible that one man could play two such divergent parts. He had not learned this at Washurst. But no; the world was not such a bed of putrefaction. He would not believe it; he would not believe it.

After adventures which require great nervous endurance, it is only upon the second or third night that the common man sleeps hard. The students had expected to slumber like dogs on the first night after their trials, but none slept long. And few slept.

Coleman was the first man to arise. When he left the room the students were just beginning to blink. He took his dragoman among the shops and he bought there all the little odds and ends which might go to make up the best breakfast in Arta. If he had had news of certain talk he probably would not have been buying breakfast for eleven people. Instead, he would have been buying breakfast for one. During his absence the students arose and performed their frugal toilets. Considerable attention was paid to Coke by the others. "He made a monkey of you," said Peter Tounley with unction. "He twisted you until you looked like a wet, grey rag. You had better leave this wise guy alone."

It was not the night nor was it meditation that had taught Coke anything, but he seemed to have learned something from the mere lapse of time. In appearance he was subdued, but he managed to make a temporary jauntiness as he said: "Oh, I don't know."

"Well, you ought to know," said he who was called Billie. "You ought to know. You made an egregious snark of yourself. Indeed, you sometimes resembled a boojum. Anyhow, you were a plain chump. You exploded your face about something of which you knew nothing, and I'm damned if I believe you'd make even a good retriever."

"You're a half-bred water-spaniel," blurted Peter Tounley. "And," he added, musingly, "that is a pretty low animal."

Coke was argumentative. "Why am I?" he asked, turning his head from side to side. "I don't see where I was so wrong."

"Oh, dances, balloons, picnics, parades and ascensions," they retorted, profanely. "You swam voluntarily into water that was too deep for you. Swim out. Get dry. Here's a towel."

Coke, smitten in the face with a wet cloth rolled into a ball, grabbed it and flung it futilely at a well-dodging companion "No," he cried, "I don't see it. Now look here. I don't see why we shouldn't all resent this Nora Black business."

One student said: "Well, what's the matter with Nora B lack, anyhow?"

Another student said "I don't see how you've been issued any license to say things about Nora Black."

Another student said dubiously: "Well, he knows her well."

And then three or four spoke at once. "He was very badly rattled when she appeared upon the scene."

Peter Tounley asked: "Well, which of you people know anything wrong about Nora Black?"

There was a pause, and then Coke said: "Oh, of course—I don't know—but—"

He who was called Billie then addressed his companions. "It wouldn't be right to repeat any old lie about Nora Black, and by the same token it wouldn't be right to see old Mother Wainwright chummin' with her. There is no wisdom in going further than that. Old Mother Wainwright don't know that her fair companion of yesterday is the famous comic opera star. For my part, I believe that Coleman is simply afraid to tell her. I don't think he wished to see Nora Black yesterday any more than he wished to see the devil. The discussion, as I understand it concerned itself only with what Coleman had to do with the thing, and yesterday anybody could see that he was in a panic."

They heard a step on the stair, and directly Coleman entered, followed by his dragoman. They were laden with the raw material for breakfast. The correspondent looked keenly among the students, for it was plain that they had been talking of him. It, filled him with rage, and for a stifling moment he could not think why he failed to immediately decamp in chagrin and leave eleven orphans to whatever fate their general incompetence might lead them. It struck him as a deep shame that even then he and his paid man were carrying in the breakfast. He wanted to fling it all on the floor and walk out. Then he remembered Marjory. She was the reason. She was the reason for everything.

But he could not repress certain, of his thoughts. "Say, you people," he said, icily, "you had better soon learn to hustle for yourselves. I may be a dragoman, and a butler, and a cook, and a housemaid, but I'm blowed if I'm a wet nurse." In reality, he had taken the most generous pleasure in working for the others before their eyes had even been opened from sleep, but it was now all turned to wormwood. It is certain that even this could not have deviated this executive man from labor and management because these were his life. But he felt that he was about to walk out of the room, consigning them all to Hades. His glance of angry, reproach fastened itself mainly upon Peter Tounley, because he knew that of all, Peter was the most innocent.

Peter, Tounley was abashed by this glance. So you've brought us something to eat, old man. That is tremendously nice of you—we—appreciate it like everything."

Coleman was mollified by Peter's tone. Peter had had that emotion which is equivalent to a sense of guilt, although in reality he was speckless. Two or three of the other students bobbed up to a sense of the situation. They ran to Coleman, and with polite cries took his provisions from him. One dropped a bunch of lettuce on the floor, and others reproached him with scholastic curses. Coke was seated near the window, half militant, half conciliatory. It was impossible for him to keep up a manner of deadly enmity while Coleman was bringing in his breakfast. He would have much preferred that Coleman had not brought in his breakfast. He would have much preferred to have foregone breakfast altogether. He would have much preferred anything. There seemed to be a conspiracy of circumstance to put him in the wrong and make him appear as a ridiculous young peasant. He was the victim of a benefaction, and he hated Coleman harder now than at any previous time. He saw that if he stalked out and took his breakfast alone in a cafe, the others would consider him still more of an outsider. Coleman had expressed himself like a man of the world and a gentleman, and Coke was convinced that he was a superior man of the world and a superior gentleman, but that he simply had not had words to express his position at the proper time. Coleman was glib. Therefore, Coke had been the victim of an attitude as well as of a benefaction. And so he deeply hated Coleman.

The others were talking cheerfully. "What the deuce are these, Coleman? Sausages? Oh, my. And look at these burlesque fishes. Say, these Greeks don't care what they eat. Them thar things am sardines in the crude state. No? Great God, look at those things. Look. What? Yes, they are. Radishes. Greek synonym for radishes."

The professor entered. "Oh," he said apologetically, as if he were intruding in a boudoir. All his serious desire to probe Coleman to the bottom ended in embarrassment. Mayhap it was not a law of feeling, but it happened at any rate. "He had come in a puzzled frame of mind, even an accusative frame of mind, and almost immediately he found himself suffering like a culprit before his judge. It is a phenomenon of what we call guilt and innocence.

"Coleman welcomed him cordially. "Well, professor, good-morning. I've rounded up some things that at least may be eaten."

"You are very good "very considerate, Mr. Coleman," answered the professor, hastily. "I am sure we are much indebted to you." He had scanned the correspondent's face, land it had been so devoid of guile that he was fearful that his suspicion, a base suspicion, of this noble soul would be detected. "No, no, we can never thank you enough."

Some of the students began to caper with a sort of decorous hilarity before their teacher. "Look at the sausage, professor. Did you ever see such sausage "Isn't it salubrious "And see these other things, sir. Aren't they curious "I shouldn't wonder if they were alive. Turnips, sir? No, sir. I think they are Pharisees. I have seen a Pharisee look like a pelican, but I have never seen a Pharisee look like a turnip, so I think these turnips must be Pharisees, sir, Yes, they may be walrus. We're not sure. Anyhow, their angles are geometrically all wrong. Peter, look out." Some green stuff was flung across the room. The professor laughed; Coleman laughed. Despite Coke, dark-browed, sulking, and yet desirous of reinstating himself, the room had waxed warm with the old college feeling, the feeling of lads who seemed never to treat anything respectfully and yet at the same time managed to treat the real things with respect. The professor himself contributed to their wild carouse over the strange Greek viands. It was a vivacious moment common to this class in times of relaxation, and it was understood perfectly.

Coke arose. "I don't see that I have any friends here," he said, hoarsely, "and in consequence I don't see why I should remain here."

All looked at him. At the same moment Mrs. Wainwright and Marjory entered the room.

## CHAPTER XIX.

"Good-morning," said Mrs. Wainwright jovially to the students and then she stared at Coleman as if he were a sweep at a wedding.

"Good-morning," said Marjory.

Coleman and the students made reply. "Good-morning. Good-morning. Good-morning. Good-morning—"

It was curious to see this greeting, this common phrase, this bit of old ware, this antique, come upon a dramatic scene and pulverize it. Nothing remained but a ridiculous dust. Coke, glowering, with his lips still trembling from heroic speech, was an angry clown, a pantaloon in rage. Nothing was to be done to keep him from looking like an ass. He, strode toward the door mumbling about a walk before breakfast.

Mrs. Wainwright beamed upon him. "Why, Mr. Coke, not before breakfast? You surely won't have time." It was grim punishment. He appeared to go blind, and he fairly staggered out of the door mumbling again, mumbling thanks or apologies or explanations. About the mouth of Coleman played a sinister smile. The professor cast upon his wife a glance expressing weariness. It was as if he said "There you go again. You can't keep your foot out of it." She understood the glance, and so she asked blankly: "Why, What's the matter? Oh." Her belated mind grasped that it was an aftermath of the quarrel of Coleman and Coke. Marjory looked as if she was distressed in the belief that her mother had been stupid. Coleman was outwardly serene. It was Peter Tounley who finally laughed a cheery, healthy laugh and they all looked at him with gratitude as if his sudden mirth had been a real statement or reconciliation and consequent peace.

The dragoman and others disported themselves until a breakfast was laid upon the floor. The adventurers squatted upon the floor. They made a large company. The professor and Coleman discussed the means of getting to Athens. Peter Tounley sat next to Marjory. "Peter," she said, privately, "what was all this trouble between Coleman and Coke?"

Peter answered blandly: "Oh, nothing at Nothing at all."

"Well, but—" she persisted, "what was the cause of it?"

He looked at her quaintly. He was not one of those in love with her, but be was interested in the affair. "Don't you know?" he asked.

She understood from his manner that she had been some kind of an issue in the quarrel. "No," she answered, hastily. "I don't."

"Oh, I don't mean that," said Peter. "I only meant—I only meant—oh, well, it was nothing—really."

"It must have been about something," continued Marjory. She continued, because Peter had denied that she was concerned in it. "Whose fault?"

"I really don't know. It was all rather confusing," lied Peter, tranquilly.

Coleman and the professor decided to accept a plan of the correspondent's dragoman to start soon on the first stage of the journey to Athens. The dragoman had said that he had found two large carriages rentable.

Coke, the outcast, walked alone in the narrow streets. The flight of the crown prince's army from Larissa had just been announced in Arta, but Coke was probably the most woebegone object on the Greek peninsula.

He encountered a strange sight on the streets. A woman garbed in the style for walking of an afternoon on upper Broadway was approaching him through a mass of kilted mountaineers and soldiers in soiled overcoats. Of course he recognized Nora Black.

In his conviction that everybody in the world was at this time considering him a mere worm, he was sure that she would not heed him. Beyond that he had been presented to her notice in but a transient and cursory fashion. But contrary to his conviction, she turned a radiant smile upon him. "Oh," she said, brusquely, "you are one of the students. Good morning." In her manner was all the confidence of an old warrior, a veteran, who addresses the universe with assurance because of his past battles.

Coke grinned at this strange greeting. "Yes, Miss Black," he answered, "I am one of the students."

She did not seem to quite know how to formulate her next speech. "Er—I suppose you're going to Athens at once "You must be glad after your horrid experiences."

"I believe they are going to start for Athens today," said Coke.

Nora was all attention. "'They?'" she repeated. "Aren't you going with them?"

"Well," he said, "Well—"

She saw of course that there had been some kind of trouble. She laughed. "You look as if somebody had kicked you down stairs," she said, candidly. She at once assumed an intimate manner toward him which was like a temporary motherhood. "Come, walk with me and tell me all about it." There was in her tone a most artistic suggestion that whatever had happened she was on his side. He was not loath. The street was full of soldiers whose tongues clattered so loudly that the two foreigners might have been wandering in a great cave of the winds. "Well, what was the row about?" asked Nora. "And who was in it?"

It would have been no solace to Coke to pour out his tale even if it had been a story that he could have told Nora. He was not stopped by the fact that he had gotten himself in the quarrel because he had insulted the name of the girt at his side. He did not think of it at that time. The whole thing was now extremely vague in outline to him and he only had a dull feeling of misery and loneliness. He wanted her to cheer him.

Nora laughed again. "Why, you're a regular little kid. Do you mean to say you've come out here sulking alone because of some nursery quarrel?" He was ruffled by her manner. It did not contain the cheering he required. "Oh, I don't know that I'm such a regular little kid," he said, sullenly. "The quarrel was not a nursery quarrel."

"Why don't you challenge him to a duel?" asked Nora, suddenly. She was watching him closely.

"Who?" said Coke.

"Coleman, you stupid," answered Nora.

They stared at each other, Coke paying her first the tribute of astonishment and then the tribute of admiration. "Why, how did you guess that?" he demanded.

"Oh," said Nora, "I've known Rufus Coleman for years, and he is always rowing with people."

"That is just it," cried Coke eagerly. "That is just it. I fairly hate the man. Almost all of the other fellows will stand his abuse, but it riles me, I tell you. I think he is a beast. And, of course, if you seriously meant what you said about challenging him to a duel—I mean if there is any sense in that sort of thing—I would challenge Coleman. I swear I would. I think he's a great bluffer, anyhow. Shouldn't wonder if he would back out. Really, I shouldn't.

Nora smiled humorously at a house on her side of the narrow way. "I wouldn't wonder if he did either," she answered. After a time she said "Well, do you mean to say that you have definitely shaken them? Aren't you going back to Athens with them or anything?"

"I—I don't see how I can," he said, morosely.

"Oh," she said. She reflected for a time. At last she turned to him archly and asked: "Some words over a lady?"

Coke looked at her blankly. He suddenly remembered the horrible facts. "No—no—not over a lady."

"My dear boy, you are a liar," said Nora, freely. "You are a little unskillful liar. It was some words over a lady, and the lady's name is Marjory Wainwright."

Coke felt as though he had suddenly been let out of a cell, but he continued a mechanical denial. "No, no— It wasn't truly…upon my word…."

"Nonsense," said Nora. "I know better. Don't you think you can fool me, you little cub. I know you're in love with Marjory Wainwright, and you think Coleman is your rival. What a blockhead you are. Can't you understand that people see these things?"

"Well—" stammered Coke.

"Nonsense," said Nora again. "Don't try to fool me, you may as well understand that it's useless. I am too wise."

"Well—" stammered Coke.

"Go ahead," urged Nora. "Tell me about it. Have it out."

He began with great importance and solemnity. "Now, to tell you the truth…that is why I hate him… I hate him like anything…. I can't see why everybody admires him so. I don't see anything to him myself. I don't believe he's got any more principle than a wolf. I wouldn't trust him with two dollars. Why, I know stories about him that would make your hair curl. When I think of a girl like Marjory—"

His speech had become a torrent. But here Nora raised her hand. "Oh! Oh! Oh! That will do. That will do. Don't lose your senses. I don't see why this girl Marjory is any too good. She is no chicken, I'll bet. Don't let yourself get fooled with that sort of thing."

Coke was unaware of his incautious expressions. He floundered on while Nora looked at him as if she wanted to wring his neck. "No—she's too fine and too good—for him or anybody like him—she's too fine and too good—"

"Aw, rats," interrupted Nora, furiously. "You make me tired."

Coke had a wooden-headed conviction that he must make Nora understand Marjory's infinite superiority to all others of her sex, and so he passed into a pariegyric, each word of which was a hot coal to the girl addressed. Nothing would stop him, apparently. He even made the most stupid repetitions. Nora finally stamped her foot formidably. "Will you stop? Will you stop?" she said through her clenched teeth. "Do you think I want to listen to your everlasting twaddle about her? Why, she's—she's no better than other people, you ignorant little mamma's boy. She's no better than other people, you swab!"

Coke looked at her with the eyes of a fish. He did not understand. "But she is better than other people," he persisted.

Nora seemed to decide suddenly that there would be no accomplishment in flying desperately against this rock-walled conviction. "Oh, well," she said, with marvelous good nature, "perhaps you are right, numbskull. But, look here; do you think she cares for him?"

In his heart, his jealous heart, he believed that Marjory loved Coleman, but he reiterated eternally to himself that it was not true. As for speaking it to, another, that was out of the question. "No," he said, stoutly, "she doesn't care a snap for him." If he had admitted it, it would have seemed to him that he was somehow advancing Coleman's chances.

"Oh, she doesn't, eh?" said Nora enigmatically.

"She doesn't?" He studied her face with an abrupt, miserable suspicion, but he repeated doggedly: "No, she doesn't."

"Ahem," replied Nora. "Why, she's set her cap for him all right. She's after him for certain. It's as plain as day. Can't you see that, stupidity?"

"No," he said hoarsely.

"You are a fool," said Nora. "It isn't Coleman that's after her. It is she that is after Coleman."

Coke was mulish. "No such thing. Coleman's crazy about her. Everybody has known it ever since he was in college. You ask any of the other fellows."

Nora was now very serious, almost doleful. She remained still for a time, casting at Coke little glances of hatred. "I don't see my way clear to ask any of the other fellows," she said at last, with considerable bitterness. "I'm not in the habit of conducting such enquiries."

Coke felt now that he disliked her, and he read plainly her dislike of him. If they were the two villains of the play, they were not having fun together at all. Each had some kind of a deep knowledge that their aspirations, far from colliding, were of such character that the success of one would mean at least assistance to the other, but neither could see how to confess it. Perhaps it was from shame, perhaps it was because Nora thought Coke to have little wit; perhaps it was because Coke thought Nora to have little conscience. Their talk was mainly rudderless. From time to time Nora had an inspiration to come boldly at the point, but this inspiration was commonly defeated by, some extraordinary manifestation of Coke's incapacity. To her mind, then, it seemed like a proposition to ally herself to a butcher-boy in a matter purely sentimental. She Wondered indignantly how she was going to conspire With

this lad, who puffed out his infantile cheeks in order to conceitedly demonstrate that
he did not understand the game at all. She hated Marjory for it. Evidently it was only
the weaklings who fell in love with that girl. Coleman was an exception, but then,
Coleman was misled, by extraordinary artifices. She meditated for a moment if she
should tell Coke to go home and not bother her. What at last decided the question
was his unhappiness. She clung to this unhappiness for its value as it stood alone,
and because its reason for existence was related to her own unhappiness.

"You say you are not going back to Athens with your party. I don't suppose
you're going to stay here. I'm going back to Athens today. I came up here to see a
battle, but it doesn't seem that there are to be any more battles. The fighting will now
all be on the other side of the mountains."

Apparent she had learned in some haphazard way that the Greek peninsula was
divided by a spine of almost inaccessible mountains, and the war was thus split into
two simultaneous campaigns. The Arta campaign was known to be ended.

"If you want to go back to Athens without consorting with your friends, you had
better go back with me. I can take you in my carriage as far as the beginning of the
railroad. Don't you worry. You've got money enough, haven't you? The professor
isn't keeping your money?"

"Yes," he said slowly, "I've got money enough."

He was apparently dubious over the proposal. In their abstracted walk they had
arrived in front of the house occupied by Coleman and the Wainwright party. Two
carriages, forlorn in dusty age, stood before the door. Men were carrying out new
leather luggage and flinging it into the traps amid a great deal of talk which seemed
to refer to nothing. Nora and Coke stood looking at the scene without either thinking of the importance of running away, when out tumbled seven students, followed
immediately but in more decorous fashion by the Wainwrights and Coleman.

Some student set up a whoop. "Oh, there he is. There's Coke. Hey, Coke, where
you been? Here he is, professor."

For a moment after the bedlam had subsided, the two camps stared at each other
in silence.

## CHAPTER XX.

Nora and Coke were an odd looking pair at the time. They stood indeed as if
rooted to the spot, staring vacuously, like two villagers, at the surprising travelers.
It was not an eternity before the practiced girl of the stage recovered her poise,
but to the end of the incident the green youth looked like a culprit and a fool. Mrs.
Wainwright's glower of offensive incredulity was a masterpiece. Marjory nodded
pleasantly; the professor nodded. The seven students clambered boisterously into
the forward carriage making it clang with noise like a rook's nest. They shouted to
Coke. "Come on; all aboard; come on, Coke; we're off. Hey, there, Cokey, hurry
up." The professor, as soon as he had seated himself on the forward seat of' the
second carriage, turned in Coke's general direction and asked formally: "Mr. Coke,
you are coming with us?" He felt seemingly much in doubt as to the propriety of
abandoning the headstrong young man, and this doubt was not at all decreased by
Coke's appearance with Nora Black. As far as he could tell, any assertion of authority on his part would end only in a scene in which Coke would probably insult him
with some gross violation of collegiate conduct. As at first the young man made no
reply, the professor after waiting spoke again. "You understand, Mr. Coke, that if
you separate yourself from the party you encounter my strongest disapproval, and
if I did not feel responsible to the college and your father for your safe journey to

New York I—I don't know but what I would have you expelled by cable if that were possible."

Although Coke had been silent, and Nora Black had had the appearance of being silent, in reality she had lowered her chin and whispered sideways and swiftly. She had said: "Now, here's your time. Decide quickly, and don't look such a wooden Indian." Coke pulled himself together with a visible effort, and spoke to the professor from an inspiration in which he had no faith. "I understand my duties to you, sir, perfectly. I also understand my duty to the college. But I fail to see where either of these obligations require me to accept the introduction of objectionable people into the party. If I owe a duty to the college and to you, I don't owe any to Coleman, and, as I understand it, Coleman was not in the original plan of this expedition. If such had been the case, I would not have been here. I can't tell what the college may see fit to do, but as for my father— I have no doubt of how he will view it."

The first one to be electrified by the speech was Coke himself. He saw with a kind of subconscious amazement this volley of bird-shot take effect upon the face of the old professor. The face of Marjory flushed crimson as if her mind had sprung to a fear that if Coke could develop ability in this singular fashion he might succeed in humiliating her father in the street in the presence of the seven students, her mother, Coleman and—herself. She had felt the birdshot sting her father.

When Coke had launched forth, Coleman with his legs stretched far apart had just struck a match on the wall of the house and was about to light a cigar. His groom was leading up his horse. He saw the value of Coke's argument more appreciatively and sooner perhaps than did Coke. The match dropped from his fingers, and in the white sunshine and still air it burnt on the pavement orange colored and with languor. Coleman held his cigar with all five fingers—in a manner out of all the laws of smoking. He turned toward Coke. There was danger in the moment, but then in a flash it came upon him that his role was not of squabbling with Coke, far less of punching him. On the contrary, he was to act the part of a cool and instructed man who refused to be waylaid into foolishness by the outcries of this pouting youngster and who placed himself in complete deference to the wishes of the professor. Before the professor had time to embark upon any reply to Coke, Coleman was at the side of the carriage and, with a fine assumption of distress, was saying: "Professor, I could very easily ride back to Agrinion alone. It would be all right. I don't want to—"

To his surprise the professor waved at him to be silent as if he were a mere child. The old man's face was set with the resolution of exactly what he was going to say to Coke. He began in measured tone, speaking with feeling, but with no trace of anger.

"Mr. Coke, it has probably escaped your attention that Mr. Coleman, at what I consider a great deal of peril to himself, came out to rescue this party—you and others—and although he studiously disclaims all merit in his finding us and bringing us in, I do not regard it in that way, and I am surprised that any member of this party should conduct himself in this manner toward a man who has been most devotedly and generously at our service." It was at this time that the professor raised himself and shook his finger at Coke, his voice now ringing with scorn. In such moments words came to him and formed themselves into sentences almost too rapidly for him to speak them. "You are one of the most remarkable products of our civilization which I have yet come upon. What do you mean, sir? Where are your senses? Do you think that all this pulling and pucking is manhood? I will tell you what I will do with you. I thought I brought out eight students to Greece, but when I find that I brought out, seven students and—er—an—ourang-outang—don't get angry, sir—I don't care for your anger—I say when I discover this I am naturally puzzled for a moment. I will leave you to the judgment of your peers. Young gentlemen!"

Of the seven heads of the forward carriage none had to be turned. All had been turned since the beginning of the talk. If the professor's speech had been delivered in one of the class-rooms of Washurst they would have glowed with delight over the butchery of Coke, but they felt its portentous aspect. Butchery here in Greece thousands of miles from home presented to them more of the emphasis of downright death and destruction.

The professor called out, "Young gentlemen, I have done all that I can do without using force, which, much to my regret, is impracticable. If you will persuade your fellow student to accompany you I think our consciences will be the better for not having left a weak minded brother alone among the bypaths." The valuable aggregation of intelligence and refinement which decorated the interior of the first carriage did not hesitate over answering this appeal. In fact, his fellow students had worried among themselves over Coke, and their desire to see him come out of his troubles in fair condition was intensified by the fact that they had lately concentrated much thought upon him. There was a somewhat comic pretense of speaking so that only Coke could hear. Their chorus was law sung. "Oh, cheese it, Coke. Let up on yourself, you blind ass. Wait till you get to Athens and then go and act like a monkey. All this is no good—"

The advice which came from the carriage was all in one direction, and there was so much of it that the hum of voices sounded like a wind blowing through a forest.

Coke spun suddenly and said something to Nora Black. Nora laughed rather loudly, and then the two turned squarely and the Wainwright party contemplated what were surely at that time the two most insolent backs in the world.

The professor looked as if he might be going to have a fit. Mrs. Wainwright lifted her eyes toward heaven, and flinging out her trembling hands, cried: "Oh, what an outrage. What an outrage! That minx—" The consensus of opinion in the first carriage was perfectly expressed by Peter Tounley, who with a deep drawn breath, said: "Well, I'm damned!" Marjory had moaned and lowered her head as from a sense of complete personal shame. Coleman lit his cigar and mounted his horse. "Well, I suppose there is nothing for it but to be off, professor?" His tone was full of regret, with sort of poetic regret. For a moment the professor looked at him blankly, and then gradually recovered part of his usual manner. "Yes," he said sadly, "there is nothing for it but to go on." At a word from the dragoman, the two impatient drivers spoke gutturally to their horses and the carriages whirled out of Arta. Coleman, his dragoman and the groom trotted in the dust from the wheels of the Wainwright carriage. The correspondent always found his reflective faculties improved by the constant pounding of a horse on the trot, and he was not sorry to have now a period for reflection, as well as this artificial stimulant. As he viewed the game he had in his hand about all the cards that were valuable. In fact, he considered that the only ace against him was Mrs. Wainwright. He had always regarded her as a stupid person, concealing herself behind a mass of trivialities which were all conventional, but he thought now that the more stupid she was and the more conventional in her triviality the more she approached to being the very ace of trumps itself. She was just the sort of a card that would come upon the table mid the neat play of experts and by some inexplicable arrangement of circumstance, lose a whole game for the wrong man. After Mrs. Wainwright he worried over the students. He believed them to be reasonable enough; in fact, he honored them distinctly in regard to their powers of reason, but he knew that people generally hated a row. It, put them off their balance, made them sweat over a lot of pros and cons, and prevented them from thinking for a time at least only of themselves. Then they came to resent the principals in a row. Of course the principal, who was thought to be in the wrong, was the most resented, but Coleman believed that, after all, people always came to resent the other principal, or at least be impatient and suspicious of him. If he was a correct person, why was he in a row at all? The principal who had been in the right often brought this impatience and suspicion upon himself, no doubt, by never letting the matter end, continuing to yawp about his virtuous suffering, and not allowing people to return to the steady contemplation of their own affairs. As a precautionary measure he decided to say nothing at all about the late trouble, unless some one addressed him upon it. Even then he would be serenely laconic. He felt that he must be popular with the seven students. In the first place, it was nice that in the presence of Marjory they should like him, and in the second place he feared to displease them as a body because he believed that he had some dignity. Hoodlums are seldom dangerous to other hoodlums, but if they catch pomposity alone in the field, pomposity is their prey. They tear him to mere bloody ribbons, amid heartless shrieks. When Coleman put himself on the same basis with the students, he could cope with them easily, but he did not want the wild pack after him when Marjory could see the chase. And so be reasoned that his best attitude was to be one of rather taciturn serenity.

On the hard military road the hoofs of the horses made such clatter that it was practically impossible to hold talk between the carriages and the horsemen without all parties bellowing. The professor, however, strove to overcome the difficulties. He was apparently undergoing a great amiability toward Coleman. Frequently he turned with a bright face, and pointing to some object in the landscape, obviously tried to convey something entertaining to Coleman's mind. Coleman could see his lips mouth the words. He always nodded cheerily in answer and yelled.

The road ultimately became that straight lance-handle which Coleman—it seemed as if many years had passed—had traversed with his dragoman and the funny little carriers. He was fixing in his mind a possible story to the Wainwrights about the snake and his first dead Turk. But suddenly the carriages left this road and began a circuit of the Gulf of Arta, winding about an endless series of promontories. The journey developed into an excess of dust whirling from a road, which half circled the waist of cape after cape. All dramatics were lost in the rumble of wheels and in the click of hoofs. They passed a little soldier leading a prisoner by a string. They passed more frightened peasants, who seemed resolved to flee down into the very boots of Greece. And people looked at them with scowls, envying them their speed. At the little town from which Coleman embarked at one stage of the upward journey, they found crowds in the streets. There was no longer any laughter, any confidence, any vim. All the spirit of the visible Greek nation seemed to have been knocked out of it in two blows. But still they talked and never ceased talking. Coleman noticed that the most curious changes had come upon them since his journey to the frontier. They no longer approved of foreigners. They seemed to blame the travelers for something which had transpired in the past few days. It was not that they really blamed the travelers for the nation's calamity: It was simply that their minds were half stunned by the news of defeats, and, not thinking for a moment to blame themselves, or even not thinking to attribute the defeats to mere numbers and skill, they were savagely eager to fasten it upon something near enough at hand for the operation of vengeance.

Coleman perceived that the dragoman, all his former plumage gone, was whining and sniveling as he argued to a dark-browed crowd that was running beside the cavalcade. The groom, who always had been a miraculously laconic man, was suddenly launched forth garrulously. The, drivers, from their high seats, palavered like mad men, driving with oat hand and gesturing with the other, explaining evidently their own great innocence.

Coleman saw that there was trouble, but he only sat more stiffly in his saddle. The eternal gabble moved him to despise the situation. At any rate, the travelers would soon be out of this town and on to a more sensible region.

However he saw the driver of the first carriage suddenly pull up before a little blackened coffee shop and inn. The dragoman spurred forward and began wild expostulation. The second carriage pulled close behind the other. The crowd, murmuring like a Roman mob in Nero's time, closed around them.

.

## CHAPTER XXI.

COLEMAN pushed his horse coolly through to the dragoman's side.

"What is it?" he demanded. The dragoman was broken-voiced. "These peoples, they say you are Germans, all Germans, and they are angry," he wailed. "I can do nossing—nossing."

"Well, tell these men to drive on," said Coleman, "tell them they must drive on."

"They will not drive on," wailed the dragoman, still more loudly. "I can do nossing. They say here is place for feed the horse. It is the custom and they will note drive on."

"Make them drive on."

"They will note," shrieked the agonized servitor. Coleman looked from the men waving their arms and chattering on the box-seats to the men of the crowd who also waved their arms and chattered. In this throng far to the rear of the fighting armies there did not seem to be a single man who was not able-bodied, who had not been free to enlist as a soldier. They were of that scurvy behind-the-rear-guard which every nation has in degree proportionate to its worth. The manhood of Greece had gone to the frontier, leaving at home this rabble of talkers, most of whom were armed with rifles for mere pretention. Coleman loathed them to the end of his soul. He thought them a lot of infants who would like to prove their courage upon eleven innocent travelers, all but unarmed, and in this fact he was quick to see a great danger to the Wainwright party. One could deal with soldiers; soldiers would have been ashamed to bait helpless people; but this rabble—

The fighting blood of the correspondent began to boil, and he really longed for the privilege to run amuck through the multitude. But a look at the Wainwrights kept him in his senses. The professor had turned pale as a dead man. He sat very stiff and still while his wife clung to him, hysterically beseeching him to do something, do something, although what he was to do she could not have even imagined.

Coleman took the dilemma by its beard. He dismounted from his horse into the depths of the crowd and addressed the Wainwrights. "I suppose we had better go into this place and have some coffee while the men feed their horses. There is no use in trying to make them go on." His manner was fairly casual, but they looked at him in glazed horror. "It is the only thing to do. This crowd is not nearly so bad as they think they are. But we've got to look as if we felt confident." He himself had no confidence with this angry buzz in his ears, but be felt certain that the only correct move was to get everybody as quickly as possible within the shelter of the inn. It might not be much of a shelter for them, but it was better than the carriages in the street.

The professor and Mrs. Wainwright seemed to be considering their carriage as a castle, and they looked as if their terror had made them physically incapable of leaving it. Coleman stood waiting. Behind him the clapper-tongued crowd was moving ominously. Marjory arose and stepped calmly down to him. He thrilled to the end of every nerve. It was as if she had said: "I don't think there is great danger, but if there is great danger, why…here I am—ready—with you." It conceded everything, admitted everything. It was a surrender without a blush, and it was only possible in the shadow of the crisis when they did not know what the next moments might contain for them. As he took her hand and she stepped past him he whispered swiftly and fiercely in her ear, "I love you." She did not look up, but he felt that in this quick incident they had claimed each other, accepted each other with a far deeper meaning and understanding than could be possible in a mere drawing-room. She laid her hand on his arm, and with the strength of four men he twisted his horse into the making of furious prancing sidesteps toward the door of the inn, clanking sidesteps which mowed a wide lane through the crowd for Marjory, his Marjory. He was as haughty as a new German lieutenant, and although he held the fuming horse with only his left hand, he seemed perfectly capable of hurling the animal over a house without calling into service the arm which was devoted to Marjory.

It was not an exhibition of coolness such as wins applause on the stage when the hero placidly lights a cigarette before the mob which is clamoring for his death. It was, on the contrary, an exhibition of downright classic disdain, a disdain which with the highest arrogance declared itself in every glance of his eye into the faces about him. "Very good…attack me if you like— there is nothing to prevent it—you mongrels." Every step of his progress was made a renewed insult to them. The very air was charged with what this lone man was thinking of this threatening crowd.

His audacity was invincible. They actually made way for it as quickly as children would flee from a ghost. The horse, dancing; with ringing steps, with his glistening neck arched toward the iron hand at his bit, this powerful, quivering animal was a regular engine of destruction, and they gave room until Coleman halted him at an exclamation from Marjory.

"My mother and father." But they were coming close behind and Coleman resumed this contemptuous journey to the door of the inn. The groom, with his newborn tongue, was clattering there to the populace. Coleman gave him the horse and passed after the Wainwrights into the public room of the inn. He was smiling. What simpletons!

A new actor suddenly appeared in the person of the keeper of the inn. He too had a rifle and a prodigious belt of cartridges, but it was plain at once that he had elected to be a friend of the worried travelers. A large part of the crowd were thinking it necessary to enter the inn and pow-wow more. But the innkeeper stayed at the door with the dragoman, and together they vociferously held back the tide. The spirit of the mob had subsided to a more reasonable feeling. They no longer wished to tear the strangers limb from limb on the suspicion that they were Germans. They now were frantic to talk as if some inexorable law had kept them silent for ten years and this was the very moment of their release. Whereas, their simultaneous and interpolating orations had throughout made noise much like a coal-breaker. Coleman led the Wainwrights to a table in a far part of the room. They took chairs as if he had commanded them. "What an outrage," he said jubilantly. "The apes." He was keeping more than half an eye upon the door, because he knew that the quick coming of the students was important.

Then suddenly the storm broke in wrath. Something had happened in the street. The jabbering crowd at the door had turned and were hurrying upon some central tumult. The dragoman screamed to Coleman. Coleman jumped and grabbed the dragoman. "Tell this man to take them somewhere up stairs," he cried, indicating the Wainwrights with a sweep of his arm. The innkeeper seemed to understand sooner than the dragoman, and he nodded eagerly. The professor was crying: "What is it, Mr. Coleman? What is it?"

An instant later, the correspondent was out in the street, buffeting toward a scuffle. Of course it was the students. It appeared, afterward, that those seven young men, with their feelings much ruffled, had been making the best of their way toward the door of the inn, when a large man in the crowd, during a speech which was surely most offensive, had laid an arresting hand on the shoulder of Peter Tounley. Whereupon the excellent Peter Tounley had hit the large man on the jaw in such a swift and skilful manner that the large man had gone spinning through a group of his countrymen to the hard earth, where he lay holding his face together and howling. Instantly, of course, there had been a riot. It might well be said that even then the affair could have ended in a lot of talking, but in the first place the students did not talk modern Greek, and in the second place they were now past all thought of talking. They regarded this affair seriously as a fight, and now that they at last were in it, they were in it for every pint of blood in their bodies. Such a pack of famished wolves had never before been let loose upon men armed with Gras rifles.

They all had been expecting the row, and when Peter Tounley had found it expedient to knock over the man, they had counted it a signal: their arms immediately begun to swing out as if they had been wound up. It was at this time that Coleman swam brutally through the Greeks and joined his countrymen. He was more frightened than any of those novices. When he saw Peter Tounley overthrow a dreadful looking brigand whose belt was full of knives, and who crashed to the ground amid a clang of cartridges, he was appalled by the utter simplicity with which the lads were treating the crisis. It was to them no common scrimmage at Washurst, of course, but it flashed through Coleman's mind that they had not the slightest sense of the size of the thing. He expected every instant to see the flash of knives or to hear the deafening intonation of a rifle fired against his ear. It seemed to him miraculous that the tragedy was so long delayed.

In the meantime he was in the affray. He jilted one man under the chin with his elbow in a way that reeled him off from Peter Tounley's back; a little person in checked clothes he smote between the eyes; he received a gun-butt emphatically on the side of the neck; he felt hands tearing at him; he kicked the pins out from under three men in rapid succession. He was always yelling. "Try to get to the inn, boys, try to get to the inn. Look out, Peter. Take care for his knife, Peter—" Suddenly he whipped a rifle out of the hands of a man and swung it, whistling. He had gone stark mad with the others.

The boy Billy, drunk from some blows and bleeding, was already staggering toward the inn over the clearage which the wild Coleman made with the clubbed rifle. The others followed as well as they might while beating off a discouraged enemy. The remarkable innkeeper had barred his windows with strong wood shutters.

He held the door by the crack for them, and they stumbled one by on through the portal. Coleman did not know why they were not all dead, nor did he understand the intrepid and generous behavior of the innkeeper, but at any rate he felt that the fighting was suspended, and he wanted to see Marjory. The innkeeper was, doing a great pantomime in the middle of the darkened room, pointing to the outer door and then aiming his rifle at it to explain his intention of defending them at all costs. Some of the students moved to a billiard table and spread themselves wearily upon it. Others sank down where they stood. Outside the crowd was beginning to roar. Coleman's groom crept out from under the little Coffee bar and comically saluted his master. The dragoman was not present. Coleman felt that he must see Marjory, and he made signs to the innkeeper. The latter understood quickly, and motioned that Coleman should follow him. They passed together through a dark hall and up a darker stairway, where after Coleman stepped out into a sunlit room, saying loudly: "Oh, it's all right. It's all over. Don't worry."

Three wild people were instantly upon him. "Oh, what was it? What did happen? Is anybody hurt? Oh, tell us, quick!" It seemed at the time that it was an avalanche of three of them, and it was not until later that he recognized that Mrs. Wainwright had tumbled the largest number of questions upon him. As for Marjory, she had said nothing until the time when she cried: "Oh—he is bleeding—he is bleeding. Oh, come, quick!" She fairly dragged him out of one room into another room, where there was a jug of water. She wet her handkerchief and softly smote his wounds. "Bruises," she said, piteously, tearfully. "Bruises. Oh, dear! How they must hurt you.' The handkerchief was soon stained crimson.

When Coleman spoke his voice quavered. "It isn't anything. Really, it isn't anything." He had not known of these wonderful wounds, but he almost choked in the joy of Marjory's ministry and her half coherent exclamations. This proud and beautiful girl, this superlative creature, was reddening her handkerchief with his blood, and no word of his could have prevented her from thus attending him. He could hear the professor and Mrs. Wainwright fussing near him, trying to be of use. He would have liked to have been able to order them out of the room. Marjory's cool fingers on his face and neck had conjured within him a vision at an intimacy that was even sweeter than anything which he had imagined, and he longed to pour out to her the bubbling, impassioned speech which came to his lips. But, always doddering behind him, were the two old people, strenuous to be of help to him.

Suddenly a door opened and a youth appeared, simply red with blood. It was Peter Tounley. His first remark was cheerful. "Well, I don't suppose those people will be any too quick to look for more trouble."

Coleman felt a swift pang because he had forgotten to announce the dilapidated state of all the students. He had been so submerged by Marjory's tenderness that all else had been drowned from his mind. His heart beat quickly as he waited for Marjory to leave him and rush to Peter Tounley.

But she did nothing of the sort. "Oh, Peter," she cried in distress, and then she turned back to Coleman. It was the professor and Mrs. Wainwright who, at last finding a field for their kindly ambitions, flung themselves upon Tounley and carried him off to another place. Peter was removed, crying: "Oh, now, look

here, professor, I'm not dying or anything of the sort Coleman and Marjory were left alone. He suddenly and forcibly took one of her hands and the blood stained handkerchief dropped to the floor.

# CHAPTER XXII.

From below they could hear the thunder of weapons and fits upon the door of the inn amid a great clamor of tongues. Sometimes there arose the argumentative howl of the innkeeper. Above this roar, Coleman's quick words sounded in Marjory's ear.

"I've got to go. I've got to go back to the boys, but—I love you."

"Yes go, go," she whispered hastily. "You should be there, but—come back."

He held her close to him. "But you are mine, remember," he said fiercely and sternly. "You are mine—forever—As I am yours—remember."

Her eyes half closed. She made intensely solemn answer. "Yes."

He released her and was gone. In the glooming coffee room of the inn he found the students, the dragoman, the groom and the innkeeper armed with a motley collection of weapons which ranged from the rifle of the innkeeper to the table leg in the hands of Peter Tounley. The last named young student of archeology was in a position of temporary leadership and holding a great pow-wow with the innkeeper through the medium of piercing outcries by the dragoman. Coleman had not yet understood why none of them had been either stabbed or shot in the fight in the street, but it seemed to him now that affairs were leading toward a crisis of tragedy. He thought of the possibilities of having the dragoman go to an upper window and harangue the people, but he saw no chance of success in such a plan. He saw that the crowd would merely howl at the dragoman while the dragoman howled at the crowd. He then asked if there was any other exit from the inn by which they could secretly escape. He learned that the door into the coffee room was the only door which pierced the four great walls. All he could then do was to find out from the innkeeper how much of a siege the place could stand, and to this the innkeeper answered volubly and with smiles that this hostelry would easily endure until the mercurial temper of the crowd had darted off in a new direction. It may be curious to note here that all of Peter Tounley's impassioned communication with the innkeeper had been devoted to an endeavor to learn what in the devil was the matter with these people, as a man about to be bitten by poisonous snakes should, first of all, furiously insist upon learning their exact species before deciding upon either his route, if he intended to run away, or his weapon if he intended to fight them.

The innkeeper was evidently convinced that this house would withstand the rage of the populace, and he was such an unaccountably gallant little chap that Coleman trusted entirely to his word. His only fear or suspicion was an occasional one as to the purity of the dragoman's translation.

Suddenly there was half a silence on the mob without the door. It is inconceivable that it could become altogether silent, but it was as near to a rational stillness of tongues as it was able. Then there was a loud knocking by a single fist and a new voice began to spin Greek, a voice that was somewhat like the rattle of pebbles in a tin box. Then a startling voice called out in English. "Are you in there, Rufus?"

Answers came from every English speaking person in the room in one great outburst. "Yes."

"Well, let us in," called Nora Black. "It is all right. We've got an officer with us."

"Open the door," said Coleman with speed. The little innkeeper laboriously unfastened the great bars, and when the door finally opened there appeared on the threshold Nora Black with Coke and an officer of infantry, Nora's little old companion, and Nora's dragoman.

"We saw your carriage in the street," cried the queen of comic opera as she swept into the room. She was beaming with delight. "What is all the row, anyway?

O-o-oh, look at that student's nose. Who hit him? And look at Rufus. What have you boys been doing?"

Her little Greek officer of infantry had stopped the mob from flowing into the room. Coleman looked toward the door at times with some anxiety. Nora, noting it, waved her hand in careless reassurance; "Oh, it's, all right. Don't worry about them any more. He is perfectly devoted to me. He would die there on the threshold if I told him it would please me. Speaks splendid French. I found him limping along the road and gave him a lift. And now do hurry up and tell me exactly what happened." They all told what had happened, while Nora and Coke listened agape. Coke, by the way, had quite floated back to his old position with the students. It had been easy in the stress of excitement and wonder. Nobody had any time to think of the excessively remote incidents of the early morning. All minor interests were lost in the marvel of the present situation.

"Who landed you in the eye, Billie?" asked the awed Coke. "That was a bad one."

"Oh, I don't know," said Billie. "You really couldn't tell who hit you, you know. It was a football rush. They had guns and knives, but they didn't use 'em. I don't know why Jinks! I'm getting pretty stiff. My face feels as if it were made of tin. Did they give you people a row, too?"

"No; only talk. That little officer managed them. Out-talked them, I suppose. Hear him buzz, now." The Wainwrights came down stairs. Nora Black went confidently forward to meet them. "You've added one more to your list of rescuers," She cried, with her glowing, triumphant smile. "Miss Black of the New York Daylight—at your service. How in the world do you manage to get yourselves into such dreadful Scrapes? You are the most remarkable people. You need a guardian. Why, you might have all been killed. How exciting it must seem to be regularly of your party." She had shaken cordially one of Mrs. Wainwright's hands without that lady indicating assent to the proceeding but Mrs. Wainwright had not felt repulsion. In fact she had had no emotion springing directly from it. Here again the marvel of the situation came to deny Mrs. Wainwright the right to resume a state of mind which had been so painfully interesting to her a few hours earlier.

The professor, Coleman and all the students were talking together. Coke had addressed Coleman civilly and Coleman had made a civil reply. Peace was upon them.

Nora slipped her arm lovingly through Marjory's arm. "That Rufus! Oh, that Rufus," she cried joyously. "I'll give him a good scolding as soon as I see him alone. I might have foreseen that he would get you all into trouble. The old stupid!"

Marjory did not appear to resent anything.

"Oh, I don't think it was Mr. Coleman's fault at all," she answered calmly. "I think it was more the fault of Peter Tounley, poor boy."

"Well, I'd be glad to believe it, I'd be glad to believe it," said Nora. "I want Rufus to keep out of that sort of thing, but he is so hot-headed and foolish." If she had pointed out her proprietary stamp on Coleman's cheek she could not have conveyed what she wanted with more clearness.

"Oh," said the impassive Marjory, "I don't think you need have any doubt as to whose fault it was, if there were any of our boys at fault. Mr. Coleman was inside when the fighting commenced, and only ran out to help the boys. He had just brought us safely through the mob, and, far from being hot-headed and foolish, he was utterly cool in manner, impressively cool, I thought. I am glad to be able to reassure you on these points, for I see that they worry you."

"`.Yes, they do worry me," said Nora, densely. They worry me night and day when he is away from me."

"Oh," responded Marjory, "I have never thought of Mr. Coleman as a man that one would worry about much. We consider him very self-reliant, able to take care of himself under almost any conditions, but then, of course, we do not know him at all in the way that you know him. I should think that you would find that he came off rather better than you expected from most of his difficulties. But then, of course, as. I said, you know him so much better than we do." Her easy indifference was a tacit dismissal of Coleman as a topic.

Nora, now thoroughly alert, glanced keenly into the other girl's face, but it was inscrutable. The actress had intended to go careering through a whole circle of daring illusions to an intimacy with Coleman, but here, before she had really developed her attack, Marjory, with a few conventional and indifferent sentences, almost expressive of boredom, had made the subject of Coleman impossible. An effect was left upon Nora's mind that Marjory had been extremely polite in listening to much nervous talk about a person in whom she had no interest.

The actress was dazed. She did not know how it had all been done. Where was the head of this thing? And where Was the tail? A fog had mysteriously come upon all her brilliant prospects of seeing Marjory Wainwright suffer, and this fog was the product of a kind of magic with which she was not familiar. She could not think how to fight it. After being simply dubious throughout a long pause, she in the end went into a great rage. She glared furiously at Marjory, dropped her arm as if it had burned her and moved down upon Coleman. She must have reflected that at any rate she could make him wriggle. When she was come near to him, she called out: "Rufus!" In her tone was all the old insolent statement of ownership. Coleman might have been a poodle. She knew how to call his same in a way that was anything less than a public scandal. On this occasion everybody looked at him and then went silent, as people awaiting the startling denouement of a drama. "Rufus!" She was baring his shoulder to show the fleur-de-lis of the criminal. The students gaped.

Coleman's temper was, if one may be allowed to speak in that way, broken loose inside of him. He could hardly breathe; he felt that his body was about to explode into a thousand fragments. He simply snarled out "What?" Almost at once he saw that she had at last goaded him into making a serious tactical mistake. It must be admitted that it is only when the relations between a man and a woman are the relations of wedlock, or at least an intimate resemblance to it, that the man snarls out "What?" to the woman. Mere lovers say "I beg your pardon?" It is only Cupid's finished product that spits like a cat. Nora Black had called him like a wife, and he had answered like a husband. For his cause, his manner could not possibly have been worse. He saw the professor stare at him in surprise and alarm, and felt the excitement of the eight students. These latter were diabolic in the celerity with which they picked out meanings. It was as plain to them as if Nora Black had said: "He is my property."

Coleman would have given his nose to have been able to recall that single reverberating word. But he saw that the scene was spelling downfall for him, and he went still more blind and desperate of it. His despair made him burn to make matters Worse. He did not want to improve anything at all. "What?" he demanded. "What do ye' want?"

Nora was sweetly reproachful. "I left my jacket in the carriage, and I want you to get it for me."

"Well, get it for yourself, do you see? Get it for yourself."

Now it is plainly to be seen that no one of the people listening there had ever heard a man speak thus to a woman who was not his wife. Whenever they had heard that form of spirited repartee it had come from the lips of a husband. Coleman's rude speech was to their ears a flat announcement of an extraordinary intimacy between Nora Black and the correspondent. Any other interpretation would not have occurred to them. It was so palpable that it greatly distressed them with its arrogance and boldness. The professor had blushed. The very milkiest word in his mind at the time was the word vulgarity.

Nora Black had won a great battle. It was her Agincourt. She had beaten the clever Coleman in a way that had left little of him but rags. However, she could have lost it all again if she had shown her feeling of elation. At Coleman's rudeness her manner indicated a mixture of sadness and embarrassment. Her suffering was so plain to the eye that Peter Tounley was instantly moved. "Can't I get your jacket for you, Miss Black?" he asked hastily, and at her grateful nod he was off at once.

Coleman was resolved to improve nothing. His overthrow seemed to him to be so complete that he could not in any way mend it without a sacrifice of his dearest prides. He turned away from them all and walked to an isolated corner of the room. He would abide no longer with them. He had been made an outcast by Nora Black, and he intended to be an outcast. There was no sense in attempting to stem this extraordinary deluge. It was better to acquiesce. Then suddenly he was angry with Marjory. He did not exactly see why he was angry at Marjory, but he was angry at her nevertheless. He thought of how he could revenge himself upon her. He decided to take horse with his groom and dragoman and proceed forthwith on the road, leaving the jumble as it stood. This would pain Marjory, anyhow, he hoped. She would feel it deeply, he hoped. Acting upon this plan, he went to the professor. Well, of course you are all right now, professor, and if you don't mind, I would like to leave you—go on ahead. I've got a considerable pressure of business on my mind, and I think I should hurry on to Athens, if you don't mind."

The professor did not seem to know what to say. "Of course, if you wish it— sorry, I'm sure—of course it is as you please—but you have been such a power in our favor—it seems too bad to lose you—but—if you wish it—if you insist—"

"Oh, yes, I quite insist," said Coleman, calmly. "I quite insist. Make your mind easy on that score, professor. I insist."

"Well, Mr. Coleman," stammered the old man. "Well, it seems a great pity to lose you—you have been such a power in our favor—"

"Oh, you are now only eight hours from the railway. It is very easy. You would not need my assistance, even if it were a benefit!

"But—" said the professor.

Coleman's dragoman came to him then and said: "There is one man here who says you made to take one rifle in the fight and was break his head. He was say he wants sunthing for you was break his head. He says hurt."

"How much does he want?" asked Coleman, impatiently.

The dragoman wrestled then evidently with a desire to protect this mine from outside fingers. "I—I think two gold piece plenty."

"Take them," said Coleman. It seemed to him preposterous that this idiot with a broken head should interpolate upon his tragedy. "Afterward, you and the groom get the three horses and we will start for Athens at once."

"For Athens? At once?" said Marjory's voice in his ear.

## CHAPTER XXIII

"Um," said Coleman, "I was thinking of starting."

"Why?" asked Marjory, unconcernedly.

Coleman shot her a quick glance. "I believe my period of usefulness is quite ended," he said with just a small betrayal of bitter feeling.

"It is certainly true that you have had a remarkable period of usefulness to us," said Marjory with a slow smile, "but if it is ended, you should not run away from us."

Coleman looked at her to see what she could mean. From many women, these words would have been equal, under the circumstances, to a command to stay, but he felt that none might know what impulses moved the mind behind that beautiful mask. In his misery he thought to hurt her into an expression of feeling by a rough speech. "I'm so in love with Nora Black, you know, that I have to be very careful of myself."

"Oh," said Marjory, never thought of that. I should think you would have to be careful of yourself."

She did not seem moved in any way. Coleman despaired of finding her weak spot. She was adamant, this girl. He searched his mind for something to say which would be still more gross than his last outbreak, but when he felt that he was about to hit upon it, the professor interrupted with an agitated speech to Marjory.

"You had better go to your mother, my child, and see that you are all ready to leave here as soon as the carriages come up."

"We have absolutely nothing to make ready," said Marjory, laughing. "But I'll go and see if mother needs anything before we start that I can get for her."

She went away without bidding good-bye to Coleman. The sole maddening impression to him was that the matter of his going had not been of sufficient importance to remain longer than a moment upon her mind. At the same time he decided that he would go, irretrievably go.

Even then the dragoman entered the room. "We will pack everything upon the horse?"

"Everything—yes."

Peter Tounley came afterward. "You are not going to bolt?"

"Yes, I'm off," answered Coleman recovering himself for Peter's benefit. "See you in Athens, probably."

* * * *

Presently the dragoman announced the readiness of the horses. Coleman shook hands with the students and the Professor amid cries of surprise and polite regret. "What? Going, old man? Really? What for? Oh, wait for us. We're off in a few minutes. Sorry as the devil, old boy, to' see you go." He accepted their protestations with a somewhat sour face. He knew perfectly well that they were thinking of his departure as something that related to Nora Black. At the last, he bowed to the ladies as a collection. Marjory's answering bow was affable; the bow of Mrs. Wainwright spoke a resentment for something; and Nora's bow was triumphant mockery. As he swung into the saddle an idea struck him with over whelming force. The idea was that he was a fool. He was a colossal imbecile. He touched the spur to his horse and the animal leaped superbly, making the Greeks hasten for safety in all directions. He was off; he could no more return to retract his devious idiocy than he could make his horse fly to Athens. What was done was done. He could not mend it. And he felt like a man that had broken his own heart; perversely, childishly, stupidly broken his own heart. He was sure that Marjory was lost to him. No man could be degraded so publicly and resent it so crudely and still retain a Marjory. In his abasement from his defeat at the hands of Nora Black he had performed every imaginable blockheadish act and had finally climaxed it all by a departure which left the tongue of Nora to speak unmolested into the ear of Marjory. Nora's victory had been a serious blow to his fortunes, but it had not been so serious as his own subsequent folly. He had generously muddled his own affairs until he could read nothing out of them but despair.

He was in the mood for hatred. He hated many people. Nora Black was the principal item, but he did not hesitate to detest the professor, Mrs. Wainwright, Coke and all the students. As for Marjory, he would revenge himself upon her. She had done nothing that he defined clearly but, at any rate, he would take revenge for it. As much as was possible, he would make her suffer. He would convince her that he was a tremendous and inexorable person. But it came upon his mind that he was powerless in all ways. If he hated many people they probably would not be even interested in his emotion and, as for his revenge upon Marjory, it was beyond his strength. He was nothing but the complaining victim of Nora Black and himself.

He felt that he would never again see Marjory, and while feeling it he began to plan his attitude when next they met. He would be very cold and reserved. At Agrinion he found that there would be no train until the next daybreak. The dragoman was excessively annoyed over it, but Coleman did not scold at all. As a matter of fact his heart had given a great joyous bound. He could not now prevent his being overtaken. They were only a few leagues away, and while he was waiting for the train they would easily cover the distance. If anybody expressed surprise at seeing him he could exhibit the logical reasons. If there had been a train starting at once he would have taken it. His pride would have put up with no subterfuge. If the Wainwrights overtook him it was because he could not help it. But he was delighted that he could not help it. There had been an interposition by some specially beneficent fate. He felt like whistling. He spent the early half of the night in blissful smoke, striding the room which the dragoman had found for him. His head was full of plans and detached impressive scenes in which he figured before Marjory. The simple fact that there was no train away from Agrinion until the next daybreak had wrought a stupendous change in his outlook. He unhesitatingly considered it an omen of a good future. He was up before the darkness even contained presage of coming light, but near the railway station was a little hut where coffee was being served to several prospective travelers who had come even earlier to the rendezvous. There was no evidence of the Wainwrights.

Coleman sat in the hut and listened for the rumble of wheels. He was suddenly appalled that the Wainwrights were going to miss the train. Perhaps they had decided against travelling during the night. Perhaps this thing, and perhaps that thing. The morning was very cold. Closely muffled in his cloak, he went to the door and stared at where the road was whitening out of night. At the station stood a little spectral train, and the engine at intervals emitted a long, piercing scream which informed the echoing land that, in all probability, it was going to start after a time for the south. The Greeks in the coffee room were, of course, talking.

At last Coleman did hear the sound of hoofs and wheels. The three carriages swept up in grand procession. The first was laden with students; in the second was the professor, the Greek officer, Nora Black's old lady and other persons, all looking marvelously unimportant and shelved. It was the third carriage at which Coleman stared. At first be thought the dim light deceived his vision, but in a moment he knew that his first leaping conception of the arrangement of the people in this vehicle had been perfectly correct. Nora Black and Mrs. Wainwright sat side by side on the back seat, while facing them were Coke and Marjory.

They looked cold but intimate.

The oddity of the grouping stupefied Coleman. It was anarchy, naked and unashamed. He could not imagine how such changes could have been consummated in the short time he had been away from them, but he laid it all to some startling necromancy on the part of Nora Black, some wondrous play which had captured them all because of its surpassing skill and because they were, in the main, rather gullible people.

He was wrong. The magic had been wrought by the unaided foolishness of Mrs. Wainwright. As soon as Nora Black had succeeded in creating an effect of intimacy and dependence between herself and Coleman, the professor had flatly stated to his wife that the presence of Nora Black in the party, in the inn, in the world, was a thing that did not meet his approval in any way. She should be abolished. As for Coleman, he would not defend him. He preferred not to talk to him. It made him sad. Coleman at least had been very indiscreet, very indiscreet. It was a great pity. But as for this blatant woman, the sooner they rid themselves of her, the sooner he would feel that all the world was not evil.

Whereupon Mrs. Wainwright had changed front with the speed of light and attacked with horse, foot and guns. She failed to see, she had declared, where this poor, lone girl was in great fault. Of course it was probable that she had listened to this snaky-tongued Rufus Coleman, but that was ever the mistake that women made. Oh, certainly; the professor would like to let Rufus Coleman off scot-free. That was the way with men. They defended each other in all cases. If wrong were done it was the woman who suffered. Now, since this poor girl was alone far off here in Greece, Mrs. Wainwright announced that she had such full sense of her duty to her sex that her conscience would not allow her to scorn and desert a sister, even if that sister was, approximately, the victim of a creature like Rufus Coleman. Perhaps the poor thing loved this wretched man, although it was hard to imagine any woman giving her heart to such a monster.

The professor had then asked with considerable spirit for the proofs upon which Mrs. Wainwright named Coleman a monster, and had made a wry face over her completely conventional reply. He had told her categorically his opinion of her erudition in such matters.

But Mrs. Wainwright was not to be deterred from an exciting espousal of the cause of her sex. Upon the instant that the professor strenuously opposed her she became an apostle, an enlightened, uplifted apostle to the world on the wrongs of her sex. She had come down with this thing as if it were a disease. Nothing could stop her. Her husband, her daughter, all influences in other directions, had been overturned with a roar, and the first thing fully clear to the professor's mind had been that his wife was riding affably in the carriage with Nora Black. Coleman aroused when he heard one of the students cry out: "Why, there is Rufus Coleman's dragoman. He must be here." A moment later they thronged upon him. "Hi, old man, caught you again! Where did you break to? Glad to catch you, old boy. How are you making it? Where's your horse?"

"Sent the horses on to, Athens," said Coleman. He had not yet recovered his composure, and he was glad to find available this commonplace return to their exuberant greetings and questions. "Sent them on to Athens with the groom."

In the mean time the engine of the little train was screaming to heaven that its intention of starting was most serious. The diligencia careered to the station platform and unburdened. Coleman had had his dragoman place his luggage in a little first-class carriage and he defiantly entered it and closed the door. He had a sudden return to the old sense of downfall, and with it came the original rebellious desires. However, he hoped that somebody would intrude upon him.

It was Peter Tounley. The student flung open the door and then yelled to the distance: "Here's an empty one." He clattered into the compartment. "Hello, Coleman! Didn't know you were in here!" At his heels came Nora Black, Coke and Marjory.

"Oh!" they said, when they saw the occupant of the carriage. "Oh!"

Coleman was furious. He could have distributed some of his traps in a way to create more room, but he did not move.

## CHAPTER XXIV.

THERE was a demonstration of the unequalled facilities of a European railway carriage for rendering unpleasant things almost intolerable. These people could find no way to alleviate the poignancy of their position. Coleman did not know where to look. Every personal mannerism becomes accentuated in a European railway carriage. If you glance at a man, your glance defines itself as a stare. If you carefully look at nothing, you create for yourself a resemblance to all wooden-headed things. A newspaper is, then, in the nature of a preservative, and Coleman longed for a newspaper.

It was this abominable railway carriage which exacted the first display of agitation from Marjory. She flushed rosily, and her eyes wavered over the compartment. Nora Black laughed in a way that was a shock to the nerves. Coke seemed very angry, indeed, and Peter Tounley was in pitiful distress. Everything was acutely, painfully vivid, bald, painted as glaringly as a grocer's new wagon. It fulfilled those traditions which the artists deplore when they use their pet phrase on a picture, "It hurts." The damnable power of accentuation of the European railway carriage seemed, to Coleman's amazed mind, to be redoubled and redoubled.

It was Peter Tounley who seemed to be in the greatest agony. He looked at the correspondent beseechingly and said: "It's a very cold morning, Coleman." This was an actual appeal in the name of humanity.

Coleman came squarely to the front and even grinned a little at poor Peter Tounley's misery. "Yes, it is a cold morning, Peter. I should say it to one of the coldest mornings in my recollection."

Peter Tounley had not intended a typical American emphasis on the polar conditions which obtained in the compartment at this time, but Coleman had given the word this meaning. Spontaneously every body smiled, and at once the tension was relieved. But of course the satanic powers of the railway carriage could not be altogether set at naught. Of course it fell to the lot of Coke to get the seat directly in front of Coleman, and thus, face to face, they were doomed to stare at each other.

Peter Tounley was inspired to begin conventional babble, in which he took great care to make an appearance of talking to all in the carriage.

"Funny thing I never knew these mornings in Greece were so cold. I thought the climate here was quite tropical. It must have been inconvenient in the ancient times, when, I am told, people didn't wear near so many—er—clothes. Really, I don't see how they stood it. For my part, I would like nothing so much as a buffalo robe. I suppose when those great sculptors were doing their masterpieces, they had to wear gloves. Ever think of that? Funny, isn't it? Aren't you cold, Marjory? I am. Jingo!

Imagine the Spartans in ulsters, going out to meet an enemy in cape-overcoats, and being desired by their mothers to return with their ulsters or wrapped in them."

It was rather hard work for Peter Tounley. Both Marjory and Coleman tried to display an interest in his labors, and they laughed not at what he said, but because they believed it assisted him. The little train, meanwhile, wandered up a great green slope, and the day rapidly colored the land.

At first Nora Black did not display a militant mood, but as time passed Coleman saw clearly that she was considering the advisability of a new attack. She had Coleman and Marjory in conjunction and where they were unable to escape from her.

The opportunities were great. To Coleman, she seemed to be gloating over the possibilities of making more mischief. She was looking at him speculatively, as if considering the best place to hit him first.

Presently she drawled: "Rufus, I wish you would fix my rug about me a little better."

Coleman saw that this was a beginning. Peter Tounley sprang to his feet with speed and enthusiasm.

"Oh, let me do it for you." He had her well muffled in the rug before she could protest, even if a protest had been rational. The young man had no idea of defending Coleman. He had no knowledge of the necessity for it. It had been merely the exercise of his habit of amiability, his chronic desire to see everybody comfortable. His passion in this direction was well known in Washurst, where the students had borrowed a phrase from the photographers in order to describe him fully in a nickname. They called him "Look—pleasant Tounley."

This did not in any way antagonize his perfect willingness to fight on occasions with a singular desperation, which usually has a small stool in every mind where good nature has a throne.

"Oh, thank you very much, Mr. Tounley," said Nora Black, without gratitude. "Rufus is always so lax in these matters."

"I don't know how you know it," said Coleman boldly, and he looked her fearlessly in the eye. The battle had begun.

"Oh," responded Nora, airily, "I have had opportunity enough to know it, I should think, by this time."

"No," said Coleman, "since I have never paid you particular and direct attention, you cannot possibly know what I am lax in and what I am not lax in. I would be obliged to be of service at any time, Nora, but surely you do not consider that you have a right to my services superior to any other right."

Nora Black simply went mad, but fortunately part of her madness was in the form of speechlessness. Otherwise there might have been heard something approaching to billingsgate.

Marjory and Peter Tounley turned first hot and then cold, and looked as if they wanted to fly away; and even Coke, penned helplessly in with this unpleasant incident, seemed to have a sudden attack of distress. The only frigid person was Coleman. He had made his declaration of independence, and he saw with glee that the victory was complete. Nora Black might storm and rage, but he had announced his position in an unconventional blunt way which nobody in the carriage could fail to understand. He felt somewhat like smiling with confidence and defiance in Nora's face, but he still had the fear for Marjory.

Unexpectedly, the fight was all out of Nora Black. She had the fury of a woman scorned, but evidently she had perceived that all was over and lost. The remainder of her wrath dispensed itself in glares which Coleman withstood with great composure.

A strained silence fell upon the group which lasted until they arrived at the little port of Mesalonghi, whence they were to take ship for Patras. Coleman found himself wondering why he had not gone flatly at the great question at a much earlier period, indeed at the first moment when the great question began to make life exciting for him. He thought that if he had charged Nora's guns in the beginning they would have turned out to be the same incapable artillery. Instead of that he had run away and continued to run away until he was actually cornered and made to fight, and his easy victory had defined him as a person who had, earlier, indulged in much stupidity and cowardice. Everything had worked out so simply, his terrors had been dispelled so easily, that he probably was led to overestimate his success. And it occurred suddenly to him. He foresaw a fine occasion to talk privately to Marjory when all had boarded the steamer for Patras and he resolved to make use of it. This he believed would end the strife and conclusively laurel him.

The train finally drew up on a little stone pier and some boatmen began to scream like gulls. The steamer lay at anchor in the placid blue cove. The embarkation was chaotic in the Oriental fashion and there was the customary misery which was only relieved when the travelers had set foot on the deck of the steamer. Coleman did not devote any premature attention to finding Marjory, but when the steamer was fairly out on the calm waters of the Gulf of Corinth, he saw her pacing to and fro with Peter Tounley. At first he lurked in the distance waiting for an opportunity, but ultimately he decided to make his own opportunity. He approached them. "Marjory, would you let me speak to you alone for a few moments? You won't mind, will you, Peter?"

"Oh, no, certainly not," said Peter Tounley.

"Of course. It is not some dreadful revelation, is it?" said Marjory, bantering him coolly.

"No," answered Coleman, abstractedly. He was thinking of what he was going to say. Peter Tounley vanished around the corner of a deck-house and Marjory and Coleman began to pace to and fro even as Marjory and Peter Tounley had done. Coleman had thought to speak his mind frankly and once for all, and on the train he had invented many clear expressions of his feeling. It did not appear that he had forgotten them. It seemed, more, that they had become entangled in his mind in such a way that he could not unravel the end of his discourse.

In the pause, Marjory began to speak in admiration of the scenery. "I never imagined that Greece was so full of mountains. One reads so much of the Attic Plains, but aren't these mountains royal? They look so rugged and cold, whereas the bay is absolutely as blue as the old descriptions of a summer sea."

"I wanted to speak to you about Nora Black," said Coleman.

"Nora Black? Why?" said Marjory, lifting her eyebrows.

You know well enough," said Coleman, in a headlong fashion. "You must know, you must have seen it. She knows I care for you and she wants to stop it. And she has no right to—to interfere. She is a fiend, a perfect fiend. She is trying to make you feel that I care for her."

"And don't you care for her?" asked Marjory.

"No," said Coleman, vehemently. "I don't care for her at all."

"Very well," answered Marjory, simply. "I believe you." She managed to give the words the effect of a mere announcement that she believed him and it was in no way plain that she was glad or that she esteemed the matter as being of consequence.

He scowled at her in dark resentment. "You mean by that, I suppose, that you don't believe me?"

"Oh," answered Marjory, wearily, "I believe you. I said so. Don't talk about it any more."

"Then," said Coleman, slowly, "you mean that you do not care whether I'm telling the truth or not?"

"Why, of course I care," she said. "Lying is not nice."

He did not know, apparently, exactly how to deal with her manner, which was actually so pliable that—it was marble, if one may speak in that way. He looked ruefully at the sea. He had expected a far easier time. "Well—" he began.

"Really," interrupted Marjory, "this is something which I do not care to discuss. I would rather you would not speak to me at all about it. It seems too—too—bad. I can readily give you my word that I believe you, but I would prefer you not to try to talk to me about it or—anything of that sort. Mother!"

Mrs. Wainwright was hovering anxiously in the vicinity, and she now bore down rapidly upon the pair. "You are very nearly to Patras," she said reproachfully to her daughter, as if the fact had some fault of Marjory's concealed in it. She in no way acknowledged the presence of Coleman.

"Oh, are we?" cried Marjory.

"Yes," said Mrs. Wainwright. "We are."

She stood waiting as if she expected Marjory to instantly quit Coleman. The girl wavered a moment and then followed her mother. "Good-bye." she said. "I hope we may see you again in Athens." It was a command to him to travel alone with his servant on the long railway journey from Patras to Athens. It was a dismissal of a casual acquaintance given so graciously that it stung him to the depths of his pride. He bowed his adieu and his thanks. When the yelling boatmen came again, he and his man proceeded to the shore in an early boat without looking in any way after the welfare of the others.

At the train, the party split into three sections. Coleman and his man had one compartment, Nora Black and her squad had another, and the Wainwrights and students occupied two more.

The little officer was still in tow of Nora Black. He was very enthusiastic. In French she directed him to remain silent, but he did not appear to understand. "You tell him," she then said to her dragoman, "to sit in a corner and not to speak until I tell him to, or I won't have him in here." She seemed anxious to unburden herself to the old lady companion. "Do you know," she said, "that girl has a nerve like steel. I tried to break it there in that inn, but I couldn't budge her. If I am going to have her beaten I must prove myself to be a very, very artful person."

"Why did you try to break her nerve?" asked the old lady, yawning. "Why do you want to have her beaten?"

"Because I do, old stupid," answered Nora. "You should have heard the things I said to her."

"About what?"

"About Coleman. Can't you understand anything at all?"

"And why should you say anything about Coleman to her?" queried the old lady, still hopelessly befogged.

"Because," cried Nora, darting a look of wrath at her companion, "I want to prevent that marriage."

She had been betrayed into this avowal by the singularly opaque mind of the old lady. The latter at once sat erect.

"Oh, ho," she said, as if a ray of light had been let into her head. "Oh, ho. So that's it, is it?"

"Yes, that's it, rejoined Nora, shortly.

The old lady was amazed into a long period of meditation. At last she spoke depressingly. "Well, how are you going to prevent it? Those things can't be done in these days at all. If they care for each other—"

Nora burst out furiously. "Don't venture opinions until you know what you are talking about, please. They don't care for each other, do you see? She cares for him, but he don't give a snap of his fingers for her."

"But," cried the bewildered lady, "if he don't care for her, there will be nothing to prevent. If he don't care for her, he won't ask her to marry him, and so there won't be anything to prevent."

Nora made a broad gesture of impatience. "Oh, can't you get anything through your head? Haven't you seen that the girl has been the only young woman in that whole party lost up there in the mountains, and that naturally more than half of the men still think they are in love with her? That's what it is. Can't you see? It always happens that way. Then Coleman comes along and makes a fool of himself with the others."

The old lady spoke up brightly as if at last feeling able to contribute something intelligent to the talk. "Oh, then, he does care for her."

Nora's eyes looked as if their glance might shrivel the old lady's hair. "Don't I keep telling you that it is no such thing? Can't you understand? It is all glamour! Fascination! Way up there in the wilderness! Only one even passable woman in sight."

"I don't say that I am so very keen," said the old lady, somewhat offended, "but I fail to see where I could improve when first you tell me he don't care for her, and then you tell me that he does care for her."

"Glamour, Fascination," quoted Nora. "Don't you understand the meaning of the words?"

"Well," asked the other, didn't he know her, then, before he came over here?"

Nora was silent for a time, while a gloom upon her face deepened. It had struck her that the theories for which she protested so energetically might not be of such great value. Spoken aloud, they had a sudden new flimsiness. Perhaps she had reiterated to herself that Coleman was the victim of glamour only because she wished it to be true. One theory, however, remained unshaken. Marjory was an artful minx, with no truth in her.

She presently felt the necessity of replying to the question of her companion.

"Oh," she said, carelessly, "I suppose they were acquainted—in a way."

The old lady was giving the best of her mind to the subject. "If that's the case—" she observed, musingly, "if that's the case, you can't tell what is between 'em."

The talk had so slackened that Nora's unfortunate Greek admirer felt that here was a good opportunity to present himself again to the notice of the actress. The means was a smile and a French sentence, but his reception would have frightened a man in armor. His face blanched with horror at the storm, he had invoked, and he dropped limply back as if some one had shot him. "You tell this little snipe to let me alone!" cried Nora, to the dragoman. "If he dares to come around me with any more of those Parisian dude speeches, I—I don't know what I'll do! I won't have it, I say." The impression upon the dragoman was hardly less in effect. He looked with bulging eyes at Nora, and then began to stammer at the officer. The latter's voice could sometimes be heard in awed whispers for the more elaborate explanation of some detail of the tragedy. Afterward, he remained meek and silent in his corner, barely more than a shadow, like the proverbial husband of imperious beauty.

"Well," said the old lady, after a long and thoughtful pause, "I don't know, I'm sure, but it seems to me that if Rufus Coleman really cares for that girl, there isn't much use in trying to stop him from getting her. He isn't that kind of a man."

"For heaven's sake, will you stop assuming that he does care for her?" demanded Nora, breathlessly.

"And I don't see," continued the old lady, "what you want to prevent him for, anyhow."

## CHAPTER XXV.

"I feel in this radiant atmosphere that there could be no such thing as war-men striving together in black and passionate hatred." The professor's words were for the benefit of his wife and daughter. He was viewing the sky-blue waters of the Gulf of Corinth with its background of mountains that in the sunshine were touched here and there with a copperish glare. The train was slowly sweeping along the southern shore. "It is strange to think of those men fighting up there in the north. And it is strange to think that we ourselves are but just returning from it."

"I cannot begin to realize it yet," said Mrs. Wainwright, in a high voice.

"Quite so," responded the professor, reflectively.

"I do not suppose any of us will realize it fully for some time. It is altogether too odd, too very odd."

"To think of it!" cried Mrs. Wainwright. "To think of it! Supposing those dreadful Albanians or those awful men from the Greek mountains had caught us! Why, years from now I'll wake up in the night and think of it!"

The professor mused. "Strange that we cannot feel it strongly now. My logic tells me to be aghast that we ever got into such a place, but my nerves at present refuse to thrill. I am very much afraid that this singular apathy of ours has led us to be unjust to poor Coleman." Here Mrs. Wainwright objected. "Poor Coleman! I don't see why you call him poor Coleman.

"Well," answered the professor, slowly, "I am in doubt about our behavior. It—"

"Oh," cried the wife, gleefully," in doubt about our behavior! I'm in doubt about his behavior."

"So, then, you do have a doubt of his behavior?"

"Oh, no," responded Mrs. Wainwright, hastily, "not about its badness. What I meant to say was that in the face of his outrageous conduct with that—that woman, it is curious that you should worry about our behavior. It surprises me, Harrison."

The professor was wagging his head sadly. "I don't know I don't know It seems hard to judge— I hesitate to—"

Mrs. Wainwright treated this attitude with disdain. "It is not hard to judge," she scoffed, "and I fail to see why you have any reason for hesitation at all. Here he brings this woman—"

The professor got angry. "Nonsense! Nonsense! I do not believe that he brought her. If I ever saw a spectacle of a woman bringing herself, it was then. You keep chanting that thing like an outright parrot."

"Well," retorted Mrs. Wainwright, bridling, "I suppose you imagine that you understand such things, Men usually think that, but I want to tell you that you seem to me utterly blind."

"Blind or not, do stop the everlasting reiteration of that sentence."

Mrs. Wainwright passed into an offended silence, and the professor, also silent, looked with a gradually dwindling indignation at the scenery.

Night was suggested in the sky before the train was near to Athens. "My trunks," sighed Mrs. Wainwright. "How glad I will be to get back to my trunks! Oh, the dust! Oh, the misery! Do find out when we will get there, Harrison. Maybe the train is late."

But, at last, they arrived in Athens, amid a darkness which was confusing, and, after no more than the common amount of trouble, they procured carriages and were taken to the hotel. Mrs. Wainwright's impulses now dominated the others in the family. She had one passion after another. The majority of the servants in the hotel pretended that they spoke English, but, in three minutes, she drove them distracted with the abundance and violence of her requests. It came to pass that in the excitement the old couple quite forgot Marjory. It was not until Mrs. Wainwright, then feeling splendidly, was dressed for dinner, that she thought to open Marjory's door and go to render a usual motherly supervision of the girl's toilet.

There was no light: there did not seem to be anybody in the room.

"Marjory!" called the mother, in alarm. She listened for a moment and then ran hastily out again. "Harrison!" she cried. "I can't find Marjory!"

The professor had been tying his cravat. He let the loose ends fly.

"What?" he ejaculated, opening his mouth wide. Then they both rushed into Marjory's room. "Marjory!" beseeched the old man in a voice which would have invoked the grave.

The answer was from the bed. "Yes?" It was low, weary, tearful. It was not like Marjory. It was dangerously the voice of a heartbroken woman. They hurried forward with outcries.

"Why, Marjory! Are you ill, child? How long have you been lying in the dark? Why didn't you call us? Are you ill?"

"No," answered this changed voice, "I am not ill. I only thought I'd rest for a time. Don't bother."

The professor hastily lit the gas and then father and mother turned hurriedly to the bed. In the first of the illumination they saw that tears were flowing unchecked down Marjory's face.

The effect of this grief upon the professor was, in part, an effect of fear. He seemed afraid to touch it, to go near it. He could, evidently, only remain in the outskirts, a horrified spectator. The mother, however, flung her arms about her daughter.

"Oh, Marjory!" She, too, was weeping.

The girl turned her face to the pillow and held out a hand of protest.

"Don't, mother! Don't!"

"Oh, Marjory! Oh, Marjory!"

"Don't, mother. Please go away. Please go away. Don't speak at all, I beg of you."

"Oh, Marjory! Oh, Marjory!"

"Don't." The girl lifted a face which appalled them. It had something entirely new in it. "Please go away, mother. I will speak to father, but I won't—I can't—I can't be pitied."

Mrs. Wainwright looked at her husband.

"Yes," said the old man, trembling. "Go!"

She threw up her hands in a sorrowing gesture that was not without its suggestion that her exclusion would be a mistake. She left the room.

The professor dropped on his knees at the bedside and took one of Marjory's hands. His voice dropped to its tenderest note. "Well, my Marjory?"

She had turned her face again to the pillow. At last she answered in muffled tones, "You know." Thereafter came a long silence full of sharpened pain. It was Marjory who spoke first. "I have saved my pride, daddy, but—I have—lost—everything—else." Even her sudden resumption of the old epithet of her childhood was an additional misery to the old man. He still said no word. He knelt, gripping her fingers and staring at the wall.

"Yes, I have lost everything else."

The father gave a low groan. He was thinking deeply, bitterly. Since one was only a human being, how was one going to protect beloved hearts assailed with sinister fury from the inexplicable zenith? In this tragedy he felt as helpless as an old grey ape. He did not see a possible weapon with which he could defend his child from the calamity which was upon her. There was no wall, no shield which could turn this sorrow from the heart of his child. If one of his hands loss could have spared her, there would have been a sacrifice of his hand, but he was potent for nothing. He could only groan and stare at the wall. He reviewed the past half in fear that he would suddenly come upon his error which was now the cause of Marjory's tears. He dwelt long upon the fact that in Washurst he had refused his consent to Marjory's marriage with Coleman, but even now he could not say that his judgment was not correct. It was simply that the doom of woman's woe was upon Marjory, this ancient woe of the silent tongue and the governed will, and he could only kneel at the bedside and stare at the wall.

Marjory raised her voice in a laugh. "Did I betray myself? Did I become the maiden all forlorn? Did I giggle to show people that I did not care? No—I did not—I did not. And it was such a long time, daddy! Oh, such a long time! I thought we would never get here. I thought I would never get where I could be alone like this, where I could—cry—if I wanted to. I am not much of—a crier, am I, daddy? But this time—this—time—"

She suddenly drew herself over near to her father and looked at him. "Oh, daddy, I want to tell you one thing, just one simple little thing." She waited then, and while she waited her father's head went lower and lower. "Of course, you know—I told you once. I love him! I love him! Yes, probably he is a rascal, but, do you know, I don't think I would mind if he was a—an assassin. This morning I sent him away, but, daddy, he didn't want to go at all. I know he didn't. This Nora Black is nothing to him. I know she is not. I am sure of it. Yes—I am sure of it…. I never expected to talk this way to any living creature, but—you are so good, daddy. Dear old daddy—"

She ceased, for she saw that her father was praying.

The sight brought to her a new outburst of sobbing, for her sorrow now had dignity and solemnity from the bowed white head of her old father, and she felt that her heart was dying amid the pomp of the church. It was the last rites being performed at the death-bed. Into her ears came some imagining of the low melancholy chant of monks in a gloom.

Finally her father arose. He kissed her on the brow. "Try to sleep, dear," he said. He turned out the gas and left the room. His thought was full of chastened emotion.

But if his thought was full of chastened emotion, it received some degree of shock when he arrived in the presence of Mrs. Wainwright. "Well, what is all this about?" she demanded, irascibly. "Do you mean to say that Marjory is breaking her heart over that man Coleman? It is all your fault—" She was apparently still ruffled over her exclusion.

When the professor interrupted her he did not speak with his accustomed spirit, but from something novel in his manner she recognized a danger signal. "Please do not burst out at it in that way."

"Then it Is true?" she asked. Her voice was a mere awed whisper.

"It is true," answered the professor.

"Well," she said, after reflection, "I knew it. I always knew it. If you hadn't been so blind! You turned like a weather-cock in your opinions of Coleman. You never could keep your opinion about him for more than an hour. Nobody could imagine what you might think next. And now you see the result of it! I warned you! I told you what this Coleman was, and if Marjory is suffering now, you have only yourself to blame for it. I warned you!"

"If it is my fault," said the professor, drearily, "I hope God may forgive me, for here is a great wrong to my daughter."

Well, if you had done as I told you—" she began.

Here the professor revolted. "Oh, now, do not begin on that," he snarled, peevishly. Do not begin on that."

"Anyhow," said Mrs. Wainwright. "It is time that we should be going down to dinner. Is Marjory coming?"

"No, she is not," answered the professor, "and I do not know as I shall go myself."

"But you must go. Think how it would look! All the students down there dining without us, and cutting up capers! You must come."

"Yes," he said, dubiously, "but who will look after Marjory?"

"She wants to be left alone," announced Mrs. Wainwright, as if she was the particular herald of this news. "She wants to be left alone."

"Well, I suppose we may as well go down." Before they went, the professor tiptoed into his daughter's room. In the darkness he could only see her waxen face on the pillow, and her two eyes gazing fixedly at the ceiling. He did not speak, but immediately withdrew, closing the door noiselessly behind him.

## CHAPTER XXVI.

If the professor and Mrs. Wainwright had descended sooner to a lower floor of the hotel, they would have found reigning there a form of anarchy. The students were in a smoking room which was also an entrance hall to the dining room, and because there was in the middle of this apartment a fountain containing gold fish, they had been moved to license and sin. They had all been tubbed and polished and brushed and dressed until they were exuberantly beyond themselves. The proprietor of the hotel brought in his dignity and showed it to them, but they minded it no more than if he had been only a common man. He drew himself to his height and looked gravely at them and they jovially said: "Hello, Whiskers." American college students are notorious in their country for their inclination to scoff at robed and crowned authority, and, far from being awed by the dignity of the hotel-keeper, they were delighted with it. It was something with which to sport. With immeasurable impudence, they copied his attitude, and, standing before him, made comic speeches, always alluding with blinding vividness to his beard. His exit disappointed them. He had not remained long under fire. They felt that they could have interested themselves with him an entire evening. "Come back, Whiskers! Oh, come back!"

Out in the main hall he made a gesture of despair to some of his gaping minions and then fled to seclusion.

A formidable majority then decided that Coke was a gold fish, and that therefore his proper place was in the fountain. They carried him to it while he struggled madly. This quiet room with its crimson rugs and gilded mirrors seemed suddenly to have become an important apartment in hell. There being as yet no traffic in the dining room, the waiters were all at liberty to come to the open doors, where they stood as men turned to stone. To them, it was no less than incendiarism.

Coke, standing with one foot on the floor and the other on the bottom of the shallow fountain, blasphemed his comrades in a low tone, but with intention. He was certainly desirous of lifting his foot out of the water, but it seemed that all movement to that end would have to wait until he had successfully expressed his opinions. In the meantime, there was heard slow footsteps and the rustle of skirts, and then some people entered the smoking room on their way to dine. Coke took his foot hastily out of the fountain.

The faces of the men of the arriving party went blank, and they turned their cold and pebbly eyes straight to the front, while the ladies, after little expressions of alarm, looked as if they wanted to run. In fact, the whole crowd rather bolted from this extraordinary scene.

"There, now," said Coke bitterly to his companions. "You see? We looked like little schoolboys—"

"Oh, never mind, old man," said Peter Tounley. "We'll forgive you, although you did embarrass us. But, above everything, don't drip. Whatever you do, don't drip."

The students took this question of dripping and played upon it until they would have made quite insane anybody but another student. They worked it into all manner of forms, and hacked and haggled at Coke until he was driven to his room to seek other apparel. "Be sure and change both legs," they told him. "Remember you can't change one leg without changing both legs."

After Coke's departure, the United States minister entered the room, and instantly they were subdued. It was not his lofty station—that affected them. There are probably few stations that would have at all affected them. They became subdued because they unfeignedly liked the United States minister. They, were suddenly a group of well-bred, correctly attired young men who had not put Coke's foot in the fountain. Nor had they desecrated the majesty of the hotelkeeper.

"Well, I am delighted," said the minister, laughing as he shook hands with them all. "I was not sure I would ever see you again. You are not to be trusted, and, good boys as you are, I'll be glad to see you once and forever over the boundary of my jurisdiction. Leave Greece, you vagabonds. However, I am truly delighted to see you all safe."

"Thank you, sir," they said.

"How in the world did you get out of it? You must be remarkable chaps. I thought you were in a hopeless position. I wired and cabled everywhere I could, but I could find out nothing."

"A correspondent," said Peter Tounley. "I don't know if you have met him. His name is Coleman. He found us."

"Coleman?" asked the minister, quickly.

"Yes, sir. He found us and brought us out safely."

"Well, glory be to Coleman," exclaimed the minister, after a long sigh of surprise. "Glory be to Coleman! I never thought he could do it."

The students were alert immediately. "Why, did you know about it, sir? Did he tell you he was coming after us?"

"Of course. He came to me here in Athens and asked where you were. I told him you were in a peck of trouble. He acted quietly and somewhat queerly, and said that he would try to look you up. He said you were friends of his. I warned him against trying it. Yes, I said it was impossible, I had no idea that he would really carry the thing out. But didn't he tell you anything about this himself?"

"No, sir," answered Peter Tounley. "He never said much about it. I think he usually contended that it was mainly an accident."

"It was no accident," said the minister, sharply. "When a man starts out to do a thing and does it, you can't say it is an accident."

"I didn't say so, sir," said Peter Tounley diffidently.

"Quite true, quite true! You didn't, but—this Coleman must be a man!"

"We think so, sir," said be who was called Billie. "He certainly brought us through in style."

"But how did he manage it?" cried the minister, keenly interested. "How did he do it?"

"It is hard to say, sir. But he did it. He met us in the dead of night out near Nikopolis—"

"Near Nikopolis?"

"Yes, sir. And he hid us in a forest while a fight was going on, and then in the morning he brought us inside the Greek lines. Oh, there is a lot to tell—"

Whereupon they told it, or as much as they could of it. In the end, the minister said: "Well, where are the professor and Mrs. Wainwright? I want you all to dine with me tonight. I am dining in the public room, but you won't mind that after Epirus."

"They should be down now, sir," answered a Student.

People were now coming rapidly to dinner and presently the professor and Mrs. Wainwright appeared. The old man looked haggard and white. He accepted the minister's warm greeting with a strained pathetic smile. "Thank you. We are glad to return safely."

Once at dinner the minister launched immediately into the subject of Coleman. "He must be altogether a most remarkable man. When he told me, very quietly, that he was going to try to rescue you, I frankly warned him against any such attempt. I thought he would merely add one more to a party of suffering people. But the boys tell me that he did actually rescue you."

"Yes, he did," said the professor. "It was a very gallant performance, and we are very grateful."

"Of course," spoke Mrs. Wainwright, "we might have rescued ourselves. We were on the right road, and all we had to do was to keep going on."

"Yes, but I understand—" said the minister. "I understand he took you into a wood to protect you from that fight, and generally protected you from all, kinds of trouble. It seems wonderful to me, not so much because it was done as because it was done by the man who, some time ago, calmly announced to me that he was going to do it. Extraordinary."

"Of course," said Mrs. Wainwright. "Oh, of course."

"And where is he now?" asked the minister suddenly. "Has he now left you to the mercies of civilization?"

There was a moment's curious stillness, and then Mrs. Wainwright used that high voice which—the students believed—could only come to her when she was about to say something peculiarly destructive to the sensibilities. "Oh, of course,

Mr. Coleman rendered us a great service, but in his private character he is not a man whom we exactly care to associate with."

"Indeed" said the minister staring. Then he hastily addressed the students. "Well, isn't this a comic war? Did you ever imagine war could be like this?" The professor remained looking at his wife with an air of stupefaction, as if she had opened up to him visions of imbecility of which he had not even dreamed. The students loyally began to chatter at the minister. "Yes, sir, it is a queer war. After all their bragging, it is funny to hear that they are running away with such agility. We thought, of course, of the old Greek wars."

Later, the minister asked them all to his rooms for coffee and cigarettes, but the professor and Mrs. Wainwright apologetically retired to their own quarters. The minister and the students made clouds of smoke, through which sang the eloquent descriptions of late adventures.

The minister had spent days of listening to questions from the State Department at Washington as to the whereabouts of the Wainwright party. "I suppose you know that you are very prominent people in, the United States just now? Your pictures must have been in all the papers, and there must have been columns printed about you. My life here was made almost insupportable by your friends, who consist, I should think, of about half the population of the country. Of course they laid regular siege to the department. I am angry at Coleman for only one thing. When he cabled the news of your rescue to his newspaper from Arta, he should have also wired me, if only to relieve my failing mind. My first news of your escape was from Washington—think of that."

"Coleman had us all on his hands at Arta," said Peter Tounley. "He was a fairly busy man."

"I suppose so," said the minister. "By the way," he asked bluntly, "what is wrong with him? What did Mrs. Wainwright mean?"

They were silent for a time, but it seemed plain to him that it was not evidence that his question had demoralized them. They seemed to be deliberating upon the form of answer. Ultimately Peter Tounley coughed behind his hand. "You see, sir," he began, "there is—well, there is a woman in the case. Not that anybody would care to speak of it excepting to you. But that is what is the cause of things, and then, you see, Mrs. Wainwright is—well—" He hesitated a moment and then completed his sentence in the ingenuous profanity of his age and condition. "She is rather an extraordinary old bird."

"But who is the woman?

"Why, it is Nora Black, the actress."

"Oh," cried the minister, enlightened. "Her Why, I saw her here. She was very beautiful, but she seemed harmless enough. She was somewhat—er—confident, perhaps, but she did not alarm me. She called upon me, and I confess I—why, she seemed charming."

"She's sweet on little Rufus. That's the point," said an oracular voice.

"Oh," cried the host, suddenly. "I remember. She asked me where he was. She said she had heard he was in Greece, and I told her he had gone knight-erranting off after you people. I remember now. I suppose she posted after him up to Arta, eh?"

"That's it. And so she asked you where he was?

"Yes."

"Why, that old flamingo—Mrs. Wainwright insists that it was a rendezvous."

Every one exchanged glances and laughed a little. "And did you see any actual fighting?" asked the minister.

"No. We only beard it—"

Afterward, as they were trooping up to their rooms, Peter Tounley spoke musingly. "Well, it looks to me now as if Old Mother Wainwright was just a bad-minded old hen."

"Oh, I don't know. How is one going to tell what the truth is?"

"At any rate, we are sure now that Coleman had nothing to do with Nora's debut in Epirus."

They had talked much of Coleman, but in their tones there always had been a note of indifference or carelessness. This matter, which to some people was as vital and fundamental as existence, remained to others who knew of it only a harmless detail of life, with no terrible powers, and its significance had faded greatly when had ended the close associations of the late adventure.

After dinner the professor had gone directly to his daughter's room. Apparently she had not moved. He knelt by the bedside again and took one of her hands. She was not weeping. She looked at him and smiled through the darkness. "Daddy, I would like to die," she said. "I think—yes—I would like to die."

For a long time the old man was silent, but he arose at last with a definite abruptness and said hoarsely "Wait!"

Mrs. Wainwright was standing before her mirror with her elbows thrust out at angles above her head, while her fingers moved in a disarrangement of her hair. In the glass she saw a reflection of her husband coming from Marjory's room, and his face was set with some kind of alarming purpose. She turned to watch him actually, but he walked toward the door into the corridor and did not in any wise heed her.

"Harrison!" she called. "Where are you going?"

He turned a troubled face upon her, and, as if she had hailed him in his sleep, he vacantly said: "What?"

"Where are you going?" she demanded with increasing trepidation.

He dropped heavily into a chair. "Going?" he repeated.

She was angry. "Yes! Going? Where are you going?"

"I am going—" he answered, "I am going to see Rufus Coleman."

Mrs. Wainwright gave voice to a muffled scream. "Not about Marjory?"

"Yes," he said, "about Marjory."

It was now Mrs. Wainwright's turn to look at her husband with an air of stupefaction as if he had opened up to her visions of imbecility of which she had not even dreamed.

"About Marjory!" she gurgled. Then suddenly her wrath flamed out. "Well, upon my word, Harrison Wainwright, you are, of all men in the world, the most silly and stupid. You are absolutely beyond belief. Of all projects! And what do you think Marjory would have to say of it if she knew it? I suppose you think she would like it? Why, I tell you she would keep her right hand in the fire until it was burned off before she would allow you to do such a thing."

"She must never know it," responded the professor, in dull misery.

"Then think of yourself! Think of the shame of it! The shame of it!"

The professor raised his eyes for an ironical glance at his wife. "Oh I have thought of the shame of it!"

"And you'll accomplish nothing," cried Mrs. Wainwright. "You'll accomplish nothing. He'll only laugh at you."

"If he laughs at me, he will laugh at nothing but a poor, weak, unworldly old man. It is my duty to go."

Mrs. Wainwright opened her mouth as if she was about to shriek. After choking a moment she said: "Your duty? Your duty to go and bend the knee to that man? Your duty?"

"'It is my duty to go,'" he repeated humbly. "If I can find even one chance for my daughter's happiness in a personal sacrifice. He can do no more than he can do no more than make me a little sadder."

His wife evidently understood his humility as a tribute to her arguments and a clear indication that she had fatally undermined his original intention.

"Oh, he would have made you sadder," she quoth grimly. "No fear! Why, it was the most insane idea I ever heard of."

The professor arose wearily. "Well, I must be going to this work. It is a thing to have ended quickly." There was something almost biblical in his manner.

"Harrison!" burst out his wife in amazed lamentation. You are not really going to do it? Not really!"

"I am going to do it," he answered.

"Well, there!" ejaculated Mrs. Wainwright to the heavens. She was, so to speak, prostrate. "Well, there!"

As the professor passed out of the door she cried beseechingly but futilely after him. "Harrison." In a mechanical way she turned then back to the mirror and resumed the disarrangement of her hair. She addressed her image. "Well, of all stupid creatures under the sun, men are the very worst!" And her image said this to her even as she informed it, and afterward they stared at each other in a profound and tragic reception and acceptance of this great truth. Presently she began to consider the advisability of going to Marjory with the whole story. Really, Harrison must not be allowed to go on blundering until the whole world heard that Marjory was trying to break her heart over that common scamp of a Coleman. It seemed to be about time for her, Mrs. Wainwright, to come into the situation and mend matters.

## CHAPTER XXVIL

WHEN the professor arrived before Coleman's door, he paused a moment and looked at it. Previously, he could not have imagined that a simple door would ever so affect him. Every line of it seemed to express cold superiority and disdain. It was only the door of a former student, one of his old boys, whom, as the need arrived, he had whipped with his satire in the class rooms at Washurst until the mental blood had come, and all without a conception of his ultimately arriving before the door of this boy in the attitude of a supplicant. He would not say it; Coleman probably would not say it; but—they would both know it. A single thought of it, made him feel like running away. He would never dare to knock on that door. It would be too monstrous. And even as he decided that he was afraid to knock, he knocked.

Coleman's voice said, "Come in."

The professor opened the door. The correspondent, without a coat, was seated at a paper-littered table. Near his elbow, upon another table, was a tray from which he had evidently dined and also a brandy bottle with several recumbent bottles of soda. Although he had so lately arrived at the hotel he had contrived to diffuse his traps over the room in an organized disarray which represented a long and careless occupation if it did not represent the scene of a scuffle. His pipe was in his mouth.

After a first murmur of surprise, he arose and reached in some haste for his coat. "Come in, professor, come in," he cried, wriggling deeper into his jacket as he held out his hand. He had laid aside his pipe and had also been very successful in flinging a newspaper so that it hid the brandy and soda. This act was a feat of deference to the professor's well known principles.

"Won't you sit down, sir?" asked Coleman cordially. His quick glance of surprise had been immediately suppressed and his manner was now as if the professor's call was a common matter.

"Thank you, Mr. Coleman, I—yes, I will sit down," replied the old man. His hand shook as he laid it on the back of the chair and steadied himself down into it. "Thank you!"

Coleman looked at him with a great deal of expectation.

"Mr. Coleman!"

"Yes, sir."

"I—"

He halted then and passed his hand over his face. His eyes did not seem to rest once upon Coleman, but they occupied themselves in furtive and frightened glances over the room. Coleman could make neither head nor tail of the affair. He would not have believed any man's statement that the professor could act in such an extraordinary fashion. "Yes, sir," he said again suggestively. The simple strategy resulted in a silence that was actually awkward. Coleman, despite his bewilderment, hastened into a preserving gossip. "I've had a great many cables waiting for me for heaven knows how long, and others have been arriving in flocks tonight. You have no idea of the row in America, professor. Why, everybody must have gone wild over the lost sheep. My paper has cabled some things that are evidently for you. For instance, here is one that says a new puzzle-game called Find the Wainwright Party has had a big success. Think of that, would you." Coleman grinned at the professor. "Find the Wainwright Party, a new puzzle-game."

The professor had seemed grateful for Coleman's tangent off into matters of a light vein. "Yes?" he said, almost eagerly. "Are they selling a game really called that?"

"Yes, really," replied Coleman. "And of course you know that—er—well, all the Sunday papers would of course have big illustrated articles—full pages—with your photographs and general private histories pertaining mostly to things which are none of their business."

"Yes, I suppose they would do that," admitted the professor. "But I dare say it may not be as bad as you suggest."

"Very like not," said Coleman. "I put it to you forcibly so that in the future the blow will not be too cruel. They are often a weird lot."

"Perhaps they can't find anything very bad about us."

"Oh, no. And besides the whole episode will probably be forgotten by the time you return to the United States."

They talked on in this way slowly, strained, until they each found that the situation would soon become insupportable. The professor had come for a distinct purpose and Coleman knew it; they could not sit there lying at each other forever. Yet when he saw the pain deepening in the professor's eyes, the correspondent again ordered up his trivialities. "Funny thing. My paper has been congratulating me, you know, sir, in a wholesale fashion, and I think—I feel sure—that they have been exploiting my name all over the country as the Heroic Rescuer. There is no sense in trying to stop them, because they don't care whether it is true or not true. All they want is the privilege of howling out that their correspondent rescued you, and they would take that privilege without in any ways worrying if I refused my consent. You see, sir? I wouldn't like you to feel that I was such a strident idiot as I doubtless am appearing now before the public."

"No," said the professor absently. It was plain that he had been a very slack listener. "I—Mr. Coleman—" he began.

"Yes, sir," answered Coleman promptly and gently.

It was obviously only a recognition of the futility of further dallying that was driving the old man onward. He knew, of course, that if he was resolved to take this step, a longer delay would simply make it harder for him. The correspondent, leaning forward, was watching him almost breathlessly.

"Mr. Coleman, I understand—or at least I am led to believe—that you—at one time, proposed marriage to my daughter?"

The faltering words did not sound as if either man had aught to do with them. They were an expression by the tragic muse herself. Coleman's jaw fell and he looked glassily at the professor. He said: "Yes!" But already his blood was leaping as his mind flashed everywhere in speculation.

"I refused my consent to that marriage," said the old man more easily. "I do not know if the matter has remained important to you, but at any rate, I—I retract my refusal."

Suddenly the blank expression left Coleman's face and he smiled with sudden intelligence, as if information of what the professor had been saying had just reached him. In this smile there was a sudden betrayal, too, of something keen and bitter which had lain hidden in the man's mind. He arose and made a step towards the professor and held out his hand.

"Sir, I thank you from the bottom of my heart!" And they both seemed to note with surprise that Coleman's voice had broken.

The professor had arisen to receive Coleman's hand. His nerve was now of iron and he was very formal.

"I judge from your tone that I have not made a mistake—something which I feared."

Coleman did not seem to mind the professor's formality. "Don't fear anything. Won't you sit down again? Will you have a cigar? No, I couldn't tell you how glad I am. How glad I am. I feel like a fool. It—"

But the professor fixed him with an Arctic eye and bluntly said: "You love her?"

The question steadied Coleman at once. He looked undauntedly straight into the professor's face. He simply said: "I love her!"

"You love her?" repeated the professor.

"I love her," repeated Coleman.

After some seconds of pregnant silence, the professor arose. "Well, if she cares to give her life to you I will allow it, but I must say that I do not consider you nearly good enough. Good-night."

He smiled faintly as he held out his hand.

"Good-night, sir," said Coleman. "And I can't tell, you, now—"

Mrs. Wainwright, in her room was languishing in a chair and applying to her brow a handkerchief wet with cologne water. She, kept her feverish glance upon the door. Remembering well the manner of her husband when he went out she could hardly identify him when he came in. Serenity, composure, even self-satisfaction, was written upon him. He paid no attention to her, but going to a chair sat down with a groan of contentment.

"Well?" cried Mrs. Wainwright, starting up. "Well?"

"Well—what?" he asked.

She waved her hand impatiently. "Harrison, don't be absurd. You know perfectly well what I mean. It is a pity you couldn't think of the anxiety I have been in." She was going to weep.

"Oh, I'll tell you after awhile," he said stretching out his legs with the complacency of a rich merchant after a successful day.

"No! Tell me now," she implored him. "Can't you see I've worried myself nearly to death?" She was not going to weep, she was going to wax angry.

"Well, to tell the truth," said the professor with considerable pomposity, "I've arranged it. Didn't think I could do it at first, but it turned out"

"I Arranged it,'" wailed Mrs. Wainwright. "Arranged what?"

It here seemed to strike the professor suddenly that he was not such a flaming example for diplomatists as he might have imagined. "Arranged," he stammered. "Arranged."

"Arranged what?"

"Why, I fixed—I fixed it up."

"Fixed what up?"

"It—it—" began the professor. Then he swelled with indignation. "Why, can't you understand anything at all? I—I fixed it."

"Fixed what?"

"Fixed it. Fixed it with Coleman."

"Fixed what with Coleman?

The professor's wrath now took control of him. "Thunder and lightnin'! You seem to jump at the conclusion that I've made some horrible mistake. For goodness' sake, give me credit for a particle of sense."

"What did you do?" she asked in a sepulchral voice.

"Well," said the professor, in a burning defiance, "I'll tell you what I did. I went to Coleman and told him that once—as he of course knew—I had refused his marriage with my daughter, but that now—"

"Grrr," said Mrs. Wainwright.

"But that now—" continued the professor, "I retracted that refusal."

"Mercy on us!" cried Mrs. Wainwright, throwing herself back in the chair. "Mercy on us! What fools men are!"

"Now, wait a minute—"

But Mrs. Wainwright began to croon: "Oh, if Marjory should hear of this! Oh, if she should hear of it! just let her. Hear—"

"But she must not," cried the professor, tigerishly. "Just you dare!"

And the woman saw before her a man whose eyes were lit with a flame which almost expressed a temporary hatred.

The professor had left Coleman so abruptly that the correspondent found himself murmuring half-coherent gratitude to the closed door of his room. Amazement soon began to be mastered by exultation. He flung himself upon the brandy and soda and negotiated a strong glass. Pacing the room with nervous steps, he caught a vision of himself in a tall mirror. He halted before it. "Well, well," he said. "Rufus, you're a grand man. There is not your equal anywhere. You are a great, bold, strong player, fit to sit down to a game with the best."

A moment later it struck him that he had appropriated too much. If the professor had paid him a visit and made a wonderful announcement, he, Coleman, had not been the engine of it. And then he enunciated clearly something in his mind which, even in a vague form, had been responsible for much of his early elation. Marjory herself had compassed this thing. With shame he rejected a first wild and preposterous idea that she had sent her father to him. He reflected that a man who for an instant could conceive such a thing was a natural-born idiot. With an equal feeling, he rejected also an idea that she could have known anything of her father's purpose. If she had known of his purpose, there would have been no visit.

What, then, was the cause? Coleman soon decided that the professor had witnessed some demonstration of Marjory's emotion which had been sufficiently severe in its character to force him to the extraordinary visit. But then this also was wild and preposterous. That coldly beautiful goddess would not have given a demonstration of emotion over Rufus Coleman sufficiently alarming to have forced her father on such an errand. That was impossible. No, he was wrong; Marjory even indirectly, could not be connected with the visit. As he arrived at this decision, the enthusiasm passed out of him and he wore a doleful, monkish face.

"Well, what, then, was the cause?" After eliminating Marjory from the discussion waging in his mind, he found it hard to hit upon anything rational. The only remaining theory was to the effect that the professor, having a very high sense of the correspondent's help in the escape of the Wainwright party, had decided that the only way to express his gratitude was to revoke a certain decision which he now could see had been unfair. The retort to this theory seemed to be that if the professor had had such a fine conception of the services rendered by Coleman, he had had ample time to display his appreciation on the road to Arta and on the road down from Arta. There was no necessity for his waiting until their arrival in Athens. It was impossible to concede that the professor's emotion could be anew one; if he had it now, he must have had it in far stronger measure directly after he had been hauled out of danger.

So, it may be seen that after Coleman had eliminated Marjory from the discussion that was waging in his mind, he had practically succeeded in eliminating the professor as well. This, he thought, mournfully, was eliminating with a vengeance. If he dissolved all the factors he could hardly proceed.

The mind of a lover moves in a circle, or at least on a more circular course than other minds, some of which at times even seem to move almost in a straight line. Presently, Coleman was at the point where he bad started, and he did not pause until he reached that theory which asserted that the professor had been inspired to his visit by some sight or knowledge of Marjory in distress. Of course, Coleman was wistfully desirous of proving to himself the truth of this theory.

The palpable agitation of the professor during the interview seemed to support it. If he had come on a mere journey of conscience, he would have hardly appeared as a white and trembling old, man. But then, said Coleman, he himself probably exaggerated this idea of the professor's appearance. It might have been that he was only sour and distressed over the performance of a very disagreeable duty.

The correspondent paced his room and smoked. Sometimes he halted at the little table where was the brandy and soda. He thought so hard that sometimes it seemed that Marjory had been to him to propose marriage, and at other times it seemed that there had been no visit from any one at all.

A desire to talk to somebody was upon him. He strolled down stairs and into the smoking and reading rooms, hoping to see a man he knew, even if it were Coke. But the only occupants were two strangers, furiously debating the war. Passing the minister's room, Coleman saw that there was a light within, and he could not forbear knocking. He was bidden to enter, and opened the door upon the minister, carefully reading his Spectator fresh from London. He looked up and seemed very glad.

"How are you?" he cried. "I was tremendously anxious to see you, do you know! I looked for you to dine with me tonight, but you were not down?"

"No; I had a great deal of work."

"Over the Wainwright affair? By the way, I want you to accept my personal thanks for that work. In a week more I would have gone demented and spent the rest of my life in some kind of a cage, shaking the bars and howling out State Department messages about the Wainwrights. You see, in my territory there are no missionaries to get into trouble, and I was living a life of undisturbed and innocent calm, ridiculing the sentiments of men from Smyrna and other interesting towns who maintained that the diplomatic service was exciting. However, when the Wainwright party got lost, my life at once became active. I was all but helpless, too; which was the worst of it. I suppose Terry at Constantinople must have got grandly stirred up, also. Pity he can't see you to thank you for saving him from probably going mad. By the way," he added, while looking keenly at Coleman, "the Wainwrights don't seem to be smothering you with gratitude?"

"Oh, as much as I deserve—sometimes more," answered Coleman. "My exploit was more or less of a fake, you know. I was between the lines by accident, or through the efforts of that blockhead of a dragoman. I didn't intend it. And then, in the night, when we were waiting in the road because of a fight, they almost bunked into us. That's all."

"They tell it better," said the minister, severely. "Especially the youngsters."

"Those kids got into a high old fight at a town up there beyond Agrinion. Tell you about that, did they? I thought not. Clever kids. You have noted that there are signs of a few bruises and scratches?"

"Yes, but I didn't ask—"

"Well, they are from the fight. It seems the people took us for Germans, and there was an awful palaver, which ended in a proper and handsome shindig. It raised the town, I tell you."

The minister sighed in mock despair. "Take these people home, will you? Or at any rate, conduct them out of the field of my responsibility. Now, they would like Italy immensely, I am sure."

Coleman laughed, and they smoked for a time.

"That's a charming girl—Miss Wainwright," said the minister, musingly. "And what a beauty! It does my exiled eyes good to see her. I suppose all those youngsters are madly in love with her? I don't see how they could help it."

"Yes," said Coleman, glumly. "More than half of them."

The minister seemed struck with a sudden thought. "You ought to try to win that splendid prize yourself. The rescuer! Perseus! What more fitting?"

Coleman answered calmly: "Well…I think I'll take your advice."

## CHAPTER XXVIII.

The next morning Coleman awoke with a sign of a resolute decision on his face, as if it had been a development of his sleep. He would see Marjory as soon as possible, see her despite any barbed-wire entanglements which might be placed in the way by her mother, whom he regarded as his strenuous enemy. And he would ask Marjory's hand in the presence of all Athens if it became necessary.

He sat a long time at his breakfast in order to see the Wainwrights enter the dining room, and as he was about to surrender to the will of time, they came in, the professor placid and self-satisfied, Mrs. Wainwright worried and injured and Marjory cool, beautiful, serene. If there had been any kind of a storm there was no trace of it on the white brow of the girl. Coleman studied her closely but furtively while his mind spun around his circle of speculation. Finally he noted the waiter who was observing him with a pained air as if it was on the tip of his tongue to ask this guest if he was going to remain at breakfast forever. Coleman passed out to the reading room where upon the table a multitude of great red guide books were crushing the fragile magazines of London and Paris. On the walls were various depressing maps with the name of a tourist agency luridly upon them, and there were also some pictures of hotels with their rates—in francs—printed beneath. The room was cold, dark, empty, with the trail of the tourist upon it.

Coleman went to the picture of a hotel in Corfu and stared at it precisely as if he was interested. He was standing before it when he heard Marjory's voice just without the door. "All right! I'll wait." He did not move for the reason that the hunter moves not when the unsuspecting deer approaches his hiding place. She entered rather quickly and was well toward the centre of the room before she perceived Coleman. "Oh," she said and stopped. Then she spoke the immortal sentence, a sentence which, curiously enough is common to the drama, to the novel, and to life. "I thought no one was here." She looked as if she was going to retreat, but it would have been hard to make such retreat graceful, and probably for this reason she stood her ground.

Coleman immediately moved to a point between her and the door. "You are not going to run away from me, Marjory Wainwright," he cried, angrily. "You at least owe it to me to tell me definitely that you don't love me—that you can't love me—"

She did not face him with all of her old spirit, but she faced him, and in her answer there was the old Marjory. "A most common question. Do you ask all your feminine acquaintances that?"

"I mean—" he said. "I mean that I love you and—"

"Yesterday—no. Today—yes. Tomorrow—who knows. Really, you ought to take some steps to know your own mind."

"Know my own mind," he retorted in a burst of indignation. "You mean you ought to take steps to know your own mind."

"My own mind! You—" Then she halted in acute confusion and all her face went pink. She had been far quicker than the man to define the scene. She lowered her head. Let me past, please—"

But Coleman sturdily blocked the way and even took one of her struggling hands. "Marjory—" And then his brain must have roared with a thousand quick sentences for they came tumbling out, one over the other.... Her resistance to the grip of his fingers grew somewhat feeble. Once she raised her eyes in a quick glance at him.... Then suddenly she wilted. She surrendered, she confessed without words. "Oh, Marjory, thank God, thank God—" Peter Tounley made a dramatic entrance on the gallop. He stopped, petrified.

"Whoo!" he cried. "My stars!"

He turned and fled. But Coleman called after him in a low voice, intense with agitation.

"Come back here, you young scoundrel! Come back here I—"

Peter returned, looking very sheepish. "I hadn't the slightest idea you—"

"Never mind that now. But look here, if you tell a single soul—particularly those other young scoundrels—I'll break—"

"I won't, Coleman. Honest, I won't." He was far more embarrassed than Coleman and almost equally so with Marjory. He was like a horse tugging at a tether. "I won't, Coleman! Honest!"

"Well, all right, then." Peter escaped.

The professor and his wife were in their sitting room writing letters. The cablegrams had all been answered, but as the professor intended to prolong his journey homeward into a month of Paris and London, there remained the arduous duty of telling their friends at length exactly what had happened. There was considerable of the lore of olden Greece in the professor's descriptions of their escape, and in those of Mrs. Wainwright there was much about the lack of hairpins and soap.

Their heads were lowered over their writing when the door into the corridor opened and shut quickly, and upon looking up they saw in the room a radiant girl, a new Marjory. She dropped to her knees by her father's chair and reached her arms to his neck. "Oh, daddy! I'm happy I I'm so happy!"

"Why—what—" began the professor stupidly.

"Oh, I am so happy, daddy!

Of course he could not be long in making his conclusion. The one who could give such joy to Marjory was the one who, last night, gave her such grief. The professor was only a moment in understanding. He laid his hand tenderly upon her head "Bless my soul," he murmured. "And so—and so—he—"

At the personal pronoun, Mrs. Wainwright lumbered frantically to her feet. "What?" she shouted. Coleman?"

"Yes," answered Marjory. "Coleman." As she spoke the name her eyes were shot with soft yet tropic flashes of light.

Mrs. Wainwright dropped suddenly back into her chair. "Well—of all things!" The professor was stroking his daughter's hair and although for a time after Mrs. Wainwright's outbreak there was little said, the old man and the girl seemed in gentle communion, she making him feel her happiness, he making her feel his appreciation. Providentially Mrs. Wainwright had been so stunned by the first blow that she was evidently rendered incapable of speech.

"And are you sure you will be happy with him?" asked her father gently.

"All my life long," she answered.

"I am glad! I am glad!" said the father, but even as he spoke a great sadness came to blend with his joy. The hour when he was to give this beautiful and beloved life into the keeping of another had been heralded by the god of the sexes, the ruthless god that devotes itself to the tearing of children from the parental arms and casting them amid the mysteries of an irretrievable wedlock. The thought filled him with solemnity.

But in the dewy eyes of the girl there was no question. The world to her was a land of glowing promise.

"I am glad," repeated the professor.

The girl arose from her knees. "I must go away and—think all about it," she said, smiling. When the door of her room closed upon her, the mother arose in majesty.

"Harrison Wainwright," she declaimed, "you are not going to allow this monstrous thing!"

The professor was aroused from a reverie by these words. "What monstrous thing?" he growled.

"Why, this between Coleman and Marjory."

"Yes," he answered boldly.

"Harrison! That man who—"

The professor crashed his hand down on the table. "Mary! I will not hear another word of it!"

"Well," said Mrs. Wainwright, sullen and ominous, "time will tell! Time will tell!"

When Coleman bad turned from the fleeing Peter Tounley again to Marjory, he found her making the preliminary movements of a flight. "What's the matter?" he demanded anxiously.

"Oh, it's too dreadful!"

"Nonsense," lie retorted stoutly. "Only Peter Tounley! He don't count. What of that?"

"Oh, dear!" She pressed her palm to a burning cheek. She gave him a star-like, beseeching glance. Let me go now—please."

"Well," he answered, somewhat affronted, "if you like—"

At the door she turned to look at him, and this glance expressed in its elusive way a score of things which she had not yet been able to speak. It explained that she was loath to leave him, that she asked forgiveness for leaving him, that even for a short absence she wished to take his image in her eyes, that he must not bully her, that there was something now in her heart which frightened her, that she loved him, that she was happy—

When she had gone, Coleman went to the rooms of the American minister. A Greek was there who talked wildly as he waved his cigarette. Coleman waited in well-concealed impatience for the evaporation of this man. Once the minister, regarding the correspondent hurriedly, interpolated a comment. "You look very cheerful?"

"Yes," answered Coleman, "I've been taking your advice."

"Oh, ho!" said the minister.

The Greek with the cigarette jawed endlessly. Coleman began to marvel at the enduring good manners of the minister, who continued to nod and nod in polite appreciation of the Greek's harangue, which, Coleman firmly believed, had no point of interest whatever. But at last the man, after an effusive farewell, went his way.

"Now," said the minister, wheeling in his chair tell me all about it."

Coleman arose, and thrusting his hands deep in his trousers' pockets, began to pace the room with long strides. He, said nothing, but kept his eyes on the floor.

"Can I have a drink?" he asked, abruptly pausing.

"What would you like?" asked the minister, benevolently, as he touched the bell.

"A brandy and soda. I'd like it very much. You see," he said, as he resumed his walk, "I have no kind of right to burden you with my affairs, but, to tell the truth, if I don't get this news off my mind and into somebody's ear, I'll die. It's this—I asked Marjory Wainwright to marry me, and—she accepted, and—that's all."

"Well, I am very glad," cried the minister, arising and giving his hand. "And as for burdening me with your affairs, no one has a better right, you know, since you released me from the persecution of Washington and the friends of the Wainwrights. May good luck follow you both forever. You, in my opinion, are a very, very fortunate man. And, for her part she has not done too badly."

Seeing that it was important that Coleman should have his spirits pacified in part, the minister continued: "Now, I have got to write an official letter, so you just walk up and down here and use up this surplus steam. Else you'll explode."

But Coleman was not to be detained. Now that he had informed the minister, he must rush off somewhere, anywhere, and do—he knew not what.

All right," said the minister, laughing. "You have a wilder head than I thought. But look here," he called, as Coleman was making for the door. "Am I to keep this news a secret?"

Coleman with his hand on the knob, turned impressively. He spoke with deliberation. "As far as I am concerned, I would be glad to see a man paint it in red letters, eight feet high, on the front of the king's palace."

The minister, left alone, wrote steadily and did not even look up when Peter Tounley and two others entered, in response to his cry of permission. How ever, he presently found time to speak over his shoulder to them. "Hear the news?"

"No, sir," they answered.

"Well, be good boys, now, and read the papers and look at pictures until I finish this letter. Then I will tell you."

They surveyed him keenly. They evidently judged that the news was worth hearing, but, obediently, they said nothing. Ultimately the minister affixed a rapid signature to the letter, and turning, looked at the students with a smile. "Haven't heard the news, eh?"

"No, Sir."

"Well, Marjory Wainwright is engaged to marry Coleman."

The minister was amazed to see the effect of this announcement upon the three students. He had expected the crows and cackles of rather absurd merriment with which unbearded youth often greets, such news. But there was no crow or cackle. One young man blushed scarlet and looked guiltily at the floor. With a great effort he muttered: "She's too good for him." Another student had turned ghastly pate and was staring. It was Peter Tounley who relieved the minister's mind, for upon that young man's face was a broad jack-o-lantern grin, and the minister saw that, at any rate, he had not made a complete massacre.

Peter Tounley said triumphantly: "I knew it!"

The minister was anxious over the havoc he had wrought with the two other students, but slowly the color abated in one face and grew in the other. To give them opportunity, the minister talked busily to Peter Tounley. "And how did you know it, you young scamp?"

Peter was jubilant. "Oh, I knew it! I knew it I—I am very clever."

The student who had blushed now addressed the minister in a slightly strained voice. "Are you positive that it is true, Mr. Gordner?,"

"I had it on the best authority," replied the minister gravely.

The student who had turned pale said: "Oh, it's true, of course."

"Well," said crudely the one who had blushed, she's a great sight too good for Coleman or anybody like him. That's all I've got to say."

"Oh, Coleman is a good fellow," said Peter Tounley, reproachfully. "You've no right to say that—exactly. You don't know where you'd be now if it were not for Coleman."

The, response was, first, an angry gesture. "Oh, don't keep everlasting rubbing that in. For heaven's sake, let up. Supposing I don't know where I'd be now if it were not for Rufus Coleman? What of it? For the rest of my life have I got to—"

The minister saw that this was the embittered speech of a really defeated youth, so, to save scenes, he gently ejected the trio. "There, there, now! Run along home like good boys. I'll be busy until luncheon. And I dare say you won't find Coleman such a bad chap."

In the corridor, one of the students said offensively to Peter Tounley: "Say, how in hell did you find out all this so early?"

Peter's reply was amiable in tone. "You are a damned bleating little kid, and you made a holy show of yourself before Mr. Gordner. There's where you stand. Didn't you see that he turned us out because he didn't know but what you were going to blubber or something? You are a sucking pig, and if you want to know how I find out things, go ask the Delphic Oracle, you blind ass."

"You better look out or you may get a punch in the eye!"

"You take one punch in the general direction of my eye, me son," said Peter cheerfully, "and I'll distribute your remains, over this hotel in a way that will cause your, friends years of trouble to collect you. Instead of anticipating an attack upon my eye, you had much better be engaged in improving your mind, which is at present not a fit machine to cope with exciting situations. There's Coke! Hello, Coke, hear the news? Well, Marjory Wainwright and Rufus Coleman , are engaged. Straight? Certainly! Go ask the minister."

Coke did not take Peter's word. "Is that so?" he asked the others.

"So the minister told us," they answered, and then these two, who seemed so unhappy, watched Coke's face to see if they could not find surprised misery there. But Coke coolly said: "Well, then, I suppose it's true."

It soon became evident that the students did not care for each other's society. Peter Tounley was probably an exception, but the others seemed to long for quiet corners. They were distrusting each other, and, in a boyish way, they were even capable of malignant things. Their excuses for separation were badly made.

"I—I think I'll go for a walk."

"I'm going upstairs to read."

"Well, so long, old man."

"So long." There was no heart to it.

Peter Tounley went to Coleman's door, where he knocked with noisy hilarity. "Come in I "The correspondent apparently had just come from the street, for his hat was on his head and a light top-coat was on his back. He was searching hurriedly through some, papers. "Hello, you young devil What are you doing here?

Peter's entrance was a somewhat elaborate comedy which Coleman watched in icy silence. Peter after a long and impudent pantomime halted abruptly and fixing Coleman with his eye demanded: "Well?"

"Well—what?" said Coleman, bristling a trifle.

"Is it true?"

"Is what true?"

"Is it true?" Peter was extremely solemn. "Say, me bucko," said Coleman suddenly, "if you've come up here to twist the beard of the patriarch, don't you think you are running a chance?"

"All right. I'll be good," said Peter, and he sat on the bed. "But—is it true?

"Is what true?"

"What the whole hotel is saying."

"I haven't heard the hotel making any remarks lately. Been talking to the other buildings, I suppose."

"Well, I want to tell you that everybody knows that you and Marjory have done gone and got yourselves engaged," said Peter bluntly.

"And well?" asked Coleman imperturbably.

"Oh, nothing," replied Peter, waving his hand. "Only—I thought it might interest you."

Coleman was silent for some time. He fingered his papers. At last he burst out joyously. "And so they know it already, do they? Well—damn them—let them know it. But you didn't tell them yourself?"

"I!" quoth Peter wrathfully. "No! The minister told us."

Then Coleman was again silent for a time and Peter Tounley sat on the bed reflectively looking at the ceiling. "Funny thing, Marjory 'way over here in Greece, and then you happening over here the way you did."

"It isn't funny at all."

"Why isn't it?"

"Because," said Coleman impressively, "that is why I came to Greece. It was all planned. See?"

"Whirroo," exclaimed Peter. "This here is magic."

"No magic at all." Coleman displayed some complacence. "No magic at all just pure, plain—whatever you choose to call it."

"Holy smoke," said Peter, admiring the situation. "Why, this is plum romance, Coleman. I'm blowed if it isn't."

Coleman was grinning with delight. He took a fresh cigar and his bright eyes looked at Peter through the smoke. "Seems like it, don't it? Yes. Regular romance. Have a drink, my boy, just to celebrate my good luck. And be patient if I talk a great deal of my—my—future. My head spins with it." He arose to pace the room flinging out his arms in a great gesture. "God! When I think yesterday was not like today I wonder how I stood it."

There was a knock at the door, and a waiter left a note in Coleman's hand

Dear Rufus:—
We are going for a drive this afternoon at three, and mother wishes you to come, if you care to. I too wish it, if you care to.
Yours,
MARJORY.

With a radiant face, Coleman gave the note a little crackling flourish in the air. "Oh, you don't know what life is, kid."

"S-steady the Blues," said Peter Tounley seriously. You'll lose your head if you don't watch out."

"Not I!" cried Coleman with irritation. "But a man must turn loose some times, mustn't he?"

When the four, students had separated in the corridor, Coke had posted at once to Nora Black's sitting room. His entrance was somewhat precipitate, but he cooled down almost at once, for he reflected that he was not bearing good news. He ended by perching in awkward fashion on the brink of his chair and fumbling his hat uneasily. Nora floated to him in a cloud of a white dressing gown. She gave him a plump hand. "Well, young man? "she said, with a glowing smile. She took a chair, and the stuff of her gown fell in curves over the arms of it.

Coke looked hot and bothered, as if he could have more than half wanted to retract his visit. "I—aw—we haven't seen much of you lately," he began, sparing. He had expected to tell his news at once.

No," said Nora, languidly. "I have been resting after that horrible journey—that horrible journey. Dear, dear! Nothing will ever induce me to leave London, New York and Paris. I am at home there. But here I Why, it is worse than living in Brooklyn. And that journey into the wilds! No, no; not for me!"

"I suppose we'll all be glad to get home," said Coke, aimlessly.

At the moment a waiter entered the room and began to lay the table for luncheon. He kept open the door to the corridor, and he had the luncheon at a point just outside the door. His excursions to the trays were flying ones, so that, as far as

Coke's purpose was concerned, the waiter was always in the room. Moreover, Coke was obliged, naturally, to depart at once. He had bungled everything.

As he arose he whispered hastily: "Does this waiter understand English?"

"Yes," answered Nora. "Why?"

"Because I have something to tell you—important."

"What is it?" whispered Nora, eagerly.

He leaned toward her and replied: "Marjory Wainwright and Coleman are engaged."

To his unfeigned astonishment, Nora Black burst into peals of silvery laughter, "Oh, indeed? And so this is your tragic story, poor, innocent lambkin? And what did you expect? That I would faint?"

"I thought—I don't know—" murmured Coke in confusion.

Nora became suddenly businesslike. "But how do you know? Are you sure? Who told you? Anyhow, stay to luncheon. Do—like a good boy. Oh, you must."

Coke dropped again into his chair. He studied her in some wonder. "I thought you'd be surprised," he said, ingenuously.

"Oh, you did, did you? Well, you see I'm not. And now tell me all about it."

"There's really nothing to tell but the plain fact. Some of the boys dropped in at the minister's rooms a little while ago, and, he told them of it. That's all."

Well, how did he know?

"I am sure I can't tell you. Got it first hand, I suppose. He likes Coleman, and Coleman is always hanging up there."

"Oh, perhaps Coleman was lying," said Nora easily. Then suddenly her face brightened and she spoke with animation. "Oh, I haven't told you how my little Greek officer has turned out. Have I? No? Well, it is simply lovely. Do you know, he belongs to one of the best families in Athens? He does. And they're rich—rich as can be. My courier tells me that the marble palace where they live is enough to blind you, and that if titles hadn't gone out of style—or something—here in Greece, my little officer would be a prince! Think of that! The courier didn't know it until we got to Athens, and the little officer—the prince—gave me his card, of course. One of the oldest, noblest and richest families in Greece. Think of that! There I thought he was only a bothersome little officer who came in handy at times, and there he turns out to be a prince. I could hardly keep myself from rushing right off to find him and apologize to him for the way I treated him. It was awful! And—" added the fair Nora, pensively, "if he does meet me in Paris, I'll make him wear that title down to a shred, you can bet. What's the good of having a title unless you make it work?"

## CHAPTER XXIX.

Coke did not stay to luncheon with Nora Black. He went away saying to himself either that girl don't care a straw for Coleman or she has got a heart absolutely of flint, or she is the greatest actress on earth or—there is some other reason."

At his departure, Nora turned and called into an adjoining room. "Maude I "The voice of her companion and friend answered her peevishly. "What?"

"Don't bother me. I'm reading."

"Well, anyhow, luncheon is ready, so you will have to stir your precious self," responded Nora. "You're lazy."

"I don't want any luncheon. Don't bother me. I've got a headache."

"Well, if you don't come out, you'll miss the news. That's all I've got to say."

There was a rustle in the adjoining room, and immediately the companion appeared, seeming much annoyed but curious. "Well, what is it?"

"Rufus Coleman is engaged to be married to that Wainwright girl, after all."

"Well I declare!" ejaculated the little old lady. "Well I declare." She meditated for a moment, and then continued in a tone of satisfaction. "I told you that you couldn't stop that man Coleman if he had really made up his mind to—"

"You're a fool," said Nora, pleasantly.

"Why?" asked the old lady.

"Because you are. Don't talk to me about it. I want to think of Marco."

"'Marco,'" quoted the old lady startled.

"The prince. The prince. Can't you understand? I mean the prince."

"'Marco!'" again quoted the old lady, under her breath.

"Yes, 'Marco,'" cried Nora, belligerently. "'Marco,' Do you object to the name? What's the matter with you, anyhow?"

"Well," rejoined the other, nodding her head wisely, "he may be a prince, but I've always heard that these continental titles are no good in comparison to the English titles."

"Yes, but who told you so, eh?" demanded Nora, noisily. She herself answered the question. "The English!"

"Anyhow, that little marquis who tagged after you in London is a much bigger man in every way, I'll bet, than this little prince of yours."

"But—good heavens—he didn't mean it. Why, he was only one of the regular rounders. But Marco, he is serious I He means it. He'd go through fire and water for me and be glad of the chance."

"Well," proclaimed the old lady, "if you are not the strangest woman in the world, I'd like to know! Here I thought—"

"What did you think?" demanded Nora, suspiciously. "I thought that Coleman—"

"Bosh!" interrupted, the graceful Nora. "I tell you what, Maude; you'd better try to think as little as possible. It will suit your style of beauty better. And above all, don't think of my affairs. I myself am taking pains not to think of them. It's easier."

Mrs. Wainwright, with no spirit of intention whatever, had sit about readjusting her opinions. It is certain that she was unconscious of any evolution. If some one had said to her that she was surrendering to the inevitable, she would have been immediately on her guard, and would have opposed forever all suggestions of a match between Marjory and Coleman. On the other hand, if some one had said to her that her daughter was going to marry a human serpent, and that there were people in Athens who would be glad to explain his treacherous character, she would have haughtily scorned the tale-bearing and would have gone with more haste into the professor's way of thinking. In fact, she was in process of undermining herself and the work could have been retarded or advanced by any irresponsible, gossipy tongue.

The professor, from the depths of his experience with her, arranged a course of conduct. "If I just leave her to herself she will come around all right, but if I go 'striking while the iron is hot,' or any of those things, I'll bungle it surely."

As they were making ready to go down to luncheon, Mrs. Wainwright made her speech which first indicated a changing mind. "Well, what will be, will be," she murmured with a prolonged sigh of resignation. "What will be, will be. Girls are very headstrong in these days, and there is nothing much to be done with them. They go their own roads. It wasn't so in my girlhood. We were obliged to pay attention to our mothers wishes."

"I did not notice that you paid much attention to your mother's wishes when you married me," remarked the professor. "In fact, I thought—"

"That was another thing," retorted Mrs. Wainwright with severity. "You were a steady young man who had taken the highest honors all through your college course, and my mother's sole objection was that we were too hasty. She thought we ought to wait until you had a penny to bless yourself with, and I can see now where she was quite right."

"Well, you married me, anyhow," said the professor, victoriously.

Mrs. Wainwright allowed her husband's retort to pass over her thoughtful mood. "They say—they say Rufus Coleman makes as much as fifteen thousand dollars a year. That's more than three times your income.... I don't know.... It all depends on whether they try to save or not. His manner of life is, no doubt, very luxurious. I don't suppose he knows how to economies at all. That kind of a man usually doesn't. And then, in the newspaper world positions are so very precarious. Men may have valuable positions one minute and be penniless in the street the next minute. It isn't as if he had any real income, and of course he has no real ability. If he was suddenly thrown out of his position, goodness knows what would become of him. Still—still, fifteen thousand dollars a year is a big income while it lasts. I suppose he is very extravagant. That kind of a man usually is. And I wouldn't be surprised if he was heavily in debt; very heavily in debt. Still—if Marjory has set her heart there is nothing to be done, I suppose. It wouldn't have happened if you had been as wise as you thought you were. I suppose he thinks I have been very rude to him. Well, some times I wasn't nearly so rude as I felt like being. Feeling as I did, I could hardly be very amiable.... Of course, this drive this afternoon was all your affair and Marjory's. But, of course, I shall be nice to him."

"And what of all this Nora Black business?" asked the professor, with, a display of velour, but really with much trepidation.

"She is a hussy," responded Mrs. Wainwright with energy. "Her conversation in the carriage on the way down to Agrinion sickened me!"

"I really believe that her plan was simply to break everything off between Marjory and Coleman," said the professor, "and I don't believe she had any grounds for all that appearance of owning Coleman and the rest of it."

"Of course she didn't" assented Mrs. Wainwright. "The vicious thing!"

"On the other hand," said the professor, "there might be some truth in it."

"I don't think so," said Mrs. Wainwright seriously. I don't believe a word of it."

"You do not mean to say that you think Coleman a model man?" demanded the professor.

"Not at all! Not at all!" she hastily answered. "But...one doesn't look for model men these days."

"Who told you he made fifteen thousand a year?" asked the professor.

"It was Peter Tounley this morning. We were talking upstairs after breakfast, and he remarked that he if could make fifteen thousand, a year: like Coleman, he'd—I've forgotten what—some fanciful thing."

"I doubt if it is true," muttered the old man wagging his head.

"Of course it's true," said his wife emphatically. "Peter Tounley says everybody knows it."

Well—anyhow—money is not everything."

But it's a great deal, you know well enough. You know you are always speaking of poverty as an evil, as a grand resultant, a collaboration of many lesser evils. Well, then?

"But," began the professor meekly, when I say that I mean—"

"Well, money is money and poverty is poverty," interrupted his wife. "You don't have to be very learned to know that."

"I do not say that Coleman has not a very nice thing of it, but I must say it is hard to think of his getting any such sum, as you mention."

"Isn't he known as the most brilliant journalist in New York?" she demanded harshly.

"Y-yes, as long as it lasts, but then one never knows when he will be out in the street penniless. Of course he has no particular ability which would be marketable if he suddenly lost his present employment. Of course it is not as if he was a really talented young man. He might not be able to make his way at all in any new direction."

"I don't know about that," said Mrs. Wainwright in reflective protestation. "I don't know about that. I think he would."

"I thought you said a moment ago—" The professor spoke with an air of puzzled hesitancy. "I thought you said a moment ago that he wouldn't succeed in anything but journalism."

Mrs. Wainwright swam over the situation with a fine tranquility. "Well—I—I," she answered musingly, "if I did say that, I didn't mean it exactly."

"No, I suppose not," spoke the professor, and despite the necessity for caution he could not keep out of his voice a faint note of annoyance.

"Of course," continued the wife, "Rufus Coleman is known everywhere as a brilliant man, a very brilliant man, and he even might do well in—in politics or something of that sort."

"I have a very poor opinion of that kind of a mind which does well in American politics," said the professor, speaking as a collegian, "but I suppose there may be something in it."

"Well, at any rate," decided Mrs. Wainwright. "At any rate—"

At that moment, Marjory attired for luncheon and the drive entered from her room, and Mrs. Wainwright checked the expression of her important conclusion. Neither father or mother had ever seen her so glowing with triumphant beauty, a beauty which would carry the mind of a spectator far above physical appreciation into that realm of poetry where creatures of light move and are beautiful because they cannot know pain or a burden. It carried tears to the old father's eyes. He took her hands. "Don't be too happy, my child, don't be too happy," he admonished her tremulously. "It makes me afraid—it makes me afraid."

## CHAPTER XXX

It seems strange that the one who was the most hilarious over the engagement of Marjory and Coleman should be Coleman's dragoman who was indeed in a state bordering on transport. It is not known how he learned the glad tidings, but it is certain that he learned them before luncheon. He told all the visible employees of the hotel and allowed them to know that the betrothal really had been his handiwork He had arranged it. He did not make quite clear how he had performed this feat, but at least he was perfectly frank in acknowledging it.

When some of the students came down to luncheon, they saw him but could not decide what ailed him. He was in the main corridor of the hotel, grinning from ear to ear, and when he perceived the students he made signs to intimate that they possessed in common a joyous secret.

"What's the matter with that idiot?" asked Coke morosely. "Looks as if his wheels were going around too fast."

Peter Tounley walked close to him and scanned him imperturbably, but with care.

"What's up, Phidias?"

The man made no articulate reply. He continued to grin and gesture.

"Pain in 'oo tummy? Mother dead? Caught the cholera? Found out that you've swallowed a pair of hammered brass-and-irons in your beer? Say, who are you, anyhow?"

But he could not shake this invincible glee, so he went away.

* * * *

The dragoman's rapture reached its zenith when Coleman lent him to the professor and he was commissioned to bring a carriage for four people to the door at three o'clock. He himself was to sit on the box and tell the driver what was required of him. He dashed off, his hat in his hand, his hair flying, puffing, important beyond everything, and apparently babbling his mission to half the people he met on the street. In most countries he would have landed speedily in jail, but among a people who exist on a basis of jabbering, his violent gabble aroused no suspicions as to his sanity. However, he stirred several livery stables to their depths and set men running here and there wildly and for the most part futility.

At fifteen minutes to three o'clock, a carriage with its horses on a gallop tore around the corner and up to the front of the hotel, where it halted with the pomp and excitement of a fire engine. The dragoman jumped down from his seat beside the driver and scrambled hurriedly into the hotel, in the gloom of which he met a serene stillness which was punctuated only by the leisurely tinkle of silver and glass in the dining room. For a moment the dragoman seemed really astounded out of speech. Then he plunged into the manager's room. Was it conceivable that Monsieur Coleman was still at luncheon? Yes; in fact, it was true. But the carriage, was at the door! The carriage was at the door! The manager, undisturbed, asked for what hour Monsieur Coleman had been pleased to order a carriage. Three o'clock! Three o'clock? The manager pointed calmly at the clock. Very well. It was now only thirteen minutes of three o'clock. Monsieur Coleman doubtless would appear at three. Until that hour the manager would not disturb Monsieur Coleman. The dragoman clutched both his hands in his hair and cast a look of agony to the ceiling. Great God! Had he accomplished the herculean task of getting a carriage for four people to the door of the hotel in time for a drive at three o'clock, only to meet with this stoniness, this inhumanity? Ah, it was unendurable? He begged the manager; he implored him. But at every word the manager seemed to grow more indifferent, more callous. He pointed with a wooden finger at the clock-face. In reality, it is thus, that Greek meets Greek.

Professor Wainwright and Coleman strolled together out of the dining room. The dragoman rushed ecstatically upon the correspondent. "Oh, Meester Coleman! The carriage is ready!"

"Well, all right," said Coleman, knocking ashes from his cigar. "Don't be in a hurry. I suppose we'll be ready, presently." The man was in despair.

The departure of the Wainwrights and Coleman on this ordinary drive was of a somewhat dramatic and public nature, No one seemed to know how to prevent its being so. In the first place, the attendants thronged out en masse for a reason which was plain at the time only to Coleman's dragoman. And, rather in the background, lurked the interested students. The professor was surprised and nervous. Coleman was rigid and angry. Marjory was flushed and some what hurried, and Mrs. Wainwright was as proud as an old turkey-hen.

As the carriage rolled away, Peter Tounley turned to his companions and said: "Now, that's official! That is the official announcement! Did you see Old Mother Wainwright? Oh, my eye, wasn't she puffed up! Say, what in hell do you suppose all these jay hawking bellboys poured out to the curb for? Go back to your cages, my good people—"

As soon as the carriage wheeled into another street, its occupants exchanged easier smiles, and they must have confessed in some subtle way of glances that now at last they were upon their own mission, a mission undefined but earnest to them all. Coleman had a glad feeling of being let into the family, or becoming one of them

The professor looked sideways at him and smiled gently. "You know, I thought of driving you to some ruins, but Marjory would not have it. She flatly objected to any more ruins. So I thought we would drive down to New Phalerum." Coleman nodded and smiled as if he were immensely pleased, but of course New Phalerum was to him no more nor less than Vladivostok or Khartoum. Neither place nor distance had interest for him. They swept along a shaded avenue where the dust lay thick on the leaves; they passed cafes where crowds were angrily shouting over the news in the little papers; they passed a hospital before which wounded men, white with bandages, were taking the sun; then came soon to the and valley flanked by gaunt naked mountains, which would lead them to the sea. Sometimes to accentuate the dry nakedness of this valley, there would be a patch of grass upon which poppies burned crimson spots. The dust writhed out from under the wheels of the carriage; in the distance the sea appeared, a blue half-disc set between shoulders of barren land. It would be common to say that Coleman was oblivious to all about him but Marjory. On the contrary, the parched land, the isolated flame of poppies, the cool air from the sea, all were keenly known to him, and they had developed an extraordinary power of blending sympathetically into his mood. Meanwhile the professor talked a great deal. And as a somewhat exhilarating detail, Coleman perceived that Ms. Wainwright was beaming upon him.

At New Phalerum—a small collection of pale square villas—they left the carriage and strolled, by the sea. The waves were snarling together like wolves amid the honeycomb rocks and from where the blue plane sprang level to the horizon, came a strong cold breeze, the kind of a breeze which moves an exulting man or a parson to take off his hat and let his locks flutter and tug back from his brow.

The professor and Mrs. Wainwright were left to themselves.

Marjory and Coleman did not speak for a time. It might have been that they did not quite know where to make a beginning. At last Marjory asked: "What has become of your splendid horse?"

"Oh, I've told the dragoman to have him sold as soon as he arrives," said Coleman absently.

"Oh. I'm sorry…I liked that horse."

"Why?"

"Oh, because—"

"Well, he was a fine—" Then he, too, interrupted himself, for he saw plainly that they had not come to this place to talk about a horse. Thereat he made speech of matters which at least did not afford as many opportunities for coherency as would the horse. Marjory, it can't be true— Is it true, dearest… I can hardly believe it. I—"

"Oh, I know I'm not nearly good enough for you."

"Good enough for me, dear?

"They all told me so, and they were right! Why, even the American minister said it. Everybody thinks it."

"Why, aren't they wretches To think of them saying such a thing! As if—as if anybody could be too—"

"Do you know—" She paused and looked at him with a certain timid challenge. "I don't know why I feel it, but—sometimes I feel that I've been I've been flung at your head."

He opened his mouth in astonishment. "Flung at my head!

She held up her finger. "And if I thought you could ever believe it!"

"Is a girl flung at a man's head when her father carries her thousands of miles away and the man follows her all these miles, and at last—"

"Her eyes were shining. "And you really came to Greece—on purpose to—to—"

"Confess you knew it all the time! Confess!" The answer was muffled. "Well, sometimes I thought you did, and at other times I thought you—didn't."

In a secluded cove, in which the sea-maids once had played, no doubt, Marjory and Coleman sat in silence. He was below her, and if he looked at her he had to turn his glance obliquely upward. She was staring at the sea with woman's mystic gaze, a gaze which men at once reverence and fear since it seems to look into the deep, simple heart of nature, and men begin to feel that their petty wisdoms are futile to control these strange spirits, as wayward as nature and as pure as nature, wild as the play of waves, sometimes as unalterable as the mountain amid the winds; and to measure them, man must perforce use a mathematical formula.

He wished that she would lay her hand upon his hair. He would be happy then. If she would only, of her own will, touch his hair lightly with her fingers—if she would do it with an unconscious air it would be even better. It would show him that she was thinking of him, even when she did not know she was thinking of him.

Perhaps he dared lay his head softly against her knee. Did he dare?

As his head touched her knee, she did not move. She seemed to be still gazing at the sea. Presently idly caressing fingers played in his hair near the forehead. He looked up suddenly lifting his arms. He breathed out a cry which was laden with a kind of diffident ferocity. "I haven't kissed you yet—"